VASILY GROSSMAN

Vasily Grossman (1905–64) is best known as the author of *Life and Fate*, regarded by many as the greatest Russian novel of the twentieth century.

Among his most acclaimed works of fiction are *Life and Fate*, *Everything Flows* and the short stories collected in *The Road*. *A Writer at War* collects Grossman's notebooks, war diaries, personal correspondence and newspaper articles from his time as a war reporter.

ROBERT AND ELIZABETH CHANDLER

Robert Chandler translated *Life and Fate* nearly forty years ago, and other works by Vasily Grossman more recently. He has written a short biography of Pushkin and compiled three anthologies of Russian literature for Penguin Classics. He is also the main English translator of Andrey Platonov and Teffi.

Elizabeth Chandler has worked closely with her husband on all his recent translations of Russian prose.

ALSO BY VASILY GROSSMAN

Life and Fate
Everything Flows
The Road: Short Fiction and Essays
An Armenian Sketchbook

By Vasily Grossman, edited and
translated by Antony Beevor
and Luba Vinogradova

A Writer at War:
Vasily Grossman with the Red Army 1941–1945

VASILY GROSSMAN

Stalingrad

TRANSLATED FROM THE RUSSIAN BY
Robert and Elizabeth Chandler

EDITED BY
Robert Chandler and Yury Bit-Yunan

VINTAGE

1 3 5 7 9 10 8 6 4 2

Vintage
20 Vauxhall Bridge Road,
London SW1V 2SA

Vintage Classics is part of the Penguin Random House
group of companies whose addresses can be found at
global.penguinrandomhouse.com.

Penguin
Random House
UK

First published in the UK by Harvill Secker in 2019
First published by Vintage Classics in 2020

First published in Russian in serial form by *Novy Mir* in 1952
and as a book by *Voenizdat* in 1954

penguin.co.uk/vintage

A CIP catalogue record for this book is available from the
British Library

ISBN 9780099561361

Printed and bound in Great Britain by Clays Ltd, Elcograf S.p.A.

Penguin Random House is committed to a sustainable future for our
business, our readers and our planet. This book is made from Forest
Stewardship Council® certified paper.

This translation is dedicated to the translator's father,
Colonel Roger Elphinstone Chandler (1921–68)

Contents

Introduction   xi

Stalingrad   1

Timeline of the War   893

Afterword   897

Note on Russian Names and List of Characters   927

Further Reading   933

Acknowledgements   935

Notes   937

Maps   962

Introduction

1.

Vasily Grossman's novel *Life and Fate* (completed in 1960) has been hailed as a twentieth-century *War and Peace*. It has been translated into most European languages, and also into Chinese, Japanese, Korean, Turkish and Vietnamese. There have been stage productions, TV series and an eight-hour BBC radio dramatization. Most readers, however, have been unaware that Grossman did not originally conceive of *Life and Fate* as a self-contained novel. It is, rather, the second of two closely related novels about the Battle of Stalingrad that it is probably simplest to refer to as a dilogy. The first of these two novels was first published in 1952, under the title *For a Just Cause*. Grossman himself, however, had wanted to call it *Stalingrad* – and that is how we have titled it in this translation.

The characters in the two novels are largely the same and so is the storyline; *Life and Fate* picks up where *Stalingrad* ends, in late September 1942. Ikonnikov's essay on senseless kindness – now a part of *Life and Fate* and often seen as central to it – was originally a part of *Stalingrad*. Another of the most memorable elements of *Life and Fate* – the letter written by Viktor Shtrum's mother about her last days in the Berdichev ghetto – is of central importance to *both* novels. The actual words of the letter were probably always intended for *Life and Fate*, but it is in *Stalingrad* that Grossman tells us how the letter reached Viktor and what he felt when he read it.

Grossman completed *Life and Fate* almost fifteen years after he first started work on *Stalingrad*. It is, amongst other things, a considered statement of his moral and political philosophy – a meditation on the nature of totalitarianism, the danger presented by even the most seemingly benign of ideologies, and the moral responsibility of each individual for his own actions. It is this philosophical depth that has led many readers to speak of the novel as having changed their lives. *Stalingrad*, in contrast, is less philosophical, but more immediate; it presents us with a richer, more varied human story.

Grossman worked as a front-line war correspondent throughout nearly all the four years of the Soviet–German war. He had a powerful memory and an unusual ability to get people from every walk of life to talk openly to him; he also had relatively free access, during the war years, to a wealth of military reports. His wartime notebooks include potted biographies of hundreds of individuals, scraps of dialogue, sudden insights and unexpected observations of all kinds. Much of this material found its way into *Stalingrad* and it endows the novel with great vitality and a certain democratic quality; Grossman writes with equal delicacy and respect about the experiences of a senior Red Army general, a newly recruited militiaman or a terrified housewife. And he devotes more space than other Soviet writers to the effects of the Battle of Stalingrad on the lives of dogs, cats, camels, rodents, birds, fish and insects in the surrounding steppe.

Few war correspondents can, in only a few years and without becoming desensitized, have experienced so many aspects of war. Grossman's extended analysis of the mood of a retreating army is subtle and penetrating. His evocation of the thoughts and feelings of the inhabitants of a large city subjected to a massive bombing raid is almost encyclopaedic. And the account of the defence of the Stalingrad railway station can stand comparison with the *Iliad*; Grossman's evocation of the inner life of young men who know they are certain to die within the next twenty-four hours is remarkably convincing.

Grossman is a master of character portrayal, with an unusual gift for conveying someone's feelings through some tiny but vivid detail. The quiet, modest Major Berozkin, for example, has lost touch with his wife and does not know if she is still alive. Grossman tell us that, on sitting down to an unusually lavish meal, Berozkin 'touched the tomatoes, hoping to find one that was fully ripe but not going soft. Then he felt embarrassed, thinking sadly how Tamara used to tell him off for doing exactly this. She didn't like him fingering the tomatoes or cucumbers on a shared dish.'

Grossman is equally deft in his shifts of perspective, moving between the microscopic and the epic and showing the same generous understanding towards his German characters as towards his Russians. One of his most interesting creations is Lieutenant Bach, an intellectual and former dissident now yielding to the seductions of Nazi ideology. A company commander in one of the first divisions to cross the Don, he feels he is taking part in a venture of epic grandeur: 'He rose to his full height and stamped his foot against the ground. He felt as if he were kicking the sky [...] He could feel, it seemed, with his skin, with his whole body the furthest reaches of this alien land he had crossed.' A thousand pages later, in the last part of *Life and Fate*, Lieutenant Bach realizes he has been deluded. This, perhaps, will come as no surprise to the reader; what is astonishing is Grossman's ability to enable us to sense how easily we too might have been deluded.

Stalingrad is one of the great novels of the last century. If it has been overshadowed by its sequel, this is probably for two main reasons. First, we are still in thrall to Cold War thinking; people have been unable to conceive that a novel first published during Stalin's last years, when his dictatorship was at its most rigid, might deserve our attention. Eminent figures have been dismissive of *Stalingrad* and it has been easy to assume that there must be good reason for this. I too made this lazy assumption for many years and I am grateful to the historian Jochen Hellbeck for persuading me – albeit belatedly – to read the novel and judge for myself.

A second reason is that none of the published editions of *Stalingrad*, in Russian or any other language, do justice to Grossman's original vision of the novel. There are many bold, witty, vivid and perceptive passages in his early typescripts that have never been published and have probably only been read by a few dozen people. Grossman's editors – who, like all Soviet editors, also played the role of censors – required him to delete them and scholars have been slow to study and publish the wealth of material preserved in his archive. In this translation we have, wherever possible, restored these passages. It is an honour to be in a position to publish some of Grossman's finest writing for the first time. My hope is that this may allow readers to recognize the full breadth, humour and emotional generosity of another of Grossman's masterpieces.

2.

War and Peace has probably never been as widely read as in the Soviet Union during the Second World War. The authorities had every reason to promote the novel. Tolstoy was seen as a forerunner of Soviet socialist realism and the novel's implications for the outcome of the war were obviously positive.

War and Peace was broadcast at length on the radio. The two generals who played the most important roles in the defence of Stalingrad both spoke about how much Tolstoy meant to them; General Rodimtsev said he read the novel three times, and General Chuikov said in a 1943 interview that Tolstoy's generals were the model by which he judged his own performance. According to the Soviet literary critic Lydia Ginzburg, civilians in blockaded Leningrad judged themselves in exactly the same way. The People's Commissariat for Education printed brochures with instructions on how to summarize *War and Peace* and explain the novel to soldiers.[1] In late August and early September 1941, Grossman's mother Yekaterina Savelievna used a French translation of *War and Peace* to teach French to the children of the doctor with whom she lived during her last weeks in the Berdichev ghetto, before being shot by the Nazis.[2] Grossman himself wrote, 'During the whole war, the only book that I read was *War and Peace*, which I read twice.'[3] And Grossman's daughter Yekaterina Korotkova concludes a brief summary of her volume of memoirs with the words: 'I remember a letter of his from Stalingrad: "Bombers. Shelling. Hellish thunder. It's impossible to read." And then, unexpectedly: "It's impossible to read anything except *War and Peace*."'[4]

The Soviet literary and political establishment wanted a Red Tolstoy to memorialize the war. A short article published by Grossman on 23 June 1945 testifies both to his determination to take on the challenge and to his awareness of the responsibility involved.

Grossman begins by evoking the atmosphere in an infantry-division command post during a hard-fought battle in 1944. The divisional commander is under pressure; his immediate superior is yelling at him down the field telephone and his subordinates are begging for support he is unable to offer. At one point, Grossman imagines himself in the commander's shoes, bearing such a weight of responsibility. 'Just then, as if reading my mind, the commander – who had seemed to have forgotten I was there – suddenly turned to me and smiled. Still smiling, he said with a certain *Schadenfreude*, "Well, I may be sweating now, but after the war it will be the writers' turn to sweat as they try to describe all this."' Grossman then returns to the present, late June 1945, only six weeks after the German surrender: 'And so, the time has now come for us writers to shoulder our responsibility. Do we understand the magnitude of this noble and far from simple task? Do we understand that it is we who, more resolutely than anyone, must now enter into battle against the forces of forgetfulness, against the slow and implacable flow of the river of time?' Grossman concludes: 'Are our labours worthy to stand beside the great literature of the past? Can they serve as an example to the future? Today we can only answer in the negative. And this makes it all the more painful when, in our literary milieu, we sometimes encounter a certain boastful presumptuousness, a lazy, self-satisfied contentment with the paltry results of hurried and superficial work.'[5]

Structurally, the Stalingrad dilogy is clearly modelled on *War and Peace*, and Grossman directly refers to Tolstoy several times. It would have been unlike Grossman, however, to imagine he could simply copy his predecessor. His first step was to question him. Grossman visited Tolstoy's Yasnaya Polyana estate in autumn 1941 and the following paragraphs from *Stalingrad* convey his own thoughts and feelings, as recorded in his wartime notebooks. Here, as in several other chapters, Commissar Krymov is Grossman's mouthpiece.

The storm that had flung open every door in Russia, that had driven people out of their warm homes and onto black autumn roads, sparing neither peaceful city apartments, nor village huts, nor hamlets deep in the forest, had treated Lev Tolstoy's home no less harshly. It too was preparing to leave, in rain and snow, along with the entire country, the entire people. Yasnaya Polyana was a living, suffering Russian home – one of thousand upon thousand of such homes. With absolute clarity, Krymov saw in his mind Bald Hills and the old, sick prince. The present merged with the past; the events of today were one with what Tolstoy described with such truth and power that it had become the supreme reality of a war that ran its course 130 years ago.

[...] And then Tolstoy's granddaughter Sofya Andreyevna came out of the house, calm, downcast, shivering a little in spite of the coat thrown over her shoulders. Once again Krymov did not know whether this was Princess Maria, going out for a last walk around the garden before the French arrived, or whether it was Lev Tolstoy's elderly granddaughter scrupulously fulfilling the demands of her fate: applying all her heart and soul, as she prepared to leave, to checking the accuracy of her grandfather's account of the princess's earlier departure from this same house.

At this point Krymov seems to see little difference between the two wars. Later, however, he comes to understand that the atrocities of the Second World War were on a different scale from anything imagined by Tolstoy:

Krymov looked at the wounded who had fallen by the wayside, at their grim, tormented faces, and wondered if these men would ever enter the pages of books. This was not a sight for those who wanted to clothe the war in fine robes. He remembered a night-time conversation with an elderly soldier whose face he had been unable to see. They had been lying in a gully, with only a great-coat to cover them. The writers of future books had better avoid listening to conversations like that. It was all very well for Tolstoy – he wrote his great and splendid book decades after 1812, when the pain felt in every heart had faded and only what was wise and bright was remembered.

Grossman, of course, knew only too well how very different his position was from Tolstoy's. Tolstoy had relatively few problems with censors, whereas Grossman battled editors and censors throughout his career. Much of what he wrote in the 1930s was bowdlerized. And from 1943 to 1946, along with the poet, journalist and novelist Ilya Ehrenburg, he had worked for the Jewish Anti-Fascist Committee on *The Black Book*, a collection of eyewitness accounts of the Shoah on Soviet and Polish soil. A Soviet edition of *The Black Book* had been ready for production in 1946, but it was never published; the first Russian-language edition was published only in 1980, in Jerusalem. Admitting that Jews constituted the overwhelming majority of those shot at Babi Yar and elsewhere might have led people to realize that members of other Soviet nationalities had been accomplices in the genocide. In any case, Stalin had no wish to emphasize Jewish suffering; anti-Semitism was a force he could exploit in order to bolster support for his regime.

In late spring 1945 Grossman had taken over from Ehrenburg as head of the editorial board of *The Black Book*. Grossman's mother had been shot at Berdichev and he himself had written the first pub-lished account of the Treblinka death camp. What he must have felt when *The Black Book* was aborted is hard to imagine. That he contin-ued doggedly working on *Stalingrad* – his other great post-war project – testifies to an extraordinary strength of character.

3.

It should come as no surprise that *Stalingrad* – written during the increasingly repressive and anti-Semitic last years of the Stalin regime – is haunted by the presence of what cannot be spoken about. During a meeting at Viktor Shtrum's institute, his colleague Maximov talks about his recent visit to German-occupied Czechoslovakia; he is appalled by what he has seen of the reality of fascism. The Nazi–Soviet non-aggression pact is still in force, and so the institute director and a colleague try to silence him. In the early typescripts of *Stalingrad* Viktor then encourages Maximov to write an article about fascism; Viktor hopes, audaciously, to publish it in the institute bulletin. Maximov writes no less than eighty pages and brings them round to Viktor's dacha. But Hitler invaded the Soviet Union only a week later, and neither Viktor nor Grossman's readers ever get to see so much as a word of this article. Viktor and Maximov do not even manage to talk about fascism together, even though both desperately want to.

A still more important document we never read is the last letter Viktor Shtrum receives from his mother Anna Semyonovna. This is as powerful a presence in *Stalingrad* as in *Life and Fate*. We do not – in *Stalingrad* – get to read Anna's words, but we read *about* her letter again and again. Grossman describes each stage of the letter's journey from the Berdichev ghetto to Viktor's dacha. Altogether, the letter is passed from hand to hand seven times. There are moments of black humour along the way. At one point the Old Bolshevik Mostovskoy takes the letter to the Stalingrad apartment of Viktor Shtrum's mother-in-law Alexandra Vladimirovna. When he hands it to Tamara, the young friend of the family who opens the door to him, she responds, 'Heavens, what filthy paper – anyone would think it's been lying in a cellar for the last two years.' And she promptly wraps it up 'in a sheet of the thick pink paper people use to make decorations for Christmas trees'.

Tamara then gives the package to Colonel Novikov, who is about to fly to Moscow. Novikov goes to Viktor's apartment, where he happens to interrupt a romantic tête-à-tête between Viktor and a pretty young neighbour by the name of Nina. Viktor drops the package into his briefcase, then forgets about it. Twenty-four hours later, at his dacha, he momentarily mistakes it for a bar of chocolate – intended, at least in the early typescripts, as a present for this same Nina.

The morning after finally reading the letter Viktor looks at himself in the mirror, expecting 'to see a haggard face with trembling lips'. He is surprised to find that he looks much the same as he did the day before.

From then on Viktor carries the letter about with him wherever he goes, but he is unable to talk about it. He can hardly even talk about it to himself: 'Viktor reread the letter again and again. Each time he felt the same shock as at the dacha, as if he were reading it for the first time. Perhaps his memory was instinctively resisting, unwilling and unable fully to take in something whose constant presence would make life unbearable.'

After the suppression of *The Black Book*, Grossman must have been well aware that he could not write freely about the events Viktor's mother describes. It seems likely that, rather than toning her letter down to make it acceptable, he took a conscious decision simply to leave a blank space, to replace her letter by an explicit, audible silence. If so, this is a powerful example of Grossman's unusual ability to make creative use of editorial interference.

On the surface, the Stalingrad dilogy has much in common with *War and Peace*. Both include general reflections on history, politics and philosophy. Both are divided between accounts of military and civilian life. The Stalingrad dilogy is structured around a single extended family much as *War and Peace* is structured around a group of families who become linked by marriage. There is, however, a fundamental difference. For all his appearance of being an omniscient and dispassionate narrator, Grossman's dilogy is more personal than *War and Peace*. Grossman, unlike Tolstoy, lived through the war he describes. He felt profoundly guilty about having allowed his mother to stay in Berdichev rather than insisting that she join him and his wife in Moscow. Her death troubled him for the rest of his life and the last letter from Anna Semyonovna – who is clearly a portrait of Grossman's mother – lies at the centre of *Stalingrad* like a deep hole. Or, in Viktor Shtrum's words, 'like an open grave'.

4.

Stalingrad is, amongst much else, an act of homage. One of Grossman's aims was to honour the dead – especially those who had been forgotten. He writes of those who died in the many small battles of the war's first months, 'There were men who, recognizing they were hopelessly outnumbered, fought only the more fiercely. These are the heroes of the first period of the war. Many are nameless and received no burial. It is to them, in large part, that Russia owes her salvation.' This may sound like orthodox Soviet rhetoric, but Grossman is, in fact, courting controversy. The brutality with which the Soviet authorities treated their own soldiers and their soldiers' families is hard for a Western reader to comprehend. Most of the men Grossman calls heroes would have been officially classified as 'missing' rather than 'killed in action'. If there were no witnesses to their death, they might – in the eyes of the authorities – simply have been deserters. Their families, therefore, would have received no pension and would have lived under a shadow for the rest of their lives.

Grossman also remembers more famous figures. In particular, he pays homage to the biologist and plant breeder Nikolay Vavilov, one of the most important scientists to fall victim to Stalin's purges. With surprising straightforwardness – hiding him, perhaps, in plain sight – Grossman gives his name to one of his most appealing characters, the wise and heroic Pyotr Vavilov whom we see receiving his call-up papers and setting out for the war in one of the novel's first chapters. The similarities between the famous scientist and Grossman's peasant soldier are clear, though they seem to have gone unnoticed. The cultural historian Rachel Polonsky writes of Nikolay Vavilov, 'He wanted [...] to improve the quality of grain, make better harvests, feed the Soviet people. [...] He believed in global research; he wanted to understand the plant world of the whole planet, the cultivation and migration of grain varieties – rye, wheat, rice and flax.'[6] Another historian writes, 'Vavilov was one of the first scientists to really listen to farmers – traditional farmers, peasant farmers around the world – and why they felt seed diversity was important in their fields.'[7] And Grossman says of his peasant soldier, 'Vavilov thought of the terrestrial globe as a single vast field that it was the people's responsibility to plough and sow [...] [He] would ask people about their lives in peacetime: "What's your land like? Does your wheat grow well? Are there droughts? And millet – do you sow millet? Do you get enough potatoes?"'

Later, in *Life and Fate*, Viktor Shtrum laments 'dozens of people who had left and never returned'; among them is Nikolay Vavilov. In *Stalingrad*, Grossman has to write more obliquely. Nevertheless, he takes pains to draw our attention to the significance of the name Vavilov. Soon after he has begun his training, one of Pyotr Vavilov's fellow soldiers asks him if he is related to yet another Vavilov, a regimental commissar. Pyotr replies that he just happens to have the same surname. The function of this seemingly rather pointless exchange is, of course, to summon up the memory of the murdered scientist.

Another of Grossman's allusions to Nikolay Vavilov is more complex. The manager of a prestigious Moscow hotel is proud that famous scientists have visited his hotel and he even remembers which room each stayed in, but he gets oddly confused when he mentions Vavilov, failing to remember that he was a biologist. Vavilov's ambition was to end world hunger, but in 1943 he died in prison of starvation. It is no wonder that the hotel manager gets confused – as if there is something he is unable to take in, or that he half-realizes it might be best not to remember.

Nikolay Vavilov remained well known; it was impossible for the authorities to erase his memory. There is another historical figure, however, of still greater importance to the Stalingrad dilogy, who has emerged from oblivion only recently. The German–Ukrainian scholar Tatiana Dettmer has established that Viktor Shtrum, Grossman's fictional nuclear physicist, is modelled on a real-life figure – Lev Yakovlevich Shtrum, one of the founders of Soviet nuclear physics. Lev Shtrum was born in 1890 and executed in 1936; like many of the victims of Stalin's purges, he was accused of 'Trotskyism'. After his death, his books and papers were removed from libraries and he was deleted from the historical record.

During the years Grossman lived and studied in Kiev (1914–19 and 1921–3), Lev Shtrum taught physics and mathematics at several Kiev educational institutes. Eventually he became the head of the Kiev University Department of Theoretical Physics. Historians of science have been surprisingly slow to resurrect such figures and it was only in 2012 that a group of Ukrainian and Russian scholars published an article about Lev Shtrum, drawing attention to a theory he formulated in the 1920s about particles moving at speeds faster than that of light. Until then, it had been believed that such particles were first hypothesized only in 1962.

Grossman calls our attention to the name Shtrum, much as he calls our attention to the name Vavilov. During a visit to Moscow, Colonel Novikov telephones a friend with whom he is staying. The friend, Colonel Ivanov, says there is a postcard for him. Novikov asks him to look at the signature and say who it is from. After a brief silence, 'clearly struggling to decipher the handwriting', Ivanov replies, 'Shturm, or maybe Shtrom, I'm not quite sure.' And in a memorable passage of *Life and Fate*,[8] Viktor Shtrum ponders a long, intimidating questionnaire: '1. Surname, name and patronymic ... Who was he, who was this man filling in a questionnaire at the dead of night? Shtrum, Viktor Pavlovich? His mother and father had [...] separated when Viktor was only two; and on his father's papers he had seen the name Pinkhus – not Pavel. So why was he Viktor Pavlovich? Did he know himself? Perhaps he was someone quite different – Goldman ... or Sagaydachny?' Sagaydachny (the name both of a seventeenth-century Cossack hetman and of an artist living in Kiev in the early 1920s) may be little more than a random name, but Alexander Goldman was another professor of physics, working in Kiev in the 1920s and 1930s. He was Lev Shtrum's supervisor and he taught at the institute where Grossman studied from 1921 to 1923.

Goldman was arrested in 1938, two years after Lev Shtrum. Unlike Lev Shtrum, however, he survived and was able to return to physics after the war. In Tatiana Dettmer's words, 'If we assume that Grossman knew the eventual fates of Lev Shtrum and Goldman, then Viktor's words in the novel about whether he was Shtrum, rather than Goldman, take on a deeper significance. Both Goldman and Lev Shtrum were victims of Stalin's Terror. Goldman, however, survived, while Lev Shtrum did not – except in so far as he is resurrected in the pages of Grossman's novel.'

There are many parallels between the lives of the fictional Shtrum and the historical Shtrum. Both were nuclear physicists with a particular interest in Relativity; both were also concerned with broader social and political questions. Like Viktor Shtrum, Lev Shtrum had two children – a son (called Viktor!) from his first marriage and a daughter from his second marriage. Lev Shtrum would have certainly known most of the physicists whom Viktor Shtrum meets or thinks about in the pages of *Life and Fate*.[9] And the conflicts Grossman describes in Viktor's Physics Institute – the demotion of important scientists and laboratory workers and the promotion of less talented but more servile figures – seem to be closely modelled on real conflicts in the Moscow University Physics Faculty in 1944.

We know that Grossman himself was deeply interested in physics from his teenage years to his death. In a letter to his father he wrote, 'From when I was fourteen to when I was twenty [i.e. when he was living and studying in Kiev], I was a passionate devotee of the exact sciences and was not interested in anything else.'[10] Grossman's wartime notebooks include a diagram of a chain reaction.[11] Like Lev Shtrum, Grossman passionately admired Einstein; an illustration in John and Carol Garrard's biography of Grossman shows two photographs of Einstein on a bookshelf in his study. Similarly, one of the few surviving photographs of Lev Shtrum shows him in *his* study, where there is one photograph of Einstein and one of Max Planck.

Two of Grossman's school friends, Lev and Grigory Levin, were cousins of Lev Shtrum. And in a letter to his father in 1929, Grossman mentions visiting Lev Shtrum and borrowing money from him – which suggests that he knew Lev Shtrum very well. There is, as yet, no incontrovertible documentary evidence for this, but it is highly probable that, when Grossman was still living and studying in Kiev, Lev

Shtrum was one of his teachers. This vivid passage from *Stalingrad*, an account of lectures given by Viktor Shtrum's mentor Chepyzhin, may well be Grossman's evocation of lectures that he himself was inspired by: 'These formulae seemed full of human content; they could have been passionate declarations of faith, doubt or love. Chepyzhin reinforced this impression by scattering question marks, ellipses and triumphant exclamation marks over the board. It was painful, when the lecture was over, to watch the attendant rub out all these radicals, integrals, differentials and trigonometric signs, all these alphas, deltas, epsilons and thetas that human will and intelligence had marshalled into a single united regiment. Like a valuable manuscript, this blackboard should surely have been preserved for posterity.' If Grossman did indeed have Lev Shtrum in mind, this last sentence is all the more poignant; Grossman *has* preserved this blackboard for posterity.

Grossman bestowed on the central figure of his dilogy the name, the profession, the family, the interests and even the friends of an 'enemy of the people'. Grossman was anything but naive; he would have known the danger to which he was exposing himself and his novel. One can only conclude that Lev Shtrum must have been a figure of extraordinary importance to him, that he must have felt deeply indebted to him.[12]

5.

In the aftermath of the war, Grossman may have hoped that his novel would play a healing, conciliatory role. Bitter arguments had erupted as to whether it was the Soviet infantry or the Soviet artillery that saved Stalingrad. Grossman goes to some length to establish that neither could have achieved anything without the other.

Grossman takes a similarly balanced line with regard to a more important and still unresolved question. He insists that the Red Army's absolute determination not to retreat any further arose spontaneously among the rank-and-file soldiers *at the same time* as Stalin issued his draconian 'Not One Step Back' Order of 28 July 1942. Grossman sees the soldiers' courage and patriotism as genuine; he would certainly not agree with those Western historians who have suggested that they fought with such desperation simply because they were terrified of being shot by the Soviet security police if they were seen to desert. But Grossman also sees Stalin's Order as crucial; he sees Stalin as giving voice to the soldiers' patriotism and so reinforcing it.

In other respects, however, Grossman is more challenging. His most sustained argument in *Stalingrad* is with Maxim Gorky. In 1932, Grossman was struggling to publish his first novel, *Glückauf*, set in a mining community in the Donbass; an editor had recently told him that some aspects of the novel were 'counter-revolutionary'. Gorky was, at the time, the most influential figure in the Soviet literary establishment, and Grossman tried to enlist his support. In his first letter to Gorky, Grossman wrote, 'I described what I saw while living and working for three years at mine Smolyanka-11. I wrote the truth. It may be a harsh truth. But the truth can never be counter-revolutionary.' Gorky replied at length, clearly recognizing Grossman's gifts but criticizing him with regard to his attitude to truth: 'It is not enough to say, "I wrote the truth." The author should ask himself two questions: "First, which truth? And second, why?" We know that there are two truths and that, in our world, it is the vile and dirty truth of the past that quantitatively preponderates. But this truth is being replaced by another truth that has been born and continues to grow [...] The author sees the truth of the past quite well, but he doesn't have a very clear understanding of what to do with it. The author truthfully depicts the obtuseness of coal miners, their brawls and drunkenness, all that predominates in his – the author's – field of vision. This is, of course, truth – but it is a disgusting and tormenting truth. It is a truth we must struggle against and mercilessly extirpate.'[13]

In *Stalingrad*, Marusya – a candidate member of the Communist Party – comes out with precisely the same thoughts while arguing with her younger sister Zhenya, who is an artist: 'Instead of strange daubs no one can understand, you should paint posters. But I know what you'll say next. You'll start going on about truth to life ... How many times do I have to tell you that there are two truths? There's the truth of the reality forced on us by the accursed past. And there's the truth of the reality that will defeat that past. It's this second truth, the truth of the future, that *I* want to live by.' At this point, Sofya Osipovna, a surgeon and friend of the family, intervenes. 'No, Marusya [...] You're wrong. I can tell you as a surgeon that there is one truth, not two. When I cut someone's leg off, I don't know two truths. If we start playing at two truths, we're in trouble. And in war too – above all, when things are as bad as they are today – there is only one truth. It's a bitter truth, but it's a truth that can save us. If the Germans enter Stalingrad, you'll learn that if you chase after two truths, you won't catch either. It'll be the end of you.'

Despite his earlier criticisms, Gorky evidently played a central role in orchestrating Grossman's remarkably successful literary debut in 1934.[14] Like Lev Shtrum, he is a mentor to whom Grossman felt deeply indebted. Unlike Lev Shtrum, however, Gorky is a very ambiguous figure. In the aftermath of the Revolution his publishing projects rescued many writers from starvation, yet from 1928 until his death in 1936 he was complicit in the most brutal aspects of Stalinism. It is possible that Grossman's awareness of his debt to Gorky made him all the more determined to continue to write truthfully himself – not, like Gorky, to be seduced by the privileges that accompany power and success. David Ortenberg, the editor of *Red Star*, the main Soviet army newspaper, remembers arguing with Grossman about whether or not it was really necessary for the hero of one of his works to die. Grossman replied, 'We have to follow the ruthless truth of war.'[15]

6.

The Soviet regime needed a Soviet Tolstoy. After 1945, however, Stalin also needed a new, preferably internal, enemy to help justify his dictatorship. The choice of enemy was simple enough; anti-Semitism had always been widespread in Russia and Ukraine. Grossman – both a Jew and a candidate for the role of the new Tolstoy – was positioned on a dangerous fault line.[16]

The question of who to choose as the Soviet Tolstoy was, in any case, fraught. There had always been rivalry between the Soviet Writers' Union and the Agit-Prop Department (the Department of Agitation and Propaganda) of the Communist Party's Central Committee. In this instance the Agit-Prop Department was backing the now-forgotten novelist Mikhail Bubyonnov, while Alexander Fadeyev (chairman of the Writers' Union) and Alexander Tvardovsky (chief editor of the journal *Novy Mir*) were backing Grossman. For all their political acumen, Fadeyev and Tvardovsky evidently underestimated how fiercely the anti-Jewish campaign would intensify. They began publishing *For a Just Cause* during the very month – July 1952 – when most of the leading members of the Jewish Anti-Fascist Committee were undergoing secret trial, before their execution in August.

Initial reviews of *For a Just Cause* were enthusiastic and on 13 October 1952 the Prose Section of the Soviet Writers' Union nominated the novel for a Stalin Prize.[17] On 13 January 1953, however, an article appeared in *Pravda* titled 'Vicious Spies and Killers Passing Themselves off as Doctors and Professors'. A group of the country's most eminent doctors – most of them Jewish – had allegedly been plotting to poison Stalin and other members of the political and military leadership. These ludicrous accusations were intended to serve as a prelude to a more general purge of Soviet Jews.

A month later, on 13 February, Bubyonnov published a denunciatory review of *For a Just Cause*. A campaign against Grossman swiftly gathered momentum. Major newspapers printed articles with such titles as 'A Novel that Distorts the Image of Soviet People', 'On a False Path' and 'In a Distorting Mirror'. In response, Tvardovsky and the *Novy Mir* editorial board as a whole duly acknowledged that publication of the novel had been a grave mistake.

Soon after this Grossman committed an act of betrayal that troubled him for the rest of his life: he agreed to sign a letter calling for the execution of the 'Killer Doctors'. He may have thought – perhaps not unreasonably – that the doctors were certain to be executed anyway and that the letter was worth signing because it affirmed that the Jewish people *as a whole* were innocent. Whatever his reasons, Grossman at once regretted what he had done. A passage in *Life and Fate* based on this incident ends with Viktor Shtrum (who has just signed a similar letter) praying to his dead mother to help him never to show such weakness again.

Grossman's act of betrayal did nothing to ease his position. The campaign against him intensified. Mikhail Sholokhov, the most eminent Soviet writer of the time, had previously expressed admiration for *Stalingrad*.[18] Now, however, he allowed Bubyonnov to quote him at an important meeting as saying, 'Grossman's novel is spittle in the face of the Russian people.'[19] Fadeyev published an article full of what Grossman described as 'mercilessly severe political accusations'. *Voenizdat*, the military publishing house that had agreed to publish *For a Just Cause* in book form, asked Grossman to return his advance – in view of what Grossman caustically referred to as 'the book's now unexpectedly discovered anti-Soviet essence'.[20] Fortunately for Grossman, Stalin died on 5 March 1953. But for this, he too – like many other writers with links to the Jewish Anti-Fascist Committee – might well have been executed.

Denunciations of Grossman and his novel continued for another few weeks, but then the campaign petered out. In mid-June *Voenizdat*, with Fadeyev's encouragement, repeated their original offer to publish *For a Just Cause*. Grossman had clearly known very well, from the beginning, how difficult it would be to publish the novel and he recorded all relevant official conversations, letters and meetings in a fifteen-page document titled 'Diary of the Journey of the Manuscript of the Novel *For a Just Cause* through Publishing Houses'. The final, laconic entry in this diary reads '26 October 1954. The book is on sale on the Arbat, in the shop "The Military Book".'

7.

Almost every step of Grossman's career – even after his death – has been marked by long delays and protracted battles. Editors, scholars and literary critics seem to have responded to the painful and intractable nature of much of Grossman's subject matter with an equal intractability of their own. A Russian edition of *Everything Flows* was published in Frankfurt in 1970; a first English translation was published in 1972. Both attracted little attention – though *Everything Flows* is one of Grossman's finest works, remarkable, above all, for its searing account of the Terror Famine in Ukraine in 1933 and its bold reinterpretation of several centuries of Russian history.

Life and Fate is now well known, but it too was slow to reach the reader. Even after the satirist Vladimir Voinovich had smuggled a microfilmed text to the West, it took almost five years to find a publisher for the first Russian-language edition – mainly, it seems, because of personal and political rivalries among Russian émigrés. Grossman's friends and admirers were bewildered and shocked. In 1961, after what he always referred to as the 'arrest' of *Life and Fate*, Grossman said it was as if he had been 'strangled in a dark corner'. Dismayed at being unable to find a publisher in the late 1970s, Voinovich said it was as if Grossman were being strangled a second time.

In 1980, however, the Russian text of *Life and Fate* was finally published, by L'Age d'Homme in Lausanne. At a conference in 2003 in Turin, Vladimir Dimitrijevic, the editor who accepted the novel, said he had sensed at once that Grossman was portraying 'a world in three dimensions' and that he was one of those rare writers whose aim was 'not to prove something but to make people live something'. He could equally well have said this of *Stalingrad*.

The microfilms of *Life and Fate* were made from a copy of the typescript that Grossman had entrusted to the poet Semyon Lipkin and which Lipkin had kept in his dacha near Moscow. There is a curious parallel between the slow, faltering journey made by the text of *Life and Fate*, from a dacha near Moscow to a Swiss publishing house, and the journey made in *Stalingrad* by Anna Semyonovna's letter, from the Berdichev ghetto to a dacha near Moscow. In each case there were delays and misunderstandings, and a strange lack of interest – at least initially – when the document first reached its destination. Even after the first publication of translations of *Life and Fate* in the mid-1980s, Grossman's international reputation grew only slowly.

Grossman is now seen as one of the greatest novelists of the last century – and Anna Semyonovna's letter is probably the best-known chapter in his entire *oeuvre*. Nevertheless, there is still much about Grossman and his work that we do not know. Few of his works are available – even in Russian – in definitive texts. His first novel, *Glückauf* (1934), is generally considered dull and has never been republished. It is entirely possible, however, that Grossman's original manuscript is more interesting than the published text. We know that the novel was heavily censored and that this appalled Grossman, yet no one – as far as I know – has seriously studied the manuscript.

Even more surprisingly, there is still no definitive Russian text of *Life and Fate*. In 2013, to much fanfare, the Russian security services released the typescripts confiscated by the KGB in 1961. These typescripts, too, have hardly been studied.

I hope one day to revise my translation of *Life and Fate* in the light of a definitive Russian text. For now, though, it is a joy to be able to bring out a version of *Stalingrad* that is more complete than any existing edition, in Russian or in any other language. This version is by no means definitive, but it includes a great deal of important material, from the earliest and boldest of Grossman's typescripts, that has never before been published.

Robert Chandler
London, 2018

PART I

1

On 29 April 1942 Benito Mussolini's train pulled into Salzburg station, now hung with both Italian and German flags.

After the official welcome in the station building, Mussolini and his entourage were driven to Schloss Klessheim, former summer residence of the archbishops of Salzburg.

There, in huge chilly halls newly refurnished with loot from France, Hitler and Mussolini were to hold another of their meetings – along with Ribbentrop, Marshal Keitel, General Jodl, Galeazzo Ciano, Marshal Cavallero, Dino Alfieri the Italian ambassador in Berlin, and other senior German and Italian officers, diplomats and politicians.

The two dictators, the self-styled masters of Europe, had met each time Hitler was preparing some new human catastrophe. Their tête-à-tête meetings, on the border between the Austrian and Italian Alps, heralded major political developments and the movements of vast motorized armies. The brief newspaper bulletins about these meetings filled every heart with foreboding.

Fascism had enjoyed seven years of triumph, in Africa as well as in Europe, and both dictators would probably have found it difficult to list the many major and minor victories thanks to which they now ruled over vast expanses of territory and hundreds of millions of people. Without bloodshed, Hitler had reoccupied the Rhineland and then annexed Austria and the Sudetenland. In 1939 he had invaded Poland and routed the armies of Marshal Rydz-Śmigły. In 1940 he had defeated France, avenging Germany's defeat in the First World War; he had also occupied Luxembourg, Belgium and the Netherlands, and crushed Denmark and Norway. He had expelled Britain from the European mainland, driving her troops out of both Norway and France. In the first months of 1941, Hitler had defeated both Greece and Yugoslavia. Measured against these extraordinary successes, Mussolini's brigandry in Albania and Abyssinia looked petty and provincial.

The fascist empires had further extended their power in Africa, seizing Algeria, Tunisia and ports on the Atlantic Ocean. To the east, they threatened Cairo and Alexandria.

Japan, Hungary, Romania and Finland were all in military alliance with Germany and Italy. Powerful elements in the ruling circles of Spain, Portugal, Turkey and Bulgaria were also complicit in fascism.

In the ten months since Germany had first invaded the Soviet Union, Hitler's forces had seized not only Estonia, Latvia and Lithuania but also Belorussia, Moldavia and Ukraine. They were in control of all the provinces of Pskov, Smolensk, Oryol and Kursk, and large parts of the provinces of Leningrad, Kalinin, Tula and Voronezh.

The military-industrial machine created by Hitler had absorbed vast riches: French steelworks, French engineering and car factories, the iron mines of Lorraine, Belgian coal mines and steel furnaces, Dutch precision mechanics and radio factories, Austrian metalworking companies, the Skoda arms manufacturer in Czechoslovakia, the Romanian oil industry, Norwegian iron mines, Spanish tungsten and mercury mines, and the textile factories of Łódź. And all over occupied Europe the long drive belt of the 'new order' was spinning the wheels of hundreds of thousands of smaller businesses of every kind.

In twenty countries, mills were grinding barley and wheat, and ploughs turning over fields, for the fascist occupiers. In three oceans and five seas fishermen were catching fish to supply fascist cities. Hydraulic presses were at work in plantations throughout Europe and northern Africa, pressing grape juice, olive oil, and flax and sunflower oil. A fine harvest was ripening on the branches of millions of apple, plum, orange and lemon trees; fruit already ripe was being packed into wooden crates stamped with a black eagle. The Reich's iron fingers were milking Danish, Dutch and Polish cattle, shearing sheep in Hungary and the Balkans.

Dominion over vast areas of Europe and Africa appeared to be strengthening the power of fascism with every year, every day, every hour.

With sickening servility, those who had betrayed freedom, goodness and truth were predicting the defeat of all Hitler's opponents and proclaiming Hitlerism to be a truly new and higher order.

The new order established by Hitler throughout conquered Europe had seen the modernization and renewal of all the methods and techniques of violence that had arisen in the course of thousands of years of the rule of the few over the many.

This meeting in Salzburg heralded a major German offensive in southern Russia.

3

2

Hitler and Mussolini began their meeting in their usual way, displaying all the gold and enamel of their false teeth in broad, friendly smiles and saying how delighted they were that circumstances once again allowed them to meet.

Mussolini at once thought that the past winter and the cruel defeat outside Moscow had left their mark on Hitler. There was more grey in his hair, and not just at his temples. The dark rings under his eyes had become more pronounced and his general complexion was pale and unhealthy; only his trench coat still looked fresh. All in all, the Führer looked grimmer and harsher than ever.

Hitler for his part thought that in another five or six years the Duce would be looking wholly decrepit. His short legs would grow still shorter, his heavy jaw still heavier and his old man's belly would protrude still further. There was a terrible mismatch between his dwarf's body and his huge chin, face and forehead. His intelligent dark eyes, however, remained cruel and penetrating.

The Führer, still smiling, complimented the Duce, saying he looked younger than ever. The Duce, in turn, complimented the Führer; he could see at once that he was in excellent health and good spirits.

They began to talk about the winter campaign. Mussolini, rubbing his hands, as if the mere thought of the Moscow winter had been enough to chill them, congratulated Hitler on his victory over the Russian snow and ice, over those three great Russian generals: December, January and February. His voice was solemn; he had clearly prepared his words in advance, just as he had prepared his fixed smile.

They agreed that, despite the losses of both men and equipment during what, even by Russian standards, had proved an unprecedentedly severe winter, the German divisions had suffered no repeat of Napoleon's experience at Berezina; the invader of 1941 was evidently a superior strategist to the invader of 1812.[21] The two leaders went on to discuss the overall outlook.

Now that winter was over, there was nothing that could save Russia – the only remaining enemy of the new order on the European continent.

The impending offensive would bring the Soviets to their knees; it would cut off the supply of oil to factories in the Urals and would leave Soviet agriculture, the Soviet air force and the Red Army without fuel. It would bring about the fall of Moscow. Soon after the defeat of Russia, the British would capitulate too, overwhelmed by air raids and submarine warfare. The United States would do little to help them. General Motors, US Steel and Standard Oil had no wish to increase production. On the contrary, it was in their interests to limit production and so be in a position to increase prices. It was the same with every other company producing steel, magnesium, artificial rubber, aircraft and engines for military vehicles. And Churchill, in any case, hated his Russian ally more than his German enemy; in his senile mind he no longer understood who he was fighting. Neither Hitler nor Mussolini had anything to say about Roosevelt, that 'absurd paralytic'. They did, however, have something to say about the situation in France – and their views were identical. Although Hitler had recently reorganized the Vichy cabinet, anti-German sentiment was intensifying and there was the possibility of French treachery. But this was no cause for alarm: once Germany had its hands free in the east, it would be able to establish peace and order in the rest of Europe.

Hitler said with a little smile that he would, in any case, soon recall Heydrich from Czechoslovakia and send him to France to restore order there.[22] He then turned to African matters. Without a hint of reproach, he listed the various units comprising Rommel's now reinforced Afrika Korps, sent to support the Italians.[23] Mussolini understood that Hitler was clearing the ground, that he was about to move on to the main topic of their meeting – the impending offensive in Russia – but that he had felt obliged first to emphasize his readiness to support the Italians in Africa.

And Hitler did indeed soon begin to talk about Russia and the coming offensive. What he did not say – and evidently preferred not to admit even to himself – was that the hard battles and cruel losses of the previous winter had made it impossible for the German army to conduct a simultaneous offensive along all three axes: in the south, in the north and in the centre. Hitler believed his plans for a southern campaign to be the product of his own free will; he still thought that he and he alone was determining the course of events.

He told Mussolini that the Soviets had suffered huge losses. They no longer received supplies of Ukrainian wheat. Leningrad was under continuous artillery bombardment. The Baltic States had been wrested from Russia's grasp once and for all. German armies had already advanced far beyond the Dnieper. The coal mines, the chemical and metal-processing plants of the Donbass were in the hands of the Fatherland. German fighters now flew over Moscow. The Soviet Union had lost Belorussia, most of Crimea, and many provinces in the heart of the country that had been part of Russia for a thousand years. Russia had been driven from such ancient cities as Smolensk, Pskov, Oryol, Kursk, Vyazma and Rzhev. All that remained – Hitler continued – was to deliver the final blow. But if it were truly to be a final blow, then it must be delivered with fantastic strength. The generals in the strategy department thought it would be a mistake to advance simultaneously on both Stalingrad and the Caucasus. But he himself thought otherwise: if, during the previous year, he had had the strength to wage war in Africa, to pound Britain from the air, to paralyse American shipping with his submarine fleet and at the same time to advance swiftly into the heart of Russia along the whole of a 3,000-kilometre front, why should he hesitate today? Why should he hesitate when the supine weakness of Britain and America freed him to concentrate such vast power against a single section of a single front? The new offensive had to be overwhelming. Once again, Hitler would redeploy large forces from France, Belgium and the Netherlands, leaving only the divisions required to patrol the Atlantic and North Sea coasts. The troops transferred to the east would be regrouped; the Northern, North-western and Western Army Groups would be playing a passive role – the force of the impact was to be concentrated in the south-east.

Never, perhaps, had so much artillery, so many tank and infantry divisions, so many bomber and fighter aircraft been brought together. This seemingly limited offensive would acquire universal significance. It was the final, definitive stage of the advance of National Socialism. It would determine for ever the fate not only of Europe but of the world. The Italian army, therefore, should play a worthy role in the offensive. And not only the Italian army, but also Italian industry, Italian agriculture and the whole Italian people.

Mussolini was well aware that these amicable meetings were always accompanied by considerable material demands. Hitler's last sentences meant the despatch to the Eastern front of hundreds of thousands of Italian soldiers, a sharp increase in the Wehrmacht's requirement for Italian grains and other foods, and additional forced recruitment of Italian workers for German companies.

After their tête-à-tête, Hitler followed Mussolini out of the room and walked beside him through the large hall. Mussolini glanced with a pang of envy at the German sentries. Their shoulders and uniforms seemed cast from steel – though their eyes took on a look of ecstatic tension as the Führer walked past. Somehow the splendid colours of the Italian army paled before the grey of these sentries' uniforms and of Hitler's trench coat – a dull monotone grey, similar to that of military vehicles or the hull of a battleship, that appeared to embody the power of the German army. Was this self-assured commander-in-chief really the same man as the awkward figure who, during their first meeting in Venice eight years ago, had made the crowd laugh as he stumbled during a parade of the Guardia and Carabinieri? Wearing a white raincoat, old shoes and a crumpled black hat, the Führer had looked like some provincial actor or painter – while the Duce himself had worn an officer's cloak, a plumed helmet and the silver-embroidered uniform of a Roman general.

Hitler's power and success never ceased to astonish Mussolini. There was something unreal, something that didn't make sense, about the triumph of this Bohemian psychopath. In his heart of hearts Mussolini saw Hitler's success as a bizarre freak, an aberration on the part of world history.

That evening Mussolini talked for a few minutes with his son-in-law, Galeazzo Ciano. The two men had gone out for a short walk in the charming garden – it was, after all, possible that their friend and ally might have installed secret Siemens microphones in the rooms of the schloss. Mussolini expressed his irritation: once again, he had had no choice but to comply with Hitler. It was events in the godforsaken Don or Kalmyk steppes – rather than in the Mediterranean or in North Africa – that would now determine his own success or failure in establishing the Great Italian Empire. Ciano asked about the Führer's health. Mussolini replied that he seemed strong, though somewhat exhausted – and, as always, had been unbelievably verbose.

Ciano said that Ribbentrop had been courteous and solicitous, to the point of seeming almost unsure of himself. Mussolini replied that the war's final outcome would soon be decided; everything would be clear by the end of the summer.

'I fear,' said Ciano, 'that any failure of the Führer's will be our failure too. But whether or not we will share in any final and definitive success of the Führer's is another matter. I have my doubts, and have done for some time.'

Mussolini said he considered such scepticism unjustified. He then retired to his room.

On 30 April, after breakfast, Hitler and Mussolini met for a second time, in the presence of generals, field marshals and both countries' ministers of foreign affairs. Hitler was in an excited state. Without so much as a glance at the papers in front of him, he cited details about the deployment of German divisions and statistics showing the power of German industry. He spoke for an hour and forty minutes without a pause, occasionally licking his lips with his large tongue, as if his own words tasted sweet to him. He touched on a huge variety of questions: *Krieg, Frieden, Weltgeschichte, Religion, Politik, Philosophie, deutsche Seele* ...[24] He spoke quickly and forcefully, but calmly, seldom raising his voice. He smiled only once, his face twitching as he said, 'Soon the laughter of Jews will fall silent forever.' He raised his fist for a moment but quickly unclenched it and let his hand drop to the table. Mussolini frowned; the Führer's rages scared him.

Hitler moved several times to questions about life after the war. Expecting a successful summer offensive to put a quick end to the war on the European mainland, he was devoting much thought to questions about the peace that would follow: to questions about social laws and the position of religion – and about the National Socialist science and art that would at last be free to develop in a new, purified Europe, now purged of Communists, Democrats and Jews.

And it was indeed time to consider such matters. In September or October, when the final collapse of Soviet Russia marked the beginning of a new era of peace, when the last blaze was extinguished and the dust of the last battle in Russian history had settled, there would be countless questions demanding urgent resolution: about the peacetime organization of German life, about the administrative divisions and political status of the defeated countries, about restrictions to be placed on the legal rights and entitlement to education of inferior nations, about breeding and reproduction control, about the transfer of human masses from the former Soviet Union to carry out restoration and reconstruction work in the Fatherland and the organization of long-term camps for these masses, about the dismantling and liquidation of industrial units in Moscow, Leningrad and the Urals, and even such minor but inescapable tasks as the renaming of Russian and French cities.

There was one peculiarity about the Führer's manner of speech: he seemed hardly to care whether or not people were listening to him. He spoke with relish, as if taking pleasure in moving his large lips, his gaze directed at some point between the ceiling and the top of the white satin drapes hanging over the dark oak doors. Now and then he would come out with a resonant sentence: 'The Aryan is the Prometheus of mankind'; 'Violence is the mother of order and the source of all true greatness – I have restored to violence its true meaning'; 'We have now established the eternal dominion of the Aryan Prometheus over all human and other earthly beings.'

He would say these things with a radiant look, gasping excitedly, almost convulsively.

Mussolini frowned. He made a quick movement of his head, looking to one side, as if trying to see his own ear. He twice looked anxiously at his wristwatch – he too liked to have his say. During these meetings it was always the younger man, the disciple, who played the leading role; the Duce's only consolation lay in his awareness of the superiority of his own intelligence, but this made it all the more painful to have to remain silent for long periods. He was constantly aware that Ribbentrop was watching him; the look in the German diplomat's eyes was friendly and respectful, but also penetrating. Sitting next to Ribbentrop was Ciano. He was leaning back in his armchair and watching the Führer's lips: might he say something about the North African colonies and the future Franco-Italian frontier? On this occasion, however, the Führer did not descend to such details. Alfieri, who had heard Hitler speak more often than most Italians, was looking up at the same spot as the Führer – just above the top of the white drapes, with an expression of quiet submissiveness. General Jodl, sitting on a distant couch, was dozing, while somehow maintaining a look of delicate attentiveness. Marshal Keitel – who was sitting directly opposite Hitler and so could not afford to fall asleep – kept throwing back his massive head, adjusting his monocle and, without looking at anyone, scowling morosely. Marshal Cavallero seemed to be drinking in every word Hitler said. He was craning his neck, his head cocked a little to one side, and listening with an expression of obsequious joy. From time to time he gave a quick nod.

To all those who had already attended one of these occasions, this meeting in Salzburg seemed in no way exceptional.

As during previous meetings, the main topic of discussion was European politics and the progress of the war. And the Führer and the Duce behaved the same as always: those close to them were well aware of each man's attitude – by now only too settled and fixed – towards the other. They knew that Mussolini felt he was now the subordinate partner and that he resented this. It upset him that new initiatives and decisions always came from Berlin, rather than from Rome. It upset him never to be asked in advance for his thoughts about the joint declarations he was so solemnly and respectfully asked to sign. It upset him to be woken just before dawn, when he was soundly asleep, by telephone calls from the Führer, whose attitude towards the patriarch of fascism seemed surprisingly casual.

Galeazzo Ciano also understood that Mussolini looked down on Hitler. It comforted him to consider the Führer a fool. The Führer's power derived merely from numbers, from statistical superiority: German industry and the German army were bigger than Italian industry and the Italian army. Mussolini's strength, on the other hand, came from Mussolini himself. The Duce even enjoyed making fun of Italian weakness and pusillanimity; these qualities set off all the more clearly the personal power of a leader who was fighting to make a hammer out of a people who for sixteen centuries had played the role of an anvil.

The members of the two leaders' entourages, alert to their masters' every look and gesture, noted that nothing had changed between the Führer and the Duce; both superficially and at a deeper level, their relations were the same as during previous meetings. The external surroundings appeared equally similar: Schloss Klesshcim, like other buildings where the leaders had met, was endowed with a severe grandeur appropriate to the protagonists' extraordinary power and military might. Hitler's speeches, admittedly, differed in one small respect: here in Salzburg he was talking for the first time about a final, decisive military operation. Apart from Soviet armies that had already retreated a huge distance, Hitler now had no armed adversary on the European mainland. This difference might have been noted by some future National Socialist historian. This historian might also have noted that Hitler seemed more self-confident than ever.

Nevertheless, there was a difference of far greater significance. The Führer had always been eager for war; he had always been intoxicated by war. In Salzburg, however, he spoke insistently and with remarkable confidence about peace, so betraying an unconscious fear of the war he had himself unleashed. For six years Hitler, through a combination of satanic violence and astute bluffing, had won victory after victory. He had been certain that the only real force, the only true strength in the world was that of his own army and his own empire; everything opposed to him was imaginary, arbitrary and insubstantial. Only his own fist possessed weight and reality. His powerful fist had smashed through the military, political and constitutional settlements agreed at Versailles; these proved no stronger than gossamer. Hitler sincerely believed that by giving free rein to primitive brutality he had opened

10

up new avenues of history. And he had demonstrated all too clearly the impotence of the Treaty of Versailles, first violating individual clauses, next trampling the whole treaty into the ground, and then rewriting it in front of the American president and the prime ministers of Britain and France.

He reintroduced compulsory military service and began to recreate the navy, army and air force forbidden by Versailles. He remilitarized the Rhineland, bringing in 30,000 soldiers. These 30,000 men turned out to be enough to alter the apparently decisive outcome of the First World War; there had been no need for an army of millions or masses of heavy weapons. Hitler then struck blow after blow. One after another, he destroyed the new states of post-Versailles Europe: first Austria, then Czechoslovakia, Poland and Yugoslavia.

But the greater Hitler's success, the blinder he became. He was unable to conceive that not everything in the world was propaganda or political posturing, that there might be other real forces in the world and that there might exist governments able to do more than transmit their own impotence to their workers, soldiers and sailors. Hitler was unable to conceive that his fist could not smash through everything.

German armies had invaded Soviet Russia on 22 June 1941. Hitler's initial success blinded him to the true nature of the granite, of the spiritual and material forces, that he had chosen to attack. These were not imaginary forces; they were the forces of a great nation that had already laid the foundations of a future world. That first summer offensive, followed by the winter's devastating losses, bled the German army and placed overwhelming demands on the military-industrial complex. Hitler was therefore unable, in 1942, to do as he had done the previous year, to advance simultaneously in the south, in the north and in the centre. War had become slow and heavy; it was no longer a pleasure. But it was impossible for Hitler not to advance; far from being a strength, this was what doomed him. He began to tire of the war, to feel afraid of it, yet it went on growing and growing. He himself, ten months earlier, had ignited this war, but he no longer had any power over it; it was impossible for him to extinguish it. The war was spreading like a forest fire; its scope, its rage, its strength and duration were constantly growing. No matter what the price, Hitler had to bring it to an end, but it is easier to achieve initial success in a war than to bring it to a successful conclusion.

This new note in his speeches was a clear pointer to the true course of the historical forces that in time led to the death of almost everyone who took part in this fateful Salzburg meeting.

3

Pyotr Semyonovich Vavilov's call-up papers arrived at the worst possible moment. Had the commissariat given him another six weeks, or a couple of months, he would have been able to leave his family with enough wheat and firewood to see them through the coming year.

When he looked out and saw Masha Balashova crossing the street with a slip of white paper, walking straight towards his house, he felt something go tight inside him. Without even pausing, she went past the window. For a second Vavilov thought she must be going somewhere else, but then he remembered that there were no young men left in any of the neighbouring houses and that old men do not receive call-up papers. And he was right – the next thing he heard was a loud crash in the entrance room.[25] Masha had stumbled in the half-dark. She had knocked against the yoke – and it had fallen onto the bucket.

Masha sometimes came round in the evenings. It wasn't long since she'd finished school; she'd been in the same class as his daughter Nastya, and the two girls often went around together. Usually she addressed Vavilov as 'Uncle Pyotr', but this morning she merely said, 'Please sign in receipt of this letter.' And she did not ask to speak to Nastya.

Vavilov sat down and signed his name.

'So that's that,' he said, as he got to his feet.

These three syllables related not only to his signature in Masha's delivery book. Vavilov was thinking of his whole life here in this hut, his life with his family – a life now suddenly ended. The home he now had to leave seemed good and kind. The stove – which had let out a lot of smoke in the raw days of March, with one side now convex, swollen from old age, with bare bricks that had lost their whitewash – seemed splendid and glorious, a living being who had spent her whole life beside him.[26] Entering the house in winter, he had often stood in front of the stove, breathing in her warmth as he stretched out his numb fingers, and at night, spreading his sheepskin coat across her, he had lain on her warm bricks, knowing where would be hotter and where cooler. Getting up early to go out to work, he had gone up to the stove in the dark and felt, with practised hands, for his matchbox and his foot cloths, which he had left there to dry overnight.[27] And everything – the white curtains on the windows, the table with its black half-moons left by hot pans, the little bench by the door where his wife sat to peel potatoes, the chinks between floorboards through which the children spied on the lives of the mice and cockroaches below, the flatiron, so black from soot that in the morning you couldn't make it out at all inside the warm dark of the stove, the windowsill, where there was a towel on a nail and a little red houseplant in a pot – everything was now dearer than ever to him, dear and precious in a way that only living beings can be dear and precious.

Vavilov had three children. Alyosha, the eldest, had already left for the war. Still living at home were his daughter Nastya and little four-year-old Vanya, who was both very wise and very silly and whom Vavilov called 'Mister Samovar'. Puffing and snuffling as he went about the house, with red cheeks, a pot belly and a little spigot often visible through unbuttoned trousers, he really did resemble a samovar.

Sixteen-year-old Nastya was now working for the kolkhoz.[28] With her own money she had bought a dress, a pair of shoes and a little red cloth beret that she thought very smart. She would put on this beret and look at herself in a hand mirror. This mirror had lost half its silver, and Nastya saw not only her beret but also her fingers holding the mirror – her face and her beret in reflection, her fingers as if through a window. She'd have gladly slept in this beret, only she was afraid of crushing it; instead, she put it beside her and stroked it when she woke up. When he saw his daughter walking down the street with her girlfriends, looking merry and excited and wearing her beloved beret, Vavilov would think sadly about how, when the war was over, there were sure to be many more young women than young men.

Yes, much had happened in this house. Alyosha had sat at this table at night with his friends, going through algebra, geometry and physics problems with them as they all prepared for the entrance exams to the agronomy institute. Nastya had sat at this same table with her girlfriends and studied the textbook *Literature of the Motherland*. His neighbours' sons, visiting from new homes in Moscow and Gorky, had sat here and talked about their new lives and work. Vavilov's wife Marya had responded, 'Well, our children will soon be studying in the city too. Soon it will be their turn to become technical experts and engineers.'

Vavilov took from a chest the red scarf that he used as a wrapper for important documents and found his military service record. He then put the red bundle with his little boy's birth certificate and his wife's and his daughter's work records back into the chest, slipped his own document into his jacket pocket – and felt as if he had severed himself from his family. His daughter was looking at him with a new, questioning look. During these last moments he seemed to her to have changed, as if an invisible veil now hung between them. His wife would not be coming back until late; she and the other women had been sent to level the road to the station – army trucks now used this road to take hay and grain to trains bound for the front.

'Well, my daughter,' he said, 'now it's my turn.'

And she replied quietly, 'Don't worry about me and Máma. We'll keep working. Just be sure to come back in one piece.' Looking up at him, she added, 'Maybe you'll come across our Alyosha. That would be good. Then neither of you will be lonely.'

Vavilov was not yet thinking about what lay ahead. He was still thinking about his home and the various tasks at the kolkhoz that he had left unfinished. Nevertheless, his thoughts had changed; they were no longer the thoughts of a few minutes earlier. His intention this morning had been to patch a felt boot, to solder a leaking bucket, to adjust and set the saw, to mend his sheepskin coat, and to re-heel his wife's boots. What mattered now, though, were the jobs his wife would be unable to manage on her own. He had to be at the office in the district town, eighteen kilometres away, by nine o'clock the following morning.

He began with the very simplest job; he replaced the haft of his axe – he had a spare ready and waiting. Then he replaced a shaky rung in the ladder and went up to repair the roof, taking with him a few new planks, the axe, a hacksaw and a small bag of nails. For a moment he felt as if he were not a forty-five-year-old man, the head of a family, but a naughty boy who had climbed up onto the roof for fun. Soon his mother would come out of the house. Shading her eyes from the sun with the palm of one hand, she would look up and shout, 'Get down, you little rascal!' And she would stamp her foot impatiently, wishing she could grab hold of him by the ear, and repeat, 'Petya, I'm telling you to get down!'

Without thinking, he glanced at the hill behind the village. It was overgrown with elders and rowans and the few crosses still visible had sunk into the ground. For a moment he felt guilty before everyone and everything. He felt guilty before his late mother – there would be no time now to mend the cross on her grave. He felt guilty before his eldest son Alyosha – the kolkhoz chairman had found his own son a job in a military factory where he'd be exempt from conscription, but

14

he himself hadn't managed to get Alyosha exempted. He felt guilty before the earth – before the fields he would no longer be able to plough this autumn; and he felt guilty before his wife, on whose shoulders he would be laying a burden he had until then borne himself. He looked up and down the village – at its one wide street, at its huts and yards, at the high clear sky, and at the dark forest in the distance. Yes, this was where his life had gone by. The new school was a vivid splash of white, the sun shining on its large expanse of glass. The long wall of the kolkhoz cattle-yard was equally white.

How hard he had worked, without ever a break. At the age of four, plodding about on his bandy legs, he had looked after the geese. A year or two later, when his mother was digging up potatoes, he had searched for the ones she'd missed and brought them along to the main pile. When he was older still, he'd taken the cows to pasture, and then he'd dug the vegetable garden, fetched water from the well, harnessed the horse and chopped firewood. Then he'd become a ploughman, and he had learned to scythe and work the combine harvester.

He had worked as a carpenter. He had put in windows; he had sharpened tools; he had done the plumbing; he had made felt boots and repaired leather boots; he had flayed horses and sheep and tanned their skins; he had made sheepskin coats; he had sown tobacco; he had built a stove. And then there had been all the voluntary work. Standing in cold September water, he had constructed a dam. He had helped build a mill; he had paved a road; he had dug ditches; he had kneaded clay; he had crushed stone when they were building the kolkhoz stockyard and barn; and he had dug trenches for the kolkhoz potatoes. And there was all the land he had ploughed, all the hay he had mown, all the grain he had threshed, all the sacks he had carried. There were all the planks he had transported to the new school, all the forest oaks he had felled and rough-hewn, all the nails he had hammered, all the blows he had struck with an axe, all the work he had done with a spade. He had spent two summers digging peat, turning out 3,000 bricks a day – and what had he and his two mates been given to eat? A kilo of bread, a bucket of *kvas*[29] and a single egg for the three of them, while the mosquitoes buzzed so loudly that they drowned the sound of the diesel engine. And there were all the bricks he had moulded – bricks for the hospital, and the school, and the club, and the village soviet,[30] and the kolkhoz administration building, and even for buildings in the district town. And he had worked two summers as a boatman, taking materials to the factory. The current had been too strong to swim

15

against – and there they were taking eighty-ton loads. They had had to row for all they were worth.

He looked around him: at the buildings, the vegetable patches, the street and the paths. He looked at the whole village – and it was as if he were looking back at his life. Two old men – Pukhov, who was cross and quarrelsome, and Vavilov's neighbour Kozlov, known behind his back as 'Billy Goat'[31] – were on their way to the administration building. Another neighbour, Natalya Degtyarova, came out of her hut, went up to her gate, looked first to the right and then to the left, shook an arm threateningly at the chickens and went back into the house.

Yes, traces of his work would remain.

He had seen tractors and combine harvesters, mowing machines and threshing machines invade this village where his father had known only sickle and scythe, only the wooden plough and the flail. He had seen young men and women leave the village to study, then return as agronomists, teachers, mechanics and livestock experts. He knew that the son of Pachkin the blacksmith had become a general, and that other young men who'd come back to the village to see their parents were now engineers, factory directors, and officials in the provincial party apparatus.

Sometimes people used to gather in the evenings and talk about how life had changed. Old Pukhov thought that life had got worse. He had worked out how much grain had cost in the days of the tsar, what you could buy in the village shop, the price of a pair of boots, and how much meat people had put in their cabbage soup. From all this it appeared that life had been easier in the old days. Vavilov disagreed. The more the people helped the state, he argued, the more the state would be able to help the people.

Old women said that peasants were now treated as human beings like any others; their children could get on in the world and become important. Maybe boots had been cheaper in the old days, but the peasants themselves were seen as worthless.

Pukhov replied that the peasants had always had to support the state and that the state was a heavy burden. There had been hunger in the days of the tsar – and there was hunger today. They had had ways of fleecing the peasant in the old days – and today's taxes were no different. Peasants were looked down on in the past – and they still were. The kolkhozes might help the state, but they didn't help people.

When the war began, Pukhov had thought that life would be better under the Germans. There'd be trade and smallholdings. There'd be clothes, tea, sugar, spiced breads, shoes, boots and coats. But the

16

Germans had killed his three sons and his son-in-law. No one in the village had suffered more than Pukhov.

Vavilov saw the war as a catastrophe. He knew that war destroys life. A peasant leaving his village for the war does not dream of medals and glory. He knows he is probably on his way to die.

Vavilov looked around him once more. He had always wanted the life of mankind to be spacious and full of light like the sky today, and he had done what he could to build such a life. And he and millions like him had not worked in vain. The kolkhoz had achieved a great deal.

When he had finished, Vavilov got down from the roof and walked towards the gate. He remembered the last night of peace, the night before Sunday, 22 June: the whole of the vast young country, the whole of workers' and peasants' Russia had been singing and playing the accordion – in little city gardens, on dance floors, in village streets, in groves and copses, in meadows, beside streams.

And then everything had gone quiet; the accordions had suddenly broken off.

For nearly a year now there had been only stern, unsmiling silence.

4

Vavilov set off towards the kolkhoz office. On the way, he saw Natalya Degtyarova again.

Usually she looked at Vavilov with sullen reproach – *her* husband had been called up some time ago, as had her son. Now, though, she was looking at him thoughtfully and with sympathy. She must have known that he had now received his papers.

'You too, Pyotr Semyonovich?' she asked. 'Does Marya know yet?'

'She will soon enough,' he replied.

'That she will,' said Natalya. And she went back into her hut.

The kolkhoz chairman turned out to be away for a couple of days; he had gone to the district town. Vavilov went up to Shepunov, the one-armed accountant, and handed over the kolkhoz money he had collected the day before from the district office of the state bank. He took the receipt, folded it twice and put it in his pocket. 'There you are,' he said. 'Every last kopek due.'

Lying on the table was a copy of the district newspaper. Shepunov pushed it towards Vavilov, his 'For Military Merit' medal jingling against a metal button on his soldier's tunic. 'Comrade Vavilov,' he asked, 'have you read the latest news from the Sovinform Bureau?'

'No,' said Vavilov.

Shepunov began reading: 'On 12 May our troops launched an offensive in the Kharkov area, broke through the German defences and, repelling counter-attacks by motor infantry and major tank formations, are continuing their drive west.' He raised a finger and winked at Vavilov. 'Our troops have covered from twenty to sixty kilometres of ground and liberated more than 300 inhabited localities. Yes, and this too! Around 365 artillery pieces, twenty-five tanks and 1 million rounds of ammunition have now been captured.'

Looking at Vavilov with the benign interest an old soldier shows in a new recruit, he said, 'Understand now?'

Vavilov showed him his call-up papers. 'Of course I understand. Why wouldn't I? And I also understand that this is only the beginning.

18

I'll be there in time for what really counts.' He smoothed his call-up papers between his hands.

'Anything I should say to Ivan Mikhailovich?' asked the bookkeeper.

'What's there to say? He knows everything already.' They began talking about kolkhoz matters, and Vavilov, forgetting that the chairman knew everything already, began giving instructions for Shepunov to pass on to him: 'Tell Ivan Mikhailovich not to allow the boards I brought from the sawmill to be used for repairs, only for construction. Yes, you must tell him that. Now, as for our sacks – the ones still in town – we must send someone to fetch them. Otherwise they'll disappear, or we'll be palmed off with who knows what. And the papers about the loan, just say that Vavilov …'

Vavilov did not like the chairman. He was sly, out only for himself. He had lost touch with the earth. He drew up reports making out that the kolkhoz had overfulfilled its plan when everyone knew this was nonsense. He would think up spurious reasons to visit the district town and even the provincial capital, and he always made sure he had presents to give to the people he met there – sometimes honey, sometimes apples. Once he had even taken someone a piglet.

His reports to the authorities naturally contained no mention of the sofa, the large lamp and the Singer sewing machine he had once brought back from the city. When their province received some award, he was awarded a medal 'For Excellence in Labour'. In summer he had worn it on his jacket and in winter he had pinned it to his fur coat. When he came into a heated room after being out in the cold, the medal would look as if it were covered in little droplets of dew.

What really mattered in life, to the chairman's mind, was not work but knowing how to cultivate the right people. He would say one thing and do something quite different. His attitude to the war couldn't have been simpler: he understood immediately that there were few people more important than the district military commissar. And his son Volodya did indeed start work in a military factory, which made him exempt from conscription; sometimes he came home to pick up supplies of fatback and moonshine to pass on to the appropriate people.

The chairman, for his part, disliked Vavilov and was afraid of him, telling him that he was contrary and that he had no manners. The chairman preferred to spend time with people who were useful to him, people who understood what was what. Some people in the kolkhoz were a little wary of Vavilov, finding him sullen and taciturn. Nevertheless, Vavilov was a trusted figure and, whenever the village was engaged in some communal enterprise, it was he who was asked to receive and take care of the money. Any voluntary work, anything for which the villagers had to club together – it was Vavilov who was chosen as treasurer. He had never been interrogated or involved in any legal proceedings and he had only once been inside a police station. A stupid little incident, a year before the war.

One evening an elderly man had knocked at the window of his hut and asked if he could stay the night. His face was covered by an unkempt black beard. Vavilov had looked at him in silence, taken him to the hay barn, spread out a sheepskin coat for him to lie on, and brought him some milk and a piece of bread.

During the night some young men in yellow leather jackets had appeared. They had arrived in a car and gone straight to Vavilov's barn. They then set off again in their car, taking both Vavilov and the stranger. In the police station a senior officer asked Vavilov why he had let this bearded man sleep in his barn. Vavilov had thought for a moment, then said, 'I felt sorry for him.'

'But didn't you ask him who he was?' asked the officer.

'Why?' Vavilov replied. 'I could see. He was a human being.'

Without uttering a word, the officer looked for a long time, for what seemed a very long time indeed, into Vavilov's eyes. And then he said, 'All right then, go back home.'

Everyone in the village had had a good laugh about all this, asking Vavilov if he had enjoyed his ride in a car. The chairman, though, had shaken his head and said, 'You're a fool.'

*

Vavilov went down the empty village street, walking more and more quickly. He couldn't wait to see his home and children again; it was as if not only his mind but his entire body felt the anguish of the imminent separation.

He stood for a moment by the open door of his hut. His life there had not been easy. His children were badly dressed, and they did not always have enough to eat. His boots were worn out. There was no kerosene for the lamp, and it was dim even when it was lit. It had no glass and it smoked. Sometimes they did not even have bread. He seldom ate meat. There had been meat once, but it would have been better if there hadn't. Their cow had fallen into a pit that wasn't fenced off and had broken both her front legs. They had slaughtered her and

20

eaten meat every day for the next week, their eyes swollen with tears. Vavilov seldom ate fatback. And he never ate white bread.

He went into his hut, where everything was familiar – and these long-familiar things seemed strangely new. His heart was touched by all of them: the chest of drawers covered by a knitted tablecloth; the felt boots he had resoled and repaired with black patches; the pendulum clock above the wide bed; the wooden spoons with edges nibbled away by impatient childish teeth; the picture frame with the family photographs; a small heavy mug made from dark copper; a large light mug made from fine white tin; and little Vanya's tiny trousers, all colour now washed out of them except for a sad, hazy, pale blue. And the hut itself was endowed with an astonishing quality unique to Russian huts: the interior was at once cramped and spacious. It was well lived-in, warmed by the breath of its owners and the breath of its owners' parents, as deeply imbued with human presence as any dwelling can possibly be – and at the same time it was as if no one had meant to stay for long, as if a few people had come in, put their things down for a minute and would be off again straightaway, leaving the door wide open behind them ...

How beautiful children seemed in this hut! Early in the morning, when little fair-headed Vanya came running across the floor on his bare feet, he was like a warm, moving flower.

*

Vavilov helped Vanya up onto a high chair and sensed, through his rough calloused hand, the precious warmth of Vanya's little body. The child's clear bright eyes looked at him with a trust that was pure and absolute – and the voice of a very small human being who had never uttered a single coarse word, never smoked a single cigarette or drunk even one drop of vodka, asked, 'Pápa, are you really going to the war tomorrow?'

Vavilov smiled, and his eyes moistened.

21

5

——◆——

That night Vavilov stood in the moonlight, chopping up the tree stumps stacked under an awning behind the shed. He had collected these stumps over many years and they had long been trimmed and stripped of their bark. Really, they were little more than bundles of twisted roots; he couldn't split them or chop them cleanly – all he could do was hack at them and then tear them apart.

Marya – tall, broad-shouldered and dark-skinned like her husband – was standing nearby. Now and again she bent down to pick up stray pieces of wood and occasionally she gave her husband a sideways look. And he too caught glimpses of her as he worked away with his axe. As he bent down, he saw her legs or the hem of her dress; straightening up, he would see her large, thin-lipped mouth, her intent dark eyes, or her high, clear, convex forehead, without a single wrinkle. Standing beside each other, they could have been brother and sister. Life had forged them in the same fashion, beaten them into the same shape; hard labour had not bowed them but straightened them. Neither was speaking, which was their way of saying farewell. Vavilov struck with his axe at the springy wood. It was soft, yet unyielding, and the blows resonated both in the earth and in Vavilov's own chest. The axe blade shone blue in the moonlight, flaring as he lifted it into the air, fading as it moved nearer the ground.

All around was silence. Like soft linseed oil, the moonlight covered the ground, the grass, the broad fields of young rye and the roofs of the huts, dissolving in the puddles and little windows.

Vavilov wiped his sweaty forehead with the back of his hand and looked at the sky. It was as if he were out in the hot summer sun, though the light shining down on him was from the bloodless luminary of the night.

'That'll do,' said his wife. 'You're not going to lay in enough firewood for the whole of the war.'

Vavilov glanced at the mountain of wood he had chopped.

'All right – but the moment we get back, Alyosha and I will chop you some more.' And he drew the back of his hand across the axe blade, just as he had wiped it across his sweaty forehead a moment before.

Vavilov took out his tobacco pouch, rolled a cigarette and lit up; the smoke from the coarse tobacco drifted slowly away in the still air.

They went back inside. He felt the hut's warmth on his face, and he could hear the breathing of his sleeping children. This quiet, this warmth, these two fair heads in the half-dark – here beside him was his life, his love, his good fortune. He remembered how he had lived here as a young bachelor – how he had gone about in blue riding breeches and a pointed Red Army helmet from the time of the Civil War, how he had smoked a pipe with a little lid that his elder brother had brought back from the imperialist war, that earlier war against the Germans. He had been proud of this pipe. It had made him look dashing, and people had held it in their hands and said, 'It's beautiful, it's so interesting.' Shortly before getting married, he had lost it.

Nastya was asleep. He saw her face and the dark shape of her beret. He looked round at his wife – and felt that there could be no greater happiness in the world than to stay here in this hut, never to leave it. Never had he known a moment more bitter; in the sleepy silence before dawn he could sense the power of a harsh whirlwind that was entirely indifferent to Vavilov and all that he loved and desired – and he could sense this power in every cell of his body, on his skin and in the marrow of his bones. He felt the horror that a splinter of wood might feel if it suddenly realized that it was not moving of its own accord past the river's green banks but was being carried by the insuperable power of the water. The whirlwind had snatched him up and he no longer belonged either to himself or to his family. For a moment he forgot that his own fate and that of the children asleep on the bed were bound to the fate of the country and all its inhabitants, that the fate of his kolkhoz and the fate of the huge stone cities with their millions of citizens were one and the same. In this bitter hour his heart was gripped by a pain that neither knows nor wants consolation or understanding. He wanted only one thing: to go on living here – in the wood that his wife would put into the stove in winter, in the salt with which she would season the potatoes and bread, in the grain she would receive in return for his many workdays on the kolkhoz. And he knew that this was impossible, that it would be need and shortage, not plenty, that would make him live in their thoughts. They would think of him as they looked at the empty salt cellar, when they asked a neighbour for a measure of flour, as they tried to persuade the chairman to allow them a horse to drag a sledge-load of firewood from the forest.

'We'll run out of potatoes before spring. Same with bread. Same with firewood. The only thing we won't be short of is grief.' Quickly, quietly but bitterly, Marya listed what they would run out of before winter, what before Christmas, what before the beginning of Lent and what before Easter.³² Pointing to the sleeping children, she went on, 'It's all very well for you, you won't need to worry about bread. But what about me? Where am I going to find bread for *them*?' And she picked up a towel that had been dropped on the floor.

This upset Vavilov. It wasn't as if he were going away for his own pleasure. But he understood that his wife was in pain and that she was trying to stop this pain from bursting out into the open.

When she had had her say, he said, 'And my knapsack? Have you put everything in?'

She put his knapsack on the table and said, 'Yes, but it's not much. The knapsack itself weighs more than everything I've put in it.'

'All the easier for me to carry,' he said gently. The knapsack was indeed very light: bread, some rye rusks, some onions, a tin mug, a needle and thread, two pairs of clean foot cloths, a penknife with a wooden handle.

'Mittens?' she asked angrily.

'No. *You* need them more.'

'That's for me to say,' Marya replied sharply. She knew she was being unkind and this made her angrier still.

'Pápa!' came Nastya's sleepy voice. 'Your jacket. I don't need your jacket. Take it with you!'

'Jacket, your jacket,' said her mother, imitating Nastya's sleepy voice. 'You go back to sleep. What if they send you out in midwinter to dig trenches? What'll you wear then?'

'My darling, my silly darling,' Vavilov said to his daughter. 'I love you, my silly girl. I love you. Don't think I'm strict with you because I don't care.'

And the girl began to cry. Pressing her cheek against his hand, she sobbed, 'Dearest Pápenka! Do at least write to us!'

'Maybe you *should* take your padded jacket with you,' said Marya.

There was so much more that Vavilov could have said. He wanted to say that it was no use his taking the mittens because he'd be dead before winter anyway, and they'd simply be wasted. He wanted to say dozens of things, both important and unimportant, that would have served to express not only his concern over practical matters but also his love for his family. The potatoes needed sorting – they were beginning to rot. The young plum tree needed protecting from the frosts. His wife should have a word with the kolkhoz chairman about getting the stove repaired. And he wanted to talk about the war, this war that had mobilized the entire nation. Their son was already fighting, and now he himself would be fighting too.

But there was so much to say that he said nothing at all. Otherwise he'd be talking all night.

'Well, Marya,' he said. 'Before I go, let me fetch you some water.'

He took the buckets and walked to the well. He lowered the first bucket and it clattered against the slimy walls of the well frame. Vavilov leaned over and looked down. There was a smell of something cold and damp, and the absolute dark was as blinding as bright sunlight. 'There it is,' he thought. 'My death.'

The bucket quickly filled to the brim. As it came up again, Vavilov heard the sound of water falling on water. The closer the bucket came to the surface, the louder the sound. Then the bucket emerged from the darkness. Swift streams of water were flowing down its sides, eager to return to the dark below.

Going back into the entrance room, he found his wife sitting on the bench. In the half-dark he couldn't make out her face, but this didn't matter; her feelings were not hard to guess.

She looked up and said, 'Sit down for a few minutes. Have a rest and a bite to eat.'

'All right,' he said. 'There's no hurry.'

It was already getting light. He sat down at the table. On it stood a bowl of potatoes, a saucer with a little white, crystallized honey, some slices of bread and a mug of milk. He ate slowly. His cheeks were stinging, as if he'd been out in the winter wind, and his head felt as if full of smoke. He thought, talked, chewed and shifted about on his chair. Any moment now the smoke would blow away and he'd be able to see things clearly again.

His wife pushed a bowl towards him and said, 'Eat these eggs. I'll put another dozen in your bag. I've boiled them already.'

In answer he smiled such a clear and shy smile that she felt almost burned. He had smiled in exactly the same way when she entered this hut aged eighteen. And what she felt now was the same as what thousands upon thousands of other women were feeling. Her heart clenched, and all she really wanted was to let out a scream – to silence her grief by giving voice to it.

But she merely said, 'I should have baked lots of pies. I should have bought a few bottles of vodka. But … with it being wartime …'

25

And he just got to his feet, wiped his mouth and said, 'Yes.' And got ready to leave.

They embraced.

'Petya,' she said slowly, as if trying to persuade him to come back to his senses and change his mind.

'I have to,' he said.

His movements were slow. And he was trying not to look in her direction.

'We must wake the children,' said Marya. 'Nastya's gone back to sleep.' She wasn't sure what to do. It was for her own sake that she wanted to wake the children, so she would have someone to share her pain with.

'There's no need. We've already said our goodbyes,' he replied. And he listened for a moment to his sleeping daughter's slow breathing.

He adjusted his knapsack, took his hat, stepped towards the door and glanced quickly back at his wife.

Both looked around the room – but how very differently they each saw it, at this last moment, as they stood together on the threshold ... She knew that these four walls would witness all her loneliness, and to her they seemed bleak and empty. He, on the other hand, wanted to carry away in his memory what he saw as the kindest home on this earth.

He set off down the road. Standing by the gate, she watched him walk away. She felt that she would survive, that she would be able to endure everything – if only he would come back again and stay for another hour, if only she could look at him one more time.

'Petya, Petya,' she whispered.

But he didn't look round. He didn't stop. He just carried on walking towards the dawn. It was reddening over land that he had ploughed himself. A cold wind was blowing straight into his face, blowing the last vestige of warmth, the last breath of hearth and home, out of his clothes.

6

It was the birthday of Alexandra Vladimirovna Shaposhnikova, the widow of an eminent specialist in bridge construction, but this was not the only reason why her family were giving a party.

There is something moving about a family sitting together around a table in order to be with a loved one about to go on a long journey. This custom answers a deep need; it is not for nothing that – unlike many other old customs – it is still so widely observed.

The country was at war. Friends, family – everyone understood that this might be their last gathering. There was no knowing how many of them would meet again.

It had been decided to invite Mikhail Mostovskoy and Pavel Andreyev, family friends of long standing. As a nineteen-year-old polytechnic student, Alexandra Vladimirovna's late husband had gone to Stalingrad for a few months to work as an engineer on a tugboat on the River Volga. Andreyev had been a stoker on the same boat, and he and the young Shaposhnikov had often chatted together on deck. Andreyev had later become a friend to the whole family. When Alexandra moved to Stalingrad with her children, he became a regular visitor.

Zhenya, the youngest of Alexandra's three daughters, had joked, 'Clearly one of Máma's admirers.'

The Shaposhnikovs had also invited Tamara Berozkina, whom they had got to know only recently. Tamara and her children had seen so many burning buildings, air raids and hurried evacuations that the Shaposhnikovs had got into the habit of referring to her as 'poor Tamara': 'What's happened to poor Tamara?'; 'How come poor Tamara hasn't been round?'

For many years, this three-room apartment in Stalingrad had felt spacious – home only to Alexandra Vladimirovna and her grandson Seryozha. Now, though, it was crowded. First, Zhenya had moved in. And then, after the German summer offensive, Alexandra's middle daughter, Marusya, had moved in, along with her husband Stepan Spiridonov and her daughter Vera. Until then the three of them had lived a few miles away, near Stalgres, the central power station.

Anticipating night air raids on Stalgres, most of the engineers with relatives in the city had sent their wives and children to join them. Spiridonov had installed not only his family but also a piano and several items of furniture.

When she wasn't on night shift, another old friend, Sofya Osipovna Levinton, would sleep at the Shaposhnikovs. She had first got to know Alexandra long ago, in Paris and Bern. She now worked as a surgeon in one of the city hospitals.

And only the previous day, Tolya had arrived unexpectedly. He was another of Alexandra Vladimirovna's grandchildren, the son of her eldest daughter Ludmila, and he was on his way from military school to his new unit. He had come to the apartment with his travelling companion, a lieutenant on his way back to the front after a spell in hospital. When they first appeared, his grandmother had failed to recognize Tolya in his army uniform and had asked rather severely, 'Who is it you're looking for, comrades?' And then she had yelled, 'Tolya!'

Zhenya had said that they absolutely must celebrate this family reunion.

The pie dough had already been mixed. Spiridonov had come in his car, bringing a large bag of white flour and a yellow briefcase full of butter, sturgeon and caviar. Zhenya had got hold of three bottles of sweet wine through her artistic contacts. Marusya had sacrificed part of her inviolable fund of emergency bartering currency – two half-litre bottles of vodka.

It was usual in those days for guests to bring supplies of their own when they came round; it was difficult for anyone to lay their hands on enough food for a large group.

Zhenya's cheeks and temples were moist from the heat. In a dressing gown thrown over a smart summer dress, her dark curls peeking out from under a headscarf, she stood in the middle of the kitchen, holding a knife in one hand and a kitchen towel in the other.

'Heavens, is Máma still not back?' she asked Marusya. 'Should I be turning the pie round by now? I don't know the oven and I'm afraid of it burning.'

At this moment she had no thought for anything except the pie she was baking. Amused by her younger sister's zeal, Marusya said, 'I don't know this oven any better than you do, but there's no need to get so worked up. Máma's already here, and so are one or two of the guests.'

'Marusya, why are you wearing that hideous brown jacket?' asked Zhenya. 'You're beginning to stoop anyway – and that jacket makes you look a real hunchback. And your dark scarf makes your hair look even greyer. Someone as thin as you needs to wear something brighter.'

'Who cares?' replied Marusya. 'It won't be long before I'm a granny. Vera's already eighteen now – would you believe it?'

Someone had started to play the piano. Marusya frowned. Staring angrily at Zhenya with her large dark eyes, she said, 'Trust you! Who else could have dreamed up something like this? What will the neighbours think? It's embarrassing. This really isn't the time for music and feasting!'

Zhenya often took decisions on the spur of the moment, and some of these decisions ended up causing her and her family a great deal of grief. While still at school, she had neglected her studies because of her passion for dance – and then she had taken it into her head that she was an artist. In friendship she was inconstant. One day she would be telling everyone that some friend or other was truly noble and extraordinary; the next day she would be bitterly denouncing this same friend. She had studied at the Moscow Art Institute, graduating from the Faculty of Painting. Sometimes she felt she was an accomplished master and was full of enthusiasm both for her finished works and for her future projects; but then she would remember some indifferent look or mocking remark and tell herself she was a useless old cow without the least hint of talent. And she would wish she had studied some applied art, like painting on fabric. At the age of twenty-two, still in her last year at the Arts Institute, she had married a Comintern[33] official, Nikolay Krymov. He was thirteen years older than her and she was drawn to almost everything about him: his contempt for bourgeois comfort, his romantic past in the battles of the Civil War, his work in China and his Comintern friends. Nevertheless, in spite of Zhenya's admiration for him, and in spite of his apparently deep and sincere love for her, their marriage did not last. One day in December 1940 Zhenya had packed her belongings into a suitcase and gone back to live with her mother.

Zhenya's explanations to her family had been so confusing that no one understood anything at all. Marusya called her a neurasthenic. Her mother kept asking if she had fallen in love with someone else. Vera had argued with the fifteen-year-old Seryozha, who believed that Zhenya had done the right thing.

'It's very simple,' he'd insisted. 'She's fallen out of love – and that's all there is to it. How can you not understand?'

'Quite the little philosopher! Into love, out of love … What do you know about love, you little brat?' Vera had replied. Then in her ninth year at school, she considered herself experienced in matters of the heart.

The neighbours and some of Zhenya's acquaintances had their own rather straightforward explanations. Some thought that Zhenya had been very sensible. Things were not going well for her husband. Several of his friends were in trouble; some had been dismissed from their positions; a few had been arrested. Zhenya had decided to leave before it was too late, so as not to be dragged down by her husband. Others, who preferred more romantic gossip, affirmed that Zhenya had a lover. Her husband had set out on a trip to the Urals but had been called back by a telegram and had found Zhenya in her lover's arms.

There are people who like to ascribe only the basest of motives to the actions of others. This is not always because they act basely themselves; often they would not dream of acting as they suspect others of doing. They talk like this because they think that cynical explanations testify to their knowledge of life. A readiness to believe that others are acting honourably, so they imagine, is a sign of naiveté.

Zhenya had been appalled when she heard what was being said about her divorce.

But that had been before the war. None of these things troubled her now.

7

The younger generation had gathered in Seryozha's little room, where Spiridonov had somehow managed to squeeze in his piano.

They were joking about who did, and who didn't, look like who else in the family. With his dark eyes and slender build, Seryozha looked like his mother, the wife of Alexandra's son Dmitry. He had her dark hair, her olive skin and her nervy movements. He also had the same quick look in his eyes, a look that could be both timid and bold. Tolya was tall and broad-shouldered. He had a broad face and a broad nose, and he was constantly looking in the mirror and smoothing his straw-blond hair. When he took from his tunic pocket a photograph of himself next to his half-sister Nadya, a small thin girl with long fine plaits, everyone burst out laughing – so little did the two resemble each other. Nadya was now with her parents in Kazan; they had been evacuated from Moscow. As for Vera – tall, rosy-cheeked and with a short, straight nose – she had nothing in common with any of her three cousins; she did, however, have the quick, fiery brown eyes of her young Aunt Zhenya.

Such a lack of external resemblance between members of a single family was especially common in the generation born just after the Revolution, a time when marriages were entered into simply for love, regardless of differences of blood, nationality, language and social class. The inner, psychological differences between family members were equally great; the products of these unions were endowed with rich and complex characters.

That morning Tolya and his travelling companion, Lieutenant Kovalyov, had gone to the Military District HQ. Kovalyov had learned that his division was still being held in reserve, somewhere between Kamyshin and Saratov. Tolya had also received instructions to join one of the reserve divisions. The two lieutenants had resolved to stay an extra day in Stalingrad. 'We'll be seeing more than enough of the war,' Kovalyov had said sensibly. 'It won't run away from us.' But they had decided not to wander about on the streets, in case they were picked up by a patrol.

Throughout the difficult journey to Stalingrad, Kovalyov had helped Tolya in all kinds of ways. Kovalyov had a mess tin, while Tolya's had been stolen the day he graduated from military school. Kovalyov always knew at which stations they would be able to find boiled water, and which of the army canteens would provide them with smoked fish and mutton sausage and where they would only get pea and millet concentrate.[34]

At Batraki he had managed to get hold of a bottle of moonshine, and he and Tolya had drunk it together. Kovalyov had told Tolya how he loved a girl from his village and would marry her as soon as the war was over. This had not prevented him from talking about his front-line liaisons with a frankness that took Tolya's breath away and made his ears burn.

Kovalyov also told Tolya many things about war that you can never learn from books or service regulations and that are important only to those who are actually fighting, with their backs against the wall – not to those trying to imagine the reality of the war many years later.

This good-natured friendship, on the part of a lieutenant who had seen his share of action, was flattering to Tolya. He had pretended to be older than his years, to be a young man who knew the ways of the world. 'That's women for you,' he had said when the conversation turned to girls. 'Best just to love 'em and leave 'em.'

Now, though, Tolya wanted more than ever to talk freely to his cousins, but, without understanding why, he felt embarrassed. If it weren't for Kovalyov, he'd have talked about all the things he usually talked about with them. There were moments when he felt burdened by Kovalyov's presence, and this made him feel ashamed: Kovalyov had, after all, been a loyal travelling companion.

He had lived his whole life in a world he shared with Seryozha, Vera and his grandmother, but this family reunion now seemed like something chance and ephemeral. He was now fated to live in a different world, in a world of lieutenants, political instructors,[35] sergeants and corporals, of triangles, diamonds and other badges of rank, of travel warrants and military ration cards. In this world he had met new people; he had made new friends and new enemies. Everything was different.

Tolya had not told Kovalyov that he wanted to enter the Faculty of Physics and Mathematics and that his ambition was to bring about a scientific revolution that would eclipse both Newton and Einstein. He had not told him that he had already made a short-wave radio receiver and that, shortly before the war, he had begun building a television. Nor did he say that he used to go to his father's institute after school and help the laboratory assistants assemble complex apparatus or that his mother used to joke, 'How the boy's managed to inherit Viktor's scientific gifts I really can't understand!'

Tolya was tall and robust-looking. His family liked to call him a 'heavyweight', but at heart he was timid and sensitive.

The conversation was not flowing. Kovalyov was at the piano, playing 'The town I love can sleep peacefully' with one finger.[36]

'And who's that?' he asked with a yawn, pointing to a portrait hanging above the piano.

'That's me,' said Vera. 'It was painted by Auntie Zhenya.'

'It's not like you at all,' said Kovalyov.

The worst embarrassment of all was Seryozha. Any normal boy would have been full of admiration for two young lieutenants – especially for Kovalyov, with his scar and his two medals 'For Bravery' – but Seryozha was just supercilious and mocking. He didn't ask even a single question about military school. This was particularly upsetting; Tolya was longing to talk about their sergeant, about the shooting range, and about the cinema he and his mates had managed to visit without authorization.

Everyone knew Vera's habit of bursting into laughter for no apparent reason, simply because laughter was always there within her. Now, though, she was sullen and silent. And she kept staring at Kovalyov, as if sizing him up. As for Seryozha, anyone would have thought he was taking a malicious pleasure in being unfailingly tactless.

'Vera, why are you being so silent?' Tolya asked crossly.

'I'm not being silent.'

'The wounds of love,' said Seryozha.

'Imbecile!' said Vera.

'She blushed – and that's a fact!' said Kovalyov, giving Vera a roguish wink. 'No doubt about it, she's in love. With a major, yes? Every young woman today complains about lieutenants and says they get on her nerves.'

'Lieutenants do not get on my nerves,' said Vera, looking Kovalyov straight in the eye.

'So it's a lieutenant, is it?' said Kovalyov. He was a little upset, since no lieutenant likes a young woman to fall for another lieutenant. 'Well then,' he went on after a pause, 'I think we should drink to the two of them. I've got the necessary here in my water bottle.'

'Yes!' said Seryozha with sudden animation. 'Let's drink to them!'

Vera demurred, but ended up downing her vodka in one. And then, just as if she were a soldier too, she took a hunk of dried bread from a green bag.

'You're the kind of companion a soldier needs,' said Kovalyov.

And Vera began laughing like a little girl, wrinkling her nose, tapping her foot and tossing her mane of fair hair.

Seryozha became tipsy straightaway. First, he launched into a critique of Soviet military operations; then he began reciting poems. Tolya kept glancing at Kovalyov, afraid he would be laughing at Seryozha, that he would think it ridiculous for a young man to be waving his arms about and reciting Yesenin, but Kovalyov was listening attentively. Now less like a lieutenant and more like an ordinary young man from a village, he opened his knapsack and said, 'Stop. Let me write it down!'

As for Vera, she frowned, fell into thought and then turned to Tolya. Stroking him on the cheek, she said, 'Oh Tolya, dear Tolya, what do *you* know about anything?'

She sounded more like a sixty-year-old than an eighteen-year-old.

8

Many years before the Revolution, Alexandra Vladimirovna Shaposhnikova – now a tall, imposing old woman – had studied natural sciences at a women's college. After her husband's death, she had worked first as a teacher and then as a chemist in a bacteriological institute. For the last few years she had been head of a small laboratory that monitored working conditions in factories. She had never had many members of staff and now, with the war, she had still fewer; she herself had to visit factories, railway depots, grain silos, shoe factories and clothes factories in order to collect dust samples and check the quality of the air. She loved her work and in her small laboratory she had constructed her own apparatus for the quantitative analysis of air pollution in industrial enterprises. She could analyse metallic dust, drinking water, water for industrial use and a variety of lead compounds and alloys. She could detect the presence of mercury and arsenic vapours, carbon bisulphite, nitric oxides and harmful levels of carbon monoxide. And she loved people no less than her work; during her visits she made friends with lathe-operators, seamstresses, millers, blacksmiths, electricians, stokers, tram conductors and engine drivers.

A year before the war she had begun working during the evenings in a library for the applied sciences, doing translations for herself and for engineers in various Stalingrad factories. She had learnt English and French as a child, and German when she and her husband were political exiles, living in Bern and Zurich.

When she got home on the day of the family party, she spent a long time in front of the mirror, arranging her white hair and pinning a small brooch – two enamel violets – to the collar of her blouse. She looked once again in the mirror, thought for a moment, unpinned her brooch with an air of decision and placed it on the bedside table. The door half-opened and Vera announced in a loud whisper, 'Hurry up, Granny! That scary old man's here – Mostovskoy!'

After another moment of uncertainty, Alexandra put her brooch back on again and walked quickly towards the door.

She found Mostovskoy in the tiny hall, which was piled high with baskets, old suitcases and sacks of potatoes.

Mikhail Sidorovich Mostovskoy was a man of inexhaustible vitality – the kind of man of whom others say, 'He's a breed apart.'

Before the war, he had lived in Leningrad. After surviving four months of the Blockade, he had been flown out in February 1942. He was still light on his feet. He had good sight and good hearing. His memory and mental faculties were intact and he retained a genuine, lively interest in life, the sciences and people. All this in spite of the fact that the experiences he had been through were enough for several more ordinary lives: forced labour and exile, persecution, disillusion, bitterness, joys and sorrows, deprivations of every kind, and endless nights of unceasing work. Alexandra had first met Mostovskoy before the Revolution, when her late husband was working in Nizhny Novgorod. Mostovskoy, who had gone there to help organize clandestine political activities, had stayed in their apartment for a month.

Mostovskoy stepped into the main room and looked around: at the wicker armchairs and stools by the table, at the white tablecloth spread out in anticipation of guests, at the wall clock, the wardrobe and the folding Chinese screen on which an embroidered silk tiger was moving stealthily through yellow-green bamboo.

'If your room were to be dug up in a thousand years,' he said, 'an archaeologist could learn a great deal about the juxtaposition of different social strata in our time.' There was a hint of laughter in his eyes; the little wrinkles around them appeared, disappeared and reappeared. Pointing to the plain wooden shelves, he went on, 'Look. Here we have *Das Kapital* and Hegel in German. And on the wall – portraits of Nekrasov and Dobrolyubov.[37] That's your revolutionary past. But the silk tiger must be from your merchant father. And the huge wall clock too. And then there's a cupboard, a vase as big as a cupboard and a huge dining table – they're all symbols of our new prosperity, the prosperity of the present day. They must have been brought here by your chief engineer son-in-law.' Then he raised an admonitory finger. 'Oh! Judging by the number of place settings, this is going to be a real banquet. Why didn't you say? I'd have got out my best tie!'

Alexandra always felt uncharacteristically unsure of herself in Mostovskoy's presence. Now too, thinking he was criticizing her, she blushed – the sad, touching blush of an old person.

'I yielded to the demands of my daughters and grandsons,' she said. 'After a winter in Leningrad, I fear all this must seem strange and excessive.'

'Far from it, far from it,' Mostovskoy replied. He sat down at the table, began filling his pipe and then held out his tobacco pouch, saying, 'You enjoy a smoke too. See what you think of this!' He looked at her tobacco-stained fingers and added, 'But you really should use a cigarette holder.'

'It's better without,' she replied. Once again, she felt the need to justify herself. 'I started when we were in exile, in Siberia. Goodness knows how many times Nikolay and I argued about it. But I'm hardly likely to stop now.'

Mostovskoy took a flint from his pocket, along with a piece of thick white string and a steel file. 'I'm having trouble with my Katyusha,'[38] he said. He and Alexandra smiled at each other. His Katyusha truly was refusing to light.

'Let me get some matches,' said Alexandra.

'No,' said Mostovskoy, with a dismissive wave. 'Why waste precious matches?'

'Yes, nowadays people like to hang on to their matches. I've got a tiny night light in my kitchen and my neighbours are always coming round "to borrow a light".'

'It's the same everywhere. People tend their little flames like cave dwellers thousands of years ago. And the old like to keep two or three matches in reserve. They're afraid the war may bring them some night-time surprise.'

She went to the cupboard, came back to the table and said with mock solemnity, 'Allow me, from the bottom of my heart ...' And she held out an unopened box of matches.

Mostovskoy accepted her gift. They both lit up, drew on their pipes and exhaled at the same time. The two curls of smoke met and drifted lazily towards the window.

'Are you thinking about leaving?' asked Mostovskoy.

'Yes, of course. Who isn't? But we haven't yet talked about it at all seriously.'

'And where might you go, if it's not a military secret?'

'To Kazan. Part of the Academy of Sciences has been evacuated there. And Ludmila's husband's a professor, or rather, he's a corresponding member of the Academy of Sciences,[39] and so they've been given an apartment. Well, two rooms, anyway – and he's asking us to go and join them. But don't worry – you'll be all right. I'm sure the authorities will take proper care of you.'

Mostovskoy looked at her and nodded.

'Are they really so unstoppable?' asked Alexandra. There was a note of despair in her voice that somehow didn't fit with the confident, even haughty expression of her handsome face. Slowly, with effort, she began again, 'Is fascism really so very powerful? I don't believe it. For the love of God, tell me what's happening! This map on the wall – sometimes I just want to take it down and hide it. Day after day Seryozha keeps moving the little flags. Day after day – the same as last summer – we hear about some new German offensive. Towards Kharkov. Then, all of a sudden, Kursk. Then Volchansk and Belgorod. Sevastopol has fallen. I keep asking, "What's happening?" None of our soldiers can tell me.'

She fell silent for a moment and then, moving one hand as if to push away some frightening thought, she went on, 'I go over to the book shelves you were just talking about. I say to Lenin, Chernyshevsky, and Herzen,[40] "Can we really not defend you? Is this really going to be the end of you?" And then I say, "Defend us! Help us! Some kind of darkness has fallen on us."'

'What *do* our soldiers tell you?' said Mostovskoy.

Just then, from behind the kitchen door, came the sound of a young woman's voice – half amused, half angry: 'Máma! Marusya! Where are you? The pie's burning.'

'A pie!' said Mostovskoy, clearly glad to evade Alexandra's questions. 'Seems this is going to be quite a dinner!'

'A feast in time of plague,'[41] Alexandra replied. Pointing towards the door, she went on, 'Zhenya, my youngest ... you've met her. Really all this was her idea. She arrived just a week ago, unexpectedly. Everyone else is parting from their nearest and dearest – while here we have this surprise reunion. And there's another of my grandchildren, Ludmila's son Tolya. He's on his way to the front, he's just passing through. So we decided to celebrate both meetings and partings.'

'It's all right,' said Mostovskoy. 'No need for explanations. Life goes on.'

'It's harder when you're old,' Alexandra said quietly. 'I feel the country's tragedy differently from the young. Forgive me weeping, but who else can I say these things to? Nikolay so loved and respected you. And then we're all ...' Looking straight at Mostovskoy, she went on, 'Sometimes I just want to die. And then I think not – that I've still got the strength to move mountains.'

Mostovskoy stroked her hand and said, 'Quick – or the pie really will burn.'

*

'And now – the moment of truth,' said Zhenya, bending down towards the half-open oven door. Glancing at Alexandra and then putting her lips to her ear, she said very quickly, 'I got a letter this morning … Long ago, before the war … Remember, I told you about him … A commander I once met, Novikov … We met again on a train. Such a strange coincidence. And then today … Just imagine, I was thinking about him as I woke up. He's probably no longer alive, I said to myself. And an hour later there was a letter from him. And our meeting in the train, when I was on my way here from Moscow, that was extraordinary too.'

Zhenya put her arms around Alexandra's neck and began kissing her – first on the cheek and then on the white hair falling over her temples.

When Zhenya was studying at the Art Institute, she had been invited to some gala at the Military Academy. There she met a tall, slow, heavy-footed man, the 'elder' for his year. He had escorted her to her tram and then called on her several times. He graduated from the academy in the spring and then left Moscow. He wrote to her two or three times, asking her to send him a photograph but not saying anything about his feelings. She sent a very small photo she had had taken for her passport. And then, around the time she finished at the Art Institute and got married, he stopped writing.

But when she left Krymov and was on her way to her mother's, the train had stopped in Voronezh and a tall, fair-haired commander had entered her compartment.

'Do you remember me?' he asked, holding out a large, pale hand.

'Comrade Novikov,' she replied, 'of course I remember you. Why did you stop writing?'

He smiled, silently took a small photograph out of an envelope and showed it to her.

It was the photograph she had sent him long ago.

'The train was just coming to a stop,' he said, 'and I saw your face in the window.'

The two elderly women doctors sitting in the compartment with them listened avidly to every word she and Novikov said. For them, this meeting was an unexpected diversion; after a while, they joined in the conversation. One of them, with a spectacle case sticking out of her jacket pocket, talked almost without stopping, recalling all the unexpected meetings she could think of – in her own life and in the lives of her friends and family. Zhenya felt grateful to her; Novikov – evidently seeing this meeting as deeply significant – seemed to be wanting a heart-to-heart conversation, whereas she just wanted to be quiet. Novikov got out at Liski, promising to write, but he never did. And now she had suddenly received a letter from him, which had reawoken thoughts and feelings from a time she had thought gone forever.

As Alexandra watched Zhenya working away in the kitchen, she admired her fine gold chain, thinking how it looked just right against her pale neck. She noticed how her perfectly chosen comb brought out faint gleams of gold in her dark hair. But, had they not been touched by the living beauty of a young woman, the comb and the gold chain would have been nothing. There was a sense of warmth, she thought, that emanated not from her daughter's flushed cheeks or half-parted lips but from somewhere deep in her clear brown eyes – eyes that had seen so much, that were now so much older and wiser, yet still as immutably childlike as two decades earlier.

9

Towards five o'clock they sat down at table. Alexandra Vladimirovna offered the wicker armchair to Mostovskoy, the guest of honour, but he chose instead to sit down beside Vera on a little stool. To his left was a young lieutenant with bright, clear eyes. He had two cherry-coloured diamonds on his collar tabs.

Alexandra then turned towards Spiridonov. 'As our chief supplies officer,' she said, gesturing towards the armchair, 'you, Stepan, must sit here.'

'Pápa is the source of all light, warmth and pickled tomatoes,' said Vera.

'My uncle,' said Seryozha, 'is the boss of the home repairs company.'

Spiridonov had indeed provided Alexandra not only with a good supply of firewood but also with enough potatoes and pickled tomatoes to last the winter. He knew how to mend everything: from kettles and electric irons to taps and chair legs. And he had even handled the negotiations with a furrier over repairs to her squirrel-fur coat.

After sitting down, Spiridonov glanced now and again at Vera. Tall, fair-haired and rosy-cheeked, she looked very like him. Sometimes he expressed regret that she did not look more like Marusya. But deep down he was happy to recognize in his daughter some of the physical traits of his brothers and sisters.

Like more than a few of his contemporaries, Stepan Fyodorovich Spiridonov had followed a path that only a few decades earlier would have seemed astonishing.

Chief engineer – and then director – of the Stalgres power station, Spiridonov had, thirty years ago, been grazing goats on the outskirts of a small factory settlement near Naro-Fominsk. Today, with the Germans now moving south from Kharkov towards the Volga, he had been thinking about the course of his life, who he had been and who he had become. He had a reputation for coming up with bold ideas. He had several new inventions and innovations to his credit, and his name had even been mentioned in an important electrical engineering manual. He was in charge of a major power station. Some said he was a poor administrator – and there had indeed been times when he'd spent all day on the shop floor, leaving his secretary to deal with the endless telephone calls. Once he had even made a formal request to be transferred from administrative work, but he had felt relieved when the people's commissar refused this request; there was much that he found interesting and enjoyable even in administrative work. He was not afraid of responsibility; he enjoyed the tension that went with being in charge of things. The workers admired him, though he was sometimes severe and quick-tempered. He liked to eat and drink well. He liked going to restaurants and he kept a large secret cache of two- and three-rouble notes – his 'subcutaneous store', as he called it. He let himself go if he had a free evening during one of his trips to Moscow – and some of what he got up to also had to be kept secret from his family. Nevertheless, he loved his wife and took pride in her being so well educated – and there was nothing he would not have done for her, for his daughter and for all his extended family.

Sitting beside Spiridonov was Sofya Osipovna, the head of a hospital surgery department. She was middle-aged and she had broad shoulders, red fleshy cheeks and the two bars of a major on her collar tabs. She frowned a lot and had an abrupt manner of speech. According to Vera, who worked in the same hospital, the other members of staff were afraid of her – not only the nurses and orderlies but even the other doctors. She had been a surgeon since before the war. Her character may have influenced her choice of profession, but her profession had, in turn, left a certain imprint on her character.

She had taken part, as a doctor, in expeditions organized by the Academy of Sciences; she had been to Kamchatka and Kirghizia and had spent two whole years in the Pamir Mountains. Occasional words of Kazakh and Kirghiz had become a part of her everyday speech. After a while, Vera and Seryozha came to adopt one or two of these words. Instead of 'good', they would say 'jakhshi'; instead of 'all right' – 'hop'.

She loved music and poetry. Returning from a twenty-four-hour shift, she would lie down on the sofa and tell Seryozha to recite Pushkin and Mayakovsky. Sometimes she would quietly sing Gilda's aria from *Rigoletto*, half-closing her eyes and gesturing with one hand as if she were a conductor. Her face would take on such a strange look that Vera would have to run out into the kitchen, her cheeks swollen with laughter.

She also loved card games. She would play a couple of rounds of blackjack with Spiridonov, but really she preferred to play something simpler, 'just for fun', with Vera and Seryozha. Sometimes, though, she would feel suddenly agitated; she would throw down her cards and say, 'No, I'm not going to be able to sleep tonight. I'd do better to go back to the hospital.'

On the other side of Sofya Osipovna was Tamara Berozkina. Her husband was a Red Army commander, but she had heard nothing from or about him since the war began. She dressed with the particular care of someone ashamed of their poverty. She was thin; she had sad, beautiful eyes and her delicate face looked pale and exhausted. She seemed the kind of person simply unable to cope with life's cruelties.

She and her husband had lived close to the frontier. On the first day of the war their house had caught fire; she had rushed outside in her dressing gown and slippers, holding in her arms her little daughter Luba, who had measles. Her son Slava had run along beside her, clutching her gown.

With her sick little Luba and her barefoot boy, she had been put on a truck – and so her long months of sorrows and homelessness had begun. She had ended up in Stalingrad, where she at last managed to find some kind of shelter for herself and her two children. The military recruitment office had helped, allocating her a dress and each of her children a pair of shoes. She had sewed and darned for the wives of important officials. In the offices of the city soviet, she got to know Marusya, who was a senior inspector for the education section – and through her she met Alexandra Vladimirovna.

Alexandra had given Tamara her own coat and boots and insisted that Marusya find little Slava a place in a children's home, where he would be sure to receive regular meals.

To the other side of Tamara was Andreyev. He was sixty-five, but there was barely a hint of grey in his thick black hair. His long thin face looked somehow sullen and surly.

Putting her hand on Tamara's shoulder, Alexandra said thoughtfully, 'It seems we too may soon be forced out of our homes, made to drink from the same bitter cup as you. Who'd have thought it – as far east as this!' Then she thumped her hand on the table and went on, 'And if that's how things turn out, then you must come with us. We can all go to Ludmila's, in Kazan. Our fate will be your fate.'

'Thank you,' said Tamara, 'but that will be a terrible burden for you.'

'Nonsense,' Alexandra replied firmly. 'Now is no time to be thinking of comfort.'

43

Marusya whispered to her husband, 'May God forgive me, but Máma truly does live in a world beyond time and space. Ludmila only has two tiny rooms in Kazan.'

'What do you expect?' Spiridonov replied genially. 'Look at the way we've all invaded her own apartment and made ourselves at home in it. She's even given you her own bed – and I haven't heard you voice any objection to *that*.'

Spiridonov admired his mother-in-law for her total lack of pragmatic self-interest. For the main part she spent her free time with people she liked but who were unlikely ever to be of any help to her; more often it was *they* who needed *her* help. This impressed Spiridonov; it was not that he made a habit of seeking out people in high places, but he understood that friends could be of practical value and he was not above, at least now and again, cultivating someone likely to be of use to him. Alexandra, on the other hand, was blind to such considerations.

Spiridonov had more than once visited Alexandra in her workplace. He enjoyed watching her sure, confident movements and the deftness with which she managed complex chemical apparatus for the volumetric analysis of gases and liquids. Having a natural gift for anything practical, he would get angry when Seryozha appeared unable to change a burnt-out fuse or Vera was slow and clumsy with her sewing and darning. Not only was he a good carpenter and metalworker, not only did he know how to build a Russian stove – but he also liked to invent more unusual things. Once he dreamed up a little gadget that allowed him, without getting up from his armchair, to light and extinguish the candles on their New Year tree. He also installed such an unusual and interesting doorbell that an engineer from the Tractor Factory came round specially to examine the mechanism and replicate it. But Spiridonov had never been handed anything on a plate. He had had to work hard to reach his present position, and he had no time for bunglers and idlers.

'Well, comrade Lieutenant,' he asked the bright-eyed young man to his left, 'will you keep Stalingrad safe from the Germans?'

As a young commander, Kovalyov was contemptuous of civilians. 'Our task is very simple,' he replied condescendingly. 'When we receive the order to fight, we will fight.'

'You received that order on the very first day of the war,' said Spiridonov, with amusement.

Kovalyov took this personally. 'It's easy enough to talk when you're safe in the rear,' he said. 'But on the front line, with mortar bombs exploding all around you and Stukas up above, you think differently. Isn't that so, Tolya?'

'Precisely,' said Tolya, with little conviction.

'Well, let me say one thing,' said Spiridonov, raising his voice. 'The Germans will never get past the Don. Our defences there are impregnable.'

'You seem to be forgetting a great deal,' Seryozha exclaimed in a thin, squeaky voice. 'Don't you remember a year ago? How everyone kept saying, "The Germans will stop when they reach the old border. They won't get any further than that!"'

'Attention! Attention!' shouted Vera. 'Air-raid alert!' And she gestured towards the kitchen door.

Zhenya came into the room, carrying a large, pale blue dish. Tamara, looking prettier for being a little flushed, was walking beside her, hurriedly adjusting the white towel thrown over the pie.

'The edge is a little burnt,' Zhenya declared. 'I got distracted.'

'It's all right,' said Vera. 'I'll eat the burnt bits.'

'Why's the girl always so greedy?' said Marusya, looking pointedly at her husband. All Vera's failings – she believed – came wholly from him.

'And I say again that they won't cross the Don,' Spiridonov declared vehemently. 'The Don will be the end of them.' Brandishing a long knife, he got to his feet. The weightiest mealtime responsibilities – dividing a watermelon, slicing up a pie – were always entrusted to him. Afraid of making the pie crumble, of failing to justify his family's trust, he said, 'But shouldn't it be left to cool down a little?'

'What do *you* think?' asked Seryozha, looking at Mostovskoy. 'Will the Germans get across the Don?'

Mostovskoy did not answer.

'They'll cross the Don soon enough. They've already taken all of Ukraine and half of Russia,' Andreyev said grimly.

'So your opinion,' said Mostovskoy, 'is that the war's lost?'

'It's not a matter of opinions,' said Andreyev. 'I'm just saying what I've seen. Opinions are for people smarter than me.'

'And what makes you think the Don will be the end of the Germans?' asked Seryozha, addressing Spiridonov in the same squeaky voice as before. 'They've crossed the Berezina and they've crossed the Dnieper. Now they're heading for the Don and the Volga. Which river's really going to be the end of them? The Irtysh? The Amu-Darya?'[42]

45

Alexandra looked at her grandson thoughtfully. Usually he was shy and silent. She thought it must be the presence of the two young lieutenants that had stirred him up. What she didn't know was that Seryozha had drunk some of Kovalyov's moonshine. He was no longer thinking clearly. To himself he now seemed uncommonly clear-headed and intelligent, but he was not certain that his many gifts were being fully appreciated.

Vera leaned over towards him and asked, 'Seryozha, are you drunk?'

'Not in the least,' he answered crossly.

'Let me explain, my friend,' said Mostovskoy, turning to Seryozha. Everyone fell silent, listening eagerly. 'I'm sure you all remember Stalin's remarks about the giant Antaeus. Each time his feet touched the ground he grew stronger. Well, what we see today is an anti-Antaeus. He imagines he's a giant and a warrior, but he isn't really. When this false warrior advances over land that is not his, each step makes him not stronger but weaker. The earth does not lend him strength; on the contrary, a hostile land saps his strength until in the end he collapses. Such is the difference between the true Antaeus and today's vulgar pseudo-Antaeus, who has sprung up overnight like some fungus or mould. And our Soviet regime is a powerful force. And we have the Party, a Party whose will calmly and rationally unites and organizes the might of the people.'

Seryozha was looking at Mostovskoy intently, his eyes dark and gleaming. Mostovskoy smiled and patted him on the head.

Marusya got to her feet, raised her glass and said, 'Comrades! Here's to our Red Army!'

Everyone turned towards Tolya and Kovalyov, all wanting to clink glasses with them and to wish them health and success.

Next came the ceremony of slicing the pie. Splendid and ruddy, this pie evoked both joy and sorrow. It conjured up a more peaceful past that, like all pasts, now seemed to embody nothing but good.

Spiridonov said to his wife, 'Marusya, remember when we were both students? Swaddling clothes hanging up to dry, little Vera screaming loud enough to bring the house down, and you and me handing round slices of pie to our guests. And great cracks in the window frames, and a cold draught coming up through the floor.'

'How could I not remember?' Marusya replied with a smile.

Also turning to Marusya, Alexandra said slowly and thoughtfully, 'And I used to bake pies in Siberia. You and Ludmila were living with Grandad, and Zhenya wasn't yet born. What didn't we live through then! Crossing

46

the Yenisey in spring, while the ice was breaking up. Being pulled on a sledge by reindeer, through a howling blizzard. It was so cold the window panes burst. We stored our milk and our water in solid form. And the nights lasted for ever and ever. I used to bake cranberry and lingonberry pies. I used to bake pies filled with Siberian salmon … Our comrades would come and join us. Heavens, how long ago that all seems.'

'Pheasant pie is delicious. We used to eat it in the Issyk-Kul valley,' said Sofya Osipovna.

'*Jakhshi, jakhshi!*' said Seryozha and Vera in one voice.

'Seems I'm the only one here with no pies to recall,' said Mostovskoy. 'I either ate in student canteens or in restaurants in foreign cities. And then, after the Revolution, it was canteens or houses of recreation.'[43] After a moment, he went on, 'No, I lie. One Easter during my time in prison we were given a slice of *kulich*. And then, for lunch, there was an excellent *kasha* and mushroom pie. It wasn't exactly home cooking, but believe me, it's still a joy to recall!'

'Dear God!' said Marusya. 'Does Hitler really want to take everything from us? Our lives, our homes, our loved ones, even our memories?'

'Let's all agree not to say another word about the war today!' said Zhenya. 'Let's just talk about pies!'

At that moment little Luba walked up to her mother, pointed at Sofya and announced triumphantly, 'Máma, look what a big sugar lump that auntie's given me!' Unclenching her fist, she exhibited a cube of sugar, moistened by the warmth of her pale yet dirty hand. 'See,' she went on in a loud whisper. 'We mustn't go yet. Maybe there'll be more!'

Everyone was looking at Luba. Luba turned to her mother and saw her embarrassment. Realizing she had betrayed their secret poverty, she buried her head in her mother's lap and burst into tears.

Sofya stroked Luba's head and sighed loudly.

After this, something changed. It was clearly impossible to make the evening into a last merry supper, with no mention of today's or tomorrow's troubles.

The conversation returned to the matters on everyone's mind: the Red Army's long retreat, the reasons for its repeated defeats, the possibility that even moving to Kazan might not be enough, that they might all have to move again – to Siberia or the Urals.

'And what if the Japanese invade through Siberia?' asked Zhenya.

Tamara looked at Luba, whose head was lying in her lap. Hiding her disfigured, work-worn hands in Luba's curly hair, she said quietly, 'Is this really the end?'

Spiridonov spoke of 'former people'[44] who, rather than planning to leave, were keenly awaiting the Germans.

'Yes,' said Sofya. 'I've met that sort too. There was a doctor yesterday who told me quite straightforwardly that he and his wife had already made up their minds. They're going to stay in Stalingrad, no matter what.'

'Yesterday I met some actors I know from Leningrad,' said Zhenya. 'I couldn't believe it. They wanted me to go to Kislovodsk with them. "Germans or not," they said, "Kislovodsk is a good place to be."'

'What of it?' said Seryozha, 'What's more surprising is how often we all get it wrong. People we think rock solid turn out to be pathetic wimps. But I've heard about one boy who was quite desperate to go to flying school. The authorities kept refusing him because of his social origin, but in the end they gave in. He graduated and they say he died the death of a hero. Like Gastello!'[45]

'Look at the young ones,' Alexandra Vladimirovna said quietly to Sofya. 'Tolya's a real man now. When he came to visit us before the war he was still a child, but now he's our defender. His voice, his mannerisms, even his eyes – everything about him is different.'

'Have you noticed how his friend can't keep his eyes off our Zhenya?' Sofya replied in her low voice.

'And Tolya even drinks like a man now. Last summer, though, when he and Ludmila were staying with us, he went out for a walk – and it started to rain. Ludmila snatched a raincoat and a pair of galoshes and went down to the Volga to look for him: "He'll fall ill, the boy's very susceptible to tonsillitis ..."'

Meanwhile, at the other end of the table, the young ones were arguing.

'The army's fleeing in panic,' said Seryozha.

'Not in the least,' Kovalyov replied angrily. 'Since Kastornoye we've fought every day.'

'Well, how come you've retreated so fast?'

'If you'd seen combat, you wouldn't ask.'

'But why do our men keep surrendering?'

'Why do you think? But as for our own regiment, it's certainly done its fair share of fighting.'

'Some of the wounded I've seen in hospital,' said Vera, 'are saying it's like the first months of the war all over again.'

'The worst part,' said Kovalyov, his irritation fading, 'is crossing the rivers. Day and night, the bombing never stops. You certainly want to move fast then. My mate was killed. I was wounded in the shoulder, bleeding like a stuck pig. At night the sky's all lit up with flares – and it rains bombs.'

'Soon it'll be the same here,' said Vera. 'I'm scared stiff.'

'You really don't need to be scared,' said Spiridonov. 'We're a long way from the front line and they say our anti-aircraft defences are very strong indeed. As strong as around Moscow. Maybe one or two planes will get through, but not more than that!'

'Oh yes,' laughed Kovalyov, 'we know your one or two planes. If the Fritzes want to set us alight, they certainly will. Isn't that so, Tolya?'

'But no bombers have got through yet,' Spiridonov replied. 'Our anti-aircraft guns can put up a wall of fire.'

'Wait till the Fritzes set their minds to it. If rivers don't stop their ground forces, they certainly won't stop their planes. First their bombers will give you a good dusting, then you'll be seeing their tanks.'

'I see,' said Spiridonov.

Kovalyov had more experience of the war, and was more sure of himself, than anyone else in the room. Every now and then he would give a little smile, conscious of the ignorance and naiveté of his listeners.

He reminded Vera of the lieutenants in her hospital. They would glance mockingly at the nurses while arguing furiously about matters comprehensible to them alone. Yet he was also similar to young boys she had known from school clubs before the war, boys who had come round to play cards or who had wanted to borrow – just for an evening, leaving as security a difficult-to-obtain school textbook – her copy of *King Solomon's Mines* or *The Hound of the Baskervilles*.[46]

'I think this may be the end,' said Sofya, pushing her plate away. 'Evil is stronger than good.'

There was a general silence.

'Time to put up the blackout curtains,' said Marusya. And, pressing her fists against her temples, as if to deaden some pain, she muttered, 'War, war, war ...'

'Time, I think, for another glass,' said Spiridonov.

'No, Stepan!' said Marusya. 'Not after the dessert!'

Kovalyov unhooked his water bottle from his belt. 'I'd been meaning to keep some for the road. Better, though, to share it with good people like yourselves! Well, Tolya, all the best. I won't stay the night. I'll be off in a moment.'

He poured out what was left of his yellowish vodka, sharing it between Tolya, Spiridonov and himself. 'All gone,' he said to Seryozha, shaking the empty bottle in front of him and making the stopper rattle.

Kovalyov staggered a few steps, then said to Zhenya, 'I'm as good as dead. Get it? People can talk all they like, but in five days I'll be back at the front. Get it? But that doesn't frighten me, I'll be killed anyway. I won't live to see an end to the war. Get it? Twenty years. Call it a lifetime. Understand?'

He was looking her straight in the face, with greedy, beseeching eyes. And she understood: he wanted her love. His days were numbered. Tears came to her eyes – she understood only too clearly.

Spiridonov put an arm around Kovalyov's shoulders, as if to accompany him on his way. Spiridonov had drunk too much, and Marusya was looking at him with pain and fury. His one glass too many seemed to have upset her as much as all the war's tragedies.

Standing in the doorway, Kovalyov burst out in sudden rage, 'What makes men surrender, I've heard people ask. Words, words, words ... Fritz is still over 200 kilometres away, but people here are already packing their things. Before the front reaches Stalingrad, bureaucrats will be eating pies in Tashkent. Do you know what it's like at the front? Lie down for a few hours – and you wake to find Fritz has advanced a hundred kilometres during the night. War's one thing – words are another. I've seen bureau-rats take fright at a puff of wind. But soldiers get taken prisoner and die – and then bureau-rats in Tashkent point the finger at them. And believe me, I know those finger-pointers. If they were encircled, you wouldn't catch them marching 500 kilometres, half-starved, to break through the German front. They'd be collaborators, they'd be *polizei*! They'd have fattened up nicely. But us soldiers have souls – and we know what it takes to keep fighting! Truth, that's what I care about. I want the truth, and I want it straight!'

Kovalyov's words were spoken somewhat at random, but there was nothing to stop any of his listeners from taking them personally. Kovalyov may well have hoped that one of them would answer him back. Then he'd have really let rip. He might have produced a weapon.

But everyone sensed that something had snapped, or broken free, deep inside Kovalyov. They knew he would be unable to control whatever this thing was. They all kept silent and avoided his eyes. His face had gone pale, with patches of skin that looked grey and dirty.

He slammed the door behind him and let out a long volley of curses as he went down the stairs.

'And there I was,' said Vera, 'thinking I'd be getting a day off from the hospital. He's shell-shocked. They're all shell-shocked.'

'There's no shell shock that shocks like the truth,' said Andreyev. He sounded so sad that everyone turned to look at him.

When Zhenya came back into the room, Mostovskoy asked, 'Have you heard anything from Krymov?'

'No,' she replied. 'But I know he's here in Stalingrad.'

'Oh, I forgot,' said Mostovskoy, looking perplexed. 'I forgot that you've separated. But it's my duty to report to you that he's a good man. I've known him a long time, since he was a boy.'

10

The moment their guests were gone, a sense of calm and peace returned to the Shaposhnikovs' apartment. Tolya volunteered to do the washing-up. The family's cups, saucers and teaspoons seemed sweet and dear to him – very different from the ones in the barracks. Vera laughed as she put an apron on him and tied a kerchief round his head.

'What a wonderful smell of home, of home and warmth, just like in peacetime,' said Tolya.

Marusya put her husband to bed and repeatedly checked his pulse. She was afraid his snoring might be a symptom of heart palpitations.

Looking into the kitchen, she said, 'Tolya, let someone else do the dishes. You should write your mother a letter. You need to take better care of those who love you.'

But Tolya didn't feel like writing to his mother. He was playing about like a mischievous child. First he called out to the cat, mimicking Marusya's voice. Then he got down on his hands and knees and pretended to headbutt the cat: 'Come on, come on, little ram! Let's see your horns!'

'If it weren't for the war,' Vera said dreamily, 'we'd be going to the beach tomorrow. We'd be taking a boat out, wouldn't we? But as it is, I haven't even felt like going for a swim. I haven't gone to the beach once.'

'If it weren't for the war,' said Tolya, 'I'd be going to the power station tomorrow, with Uncle Stepan. I really would like to see it, in spite of everything.'

Vera leaned over towards him and said very quietly, 'Tolya, there's something I want to tell you about.' But just then Alexandra Vladimirovna came in. Vera winked at Tolya and shook her head.

Alexandra began questioning Tolya: had he found military school difficult? Did he get out of breath if they had to march fast? Was he a good marksman? Were his boots the right size? Had he got photographs of his family? Had he got enough handkerchiefs, needles and thread? Had he got enough money? Was he getting regular letters from his mother? Did he ever have time to think about physics?

Tolya felt surrounded by the warmth of his family. This meant a lot to him, but it was as troubling as it was calming. It made the thought of his imminent departure all the more painful; difficulties are easier to bear when your heart is hardened.

Then Zhenya came in too. She was wearing the blue dress she used to wear when she came to visit Ludmila and Viktor in their dacha. 'Let's have tea in the kitchen,' she said. 'Tolya will like that!'

Vera went out to fetch Seryozha. A moment later she came back and said, 'He's lying in bed crying, burying his face in the pillow.'

'Oh, Seryozha, Seryozha,' said Alexandra Vladimirovna. Saying, 'Leave this to me,' she went to speak to her grandson.

11

When they left the Shaposhnikovs, Mostovskoy invited Andreyev to go and have a look at the town with him.

'Go out on the town with you?' laughed Andreyev. 'Two old fellows like us?'

'For a quiet stroll,' said Mostovskoy. 'It's a fine evening.'

'All right,' said Andreyev. 'Why not? Tomorrow I don't start till two.'

'Is your work very tiring?' asked Mostovskoy.

'At times.'

Andreyev liked this small man, with his bald head and alert little eyes.

For a while they walked in silence. It was a beautiful summer evening. The Volga was barely visible in the twilight, but it made its presence felt everywhere; every street, every little lane, lived and breathed the Volga. All the hills and slopes, the orientation of the streets – everything was determined by the river's curves and the steep cliffs of the west bank. And the monuments, the squares and parks, the giant factories, the little old houses on the outskirts, the tall new apartment blocks with blurred reflections of the summer moon in their windows – all had their eyes on the Volga, all were turned towards it.

On this warm summer evening, as the war raged not far away on the Don steppe, moving relentlessly east, everything in the city seemed strangely solemn and full of meaning: the loud tread of the patrols, the rumble of a nearby factory, the hoots of the Volga steamers, even the meek silence.

They sat down on an empty bench. Two young couples were sitting nearby. One of the young men, a soldier, got to his feet, walked over to Andreyev and Mostovskoy, his shoes squeaking on the gravel, took a quick look at them, went back again and said something in a low voice. There was the sound of girlish laughter. The two old men coughed in embarrassment.

'The young,' said Andreyev. He sounded both critical and admiring.

'I've heard that there's a factory where some of the workers are evacuees from Leningrad,' said Mostovskoy. 'I want to go and talk to them. I'm from Leningrad too.'

'Yes, the Red October steelworks. That's where I work. I don't think there are that many of your evacuees. But come along anyway. Come and visit us.'

'Were you in the revolutionary movement?' asked Mostovskoy. 'Back in the days of the tsars ...'

'Not really,' said Andreyev. 'All I ever did was read leaflets and spend a couple of weeks in prison for taking part in a strike. And I spoke now and again to Alexandra Vladimirovna's husband. I was a stoker on a steam tugboat and he was a student, getting a few months of practical experience. We used to go up on deck together and chat.'

Andreyev took out his tobacco pouch. There was a rustle of paper as they rolled their cigarettes. Mostovskoy's lighter sent up a shower of sparks, but the wick obstinately refused to catch.

'The old men are giving it their all,' one of the young soldiers said loudly. 'They're trying to operate a Katyusha!'

There was more girlish laughter.

'Damn it!' said Mostovskoy. 'I've forgotten my treasure. Alexandra Vladimirovna gave me a box of matches.'

'But tell me – what do you really make of it all?' said Andreyev. 'Things are going badly, aren't they? Say what you like about antis and Antaeuses – the Germans still keep advancing.'

'Things are going badly,' replied Mostovskoy, 'but the Germans will still lose the war. I'm sure Hitler has more than a few enemies even in Germany. Germany too has its internationalists and its revolutionary workers.'

'What makes you so sure?' said Andreyev. 'I've heard what some of our tank crew have to say – men who've taken their share of German prisoners. They say the Germans are all the same. Working class or not, it makes no difference.'

'We truly are in trouble,' Mostovskoy said quietly, 'if an old worker like yourself thinks there's no difference between the German government and the German working class.'

Andreyev turned towards Mostovskoy and said sharply, 'I understand. You want the Soviet people to fight against Hitler. And you also want them to remember the words, "Workers of the World, Unite!"[47] But the only thing that matters today is who's with us and who's against us. Your thinking's like the teachings of Christ. All very beautiful – but nobody actually lives by them. They just soak the whole earth with blood.'

'Times change,' said Mostovskoy. 'Nikolay Shaposhnikov once taught you about Marx – and *he* learned from the books I'd written. And now it's your turn to teach me.'

Too sad and exhausted to argue, Mostovskoy slumped down; he could almost have been asleep. In his mind's eye he was picturing a scene from two decades earlier: a huge congress hall, countless eyes full of excitement and joy, hundreds of faces he loved, dear Russian faces, together with the faces of fellow Communists from all over the world – France, England, Japan, India, Belgium, Africa and America, Bulgaria, Germany, China, Italy, Hungary, Latvia – who were friends of the young Soviet Republic. This huge hall had fallen silent – as if the very heart of humanity had missed a beat – as Lenin raised one hand and, with clarity and assurance, told the Comintern conference, 'Soon we will witness the foundation of an international Soviet Republic.'

Feeling a sudden surge of warmth and trust towards the man sitting beside him, Andreyev quietly lamented, 'My son is fighting on the front line, but his wife just wants to go to the cinema with her girlfriends and have a good time. And she and my wife Varvara are at each other's throats. It's a sorry story.'

12

Mostovskoy's wife had died many years ago. Living alone had taught him the importance of being orderly. He kept his large room clean and tidy. Sheets of paper, journals and newspapers were stacked in neat piles on his desk and the books on his shelves were all in their assigned places. Mostovskoy usually did most of his work in the morning. During the last few years he had been lecturing on philosophy and political economy and writing entries for an encyclopedia and a dictionary of philosophy. His articles were mostly short but always required a lot of work and the correlation of many different sources. Each year he received several packages of books from his editors. He had already written about Heraclitus, Fichte and Schopenhauer. The beginning of the war had found him in the middle of an unusually long article about Kant. Mostovskoy usually signed his articles just with his initials: M. M. His editors kept trying to persuade him to use his full name, but Mostovskoy obstinately and crossly went on using his initials.

He did not know many people in Stalingrad. Now and again other teachers of philosophy and political economy would drop by for consultations. They were a little afraid of him; he was impatient, and unyielding in argument.

That spring Mostovskoy had contracted acute pneumonia. The doctors had thought this would be the end of him; he was an old man and he had not yet recovered from his months in besieged Leningrad. But Mostovskoy did recover. His doctor then drew up a careful programme detailing each step of the gradual transition he was to make from the sickbed back to his ordinary routine.

Mostovskoy read through the programme, put blue or red ticks against particular points – and then, during his third day of being up and about, took a cold shower and polished the parquet floor of his room.

He was determined and impassioned; he had no time for affability and good sense.

Sometimes he dreamed of the past and heard the voices of friends long dead. Or he might be giving a speech in a small hall in London.

Quick, alert eyes were watching him; he saw black ties, high starched collars and the bearded faces of friends.

Or he would wake in the middle of the night and be unable to get back to sleep. One after another, pictures and scenes came to mind: student meetings; arguments in the university park; the path to Bakunin's grave in Bern; the rectangular stone over Marx's grave; a steamer on Lake Geneva; Sevastopol and a winter storm on the Black Sea; a stifling railway carriage taking political prisoners to Siberia, the rhythmic knocking of the wheels, songs sung in unison, a guard banging a rifle butt against the door; the early Siberian twilight, snow squeaking beneath his feet, a distant yellow light in the window of his hut, the light he had walked back to through all the dark evenings of his six years of exile.

Those dark, difficult days were the days of his youth, days of unrelenting struggle in anticipation of the great future that was the purpose of his life on earth.

He remembered his never-ending labour, the many occasions during the first years of the Soviet Republic when he had worked through the night, his work for the Provincial Commissariat of Enlightenment and for the Army Political Enlightenment Committee, his contribution to the theory and practice of the Five Year Plans and the general electrification plan, his work for the State Centre for Scientific Research.

Sometimes he would let out a long sigh. Why was he sighing? What was he regretting? Or was this merely the sigh of a tired, sick heart struggling day and night to force the blood through his clogged, sclerotic arteries?

Sometimes he would go down to the Volga before dawn, then walk a long way along the deserted shore, beneath the steep cliffs. He would sit on the cold stones and observe the first stirrings of light. He liked to watch the grey night clouds swell with the rosy warmth of life while the hot smoke from the factories turned suddenly dull and ashen.

In the slant sunlight the black water would seem younger. The very tiniest of waves would creep timidly over the dense flat sand and every least grain would start to glitter.

Sometimes Mostovskoy remembered the Leningrad winter: mountains of snow and ice on the streets; the silence of death and the roar of death; a piece of bread on the table; sledges carrying water; sledges carrying firewood; sledges carrying corpses covered with white sheets; frozen paths down to the Neva; frost-covered apartment walls; his many journeys to factories and military units; the talks he gave to meetings of volunteer militia; a grey sky sliced by searchlights; dark windows with pink stains that were the reflections of burning buildings; the howl of air-raid sirens; sandbags around the equestrian statue of Peter the Great; and, everywhere in the city, the living memory of the first beats of the Revolution's young heart: the Finland station, the deserted beauty of the Field of Mars, the Smolny Institute;[48] and – over and above all this – the pale, deathly faces and living, suffering eyes of children and the patient heroism of women, workers and soldiers. And his heart would be overwhelmed by a burden that was heavier, a pain more extreme, than he felt it could bear. 'Why, why did I ever leave?' he would ask in anguish.

Mostovskoy wanted to write a book about his life. He already had a clear idea of its basic structure: childhood; his village; his father, who had been a sexton; the school he had attended as a small boy; the political underground; the years of Soviet construction.

He did not like to correspond with those of his old friends whose letters were mainly about illnesses, sanatoriums, blood pressure and loss of memory.

Mostovskoy knew one thing for sure: never in Russian history had events succeeded one another with such dizzying speed as during the last twenty-five years. Never had life's various strata been so comprehensively rearranged. Everything had, of course, always been changing and flowing. Even before the Revolution it had been impossible for one man to step into the same river twice – but in those days the river had flowed very slowly, its banks had never looked any different and Heraclitus' revelation had seemed strange and obscure.[49]

Was there anyone at all in Soviet Russia who would feel surprised by the revelation that had so struck the Greek philosopher? This truth had moved from the realm of philosophical speculation to that of common experience; it was now equally obvious to full members of the Academy of Sciences, to factory and collective-farm workers and to children still at school.

Mostovskoy had thought a great deal about all this. Precipitate, indomitable movement! There was no escaping it. Movement was everywhere: in the almost geological transformation of the landscape; in the vast campaign that had brought literacy to the entire country; in the new cities appearing all over the map; in the new districts of cities, in the new streets and buildings, in the ever-growing number of new inhabitants of these buildings. This movement had mercilessly plunged once-famous names into obscurity and at the same time – from remote and misty villages, from the vast spaces of Siberia – it had called up hundreds of new names now celebrated throughout the country.

Journals published ten years ago seemed like ancient yellowed papyri, so momentous were the events of the last decade. People's living conditions had been transformed. Soviet Russia had advanced a hundred years. With its vast landmass and forests the new country had leaped into the future, changing everything that had seemed most unchangeable: its agriculture, its roads, the beds of its rivers. Thousands of inns, taverns and cabaret venues had disappeared – as had parish schools, institutes for the daughters of the nobility, monastery lands, private estates, stock exchanges and the grand mansions of wealthy capitalists. Scattered and annihilated by the Revolution, whole classes of people had disappeared: not only the exploiters but also those who enabled them to exploit; people whose misdeeds had been castigated in popular songs but whose position had seemed unassailable; people whose characteristics had been described by the greatest of Russian writers: landlords, merchants, factory owners, stockbrokers, cavalry officers, moneylenders, chamberlains, police chiefs and police sergeants. Senators had disappeared – as had full state councillors, privy councillors and collegiate assessors – the whole of that complex and cumbersome world of Russian officialdom, divided into no fewer than seventeen different ranks. Organ grinders, footmen and butlers had disappeared. Concepts and words had disappeared: Lady, Sir, Your Grace, Your Excellency, and the like.

Workers and peasants had become the masters of life. A whole new panoply of professions had been born: industrial and agricultural planners, peasant scientists, beekeeper scientists, cattle breeders, vegetable growers, kolkhoz engineers, radio operators, tractor drivers, electricians. Russia had attained an unprecedented level of literacy and general enlightenment, a sudden leap whose power can be compared only with that of some cosmic force; if there were an electromagnetic equivalent for Russia's cultural explosion in 1917, astronomers in other galaxies would have registered the birth of a new star, a star growing ever brighter. The common people, the 'fourth estate' of workers and peasants, put their strength, their honest directness and all their unique abilities at the service of the state – they became field marshals, generals, the fathers of giant cities, important Party officials at every level, the directors of mines, factories and agricultural projects. The hundreds of new industrial enterprises brought out new and unexpected abilities in people. Pilots, flight mechanics, air navigators, radio operators, drivers of cars and trucks, geologists, industrial synthetic chemists, electro-chemists,

60

photo-chemists, thermo-chemists, specialists in the applications of high-voltage electricity, automobile- and aircraft-engineers – these were the protagonists of the new Soviet society.

Even now, in this darkest period of the war, Mostovskoy could see the might of the Soviet state. He knew it was many times greater than the strength of the old Russia; he understood the strength that its millions of working people now drew from their faith, literacy, knowledge and love for the Soviet motherland.

He believed in victory. And he had only one wish: to forget his age and join in the fighting, to take part in the struggle for the freedom and dignity of the people.

13

Agrippina Petrovna, the brisk, alert old woman who washed Mostovskoy's clothes, prepared his morning tea and brought him his meals from the Party canteen, could see how shaken he was by the way the war was going.

Often, when she came round in the morning, she found his bed as she had made it the day before. Mostovskoy would be sitting by the window in his armchair, a full ashtray on the sill beside him.

Agrippina Petrovna had known better days: before the Revolution her late husband had owned a Volga ferry. In the evening, she usually had a glass of moonshine in her room. Not wanting to dilute its effect, she didn't eat anything with it. Then she would go out and sit on a bench in the yard. Her companions would be sober, but she herself would be feeling pleasantly tipsy and she would chatter away animatedly. Usually she covered her mouth with the hem of her shawl and tried not to breathe over the others: Markovna, the severe concierge, and Anna Spiridonovna, the cobbler's widow. Agrippina did not like gossip, but her need for conversation – especially when she'd had a drink – was overwhelming.

'Well, my friends,' she said, brushing the dust off the bench with her apron before she sat down. 'There was a time when it seemed to old women like us that the Communists were closing churches.' She turned towards the open ground-floor windows and continued in a loud voice, 'This accursed Hitler is truly the Antichrist. Truly Hitler is the Antichrist – and may no good ever come to him, in this world or in the next. I've heard tell that the Metropolitan bishop is celebrating the liturgy in Saratov and that prayers are now being said in every one of the churches. Yes, the churches are packed. And it's not only the old – it's young and old alike. Everyone has risen up against Hitler, everyone has arisen as one against this accursed Antichrist.' Then she went on more quietly, 'Yes, my girls, our beloved Soviet authorities are leaving us. People in our building are packing their belongings. They're going to the market and buying suitcases. They're sewing bags and sacks. As for my dear Mostovskoy, he looks ashen. Today he's been to see that old woman he knows, to arrange to be evacuated. He hasn't even had his lunch.'

'What's he got to worry about? He's old, and he's got no family.'

'What do you mean? Really, what on earth do you mean? If anyone needs to leave, it's Mostovskoy. The Germans will make mincemeat of a man like him. He's rushing about like crazy, trying to work out what to do. Today he's been out and about all day long. After all, he's a Party member, an Old Bolshevik from Leningrad. Yes, he's in a bad way now. Stays up all night. Smokes like a chimney ... A pension of 1,500 roubles and a pass to the Party dining room. An apartment that's warm and dry. A trip to the Caucasus every summer. The man's done well for himself. No wonder he doesn't want to be liquidated by Hitler!'

It turned dark. The women went on talking – about this, that and everything. Markovna glanced up at the windows above her and said, 'I can see light again in the window of that whore on the second floor. Let's hope she's not signalling to the Germans.'

In a loud and intimidating bass, Markovna bellowed, 'Hey! You on the second floor! In a moment we'll shoot!'

The old women got up from their bench. Agrippina went back to her room.

Spiridonovna and Markovna lingered a little, to discuss Agrippina.

'She's been drinking again,' said Spiridonovna. 'You can smell it on her breath. But where does she get the money?'

'What do you think? She steals it from Mostovskoy,' Markovna replied. 'God knows how much she steals! If the Germans weren't coming, she could buy back the fine house she lost after the Revolution.' In sudden fright she went on, 'Lord, Lord, what have we done? Why this German Satan? What sins, Lord, are you punishing us for?'

14

———

Tolya was leaving on the evening train. He was tense and anxious, as if he had only just realized what lay in store for him. He wanted to appear nonchalant, but he could see that he was not fooling his grandmother, who was looking very distressed indeed. This upset him.

'Have you written to your family?' she asked.

'Heavens above!' he said crossly. 'What do you want from me? I've been writing to my mother almost every day. I didn't today, but I will tomorrow.'

'I'm sorry, please don't be angry with me,' Alexandra Vladimirovna said quickly.

This infuriated Tolya still more.

'What's got into you? Why are you talking to me as if you think I'm some lunatic?'

Now it was Alexandra's turn to feel angry.

'Please calm down,' she said brusquely. 'Get a grip on yourself.'

Half an hour before he was due to leave, Tolya called out, 'Seryozha, come here a moment!'

And he took from his knapsack an exercise book wrapped in newspaper.

'Here – these are my notes, summaries of what I've read, a few ideas of my own. I once drew up a plan for my life up to the age of sixty. I'd resolved to devote myself to science, to work every day, every hour. So ... You understand ... If I ... In a word, keep this in memory of me. So, there we are ... That's all.'

For some time they just stood there and looked at each other, shaken, unable to speak. Tolya squeezed Seryozha's hand so tightly that his fingers went white.

There was no one else at home – only Seryozha and Alexandra Vladimirovna. Tolya said his goodbyes hurriedly, afraid of giving way to his feelings. 'I don't want Seryozha to come to the station with me. I don't like being seen off.'

And in the corridor, he said to his grandmother, getting the words out as fast as he could, 'I shouldn't have come. I've been living a different life, away from everyone I love. I'd grown a hard shell. And now that shell's just melted away. If I'd known it would be like this, I wouldn't have come. That's why I haven't written to Máma today.'

Alexandra held her palms to Tolya's large flushed ears and, drawing him close, pushed his cap to one side and gave him a long kiss on the forehead. He went very still, remembering the sense of happy peace he had known long ago in her arms.

And now that his grandmother was old and weak and he was a strong young soldier, his strength and his helplessness had got suddenly confused. He pressed his whole body against her, called her his *bábushka*, his *babúsya*, his darling *babúlya* and then rushed towards the door, head bowed.

15

Vera was still in the hospital. She was on night shift. After the evening round, she made her way out of the ward.

The corridor was lit by a blue lamp. Vera opened the window and stood there, leaning her elbows on the sill.

From the third floor there was a good view of the city. The river was white and gleaming. The blacked-out windows of buildings gave off a faint, grey-blue light, the colour of mica. There was no kindness, no warmth, no life in this icy blue – a light reflected first from the dead face of the moon and then from the dust-covered windows and the cold night-time water. It was a fragile, uncertain light. You had only to turn your head a little and it would disappear; once again the windows and the Volga would be a lifeless black.

Over on the east bank Vera could see a vehicle with lit headlamps. High in the sky above her, the beams from two searchlights had crossed; it was as if someone with a pair of pale blue scissors was shearing the curly clouds. Down below, in the garden, she could hear quiet voices and see little red lights; some of the patients from the convalescent ward must have slipped out through the kitchen door to enjoy a secret smoke. The wind off the Volga brought with it the freshness of the water, a clean cool smell that sometimes got the better of the heavy smell of the hospital but sometimes yielded to it, making it seem as if not only the hospital but also the moon and the river smelled of ether and carbolic acid, and that it was not clouds scudding across the sky but dusty balls of cotton wool.

From the isolation ward, where three patients were dying, came muffled groans.

Vera knew this monotonous groan of the dying, of those who could no longer ask for anything – neither food, nor water, nor even morphine.

The door of the ward opened; two men were bringing out a stretcher. First came Nikiforov, short and pockmarked; at the other end of the stretcher was Shulepin, who was tall and thin. Because of Nikiforov, Shulepin had to take unnaturally short steps.

Without turning round, Nikiforov said, 'Slow down a bit, you're pushing me.'

Lying on the stretcher was a body covered in a blanket.

It seemed as if the dead man had pulled the blanket over his head himself, so as not to see these walls, these wards and corridors where he had suffered so cruelly.

'Who is it?' asked Vera. 'Sokolov?'

'No, it's the new one,' replied Shulepin.

For a moment Vera imagined she was an important doctor, with the rank of general, who had just flown in from Moscow. The chief surgeon would lead her into the room for the dying and say, 'This one's a goner.' 'No, you're wrong,' she would reply. 'Prepare him to be operated on straightaway. I'll carry out the operation myself.'

From the commanders' ward on the second floor came the sound of laughter and quiet singing:

> Tanya, Tatyana, Tanyusha,
> Remember that glorious May?
> I know we shall never forget –
> Such joys can't be taken away.

She recognized the voice of Captain Sitnikov, wounded in the left hand. The military prosecutor had made inquiries, but there turned out to be nothing untoward about this wound – a splinter from a German mortar bomb was indeed found in it.[50] Then someone else quietly joined in, probably Kvasyuk, the quartermaster lieutenant with a broken leg. He had been driving a small truck full of watermelons for the canteen and a three-ton ammunition truck had crashed straight into him.

Sitnikov had pestered Vera day after day, begging her to bring him some alcohol from the pharmacy. 'Even if it's only fifty grams,'[51] he had kept saying. 'How can you say no to a soldier?'

Vera had steadfastly said no – but since Sitnikov and Kvasyuk had become friends, she had smelt alcohol on their breath several times. Evidently one of the pharmacy duty nurses had proved more compassionate.

Here, standing by the window, she sensed two different worlds with apparently no points of contact between them. There was a fresh, cool world unlike anything else, a world of stars, moonlit water and ethereal pale blue light that appeared and disappeared in the windows, a world born from heroic romances and night-time dreams, a world without which she felt life was not worth living. And there was another world right beside her, advancing on her from all sides, entering her nostrils, rustling her white medicine-impregnated gown – a world of groans, coarse tobacco and clomping boots. This more prosaic world was everywhere – in the tedious registration forms she kept having to fill in, in tetchy remarks by doctors, in the bowls of millet she ate day after day, in the hospital commissar's dull lectures, in the dust of the streets and the howls of the air-raid siren, in her mother's moralizing, in conversations about shop prices, in the endless queues, in her quarrels with Seryozha, and in family discussions of the merits and faults of friends and relatives. She could sense this world's presence in her rubber-soled shoes and in her father's old coat, now re-tailored to fit her.

Behind her, Vera heard the quiet click of crutches. Her elbows on the sill, she lifted her head to look up at the sky. She was forcing herself to look at the clouds, at the stars, at the play of moonlight on windows – but all she was really aware of was the sound of crutches, coming towards her out of the dark corridor. Only one pair of hospital crutches sounded like this.

'What is it you're dreaming about?' came the voice of a young man.

'Is it you, Viktorov? I didn't hear you coming.'

And then she laughed, amused by her own little pretence, by her own unnatural voice.

'What is it?' he asked again, starting to laugh too. Whether she was feeling cheerful or sad, he wanted to show his meek readiness to join in her feelings – simply because they were hers.

'It's nothing,' said Vera. 'Nothing at all. I heard you perfectly. I knew you were coming. I wasn't really lost in a dream, only pretending.'

But here too she was only playing at telling the truth. She felt these words would help love's cause, that they would show Viktorov how strange and unusual she was, how unlike any other woman. But learning this game of love was impossible – and anyway it was unnecessary. Impossible, because it was too complex and difficult; unnecessary, because her love was growing within her all the time, like it or not.

'No!' Vera exclaimed, once Viktorov had duly told her how extraordinary she was. 'I couldn't be more ordinary. I'm dull and boring. There are tens of thousands of women in the city just like me.'

Viktorov had been brought to the hospital two weeks earlier. Some Messerschmitts had shot him down over the steppe and he had been wounded in the leg by an explosive bullet. A truck had happened to pass by and had picked him up in the middle of nowhere. His clothes and his long fair hair were full of burs, thorns and bits of dry grass and wormwood. He had lain there on his stretcher, his head turned to one side on his long thin neck. His pale face looked dirty and dusty, his mouth was open and there was a strange, touching look in his eyes – a mixture of childish fear and the anguish of the old.

Vera had remembered how, when she was little, she once saw a young turkey that had just been clubbed. Its thin neck was curved back, its beak was open and its eyes were starting to glaze over. Bits of grass and straw were stuck to its rumpled feathers.

As they got ready to put Viktorov on the operating table, he had looked at Vera. Then he had seen his soiled underwear and looked away. And Vera, who had seen hundreds of naked male bodies, had felt embarrassed; tears of pity and shame had come to her eyes.

It wasn't the first time convalescent patients had made a play for her. Some had even tried to embrace her in the corridor. One political instructor had declared his love for her in a letter and asked her to marry him. When he was being discharged, he had asked her to give him a photograph.

Senior Sergeant Viktorov had never tried to talk to her, though she had often sensed him looking when she went into the ward. It was she who had started their first conversation: 'Your unit's not far away. Why don't any of your comrades come to visit you?'

'I'd just been transferred to another regiment. And I hardly know anyone any longer in my old regiment. They're all new.'

'Does that frighten you?'

He was slow to respond. She understood that he was suppressing the wish to reply the way pilots usually reply to questions like this from a young woman. Looking very serious, he said, 'Yes.'

They were both embarrassed. Both wanted the relationship between them to be special, not just something fleeting and shallow. And for both it was as if a bell had rung out, solemnly proclaiming that their wish was being realized.

Viktorov turned out to have been born in Stalingrad. At one time he had worked as a metal fitter. Spiridonov had often visited his work-shop and had made his presence felt there.

But the two of them had no shared acquaintances. Viktorov lived six kilometres from Stalgres and had always gone straight home from work, not joining any sports teams or staying for any of the films shown in the club.

'I don't like sport,' he said. 'I like to read.'

Vera noticed that he liked the same books as Seryozha – books she didn't find very interesting.

'What I like best are historical novels. But it was difficult to get hold of them – there were only a few in the club library. I used to go into the city on Sundays and order from Moscow.'

The other patients liked Viktorov. Vera once overheard a commissar say, 'He's a good lad, someone you can rely on.'

She blushed, like a mother hearing people praise her son.

He smoked a lot. She would bring him cigarettes and loose tobacco. And soon afterwards the whole ward would be full of smoke.

On one arm he had a tattoo of an anchor and a length of cable. 'That's from when I was at factory school,' he said. 'I was quite wild. Once I was almost expelled.'

She liked his modesty. He never boasted. If he mentioned his combat experience, what he spoke about was always his comrades, his plane, the engine, the weather, the flying conditions – anything but himself. But he preferred to talk about life before the war. When the conversation did turn to the war, he usually said nothing at all – though he probably had a great deal to say. And certainly a lot more than Sitnikov, the munitions supply officer who was the ward's chief orator.

Viktorov was thin, with narrow shoulders, small eyes and a large, wide nose. Vera was fully aware that he was not handsome – but since she liked him, she saw this as not a fault but a virtue. No one but her, she believed, could understand just how special he was. His smile, his gestures and movements, the way he looked at his watch or rolled a cigarette – everything about him was special.

When Vera was twelve, she had planned to marry her cousin Tolya, and at the age of fifteen she had fallen in love with the Komsomol[52] organizer; the two of them had gone to the cinema and the beach together. She had thought there was nothing she didn't know about love and romance and she had listened with a condescending smile to talk about such matters at home. When she was in her last year at school, girls in her class had said things like, 'One should marry a man ten years older than oneself, a man who's found his place in the world.'

Life could hardly have turned out more differently.

The corridor window became their meeting place. Often, if she had a free moment, she needed only go there and think about Viktorov – and she would hear the sound of his crutches, as if she had sent him a telegram.

Sometimes, though, when he was looking thoughtfully out of the window and she was standing beside him, looking at him in silence, he would suddenly turn round and say, 'What?'

'What is it?' she would ask in bewilderment.

They often talked about the war, but sometimes it was their more casual, childish words that mattered the most.

'Senior Sergeant – I like that!' she would say. 'How senior can you be when you're only twenty!'

*

That night, after she'd pretended not to hear him coming, they went on standing side by side, their shoulders touching. They were talking all the time, though neither was really listening. More important than any words was the way he would go very still, waiting for her to touch him again, if her shoulder moved away from him. Trustingly, she would move closer. Sensing this apparently chance contact, he would look sideways at her neck, at her ear, at her cheek and at a lock of her hair.

In the blue light, Viktorov's face appeared dark and sad. Vera looked at him with a presentiment of tragedy. 'I don't understand. At first I thought I just felt sorry for you, because you'd been wounded. But now it's myself I'm starting to pity.'

He wanted to put his arms around her. He wondered if this was what she wanted too, if she was waiting patiently for him to stop being so hesitant. And then he just said, 'Why? What do you mean?'

'I don't know,' she said. And she looked up at him, the way a child looks at an adult.

Choking with emotion, he leaned towards her. His crutches fell to the floor and he let out a little cry. He hadn't actually put any weight on his wounded leg; he had simply been afraid he might do.

'What's the matter? Are you feeling dizzy?'

'Yes,' he said. 'My head's spinning.' And he put his arms around her shoulders.

'Hang on to the windowsill. Let me pick up your crutches.'

'No,' he replied. 'Let's stay like this.' And they went on embracing. To Viktorov it felt as if, rather than Vera supporting him because he was clumsy and helpless, it was he who was defending Vera, protecting her from a huge and hostile night sky.

Soon he would be fully recovered and he would be back in his Yak[53] again, patrolling the sky over Stalgres and the hospital. He could hear the roar of his engine – in his mind he was already pursuing a Junkers. Once again, he experienced that desire so difficult for anyone but a pilot to understand – the desire to get close to an enemy who may be your death. Ahead of him he could see the lilac flicker of tracer bullets and a cruel pale face – the face of a German gunner and radio operator – that he had once glimpsed during a dogfight over Chuguev.

He pulled open his hospital gown and wrapped it around Vera. She pressed herself against him.

For a few moments he stood there in silence, looking down at the floor, sensing her warm breath and the pressure of her breast against his chest. He would be happy, he felt, to stand there on one leg for the next year, holding this young woman in a dark and empty corridor.

'That's enough,' she said suddenly. 'Let me pick up your crutches.'

She helped Viktorov to sit down on the windowsill. 'Why?' she asked. 'Why does it all have to be like this? Everything could have been so good. My cousin's just left for the front. And the surgeon says you're healing unusually quickly. You'll be discharged in ten days.'

'Never mind,' he replied, with the insouciance of a young man choosing not to think about love's future. 'Come what may, what we have now is good.' And then, with a little smile, he added, 'You know … I mean … You know why I'm getting better so quickly? It's because I love you.'

Later that night, lying on a little white-painted wooden bench in the duty room, Vera thought and thought.

Was it possible, in this vast four-storey building full of groans, blood and suffering, for newborn love to survive?

She remembered the stretcher and the body covered with a blanket. She was gripped by a sharp, heart-rending pity for a man whose name she did not know and whose face she had forgotten, a man whom the orderlies had already taken out to be buried. This feeling was so powerful that she cried out and folded her legs up towards her, as if to fend off a blow.

But she knew now that this joyless world was dearer to her than the heavenly palaces of her childish dreams.

16

The next morning, Alexandra Vladimirovna, wearing her usual dark dress with a white lace collar, threw her coat over her shoulders and left the building. Krotova, her laboratory assistant, was already waiting outside. A truck was going to take the two of them to a chemical factory to test the air quality in the workshops.

Alexandra got into the cab. Krotova, who was strong and stocky, grabbed hold of the side of the truck and climbed into the back. Poking her head out of the window, Alexandra called out, 'Take good care of the apparatus, comrade Krotova. It'll be a bumpy ride!'

The driver, a puny young woman in ski trousers, a red headscarf wound round her head, put her knitting down on the seat beside her and started the engine. 'It's asphalt all the way. No ruts at all,' she said. Looking at her elderly passenger with curiosity, she added, 'Once we're on the main road, I'll be putting my foot down.'

'How old are you?' asked Alexandra.

'Oh, I'm getting on now. I'm twenty-four.'

'Much the same as me! Married?'

'I was. Now I'm on my own again.'

'Has your husband been killed?'

'No, he's in Sverdlovsk, working at the Urals Machine Factory. He's found himself another wife there.'

'Children?'

'A little girl. She's one and a half now.'

When they got to the main road, the driver, looking bright and cheerful, began asking Alexandra about her daughters and grandchildren – and then about her work: what was she going to do with all these glass cylinders, rubber hoses and angled pipes?

Next the driver said a little more about herself. She and her husband had lived together for six months. Then her husband had moved to Sverdlovsk. In his letters he had said again and again, 'Very soon they'll give me a room,' but then the war had begun. He was exempt from conscription, since his was a reserved occupation. He wrote less and less often. He'd said he was living in a hostel for unmarried workers, but then, in the winter, he wrote to say he had married again. He asked if she'd let him have their little daughter. She had kept her daughter and not answered the letter. But there had been no court proceedings – each month he sent her 200 roubles for the girl's upkeep.

'He could send me a thousand roubles, but I still wouldn't forgive him. And I'll still be able to feed the girl even if he doesn't send me anything at all. This job's well paid.'

They sped along, past orchards, past little grey wooden houses, and past factories of all sizes. Now and again, in the gaps between trees, Alexandra could see splashes of pale blue water. Then the Volga would disappear behind fences, buildings or small hills.

On reaching the factory and receiving her pass, Alexandra went straight to the head office; she wanted them to assign her a technician who could tell her about their ventilation system and the layout of the equipment. She also wanted the help of an ordinary worker, if only for an hour; it was not easy for Krotova to carry a twenty-four-litre suction apparatus all by herself.

Meshcheryakov, the factory director, lived in the same building as Alexandra and her family. In the morning she sometimes saw him going off to work. After getting into his car and closing the door, he would wave goodbye and blow theatrical kisses to his wife, who would be standing by a window in their apartment.

Alexandra would have liked to appear affable and easy-going. She wanted to say to Meshcheryakov, 'Be a good fellow. After all, we're neighbours. Meet me halfway – help me carry out my work quickly. And who knows? Maybe I'll be able to suggest one or two little improvements to your ventilation.'

But Meshcheryakov gave her no chance to say anything at all. Through a half-open office door, she heard him say to his secretary, 'I can't see her today. And you can also tell her that this is no time to be fussing about minor questions of health. On the front line our men are sacrificing not just their health but their lives.'

Alexandra went up to the door. If anyone who knew her had seen her pursed lips and angry frown, they would have thought that Meshcheryakov was in for an unpleasant few minutes. But she did not go inside. She merely stood there for a moment and then made her way to the workshop.

In the large hot workshop the men watched mockingly as the two women arranged their cylinders, took air samples from different sites, sealed their rubber tubes with screw clamps and released a little water from three of the pipettes: by the technician's desk, beside the main ventilator and above the barrels containing some strong-smelling liquid. A thin, unshaven worker in a blue gown with torn elbows said in Ukrainian, 'Measuring water! You can't get more idiotic than that!'

A young foreman, or perhaps a chemist, with a nasty, insolent look in his eyes, said to Krotova, 'Why bother? Any day now German bombers will be sorting out our ventilation for us.'

An old man with little red cheeks criss-crossed with blue veins took a good look at the young, well-developed Krotova and said a few evidently coarse words that Alexandra couldn't quite hear. Krotova blushed and turned away, looking upset.

During the lunch break Alexandra sat down on a crate near the door; she was tired, partly because of the polluted air. One of the younger workers came up to her, pointed to her apparatus and asked, 'Auntie, what *is* all this stuff of yours?'

She began to explain about noxious gases and the importance of good ventilation.

Other workers began listening too. The Ukrainian who had joked about the idiocy of measuring water saw Alexandra get out her tobacco. 'Try some of this,' he said. 'It's good and strong.' And he held out a little red pouch tied with a lace.

Very soon this became a general discussion. First, there was talk about the relative dangers of different industries. The chemical workers took a certain bitter pride in their work; their conditions were generally considered more dangerous even than those of miners, furnacemen and steelworkers.

The men told Alexandra about occasions when the ventilation had broken down and people had been poisoned or asphyxiated. They talked of the vicious powers of 'chemistry' – how it rusted metal cigarette cases and ate away the soles of boots, how old men coughed up so much phlegm that they choked to death. They joked about a certain Panchenko who had forgotten to put on his protective overall; by the end of the day large holes had been burnt in his trousers.

Then the conversation turned to the war. The men talked with pain and bitterness about the destruction of mines, large factories, sugar refineries, railways and the Stalino locomotive works.

The man who'd upset Krotova went up to Alexandra and said, 'Mother, you'll probably be coming back again tomorrow. You must get some passes for the canteen.'

'Thank you, my son,' she replied, 'but tomorrow we'll bring something with us.'

After addressing this old man as her son, she laughed. He understood – and replied, 'I got married only a month ago.'

And in no time at all they were all talking as freely and animatedly as if Alexandra had spent not just a few hours but many long days in this workshop.

At the end of the lunch break, the workers gave them a hose, to save Krotova having to carry buckets of water from one end of the workshop to the other. They also helped the two women to move the apparatus around and set it up where the air was most likely to be polluted.

During the afternoon Alexandra remembered Meshcheryakov's words several times and felt her face flush; she wanted to go to his office and give him a piece of her mind there and then, but she held herself back: 'I'll finish the work first – then I'll speak to him. I'll teach him to get on his high horse!'

After getting an earful from Alexandra Vladimirovna, many directors and chief engineers had regretted trying to brush aside her safety recommendations. Her practised eye and her sense of smell – she often used to say that a chemist's most important instrument is their nose – had at once detected that there was something wrong in Meshcheryakov's workshop. The indicator papers had quickly changed colour and her absorbent solutions had turned cloudy; the air was indeed seriously polluted. She could already feel how it was affecting her, how the heavy, greasy air was irritating her nostrils and making her cough.

For the journey back home they were given a different truck and driver, but the engine broke down after they'd gone only a short distance. The driver fiddled about for a long time, then came back to the cab and, wiping his hands slowly and thoughtfully on an old rag, said, 'We won't be going any further in this. I'll have to call a breakdown truck from the garage. The pistons have jammed.'

'We were brought here by a young girl,' said Krotova, 'but it seems that you, a man, can't get us back again. And there I was, hoping to get to the food shop this evening.'

'You won't find it hard to get a lift,' said the driver. 'It'll only be ten roubles.'

'The real problem,' Alexandra said thoughtfully, 'is what to do with the apparatus.' And then she made up her mind. 'I know. We're not far from Stalgres. I'll go and get a truck from there. You stay here, Krotova, and look after the apparatus.'

'You won't get much help from Stalgres,' the driver replied. 'I know some of the drivers there. Spiridonov signs out the trucks himself – and he's a skinflint. You won't get any joy out of him.'

'I think I will,' said Alexandra. 'Shall we bet on it?'

'What on earth's got into you?' the driver said crossly. He turned to Krotova. Winking at her, he said, 'You stay here. We'll sleep under a tarpaulin – it'll be warm and cosy. Our own little holiday resort. And you can go to your food shop tomorrow.'

Alexandra set off down the road. On the uphill slope the windscreens of trucks speeding towards the city shone dazzlingly bright. The road was a cold greyish lilac where it dipped towards the east, but the spots still in the sun were a clear blue, and there were swirls of dust from the passing trucks. After a while, she caught sight of the tall buildings of Stalgres. The office building and the great apartment blocks were pink in the setting sun; clouds of steam and smoke shone over the workshops. Walking along the side of the road, past the little houses with their flower and vegetable gardens, were young men in boots and overalls and young women in wide trousers and shoes with high heels. All were carrying some kind of little knapsack or bag; a new shift must have been about to start work.

It was a quiet, clear evening. The leaves shone in the sun's last rays.

And, as always, the calm beauty of nature made Alexandra think of her son.

Aged sixteen, Dmitry had joined the Red Army to fight against Admiral Kolchak. He had then studied at Sverdlovsk University and, young as he was, had been put in charge of an important branch of industry. In 1937 he was arrested, accused of links with conspirators and enemies of the people. His wife was arrested soon afterwards. Alexandra had gone to Moscow and returned to Stalingrad with Seryozha, her twelve-year-old grandson. She had then made two further visits to Moscow, to petition on Dmitry's behalf. His former friends, people who had once depended on him, refused to see her and did not reply to her letters.

Her husband, Nikolay Semyonovich Shaposhnikov, had died of pneumonia during the Civil War. There was just one high-placed figure, a man who remembered him, who agreed to receive her. He obtained permission for her to visit her son, now working in a labour camp, and he assured her that his case would be reviewed.

The only time that those close to Alexandra ever saw her cry was when she was recounting her subsequent meeting with Dmitry. She had stood for a long time on a jetty, waiting for the launch that would bring him. When he arrived, she walked towards him and they stood there in silence, on the shore of the cold sea. They held each other's hands and looked into each other's eyes; they might have been two small children. Afterwards she had wandered about on the empty shore; the waves had flung white foam at the rocks and seagulls had cried high above her white head … In autumn 1939 Dmitry stopped replying to her letters. She sent further petitions and made more trips to Moscow. People promised to review Dmitry's case. Time passed and the war began.

As she hurried along the road, Alexandra felt slightly dizzy. She knew that this was not only because of the passing vehicles and the sudden flashes of light; it was also from age, exhaustion, her state of constant nervous tension and the poisoned air she had been breathing. Towards the end of each day her feet swelled and her shoes started to pinch; it seemed that her heart was now finding it hard to cope.

*

Her son-in-law was walking past the main entrance to the power station. There were people all round him and he was waving a sheaf of papers about, as if trying to ward off some official making importunate requests.

'No,' he was saying. 'If I try to connect you, it'll burn out the transformers. The entire city will be without electricity.'

'Stepan Fyodorovich,' Alexandra said quietly.

Spiridonov stopped dead.

'Has something happened at home?' he asked quickly, taking Alexandra to one side.

'No, we're all well,' she replied. 'Except that Tolya left yesterday evening.' And she went on to tell him about the truck breaking down.

'So much for Meshcheryakov – not one truck in proper working order!' said Spiridonov, with a certain satisfaction. 'Well, we can sort this out for you easily enough.' He looked at his mother-in-law and added more quietly, 'You're looking very pale, that's not good.'

'I feel dizzy.'

'What do you expect? You've been on your feet all day. You haven't eaten since this morning. You should know better,' he said crossly. And Alexandra noticed that here in Stalgres, where he was the boss, her son-in-law was speaking to her in a tone of patronizing solicitude she had not heard before. Usually he was more deferential.

'I'm not letting you leave in a state like this,' he said. He thought for a moment, then continued, 'So, I'll send out a truck for your laboratory assistant and the apparatus. And as for you, you're going to rest in my office. I'll be leaving for a Party meeting in an hour and I'll take you back home in my car. But first you must have something to eat.'

Before Alexandra could say a word in reply, he was shouting out, 'Sotnikov, tell the garage superintendent to send a small truck out towards Krasnoarmeisk. After about a kilometre he'll see a broken-down vehicle by the side of the road. It's transporting some scientific apparatus. He's to take the apparatus and the laboratory assistant back into town. All right? And no dawdling! And as for that Meshcheryakov …' Next, he called to an elderly lady, probably one of the cleaners, 'Olga Petrovna, take this guest to my office. Tell Anna Ivanovna to let her in. I'll be back in quarter of an hour, as soon as I'm free.'

Alone in her son-in-law's office, Alexandra sat down in a chair and looked at the large sheets of blue tracing paper on the walls; at the couches and chairs with covers still pristine and starched, as if no one had ever sat on them; at the dust-covered water jug, standing on a dish with yellow stains, which looked as if it had hardly ever been drunk from; and at the crookedly hung paintings – probably also seldom noticed – depicting celebrating crowds at the inauguration of Stalgres. She then glanced at her son-in-law's desk. On it lay papers, technical drawings, pieces of cable, porcelain insulators, a small pile of coal on a sheet of newspaper, a set of drafting pencils, a voltmeter and a slide rule. There was an ashtray full of cigarette butts and there were phones with dials so worn that the numbers had all been erased; all you could see was white metal. It was clearly a desk on which someone carried out real work, day and night.

Alexandra wondered if she might be the first person who had ever come to this office for a rest – it seemed that no one had ever done anything here but work.

Indeed, Spiridonov had barely returned when there was a knock on the door and a young man in a blue jacket appeared. Placing a lengthy report on the desk, he said, 'For the night shift' – and went on his way. A moment later an old man with round glasses and black oversleeves handed Spiridonov a folder. 'A request from the Tractor Factory,' he announced – and he too went on his way. Then the telephone rang. Spiridonov picked up the receiver: 'Yes, of course I know your voice …

And I've told you. I can't help. Why? Because Red October has priority – you know very well what it produces. Well? Now what?' Spiridonov was clearly about to break into curses. His eyes narrowed; Alexandra had never seen him so furious. After a quick glance in her direction, he went on, 'No, don't try to scare me with talk of higher authorities. In an hour or two I'll be seeing those authorities myself. So you're going to denounce me, are you? Yet you still ask for favours? Well, I've told you – the answer's no.'

His secretary came in, a woman of about thirty, with beautiful, flashing eyes.

She bent down and whispered something in her boss's ear. Alexandra looked at her dark hair, her splendid dark eyebrows, and her large, rather masculine, ink-stained hand.

'Of course, she can come in,' said Spiridonov, and the secretary went to the door and called out, 'Nadya, come in.'

Heels clacking, a girl in a white gown brought in a tray covered with a towel.

Spiridonov opened a drawer in his desk and took out half a white loaf wrapped in newspaper and held it out to Alexandra.

'I can also offer you something stronger,' he said – and tapped on the drawer. 'Only don't go telling Marusya. You know what she's like – she'll eat me alive.' And he at once began to look like the usual Stepan, the man she had known for many years.

Alexandra took a sip of vodka, smiled and said, 'You have interesting ladies here, that young girl's a delight, and not every drawer in your desk is filled with plans and diagrams. And there I was, imagining you work round the clock, day and night.'

'Well, there is a little work to be done now and again,' he said. 'And talking of young girls – you'll never guess what our Vera's been up to. I'll tell you when we're in the car.'

Somehow it seemed very strange to Alexandra to be hearing family talk in this office.

Spiridonov glanced at his watch. 'We'll be off in half an hour, but first I must check a few things in the workshops. You stay here and have a rest.'

'Can't I come with you? This is my first time here.'

'What's got into you? There are a lot of stairs – I'll be going up to the first and second floors. Stay here and rest.' It was clear, though, that Spiridonov was pleased. Really, he very much wanted to show Alexandra Vladimirovna the power station.

They walked across the yard in the twilight. Pointing out the different buildings, Spiridonov explained, 'Those are the transformers, oil-filled transformers ... The boiler room, the cooling tower ... Here's where we're building an underground command post. Just in case ... as the phrase goes.'

He looked up at the sky and said, 'It's terrifying. What if they really do bomb us? With the equipment we have now ... With turbines like these ...'

They entered a large brightly lit hall – and at once felt caught up, gently but inescapably spellbound, by the supercharged atmosphere of a large power station. Nowhere else – neither a blast furnace, nor an open-hearth furnace, nor a rolling mill – evokes the same emotions. The vastness of the work being done in a steel-making plant is only too obvious; it can be sensed in the heat of the molten iron, in the roar of the furnace, in the dazzling brightness of the vast blocks of metal. What Alexandra saw here was very different – electric light that was clear and steady, a cleanly swept floor, white marble switchboards, the stillness of the steel and cast-iron housings, the subtle curves of the turbines and control wheels, and the workers' calm, attentive eyes and measured movements. The warm gentle breeze, the dense, low hum, the barely perceptible flicker of copper and steel – these expressions of the silent speed of the turbine blades, of the springy resilience of steam, testified to a mysterious power. The energy created by this power was something higher and nobler than mere heat.

Most overwhelming of all was the dull sheen of the silent dynamos; their apparent stillness was profoundly deceptive. Alexandra breathed in the warm breeze coming off the flywheel. This was rotating so swiftly and silently that it might not have been moving at all. The spokes appeared to have merged, as if covered by a fine grey cobweb – and only the flickering of this cobweb betrayed the speed of the wheel's movement. There was a faint, slightly bitter smell of ozone, or garlic. The atmosphere was like in a field after a thunderstorm, and Alexandra thought how different it was from the greasy atmosphere of chemical factories, the stifling heat of a forge, a cloudy dust-filled mill or the dry airless heat of sewing workshops and clothes factories.

And once again this man she thought she knew so well – who had been married for so many years to her own daughter – seemed entirely new to her.

It was not only his movements, his voice, his smile and general expression that were different; at a deeper level he seemed still more different. When she heard him talking to the workers and engineers, when she watched their faces, she could see that he and they were united by something of crucial importance to all of them. When he walked through the different halls, speaking to fitters and mechanics, listening to motors, leaning over flywheels and instruments, his face always wore the same look of quiet attentiveness. It was a look that could be born only of love; at moments like this Spiridonov and his workers and engineers seemed to have left behind all their usual thoughts and worries, all their domestic joys and sorrows.

Slowing his pace as they approached the central control panel, Spiridonov said, 'And now we come to our holy of holies.'

On a high marble column, mounted on sheets of heavy copper and glossy plastic, was an array of switches, rheostats and acorn-shaped indicator lights – some red and some pale blue.

Close by stood a thick-walled steel case, half as tall again as a human being, with a narrow observation slit.

'This is in case we get bombed – for the man on control-panel duty,' said Spiridonov. 'Armour-plated, like a battleship.'

'A Man in a Case,' said Alexandra. 'But not quite what Chekhov had in mind.'[54]

Spiridonov went up to the control panel. Patches of blue and red light fell on his face and jacket.

'Connecting the city!' he said, pretending to move a massive lever. 'Connecting the Barricades ... The Tractor Factory ... Krasnoarmeisk ...'

His voice trembled with emotion; in the strange blue and red light his face looked excited and happy. Silent and serious, the workers nearby were all watching.

A little later, in the car, Spiridonov leant over towards Alexandra and, too quietly for the driver to hear, whispered, 'Remember the cleaning woman who showed you to my office?'

'Olga Petrovna, wasn't it?'

'That's right, Olga Petrovna, she's a widow. Well, she had a young man living in her apartment who worked for me as a fitter. This young man went to flying school – and then he ended up in hospital, here in Stalingrad. And now he's written to Olga to say that the daughter of the director of Stalgres – our very own Vera – is working as a nurse in the hospital, and that the two of them want to get married. Can you believe it? And Vera hasn't yet said a word to me. I only know all this from my secretary, Anna Ivanovna. And she only knows because she heard from Olga Petrovna. Really, can you believe it?'

'Well,' said Alexandra, 'that all sounds very good. As long as he's a decent man, as long as he's kind and honest.'

'Yes, but at a time like this, for the love of God! And anyway she's still only a girl. Wait till it happens! Wait till the day you're a great-grandmother – I'd like to hear what you have to say then!'

It was too dark for Alexandra to make out his expression, but his voice was the voice she had known for many years. The look on his face, she was sure, would be no less familiar.

'And not a word to Marusya about the bottle – all right?' he said very quietly, and laughed.

Alexandra was seized by a sudden, sad, maternal tenderness towards her son-in-law.

'And you, Stepan, may soon be a grandfather,' she said gently – and patted him on the shoulder.

17

During his visit to the Tractor Factory *raikom* Spiridonov learned
something unexpected: Ivan Pavlovich Pryakhin, whom he had known
for many years, had been promoted. He was to be first secretary of the
obkom, the Party committee for the entire province.[55]

Pryakhin had once worked in the Tractor Factory's Party office.
Then he had gone to study in Moscow. Not long before the war he had
returned to the Tractor Factory, this time as Party organizer.

Spiridonov had known Pryakhin for a long time, but they had never
seen a lot of each other. He did not understand why he felt so affected
by this news, which did not directly concern him.

He went to Pryakhin's office and found him putting on his coat,
about to go out. 'Greetings, comrade Pryakhin, and my congratulations on your promotion!'

Pryakhin – large, slow and with a broad forehead – turned to look
at Spiridonov and said, 'Well, comrade Spiridonov, we'll still be seeing
each other, the same as always, perhaps more often now.'

They left the building together.

'Let me give you a lift,' said Spiridonov. 'I can drop you off on my
way back to Stalgres.'

'No, I'd rather walk,' said Pryakhin.

'Walk?' Spiridonov said in surprise. 'That'll take you three hours.'

Pryakhin smiled but didn't reply. Spiridonov looked at Pryakhin,
smiled and also didn't say anything. He realized that this taciturn man
wanted, as the war drew closer, to walk the streets of the city where
he had been born, to walk past a factory he had seen being built, past
gardens he had seen being planted, past the school he had helped to
build, past new blocks of apartments into which he had helped people
to settle.

Spiridonov stood by the main door, waiting for his driver. He
watched Pryakhin walk away.

'Now it'll be him I have to report to!' he thought. He wanted to
smile, but he was too moved. He remembered some of his previous
meetings with Pryakhin. During the official opening of the school for

the factory workers' children Pryakhin had reprimanded the foreman for the appalling state of the parquet floors in some of the classrooms; his cross voice and preoccupied look had jarred with the celebratory atmosphere of the day. Spiridonov also remembered how, long before the war, there had been a bad fire in one of the workers' settlements; seeing Pryakhin stride through the grey-blue smoke, he had said to himself with relief, 'Ah, the district committee – here to the rescue!' And then there had been an occasion when a new workshop was about to come into operation. For three days and nights Spiridonov barely slept. Then Pryakhin turned up. It was as if he were just passing by, not needing to say anything in particular, but, each time he spoke, he had said something helpful about whatever was most troubling Spiridonov at that moment. Today, hearing of Pryakhin's promotion, Spiridonov had felt the same as he had during the fire: 'Ah, the district committee – here to the rescue!'

Spiridonov now saw Pryakhin in a new light: 'The man must be feeling real anguish. He's put his whole life into building this city. He wants to look at everything one more time. Yes, Stalingrad is our life – his life and mine.'

And it seemed likely that, when they were saying goodbye, Pryakhin had guessed what Spiridonov was thinking; he had squeezed his hand very firmly, as if to thank him both for his understanding and for his reticence, for not saying, 'Ah, yes, I see. You're wanting to look once more at the places where your life has gone by, at what you've worked so hard to construct.'

Few people like it when someone digs about in their soul and then broadcasts to the world what they've discovered there.

When he got back to Stalgres, Spiridonov returned at once to his everyday concerns, but the thoughts stirred up by this chance encounter remained with him. They did not simply dissolve in the noise of the everyday.

18

In the evening Zhenya blacked out the windows, pinning together a medley of shawls, jackets and old blankets.

The room at once felt stifling. Small beads of sweat appeared on the foreheads and temples of everyone at the table. The yellow salt in the salt cellar began to look moist, as if it too were sweating. On the other hand, the blackout did at least spare everyone from the sight of the troubling wartime sky.

'Well, comrade ladies?' asked Sofya, who was out of breath. 'What's new in our glorious city?'

But the comrade ladies did not answer. They were hungry and more interested in the potatoes, which were very hot. They were carefully picking them out of the saucepan, blowing on their fingers as they did so.

Spiridonov, who had had both lunch and supper in the Party committee dining room, was the only person not eating.

'From next week I'll be sleeping at the power station,' he said. 'That's the latest from the *obkom*.' He coughed and added slowly, 'Do you know? Pryakhin's going to be the new first secretary.'

No one responded.

Marusya had just come back from a voluntary meeting for education workers. She began telling everyone about the high morale in the factory where the meeting had been held.

Marusya was considered the best-educated member of the family. As a schoolgirl, she had impressed everyone with her diligence, with her ability to keep studying all day long. Later, at the same time as attending the pedagogical institute, she obtained an external degree from the Faculty of Philosophy. Before the war, the Party publishing house printed her booklet *Women and the Economy of Socialism*. Spiridonov had one copy rebound in yellow leather with the title engraved in silver; the object of family reverence, this never left his desktop. He greatly respected Marusya's judgement; in any discussion about friends and acquaintances, no one's opinion mattered more to him.

'The moment you enter the workshop, all your worries and doubts slip away,' said Marusya, taking a potato from the saucepan but then, in her excitement, putting it back again. 'A nation so hard-working and self-sacrificing cannot be defeated. But it's only on the shop floor that I've truly sensed this determination. We should all of us stop whatever we're doing now and go and work at armament factories or kolkhozes. And to think that our Tolya's already at the front!'

'It's worst of all for us young,' said Vera. 'It's not so bad for those who are elder.'

'Not "elder",' said Marusya. 'Older.' She constantly corrected Vera's small mistakes.

'Your jacket's covered in dust!' said Spiridonov. 'It needs a good clean.'

'It's sacred, factory dust,' said Marusya.

'Do have something to eat, Marusya,' said Spiridonov, afraid lest his wife's love of exalted sentiment might lead her to neglect her share of the fried sturgeon he had brought back from the Party canteen.

'Everything Marusya says is true,' said Alexandra Vladimirovna, 'but poor Tolya! He really was very upset.'

'War's war,' said Marusya. 'The motherland requires us to make sacrifices.'

Zhenya looked quizzically at her elder sister. 'A single voluntary meeting's all very well, dear Marusya – but imagine making your way to that factory every morning, in winter darkness, knowing there may be German bombers overhead, and then hurrying back again in the dark every evening. And nothing to put on the table but salty cheese and fish that's just salt and bone.'

'And what gives *you* the right to talk with such authority?' Marusya replied. 'Have *you* been working at a factory for the last twenty years? The trouble is, you're constitutionally incapable of understanding that to be a part of a vast collective is a source of constant moral uplift. The workers make jokes, their confidence never flags. You should have seen the moment when a new gun was wheeled out of the workshop. The commander shook the hand of the old foreman, and the foreman embraced him and said, "God grant you return safe and sound from the war!" I felt such love for my country that I could have gone on working not for another six hours but for another six days.'

'Heavens!' said Zhenya with a sigh. 'We don't disagree about what's really important. Your words are very noble, and I'm with you heart and soul. But you talk about people as if it isn't women who bring them into the world but newspaper editors. I know what you say about the factory is true, but why do you always have to sound so grand and lofty? Like it or not, it comes across as false. The people you talk about

87

are figures on posters – and I don't like that. I don't want to paint posters.'

'But that's just what you should be doing!' interrupted Marusya. 'Instead of strange daubs no one can understand, you should paint posters. But I know what you'll say next. You'll start going on about truth to life … How many times do I have to tell you that there are two truths? There's the truth of the reality forced on us by the accursed past. And there's the truth of the reality that will defeat that past. It's this second truth, the truth of the future, that *I* want to live by.'

'Closing your eyes to everything around you?' said Zhenya.

'Well, you don't see very much either,' Marusya retorted. 'You don't even want to see the wood for the trees.'

'No, Marusya,' said Sofya Osipovna. 'You're wrong. I can tell you as a surgeon that there is one truth, not two. When I cut someone's leg off, I don't know two truths. If we start pretending there are two truths, we're in trouble. And in war too – above all, when things are as bad as they are today – there is only one truth. It's a bitter truth, but it's a truth that can save us. If the Germans enter Stalingrad, you'll learn that if you chase after two truths, you won't catch either. It'll be the end of you.'

'The retreat,' Vera began slowly, 'is becoming a rout. Today they brought in a new batch of wounded. The stories they tell are quite dreadful. But on the way here I met my friend Zina. She lived in Kiev for three months, under the Germans. She makes out it wasn't so bad there. There were markets, interesting films, officers who were rather well educated—'

'Vera, don't you dare talk like that!' said Spiridonov. 'You know as well as I do what you get for spreading counter-revolutionary rumours in wartime!'

'What's got into the young?' said Marusya. 'When we were your age, we knew better. And let me say for the hundredth time – you should choose better friends!'

'Dear Máma and Pápa,' Vera replied. 'You two are like little children, with all your prejudices and taboos. I'm only telling you what I've heard. *I'm* not wanting to live under the Germans. Zina also said there'd been killing in Kiev, that Jews had been killed there. And what with poor Uncle Dmitry being in a camp, she also thought that Granny might just as well stay here in Stalingrad.'

'I can't believe it!' said Marusya. 'Such cynicism from my own daughter!'

'It can't be true,' said Sofya. 'There must be tens of thousands of Jews in Kiev. It's impossible to kill all of them.'

'Whatever may have happened in Kiev,' said Alexandra, 'I can't stay here under the Germans. Nothing could be more appalling. Anyway, I'm responsible for Seryozha – I can't do anything that might endanger the boy.'

Just then Seryozha rushed in.

'At last!' Alexandra exclaimed joyfully. 'Where have you been?'

'Grandma, can you put a few things in a knapsack for me? I'm leaving the day after tomorrow with a labour battalion. We'll be digging trenches,' Seryozha announced breathlessly. He took out a slip of paper from inside his student card and put it on the table. He was like a gambler, startling the other players by suddenly producing the ace of trumps.

Spiridonov unfolded the paper and, with the air of a man who knows all there is to know about paperwork, began to examine it, starting with the date and the number of the stamp.

Confident that his document was entirely in order, Seryozha watched Spiridonov with a condescending smile.

Marusya and Zhenya forgot their quarrel and exchanged concerned looks, glancing surreptitiously at their mother.

Alexandra Vladimirovna adored her grandson. His handsome eyes, a childish directness coupled with a powerful adult intelligence, a timidity that did not preclude expressions of strong feeling, a simple trustfulness that went hand in hand with a biting scepticism, his kindness, his quick temper – all this inspired her devotion. On one occasion she had said to Sofya Osipovna, 'Here we are, Sofya, we're getting old and we're coming to the end of our lives. The life we're leaving is no garden of peace. War rages, the entire world is on fire, and I'm an old woman, but I still believe as passionately as ever in the power of the Revolution. I believe we shall defeat fascism, I believe in the strength of those holding aloft the banner of the people's happiness and freedom, and it seems to me that Seryozha is cut from the same cloth as I am. That's why I love him so much.'

But what mattered more was that Alexandra's love was unquestioning and unconditional; it was, therefore, true love.

Everyone close to Alexandra was aware of her love for her grandson. It both touched and angered them; it made them feel protective towards her but also jealous. Sometimes her daughters would say anxiously, 'If anything happens to Seryozha, Máma will never get over it.' Sometimes they would say angrily, 'Heavens, the fuss she makes over that boy!' Or, with a slight laugh, 'Yes, now and again Máma tries to be fair, to treat Tolya and Vera the same as she treats Seryozha – but she can never quite manage it.'

Spiridonov returned the slip of paper to Seryozha and said casually, 'I know it's signed by Filimonov, but don't worry. Tomorrow I'll have a word with Petrov, and we'll get you transferred to Stalgres.'

'Why?' asked Seryozha. 'I volunteered. We'll be equipped with rifles as well as spades and everyone in good health will soon be transferred to a regular battalion.'

'So … you really … you truly volunteered?' asked Spiridonov.

'Of course I did.'

'You're mad!' Marusya said furiously. 'What about your grand-mother? If, God forbid, anything happens to you, it'll be the end of her – as you well know!'

'You're not even old enough to have a passport,'[56] said Sofya. 'God, what a fool!'

'And Tolya?'

'What's Tolya got to do with it?' Sofya replied. 'Tolya's three years older than you are. Tolya's an adult. Tolya's obliged to carry out his duty as a citizen. And so is Vera – I certainly haven't tried to stop *her* from working. Your turn will come in due course. When you've done your ten years at school, you'll be called up. And that'll be that – no one will try to stop you. I can't believe they let you register. They should have just given you a good hiding!'

'There was one boy even shorter than me,' said Seryozha.

'Well,' said Spiridonov, with a smile. 'What can I say to that?'

'Máma, why aren't you saying anything?' asked Zhenya.

Seryozha looked at his grandmother and said quietly, 'Well, Granny?'

Seryozha was the only member of his family who ever made fun of Alexandra Vladimirovna. He argued with her quite often, in a tone half jocular, half touchingly indulgent. Ludmila, on the other hand, only rarely argued with her mother, even though she was naturally assertive, the eldest of the three sisters, and unfailingly certain that in all family matters she always knew best.

Alexandra looked up, as if sitting before a tribunal, and said, 'Seryozha, you must do as you … I …' She faltered, got quickly to her feet and left the room.

There was a moment of silence. Vera, whose heart that day was so open, so ready to show kindness and sympathy, scowled crossly to hold back her tears.

19

That night, the city was suddenly filled with noise: hooters, loud shouts, the sound of car and truck engines.

Everyone awoke in alarm, then lay there in silence, trying to work out what was happening.

They were all asking themselves the same questions: had something awful just happened? Had the enemy broken through somewhere? Was the Red Army retreating? Should they all get dressed as fast as they could, bundle a few things together and make a quick getaway? Now and again they felt real terror: what were those strange voices? There hadn't been a German parachute landing, had there?

Zhenya, who was sleeping in one room with Vera, Sofya and her mother, propped herself up on one elbow and said quietly, 'It's like when I was in Yelets with our artists' brigade.[57] We woke up one fine morning – and the Germans were already on the outskirts of town! We didn't get a word of warning.'

'A grim thought,' said Sofya. Then they heard Marusya, who had left the door open to make it easier to wake everyone if there were an air raid: 'Stepan, wake up! Quick, find out what's happening! Damn you and your Olympian calm!'

'Sh!' whispered Spiridonov. 'I'm not asleep. I'm listening.'

There was the rumble of a truck just beneath their window. The engine stalled. A voice – as distinct as if the speaker were there in the room with them – said, 'What's the matter with you? Are you asleep? Get the engine started again!' Then came a few furious words that momentarily embarrassed the women but left no doubt that the speaker was a bona fide Russian.

'What blessed sounds!' said Sofya.

In their relief, everyone started talking at once.

'It's all because of Zhenya,' said Marusya. 'If it weren't for her and her stories about Yelets, we'd have been all right. But my heart's still racing. I can still feel a pain under my shoulder blade.'

Spiridonov, embarrassed by his frightened whispers of a minute before, said loudly, 'Yes, how on earth could it have been the Germans?

That sort of thing just doesn't happen. Our defences are solid concrete – even as far away as Kalach. And anyway, I'd have been informed at once if it was anything serious. Oh, you women, you women!'

'Everything's all right,' said Alexandra Vladimirovna. 'And there really isn't anything to worry about, but things like that *have* been known to happen. Or so I was thinking.'

'Yes, Máma,' said Zhenya. 'They certainly have.'

Spiridonov threw his tweed coat over his shoulders, padded across the room, tugged at the blackout curtain and opened the window.

'Windows flung wide in the first days of spring,' said Sofya. Listening to the racket outside, to the cars, trucks and people, she went on, 'Clatter of wheels, patter of voices and the church bells ring.'[58]

'*Gabble* of voices,' said Marusya. 'Not *patter.*'

'Oh let them just patter,' said Sofya – and everyone laughed.

'There are a lot of cars,' said Spiridonov, looking down at the street, which was lit by a dim moon. 'I can see Emkas and even a few ZISes.'[59]

'Must be reinforcements on their way to the front,' said Marusya.

'I don't think so,' said Spiridonov. 'They're going the other way.' And then, lifting a finger: 'Sh!'

There was a traffic controller on the corner. Drivers were asking him questions, but it was impossible to make out their words. And the controller simply answered with a wave of his flag, pointing them down the right road. There were not only cars but also large trucks, piled high with tables, boxes, stools and camp beds. In the backs of some of the trucks were groups of soldiers, wearing greatcoats and waterproof capes and swaying about sleepily as their vehicles accelerated or decelerated. Then a ZIS-101 stopped beside the controller. This time Spiridonov heard every word.

'Where's the commandant?' asked a thick slow voice.

'The city commandant?'

'No! The Front HQ commandant!'

At this Spiridonov closed the window, stepped back and announced from the middle of the room, 'Well, comrades, we are now a front-line city. The Southwestern Front.[60] Stalingrad is now the location of Southwestern Front HQ.'

'Seems there's no getting away from the war,' said Sofya. 'It's always present, right on our heels. But let's get some sleep! I have to be at the hospital by six.'

She had barely said this when the bell rang.

'I'll go,' said Spiridonov. Putting his coat on properly, he went to the door. It was the fine tweed coat that he usually wore only on trips to Moscow and during the October holidays. He now kept it hanging over the bed head so as to have it to hand in case of an air raid. Next to it hung his new suit; beside the cupboard, also in combat readiness, stood a suitcase with Marusya's fur coat and dresses.

Spiridonov was not gone for long. He came back laughing. In a mock whisper he said, 'Zhenya, you've got a gentleman caller – a handsome commander! I've left him just outside our front door.'

'Me!' said Zhenya in astonishment. 'You're talking nonsense – I don't understand!' But she clearly felt agitated and embarrassed.

'*Jakhshi!*' Vera said brightly. 'Here's to our Auntie Zhenya!'

'Stepan, go outside for a moment,' Zhenya said quickly. 'I must get dressed.' Jumping to her feet like a young girl, she put the blackout curtain back in place and turned on the light.

She put on her shoes and her dress in only a few seconds, but her movements slowed when she began to apply her lipstick.

'You're mad,' Alexandra said crossly. 'Making a man wait outside while you paint your lips in the middle of the night.'

'And she hasn't washed, and she's got sleep in her eyes – and her hair's in such a tangle anyone would think she's a witch,' said Marusya.

'It's all right,' said Sofya. 'Our Zhenya knows very well that she is a young and lovely witch. Washed or unwashed, she's beautiful.'

Sofya herself was now stout and grey-haired. She was fifty-eight years old and still a virgin. In all likeliness, she had never in her life felt her heart start to race as she coloured her lips in preparation for some such encounter.

She could work like an ox; she had travelled half the world with geographical expeditions; she took pleasure in using curses and swear words; and she read the works of poets, philosophers and mathematicians. One might have expected this masculine woman to look on the beautiful Zhenya with mockery and contempt – but she showed only tender admiration and a kind of touching, very gentle envy.

Still looking agitated, Zhenya went towards the door.

'Can you guess who it is?' came a voice from outside.

'Maybe, maybe not,' said Zhenya.

'Novikov,' said the voice.

As she walked towards the door, Zhenya had felt almost certain that it was Novikov. She answered as she did because she didn't know whether or not she should reprimand him for the unceremoniousness of this visit.

And then, as if looking on from outside, she became aware of the poetry of this encounter. She saw herself – half asleep, still warm from the bed she shared with her mother – and, there at the door, this man just emerged from the threatening dark of the war, bringing with him a smell of dust, leather, petrol and the freshness of the steppe.

'I'm sorry,' he said. 'It's stupid of me to appear like this in the middle of the night.' He bowed his head, like a prisoner before an army commander.

'Well, I certainly know who you are now. Glad to see you, comrade Novikov!'

'The war's brought me here. Excuse me, I'll come back again during the day.'

'Where are you going to go now, in the middle of the night? You're staying here!'

Novikov began to make excuses. She ended up getting cross with him not for bursting in on them in the middle of the night but for not wanting to stay. And so Novikov, turning to the dark stairwell, called out quietly, in the tone of someone accustomed to giving orders and confident of being obeyed, 'Korenkov, bring up my case and my bedroll.'

'I'm glad you're alive and well,' she said. 'But I won't ask you anything now. You're tired. You'll be wanting to wash, and to have some tea and a bite to eat. There'll be time to talk in the morning. You can tell me your news then. And I'll introduce you to my mother, my sister and my niece.'

And then she took his hand, looked him in the face and said, 'You've changed a lot. Especially your eyebrows – they've grown fairer.'

'It's the dust,' he said. 'There's dust everywhere.'

'Dust and sun. And it makes your eyes look darker.' Zhenya was still holding his large hand. She felt it tremble a little. Laughing, she said, 'Well, I'll leave you for now with our menfolk. And tomorrow – the world of women.'

A bed was made up for Novikov in Seryozha's room. Seryozha showed Novikov to the bathroom, and Novikov said, 'So you've even got a working shower, have you?'

'For the time being, at least,' said Seryozha, watching their guest take off his belt, a revolver and a tunic with a colonel's four red bars, and then take a razor and a bar of soap from his little suitcase.

Tall and broad-shouldered as he was, Novikov looked as if he had been born to put on military uniform and bear weapons. In the presence of this stern son of the war, Seryozha felt puny. Yet he too would soon be a son of the war.

'Are you Zhenya's brother?' asked Novikov.

Seryozha felt embarrassed to say he was her nephew – she was too young to be the aunt of a young man about to join a labour battalion. Novikov would think either that Zhenya must be older than she looked or that her nephew was still just a whippersnapper.

As if not hearing the question, he answered, 'Here, use the rough towel!'

He did not like Novikov's way of talking to his driver, a rather hunched man who must have been in his forties.

After making tea on the little oil stove, Seryozha said, 'We can make up a bed for the comrade driver just here.'

'No,' said Novikov. 'He'll be sleeping in the car. We can't leave it unguarded.'

The driver grinned and said, 'We've reached the Volga, comrade Colonel. The car's no use now – it won't get anyone across the river.'

Novikov merely replied, 'Go back down to the car, Korenkov!'

Novikov sat down and began drinking his tea. Spiridonov, yawning and scratching his chest, sat down opposite him. He too was holding a mug of tea. He felt troubled. The arrival of the Front HQ, in the middle of the night, had unsettled him.

From the other room came the voice of Zhenya: 'Everything all right in there?'

Novikov quickly got to his feet and, as if addressing an important superior, said, 'Thank you, Yevgenia Nikolaevna.[61] And, once again, please forgive me for this night-time invasion.' His eyes took on a guilty look that seemed out of place on his imperious face with its broad forehead, straight nose and firm lips.

'Goodnight, then,' said Zhenya, 'see you tomorrow!' And Seryozha realized that Novikov was listening to the clack of her heels as she walked away.

Spiridonov, sipping his tea, offered their guest something to eat and studied him with eyes accustomed to assessing others. He was trying to decide what job Novikov would be best suited for if he were a civilian. He would certainly be out of place in a small factory; probably he ought to be in charge of some industrial enterprise of national importance.

'So, Front HQ is to be located in Stalingrad, is it?' asked Spiridonov. Novikov gave him a sideways look. He seemed a little irritated.

'A military secret, is it?' said Spiridonov. And he was unable to stop himself from boasting, 'I knew anyway because of my work. I provide power to three giant factories, and these factories supply the Front.'

But his boasting, like all boasting, stemmed from a sense of weakness and uncertainty: he was confused by the cold, calm look in Novikov's eyes. It was as if this colonel were saying to himself, 'Even if you are in the know, this isn't something you should be repeating – and certainly not in the presence of this boy. *He* isn't providing anybody with power.'

Spiridonov laughed. 'All right, let me tell you the truth. Here's how I really found out!'

And he told Novikov about the conversation between the man in the ZIS and the traffic controller.

Novikov shrugged.

Seryozha asked, 'And when did you first meet our Zhenya? Was it before the war began?'

'More or less,' Novikov replied quickly.

'Another military secret,' said Spiridonov, this time with a smile. And to himself he thought, 'Well, Colonel, you *are* tight-lipped!'

Novikov was looking at a painting on the wall, an old man in green trousers and with a green beard. 'What happened?' he asked. 'Did the old man turn green from age?'

'It's by Zhenya,' Seryozha answered. 'She thinks that old wanderer's one of her best works.'

Spiridonov suddenly took it into his head that Zhenya and this colonel must have been having an affair for a very long time, and that the entire scene – Novikov's apparently unexpected arrival, the formality with which he and Zhenya had addressed each other – had been pure theatre. And this somehow annoyed him. 'No, Mister Soldier, she's a great deal too good for you,' he said to himself.

After a brief silence, Novikov said quietly, 'You know, this city of yours is unusual. I spent a long time trying to find your street and I discovered that there are streets here named after every city in the Soviet Union. There's a Sevastopol street, and a Kursk street. There's Vinnitsa and Chernigov and Slutsk and Tula. There's Kiev and Kharkov and Moscow. There's Rzhevsk.' He smiled. 'I've seen combat in and around many of those cities. I was stationed in others before the war. Yes. And suddenly it turns out that every one of these cities is here in Stalingrad.'

Seryozha listened. The man sitting beside him seemed to have changed; he was no longer a stranger, no longer alien and incomprehensible. And Seryozha said to himself, 'I've done the right thing!'

'Yes, the streets. Our Soviet cities,' sighed Spiridonov. 'But it's time you lay down. You've been on the road a long time.'

20

Novikov was from the Donbass. The only other member of his family still alive at the beginning of the war was his elder brother Ivan, who worked at the Smolyanka mine, not far from Stalino.[62] Their father had died in a fire, deep underground; not long after that, their mother had died of pneumonia.

Since the beginning of the war, Novikov had received only two letters from his brother. The second, in February, had been sent from some mine far off in the Urals to which Ivan and his wife and daughter had been evacuated; it was clear from this letter that life as an evacuee was not easy. Novikov, then in Voronezh with the Southwestern Front, had sent his brother money and food – but there had been no reply and he did not know whether Ivan had received the parcel or whether he'd had to move yet again.

Their last meeting had been in 1940. Novikov had gone to stay with his brother for a week. Wandering around places he'd known as a child had felt strange. But love for one's birthplace, one's memory of childhood and a mother's love, is evidently so powerful that this austere and gloomy mining settlement had seemed sweet, cosy and beautiful and Novikov had not noticed the biting wind, the acrid, nauseating smoke from the coke and benzene, and the grim slag heaps that looked like burial mounds. And his brother's face, eyelashes blackened by coal dust, and the faces of the childhood friends who came to drink vodka with him, had seemed so close, so intimate a part of his life, that he had wondered how he could have lived so far away for so long.

Novikov was one of those people who never know easy successes and victories. He put this down to his inability to make quick friendships, and to a directness that sometimes made him awkward and clumsy. He thought of himself as responsive, good-natured and well meaning, but this was not at all how others saw him. Many people's view of themselves is mistaken, but Novikov was at least partly right. He appeared colder and more unfriendly than was really the case.

When he gave up chasing the village pigeons and first went to technical school in a nearby town, the other boys had thought him unfriendly; and when he began work in a fitter's shop, the other workers had thought him unfriendly; so it had been during his first days in the Red Army; and so – unfortunately – it had been throughout his life.

His father and grandfather had been workers, but his fellow commanders had thought him stuck-up and aristocratic. He hardly ever drank and he strongly disliked the smell of vodka. He never raised his voice – let alone cursed or swore – when speaking to his subordinates. People said he was as scrupulously fair as a pair of pharmaceutical scales. Nevertheless, there were occasions when the men under him had felt nostalgic for their former commanders – however loud-mouthed, capricious and dictatorial they may have been.

Novikov loved the idea of fishing and shooting, he would have liked to plant fruit trees and he enjoyed beautifully furnished rooms; but there had been no time in his nomadic life for anything but work. He had never fished, gone shooting or gardened, nor had he ever lived in comfortable, well-furnished rooms with paintings and carpets. People had seen him as indifferent to such things, as having no interest in anything but his work – and he had indeed worked unusually hard.

He had married young, when he was only twenty-three – and he was still young when his wife died.

Like most commanders, he had known difficult moments during the war. Though he had always been a staff officer, far from the front line, he had survived air raids and encirclements. In August 1941, not far from Mozyr, he had led into the attack an ad hoc detachment made up entirely of commanders from an Army HQ.

Novikov had been promoted several times, but his progress had been steady rather than dazzling. By the end of the first year of the war he had received his fourth red bar; he was a full colonel, and he had been awarded the Order of the Red Star.

He was considered an excellent staff officer: well educated, open-minded, calm, methodical and intelligent, with a gift for quick analysis of complex and confusing situations. But Novikov did not see staff work as his real calling. He saw himself as a front-line commander, a born tank man who would truly prove himself only in combat. Not only could he think logically and analytically but he would also be able to carry out swift, decisive attacks. His capacity for careful thought went hand in hand with courage and passion, with the ability to take risks.

Others saw Novikov as excessively cerebral – and he was well aware what gave them that impression. He was calm and restrained in argument and meticulous about everyday matters. He got irritated if others infringed on his routines and he never infringed on these routines himself. He was capable, during an air raid, of reprimanding a cartographer for not sharpening his pencil properly, or of saying to a typist, 'I asked you to stop using the typewriter that does such faint "t"s.'

His feelings for Zhenya Shaposhnikova did not fit with anything else in his life. His first meeting with her at the Military Academy gala had made an overwhelming impression on him. The news of her marriage to Krymov had made him jealous; the news of their separation had filled him with joy. On glimpsing Zhenya through the window of a railway carriage, he had got onto her train and travelled south for three hours when he should have been travelling north. And he did not tell her this.

Altogether, he had seen Zhenya only a very few times in his life. Nevertheless, during the first hour of the war, his thoughts had kept returning to her.

Only now, about to lie down on a bed newly made up for him on the floor, did Novikov feel any surprise. With absolutely no right to behave like this, he had called on Zhenya in the middle of the night and woken her family. He might have put her in an awkward position. No, worse than that – he had almost certainly put her in a false and very unpleasant position. How would she explain all this to her mother, and to the rest of her family? Or maybe she'd find it only too easy – she'd give an exasperated shrug and everyone would have a good laugh at his expense: 'How very strange! Bursting in on us at two in the morning ... What was he after? Was the man drunk? He charges in, has a shave, drinks some tea, then sleeps the sleep of the dead!' He could hear them making fun of him already. 'No,' he said to himself. 'I must leave an apologetic note on the table, go out as quietly as I can, wake my driver and tell him to get going.'

Barely had he decided to leave when he began to see everything in a different light. She had smiled at him. With her own sweet hands she had made up a bed for him. Come morning he'd be seeing her again. And had he come a day or two later, she might well have said, 'Oh, what a shame you didn't come round straightaway. We've got someone else sleeping here now.' But what did he have to offer her? And what right did he have to be dreaming of personal happiness at a time like this? None at all. He knew this only too well, yet somewhere deep inside him lived a different knowledge – and this other, wiser knowledge was telling him that all the movements of his heart were legitimate and had their meaning.

He took from his briefcase an exercise book with an oilskin cover and, sitting on his bedding, began to leaf through it. He was deeply agitated and his exhaustion, rather than bringing sleep nearer, was only driving it still further away.

Novikov looked at a faded pencil note: '22 June 1941. Night. The main Brest–Kobrin highway.'

He looked at his watch: four o'clock. The pain and anxiety he had got used to during the last year, and which did not prevent him from eating, sleeping, shaving or breathing, were now strangely fused with a joyful excitement that made his heart beat faster. When he entered this room, the idea of sleep had seemed as absurd as it had in the dawn of 22 June 1941.

He thought back over his conversation with Spiridonov and Seryozha; he had disliked both of them, especially Spiridonov. Then he relived the moment when, waiting out on the landing, he had heard quick, light, adorable steps.

And in spite of all this, he fell asleep.

21

———◆———

Novikov was always able to recall the first night of the war with absolute clarity.[63] He had been sent by the Military District HQ to the River Bug, to carry out some inspections. On his way there he had taken the opportunity to gather information from commanders who had taken part in the war against Finland; he wanted to write a memo about the breaching of the Mannerheim Line.[64]

He had looked calmly at the west bank of the Bug, at the bald patches of sand, at the meadows, at the little houses and gardens, and at the dark pines and groves of deciduous trees in the distance. He heard German planes whining like sleepy flies in the cloudless sky over the General Government.[65]

At the sight of puffs of smoke on the western horizon, he thought, 'The Germans are cooking their porridge,' as if it were out of the question for the Germans to be cooking up anything else. He had been reading the newspapers; he had discussed the war in Europe; and he had toyed with the thought that the hurricane raging in Norway, Belgium, Holland and France was now moving farther and farther away, from Belgrade to Athens, from Athens to Crete – and that from Crete it would cross over into Africa and blow itself out in the desert sands. Yet deep in his heart he had already understood that this silence was not that of a peaceful midsummer day but the stifling, agonizing silence before a storm.

Even now Novikov could still sense sharp, ineradicable memories that had become his constant companions for no other reason except that they were memories of 22 June 1941, the day that had put an end to the era of peace. It was like when someone has just died and those close to this person keep remembering every last detail. A momentary smile, a chance movement, a sigh, a word – everything, in retrospect, takes on significance, turns into a clear signal of the tragedy to come.

A week before the beginning of the war, in Brest, Novikov had been crossing a wide street paved with cobblestones; coming the other way was a German officer, probably a member of the commission for the repatriation of ethnic Germans.[66] Novikov could still remember his smart peaked cap with its metal band, his thin, haughty face, his steel-coloured SS uniform, his armband with a black swastika in a white circle, his cream-coloured leather briefcase and his gleaming boots – black mirrors the dust of the street did not dare to settle on. His stiff, strange gait seemed all the stranger against the backdrop of the little old one-storey houses.

Novikov crossed the street and went up to a kiosk selling seltzer water with syrup. While an elderly Jewish woman filled his glass, he said to himself three words he would remember again and again: 'Clown!' Then, correcting himself: 'Madman!' And, correcting himself once more: 'Thug!'[67]

And he had at once felt a sticky, crooked feeling, a sense of frustration and embarrassment. He had felt ashamed of his baggy tunic and his rawhide belt – and still more ashamed of drinking seltzer water with cherry syrup.

Novikov also remembered that a peasant passing by on a cart and the woman at the kiosk had both watched the Nazi officer in the same tense way. Probably they had understood the true meaning of the message brought by this lone harbinger of evil walking down the wide dusty streets of a city on the Soviet frontier.

And then, just three days before the beginning of the war, Novikov had had dinner with a commander in charge of a frontier post. It was unusually hot and the net curtains across the open windows were not stirring at all. Amid the silence beyond the river, they had heard the low boom of an artillery piece, and the commander had said crossly, 'There's that damned neighbour of ours, doing his voice exercises again!'

Later, in spring 1942, Novikov happened to learn that five days after this meal this same commander, armed only with a few machine guns, had resisted the German advance for sixteen hours. His wife and his twelve-year-old son had died beside him.

After occupying Greece, the Germans had launched an airborne invasion of Crete. Novikov could remember hearing a report about this at HQ. There had been a marked note of anxiety in many of the questions that followed: 'Please tell us in more detail about the losses suffered by the German army'; 'Has any weakening of the German forces been detected?' One of the little notes handed to the man on the rostrum asked baldly: 'Comrade speaker, if the trade agreement is violated in the near future, will there be time for the equipment on order from Germany to reach us?'[68]

He remembered a moment in the middle of that night, a few hours after he had heard this report. His heart had missed a beat and he had said to himself, 'It'll be a miracle if Russia escapes this storm – but there are no miracles in the world.'

*

The last night of peace, the first night of war.

That night Novikov was due to meet the commander of a heavy tank brigade. Novikov was in one of the regimental HQs, but the orderly was unable to connect him with Brigade HQ.

They both cursed the stupidity of telephonists. It was puzzling – usually the telephones worked perfectly.

Novikov drove to the airstrip; the airmen liaised with higher HQs, and he thought he would be able to use their wire. But he was equally unable to get through from the airstrip. There was no connection at all – neither direct, nor indirect; the wire, on this quiet summer evening, seemed to have been damaged in several different places.

The commander of the fighter regiment invited Novikov to the town theatre, to see a production of *Platon Krechet*.[69] Some of the airmen were going with their wives, others with parents who'd come to visit. There was still room in the bus. But Novikov refused; he had decided to drive to Brigade HQ.

It was a warm moonlit night. Between the two rows of dark, squat lime trees, the road seemed almost white. A moment after Novikov had got into the car, he heard the orderly call out from the brightly lit, wide-open window, 'Comrade Colonel, the line's working again!'

It was a poor line, but Novikov was able to talk. It turned out that the brigade commander had gone to the maintenance depot, where his tanks had been taken to be serviced and have their engines replaced. He would not be back until tomorrow evening.

Novikov decided to stay the night at the airstrip. In response to his request for accommodation, the orderly smiled and said, 'All right. We're certainly not short of room here.' Regimental headquarters was a large manor house.

The orderly took him to a huge room, lit by a bright 300-candlepower bulb. Against a panelled wall stood an iron bed, a stool and a small bedside table.

The narrow army bed and plywood table were out of keeping with the splendour of the oak panelling and the plaster mouldings on the ceiling. Novikov noticed that there were no bulbs in the crystal chandelier: the wire with the 300-candlepower bulb simply hung down beside it.

Then Novikov went to the grand, spacious dining room. It was almost empty; there were just two political commissars at the far table, eating sour cream. Novikov usually enjoyed his food, but he ate barely half the plentiful meal put in front of him: meat patties and fried potatoes in an enamel bowl, followed by thin pancakes with sour cream on a gilt-rimmed porcelain plate with a picture of a shepherdess in a pink dress, surrounded by white sheep. The *kvas* came in a pale blue glass, and the tea in a new aluminium mug that burnt his lips.

'How come there's hardly anyone here?' Novikov asked the waitress.

'A lot of our men are married,' she replied, in the accent of someone from the lower Volga. 'Sometimes their wives cook for them. Sometimes the men come down and take food back to their rooms.' And then she raised a finger and added, with a sweet, innocent smile, 'Some of the girls don't like it here. They complain about the young men all having wives and children. But I love it – it's like being at home, with your mother and father.'

She spoke with feeling, as if hoping for Novikov's agreement and understanding; Novikov wondered if she and a girlfriend had been arguing about this in the kitchen.

Some time later she came back and said in a tone of alarm, 'You've hardly eaten a thing! What's the matter? Don't you like our cooking?' Bending down towards him, she added confidentially, 'Will you be staying with us long, comrade Lieutenant Colonel? Whatever you do, you mustn't leave tomorrow – our Sunday lunch will be really special! We'll be serving ice cream – and the first course will be cabbage soup. We've just received a whole barrel of pickled cabbage from Slutsk. We haven't had cabbage soup for a long time, and the pilots have been complaining.'

He could feel the girl's breath on his cheek. Had her shining eyes not looked so trustful, Novikov would have thought she was flirting. As it was, he felt moved by her childlike whispering.

Not feeling in the least sleepy, he went out into the garden.

In the moonlight the wide stone steps were like white marble. The silence was absolute, somehow unusual. So still was the bright air that the trees seemed almost to be underwater, as if deep in a clear pond.

There was a strange light in the sky – moonlight, together with a faint remnant of pink in the west and a stain of colour to the east that

105

was the dawn of the year's longest day. The sky above him was whitish, opalescent, with a touch of blue.

Each leaf on the maples and lindens was sharply outlined, as if chiselled from black stone. Taken as a whole, however, the great mass of trees seemed like a flat black pattern against the bright sky. The world's beauty had surpassed itself. It was one of those moments when everyone stops to gaze in wonder – not only the idler with time on his hands but also the shift worker on his way home and the traveller half-dead on his feet.

At times like this we cease to have distinct perceptions of light, space, silence, rustlings, warmth, sweet smells, the swaying of long grass or leaves – all the millions of ingredients that make up the world's beauty.

What we perceive then is true beauty, and it tells us only one thing: that life is a blessing.

And Novikov kept walking around the garden, stopping, looking about, sitting, walking a little further, not thinking about anything or remembering anything, not realizing how sad it made him that the world's beauty is long-lived while human beings are not.

When he got back to his room, he undressed and then, in only his socks, went up to the light bulb and began unscrewing it from its socket. The hot bulb burned his fingers and he took a newspaper from the table to wrap around it.

He returned to more routine thoughts: about what he would be doing the next day, about the report he had now almost finished and would soon be handing in to the Military District HQ, about how his car battery needed changing and how it would probably be best to get this done in the tank corps maintenance depot.

In the darkness he went up to the window and glanced abstractedly, with sleepy indifference, at the sky and the quiet, night-time garden. He would remember more than once just how casually he had looked for the last time at the world of peace.

He woke up with a precise awareness that something terrible had happened, but with no idea what this might be.

He saw tiny crumbs of alabaster on the parquet floor and glimmers of orange on the crystal pendants of the chandelier.

He saw black scraps of smoke against a dirty red sky.

He heard a woman wail. He heard the cries of crows and jackdaws. He heard a crash that shook the walls and, at the same time, a faint whining sound in the sky – and though this whining was quiet and even melodic it was this that made Novikov shudder in horror as he jumped out of bed.

He saw and heard all this in a fraction of a second. Just as he was, in his underwear, he ran towards the door. Then, unexpectedly, he found himself saying, 'Steady now!' – and he walked back to his bed to get dressed.

He forced himself to do up all the buttons on his tunic. He adjusted his belt, straightened his holster and walked downstairs at a measured pace.

Later, in newspapers and journals, he often came across the phrase 'surprise attack'. How – he wondered – could anyone who had not experienced the war's first minutes ever understand what these words really meant?

Men were running along the corridor, some in uniform, some only half dressed.

Everyone was asking questions. No one was replying.

'Have the petrol tanks caught fire?'

'Was it a bomb?'

'A military exercise?'

'Saboteurs?'

Some of the pilots were already standing on the steps outside.

One, with no belt round his tunic, pointed towards the city and said, 'Comrades, look! Over there!'

Flames the colour of dark blood were climbing up over the railway stations and embankments, swelling and ballooning into the sky. At ground level there were the flashes of repeated explosions. Black planes were circling like gnats in the bright, deathly air.

'It's a provocation!' someone shouted.

And another quiet yet clearly audible voice pronounced with awful certainty, 'Comrades, Germany has attacked the Soviet Union. Everyone to the airstrip!'

Soon after this came a moment that lodged itself in Novikov's memory with a particular sharpness and precision. As he hurried after the pilots dashing towards the airstrip, he stopped in the middle of the garden where only a few hours earlier he had gone for a stroll. There was a silence, during which it seemed that everything was unchanged: the earth, the grass, the benches, the wicker table under the trees, a card chessboard, dominoes still lying scattered about.

In that silence, with a wall of foliage shielding him from the flames and smoke, Novikov felt a lacerating sense of historical change that was almost more than he could bear.

It was a sense of hurtling movement, similar perhaps to what someone might experience if they could glimpse, if they could sense on their skin and with every cell of their being, the earth's terrible hurtling through the infinity of the universe.

This change was irrevocable, and although only a millimetre lay between Novikov's present life and the shore of his previous life, there was no force that could cancel out this gap. The gap was growing, widening; it could already be measured in metres, in kilometres. The life and time that Novikov still sensed as his own were already being transformed into the past, into history, into something about which people would soon be saying, 'Yes, that's how people lived and thought before the war.' And a nebulous future was swiftly becoming his present. At that instant, he remembered Zhenya, and it seemed to him that his thoughts about her would accompany him throughout this new life.

Taking a shortcut to the airstrip, he climbed over a fence and began to run down a gap between two rows of young firs. Outside a little house – probably once the home of the landowner's gardener – he saw a group of Poles, men and women. As he ran past them, a woman called out excitedly, 'Who is it, Staś?'

And in a clear strong voice a child replied, 'A Russky, Máma. A soldier Russky.'

Novikov ran on. Out of breath, deeply shaken, he kept repeating these words, now somehow stuck in his mind: 'Russian soldier, Russian, Russian soldiers.'

The words sounded different from how they had sounded before – both bitter and proud, new and joyful.

The following day, he again and again heard Polish voices say, 'Some dead Russians … We saw the Russians pass by … Some Russians stayed the night …'

During the first months of the war it was always: 'Yes, only we Russians …' Or 'Yes, that's our Russian organization for you …' Or 'Our Russian *let's hope for the best* … Our Russian *by guess or by God* …' But this 'Russian soldier', this bitterness that became a part of Novikov, that wove itself into his being, that took root in his soul along with the pain of the long retreat – this bitterness was awaiting the day of victory. Then the words would sound sweet.

Novikov had barely reached the airstrip when he saw planes peeling away from the tops of the nearby trees. One, two ... Three more ... Another three ... Something tore at the air. Something somewhere missed a beat. The earth began to smoke. It began to boil, almost like water. Without meaning to, Novikov closed his eyes. A burst of machine-gun fire tore into the ground a few steps away from him. And then he was being deafened by the roar of an engine, and he could make out the crosses on the plane's wings, the swastika on its tail and the helmeted head of the pilot, briskly assessing what he had accomplished. And then came another roar, the growing roar of a second ground-attack aircraft. And a third, skimming the ground.

Three of the planes on the airstrip were in flames. People were running, falling, jumping to their feet, running again ...

Looking resolute and vengeful, a pale young pilot got into his cockpit, waved his mechanic away from the propeller and took the quivering plane onto the runway. Barely had this plane, the draught from its propeller flattening the still dew-white grass, got up speed – barely had it leapt from the ground and begun to climb into the sky when the propeller of a second fighter began to spin. Taking heart from the roar of its engine, this second MIG made a little jump, as if flexing its leg muscles, ran a short distance along the ground and launched itself into the sky. These were the first airmen, the first Soviet soldiers of the air, to try to shield with their bodies the body of the people.

Four Messerschmitts swooped down on the first MIG. Whistling, howling, letting out short bursts of machine-gun fire, they hung on its tail. The MIG already had holes in its fuselage. It smoked and spluttered. It was struggling to gain speed and break away from the enemy. It soared over the forest, disappeared and no less suddenly reappeared. Trailing black smoke, as if in mourning, it was trying to get back to the airstrip.

The dying man and the dying plane had merged; they were a single being. And everything that the young pilot felt, high in the sky, was now being accurately registered by the wings of his plane. The plane swayed and trembled; it was in spasm, just as the pilot's fingers were in spasm. Lit by the dawn sun, the plane lost all hope – and then, now free of hope, returned to the struggle. Everything in the young man's consciousness – hatred, suffering, the longing to defeat death – everything in this man's eyes and heart was conveyed to the men down below by the death throes of his plane. And then the most heartfelt wish of these men was granted. On the tail of the

Messerschmitt that was finishing off this first Soviet fighter appeared the second Soviet fighter, which everyone had forgotten about. The men on the ground saw tongues of yellow fire mingle with the yellow of the Messerschmitt's fuselage – and then this swift and mighty demon, which only a moment ago had seemed invincible, broke into pieces and fell through the air, a shapeless heap on the tree-tops. At the same time, spreading black, corrugated smoke through the morning sky, the first Soviet fighter crashed to the ground. The three remaining Messerschmitts disappeared to the west. The second Soviet fighter circled upwards, as if climbing invisible steps, and flew off towards the city.

The pale blue sky was now empty. Only two black columns of smoke rose over the forest, trembling, swelling, growing thicker and thicker.

A few minutes later an exhausted plane landed heavily on the airstrip. A man climbed out and shouted hoarsely, 'Comrade Regimental Commander, to the glory of our Soviet homeland – I shot down two of them!'

And in his eyes Novikov saw all the happiness, all the fury, all the madness and clear logic of what had just taken place in the sky, everything a pilot can never find words for but that can still be glimpsed – glimmering in his bright, dilated eyes – during his first moments back on the earth.

At noon, at the regimental HQ, Novikov heard Molotov's speech on the radio: 'Our cause is just. We will be victorious!' He went up to the commander and embraced him. They kissed.

Later that day Novikov was at an Infantry division HQ.

Brest was now beyond reach. Apparently German tanks had already entered the city, simply bypassing the Soviet fortresses to the west.

The ceaseless roar of the heavy artillery from these fortresses shook the little house where the division was headquartered.

The differences between people were remarkable. Some were entirely calm, rock-steady; others could barely speak, and their hands were trembling.

The chief of staff, a lean elderly colonel, his hair streaked with grey that seemed to have appeared overnight, remembered Novikov from a training exercise the previous year. Seeing him come in, he slammed down the dead telephone receiver and said, 'A far cry from last year's "reds" and "blues"! An entire battalion wiped out in just half an hour! To the last man! Not one survivor!' Banging his fist on the table, he yelled, 'Bastards!'

Pointing through the window, Novikov said, 'Only a hundred metres from here some shit of a saboteur took a couple of shots at my car. He's there in those bushes. You should send out a few of your men.'

'It's no good,' the chief of staff replied with a dismissive wave of the hand. 'There's just too many of them.'

Screwing up one eye, as if there were a speck of dust in it that might prevent him from seeing everything clearly, the chief of staff went on: 'The moment this all began, the divisional commander rushed off to the regimental HQs. I stayed here. Then one of the regimental commanders phones me, icy calm: "I've engaged with the enemy. My tanks and my infantry are in action. We've repelled two attacks with artillery fire." And then another of the commanders reports: "A German tank column has overwhelmed our frontier post. A large number of tanks are now advancing along the main highway. I've opened fire."'

The chief of staff jabbed at the map. 'Here to the left their tanks have already outflanked us. Our frontier troops don't even think of retreating, they're fighting to the last man. But what about their wives and children? What about all the babies in crèches? How are we supposed to evacuate them? We've put them in trucks and driven them away, but God knows where to. For all I know, they may be right in the path of these same tanks. And what about ammunition supplies? Should we be sending our ammunition back to the rear? Or asking for more? It's anyone's guess.' He let out a few curses, lowered his voice and added, 'At dawn I phoned Army Corps HQ. Some bright fellow ordered me to sit still and do nothing. "Don't fall for this provocation!" he said. 'The cretin!'

'And this?' asked Novikov, pointing to a sector adjacent to the highway.

'This is where the battalion was massacred,' the chief of staff shouted. 'And the divisional commander with them. I've never known anyone like him – pure gold!'

He wiped his hands across his face, as if he were washing, then pointed to some bamboo fishing rods, a dragnet and a landing net standing in one corner of the room. 'We were meaning to go out at six o'clock this morning, just the two of us. He said there'd been good fishing here a week ago – the tench had been biting . . . Pure gold – and now it's as if he'd never lived! His new deputy's on his way from Kislovodsk and I was due to leave on the first. My travel warrant's already been issued.'

'What orders are you giving the regiments?' asked Novikov.

111

'The only orders I can. I encourage them to carry out their duty. A regimental commander says, "I'm opening fire." I say, "That's right – open fire!" Men are digging trenches. "Go on," I say, "keep digging!" After all, we all want the same thing: to stop the enemy, to fight him off!' He looked Novikov calmly in the eye. His own eyes were intelligent and alert.

Even far to the east the Germans seemed to have seized control of the sky. All around, the earth was shaking; there were explosions both nearby and in the distance. Then the earth trembled, as if in some death agony, and the sun disappeared behind a veil of smoke. From all sides came the hammering of rapid-fire cannon and the now all too familiar sound of heavy machine guns. For all the chaos of movement and sound, the thrust of the Germans' deadly work was painfully clear. Some pilots were heading due east, paying no attention to anything below them; each must have had his precise mission. Some were roaming about like bandits over the Soviet border units. And some were simply returning to their own airfields, west of the Bug.

The other commanders' faces looked very different on this day; pale, drawn, with large serious eyes, they were the faces not of colleagues but of brothers. Novikov did not see a single smile, nor did he hear a single lightly spoken or humorous word. Never before, perhaps, had he looked so far into people's most hidden depths – depths that can be glimpsed only at moments of extreme trial. He saw stern concentration and unshakeable will. Many of those who were usually most timid and silent, seemingly untalented men whom nobody noticed, revealed a wonderful strength. And sometimes he glimpsed an unexpected void in the eyes of commanders who only the day before had seemed the loudest, most energetic and self-confident; now they seemed lost, crushed and pathetic.

There were times when everything around him seemed a mirage; in a moment there would be a breath of wind – and yesterday's quiet evening would return, bringing with it days, weeks and months of peace. But then it would be the turn of the moonlit garden, of the sweet waitress, of his dinner in the half-empty dining room and the whole of the previous week or month to seem no more than a dream; the only reality was fire, smoke and this constant rumble.

That evening Novikov was in an infantry battalion command post, and then in the HQ of a nearby artillery regiment. By then he had had time to draw some conclusions. The greatest misfortune of the first few hours, he believed, had been the breakdown of communications.

With proper communications everything would have been different. He decided that, when he came to write his report, he would use as an example the infantry division he had visited in the afternoon. The regiments that remained in contact with the chief of staff had fought well, while the regiment that lost contact with HQ at the very beginning had been wiped out.

Novikov did indeed say all this in his subsequent report. But in fact it had been the other way round: the regiment was unable to communicate with the chief of staff because it had been wiped out – it was not wiped out because of its lack of communications. Novikov's conclusions had been drawn from only a few isolated observations.

The simple truth of those first tragic hours was that those who carried out their duty were those able to find within their own hearts and minds the necessary faith, strength, courage, calm and intelligence to keep fighting. Often it was those left without orders who fought most successfully. Orders are born from foresight and analysis – and there had been no time for foresight or analysis. Those who usually issued orders and those who usually carried them out were all equally unprepared.

An hour later, Novikov was with a heavy howitzer regiment. Their commander was on leave, and the acting commander was a young Major Samsonov. His long, thin face looked pale.

'How are things going?' asked Novikov.

'Not so badly,' said the major, with a shrug.

'What decisions have you taken?'

'Well,' said the major, 'they're preparing to cross the Bug. They're concentrating their forces close to the bank. I've opened fire, using everything we've got.' As if apologizing for some foolish act, he went on, 'We're doing pretty well, I think. I've had a look through the OP telescope. The fountains of earth from our shells are quite something. We came first in the Military District shooting competition, you know.'

'And after that?' Novikov asked sternly. 'Remember, you're responsible for both men and equipment.'

'We'll keep on shooting,' said the major, 'for as long as we can.'

'Got plenty of shells?'

'Enough,' said Samsonov. He added, 'My radio operator heard that we're now being attacked by Finland, Romania and Italy. All of them – but I shall keep shooting. I won't retreat!'

Novikov went to look at the nearest battery. Despite the roar of the guns, and the intent seriousness of the gunners' faces, there was a sense of calm. All the regiment's controlled power was now trained on the crossing, focused on destroying the German tanks and motor infantry gathering on the far bank.

One of the loaders came out with almost the same words as Samsonov. Turning towards Novikov, his face tanned and sweaty, he said with grim calm, 'We'll shoot till we've no more shells. Then we'll decide what to do next.' It was as if, after due consideration, he himself had taken the decision not to retreat.

Surprisingly, it was here, with a regiment he thought doomed, that Novikov for the first time that day felt a sense of calm. Battle had been joined; the Germans were being met with Russian fire.

The gunners quietly carried on with their work.

'Well, comrade Colonel, it's started now!' said a gun-layer. It was as if he had known all along what this morning would bring.

'Hard to get used to, isn't it?' said Novikov.

The gun-layer smiled. 'Will we ever get used to it? It'll be the same in a year's time as it is today. The mere sight of their planes makes me feel sick.'

Soon afterwards Novikov drove off, thinking he would never see any of these men again.

That winter, on the Donets, near Protopopovka, Novikov happened to meet a senior artillery commander he knew, and this man told him that the regiment had fallen back to the Berezina almost without casualties – and fighting all the way. Samsonov had prevented the Germans from crossing the Bug on 22 June, destroying a large amount of German equipment and inflicting considerable casualties. He had died only that autumn, on the Dnieper.

The war did indeed have a logic all its own.

Novikov saw a great deal on that first day of the war. Though he saw much that was sad and painful, though he saw confusion, cowardice and cynicism, this most difficult day in the history of his people filled his heart with faith and pride. What impressed him most deeply of all were the calm, serious eyes of the gunners – and the spirit of strength and endurance that he glimpsed in them. The roar of the Soviet guns also stayed with him, as did the distant rumble of the heavy artillery in the vast concrete pillboxes of the Brest fortress. Even many days later, as the German avalanche approached the Dnieper, the Soviet soldiers there would still be keeping up their brave fight.

Towards evening, after a roundabout journey on back roads through villages, Novikov came out onto the main highway. Only then did he begin to grasp the scale of the day's disaster.

Vast numbers of people were making their way east. The roads were full of trucks carrying men, women and children – many of the children still half-naked. All these people were doing the same thing – constantly looking back, and then up at the sky. There were tankers, covered trucks and ordinary cars, all moving as fast as they could. Walking along the verges, and through the fields on either side of the road, were more people; some, near the end of their strength, would collapse onto the ground for a while, then get up again and walk on. There were men and women of every age, some pushing prams and carts, some carrying bundles and suitcases. Soon Novikov ceased to distinguish the looks on people's faces. His memory registered only a few of the more unusual pictures: a grey-bearded old man with a small child in his arms, sitting by the road with his feet in a ditch and watching the passing vehicles with meek resignation; a crocodile of small boys and girls, in sailor suits and red ties – evidently a pioneer summer camp; a long line of blind men and women, tied to one another by towels and following their guide, an elderly woman with round spectacles and tousled grey hair.

When they stopped at a petrol pump and his driver was refilling the tank, Novikov heard any number of outlandish stories: Slutsk had supposedly been captured by parachute troops; Hitler, at dawn, had come out with some frenzied and mendacious speech; and there were absurd rumours about how Moscow, that same dawn, had been destroyed by a German air raid.

Novikov stopped at the HQ of a tank corps, not far from Kobrin, in which he had served until autumn 1940.

'You've just come from *there*?' people asked. 'Is it true the Germans will soon be on the main highway?'

In Kobrin he was no longer surprised by the crowds of people with bundles, the weeping mothers who had lost their children in the general chaos, or the exhausted look in the eyes of the older women. What struck him now were the smart little houses with their red tiles, curtained windows and neat lawns and flower beds. He was already, he realized, seeing the world through the eyes of war.

The further east they drove, the less clearly anything imprinted itself on his memory. Faces and events blurred together. Novikov had no subsequent recollection of where he had nearly been burnt alive during a night-time air raid or where he had seen two dead Red Army soldiers, their throats cut by saboteurs while they lay asleep in a chapel. Kobrin? Beroza-Kartuska?

But he did remember a night he had spent in a small town near Minsk. It was dark when they got there. The town was full of cars and trucks. Novikov was exhausted. He let his driver go off on his own while he himself went to sleep in the car, in the middle of a noisy, crowded square. And then, later that night, he woke to discover that his car was alone in the middle of a square that now seemed vast and deserted. All around him houses were quietly burning. The town was in flames.

He had grown so tired, so used to the deafening thunder of war, that he had slept through an air raid. What woke him was the silence that followed.

What remained from those days was one lasting image. He had seen hundreds of fires. Red, smoky flames had swallowed up the schools, factories and tall apartment blocks of Minsk; barns, sheds and thatched peasant huts had burned with pale, light flames; clouds of blue smoke had drifted over burning pine forests.

In Novikov's mind these fused into a single blaze.

His country seemed to him like a single huge house, and everything in this house was infinitely dear to him: small whitewashed rooms in villages; rooms in towns and cities, with colourful lampshades; quiet reading rooms; brightly lit halls; the Red Corners of army barracks.[70]

Everything he loved was in flames. The Russian earth was on fire; the Russian sky was cloaked in smoke.

22

In the morning Zhenya introduced Novikov to her mother, her sister and her niece.

Spiridonov had left at six o'clock, and Sofya Osipovna had set off for the hospital still earlier, while it was still dark.

Everything went easily and straightforwardly. Novikov very much liked the women sitting at the table with him: swarthy Marusya, with her greying hair; rosy-cheeked Vera, gazing at him with round clear eyes that somehow seemed both gay and cross; and especially Alexandra Vladimirovna, whom Zhenya resembled. He looked at Zhenya's broad pale forehead, at her alert eyes, at her pink lips, at her casual, 'first thing in the morning' plaits – and the word 'wife', which he must have pronounced thousands of times in his life, suddenly took on a new meaning for him. As never before, he sensed his own loneliness. He understood that it was to her, and to her alone, that he needed to recount all he had lived through, all he had thought about during this last difficult year; he realized that he had been looking for her, and thinking about her at painful moments, because he longed for real closeness, for an end to his loneliness. And he also had a feeling as pleasant as it was awkward; it was as if he had made a proposal of marriage and was now being scrutinized by members of the family he was hoping to enter.

'The war has been unable to break up your family,' he said to Alexandra.

'Maybe,' she replied with a sigh. 'But the war can certainly kill a family. It can kill a great many families.'

Noticing that Novikov was looking at the paintings on the wall, Marusya said, 'The one by the mirror. Pink earth. Dawn in a burnt-out village. That's Zhenya's work. Do you like it?'

Novikov was embarrassed. 'It's difficult for someone who isn't an expert.'

To which Zhenya replied, 'Last night, I've heard, you were more forthcoming with your judgements.'

117

Novikov realized that Seryozha must have reported to the appropriate authorities his words about the man who had turned green from old age.

'But anyone can enjoy Repin and Surikov,' said Marusya. 'You don't have to be an expert to admire painters like them. I keep telling Zhenya that she ought to paint posters for factories, for Red Corners and hospitals.'

'Well, I like Zhenya's paintings,' said Alexandra, 'even if I am an old woman who probably knows less about these things than any of you.'

Novikov asked if he could come back again in the evening – but he did not return either then or during the following day.

23

During the summer of 1942, after a relatively calm winter in Voronezh, Southwestern Front HQ had been constantly on the move, in the state of frenzied activity that is often as ineffectual as complete idleness; no matter what orders HQ commanders issued to their front-line units, the retreat continued.

In the spring of 1942, after receiving reinforcements, they had launched the Kharkov offensive. Gorodnyansky's army crossed the Donets and, moving through the narrow corridor between Izyum and Balakleya, advanced swiftly in the direction of Protopopovka, Chepel and Lozovaya.

In response, the Germans deployed a large concentration of troops and attacked both flanks of the Soviet army that had advanced so recklessly through the breach in their lines. The gate that Marshal Timoshenko had edged open as he advanced on Kharkov was slammed shut. Gorodnyansky's army was encircled and destroyed.[71] And once again, through dust, smoke and flame, Soviet forces were on the retreat. To the previous year's list of lost towns and cities were added new names: Valuiki, Kupyansk, Rossosh, Millerovo. To the grief of losing Ukraine was added a new grief: Southwestern Front HQ was now located on the Volga. Any further retreat – and it would be in the steppes of Kazakhstan.

The quartermasters were still assigning the commanders their new billets, but in the operations department telephones were ringing, typewriters were clattering and maps had already been spread out on the table.

Everyone in the department was going about their work as if they had been living in the city for months. Pale from lack of sleep, they hurried around abstractedly, hardly noticing Stalingrad itself. To them it made no difference whether HQ was located in a forest dugout, with amber-coloured resin dripping onto the table from a pine-log ceiling; in a village hut, with a cockroach scuttling across the map and geese following the signals officers indoors as they searched timidly for their mistress; or in a small house in some district town, with rubber plants in the windows and a smell of mothballs and wheat muffins. No matter where they were billeted, the staff officers' reality was unchanging: a dozen telephone numbers, some signals corps pilots and motorcyclists, a signals office, a teleprinter, a message despatch point, a radio and – laid out on the table – a map of the war, densely covered with blue and red pencil marks.

During the summer of 1942 the demands on the staff had been greater than ever. Positions were changing from one hour to the next. In a hut that only two days before had seen a meeting of the military soviet, where a staid, pink-cheeked secretary, sitting at a table covered in red felt, had conscientiously minuted decisions never to be put into effect, since German bombers and tank columns took little account of them – in this same hut a battalion commander would be yelling into the receiver, 'Comrade One, the enemy is breaking through,' while scouts in camouflage overalls slowly finished their tinned food and urgently reloaded their sub-machine guns.

The speed of the retreat meant that they kept having to change from one 1:100,000 map to another. To Novikov it sometimes felt as if he were a cinema operator furiously, day and night, turning the handle of a portable film projector while a kaleidoscope of images sped past his inflamed eyes. He suggested to his exhausted staff that they should change to 1:1,000,000 maps.

The information on the intelligence-section maps seldom fitted with the information provided by the operations section, while the artillery-HQ maps always provided the most optimistic view of the situation. The air-force data, on the other hand, always provided the most 'eastern' view of the front line – and it was their data that Novikov found of most practical use. Air reconnaissance was usually more accurate, quicker to reassess a constantly changing military position.

On the air-force maps, the symbols for Soviet bomber airfields were swiftly replaced by the symbols for front-line fighter and ground-attack airfields, just as the infantry's symbols for corps and divisional HQs were replaced by those for regimental and company command posts. And only a few days later these same airfields, now bases for German planes, would be marked as targets for Soviet bombers.

Novikov's daily task of marking in the front line was extremely difficult. Novikov loved precision and he had no doubt that inaccurate information was one of the reasons for the many Soviet defeats. He found it painful to see in front of him the contradictory data received from Army HQ, Front HQ reconnaissance section and Air Force HQ. Often his most accurate source about troop positions would be a commander who had come to HQ on some business of his own and whom he happened to have a word with at breakfast. Correlating these different sources and distinguishing truth from falsehood required enormous mental effort. Deep down, even he himself was surprised by his ability to make sense of a chaos that often seemed beyond understanding.

Novikov had had to report to the chief of staff frequently. He had also been summoned to meetings of the military soviet and he had a clear and complete grasp of the details of the Soviet retreat, something most people understood only partially and through guesswork. He knew the intelligence map of the German front; he knew the precise positions of the flat irons that symbolized the German army groups. He knew the names of the generals and field marshals who commanded these army groups: Busch, Leeb, Rundstedt, Kluge, Bock, List. These alien names were now linked to the names of cities he loved: Leningrad, Moscow, Stalingrad, Rostov.

The elite divisions of the army groups commanded by Bock and List had moved onto the offensive.

The Southwestern Front had been torn open, and two German mobile armies – the 4th Panzer and the 6th Army – were heading towards the Don, widening the breach in the Soviet front line as they advanced. Out of the dust and smoke a new name came to the fore – that of Colonel General Paulus, commander of the 6th Army.

All over the map were small black numbers representing German tank divisions: the 9th, 11th, 3rd, 23rd, 22nd and 24th. During the previous summer the 9th and 11th divisions had been deployed on the Minsk and Smolensk axes; evidently they had been moved south to take part in the Stalingrad offensive.

Sometimes it seemed that all this was simply a continuation of the summer offensive with which the war had begun; the German divisions moving across the map still bore the same numbers. In reality, however, these were entirely new divisions, manned by soldiers from the reserves called up to replace the dead and the wounded.

Meanwhile Richthofen's 4th Air Fleet was doing its work: massive air raids, terror on the roads, attacks against columns of vehicles and even against men on foot or on horseback.

And all this continual movement of vast armies, the bitter fighting, the repeated relocations of HQs, airstrips, maintenance and supply dumps, the abandoned fortified points, the sudden breakthroughs by German mobile units, this fire that had blazed across the steppe from

Belgorod and Oskol as far as the Don – day after day every detail of this grim picture had been clearly presented on the map for which Novikov was responsible.

There was one question that perplexed Novikov: why was this current German offensive so very different from that of the summer before? Even in the din and chaos of the first day of the war he had felt able, if more through intuition than logic, to grasp the Germans' overall strategy; it had been possible to understand a great deal simply from the flight paths of their planes. And Novikov's reflections during the winter had, he believed, deepened his understanding. Studying the map, he had seen what care the Germans had always taken not to expose their flanks. The left flank of Rundstedt's Army Group South had been covered by Bock, who was advancing on Moscow with their greatest concentration of forces; Bock's left flank had been covered by Leeb, who was advancing on Leningrad; and Leeb's left flank had been covered by the waters of the Baltic.

This year the Germans had adopted a very different strategy, advancing as swiftly as they could to the south-east, leaving their left flank exposed to the entire mass of Soviet Russia. This was hard to understand.

Why was it only in the south that the Germans had launched an offensive? Was this a sign of weakness? Or of strength? Or was it some kind of bluff?

These were questions Novikov was unable to answer. He needed to know more than can be read from an operations map.

Novikov had not yet realized that the Germans were simply no longer strong enough to advance simultaneously across the entire front; they had achieved their breakthrough in the south-east only at the price of enforced inaction on the Moscow and Leningrad axes. Nor could he know that even this one and only possible offensive had been launched without the necessary reserves. Several months later, when the fighting in Stalingrad reached its greatest intensity, the German High Command would find itself unable to transfer any forces at all from the Moscow and Leningrad axes; the Soviet armies in the centre and north-west posed too great a threat.

*

Novikov dreamed of something other than staff work. It was as a front-line commander, he believed, that he would be able to make best

122

use of the experience he had accumulated in the course of a year of intensive thought and careful analysis of military operations that he himself had helped plan.

He had filed a memorandum to the chief of staff and handed in a written application to his section head, asking to be released from his work at the Front HQ. His application had been rejected, and he knew nothing about the fate of his memorandum.

Had it been read by the general in command of the Front?

This was a question of great importance to Novikov; he felt he had put all the strength of his mind and soul into his memorandum. In it he had outlined a plan for a defence in depth at three different levels: regimental, divisional and corps.

Open steppe grants the attacker great freedom of manoeuvre, allowing him to concentrate his forces and make lightning strikes. While the defender is regrouping, while he brings up reinforcements along roads parallel to the front line, the attacker can break through, seize important junctions and sever communication lines. Defensive fortifications, however impregnable, become mere islands amid a vast flood. Heraclitus said, 'Everything flows, everything changes.' The Germans had rephrased this: 'We can go around everything, we can flow around everything.' Anti-tank ditches had proved worthless. Mobility could be resisted only by means of mobility.

Novikov had set out careful plans for the defence of steppe regions, taking into full account details specific to warfare in areas with a complex network of small roads and tracks that, during dry summers, are easily negotiable. He had included in his considerations the speeds of various kinds of motorized weaponry and other vehicles, the speeds of fighters, bombers and ground-attack aircraft, comparing all these with the speeds of corresponding enemy vehicles and aircraft.

Even during a strategic retreat, a mobile defence offered enormous potential. It was not simply a matter of being able to bring about a swift concentration of forces in the axes of a German offensive. Novikov also envisaged swift deployments that would make it possible to achieve sudden breakthroughs at points where they were least expected. Flanking counter-attacks could impede an advancing enemy and prevent him from carrying out encirclements. Soviet forces could even break through to the rear of an advancing enemy, sever his communications and carry out encirclements themselves.

There were moments when Novikov felt that his analysis of steppe warfare was extraordinarily clear and important. His heart would tremble with joy and excitement.

Novikov, however, was not the only commander to be elaborating plans of this nature. And he did not yet know about some of the regiments already being formed in the deep rear. Ultra-mobile anti-tank regiments were preparing to go into battle on the distant approaches to Stalingrad. Whole regiments and divisions had been equipped with the latest anti-tank guns. High-speed trucks made it possible to deploy these regiments anywhere in the vast arena of the steppe. At the first reports of a German tank breakthrough, these anti-tank regiments could deliver crushing blows, striking swiftly and decisively.

Novikov did not and could not know that his dream of an ultra-mobile defence was already being realized. Still less could he know that such a defence would turn out to be the precursor to infantry fighting of unprecedented violence on the outskirts of Stalingrad, on the cliffs of the Volga and in the streets and factories of the city itself. Nor, of course, could he know that this very street fighting, this dogged defence of the city streets by Soviet foot soldiers, would in turn be the precursor to a swift and decisive Soviet offensive.

Novikov now had a firm grasp of many things that, before the war, he had understood only theoretically. He knew about infantry and tank operations under cover of darkness, about the interaction of infantry, artillery, tanks and aircraft, about cavalry raids and operational planning. He knew the strengths and weaknesses of heavy and light artillery, of heavy and light mortars. He understood Yaks, LaGGs and Ilyushins,[72] heavy bombers, light bombers and dive-bombers. But what interested him most were tanks; he believed he knew all there was to know about every possible kind of tank operation: daytime and night-time, in forest, steppe and populated areas, in ambush and in attack, and in response to a breach of a defensive line.

For all his excitement about the advantages of ultra-mobility, Novikov was well aware of the extraordinary tenacity with which Soviet forces had stood their ground in Sevastopol and Leningrad; he knew what a vast number of German lives had been lost, week after week and month after month, in struggles for a single small patch of land, for a single hilltop, bunker or trench.

Novikov longed to correlate and make overall sense of the countless engagements that had taken place over the whole of the Soviet–German front. There had been battles in open country and in marshy forests, on the vast Don steppes and in the tiny Hanko peninsula.[73] On plains and steppes the Germans had made rapid advances of thousands of kilometres; in marshes and forests, and amid the rocks of Karelia, there had been times when the front line had moved only tens of metres in the course of a year.

Novikov's mind was constantly at work. Nevertheless, the war as a whole remained too vast, too complex for him to take in; his experience, after all, was only that of a single individual.

This, however, only made him still more determined to arrive at a broader and deeper understanding. He knew that the sole true judge of formulas and theories was the flow of reality.

24

Novikov hurried down the street. He had not needed to ask where HQ was located; it had been enough for him to see familiar faces in windows and familiar sentries outside doors.

In a corridor he chanced upon Lieutenant Colonel Usov, the HQ commandant. Red-faced, with small narrow eyes and a hoarse voice, he was not a man of great sensitivity – nor was his a position likely to encourage sensitivity. His usual expression was one of imperturbable calm; now, though, he looked pained.

'I've been across the Volga, comrade Colonel,' he said in an agitated voice. 'I flew to Lake Elton in a U-2.[74] Some of my supplies are being kept there. All I saw was camels, steppe and salt plains. There certainly wasn't much in the way of crops. What if we end up being stationed there? I said to myself. Where am I going to put the Artillery HQ? Or the engineers? Our intelligence, our commissars, our second line? I really don't know.' He let out a sigh of despair. 'The only thing anyone can grow over there is melons. I brought so many back with me the plane could hardly fly. I'll send you a couple this evening. They're wonderfully sweet.'

Novikov was greeted as if he'd been caught in an encirclement and been absent for a whole year. Apparently the deputy chief of staff had asked for him twice in the course of the night, and Battalion Commissar Cheprak, the secretary of the military soviet, had telephoned about two hours ago.

Novikov crossed the large room. The familiar desks, typewriters and telephones were already in place.

A woman with full breasts and dyed hair put down her cigarette and called out, 'A wonderful city, isn't it, comrade Colonel? Somehow it reminds me of Novorossiisk.' This was Angelina Tarasovna, the best of the HQ typists.

The cartographer, a sallow-faced major who suffered from eczema, welcomed Novikov back and then said, 'Last night I slept on a sprung mattress. It was like being a civilian again.'

The draughtsmen, who were junior lieutenants, and the young tele-printer operators with perms all jumped to their feet and called out merrily, 'Good morning, comrade Colonel!'

Gusarov, curly-haired and always smiling, was a favourite of Novikov's. Well aware of this, he asked, 'Comrade Colonel, I was on duty last night. May I go to the bathhouse after lunch?' Gusarov was also aware that senior commanders are usually more ready to allow someone to go to the bathhouse than to allow him to call on relatives or simply to catch up on his sleep after working all night.

Novikov inspected the room. His desk, his telephone and his locked metal box of important documents were all there.

Bobrov, a bald lieutenant, formerly a geography teacher and now another of the cartographers, brought Novikov a batch of new maps and said, 'Well, comrade Colonel, let's hope we'll be changing maps as often as this when it's our turn to take the offensive!'

'Send an orderly to the intelligence section and don't let anyone in to see me,' said Novikov. He took the new maps to his desk and began to open them out.

'Lieutenant Colonel Darensky has telephoned twice.'

'Tell him to come round at two.'

Novikov got down to work.

Infantry units, supported by both artillery and tanks, had halted the enemy's movement towards the Don. But alarming reports had come in during the last few days. Intelligence sections were report-ing a major concentration of German tanks, infantry and motor rifle divisions.

The question of supplies had become more critical than ever.

Novikov discussed these reports with his section head, General Bykov.

With the characteristic mistrust of a strategist for intelligence offi-cers, Bykov said, 'Where do they get all these ideas from? Who tells them the size of all these supposed new German divisions? Scouts do like to fantasize.'

'But it's not only our scouts. Our division and army commanders are under a lot of pressure. They're saying exactly the same about these new German units.'

'Commanders are no better. They like to exaggerate the enemy's strength too. But when it comes to their own strength, they're only too modest. Their only concern is how to get more reinforcements out of the commander-in-chief.'

The front line was hundreds of kilometres long, and the Soviet dispositions were too shallow to contain a powerful thrust from an enemy who could swiftly concentrate large forces wherever he chose. Novikov understood this, though deep down he hoped that the front might be stabilizing. He hoped and believed – and was afraid to hope and believe. The Soviet front line was all too thin.

Soon the scouts' reports were confirmed. The enemy was attacking in force.

German divisions had breached the Soviet front line and their tanks were now advancing rapidly. Novikov read the reports, correlated them and entered new data onto his map. This was anything but reassuring.

The main breakthrough had been from the south; other divisions were advancing to the north. There were signs of new pincer movements; several Soviet divisions were in danger of being encircled.

Novikov knew these curving blue fangs only too well. They grew so quickly on a map. He had seen them on the Dnieper and on the Donets. And now here they were again.

Today he felt more anguished than ever. For a second he was gripped by a mad rage. He clenched his fist. He wanted to scream, to strike out with all his strength, to bring his fist down on these blue fangs now threatening the sinuous, tender, pale blue curves of the Don.

'What's the joy of seeing Zhenya,' he said to himself, 'if it's only because we've retreated all the way to the Volga? No, it's not my idea of joy.'

He smoked cigarette after cigarette, wrote, read and thought, and once again bent forward over the map.

There was a quiet knock at the door.

'Yes!' Novikov shouted crossly. He looked at his watch, then at the now open door, and said, 'Ah, Darensky, come in!'

A lean lieutenant colonel with a thin, dark face, his hair brushed back, walked briskly up to Novikov and shook his hand.

'Sit down, Vitaly Alexeyevich,' said Novikov. 'Welcome to our new home!'

Darensky sat down in an armchair by the window, lit the cigarette Novikov offered him and inhaled. He appeared to have settled down comfortably but, after another drag, he got to his feet and began to stride about the room in his smart, squeaking boots. No less abruptly, he sat down on the windowsill.

'How are things?' asked Novikov.

'How things are at the front,' Darensky replied, 'you know better than I do. But as for me personally, they're not going well.'

'Same as before?'

'I'm being dismissed, posted to the reserves. I've seen Bykov's order. It's a bad business. The director of cadres has even said to me, "I know you've got a stomach ulcer. You can have six weeks' leave to get yourself treated." "But I don't want to be treated," I said. "I want to work!"' Darensky was speaking quickly and quietly, yet articulating each word distinctly. And then he went on, 'Since we've been here in the city, I can't stop thinking about the first day of the war. It keeps coming back to me.'

'Go on,' said Novikov. 'I've been thinking about that day too.'

'Seems like we're going through it all over again.'

'I don't think so,' said Novikov, shaking his head.

'I don't know. I feel I've seen it all before … Blocked roads, streams of vehicles. Anxious senior commanders. All asking which are the best roads, where they're least likely to get bombed … But then I see an artillery regiment, all spick and span, as if it's just out on exercise – and it's advancing west! Scouts, advance parties – all present and correct. I stop a car and ask, "Who's the commander?" A lieutenant replies, "Major Berozkin." "Under whose orders are you advancing?" I ask. The lieutenant demands my documents. After seeing the general's signature, he replies in a ringing voice, "The regiment is advancing, under orders from Major Berozkin, to engage with the enemy." That's what I'd like to see more of. While everyone else wants to retreat, Berozkin advances. His men just look down at the ground, while the women gaze at them as if they're holy martyrs. I never saw Berozkin himself – he was further forward. And now … why is it I can't forget this Berozkin? I want to meet him, to shake him by the hand. And meanwhile, I'm being packed off to the reserves. Why? It's not right, comrade Colonel, is it?'

Darensky went on to explain that, a few weeks earlier, he had had a disagreement with Bykov. Before the beginning of a Soviet offensive on a particular sector of the front, Darensky had reported that the Germans were deploying large forces just to the south of this sector; he had provided sound evidence that they were preparing to attack.

Bykov had referred to his report as balderdash. Darensky had lost his temper. Bykov reprimanded him, but Darensky continued to argue his case. Bykov had sworn at him and ordered him to be dismissed from his post and sent to the reserves.

'You know I'm not easy to please,' Novikov replied, 'but I can tell you one thing for sure. If I were given command of a unit, you're the man I'd choose as my chief of staff. You've got intuition – and that's what one needs to make sense of a map. And as for you and the ladies, don't we all have our weaknesses?'

Darensky gave Novikov a quick look, his brown eyes twinkling. Showing a gold tooth as he smiled, he said, 'It's a great shame they haven't given you a division of your own.'

Novikov went up to the window, sat down beside Darensky and said, 'I'll have a word with Bykov today, without fail.'

'Thank you.'

'No need for thanks.'

As Darensky was leaving the room, Novikov asked, 'Vitaly Alexeyevich, do you like modern art?'

Darensky looked at him in surprise, laughed and said, 'Modern art? No. Certainly not.'

'But it is, at least, modern. It's new.'

'So what?' said Darensky with a shrug. 'People don't argue about whether Rembrandt's old or new. They just say he's eternal. Permission to leave?'

'Please do,' said Novikov abstractedly, and bent forward over the map.

A few minutes later Angelina Tarasovna the chief typist came in. Wiping her tear-stained eyes, she asked, 'Is it true, comrade Colonel, that Darensky's been dismissed from his post?'

'Unless it concerns your work,' Novikov replied sharply, 'you are not to disturb me.'

At five o'clock Novikov reported to Major General Bykov.

'So what do you have to report?' asked Bykov, looking crossly at the inkpot in front of him on his desk. The sight of Novikov was always an irritation; it was as if this daily bringer of bad news were responsible for all the disasters of the retreat.

The summer sun shone brightly on the map – on steppes, valleys and rivers, and on the general's pale hands.

Calmly and methodically, Novikov began to go through a list of place names. Bykov marked them on the map with his pencil, nodding his head and repeating, 'Yes, yes …'

By the time Novikov finished, the pencil in the general's hand had moved down as far as the mouth of the Don.

Bykov looked up and asked, 'Is that it?'

'Yes.'

The general was composing a report about events that had taken place several weeks ago. Novikov could see that this was of far more concern to him than the alarming situation developing right now.

Bykov began explaining the movements of the various armies, repeatedly emphasizing the words *axis* and *momentum*. 'You see,' he said, moving the other end of his pencil over the map, 'the axis of movement of our 38th Army is a straight line, from Chuguev to Kalach. And the 21st Army's momentum of retreat is constantly decreasing.'

He demonstrated this too, with the help of a ruler. From his tone one might have thought that he had foreseen all this and was pleased to have been proved right. It might even have been he himself who determined the axis and momentum of the Soviet armies.

Annoyed by all this and incapable of playing the role of a meek subordinate, Novikov said, 'Comrade General, you sound like a scientist in a sinking boat, explaining why the bow is under water, the stern is up in the air and the boat is keeling over. The important thing is to plug the holes, not to say why the boat is going under. With this axis and this momentum we won't hold out even if we fall back as far as the Volga. And there's no sign of reinforcements.'

After attempting with an India rubber to erase a spot of sunlight creeping across a red axis of movement, Bykov came out with words Novikov had heard from him many times before, 'That's none of our business. The disposition of the reserves is a matter for the Stavka to determine.[75] We too depend on our superiors.' He contemplated the fingernails of his left hand for a moment, then added crossly, 'The general's reporting to the commander-in-chief today. You must remain in your section, comrade Colonel. But until you're summoned, you're free to do as you wish.'

Novikov understood Bykov's dissatisfaction. Bykov did not like him. When Novikov was being considered for the position of Bykov's second in command, Bykov had said, 'Well, I can't say that would be wrong. Novikov knows what he's doing. Still, he is rather quarrelsome. And conceited. Not a man who knows how to get the best out of people.'

And when Novikov was put forward for the Order of the Red Banner, Bykov had said, 'Give the man a star – that'll do.' And Novikov had indeed only been awarded the Order of the Red Star. But in winter, when there was talk of Novikov being transferred to one of the Army HQs, Bykov had been very upset, saying he'd never be able to get by

131

without him. And when Novikov asked to be transferred to a front-line unit, Bykov's refusal had been no less categorical.

Whenever anyone in the section was asked a difficult question, they always replied without hesitation, 'Go straight to Novikov. Bykov will just keep you for an hour and a half in his anteroom. He'll be in a meeting, or listening to a report, or having a rest. And when you get to speak to him, he'll just say, "Ask Novikov. I've delegated this to him."'

It was out of respect for Novikov's abilities rather than for his rank that the commandant usually assigned him one of the best billets at each new location. The head of the service section, a man with few illusions about people, always gave Novikov the best cigarettes and the best gabardine for his uniform. And even the waitresses in the canteen used to serve him out of turn, saying, 'The colonel never has a spare moment. We mustn't keep him waiting.'

Battalion Commissar Cheprak, the secretary of the military soviet, once told Novikov that the Front second in command, looking through the list of commanders to be called to an important meeting, had said, 'You know what Bykov's like. Get hold of Novikov.'

Bykov was clearly aware of incidents like this, and he did not like it when Novikov was invited to meetings of the military soviet. Recently he had been more irritated than ever; he had heard about the memorandum Novikov had filed. As well as outlining plans and ideas of his own, Novikov had volunteered his criticisms of an important operation – and Bykov knew that the commander-in-chief had been impressed. He felt upset that Novikov had not even consulted him; he should not have bypassed his immediate superior.

Bykov saw himself as an experienced and valuable commander, with an exceptional knowledge of military regulations and an equally fine grasp of the complex system for the classification of documents. His files and archives were in perfect order and his staff carried out their duties with impeccable discipline. Making war, Bykov believed, was simple enough; getting people to understand the rules of war was a great deal harder.

Some of the questions Bykov asked were very strange indeed: 'But how come they had no ammunition?'

'Their own dump was blown up and there had been no deliveries to the support services dump.'

'Well, it makes no sense to me. It's just not the way to go about things,' Bykov had replied with a shrug. 'It's every commander's duty to keep a full stock and half as much again in reserve.'

Noticing Bykov's sullen expression, Novikov thought about how, in matters of more personal concern, this man could show considerable flexibility and resourcefulness. When it came to imposing his own authority, he adapted only too well to changing circumstances. Military regulations might have nothing to say about such things, but he certainly knew how to get rid of someone unwanted, how to find an opponent's weak spot and how to present himself in the best possible light.

After quickly sizing him up, Novikov concluded that even Bykov's areas of expertise were of doubtful value.

'Afanasy Georgievich,' Novikov began, 'may I ask you about another matter?'

By using Bykov's first name and patronymic, he was intimating that he now wanted to speak about something quite different. Bykov gestured to him to sit down.

'Please do. I'm listening.'

'Afanasy Georgievich, it's about Darensky.'

'Darensky?' replied Bykov, raising his eyebrows. 'And what exactly about Darensky?'

Novikov could see at once that he was not going to get anywhere. This angered him.

'I think you already know. He's a gifted commander. Why have him kicking his heels in the reserves when he could be doing something useful?'

Bykov shook his head. 'I don't need him myself, and I think you can get by without him too.'

'But Darensky did, the other day, prove to be right as regards the point under discussion.'

'That's beside the point.'

'But it's *precisely* the point. Darensky has a remarkable gift for divining the enemy's intentions from only minimal data.'

'Then he should transfer to intelligence. I'm not interested in fortune-telling.'

Novikov let out a sigh. 'I don't understand. The man's a born staff officer – and you don't want to use him. And I'm not a staff officer at all. I'm a tank man – I apply for a transfer, and you won't release me.'

Bykov grunted, took out his gold pocket watch, wrinkled his brow in surprise and held his watch to his ear.

'He wants his supper,' thought Novikov.

'Well, that's all,' said Bykov. 'You can go now.'

25

Novikov was summoned towards eleven o'clock in the evening.

A tall guard with a sub-machine gun asked in a friendly yet respectful voice, 'Whom do you wish to see, comrade Colonel?'

Whether Front HQ was in the sombre halls of some old palace or in a little cottage with a pretty front garden, the atmosphere in the commander-in-chief's anteroom was always the same. The curtains were always drawn, it was always half dark and everyone always spoke in a whisper, glancing every now and then at the inner door. The waiting generals would be looking anxious and even the telephones would seem to have a muted ring, as if afraid of disturbing the general solemnity.

Novikov was first to arrive. Cheprak, the secretary of the military soviet, was sitting at his desk; frowning a little, he was reading a book. He had the sallow face of a man who works all night and sleeps during the day.

An orderly covered in medals was eating his supper, his plate on the windowsill. Seeing Novikov, he sighed and got to his feet. Taking his plate with him, his medals tinkling sadly, he walked lazily into an adjoining room.

'Not here yet?' asked Novikov, nodding in the direction of the inner door.

'No, he's here all right,' said Cheprak, speaking normally, as if they were in the canteen – not in his usual anteroom voice. He slapped his hand down on his book and said, 'What a life we once had, back in the days of peace!'

Cheprak stood up and walked about the room. He went over to the windowsill and beckoned Novikov to join him. Then he switched into Ukrainian, which Novikov had never heard him speak before, and asked, 'What do you make of it all?'

Novikov looked at him questioningly. Cheprak returned his look. His eyes, as always, were intelligent and sardonic. 'Do you happen to know,' Cheprak continued, 'who's the commander-in-chief of the Southern Front?'

'I do.'

'You may have known once, but you don't know any longer. The commander-in-chief has just been replaced.' Cheprak went on staring at Novikov, as if wondering whether he would be taken aback by this news. Novikov was not taken aback, but he could see that Cheprak was agitated and he understood why.

He could also see that Cheprak was expecting him to ask questions. But he did not respond.

'Goodness knows what we're in for now,' Cheprak continued, looking bewildered. 'Apparently we've all got too used to yielding ground: all the way from Tarnopol to the Volga. Retreat, retreat, retreat – they say we've developed *a psychology of retreat*. Our Front's been renamed now. Since the twelfth of the month, it's no longer the Southwestern Front but the Stalingrad Front. There's no longer any such thing as a south-western axis.'[76]

'Who told you all this?' asked Novikov.

Cheprak smiled. Without answering, he went on, 'We may all get sent back beyond the Volga. The Don may be entrusted to a new Front, with an entirely new HQ.'

'Is that what you think?'

'Well, there was a radio communication, but just who said what I can't tell you.'

Cheprak looked around him. Perhaps aware that he too might soon be transferred to some other position, he said, 'Remember how you came out from the operations room in Valuiki and said cheerily, "We've won the battle for Kharkov!" And it was just then that the Germans broke through from Barvenkovo and attacked Balakleya.'

'What makes you bring *that* up?' Novikov retorted. 'Anything can happen, as you well know. And I was hardly alone – one or two people rather more important than me were saying just the same.'

Cheprak shrugged. 'It just came to mind … And we had some fine men. Gorodnyansky, and Lieutenant General Kostenko the Front C-in-C … And divisional commanders Bobkin, Stepanov and Kuklin. And there was a splendid journalist, Rozenfeld – he could tell stories all day and all night. Not one of them still with us – it hurts to think of them.'

The meeting of the military soviet was clearly going to start late.

There were so many important figures in the anteroom that even major generals remained on their feet. Not daring to sit on the chairs and sofas, they stood by the windows, chatting quietly and glancing now and again at the commander-in-chief's closed door. Ivanchin, the soviet's political member, walked briskly in, merely nodding in response to greetings. He looked troubled and exhausted.

In a loud voice, he asked Cheprak, 'Is he in?'

Cheprak replied hurriedly, 'Yes, but he's asked you to wait for a few minutes.' He said this with the respectful look of a subordinate obliged to repeat the words of his boss: had it depended on him alone, he would, naturally, have shown Ivanchin in straightaway.

After looking around the waiting room, Ivanchin turned to an artillery general. 'Well, are you all right in your city billet?' he asked. 'No problems with malaria?'

The artillery general was the only man present not to be speaking in a hushed voice. Another general, recently arrived from Moscow, had been whispering something to him and he was laughing loudly. 'Everything's all right so far,' he replied to Ivanchin. With a nod towards the general standing beside him, he went on, 'And I've met a friend. The two of us served together in Central Asia.'

He walked over to Ivanchin and they exchanged a few more words – the kind of brief remarks that make sense only to people who see each other at work day after day.

'And yesterday's?' Novikov heard the artillery general ask.

'To be concluded in the next issue, as they say,' Ivanchin replied. The artillery general laughed once again, covering his mouth with a large, broad hand.

People were, of course, trying to guess what the two men were talking about – but it could have been almost anything. Before an important meeting, no one wants to talk prematurely about what really matters; they prefer to discuss trivialities.

'And as for the local hospitality!' said a deep voice. 'I heard my men say that the Military District canteen was checking their ration cards and refusing to serve them. "If you're from the front line," I kept hearing, "they turn you away. But if you've been safe in the rear all the time, that's fine!"'

'It was scandalous,' said someone else. 'I telephoned Ivanchin. It turned out that everything had, in fact, been agreed with Gerasimenko, the Military District commander. But those idiots in the canteen had ideas of their own. And they made out they couldn't cope with the numbers – it meant that commanders were getting back late from their lunch break!'

'So, how does the story end?' asked a short, pink-cheeked intelligence general. He had returned from the front only an hour ago and all this was new to him.

'Simply enough,' replied the previous speaker. 'A certain person,' he gestured discreetly towards Ivanchin, 'picked up his phone and said a few words to Gerasimenko. And after that the commandant was waiting in the doorway, greeting everyone from the front with bread and salt!'[77]

The intelligence general asked Bykov, 'How's your new billet? All right?'

'Yes,' replied Bykov. 'There's a bath – and south-facing windows.'

'I'd forgotten what it's like to sleep in a city apartment. It seems strange now. As for baths – who needs baths? The moment we got here, I went straight to the bathhouse. That's good enough for us soldiers!'

'So, how was your journey, comrade General?' asked the commander with the deep voice.

'All I can say,' the intelligence general replied, 'is that it's the last time I'll be driving anywhere in the daytime.'

'What, did you have to bale out into the ditch – as my driver likes to put it?'

'Don't ask,' the general replied with a laugh. 'Especially as we were approaching the Don. They could hardly have flown any lower. I had to leap out of the car three times. I really thought I was done for.'

Just then the inner door opened, and a quiet, slightly hoarse voice said, 'Comrades, this way.'

Everyone fell silent, looking intent and severe. The banter of the last few minutes had provided a necessary respite, but it was instantly forgotten.

Marshal Timoshenko's head was closely shaved. Even in the brightly lit room it was impossible to tell where his bald patch ended and the shaved parts began.

He walked around the room, glanced quickly but keenly into the faces of the generals standing to attention before him, reached out to touch the blackout curtain, paused and sat down. Resting his large peasant hands on the map, he thought for a moment, shook his head a little impatiently – as if, rather than him keeping the generals waiting, it had been the other way round – and said, 'Well, it's time we got started!'

The first speaker was Bykov, his deputy chief of staff.

'A pity it's not Bagramyan,' whispered the intelligence general, who was sitting beside Novikov.[78]

Bykov began with the question of supplies. The railway lines across the steppe were being bombed regularly and German planes had also begun laying mines in the Volga. A cargo ship had been lost between Stalingrad and Kamyshin. It was, in principle, possible to transport both supplies and reinforcements along the Saratov–Astrakhan railway, the far side of the Volga. But this too was within range of the German bombers. Moreover, everything would need to be conveyed in three stages: along the railway to the Volga, across the Volga into Stalingrad, and from Stalingrad to the front line. The various crossing points on the Don were also being bombed repeatedly. There would clearly be problems with transport for some time to come.

'All too true,' said Ivanchin with a sigh.

Bykov was not spouting platitudes; he was speaking the language of a professional soldier. Everything he had to say about the situation of the Soviet people and state was concrete and specific and his analysis of the military situation was unsparing. Nevertheless, Novikov frowned. Bykov was still not hitting the nail on the head.

'When, in the late afternoon of the day before yesterday, enemy mobile units appeared in his rear, the army commander took up a defensive position on the banks of the watercourse,' Bykov went on calmly. Turning to the map, he casually outlined the combat zone with a pale, short-nailed finger. 'But the army commander's HQ had been subjected to intensive air raids for the previous twenty-four hours, his telephone lines had been severed and his radio transmitter had also been out of action for four hours; as a result his orders failed to reach the commander of the division constituting his left flank. The army commander also sent signallers, but they too were unable to get through. The only line of communication had been straddled not only by enemy tanks but also by infantry, evidently brought up in trucks.'

'Anything new to report?' Timoshenko asked curtly.

'Yes, comrade Commander-in-Chief, there is something new.' Bykov glanced quickly at Novikov, who had briefed him an hour earlier. 'Permission to continue, comrade Commander-in-Chief?'

Timoshenko nodded.

'The divisional staff lost contact with the regiments yesterday morning. German tanks broke through to the command post. The commander suffered severe concussion, but he was evacuated by air ambulance. The chief of staff had his legs crushed; he died then and there. There was no further communication with the regiments.'

'Hardly surprising,' said Ivanchin, 'given that the divisional command post no longer existed.'

'What was the name of that chief of staff?' asked Timoshenko.

'Comrade Commander-in-Chief, he hadn't been here at all long,' said Bykov. 'He'd just been transferred from the Far East.'

Timoshenko went on looking at Bykov expectantly.

Bykov narrowed his eyes. His face took on the suffering look of a man struggling to find the right word. He fluttered his hand and tapped his foot on the floor, but this did not help.

'Colonel … Colonel … The name's on the tip of my tongue … A new division.'

'The division no longer exists, the men are all dead, but you still think of it as a new division,' said Timoshenko. With a weary smile he went on, 'Names, names – how many times must I say this? You must know your men's names!' Turning to Novikov, he asked, 'Do you know his name, Colonel?'

Novikov named the man who had died: 'Lieutenant Colonel Alferov.'

'Memory eternal!' said Timoshenko.[79]

After a brief silence, Bykov gave a little cough and asked, 'Permission to continue?'

'Please do!'

'And so, with this division now dispersed and fragmented, the army was severed from immediate contact with the army on its left flank.' This was Bykov's delicate way of saying that the Germans had breached the Soviet front line and that their tanks and infantry had then streamed through this breach. 'Twenty-four hours later, however,' Bykov continued, now speaking a little more loudly, 'the integrity of the front line was re-established thanks to a skilful and energetic counter-attack by an infantry division under the command of Colonel Savchenko.' Bykov looked Timoshenko in the eye as he pronounced the name Savchenko, as if hoping to compensate for having forgotten Alferov. Pointing to the map, he then said, 'And this was the configuration of the front line at sixteen hundred hours.'

'Configuration?' Timoshenko repeated.

'The disposition of our various units,' said Bykov, realizing that Timoshenko was irritated by the word *configuration*. 'The enemy, however, then began to pressure an adjacent sector, achieving at two points a tactical success that could have led to the encirclement of the army's right wing. Chistyakov therefore ordered a withdrawal to a new defensive line, thus forcing our army to retreat.'

'So it was Chistyakov who made us retreat, was it?' said Timoshenko with a smile. 'And there was I thinking it had been the enemy. But how are things going further south?'

'The front line has been stabilized, but it seems as if the enemy, after encountering strong resistance and suffering significant losses, is now concentrating his forces to the north.' Bykov then began listing dates, battlefronts and the names of towns and villages. Everything he said bore witness to his military experience and ability to cross-check and organize information – yet his report did not satisfy his listeners. The extraordinary difficulty of their position made them want to hear something equally extraordinary. To Novikov it seemed that this was the time for them to be discussing the strategy of swift, fluid, highly mobile warfare he had advocated in his memorandum.

Glancing every now and then at Timoshenko, he kept wondering, 'Has he read my memo?'

After the report, Timoshenko asked a few questions. Several generals spoke about mistakes they had made. There was talk about how things might turn out on the new defensive lines, on the approaches to the Don.

There was talk about a commander's responsibilities towards the commander-in-chief – for a retreat from an agreed line of defence, for the loss of valuable ordnance, for abandoning a bridge to the enemy instead of blowing it up. This kind of responsibility – the responsibility of one commander before another – was discussed openly. Deep down, however, everyone felt that what mattered now was another, still more onerous responsibility: that of a son before his mother, of a soldier before his conscience and his people.

'We've been trapped by our own strongpoints, by our fortified zones,' said the artillery general. Everyone looked at him, then at Marshal Timoshenko.

'Say more,' said Timoshenko, turning towards him.

'We need mobility!' said the artillery general, his face flushing. 'We need freedom of manoeuvre. As for positional warfare, look where it's got us.' He flung out his hands. 'We simply don't have an intact front line any longer.'

'Freedom of manoeuvre all the way from Chuguev to Kalach!' said Bykov, smiling sceptically.

'Yes!' said Timoshenko. 'From the Donets to the Don. There's no denying it. Warfare today is mobile warfare!'

Novikov's palms were tingling. The artillery general had given voice to his most cherished dream. But neither he, nor Timoshenko, nor anyone else at this meeting had any conception of what the next months would bring, of the events that time was already beginning to shape, if only in secret.

The city of Stalingrad, where even the most conservative commanders had finally come to recognize the absolute triumph of mobile warfare, was to become the theatre for months of positional warfare such as the world had never seen – a battle more grinding, more relentless than Thermopylae or even the Siege of Troy.

With some irritation, Timoshenko said, 'We're talking a lot about tactics. What matters is initiative. Whoever holds the initiative turns out to have the right tactics.'

Novikov immediately wondered if he had been like a novice chess player watching a master and desperately, overexcitedly wanting to give him advice. Had he only been imagining he could see the decisive move? Had he, perhaps, failed to realize that the master had considered this move long ago – and dismissed it for good reason?

'Everything comes down to one thing,' said Timoshenko. 'Each of us must carry out his duty in the position assigned to us by the Supreme Command.'

The general in charge of transport had been speaking, but Timoshenko had interrupted him. Timoshenko now asked this general to continue.

'I wanted to say a few words about repairs to trucks and the availability of spare parts,' the general began. He felt awkward, concerned that, after a discussion of such important matters, his report would appear banal.

Timoshenko turned towards him, listening attentively.

At other times, when he was the one initiating events, Timoshenko could be harsh and impatient, only too aware of his subordinates' incompetence, lazy thinking and readiness to talk too much. Now too he was probably well aware of their failings, but at present it was the enemy who held the initiative and the last thing he wanted was to criticize. He had no wish to blame the swiftness of the Soviet retreat on the failings of his subordinates.

When the meeting was over and the generals all put their papers together, closed their files and got to their feet, the commander-in-chief went up to each of them in turn to shake his hand. His calm, broad face was quivering. It was as if he were struggling against something alarming, something that had suddenly burnt him inside.

The generals' drivers woke with a jolt and started their engines. Like a series of gunshots, car doors slammed shut. The dark and deserted street filled with noise and light – with the roar of engines and the blue beams of headlamps – then swiftly returned to darkness and silence. The road and the walls of the buildings still gave off the warmth accumulated during the day, but now and again there was a cool breath from the Volga.

Clicking his heels against the pavement so as not to arouse the suspicions of a patrol, Novikov made his way back to his billet.

Unexpectedly, he found himself thinking of Zhenya. In spite of everything, deep in his heart lay an expectation of something good, of happiness. He had no idea where this obstinate, irrational certainty of happiness had sprung from.

It seemed to be the intensity of his own thoughts that was making it hard to breathe, making the streets feel hot and stifling.

The following morning, in the canteen, Cheprak said quietly to Novikov, 'What I told you yesterday's been confirmed. A new Front has been created. The C-in-C flew off to Moscow at dawn, by Douglas.'[80]

'Oh!' said Novikov. 'In that case I'll apply again to be transferred to a combat unit. To the front line.'

'That'll be the end of you,' said Cheprak. He sounded calm and serious.

'What do you mean?' Novikov replied with a laugh. 'I also intend to get married.'

Hearing his own words, which were meant to sound like a little joke, he blushed.

26

The Southwestern Front's long retreat, from Valuiki to Stalingrad, was now over.

People say that on his first day in Stalingrad, Marshal Timoshenko bathed in the Volga, washing away the dust of this long, agonizing retreat. Thick dust had penetrated men's veins and coated their hearts. The task entrusted to Timoshenko – to save his men and equipment from the Germans – had been sad and painful.[81]

The enemy had done everything they could to turn a retreat into a rout. There had been times when the front line had fragmented, when German tanks had broken through to the Soviet rear. There had been times when German tank columns and Soviet columns of trucks carrying people, arms and equipment had moved within sight of each other, in clouds of dust, with no shots being fired, along parallel roads. The same had happened in June 1941, around Kobrin, Beroza-Kartuska and Slutsk. It had also happened in July 1941 on the Lvov highway, when German tanks moving from Rovno to Novograd-Volynsky, Zhitomir and Korostyshev overtook columns of Soviet troops retreating towards the Dnieper.

Marshal Timoshenko saved many divisions from encirclement, getting them safely across the Don. This success, however, was achieved at a cost that went largely unnoticed. Neither the main commissariat, nor the medical section, nor the cadres section was able to register that the tens of thousands of soldiers who crossed the Don had lost all faith in themselves and their future. It was impossible to appreciate the seriousness of this loss unless you had seen with your own eyes those vast columns of worn-out men marching east, day and night.

Marshal Timoshenko carried out the task entrusted to him. And on reaching Stalingrad, he spent several hours down by the Volga. He and his deputies and adjutants stood in the river, up to their waists in the flowing water, letting out little moans and grunts as they soaped their shaven heads and red necks.

Thousands of other Red Army soldiers did the same. They went carefully down the steep slope towards the water. They saw the sand in front of them shining with quartz grains and fragments of mother-of-pearl. Sometimes they winced as they walked over sharp, prickly blocks of sandstone that had fallen from the cliff.

The breath of the river touched their inflamed eyelids. Slowly and carefully they took off their boots. Many of these men had marched all the way from the Donets and their feet hurt badly; even a faint gust of wind could make the pain worse. They unwound their foot cloths as delicately as if they were bandages.

The more fortunate washed with slivers of soap; the less fortunate rubbed their skin with handfuls of sand or scratched at it with their fingernails.

Blue and black clouds of dust and dirt spread through the water. Like their commanders, the men moaned with pleasure as they peeled off a thick, ingrained crust as dry and abrasive as sandpaper.

Newly washed tunics and underwear were spread out to dry in the sun, protected by small yellow stones from the merry Volga breeze that wanted to snatch them up and toss them back into the water.

We do not know Marshal Timoshenko's thoughts. We do not know whether he, or any of these thousands of men throwing water over themselves, understood that they were performing a symbolic ritual.

This mass baptism, however, was a fateful moment for Russia. This mass baptism before the terrible battle for freedom on the high cliffs of the west bank of the Volga may have been as fateful a moment in the country's history as the mass baptism carried out in Kiev a thousand years earlier, on the banks of the Dnieper.

When they had finished washing, the men sat on the shore, beneath the steep cliff, and looked at the dismal, sandy semi-desert stretching beyond the far bank. Whoever they were – elderly drivers, spirited young gun-layers or Marshal Timoshenko himself – their eyes filled with sadness. The foot of the cliff was Russia's eastern boundary; the far bank marked the beginning of the Kazakh steppe.

Should future historians wish to understand the turning point of this war, they need only come to this shore. They need only imagine a soldier sitting beneath this high cliff; they need only try, for a moment, to imagine the thoughts of this soldier.

27

Ludmila Nikolaevna, Alexandra Vladimirovna's eldest daughter, did not see herself as one of the younger generation. Hearing her talk to her mother about Marusya and Zhenya, anyone would have thought this was a conversation between two friends, or two sisters – not between mother and daughter.

Ludmila took after her father. She had broad shoulders, blonde hair and clear, pale blue eyes set far apart. She was selfish yet sensitive, hard-working yet sometimes happy-go-lucky, pragmatic yet capable of carefree generosity.

Ludmila had married when she was eighteen but had not stayed long with her first husband; they separated soon after Tolya's birth. She got to know Viktor Pavlovich Shtrum when she was a student in the Faculty of Physics and Mathematics, and she married him a year before finishing her degree. She had specialized in chemistry and begun to study for a doctorate, but she never completed this. She often blamed this on material difficulties, on the difficulties of looking after a household and feeding her family. The true reason, however, may have been almost the opposite; Ludmila abandoned her experiments in the university laboratory at a time when her husband was doing well in his career and they were better off than ever. They had been given a large apartment in a new building in Kaluga Street and a dacha in Otdykh with a plot of land. Ludmila had been swept up by the excitement of managing all this. She had gone on long shopping trips, buying china and furniture. Come spring, she had started working in the garden, planting tulips, asparagus, pineapple tomatoes and Michurin apple trees.[82]

*

On 22 June 1941, when she first heard the news of the German invasion, Ludmila had been on the corner of Theatre Square and Okhotny Ryad. She had stood there in the crowd, near the loudspeaker. Women were crying; she felt tears running down her own cheeks too.

The first air raid on Moscow had been on 22 July, exactly a month after the beginning of the war. Ludmila had spent the night on the roof of their building, together with her son Tolya. She had extinguished an incendiary bomb and in the pink light of dawn she had stood beside Tolya on the flat roof that had been their solarium. She was pale and covered in dust. Though clearly shaken, she looked proud and resolute. To the east the sun was rising in a cloudless summer sky; to the west stood a wall of dense black smoke – from the tarpaper factory at Doro-gomilovo and the depot beside the Belorussky station. Ludmila looked at the sinister fire without fear; her only anxieties were on behalf of her son. She was holding him close, her arms around his shoulders.

Regularly keeping watch on the roof, she became a living reproach to those who went off to spend the night with friends and relatives living near metro stations. She was particularly scornful of an eminent scientist who took shelter in a cellar after saying that his life was essential to science. She also talked about a well-known writer, a middle-aged man, who had quite lost his head during an air raid, rushing about the bomb shelter, crying out and wailing. During those summer months she made friends with firemen, house managers, schoolchildren with no fear of death and young vocational-school students. In the second half of August she left for Kazan with Tolya and Nadya. When Viktor suggested she take some of their most valuable possessions with her, she looked at the fine china dinner service she had bought from an antique shop and said, 'What do I need all this junk for? Goodness knows why I wasted so much time on it all.'

Viktor had looked at her, and at the china in the glass-fronted cup-board. Remembering her excitement on first acquiring these cups, bowls and plates, he had laughed and said, 'That's wonderful. If you don't need any of this, I can certainly get by without it myself!'

In Kazan, Ludmila, Tolya and Nadya were put in a small two-room apartment not far from the university. But when Viktor arrived a month later, he found that Ludmila was no longer there: she had gone to work on a Tatar kolkhoz, in the Laishev district. He wrote to her, remind-ing her of all her various illnesses – myocarditis, metabolic problems, bouts of vertigo – and begged her to return to Kazan.

Only in October had she finally joined him. She was slim and tanned. Working on a kolkhoz had evidently done more for her health than consultations with four eminent professors, dietary regimes, spa cures in Kislovodsk, massage and pine-needle baths, or courses of photo-, electro- and hydrotherapy.

She had resolved to go out to work. Viktor found her a position in the Institute of Inorganic Chemistry, but Ludmila said, 'No, I don't want special treatment. I'd rather go and work on the shop floor.'

She got a job as a factory chemist. And in due course it emerged how diligently she had worked at the kolkhoz; at the end of December a sledge drew up outside their building and an old Tatar, along with a young boy, brought in four sacks of wheat – Ludmila's payment for the days she had worked there. Throughout the next four or five months Varya, their domestic worker,[83] made weekly trips to the market and bartered this wheat for apples, milk and sour cream. Varya liked to talk and she told everyone proudly that it was the wife of a member of the Academy of Sciences who had earned this wheat through her work on a kolkhoz. 'There she is,' the Tatars at the market used to say, 'the academician's old woman, come for her sour cream!'

It was a harsh winter. Tolya was called up and sent to military school in Kuibyshev. Ludmila caught a cold in the factory and fell ill with pneumonia. She was in bed for over a month. Instead of going back to the factory, she set up a collective to knit gloves, socks and sweaters to be given to wounded soldiers being discharged from hospital. Then the political commissar of one hospital invited her to join his women's committee. Ludmila read books and newspapers to the wounded and, being on good terms with most of the scholars and scientists evacuated from Moscow, she arranged for professors and members of the Academy of Sciences to give lectures to the convalescent patients.

But she often reminisced about her nights on duty on her Moscow rooftop. 'If I didn't have you and Nadya to think about,' she would say to her husband, 'I'd be going back to Moscow tomorrow!'

28

Ludmila's first husband – Tolya's father – had been a fellow student called Abarchuk. Ludmila had married him during her first year at university and separated from him at the beginning of her third year. He had been a member of the university commission responsible for checking the social background of students and exacting payment from those of non-proletarian origin for the right to matriculate.

The sight of this lean, fine-lipped university Robespierre in his worn leather jacket had often provoked outbursts of excited whispering from the female students. To Ludmila he had once said that it was unthinkable – even criminal – for a proletarian student to marry a young woman of bourgeois background. And if he had to choose between a sexual liaison with a bourgeois girl or a human-like monkey, he would not hesitate to choose the monkey.

He was uncommonly hard-working. He was busy with student affairs from morning till late at night. He gave talks, which he always prepared scrupulously; he set up links between the university and the new workers' faculties; and he waged war against the last devotees of Tatyana's Day and its drunken celebrations.[84] None of this got in the way of his conducting experiments in the chemistry laboratory – in quantitative and qualitative analysis – and getting high marks in all his tests and exams. He never slept for more than four or five hours. He had been born in Rostov-on-Don, where his sister still lived, now married to a factory administrative worker. His father, a medical assistant, had been killed by a shell during the Civil War, when the White artillery was bombarding Rostov; his mother had died before the Revolution.

When Ludmila asked Abarchuk about his childhood, he would frown and say, 'What's there to tell you? There wasn't much about my childhood that was good. The family was quite comfortably off, not so far from being bourgeois.'

On Sundays he visited students in hospital, bringing them books and newspapers. He gave nearly all his student grant to the International Organization of Aid for the Fighters of the Revolution,[85] to help foreign Communists suffering under the yoke of capital.

Confronted with even the slightest infringement of the ethics of proletarian studenthood, he was implacable. He insisted that a young woman who put on perfume and lipstick before the First of May international workers' holiday should be excluded from the Komsomol. He demanded that a 'Nepman'[86] student who once rode in a cab, wearing a jacket and tie, to the Livorno restaurant, should be expelled from the university. In one of the student hostels he publicly shamed a girl for wearing a cross round her neck.

Bourgeois tendencies were, he believed, ineradicable; they were etched in someone's blood cells and brain cells. If a working-class girl married a man of bourgeois origin – even if he had tried to cleanse himself through factory work – their children would be carriers of bourgeois ideology. Even their children's children would carry a dangerous contagion in the depths of their psyche. When asked what should be done with such people, he would reply sombrely, 'First they must be isolated. Once they've been removed from social circulation, there'll be time enough to decide.'

Anyone of bourgeois origin inspired in him a sense of physical disgust; if he happened, in a narrow corridor, to brush against a pretty, elegant girl student whom he suspected of being bourgeois, he instinctively shook his arm, as if to remove any least trace of her from the sleeve of his military jacket.

He married Ludmila in 1922, a year after the death of her father. The hostel commandant allocated them a room of their own, six square metres. Ludmila became pregnant. In the evenings she began sewing swaddling clothes. She bought a teapot, two saucepans and some large dishes. These acquisitions upset Abarchuk, who believed that a modern family should be liberated from the bondage of the kitchen. Husband and wife, in his view, should eat in a communal canteen and their children should be fed in nurseries, kindergartens and boarding schools. Their room should have only the simplest of furniture: two writing desks; two beds that folded up against the wall; some bookshelves; and a small recessed cupboard.

Around this time Abarchuk fell ill with tuberculosis. His comrades managed to arrange for him to spend two months at a sanatorium in Yalta, but he refused to go. Instead he gave his place to a sick student from one of the workers' faculties.

He could be kind and generous, but the moment anything became a matter of principle he turned pig-headed and cruel. He behaved honourably in his work and he despised money and everyday comforts,

149

but he sometimes read other people's letters, looked at the diary Ludmila kept under her pillow and failed to return books he borrowed from friends.

Ludmila thought her husband unique; there could never be anyone like him. But once, when she was singing his praises, her mother interrupted, 'No, no, I've seen too many young people like that – both when I was a student in Petersburg and when I was in exile in Siberia. They just don't know how to reconcile love of humanity and love for an actual person.' 'No,' said Ludmila, 'you don't understand. He's not like that at all.'

Until their child came into the world, Ludmila subordinated herself to Abarchuk without reservation. But when this new little human being appeared, the relationship between husband and wife began to deteriorate. Abarchuk spoke less about the achievements of Ludmila's revolutionary father and reproached her more and more often with regard to her bourgeois maternal grandfather. As he saw it, the birth of the little boy had awoken petty-bourgeois instincts that, until then, had lain dormant within her. He watched sullenly as his wife put on a white apron and wound a kerchief around her head before making a pan of *kasha*. He noticed how deftly she embroidered initials and delicate patterns on the boy's clothes and bed linen, how intently she gazed at the embroidered coverlet on top of his tiny cot. A torrent of alien, hostile objects was invading their room; the apparent innocence of these objects only made the struggle against them still harder.

Abarchuk's idea of a nursery, his plans for the boy to be brought up in a workers' commune in an iron and steelworks – all came to nothing.

Ludmila said she wanted to go for the summer to her brother Dmitry's dacha. There was plenty of space, and her mother and her two sisters would come and help her look after the boy. But around the time she was due to leave, a bitter argument erupted between her and her husband: she would not agree to have the boy named 'October'.[87]

During his first night on his own, Abarchuk stripped the walls bare and restored the room to its previous, non-bourgeois state. He then sat until morning at his desk, from which he had removed the tasselled cloth, and wrote a six-page letter to Ludmila, painstakingly outlining his decision to separate from her. He himself was one of the now ascendant class; he would eradicate within him all that was personal and egotistic. She, for her part – and he now had no doubt of this – was

150

psychologically and ideologically inseparable from the class that history had made redundant. Her individualistic instincts held sway over any sense she might have of society. He and she were not following the same path; worse, they were following entirely opposed paths. He refused to allow the boy to bear his surname; it was already clear that the boy's psychology would be that of the bourgeoisie. Ludmila found these last words particularly wounding; she wept as she read them. Later, though, when she reread them, she felt furious – which partly healed her wounds. Towards the end of the summer, Alexandra Vladimirovna took little Tolya back to Stalingrad with her, and Ludmila returned to her studies.

After one of the first lectures of the new term, Abarchuk went up to her, held out his hand and said, 'Greetings, comrade Shaposhnikova!' She quietly shook her head and put her hand behind her back.

In 1924 there was a purge of the student body; students of bourgeois origin were to be excluded. Ludmila heard from a friend that Abarchuk had demanded that she herself be excluded. He told the commission about their marriage and the reasons for their divorce. This was a time when students used to joke, 'Vanya was lucky with his parents – he's the son of two peasant women and one factory worker!' And there was a little ditty:

> Oh tell me where I can go
> To buy a factory-worker dad
> And a mother who pulls the plough!

In the event Ludmila was not excluded. There were, however, two young men – Pyotr Knyazev and Viktor Shtrum – who had not worked before entering university and had not even been members of a trade union. These two, dubbed 'inseparable companions', *were* excluded. Their teachers, however, intervened on their behalf, asserting that both these young men were exceptionally talented. Three months later the Central Commission rescinded the faculty's decision and Shtrum and Knyazev were reinstated. But Knyazev fell ill and did not re-enter the university even after he got better; instead he went back to live with his parents, somewhere far from Moscow.

While the purge was being conducted, Ludmila was interviewed several times, and she crossed paths with Viktor. When Viktor reappeared in the middle of the third term, she congratulated him and said how glad she was to see him.

They talked for a long time in the half-dark anteroom to the dean's office. Then they went to the canteen and had some buttermilk; then they sat together on a bench in the little university park.

Viktor turned out to be very different from how Ludmila had imagined him – far from being a mere bookworm. His eyes were nearly always laughing, only entirely serious when he talked about something funny. He loved literature, went regularly to the theatre and didn't miss a single concert. He often went to beer houses, enjoyed listening to gypsy singers and adored the circus.

It emerged that at some time in the past their parents had been friends. Viktor's mother had studied medicine in Paris when Alexandra Vladimirovna and her husband had been living in exile there. Ludmila said, 'I heard my mother come out with the name "Shtrum", but it never entered my head that you could be the son of the woman she once stayed with for a whole month.'

That winter Ludmila and Viktor went together to theatres and to the 'Giant' cinema in the Conservatory. In the spring they went on outings to Kuntsevo and the Sparrow Hills or for boat trips on the River Moscow. A year before graduating, they married.

Alexandra Vladimirovna was astonished to see her old friendship with Anna Semyonovna Shtrum being reaffirmed by the young couple. The two mothers wrote letters to each other, repeatedly expressing their surprise and delight.

Ludmila's second marriage was very different from her first. Viktor had never gone out to work, nor did he have to support himself during his studies; his mother sent him eighty roubles a month, and three substantial parcels each year. It was clear from these parcels that she still saw her son as a little boy. The plywood box usually contained apples, sweets, an apple strudel, some underwear and a few pairs of socks embroidered in red with Viktor's initials. Beside Abarchuk, Ludmila had felt like a little girl, but now she felt like a woman of the world, treating her young child of a husband with condescending indulgence. Viktor wrote to his mother once a week. If ever he missed a week, Ludmila would receive a telegram: was Viktor in good health?

If Viktor asked her to add a few lines at the end of one of his letters, she would reply crossly, 'Heavens, I don't write this often even to my own mother. Sometimes I don't write for two months on end. Who am I married to – you or your mother?'

Abarchuk completed his degree a year after Ludmila and Viktor, having taken time off because of his work as an activist. Ludmila gradually forgot her resentment and came to take an interest in her first husband's career. He was doing well – publishing articles, giving lectures and, at one point, even occupying an important position in the Science and Scholarship section of the Commissariat of Enlightenment.

At the beginning of the first Five Year Plan, Abarchuk, now an industrial manager, moved to western Siberia. Ludmila came across his name now and then in articles about the construction of some huge factory, but he never wrote to her or asked after Tolya. Then came a period when she heard nothing at all. She saw newspaper articles about the official inauguration of the factory he had been in charge of constructing, but he was not mentioned even in passing. A year later, Ludmila learned that he had been arrested as an enemy of the people.

In 1936 Viktor Pavlovich Shtrum – the youngest of that year's candidates – was elected a corresponding member of the Academy of Sciences.[88] After the celebratory dinner, when all the guests except Zhenya and Krymov had left, Krymov said something that Viktor and Ludmila would never forget.

Viktor, still jealous of Abarchuk, had said boastfully, 'Here's a story for you, a simple little tale. Once there were two students. The first wanted to decide the fate of the second. He pronounced that the second had no right to be studying in the Faculty of Physics and Mathematics. And now, today, that second student has been elected to the academy. While the first student ... What has *he* achieved in the world?'

'No,' Krymov had replied. 'Your little tale is more complicated than you think. I've met that first student several times. Once, in Petersburg, he was leading a platoon attacking the Winter Palace. He was full of fire and passion. I saw him a second time in the Urals. Kolchak's men had stood him in front of a firing squad, but somehow he got away with his life. He lay in a pit till nightfall, then crawled out and made his way, covered in blood, to our revolutionary committee. Just as before, he was full of fire and passion ... No, the laws that govern our lives are far from simple. That first student carried out his duty when the revolutionary future of Russia – and perhaps of the entire world – was being decided. He carried out his duty honourably – and he paid with his sweat and blood.'

'Maybe,' Viktor had said lamely, 'but he almost ate me alive.'

'Things happen,' Krymov had replied.

153

29

The Shtrums' Kazan apartment was a typical evacuee home. In the first room, as if to indicate that the inhabitants were nomads, suitcases had been piled against the wall and a long line of boots and shoes stretched out beneath the bed. Poking out beneath the tablecloth were the lower halves of crudely planed pine table legs. The space between the table and the bed was filled with stacks of books. And in Viktor's room, beside the window, stood a large writing desk, its surface as empty as a runway for a heavy bomber; Viktor liked to keep his working space free of clutter.

Ludmila had written to her family in Stalingrad, inviting them – if they had to leave the city – to come 'en masse' and join her and Viktor in Kazan. She had already worked out how to arrange the camp beds. There was only one corner she was determined to keep clear. This was for Tolya: one day he would return from the army and she would bring his bed down from the attic. There was also a suitcase in which she kept his underwear, a supply of his favourite tinned sprats and a small pile of letters from him, tied with a ribbon. The uppermost was a page from a child's exercise book, almost filled by the four words, 'Hello Mama Come Soon.'

Ludmila often woke during the night and lay there thinking about Tolya. She wanted passionately to be with him, to protect him from danger with her own body, to work day and night digging deep trenches for him in heavy clay or in stone – but she knew this was impossible.

Her love for her son was, she believed, something extraordinary, different from the love of any other mother. She loved her son for not being handsome, for his large ears, for his awkward gait and general clumsiness, for being so shy. She loved him for not daring to learn to dance, for the way he snuffled as he got through twenty sweets, one after another. When, looking down at the floor, he told her about a low mark he had got for a literature exam, she felt a still greater tenderness towards him than when, muttering, 'It's nothing' and frowning in embarrassment, he showed her his physics or trigonometry work with its unvarying 'Excellent!'

Before the war, Viktor had sometimes got angry with her for allowing Tolya to go to the cinema instead of helping about the home. 'That's not the way *I* was brought up,' he would say. '*I* was certainly never mollycoddled like that!' He seemed unaware that his mother had been at least as protective of him as Ludmila was of Tolya, and that she had spoiled him in just the same way.

When she was cross, Ludmila would sometimes make out that Tolya did not love his stepfather, but she knew that this was not true.

Tolya's love of the exact sciences had become quickly apparent. He had no interest in literature, nor did he care for the theatre.

And yet, one day not long before the war, Viktor had found Tolya in front of the mirror. Wearing his stepfather's hat, tie and jacket, he was dancing, then bowing to someone and smiling graciously.

'I feel I hardly know the boy,' Viktor said to Ludmila.

Tolya's half-sister Nadya was very devoted indeed to her father. Once, when she was ten, she had gone with her parents to a shop. Ludmila wanted a length of velvet for curtains and she asked Viktor to calculate how many metres she needed. Viktor began multiplying the length, width and the number of curtains but instantly got in a muddle. The shop assistant did the calculation in a few seconds, smiled condescendingly and said to Nadya, who was deeply embarrassed, 'Your pápa doesn't seem to be much of a mathematician.'

Ever since, Nadya had believed deep down that her father's work did not come easily to him. Once, looking at sheets of manuscript covered from top to bottom with signs and formulae, with countless deletions and corrections, she had said with genuine compassion, 'Poor Pápa!'

Ludmila sometimes saw Nadya go into her father's study, steal up to his armchair on tiptoe and cover his eyes with her hands. For a few seconds he would remain motionless; then he would turn, put his arms round his daughter's shoulders and kiss her. When they had guests in the evenings, Viktor would sometimes look round and find he was being observed by two large sad and attentive eyes. Nadya read a great deal, and quickly, but there was much she did not take in. Sometimes she was strangely absent-minded. Lost in thought, she would answer questions in a way that made no sense at all. Once she had gone to school in socks that didn't match; after that, their cleaning woman used to say every now and then, 'Our Nadya seems a little melancholical.'

If Ludmila asked Nadya what she wanted to be when she grew up, Nadya would reply, 'I don't know. Nobody.'

She and Tolya were very unlike each other and, when they were little, they quarrelled constantly. Nadya knew how easy it was to tease Tolya and she tormented him mercilessly. He would get angry and pull her long plaits. This upset her but did not silence her. Doggedly, sullenly, in tears, she would carry on mocking him, calling him 'Our blue-eyed baby' or by a strange nickname that particularly enraged him: 'Pigsty!'

Not long before the war Ludmila realized that her children had, at last, made peace. She mentioned this to two elderly friends of hers. They smiled sadly and, with one voice, replied, 'They're getting older.'

*

One day, on her way back from the special store,[89] Nadya found the postman outside their door. In his hand was a triangular letter addressed to Ludmila.[90] Tolya wrote proudly that he had, at last, completed military school and was now being sent to an active unit, probably not far from the city where his grandmother lived.

Ludmila stayed awake half the night, clutching the letter. Again and again she relit the candle and slowly reread each word, as if these brief, hurriedly written lines contained the secret of her son's fate.

30

A telegram came for Viktor, summoning him to Moscow. One of his colleagues, Academician Postoev, received a similar telegram. Viktor felt unsettled, assuming this summons had to do with his work plan, which had yet to be granted official approval.

This work plan was ambitious, focusing on theoretical problems that could be investigated only at considerable expense.

In the morning Viktor showed the telegram to his friend and colleague, Pyotr Lavrentievich Sokolov. Fair-haired and stocky, with a massive head, Sokolov could hardly have looked more different from Viktor. Sitting in a small office beside the lecture theatre, the two men went through the pros and cons of the work plan they had drawn up the previous winter.

Sokolov was eight years the younger. He had been awarded his higher doctorate shortly before the war and his first publications had attracted interest throughout the Soviet Union and even abroad.

A French journal had published a short article about him, along with a photograph. The author had expressed surprise that someone who, as a young man, had worked as a stoker on a Volga steamer, should have completed a degree at Moscow University and gone on to explore the theoretical foundations of one of the most complex areas of physics.

'Our plan's unlikely to be approved in full,' Sokolov said. 'I'm sure you can remember our conversation with Sukhov. Anyway, who's going to develop the steel we need when every high-quality producer is struggling to meet the demands of the war? Our steel would require trial melts – and every furnace in the country has been turned over to producing steel for tanks and guns. How could anyone approve a plan like ours? Who's going to set up a furnace to make a mere few hundred kilograms of steel?'

'Yes,' said Viktor. 'I know all this. But Sukhov's no longer our director. He's been gone for two months now. As for the steel, no doubt you're right, but that's just a general consideration. What's more, Chepyzhin has approved the general thrust of our work. I read you his letter. You do have a way, Pyotr Lavrentievich, of forgetting about concrete details.'

'Excuse me, Viktor Pavlovich!' replied Sokolov. 'But it's you who's forgetting concrete details. Is the war not concrete enough for you?'

Both men were agitated. They were unable to agree how Viktor should respond if their plan met with opposition.

'It's not for me to give you advice,' said Sokolov. 'But there are many doors in Moscow, and I'm not sure you'll be knocking at the right one.'

'We all know your worldly wisdom,' Viktor retorted. 'That's why you're still without a residence permit and why you somehow managed to register for the worst special store in the city.'

Seeing this as a compliment, each liked to accuse the other of being impractical, of being above worldly matters.

Sokolov considered it the administration's duty to sort out his residence permit. But he didn't intend to remind them; he was too proud. Nor, of course, did he say any of this to Viktor. He just shook his head nonchalantly and said, 'As you know, I'm really not bothered about things like that.'

Next, they discussed what Sokolov should work on in Viktor's absence.

Late in the afternoon a pockmarked clerk in blue riding breeches came round from the city soviet. He looked Viktor up and down in mistrustful surprise and handed him a pass and a ticket for the next day's Moscow express. Thin and round-shouldered, with dishevelled hair, Viktor did not in the least look like a professor of theoretical physics; he looked more like a composer of gypsy romances. Viktor put the ticket in his pocket and, without asking what time the train left, began saying goodbye to his colleagues.

He promised to convey both collective and individual greetings to Anna Stepanovna, the senior laboratory assistant who had stayed on in Moscow to look after the equipment they couldn't take to Kazan. He heard repeated feminine exclamations of 'Oh, Viktor Pavlovich, how I envy you. The day after tomorrow you'll be in Moscow!' And then, to a chorus of 'Good luck!', 'Come back soon!' and 'Bon voyage!' he set off home for his evening meal.

As he walked back, Viktor went on thinking about the work plan and wondering whether or not it would receive official approval. He remembered his meeting with Ivan Dmitrievich Sukhov, the institute's former director, who had come to visit them the previous December.

Sukhov had been extraordinarily affable. He had held both Viktor's hands and asked him about his health, his family and their living conditions. From his tone, one would have thought he had come not from Kuibyshev but from the front line, straight from the trenches, and that he was talking to a frail and timid civilian.

But he had nothing good to say about the work plan.

Sukhov seldom took much interest in what lay at the heart of a scientific question; what usually concerned him far more were its political ramifications. He was endowed with an accurate sense, honed by experience, of what a particular circle of people would consider most important to the state. And there had been occasions when he had been fiercely critical of something that, only the previous day, he had appeared to support wholeheartedly.

When people like Viktor got foolishly worked up, when they argued about some issue from a purely subjective point of view, seemingly unaware of its broader implications, he saw them as ignorant of the ways of the world.

In conversation he liked to point out that there was nothing personal in his attitude to someone, or to the question under discussion: his only concern was to do what was in the collective interest. But he never appeared to notice how very harmoniously his opinions, and their sudden shifts, always dovetailed with the interests of his career.

'Ivan Dmitrievich,' Viktor had said as he and Sukhov began to argue, 'how can mere mortals like ourselves know which areas of research will matter most to the Soviet people? The entire history of science ... And anyway I can hardly change the beliefs I've lived by since I was a child. Let me tell you how once, when I was little, I was given an aquarium ...'

Glimpsing Sukhov's condescending smile, he had faltered and said, 'This has nothing to do with the matter at hand, and yet, really it has everything to do with it – however strange that may seem.'

'I understand,' Sukhov had replied. 'But you too must try to understand. Your childhood aquarium is neither here nor there. We're talking about something a great deal more important than any aquarium. Now is not the time to be working on theory.'

This had upset Viktor. He had realized he was about to lose his temper. Which he did. 'For better or worse,' he had burst out, 'I'm the one here who knows about physics. How is it that a bureaucrat like you thinks he has the right to give me lessons? Doesn't really make sense, does it?'

Sukhov had gone red in the face and everyone present had frowned. 'Well,' Viktor had said to himself, 'no more hope of *him* requesting a better apartment for me. I certainly can't ask him for anything now.' To his astonishment, Sukhov had not shown the least indignation. On the contrary, he had looked rather guilty. And his eyelids had trembled, like those of a little boy about to burst into tears. But only for a second. Then Sukhov had said, 'I think you need a rest. It seems your nerves are on edge.' And he had added, 'As for your work plan, I can only repeat what I have already said. I do not consider that it answers the needs of the day. I shall speak against it.'

From Kazan, Sukhov had gone back to Kuibyshev, and then to Moscow. After another six weeks, he had sent a telegram to say he'd be coming to Kazan again soon.

But instead of going to Kazan, he had been summoned to the Central Committee, harshly criticized, removed from his position and sent off to Barnaul – to teach at a local agricultural-machinery construction institute. His acting replacement was a young scientist by the name of Pimenov, whom Viktor had once supervised. It was his imminent meeting with Pimenov that Viktor was thinking about as he walked down the street.

160

31

Ludmila greeted Viktor just inside the front door. As she got to work with her brush, removing the Kazan dust from the shoulders of his jacket, she questioned him about his coming trip to Moscow. Every detail was important to her, concerned as she was that her husband's greatness should be duly acknowledged.

She wanted to know who had sent the telegram, whether a car was being sent to take Viktor to the station, whether his train ticket was for an open-plan carriage or for one with compartments. With a little smile, she told him that Professor Podkopaev, whose wife she disliked, had not been called to Moscow. Then, as if dismissing these thoughts with a brusque wave of the hand, she said, 'But this is all nonsense. I can't stop worrying. Day and night, my heart just keeps pounding away: "Tolya, Tolya, Tolya …"'

Nadya was late coming home; she had been to see her friend Alla Postoeva.

Recognizing Nadya's light, careful tread, Viktor thought, 'She really is very skinny indeed. The sofa's springs are in a bad way, but she can sit down without it giving even the least little squeak.' Not looking round, he said, 'Good evening, my girl!' And he went on with his work; he was writing fast.

After a long silence, still not looking round, Viktor asked, 'Well, how's Postoev? Is he packing his suitcase?'

Nadya still didn't say anything. Viktor tapped on his desk, as if calling for silence. There was a mathematical problem he wanted to solve before leaving. If he didn't, it was sure to trouble him all the time he was away – he wouldn't be able to give it the concentration it demanded. He seemed to have completely forgotten about Nadya, but then he turned round and said, 'What's the matter, my little sniffler?'

Nadya looked at him angrily, then burst out, 'I don't want to go to the kolkhoz in August to work on the fields. Alla Postoeva isn't going anywhere, but Máma's put me down without even telling me. She went into school and volunteered me just like that. I won't come home till the end of the month and then it'll be straight back to lessons. And the girls say you hardly get anything to eat and they work you so hard there's barely even time to bathe in the river.'

'All right, all right, but go to bed now,' said Viktor. 'Worse things happen.'

'I know very well they do,' said Nadya. After shrugging first one shoulder, then the other, she went on, 'But I don't think you'll be going to a kolkhoz, will you?' And then, 'My dear pápa's very politically conscious, that's why he's obliged to go to Moscow.'

She got to her feet. As she was leaving the room, she stopped and said, 'Oh yes, Olga Yakovlevna told us she went to the station to take presents to the wounded. And there, in one of the hospital trains, she saw Maximov. He'd been wounded twice and was being taken to Sverdlovsk. When he's discharged from hospital, he'll be going back to his chair at Moscow University.'

'Which Maximov?' asked Viktor. 'The sociologist?'

'No, no, no! The biochemist, the man from the dacha next door. The man who came and had tea with us the day before the war began … Remember?'

'Is there a chance the train might still be in the station?' asked Viktor, upset by this news. 'Máma and I could go straightaway.'

'No, it's too late,' said Nadya. 'Olga Yakovlevna was in his carriage when the bell went. He hardly had time to tell her anything at all.'

Later that evening, just before going to bed, Viktor and Ludmila quarrelled. It began with Viktor pointing to the sleeping Nadya's thin little arms and telling Ludmila she'd been wrong to insist that Nadya go to the kolkhoz. It would be better, he said, to let her have a good rest before what was sure to be a difficult winter.

Ludmila said that girls Nadya's age were always thin, that she'd been a great deal thinner herself at that age, and that there were any number of families with children who'd be spending the summer in factories or doing heavy work out in the fields.

To which Viktor replied, 'I tell you that our daughter's getting thinner and thinner and you just spout nonsense. Look at her collarbones. Look at her pale anaemic lips. What's got into you? You seem to want *both* our children to have to suffer. Is that really going to make you any happier?'

Ludmila looked at him in pain, began to cry and said, 'You don't sound too worried about what may happen to Tolya. Sometimes I need your heart, not your logic. I want you to care.'

Slowly, with emphasis, Viktor replied, 'Ludmila, you too often seem not to care.'

'You're right,' said Ludmila. 'As always, you're right.' And she left the room, slamming the door behind her.

What lay behind Viktor's last remark was his belief that Ludmila had little love for his mother. This was the main cause of their quarrels and disagreements.

In other respects, Viktor gave little conscious thought to his marriage. He and Ludmila had reached the stage when long years of habit can make a relationship seem unimportant, when its meaning has been obscured by daily routine, when only some sudden shock can make a husband and wife realize that these long years of habit and daily closeness are the most important, most truly poetic thing of all, the force that binds two people together as they move side by side from youth to white-haired old age. And Viktor was entirely unaware of how often he made Tolya and Nadya laugh by asking, the moment he walked through the door, 'Is Máma at home? ... What do you mean, she's not here? ... Where is she? ... Will she be back soon?'

And if Ludmila got delayed somewhere, he would abandon his work and start wandering about the apartment, either complaining loudly or threatening to go out and search for her. 'Where on earth is the woman? Which way did she go? Was she feeling all right when she left? And why does she have to go out at a time when there's so much traffic?'

But the moment Ludmila appeared, he would calm down, return to his desk and answer all her questions with a preoccupied 'What is it? No, please don't disturb me. I'm working.'

Like many young people prone to melancholy, Nadya was also capable of infectious gaiety and she could act out scenes like this with consummate skill. Her impromptu kitchen performances would make Tolya explode with laughter while Varya, their domestic worker, exclaimed, 'No, no, I can't bear it – it's Viktor Pavlovich to a T!'

32

Ludmila did not like Viktor's relatives and she saw them only if she could not avoid it. They were divided into those who were still flourishing – of whom there were very few – and those who were spoken about only in the past tense: 'He was a famous lawyer, his wife was the town beauty'; 'He had a wonderful voice, in the south he was a real celebrity.' Viktor always appeared interested in family events of every kind and he treated his elderly relatives with warmth and affection – even though, when they began to reminisce, they would speak not about their own long-ago youth but about times still more mythical, when the members of some still more distant generation had been young.

Ludmila was incapable of unravelling this complex web of relationships: cousins, second cousins, aged aunts and uncles. Viktor would say, 'But what could be simpler? Maria Borisovna is the second wife of Osip Semyonovich, and Osip Semyonovich is the son of my late Uncle Ilya – I've already told you about him, my father's brother, he loved cards and he was a terrible gambler. And Veronika Grigorievna is Maria Borisovna's niece – the daughter of her sister Anna Borisovna. Now she's married to Pyotr Grigorievich Motylyov. What don't you understand?'

Ludmila would reply, 'No, I'm sorry. You may be able to understand all this. And maybe Einstein could understand some of it. But not me – I'm far too stupid.'

Viktor Pavlovich was the only son of Anna Semyonovna Shtrum.

As a young woman, Anna Semyonovna had been bright and boisterous. She had adored the theatre. Still a schoolgirl, she had more than once queued all night for tickets when Stanislavsky and his company came to Odessa. Then she had lived abroad for several years, graduating in medicine from the University of Bern and also spending time in Geneva. She had worked with renowned eye specialists in Italy. She had lived for two years in Paris. In 1903 Alexandra Vladimirovna had stayed with her for a month while her husband, along with other revolutionaries, attended the Party Congress in London; Anna Semyonovna had given her the little brooch – two enamel violets – that Alexandra still often wore.

Anna Semyonovna had been widowed when Viktor was only three. After spending the summer of 1914 on the Baltic coast, for Viktor's health, she had moved to Kiev. Her friends had marvelled at the single-minded devotion she then showed to her young son. She became a homebody, seldom going out and always taking Viktor along with her when she did. And she only visited people who had children the same age as Viktor.

One of the friends she visited most often was Olga Ignatievna, the widow of a merchant-navy captain. The captain had brought his wife a great many presents from distant countries: collections of butterflies and shells and little ivory or stone figurines. Anna Semyonovna probably never realized that these evening visits meant more to her son than any of his lessons, either at school or with his private language and music tutors.

Viktor had been especially taken with a collection of little shells from the shores of the Sea of Japan: gold and orange, like miniature sunsets; pale blue and green, milky pink, like dawn over a miniature sea. They were unusual shapes: fine, delicate swords; lace bonnets; petals of cherry blossom; stars and snowflakes made from plaster. Next to the shells was a display cabinet of tropical butterflies whose colours were still more brilliant, as if their vast chiselled wings had somehow captured tongues of red flame and puffs of violet smoke. The little boy had imagined that the shells were similar to the butterflies, that they flew through the seaweed, in the light of an underwater sun that was sometimes green and sometimes light blue.

He was fascinated by herbariums and collections of insects. His desk drawers were always full of samples of metals and minerals. Once he had almost drowned in a pond, forgetting as he jumped into the water about all the pieces of granite, quartz and feldspar in his pockets. It was only with difficulty that his friends managed to drag him back into the boat.

Olga Ignatievna also had two large aquariums. The fish grazing amid the underwater copses and forests were no less beautiful than the butterflies and ocean shells. There were lilac or mother-of-pearl gouramis; telescope-eye goldfish; red-, green- and orange-striped paradise fish with sly, catlike faces; glassy perch inside whose transparent mica bodies could be seen dark gullets and skeletons; pink veiltails

– living potatoes that liked to wrap themselves in their long delicate tails, which seemed as insubstantial as cigarette smoke.

Anna Semyonovna wanted both to indulge her son and to instil in him the habit of long, disciplined daily work. Sometimes she thought he was spoiled, capricious and lazy and, if he got bad marks at school, she would call him an idler, shouting out the German word *Taugenichts!* He liked to read, but there were times when no power on earth could make him open a book. He would eat his lunch and run out into the yard – and she wouldn't see him again until he ran home in the evening, excited, breathing heavily, as if he'd been pursued to the front door by a pack of wolves. He would bolt down his supper, go to bed and fall asleep instantaneously. Once, standing by the window, she had heard her weak, shy little son down in the yard below. Sounding like a barefoot street urchin, he was shouting, 'You rat, for that you'll get a brick through your skull!'

Once, she hit him. He had told her he was going to a friend's, so they could do their homework together, but he had gone instead to the cinema, after taking some money out of her purse. During the night he woke up as she was looking at him. Shaken by her long severe gaze, he got up onto his knees and threw his arms round her neck. She pushed him away.

The little boy began to grow up. His body changed, and so did his clothes. And as his bones grew thicker, as his voice deepened, so his inner world changed too. His love of nature changed; he developed new passions.

Towards the age of fifteen he fell in love with astronomy. He got hold of some lenses and set about making himself a telescope.

There was a constant struggle within him between his desire for practical experience and a pull towards the abstract, towards pure theory. Even then, it was as if he were unconsciously trying to reconcile these two worlds. His interest in astronomy went with dreams of building an observatory high in the mountains; the discovery of new stars was linked in his imagination to difficult and dangerous journeys. The conflict between his romantic desire for activity and his abstract, monastic cast of mind was deep-rooted; it was many years before he even began to understand it.

As a child, he had admired things greedily. He had split stones with a hammer; he had stroked the smooth facets of crystals; he had sensed with amazement the extraordinary weight of lead and mercury. Observing a fish had not been enough for him; he used to turn

166

up his sleeve and put his hand into the water to seize the fish, holding it carefully and not taking it out of the water. He wanted to catch the wonderful, shining world of material objects in the nets of touch, smell and vision.

Aged seventeen, he felt excited and moved by books on mathematical physics. There were pages with almost no words – only a dozen pallid conjunctions: 'thus', 'therefore', 'and so on'. The real thrust of the thought was expressed entirely through differential equations and transformations as unexpected as they were inevitable.

It was at this time that Viktor became friends with Pyotr Lebedev. Pyotr was at the same school, though a year and a half older, and he shared Viktor's love of mathematics and physics. They read textbooks together and dreamed of making discoveries about the structure of matter together. Lebedev passed the university entrance exam but then joined a Komsomol detachment to fight in the Civil War. Soon after this he was killed, in a battle near Darnitsa. Viktor was deeply shaken; he never forgot his friend who had chosen the path of a soldier of the Revolution over that of a scientist.

A year later, Viktor began his studies at Moscow University, in the Faculty of Physics and Mathematics. What interested him most were the laws governing the behaviour of atomic nuclei and electrons.

There was poetry in nature's deepest mysteries. Little violet stars flickered for a second on a dark screen; invisible particles hurtled by like comets, leaving behind them only misty tails of condensed gas; the fine needle of an ultra-sensitive electrometer shivered in response to the upheaval brought about by invisible demons endowed with insane energy and velocity. Seething beneath the surface of matter were enormous powers. These flashes on a dark screen, the mass spectrograph readings that made it possible to figure out the charge of an atomic nucleus, the dark spots on a photographic film – these were the first scouts, the first prospectors for tremendous forces now beginning to stir, if only for a moment, in their sleep.

Sometimes Viktor imagined these flashes and dark spots as a fine cloud of breath, exhaled by a huge bear asleep in its lair. Sometimes he imagined them as the splashes of tiny fish over a bottomless pool where monstrous pike and catfish had been dozing for centuries. He wanted to glance beneath the pool's green surface, to disturb its silty bottom and compel the great fish to the surface. He wanted to find the long pliant withe that would make the bear roar, that would make it emerge from its dark lair, shaking its shaggy shoulders.

167

A two-way passage across the boundary that both bound matter to quanta of energy and separated it from them, within the framework of a single mathematical transformation! And the bridge between the high cliff of our ordinary, common-sense picture of the world and the still mist-shrouded, silent realm of nuclear forces was an experimental apparatus that – for all its apparent complexity – was in its basic principles absurdly simple.

It was strange and surprising to think that it was here, in this deaf-mute realm of protons and neutrons, that the material essence of the world was to be discovered.

At one point, Viktor suddenly informed his mother that study alone was no longer enough for him. He got himself a job at the Butyrsky chemical factory, in the paint-grinding workshop, where conditions were particularly harsh. During the winter he both worked and studied; during the summer he worked full-time, not taking any holiday.

On the face of it, Viktor appeared to have changed a great deal over the years. Yet whenever a new theory appeared to him – amid contradictory hypotheses, amid the inaccurate experiments that can lead a researcher towards sound conclusions, amid the subtle, sophisticated experiments that can throw one against a wall of absurdity – he felt the same as he had in childhood. He had glimpsed a small gleaming miracle in the dense green water. Soon he would seize hold of this miracle.

Matter was no longer something to be seen or grasped – but the reality of its being, this reality of atoms, protons and neutrons, shone no less bright than that of the earth and the oceans.

There was one other constant in Viktor's life, a quiet light that illuminated his whole inner world. It was his mother who had given him this light, but he did not realize this. She felt Viktor's life was more important than her own; nothing made her happier than to sacrifice herself for her son's happiness. For Viktor, however, nothing was more important than the science he served. He appeared gentle, incapable of saying a harsh word or acting coldly and brutally. Nevertheless, like many people with a sincere belief in the absolute importance of their work, he could be harsh and unfeeling, even merciless. He saw his mother's love, and the sacrifices she made for him, as entirely right and natural. One of his mother's cousins once told him that, when she was a young widow, a man she very much liked had tried for several years to persuade her to marry him. She refused, afraid this would prevent her from devoting all her love and attention to her son. She had doomed herself to loneliness. And she had said to this cousin, 'It doesn't matter. When Viktor's grown up, I'll live with him. I won't be alone as an old woman.' Viktor was touched by this story, yet it did not move him at all deeply.

Viktor appeared to have realized the dreams of his youth. And yet, deep down, he remained unsatisfied. There were moments when he felt that the main flow, the central current of life was passing him by and he wanted to find a way to fuse his research with the work being carried out in the country's factories, mines and construction sites. He wanted to build a bridge that would bring together his theoretical research and the difficult, noble labour of the country's millions of workers. He remembered his friend Lebedev, wearing the helmet of a Red Army soldier and with a rifle on his shoulder. This memory burned into him.

33

Dmitry Petrovich Chepyzhin, Viktor's teacher, played an important role in his life.

One of the most gifted of Russian physicists, a scientist with a worldwide reputation, he had big hands, broad shoulders and a broad forehead; he looked like an elderly blacksmith.

At the age of fifty, with the help of his two student sons, he had built a log house out in the country. He trimmed the heavy logs himself. He dug a well nearby. He built a bathhouse and cleared a track through the forest.

He enjoyed telling people about an old man, a village doubting Thomas who had, for a long time, refused to recognize Chepyzhin's competence as a carpenter. And then one day this old man had clapped him on the shoulder, as if acknowledging him as a brother, as a fellow skilled labourer, and said slyly, 'All right, my boy, you come and build me a little shed. And don't worry – I'll pay you fair and square.'

But Chepyzhin preferred not to spend his summers in this house. Usually he and his wife Nadezhda Fyodorovna went on long, two-month journeys together. They had been to Lake Baikal and to the far-eastern taiga; they had been in the heights of Tian Shan near Naryn and on the shore of Lake Teletskoye in the Altay Mountains. They had set off from Moscow in a rowing boat and gone down the Moscow, Oka and Volga rivers as far as Astrakhan. They had explored the Meshchersk forest beyond Ryazan and they had walked through the Bryansk forest from Karachev to Novgorod-Seversky. They had gone on journeys like this as students, and they had continued even after reaching the age when you are expected to stay in a sanatorium or a dacha rather than to be trekking through forests or mountains with a pack on your back.

Chepyzhin did not like hunting and fishing, but he always kept a detailed diary during these journeys. One section, titled 'Lyric', was devoted to the beauty of nature, to sunsets and sunrises, to night-time storms in forests, to starry and moonlit nights. The only person to whom he ever read these descriptions was his wife.

170

In the autumn, when he chaired meetings in the Physics Institute or sat on the presidium during sessions of the Academy of Sciences, Chepyzhin looked strangely out of place amid white-haired colleagues and already greying students who had spent the summer in a house of recreation – in Barvikha or Uzkoye – or in a dacha in Luga, in Sestroretsk on the Gulf of Finland or in the countryside not far from Moscow. He still had barely a strand of grey in his dark hair, and he would sit there frowning severely, supporting his large head on a brown, sinewy fist while he ran his other hand over his broad chin and thin, sunburnt cheeks. His was the kind of deep tan more often seen on navvies, soldiers or turf cutters. It was the tan of someone who seldom sleeps beneath a roof, that comes from exposure not only to the sun but also to frosts, chilling night winds and the cold mist just before dawn. Compared with Chepyzhin, his sickly-looking colleagues, with their pink, milky skin threaded by deep blue veins, seemed like silly old sheep or blue-eyed angels beside a huge brown bear.

Viktor remembered how, long ago, he and Pyotr Lebedev had often talked about Chepyzhin.

Studying with Chepyzhin had been one of Pyotr's cherished dreams. He had longed both to work under his supervision and to argue with him about the philosophical implications of modern physics.

Both opportunities were denied him.

People who knew Chepyzhin did not find it surprising that he enjoyed hiking through forests, that he liked working with an axe or a spade, that he wrote poetry and enjoyed painting. What astonished people, what they wondered at more than anything, was that, for all his extraordinarily wide range of interests and enthusiasms, he was a man with a single guiding passion. People who knew him well – his wife and his close friends – understood that all his interests had one and the same foundation: his love for his native land. His love for Russian fields and forests, his collection of paintings by Levitan and Savrasov,[91] his friendships with old peasants who would come to visit him in Moscow, the huge amount of work he had done in the 1920s to help establish workers' faculties, his knowledge of folk songs, his interest in the development of new branches of industry, his passionate love of Pushkin and Tolstoy, his touching concern (a source of amusement to some of his colleagues) for some of the lesser inhabitants of his beloved fields and forests, for the hedgehog and the blue tits and finches that chose his house as their dwelling – all this constituted a foundation, the one and only possible foundation for the apparently supraterrestrial edifice of his scientific thought.

An entire universe of abstract thought – of thought that had reached an altitude from which it was impossible even to make out the terrestrial globe, let alone its seas and continents – this whole universe had solid roots in the soil of his native land. It drew vital nourishment from this land and could probably not have survived without it.

From their early youth people like Chepyzhin are moved by a single powerful sentiment. This feeling, this consciousness of a single aim, accompanies them to the end of their days. Nikolay Nekrasov evokes just such a feeling in his poem 'On the Volga', about the vows he made as a boy, when he first saw a group of barge haulers. And it is this kind of feeling that moved the young Herzen and Ogaryov when they swore their famous vow on the Sparrow Hills.[92]

There are people to whom this sense of an overriding aim seems a naive vestige of the past, something that just happens to have survived for no good reason. These, however, are people whose inner world is filled by the trivia of the day; enthralled by the bright colours of life's surface, they are blind to the unity that lies beneath them. Such people often achieve small material successes, but they never win life's real battles. They are like a general who fights without any real aim, without the inspiration of love for his people. He may capture a town, he may defeat a regiment or a division, but he cannot win the war.

Only in their last days and hours do such people realize that they have been deceived. Only then do they see the simple realities they had previously dismissed as irrelevant. But this does them little good. 'Oh, if only I could begin life afresh!' – these words, pronounced bitterly as one draws up the balance sheet of one's days, change nothing.

The simple wish for working people to live freely and happily and comfortably, for society to be ordered freely and justly – this simple desire determined the lives of many of the most remarkable revolutionary thinkers and fighters. And there were many other important Soviet figures – scientists, travellers, agriculturalists, engineers, teachers, doctors, builders and reclaimers of deserts – who were guided, until their last days, by an equally clear, childishly pure sense of purpose.

*

Viktor never forgot Chepyzhin's first lecture. He had not sounded like a professor of physics; his deep, slightly hoarse way of speaking,

172

at times slow and patient but more often quick and impassioned, had seemed more like that of a political agitator. Similarly, the formulae he wrote on the blackboard were far from being cold, dry expressions of the new mechanics of an invisible world of extraordinary energies and velocities; they sounded more like political appeals or slogans. The chalk squeaked and crumbled. Chepyzhin's hand was as accustomed to axes and spades as to a pen or to delicate instruments made from quartz or platinum. Sometimes, when he nailed in a full stop or sketched the graceful swan's neck of an integral – $\int$ – it was as if he were firing a series of shots. These formulae seemed full of human content; they could have been passionate declarations of faith, doubt or love. Chepyzhin reinforced this impression by scattering question marks, ellipses and triumphant exclamation marks over the board. It was painful, when the lecture was over, to watch the attendant rub out all these radicals, integrals, differentials and trigonometric signs, all these alphas, deltas, epsilons and thetas that human will and intelligence had shaped into a single united regiment. Like a valuable manuscript, this blackboard should surely have been preserved for posterity.

And although many years had passed since then, although Viktor now gave lectures and wrote on a blackboard himself, the feelings with which he had listened to his teacher's first lecture were still present within him.

Viktor felt a sense of excitement every time he went into Chepyzhin's office. And when he got back home, he would boast, just like a child, to his family and friends, 'I went for a walk with Chepyzhin. We went all the way to the Shabolovka radio tower'; 'Chepyzhin's invited me and Ludmila to see in the New Year with him'; 'Chepyzhin approves of the path we're following in our research.'

Viktor remembered a conversation about Chepyzhin with Krymov, a few years before the war. After a long period of particularly intensive work, Krymov and Zhenya had come to visit Viktor and Ludmila in their dacha.

Ludmila had persuaded Krymov to take off his rough tunic and put on a pyjama top of Viktor's. Krymov had been sitting in the shade of a flowering linden. On his face was the blissful look of a man who has just got away from the city, a man who has spent long hours in hot smoke-filled rooms and to whom fresh, fragrant air, cool well water and the sound of the wind in the pines have brought a sense of simple and complete happiness.

Nothing, it appeared, could have disturbed such a sense of peace. And so the sudden change in Krymov – the moment the conversation turned from the joys of strawberries with cold milk and sugar to more work-related themes – was all the more startling.

Viktor had talked about how he had seen Chepyzhin the previous day. Chepyzhin had discussed the tasks of the new laboratory that had just been set up in the Institute of Mechanics and Physics.

'Yes, he's an impressive figure,' said Krymov. 'But when he leaves the world of physics and tries his hand at philosophizing, he ends up contradicting everything he knows as a physicist. He has no understanding of Marxist dialectics.'

This enraged Ludmila. 'What do you mean? How can you talk like that about Dmitry Petrovich?'

Krymov had retorted, 'Comrade Luda, what else can I say? When it comes to matters like this, there's only one thing a revolutionary Marxist can say – whether he's talking about his own father, about Chepyzhin or about Isaac Newton himself.'

Viktor had known that Krymov was right. His friend Pyotr Lebedev had more than once made the same criticism of Chepyzhin.

But he had been upset by Krymov's harsh tone. 'Nikolay Grigorievich,' he had said, 'however right you may be, you need to think a bit more about how people with such a weak grasp of the theory of knowledge can be so very strong when it comes to actual knowledge.'

Glaring furiously at Viktor, Krymov had replied, 'That is hardly a philosophical argument. You know as well as I do that there are many scientists who, in their laboratories, have been disciples and propagandists of dialectical materialism, who would have been helpless without it, but who then start cobbling together some homespun philosophy and become unable to explain anything at all. Without realizing it, they undermine their own remarkable scientific discoveries. If I am uncompromising, it is because men like Chepyzhin – and his remarkable work – are as precious to me as they are to you.'

Years had gone by, but Chepyzhin's connection to his students, who were now doing independent research of their own, had in no way weakened. These connections were free, vital and democratic. They bound teacher and student together more firmly than any other tie that man has created.

34

It was a cool, clear morning. Viktor was about to leave for Moscow.

Looking out through the wide-open window, he was listening to his wife's last instructions. In those grim wartime days people going on long journeys equipped themselves as if they were polar explorers.

Ludmila was explaining exactly how she had arranged everything in his suitcase: the aspirin, the pyrethrum, the iodine and the sulfonamide,[93] the tins of butter, honey and lard; the little packets of salt, tea and powdered egg; the bread, the dried rusks, the five onions and the bag of buckwheat; the piece of soap, the reels of black and white cotton; the matches and the old newspapers he could use for rolling cigarettes; the spare batteries for his flashlight; the large thermos of boiled water; and the two half-litre bottles of vodka in case he needed to pay for important favours. She told him which foods he should eat first and which he could leave till the end of his stay. She also asked him to bring back the empty tins and bottles, since these were not easy to obtain in Kazan.

'And don't forget,' she added. 'The list of things to bring back from the dacha and the apartment is in your wallet, next to your passport.'

'I remember the first train journey I ever made on my own, during the Civil War,' Viktor replied. 'Máma put some money into a special pouch and sewed it to the inside of my shirt. Then she sprinkled me from head to toe with tobacco, to keep off the lice, and told me again and again not to buy raw milk or sunflower seeds at any of the stations, and not to eat unwashed apples. The main dangers then were typhus and criminals.'

Ludmila didn't reply. It annoyed her that Viktor was reminiscing, rather than thinking about their imminent parting. She felt that he was too casual about her well-being and that he didn't appreciate all the trouble she went to over practical, domestic matters.

Then she put her arms around him and said, 'Don't get overtired, and give me your word to go straight down into the cellar if you hear an air-raid alert.'

Once the car had set off, Viktor forgot all his wife's words of advice. The morning sun was shining on the trees, on the roadway still gleaming with dew, and on the brickwork, the crumbling stucco and the dusty windows of the buildings.

Postoev was already waiting out on the street. Tall, stout and bearded, he stood out from the rest of his family; he was a head taller than his wife, his daughter Alla and his thin son, a pale-faced student.

Postoev got into the car. Leaning very close to Viktor, glancing a little warily at the protruding ears of the grey-haired driver, he said, 'What do you think? Should we evacuate our families yet again? Some prudent fellows have been sending their families off to Sverdlovsk, or even to Novosibirsk.'

The driver looked back over his shoulder and said, 'I've heard that a German reconnaissance plane flew overhead yesterday.'

'So what?' said Postoev. 'We do the same – our reconnaissance planes fly over Berlin.'

The driver stopped at the railway station and the two passengers got out. They stacked their cases, ran their hands over their jacket pockets and looked suspiciously at three dishevelled, barefoot boys who had suddenly appeared. One offered to carry their belongings, but Postoev refused. One of the other boys then crossly asked for a cigarette.

A porter in a white apron appeared. He and Postoev eventually agreed on a price – fifty roubles and two kilos of bread off a ration card – and he began strapping their cases together. Postoev kept hold of one smart little suitcase, whispering to Viktor, 'Do you think he's all right? Can you see his number anywhere?'

Not even the bright morning sun could relieve the stern bleakness of the wartime railway station: children asleep on bundles and boxes; old men slowly chewing pieces of bread; women stupefied by exhaustion and the cries of their children; new recruits with large knapsacks; pale wounded soldiers; other soldiers setting off to join their new units.

In peacetime people had travelled for all kinds of reasons. There would be students on vacation or about to do a few months' work during the summer; families setting off merrily on their annual holiday; intelligent, loquacious old women on their way to visit sons who had made their mark in the world; sons and daughters wanting to pay their respects to elderly parents. Many of these people were going to places where they had been born and raised.

But the atmosphere in wartime trains and stations was very different. There was a sadness and severity about the travellers.

Viktor was trying to make his way through the main hall when he heard a loud yell; in the general commotion, a woman from a kolkhoz had had her money and documents stolen. A boy in short trousers cut from a groundsheet was pressing up against her, seeking protection. He was wanting both to console and to be consoled; as for his mother, who was carrying a small baby, she was in despair: what was she to do – she was crying out – with no ticket, no money and no document from her kolkhoz?

A few people told her off, saying she should have kept her eyes peeled. Others said they'd have gladly given the thief a good kicking, or beaten him to death; when everyone is suffering, it's easier to curse a pickpocket than to comfort his victim. Others told her to go and look in the rubbish bins, in case her documents had been thrown away. Most people simply tried not to notice her.

As Viktor walked by, following the porter, the woman looked at him and, for a moment, fell silent. She might have been thinking, as her eyes met Viktor's, that this man in a hat and a white raincoat had come to help her, to provide her with a ticket and fresh documents.

In the second hall there was a drunk, staggering to and fro. He was bored, his bulging eyes full of hatred and anguish. He sang and swore, tried to dance, shouted out threats and knocked into people. He was alone in the crowd. No one wanted to join in and sing with him; no one even bothered to take offence. He wanted to escape from his own anguish – that was why he had got drunk. He wanted to hit someone or be hit by them, anything to get away from himself, but no one was willing to co-operate.

The drunk caught sight of the porter with the suitcases. He saw the rosy-cheeked man with the beard and his companion with the long nose and the white raincoat. He let out a cry of joy – these were just the kind of people he needed. But once again he proved unlucky. He stumbled and fell. By the time he was back on his feet, the three men had had their tickets checked and made their way onto the platform.

'It's too much,' said Postoev. 'I can't bear all this. Next time I'm going by plane, even if I do have a weak heart.'

A locomotive under full steam laboured into the station, followed by a line of dust-covered carriages. An attendant, mistrustful of passengers wanting to board at intermediate stations, began examining tickets. The already-established passengers – engineers from factories in the Urals and commanders just discharged from hospital – were jumping out onto the platform and asking, 'Where's the market – is it far? Where can I get drinking water? Heard any news bulletins? Where can I buy salt? How much are apples here?' And they rushed off into the main building.

Postoev and Viktor got into their carriage; the moment they glimpsed the strip of carpet, the dusty mirrors and the seats' pale blue covers, they felt calmer. The racket outside was no longer audible. Nevertheless, their peace and comfort was by no means untroubled; here in the carriage it might seem like peacetime, but everything outside still spoke of disaster and lacerating grief. A few minutes later there were some slight jolts as a new locomotive was coupled on. The commanders and the Urals engineers came hurrying back, some gripping the handles of kettles and mugs, some with armfuls of tomatoes or cucumbers, some pressing parcels of flatbreads and fish to their chests.

And then came the painful moment when everybody was impatient for the train to get under way, when even those now leaving their home and their loved ones wanted to move – as if anything were better than staying where they were.

A woman out in the corridor, having already lost all interest in Kazan, said thoughtfully, 'The attendants say we'll be in Murom by this afternoon. I've heard onions are very cheap there.' 'Read the latest news bulletin?' came a man's voice. 'I saw the names of places I know. Any day now the Germans will get to the Volga.'

Postoev changed into his pyjamas, put an embroidered skullcap over his bald patch, cleaned his hands with eau de cologne from a faceted flask with a nickel top, combed his thick grey beard, fanned his cheeks with a chequered handkerchief, leaned back in his seat and said, 'Well, it seems we're on our way now.'

Weighed down by anxiety, Viktor tried to distract himself by looking first out of the window and then at the pink cheeks of Postoev. Postoev had received greater official recognition than his younger colleague. His mannerisms, his booming voice, the little jokes with which he put people at ease, the stories he told about well-known scientists, referring to them simply by their name and patronymic – all these never failed to impress. The nature of his work meant that he was often – more often than any of his colleagues – called upon to meet people's commissars and the directors of famous factories, public figures on whom the country's economy depended. His name was known to thousands of engineers; many institutes of higher education used his textbook. When they met at conferences and important meetings, he treated Viktor as a friend – and Viktor enjoyed this, gladly taking

178

the opportunity to sit down next to him or to go for a walk with him during a break. When Viktor admitted this to himself, he would feel angered by his own pettiness and vanity, but it's difficult to remain angry with oneself for long and so he would start to feel angry with Postoev instead.

'Remember that woman with the two children, back at the station?' Viktor asked.

'Yes, I can almost see the poor soul right now,' Postoev replied, as he took his suitcase down from the rack above. In the sincere, serious tone of a man who fully understands someone else's feelings, he added, 'Yes, my friend, things are difficult, very difficult – but we need to preserve our strength.' And then, wrinkling his brow, 'How do you feel about a bite to eat? I have some roast chicken.'

'That sounds good,' Viktor replied.

The train reached the bridge over the Volga. It began to clatter and rumble like a village cart passing from a dirt track onto a cobbled road.

Down below lay the river – pitted from the wind, all sandbars and shallows; it was impossible even to make out which way it was flowing. From up above, it seemed grey, ugly and turbid. Long-barrelled anti-aircraft guns had been mounted in gulleys and on small hillocks. Two Red Army soldiers were carrying mess tins along the trenches; they didn't so much as glance at the train.

'Probability theory tells us that the chances of a German pilot managing to drop a bomb on our bridge from a plane flying in a gusty wind at high speed and high altitude are almost zero. So there's nowhere safer during an air raid than on a strategic bridge,' said Postoev. 'But I do hope we don't get caught in an air raid in Moscow. To be honest with you, that's something I'd rather not even think about.' Postoev looked down at the river, thought for a moment and added, 'The Germans are nearing the Don. Will they soon be looking down at the Volga just like we are? The mere thought of it makes my blood run cold.'

In the next-door compartment someone began playing the accordion:

> From beyond the wooded island
> To the river wide and free.[94]

Their neighbours, it seemed, had also started thinking about the Volga. And after Stenka Razin, there was no stopping them. Next came:

179

I've planted my garden –
It's for me to water it.
I've loved my beloved –
It's for me to forget him.

Postoev glanced at Viktor and said, 'Russia is baffling to the mind.'[95]
After talking about his children and life in Kazan, Postoev said, 'I like to study my travelling companions, and there's something I've often noticed: during the first part of the journey people talk about their domestic concerns, about life in Kazan. But when we reach Murom something changes. From then on people talk not about what lies behind them but about what lies ahead in Moscow. A man on a journey, like any solid body moving through space, moves from the sphere of gravitational attraction of one system to that of another. You can verify this by observing my own behaviour. In a minute or two I'll probably fall asleep. When I wake up, I'm sure to start talking about Moscow.'

And he did indeed fall asleep. Viktor was surprised to discover that he slept like a baby – without the least sound. Postoev was built like a warrior; Viktor would have expected him to snore loudly.

Viktor looked out of the window. He felt more and more excited. This was his first journey since leaving Moscow in September 1941. He was deeply moved by what in peacetime would have seemed ordinary enough: he was on his way back to Moscow.

Viktor's everyday concerns had faded away and the tension of his thoughts about his own work – a tension that seldom left him – had relaxed, but this did not grant him the sense of peace he usually experienced during a long and comfortable journey. Instead, he felt troubled by thoughts and feelings that had previously been crowded out.

He felt bewildered, taken aback by the force of feelings still not fully felt and thoughts he had yet to think through. Had he expected this war? What kind of man had he been when it began? And he thought about two men to whom his memories of the last weeks of peace were closely linked: Academician Chepyzhin and Professor Maximov, whom Nadya had mentioned the previous evening.

A whole year had gone by, the longest year of his life – and now he was on his way to Moscow. But he still felt anxious at heart, and the news bulletins were very grim indeed, and the war was now nearing the Don.

Then Viktor thought about his mother. Whenever he had told himself that she had perished, it had been without his truly believing it, without his believing it in his heart of hearts … He closed his eyes and tried to imagine her face. For some strange reason, the faces of those closest to you can be harder to imagine than the faces of distant acquaintances. The train was going to Moscow. He himself was on his way to Moscow!

With a sudden sense of joy, Viktor felt certain that his mother was alive, that in time he would see her again.

35

Anna Semyonovna's home was a quiet, green town in Ukraine. She had not seen Viktor often, going to stay with him and Ludmila only once every two or three years. She wrote to him three times a week and he always replied with a postcard. She also sent telegrams every New Year and on Viktor's, Nadya's and Tolya's birthdays. Viktor intended each summer to send his mother a telegram on her own birthday, but he never remembered; he usually chanced upon the right notebook only two or three weeks after the day.

She did not correspond with Ludmila, but she always asked after her health and asked Viktor to pass on her greetings. And Viktor, as people often do, failed to pass on these greetings and, without even mentioning it to Ludmila, wrote in every letter, 'Ludmila sends her greetings.'

Anna Semyonovna worked in a clinic, seeing people with eye problems twice a week. Now in her late sixties, she was no longer strong enough to work full-time. On the days she didn't go to the clinic, she gave French lessons in her home to children from local families. Viktor used to beg her to give up work altogether, saying he would send her 200 or 300 roubles each month, but she said this might be difficult for him. And anyway, she liked to feel financially independent. She liked to be able to send little presents to him and his family; this reminded her of when she had been a young mother. The main thing, though, was that she *needed* to work. She had worked all her life, and without work she would go out of her mind. Her dream was to go on working until the end of her life.

Sometimes she used to quote amusing Yiddish expressions she had heard from her neighbours; most of the town's population was Jewish. She wrote the words in Cyrillic letters, but Viktor knew very few words of Yiddish and usually had to ask for a translation. She also used to tell Viktor about her patients and her young pupils, about their relatives, about local events and about the books she had been reading.

There was an old wild pear tree just outside her window, and she used to tell her son every detail of this tree's life – branches broken by winter storms, the appearance of new buds and leaves ... In the autumn she would write, 'Will I ever again see my old friend in blossom? Her leaves are turning yellow. They're falling now.'

Her letters were always very calm. There was just one occasion when she wrote that she felt so lonely she wanted to die. Viktor replied at length, asking if he should come and visit. She then assured him that everything was all right, that she was in good health and had simply been feeling low on that day.

But in March 1941 she wrote another strange letter. 'First, it turned unseasonably warm – as if it were already May. The storks arrived – there have always been a lot of them around here. But the day they came, the weather changed for the worse. In the evening, as if sensing the approach of misfortune, the storks all huddled together in a bog on the outskirts of town, not far from the tannery. And then, that night, there was a terrible snowstorm. Dozens of the storks perished. Many staggered out onto the highway, dazed and half-dead, as if seeking help from mankind. Some were run over by trucks. The local boys beat others to death in the morning, perhaps for fun, perhaps wanting to put an end to their misery. The milkwoman said there were frozen birds all along the road, their beaks half-open and their eyes glazed over.'

In the same letter, she also said that she missed him very badly and dreamed of him almost every night. She would, without fail, come to visit him in the summer. She now thought that war was inevitable. Every time she turned on the radio, it was with trepidation. 'My only support is the letters and cards we send each other – the thought of being cut off from you is terrifying … You have no idea what anxious thoughts I have as I lie in bed at night and look into the darkness and think. I think and think. I can't sleep …'

In reply Viktor had written that he thought her fears were exaggerated. Soon after this she had written to say that it had now turned warm again. Her tone had been calm and quietly humorous. She had told little stories about her pupils and, along with the letter itself, she had sent him a violet, a blade of grass and a few petals from her pear tree.

Viktor had expected his mother to join him and his family in their dacha in early July, but the war had intervened. The last card he received had been dated 30 June. She had written only a few lines, evidently hinting at air raids, 'Several times a day we are deeply agitated and my neighbours help me down into the cellar. But whatever happens, my dearest son, it'll be the same for all of us.' In a postscript, in a trembling hand, she asked him to convey her greetings to Ludmila and Tolya. And she asked after Nadya, her favourite, telling him to kiss 'her sweet, sad eyes …'

36

Once again, as the train headed towards Moscow, Viktor's thoughts returned to the months before the German invasion. He was trying to bring together the vast events of world history and his own life – his own worries, his own grief, his own loved ones.

Hitler had conquered a dozen West European countries, and it was clear that he had achieved this at almost no cost, expending hardly any of his military strength. His huge armies were now concentrated in the east. Every day brought rumours of some new political or military manoeuvring. Everyone was waiting, expecting to hear something important on the radio, but all they heard were long and solemn accounts of children's Olympics in Bashkiria; the announcers said barely a word about fires in London or air raids on Berlin. Owners of good radios listened at night to foreign broadcasts and heard Hitler's words about how the fate of Germany and the world was at this moment being determined for a thousand years to come.

In Soviet family circles, in houses of recreation and higher-education institutes, almost every conversation had touched on politics and war. The storm was approaching; world events were bursting into people's everyday lives. Questions of every kind – about going for a summer holiday by the sea, about whether to buy a winter coat or some item of furniture – were being decided according to military news bulletins or newspaper accounts of speeches and treaties. Decisions about marriages, about having a baby, about which institute of higher education a child should apply to – everything was considered in the light of Hitler's successes or failures, speeches by Roosevelt or Churchill, or the laconic statements or denials of Tass, the main Soviet news agency.

People had quarrelled a great deal, and nearly always hysterically. Long-established friendships were abruptly severed. There was no end to the arguments about Germany. Just how strong was Hitler's Germany? And if Germany *was* strong, was this a good thing or a bad thing?

Around this time, Maximov the biochemist had returned from a working trip to Austria and Czechoslovakia. Viktor did not especially like Maximov. To Viktor, this man with pink cheeks and grey hair, with his rounded movements and quiet way of speaking, seemed timid, weak-willed and starry-eyed. 'With a smile like his, you wouldn't need to put sugar in your tea,' Viktor used to say. 'Just two smiles per glass.'

Maximov had reported to a small meeting of professors but had said next to nothing about the scientific aspect of his visit, speaking more about his conversations with colleagues and his general impressions of life in German-occupied cities.

When he spoke about the predicament of science in Czechoslovakia, his voice began to quaver. Then he shouted, 'It's impossible to describe, you have to see it with your own eyes! Scientific thought is in fetters. People are afraid of their own shadows. They're afraid of their fellow workers. Professors are afraid of their students. People's thoughts, their inner lives, their families and friendships – everything is under fascist control. A man I once studied with – we sat at the same table and worked through eighteen organic chemistry syntheses together, we've known each other for thirty years – this friend of mine begged me not to ask him any questions whatsoever. He's the head of an important faculty, but he behaves like some petty criminal, afraid the police might collar him at any moment. "Don't ask me anything at all," he said. "It's not only my colleagues I'm afraid of. I'm afraid of my own voice. I'm afraid of my own thoughts." He was petrified I might quote something he'd said and that even if I didn't mention his name – or his university or even his city – the Gestapo would be able to trace this back to him. You can learn more from simple people – from chambermaids and porters, from drivers and footmen. They think they're anonymous and so they have less to fear from talking to a foreigner. But intellectuals and scientists have lost all capacity for freedom of thought – they've lost the right to call themselves human beings. In science, fascism now rules. Its theories are terrifying, and tomorrow these theories will become practice. They already *have* become practice. People talk seriously about sterilization and eugenics. One doctor told me that the mentally ill and the tubercular are being murdered. People's hearts and minds are going dark. Words like *freedom*, *conscience* and *compassion* are being persecuted. People are being forbidden to speak them to children or to write them in private letters. That's fascism for you – and may it be damned!'

He yelled out these last words and, swinging his arm, thumped his fist hard down on the table; he seemed more like an enraged Volga sailor than a quiet-spoken professor with grey hair and a saccharine smile.

His speech made a strong impression.

185

The director of the institute broke the silence, saying, 'Ivan Ivanovich, if you are not too tired, perhaps you should tell us about the scientific fruits of your visit.'

Viktor interrupted angrily. 'Ivan Ivanovich has already told us the most important fruits of his visit. Nothing else is of any account. Ivan Ivanovich, you must write down your observations and publish them. That is your duty.' He paused, then added, 'I'm willing to publish them in the Physics Institute bulletin, along with your scientific findings.'

In the voice of an adult quietly addressing a child, someone else said, 'None of this is new, it's all somewhat exaggerated, and no one is likely to publish it now. It's in our interest to reinforce the politics of peace, not to undermine them.'[96]

Viktor had argued a great deal during these months with Yakovlev, a professor of theoretical mechanics he had known a long time. Yakovlev asserted that Germany had hit upon a perfect form of social organization and was now the strongest power in the world. He told Viktor he was stuck in an old-fashioned world view and had no understanding of anything.

Viktor had begun to wonder if this might be true. He wished he could have a good talk with Krymov. Krymov always spoke intelligently about politics and usually knew a great deal more than was written about in the newspapers. 'I really can't understand why Zhenya left Krymov,' he said crossly to Ludmila. 'Now I don't know how to find him. Anyway, I'd feel awkward. I can't help feeling guilty because of your beautiful idiot of a sister.'

*

On Sunday, 15 June 1941, Viktor and his family had gone to their dacha. They had been expecting Viktor's mother to come and stay, along with Alexandra Vladimirovna and Seryozha. Over lunch, Viktor and Ludmila had quarrelled about where to put their three guests. Viktor wanted to put 'the two mámas' on the ground floor. Tolya and Seryozha – he added – would enjoy being together on the first floor. Ludmila wanted Alexandra Vladimirovna and Seryozha on the ground floor and Viktor's mother on the first floor.

'But you know Máma finds it hard to climb those steep stairs,' said Viktor.

'She'll be more comfortable up there. No one will disturb her. And she likes having a balcony.'

'You *are* being thoughtful. Might there, perhaps, be something you're not quite saying?'

'Well, yes, I suppose I *would* like Tolya to have a room to himself. He's worn out from his exams and he needs to prepare for next year. Seryozha will get in his way.'

'Ah, so now, at last, we get to the true reason. A threat to the sovereignty of the dauphin!'

'For the love of God!' said Ludmila. 'When *my* mother comes to stay, it's all quite straightforward. But if it's Anna Semyonovna, then everything becomes a matter of principle. There's more than enough space – the old woman will be happy wherever we put her.'

'Why *the old woman*? Doesn't my mother have a name?' Aware that he might be about to start shouting, Viktor closed the window looking out towards their neighbours.

'Your mother's hardly a young girl,' Ludmila retorted. She knew that Viktor was getting angry, but she wanted to needle him. She too was feeling angry, upset that her husband was not giving enough thought to Tolya.

Tolya had done his last school exam two days before this. Viktor had congratulated him on completing his ten years of schooling – but only in the most casual of manners. And he had forgotten to buy him a present, even though she had reminded him twice, saying that finishing school was, perhaps, still more important than completing one's higher education.

What mattered still more was Tolya's future. He had told her he was interested in the subject of radio communication with planes and that he wanted to study at the Electro-Technical Institute. This upset Ludmila, who saw the applied sciences as unworthy of her gifted son. Since Viktor was the only person whose authority Tolya recognized, she wanted him to intervene, but he was failing to do this.

Tolya found his parents' quarrels deeply tedious. He would yawn uncontrollably and mutter, 'I won't ever marry, I won't ever marry.' But when Viktor shouted and blustered, his voice shaking, he had to look the other way; he found it hard not to laugh. Nadya's response was very different. She would turn pale. Her eyes would open very wide, as if she were afraid of something terrifying and beyond her understanding. During the night, she would weep and ask, 'Why? Why?'

*

Viktor, Tolya and Nadya had been sitting in the garden when Nadya heard the squeak of the little gate and shouted out joyfully, 'Someone's coming. Ah, it's Maximov!'

Maximov could see that Viktor was pleased to see him. Nevertheless, he asked anxiously, 'I'm not disturbing you? Are you sure you weren't about to lie down for a rest?'

Next, he tried to make sure that Viktor hadn't been meaning to visit anyone or to go out for a walk. There was an imploring note in his voice. Viktor began to get angry. 'I assure you I'm glad to see you. Glad, glad, glad. Please don't say any more.'

In the same uncertain tone, Maximov went on, 'Remember what you said after my little report? Well, I've written down my impressions.' He took out a thick manuscript, rolled into a tube, smiled apologetically and said, 'It's ended up eighty pages long. I'd very much like to know what you think of it ... If you're still interested and you can find a spare hour. Only please don't think it's anything urgent ... What I'm giving you is a copy, you can hang on to it as long as you like ...'

This marked the beginning of another long and exhausting argument. The more Viktor insisted that he was genuinely interested, the more obstinately Maximov begged him to wait until he had an unusual amount of free time. Once again Viktor felt exasperated. 'Ivan Ivanovich, I really don't quite understand why you've brought me these pages. If you'd rather I didn't read them, you could have left them at home.'

They sat down on a bench in the shade. Viktor began asking, in an undertone, about important matters that Maximov would have been unlikely to mention in writing.

But just then Ludmila came out into the garden. Maximov hurried towards her, launched into a lengthy greeting, kissed her hand, apologized again for his intrusion and repeatedly insisted that he didn't want any tea.

After the three of them had finished their tea, Ludmila took Maximov to see her strawberry bed, with its six kinds of strawberries, and her little apple tree that bore up to 500 apples each year. To buy this apple tree, she had made a special journey to an elderly disciple of Michurin's in Yukhnov.[97] Then she showed Maximov her gooseberry bush, which bore gooseberries as big as plums, and her plum tree, which bore plums as big as apples.

The two of them evidently got carried away. Maximov was a keen gardener too. He promised to bring Ludmila some flame phlox and a special kind of lily, rather like an orchid.

'What you've got here is remarkable,' Maximov said to Ludmila as he got ready to go. 'If everyone had two little apple trees like this, I believe there'd be no need for wars. Fascism would be impotent. These knobbly little branches are like honest arms and hands. They could save the world from war, savagery and disaster.'

Once again Maximov apologized to Viktor and Ludmila for disrupting their day and all the inconvenience he had caused. He begged Viktor not to look at his notes until he truly had nothing better to do. And the conversation about fascism never took place.

After Maximov had left, Viktor launched into a tirade against the Russian intelligentsia. All too many of them talked too much, did too little, had no strength of will and were oversensitive to the point that their sensitivity was an excruciating burden to others.

When he went back to Moscow, Viktor left Maximov's article in the dacha, intending to read it the following Sunday.

But the following Sunday, there was no time for thoughts of Maximov.

And a month later Viktor heard from someone he knew that this fifty-four-year-old professor had given up his chair, joined a division of Moscow militia and gone to the front line, as a rank-and-file soldier.

*

Would Viktor ever forget those June and July days? Dark smoke hanging over the streets. Black ash falling on Red Square and Sverdlov Square as offices and commissariats burned their archives. It had seemed to many people that there was no future and that there could no longer be any plans.

All memory of the Revolution's first years was being destroyed. The memory of the first Five Year Plan, of the difficulties and enthusiasm of those years, was also being turned to black ash. Trucks rumbled by all through the night, and in the morning people whispered gloomily about yet another commissariat being evacuated to Omsk. The advancing tide was still far away, nearing Kiev, Dnepropetrovsk, Smolensk and Novgorod, but in Moscow disaster already felt inescapable.

Every evening the sky had taken on an ominous look. Nights passed in painful expectation of the morning light, and the six o'clock radio bulletin invariably brought grim news.

Now, a year later, in the train taking him to Moscow, Viktor remembered that first bulletin from the Red Army Supreme Command, those words for ever engraved in his memory: 'On 22 June 1941, at dawn, regular troops of the German army attacked our border units along a front stretching from the Baltic to the Black Sea.'

The twenty-third of June brought reports of battles along the whole of that vast front – on the axes of Shavli, Kaunas, Grodno-Volkovyssk, Kobrin, Vladimir-Volyn and Brody.

And every day after that, at home, on the street, or in the institute, there was talk of some new German offensive. Comparing the different bulletins, Viktor would wonder gloomily, '"Fighting in the Vilnius region" – but what does that mean? To the east of Vilnius? Or to the west?' And he would stare blankly at the map or newspaper.

In the course of three days, apparently, the Soviet Air Force had lost 374 aircraft, and the enemy 381. And Viktor would try to divine something from these numbers, to find some clue in them as to the future course of the war.

A German submarine had been sunk in the Gulf of Finland. A prisoner of war, a German pilot, had said, 'We're sick of the war. No one has any idea why we're fighting.' Captured German soldiers had said that they were being given vodka immediately before each battle. Another German soldier had deserted and written a flyer calling for the overthrow of the Nazi regime.

For a while Viktor was seized by a kind of feverish joy. Another day, another two days – and the German advance would be slowed. It would be halted. It would be repelled.

The 26 June bulletins spoke of a new German advance – towards Minsk; German tanks had effected a breakthrough. On 28 June there was news of a major tank battle near Lutsk; nearly 4,000 Soviet and German tanks had taken part. On 29 June Viktor read that the enemy were attempting to break through towards Novograd-Volynsky and Shepetov; then he read about fighting not far from the Dvina. There were rumours that Minsk had been taken and that the Germans were now moving down the highway towards Smolensk.

Viktor was in anguish. No longer was he keeping a tally of destroyed German tanks and German planes that had been shot down. Nor did he keep telling his family and colleagues that the Germans would be halted when they reached the old, pre-1939 frontier. Nor did he continue to calculate the German tank corps' supplies of petrol and oil, dividing their estimated total reserves by their likely consumption per day.

Any moment now, he feared, he would hear that the Germans were advancing on Smolensk. And then on Vyazemsk. He would look at the faces of his wife and children, of his colleagues, of passers-by, and think, 'What will become of us all?'

On the evening of Wednesday, 2 July Viktor and Ludmila went to their dacha. Ludmila had decided that they should collect their most important belongings and take them to Moscow.

They sat outside in silence. The air was cool and the garden flowers shone bright in the twilight. It seemed as if a whole eternity had passed since that last Sunday of peace.

'It's very strange,' Viktor said to Ludmila, 'but my thoughts keep returning to my mass-spectrometer and my research into positrons. Why? What's the use? It's crazy. Am I just an obsessive?'

Ludmila did not reply. They went back to looking into the darkness.

'What are you thinking about?' Viktor asked.

'I can only think about one thing. Soon Tolya will be called up.'

In the darkness Viktor found his wife's hand and squeezed it.

That night Viktor dreamed he entered a room full of pillows and sheets thrown onto the floor. He went up to an armchair that still seemed to preserve the warmth of whoever had just been sitting in it. The room was empty; the people who lived there must have left all of a sudden in the middle of the night. He looked for a long time at a shawl hanging over the chair and almost down to the floor – and then understood that it was his mother who had been sleeping in this chair. Now the chair was empty, standing in an empty room.[98]

Early the next morning, Viktor went downstairs, took down the blackout curtain, opened the window and turned on the radio.

He heard a slow voice. It was Stalin.

'This war against fascist Germany,' he said, 'cannot be considered an ordinary war. It is not only a war between two armies. It is also a war for the Fatherland, a great war fought by the entire Soviet people against the fascist German forces.'

Stalin had then asked whether the fascist forces were truly as invincible as their propaganda boasted. Catching his breath, Viktor had moved closer to the radio, wondering how Stalin would answer his own question.

'Of course not!' he had said. 'History shows us that there have *never* been invincible armies.' These simple words had helped Viktor and others to glimpse what lay far off in the future, to see beyond the dense clouds of dust raised over Soviet soil by the boots of millions of invading fascist soldiers.

Viktor had been through a great deal since that morning, but never, after Stalin's speech, had he felt the fear and heartache of those first ten days of the war.

*

In the middle of September 1941 Viktor had been due to leave Moscow for Kazan, on an Academy of Sciences special train.

On the scheduled day there was a terrible air raid. The train was unable to leave and the passengers were led down into the metro. They spread newspapers over the rails and oil-stained stones and sat there until dawn.[99]

In the morning, sticky with sweat and half-dead from the lack of air, pale figures had emerged from underground. The instant they reached the surface, each experienced a brief explosion of happiness, a happiness seldom felt or appreciated by living beings accustomed to being alive; they had seen daylight and breathed air. They had sensed the warm morning sun.

All day long their train remained in a siding. By evening, everyone's nerves were fraying.

The barrage balloons[100] had already gone up, the sky's blue was fading and the clouds were turning pink – but these peaceful colours inspired only anguish and fear.

At eight o'clock, grating and grinding, as if the carriages no longer believed in the possibility of movement, the train moved away from the heat of the station and into the cool of the fields.

Viktor stood at the end of the carriage, watching the telegraph wires, the Moscow buildings and streets, the last suburban trams, the smoky pink of the city sky – all slipping more and more swiftly away from him. He was leaving Moscow, perhaps for ever. For a moment he wanted to throw himself under the wheels of the train.

Forty minutes later there was an air-raid alert. The train stopped and the passengers got out into the forest. Over the city, swaying anxiously, almost as if it were breathing, hung a pale blue tent of searchlight beams. The trajectories of anti-aircraft shells – coloured threads drawn by an invisible steel needle – embroidered the sky with living patterns of red and green. There were the flashes of the exploding shells, and the roar of the guns themselves. Now and again there was a slow, sullen, muted rumble – a high-explosive bomb falling on some Moscow building. And then – rising slowly into the air – something yellow and heavy, like the slow flapping of wings.

It was cool in the forest. The slippery, prickly pine needles smelled of the sadness of autumn. The trunks of the pines were like quiet, kind old men, standing about in the evening stillness. It was beyond anyone's ability to take in such complex and contradictory impressions: the evening freshness, a sense of peace and safety – and the fire, smoke and death now raging through Moscow. One and the same space somehow contained both silence and thunder, the body's instinctive wish to move eastwards and an ache of shame in response to this wish.

It was a difficult journey – what with the train's slow progress, the lack of air, and long waits in Murom and Kanash.

During these long stops there were hundreds of people – clerks, scientists, writers, composers – wandering over the tracks, talking mainly about potatoes and where to find water that had been boiled ... Viktor was astonished by the behaviour of people he had met previously at art exhibitions, at concerts in the Conservatory and during summer holidays in Crimea or the Caucasus.

A lover of Mozart, who had made a special trip to Leningrad to hear a performance of his Requiem, turned out to be selfish and quarrelsome; he installed himself on the top bunk of his compartment and refused to yield it to a woman with a small baby.

On one of the top bunks in his own compartment there was someone Viktor knew quite well; during Intourist excursions to Bakhchisaray, Chufut-Kale and other sites in Crimea he had seemed kind and obliging. On the train, however, he didn't let anyone see his supplies of food. During the night Viktor heard the rustle of paper and the sound of interminable chewing. And come morning, he found cheese rind in one of his shoes.

There were also people who astonished Viktor by their kindness and selflessness.

And there was anxiety – an ever-deepening anxiety, and a sense that what lay ahead was dark and murky.

Watching a freight train pass slowly by, Viktor had pointed to a truck bearing the words 'Mosc. Vor. Kiev. Rail.' and said to Sokolov, '*Perfectum.*' And Sokolov had nodded and pointed to another truck with the words 'Cent. Asia. Rail.' and said, '*Futurum.*'[101]

Viktor remembered the crowds at the stations. He remembered people he knew, striding between the lines of freight trucks, among piles of filth and rubbish – one man carrying some boiled potatoes, another holding with both hands a large bone he had been gnawing.

*

Now that he was, at last, on his way back to Moscow, Viktor thought about those bleak days – and he understood that he had been wrong. The people he had seen then had not, after all, been weak and helpless. He had failed to understand the power that united them, that brought together their knowledge, their capacity for labour and their love of freedom. Their strength had kindled a war of liberation.

And in spite of his anxiety and bitterness, somewhere in the depth of his consciousness was a spark of joy. Once again he thought, 'Those forebodings of mine were wrong. My mother's alive. I'll see her again.'

37

They arrived towards evening. During those summer months, evening Moscow was endowed with a sad, troubled charm. The city did not fight the coming of darkness; it did not light up its windows or illuminate its streets and squares. Like a mountain or valley, Moscow moved smoothly from dusk into darkness. Those who did not witness those evenings will never know how calmly and surely darkness descended on buildings, how pavements and asphalt-covered squares faded into the night. The water beside the Kremlin quay shone as peacefully in the moonlight as some village stream flowing timidly through clumps of rushes. The night-time boulevards, parks and squares seemed impenetrable, devoid of paths or tracks. Not even the faintest ray of city light hindered the evening and its unhurried work. And there were moments when the barrage balloons in the pale blue sky seemed like silvery night-time clouds.

'What a strange sky,' said Viktor, striding along the station platform.

'Yes,' said Postoev, 'it *is* strange. But what will really surprise me is if they've done as they said and sent a car to collect us.'

Quickly, in silence, the passengers went their separate ways. It was wartime; no one had come to meet the train, and there were no women or children among the passengers. Most of the men getting out of the carriages were army commanders, wearing raincoats and greatcoats and with green haversacks on their backs. They hurried along without a word, glancing up now and again at the sky.

In the Hotel Moscow, Postoev asked for a room no higher than the third floor, saying he had a weak heart. The receptionist said the lower floors were fully occupied, but that he needn't worry – the lift was working perfectly. 'Everyone has a weak heart now,' she added with a smile. 'No one likes air raids.'

'What do you mean?' Postoev replied. 'I like them very much.' He then questioned her about the times of meals, the system of meal coupons and whether or not the restaurant was supplied with vodka and wine.

'But you have a weak heart, comrade Academician. Why do you want to know about vodka and wine?'

195

The hotel corridors were full of commanders, and there were a few beautiful women. Postoev – a grey-haired Hercules – attracted attention.

Through the half-open doors they could hear loud voices and, now and again, an accordion. Elderly waiters were carrying trays of the simple diet of the year 1942: soup, buckwheat *kasha* and grey, frozen potatoes. The glitter of the massive nickel-plated dishes served only to underline the frugality of the meals. Each tray, however, was graced with a pot-bellied carafe of vodka. This was one of Moscow's biggest pluses – it always had supplies of vodka. Muscovites used to go with empty cans and flasks and ask the waiters to fill them with this precious liquid.

Postoev and Viktor entered their room and took off their raincoats. Postoev inspected the beds, felt the blackout curtains and reached for the telephone. 'I must call the manager,' he said. 'I don't like this room, and I need to have a word with him about our meals.'

'Leonid Sergeyevich,' Viktor replied. 'The manager's hardly going to want to come up to the seventh floor. Better to find out when he'll be in his office and call on him there.'

Postoev shrugged and picked up the receiver.

They had barely managed to wash before an important-looking man with a dark complexion knocked at the door and entered.

'Leonid Sergeyevich?' he asked.

'Yes, yes, that's me,' said Postoev, walking towards him. 'And this is Viktor Pavlovich Shtrum.' But the manager merely nodded at Viktor; his attention was all on Postoev.

The manager quickly agreed to provide them with superior meals. Postoev went on to explain that they would like a two-room suite no higher than the second floor.

The manager nodded, noted this down and said, 'Tomorrow I'll be able to provide you with everything. And I'll come round in person.'

Viktor realized that Postoev's magic sprang from his absolute and unshakeable self-assurance. Everyone who encountered him understood at once that his privileges – to travel first class, to eat veal rather than potatoes, to sit in a comfortable chair at the very front of a conference hall – were guaranteed not by law, but by his very nature. Postoev's self-assurance when speaking with receptionists, ticket collectors or hotel managers was all one with his general certainty as to the importance of his work, the uniqueness of his erudition and the value of his scientific and technical experience. And as the country's most senior adviser on the production of high-quality steel, he did indeed have reason to feel sure of himself.

The manager began to name the various academicians and other scientific luminaries who had stayed in the hotel. He could remember with astonishing exactness the numbers of the rooms in which Vavilov, Fersman, Vedeneyev and Alexandrov had stayed, though he seemed to have little idea which of them was a geologist, which a physicist and which a metallurgist.[102] The manager was used to dealing with important people; he had a calm, confident manner, and this allowed him to tread the fine line between offering a respectful welcome and delicately allowing it to become apparent that he was tired and busy. He evidently ranked Postoev very high indeed; he showed only the most minimal sign of being tired or busy, and he could hardly have been more respectful or welcoming.

When the manager left, Viktor flung up his hands in astonishment and said, 'Leonid Sergeyevich, another minute and he'd have arranged for a choir of maidens in white tunics to be brought to our room, with garlands of roses.'

Postoev burst out laughing. His beard, his heavy shoulders and even his armchair all began to shake. The glass beside the water carafe tinkled, yielding to the power of this large, laughing body.

'Heavens!' he said. 'The things you say! But then there's something about hotel air – it always contains a microbe of student frivolity.'

Tired though they were, both men took a long time to get to sleep that night. But, rather than talking, they chose to read. Strangely, they had each brought the same book: *The Adventures of Sherlock Holmes*.[103] Postoev kept getting up, pacing about the room, then taking different medicines. 'You're not asleep?' he said quietly. 'I feel a weight on my heart. I was born in Moscow, on Vorontsovo Field. My whole life's been in Moscow, everything near and dear to me is in Moscow. Both my mother and father are buried in the Vagankovo cemetery, and I'd like to … I'm an old man. But Hitler and his Nazis, damn them, they just keep on advancing …'

In the morning Viktor changed his mind. Instead of going with Postoev to the Party committee, he decided to go on foot to his own apartment, and from there to the institute.

'I'll be at the committee by two,' said Postoev. 'Ring me then. First I must visit the commissariats.'

He looked bright-eyed, animated, as if he were looking forward to his various meetings. It was hard to imagine that this was the same man who, during the night, had spoken of death, old age and the war.

38

Viktor set off to the telegraph office to send a telegram to his wife. He walked up Gorky Street, along the spacious, deserted pavement, past shop windows that had been boarded up and packed with sandbags.

After sending the telegram, he went back down to Okhotny Ryad, meaning to walk across Kamenny Bridge and then go through Yakimanka to Kaluga Square.

An infantry unit was crossing Red Square.

Past and present suddenly met. There before him were the Kremlin and the Lenin mausoleum. Viktor could see today's sky and the soldiers' severe, exhausted faces. And, at the same time, he was standing at the end of a railway carriage, on an autumn evening, thinking he was leaving Moscow for ever.

The clock on the Kremlin tower struck ten.

Viktor walked on, moved by every new detail, every smallest thing that he saw. He looked at windows masked with strips of blue paper, at the remains of a building – now fenced off – that had been hit by a bomb, and at barricades made from pine logs and sacks of earth, with slits for guns and machine guns. He looked at tall new buildings with shining windows, at old buildings with crumbling stucco, at newly painted signs: the words 'AIR-RAID SHELTER', with a bright white arrow beneath them.

He looked at what passed for crowds in this city now almost on the front line: commanders and soldiers, women in boots and tunics. He looked at half-empty trams, at army trucks packed with soldiers, at cars camouflaged with splodges of black and green. Some of the windscreens had been holed by bullets.

He looked at silent women standing in queues, at children playing in small squares and yards – and he imagined that they all knew he had only come back from Kazan the day before and that he had not spent the cruel, cold Moscow winter alongside them.

*

As he fumbled with his key, the door of the neighbouring apartment half-opened. The animated face of a young woman peered out, and a laughing yet stern voice asked, 'Who are you?'

'Me? Somebody who lives here, I suppose,' said Viktor.

He went inside and breathed in the stale, musty air. The apartment had barely changed since the day they left. The piano and the book-shelves, though, were grey with dust, while a piece of bread left on the dining table had grown a fluffy layer of greenish-white mould. Nadya's white summer shoes and tennis racket were peeping out from under the bed, and Tolya's dumb-bells were still lying in a corner.

Things that had changed, things that had not changed – all were equally sad.

Viktor opened the sideboard and felt around inside it. There in a dark corner was a bottle of wine. He took a glass from the table and found the corkscrew. He wiped the dust from the bottle and glass with his handkerchief, then drank some wine and lit a cigarette.

He drank only rarely, and wine had a strong effect on him. Instead of seeming close and stuffy, the room at once felt bright and elegant.

He sat down at the piano and tried out the keys, listening intently.

His head was spinning. To be back in his own home felt both sad and joyful. It was all very strange. He had returned, yet he felt aban-doned. He was alone, yet in the presence of his family. He was con-scious of his ties and obligations, yet unusually free.

Everything was as it always had been – yet also, somehow, unfamil-iar and strange. And he felt different in himself; he was not the man he understood and was accustomed to.

Viktor wondered about his neighbour. Could she hear him? Who *was* this bright-eyed young woman next door? The Menshovs had left Moscow long ago, before Viktor and his family, only a few weeks after the German invasion.

When Viktor stopped playing, he felt anxious – the silence was oppressive. He felt the need to move about. He walked around the apartment, had a look in the kitchen and decided to go back outside.

On the street he met the house manager. They talked about how cold the winter had been, about burst central-heating pipes, about rent payments and empty apartments – and Viktor asked, 'By the way, who's the young woman in the Menshovs' apartment? They're all still in Omsk, aren't they?'

'Don't worry,' the man replied. 'She's a friend of theirs from Omsk. She's here on business. I registered her for two weeks – she'll be leaving in a few days.' And then, looking Viktor in the eye, he winked slyly and said, 'But she's quite a beauty, isn't she, Viktor Pavlovich?' He laughed and added, 'A pity Ludmila Nikolaevna hasn't come back with you. We put out a lot of fires together. The yardmen and I often remember her and all the incendiaries she helped us to deal with.'

On his way to the institute Viktor suddenly thought, 'I'd rather stay in my own home – I'll have to go back and fetch my case.'

39

But when Viktor went into the institute, when he saw the familiar lawn and bench, the poplars and lindens in the yard and the windows of his own office and laboratory – he immediately forgot everything else.

The institute had not been damaged by bombs; this he already knew. He also knew that all the equipment on the main floor – the first floor, where his laboratory was located – had been entrusted to the care of senior laboratory assistant Anna Stepanovna.

Anna Stepanovna was the only senior laboratory assistant without a degree. Shortly before the war, there had been a proposal to replace this elderly woman with someone with higher formal qualifications. But both Viktor and Pyotr Sokolov had opposed this – and she had been allowed to stay.

The watchman told Viktor that Anna Stepanovna kept all the keys to the first-floor rooms in her own apartment. The laboratory door, however, turned out not to be locked.

The main room seemed very bright. The huge, wide windows were clean and shining and the entire laboratory, full of glass, copper and nickel, glittered in the summer sun. The absence of the most valuable apparatus, moved the previous autumn first to Kazan and then to Sverdlovsk, was not immediately noticeable.

Viktor was breathing fast and he had lit a cigarette. His head was spinning – perhaps from excitement, perhaps from the wine he had drunk earlier. Still close to the door, he leant against the wall and looked slowly around him. This was the one place where he was never absent-minded. He was absent-minded in every other part of his life – at home, with his friends, during boat trips, in the theatre, and in the letters he wrote – because all his energy was taken up with what went on in these rooms. Here he noticed everything. As he crossed the threshold of his laboratory, his vision, his hearing and every aspect of his attention became precise and tenacious; there was nothing so small that it escaped his notice.

Now, too, he saw everything: the polished parquet, the spotless glass, and the noble, tender metal of the remaining equipment, which gave off a sense of health and cleanliness. He looked at the temperature chart on the wall; during the winter it had not once fallen below 10°C.

His vacuum pump had been placed beneath a bell jar. A special measuring apparatus – one particularly sensitive to damp – was in a glass cupboard sprinkled with fresh granules of calcium chloride. An electric motor on a vast frame had been installed exactly where he had meant to install it before the war.

Hearing quick, light footsteps, he turned round.

'Viktor Pavlovich!' a woman shouted as she ran towards him.

Viktor looked at Anna Stepanovna and was astonished at how much she had changed. Yet nothing in the laboratory had changed at all; everything entrusted to her was exactly as he had left it.

Viktor struck a match and began lighting a cigarette he had already lit. Anna Stepanovna's hair had turned white. Her once full, pink face was thin and haggard. Her skin looked grey, and two deep furrows had appeared on her forehead, in the form of a cross.

He took her hand. It was densely callused and the skin was dark brown and rough as sandpaper.

What Anna Stepanovna had achieved, and what she had endured during the winter, were only too clear – even before she spoke. What could he say to her? Should he thank her on behalf of the institute, on behalf of the professors as a whole? Or even in the name of the president of the Academy of Sciences?

Without saying a word, he bowed low and kissed her hand.

She hugged him and kissed him on the lips.

They walked round the room arm in arm, talking and laughing, while the old watchman stood in the doorway and smiled.

Then the three of them went into Viktor's office.

'How did you get that vast frame up from the ground floor?' Viktor asked. 'It must have taken at least seven or eight strong men.'

'That was the easy part,' Anna Stepanovna replied. 'During the winter we had an anti-aircraft battery stationed in the square. The gunners helped out. But getting six tons of coal through the yard on a sledge – that was hard work.'

Then old Alexander Matveyevich, the watchman, brought a kettle of boiling water and Anna Stepanovna took from her bag a little packet of red caramels stuck together into a ball. She spread out a sheet of newspaper, so she could cut some bread into tiny rectangular slices

– and the three of them sat together, chatting and drinking tea out of chemical measuring beakers.

As she offered Viktor the caramels, Anna Stepanovna said, 'Feel free, Viktor Pavlovich! I collected them this morning on my academy sugar ration.'

And old Alexander Matveyevich picked up little crumbs of bread between his fingers – which looked pale and bloodless despite being stained with nicotine – ate them slowly and thoughtfully and said, 'Yes, Viktor Pavlovich, it wasn't an easy winter for the old. It's a good thing the gunners were there to give us a hand now and then.'

Realizing that Viktor might interpret this as a hint not to eat any more of their bread and sweets, he added, 'But everything's a lot easier now. This month I'll be getting better rations – there'll be sugar on my card too.'

The care with which Anna Stepanovna and Alexander Matveyevich held their tiny pieces of bread, their quiet, measured movements, their seriousness and concentration as they chewed – all this told Viktor a great deal. More clearly than ever, he understood how difficult this last winter in Moscow had been.

When they'd finished their tea, Viktor and Anna Stepanovna went round the offices and laboratories once again.

Anna Stepanovna brought up the question of the laboratory's work plan. She had seen a draft during the winter, when Sukhov was still the director.

'Yes,' Viktor replied. 'Sokolov and I were talking about Sukhov just before I set off for Moscow. He came to Kazan a few months ago, to discuss the plan with us.'

Anna Stepanovna then told him about her own meetings with Sukhov during the winter. 'I went to the committee to ask for more coal. He couldn't have been kinder or more cordial. I was very pleased, of course, but there was still something depressing and bureaucratic about him. Things were looking bad for us, I thought. And then I happened to meet him in the spring, by the entrance to the main building, and he seemed a different person. I sensed it at once. His attention wandered and he treated me coldly. But, would you believe it, I felt glad. I thought things must be looking up for us.'

'Yes,' said Viktor. 'Though they're certainly not looking up for him any longer. But tell me, is our telephone working?'

'Of course it is.'

With the words 'So help me God!', Viktor picked up the receiver and began to dial. He had kept putting off this conversation with the new director, though he had taken out his notebook and checked the number several times while still on the train. Now, hearing the phone ring, he felt agitated. He was hoping to hear the secretary reply, 'Pimenov's away. He'll be back in a few days.'

Instead, he heard Pimenov himself.

Anna Stepanovna understood this at once, from the look on Viktor's face.

Pimenov said how glad he was to hear from Viktor. He asked how the journey had gone and if he was comfortable in his hotel room. He said he'd have come to see Viktor himself but hadn't wanted to interrupt his first reunion with his laboratory. Finally, he came out with the words Viktor had been waiting for so anxiously and had feared he would never hear: 'The academy fully guarantees to fund all the work. That applies to all our institutes, and to your laboratory in particular, Viktor Pavlovich. Your research themes have been officially approved. Your work plan has also been approved by Academician Chepyzhin. Any day now, by the way, we're expecting him here from Sverdlovsk. There is really only one remaining concern: will it be possible for us to obtain the grade of steel your apparatus requires?'

As soon as he'd put the phone down, Viktor went up to Anna Stepanovna, took both her hands and said, 'Moscow, magnificent Moscow …'

And she laughed and said, 'See how we're greeting you!'

40

The summer of 1942 was an extraordinary time for Moscow.

Only during the most terrible of foreign invasions had the state's frontiers been pushed back so far. There had been a time when a courier could gallop in one night from the Kremlin to the boundary of the Russian state, pass on a message from the Grand Prince of Moscow to his military commander and then look down from a hilltop at Tatar horsemen, in ragged fur hats and sweat-drenched tunics, riding without a care over devastated Russian fields.

And in the dark, troubled days of August 1812, a courier sent by Rostopchin, governor of Moscow, could ride by night to Kutuzov's HQ, have time for a few hours' rest and a meal, and be back in Moscow by evening with the latest despatches. He could tell a friend in the governor's house how, only that morning, from one of the forward positions, he'd been able to see the French uniforms 'as clearly as I can see you this minute!'

And in the summer of 1942 a signals officer in an armoured car could set out in the morning from the General Staff, deliver a message to the commander of the Western Front, ask a colleague to give him a lunch coupon, eat in the canteen and return straightaway to the general-staff signals section. 'Only an hour and a half ago,' he could say to his comrades, 'I was listening to the rumble of German field artillery.'

And a fighter pilot could take off from Moscow's central aerodrome, reach the front line in thirteen or fourteen minutes, fire a few rounds at the German uniforms dotting the aspen and birch copses around Mozhaisk and Vyazemsk, shake his fist as he banked over a German regimental HQ, be back in Moscow within quarter of an hour and go by tram, past the Belorussian station, to the Pushkin monument, where he and a woman he knew had arranged to meet.

Mtsensk to the south of Moscow, Vyazma to the west and Rzhev to the north-west were all in German hands. The provinces of Kursk, Oryol and Smolensk were occupied by the rear support services of Field Marshal Kluge's Army Group Centre. Four German infantry and two German tank armies, along with their ordnance and supplies, were within two days' march of Red Square, the Kremlin, the Lenin Institute, the Moscow Art Theatre and the Bolshoy – and of the Razguliay, Cheryomushki and Sadovniki districts,[104] of Moscow schools and maternity homes, and of the monuments to Pushkin and Timiryazev.[105]

The Western Front's support services' HQs – the supplies, quartermasters and army newspaper editorial offices – were located within the city itself. Muscovites among the staff were simultaneously at home and at war. They spent the night alone in their apartments, transferred food from their mess tins to their usual plates and bowls and slept in their boots not in dugouts and bunkers but on their usual beds. Their apartments bore witness to a strange blend of war and domestic life. Hand-grenade fuses and cartridge magazines lay on the floor beside children's toys and women's berets and dressing gowns. Sub-machine guns stood against sofas, and windows were blacked out with tarpaulin groundsheets. It was strange to hear only the squeak of heavy boots in the evenings – not the quick tread of children or the shuffle of a grandmother's slippers.

The front line lay close by, only a little further away than in the terrible days of October 1941. Nevertheless, as the German armies advanced deeper into the south-eastern steppe, the Moscow front grew ever quieter, ever more static. The war, it seemed, was moving away from Moscow.

There were days, even weeks when German bombers did not appear over Moscow at all. Muscovites ceased to pay attention to the Soviet fighters buzzing about the sky. They had grown so used to them that a few minutes of silence would make them look up in surprise, wondering what was going on.

There was space in the trams and the metro. Even during the busiest times of day there was none of the usual pushing and jostling around Theatre Square and the Ilinsky Gates. In the evenings, with practised efficiency, young women Air Defence volunteers sent silvery barrage balloons up into the sky from Chistye Prudy and from the Tverskoy, Nikitsky and Gogol boulevards.

But, even though hundreds of factories, schools, higher-education institutes and other establishments had been evacuated, Moscow was not empty.

Muscovites gradually got used to the proximity of the front line. They returned to their routine tasks. They prepared for the winter, laying in stores of potatoes and firewood.

There were several reasons why people felt calmer. One was a some-what inaccurate sense that the danger had now moved elsewhere. Another was that it is impossible to remain very long in a state of extreme nervous tension; nature simply doesn't allow this.

One can get used to particular conditions and start to feel calmer not because there has been any real improvement but simply because one's sense of tension has been dissipated by everyday tasks and concerns. A sick person can start to feel calmer not because he is recovering but simply because he has got used to his illness.

Last, and most important of all – people truly began to believe, consciously or not, that Moscow would never be allowed to fall to the Germans. This faith was reaffirmed when the German forces, after appearing poised to encircle the city, were driven out of Klin and Kalinin and back to Mozhaisk; this faith was reaffirmed by the way that Leningrad refused to yield, even after 300 days of fire, ice and hunger. This faith constantly strengthened and deep-ened, supplanting the anguish Muscovites had felt in September and October 1941.

By summer 1942 Muscovites had come to feel that the tone of offi-cial bulletins and newspapers was excessively grim, even alarmist. Changing circumstances had brought about remarkable changes in the way people thought; they had even come to an entirely new under-standing of their own past behaviour.

In October 1941 some Muscovites, concerned only about their worldly belongings, had refused to get on trains that could have taken them east. When asked why, they had looked away in embarrassment.

At the time it had been thought that those who abandoned their belongings to fate, who left their apartments and moved with their factory or institute to Bashkiriya or the Urals, were acting patriotically. Anyone who refused to leave the city because their mother-in-law was ill, or because they couldn't take a beloved piano or dressing-table mirror with them, was considered petty-minded or worse.

But by the summer of 1942 some such people had managed to for-get the real reasons behind their decision to stay. They now saw the evacuees as deserters and themselves as Moscow's defenders. They had no conception of how little they had in common with the city's true defenders – the fighter pilots, the volunteers manning the anti-aircraft defences, the soldiers, workers and militia defending the city with their own blood.

These people now felt that the city belonged to them. They talked about how good it would be if the government forbade evacuees to return to the capital.

Conditions had changed, and so had people's attitudes. An extreme flexibility of thought, to keep up with the demands of the moment, is the defining characteristic of the philistine and the petty-minded.

Those who had left in October 1941, taking only a pair or two of felt boots, a few changes of underclothes and a few loaves of bread, those who had been reluctant even to lock their apartments, in case their belongings might be of some use to the city's defenders – these same people were now writing to neighbours, yardmen and house managers, asking them to keep a close eye on their belongings. Some of the evacuees were even writing to public prosecutors and the heads of district police stations, complaining that yardmen and house managers were failing to protect their property. And those who had stayed in Moscow now professed surprise at the evacuees' petty-mindedness.

More important, however, than such small paradoxes was the determination with which Moscow's defenders – strong, self-sacrificing working people – continued to work. They dug trenches, built barricades and then returned to their factories.

The evacuees imagined that they had taken away with them all Moscow's life and warmth. They imagined factory workshops now covered in snow, cold boilers, empty bays with no lathes or machine tools, buildings that had died, that had become mere slabs of stone. They thought that all the energy of life had left Moscow and reappeared far away, in the new construction sites of Bashkiriya, Uzbekistan, Siberia and the Urals. But the life force of the great Soviet city was stronger than these people realized. Moscow's strength proved inexhaustible; her shop floors returned to life and her factory chimneys began to smoke once again. Her citizens' capacity for work appeared to have doubled; Moscow's industrial life was strong enough both to put down new roots in the harsh ground of the new construction sites to the east, and to spring up anew from the roots left behind.

And this engendered yet another paradox.

Those who had left began to feel unhappy and anxious. Even without them Moscow was still well and strong, and this made them want to return. They petitioned to be allowed back. Forgetting how only the previous autumn they had struggled to obtain permission to leave, they talked of the wisdom of those who had stayed behind. And those who had moved to Saratov and Astrakhan said, 'Yes, it's a lot quieter now in

Moscow than it is on the Volga!' They seemed not to understand that the fate of Moscow and the fate of the Volga were one and the same.

Moscow – city of makeshift iron chimneys installed in air vents and ventilation panes, city of hastily built barricades and daytime air raids, city whose leaden sky was lit by blazing buildings and the flashes of exploding bombs, city where the bodies of women and children killed during air raids could be buried only at night – in the summer of 1942 this city became elegant and beautiful. Even shortly before the curfew couples would be sitting on the benches of Tverskoy Boulevard, and after warm summer showers the linden blossom seemed to smell sweeter and more splendid than ever it had smelled in peacetime.

41

On his second morning in Moscow Viktor packed his belongings and left the hotel, where there was hot water in the bathroom and where both wine and vodka were available every day.

Back in his apartment, he opened the windows and went into the kitchen to add some water to the dried-up ink in the inkwell. A rust-coloured fluid flowed lazily from the tap and he waited a long time for it to run clear.

He sat down to write a postcard to Ludmila and then began a letter to Sokolov – a detailed account of his conversation with Pimenov. He thought it would now take him about ten days to get through the various formalities required for the official approval of the institute's work plan.

Viktor addressed the envelope and fell into thought. It was all very strange. He had set off for Moscow, expecting to have to fight his corner, to have to argue passionately about his project's importance – but he had not had to argue at all. Every last one of his proposals had been accepted.

He sealed the envelope and began walking about the room. 'It's good to be back home,' he thought. 'I've done the right thing.'

After a while he sat down at his desk and turned to his work. Now and again he looked up and listened: the silence seemed extraordinary. And then he realized that he wasn't listening to the silence so much as wondering if there would be a ring at the door. And it might, perhaps, be that young woman from Omsk – and he would say, 'Come and sit down. Being on one's own can be terribly sad.'

But then he got carried away by his work and forgot about the young woman for several hours. And he was leaning over his desk, writing fast, when he really did hear a knock. It was her. She wanted to borrow two matches to light the gas: one for now, and one for the morning.

'Lending you matches is out of the question,' Viktor replied, 'but I'll gladly give you a box. But why are you standing out there in the corridor? Come in!'

'You're very kind,' she said with a laugh. 'Matches are hard to come by.' And she came in. Seeing a crumpled collar on the floor, she picked it up, put it on the table and said, 'There's dust everywhere. The place is a mess.'

Her face looked especially pretty when she was bending down, glancing up at Viktor.

'Goodness,' she said. 'You've got a piano. Do you know how to play?' Wanting to appear light-hearted, she answered on his behalf, 'A few simple pieces, maybe, like "Where have you been, little finch?"'[106]

Viktor couldn't think what to say.

He was awkward and shy with women.

Like many shy men, he saw himself as cool and experienced, imagining that this young woman had no idea that her neighbour with the matches fancied her, that he was admiring her slender fingers, her tanned feet in sandals with red heels, her shoulders, her small nose, her breasts and her hair.

He had still not managed to ask her name.

Then she asked him to play something. He began with pieces he thought she might know: a Chopin waltz, a Wieniawski mazurka. Then he gave a little snort, shook his head and began some Scriabin, glancing at her now and again out of the corner of his eye. She listened intently, slightly wrinkling her brow.

'Where did you learn to play?' she asked, after he'd closed the piano lid and wiped his palms and his forehead.

Instead of answering, he asked, 'What's your name?'

'Nina,' she answered, 'and you're Viktor.' And she pointed to a large picture, lying flat on his desk, with the inscription 'Viktor Pavlovich Shtrum – from the postgraduate students of the Institute of Mechanics and Physics.'

'And your patronymic?' he asked.

'Just call me Nina.'

Viktor offered her some tea and invited her to stay and eat with him. Nina agreed and then laughed, amused by how awkwardly he began preparing the meal.

'What a strange way to cut bread!' she said. 'Let me do it. And you don't need to open any tins – there's more than enough on the table as it is! Wait, wait – first you have to shake the dust from the tablecloth!'

There was a touching charm in the way this pretty young woman took charge of the large empty apartment.

While they were eating, Nina told Viktor that she lived in Omsk, where her husband worked in the district consumers' union. She had come to deliver a consignment of linen from Omsk to some of the Moscow hospitals, but she had been held up by administrative problems. In a few days she'd be going to Kalinin – materials intended for Omsk had been sent there by mistake. 'And then I'll have to go home,' she added.

'Why *I'll have to*?' asked Viktor.

'Why?' she repeated. With a sigh, she added, 'Because ...'

Viktor offered her some wine.

Nina drank half a glass of Madeira – the Madeira that Ludmila had told Viktor to bring back to Kazan with him.[107] Above her upper lip there were now shiny little beads of sweat, and she began to fan her neck and cheeks with her handkerchief.

'You don't mind the window being open?' asked Viktor. 'But tell me what made you say "I'll have to go home"? Usually it's the opposite – people complain about having to *leave* home.'

She laughed and gently shook her head.

'What's that on your little chain?' he asked.

'A locket. A photograph of my late mother.' She took the chain from her neck and held it out to him. 'Have a look.'

Viktor looked at the small yellowing photograph of an elderly woman with a white peasant kerchief tied round her head. Then he carefully handed the locket back to his guest.

Nina walked around the room and said, 'Heavens – what a huge space – you could get lost in it!'

'I'd love you to get lost here,' he said – and at once felt embarrassed by his own boldness. But she seemed not to have understood.

'You know what?' she said. 'Let me help you dust the room and wash the dishes.'

'What on earth do you mean?' said Viktor, somewhat alarmed.

'What's the matter?'

Nina wiped the oilskin tablecloth and then, as she went on to wash the glasses, began to say a little more about herself.

Viktor stood at the window and listened.

How strange she was – quite different from any other woman he knew! And so beautiful! And how, without hesitation and with such heart-rending frankness, could she talk like this about such personal matters – about her late mother, about her unkind husband and the wrongs he had done her?

Her stories were a strange mixture of childishness and worldly wisdom.

She told him about a 'wonderful man' – an electrician – who had been in love with her. Back then she'd been working as a fitter. Now she couldn't understand why she'd refused to marry him. Instead, just before the war, she had married a handsome neighbour with an important job in the food industry. He was now 'clinging' – as she herself put it – to the exemption from military service to which this entitled him.

Nina looked at her watch. 'Well, it's time I left. Thank you for the meal.'

'Thank *you*. I really can't thank you enough.'

'It's wartime,' she said. 'We all need to help one another.'

'No, not just for that. For such a wonderful, remarkable evening. And for your trust in me. Believe me, I'm moved by the way you've spoken to me.' Viktor put his hand to his heart.

'You're very strange,' she said, and looked at him with curiosity.

'Unfortunately,' he replied, 'I'm not strange at all. I'm as ordinary as can be. You're the unusual one. Will you allow me to go with you to your door?' And he bowed respectfully.

For several seconds she looked him straight in the eye. There was not one blink of her lashes. Her eyes were wide open, intent, surprised.

'You're very …' she said – and sighed, as if about to cry.

He would never have guessed that this beautiful young woman had lived through so much. 'Yet she's so pure and trusting,' he thought.

*

In the morning, as he went past the old lift attendant, sitting in her wicker armchair, Viktor asked, 'How are you doing, Alexandra Petrovna?'

'The same as every one else,' she replied. 'My daughter's ill. We wanted to send her children away, to stay with my son – but on Thursday I got a letter from her. My son's been called up. What can we do with the children now? My daughter-in-law's got her hands full already – one girl and a very young boy.'

42

Later that day, at the committee, Viktor heard that Chepyzhin was already in Moscow. Pimenov's secretary, a stout old matron in her sixties who seemed to look equally critically at every man from first-year student to grey-haired professor, said, 'Viktor Pavlovich, Academician Chepyzhin asked you to wait for him. He'll be here by six.'

She looked at Viktor and said severely, 'You absolutely must wait. Tomorrow he's leaving for Sverdlovsk.' After a little laugh she added quietly, 'And you'll have to wait a long time, since he's sure to be late.'

This was her way of saying that not even a famous academician is exempt from the usual male weaknesses, since the male sex is flighty and hard to educate.

But she turned out to be right. Chepyzhin arrived only after seven o'clock, when the offices and other rooms were already empty and the night watchman was keeping a stern eye on Viktor as he strode anxiously up and down the corridor. One of the other secretaries, also on night duty, was arranging his armchair beside his boss's desk, making his preparations for a peaceful night.

When Viktor heard Chepyzhin's footsteps, when he looked round and glimpsed his familiar, stocky figure at the end of the corridor, he felt a surge of excitement and joy.

Chepyzhin immediately held out his hand and hurried towards Viktor, saying in a loud voice, 'Viktor Pavlovich! At last! And in Moscow!'

His questions were quick and abrupt: 'How are things in Kazan? Difficult? Do you think of me now and again? What exactly have you and Pimenov agreed on? Do the air raids scare you? Is it true that Ludmila Nikolaevna worked on a kolkhoz during the summer?'

Listening to Viktor's replies, he cocked his head to one side. His eyes were serious yet cheerful, shining from underneath his broad forehead.

'I've read your work plan,' he said. 'I think you're making the right choices.' He thought then quietly went on, 'My sons are in the army. Vanya's been wounded. You've got a son in the army too, haven't you? What do you think? Should we forget about science and volunteer for

214

the front ourselves?' He looked around the room and said, 'It's stifling in here – dusty and smoky. Look – let's go for a walk. You can come back home with me. It's not far. Only four kilometres. There'll be a car to take you back afterwards. All right?'

'Of course,' Viktor replied.

In the still twilight Chepyzhin's tanned, weather-beaten face was a dark brown and his large, bright eyes seemed keen and alert. This was probably how he had looked during his long summer hikes, as the path began to disappear in the twilight and he walked swiftly towards the spot where he planned to stop for the night.

As they crossed Trubnaya Square, Chepyzhin paused and took a long hard look at the grey-blue evening sky. His gaze was not like that of other people. There it was – the sky of his childhood dreams, a sky that prompted sad contemplation, or irrational sorrow ... But no, that was not what Chepyzhin saw. The sky Chepyzhin saw was a universal laboratory, a place where his mind could settle down to serious labour; Chepyzhin the scientist was looking at the sky the way a peasant inspects a field where he has worked and sweated.

These first flickering stars were perhaps giving birth in his mind to thoughts of proton explosions, of developmental phases and cycles, of super-dense matter, of cosmic showers and storms of varitrons,[108] of different theories of cosmogony, including his own, of instruments for recording invisible streams of stellar energy ...

Or perhaps these first stars had made him think of something entirely different.

Of a bonfire, of crackling twigs, of a blackened pan in which millet porridge was quietly steaming, of dark leaves up above him, silhouetted against the night sky?

Or of a quiet evening when he was little, when he had sat on his mother's lap and, sensing her warm breath and her warm hands stroking his head, had gazed up at the stars, sleepy yet full of wonder?

Amid the few stars and the fragile little tin clouds Viktor could see barrage balloons and the broad, sweeping beams of searchlights. The war had burst into Russian cities and the fields of Russian farmers – and it was no less present in the Russian sky.

They walked slowly and in silence. There were many questions Viktor wanted to ask, but he did not ask anything about the war, nor about Chepyzhin's own work, nor about the discoveries of Professor Stepanov, who had recently gone to consult Chepyzhin. Nor did Viktor ask Chepyzhin what he thought about the work he was doing himself, nor about the conversation between Chepyzhin and Pimenov that Pimenov had mentioned to him a few hours earlier.

He knew there was some other, more important question to discuss, something that related at one and the same time to the war, to their work, and to the anguish deep in their hearts.

Chepyzhin looked at Viktor and said, 'Fascism! What's happened? What has become of the Germans? Reading about the fascists' medieval brutality makes your blood run cold. They burn villages, they build death camps, they organize mass executions of prisoners of war, massacres of peaceful civilians we haven't seen since the dawn of history. Everything good seems to have disappeared. Are there no longer any good, noble or honest Germans? How can that be? You and I know Germans. We know their science, their literature, their music, their philosophy! And their working classes? And their progressive movement – what's happened to that? Where have so many evil people sprung from? People tell us the Germans have changed – or, rather, degenerated. People say Hitler and his Nazis have transformed them.'

'Maybe,' Viktor replied, 'but Nazism didn't appear out of nowhere. Muhammad went to the mountain – *and* the mountain went to Muhammad. "Deutschland, Deutschland über alles" was sung long before Hitler. Not long ago I was rereading the letters of Heinrich Heine. A hundred years ago he wrote *Lutezia* – about what he called the ghastly falsity of German nationalism, about the idiotic German hostility towards their neighbours, towards other nations.[109] And then, fifty years later, Nietzsche started preaching his superman – a blond beast to whom everything is permitted. And in 1914 the flower of German Science welcomed the kaiser's invasion of Belgium; Ostwald was one such scientist, but there were others even more important.[110] As for Hitler himself, he has always known very well that there's no lack of demand for the goods he sells; he has friends among the captains of industry and among the Prussian nobility, among army officers and among the petty bourgeoisie. Yes, there's been no shortage of takers! Who do you think mans the regiments of the SS? Who has turned the whole of Europe into a huge concentration camp? Who has forced tens of thousands of people into mobile gas chambers?[111] Fascism comes out of the whole of Germany's reactionary past, even if it has its own particular features and is more terrible than anything before it.'

'All very well,' said Chepyzhin, with a dismissive wave of the hand. 'Fascism may be strong, but we mustn't forget that its power over people is not unlimited. All Hitler has really changed is the pecking

216

order – who occupies what position in German society. The relative proportions of the various elements remain the same – but fascism has brought to the surface all the sediment, all the inevitable dregs of capitalist life, all the filth that had previously lain hidden. Fascism has brought all this into the light of day, while everything good and wise, everything most truly of the people has been forced underground. Nevertheless, what is good and wise is still alive. This bread of life still exists. Many souls, it goes without saying, have been distorted and perverted by fascism, but the German people remain. And the German people always will remain.'

He looked at Viktor animatedly, took him by the hand and went on, 'Imagine a city where there are some men and women whom everyone recognizes as honest, kind-hearted and educated, as true benefactors of humanity. Every old man, every small child knows who they are. They are central to the city's life and they give it meaning and beauty. They teach in its schools and universities. They write books, they contribute to its scientific journals and workers' newspapers. They work and struggle for the working class. They are in the public eye from morning until late in the evening. They are everywhere: in schools, factories and lecture halls, on the streets, in the main squares. At night other people appear, but hardly anyone knows about them. Their lives and work are secret and murky. They are afraid of the light. They are used to stealing through darkness, in the shadow of large buildings. But then something changes – and Hitler's dark power bursts into the world. Those who are honest and kind, those who bring light to the world are flung into camps and prisons. Some die fighting, others go underground. These people are no longer to be seen in schools, factories and lecture halls, or taking part in workers' demonstrations. Their books are cast into the flames. And of course, a few turn out to be traitors. A few become Brownshirts, followers of Hitler. As for those who used to lurk in the shadows, they become prominent figures. Their deeds fill the newspapers. And it seems as if reason, science, humanity and honour have all died, as if they have vanished from the face of the earth. It seems as if the nation has degenerated, as if it has lost all sense of goodness and honour. But that's not true! It's simply not true! The strength and good sense of the people, their morality, their true wealth – all this will live forever, no matter how hard fascism tries to destroy it.'

And without waiting for an answer, he went on, 'And it's the same with individuals. There's a great deal in all of us that is false, coarse and primitive, an unholy mixture of stuff usually kept under wraps. Many people living in normal social conditions have no idea of the cellars and basements of their own being. But there has been a catastrophe – and vermin of every kind have escaped from the cellars. Now they are at large, scuttling through rooms that were once bright and clean.'

'Dmitry Petrovich,' Viktor replied, 'you say everyone's this unholy mixture. But you yourself, by your very existence, are enough to refute your own words. Everything in you is pure and clear – you have no dark cellars or basements. Yes, I know one's not supposed to speak of present company – but to prove you wrong, I really don't need to invoke the memory of such great figures as Giordano Bruno and Nikolay Chernyshevsky.[112] All I need do is look around me. Your explanation simply doesn't hold water. You say a bunch of villains led by Hitler has burst into German life. But there have been far too many times in German history when, at the decisive moment, reactionary forces have been able to seize control. There's always been some Wilhelm or Friedrich or Wilhelm-Friedrich, ready to do their bidding.

'So, we're not just talking about a bunch of villains led by Hitler – we're talking about Prussian militarism, about the Prussian Junkers who always push these villains and super-villains to the fore.

'Someone close to me, Nikolay Krymov – he's a commissar now, at the front – once quoted some words of Marx about the role played by the forces of reaction in German history. I remember them to this day: "Led by our pastors, we have never known liberty. Only when she was being buried have we been in her company."[113] And in the epoch of imperialism these same forces have spawned Hitler – a monster of monsters – and 13 million Germans have voted for him in elections.'

'Yes, that's how it is today,' said Chepyzhin. 'Hitler has conquered in Germany. I understand what you're saying. But you can't deny that the people's morality, the people's true wealth and goodness are indestructible, stronger than Hitler and his axe. Fascism will be destroyed, and human beings will remain human beings. Everywhere – not only in Nazi-occupied Europe, but even in Germany itself! The morality of the people – this is the measure of free, useful, creative labour. Its essence, its foundation is the belief in the right to equality, to the freedom of all living people. The morality of the people is simple: the sanctity of my own right is inseparable from the sanctity of the rights of all other working people on earth. But fascism asserts the opposite. And Hitler himself, with a frenzy all of his own, claims, "My right is to deprive all others of rights. I have the right to make the whole world submit to me."'

218

'Yes, Dmitry Petrovich, yes, of course you are right. Fascism will be destroyed, and human beings will remain human beings. Unless one believes this, it is impossible to go on living. Like you, I believe in the strength of the people. It is from you, amongst others, that I have absorbed this belief. And like you, I know that the chief source of this strength is humane, progressive, working people brought up on the ideas of Marx, Engels and August Bebel.[114] But where's this strength now? Where is it in today's Germany, in the country's everyday life? Where is it to be found – with hordes of Germans laying waste to our country, burning our towns, fields and villages?'

'Viktor Pavlovich,' said Chepyzhin reproachfully, 'everyday life and scientific theory should never part company. Practice and theory can't exist separately. What we have been talking about relates not only to the war but also to the work you and I do today. Physical science has, in a sense, progressed very little. The first era, which lasted 100,000 years, was concerned only with changing the shape and position of matter; primitive man threw sticks or used a length of sinew to tie a lump of ore to a cudgel. He didn't alter the chemistry of matter; he didn't infringe on the integrity of its molecules. During the second era, which lasted another 100,000 years, man worked on the outer ring of electrons. This era began with the first bonfire, with the chemistry of wine and vinegar, with the extraction of metals from their ore in simple furnaces, and it ends with achievements like the separation of nitrogen from air and the synthesis of paint and rubber. Now we are on the verge of a third era – the era of breaking into the atomic nucleus. A new technology is being created. Soon, our existing technology will appear as primitive as a flint attached to a stick in comparison with today's steam and mercury turbines.

'In the course of hundreds of thousands of years we have moved from physics to chemistry and then back again to physics – the physics of the nucleus instead of the physics of stone. During this time we have progressed a tiny fraction of a millimicron. And so it may appear that science does not acknowledge our everyday world, our world full of labour, grief, blood, slavery and violence. It may seem as if science is only a matter of abstract reason, penetrating from the outer ring of electrons to the nucleus, while the entire bitter world of human existence comes and goes like smoke, disappearing without a trace. Well, if that's what a scientist thinks, then his science is worthless. Nothing he does is worth even a kopek. Science is on the verge of discovering enormous sources of energy. It is the working people who must control these sources – in the hands of fascism their destructive force could turn the whole world to ashes. We cannot understand the reality of today unless we look ahead, unless we try to predict what tomorrow will bring. War is war – but we need to understand how wrong it is to see the temporary triumph of fascist villainy as the destruction, once and for all, of the German people and the inauguration of an eternal kingdom of Hitlerian darkness.'

Tracing a large circle in the air with one hand, Chepyzhin went on slowly and solemnly, 'No matter what is done to destroy it, energy is eternal. The energy of the sun, radiating out into space, passes through deserts of darkness to come to life again in the leaves of a poplar or the living sap of a birch tree. It lies hidden in a lump of coal, in the intra-molecular tension of crystals. It is the leaven of life ... And the spiritual energy of a people is no different. It too may lie hidden and dormant, but it cannot be destroyed. After a period of lying hidden it gathers again and again into massive clumps, radiating light and heat, giving meaning to human life. And do you know? One of the proofs of the indestructibility of this spiritual energy is the fact that even the most evil of fascist leaders feel obliged to pose as the champions of justice and the greater good. They commit their greatest crimes in secret. They know from experience that evil does not only engender evil; they know that, although it may sometimes suppress what is good, evil can also call good into being. These leaders don't have the power openly to pro-claim their central, amoral principle – that the freedom of a favoured person, race or state is to be achieved through the bloody negation of the freedom of other persons, races or states. They have the power to confuse people, to deceive and intoxicate them for a while, but they cannot refashion the soul of the people. They cannot alter the people's fundamental convictions.'

With a little smile, Viktor said, 'So, Dmitry Petrovich, are you telling me that without darkness we cannot perceive light? That the eternal struggle to assert good is inconceivable without the eternal existence of evil? Is that what you're saying?'

Remembering his conversation with Krymov just before the war, Viktor went on, 'Dmitry Petrovich, here too I disagree: the study of social relations requires the same degree of scientific rigour as the study of the natural world. You know you can't bring your own subjective ideas into the laws of thermodynamics. In physics you have always been a defender of the laws of causality, of objective principles. But if I accept the theory you have just outlined, I become, willy-nilly, not an optimist but a pessimist. Your talk of unholy mixtures, of cellars and basements, denies any possibility of progress, of forward movement. I understand, of course: you think that this theory of yours limits fascism's ability to change the social structure, to cripple humanity. But see what happens if you apply your theory not to fascism, which will rot away of itself, but to progressive phenomena, to revolutions that bring liberation. You will see that your theory promises only stagnation. According to your theory, revolutionary struggle cannot change society. It cannot raise human beings to a higher level – all it can do is reorder the various elements that make up a given society. But that is not the way it is. During the years of Soviet power the country, the economy, our society as a whole, and individual people have changed a great deal. Whatever anyone does now, we can never return to where we were before. But you, Dmitry Petrovich, seem to think of society as something more like a keyboard. One person plays one kind of music, another person plays some other kind – but the keyboard itself remains unchanged. I share your optimism. I share your faith in mankind, in our victory over fascism. But we need to do more, when we have defeated fascism, than just blindly return German society to the way it was before the war. We need to change German society, to restore health to the soil that has given birth to wars, to atrocities, and now to the nightmares of Hitlerism.'

'Well, that's certainly put me in my place,' said Chepyzhin. 'But who first taught you to argue like that? I must have done a good job!'

'Dmitry Petrovich,' said Viktor, 'please forgive me for being passionate. But you know better than me that physicists love you not only because you are an authority but also because you never use your authority to silence others. The joy of working with you lies in the possibility of escaping from dogmatism into the realm of living, impassioned discussion. When I glimpsed you in the institute corridor, I felt real joy – because I love you and because you are someone I can talk to about what truly matters. But I knew that you wouldn't be coming to me bearing tablets of stone. I knew that you and I agree on the main things, but I also knew that I might end up arguing with you – and that there is no one I argue with as passionately as I do with you, my teacher, my friend.'

'Very good,' said Chepyzhin. 'So be it. We've argued, and we shall argue again. What you've just said is serious, and serious matters demand serious thought.'

Chepyzhin took Viktor by the arm. Stirred and excited by their conversation, they set off, taking long fast strides.

43

Nikolay Krymov, now the commissar of an anti-tank brigade, had gone several nights without sleeping. Immediately after being in combat, the brigade had been ordered to move along the front to a sector where German tanks had once again broken through.

Barely had the brigade taken up position when it came under attack. This time they were in combat for four hours. The German tanks then continued their advance in a different direction.

Ordered to retreat to the Great Bend of the Don, the brigade came under attack yet again. It was forced to fight in unfavourable conditions.

They suffered heavy losses. The army commander ordered the brigade to cross the Don, repair their tanks away from the combat zone, get their vehicles and equipment in order and prepare to defend another area now seen as vulnerable to attack. He made it clear that this period of rest would be short, forty-eight hours at most, but not even twenty-four hours had passed before the brigade was ordered to advance forthwith. After effecting a breakthrough along back roads, enemy tanks were moving rapidly north-east.

This was in mid-July 1942, perhaps the most searing, difficult days of this difficult period of the war.

The orderly to the brigade chief of staff went into the bright, spacious house of the chairman of the village soviet, where Krymov was billeted. He found Krymov asleep on a wide bed, a sheet of newspaper over his face to keep off the sun.

The newspaper was rising and falling with Krymov's breathing. The orderly glanced at it hesitantly and read a few lines from a Sovinform Bureau bulletin, 'After fierce fighting around Kantemirovka ...'

An elderly woman, the mistress of the house, said quietly, 'No, don't wake him – he's only just gone to sleep.'

The orderly shook his head sorrowfully and said in a plaintive whisper, 'Comrade Commissar, comrade Commissar, you're wanted at HQ.'

The orderly expected Krymov to grunt and groan, to tell him to go away. He thought it would take a long time to rouse him. But the moment the orderly touched his shoulder, Krymov sat up, pushed the newspaper aside, looked around with his inflamed, bloodshot eyes, and began to pull on his boots.

At Brigade HQ, Krymov learned that they had been ordered to cross the Don yet again and take up defensive positions on the west bank. The brigade commander had already set off for the artillery, now located in a neighbouring village. He had telephoned to say that he would cross the river with the artillery and then go on to Army HQ to learn about any recent developments. Lieutenant Sarkisyan's mortar unit had already received their instructions and was to advance in three hours. Brigade HQ would follow.

'Well, comrade Commissar, so much for our two days on the east bank,' said the chief of staff. Seeing Krymov's bloodshot eyes, he added, 'Maybe you should rest a little longer. The lieutenant colonel and I have already had a few hours' sleep, but you've been up and about all night with the units.'

'No,' said Krymov. 'I'll go on ahead and see how the ground lies. Give me the route – we can meet up later.'

An hour later, after checking that the units were ready for action, Krymov said to the orderly, 'Tell my driver to call at my billet, collect my things and then pick me up from HQ.'

The chief of staff said sadly, 'And there was I thinking we could all go to the bathhouse this evening and then have a drink together. Seems the Germans can't do without us for even twenty-four hours!'

Krymov looked at the chief of staff's round, good-natured face.

'All the same, Major, you haven't got any thinner these last few days.'

'That really would be too much – getting thin because of the Germans!'

Krymov smiled. 'Yes, you're right. And maybe you've even put on a little weight.'

'Not a gram,' said the chief of staff. 'My weight hasn't changed since 1936.' A map was lying open on the table and he pushed it towards Krymov. 'See our new line of defence? Almost ninety kilometres east of where we were fighting yesterday. The Germans are moving fast. I may not be losing weight, but my thoughts keep gnawing away at me: when are we going to stop them? Where are our reserves? Our brigade is worn thin – people and equipment alike.'

The orderly came in to report that Krymov's car was waiting outside.

'See you this evening. In an hour or so I'll be getting ready to leave too,' said the chief of staff. He went out to the car with Krymov, map in hand. When Krymov had got in, he added, 'But I'd advise you to avoid the main crossing – the Germans are bombing it day and night. You'd do better to cross here, on this pontoon bridge. That's the way I'll be taking our HQ equipment.'

'All right, let's get going,' said Krymov.

The air, the sky, the houses surrounded by trees – here in this Cossack village everything seemed calm and peaceful. But once they were back on the main road, this peace was eclipsed by the dust and noise of a major military artery.

Krymov lit a cigarette and passed his cigarette case over to Semyonov, his driver. Not taking his eyes off the road, Semyonov took a cigarette with his right hand, just as he had hundreds of times before, day and night, west and east of the Dnieper, west and east of the Donets, and now west and east of the Don.

Krymov barely noticed the front-line road, which somehow always looked much the same, whether it was near Oryol or whether it was in Ukraine, beyond the Donets. He was thinking about the battles ahead, wondering what orders they would receive next.

44

They were nearing the Don.

'We'd have done better to wait till night, comrade Commissar,' said the driver. 'There's nowhere to shelter, only open steppe – and the Messers like going for cars. They get a reward for every car they destroy.'

'The war's got its own ideas, comrade Semyonov. It's not going to just stop and wait for us.'

Semyonov opened the door a little, leaned out so he could look behind him and said, 'That's all we need. A flat tyre. That certainly isn't going to stop and wait.' He began to slow down, leaving the road and heading for the shelter of some dusty trees.

'Don't worry,' said Krymov. 'Better here than at the crossing.'

Semyonov glanced at a shallow trench someone had dug and smiled. 'Our drivers are never at a loss,' he said. 'They'll always find a way out. I know one whose condenser broke. And he'd lost his spare. So, till he got back to the repair shop, he made do with frogs. He caught a whole bunch of them. Each frog lasted him five kilometres. And I've heard someone else did the same with field mice.' And he burst into laughter. 'Yes, there's no defeating a Russian driver!'

The trees they had stopped by were still young, but their leaves looked aged. They were grey with dust. And they were close to an important fork in the road – during the last weeks these trees had clearly seen a great deal.

There were columns of vehicles and caravans of horses and carts heading east. There were wounded marching along in dust-covered bandages; some had hung their belts around their necks, using them as slings for their bandaged arms. Some could walk only with the help of a stick; others carried a mug or an empty tin. No one on this road needed even the most precious of personal possessions. All anyone needed was bread, a mug of water, and tobacco and matches; everything else, even a pair of new box-calf boots, was useless.

There were men who'd been wounded in the arm, and in the head. There were a few who'd been wounded in the neck. A still smaller number had been wounded in the chest; their white bandages stood out beneath their unbuttoned tunics, which were spattered with black, congealed blood.

Those wounded in the belly, groin, thigh, knee, calf and foot were out of sight – being transported in open-sided trucks with a plywood roof. To an onlooker it seemed as if men got wounded only in the head, hands and arms.

From time to time – though not often – the wounded would glance from side to side, checking if there was anywhere they could fill their water mug without going far from the road. Everyone was silent, not saying even a word either to those they overtook or to those who over-took them. Their own pain and their worries about their own wounds isolated them from the pain of those around them.

Not far from the road, defences were being constructed. Beneath the wide steppe sky women in white kerchiefs were digging trenches and building small pillboxes, looking up now and again in case 'those vermin' were on the wing. The Don steppe was studded with fortifica-tions, though not one of them was being defended.

The soldiers walking east glanced at the anti-tank ditches, at the barbed wire, at the trenches, dugouts and gun emplacements – and walked on.

HQs of all kinds were also heading east; they were easy to distin-guish. In the backs of trucks, amid tables, mattresses and black type-writer cases sat dust-coated clerks and sad-looking young girls in side caps, holding kerosene lamps and files of documents and gazing up at the sky.

There were mobile repair units, huge aerodrome support trucks and supply trucks carrying everything from uniforms to plates and cutlery. There were walkie-talkie sets and portable engines; there were refuel-ling trucks; there were three-tonners carrying bombs in wooden crates. A tractor was towing a trailer with a fighter aircraft that had been shot down. The plane's wings were twitching – the tractor could have been an industrious black beetle dragging along a half-dead dragonfly.

Artillery too was heading east. Soldiers sat astride their guns, hug-ging the dust-covered green barrels as they rumbled over potholes. Tractors were pulling trailers with large metal barrels.

Foot soldiers were heading east. No one that day was heading west.

Krymov looked around him. He had seen this eastward flow of life all too often: near Kiev, Priluki and Shtepovka, near Balakleya, Valuiki and Rossosh.

It seemed that this steppe would never know peace again.

226

'But the day will come,' Krymov said to himself, 'when the dust raised by the war will fall to the ground, when silence will return, when these fires will be extinguished and their ash will settle, when the smoke clears and this whole world of war – its smoke, flames, tears and thunder – becomes history.'

The previous winter, in a hut not far from Korocha, his orderly Rogov had said with surprise, 'Look, comrade Commissar, the walls are papered with newspapers from before the war!'

Krymov had laughed and replied, 'Yes indeed – and soon they'll be papering the walls with today's newspapers. We'll come back when the war's over, and you, Rogov, will say, "Look, Commissar – wartime newspapers, bulletins from the Sovinform Bureau!"'

Rogov had shaken his head sceptically, and he had been right: he had been killed in an air raid. He had not lived to see peace. Nevertheless, all this would pass; people would reminisce about these years and writers would write books about this great war.

Krymov looked at the wounded who had fallen by the wayside, at their grim, tormented faces, and wondered if these men would ever enter the pages of books. This was not a sight for those who wanted to clothe the war in fine robes. He remembered a night-time conversation with an elderly soldier whose face he had been unable to see. They had been lying in a gully, with only a greatcoat to cover them. The writers of future books had better avoid listening to conversations like that. It was all very well for Tolstoy – he wrote his great and splendid book decades after 1812, when the pain felt in every heart had faded and only what was wise and bright was remembered.

Semyonov put away the jack, the spanner and a black inner tube with red patches; he had a space for them under his dusty seat. Then he listened to the peals of thunder; rather than coming down from above, they were climbing upwards – from a storm-gripped earth into a cloudless sky.

He looked at the quiet, grizzled trees with regret; he had already come to feel at home in this place, where for twenty long minutes nothing bad had happened to him. 'Fritz is pounding away at the crossing,' he said. 'We'd do better to wait till things quieten down.' Knowing only too well what Krymov would reply, he started the engine.

The general sense of danger was intensifying.

'Comrade Commissar,' he said, 'there are burning vehicles on the bridge.' Pointing up at the sky, he began counting the German planes: 'One, two, three!'

227

The water was glittering in the sunlight – and this glitter was like the vicious grey gleam of a knife. Cars and trucks that had just crossed over were skidding on the slippery sand of the east bank. Men were pushing them on – with their arms, with their shoulders, with their chests – putting all their will to live into helping the vehicles on their way. The drivers kept changing gear, staring fixedly, listening intently to the sound of their engines: would they, or wouldn't they, reach the top of the slope? To stall, to get stuck in a spot like this, would mean to squander the lucky chance they had just wrested from fate.

Sappers were laying green branches and boards under the vehicles' wheels. When a truck reached the top of the slope and got out onto the road, the sappers' dark faces brightened – as if they too were now free to drive away from this bridge. A moment later, though, they would be laying boards and branches under the wheels of the next vehicle.

Once on the road, the trucks quickly picked up speed. The more agile passengers clung to the trucks' sides and, legs dangling, hoisted themselves up and tumbled into the truck's bodies. Other passengers just kept running, lurching across the sand in their heavy boots and shouting, 'Keep going! Keep going!' – as if they truly believed the driver might suddenly brake for them.

Later, when their truck came to a stop further away, they would climb on board. Out of breath and laughing, they would look back at the river, scatter crumbs of tobacco as they rolled their cigarettes, and call out, 'Time to get going again!'

But their exhilaration soon dissipated; the longed-for east bank had nothing to offer but the same steppe and the same gloomy faces. There were wrecked cars and trucks. Amid dusty feathergrass shone the pale blue wing of another downed plane.

Krymov told Semyonov to stop, then walked slowly along to the bridge. He stumbled; the steppe grass, coarse and thick as rope, was catching at his feet. He made no attempt to walk faster. He didn't look up, nor did he look to either side – only down at the dust-covered toes of his boots.

There was the crack of an anti-aircraft gun and, high in the sky, the quiet sound of a German plane. And all of a sudden, unbelievably loud, unbelievably piercing – the ear-splitting screech of a Stuka gone into a dive. And then three terrible groans – like three huge axe-blows – that seemed to come from deep in the earth.

There was a pitiful cry – maybe a man, maybe a woman. The ack-ack gun started up again, like a small guard dog intrepidly trying to bite the ankles of thugs too intent on their business to notice it.

Krymov walked on, still looking at the grey dust and the grey leather of his boots, now being burnt by the hot sand.

Krymov's face took on a look of cool disdain. This disdain was directed at the Germans bombing the crossing, at the panicking Red Army soldiers and commanders, and, still more, at the life instinct itself, which he could feel raging within him. This instinct was crying out, 'Look round! Run! Throw yourself down on the ground! Hide your head in the sand!'

But Krymov knew that there is a force still more obstinate than the life instinct. He carried on walking towards the crossing, not looking round, not quickening his step, putting his faith in this cruel force of reason.

Time and again he had stayed on his feet when everything within him was crying out, 'Lie down!' Time and again he had walked forward when this instinct for life was furiously urging him to run back. What was astonishing – and he was thinking about this as he walked towards the bridge – was that this life instinct never admitted defeat. Stubbornly and methodically, it went on trying to make Krymov turn back when he was walking forward or drop to the ground when he was standing upright. It was possible, it seemed, to suppress this instinct but not to defeat it. It was invincible and importunate. It was both senseless and wise. It was as irritating as a mother's insistent admonitions; it was as sweet as these same admonitions, born of a love that has nothing to do with reason.

Swift black smoke and slow yellow dust covered the carts, trucks and crowds of people on the west bank. The bridge suddenly emptied. Then a hunched-over man without a side cap ran across it. There was no colour in his face and he was using both hands to keep his guts in place, pressing his shredded tunic against his body. His fading consciousness was driven by a single desire – to reach the east bank. He was almost dead, but he kept going – so powerful was his will to flee. He reached the bank, then collapsed. As he fell, others got to their feet. They ran straight past him.

As Krymov reached the bridge, a puny-looking young lieutenant with a red band on his sleeve ran up to the cars and trucks, pistol in hand, and shouted, 'Attention! Keep back! No one to drive onto the bridge till I give the order!' It was clear from the lieutenant's voice that this was not his first day on the bridge and that he had already yelled these words many times.

Not bothering to shake the dust and sand from their clothes, the drivers climbed out of the trenches where they had taken shelter, returned to their vehicles and hurriedly started their engines. The vehicles shuddered but did not move forward.

The drivers were all keeping an eye on the bridge commandant, who did indeed look capable of using his pistol. They also kept an eye on the sky, in case the planes returned. The moment they were sure the commandant was looking away, they would nudge their vehicles a little closer to the bridge – the wooden planks laid across the river had a hypnotic power.

It was like some children's game. Each time a vehicle moved even half a metre forward, the vehicle behind would at once do the same. And then a third, and a fourth, and a fifth. Had the first driver wished to move back, he would have found it impossible.

'Back!' yelled the enraged commandant. 'Get back – or no one's going past!' To prove he meant what he said, he raised his pistol in the air.

Krymov got up onto the bridge. After the difficult sand, it was a relief to be walking on planks. The river's moist freshness reached up to touch his face.

Krymov walked slowly on. The soldiers hurrying in the opposite direction slowed their pace, straightened their tunics and saluted. A proper salute, at a moment like this, was not without meaning – and Krymov understood this. Two days earlier, on this same bridge, he had seen a general open his car door and shout into a crowd of soldiers marching in the same direction, 'Where d'you think you're going? Make way! Make way!'

And an elderly soldier, forced by the wing of the general's car to the very edge of the bridge, said with only the slightest hint of reproach, 'Where d'you think we're going? We're going the same way as you are. We want to stay alive too.' He spoke in the most genial of tones, like one fleeing peasant to another.

And the general had slammed his door shut, disconcerted by this soldier's straightforwardness.

Here, on this bridge, Krymov at once sensed his own power – the power of a man going slowly and calmly west when everyone else is going east.

Krymov went up to the young commandant, the dictator of the crossing. His face showed the extreme fatigue of a man who understands that any kind of rest is out of the question. No matter what, he must see his task through. Duty was duty, though it would be easier if a bomb put an end to his life there and then.

The commandant gave Krymov a hostile look, ready to say no to all his demands, imagining he already knew what Krymov was about to say: that he was accompanying a seriously wounded colonel, or he had an unusually important document to deliver, or he had an urgent meeting – one that couldn't be put off for even an hour – with the Front commander, the colonel general himself.

'I'm going west,' said Krymov, pointing to where he wanted to go. 'Can you let me across?'

The commandant put his pistol back in its holster and said, 'West? All right – just a moment.'

A minute later, two controllers waving small flags were clearing the way for Krymov's car. Truck drivers, leaning out of their cabs, were saying to one another, 'Just go back a little – then I can reverse too. There's a commander here. He needs to get to the front quick.'

Seeing how swiftly the jammed-together vehicles somehow made way, Krymov thought about the strength of the desire to regain the offensive – how this desire was still alive in the retreating army. For the time being, though, it was apparent only in small things, in the readiness with which the drivers, the two traffic controllers and this exhausted young lieutenant, half-crazed from the general din and his own endless shouting, had cleared the way for a solitary light vehicle heading towards the front line.

Krymov went back onto the bridge, waved one hand in the air and shouted, 'Semyo-o-onov!'

Just then they heard a shout: 'Air alert!' Several other voices followed suit, 'There, up there! Back again! And coming straight for us!'

Hundreds of men rushed away from their vehicles – into the bushes, into the steppe, along the bank, into pits and ditches they'd made a mental note of beforehand.

Krymov didn't so much as turn his head. He just yelled angrily, 'This wa-a-ay!'

He knew that Semyonov must also be wanting to flee. But he could see a small cloud of dust behind his car. Semyonov, probably cursing his boss, was driving towards the bridge.

By now everyone else was running. They were no longer soldiers – only a panicking crowd. More clearly than ever before, Krymov – alone on an empty bridge – understood the law that made a human mass either disintegrate into a mere crowd or take shape as a collective, as a true army. In this crowd on the bank of the Don everyone was thinking only of himself; everyone was driven only by the instinct for self-preservation. The size of the crowd only made this instinct all the more powerful, all the more overwhelming. Krymov's task, as a commissar, was to waken other, higher feelings in these men, to help them to understand that they were part of a whole, of a nation.[115]

But this was not a duty he could fulfil at this moment.

'Semyo-o-onov!' he shouted, stamping his foot. 'Quick!'

Standing on the flat pontoons, their chests against the surface of this floating bridge, were two soldiers. Pontoon duty was considered particularly dangerous – even by the sappers and traffic controllers. More shells and splinters came the pontooners' way than anyone else's. And a thin-sided pontoon in the middle of a river was no protection against anything.

Watching the constant flow of fleeing troops had left these two men with a poor opinion of the human race. Resigned to their impending death, they looked on everything in the world with a mocking indifference. This mockery was their last consolation; they had seen people at a time of terrible weakness and they did not share Maxim Gorky's belief that the word 'mankind' has a proud ring.[116]

When there was a particularly pathetic look on the face of someone running or driving past, one would simply say, 'Did you see?'

Certainty of their own death had made them careless about many things. Their faces were covered in stubble. They did not even bother to use each other's names.

Hearing Krymov call out to Semyonov, one had said to the other, 'A real flighter!'

This, evidently, was their word not only for everyone driving about in a car but also for everyone still hoping to survive the war and enjoy life afterwards.

In a matter-of-fact tone, his companion agreed: 'Yes, flighting to live!'

Krymov heard all this. When his car reached the bridge, instead of simply jumping in as Semyonov slowed down, he stood in the middle of the road and raised one hand. The car skidded and stopped at an angle. Krymov then went slowly up to the pontooners, squatted down, took out his cigarette case and held it out to them with the words, 'Hang on a moment and I'll give you a light.'

Krymov could feel his heart beat faster. Stopping on an empty bridge while dive-bombers approached was, of course, an act of senseless bravado.

And then came an angry voice, carrying over the water. A stocky young peasant woman, standing in a cart with a group of other refugees, was waving her fist in the air and shouting, 'Cowards! You fucking crowd of cowards! They're cranes, just a few cranes!'

To Krymov, her thin, furious face seemed to be the face of his country.

And the men cowering in the pits and ditches now saw a triangle of birds, high in the blue sky, flying calmly towards the river. One bird slowly flapped its wings, then a second, and a third – and they glided smoothly on.

'It's the wrong month,' said the commandant, looking up at the sky with childlike curiosity. 'Those cranes shouldn't be relocating now. Don't say they've been displaced by the war too!'

Krymov walked on beside his car, picking his way between the carts and trucks. Back on the road, in the steppe, among the reeds by the river, everyone was laughing in embarrassment. They were laughing at one another; they were laughing about the woman who had sworn at them from her cart; and they were laughing at the thought of refugee cranes.

A few minutes later, when they had driven about a kilometre and a half from the river, Semyonov touched Krymov on the arm and pointed upwards. There were a number of black spots in the sky. This time it was a squadron of dive-bombers, making for the bridge.

45

Evening was already drawing in. The steppe sunsets that summer were especially splendid. The dust raised by countless explosions – and by millions of feet, wheels and tank treads – hung high in the upper air, suspended in the crystalline strata bordering the cold of cosmic space.

Refracted by this fine dust, the evening light took on a whole range of colours before reaching the earth. The steppe is immense, like the sky and the sea. And like the sky and the sea, so the hard, dry steppe – grey-blue or yellowy-grey during the day – takes on many different colours at sunset. Like the sea, it can turn from pink to deep blue, and then violet-black.

And the steppe gives off wonderful scents; fragrant oils in the sap of herbs, flowers and bushes, vaporized by the summer sun, cling to the gradually cooling earth and move through the air in slow distinct streams.

The warm earth gives off a smell of wormwood or of still-damp hay. Going down into a hollow, you meet the heavy scent of honey. From some deep ravine comes first the smell of young herbs and grasses, then of dry, dusty, sun-baked straw, and then, all of a sudden, something neither grass, nor smoke, nor wormwood, nor watermelon, nor the bitter leaves of the wild steppe-cherry but what must be the very flesh of the earth: a mysterious breath, in which you sense, all at once, the lightness of the earth's dust, the heaviness of the layers of stone fixed in the lower darkness and the piercing cold of deep underground springs and rivers.

Not only is the evening steppe full of smells and colours; it also sings. The steppe's sounds cannot be perceived separately. Barely touching the ear, they go straight to the heart, bringing not only calm and peace but also sorrow and a sense of alarm.

The tired, indecisive creak of crickets, as if asking whether or not it is worth making sound of an evening; the calls of the grey steppe partridges just before dark; a distant squeak of wheels; the whispering of grass as it quietens down for the night, rocked by a cool breeze; the constant hurrying of field mice and ground squirrels; the scraping sound of beetles' hard wings. And then, alongside these peaceful signs of the day's retreating life: the brigand-like cries of owls; the sombre hum of night hawk moths; the rustle of yellow-bellied sand boas; the sounds of predators emerging from burrows, holes and gullies, from crevices in the dry earth. And over the steppe rises the evening sky, and the earth is reflected in it; or maybe it is the sky that is reflected in the earth, or maybe earth and sky are two huge mirrors, each enriching the other with the miracle of the struggle between light and dark.

In the sky, at a terrible height, in the indifferent astronomical silence, without smoke, without the constant din of explosions, fires light up one after another. First it is only the very edge of one calm grey cloud – but a minute later this entire high cloud is ablaze, like a multistorey building, all red brick and dazzling glass. Then more and more clouds catch fire. Huge or small, cumulus or flat as a slab of slate – all catch fire alike; they crumble, collapse, fall on top of one another.

Nature is eloquent. Moist earth, covered in tiny shoots of young aspen and splinters from recent felling; a bog, overgrown with sharp-leaved sedge that cuts your fingers; small woods and glades on the edges of cities, threaded by roads and paths that have gone bald from the many feet passing over them; a small river losing its way amid marshy tussocks; the sun, peeping out from behind clouds to look at a freshly harvested field; misty, snow-covered mountains, more than five days' walk away – all this speaks about friendship and loneliness, about fate, about happiness and sadness …

Wanting to save time, Krymov told Semyonov to take a shortcut, turning off the main road onto a barely visible track, overgrown with grass, that looked as if it ran from north to south and so would cross all the roads running west from the Don.

Squat stems of grey-blue feathergrass and silvery wormwood beat against the sides of the car, brushing away the dust and releasing small clouds of pollen. Krymov had hoped to save time, but this track merely passed the far side of a small hollow and then rejoined the main road – the road being taken by everyone now retreating from Chuguev, Bala-kleya, Valuiki and Rossosh. Other roads and tracks, from all the nearby towns and Cossack villages, also kept joining this road.

'We'll never get through here,' Semyonov pronounced authorita-tively – and braked.

'Keep going,' said Krymov. 'Soon we'll be able to turn off.'

Also making their slow way through the steppe were long herds of exhausted, stumbling cows, shaking their heavy heads, and flocks of sheep that had fused into a single grey mass, a living, flowing stain of grey.

Both on and off the road were people on foot, carrying green ply-wood suitcases and bundles and sacks of every kind; on their faces was a look of calm, habitual fatigue. There were slow, creaking trains of farm carts, carrying refugees in makeshift cabins covered by plywood, by bright-coloured Ukrainian sackcloth or by sheets of tin, painted red or green, from the roofs of houses.

Within these cabins could be seen biblical beards, children's heads of hair – pale blonde, gold and black – and women's faces, seemingly stone-calm. Old men, women and girls, children – all appeared still and silent. They had lost homes and loved ones; they had lost everything they owned. They had known heat, thirst and hunger. They were covered in dust that penetrated their bread, their clothes, their hair and each cell of their body, that grated against their teeth and scratched their reddened eyes. Their ordeals had taken away all hope of anything good but left them afraid of something still worse. They were dissolving in the vastness of this slow movement amid yellowish clouds of dust, across the hot grey-blue steppe. Everything around them was creaking, grinding and humming; it was impossible for anyone to step away from the general flow, to make a fire, take a rest or wash in some stream or pool. People still sensed the cart in front of them, the oxen's heavy breathing and the pressure of those walking behind them, but they sensed even their own selves only as particles of a single mass moving slowly and laboriously eastwards.

Those in front raised clouds of dust that settled on those behind. 'How come they kick up so much dust?' asked those behind. 'Why do they always have to keep pushing at us?' asked those in front.

Like migrating birds or animals, the individuals in this slow-moving stream had lost much of what made them individuals. Their world had become simpler, a matter of bread, water, dust, heat and river crossings. Even their sense of self-preservation and their fear of being bombed had become muted; they were subsumed in a stream now too vast to be blocked or erased.

Krymov's heart clenched tight with pain.

Fascism wanted to subordinate all human life to rules similar in their soulless, senseless and cruel uniformity to those that govern dead, inanimate nature, the laying down of sediments on the seabed or the erosion of mountain ranges. Fascism wanted to enslave the mind, soul, labour, will and acts of mineralized human beings. Fascism wanted its

236

slaves, deprived of freedom and happiness, to be both cruel and obedient; it wanted their cruelty to be like that of a brick falling off a roof onto a child's head.

Krymov felt his heart take in the whole of this vast picture. The sunset of ancient Egypt and ancient Greece, Oswald Spengler's *Decline of the West*[117] – these were nothing compared with the tragedy now threatening humanity's most sacred dream. The struggle to realize this dream had occasioned incalculable suffering; its victorious embodiment held out the promise of happiness.

Soon the twilight thickened, as if cold grey-black ash were falling onto the earth. Only in the west did the long white summer lightning of artillery salvoes stubbornly continue to disturb the gloom, while high in the sky shone a few stars, as white as if cut from the bark of a young silver birch.

46

Krymov and Semyonov passed a major crossroads and continued on their way west.

They climbed a small hill.

'Comrade Commissar, look, vehicles are heading this way from the main bridge,' Semyonov said excitedly. 'Our brigade must be moving up!'

'No,' Krymov replied. 'That can't be our brigade.' He ordered Semyonov to stop and they got out of the car. There was a good view from the top of the hill.

The setting sun looked out for a moment from behind the dark blue and red clouds massing in the west. Rays of light fanned out onto the evening earth.

A stream of vehicles was heading west from the bridge, moving swiftly across the plain.

Hauled by powerful three-axle trucks, the long-barrelled guns seemed to be creeping across the earth. They were followed by trucks carrying white cases of shells and vehicles armed with quadruple-mounted anti-aircraft guns.

Swirling over the bridge was a wall of dust.

'Our reserves are moving up to the front line, comrade Commissar,' said Semyonov. 'The steppe to the east looks as if it's covered in smoke.'

That night, Krymov's brigade took up its line of defence.

Krymov spoke to the brigade commander, Lieutenant Colonel Gorelik. Gorelik, rubbing his hands together and shivering from the night cold and damp, told Krymov why the brigade had been brought up again so soon, without being given time to rest and refit.

The Supreme Command had ordered two armies – complemented with tanks, heavy artillery and several of the new anti-tank regiments – to be brought forward from the reserves. The brigade's mission was to cover the infantry units' flank as they advanced; there was a point where they were vulnerable to attack by enemy tanks.

'It was as if they'd all just sprung up out of the earth,' said Gorelik. 'I took a different road from you, I was on the road from Kalach. At times there were eight columns of vehicles moving side by side. The

238

infantry had to keep to the steppe. Strong young men. New equipment – sub-machine guns, anti-tank rifles aplenty. Fully equipped new units. I also saw a whole tank brigade.' Gorelik thought for a moment and added, 'So you didn't get any sleep?'

'No, there wasn't much time for that.'

'Well, never mind. The army deputy commander said to me, "Soon we'll be ordering your brigade back to Stalingrad to regroup and refit." We'll get some sleep then. But back at Army HQ the gunners were making fun of me. "You lot are out of date," they kept saying. "Nowadays everyone's pinning their hopes on these new anti-tank regiments!"'

'So, it's true there's going to be a new Front?' asked Krymov. 'A Stalingrad Front?'

'Yes, but who cares what it's called? What matters is how well we fight.'

The noise of vehicles, the distant roar of tank engines went on until dawn. The reserve units were deploying, taking up their positions the length of the front. Bringing life to the cold steppe night, new forces were preparing to defend the approaches to the Don.

By morning, Brigade HQ had re-established communications with Division HQ, which had also taken up its new position in the steppe; and Division HQ was in contact with Army HQ.

Krymov was called to the phone to speak to the member of the army military soviet. The duty officer handed Krymov the receiver and said, 'Please wait – don't hang up. He's taking an urgent call on another line.'

Krymov held the receiver to his ear for a long time. He loved listening, down the long lines of field telephones, to the sleepless life of the front. Girl telephonists called out to one another; their bosses shouted and blustered. Someone said, 'Forward, forward! I've already said – there are to be no halts or rests till you've reached your position.' A voice, clearly a novice doing his best to observe the requirements of secrecy, asked, 'Well, have you received the boxes? Are you well supplied with water and cucumber now?' A deep voice reported, 'I've taken up position on my assigned sector.' A fourth pronounced very distinctly, 'Comrade Utvenko, allow me to report that the artillery is now all in position.' A fifth asked sternly, 'What's up with you? Been asleep, or what? Are my orders clear now? Then get going!' A hoarse voice said, 'Luba, Luba, you promised to connect me to fuel supply HQ! You gave me your word! What do you mean – *it wasn't you*? I may never have seen your face, but I know your voice all right. I'd recognize it among a thousand.' An Air Force commander was saying, 'Air Support HQ, Air Support HQ – 200-kilo bombs now received. Our bombers now overhead. Request permission to attack at six-zero-zero.' 'Map in front of you?' asked an infantry commander, speaking extremely fast. 'The enemy's exact position? Specify your reconnaissance data.'

Kostyukov, the brigade chief of staff, then asked, 'Why are you smiling like that, comrade Commissar?'

Putting one hand over the receiver, Krymov replied, 'Everyone's talking about bombs and tanks, asking about the enemy's precise position – and suddenly I hear a crying baby. It must have been asleep in one of the huts with a telephone. And now it's hungry.'

'No getting away from nature,' said the duty officer.

Then the member of the military soviet came on the line. He asked a few questions to which Krymov gave brief replies: 'The brigade is fully supplied with fuel and ammunition. No, the enemy has not been sighted on this sector.'

Then he asked if the brigade had any other needs. Krymov said that vehicles on the way to the front had been delayed more than once by punctures. The member replied that he would order a truckload of new tyres to be delivered immediately to the support services dump in Stalingrad.

After he had put the phone down, Krymov said to Kostyukov, 'There we were, only yesterday morning, wondering if we'd get any reinforcements. And now a whole new Front has come into being – there hasn't been a moment's quiet all night.'

'Yes,' said Kostyukov. 'It's impressive.'

As the sun rose, Krymov and Gorelik drove off to inspect the gun emplacements.

Camouflaged by bunches of dust-covered feathergrass, the gun barrels were all pointing determinedly west. In the dawn sun's slant light, people seemed to be frowning. Cool, clean and fresh, the steppe shone with dew. There was not a speck of dust in the clear air. From horizon to horizon the sky was the calm, pale blue only to be seen early on a summer's morning. There were just a few pink clouds, warmed by the sun.

While Gorelik talked to his battery commanders, Krymov went to have a word with the gunners.

Seeing their commissar approach, the men stood to attention. Their eyes were smiling.

'At ease, stand at ease!' said Krymov, and leaned his elbow on one of the gun barrels. The gunners gathered around him. 'Well, Selidov,' he said to a gun-layer, 'You must have had another night without sleep. Here we are again, back on the front line.'

'Yes, comrade Commissar,' Selidov replied. 'There was no end to the racket. A lot of fresh troops have come up. But we kept thinking the Germans were about to attack. We got through a lot of tobacco – now we've run out.'

'A quiet night – and not a sign of the enemy,' said Krymov. 'And what a splendid morning!'

'First thing in the morning's the best time to be fighting, comrade Commissar!' said a very young gunner. 'When the enemy fires, you can see where they're firing from.'

'True,' said Selidov. 'You can see everything, especially if they fire tracer.'

'So you're ready for battle?' said Krymov.

'You won't see any of us abandoning our guns, comrade Commissar! There was a moment a few days ago when there were German sub-machine-gunners only a few metres away. Our infantry turned tail, but we kept on firing.'

'And a lot of good *that* did us!' said the very young gunner. 'We're still retreating. Any day now we'll be crossing the Volga.'

'It hurts to yield our own soil,' said Krymov. 'But there's a new Front now, the Stalingrad Front. New equipment of every kind, tanks, new anti-tank regiments. No one should have any doubt at all – the Germans will advance no further! More than that, we'll drive them back! And we'll take no prisoners! We've retreated enough. I mean what I say – behind us lies Stalingrad!'

The gunners listened in silence, watching a small brightly coloured bird circling above the barrel of the farthest gun.

The bird appeared about to settle on the sun-warmed steel. But then, suddenly alarmed, it flew away.

'She doesn't like guns,' said Selidov. 'She's flown off to the mortars, to Lieutenant Sarkisyan.'

'Look, look!' someone shouted.

Heading west, spreading across the whole breadth of the sky, were squadrons of Soviet dive-bombers.

Within an hour the morning sun had lost its brilliance. Soldiers with dust- and sweat-covered faces were dragging up shells, reloading their guns and adjusting the aim, pointing the guns' muzzles at German tanks racing towards them in swirls of dust. And far above the dust raised by these tanks, the thunder of terrestrial combat echoed high in the pale blue sky.

47

On 10 July 1942 the 62nd Army – now one of the units constituting the south-eastern part of the Soviet front – was ordered to take up defensive positions in the Great Bend of the Don, to prevent any further German advance to the east.

At the same time the Supreme Command brought forward from the reserves an additional large formation, deploying it on the left flank of the 62nd Army. This created a new line of defence against the German divisions threatening to break through to the Don.

The first shots fired on 17 July marked the beginning of the defensive battle on the far approaches to Stalingrad.

The next few days saw only insignificant clashes between the German vanguard and small Soviet tank or infantry reconnaissance detachments. These minor but still fierce battles – most of them fought by individual companies and battalions – allowed the newly deployed units to test their weapons and to get a sense of the enemy's strength. In the meantime the main forces were working twenty-four hours a day to reinforce their positions.

On 20 July the German forces attacked. Major tank and infantry formations were ordered to advance to the Don, to force a crossing, to cover the short distance from there to the Volga, occupying the area between the two rivers that the German staff officers referred to as 'the bottle's neck' – and to enter Stalingrad by 25 July.

So Hitler ordered.

The German High Command, however, soon grasped that there was no 'vacuum' on the approaches to the Don, only in the strategic imagination of those who thought it a simple matter to capture a major city and who believed they could set a precise date by which this must be done.

The fighting was fierce, with no let-up day or night. The Soviet anti-tank defence proved both strong and mobile. Soviet bombers and ground-attack aircraft carried out powerful strikes against the advancing Germans. Small infantry detachments armed with anti-tank rifles fought tenaciously.

The Soviet defence was active. Their sudden counter-attacks in individual sectors made it difficult for the Germans to deploy their forces.

These three weeks of fighting did not, in the end, halt the Germans, who had concentrated a massive strike force. Nevertheless, these battles slowed the German advance. The Germans suffered considerable losses of both men and equipment. They failed to execute their grand plan; they were unable, in a single operation, to cross the Don, continue their advance and capture Stalingrad.

48

Krymov's life had not been going well when the war began. Zhenya had left him the previous winter and had been living since then with her mother, her elder sister Ludmila or a friend in Leningrad. She wrote letters telling him about her plans, about her work, about her meetings with people they knew. Her tone was calm and friendly, as if she were simply visiting friends or family and would soon be back home.

One day she asked him to send her 2,000 roubles, and he did this gladly. It upset him when she returned the money to him a month later by wire transfer.

Krymov would have found it easier if Zhenya had stopped writing to him altogether. Her letters, which came every seven or eight weeks, were a torment; he waited for them eagerly, but Zhenya's friendly tone only made these letters all the more painful. When she wrote that she had been to the theatre, he was not interested in what she had to say about the play, the stage design or the actors; what he wanted to know was who she had gone with, who had sat next to her, or who had seen her back home. Zhenya, however, did not tell him any of this.

Krymov's work brought him no satisfaction, though he was diligent and always stayed in the office until late at night. He was a department head in a publishing house that specialized in economics and the social sciences; there were many meetings, and there was a lot to read and edit.

Krymov's move to the publishing house meant that his former Comintern colleagues had less reason to visit, or even telephone him; they no longer needed to ask for advice or share their news and concerns. And since Zhenya's departure, still fewer people had been coming to his now rather bleak apartment, with its strong smell of cigarette smoke. On Sundays he would keep looking at the phone – but sometimes the whole day would pass by without it ringing at all. Or if it finally did ring, and he joyfully picked up the receiver, it would turn out to be someone from the office wanting to talk about work, or the translator of some book or other wanting to discuss his manuscript in exhausting detail.

Krymov wrote to his younger brother Semyon in the Urals, suggesting that he should move to Moscow with his wife and daughter; he could give them one of his rooms. Semyon was a metals engineer. For several years after his graduation, he had worked in Moscow but had been unable to find a room anywhere. He had lived first in Pokrovskoye-Streshnevo, then in Veshnyaki and then in Losinka; to get to work on time he had to get up at half past five in the morning.

In the summer, when many Muscovites left for their dachas, Semyon had rented a room in the city and his wife Lusya had enjoyed the delights of a comfortable apartment – gas, electricity and a bathroom. For three months they would have a break from smoking stoves, snow-drifts, wells that froze over in January, and having to walk to the station every morning in the dark.

'Semyon's an unusual kind of aristocrat,' Krymov had joked. 'He winters in the country and spends his summers in the city.'

Semyon and Lusya would sometimes come round. Krymov could see that they imagined he led a life of extraordinary interest and importance. He would ask them to tell him about themselves – and Lusya would smile in embarrassment, look down at the floor and say, 'But we've got nothing to tell you. Our lives are very dull.' And Semyon would add, 'Yes, I just do ordinary engineering work, on the shop floor. But I hear you've been on a long journey, to a congress of Pacific Ocean trade unions.'

In 1936, when Lusya was pregnant, Semyon decided that they should move to Chelyabinsk.[118] From there he wrote regularly to Krymov. He said barely a word about his own work and it was clear that his love and admiration for his elder brother were as strong as ever. Nevertheless, when Krymov suggested he return to Moscow, Semyon replied that this was impossible, and anyway he didn't want to – he was now deputy chief engineer of a huge factory. He invited Krymov to come and stay for a few days, to see his new niece. 'You'll be well looked after,' he wrote. 'We have a house of our own in a pine forest, and Lusya has created a splendid garden.'

Krymov was glad to hear that Semyon was doing so well, but he realized that he and his family were now unlikely ever to return to Moscow. This made him sad. He had dreamed of a kind of family commune, picturing himself, in a few years' time, taking his niece to the zoo every Sunday morning and carrying her about on his shoulders when he got home from work.

A few days after the beginning of the war Krymov wrote to the Party Central Committee, volunteering to join up. He was enlisted as a commissar and posted to the Southwestern Front.

On the day he locked his apartment and, with a green kitbag on his shoulder and a small case in his hand, caught a tram to the Kiev station, he felt a new confidence and peace of mind. His loneliness, he felt, was now locked away in his apartment. He was, at last, liberated from it; the nearer the train got to the front, the calmer he felt. 'This rebel, alas, seeks storms, as if in storm lies peace,' he said to himself. Day and night, the lines written by the young Lermontov kept coming back to him.[119]

Through the carriage window he saw Bryansk freight station, all crumpled metal, splintered stone and lacerated earth – the work of German bombers. Still standing there on the tracks were the fragile black and red skeletons of freight wagons. From loudspeakers over empty platforms he could hear Moscow radio resonantly denying the latest lies put out by the Transozean German news agency.

The train passed through stations Krymov remembered from the Civil War – Tereschenko, Mikhailovsky Hamlet, Krolevets, Konotop ...

The meadows, the oak groves, the pine forests, the fields of wheat and buckwheat, the tall poplars and the white huts that seemed in the twilight like pale, deathly faces – everything both on the earth and in the sky looked sad and anxious.

In Bakhmach the train was bombed; two carriages were destroyed. Locomotives whistled and hooted, their iron voices full of living despair.

On one stretch of track the train stopped twice; flying low overhead was a twin-engine Messerschmitt 110, with a cannon and a heavy machine gun. The passengers ran out into the fields, looked around in confusion, and then returned to their carriages.

They crossed the Dnieper shortly before dawn. The train seemed fearful of the echo sent back by the dark river with its white sandbanks.

In Moscow, Krymov had assumed that the main fighting was taking place around Zhitomir, where in 1920 he had been wounded in a battle with the Poles. At Southwestern Front HQ he learned that the situation was a great deal worse than the newspapers made out or than he or any of his fellow passengers had imagined: the Germans had already almost reached Kiev. They were close to Svyatoshino; in an attempt to break through to Demievka, they had engaged with Rodimtsev's Airborne Brigade. The Soviet rear was threatened by Guderian's tanks, which were moving down from the north-east, towards Gomel – while

Kleist's Army Group was moving up from the south, along the east bank of the Dnieper. Huge pincers looked set to close, isolating the Soviet troops still in Kiev and on the west bank.

The most senior political officer, a divisional commissar, was calm and methodical, with a slow, quiet manner of speech. Krymov was impressed by the straightforwardness with which he emphasized the gravity of the situation, while still showing the confidence expected of a leader. He could, it seemed, have continued calmly signing orders and listening to reports even if his Political Administration had been located in the mouth of an active volcano.

Krymov was ordered to one of the armies on the right flank, to give political information talks to the soldiers. The army's most distant division was, at the time, positioned in the forests and swamps of Belorussia.

First, though, Krymov went to the Front operations section. There he found a group of senior commanders standing around a map. A middle-aged general, with a wrinkled face and glasses, was running his hand over his greying hair and saying languidly, with a slight smile, 'It's only too clear that the German High Command has begun a colossal encirclement, on a historically unprecedented scale.' Pointing to the German positions on the map, he added, 'You can see the horseshoe – and it's a horseshoe that wants to crush us. In the last war, they encircled Samsonov's corps. This time they intend to encircle an entire Front.'

Someone said a few words Krymov was unable to make out. The general shrugged and said. 'The German High Command has a strategy. Russian-style hoping for the best will get us nowhere. We need to do more than that if we're to outmanouevre them.'

Krymov made his way into the next room. An out-of-breath major collided with him in the doorway. 'Is General Vlasov in there?' he asked – and rushed past without waiting for an answer.[120]

*

On the sector of the front Krymov was posted to, there was a general sense of calm. Many of the political-section strategists seemed strangely serene. 'The Germans have exhausted themselves. They've got no more aircraft, no fuel, no tanks, no shells. It's two whole weeks since we last saw one of their planes.'

This was neither the first nor the last of Krymov's encounters with such optimists. He knew very well how quickly they panicked in any difficult situation, wandering about in bewilderment and muttering, 'Who'd have thought it!'

Many of the soldiers in one of the infantry divisions were from Chernigov and happened to have been deployed very close to their own villages, which were now occupied by the Germans. The Germans evidently knew this, no doubt from interrogating prisoners. Looking at the stars as they lay at night in their trenches – in quiet oak groves or amid tall hemp or maize – these soldiers would suddenly hear an amplified woman's voice. Treacherously authoritative, this voice would repeat, in Ukrainian, 'Iva-an! Come ho-o-ome! Iva-an! Come ho-o-ome!' This iron woman's voice, which seemed to come from the sky itself, was followed by a brief businesslike speech pronounced with a foreign accent. The 'brothers from Chernigov' should return at once to their homes – or else, within a day or two, they would be burned to death by flamethrowers, or crushed under the treads of tanks.

Once again, the loud voice: 'Iva-an! Iva-an! Come ho-o-ome!' Then the sullen roar of motors – the soldiers thought that the Germans possessed a special wooden rattle that mimicked the sound of a tank engine.

There were mornings when men turned out to have gone missing. Only their rifles remained, lying on the bottom of trenches.[121]

Two weeks later, Krymov was on his way back from this quiet army to Front HQ.

The driver who had given him a lift stopped just outside Kiev. Krymov continued on foot. He walked past a long, deep ravine with clay sides and then stood still for a moment, taking involuntary delight in the peace and charm of the early morning. The ground was covered by yellow leaves, and the leaves still left on the trees shone in the low sun. The air felt unusually light. Bird calls were only the faintest of ripples on the clear surface of a deep, transparent silence. Then the sun reached the upper slopes of the ravine. The light and the half-light, the silence and the bird calls, the sun's warmth and the still-cool air created a sense of something extraordinary: any moment now, perhaps, some kind-hearted old men from a fairy tale would appear, quietly climbing the slope.

Krymov left the road and walked through the trees. Then he saw an elderly woman in a dark blue coat, a white canvas sack over her shoulders.

Catching sight of Krymov, she screamed.

'What's the matter?' he asked.

248

She ran her hand across her eyes, smiled wearily and said, 'Oh, my God, I took you for a German.'

Krymov asked the way to Kreshchatik,[122] and the woman replied, 'You're going the wrong way. From the ravine, from Babi Yar, you should have gone left – but the way you're going now will take you to Podol. You must go back to Babi Yar, then past the Jewish cemetery, then along Melnik Street, then Lvov Street.'[123]

As he made his way down towards Kreshchatik, he thought he had stumbled into hell.

Soviet troops were leaving the Ukrainian capital. Taking up the whole width of the street, infantry, cavalry, guns and transport carts were moving slowly along Kreshchatik.

The entire army seemed to have been struck dumb. Heads were bowed. Everyone was looking down at the ground.

Vehicles and guns were camouflaged with branches of birch, maple, aspen and hazel, and millions of autumn leaves fluttered in the air, recalling the fields and forests now being abandoned.

And all the variety of colours, of weapons, insignia and uniforms, every distinction of face and age was erased by a single common expression of sorrow; this sorrow could be seen in the eyes of the soldiers, in the commanders' bowed heads, in the banners now rolled up in their green cases, in the horses' slow steps, in the muted rumble of engines, in the knocking of wheels that sounded like a funereal drumbeat.

Krymov saw a stout young woman with a baby in her arms, forcing her way through the crowd. She wanted to throw herself under the wheels of one of the guns, to halt this fateful retreat. People still only half-clothed were rushing after her, weeping, shouting, begging the soldiers to stop her.

Hundreds of women and children in autumn and winter coats, carrying bundles and suitcases, were trying to make their way to the Dnieper, exhausted and out of breath before they had even left the city.[124] Detachments of policemen, firemen and apprentices were marching in the same direction. Old men stared at them glassily, as if hoping for some miracle. Nothing in the world, it seemed, could be more terrible than the wrinkled, yet childishly helpless faces of these old men, each alone in the crowd.

The Red Army soldiers were all gripped by a tight silence.

They knew, with an absolute, physical clarity, that every step they took to the east brought the still unseen Germans closer. Every step they took towards the Dnieper drew Hitler's divisions closer to Kiev.

And – as if summoned by the approaching dark forces – shifty-eyed, hostile-looking people began to appear in the yards and alleys. Their whispering grew ever louder. Keeping a sly eye on the retreating soldiers, they were preparing to meet those now approaching. It was here, in a narrow alley, that Krymov first heard words of Ukrainian he would all too soon hear again: 'What's been, we have seen. What's to be, we shall see.'[125]

Later, whenever he remembered this last day in Kiev – the cloudless blue sky, the gleaming windows, the streets carpeted with gold leaves – Krymov felt as if an axe were cleaving his heart; the pain was as sharp as his ever-present sense of personal loss.

In the following months there were many other times when he was among the last to leave as the Red Army abandoned a city or town to the Germans. Rather than lessening, the pain only grew still harder to bear. These towns and cities were like helpless people – people near and dear to him being taken away to some other life that was terrible, beyond understanding and infinitely distant.

Krymov had barely crossed to the east bank before the Germans, after knocking out the Soviet anti-aircraft defences, carried out a massive air raid on Brovary. Ninety bombers took part. This brought home to Krymov the full, awful meaning of the words 'air supremacy'.

Guderian's panzer divisions, moving down from the north, towards Gomel and Chernigov, were now securely positioned on the east bank of the Dnieper, to the rear of the Soviet forces in and around Kiev. It was clear that Guderian's aim was to link up with Kleist's Army Group South, which had broken through the Soviet front near Dnepropetrovsk.

A week later the pincers closed. Krymov was now behind the front line, in territory occupied by the Germans.

*

On one occasion Krymov saw dozens of enemy tanks move onto a plain crowded with families from Kiev fleeing east on foot. On the lead tank sat a German officer, waving a branch of orange autumn leaves in the air. Some of the tanks tore, at speed, into the midst of the women and children.

On another occasion a German tank passed slowly by only ten metres away from Krymov. It looked like some ferocious beast with bloodstained jaws. Now, Krymov felt that he had fully taken in the meaning of the words 'ground supremacy'.

Day and night Krymov walked east. He heard about the death of Colonel General Kirponos.[126] He read German propaganda leaflets making out that Moscow and Leningrad had already fallen and that the Soviet government had fled by plane to the Urals. He saw men who had buried their medals and Party membership cards; he saw betrayal and steely loyalty, despair and unwavering faith.

With him, under his leadership, were 200 soldiers and commanders whom he had met on his way. It was a motley squad, made up of Red Army soldiers, sailors from the Dnieper flotilla, village policemen, district Party committee workers, a few elderly Kiev factory workers, cavalrymen without horses and pilots who had lost their planes.

There were moments afterwards when Krymov felt he must have dreamed this entire journey – it was so full of extraordinary events and experiences. He remembered night-time bonfires in the forest, swimming across swollen autumn rivers under icy rain, long days of hunger, brief feasts in villages where they had eliminated detachments of Germans. Sometimes he had to judge village elders and *polizei*;[127] this did not take him long. He remembered the look in the eyes of these traitors just before they were shot. He remembered a peasant woman who, with tears in her eyes, had begged him to give her a rifle and allow her and her two children to join his men on their journey east. He remembered the cruel execution of the mistress of the commander of a German punitive detachment. He remembered an old woman who, one night, had burned down her own house and the drunken *polizei* – one of them her son-in-law – who were asleep inside. And he remembered giving a lecture in a forest, immediately after a brief battle with a detachment of *polizei*, about the principles of the construction of a Communist society.

More than anything, he remembered the sense of togetherness that came into being between his men.[128] Everyone had spoken openly about their whole lives, from their earliest childhood, and everyone's path through life had seemed clearly marked out; people's characters, their strengths and weaknesses – everything about them became manifest, in word and deed.

Sometimes Krymov had felt bewildered, unable to understand where he and his comrades were finding the strength to endure these long weeks of hunger and deprivation.

And the earth was so heavy, so difficult. To pull one boot out of the mud, to lift one foot and take one step, to lift the other foot – this alone was an immense labour. There was nothing during those autumn days that wasn't difficult. Day and night it went on drizzling – and the cold drizzle was as heavy as mercury. Impregnated with this drizzle, a cloth side cap seemed heavier than a metal helmet; greatcoats became so sodden that they dragged you towards the ground; tunics and torn shirts were like clamps, clinging so tight to your chest that it was hard to breathe. Everything was a struggle.

The branches they gathered for the fire could have been made of stone. The dense, damp smoke merged with the equally dense grey mist and lay heavily on the ground.

Day and night the men's aching shoulders felt like great weights; day and night the cold and dirt penetrated their torn boots. They would fall asleep on wet ground, under rough rain-heavy branches of hazel. At dawn, they awoke in the rain, feeling as if they had not slept at all.

In areas of German troop concentration there was ceaseless activity on the roads: columns of trucks, artillery and motor infantry. German soldiers were quartered in almost every village, and there were always sentries. In these areas Krymov and his men could move only at night.

It was their own land they were walking across, but they had to take cover in woods, to hurry across railways, to avoid asphalt roads where the sound of their footsteps might give them away. Black German cars swept past in the rain; self-propelled artillery drove past more slowly; tanks exchanged signals in metallic voices. Sometimes Krymov's men heard strange, jarring sounds, carried by the wind from tarpaulin-covered trucks: snatches of German songs and the strains of an accordion. They saw bright headlights and heard the laboured, submissive breathing of locomotives at the head of trains carrying German troops further east. They saw peaceful lights in the windows of houses and friendly smoke rising up from chimneys – yet they had to hide away in deserted forest ravines.

Nothing during this difficult time was more precious than faith in the justice of the people's cause, faith in the future. This made the rumours spread by the enemy – vague, grey, penetrating as the autumn mist – still harder to bear.

In some strange way, alongside his exhaustion, Krymov felt something very different – a sense of confidence and ardent strength. A sense of passion, of revolutionary faith; a sense of his own responsibility for the men trudging along beside him, for their lives and spiritual strength, for all that was happening on this cold autumn earth.

There was probably no heavier responsibility in the world, yet this sense of responsibility was the source of Krymov's strength.

Dozens, hundreds of times every day men turned to him with the words, 'Comrade Commissar!'

In these two words Krymov sensed a particular warmth, a warmth that came from the heart. The men walking beside him knew of Hitler's decree about the summary execution of all commissars and political instructors. These two words contained much that was good and pure.

It felt entirely natural and inevitable that Krymov should be leading this ad hoc detachment.

'Comrade Commissar,' Svetilnikov, his chief of staff, would ask, 'what route will we be taking tomorrow?'

'Comrade Commissar, where should we send our scouts?'

Krymov would unfold the map, now wind-damaged, yellow and faded from the sun and rain, half-erased by the touch of many hands. Krymov understood that the route he chose might determine the fate of 200 men. And Air Force Major Svetilnikov knew this too; his yellow-brown eyes, usually bright and mischievous, would turn serious and his ginger eyebrows would meet in a frown.

Their choice of route depended not only on the map and the reports of their scouts. Everything was important: car and cart tracks at a fork in the road, a chance word from an old man they happened upon in the forest, the height of the bushes on a particular hillside, and the state of the unharvested wheat: had it been beaten to the ground or was it standing up like a wall?

'Comrade Commissar – Germans!' Sizov, their chief scout – a man with a long face who seemed to know no fear of death – was a little out of breath. 'On foot, not more than a company, behind that little wood over there, heading north-west.'

And Sizov, who had been close to death more often than any of them, looked into Krymov's eyes, hoping to read there the order, 'Attack immediately!' He knew that Krymov was always eager to attack, whenever an opportunity arose.

These short fierce clashes brought about sudden transformations. Rather than exhausting the men, combat lent them more strength, enabled them to stand straighter.

'Comrade Commissar, what will we be eating tomorrow?' Skoropad, their provisions manager, would ask. He knew that Krymov had to take many different factors into account. One day they would have only burnt, half-cooked wheat that smelled of kerosene; another day, foreseeing a particularly difficult march, he would say, 'Goose and tinned meat – one tin for every four men.'

253

'Comrade Commissar, what are we to do with the severely wounded? Today we've got eight of them,' Petrov would ask in his hoarse voice. A military doctor, Petrov suffered from asthmatic bronchitis and his lips always looked pale and anaemic. He would wait intently for Krymov's reply, staring at him through bloodshot eyes. He knew that Krymov would never agree to leave the wounded behind, even in the care of the most loyal and dependable of villagers, but Krymov's reply always brought joy to his heart. A little colour would return to his cheeks.

It was not that Krymov could read a map better than his chief of staff, or that he understood more about military operations than the regular soldiers. Nor did he know more about provisioning than the wise Skoropad or have a clearer idea than Petrov about how best to treat the wounded. The men who asked him these questions had a sense of their own worth; they knew the value of their own expertise, combat experience and knowledge of life. They knew that Krymov was sometimes wrong, that he might not be able to answer their questions. But they all understood that Krymov made no mistakes when it came to the single most important struggle of all – the struggle to preserve what was most essential and precious in a human being, to protect this central core at a time when it was all too easy to lose not only your life but also all sense of conscience and honour.

During this period Krymov grew accustomed to answering the most unexpected questions. During a night march through the forest, a former tractor driver, now a tank driver with no tank, would suddenly ask, 'What do you think, comrade Commissar? Do the stars have Black Earth regions too?'[129] Or a fierce argument would flare up around the fire: when Communism was established, would both bread and boots be distributed to everyone free of charge? A little out of breath, the soldier delegated by the debaters would go up to Krymov and say, 'Comrade Commissar, are you still awake? The lads have got in rather a muddle. They need you to sort things out for them.' Or a sullen, taciturn old greybeard would pour out his soul to Krymov, telling him about his wife and children, about what he had done right in his dealings with others – everyone from close family to distant acquaintances – and where he had gone wrong.

Once, two of his men decided to go to ground. One pretended to be ill and the second shot himself in the calf; both intended to stay behind in a village, making out to the Germans that they had married into peasant families. Krymov had to judge them. And there were

254

also moments of comedy, moments that everyone – even the sick and wounded – could laugh about together. In one village a soldier, without saying a word to the elderly mistress of the house, took five eggs and hid them inside his hat; a little later, he went and sat on this hat. The old woman shrieked abuse at him, then brought him some hot water and a cloth and helped him to regain his military dignity.

Krymov noticed that people liked telling him funny stories – as if they wanted even their commissar to be able to enjoy a little fun and laughter. During this autumn he seemed to be reliving all the hardest days of his life as a revolutionary and a Bolshevik. He was being tested – just as he had been tested during his time in the political under- ground, and during the Civil War. Krymov could feel on his cheeks the fresh breeze of his youth – and this was something so splendid that no difficulties, no ordeals could make him lose heart. There was no one who did not sense his strength.

Just as progressive workers had followed revolutionary fighters in the days of the tsars, in spite of prison sentences and forced labour, in spite of the whips of the Cossack soldiers, so now men brought up and educated by the Revolution were following their commissar through field and forest, regardless of hunger, suffering of all kinds and the ever-present danger of death.

Most of these men were young. They had learned to read and write from Soviet textbooks and had been taught by Soviet teachers. Before the war they had worked in Soviet factories and kolkhozes; they had read Soviet books and spent their holidays in Soviet houses of recre- ation. They had never seen a private landowner or factory-owner; they could not even conceive of buying bread in a private bakery, being treated in a private hospital, or working on some landowner's estate or in factories that belonged to some businessman.

Krymov could see that the pre-revolutionary order was simply incomprehensible to these young men. And now they found themselves on land occupied by German invaders, and these invaders were prepar- ing to bring back those strange ways, to reintroduce the old order on Soviet soil.

Krymov had understood from the first days of the war that the Ger- man fascists were not only behaving with extraordinary cruelty; they also, in their blind arrogance, looked down on the Soviet people. Their attitude was one of mockery and contempt.

Old men and women, schoolgirls, young boys – everyone in the Soviet villages had been shocked by this colonialist arrogance. People brought up to believe in internationalism, in the equality of all workers, were not used to feeling themselves to be an object of scorn.

What Krymov's men needed more than anything was certainty. So strong was their desire to overcome all doubt that they often chose to devote their short, precious hours of rest to serious discussion rather than to sleep.

There was one day when their position seemed hopeless; they were caught in a forest, encircled by a German infantry regiment. Even the bravest men were saying to Krymov that there was nothing for it but to scatter; each would have to try to make his own escape.

Krymov gathered his men in a forest clearing, stood on the trunk of a fallen pine and said, 'Our strength comes from being together. The aim of the Germans is to separate us. We're not an isolated particle, forgotten in a forest far behind German lines. Two hundred million hearts beat with us – the hearts of our 200 million brothers and sisters. We will fight our way through, comrades!' Holding his Party membership card high above his head, he shouted, 'Comrades, I swear to you that we will get through!'

And so they did – and continued on their way east.

And so they marched on – ragged, with swollen feet, suffering from bloody dysentery, but still carrying rifles and grenades, dragging along their four machine guns.

One starry autumn night, they fought their way across the German front line. When Krymov looked around at his troops, staggering from weakness yet still a force to be reckoned with, he felt both pride and joy. These men had walked hundreds of miles with him; he loved them with a tenderness beyond words.

49

They crossed the front line to the north of Bryansk, near the large village of Zhukovka, on the River Desna. Krymov said goodbye to his comrades, who were assigned straightaway to different regiments.

He went first to a Division HQ, and from there, by horse, to a small farm in the forest where he was told he would find the army commander.

There, in the HQ of the 50th Army, Krymov learned what had happened during the days of his wanderings.

Krymov was called to see Brigade Commissar Shlyapin,[130] the member of the army military soviet, a stout, enormously tall man who moved very slowly. He received Krymov in a wooden barn where there was a small table and two chairs, and piles of hay by the wall.

Shlyapin rearranged the hay, told Krymov to sit down and then lay down beside him, grunting and wheezing. He said that he too had been in encirclement that July; together with General Boldin, he had broken through the German front line and joined the forces under the command of General Konev.

There was a calm and simple strength in Shlyapin's unhurried speech, in his pleasant smile and his humorous, good-natured eyes. A cook in a white apron brought them two plates of mutton with potatoes and warm rye bread. Seeing the look on Krymov's face, Shlyapin smiled and said, 'Russian soul, Russian smells.'[131]

The smell of hay and warm bread seemed somehow connected to this huge, unhurried man.

Soon after this, they were joined by Major General Petrov, the army commander. He was a small, red-haired man who was starting to go bald. On his worn general's jacket was the gold star of a Hero of the Soviet Union.

'No, no,' he said, 'don't go getting up. I'll sit down beside you – I've only just come from Division HQ.'

His bulging, pale blue eyes were alert and penetrating, his manner of speaking quick and staccato.

With him, he brought all the tension of war into the calm half-dark of this fragrant barn. Messengers kept coming and going. An elderly major came in twice to report. The silent telephone came to life.

An adjutant reported that the army tribunal chairman had arrived from HQ to confirm the sentences passed by the military soviet. Petrov had him called in. When he appeared, Petrov offered him some tea, which he refused, and then asked, 'Are there many?'

'Six,' the chairman replied, and opened a folder.

Petrov and Shlyapin listened to a report about the six traitors and deserters. In capital letters, and using a child's green pencil, Petrov wrote 'CONFIRMED', then handed the pencil to Shlyapin.

'And this?' asked Petrov, raising his eyebrows. The chairman explained that an elderly woman from the town of Pochep had been distributing German propaganda among the troops and the general population. He added that she was an old maid and a nun.

Petrov pursed his lips and said in a serious tone, 'An old maid? Well, perhaps we should show leniency.' And he began to write.

'Sure you're not being overindulgent?' asked the good-natured Shlyapin. Petrov returned the folder to the chairman and said, 'You may leave, comrade. There's someone I need to talk to, so I won't invite you to dinner. Next time you're at HQ, tell them to send us some cherry jam.'

Petrov then turned to Krymov, 'I know you, comrade Krymov – and maybe you remember me too.'

'I've forgotten, comrade Army Commander,' Krymov replied.

'Do you remember a cavalry platoon commander whom you accepted as a Party member in 1920, when you were with the 10th Cavalry Regiment?'

'I'm afraid not,' said Krymov. Looking at Petrov's uniform, and his general's green stars, he added, 'Time flies.'

Shlyapin laughed, 'Yes, Battalion Commissar, it's hard to outrun it.'

'Are the enemy getting short of tanks?' asked Petrov.

'They have a great many tanks,' said Krymov. 'Only two days ago, I heard from some peasants that transport trains had arrived in the Glukhov district and delivered around 500 tanks.'

Petrov shrugged. 'I doubt it,' he said. 'That sounds like quite an exaggeration.' He went on to say that his army had crossed the Desna at two points, taken eight villages and reached the Roslavl highway. As before, he spoke quickly, avoiding long words.

'Another Suvorov!'[132] said Shlyapin, smiling. It was clear that he and Petrov were on the best of terms and worked well together.

Early the next morning a car arrived to take Krymov to Front HQ. Colonel General Yeromenko, the Front commander, wanted to talk to him. Krymov left, still feeling the warmth of what had been a blessed day.

Front HQ was in the forest between Bryansk and Karachev. The various sections were located in spacious dugouts lined with fresh, still-damp boards. The commander's billet was a small house in a clearing.

A tall, pink-faced major met Krymov on the porch. 'I know why you're here,' he said, 'but you'll have to wait. The commander was working all night. He only went to bed an hour ago. You can sit here on this bench.'

Attached to a nearby tree was a washbasin. Two corpulent, large-boned men went up to it. Both were bald; both were wearing braces over shirts as white as snow; both were in blue breeches, but one was wearing boots while the other was in soft leather slippers, his socks looking rather tight on his fleshy calves.

Grunting and snorting, they dried the backs of their heads and their stout necks with shaggy towels. Their orderlies then handed them their tunics and yellow belts; Krymov saw that one was a major general, the other a divisional commissar. The latter strode quickly towards the house.

The major general looked at Krymov. The adjutant, who was on the terrace above, said, 'It's the man Petrov told us about – the battalion commissar from the Southwestern Front. He's been called here by the commander.'

'The commissar from the Kiev encirclement,' the general said with a contemptuous smirk – and went up onto the terrace.

The low clouds were grey and ragged, and the patches of blue sky looked chilly and hostile, like winter waters.

It began to rain. Krymov took refuge under the awning. The adjutant came out and said gravely, 'The commander wishes to speak to you, comrade Battalion Commissar.'

Yeromenko was tall and stout, with high cheekbones, a broad face and a broad wrinkled forehead. He was wearing glasses. He gave Krymov a quick yet attentive look and said, 'Sit down, sit down, I can see you've had a hard time of it. You've lost a lot of weight.' He spoke as if he had known Krymov from before his time in encirclement.

Krymov noticed that three of the four green stars on the turndown of his tunic collar were markedly dimmer than the fourth, which must have been added only recently.[133]

'Bravo, my good man from Kiev,' said Yeromenko. 'You've brought me 200 armed men. Petrov's told me about you.'

He then moved straight to the question that clearly concerned him more than anything else in the world.

'Well,' he said, 'did you see anything of Guderian? Did you see his tanks?'[134]

He gave a little smile, as if embarrassed by his own impatience, and ran one hand through his thick, close-cut, greying hair.

Krymov reported in detail. Yeromenko listened, leaning right forward, his chest against the table. Then his adjutant hurried in, saying, 'Comrade Colonel General – the chief of staff, with urgent information!'

He was followed by the major general whom Krymov had seen earlier. The major general went up to the table, a little out of breath, and Yeromenko asked, 'What's up, Zakharov?'

'Andrey Ivanovich, the enemy has gone on the offensive. His tanks have broken through towards Oryol, from Krom. And on the right flank Petrov's front line was breached forty minutes ago.'

Yeromenko swore, soldier-style, got heavily to his feet and went to the door, without another glance at Krymov.

In the Front Political Administration Krymov was issued with a greatcoat and coupons for the canteen, but no one asked him anything at all – any interest people might have taken in his experiences was eclipsed by the day's ominous new developments.

The canteen was in a glade in the forest. Under the open sky were long tables and benches resting on blocks of wood sunk into the ground. The dark ragged clouds looked as if they were being torn by the sharp tops of the pines. The friendly clatter of spoons mingled with the melancholy voice of the forest.

Then all these sounds were drowned out; above and between the clouds were German twin-engine bombers, heading towards Bryansk.

Several people jumped up and ran under the trees. In a resonant, authoritative voice, forgetting that he was no longer in command, Krymov shouted, 'No! No running!'

Soon afterwards, the earth was trembling from explosions.

That night Krymov saw an operations map. Advance units of German tanks threatened Bolkhov and Belyov. Other units, leaving

Ordzhonikidzegrad and Bryansk to their left, were moving north-east, towards Zhizdra, Kozelsk and Sukhinichi.[135]

Once again, as in Kiev, Krymov saw two vast German claws, now closing around the Bryansk Front.

The young staff commander who showed Krymov this map was thoughtful and sensible. He said that Petrov's army had suffered a particularly heavy blow. Kreizer's army was now retreating, but still fighting stubbornly.[136] From information received that afternoon it was clear that the Germans had also launched an offensive against the Western Front; from Vyazma they were advancing on Mozhaisk.

The goal of this new offensive was only too clear: Moscow. Moscow was the word now in everyone's heads and hearts.

Each month people's thoughts and feelings, their hopes and plans, had coalesced around different words. In June the words in the minds of workers and peasants, in the minds of women, feeble old men and self-assured generals, had been 'the old border with Poland'. In July the word in their minds had been 'Smolensk'; in August, 'the Dnieper'; and in October, 'Moscow'.

HQ was in a state of near-panic. Krymov saw signallers removing cables and soldiers piling stools and tables into trucks. He overheard clipped conversations:

'Which section are you? Who's in charge of this truck? Note down the route – I've heard it's a difficult road through the forest.'

At dawn, on a truck from the Bryansk Front HQ, Krymov set off towards Belyov. Once again he observed the broad road of Russia's retreat; once again, among the soldiers' greatcoats, he glimpsed women's kerchiefs, old grey heads and the skinny legs of children.

In the last two months he had seen Belorussians from the forests on the border with Poland, and Ukrainians from around Chernigov, Kiev and Sumy. Now it was Russians from Oryol and Tula who were fleeing the Germans, trudging along the autumn roads with their bundles and plywood suitcases.

From the Belorussian forests he remembered the calm glimmer of lakes and the gentle smiles of children. He remembered their parents' shy tenderness and the anxiety with which they looked at these children. He remembered quiet huts, unhurried suppers of potatoes and the bent backs of men and women working in potato fields until dusk. He remembered a people who lived far from cities and roads and seldom visited fairs, who knew how to spin and sew, to make shoes, dresses, fur coats and sheepskin jackets. Their souls still echoed the passing seasons: blizzards and thaws, the burning heat of their sandy plains, birdsong and buzzing mosquitoes, the smoke of forest fires and the rustle of autumn leaves.

Then Krymov and his men had marched through Ukraine.

The nights were filled with the buzz of German bombers, with the smoky light of night-time fires. During the day Krymov and his men saw orchards and kitchen gardens full of huge pumpkins, splendid white cabbages and red tomatoes full of the warmth of life; beside the white walls of the huts, climbing high as their thatched roofs, were dahlias and sunflowers. Nature rejoiced in this wealth, but it had brought little joy to those who had cultivated it.

In one village Krymov attended a farewell party for an old man who had served forty years in the naval artillery and had now resolved to leave his family and his magnificent orchard and slip away into the forest with only a rifle. Many of the other guests were inconsolable, but they still believed that the sun would continue to shine on the earth. The old woman whose husband was leaving was distraught. For her, this was the end of the world, the last day of her life – yet she had gone on making cheese dumplings and poppy-seed biscuits with as much care and love as if the world were at peace.

Krymov saw people laughing through tears and people who first laughed, then wept. Now and again he sensed a sly reserve hiding behind loud eloquence. Once more he heard the treacherous words, 'What's been, we have seen. What's to be, we shall see.' And he met people who hoped that the Germans would soon put an end to the collective farms.

Krymov also spoke to people who were strong, hard-working and talented, who understood that life on this rich earth is a precious gift and who were now ready to give up their lives to defend the fruits of their peaceful labour.

And now, in October, he was being driven through the fields of the province of Tula, among birches already bare, among squat village houses built of red brick, over ground that rang with frost in the early morning yet turned hot and damp as the day went on.

And the wonderful beauty of the region where he was born and raised revealed itself to him anew – in rolling fields already harvested, in bunches of rowan berries above the moss-covered frame of a well, in the huge smoky-red moon struggling to raise its chilly, stony body over the bare night-time countryside. Everything here was majestic:

the earth; a sky that held within it all the cold and lead of autumn; and, stretching from horizon to horizon, even darker than the black earth, the road itself. Krymov had seen many autumns in the Russian countryside and usually the season evoked in him only a calm sadness, mediated through poems he had known since childhood: 'Boredom and sadness, clouds without end ... a stunted mountain ash ...'[137] These, though, were the feelings of people who had beds in a warm, comfortable home and who were gazing through the window at trees they had known all their lives. What Krymov felt now was very different. The autumn earth was neither poor, nor sad and boring. He did not see mud or puddles; he did not see the damp roofs or the rickety fences. What he saw in these empty autumn spaces was a fierce beauty and grandeur. He could feel the vastness of the Russian lands in all their indissoluble unity. The penetrating autumn wind had gathered its strength from expanses that measured thousands of kilometres. This wind now blowing over the fields of Tula had blown over Moscow. Before that, it had blown over the forests of Perm, over the Ural Mountains and the Baraba steppe; it had blown over taiga and tundra, and over the sullen gloom of Kolyma. Krymov could now, with his entire being, sense the unity of the tens of millions of his brothers and sisters who had risen to fight for the people's freedom. The whole country was at war – and no matter where the enemy appeared to break through, he would be met by a living dam of Red Army regiments newly brought up from reserve. Tanks just transported from factories in the Urals were waiting in ambush; new artillery regiments were meeting the enemy with their fire. And those who had retreated along high roads and back roads, those who had broken out of encirclement and forced their way east – they too had returned to the ranks. Once again they formed part of the living dam blocking the invaders' path.

Krymov went on from Belyov in the same truck as before.

The junior lieutenant in charge of the truck respectfully offered him his place in the cab, but Krymov refused. Along with commanders from Front HQ, Political Administration staff and ordinary soldiers, he climbed into the back.

They stopped for the night in a village near Odoev. The old woman in whose large cold hut they were billeted greeted them warmly and cheerfully.

She told them that her daughter, who worked in a Moscow factory, had brought her here at the beginning of the war, to live with her son. The daughter had then returned to Moscow.

Her son's wife, however, had not wanted to share her home with her mother-in-law. And so her son had settled her here, in this large hut. He regularly brought her a little millet, or some potatoes, not mentioning this to his wife.

Her younger son, Vanya, had been working in a factory in Tula, but he had volunteered for the Red Army and was now fighting near Smolensk.

'So you're all on your own?' Krymov said to her. 'Even at night, when it's cold and dark?'

'It's all right,' she replied. 'I sit in the dark and sing. Or I tell myself old tales.'

The soldiers boiled a large pot of potatoes and they all ate. Then the old woman stood by the door and said, 'Now I'm going to sing for you.'

She sang in a rough, hoarse voice that could have been an old man's. Then she said, 'Yes, there was a time when I was strong as an ox.' After a pause, she went on, 'Last night I dreamed of the Devil. He appeared before me and dug his nails into the palm of my hand. I began to pray: "Let God arise, let his enemies be scattered."[138] But the Devil didn't take the least notice. Then I cursed and swore at him – and he was off like a shot. The day before yesterday I dreamed of my Vanya. He sat down at the table and just kept looking through the window. I kept calling out, "Vanya! Vanya!" But he didn't say a word. He just kept on looking out of the window.'

She offered her guests all she had: firewood, a pillow, a straw-filled mattress, the blanket off her own bed. She held nothing back; she even gave them a pinch of salt for the potatoes – and Krymov knew very well how reluctant village women were to use up their last stores of salt.

Then she brought an oil lamp without any glass and a small bottle with what must have been her last, cherished reserve of kerosene, and filled the lamp.

A true mistress of life and of a great land, she did all this with cheerful generosity, then retired behind the partition to her cold room. She was a mother; she had given her guests love, warmth, food and light.

That night Krymov slept on straw. He remembered lying on straw in a hut in a Belorussian village near the border with Ukraine, close to Chernigov. A tall, thin old woman with dishevelled grey hair had appeared out of the dark, carefully replaced his blanket, which had slipped off him while he was asleep, and made the sign of the cross over him.

He remembered a September night in Ukraine when a Chuvash soldier had somehow crawled into the village. He had been wounded in the chest. Two elderly women had dragged him into the hut where Krymov was spending the night. The bandages tied round the soldier's chest had soaked up a great deal of blood. First they had swollen; then they had dried and gone tight. They had become like iron bands.

The soldier began to choke and wheeze. The women cut the bandages and got him to sit up. He began to breathe more easily.

They stayed with him until morning. He was delirious, calling out in Chuvash. All night long they held him in their arms, crying and wailing, 'My child, my child, dear child of my heart!'

Krymov closed his eyes. He suddenly remembered his childhood, and his dead mother. He remembered how painfully lonely he had felt after Zhenya had left him. He realized with surprise that during these months in fields and forests, when so many were being orphaned by the storms of war, he had not once felt lonely.

Rarely in his life had the essence of Soviet unity seemed so clear to him. He understood that, by stirring up racial hatred, the Nazis hoped to undermine this unity – as if a stinking stream could undermine a deep ocean. One image troubled him day and night – the sight of the spattered blood and scraps of women's clothing on the front of a German tank. How, he kept asking, could this have happened? The driver, after all, was an ordinary soldier. No one had been giving him orders; nobody had been standing over him when, on the fringes of the Priluki forest, he had turned his tank against defenceless women and children.

Krymov's life had taken shape in a world of Communist ideals; more than that, it was woven from these ideals. Long years of work and friendship had united him with Communists from all over Europe, America and Asia.

It had been true work and true friendship, a true journey.

They used to meet in Moscow, on Sapozhkovskaya Square opposite the Alexander Garden and the Kremlin wall. He remembered Vasil Kolarov, Maurice Thorez and Ernst Thälmann. He remembered Sen Katayama, with his brown eyes, his lovable wrinkles and his good-natured smile – the smile of a man who had lived through a great deal.[139]

One memory was especially vivid. He had been with a large group – Italians, Englishmen, Germans, French, Indians and Bulgarians. They had come out of the Hotel Lux[140] and walked arm in arm down Tver-skaya, singing a Russian song. It had been in October: twilight, mist, cold rain about to turn into damp grey snow. Passers-by were turning up their collars; cabs rattled past.

Arm in arm they had walked on, through the hazy glow of the dim street lamps. Beside the little white church on Okhotny Ryad, the blue-black eyes of one of the Indians had looked startling.

Who among them still remembered that song? Who among them was still alive? Where were they all now? Which of them was taking part in the battle against fascism?

> O sacrifice to reckless thought,
> It seems you must have hoped
> Your scanty blood had power enough
> To melt the eternal Pole.
> A puff of smoke, a silent flicker
> Upon the age-old ice –
> And then a breath of iron winter
> Extinguished every trace.[141]

Krymov understood that he had not simply dreamed up the contra-dictions that so troubled him. These contradictions had an objective existence; they were wreaking havoc in a world now gone mad. Grit-ting his teeth, he repeated to himself what Lenin had said about the teachings of Karl Marx: they were invincible because they were true.[142]

50

On the road to Tula, Krymov stopped at Yasnaya Polyana.[143] The house was in the grip of feverish departure preparations. The paintings had been taken down from the walls; tablecloths, dishes and books had all been packed. The hall was full of boxes, ready to be transported east.

In peacetime Krymov had once spent a day there with a group of foreign comrades. The museum staff had done what they could to create the illusion that this was a house where people still went about their daily lives. There were fresh flowers everywhere and the dining-room table was neatly laid. And yet, the moment they all went inside, the moment Krymov put on the obligatory cloth overshoes and heard the pious voice of the guide, it became only too obvious that the master and mistress of the house were dead. This was not a house but a museum, a sepulchre.

But when he went inside this second time, Krymov felt that this was a Russian house like any other. The storm that had flung open every door in Russia, that had driven people out of their warm homes and onto black autumn roads, sparing neither peaceful city apartments, nor village huts, nor hamlets deep in the forest, had treated Leo Tolstoy's home no less harshly. It too was preparing to leave, in rain and snow, along with the entire country, the entire people. Yasnaya Polyana was a living, suffering Russian home – one of thousand upon thousand of such homes. With absolute clarity, Krymov saw in his mind Bald Hills and the old, sick prince.[144] The present merged with the past; today's events were one with what Tolstoy described with such truth and power that it had become the supreme reality of a war that ran its course 130 years ago.

Tolstoy, no doubt, had found it painful to describe the long and bitter retreat of the first months of that distant war; he might well have wept as he described how the old prince, close to death, had muttered, 'My soul aches' – and had been understood only by his daughter Maria.

And then Tolstoy's granddaughter Sofya Andreyevna came out of the house, calm, downcast, shivering a little in spite of the coat thrown

267

over her shoulders. Once again Krymov did not know whether this was Princess Maria, going out for a last walk around the garden before the French arrived, or whether it was Lev Tolstoy's elderly granddaughter scrupulously fulfilling the demands of her fate: applying all her heart and soul, as she prepared to leave, to checking the accuracy of her grandfather's account of the princess's earlier departure from this same house.

Krymov went to Tolstoy's grave. Damp, sticky earth; damp, unkind air; the rustle of autumn leaves underfoot. A strange sense of heaviness. The loneliness of this little mound of earth covered in dry maple leaves – and the living, throbbing connection between Tolstoy and all that was happening today. It was agonizing to think that in a few days German officers might come to this grave, laughing, smoking, talking in loud voices.[145]

Suddenly the air above him was shattered. Junkers, with an escort of Messerschmitts, were passing overhead, about to bomb Tula. A minute later, from a few miles to the north, came the dull roar of dozens of anti-aircraft guns. Then the earth trembled too, shaken by the explosions of bombs.

To Krymov it seemed as if Tolstoy's dead body must have felt this trembling.

*

By evening Krymov had reached Tula, which was in panic. On the outskirts, beside the red-brick buildings of the distillery, soldiers and workers were digging trenches and ditches, constructing barricades, positioning long-barrelled anti-aircraft guns along the Oryol road, evidently expecting to be using these guns not against aircraft but against the tanks that might soon approach from Yasnaya Polyana and Kosaya Gora.

Thick, damp snow was falling, changing suddenly to icy rain. One moment the streets were white; then they were black – just mud and dark puddles.

Krymov went into the army canteen. Three or four men were standing by each table, silently observing those who were seated.

A larger group of men was standing around the canteen manager, demanding meal coupons for lunch. The manager was insisting that they first bring him a note from the commandant. A captain was saying, 'But don't you understand? It's impossible even to get to speak to the commandant. I haven't eaten for twenty-four hours. Give me a bowl of soup!'

The captain looked about for support. A major standing beside him said, 'Comrade Captain, there are a lot of us – and only one canteen manager. If we're not careful, we'll drive the poor man round the bend.' Smiling ingratiatingly, he then turned to the manager. 'Isn't that so, comrade manager?'

'Absolutely!' said the manager. And he gave the major a meal coupon.

There was borsch all over the tables, along with burnt crusts of bread, saucers with traces of dried mustard, and empty salt cellars and pepper pots.

An elderly lieutenant colonel was saying to a waitress, 'But why did you bring me my soup in a shallow bowl and my *kasha* in a deep bowl? That's the wrong way round.'

Someone standing behind him said, 'Never mind, comrade Colonel, better simply to eat the food as it comes. People are waiting.'

There were pretty white curtains beside the windows. The paintings on the walls had been decorated with paper roses. One section of the large room – 'For Generals' – was partitioned off by yet more curtains. Two very young junior quartermasters entered this section.

A senior political instructor standing next to Krymov said aloud to himself, 'White curtains, paper flowers – and they complain that we're not being orderly enough. They haven't yet grasped that we're at war. And war's about more than paper roses.'

Commanders waiting their turn were exchanging quiet words.

Krymov learned that the 50th Army had been smashed and that General Petrov and Brigade Commissar Shlyapin had been killed in hand-to-hand fighting with German sub-machine-gunners.

He heard that the German advance on Mtsensk had been halted by Colonel Katukov's tank unit, recently brought forward from the reserves.[146]

The following morning, while it was still dark, he went to the garrison commander to find out the location of Southwestern Front HQ. An elderly major replied in a tired voice, 'Comrade Battalion Commissar, you're in Tula. No one here knows anything about the Southwestern Front. Ask in Moscow.'

51

Krymov arrived in Moscow at night. No sooner had he walked out of the Kursk station than the extreme tension of the last two months fell away: he was physically exhausted and, once again, he felt lonely. There would be no one waiting for him at home.

The square was deserted. The snow was damp and heavy. Krymov wanted to lift up his head and howl – like a wolf alone in the steppe.

The thought of his empty home – of listening to his own footsteps as he walked from room to room – was terrifying. He returned to the station building. Amid tobacco smoke and the hum of quiet conversation he felt more comfortable.

In the morning he went round to call on Viktor Shtrum, but the yardwoman told him that the Shtrums were now in Kazan.

'Do you happen to know if Ludmila Nikolaevna's sister is with them there? Or is she in Stalingrad with her mother?'

'That I don't know,' said the yardwoman. 'Even my own son hardly tells me anything – all I know is that he's at the front.'

Few months in Moscow's 800 years can have been as difficult as October 1941. Day and night, the fighting around Mozhaisk and Maloyaroslavets was unremitting.[147]

In the Main Political Administration Krymov was questioned at length about the situation near Tula. He was told he could be taken back to the Southwestern Front on a transport plane carrying newspapers and information leaflets. But he would have to wait; these planes flew only once every three or four days.

On his second morning in Moscow, Krymov saw large crowds making their way through dense snow, heading for the nearest railway station.

Breathing heavily, a man put down his suitcase, took a crumpled copy of *Pravda* from his pocket and said to Krymov, 'Have you read this, comrade? It's the worst so far.' And he read aloud, 'During the night of 14/15 October, the position on the Western front deteriorated. The German fascists hurled motor infantry and large numbers of tanks against our forces and, on one sector, broke through our defences.'

His fingers trembling, the man rolled a cigarette, took a drag, threw the cigarette away, grabbed his case and said, 'Zagorsk – I'll walk to Zagorsk.'

On Mayakovsky Square Krymov came across an editor he knew. From him he learned that many government institutions had already been evacuated to Kuibyshev, that there were huge crowds waiting on Kalanchovskaya Square,[148] hoping to board trains, that the metro was no longer running and that an hour ago someone just back from the front had told him that there was now fighting on the outskirts of Moscow.

Krymov wandered about the city. His face was burning and from time to time he felt his head spin. He had to lean against a wall in order not to fall over. Somehow he did not realize that he was ill.

He phoned a colonel he knew, who taught in the Lenin Military-Political Academy; he was told that the colonel had left for the front, with all his students. He phoned the Main Political Administration and asked to speak to the section head who had promised to get him onto a transport plane. The duty officer replied, 'He and his entire section were evacuated this morning.'

When Krymov asked if the section head had left any message for him, the duty officer asked him to wait and then disappeared for a long time. Listening to the crackling line, Krymov decided that the section head – probably overwhelmed by the chaos of the evacuation – had evidently left no message at all. The best thing he could do now was go either to the Moscow Party committee or to the head of the Moscow garrison. He could ask to be posted to one of the units defending the city; transport planes were clearly out of the question. But then the duty officer returned to the phone and informed Krymov that he was to collect his personal belongings and go to the People's Commissariat of Defence.

It was dark by the time Krymov reached the commissariat. By then, instead of feeling hot, he was shivering. His teeth were chattering. He asked if there was a first-aid station in the building. A duty officer took him by the hand and led him down the dark, empty corridor.

The nurse looked troubled, shaking her head after one look at Krymov. The thermometer seemed icy, and he realized he must have a very high fever indeed. The nurse said down the phone, 'Send a car. He has a temperature of 40.2.'

Krymov was in hospital for three weeks with acute pneumonia. During the first days, apparently, he had cried out in delirium,

'Moscow! Don't make me leave Moscow! Where am I? … I want to go to Moscow …' He had tried to leap out of bed and the nurses had had to restrain him, pinning him down by the arms as they tried to persuade him that he was already in Moscow.

Krymov left the hospital at the beginning of November.

He understood at once that Moscow had changed. There was a grim severity about the wartime city. Gone were the anxiety and fears of October; gone the feverish bustle and the troubled voices. People were no longer jostling one another in shops and trams, no longer dragging heavily laden carts and sledges to railway stations.

In this hour of looming disaster, when the rumble of guns forged in the Ruhr could be heard from the city's outskirts, when black Krupp tanks were smashing through aspen and pine groves near Maloyaroslavets, when German rocket engineers illuminated the winter sky over the Kremlin with ominous aniline lights from the BASF chemical factory, when German words of command echoed in forest clearings and Prussian, Bavarian, Saxon or Brandenburg voices could be heard on short-wave radio, saying '*Folgen … freiweg … richt, Feuer … direkt richt*'[149] – in this hour Moscow was calm, severe and formidable. She was the military leader of Russian cities, towns and villages, of all the Russian lands.

There were few ordinary people on the streets, only patrols. Shop windows were packed with sandbags. There were trucks carrying troops, and tanks and armoured cars now painted snow-white. The streets were covered with barricades built from thick red pine logs and yet more sandbags. Anti-tank hedgehogs wreathed in barbed wire blocked the approaches to the city's main gates. Military traffic controllers with rifles stood at all the junctions and crossroads. Wherever Krymov went, he saw more defences under construction. Moscow was preparing for battle.

This was a scowling city, a soldier city, a militiaman city. 'The new face of Moscow,' Krymov said to himself, 'the face of our capital.'

On the dark foggy morning of 7 November Krymov was on Red Square – the Moscow Party committee had given him a pass for the celebrations.[150]

Had the world ever seen so austere and majestic a picture? Somehow both massive and slender, the strong, stone-patterned breast of the Spassky Tower took up much of the sky to the west. The cupolas of St Basil's were veiled in mist; it was as if they were not of this earth but had been born from something light and celestial.

New and surprising, no matter how long you looked, these forms could have been anything – doves, clouds, human dreams turned to stone, or stone transformed into the living thoughts and dreams of a human being.

The fir trees around the Lenin Mausoleum were motionless. The very faintest hint of living blue shone through the stony sadness of their heavy branches, while up above them rose the Kremlin wall, its starkly chiselled crenellations softened by white hoar frost. Every now and then the snow stopped; then it tumbled down again in soft flakes, hiding the merciless stone of Lobnoye Mesto and causing Minin and Pozharsky to disappear into a murky gloom.[151]

Red Square itself was like a living and breathing breast, the broad breast of Russia, with warm mist rising up from it. And the sky now hanging low over the Kremlin was the same broad sky that Krymov had seen over the Bryansk forest – imbued with both the cold of the war and the cold of autumn.

The soldiers wore greatcoats, large *kirza* boots[152] and crumpled fur hats with earflaps. They had come to Red Square not after long months of training in barracks but straight from gun emplacements, combat units or combat reserves.

These were the troops of a people's war. Now and again, furtively, they brushed the melting snow from their faces – with a wet tarpaulin mitten, with a handkerchief, with the palm of a hand. Krymov wondered if those to the rear might be discreetly taking a piece of dried bread from their pockets and slipping it into their mouths.

Crowded together on the tribunes were men in greatcoats and leather jackets, women in quilted jackets and headscarves and senior commissars with diamonds on their collar tabs. The collar tabs of the front-line commanders now bore green bars.[153]

'Perfect weather!' said a woman standing near Krymov. 'We won't see any German bombers today.' And, with a handkerchief, she wiped the rain and snow from her forehead.

Still weak from his illness, Krymov sat down on a barrier.

Words of command echoed over the square. Marshal Budyonny began reviewing and greeting the troops.[154] After completing his review, he climbed quickly up onto the mausoleum.

Stalin went up to the microphone. In the murk Krymov was unable to make out his face. But his words were entirely clear. Towards the end of his speech, he wiped the snow from his face just as the rank-and-file soldiers had done, looked around the square and said, 'Can anyone doubt that we can and must defeat the German invaders?'

Krymov had heard Stalin speak before, but he now understood more clearly than ever why he spoke so very simply, without rhetorical flourishes. 'His calm,' Krymov said to himself, 'springs from his confidence in the good sense of the millions he is addressing.'

'The war you are fighting is a just war, a war of liberation,' Stalin concluded. 'Death to the German invaders!' And then, raising one hand: 'Forward to victory!'

On a day when Hitler's hordes were almost at the gates of Moscow, the combat troops of a people's army began to march sternly and solemnly past the Lenin Mausoleum.

52

On 12 November 1941 Krymov managed to rejoin Southwestern Front HQ and was appointed commissar of a motor infantry regiment. Soon afterwards, when his regiment took part in the liberation of Yelets, he experienced the sweetness of victory. He saw piles of pink and blue papers – from what had once been the HQ of General Sixt von Armin – being blown across a snowy field. He saw prisoners with sacks tied around their legs and wadded blankets thrown over their shoulders, their heads bandaged with towels and women's headscarves. The white shroud of the Voronezh winter fields was dotted with smashed trucks and cars, black Krupp cannon, and the dead bodies of Germans clothed only in thin grey sweaters and overcoats.

The news of the German defeat outside Moscow was like the peal of a joyful, celebratory bell, heard all the way from the Southern Front to the Karelian Front.

The night Krymov heard the news, he felt a joy he had never known before. He left the dugout where he and the regimental commander were quartered; the harsh January cold chilled his nostrils and burnt his cheekbones. Beneath the clear, starry sky, the snow-covered valley, with its little mounds and hillocks, shone with an unearthly light. The twinkling of the stars created a sense of swift motion in every direction at once. The news was being passed from star to star; the whole sky, it seemed, was gripped by a joyful excitement. Krymov took off his hat and stood there, no longer feeling the cold.

Again and again he reread the radio operator's transcript: forces under the command of generals Lelyushenko, Kuznetsov, Rokossovsky, Govorov, Boldin and Golikov had smashed the German flanks. Abandoning weapons and equipment, German armies were now in flight.

The names of the liberated towns – Rogachov, Klin, Yakhroma, Solnechnogorsk, Istra, Venyov, Stalinogorsk, Mikhailov and Epifan – had a joyful, springlike ring to them. It was as if they had been resurrected, reborn, wrested from beneath a cloak of darkness.

Again and again during the retreat Krymov had dreamed of the hour of vengeance – and now it had come.

He pictured the forests near Moscow that he knew so well. Now they must be full of abandoned German bunkers, heaps of rifles and mangled machine guns. Tanks, seven-ton trucks and heavy guns on massive wheels would now be in the hands of the Red Army.

Krymov, who had always enjoyed talking with the soldiers, spent long hours in infantry units and with mortar and gun crews. He quickly realized that everyone already understood the immense importance of the victory outside Moscow. Every Red Army soldier had felt personally involved in the fate of Moscow. During the German advance their pain and anxiety had grown sharper and more bitter. When they learned of the German defeat, there was a sigh of relief from millions of breasts.

It was at this time that attitudes to the Germans began to change. Instead of feeling only hatred for the invaders, people also began to feel contempt and scorn.

In bunkers and trenches, in tanks and gun emplacements, they stopped referring to the enemy simply as 'he' and began mockingly using the names 'Fritz', 'Hans' or 'Karlusha' (little Karl).

Countless little stories and jokes about Hitler's stupidity and the cowardly arrogance of his generals began to do the rounds. These stories arose spontaneously and soon became common property, throughout the whole of the front and even far back into the rear.

Even the German planes acquired nicknames: 'The Humpback', 'The Camel,' 'The Guitar', 'The Crutch', 'The Squeaker'.

And people began repeating, 'Fritz's gun is a goon.'

The sudden appearance of these jokes, stories and nicknames was a sign of the final crystallization of a sense of moral superiority over the enemy.

In May, Krymov was appointed commissar of an anti-tank brigade.

The German army went on the offensive again. They destroyed the Soviet forces defending the Kerch Peninsula. Manstein trapped Gorodnyansky as he tried to advance on Kharkov; he encircled the 6th and 57th armies.

These terrible days saw the deaths of both General Gorodnyansky and General Kostenko. Kuzma Gurov, the member of the Front military soviet, whom Krymov remembered from Moscow, managed to break out of the encirclement in a tank. Once again, the air was filled with the buzz of German bombers. Once again villages were burning, unharvested grain stood in the fields, and grain silos and rail bridges were being destroyed.

But this time the Soviet forces were not retreating towards the Bug or the Dnieper. What lay behind them now was the Don, the Volga, and the steppes of Kazakhstan.

53

What brought about the disasters of the first months of the war? First, the Germans were fully mobilized; the 170 divisions Hitler had brought to the Soviet frontier were ready to strike, waiting only for the order. The Soviet troops, on the other hand, were poorly equipped, only partially mobilized and generally unprepared – even though the imminence of the German attack had been obvious enough. Also, there was no second front; considering their rear secure, the Germans were free to throw all their troops and those of their allies against the Soviet Union.

While Muscovites told one another stories about Soviet troops reaching Königsberg, Soviet paratroopers seizing Warsaw, and brigades of Soviet railwaymen being despatched to convert the track to broad gauge as far as Bucharest – while Muscovites entertained one another with fairy tales, hundreds of thousands of people from Ukraine started a long journey east, on foot, in carts and on tractors, in trucks and freight cars. People came to understand the reality of war; that it differed from the reality of the novels they had read and the films they had seen.

What very few understood, however, was that the swiftness of the German advance disguised the true nature of what was now a people's war. The Germans' apparent strength disguised a deeper weakness, while the weakness shown by the retreating Red Army was gradually being transformed into strength.

The battles of 1941, the battles fought during this long retreat, were the grimmest and most difficult of the war. Nevertheless, the balance of strength was shifting.[155] In these tragic, hard-fought battles the future victory was slowly germinating.

A nation's character has many facets. Military valour is no less complex; it can declare itself in many ways. There were men ready to march forward to their death even when vast spaces lay free and empty behind them; and there were men who, recognizing they were hopelessly outnumbered, fought only the more fiercely. These are the heroes of the first period of the war. Many are nameless and received no burial. It is to them, in large part, that Russia owes her salvation.

The war's first year showed how many such men there were in Soviet Russia. That year saw countless small battles, some swift, some long and obstinate, on unnamed heights, outside villages, in forests, on grassy cart-tracks, in swamps, on unharvested fields, on the slopes of gullies and ravines, by the landing stages of river ferries.

It was these battles that destroyed the foundations of Hitler's blitz-krieg strategy, a strategy based on the assumption that it would take the German army eight weeks to cross European Russia. Hitler arrived at this length of time by the simplest of calculations: he divided the distance from the western frontier to the Urals by the average distance that German tanks, self-propelled artillery and motor infantry could cover in one day. This calculation, however, proved mistaken – and this undermined Hitler's other central assumptions: that Soviet heavy industry could be entirely destroyed and that the Red Army command would be unable to mobilize reserves.

In the course of this year, Russia retreated a thousand kilometres. Train after train went east carrying not only people but also machine tools, cars, boilers, motors, ballet scenery, libraries, collections of rare manuscripts, paintings by Repin and Raphael, microscopes, mirrors from astronomical observatories, millions of pillows and blankets, household items of all kinds, and millions of photographs of parents, grandparents and great-grandparents long sleeping their eternal sleep in Ukraine, Belorussia, Crimea and Moldavia.

But, however it may have seemed at the time, this was not only a period of retreat and disaster. The state's centralized power – the State Defence Committee – successfully organized the movement of millions of people and vast amounts of industrial equipment to the Urals and Siberia, where a powerful coal and steel industry was quickly established.

Members of the Party Central Committee and Party leaders and members at all levels directed the construction of new mines, factories and workers' barracks; they enabled labour battalions to achieve remarkable feats in the darkness of the Siberian nights, in blizzards and deep snow.

During this year, in these hundreds of new factories, workers and engineers multiplied the military might of the Soviet state. At the same time, the energy of millions of people previously working in china, cardboard, pencil, furniture, footwear, hosiery and confectionery factories, in workshops and collectives of every kind, was redirected to the defence industry; tens of thousands of small enterprises became, in effect, army units, just as countless thousands of farmers, agronomists, teachers and accountants – people who had never dreamed of doing military service – became soldiers. If this vast amount of work has, to many, seemed insignificant, it is because it is the vastest things that most often escape our notice. The people's rage, the people's pain and suffering, was transformed into steel, into gun barrels, into explosives and armour, into the engines of bombers.

In December 1941, America entered the war, with all its colossal industrial might. England, no longer under immediate threat, went on rapidly increasing its production of armaments. And thousands of kilometres behind the front line, Soviet workers and engineers were winning the battle over both the quantity and quality of military engines of every kind.

*

The balance of military and industrial might was shifting.

Nevertheless, in 1942 Hitler was able to deploy 179 German divisions on the Soviet–German front. Also deployed against the Soviet Union were sixty-one divisions from the various countries then allied to Germany. All in all, 240 divisions, more than 3 million men, were sent against the Red Army. This was twice the total number of troops that Germany, Turkey and the Austro-Hungarian Empire had deployed against Russia in 1914.

Hitler concentrated the greatest number of these troops on a 500-kilometre sector of the front between Oryol and Lozovaya. In late May 1942, the Germans began to advance on the Kharkov sector. In late June, they began to advance on Kursk. On 2 July, German tanks and infantry went on the offensive on the Belgorod and Volchansky axes. Sevastopol fell on 3 July.

Once again the Germans breached the Soviet front. They captured Rostov and broke through to the Caucasus. Not only to Hitler, but also to many of those caught in the whirlwind, this seemed like another chapter in their victorious blitzkrieg.

But these German victories only paved the way for their eventual defeat. The reality of the war – everything except Hitler's strategy – had changed.

54

After Seryozha's departure, the Shaposhnikovs' home became sad and silent. Alexandra Vladimirovna worked long hours, inspecting the factories and workshops preparing the mixture for Molotov cocktails. She came home only late in the evening. Her workplace was far from the city centre and there were no buses; she often had to wait a long time for a lift from a passing vehicle, and more than once she ended up walking all the way home.

One evening Alexandra was so exhausted that she telephoned Sofya Osipovna. Sofya sent a truck from the hospital to take her back home. On the way she asked the driver to stop at Beketovka, at Seryozha's barracks.

The barracks turned out to be empty; everyone had been taken off to the steppe. When she got back home and passed this news on, her daughters looked at her anxiously, but she seemed entirely calm. She even smiled as she repeated the truck driver's reply when she asked him about Sofya Osipovna: 'Comrade Levinton,' he had said, 'is a famous surgeon, and she is always fair and just. But her character is sometimes a little difficult.'

Sofya had indeed become more edgy and difficult over the last few months. She came to the Shaposhnikovs less often – she had ever more wounded to treat. Day and night an enormous battle was being fought on the western approaches to the Don, and the wounded were being taken to Stalingrad.

Once Sofya had said, 'It isn't easy for me. For some reason everyone thinks I'm made of iron.' And another time, after coming to the Shaposhnikovs straight from work, she had burst into tears and said, 'That poor boy who died an hour ago on the operating table … Such eyes, such a sweet, touching smile.'

The last few weeks had seen more and more air-raid alerts.

In daytime the German planes flew high, leaving long fluffy spirals behind them, and everyone knew that these were reconnaissance planes photographing factories and port facilities. And then, almost every night there would be the sound of solitary bombers – and loud explosions over the still city.

Spiridonov now hardly saw anything of his family; the power station was on a war footing. He would telephone after an air raid and ask, 'Is everyone all right?'

Vera was often sullen and irritable when she got back from hospital. Bewildered by her anger and rudeness, Marusya would sometimes look around in search of sympathy. One day she complained to Sofya, 'It's stupid. She refuses point blank to help me – her own mother – with ordinary housework. And then she's extraordinarily kind and helpful to people she doesn't know at all.'

Sofya replied crossly, 'If someone as bad-tempered as Vera came to work for me, I assure you I'd throw them out within twenty-four hours.'

But Marusya reserved for herself the right to complain about her daughter. Not even her husband was allowed to usurp this prerogative – and so she immediately took Vera's side: 'Well, partly it's a matter of heredity. Stepan's father was uncouth and ill-mannered. Anyway, all *I* ever think or talk about at home is my work. It's not surprising if Vera's offhand, if she has to look for friendship elsewhere. Really she couldn't be more hard-working and pure. If she's in a bad mood, I admit, you can't even get her to go and buy some bread – but another day she'll scrub all the floors without being asked and then stay up all night washing piles of laundry.'

Sofya burst out laughing: 'Oh, you mothers, you're all the same!'

In late July and early August all-too-familiar names began to appear in Sovinform Bureau bulletins: Tsimlyanskaya, Kletskaya, Kotelnikovo – towns and villages on the outskirts of Stalingrad that were almost a part of the city.

But refugees from Kotelnikovo, Kletskaya and Zimovniki had, in fact, begun to appear in Stalingrad some time before this; they had heard the roar of the approaching avalanche. And new wounded were being brought to Vera and Sofya Osipovna every day. Only a few days before, these men had been fighting on the west bank of the Don, and their stories filled everyone with alarm. The war knew no rest; day and night, it was drawing nearer the Volga.

It was impossible to get away from the war. If the Shaposhnikovs tried to talk about Viktor's work, this at once led them to think of his mother; if they mentioned Ludmila, the conversation would soon turn to Tolya – was he, or wasn't he, still alive? Grief was lurking outside, ready to fling open every door of the house.

And it seemed that the only pretext for jokes and laughter was Colonel Novikov's unexpected visit.

'All he could talk about,' said Alexandra Vladimirovna, 'was the "Russian soul" or the "spirit of Russia". To me it felt as if we were back in 1914.'

'No, Máma, you don't understand,' said Marusya. 'Thanks to the Revolution these concepts have assumed an entirely new meaning.'

Over supper one evening, at Sofya Osipovna's instigation, they embarked on a 'critical examination' of Novikov.

'Somehow he's very tense,' said Alexandra. 'He makes me feel awkward. I keep thinking he's about to take offence for some reason – or else say something offensive. I'm not sure I'd want our Seryozha to be under the command of a man like him.'

'Women, women,' said Sofya with a sigh – as if she weren't one herself and the failings of her sex had nothing to do with her. 'What, do you think, is the secret of Novikov's success? He's a hero of his time – and women love heroes of their time. There are fashions in marriages, just like in dresses. In the decade before the First World War, smart young ladies fell in love with poets and dreamers, with Symbolists of all kinds. Next, they were all marrying engineers – the mystics and Symbolists vanished into thin air. The hero of the 1930s was the director of a major construction site and today's hero's a colonel. But that said, it's a whole week since the man last put in an appearance. What's he playing at?'

'You've got nothing to worry about, Auntie Zhenya,' said Vera. 'You've bewitched him – he'll be back soon enough.'

'Yes, of course,' added Sofya, to general laughter. 'And he's even left his suitcase with us.'

At first, Zhenya would feel annoyed; then she would join in the laughter. 'You know, Sofya Osipovna,' she said, 'I think you talk about Novikov more than anyone – and certainly more than I do.' But Zhenya could not quite admit, even to herself, that she had not merely learned to put up with this banter – she truly enjoyed it.

Zhenya lacked the arrogance and calm rationality usually to be found in very beautiful women who can always be certain of their success. She took little care of her appearance; she often failed to do her hair properly and she was capable of putting on an old baggy coat and shoes with worn heels. Her sisters blamed all this on Krymov's bad influence. 'The steed and the quivering doe,' Ludmila had once laughed. 'With me as the steed,' Zhenya had replied. When men fell in love with her, which happened only too often, she would feel upset and say, 'Now I've gone and lost another good comrade.'

She used to feel a strange sense of guilt before her 'suitors', and Novikov was no exception. A strong, severe man, entirely taken up by his demanding and important work – and suddenly she would see in his eyes a look of bewilderment.

She had been thinking recently about her life with Krymov. She felt sorry for him, and this confused her. She did not realize that what evoked her pity was her feeling – now stronger than ever – that their separation was irrevocable.

When Krymov had stayed at Viktor and Ludmila's dacha and gone for a walk in the garden, Ludmila had always taken care to walk beside him, knowing from experience that he would be sure to trample her phlox and other treasures 'with his great hooves'.

Ordinary Russian cigarettes were too weak for him. He preferred to roll his own, which were huge and very strong. When he waved his arms about, sparks flew through the air. As they drank tea together, he sometimes got carried away by his own eloquence. Everyone would laugh as Ludmila removed her favourite Chekhonin cups and spread a small towel over the embroidered tablecloth.[156]

Krymov did not like music and was entirely indifferent to *objets d'art*, but he felt nature deeply and could speak about it well. He had no time, however, for the splendid resorts of Crimea and the Black Sea coast. Once, on holiday in Miskhor, he barely left his room for an entire month; lowering the blinds against the sun, he simply lay on the couch and read, showering grey ash over the parquet floor. But one day when the wind picked up and the sea turned rough, he went down to the shore. Returning late in the evening, he said to Zhenya, 'It's splendid out there – like the Revolution!'

He also had strange tastes in food. One day, when a comrade from Vienna was coming to eat with them, Krymov said to Zhenya, 'It would be good to have something tasty.'

'What are you thinking of?' Zhenya replied. 'Just say what you want.'

'Well, I'm not sure, but pea soup would certainly be good – and then liver and onion.'

There was no doubting Krymov's moral strength. Once she had heard him give a talk, in a large Moscow factory, on the anniversary of the Revolution. When he raised his calm, quiet voice and at the same time hammered his fist down on the table, a breath of excitement passed through the hall and Zhenya felt a tingle down to her fingertips.

Now, though, her feeling of pity for him was overwhelming. In the evening, after yet more banter initiated by Sofya Osipovna, Zhenya went into the bathroom and locked the door, saying she was going to wash her hair.

But the hot water in the saucepan turned gradually cold, and Zhenya was still sitting on the edge of the bath, thinking, 'Why is it that people close to me can seem so distant? Why do none of them – even Máma – understand anything?'

They imagined that her only interest was in this chance-met Novikov, but her thoughts were with someone else.

For Zhenya, Krymov had once had a romantic aura, an air of wisdom about him. His eccentricities, his past, his friends – everything had excited her. He had been working back then for journals devoted to the international workers' movement. He often took part in congresses and wrote a great deal about the revolutionary movement in Europe.

Foreign comrades, delegates to these congresses, would come and visit him. They would try to speak to Zhenya in Russian and – without fail – mangle the Russian words.

Krymov's conversations with these foreign comrades were long and animated, often going on until two or three in the morning. Sometimes they were conducted in French, which Zhenya had known since childhood. She would listen intently but, after a while, their stories and arguments began to bore her. She hadn't heard of the people they talked about, nor read the books they argued about.

Once she said to Krymov, 'You know, when I talk to them, I feel as if I'm accompanying people who have no musical ear. They can distinguish tones, but not semitones or quartertones. I don't think it's a matter of language. We're probably just too different.'

This made Krymov angry. 'That's your fault, not theirs. You're narrow-minded. Maybe you're the one with no musical ear.'

She replied, quietly and simply, 'You and I have little in common.'

Once they had a large party of guests – 'a whole band', as Krymov liked to say. Two short, stout women with round faces from the Institute of World Economics; an Indian whom they called Nikolay Ivanovich; a Spaniard, a German, an Englishman and a Frenchman.

Everyone was in a good mood. They asked Nikolay Ivanovich to sing for them. His voice turned out to be rather strange – high and sharp, with a certain melancholy.

This Indian in gold spectacles, with a cool, polite smile, had degrees from two universities. He was a regular speaker at European congresses and was the author of a large book that Krymov kept on his desk. Now, as he sang, he was transformed.

Zhenya listened to the unfamiliar sounds and looked at him out of the corner of her eye. His legs tucked in beneath him, he was sitting in a pose she had previously seen only in geography textbooks.

As he took off his glasses and wiped them with a white handkerchief, she saw that his thin, bony fingers were trembling. There were tears in his short-sighted eyes, which now seemed kind and sweet.

It was agreed that everyone should sing in his or her own language. The next person to sing was Charles, a journalist friend of Henri Barbusse.[157] He was wearing a crumpled jacket and he looked dishevelled, with a tangle of hair hanging down over his forehead. In a thin, quavering voice, he sang a song once sung by women factory workers; its sad, naive words were a moving expression of these women's bewilderment.

Next was Fritz Hakken, a tall, long-faced professor of economics who had spent half his life in prison. Clenched fists resting on the table, he sang 'The Peat Bog Soldiers', a song they all knew from the recording by Ernst Busch.[158] A song without hope, sung by those who had been condemned to death. The longer Fritz sang, the grimmer he looked. He clearly felt he was singing about himself, about his own life.

Henry, a handsome young merchant sailors' delegate invited by the Central Trade Union Council, rose to his feet to sing, keeping his hands in his pockets. He sang a song that at first sounded jolly and lively, but the words were full of anxiety: a sailor was wondering what the future held in store for him, and what would happen to those he had left behind.

When the Spaniard was invited to sing, he coughed a little, then stood, as if to attention, and sang the Internationale.

The others rose to their feet and joined in. Everyone was singing their own words but, since the words were hard to make out, it sounded as if they were all singing in the same language. They were all standing tall and it was clear that they were deeply moved. The two women had fine voices. Nevertheless, there was something a little comic about the look on their faces and the way they thrust out their imposing busts. One was tapping her stout leg and shaking her curls; the other was waving a short, plump arm about, as if conducting a choir. Zhenya had been caught up by the atmosphere of intense solemnity, but all of a sudden she wanted to laugh; she had to pretend to clear her throat to disguise this. When she saw two little tears run down Krymov's cheeks, she felt awkward and embarrassed, though without quite knowing why – whether on her account or on his.

Everyone said goodbye to the two women, who didn't want to go out to eat, and then went together to a Georgian restaurant. After they had eaten, they set off down Tverskoy Boulevard.

Krymov suggested going down Malaya Nikitskaya to the new part of the Moscow zoo. Henry, who was following a carefully organized sightseeing plan, enthusiastically agreed.

Among the other visitors was one couple they all took a liking to: a forty-year-old man and an elderly woman in a brown peasant jacket, with a smart white kerchief over her grey hair. The man had a calm though tired-looking face and large, dark hands – he was probably a factory worker. He was walking with one hand under the old woman's elbow. Probably he was her son, and she had come to Moscow to stay with him.

But for the bright sparkle in her eyes, the old woman's wrinkled face would have seemed lifeless. Looking at a large elk, she said, 'What a clown – and he certainly looks well fed. He'd make a fine tractor!'

She took an interest in everything, and she kept looking round at people, clearly proud to be seen with her son.

For some time Krymov's 'band' walked behind this couple, watching them and not noticing that they were themselves being watched by dozens of people. A crowd of spellbound young boys were following them from one enclosure to another, clearly more interested in Nikolay Ivanovich than in the elk, or in a reindeer licking a lump of salt.

The band turned off towards the pen for the young animals,[159] but the sky suddenly went dark and it began to rain. Henry took off his jacket and held it over Zhenya's head. Turbid water streamed noisily along the ditch beside the path. Everyone now had wet feet. There was a particular charm about these small discomforts; they all felt happy and carefree, as if they were children.

The sun came out again. The water in the puddles now sparkled, and the trees looked brighter and greener than ever. In the cubs' pen they could see daisies, with trembling droplets of water on each little flower.

'Paradise,' said the German.

A bear cub began awkwardly climbing a tree; drops of water fell from the branches. Meanwhile, a game started up in the grass below – some sinewy red dingo pups, their tails curled, were teasing a second bear cub. Some wolf cubs joined in, their shoulder blades rotating almost like wheels. The bear cub, who was standing on his hind legs, tried to slap one of them on the snout with a plump, childish paw. The first bear cub fell from the tree – and the animals all merged into a single merry, motley ball of fur rolling about on the grass.

Just then a fox cub emerged from the bushes. He looked anxious and troubled; his face looked baleful and his tail was sweeping from side to side. His eyes shone, and his thin, moulting flanks were rising and falling very rapidly. He was longing to take part in the game; he would steal forward a few steps and then, overcome by fear, flatten himself against the ground and freeze. All of a sudden he leaped forward and threw himself into the fray with an odd little squeal, playful yet somehow pitiful. The dingo pups knocked him off his feet, and he lay there on one side. His eyes still shone and he was trustfully exposing his belly. Then he let out a piercing cry of reproach – one of the dingo pups must have bitten him too hard. This was the end of him: the dingo pups went for his throat, and the game on the grass turned into a murder. A keeper ran up, plucked the dead creature out of the melee and carried it away; hanging down from the keeper's hand were a skinny dead tail and a dead snout, with one open eye. The red dingo pups responsible for this murder followed the keeper, their curled tails quivering with intense excitement.

The Spaniard's black eyes filled with fury. Fists clenched, he yelled, 'Hitler Youth!'

Then everyone began talking at once. Zhenya heard Nikolay Ivanovich pronounce very clearly, with a look of distaste, '*Es ist eine alte Geschichte, doch bleibt sie immer neu.*'[160]

In Russian, in a voice that allowed no argument, Krymov said, 'All right, brothers! That's enough! There is no such thing as an instinct to kill – and there never has been!'

In many respects, this had been one of the most pleasant of the days Zhenya had spent in Krymov's company: moving songs, a cheery meal, the scent of lindens, a brief shower, and the mother and son they had found so touching ... But what she recalled most vividly was that last poignant scene: the pitiful fox cub and the suffering and rage in the eyes of the Spaniard.

During Zhenya's last months with Krymov the good days had been few and far between. She noticed that she was starting to feel pleased whenever she heard something bad about his friends. Hakken had haggled unpleasantly over his pay for an article in the journal *World Economics*. Henry had had an affair with an interpreter, then treacherously abandoned her. Charles had travelled to the Black Sea to write a book, but not written a single word. Instead, he had just lazed about, drinking and swimming. She considered Krymov to blame for all these men's failings. 'See what your friends are really like!' she once said.

Sometimes he went out every evening, returning only late at night. Sometimes he didn't want to see anyone at all; he came home from work and either switched off the phone or said, 'If Pavel calls, tell him I'm out.' Sometimes he was sullen and taciturn; sometimes chatty and light-hearted, reminiscing, laughing and playing the fool.

But what mattered was not Krymov's bad moods or his late nights with friends. What troubled Zhenya more was that she did not feel lonely when Krymov went out, nor did she feel any particular joy when he was being cheerful, chatting away and telling her stories from his past. It was possible that, when she thought she was feeling cross with Krymov's friends, she was really feeling cross with Krymov himself.

What had once seemed romantic now seemed simply unnatural; everything once most appealing about him had somehow lost its appeal. His thoughts about painting, his comments on her own work, had of course always been infuriatingly vapid ... How hard it can be to answer the simplest questions. Why had she stopped loving him? Was it he who had changed, or her? Had she come to understand him better, or was it that she no longer understood him?

Once used to you, I'll cease to love
The one I could not love enough.[161]

No, it was more than that. There had been a time when she thought Krymov knew everything; now she found herself saying again and again, 'No, you don't understand!'

When he made predictions about revolutions in other countries, she mockingly repeated, 'Dreams, dreams, where is your sweetness?' Once she had thought him truly progressive, but now he seemed naive and behind the times, like some pious old woman in a bonnet.

His success or failure in the public world was neither here nor there. Zhenya was, of course, aware that people who had once phoned him often, and without ceremony, now phoned only occasionally – and that when he phoned them himself, their secretaries often refused to put him through. She knew that he no longer received invitations to premieres at the Maly and Moscow Art theatres. Not long ago, when he called the Conservatory's administrative director, to ask for tickets to hear a famous pianist, the secretary had replied, 'I'm sorry, which Krymov is this?' – and then, a minute later, 'I regret to say there are no tickets left.' She knew that he was no longer able to obtain medicines for Alexandra Vladimirovna from the Kremlin pharmacy and that he was now taken to work not in a Mercedes but in an Emka that spent ten days each month in the repair workshop. But none of this mattered to her, just as it didn't matter whether she wore clothes specially made for her by the best-known dressmakers in Moscow or purchased by coupon from the Moscow Tailoring Combine.[162] She knew that, after giving a talk at one very important meeting, he had been harshly criticized. He was, apparently, 'failing to develop'; he was 'stuck in his ways'. But these things were not important: she no longer loved him, and that was all there was to it. Everything else was secondary. Any other way of understanding what had happened was inconceivable.

And then Krymov had been transferred. Instead of working for the Party, he was to work in publishing. In a buoyant tone, he had said, 'Now I'll have more free time. I'll be able to get down to my book at last. In all this whirlwind of meetings I've hardly been able to snatch a minute for it.'

He must have sensed that something had changed between them. 'One day,' he had joked, 'I'll come round in my ragged clothes, in a leather jacket with holes in it. Your husband, a famous academician or perhaps a people's commissar, will ask, "Who is that, *ma chère*?" And you'll say with a sigh, "It's not important. A mistake from my youth. Tell him I'm busy today – he can come round on Monday."'

Zhenya could still remember the sadness in Krymov's eyes as he said this. And she wanted to see him and explain one more time that it was all the fault of her heart. Her stupid heart was to blame for everything. She had simply stopped loving him, it wasn't for any particular reason, and he must never, for even a second, think anything bad about her.

All this troubled her deeply; even during these most desperate days of the war, she was unable to stop thinking about Krymov.

That night, when she thought everyone had gone to sleep, she began to cry, overwhelmed with pity for a life now irrevocably lost. Thoughts, feelings and conversations from that time all seemed splendid and lofty. Krymov's friends now seemed kind and sweet. And he himself evoked in her the same piercing sense of love and pity as the fox cub she had heard give a trusting little squeal as it entered that cruel, merry fray.

Why was love so bound up with pity? Her pity was so intense that pity and love seemed one and the same thing.

As she wept, she held her hands close to her face. In the blacked-out room, she could barely see the hands that Krymov had once kissed – and everything about her life seemed as incomprehensible as the stifling darkness around her.

'Don't cry,' her mother said in a quiet voice. 'Your knight will come soon. He'll dry your tears.'

'Heavens!' Zhenya exclaimed, throwing up her hands in despair. Forgetting that she might wake the others, she went on, 'No, it's not that, it's really not that at all. Why doesn't anyone understand? Not even you, Máma, not even you!'

Her mother replied quietly, 'Zhenya, Zhenya, believe me, I wasn't born yesterday. I think I understand you better, right now, than you understand yourself.'

55

Vera came back home from work, said she didn't want anything to eat and began to wind up the gramophone. This surprised Zhenya. Usually Vera called out, 'Will we be eating soon?' before she had even closed the door behind her.

Vera was sitting with her elbows on the table and her fists against her cheekbones, watching the spinning record with obstinate concentration – the way a depressed person stares at some random object while their mind is elsewhere.

'Everyone's going to be late back tonight. Wash your hands and sit down to dinner with me.'

Vera merely stared at Zhenya, not saying a word.

Zhenya looked round as she went out. She saw that Vera was listening to the record with her hands over her ears.

'What's the matter?' she asked.

'Kindly leave me alone!'

'Stop it, Vera, it doesn't help.'

'Please leave me alone. All dolled up, are you, waiting for your brave paper pusher?'

'What's got into you? Talking to me like that – you should be ashamed of yourself!' said Zhenya, astonished by the pain and hate in her niece's eyes.

Vera had taken a dislike to Novikov. In his presence, she either kept silent or asked barbed questions.

'Have you been wounded many times?' she once asked. After receiving the answer she expected, she put on a look of surprise and exclaimed, 'What? Not even once? I can't believe it!' Novikov ignored her gibes, which made her still more angry.

'Ashamed?' said Vera. 'Me feel ashamed? It's you who should be ashamed of yourself! Don't *you* speak like that to *me*!' She seized the record, hurled it against the floor, rushed to the door, then turned round and shouted, 'I won't be coming back home, I'm going to Zina Melnikova's for the night.'

Vera somehow looked both vicious and pathetic. Zhenya had no idea what was troubling her.

Zhenya had meant to work all day long and through into the evening. Now, though, she no longer felt like working.

Vera's rudeness and bad temper came not from her paternal grandfather, as Marusya liked to make out, but from Marusya herself. Marusya was sometimes very stupid indeed. She would go up to an unfinished painting and, in a condescending tone, pronounce judgement: 'Ah, I see.' It was as though she were a tank man and Zhenya a child, playing some little childish game. But it was, surely, generally accepted by now that mankind needed more than just bread and boots – did Marusya really not understand that people need paintings too? Yesterday Marusya had said, 'Next thing, you'll be painting pretty little views of the city: views of the Volga, little squares, children with their nannies. There you'll be with your easel. Soldiers and workers will go marching past. They'll laugh at you!' This was all very stupid indeed – all the more so because views of the wartime city might in fact be very interesting. The sun, the glitter of the Volga, the huge leaves of the canna lilies, children playing in the sand, the white buildings – and through all this, above all this, within all this, the war, the war … Stern faces, camouflaged ships, dark smoke over factories, tanks moving up to the front, the glow of fires. All fused together, not just a matter of contrasts, but also a unity – the sweetness of life and its bitterness, the looming darkness and immortal light triumphing over this darkness.

Zhenya decided to go out for a walk and try to imagine this new painting more clearly.

As she put on her hat, the bell rang. She opened the door – and saw Novikov.

'You!' she said, and burst out laughing.

'What is it?'

'Where have you been all this time?'

'The war,' he replied, with a helpless shrug.

'And there we were, about to arrange for the sale of your possessions.'

'You look as though you're just going out.'

'Yes, I absolutely must. Will you come with me?'

'Only too glad!'

'You're not too exhausted?'

'Certainly not!' Novikov replied with absolute sincerity, although in the last three days he had slept less than five hours. Smiling broadly, he added, 'Today I got a letter from my brother.'

They came to a corner. 'Which way?' Novikov asked.

Zhenya looked back. 'Doesn't matter. What I was going to do can wait till later. Let's go down to the river.'

They walked past the theatre, through the park and down to the statue of Viktor Kholzunov.[163]

'I knew him in Moscow,' said Novikov, pointing up at the statue. 'He was a good man. Strong, intelligent. We need him now – a shame he's no longer with us.'

They walked to and fro along the waterfront, looking out at the river. Each time they passed the bronze airman, they spoke more loudly, as if wanting him to hear them.

It turned dark. They were still walking and talking.

'I'm glad it's got dark,' said Zhenya. 'You won't have to keep on saluting. It must be exhausting.'

Novikov was in the excited, euphoric state that sometimes comes over people who are usually very reserved. It wasn't merely that he was being open and straightforward; he was speaking the words of a hitherto silent man who now believes that his life is of interest to someone else.

'I've been told I'm a born staff officer, but really I'm a combat officer, a tank man. My place is on the front line. I have the knowledge and the experience, but there always seems to be something holding me back. It's the same when I'm with you – I don't seem able to say anything that makes sense.'

'Look at that strange cloud,' Zhenya said quickly, afraid that Novikov was about to come out with a declaration of love.

They sat down on a broad stone parapet. The rough stone was still hot. Panes of glass in buildings on the grassy slope still shone in the sun's last rays, but there was already a cool breath coming from the Volga and the pale new moon. A soldier and a young girl were whispering together on a nearby bench. The girl was laughing – and from the sound of her laughter, from her slow, half-hearted way of fending off her admirer, it was clear that nothing else in the world existed for her at this moment but the evening, the summer, youth and love.

'How good everything is, yet how troubling,' said Zhenya.

A nearby pavilion housed a military canteen. The door opened wide, and a woman in a white gown came out, holding a bucket. Bright light immediately fell on the pavement and roadway, and it seemed to Zhenya

294

as if the young woman had poured out a bucket of light and that weightless, sparkling light was now flowing across the asphalt. Then a group of soldiers came out. One of them, probably imitating someone they knew, began to sing in a silly voice, 'Ju-une night, whi-ite night ...'

Novikov wasn't saying anything, and this made Zhenya apprehensive: any moment now he would clear his throat, turn to her and say helplessly, 'I love you.' She was getting ready to put a hand on his shoulder and gently admonish him: 'No, really, it's best not to say such things.'

Then Novikov said, 'I got a letter today from my older brother. He works in a mine, far beyond the Urals. He says he gets good pay, but that his daughter keeps falling ill. She can't get used to the climate. I hope it isn't malaria.'

Zhenya sighed, watching Novikov warily. And then he really did clear his throat, turn abruptly towards her and say, 'I'm in a difficult position now. I filed a memo, asked for a transfer, and then I quarrelled with my boss. He said, "I am not giving my approval to your transfer, and I appoint you head of my archive section." I replied, "I do not accept your orders." Then he threatened to send me before a tribunal. He was just trying to frighten me, of course, but still, it's a bad business. After that, I came straight round to see you.'

Now Zhenya felt upset and angry. What had been troubling Novikov, it turned out, was his work.

'You know what I've just been thinking?' she said, with a mocking look. 'The days of great romantic love are now gone for ever. A love like Tristan and Isolde's. Do you know the story? For her sake he abandoned everything – his native land and the friendship of a great king. He disappeared into the forest, slept on branches and felt happy. And she, the queen, lived happily in the forest with him. That's how the story goes, isn't it? Centuries of literature glorified those who gave up fame for love – who, for love's sake, renounced all earthly and heavenly joys. Now all that just seems funny, and hard for us to understand. Not only Tristan, but even a story like Lermontov's "Taman".[164] Read it again and you'll find yourself saying, "It's impossible. An officer, on active service – and he loses his head, falls in love, forgets his duties and sails off with a pretty young smuggler. All utterly inconceivable." Either we've all lost the capacity we once had for love, or else our passions now take a very different form.'

She spoke quickly and with feeling, as if she had prepared this whole speech in advance. She was surprised at herself, unable to understand what lay behind her vehemence. But she continued, with barely a pause, 'No, no one loves like that now! You, for example, could you slip away from work for a day for the sake of the woman you love? Would you be willing to incur the wrath of your general? No, you wouldn't want to be even two hours late for him – not even twenty minutes! And as for sacrificing a kingdom!'

'It's not just fear of the authorities,' Novikov replied. 'It's a matter of duty.'

'Say no more. I've heard it already. Nothing can be more important, more sacred, than one's public duty. All quite true.' Zhenya looked at Novikov condescendingly. 'And yet ... between you and me ... What you say is true – but all the same, people really have forgotten how to love madly, blindly, absolutely. Love like that has been replaced by something else, by something new maybe, and good, but all too safe and reasonable.'

'No,' said Novikov, 'you're wrong. True love does exist.'

'Yes,' she said angrily, 'but it's no longer a question of fate. Love is no longer a whirlwind.' Momentarily putting on the voice of a very sensible schoolteacher, she went on, 'Yes, of course, love is a very good thing. Shared thoughts, shared lives, true love outside working hours.' And then, more sharply, 'Rather like going to the opera – when did you last hear of an opera-lover absconding from his workplace for the sake of his beloved music?'

Novikov frowned. He looked at her and then, smiling trustfully, said, 'If I could believe you're angry with me for not coming to see you for so long—'

'What's got into you? Don't think anything of the sort. I'm talking in general. I'm no romantic either.'

'Yes, yes, I understand,' he said, eager to show his readiness to obey.

She looked up. She could hear a mournful sound – air-raid sirens from the railway station and the factories.

'The sound of life's prose,' she said. 'Let's go back home.'

56

Zina Melnikova was aware that Vera's family disliked her and disapproved of Vera's friendship with her. Zina was only three years the older, but to Vera she seemed a model of worldly wisdom. She had been married for two years, she had visited Moscow several times, and she and her husband had lived not only in Kiev and Rostov but also in Central Asia. In 1940 she had managed to travel to Lvov[165] and had come back with shoes and dresses, white rubber boots, a transparent pale blue raincoat, round sunglasses to wear on the beach and some fashionable check scarfs. She had also brought back an unusual hat, shaped rather like a large telescope. Her girlfriends, however, had rolled about laughing when she showed it to them, and so she had never worn it.

In the course of the last year Zina had seen a great deal. In autumn 1941 she had been in Rostov with her mother. She had failed to leave the city in time and had lived for a while under the Germans, before the Red Army recaptured the city in late November. During those weeks, Zina had travelled to Kiev and Kharkov. She had intended to go on to the Baltic republics, but she had returned to Rostov with supplies of food for her mother, meaning to stay for only a day or two – and just then the Red Army had retaken the city.

In late July 1942, when Zina, once more in Stalingrad with her husband, heard that the Germans had captured Rostov a second time, she had said to Vera, 'It doesn't matter. The trains will be up and running again in a couple of months. Either I'll bring my mother here or I'll go and visit her again in Rostov.'

'You really think the Red Army will retake Rostov?' Vera had asked in surprise.

'I can't say I'm counting on it,' Zina replied, with a mischievous smile.

'You're not meaning to stay here in Stalingrad under the Germans, are you? There'll be terrible fighting. If it were me, I'd die of fear alone.'

'I've seen fighting. Last year in Rostov. It's not as bad as you think.'

'Well, I certainly feel terrified myself. I can't bear the thought of bombs and blazing buildings. I'd panic. I'd drop everything and run.'

'You've been reading too many newspapers,' Zina said with a patronizing smile. 'It's not like that in real life. And anyway, it's people one should be afraid of. They're more dangerous than any incendiaries.'

The evening she'd shouted at Zhenya and thrown a gramophone record on the floor, Vera had gone straight round to Zina's. Viktorov had been discharged from hospital that very morning, sooner than expected, and sent on to the transfer point in Saratov. After completing her shift, Vera had happened to see a list of names signed by the hospital director. The original list of twelve had been typed out, in alphabetical order, but then one more name had been written in by hand: Viktorov. They had not even been able to say a few last words in private; she'd rushed straight to his ward, but he was already making his way down the stairs with eight other patients. The hospital bus had been waiting below.

Vera had never known such grief in her life. The only person she felt able to confide in was Zina. They talked until two in the morning. Then Zina made up a bed for Vera on the sofa, turned out the light and said, 'Let's go to sleep!'

Vera lay there in silence, sleepless, gazing into the darkness with wide-open eyes. She thought Zina was asleep, but after an hour or so Zina suddenly said, 'Are you awake?'

'Yes,' Vera replied – and they carried on talking till dawn.

After that, Vera called round every evening, sitting and talking with Zina until shortly before the curfew.

Sometimes people become friends because they are similar, but often it is because they are different.

Vera saw Zina as a striking and romantic figure, a woman of great heart and soul. As for her brightly coloured dresses, her dozens of unusual items of clothing that made men say 'What a woman!' while more plainly dressed girls looked on in envy – these were merely a fitting backdrop, an appropriate outer expression of Zina's emotional depths. It never occurred to Vera that it might be the other way round, that Zina's romantic talk and extravagant behaviour might be no more than a carefully chosen accompaniment to her striking looks.

For her part, Zina was both attracted and amused by Vera's evident purity and simplicity. She saw in Vera a kind of essential salt – a clarity of thought and feeling – that she valued in others but was unable to find in herself.

People who are very similar often feel a mutual dislike; their similarities engender only envy and ill will. And polar opposites are

sometimes united by their very differences. It is the same with understanding; it too does not always bring people closer. Sometimes, one
person sees another's secret failings all too clearly; the second person is
aware of this and resents it. Conversely, people sometimes feel grateful
and affectionate towards those who do not understand them, who are
blind to their weaknesses.

Zina Melnikova may not have understood Vera, but she understood
very well how Vera imagined her. And she took care to show Vera the
particular qualities – the freedom from calculation and convention –
that she knew Vera most wanted to see in her.

*

One day Vera came round to find Zina lying on a sofa and reading.

She was young and beautiful – and she saw it as her duty to be
young and beautiful. This was clear from her every look and gesture.

She put down her book and moved up a little to make room for Vera
to sit down. Taking Vera's two hands between her palms, as if they
were icy cold and needed warming, she said, 'Life's a struggle, isn't it?'
And without giving Vera a chance to answer, she went on, in the tone
of an experienced doctor resolved to tell the whole truth to a patient,
'I'm afraid it's not going to get any easier.'

'If only I'd known earlier! Then I could have said a proper goodbye
to him. It's awful – I just can't think about anything else.'

'He'll write as soon as he gets to the hospital in Saratov.'

'What do you mean? He'll be sent straight to the front. He'll be flying again in a week. I know it – I'll never see him again.'

'No!' said Zina. 'None of us knows anything. I've seen so much
that is extraordinary. I've seen miracles. More than miracles, really.
Love cannot be calculated or predicted.' And she went on to tell Vera
about a German officer who had fallen in love with a young Russian
girl. The day the Germans withdrew from Rostov, this officer had been
elsewhere. He had been unable to take the girl with him. The two had
been separated. And then, a month after this, someone had knocked at
the young woman's door. It was the German officer. For the sake of the
girl he loved, he had abandoned everything – uniform, medals, family
and country. He was not afraid of being cursed by his parents. The girl
had fainted. Then they had spent the night together. Come morning,
he had gone to the commandant's office and given himself up. He said
he had crossed the front line for the love of a Russian woman. They

299

had asked him to name her, but he had refused. They had accused him of espionage, saying that if he named the woman, he'd be treated as a prisoner of war – but if not, he'd be shot as a spy. He had remained silent. And then, just before he was shot, he had said, 'Oh, if only I could let her know that I have no regrets!'

Zina's story made a deep impression on Vera. Wanting to hide this, she said, 'No, that kind of thing doesn't happen. It's just a story someone's made up.'

Zina smiled such a strange, sad smile that Vera's heart missed a beat. She suddenly wondered if the story might have been about Zina herself, but she didn't dare ask – and a moment later Zina was talking about something else.

Then Zina showed Vera some stockings she had bought in the market, in exchange for sugar off her ration card. Vera looked at Zina's delicate fingers, at her almond-shaped eyes and her slim legs – still slimmer in these semi-transparent stockings – and thought that the German who had given up his life for her love had done right.

'If there's one person I can't understand,' Zina suddenly began, 'it's your Aunt Zhenya. She must be blind to her own power. Why on earth doesn't she dress better? With a face and a figure like hers, and her wonderful hair, she could be quite something! She could have whatever she wants in life.'

'I believe she intends to marry a colonel,' Vera replied quietly. 'A staff officer.'

Zina failed to understand that this was meant as a criticism. She took it as a sign not of excessive pragmatism but of Zhenya's naiveté, of her repeated failure to make the most of her opportunities. 'I don't believe it,' she said. 'She could marry someone from one of the embassies. She could live wherever she chooses, somewhere without blackouts, without ration cards and endless queues for every least item of clothing. As it is, she'll be sent off to some dump like Chelyabinsk. She'll be living on a thousand roubles a month and have to stand in a queue to buy milk for her baby.'

'Oh!' said Vera. 'There's nothing I want more than to stand in a queue to buy milk for my baby.'

They both laughed. But once again Zina failed to understand her friend. She thought Vera was joking; she did not realize that Vera was trying not to show that she had tears in her eyes.

Vera had a burning desire to become a mother, to give birth to a child with Viktorov's eyes, with his slow smile, with the same delicate neck, and – despite poverty, despite deprivation – to tend this child as one tends a flame in the dark. Never before had Vera known such feelings, and they were both bitter and sweet, a source of both joy and shame. But there was no law forbidding a young girl to love and be happy. No! She had no regrets and she never would have regrets; she had acted as it was right and proper to act.

All of a sudden, as if reading Vera's mind, Zina asked, 'Are you expecting?'

'Don't ask,' Vera said quickly.

'All right, all right, I just wanted to take advantage of being older and wiser and say one thing. Being with a pilot is no joke. Alive today, dead tomorrow – and there you are on your own with a baby. A grim business!'

Vera put her hands over her ears and shook her head. 'No, no, I'm not listening!'

On her way home, Vera thought about Zina's story. Now that Viktorov had been discharged and would soon be flying again, wild, reckless love felt like the only real and meaningful thing in the world. At night, she imagined all kinds of fantastic scenarios. Viktorov would be lying on the ground wounded. She would rescue him and take him away to safety, further and further east. Remembering books she had read as a child, she dreamed of a little house in a northern forest or a hut on an uninhabited island. Life in a wilderness, in a hut surrounded by bears and packs of wolves, seemed an idyll compared with life in a city soon to be attacked by the Germans.

Vera believed that Zina lived in a different world to other people. For Zina, the laws of feeling were the laws of existence. After talking to Zina, Vera always felt more clearly than ever that love was the mightiest power in the world. Love took no account of tanks, guns, aeroplanes or blazing buildings. Love crossed trenches, did not recognize frontiers and feared no suffering or sacrifice.

She felt certain that Viktorov's life would end tragically. In his eyes she had seen a look of sadness, a recognition of an inescapable fate. The thought of their fleeing together to the peace of a northern forest was no more than a foolish dream. In his MIG, Viktorov was like a twig being swept away by a storm, through a sky full of dark flames.

At home she found Zhenya, Novikov and Sofya Osipovna. She wanted very much to tell Zhenya the story of the German officer. She wanted Zhenya to understand the triviality of the calm, comfortable love known by those who prosper in life. She wanted her to recognize

that there is another kind of love, a love that knows neither good fortune nor boundaries.

She recounted the story. She spoke quickly and with feeling, looking
Zhenya straight in the eye. She was like a preacher, castigating human
vices.

Everyone was deeply shocked.

Sofya was first to respond. 'It's true that Homer tells of a girl who
was going to live with Achilles, even though he had killed her father
and three brothers and burned down her city. But in those days people
lived by a different code. And pirates and brigands like Achilles were
respected figures, admired by everyone. It's not like that today.'

'What on earth's the *Iliad* got to do with it?' said Zhenya. She said
this quietly, but in a way that made everyone look at her. And then she
struck the rim of her glass with her spoon. Her face had turned white
and her lips were tight and trembling, but it was the high-pitched ring
of the glass that most truly expressed her fury. 'Idiot girl!' she added,
more shrilly.

'Maybe I am – but I understand what I need to understand.'

'How dare you use the word love about such vulgar, obscene filth!
Look around you! Look at all the grey hairs and haggard faces! The
graves! The burning buildings! The ashes! Look at all the broken families, all the orphans, all the people going hungry! Love has meaning
when it inspires people to sacrifice – otherwise it's just base passion.
When two people love, their love elevates them. They become willing
to sacrifice their strength, their beauty, even their lives. Love knows
everything – joy, torment, and sacrifice. Love knows great deeds. Love
is ready to meet death. But this ... This thing you've just told us ... It's
petty, foul, dirty. What you've just told us is contemptible. You call it
love, but I call it a sickness. It's vile. It's like an addiction to cocaine or
morphine. I want to spit in its eyes.'

Vera was looking at her with sullen obstinacy. Her jaw dropped
open; she could have been a schoolgirl dumbfounded by an unexpectedly fierce telling-off from a teacher. She looked helpless – and Zhenya
seemed to feel it wrong to expend any more of her fury on her. She
turned to Sofya and went on, in the same shrill voice, 'And you should
be ashamed of yourself too, Sofya! What's Homer got to do with any
of this? What Vera's told us is filth – and that's clear enough to anyone
with a Russian heart. There's no need to drag Homer and Achilles into
it. I know it's not for me to give you lectures, but really, you ought to
know better ...'

Sofya agreed with every word Zhenya had said to Vera. But being quick-tempered, she took offence at Zhenya's mention of a Russian heart. She gasped. Her broad chest swelled. Her cheeks, her ears and even her forehead turned a bright red. The locks of grey hair across her forehead seemed about to catch fire.

'Yes. Of course. A Russian heart. Mine, of course, is a mere Jewish heart. Yes, I understand.' She pushed her chair back, scraping the legs on the floor, and left the room.

'What's got into you, Sofya Osipovna?' said Zhenya. 'Has the war damaged your mind too?' Then she turned back to Vera. 'Yes, you should be ashamed of yourself. You've been brought up as a revolutionary, as a member of the intelligentsia. How dare you talk like that! Thank God Granny's not here. She wouldn't have forgiven you till the end of her days.'

Zhenya was speaking more quietly, but it was these last words that upset Vera most of all. Zhenya's first outburst had made her shrink into herself. Now, though, Zhenya sounded less out of control – and so Vera began to feel more angry. She was like a blade of grass, returning to the upright after being flattened by a blast of wind.

'Don't bring Granny into it. It's not as if *you've* got much in common with either her or Grandad. Granny was first imprisoned at the age of eighteen. You're twenty-six now – and what have you got to show for yourself? Only a failed marriage – though it seems there may be a second one on the way!'

'Don't talk nonsense,' Zhenya said coldly. 'Just try to get it into your head that love and morphine are different things. A drug addict ready to suffer or die for their fix is not a hero. They're more like a prostitute. If you can't understand that, then there's nothing more to be said.'

She made a gesture of dismissal, like a haughty queen exiling a disgraced courtier.

Vera left the room.

Zhenya and Novikov remained silent for a while. Then Zhenya said, 'Vera thinks it's just her I'm cross with, but really I'm more cross with myself. Remember our conversation down by the river?'

Novikov replied quietly, 'Zhenya, there's something I have to tell you: I'm going to Moscow very soon. I've been called to the Central Cadres Administration. I'm to be given a new posting.'

Zhenya looked at him in astonishment, not understanding.

'When are you going?'

'Any day now, by plane.'

'Why didn't you tell me sooner?'

'I was afraid you'd be angry. But after hearing the way you spoke to Vera just now, I felt bolder.'

'The only person I have any right to be angry with is myself. Embarking on any serious relationship at a time like this is sheer madness. I can't believe I was such an idiot as not to see that!'

'Madness isn't such a bad thing,' said Novikov, thinking how beautiful Zhenya looked when her feelings were roused. 'As long as it's madness about something that matters.'

'We seem to be exchanging roles,' Zhenya replied. 'You've started preaching the things I said down by the river, and I'm coming out with the boring good sense I was complaining about.'

'To be honest,' said Novikov, 'I already have committed a tiny, infinitesimal act of madness. Remember when I sat in the train with you, from Voronezh to Liski? Really, I should have been on my way north, to Kashira, but I saw your face in the window and got in a train going south, or rather south-east. When I got out at Liski I had to wait twenty-four hours for a train back.'

Zhenya gave him an intent look and started to laugh.

57

Mikhail Sidorovich Mostovskoy woke up, raised the blackout blind, opened the window and breathed in the freshness of a cool clear morning. Then he went to the bathroom and shaved, noting with annoyance that his beard was now entirely grey. He could no longer distinguish his beard trimmings from the soapsuds.

'Did you hear today's bulletin?' he asked Agrippina Petrovna when she came in with his tea. 'My radio's broken.'[166]

'Good news!' said Agrippina Petrovna. 'We've destroyed eighty-two tanks and two infantry battalions, and we've set fire to seven of their petrol tankers.'

'Nothing about Rostov?'

'No, I don't think so.'

Mostovskoy drank his tea and sat down at his desk to work. But then Agrippina Petrovna knocked at his door again.

'Mikhail Sidorovich, it's Gagarov. But if you're busy, he says he can come back in the evening.'

Mostovskoy was delighted to see someone, even if it was irritating to be disturbed during working hours.

Gagarov was a tall old man with a long, narrow face. He had long thin arms, long hands with slender and unusually pale fingers, and long legs which – judging by the way his trousers flapped about – must have been equally thin. As he came through the door, he said, 'Did you hear the bulletin? Rostov and Novocherkassk have both fallen.'

'Is that so?' said Mostovskoy, and brushed one hand over his eyes. 'And there was Agrippina Petrovna saying she'd heard good news: that we'd destroyed eighty-two tanks and two battalions of infantry, and taken prisoners.'

'Oh God, what a stupid old woman,' said Gagarov, with a nervous twitch of his shoulders. 'I've come to you for comfort and reassurance, as a sick man turns to a doctor. And I do also have some business to discuss.'

The air filled with the howl of an engine. Drowning out every other sound, a fighter up above them was looping the loop. When it grew quiet again, Mostovskoy said, 'I've not much comfort to offer. I can only say one thing: that there are, in fact, grounds for optimism in what we hear from silly old Agrippina Petrovna. What really matters is what seems least important. Rostov is a great blow, it's a tragedy – but it won't decide the outcome of the war. The final outcome depends on the small print in those bulletins – and the small print's on our side, day after day, hour after hour. For more than a year now, the fascists have been fighting on a 3,000-kilometre front. What seldom gets mentioned is that, as they advance, the fascists are losing not only lives and blood. They get through thousands of tons of fuel, they wear out a certain proportion of their engines, a certain amount of their tyre rubber. And any number of smaller things. The final outcome of the war depends more on these seemingly unimportant matters than on the big events we all hear about.'

Gagarov shook his head sceptically. 'But look at the way they keep advancing. They clearly have a definite strategy.'

'Nonsense! They did have a plan once, as you know, and that was to destroy Soviet Russia in eight weeks. But this war has already been going on for fifty-six weeks. This miscalculation matters. The war was supposed to paralyse our industry. It was supposed to trample our wheat to the ground, to destroy any possibility of a harvest. But Siberia, the Urals, everywhere to the east is working day and night. There's enough kolkhoz bread both for our front line and for the rest of the country – and there always will be. What, I ask you, has become of Hitler's elegant plan? What's so well planned about this wild rush across the southern steppe? Do you think their evil acts are making the fascists stronger? Far from it. Their evil acts guarantee their collapse. Agrippina Petrovna with her simple good sense is right. You're the one I'd call silly.'

Mostovskoy had made several brief visits to Nizhny Novgorod before the Revolution. He had gone there to do archival research on the region's history, and now and again he had written for the liberal newspapers; it was then that he had first got to know Gagarov. Here in Stalingrad, the war had brought the two men together again. Gagarov was no longer young; it was several years since he had last worked. But in his day he had been renowned for his sharpness of mind; even now there were still a fair number of old people around who treasured his letters and remembered his thoughts.

Gagarov had an uncommonly powerful memory. His knowledge of Russian history was extraordinary. He knew more small details, important and unimportant, than one would think there was room for in a single head. He could effortlessly list several dozen people present at the funeral of Peter the Great, or tell you on what day and at what time Chaadaev had arrived at his aunt's home in the country and how many horses had pulled his carriage and the colour of each of them.[167]

If people talked to him about material hardships, he soon allowed his boredom to show. But the moment a conversation touched on questions he thought more significant, he would come to life, licking his lips and swallowing his saliva as if he were a gourmet in a famous restaurant, watching a waiter carefully and unhurriedly laying his table.

'Mikhail Sidorovich,' he said, 'I've not once heard you say "the Germans". It's always "the fascists". It seems you still draw a distinction. But aren't they one and the same by now?'

'Most certainly not,' Mostovskoy replied. 'As you well know. Take the last war. We Bolsheviks drew a very clear distinction between the Prussian imperialists around the kaiser and the German revolutionary proletariat.'

'I do indeed remember,' said Gagarov, laughing. 'How could I not? But you can hardly say it's a distinction that bothers many people today.' Seeing Mostovskoy frown, he quickly added, 'Look, this isn't something to quarrel over.'

'Why not?' said Mostovskoy. 'Perhaps it should be.'

'No, no,' said Gagarov. 'Remember what Hegel said about the cunning of universal reason? While the passions it has unleashed are raging, it departs from the stage. Only when those passions have done their work, only when they leave the stage, does universal reason – the true master of history – choose to reappear. Old men should attend to the reason of history, not to its passions.'

This enraged Mostovskoy. His fleshy nostrils twitched. Still frowning, but no longer looking at Gagarov, he said pugnaciously, 'I may be five years older than you, my good objectivist, but I shan't abandon the struggle until my last breath. I can still march thirty-five miles, and I can still manage a bayonet or a rifle butt.'

'Well, there's certainly no compromising with you,' said Gagarov. 'Anyone would think you're going to join the partisans tomorrow. Now, remember I once told you about someone I know called Ivannikov?'

'Yes, I do.'

'Ivannikov asks you to give this envelope to Alexandra Vladimirovna. It's for her son-in-law, Professor Shtrum. It's from behind German lines. Ivannikov brought it across the front himself.'

He handed Mostovskoy a small package wrapped in torn, dirty, brown-stained paper.

'Wouldn't it be better if Ivannikov gave it to her himself? There'll be things the Shaposhnikovs want to ask him about.'

'Yes, of course there will. But Ivannikov says he knows nothing about this envelope. It's pure chance that it ended up in his hands. He was given it by some woman in Ukraine. He has no idea how it reached her, and he doesn't know her name or address. And he'd rather not have to go to the Shaposhnikovs.'

'All right,' said Mostovskoy with a shrug. 'I'll pass it on.'

'Thank you,' said Gagarov, watching Mostovskoy slip the package into his pocket. 'This Ivannikov, by the way, is a rather unusual man. First he studied at the Forestry Institute, and then he studied humanities. He used to spend whole months wandering about the Volga provinces. That's when we first met, he used to come and see me in Nizhny Novgorod. In 1940 he was in western Ukraine for a long time, inspecting the mountain forests. And he was there again when the war started. Living with a forester, with no radio and no newspapers. And when he finally emerged from the forest, he found the Germans already in Lvov. At this point his story becomes quite remarkable. He took refuge in the cellars of a monastery; the prior gave him a job, sorting through their store of medieval manuscripts. And without telling the monks, Ivannikov helped other people to hide there: a wounded colonel, two Red Army soldiers, and an old Jewish woman along with her grandson. Someone denounced him to the Germans, but he got everyone out in time and then slipped away into the forest. The colonel decided to try to escape through enemy lines, and Ivannikov chose to go with him. So they walked a thousand *versts*.[168] The colonel was wounded as they crossed the front. Ivannikov had to carry him in his arms.'

Then Gagarov got to his feet and said in a very serious voice, 'Before I go, I want to pass on some news – very important news, at least to me. Believe it or not, I'll soon be leaving Stalingrad – and in an official capacity.'

'You've been appointed as an ambassador?'

'Don't make fun of me. It's astonishing. I've been called to Kuibyshev all of a sudden. Would you believe it? I'm to be official consultant for a major historical work on famous Russian generals. People have

308

remembered that I exist. There have been whole years when I haven't received a single letter from anyone. And now, well, I've heard women in the building say, "The telegram? Who do you think it's addressed to? Gagarov – who else?" Mikhail Sidorovich, I haven't felt so happy since I was a little boy. It makes me want to weep. My life was so lonely – and suddenly, at a time like this, people have remembered me. Unimportant as I am, I seem to be needed.'

As he saw Gagarov out, Mostovskoy asked, 'How old is this Ivannikov?'

'You want to know whether an old man can become a partisan?'

'There are many things I want to know,' said Mostovskoy.

That evening, after finishing his work, Mostovskoy took Gagarov's package and went out for a walk. He walked fast, swinging his arms, breathing freely and easily.

After completing his usual circuit, he went to the city gardens and sat down on a bench, glancing now and again at two soldiers sitting nearby.

The sun, wind and rain had coloured their faces the dark, rich brown of well-baked bread, while the same sun, wind and rain had bleached all colour from their tunics, now white with just the merest hint of green. The soldiers seemed to be enjoying their view of the city and its calm, everyday life. One of them took off a boot, unwound his foot cloth and anxiously examined his foot.

His mate sat down on the grass, opened a green knapsack and took out some bread, some fatback and a small flask. A park attendant with a broom walked over and said sadly, 'Comrade, what are you doing?'

The soldier seemed surprised. 'Can't you see?' he said. 'We're hungry.'

Shaking his head, the attendant walked off down the path.

'Well, it's clear enough *he's* never seen war,' the soldier said with a sigh. Putting his boot on the bench, the first soldier sat down on the grass beside him and said, in a teacherly voice, 'That's just the way it is. None of them have a clue – not till they've had a few bombs smash up their lives for them.'

In a very different voice, he then called out to Mostovskoy, 'Come and join us, Grandad. Have a bite to eat with us, and a drop to drink.'

Mostovskoy sat down on the bench, beside the boot, and the soldier gave him a glass of vodka, and some bread and fatback. 'There, Grandad – you'll have been getting thin back here in the rear.'

Mostovskoy asked how long it was since they'd been at the front.

'We were there this time yesterday, and we'll be back there tomorrow. We've been to the support-services dump, to collect a consignment of tyres.'

'How *are* things going there?' asked Mostovskoy.

The soldier who'd taken off his boot said, 'War's a grim business out in the steppe. The Fritzes are giving us a hard time.'

'It's a joy being back here,' said his mate. 'It's so quiet. Everyone's so calm. No weeping and wailing.'

'It'll be another story when the war's moved a bit closer,' said the soldier wearing only one boot. Two boys in bare feet had appeared and were gazing in thoughtful silence at the bread and the fatback. The soldier looked at them. 'What's up, lads? Looking for something to get your teeth into? Here you are! In heat like this a man doesn't much feel like eating,' he said, as if ashamed of his generosity.

Mostovskoy said goodbye to the two soldiers and set off to the Shaposhnikovs.

It was Tamara Berozkina who opened the door to him. She asked him to come in and wait – the family were all out, and she had come round to use Alexandra Vladimirovna's sewing machine. Mostovskoy handed her the package for Professor Shtrum and said it would be best if he just went on his way. Everyone would be tired when they got back, and they wouldn't be wanting visitors.

Tamara said he couldn't have come at a better time. The post was no longer reliable, but Colonel Novikov was flying to Moscow first thing tomorrow. Mostovskoy had never heard of this Colonel Novikov, but Tamara spoke as if he'd known him for years. And most likely, she added, Novikov would be staying in the Shtrums' apartment.

She took the envelope between her thumb and finger and said in horror, 'Heavens, what filthy paper – anyone would think it's been lying in a cellar for the last two years.'

There and then, standing in the corridor, she wrapped the envelope in a sheet of the thick pink paper people use to make decorations for Christmas trees.

58

Viktor went to see Postoev in the hotel.

In the room with him was a group of engineers. Amid the tobacco smoke, in green overalls with large protruding pockets, Postoev looked like a huge construction superintendent surrounded by technicians, foremen and brigade leaders. Only his fur-lined slippers were out of keeping.

He was clearly excited and he was arguing a great deal. Viktor was impressed – he had never seen Postoev so animated.

There was one very important figure present – a member of the board of the People's Commissariat, or maybe even a deputy people's commissar. A short man, with curly blond hair and a pale face with high cheekbones, he was sitting at the table in an armchair. The others addressed him by name and patronymic: Andrey Trofimovich.

Sitting close to Andrey Trofimovich were two rather thin men – one with a short straight nose, the other with a slender face and greying temples. The man with the short nose was Chepchenko, director of a metals factory recently evacuated from the south of the country to the Urals. He spoke with a soft, melodious Ukrainian accent, but this did not diminish the impression he gave of extraordinary obstinacy; on the contrary, it only intensified this impression. When people argued with him, a guilty smile would appear on his lips, as if to say, 'I'd be only too glad to agree with you, but I'm afraid this is just the way I am. There's nothing I can do about it.'

The man with the slender face and grey hair was Sverchkov; he had a Urals accent and had clearly been born and bred there. He was the director of a well-known factory. Newspapers often carried accounts of receptions held there for delegations of gunners and tank commanders.

Sverchkov was a Urals patriot. A sentence he liked to repeat was 'Yes, that's how we do things in the Urals.' He appeared to dislike Chepchenko. Whenever the latter spoke, Sverchkov's bright blue eyes narrowed and his fine upper lip lifted a little, revealing his yellow tobacco-stained teeth.

Next to Postoev sat a short stocky man in a general's tunic, with yellow-grey eyes that moved slowly from person to person. Everyone referred to him simply as 'the general', often addressing him indirectly: 'Well, what does the general think?'

Near the window, sitting the wrong way round on his chair, his chin on its back, was a completely bald, pink-faced, independent-looking young man. Viktor never got to hear his name; everyone addressed him, for some reason, simply as 'Smezhnik' ('Partner Factory'). On his chest, Smezhnik wore three medals.

The engineers all sat in a row on a long sofa: factory chief engineers, power engineers, heads of experimental workshops – all frowning with concentration, all bearing the mark of long months of hard labour and little sleep.

There was one elderly man, probably a former worker who had been promoted; he had pale blue eyes, a cheerful, inquisitive smile and – shining brightly against his dark jacket – two Orders of Lenin. Sitting next to him was a young man in glasses who reminded Viktor of one of his postgraduates, worn out by too many late nights of study.

These men were the big shots, the leading lights in the field of Soviet quality-steel production.

*

As Viktor entered the room, Andrey Trofimovich had been saying in a loud voice, 'Who says your factory can't produce armour plating? You've received more from us than anybody. Why can't your factory deliver what you promised to the State Defence Committee?'

The man being criticized replied, 'But Andrey Trofimovich, don't you remember—'

'That's enough of your *buts*,' Andrey Trofimovich interrupted angrily. '*Buts* don't kill Germans and you can't fire shells from them. We've given you all the metal and coke you need. We've given you meat, tobacco and sunflower oil – and all we get in return is *buts*.'

Seeing all these strangers engaged in serious discussion, Viktor took a step back. He would have left, but Postoev asked him to stay, saying their business was nearly finished.

Viktor was surprised to discover that everyone present knew who he was. He had thought that his name was known only to professors, postgraduates and the more senior Moscow students.

Postoev quietly explained to Viktor that he had been expected at a meeting that morning in the People's Commissariat but had been feeling poorly. His heart had been giving him trouble. And so Andrey Trofimovich, who didn't like to waste time, had decided to hold the meeting in the hotel. They had already reached the last item on the agenda: the use of high-frequency electric currents in the processing of quality steel.

Now addressing the meeting as a whole, Postoev said, 'Viktor Pavlovich has elaborated a number of hypotheses of considerable import for contemporary electrical engineering. Chance has brought him to us just as we prepare to address questions closely related to his work.'

'Sit down, Viktor Pavlovich,' said Andrey Trofimovich. 'We will certainly trouble you for a free consultation.'

The young man in glasses who reminded Viktor of one of his postgraduates said, 'Professor Shtrum can have no idea what a struggle it was for me to obtain a copy of his latest work – in the end I had to get someone to make a special trip by plane to deliver it to me in Sverdlovsk.'

'And did you find it useful?' said Viktor.

'How can you ask?' the young man replied. It did not, for even a moment, occur to him that Viktor honestly did doubt the usefulness of his work to scientists and engineers struggling with real, practical difficulties. 'Needless to say, I didn't find it easy reading. I had to sweat over it.' At this point he looked more than ever like Viktor's postgraduate student. 'But I'm glad I did. I'd made several mistakes, and you showed me how and where I'd gone wrong.'

'You also made a mistake just now, when we were discussing the programme,' said the general, without the least humour or irony. He was looking at the young man intently, his eyes now appearing entirely yellow. 'But I've no idea which academy will rescue you this time.'

Then everyone forgot about Viktor and carried on as if he weren't there.

Sometimes they used a factory jargon all of their own and Viktor was unable to understand what they were saying.

The young man in glasses got so carried away and began to talk about his research in such detail that Andrey Trofimovich had to ask him to stop, saying pleadingly, 'Have a heart! You're giving us a year's worth of lectures, but we've only got forty minutes to cover everything else on the agenda.'

Soon after this they moved on to more practical matters – the overall programme, the workforce, the relationship of individual factories to

313

the association as a whole and to the People's Commissariat. Viktor found all this fascinating.

Andrey Trofimovich did not mince his words. Viktor was struck by how often he came out with phrases like 'All right, that's enough of you and your so-called "objective conditions" ... Every one of your requests was granted ... You received everything in person ... The State Defence Committee gave you everything ... No other factory was allocated more coke ... You were awarded the Order of the Badge of Honour – but there's no honour that can't be revoked.'

At first it seemed strange that the common cause, the cause that bound these men so closely together, should give rise to so much ill will and mockery.

What lay behind their arguments, however, was shared passion – their love for a cause that mattered more to them than anything else in the world.

These men were very different from one another; some were wary of innovation, others loved nothing more. The general was proud that he had overfulfilled the Defence Committee's plan using only ancient furnaces built by self-taught craftsmen in the days of the tsars. Sverchkov, on the other hand, read out a telegram he had received a month earlier: official approval from Moscow of his innovations – the outstanding success he had achieved with new installations he had constructed with startling boldness.

The general cited the opinions of old workers and craftsmen; Chepchenko relied on personal experience; Smezhnik preferred to rely on decisions taken by his superiors. Some of those present were naturally cautious; others, more audacious, said things like 'What do I care how they do things abroad? My design office has followed its own path, and the results have been excellent in all respects.'

Some were almost plodding, others quick and brusque. The young man in glasses teased Andrey Trofimovich and seemed not to care about his approval. Smezhnik glanced up at him after every word and asked, 'What does Andrey Trofimovich think?'

When Smezhnik boasted that he had overfulfilled the plan, Sverchkov, the Urals patriot, said, 'I had a visit from your Party organizer. I know that your workers have been freezing in tents and shoddily built barracks. You've had men swell up from hunger and you've had one member of a national minority drop dead on the shop floor from scurvy. Yes, you're certainly not a man for half-measures – though you don't look undernourished yourself!'

314

And Sverchkov pointed a long bony finger towards Smezhnik's rosy face.

'And *I* know,' Smezhnik retorted, 'that you had a children's canteen built at your factory, with white tiles on the walls and marble tabletops – and then in February you were criticized for failing to supply metal to the front.'

'You're lying,' Sverchkov shouted back. 'It's true I got it in the neck in February, but that was before the canteen even had walls. In June, I received an expression of gratitude from the State Defence Committee. By then the kitchen was fully functioning. We've achieved a hundred and eighteen per cent of the norm. Do you really think that the only way to do that is to give the workers' children so little food that they all get rickets?'

But it was Andrey Trofimovich whom Viktor found most interesting of all. 'Go on, take risks, we're all in this together – and we'll answer for it together!' he said more than once. 'Yes, go on! Have a go!' he said to one director. 'Being scared gets you nowhere. There's no ignoring a Party directive, but life's a directive too. Today's directive will be out of date tomorrow – it's you who must give the signal. Steel production – that's your only true directive!' He looked round at Viktor, smiled and asked, 'What do *you* think, comrade Shtrum? Am I talking sense?'

'You most certainly are!' Viktor replied.

Andrey Trofimovich looked at his watch, shook his head sadly and turned to Postoev. 'Leonid Sergeyevich, please summarize the technical issues.'

Listening to Postoev's response, Viktor was filled with admiration. The clarity with which he summarized complex ideas made his habitual self-assurance seem right and legitimate. He emphasized the value of true understanding and the danger of chasing after spectacular short-term results that would, in the end, bring no real benefits. He clearly had a natural ability to focus on what really mattered.

Then it was Andrey Trofimovich's turn to speak: 'There can be no doubt now of the importance of our quarterly plan. Remember last November, when the Germans were just outside Moscow and the factories to the west had all ceased production? Every factory was either on a train or else lying in the Siberian snow, waiting to be reassembled. There were many of us, back then, who thought we could afford to invest energy and resources only into what would yield immediate results – into what would bring us high-quality steel if not within twenty-four hours, at least within the next week. It was during those grim months that Stalin resolved to construct an entirely new iron and steel industry. But now that we have thousands of new machine tools at work in Siberia, Kazakhstan and the Urals, now that we have tripled our production of quality steel, where would we be without all those newly constructed blast furnaces and open-hearth furnaces? What would we be doing with all our fine lathes, hammers, rolling mills and blooming mills? That kind of thinking is what I call leadership – true leadership! It's not enough to think about what your factory will be doing tomorrow – you need to be thinking about what your factory will be doing a year from tomorrow.'

And then, evidently wanting, at least for a moment, to give these hard-working men an overview, to remind them how much they had already achieved, Andrey Trofimovich said, 'Remember October, November and December last year? During those three months our output of non-ferrous metals was less than three per cent of our pre-war output. And our output of ball bearings was only slightly higher – about five per cent.'

He got to his feet and held up one hand. His face was glowing. He was no longer chairing a technical discussion – he looked more like a seasoned orator addressing a workers' demonstration. 'Think for a moment, comrades, about what we have built in the snows of the Volga basin, Siberia and the Urals. Whole divisions have sprung up – divisions of machine tools, hammers and furnaces! Whole armies! Machine tools, furnaces of every kind, blooming mills turning out more and more armour plating – these are the battleships of our industry! In the Urals alone there are now 400 new factories. It's like the year's first flowers, coming back to life, fighting their way through the snow. Understand?'

Viktor was listening intently.

All the documentary films, all the poems, books and articles he had read about Soviet industry – all these images now merged. It was as if they were a single living memory, something he had witnessed himself.

In his mind he could see a clear picture: smoky shop floors; open furnaces, white-hot as the flame of an electric arc; grey armour plating, as if stiff and congealed; workers in clouds of smoke, amid beating hammers, amid the whistle and crackle of long electric sparks. The vast power of iron and steel seemed to fuse with the vastness of the Soviet Union itself. And Viktor could sense this power in the words of these men who talked about millions of tons of steel and cast iron, about billions of kilowatt-hours, about tens of thousands of tons of high-quality rolled steel.

But for all his lyrical talk of flowers pushing through the snow, Andrey Trofimovich was clearly no dreamer. Nor was he in the least easy-going. When one of the chief engineers asked him to explain a directive sent to his factory, Andrey Trofimovich interrupted, saying sternly, 'I've done enough explaining. Now I'm giving orders!' And he thumped his palm down on the table, as if stamping some document with a huge state seal.

When the meeting was over and everyone was saying goodbye to Postoev, the young engineer in glasses came up to Viktor and asked, 'Do you have any news of Nikolay Grigorievich Krymov?'

'Krymov?' Viktor repeated in surprise. Realizing why the engineer's long thin face seemed oddly familiar, he asked, 'Are you a relative?'

'I'm Semyon, his younger brother.'

The two men shook hands.

'I often think about Nikolay Grigorievich. I love him,' said Viktor. With feeling, he added, 'As for that Zhenya, I'm still furious with her.'

'But how is she? Is she in good health?'

'Yes, of course she is,' Viktor said crossly, as if wishing she weren't.

They went out into the corridor together and walked up and down for a while, talking about Krymov and reminiscing about life before the war.

'Zhenya's told me about you,' said Viktor. 'You've been promoted very fast since you moved to the Urals. You're already the deputy chief engineer.'

'Chief engineer, now.'

Viktor began questioning him: Might he be able to carry out a trial smelt and produce a small amount of the grade of steel Viktor required for his special apparatus?

Semyon considered this for a moment and said, 'It'll be difficult, very difficult indeed, but let me think about it.' With a mischievous smile, he added, 'Science helps industry, but sometimes it's the other way round. There are times when industry can help science.'

Viktor invited Semyon back to his apartment. With a shake of the head, Semyon answered, 'No, I'm afraid that's out of the question. My wife wants me to go and see her family in Fili – they don't have a telephone – and it looks like I won't even have time to do that. I have to be at the People's Commissariat in an hour. There's a meeting at the State Defence Committee at half past eleven, and then at dawn

I fly back to Sverdlovsk. But let me write down your telephone number anyway.'

They said goodbye.

'Come and visit us in the Urals,' said Semyon. 'Please – you really must!'

The engineer looked like his elder brother in many ways; they both had long hands and arms, a shuffling gait and a slight stoop. The only difference was that Semyon was a little less tall.

Viktor went back into the room. The meeting had tired Postoev, but he was pleased how well it had gone.

'They're an interesting lot,' he said. 'All the kingpins of heavy industry. You were lucky to see them all together. They were all summoned by the State Defence Committee.'

He was sitting at the table with a napkin on his lap. The waiter cleared away the cigarette ends, opened the windows and laid the table.

'Will you have lunch with me?' asked Postoev. 'You're not getting thin back in your apartment?'

'Thank you, I'm not hungry,' said Viktor.

'I won't insist,' said Postoev. 'Not at a time like this.'

The waiter smiled and left the room. Postoev began to talk more seriously. 'Here in Moscow there seem to be a lot of people who have no idea of the gravity of the military situation. Kazan may be a thousand kilometres further east, but people there are more jumpy. But where I was yesterday,' and he pointed toward the ceiling, 'up at the very top, they can see things as a whole. They know what's going on. And I have to tell you, they're very anxious indeed. I asked directly, "What's the situation on the Don? Is it serious?" And someone said, "The Don's the least of it. The Germans may well break through to the Volga."' Looking Viktor in the eye and clearly articulating each word, he added, 'Do you understand, Viktor Pavlovich? These aren't just ignorant rumours.' And then, abruptly, 'Our engineers are a good lot, aren't they? Truly remarkable!'

'Yesterday,' said Viktor, 'I was asked what I thought about returning the institute to Moscow. Did I think it best to do this all in one go, or gradually, one step at a time? There was no mention of dates. Nevertheless, I was asked my opinion. How do you square that with what you've just been saying?'

They were both silent.

'I think,' said Postoev, 'that the answer lies in what you've heard today from our engineers. Bear in mind what Stalin said last November – that modern warfare is motorized warfare. Someone up at the top must have calculated who's producing the most engines – us or the Germans. You know that we have six lathe operators now for every one we had before the Revolution. For every tool fitter we had before the Revolution we now have twelve. Where the tsar had one mechanic, we have nine. And so on and so on, across the board.'

'Leonid Sergeyevich,' said Viktor, 'I have never before felt envious. Never! But listening to all of you today, I felt I could give up everything in order to work where workers are making engines, where they produce steel for tanks.'

Postoev replied half-jokingly, 'That's all very well, but I know what you're like. You're an obsessive. Take you away for a month from your quanta and your electrons – and you'll be like a tree without sunlight. You'll fall ill.'

He paused, then asked with a smile, 'But tell me what you're doing for meals, great family man and homebody that you are?'

59

Viktor had a great deal to do in Moscow. There were many complex administrative matters to attend to.

In spite of this, he saw Nina almost every evening. They would go for a walk along Kaluga Street or visit the Neskuchny Garden. One evening they went to see the film *Lady Hamilton*.[170] During these walks it was Nina who did most of the talking. Viktor usually walked beside her and listened; now and again he would ask a question. Viktor already knew a great deal about Nina: that she worked in a sewing co-operative; that she had moved to Omsk after her marriage; that her elder sister was married to a section head at one of the Urals factories. Nina had also told him about her brother, the commander of an anti-aircraft unit, and about how angry all three of them had felt when their father remarried after the death of their mother.

Everything Nina told him so trustingly and straightforwardly was important to Viktor. He remembered the names of Nina's friends and relatives. Now and again he would say something like 'I'm sorry. Please remind me of the name of Claudia's husband.'

What moved Viktor most, however, was what Nina told him about her marriage. Her husband was clearly a bad man. He sounded rude, ignorant and egotistical, a careerist and a drunkard.

Sometimes Nina came and helped Viktor prepare dinner. He was touched when she said, 'Maybe you like peppers. Let me bring you a few – I've got some next door.' One day she said, 'You know, I'm so glad to have got to know you. And it's very sad that I'll soon be leaving.'

'I promise to come and visit you,' he replied.

'So people always say.'

'No, no, I mean it. I'll stay in a hotel.'

'No, you won't. You won't even send me a postcard.'

One evening, getting home late after being delayed at a meeting, he thought sadly as he went past Nina's door, 'Today I won't see her at all – and soon I'll be leaving.'

The following morning Viktor went to see Pimenov, who greeted him with the words, 'Everything's done now. Yesterday your plan received the approval of the redoubtable comrade Zverev. You can send a tele-gram to your family and let them know you'll be back soon!'

That evening Viktor was supposed to be seeing Postoev, but he phoned him to say that he had to deal with an unexpected problem and was no longer able to come. Then he went straight back home.

On the landing he caught sight of Nina. His heart began to race. He was almost gasping for breath.

'Why? What is it?' he said to himself, though the answer, of course, was obvious.

He saw Nina's face light up, and she called out, 'Wonderful – how good that you've come back early! I've just written you this little note.' And she handed him a letter, folded into a triangle.[171]

Viktor opened the note, read it and put it in his pocket.

'Are you really leaving this instant?' he asked. 'I was hoping we could go for a walk.'

'I don't want to go to Kalinin,' Nina replied, 'but I have to.' Seeing the disappointment on Viktor's face, she added, 'I'm definitely coming back on Tuesday morning and I'll stay here in Moscow till the end of the week.'

'I'll go to the station with you.'

'No, that would be awkward. I'm travelling with another woman from Omsk. I'm sorry.'

'In that case you must come round for a moment right now. We can drink to your speedy return!'

As Nina went in with him, she said, 'Oh, I quite forgot! Yesterday some commander came round and asked for you. He said he'd come again this evening.'

They drank a little wine.

'Does it make your head spin?' asked Nina.

'My head's spinning, but not from the wine,' he said – and began to kiss her hands. Just then the bell rang.

'Probably yesterday's commander,' said Nina.

'I'll have a word with him outside,' Viktor said determinedly. A few minutes later he came back, accompanied by a tall figure.

'Let me introduce you,' said Viktor. Almost apologetically, he said, 'This is Colonel Novikov. He's just come from Stalingrad. He's brought messages from my family.'

Novikov gave a slight bow, maintaining the impassive, blind polite-ness that war imposes on people who regularly have no choice, at any time of day and night, but to burst in on the private lives of others.

Novikov's blank eyes said that Viktor's private life was nothing to do with him, and that he was not in the least interested in the nature of the relationship between the professor and this beautiful young woman.

Behind these blank eyes, however, Novikov was thinking, 'Oh, so you soldiers of science are no different from the rest of the world. You have your campaign wives too!'

'I've brought you a little package,' he said, opening his bag. 'And everyone sends their warmest greetings – Alexandra Vladimirovna, Marya Nikolaevna, Stepan Fyodorovich and Vera Stepanovna.' As he went through these names – somehow failing to mention Zhenya – Colonel Novikov no longer had the air of an important senior commander; he seemed more like an ordinary Red Army soldier, passing on messages to the families of those with whom he had been sharing a dugout.

Viktor absent-mindedly dropped the package into an open briefcase that was lying on the table. 'Thank you, thank you!' he said, 'And how is everyone in Stalingrad?' Afraid that Novikov might launch into a protracted account, he at once asked more questions: 'Are you here in Moscow for long? Is it just a quick visit, or will you be staying for some time?'

'Heavens,' said Nina. 'I'd quite forgotten. My colleague will be here any moment. We're going to the station together.'

Viktor saw Nina to the door. Novikov heard him follow her out onto the landing.

Viktor returned. Not knowing where to begin, he asked, 'You haven't said anything about Zhenya. She hasn't left Stalingrad already, has she?'

Clearly embarrassed, Novikov barked out in his most official voice, 'Yevgenia Nikolaevna asked me to pass on her greetings. I forgot to say this.'

Just then something passed between them. It was what happens when two electric wires are brought together, when two prickly, bristling angry wire-ends are finally united – when a current begins to flow, when a lamp lights up and all that in the twilight looked alien and hostile becomes sweet and welcoming.

After exchanging quick looks, they both smiled. 'You must stay the night,' said Viktor.

Novikov thanked Viktor but said that he might be called any moment to the People's Commissariat of Defence and that he had already given them a different address. It was impossible for him to stay at Viktor's.

'How are things around Stalingrad?' asked Viktor.

Novikov was silent. Then he said, 'Bad.'

'What do you think? Will we stop them?'

'We have to stop them. And so we will.'

'Why *have to*?'

'If we don't, we're finished.'

'A compelling reason. Here in Moscow, I have to say, people seem calm and confident. There's even talk about bringing back factories and institutes that have been evacuated. Some say the situation is improving.'

'They're wrong.'

'What do you mean?'

'The situation is not improving. The Germans are still advancing.'

'And our reserves? Do we have many? And where are they positioned?'

'That is something neither you nor I are supposed to know about. That is a matter for the Stavka.'

'Yes,' Viktor said thoughtfully. He lit a cigarette. Then he asked if Novikov had seen Tolya during his two days in Stalingrad. He asked for news of Sofya Osipovna and Alexandra Vladimirovna.

And in the course of this conversation – though less from what he said and more from his smile or from a sudden serious look in his eyes – Viktor came to feel that Novikov already understood these people he had known for so long and whose behaviour he had puzzled over so very often.

Novikov said with a laugh that Marusya was educating all the children in the province – including her husband and daughter. He said that Alexandra Vladimirovna worried about everyone – and above all, about Seryozha – but that she got through as much work as any two normal people half her age. And he said of Sofya Osipovna, 'Sometimes she recites poetry to me, but she's as tough as they come. She could even cope with our general.'

He said nothing more about Zhenya, and Viktor did not ask. It was as if they had an unwritten agreement.

Gradually they slipped back into talking about the war. The war in those days was like some great sea where every river had its source and into which every river flowed back.

Novikov spoke of field commanders and staff officers who showed real initiative, and then he would begin cursing some bureaucrat who never missed an opportunity to play safe or pass the buck. From his gestures and tone of voice when he began to repeat this bureaucrat's words about 'the axis of movement' and 'the tempo of the advance', Viktor felt he could almost have been talking about Sukhov, the institute's former director.

Novikov's unexpected arrival had upset Viktor. Now he felt full of goodwill, even tenderness, towards him.

He remembered a thought that had first occurred to him many years ago, about how the apparently striking differences between Soviet people – their looks, their professions and interests – were often only superficial. The unity these things obscured was far deeper. There might seem little in common between Viktor Shtrum, an expert in mathematical theories of physics, and a front-line colonel, a man who could begin sentences with the words 'As a professional soldier ...'

But he and Novikov turned out to have a great deal in common. Many of their thoughts were similar. They loved the same things and were pained by the same things. In many ways they were brothers.

'Really, everything's very simple,' he said to himself, somewhat mistakenly.

Viktor told Novikov about the meeting with Postoev and said what he'd been thinking about the future course of the war. When Novikov was about to leave, he said, 'I'll go with you. I need to send a telegram.'

They said goodbye on Kaluga Square. Viktor went to the post office and sent a telegram to his family in Kazan, saying he was in good health, that things were going well with the work plan, and that he should be able to return at the end of the following week.

60

On Saturday evening Viktor set off by train for the dacha. Sitting in the carriage, he began to mull over the events of the last few days.

It was sad that Chepyzhin had already left. As for Colonel Novikov, Viktor liked him very much; he was glad they had met. Better still, of course, if they had met half an hour later and their meeting had not got in the way of his saying goodbye to Nina. But it didn't matter – Nina would be back on Tuesday. Once again he would be with this young, sweet and beautiful creature.

He was no less preoccupied by his thoughts about Ludmila. He imagined the intensity of her anxiety about Tolya and how lonely she must feel; he thought about the many years he and she had now been together. Combing her hair in the morning, she had said many times, 'Vitya, we're getting older.' After a vicious quarrel, she had sometimes come into his study with tears in her eyes. Once she had said, 'You know, I'm so used to you that I enjoy looking at you even when we're arguing. And when you're away from home, I just don't know what to do with myself.'

So many living ties. So many shared successes. So many anxieties, griefs and disappointments. So much hard work.

People's relationships had always seemed so clear and simple. It had always seemed so easy to explain other people's behaviour to Tolya and Nadya, but his own feelings now seemed beyond understanding.

The logic of thought was something he could trust. His study and his laboratory had always been on good terms; only occasionally had his theories and his laboratory experiments collided. There had been brief periods of bewilderment, of confused standstill, but these had always ended with reconciliation. Together, theory and practice could make progress; separated, they were powerless. Practice never tired; it could march on for ever, carrying sharp-eyed, winged theory on its steady shoulders.

In Viktor's personal life, however, everything was now confused. A man with one leg was trying to lift a blind companion onto his shoulders while asking him to point out the way.

All logic did was confuse Viktor still further. It was a logic born of emotion, not of any aspiration towards truth. It was, in its very essence, a lie. It was not seeking truth but trying to defend an error. Worse than that, this logic was simply trying to defend the wishes of the man who was exercising it.

Viktor could sense within him a multitude of logics: a logic of pity, a logic of passion, a logic of duty, a logic of kindness and a logic of selfish desire.

He remembered a phrase of Martin Luther's that had once bewildered and enraged him: 'Reason is the Devil's first harlot.'

He wanted, dear God, to kiss a young woman. How could he help it?

It was strange. The more insistent the arguments put forward by the logic of duty, the more single-mindedly the logic of selfish desire worked to turn him against Ludmila.

He remembered his quarrels with her. He remembered her rudeness, her total irrationality in argument, her extraordinary and invincible obstinacy, her constant, sullen ill will towards his relatives, her coldness towards his mother, her sudden fits of meanness, the way she shouted at beggars as she shooed them away from the dacha fence.

People said she worshipped her husband's work. Was this true? Once, seven years ago, she had said, 'I've been wearing the same fur coat for the last four years, and Tolya's worse dressed than anyone else in his school. You really shouldn't be refusing to take on a second chair. Everyone else we know holds more than one office. Everyone else thinks about their family, not just about their research.'

All too many sins had accumulated over twenty years – all too many wrongs, hurts and thoughts he'd kept hidden. Like a prosecuting lawyer, he catalogued all the wrongs she had done. He was preparing an indictment. He wanted only one thing – to indict. And indict he did.

Deep in his heart he knew that his indictment was unfair and partial, false and mendacious. Not only had falsehood, which he had detested all his life, penetrated his relations with his family and friends, but it had also clouded the cool, clear spring of his reason.

As he got out of the train, he asked himself, 'But then, what's so wrong about falsehood? Why, when it comes down to it, are lies worse than truth?'

*

326

Viktor opened the little gate and entered the garden. The setting sun was reflected in the windows of the verandah.

The garden was full of phlox and campanula – splashes of bright colour among the tall wild grass now growing densely and greedily in flower beds and strawberry beds, beneath the dacha's windows, everywhere Ludmila had never allowed it to grow. There were blades of grass on the paths, piercing through the sand and the packed earth; there were blades peeping out from beneath the first and second steps of the porch.

The fence was no longer upright. Some of the planks had been ripped out and the raspberry canes from next door were stealing in through the gaps. There were traces on the verandah floor of a small bonfire someone had made on a sheet of corrugated iron. And people must have been living in the house during the winter – Viktor could see bits of straw, a worn-out padded jacket, some tattered foot cloths, the crumpled bag from a gas mask, yellow scraps of newspaper and a few wrinkled potatoes. The cupboard doors were all open.

Viktor went up to the first floor. Their guests had evidently been there too – the doors were all wide open. The sight of the empty rooms and cleaned-out cupboards did not in the least upset Viktor. On the contrary, he felt only too glad to be freed from Ludmila's excruciatingly complicated demands. No longer would he have to find the items she wanted, pack them, struggle to get hold of a car, and take all this extra luggage to the station.

'Wonderful!' he said to himself,

Only his own room was still locked. Before leaving, Ludmila had blocked the narrow little corridor with broken chairs and old buckets, and she had disguised the door with sheets of plywood.

There were thumps and crashes as he dismantled the barricade. This took him some time. Finally, he was able to unlock the door. The orderly appearance of his untouched room was somehow more startling than the chaos elsewhere; it was as if only a week had passed since that last Sunday before the war.

He had argued with Ludmila about where his mother should sleep. And Maximov had come round – his unread manuscript still lay on the floor, close to the bed.

There were chess pieces on the desk. Around a vase lay the remains of some flowers – a circle of blue-grey dust. Their rough stalks were like a small dusty broom, sticking up into the air.

On that last peacetime Sunday, Viktor had sat there at his desk, working on some troublesome problem. And then he had solved the problem, written an article, typed it out and given copies to his colleagues in Kazan. The problem itself no longer concerned him, but the memory of that Sunday was now unbearably painful.

He took off his jacket, put his briefcase on the desk and went downstairs. The wooden staircase creaked beneath his feet. Usually Ludmila heard this from her room and asked, 'Where are you going, Vitya?'

But no one could hear his footsteps now. The house was empty.

Then came the sound of rain. In the windless air the large drops fell generously and abundantly. The setting sun was still shining; as they passed through its slant rays, the drops flared, then faded. It was a very small rain cloud, and it was passing right over the dacha; its smoky leading edge was already floating away towards the forest. The sound of the drops had not yet tired the ear. Rather than a dull monotone, it was a polyphony in which every drop was a conscientious and impassioned musician, fated to play only a single note in its whole life. The drops pattered to the ground, bouncing off the strong, taut burdock leaves, breaking up against the silky pine needles, dully tapping the wooden steps of the porch, drumming on thousands of birch and linden leaves and sounding the iron tambourines of the roofs.

The rain passed, yielding to a wonderful silence. Viktor went out into the garden. The moist air was warm and clean; every strawberry leaf, every leaf on every tree, was adorned with a drop of water – and each of these drops was a little egg, ready to release a tiny fish, a glint of sunlight, and Viktor felt that somewhere in the depth of his own breast shone an equally perfect raindrop, an equally brilliant little fish, and he walked about the garden, marvelling at the great good that had come his way: life on this earth as a human being.

The sun was setting, twilight was coming down over the trees, but the drop of light in his breast did not want to be extinguished with the light of day. It was gleaming more and more brightly.

He went back inside and up to his room, opened his briefcase and began to look inside it for a candle. He found a small package and thought it was a bar of chocolate he had bought for Nina. Then he remembered that it had been given to him by Novikov. He had forgotten about it, and the package had lain there all day unopened.

Viktor found a candle and hung a blanket over the window. The candlelight brought a sense of peace to the room.

He undressed, got into bed and began to open the little package from Stalingrad. Written in a firm, clear hand were the words 'Viktor Shtrum', followed by his Moscow address.

Recognizing his mother's handwriting, he threw off the blanket and put his clothes back on again. It was as if a calm, clearly audible voice had called to him out of the dark.

Viktor sat down and glanced through the long letter. It was his mother's record of her last days – from the beginning of the war until the eve of her inevitable death behind the barbed wire of the Jewish ghetto. It was her farewell to her son.

All sense of time disappeared. Viktor did not even ask himself how this child's exercise book had found its way to Stalingrad, how it had crossed the front line.

He got to his feet, removed the blackout curtain and opened the window. There was a white morning sun over the fir tree by the fence. Leaves, flowers and grass were all covered in dew; it was as if a dense shower of finely ground glass had fallen on the entire garden. There were explosions of birdsong from the trees in the orchard – sometimes from a single tree, sometimes a sudden volley from every tree at once.

Viktor went up to the mirror hanging on the wall. He was expecting to see a haggard face with trembling lips and crazed eyes, but his face looked just as it had the day before. His eyes were dry and there was no red on their lids.

'So that's it,' he said aloud.

Feeling hungry, he broke off a piece of bread and slowly, with effort, began to chew it, looking intently all the time at a twisted pink thread quivering on the edge of the blanket.

'It's as if it's being rocked by the sunlight,' he said to himself.

61

On Monday evening Viktor was sitting in the dark on the sofa in his Moscow apartment. He had not put up the blackout curtain and he was looking out through an open window. Suddenly, the air-raid sirens sounded and searchlights lit up the sky.

A few minutes later the sirens stopped and he could hear a few of the other tenants shuffling slowly down the stairs in the dark. Then he heard an angry voice outside, 'Why hang about in the yard, citizens? Everything in the shelter's as it should be. There are cots and benches and water that's just been boiled.'

But the citizens evidently had ideas of their own. They did not want to go down into a hot airless cellar until they were certain they needed to.

Children called out to one another. Someone said, 'Yet another false alarm – they'd do better to let us have some sleep!'

Then came the chatter of distant anti-aircraft guns.

And then – the malevolent drone of a bomber. The roar of Soviet fighters. A brief hubbub out in the yard, a distant thump and more anti-aircraft fire. But there were no longer any voices in the intervals between shots.

Human life had now flowed down into the bomb shelter. There was no one left in the buildings and yards. The pale blue brooms of search-lights went on silently and diligently sweeping the cloudy night sky.

'Good,' said Viktor. 'Now I'm alone.'

An hour passed. Viktor still sat in the same position, as if in a dream, staring out of the window, his brows furrowed, listening to the ack-ack fire and the explosions of bombs.

Then came a silence. The raid seemed to be over. There was the sound of people emerging from the shelter. The searchlights went out and the dark returned.

All of a sudden the phone rang, abrupt and unrelenting. Without turning on the light, Viktor picked up the receiver. The operator said there was a call for him from Chelyabinsk. Viktor thought it was some muddle, and he almost hung up. But it turned out to be Nikolay

Krymov's brother, the engineer he had spoken to at the end of Posto-ev's meeting. The line from Chelyabinsk was very good. Semyon began by apologizing to Viktor for disturbing him during the night.

'I wasn't asleep,' Viktor replied.

It turned out that an entirely new electronic control apparatus had been installed in Semyon's factory. They had encountered serious problems while trying to put it into operation and this was greatly slowing the entire production process. Semyon wanted Viktor to send him one of his research assistants – it was, after all, Viktor's laboratory that had worked out the principles behind this equipment. Viktor's assistant could leave Moscow at dawn on a factory plane. He should, however, be warned that it would be a difficult journey – it would be a heavily loaded transport plane, not a passenger aircraft. The factory's representative in Moscow had been put in the picture. If Viktor agreed, then he could send a car to collect the assistant – Viktor needed only to make one phone call to this representative.

Viktor replied that his colleagues were all in Kazan – there was no one except him in Moscow. Semyon begged Viktor to send a telegram to Kazan. The problem was both complex and urgent; only a scientist with a sound theoretical understanding would be able to help them.

Viktor thought.

'Hello, hello!' said Semyon. 'Are you still there, Viktor Pavlovich?'

'Give me your representative's phone number,' said Viktor. 'I'll come myself. I'll see you this evening.'

He called the representative, gave him his address and warned him that he would be taking two suitcases with him – from Chelyabinsk he would return not to Moscow but straight to Kazan. The representative said he would arrange for a car to collect Viktor at five o'clock.

Viktor went to the window and looked at the clock – it was a quarter to four.

The beam of a searchlight moved past in the dark. Viktor watched it, wondering whether it would disappear into the blackness as suddenly as it had appeared. The beam trembled, darted to the right, then to the left, and then froze – a vertical pale blue pillar between the dark of the earth and the dark of the sky.

62

The fighting to the west of the Don lasted for about three weeks. The first stage was the German attempt to break through to the river and surround the divisions defending the line Kletskaya–Surovikino–Suvorovskaya.

Had they succeeded, the Germans would have crossed the Don and headed straight for Stalingrad, but despite their numerical superiority, and although they managed to penetrate the Soviet defences in several places, the offensive failed. The battle begun on 23 July turned into a stalemate, tying down large numbers of German troops. Soviet counter-attacks paralysed the advance of the German tanks and motor infantry.

The Germans then attacked from the south-west. This too proved unsuccessful.

Then the German command decided to launch simultaneous attacks from north and south.

This time they outnumbered the Soviet forces two to one, and they enjoyed a still greater superiority in tanks, artillery and mortars.

Paulus's troops began their advance on 7 August and reached the Don two days later, taking control of a broad area on the west bank and encircling a number of Soviet units. Now in a precarious position, the Red Army troops still on the west bank began crossing the river.

In the first days of August 1942 the Supreme Command ordered Krymov's anti-tank brigade, which had suffered heavy losses, to withdraw to Stalingrad to regroup and refit.

On 5 August the brigade's main units, along with its HQ, crossed the Don near Kachalin and set off towards their regrouping point – the Tractor Factory on the city's northern outskirts.

Krymov accompanied the brigade as far as the ferry, said goodbye to the commander, and then drove to the HQ of the army on the right flank; there he was to meet Sarkisyan, the commander of the mortar unit to which he was now being posted.

The mortar unit had been delayed because their petrol tanker had been bombed during the night and their vehicles had been left without fuel. Sarkisyan had to go to Army HQ to obtain a warrant for petrol.

Wanting to shorten the journey, Krymov set off along a back road. Knowing from experience how easy it is to lose one's bearings in the steppe, he kept stopping the car and looking intently all around him. The Germans might be very close and he had no wish to get lost in the spider's web of steppe roads and tracks.

He could see he must be near to HQ: there were telephone cables alongside the road and he was overtaken by an armoured car from a signals unit. Then a camouflaged ZIS-101 with crumpled sides sped past, followed by a green Emka staff car with shattered windows.

Krymov told Semyonov to follow the Emka and they continued on their way, sometimes lagging a little behind it, sometimes driving within the cloud of dust raised by the vehicles ahead. They came to a barrier. After it had been raised to allow the first two vehicles through, Krymov held out his pass. As the sentry leafed through it, Krymov asked, 'Is this the 21st Army HQ?'

'It is indeed,' the sentry replied. He handed back Krymov's pass and smiled, knowing how relieved someone feels when, amid the confusion of war, he finds the place he's been searching for.

Krymov left his car by the aspen pole that served as a barrier and made his way into a small village, plodding through deep sand the warmth of which he could feel even through his boots.

The HQ was clearly preparing to move. Instead of being hidden beneath camouflage awnings, trucks were parked beside huts. Soldiers were loading tables, stools, typewriters and crates of documents. They were working quickly, quietly and with casual efficiency. It was easy to see that, during the last year, they had loaded and unloaded the HQ's furniture and equipment dozens of times.

Krymov went straight to the canteen – a canteen during the lunch hour was usually the easiest place to find the people you needed. A specific HQ way of life had developed in the course of the last year, and this way of life was much the same in all the different Army HQs Krymov had seen.

He used to joke that life in a Front HQ was like life in the capital of one of the Soviet republics, that life in an Army HQ was like being in a provincial capital, that a divisional HQ was like a district town and a regimental HQ like a large village, while battalion and company command posts were like field camps caught up in the sleepless frenzy of harvest time.

The canteen staff were also preparing to move on. Waitresses were packing cups and plates in trunks lined with straw. The admin clerk was stacking meal coupons and ration-card stubs in a metal box.

The canteen was located in the village school. Commanders and political workers were standing by the main door, waiting to be issued with their field rations. Desks removed from the classrooms took up almost half the yard; a pockmarked captain was sitting at one of these desks and rolling a cigarette. Opposite him stood a blackboard. It was a long time since it had last rained in the Don steppe and the children's arithmetic was still clearly visible. The waiting commanders went on talking, paying no attention to the new arrival. It was in any case obvious from Krymov's gait, from the way he headed straight to the canteen, and from the layers of dust covering his face and his clothes, that this man was simply another comrade, a brother fighter.

'So you never got a new tunic sewn for you, Stepchenko?' said one man.

'Which truck are you going in? With the scouts, or the operations section?'

'Once again,' said a third man, 'the canteen boss has given us concentrate instead of sausage. And I bet he'll be having fried chicken himself – the bastard eats as well as the army commander.'

'Look, there's Zina. She's not even going to glance at us. And she's wearing smart little new boots, made to measure.'

'What does Zina want with a lowly captain? She'll be doing the journey by car – while you'll be bouncing about at the back of a one-and-a-half-tonner, like a mere mortal.'

'You can stay with me at our next stop – the commandant's promised me a billet near the canteen!'

'I'd rather stay away from the canteen, my friend. What if Fritz sees the crowds outside and drops a bomb on it? Remember the pounding we got on the Donets, when we were quartered in ... What was the name of that village?'

'The Donets was nothing. Do you remember Chernigov last autumn? Major Bodridze was killed, along with six others.'

'Was that when your greatcoat got burnt?'

'That greatcoat! I had it made for me in Lvov. The cloth was good enough for a general.'

Several men were listening to a young black-haired political instructor. There was a restrained happiness about his entire being – it was clear that he had just returned to safety after being under fire. His animated tone of voice was at odds with the painful story he was telling.

'We were still deploying. The Messers were flying low, almost scratching our heads with their wheels. Some of our units showed true

334

heroism. There was one anti-tank battery where not a single gunner survived. Not one man abandoned his gun. But what's the use when the enemy's broken through all around you?'

'Do you have eyewitness accounts of acts of heroism?' a battalion commissar – evidently the head of the information section – asked severely.

'Of course,' said the political instructor, patting his knapsack. 'I nearly got killed on my way to speak to the battery commander, but I wrote down the names of all the dead gunners. Well, it's a good thing I found you here. No one, needless to say, had thought to put my knapsack in the car. And no one had bothered to put me down on the list for field rations. Really, comrades!'

'And the situation in general?' asked someone else. His face was covered in stubble and he wore the green cap of a quartermaster.

The political instructor shrugged. 'Chaos. No one even knows where the command posts are any longer. I nearly ended up in a gully occupied by German tanks.'

Krymov had heard any number of conversations like this. Now, however, they felt blasphemous – all the more blasphemous for their apparent normality. He ran his tongue over his dry lips, gasped with indignant fury and said, 'You, a senior political instructor, speak of the death of entire gun crews, and about the retreat of the Red Army, as if you're a tourist from Mars. It's as if you've flown here for a quick look and in a minute you'll be going back home.'

Instead of cursing and swearing as Krymov expected, the political instructor merely blinked and muttered, 'Yes, yes, I'm sorry. I was just glad to have found my comrades. Otherwise I'd have had to beg for a lift on some passing truck.'

Krymov had been ready to come out with some cutting response. Taken aback by this mild reply, he answered more gently, 'Yes, of course, I know what it's like to have to beg for a lift.'

He knew the laws of army life. He knew how often people's acts of petty selfishness are redeemed with the sacrifice of their lives. He knew how often such sacrifices are made, calmly and straightforwardly, by the very people who, as they leave a burning city, feel most upset by the thought of a soap dish or packet of tobacco left behind on a kitchen windowsill.

And yet anything normal and natural was already hard to imagine. The coming weeks – or even the coming days – were likely to prove critical.

Krymov could see that, for many people, retreat had become almost a habit. The retreat had developed its customs and routines; it had become a way of life. Army tailors, bakeries, food shops and canteens had all now adapted to it. Men thought they could keep retreating, yet carry on with all their usual activities. They could work, eat, chase after women, listen to the gramophone, get promoted, go on leave, or send packages of sugar and tinned food back to their families in the rear. But soon they would be on the edge of the abyss; even one more step back would be impossible.

Suddenly the air was filled with the drone of engines. Several voices at once shouted, 'It's our Ilyushins! They're going to attack!'

At the same time, Krymov caught sight of Senior Lieutenant Sarkisyan, the short, massive-shouldered commander of the heavy-mortar unit. Sarkisyan was running towards him, gesticulating excitedly and shouting, 'Comrade Commissar! Comrade Commissar!' He carried on shouting until he was only a few feet away.

On his face was a look of joy. He was like a little boy who has got lost in a crowd and then, all of a sudden, glimpsed the angry, yet radiant face of his mother.

'I knew it, I knew it deep in my heart,' he said, a smile across the whole of his broad face and even his thick black eyebrows. 'That's why I've been hanging about all day by the canteen.'

Sarkisyan had arrived at Army HQ early that morning and asked for a fuel warrant from the major in charge of the fuel-supply section.

'Your unit has been transferred to the Front reserves,' the major had replied. 'You have received your assigned quota of fuel and you have been deleted from my list. You must apply to the fuel-supply section of the Stalingrad Front.'

Sarkisyan's face took on one expression after another as he recounted this conversation: first horror, then pleading, then fury.

The major had remained intransigent.

'So then I looked at him like this,' said Sarkisyan.

Sarkisyan's impassioned, unwavering gaze encapsulated the eternal resentment felt by front-line soldiers towards administrators safe in the rear.

Krymov and Sarkisyan set off together to ask the major to reconsider his decision. On the way Sarkisyan told Krymov about his unit's recent engagements.

In the evening, after the brigade had withdrawn, he had taken up defensive positions, even though his unit was some distance from the front line. And in the event he really did have to engage in combat – a nearby infantry unit had left its assigned sector and a German mobile detachment ran into Sarkisyan's outposts. He was able to repel this attack with ease, since he had been issued with two complete ammunition allowances for his mortars.

After losing two small tanks and an armoured personnel carrier, the Germans had retreated. Only at two in the morning did the Soviet infantry unit return to its sector. Had it not been for Sarkisyan, this sector would have fallen into enemy hands.

During the night the Germans had attacked again. After helping the infantry to fight them off, Sarkisyan asked the regimental commander for 150 litres of fuel. The commander, with surprising niggardliness, had given Sarkisyan only seventy litres, but this had at least allowed Sarkisyan and his eight vehicles to reach Army HQ. He had halted in the steppe, five kilometres to the east of the village, taken up defensive positions once again and hitched a lift to Army HQ to petition for fuel.

The two men came to a small white house with a battered lorry standing in front of it. 'Well then,' said Sarkisyan, 'here we are!' Pressing his fists to his chest, he said pleadingly, 'I feel timid, comrade Commissar. I'll only annoy the man. It'll be better if you speak to him on your own. I'll wait for you outside the canteen.'

He truly did seem very timid. Krymov was amused by the lost, confused look in the eyes of this strong, stocky man who knew everything there was to know about firing heavy mortar bombs at enemy tanks and motor infantry.

The major in charge of the army fuel-supply section was making his last preparations for departure. He was watching a clerk wrapping straw around an oil lamp and tying lengths of twine around pink and yellow folders full of documents. To all Krymov's arguments he replied politely but unshakeably, 'It's impossible, comrade Commissar. I understand your position, believe me – but I cannot contravene orders. I must answer for each drop of fuel with my own head.' And he slapped himself on the forehead.

Krymov realized that the major was not going to give in. 'In that case,' he said, 'please advise me what I should do.'

Sensing that his importunate visitor was about to leave him in peace, the major replied, 'Speak to the general in command of support services. He decides everything. There's a fuel depot thirty kilometres away, the same size as our own – the general will be able to give you permission. Here, let me point you in the right direction. At the end of the street you'll see a little house with pale blue shutters. There's a sentry outside with a sub-machine gun – it's easy to recognize.'

As he went with Krymov to the door, he said, 'I'd have been only too glad to help, but orders are orders. I can't exceed my quarterly limit, and you've been transferred to the reserves – you're no longer on our list.'

For a moment Krymov thought that the major might relent. 'All very well to say we've been transferred,' he replied, 'but the unit was fighting all night long.'

But the major already had his mind on other things. He said to his clerk, 'Not even a week living in normal human conditions, and the commandant certainly won't be allocating us a proper billet at our next location. No, we'll be back in a dugout – like the lowest of nobodies.'

'Dugouts are safer, comrade Major,' the clerk said consolingly. 'Less chance of being bombed.'

Krymov found the little house with pale blue shutters. The sentry with the sub-machine gun called to the adjutant, a young man in a gabardine tunic. The adjutant heard Krymov out, shook his chestnut curls and said that the general was now resting – he had been working all night. Krymov would do better to come back another day, after they'd relocated. 'You can see for yourself,' he said. 'We're packing up. The only thing left is the telephone – in case there's a call from the commander of the temporary admin post.'

Krymov emphasized the urgency of his request: important vehicles were now stranded without fuel. With a sigh, the adjutant allowed Krymov to enter the building.

Watching an orderly roll up the carpet and take down the curtains while a young girl with neatly curled hair packed the china into suitcases, Krymov again fell into despair.

These pretty white curtains, this carpet, this red tablecloth and this silver glass-holder had all had brief airings in Tarnopol, Korostyshev and Kanev on the Dnieper, only to return time and again to their boxes and suitcases to continue their journey east.

'That's a fine carpet you've got here!' said Krymov. Conscious how little his words reflected his true thoughts, he smiled.

In a whisper, so as not to disturb the general resting behind a plywood partition, the adjutant replied, 'It's nothing special. But our old carpet was a museum piece. We lost it in Voronezh, during the bombing.'

The young girl, the only person not speaking in a hushed voice, said to the soldier doing the packing, 'No, don't put the samovar down at the bottom – it'll get dented. And the teapot needs to be in a separate box, how many times do I need to tell you? The general has mentioned this more than once.'

The soldier looked at her with meek reproach, the way an elderly peasant looks at a city beauty who has never in her life known real trouble.

'Kolya,' the girl said to the adjutant, 'don't forget about the barber. The general wants a shave before we set off.'

Krymov looked at the girl. She had rosy cheeks and the shoulders of a grown woman, but her fresh blue eyes, her small nose and her chubby lips were those of a child. She had large hands, the hands of a worker, and she had painted her nails red. Her smart side cap and neatly curled hair did not suit her; she would have looked better in plaits and a calico kerchief.

'Poor girl,' Krymov said to himself – and then returned to his bitter reflections. He had always seen the desire for petty-bourgeois well-being as a bitter enemy to the Revolution and all progress. This desire was dangerous because it was nourished by the powerful instinct of self-preservation. This pettiness and this hunger for personal well-being were branches of the tree of life. The life instinct fed them with its sap and helped them to grow. Nevertheless, these branches were also enemies of life. They went crazy; they wanted to grow and develop, and in their hunger they crushed and choked one another. They sucked dry the trunk that bore them; they exhausted the roots that nourished them.

Krymov well knew the power of this instinct. He had felt it the day before, while crossing the pontoon bridge, and he had refused – as he had refused on many previous occasions – to yield to it.

Somehow, it had to be made clear to the 'flighters' that their fate was inseparable from that of their brothers who had been taken prisoner. There was an insidious force that was capable of fragmenting the nation. A man with a car and plenty of petrol could drive further and further east; he could leave behind him one blazing town after another yet barely take in what was happening. He had saved his personal belongings from fire and they were safe in his car. He no longer noticed the vast load that could not be shifted by even the biggest of trains and trucks. He no longer thought about the fate of the people; he no longer thought about the past or about generations to come. His own small fate, he believed, was entirely separate from the greater fate, the fate of the people. He no longer felt any sense of responsibility. Since he was slipping safely away, taking his own little world with him, he thought that nothing terrible was happening.

It occurred to Krymov that these men ought to be taught, in material terms, that no part can survive without the whole. They needed what could be called *an object lesson*. The first time they retreated, their curtains would be confiscated. The second time, they'd lose their samovar; the third – their pillows; the fourth – their teacups and glasses. They'd have to make do with tin mugs. It should be made clear to everyone that each retreat would cost them more than the retreat before. In time, a man would be stripped of his decorations. Then he'd be demoted. And then he'd be shot.

All somewhat primitive, perhaps – but it would put an end to the smug, philosophical calm Krymov had witnessed all too often. No commander would take any further retreat for granted.

Krymov got to his feet and began pacing about the room. He wanted to smash his fist down on the table. He wanted – like a sentry he had once heard outside a brigade command post – to shout out, 'Quick! Alarm! Germans nearby!'

Puffing on his pipe, a captain came in and went up to the adjutant.

'Well?' he asked in a solicitous whisper, as if inquiring about a sick patient.

'I've already told you, comrade correspondent, not before fourteen hundred,' said the adjutant.

Then the captain looked round and said, 'Comrade Krymov?'

'Yes.'

'Yes, I thought so,' said the captain. 'My name's Bolokhin,' he continued in the same clipped manner. 'You won't remember me, no, you never knew me at all. But do you remember giving two lectures at the Trade Union School on the Treaty of Versailles and the German working class?'

'1931. Yes, I remember.'

'And later you gave a talk at the Institute of Journalism. Wait, now, what was the subject? Revolutionary forces in China … Or, was it the workers' movement in India?'

'Yes, something like that,' said Krymov, laughing with pleasure.

Bolokhin winked and put his finger to his lips. 'And, between you and me, you asserted that fascism would never take hold in Germany. Yes, you proved it definitively, with statistics of every kind to back you up.'

He laughed, his large grey-blue eyes looking straight at Krymov. Like his speech, his gestures and movements were quick and abrupt.

'Comrade, keep your voice down!' said the adjutant.

'Let's go out into the yard,' said Bolokhin. 'There's a bench there. Can you call us, comrade Lieutenant, when the general wakes up?'

'Without fail,' said the adjutant, 'the moment he wakes up. Yes, there you are – under that tree!'

'It's extraordinary,' Krymov said with a sigh. 'People from combat units come to HQ – and it's as if all we do is get in HQ's way! But it's for the combat units that HQ exists ...'

Bolokhin shrugged. 'Don't worry about why things exist. Just be sure to get hold of your petrol!'

Bolokhin worked for a military newspaper and was clearly well informed. Three hours before this he had been at the HQ of their neighbours, the 62nd Army.

'And how are the 62nd doing?' asked Krymov.

'They're crossing the Don, withdrawing to the east bank,' said Bolokhin. 'They put up a good fight, they held out for a long time, but they had too much ground to defend. So they're retreating. The only thing is, they haven't yet learned the right way to retreat. They get nervy and jittery, and then things go wrong.'

'I'd say it's a good thing they haven't learned how to retreat. Our own lot have learned that lesson only too well,' Krymov said bitterly. 'We do it calmly and quietly and no one gets the least bit jittery.'

'Yes,' said Bolokhin. 'And there were days when the Germans were hurling themselves against the 62nd. Yes, like waves against a rock.'

He looked closely at Krymov. Then he laughed and said with a shrug, 'So strange. It's all so strange.'

And Krymov understood that Bolokhin was remembering the time when an earlier Krymov – a man very different from this battalion commissar sitting beside him in dust-covered boots and a faded side cap – had come to lecture to the students about the class struggle in India. There had been a poster advertising these lectures by the main entrance to the Polytechnic Museum.

The adjutant appeared on the porch. 'This way, comrade Battalion Commissar. The general knows you're here.'

The general was middle-aged, with a broad face. Sitting at his desk, he was getting ready for his shave; where they crossed his shoulders, his braces looked like inlays, almost a part of the white cloth of his shirt.

'Well, comrade Battalion Commissar, what can I do for you?' he asked. Still with his back to Krymov, he was now examining the papers on his desk.

Krymov began, but the general went on looking at his papers. Uncertain whether the general had taken in anything at all, Krymov hesitated: should he go into greater detail – or should he start again from the beginning?

'Carry on!' said the general.

Seen from behind, with no field jacket and in his braces, the general did not look in the least like a senior military figure. Krymov sat down on a stool, inadvertently contravening military etiquette. The general, still leaning over his desk, evidently heard the stool creak. He interrupted Krymov mid-sentence: 'Have you been in the army long, comrade Battalion Commissar?'

Not realizing what lay behind it, Krymov took the general's question as a sign that things were going well.

'I fought in the Civil War, comrade General.'

Just then, the adjutant brought in a mirror. The general leaned forward and began to examine his chin. 'What have you done with that barber?' he asked. 'Don't tell me you panic-mongers have packed him away in a box too!'

'The barber is waiting outside, comrade General,' said the adjutant, 'and your hot water has been prepared.'

'Then what are you waiting for? Send the man in!'

Still looking in the mirror, the general said icily to Krymov, 'I'd never have guessed you've been in the army for long. I took you for a reservist. You sat down without asking permission. We consider that impolite.'

A reprimand like this leaves a subordinate confused: is that the end of it, or will these words be followed by a menacing 'Attention! About turn, march!'? Krymov stood up. Standing to attention, he replied with the stolid, weighty calm he could always call upon when needed: 'I apologize, comrade General – but to receive a seasoned commissar without turning to face him is also considered impolite.'

The general turned his head and, narrowing his pale grey eyes, looked at Krymov intently.

'Well, so much for Sarkisyan's fuel!' thought Krymov.

The general banged his fist on the desk and roared out, 'Somov!'

The barber came in with his brushes and razors. Glimpsing the anger on the general's red face, he took a step back.

'Beg to report!' came the loud, clear voice of Lieutenant Somov, the adjutant. Sensing the approaching storm, he too froze in the doorway.

In the soft voice of a commander issuing an order that is not to be questioned, the general said to his adjutant, 'Summon Malinin this instant and tell the son of a bitch I'll have him shot if he ever humiliates front-line commanders again. He knows very well that we have received orders to blow up our underground fuel tanks. We don't have the tankers to transport the fuel. If he doesn't issue it to fighting units, in forty-eight hours it'll go up in flames. He's to give the commissar every last drop of petrol he needs – enough to fill every vehicle and an extra five 200-kilogram barrels. And, till these orders have been carried out, he's not to move an inch.'

The general, now on his feet, looked deep into Krymov's eyes. In his intent gaze Krymov glimpsed cunning, intelligence and true soul.

'I don't know how to thank you, comrade General.'

'Very good, very good,' said the general, holding out his hand in farewell. 'One angry man meets another.' And then, very quiet, and with real anguish, 'But we keep retreating, comrade Battalion Commissar, we keep retreating.'

63

Sometimes a man can be unlucky for a long time, and unable to achieve even the smallest of things – and then something changes: after one success, everything starts to work out of its own accord, as if fate had already prepared quick, easy and convenient solutions for every difficulty.

Krymov had barely left the general's office when he saw a messenger from the fuel-supply section hurrying towards him. And he had barely left the head of the fuel-supply section's office, with a fuel-entitlement order made out and signed in only a few minutes, when he caught sight of Sarkisyan. The stocky senior lieutenant was running towards him, his large brown eyes shining:

'Well, comrade Commissar?'

Krymov handed him the order. During the last forty-eight hours fuel had been a matter of torment for Sarkisyan. If only he had been more diligent, long ago, in his studies of mathematics – then he might have been able to solve the insoluble. He and his sergeant had covered every sheet of paper they had with signs and numbers. In his large, round handwriting he had added, multiplied and divided kilograms, kilometres and the capacities of various fuel tanks, sighing, frowning and wiping the sweat from his forehead.

'Well, now we're alive and kicking!' he kept saying, laughing out loud and repeatedly scrutinizing the fuel order.

Even Krymov yielded for a moment to what he sometimes called 'the euphoria of retreat' – a state he was quick to detect in others and that upset him deeply. He knew only too well the look on the faces of men ordered to withdraw from positions where they had been under heavy fire; he knew the bright eyes of the lightly wounded, men legitimately walking away from the hell of the trenches.

He understood the preoccupied bustle of those about to set off east yet again; how a leaden weight in the heart could suddenly give way to a sense of invulnerability.

But he also knew that there was no getting away from the war. It followed men like a black shadow. The faster they fled the war, the faster it pursued them. Those who retreated brought the war with them, close

344

on their heels. The vast spaces to the east were a dangerous lure. The limitlessness of the Russian steppes was treacherous; it seemed to offer the possibility of escape, but this was an illusion.

The retreating troops came to peaceful orchards and villages. The peace and quiet were a joy to them – but an hour or a day later the black dust, the flames and thunder of war would burst in after them. The troops were bound to the war by a heavy chain, and no retreat could snap this chain; the further they retreated, the heavier the chain grew and the more tightly it bound them.

Krymov went with Sarkisyan to the western edge of the village, to the gully where the mortar unit had halted. The vehicles and equipment had been dispersed, hidden beneath the slope or camouflaged by branches. The men seemed sullen and idle; there was no sign of the usual businesslike behaviour of soldiers deftly and confidently establishing themselves in a new place – cooking, making straw beds, washing and shaving, and checking their weapons.

After a few brief conversations, it became clear that the men were depressed. Seeing Krymov approach, they got to their feet only slowly and reluctantly. If he made a joke, they replied with obstinate silence or a sullen question; if he tried to speak seriously, they answered with a joke. Krymov's connection with the men had broken – and he sensed this at once. Generalov, a man known for his cheerful courage, asked, 'Is it true, comrade Commissar, that the whole brigade's going to the city for a good rest? People say you've been telling everyone that our unit's been singled out, that it's just us who've been ordered not to retreat.'

Krymov was angered by the veiled reproach.

'Are you dissatisfied, Generalov? Have you changed your mind about defending your Soviet motherland?'

Generalov straightened his belt.

'I said no such thing, comrade Commissar. Why put words like that in my mouth? The section commander will tell you that my crew was the last to leave their position the day before yesterday. Everyone else had withdrawn, but we were still firing.'

A young ammunition-bearer, with a cross, mocking look on his face, said, 'Last to leave, first to leave – what's the difference? We still end up tramping across the whole of Russia.'

'Where are you from?' asked Krymov.

'I'm from Omsk, comrade Commissar. The Germans aren't there yet.' Evidently he was trying to forestall lectures about what the Germans might do to his birthplace.

From behind a car a voice asked, 'Is it true, comrade Commissar, that the Germans are already bombing Siberia?'

'And how do things stand with fuel, comrade Commissar? Apparently the infantry are already well on their way east.'

The mortarmen listened in silence to Krymov's angry reply. Then the voice from behind the car said sadly, 'So it's all our fault again. It's not the Germans advancing – it's just us retreating.'

'Who is it back there?' asked Krymov. He went over to the car. But whoever it was had disappeared.

64

Krymov ordered Sarkisyan to take all his vehicles to the fuel depot, since they did not have enough containers to transport the fuel.

Sarkisyan expected to be back by evening, and Krymov decided to wait for him in the village.

But Sarkisyan was delayed. First, to get enough petrol to drive to the Front fuel depot, he had to wait for a long time at the Army fuel depot. Then he took the wrong road. Finally it turned out that it was forty-two kilometres to the Front depot, not thirty as he had been led to believe.

It was still daylight when he got there, but he was told that fuel could be delivered to vehicles only at night. The depot was near the main highway, and German planes were patrolling the sky all day long.

As soon as a vehicle appeared, the Germans would swoop down, drop a few small bombs and rattle away with their machine guns.

The watchman reckoned that they were being bombed as often as eleven times in a single day.

The depot manager and his subordinates kept to their dugout. If anyone went outside, they would call after him, 'What's it like up there?'

'Only a single plane,' the man would answer. 'Circling about – as if the bastard's on sentry duty.'

Or: 'Coming straight at us, damn him! In a dive!'

At the sound of an explosion they would all throw themselves to the floor, cursing and swearing. Then one of them would shout to the man up above, 'What are you doing, parading about up there? You'll lure him back. Next time it'll be an armour-piercing incendiary.'

The day Sarkisyan came, they hadn't even been able to cook dinner, in case the Germans noticed the smoke. They had eaten only dry rations.

Sarkisyan had been stopped by sentries a kilometre before the depot. 'From here you must walk, comrade Senior Lieutenant. Until dark, vehicles are not allowed further.'

The depot manager, who had thistle heads, wisps of straw and bits of clay sticking to his uniform, advised Sarkisyan to take a good look

347

around while it was still light. He should memorize the way – and then return with his vehicles as soon as it got dark.

'But make sure that your drivers understand. They must not switch on their headlamps for even a second. If they do, we'll fire on them.'

Sarkisyan was to arrive with his vehicles at twenty-three hundred. Neither earlier nor later.

'He's out of the way then – seems that's when he likes to have supper,' the depot manager explained, pointing up at the dusty blue sky. 'And then just before midnight he litters the sky with signal flares, like an old woman putting her pots out to dry.'

German bombers were clearly no laughing matter.

65

Realizing that Sarkisyan was being badly delayed, Krymov ordered his driver to look for a billet in the village.

Semyonov was awkward and impractical. When they stayed the night in a village he was embarrassed to ask the peasant women for a glass of water, let alone milk. He slept hunched up in the car, too timid to enter someone else's hut. There appeared to be only one person whom he did not fear: the stern commissar. With Krymov, he did little but argue and grumble. In response Krymov would say, 'But one day I'll be transferred – and then you'll find yourself dying of hunger!'

Krymov was not simply joking. He felt a fatherly tenderness towards Semyonov and was truly concerned about his well-being.

On this occasion, however, Semyonov got everything right: he found an excellent billet – spacious, high-ceilinged rooms that until a few hours before had housed the Support Services HQ secretariat.

Only that morning the house's elderly owners – along with a tall, handsome young woman and the little fair-haired, dark-eyed toddler who was always there at her heels – had stood beneath the awning of their summer kitchen and watched the secretariat staff make their final departure preparations.

After lunch the last HQ sections had gone on their way, the guard battalion had followed – and the village had been left empty. Evening had set in and once again the flat steppe had taken on the moist colours of sunset. Light and dark had once again fought their silent battle high in the sky. Once again there had been a note of sadness and anxiety in the evening scents, in the muted sounds of the earth now condemned to darkness.

There are intoxicating yet bitter hours, sometimes whole days, when villages are deserted by the powers that be and are left in expectant silence. HQ had simply got to its feet and walked away; many huts now stood empty.

All that remained were tyre tracks; scraps of newspaper; empty tins outside huts; mountains of potato peelings beside the village school, which had housed the HQ canteen; narrow, carefully dug slit trenches, their walls lined with withered wormwood; and an aspen pole barrier, now raised to the vertical: the road was open – anyone could drive wherever they wished.

People felt both free and orphaned. Children roamed about the school premises: had the canteen staff left any tins of food behind, any candle ends or bits of wire, or even a bayonet? Sharp-eyed old women were checking whether their time-pressed guests had gone off with their scissors, their bits of rope, their cans of kerosene or their glass lamp-cover. An old man wanted to know how many apples had been stolen from his orchard, how much of his firewood had been consumed and whether or not his stock of dry boards was still intact. After looking around, he muttered crossly but without malice, 'Well, they're gone now, the devils ...'

And then his wife came in and said, 'That dratted cook really has gone off with my tub.'

A young woman looked thoughtfully at the empty road. Her mother-in-law, who had been keeping her under constant observation, said angrily, 'I see, missing that driver already, are you?'

Once again the village felt quiet, spacious and comfortable – but from the sudden sense of sadness and anxiety one might have thought the soldiers had lived their whole lives there, not just a day or two.

The villagers called to mind the commanders who had just left. One was quiet and diligent and always scribbling away; another, scared stiff of aeroplanes, was always first to enter the canteen and last to leave; a third, pleasant and straightforward, liked to have a smoke with the old men; a fourth was always bartering tinned meat for moonshine and pestering the young women; a fifth was arrogant and hardly ever spoke, but he had a good voice and played the guitar beautifully; and the sixth was the worst of all – you only had to look at him the wrong way and he'd accuse you of waiting impatiently for the Germans. And there was little about the commanders that the villagers didn't know; drivers, orderlies, messengers and sub-machine-gunners – Vanka, Grishka and Mitya to the villagers – had told them about the commanders' idiosyncrasies, where they were all from, and which of them was sleeping with which of the telephonists and secretaries.

But in less than an hour, every trace of these men would be gone, shrouded in dust by the wind. And then some stranger would turn up, and everyone would be shaken by the news they brought: that there was no sign of the Red Army, that the road was empty and that the Germans were approaching.

350

Semyonov said in a whisper that he didn't much like the owners but that the rooms were good. The old woman made and sold her own vodka. A neighbour had told him that before collectivization the old couple had made their living not only from the land but also from trade. Still, it wasn't as if he and Krymov were going to be staying with them for the next year. And as for the young woman, she was a real beauty!

Semyonov's sunken cheeks went a little pink. He was evidently very taken with this tall, high-breasted young woman, with her strong legs and strong, bronzed hands, with the bold, clear look in her eyes that makes a man's heart tremble.

Semyonov had learned that she was a widow. She had been married to the old couple's son, who was now dead. He had fallen out with his parents and so they had lived in another village, where he worked as a tractor-station mechanic. The young woman had come to her in-laws for a brief visit, to collect a few belongings. She would soon be leaving.

The smells brought by their recent guests had already evaporated. The freshly washed floor had been sprinkled with fragrant wormwood to get rid of the soldiers' fleas. The brightly blazing stove had absorbed the scents of light tobacco, city food and box-calf leather. Now there was only the powerful smell of the old man's home-grown tobacco.

Not far from the stove stood a large bowl of dough, protected from draughts by a little blanket.

Wormwood, home-grown tobacco, the stove, the moist cool of the newly washed floor – these smells had already blended together.

The old man put on his glasses and, looking round at the door, read in an undertone a German propaganda leaflet he had picked up in a field. Beside him, his chin touching the table, stood his fair-haired grandson, frowning severely.

'Grandad,' he asked very seriously, 'why does everyone keep liberating us? First we were liberated by the Romanians and now it's going to be these Germans.'

'Quiet!' said the old man, waving the boy away. And he went back to his reading. Figuring out the words was clearly a struggle. He was like a horse pulling a cart up an icy hill; if he stopped for even a moment, he'd never get started again.

'Grandad, who are these Yids?' asked his four-year-old listener, still severe and attentive.

When Krymov and Semyonov came in, the old man put down the leaflet, took off his glasses, looked straight at them and asked, 'So, just who *were* you two? How come you haven't left yet?'

351

It was as if Krymov and Semyonov no longer had a real, material existence. They were insubstantial, imaginary, no longer creatures of flesh and blood. And so, when he addressed them, the old man used the past tense.

'Whoever we were, we're no different now,' Krymov said with a smile. 'And if we haven't left, it's because we've been ordered to stay.'

'Why ask questions?' the old woman said to her husband. 'They'll leave when they need to.' And then, addressing their visitors: 'Sit down now and have a bite to eat.'

'No, thank you,' said Krymov. 'We've eaten already – but don't let that stop you.'

Then the young woman came in. She glanced at the new arrivals, wiped the back of her hand across her lips and laughed. As she walked past Krymov, she looked him straight in the eye. He felt as if he had been burned, and he didn't know whether this was from the intensity of her gaze or from the warmth and smell of her body.

'I had to call our neighbour round to milk the cow,' she said to Krymov in a slightly husky voice. 'My mother-in-law shares a cow with her neighbour, but I can hardly get near the animal. No, she's not one to let herself be milked by some stranger. Seems it's easier now to get a woman to do what you want than a cow.'

The old woman put a green bottle of moonshine down on the table.

'Pour yourself a glass, comrade Commander,' said the old man, bringing some stools up to the table.

There was a casual mockery in his use of the word *Commander*. Obliquely, he was saying, 'I'm not going to bother to find out what kind of commander you are. You may be a high-ranking commander or you may be a lowly commander, but really you no longer command anything at all – you can neither help me nor harm me. There's only one real commander in life – and that's the peasant. But if you want to be called *Commander*, if that's what you're used to, then I'll play along. I'll do as you wish.'

Like many people with an excess of inner energy, Krymov drank only occasionally, when he felt the need – as he liked to put it – to give himself a good shake. In reply to the old man, he shook his head.

'It's not just from beetroot,' said the old man. 'It's top quality, from real sugar.'

The old woman quietly put out glasses for all five of them and then a large dish with a mountain of tomatoes and cucumbers. She sliced some bread and carefully sprinkled a little salt over it, then threw down two forks and a knife with an unusually fine blade. One fork had a thick black wooden handle; the other, evidently acquired during the war, was made of silver.

She did all this in a few seconds, with remarkable deftness. It was as if she were simply flinging things onto the table, but each glass landed in just the right place. Tomatoes, knife, forks – everything appeared in the blink of an eye.

After muttering 'Your good health!', the old couple emptied their glasses, then ate a few mouthfuls. Without another word, the old woman refilled the glasses.

When it came to food and drink, the two of them clearly knew what they were doing.

It was good vodka, with a real kick, burning hot but not in the least acrid. Krymov was impressed. 'This place isn't a hut!' he said to himself. 'It's a temple to moonshine.'

The old woman glanced at Krymov and, as if sensing his confusion, said, 'Go on, have a bite to eat. After vodka like this, you need more than tobacco!'

As for the young woman, the way she looked at Krymov seemed to keep changing. One moment, her eyes were young and wild; next, they seemed kind and wise.

Then the old man said, 'In 1930 we slaughtered all the pigs and we drank for two weeks on end. Two men went mad. And there was one old man who drank two litres, went out into the steppe, lay down in the snow and fell asleep. They found him in the morning with a broken bottle beside him. The night was so cold that even the moonshine had frozen solid.'

'The moonshine I make wouldn't have frozen,' said the old woman. 'It's like pure spirit.'

The old man was already a little tipsy. 'You don't understand,' he said. 'That's not what I'm talking about.' And he tapped the German propaganda leaflet.

And the conversation suddenly turned, with awful frankness, to what had been and what would be. The old man did not see the Soviet retreat as a temporary setback; he believed that the Soviet regime was finished. The retreat confirmed what he had always believed.

'A Party member, are you?' he asked Krymov.

'Yes,' Krymov replied. 'My hair's going grey now, but I've been a Communist since I was a boy.'

'And what can you Communists do to me now?' asked the old man.

'My men are close by,' Krymov replied quietly.

'Glad to hear it,' the old man said good-naturedly.

The old man was drunk, and this made him want to speak out. It wasn't so much that he wanted an argument; it was more that he wanted to speak freely, no holds barred, about everything that had been forbidden.

He was, he believed, simply a witness. He was a historian.

As she listened to her husband inveigh against the kolkhozes, the blood went to the old woman's face. Wanting to help him, she said, 'And you must tell them about Luba, the woman who stole peas from our kitchen garden. And then she stuffed herself on plums in our orchard. And we didn't dare say a word against her – the moment the general went to sleep, there she was, playing cards with his adjutant ... And don't forget our kolkhoz chairman! When he left, he took all the best horses, and he went off with four whole *poods* of kolkhoz honey.[172] And the shop! Salt, kerosene and calico all got delivered there – but what good did that do us? All we ever got to see of that calico was the chairman's wife flouncing around in a new dress.'

'That was the least of it,' said the old man. 'There were things far worse than that.' He was astonished how old, long-forgotten words were now coming back to him, as if they had been engraved in his memory, and it was with intense feeling that he now pronounced these words: 'The Vineyards of the Crown Department ... Adjutant General Saltykovsky's estates ... A winery belonging to a member of the state Duma ... Company Commander Nazarov, of the Cossack Regiment of His Majesty's Life Guards ... The ataman of the *stanitsa* ...'

In the old days, everyone had lived calmly and comfortably. No one, he seemed to believe, had suffered real need.

As for this new world, with its tractors and combine harvesters, with its Magnitogorsks and its Dnieper dams, with its chairmen and brigade leaders, with everyone studying to be agronomists, doctors, teachers and engineers – nothing in this new world had brought anyone any good at all. Now people all worked like madmen. And to think of all the families deported in 1930 ... And now the Soviets had retreated to the Caucasus, now they were all on the run ...

The old couple spoke with particular anger about how hard everyone had to work for the kolkhoz. But the young woman replied, 'What are you two moaning about? The people who do the real work don't moan. When did either of you two do any work? All you ever did was make moonshine – and sell it to that same kolkhoz chairman!'

354

Krymov had long been aware of a human peculiarity he couldn't quite understand. The people who did the moaning and grumbling were not those whose lives were truly hard. This was true of individuals, and it was true of entire regions. Soviet power had done so much for the Don steppes, and for the region between the southern lakes and the Volga. Soviet power had battled against trachoma, tuberculosis and syphilis – it had healed a whole people. Soviet power had built schools. It had built a capital out in the steppe, with theatres, museums and cinemas. Huge flocks of sheep now grazed the Kalmyk steppe – but he'd heard the whole region was seething. Travelling about the steppe was dangerous. The locals murdered the wounded. They hid in the reeds and shot at you as you passed by. Whereas in the bogs and forests of Belorussia, where the soil was thin and poor and life was a thousand times harder, every escaped prisoner of war or soldier who'd broken out of encirclement was greeted as if they were long-lost sons.

'But as for the Germans!' the old woman was saying in a sing-song voice, 'We've nothing to fear from them. The Germans are releasing prisoners of war. They're giving us back our land. They're not even harming Party members – they just register them, then let them walk free. The only people with anything to fear from the Germans are the people us Russians have always had reason to fear, the people we love least of all.'

Krymov knew very well how pointless it was to argue at times like this. The twenty-five years since the Revolution had only strengthened this couple's prejudices. They had not suddenly changed. No one had suddenly cast a spell on them. It was just that they were now coming out with thoughts they had previously kept to themselves.

Krymov remembered how, in autumn 1941, near Chernigov, he had ordered a man to be shot for telling his soldiers they'd be better off if they were taken prisoner by the Germans. As if reading his mind, the old man said, 'And don't you go thinking it's just me. There are young men who think the same as me, and there are old men who think the same as me. You're not going to be able to shoot all of us.'

Krymov had fought against people like this all his life. He had fought tirelessly.

Transformed into heat, the psychic energy he had expended would have been enough to bring to a boil all the waters of Lake Baikal. When it seemed necessary, he had been merciless – but he had also been patient, more patient than the most patient of doctors, gentler than the gentlest of teachers. And at this most bitter hour of all, everything he

had fought against was still obstinately present, calmly eating tomatoes, digesting food, drinking and inviting him to drink too.

Krymov abruptly got to his feet, pushed the stool away and went
out onto the street. Semyon followed him.

It was twilight outside. The sandy track through the orchards looked
very white.

66

'What's happened to our Sarkisyan?' Krymov asked Semyonov. 'He should have been here long ago.'

Semyonov bent forward and whispered in Krymov's ear, 'A soldier passed by not long ago. He said there's no one at all to the west. Just no man's land. We need to move east – at least another twenty kilometres.'

'No,' said Krymov. 'We must wait here for Sarkisyan. But we're not staying the night with these rotgut-makers. Go and have a look in that barn over there – there'll probably be some hay we can sleep on.'

Semyonov wanted to protest: where was he going to find hay? Seeing the grim look on Krymov's face, he walked silently to the gate.

It turned dark. The street was quiet and deserted. There was a glow in the sky from some distant blaze, and an evil, uncertain light hung over the whole of this Cossack village, over its houses, barns, wells and orchards.

Dogs were beginning to howl and from somewhere to the eastern edge of the village Krymov could hear singing, wailing and drunken shouts. Above him he could hear buzzing and whining. Night-flying Heinkels were circling over the burning earth.

Looking at the sky and listening to the voices, Krymov recalled a terrible moment from the winter offensive. Lieutenant Orlov, a bold, cheerful nineteen-year-old, had asked to be released from duty for two hours – his unit had just retaken the town where he had been born and he wanted to see his family. Krymov never saw him again. After discovering that his mother had left with the Germans as the Red Army approached, Orlov had shot himself.

'Betrayal. A mother's betrayal. What could be more terrible?' Krymov said to himself.

The distant fire was still burning.

Krymov felt someone quietly draw near him, looking at him. It was the young woman. Unconsciously, not even thinking about her, he must have expected this; seeing her so close to him was no surprise. She sat down on one of the steps of the porch, her arms round her knees.

Lit by the distant glow, her eyes were shining and the now soft, now sinister light brought out her beauty to the full. She must have sensed, not with her mind or even her heart but through every inch of her skin, that he was looking at her bare upper arms, at the play of light on her legs, at the two smooth, slippery braids that fell down from her neck and curled onto her knees. She said nothing, knowing that there were no words to express what was happening between them.

This tall man with the furrowed brow and calm dark eyes looked very different from the young drivers and soldiers who, in exchange for love, had offered her tinned meat, petrol and millet concentrate.

She was not shy or submissive. These days she was having to fight for her life as roughly, as straightforwardly, as any man. She ploughed, shod horses and chopped wood; she mended roofs and walls. Little boys and old men were now doing most of the women's work – digging the garden, herding the cattle and looking after the babies – and she was doing the work usually done by the adult men.

She put out fires, chased thieves from the grain store, delivered the wheat to the district town and negotiated with the military authorities about the use of the mill. She knew how to cheat, and if anyone tried to cheat her, she knew how to outwit them, how to deceive the deceiver. And even her ways of deceit were male – more like the bold fraud of an important bureaucrat than the simple tricks of a peasant woman.

It was not her style to add water to milk or to swear that yesterday's milk, already beginning to turn, was fresh from the cow. Nor did she come out with quick, shrill, peasant-woman curses. When she was angry, she cursed and swore like a man, slowly and expressively.

And in these days of the long retreat, in the dust and thunder of war, as Heinkels and Junkers buzzed about the sky, she found it strange to remember the quiet, shy days of her youth.

The man with greying hair looked at her. There was vodka on his breath, but there was a serious look in his eyes.

It was a joy to have her sitting beside him. Krymov would have liked to go on sitting like this, beside this young and beautiful woman, for a long time, for the rest of the evening and the next day too. In the morning he would go out into the garden, then into the meadow. Come evening he would sit at table and, by the light of an oil lamp, watch her strong, bronzed hands make the bed. When she turned towards him, he would see in her fine eyes a look of gentle trust.

Still not saying a word, the young woman got to her feet and walked a little way across the bright sand.

He watched her walk away, knowing she would come back. And she soon did. 'Come along. Why sit here all on your own? Everyone's in that house over there.'

Krymov called Semyonov, ordering him to check his sub-machine gun and not to leave the car.

'Are the Germans close?' she asked. Krymov didn't answer.

He followed her into a large house. The room felt hot and airless; it was crowded and the stove was lit.

Sitting at the table were a number of women, some old men and some young, badly shaven lads in jackets.

A very pretty young woman was sitting by the window, her hands on her lap.

When Krymov spoke to her, she bowed her head and, with the palm of one hand, began to brush invisible crumbs from her knees. Then she looked at him. There was a purity in her eyes that neither hard labour nor grim need could darken.

'Don't try anything on with her!' the other women called out, laughing. 'Her man's in the Red Army. She's waiting for him. She lives like a nun. But she's got a good voice. We've asked her here so she can sing to us.'

A man with a black beard and a broad forehead, evidently the man of the house, was making sweeping gestures with his long arms and shouting hoarsely, 'Let's make it a party! It's the last day I'll be drinking with you, my friends!'

He was drunk, and he looked mad. Sweat was dripping down his forehead and into his eyes and he had to keep wiping it away, sometimes with a handkerchief, sometimes with his hand. He walked heavily, and each step he took set objects in the room trembling. Dishes, glasses and cutlery clinked on the table – as in a station buffet when a heavy freight train goes past. Women kept letting out little cries – he repeatedly seemed about to crash to the ground. Nevertheless, he kept going; he even tried to dance.

The old men had pink faces. They too were sweating – from vodka and the lack of fresh air.

Beside these old men, the young lads seemed quiet and pale. Either they weren't used to drinking and were feeling sick or else vodka wasn't enough to quell their anxieties. If your whole life still lies ahead of you, then war makes you more anxious.

When Krymov looked at these lads, they avoided his eyes; probably they had found some ruse to escape conscription.

The old men, on the other hand, came up to him and struck up conversations of their own accord. The man with the black beard said, 'You should have stood firm! Yes, by God, you should have held your ground!' He then flung up his hands in despair and hiccupped with such violence that even the old women, used to him as they were, looked startled.

There was a rich spread – everyone must have brought whatever they could. Looking at the food on the table, the women repeated, 'We must feast while we can – tomorrow the Germans will be helping themselves!'

On the table were fried eggs – in huge pans the size of the sun – and ham, pies, fatback, bowls of dumplings with cream cheese, jars of jam, bottles of wine made from grapes, and vodka made from real sugar.

The man with the black beard, gesticulating with arms that seemed to reach almost from the table to the wall, yelled out, 'Eat and drink, eat and drink! Tonight's for feasting – and then it's the Fritzes! Here's to feasting and freedom!'

Approaching Krymov, he seemed to turn suddenly sober. He offered him food and said, 'Eat, comrade chief! My eldest son's fighting too – he's a lieutenant!'

Then he went over to a very silent man sitting in an armchair beside the oak sideboard. Krymov heard him say, 'Eat, my good man, eat and drink! We've held nothing back from you – so don't hold back now! Eat all you can!' And then, with no apparent connection, 'My elder brother was in the tsar's personal bodyguard. He served with devotion till that last day in Dno.'[173]

Drunk as he was, the bearded man was still able to say the right thing to the right person; he knew who to tell about his son, who was in the Red Army, and who to tell about his elder brother.

Krymov looked at the silent man. He had foxy eyes and the face of a wolf. Sensing some hostility on his part, he asked, 'And who are you?'

'I live here in the village. I'm a Cossack,' the man replied in a slow, lazy voice. 'I've come for the feast.'

'What feast?' asked Krymov. 'Has there been a birth or a wedding? Or is it the tsar's name day?'

The man seemed to be one and the same colour all over; his skin and hair, his eyes and even his teeth were all the same dusty yellow. There was an exaggerated, almost sleepy calm about his gaze, and about his manner of speech, that reminded Krymov of the careful movements

360

of a tightrope walker treading a familiar but mortally dangerous path under the high dome of a circus tent.

Smirking a little, the man slowly got up from the table and tottered towards the door. He did not come back. He too may not have been as drunk as he seemed. There was a general silence as he made his sleepy way out, and two of the old men exchanged looks.

It was as if Krymov had happened upon a secret – some secret knowledge shared by these pink-faced, sly yet simple-minded old men.

Now and again Krymov noticed that the woman who had brought him along was looking at him. Her eyes were sad and stern, questioning.

Then, from different parts of the room, people began asking the pretty young woman by the window to sing. She smiled, straightened her hair and her blouse, laid her hands on the table, glanced at the blacked-out window and began to sing. Everyone joined in, quietly and seriously – you'd have thought not one of them had been drinking.

The man with the black beard, whose voice had been louder than anyone's while they were talking, sang so quietly that he could barely be heard. He had the air of a diligent schoolboy, and he didn't take his eyes off the young woman. She looked taller now; her white neck had grown long and fine, and her face had taken on a rare look of joy and kindness, of triumphant gentleness.

Probably nothing but song could have expressed the trouble and anguish now weighing on these people. There was one song Krymov thought he might have heard before, long ago. It touched something deeply hidden, something he had not known was still present within him. Only rarely, as if suddenly able to look down from above and glimpse the whole length of the Volga, from the hidden springs of Lake Seliger to the salty delta where it enters the Caspian Sea – only very rarely is a human being able to bring together in their heart all the different parts of their life, the sweet years of childhood, the years of labour, hopes, passions and heartbreak, and the years of old age.

Krymov saw tears running down the cheeks of their black-bearded host.

The young woman was looking at him again. 'There's little cheer,' she said, 'in our good cheer.'

You can write down the words of a song. You can describe the singer, the melody and the look in the listeners' eyes. You can write about the listeners' sorrows and longings – but will all this conjure a song into being? A song that makes people weep? Of course not. How could it?

'Yes.' said Krymov. 'Sadly little cheer.' He went outside and walked over to his car. Semyonov had moved it – it was now close up against a fence.

'Are you asleep, Semyonov?'

'No,' said Semyonov. 'I'm not asleep.' Childishly happy to see Krymov, he looked at him out of the darkness. 'It's very quiet now, and dark and frightening. That fire's burnt itself out ... I've spread out some hay for you in the barn.'

'I'll go and lie down now,' said Krymov.

*

What Krymov remembered afterwards was the half-light of the summer dawn, the smell and rustle of hay, and stars in the pale morning sky – or had it been the young woman's eyes, against her pale face?

He told her about his grief, about how hurt he had been by Zhenya. He told her things he had never even told himself.

And she whispered quickly and passionately to him, begging him to stay with her. Not far from the village of Tsimlyanskaya she had a house and garden. There was wine there, and cream, and fresh fish, and honey. No one there would betray them. They would marry in church and she swore to love no one but him. She would gladly live all her life with him – but if he tired of her, he would always be free to leave her.

She said she did not understand what had happened to her. She had known her fair share of men, had known and forgotten them. But Krymov, it seemed, had bewitched her. She was trembling all over, gasping for breath. No, she had never known anything like this.

Her words and her looks pierced his heart. 'Maybe this is it,' he thought. 'Maybe this is happiness.' And then he answered himself, 'Maybe it *is*, but it's not happiness that I want.'

He went out into the orchard. Ducking his head, he passed under the low branches of the apple trees.

Semyonov called out from the yard, 'Comrade Commissar, it's Sarkisyan, it's our mortars!'

The joy in Semyonov's voice made it clear how anxious he had felt earlier, listening to the hum of Heinkels and the rumble of Soviet bombers, looking up at the sky and the mute glow of the distant blaze.

That evening they crossed the Don yet again. Running his tongue over his dust-parched lips, Krymov said, 'It's not the same soldiers on

362

the pontoons. The two sappers from the other day must have been killed. They didn't serve long, but they served honourably.'

Semyonov did not answer; he was concentrating on steering. Once they were safely across and on their way east again, he said, 'That Cossack was a real beauty, comrade Commissar. I thought we'd be staying a day longer.'

67

That night, after accompanying the mortar unit to Stalingrad, Krymov
went to see Lieutenant Colonel Gorelik, the brigade commander.

'Well,' Krymov began, 'have you caught a few Volga sturgeon? Will
you be treating me to fish soup?'

Usually Gorelik liked to joke with his commissar. This time, however, he did not even smile. Instead, he went to the door and checked
that it was firmly closed.

'Read this, comrade Krymov,' he said, taking from his map case a
folded sheet of cigarette paper.

It was an Order from Stalin.

Krymov began to read Stalin's words to the retreating army. Full of
sorrow and rage, these words expressed Krymov's own pain, his own
sorrow, his own faith and sense of responsibility.

It was as if he were reading the words within his own being, as
if they had lived within him throughout all the dust, fire and smoke
of the retreat. Stalin's words burnt with bitter truth. They summoned
men to their highest duty. They spoke with shocking simplicity about
mortal danger. But really they said only one thing: any further retreat
would mean the end of everything. There was, therefore, no greater
crime in the world than retreat. The fate of a great country and a great
people – the fate of the world – was being decided. There could be no
further retreat.

'The very words we need!' said Krymov. He picked up the small
sheet of cigarette paper in his two hands and returned it to Gorelik.
The weightless paper felt as heavy as a slab of steel. The words were
imbued not only with sorrow and anger, but also with faith in victory.

It was as if he had heard the tocsin being rung.[174]

68

Lieutenant Kovalyov, commander of an infantry company, received a letter from Tolya Shaposhnikov, his recent travelling companion.

Tolya had been posted to an artillery unit. His letter was cheerful and spirited: his battery had come first in a shooting competition. He was eating a lot of cantaloupes and watermelons and had twice gone on fishing trips with his commander. Kovalyov understood that Tolya's unit was being held in reserve and must be positioned not far from his own unit. He too went fishing in the Volga and was eating his fill of all kinds of melons.

Kovalyov made several attempts to write back, but he was unable to say what he wanted to say. He was angered by Tolya's last line: 'My unit is a Guards unit. So, greetings from Guards Lieutenant Anatoly Shaposhnikov.'

Kovalyov imagined Tolya writing to his family in Stalingrad, to his grandmother, to his beautiful young aunt, to his cousins, and signing each letter 'With warm greetings from Guards Lieutenant Shaposhnikov.' Kovalyov wanted to write something sarcastic yet good-natured, something both mocking and protective, but he was unable to find words for his contradictory feelings. This young boy, who had barely sniffed gunpowder, was already a Guards lieutenant. This upset Kovalyov.

Kovalyov's company was part of a battalion commanded by Senior Guards Lieutenant Filyashkin. This battalion was part of a regiment commanded by Guards Lieutenant Colonel Yelin. And this regiment was, in turn, part of a division commanded by Guards Major General Rodimtsev. It was a Guards division and so all its commanders could call themselves Guards commanders. To Kovalyov it seemed wrong that a man who had not seen fighting could call himself a Guards commander simply because he had been posted to a regiment in a Guards division. The veterans in his division had fought in the battle for Kiev in the summer of 1941, when the Germans broke through to Demievka and the Goloseyevsky Forest. All through the winter of 1941–42, with its snows and harsh frosts, the division had been a part of the Southwestern Front, fighting just south of Kursk. The division had then conducted a fighting retreat back towards the Don, suffering heavy casualties. After being withdrawn to reform and refit, it had returned to the front. It was not for nothing that it was titled a Guards division. But as for becoming a Guards commander just like that, without even seeing combat ...

Wartime experiences often evoked feelings of jealousy. These feelings arose from people's sense that they had witnessed a great deal and known great suffering, from their sense of closeness to others who had fought during the first hours and days of the war, and from their knowledge that they had seen things that no one would ever see again. War, though, is ruled by the simplest of laws. Past exploits are irrelevant; what matters is a man's ability to cope with the present – the skill, strength, courage and intelligence with which he can carry out the hard work of the day.

Kovalyov understood this – and he was severe and demanding in his treatment of new recruits and reinforcements brought up from the rear. His capacity for fault-finding had become legendary. Everyone under his command had to learn the countless small ruses he himself had had to learn during the previous year. This, of course, was invaluable – thousands upon thousands of novices quickly acquired a sound grasp of wartime experience that their predecessors had acquired only at the most terrible cost.

The new recruits were of all ages and backgrounds: a young boy of a metalworker who had never touched a rifle; older men who until recently had been exempt from conscription; young kolkhoz workers; boys fresh from ten years of schooling in one of the big cities; accountants; evacuees from towns and villages to the west; volunteers who believed there was no higher calling than that of a soldier. And there were men who had been sent to the front in lieu of completing their term in a labour camp.

Among all these new recruits was a forty-five-year-old kolkhoz worker, Pyotr Semyonovich Vavilov.

69

Kovalyov's company was being held in reserve, not far from Niko-laevka, in the monotonous steppe extending east from the Volga. Like every social unit – from village to small workshop or large factory – the company had its particular way of being, not all of which was obvious to an outsider. There were men whom everyone loved – men who were bold, loyal and honest – and there were troublesome, slippery figures whom everyone complained about but who for some reason enjoyed the favour of the political instructor and the com-manders. Among these troublesome figures were Usurov – a coarse, greedy bully – and Senior Sergeant Dodonov, who was overfond of tobacco and extra rations, rude to his subordinates, obsequious to his superiors and a dangerous telltale. And then there was Rezchikov, a joker and gifted teller of stories. People liked him, but they also enjoyed making fun of him. They respected him, but this respect concealed a trace of mockery; he was treated, in short, the way Russians often treat their village and factory poets, their storytellers and domestic philosophers.

There were men whom few knew by name, faceless, silent men who remained silent even when this upset others. People addressed these men with such phrases as 'Hey, redhead!' or 'You, you idiot over there!' One such 'idiot' was Mulyarchuk, who was seldom out of trouble. If there was a large pothole on the road, Mulyarchuk would fall into it. If the company was being examined for lice, no one turned out to have more lice on him. When there was a uniform inspection, it was Mulyarchuk who had missing buttons and a side cap with no star.

There was Rysev, a bold, strong, agile paratrooper who had already taken part in twenty attacks. Everyone always spoke of Rysev with pride. When they were in a train and coming into a station, he would leap down onto the platform well before the train had come to a stop. Bucket in hand, he would run to the station boiler, turn the brass tap and lean against the boiler-room wall, bracing himself so that none of the crowd clattering after him could push him aside until he had filled his bucket with boiled water. His mates, meanwhile, would have been watching from the door of the freight wagon, calling out, 'Yes, Rysev's first again. He's left them all standing!'

After spending a little time with Kovalyov's company, after watching and listening to the men, after eating with them and marching alongside them, any observer would have understood that the company had its laws and that the men all lived by these laws. He would have noticed that the sly and the shameless were always able to gain some small but significant advantage: to ride on a supplies cart during one section of a long march, to grab a pair of new boots just the right size, or to be excused from duty at a crucial moment. But he might not have noticed the working of the most important law of all – the law that binds men together and is often the key to an army's victory or defeat.

This law, simple and natural as the beating of the heart, was unchanging and inescapable. During Hitler's years in power, for all the proclamations of fascist 'philosophy', faith in the equality of nations and love of the Soviet land did not die; this faith and love endured in the depth of soldiers' hearts, in their night-time conversations and in the speeches of their commissars. The brotherhood of all Soviet workers continued to live and breathe in the churned-up mud of the front line, in half-flooded trenches, in summer dust and winter snowdrifts. This was the law that brought men together, that united companies, battalions and regiments. The most ordinary of men had created this law and at the same time they obeyed it unquestioningly, often unaware of it yet always seeing it as the only true measure of character and deed.

Vavilov had worked all his life. He understood that labour was both a burden and a joy.

Rowing upstream against a powerful current, looking at a field he had just ploughed or at a mountain of turf he had dug out from a trench, hearing the sudden crack as he drove a wedge into a stout, gnarled log, measuring by eye the depth of a pit or the height of a wall he had just built – labour of every kind afforded him a calm sense of his own strength that he felt almost ashamed to acknowledge. It was indeed both a burden and a joy. Day after day it brought him the same reward as it brought scientists, artists and great reformers: the excitement of struggle and the satisfaction of victory.

Back on the kolkhoz, his sense of his own power and ability had merged with his sense of the unity and strength of the people and of their shared purpose. At times of year when everyone had to work together – during ploughing, harvesting and threshing – Vavilov sensed that the sheer scale of kolkhoz labour had brought something new into their lives. The hum of cars, the roar of tractors, the measured progress of the combine harvester, the determination of tractor drivers and brigade leaders – all this constituted a single communal effort towards a shared goal. All these hundreds of hands – hands dark from machine oil, hands dark from wind and sun, men's hands, young girls' and old women's hands – shared in the work of lifting layers of soil, of mowing and threshing the kolkhoz grain. And everyone there knew that his or her strength derived from the ties that gathered the strength and skills of individuals into a single collective skill.

Vavilov knew that there was much in which Soviet peasants could take just pride: tractors and combine harvesters; motors to pump water to the pig farm, the cow shed and the experimental field; portable engines and diesel engines; small hydroelectric power stations on the bank of a river. He had witnessed the first appearance in the village of bicycles, trucks and tractor stations manned by skilled mechanics – and of tarred roads, agronomists, trained beekeepers, Michurin gardens,[175] poultry farms, and stables and cowsheds with stone floors. Another ten or fifteen years of peace – and his kolkhoz could have been cultivating the finest grain on a vast expanse of fields.

But the fascists had not allowed this to happen.

The company's first hour of political instruction was held in the open air. Politinstructor Kotlov – bald, with a broad forehead – asked Vavilov, 'Who are you, comrade?'

'A kolkhoz activist,' replied Vavilov.

'Guards division kolkhoz activist,' murmured Rezchikov. Vavilov's reply had amused everyone. The correct reply was 'Red Army soldier, 3rd Company, such and such a regiment, such and such a Guards division, Order of the Red Banner.'

But Kotlov chose not to correct Vavilov. He simply said, 'Very good.'

Despite being from a village, Vavilov turned out to know more than most of his comrades. He knew about recent political developments in Romania and Hungary. He knew when Magnitogorsk had been founded, and who had commanded the defence of Sevastopol in 1855. He talked about Napoleon's invasion in 1812. When Zaichenkov the accountant made a mistake, Vavilov surprised everyone by saying, 'Hindenburg was not war minister – he was a field marshal under Kaiser Wilhelm.'

None of this passed Kotlov by. When he failed to explain something clearly and one of the soldiers had to keep asking questions, Kotlov turned to Vavilov and asked, 'Well, how would you put it, comrade Vavilov?'

That evening, the mischievous Rezchikov made everyone laugh by standing to attention before Vavilov and rattling off the words 'Comrade Kolkhoz Activist, allow me to ask if you happen to be related to Regimental Commissar Vavilov, commissar of this Guards division?'

'No,' said Vavilov. 'Seems we just have the same surname.'

At dawn, Lieutenant Kovalyov sounded the alarm; he was sleeping badly – as they all knew – because of his unrequited love for medical instructor Lena Gnatyuk. He had the company do a shooting exercise then and there. Vavilov proved to be a poor shot; he did not once hit the target.

During his first days with the company, Vavilov felt overawed by the complexity and diversity of the weaponry: rifles, sub-machine guns, hand grenades, light mortars, light and heavy machine guns, anti-tank rifles. He also went to some of the neighbouring units and inspected the larger guns, heavy mortars, anti-aircraft and anti-tank guns, anti-personnel and anti-tank mines. From a distance he glimpsed a radio post and caterpillar tractors.

A single infantry division evidently had a vast store of arms at its disposal. Vavilov said to Zaichenkov, whose place on the bedboards was next to his own, 'I can remember the old army. Russia certainly didn't have weapons like this in those days. There must be thousands of factories working non-stop!'

'And even if the tsar had been able to supply weapons like these,' Zaichenkov replied, 'no one would have known what to do with them. All a peasant knew then was how to harness and unharness a horse. While today's new recruits understand everything already. They're fitters, tractor drivers, mechanics and engineers. Look at our Usurov. In Central Asia he worked as a driver – so when he joined up, they got him to drive a caterpillar tractor.'

'But what's he doing here in the infantry?' asked Vavilov. 'Why've they put him with us?'

'Oh that's nothing,' said Zaichenkov. 'He was caught a couple of times exchanging petrol for moonshine. His regimental commissar had him transferred.'

'Not exactly nothing,' Vavilov replied quietly.

Each of the two men had already told the other his age and how many children he had. Learning that Vavilov used to go regularly on kolkhoz business to the bank in the district town, Zaichenkov felt a particular goodwill towards him – the indulgent goodwill of a senior timber-depot accountant towards his country cousin.

During their first lessons Zaichenkov did what he could to help Vavilov and even gave him a slip of paper on which he had written out the names of all the different parts of a hand grenade and a sub-machine gun.

These lessons were exceptionally important, still more important than anyone understood at the time. The instructors – commanders and soldiers alike – had already survived long months of war. They had learned more than can be learned from any military manual. They understood combat not only with their minds but also with their hearts.

No manual can tell you what it is like to lie with your face pressed against the floor of a trench while the grinding, grating caterpillar of an enemy tank passes only a foot above your fragile skull – a skull already half-covered by earth and dust. No manual can prepare you to breathe in that peculiar blend of dry dust and thick, oily exhaust gases. No manual can describe the look in men's eyes when they are woken by a night attack, as they hear the explosions of hand grenades and bursts of sub-machine-gun fire and see German flares climbing into the sky.

True knowledge of war includes knowledge of the enemy and his weapons, knowledge of war at dawn, in the mist, in bright daylight, at sunset, in the woods, on the road, in the steppe, in a village, on the banks of a river. It includes knowledge of war's sounds and whispers and – above all – knowledge of yourself, of your own strength, stamina, experience and cunning.

In field exercises, in simulated night alarms, in cruel and terrifying exercises with tanks, the new recruits assimilated all these experiences.

The commanders were not teaching schoolboys who would soon leave their classroom and return to a peaceful home; they were teaching the soldiers who would soon be fighting beside them. And they were teaching only one subject: war.

There were dozens, perhaps hundreds of methods by which the commanders passed on their knowledge. The new recruits absorbed this knowledge from the tones of voice in which commands were given, and by observing the movements, gestures and facial expressions of commanders and battle-hardened Red Army soldiers. This knowledge was embodied in the stories Rysev told at night, in his mocking tone as he asked, 'Know what Fritz enjoys more than anything?' This knowledge was present in the authority with which Kovalyov would call out, 'Run, keep running and don't fall. No one can touch you there … Why are you lying on the ground? That won't protect you from mortars … Don't expose yourself! Keep to the ravine! The valley's covered by enemy mortars ... Why leave the car there – do you want to be pounded by Junkers?'

This knowledge was present in Rezchikov's buffoonery, in his contemptuous mockery of the Germans, in his casual tone as he talked about tricks he'd played on them.

A certain capacity for contempt can be a great boon to a soldier, but in 1941 it had taken the Red Army several months to acquire this capacity.

When the fascists first invaded, everyone – city dwellers and kolkhoz workers alike – had at once understood that this was the beginning of a long and bitter struggle. People saw the Germans as a strong, wealthy and warlike nation.

The war against France was now confined to the pages of books; the last people who remembered the year 1812 had died decades ago. War against Germany, however, was still a living memory, a part of people's bitter experience.

In the summer of 1941, Vavilov had said to his wife, 'Hitler wants to take all our land. He wants to be able to plough the whole globe.'

Vavilov thought of the terrestrial globe as a single vast field that it was the people's responsibility to plough and sow.

Hitler had declared war on peasants and workers; it was the people's earth he had invaded.

*

The division kept on with its training. New contingents kept on arriving. And there was always work to be done – roads to be laid, trees to be felled, logs to be chopped, more dugouts to be constructed.

While they worked, the war would be forgotten and Vavilov would ask people about their lives in peacetime: 'What's your land like? Does your wheat grow well? Are there droughts? And millet – do you sow millet? Do you get enough potatoes?' He spoke to many people who had fled the Germans: young women and old men who had plodded east with their cattle; tractor drivers who had driven from Ukraine and Belorussia, bringing with them all the kolkhoz's most precious tools. He came across people who had lived under German occupation and then escaped across the front line; he questioned them in detail about what life had been like under the Germans.

Vavilov soon realized that the Germans were simply bandits. The only small items they brought with them were flints for cigarette lighters; the only pieces of larger machinery they brought were threshing machines. In exchange for a few flints, Hitler hoped to acquire the entire land of Russia. And Hitler's new order, with its *Gebietskommissars* and *Parteien Chefs*,[176] brought no good to anyone. The Germans did not, after all, want to plough the whole globe; they just wanted to eat other people's wheat.

Vavilov's curiosity did not escape notice. At first, the other soldiers made fun of him. 'There he goes again,' they would say. 'Our kolkhoz activist has detained yet another peasant for interrogation.' 'Hey, Vavilov!' they would shout, 'We've got some women here from Oryol. Want to organize a discussion?'

But they soon realized that they were wrong to make fun of Vavilov; he was asking about matters of vital importance to all of them.

Two incidents in particular made Vavilov into a generally liked and respected figure. The first was when the division was about to move west, towards the front. Usurov had agreed to leave his dugout to an old woman whose house had burnt down – but only in exchange for two litres of moonshine. If she brought him a bottle, he'd line the walls with new boards; if not, he'd level the whole dugout. The old woman did not possess any moonshine. When Usurov completed the work, she brought him a woollen shawl instead.

When Usurov laughed and held the shawl up in the air to show everyone, there was a general silence. Then Vavilov went up to him. In a quiet voice that made everyone present look around, he said, 'Give it back to her, you shit!' Vavilov seized the shawl with one hand, made the other into a powerful fist – and held this fist only a few inches from Usurov's face. Everyone expected a fight. They all knew that Usurov was strong, and that he had a violent temper.

But Usurov let go of the shawl and said, 'Oh all right! What do I care? Take it back to the woman.'

Vavilov threw the shawl down on the ground. 'You took it from her,' he said, 'and you'll be giving it back to her.'

The old woman had been quietly cursing Usurov, wondering why it was that German bullets finished off fine, honourable men while sparing such vile, shameless, good-for-nothing parasites. When Usurov returned her shawl, she was at a loss for words.

Back again with his comrades, Usurov tried to cover his embarrassment. 'We drivers lived quite a life in Central Asia. Yes, we did all right for ourselves! I didn't want that shawl anyway – our defender of the oppressed could have saved his breath! And I didn't steal the damned rag, it was payment for work completed. Back home, I used to earn a bit on the side too. After I'd finished work for the day, my truck would be jam-packed. My passengers paid as they could – with money, with vodka, with tobacco, even with dried apricots. There was one young woman who paid me with love. I owned three suits – all cut from the finest cloth, believe me! On my days off I'd put on a tie, a coat and my yellow shoes – no, no one would have taken *me* for a truck driver. I'd go to the cinema, then to a restaurant. I'd order lamb shashlyks, half a kilo[177] of vodka, some beer. Yes, that was the life, all right! What do I want with some peasant woman's shawl!'

The second incident, which made a still greater impression, was during an air raid. Their train was being held in a siding, outside a large junction station. The German planes appeared late in the afternoon and dropped bomb after bomb – half-tonners and even a few tonners. They were probably trying to destroy the grain silo. The raid had begun without warning and everyone simply flung themselves to the ground where they were; many did not even manage to jump out of the wagons. Dozens of men were killed or maimed. Fires broke out in several places, and shells began to explode in an ammunition train not far away. Amid the smoke and the terrible din, amid the howls of locomotive whistles, death seemed inescapable. Even the exuberant, fearless Rysev went white as a sheet. If there was the slightest lull in the bombing, everyone began rushing about, looking for safe nooks and crannies in this black, hostile earth that glistened with spilt oil. Everyone was certain that where they were was the worst place of all, that anywhere else must be safer. It was this desperate, futile toing and froing that caused the most deaths and injuries. Vavilov, meanwhile, just sat there beside a wagon, smoking a cigarette. Everyone remembered him calling out, 'Stay put! Don't panic! Think!!'

Dense and compacted as it was, the earth itself was trembling and cracking. It was ripping apart, like rotten calico.

When the raid was over, Rysev said to Vavilov, 'You're made of strong stuff, Grandad!'

Kotlov had singled out Vavilov from the first day. He had long conversations with him, entrusted more and more tasks to him and drew him into general discussions during newspaper readings and political-instruction sessions. Kotlov was intelligent and he recognized in Vavilov a clear, pure strength he knew he could rely on.

The soldiers didn't notice this happening, and Vavilov himself was still less aware of it. Nevertheless, by the time the division was ordered to the front, Vavilov had become a trusted figure, central to the company's life. It was he, above all, who brought everyone together, regardless of age or background: Rysev the former paratrooper, Zaichenkov the accountant, pockmarked Mulyarchuk, Rezchikov from Yaroslav and Usmanov the Uzbek.

Kovalyov, the young company commander, was aware of this, and so was the sergeant major.

Rysev had done active service before the war and had taken part in the first clashes by the Soviet border and the cruel battles on the outskirts of Kiev. Somehow even he did not resent Vavilov's growing authority.

Only Usurov remained hostile. When Vavilov addressed him, he frowned crossly and seemed reluctant to answer. Sometimes he did not answer at all.

The divisions held in reserve were about to enter their last stages of training. Everyone – from generals to rank-and-file soldiers – was excited to learn that their final combat-readiness exercises would be supervised by Marshal Voroshilov.

Voroshilov, who had led the miners' divisions defending Tsaritsyn[178] during the Civil War, was again being sent to the Volga – to review the people's army.

The exercises began. Thousands of men, out in the field with all their weaponry, saw the marshal's grey head.

Afterwards Voroshilov convened a meeting. In the classroom of a village school he conversed at length with the commanders of divisions and regiments, and with their chiefs of staff. Everyone was delighted by the marshal's positive assessment of their combat-readiness.

They all understood: the hour of battle was approaching.

PART II

PART II

1

At the beginning of August 1942, Colonel General Yeromenko arrived in Stalingrad. The Stavka had ordered the creation of two new Fronts: the Southeastern Front and the Stalingrad Front. The task of the former was to protect the lower Volga, the Kalmyk steppe and the southern approaches to Stalingrad; the task of the latter – to guard the north-western and western approaches to the city. The Stavka had appointed Colonel General Yeromenko to the command of the Stalingrad Front; the chief political officer – the member of the Front military soviet – was to be Nikita Khrushchev.

The position of both Fronts was critical. The Germans had considerable forces at their disposal: 150,000 men, 1,600 pieces of artillery and 700 tanks. Richthofen's 4th Air Fleet offered powerful support.

In manpower and weaponry alike, the German forces were far superior to those of the two Soviet Fronts.

There was every indication that the offensive Hitler and Mussolini had discussed in Salzburg was nearing a successful conclusion. The German army had advanced an enormous distance. Columns of German tanks had broken through the Southwestern Front. The Front's right wing had retreated towards the Don, around Kletskaya, while its left wing was retreating towards Rostov and the Caucasus. The main German forces were now advancing swiftly towards Stalingrad; their vanguard was only thirty or forty kilometres from the Volga.

In the last days of July, after regrouping, the Germans had embarked on the final stage of their offensive, aiming to capture Stalingrad.

At the time, people saw little but tragedy in the defensive battles about to be fought on the Volga cliffs. The smoke and flames of the fighting around the Don and the Volga blinded them to the changes that had taken place in the course of the year. The Stavka, however, was aware of these changes; its members knew that Soviet power was now in a position to defeat fascist violence. Soon this would become clear to the entire Soviet nation, and to the world.

In the summer of 1942, Hitler was still able to advance, but he did not realize that for all its apparent success, this offensive would bring him no real gains. Only a blitzkrieg – a lightning war – could have brought him true victory. Hitler had made a wild gamble – and the Red Army had already denied him his only chance of success.

The battle fought within the city of Stalingrad took place at a time when the Soviet Union was just beginning to produce more gun barrels and military vehicles than the Germans, when a year of struggle – in factories and on battlefields alike – had wiped out the Germans' initial superiority in weaponry and military experience. And it was at this same time that the Soviet forces first truly mastered the art of strategic manoeuvre and that the Germans, for their part, began to feel the dangerous lure of the vast spaces behind them, calling them to retreat. It was here that the Germans first learned the fear of encirclement – that cruel illness that afflicts the hearts, minds and legs of both soldiers and generals.

Throughout the grim months of the battle the Stavka was elaborating the details of the still secret Stalingrad offensive. While they struggled to keep defending the city, Soviet strategic planners could already see the red arrows soon to flash out from the middle Don and the lakes in the southern steppe and strike both flanks of the German forces.

Eventually the reserves received the order to move forward. A great iron river – the hidden energy of the Red Army and the Soviet people – split into two streams. One stream went to reinforce the divisions defending the city; the other was preparing to attack. The commanders planning the offensive already had a clear image of the moment when the two steel pincers would meet and Paulus's army would be encircled by a tight ring of artillery divisions, tank corps, Guards mortar regiments, and infantry and cavalry units newly equipped with a wealth of firepower.

The boundless river of the Soviet people's anger and grief had not been left to drain into the sand. The will of the people, the will of the Party and state had transformed it into a river of iron and steel and it was now flowing back, from east to west. Its immense weight would soon tilt the scales.

2

When people read obscure novels, when they listen to over-complex music or look at a frighteningly unintelligible painting, they feel anxious and unhappy. The thoughts and feelings of the novel's characters, the sounds of the symphony, the colours of the painting – everything seems peculiar and difficult, as if from some other world. Almost ashamed of being natural and straightforward, people read, look and listen without joy, without any real emotion. Contrived art is a barrier placed between man and the world – impenetrable and oppressive, like a cast-iron grille.

But there are also books that make a reader exclaim joyfully, 'Yes, that's just what *I* feel. I've gone through that too and that's what I thought myself.'

Art of this kind does not separate people from the world. Art like this connects people to life, to other people and to the world as a whole. It does not scrutinize life through strangely tinted spectacles.

As they read this kind of book, people feel that they are being infused with life, that the vastness and complexity of human existence is entering into their blood, into the way they think and breathe.

But this simplicity, this supreme simplicity of clear daylight, is born from the complexity of light of different wavelengths.

In this clear, calm and deep simplicity lies the truth of genuine art. Such art is like the water of a spring; if you look down, you can see to the bottom of a deep pool. You can see green weeds and pebbles. Yet the pool is also a mirror; in it you can see the entire world where you live, labour and struggle. Art combines the transparency of glass and the power of a perfect astronomical mirror.

All this applies not only to art; it is equally true of science and politics.

And the strategy of a people's war, a war for life and freedom, is no different.

3

Colonel General Yeromenko, the new commander of the Stalingrad Front, was a burly man aged about fifty. He had a round face, a short nose and quick, lively eyes. He had a crew cut and his forehead was broad and wrinkled. His spectacles looked like a village schoolteacher's – the very simplest of metal frames. He had a slight limp from a leg wound.

During the First World War, Yeromenko had served as a corporal and he liked to reminisce about those years – his aides could usually predict at what point in a conversation he would start to recount a bayonet attack during which he had stabbed twenty Germans.

Yeromenko knew a great deal about war – from the straightforward difficulties encountered by an ordinary soldier to the heights of generalship. War, for him, was everyday work, not an extraordinary event. He looked on his general's uniform as a workman looks on his tarpaulin overalls. His adjutant, Parkhomenko, wanted his general to look smarter and more impressive than any other general, but in the end he had to admit defeat; Yeromenko's chest and shoulders were always covered in cigarette ash and there was always ink and any number of other stains on his jacket.

He was massive yet stooping; his build did not make life easy for tailors.

He was both a man of the people and a highly experienced general.

In the early summer of 1941 Yeromenko had been in command of one of the sectors of the Western Front, and he had played an important part in the operation that, for some time, halted the German advance on Smolensk.

In August, he had been appointed commander of the Bryansk Front. In the course of several bitterly fought battles he had managed to prevent Guderian's tanks from breaking through towards Oryol. In the winter of 1941, while in command of the Northwestern Front, he had broken through the German front line.

Yeromenko came to Stalingrad in the grimmest days of the long Soviet retreat and it might have seemed that this soldier of bog and forest, who had spent most of the war on relatively slow-moving fronts, would have felt out of place in the southern steppe. In the course of only a year, Southwestern Front HQ had moved all the way from Tarnopol, in western Ukraine, to the Volga. The Front had had to contend with particularly difficult conditions. The broad plains and steppes, crossed by countless roads and tracks, constituted ideal terrain for the highly mobilized warfare the Germans so favoured; on open steppe their tanks and motor artillery and infantry were free to carry out pincer movements and encirclements of unprecedented swiftness and power. Conditions for Yeromenko's Northwestern Front could hardly have been more different. The swamps, the dense forest, the lack of roads – everything had combined to hinder the German advance, and for months on end the front line had barely moved.

Some staff officers, considering Yeromenko sadly inexperienced, took an absurd pleasure in recalling the many headlong retreats and disastrous encirclements.

They did not understand that Yeromenko's lack of interest in their knowledge of steppe retreat – his refusal to learn this sad art – was a sign not of weakness but of strength.

They had not yet grasped that the war was entering a new phase. Much of the knowledge accumulated during the last year was to prove invaluable – but the experience of sudden night-time evacuations, emergency HQ relocations and long wanderings through the steppe was no longer relevant.

Yeromenko chose a deep and airless tunnel as the location for his HQ. To many this seemed absurd and eccentric. Why, when he could have enjoyed the comforts and convenience of one of the city's large buildings, had Yeromenko chosen to hide away in a stifling horizontal shaft near the opening of a mine? Commanders would emerge from this tunnel out of breath, blinking for a long time in the brilliant daylight.

There was a strange contrast between this subterranean HQ and the city's elegant southern charm, still tangibly present in spite of the troubles of war and the defences now hurriedly being erected. During the day groups of young boys gathered around the pale blue kiosks selling seltzer water. There was an open-air canteen where you could sit looking out over the Volga and drink cool beer; a breeze off the river ruffled the tablecloths and the waitresses' white aprons. *The Bright Path*[179] was being shown in the cinemas, and plywood advertising boards displayed a happily smiling, rosy-cheeked young woman in a colourful dress. Both schoolchildren and Red Army soldiers would visit the zoo to see the elephant evacuated from Moscow; during the last year it too had grown thinner. Bookshops sold novels about courageous, hard-working people leading peaceful and measured lives, and schoolchildren and students bought textbooks that allowed no room for doubt about anything – even the imaginary numbers of algebra. At night, though, a bright, troubling smoke rose from the factories, spreading everywhere and blotting out the stars.

The city was bursting with people. Not only were there individuals and families from Gomel, Dnepropetrovsk, Poltava, Kharkov and Leningrad – there were also entire refugee hospitals, orphanages and institutes of higher education.

The Front HQ lived its own peculiar life, separate from that of the city. The black cables of field telephone lines hung from the branches of trees carefully trimmed by gardeners. Commanders covered in dust emerged from Emkas caked in dried mud and with bulging cracks on their windscreens; they looked up and down the streets in the same intent yet distracted way as, earlier that day, they had looked up and down the high west bank of the Don. Despatch riders, ignoring all regulations and reducing traffic controllers to despair, tore down the streets on their motorcycles; behind them, like an invisible mist, trailed all the anguish of war. Soldiers from the HQ battalion rushed out to kitchens newly installed in courtyards, clattering their mess tins just as they had in the Bryansk forest and in villages around Kharkov.

When troops are stationed in a forest, it feels as if they are bringing the mechanical breath of the city into a kingdom of birds, beasts, beetles, leaves, berries and herbs. When troops and HQs are quartered in cities, they seem to bring with them a sense of space, of field and forest, of the free life of the steppe. In the end, however, both city streets and bright forest glades are torn apart; both become mere theatres for the fury of war.

Stalingrad could already sense the breath of the war. Slit trenches had been dug in courtyards and gardens in case of air raids. Water barrels and boxes of Volga sand had been placed in hallways and stairwells. In the daytime reconnaissance planes flew high in the sky; at night there was the sound of lone German bombers. In the evenings the streets were dark; every window was blacked out by dark paper, blankets and shawls. Searchlights swept through the clouds, and from the west came the sound of distant artillery.

Some people were already packing suitcases and mending haversacks. The inhabitants of wooden houses on the city's outskirts were digging pits and burying trunks, nickel-plated bed frames and sewing machines wrapped in layers of bast matting. Some tried to acquire stores of flour, others were re-baking stale pieces of bread, making them into rusks they could pack into bags and take with them on journeys. Some slept badly, full of foreboding and frightened by the likelihood of air raids; others had total confidence in the Soviet anti-aircraft defences and felt certain that German bombers would never get through to the city. And yet life still went on as it always had, bound by all the usual ties of family, friendship and workplace.

4

A group of journalists – from Moscow newspapers, the telegraph agency and the radio committee – had gathered in the airless reception room of Colonel General Yeromenko's underground HQ. An adjutant told them that they would have to wait. Yeromenko, who had promised to brief them about the situation at the front, was being delayed by a meeting of the military soviet.

While they waited, the journalists joked about the constant squabbling between those of them who spent time on the front line and those who stayed at an Army or Front HQ. The former were often late with their articles. Their vehicles would get stuck in the sand or the mud; they would get trapped in encirclements; they would lose touch with their offices; supposedly unable to see the wood for the trees, they would fail to come up with the kind of article their editors considered appropriate. The HQ journalists provided a more general and balanced overview; they sent their articles off on time down reliable telephone lines and contemplated the hardships and misadventures of the front-line correspondents with philosophical detachment. The front-line journalists, naturally, felt resentful.

On one occasion, a repentant HQ journalist had visited an infantry company on the front line. A shell had burst nearby; he suffered severe concussion and was almost killed. In the end, he spent more than three days at the front, without sleeping. He described all this in an article – but this article, which he considered his best, was the only one of his articles never printed. His boss's response was an angry telegram: 'Grey and irrelevant, no vivid characters, and far too late.'

Zbavsky, from *The Latest Radio News*, began to talk about how he had interviewed Yeromenko when he was still in command of the Bryansk Front. Yeromenko had insisted Zbavsky stay for a meal, and then for the night.

But the others were not interested. Captain Bolokhin, the *Red Star* correspondent, brought the conversation back to the only question that really mattered: would Stalingrad hold out?

Bolokhin was an unusual man. Wherever he went, he took with him a suitcase full of books by all his favourite poets. The books lay jumbled together with army maps, newspaper cuttings, dirty underwear, torn socks and foot cloths that were almost black. During some journeys, this suitcase got shaken about so badly that it seemed as if the socks, the poems by Blok and Annensky,[180] the foot cloths and underwear might all be transformed into some ancient homogeneous material combining elements of both poetry and foot cloths. Nevertheless, when the suitcase was opened, both poetry and foot cloths would turn out to have remained themselves. At night, Bolokhin would lie on the floor of a village hut and read poems aloud, in a sing-song voice. The straw would rustle as he scratched desperately at his chest and sides.

Bolokhin was scrupulous in his dealings with others and, unlike the majority of writers, he took genuine pleasure in his colleagues' successes. They, in turn, respected him for his ability to work without respite; they had grown used to waking up in the night in a village hut and seeing his large head – lit by an oil lamp – bent over an army map.

One pessimistic photojournalist said he had equipped himself with an inflated inner tube from a car tyre: another few days and they might all have to swim to the east bank of the Volga. He was also thinking of crossing the Volga now and finding a billet near Lake Elton. There he would buy a harness for a camel, since his car would need extra traction in order to cope with the desert sands. He made out that he had begun studying Kazakh and was already drafting a future article: 'Over mounds of corpses the enemy is advancing in vain towards Tashkent.'

Most of those present, however, believed that Stalingrad would hold out.

'Stalingrad!' the *Izvestia* correspondent pronounced with reverence, before reminding everyone that the very first factory of the first Five Year Plan had been built there and that the defence of the city in 1919 was one of the most glorious chapters in Russian history.

'Yes,' said Bolokhin, 'but do you all remember Tolstoy's account of the council of war in Fili, in 1812?'

'Of course I do, it's brilliant!' Zbavsky replied, though he did not remember it at all.

'Do you remember,' Bolokhin continued, 'how someone asked, "Can we truly contemplate surrendering Moscow, Russia's ancient and sacred capital?" And how Kutuzov replied, "Moscow is indeed ancient and sacred, but I am obliged to ask a strictly military question: is it possible for us, from our present position, to defend the city?" And then Kutuzov answered his own question. "No," he said. "It can't be done." So, do you all understand me?' Bolokhin gestured towards Yeromenko's office – and everyone began to wonder if the current meeting really would come to the same decision as that council of war in 1812.

The generals then began to emerge from the office and the journalists got to their feet.

Yeromenko invited them all into his small, stuffy, brightly lit room. The journalists sat down, rather noisily, and began opening their map cases and taking out their notebooks.

'Do you remember me, comrade Colonel General?' asked Zbavsky.

'Wait a moment, where was it?' Yeromenko asked with a frown.

'In the Bryansk forest – not long ago. I ate at your table!'

'So have others,' said Yeromenko, shaking his head sadly. 'No, I don't remember.'

Zbavsky heard smothered laughs. His colleagues, he realized, would not let him forget this. He could already see the joyful mockery in their eyes.

Yeromenko walked over to the table with his usual limp. He sat down awkwardly, letting out a quiet groan. His wound from the previous winter was troubling him.

'How is your wound doing, comrade Commander?' asked the *Pravda* correspondent.

'A mortar splinter. My seventh wound – I should be used to them by now. But this one doesn't like bad weather. That's why I've come here. For a change of climate.'

'So you're expecting to stay? You don't think you'll have to change climate again?' asked Bolokhin.

Yeromenko glared at Bolokhin over the top of his spectacles and said, 'What makes you ask that? I'm certainly not leaving Stalingrad.' He thumped the table with his large palm and said sternly, addressing the room, 'Your questions please – I don't have much time.'

The journalists began asking questions.

Yeromenko outlined the military situation. The chaos of attacks and counter-attacks, of sudden thrusts and counter-thrusts, had seemed incomprehensible. But a few simple words from Yeromenko, a single gesture indicating on the map the path of the German advance, were enough to instil clarity. What had seemed most significant to an onlooker was often merely a diversionary manoeuvre; what had seemed like a German strategic success was, in reality, often a failure.

Bolokhin realized how mistaken he had been in his assessment of the major offensive launched by the Germans on 23 July. He had seen the concentric German attacks, which had led to several units of the 62nd Army being encircled, as a serious defeat for the Red Army. But Yeromenko and his staff saw this differently. Two weeks of fierce fighting on a battlefield of 70,000 square kilometres had indeed enabled the Germans to reach the Don, but the Germans had not expected such a protracted battle and they had not achieved their true aim. Numerical superiority had allowed them to break through the Soviet defences at several points, but these were only minor, tactical victories. What mattered was that their 700 tanks had failed to deliver the intended crushing blow.

Bolokhin now understood that he had been wrong to imagine a parallel between Kutuzov's abandonment of Moscow and the coming battle for Stalingrad.

Yeromenko, however, was frowning; he still seemed annoyed by Bolokhin's initial question. He had no intention whatsoever – he said crossly – of retreating or moving his HQ across the Volga. He was not, like some people, thinking about pontoon bridges, boats, rafts, boards, the inner tubes of car tyres or any other way of exchanging the west bank for the east bank.

Yeromenko had clearly had to repeat all this several times recently – and his thoughts could hardly have been more different from Kutuzov's at Fili. During the first few minutes, however, his voice sounded thin, oddly out of keeping with his massive bulk. But then someone asked about the mood of the troops. Yeromenko smiled and began talking animatedly about the battles being fought to the south. 'The 64th Army are proving real fighters! I think you all know about the battle being fought at Kilometre 74 – some of you have even been there. Yes, the 64th are an example to us all. It's them you should be having a word with – not me. You should be speaking to Colonel Bubnov, the commander of the heavy-tank brigade. And you should do more than just write a few articles – his tank men merit a full-length novel. And so do Colonel Utvenko and his infantry! The Germans sent 150 tanks against them – and they didn't waver!'

'I've been with Bubnov's brigade,' said one journalist. 'They're astonishing men, comrade General. They go to their death as if to a holiday.'

Yeromenko narrowed his eyes. 'Enough of that nonsense,' he said. 'Which of us really wants to die?' After a moment's thought, still looking at the speaker, he added, 'Death's no holiday and none of us are eager to die. Neither you, comrade writer, nor me, nor those Red Army foot soldiers.' And then, with still greater indignation, 'No, nobody wants to die. Fighting the Germans, though, that's another matter.'

Wanting to smooth over his colleague's mistake, Bolokhin said, 'Tank men, comrade Colonel General, are a young lot. They're ardent and enthusiastic. The young make the best soldiers!'

'No, comrade reporter, you're wrong. Young men the best soldiers? No, they're too hot-headed. The old, then? No – wrong again. The old think too much about their homes, about their wives and families – it's best to assign them to supplies and provisioning. The best soldiers of all are the middle-aged. War is work. And it's like any other work. A man needs some experience, he needs to have thought about life, he needs to have been knocked about a bit by the world. Do you think soldiering's just a matter of yelling "U-u-r-a-a!" and rushing into the arms of death? As if death's a holiday! No, there's more to being a soldier than being in a hurry to die. The work of a soldier is hard, complicated work. Only if duty commands does a soldier say, "Well, dying's not easy, but I'll die if I have to."'

Yeromenko looked Bolokhin in the eye and, as if concluding an argument with him, said, 'So, comrade writer, we do not want to die, we do not see death as a holiday, and we will not surrender Stalingrad. That would put us to shame before the whole people.'

Leaning his hands on the table, he half got to his feet, glanced at his watch and shook his head.

As they made their way out, Bolokhin said quietly to his colleagues, 'It seems history does not, after all, want to be repeated today.'

Zbavsky took Bolokhin's arm and said, 'Look, I know you've got more petrol coupons than you need. Please lend me a few. I give you my word to return them as soon as we get next month's issue.'

'Yes, of course,' Bolokhin replied straightaway.

He felt excited. He was happy, not upset, to discover that he had been wrong. He understood now that what he had seen as a simple question of military tactics was, in reality, something deeper and more complex.

And whose thoughts had Yeromenko been voicing?

Were they not, perhaps, the thoughts of the rank-and-file soldiers who, in sweat-whitened tunics, had climbed down the steep slope to the Volga and then looked all around them, as if to say, 'Here we are – the Volga! Can we really retreat any further?'

5

Old Pavel Andreyevich Andreyev was considered one of the best steel-workers in his factory. The engineers would ask him for advice and did not like to argue with him. He rarely looked at the data provided by the laboratory, which carried out quick, detailed and accurate analyses after each melt; he merely glanced occasionally at the page listing the basic constituents of each burden. Even this, however, he did mainly out of politeness, so as not to offend the chemist, a rather stout man who sounded constantly out of breath.

The chemist would hurry up the steep steps to the shop-floor office and say, 'Here you are, I hope I'm not too late.' He appeared to imagine that Andreyev had been waiting anxiously, worrying whether or not he would have a chance to look at the analysis before loading the furnace.

The chemist had graduated from the Steel Institute. After work, he taught at a technical school. Once he gave a public lecture, 'Chemistry in Metallurgy', in the main hall of the House of Culture. There were posters advertising this lecture beside the main entrance, and by the doors to the factory committee, the grocery store, the library, the canteen and the shop floor itself. Seeing these posters had made Andreyev smile. He could never have given a lecture about gas thermometers, methods of thermoelectric temperature measurement, and ultra-fast spectral and microchemical analysis techniques.

Andreyev had always admired educated people. He had felt proud to know such people and he believed that only they could unravel life's many complications.

The factory librarian had proudly exhibited Andreyev's library card at a conference. Andreyev was the province's number-one senior reader, both for the number of books read and for variety of subject matter. Among the books he had read in 1940 were Stalin's *Questions of Leninism*; novels by Dickens, Pisemsky, Sheller-Mikhailov, Leskov, Tolstoy, Jules Verne, Kuprin, Dostoevsky and Victor Hugo; Nikolay Ostrovsky's *How the Steel was Tempered*; works of history, geology and astronomy; and a dozen historical novels and travel books, which Andreyev especially loved.

The librarian saw him as one of her best and most honoured readers and she even allowed him to take home books the library only had one copy of, like *The Three Musketeers* and *The Count of Monte Cristo*.[181]

Andreyev never, however, read a single book about metallurgy and steelmaking, not even a popular-scientific booklet about the physics and chemistry of steel melts. Somehow this escaped the librarian's notice. Andreyev did, of course, appreciate the importance of the science that underpinned his work – but poets do not need to read textbooks about poetry. It is they, after all, who determine the birth of verse and the laws of the word.

Andreyev never tried to bypass or contradict scientific method. He was never presumptuous or opinionated and he never, like some men his age, tried to play the wise man or shaman. It was as if an understanding of physics and chemistry was present in his hearing, in the lenses of his eyes, in the sensory nerves of his hands and fingers and in a memory that stored the experience of several decades of work.

Andreyev expressed his respect for scientists, order and organization by carefully filling out at night, after completing his work, all the cards and forms he should have filled in beforehand. He made steel according to his own personal norms and proportions. He had his own preferred conditions of time, temperature and relative proportions of pig iron and scrap iron. But his personal timetable and technical norms did not always coincide with the standard timetable and technical norms. And so, out of respect for science, he entered the figures and times required by the instruction manual, doing this after his day's output of excellent steel had already been taken off to the technical and forging shops.

It was for an explanation of things he thought beyond him that Andreyev turned to books. When his wife and daughter-in-law failed to get on, he had found life at home very difficult; it seemed the two women would never stop quarrelling. His attempts at peacemaking only made matters worse. Then he had taken out a book – August Bebel's *Women and Socialism*,[182] hoping it would help him to make sense of the situation – the title looked promising. But the book turned out to be about something else altogether.

Andreyev had his own particular take on family life. To him, the relations between his wife and his daughter-in-law were the same as those within and between states. Here in his family circle he could see the imperfection of the world as a whole. 'Lack of space causes much trouble,' he would say to himself. 'If only we didn't all have to live so cheek by jowl.' He saw poverty and lack of space as the cause both of trouble within the state, and of wars between states.

At home, he was demanding, quick-tempered, severe to the point of cruelty. At the steelworks, though, he could rest from the imperfection of the world. There, people did not seek power over one another – the workers expended their energy in seeking power over iron and steel. This power engendered not slavery, but freedom.

Working at the factory, Andreyev felt ashamed that his family were so quarrelsome. Varvara, on the other hand, felt proud of her husband, knowing how much the other workers and engineers all respected him.

There were young engineers and foremen in the factory who had graduated from technical schools and special courses. Their way of working was very different from Andreyev's; they were constantly vis-iting the laboratories, sending off samples for analysis, going for con-sultations, checking the temperature and the gas supply, and glancing at the approved manual and definitions of official standards. And their work was no worse than Andreyev's.

Andreyev thought particularly highly of Volodya Koroteyev, the melter in charge of the fourth furnace. He was a young man of about twenty-five, with curly hair, thick lips and a broad nose. When he was deep in thought, he would puff out his lips. Three long wrinkles then formed on his forehead, stretching from one temple to the other.

His work always went smoothly, without any mishaps; he set about it simply and happily, as if he were playing. When Andreyev returned to the shop floor during the war, he found that Koroteyev was now a foreman; a young woman, the severe, taciturn Olga Kovalyova, had taken over his furnace. She was doing the job well – as well as the old men now in charge of the other furnaces. Once, on a day when they were following a new recipe, Kovalyova asked Andreyev for advice. After a long pause, Andreyev replied, 'I don't know. We should ask Koroteyev. He's a true scientist.' Andreyev's modesty impressed every-one. 'He's a real worker,' people said about him, 'and a good man.'

He loved his work with a love that was both calm and passionate. He saw all human labour as equally deserving of respect, and his attitude to the factory aristocracy – the melters, electricians and machine-tool operators – was no different from his attitude to the navvies, the man-ual workers on the shop floor and out in the yard, and those who did the simplest work of all, work that could be done by anyone with two hands. Of course, he sometimes made fun of people working in other

392

fields but, far from being hostile, his jokes were just a good-natured expression of friendship. For him, work was the measure of man.

His attitude towards others was always positive. His internationalism came to him as naturally as his love of work and his belief that work is the purpose of mankind's existence on earth.

When he returned to the steelworks during the war and the Party secretary said of him in a public meeting, 'Here we have a worker who thinks nothing of sacrificing his health and strength for the common cause,' he felt embarrassed. Andreyev did not in the least feel he was making a sacrifice; on the contrary, he felt happy and well. When he was registering to return to work, he had knocked three years off his age and had been afraid that this might be discovered.

'It's as if I've come back from the dead,' he once said to his friend Misha Polyakov.

He never forgot the late Nikolay Shaposhnikov and their long-ago conversations on the Volga steamer, and he had the greatest respect for all Shaposhnikov's family.

Shaposhnikov had been right to say to him that, one day, labour would become the sovereign of the world. Now, though, the country was at war. The fascists were advancing, and they threatened to destroy everything Andreyev loved. The fascists were vile and contemptible but for the time being, at least, they had might on their side.

6

Andreyev was having supper in the kitchen before going out to work on the night shift. He was eating in silence, not looking at his wife, who was standing near the table, ready to give him another helping – before leaving for work, Andreyev usually ate two plates of fried potatoes.

Varvara Alexandrovna had once been thought the most beautiful girl in Sarepta;[183] her girlfriends had regretted her choice of husband. Back then Andreyev had been a stoker on a Volga ship, and she was the daughter of an engineer; with her looks, they thought, she could have married whoever she chose – a ship's captain, a merchant or the owner of the Tsaritsyn port café.

All that had been forty years ago. Now they had both grown old, yet Andreyev – with his stoop, his sullen face and his wiry hair – still looked sadly out of place beside this tall, bright-eyed, graceful old woman.

'It's not right!' said Varvara, wiping the tablecloth with a towel. 'Natasha's on duty in the children's home – she won't be back till morning. You're about to go out, and I'll be all on my own again with little Volodya. What if there's an air raid? What will the two of us do?'

'There won't be an air raid,' Andreyev replied. 'And if there were, what help would *I* be? I've got no anti-aircraft guns.'

'That's what you always say. No, I can't bear it any longer. I'm leaving. I'll go to Anyuta's.'

Varvara was terrified of air raids. Standing in the long queues outside food shops, she had heard her fill of stories about the howl of falling bombs, about women and children buried beneath ruined buildings. She had heard of whole houses being lifted from the ground by the force of an explosion and flung dozens of metres through the air.

Constantly afraid as she was, she couldn't sleep at night.

She had no idea what made her so very afraid. Other women were afraid too, but they were still able to eat and sleep. Some said brightly, 'Well, we must just take things as they come!' Varvara, however, could not escape her fears for even a moment.

During her sleepless nights she was tormented by thoughts about her son Anatoly, who had gone missing during the first weeks of the war. And she could hardly bear even to look at her daughter-in-law Natasha – the girl just carried on as if she didn't have a care in the world. After work she went gaily off to the cinema. When she was at home she banged about and slammed doors, making such a racket that Varvara went all cold inside, thinking that the German planes had finally come.

No one, Varvara believed, loved their home as devotedly as she did. None of her neighbours kept everything so spotless; there was not a cockroach in the kitchen, not a speck of dust to be seen anywhere. Nobody else had such a splendid orchard or such a rich kitchen garden. She herself had painted the floors orange and hung wallpaper in every room. She had been saving up to buy beautiful china, new furniture, new curtains and lace pillowcases and new pictures to put on the walls. And now a devastating storm was bearing down on what her neighbours called her picture-postcard home, on these three little rooms she so loved and in which she took such pride. She felt frightened and helpless.

It was more than her heart could bear. She had made up her mind: they would pack the furniture into crates and bury everything either in the garden or in the cellar. Then they could cross the Volga and go and live with her younger sister Anyuta. The German bombers, she believed, had no reason to fly as far east as Nikolaevka.

But she and her husband had disagreed. Andreyev did not want to leave Stalingrad.

A year before the war, the medical commission had taken him off furnace work. He had been transferred to the technical supervision department, but there too the work had been difficult and he had twice suffered attacks of angina. And then in December 1941 he had returned to the furnaces. He had only to say a word and the director would have allowed him to leave. The director would even give him a truck to take his belongings as far as the Volga ferry. But Andreyev had refused to leave the steelworks.

At first Varvara hadn't wanted to go anywhere without her husband. Then it had been agreed that she would go to Anyuta's, together with Natalya and little Volodya, and that Andreyev would stay behind, at least for the time being.

That evening, as Andreyev finished his supper, she brought up this question again. For the main part she addressed her words not to her husband but either to their cat, to little dark-eyed Volodya, or – most often of all – to a listener who existed only in her imagination.

'Just look at the man,' she said, turning towards the stove, beside which this sensible, intelligent and trustworthy listener must have been standing. 'He's going to be here all on his own – so who's going to take care of everything? All our worldly goods will be hidden away – buried in the garden or down in the cellar. I'm sure you understand that this is no time to be keeping things in the house. The man's old and sick. His hair may still be black, but he's registered as category-two disabled.[184] Is it right for a sick man to work like he does? What's the very first place the Germans will bomb? What do you think? The steelworks, of course! Does that make it the right place for a disabled old man? And it's not as if the factory can't manage without him.'

The imaginary listener didn't reply. Little Volodya went out into the yard to watch the searchlights up in the sky. Her husband didn't reply either. Varvara sighed, then continued to argue her case: 'I know there are women who say, "We're not going anywhere without our belongings. Where someone's buried their things, that's where they should stay." But can that really be right? Look! Good china, a mirror wardrobe, a chest of drawers – we're leaving them all behind, we've got no choice. Those demons will soon be here with their bombs. But if the man does stay, then at least there'll be someone to keep an eye on our things. China and furniture only cost money – but you can't just go and buy yourself a new leg or a new head if that's what you've lost. All the same, if the man really *must* stay—'

'You're not making much sense,' Andreyev interrupted. 'One moment you fear for my life, the next you want to put me on guard duty.'

'I can't make much sense of myself either,' Varvara replied plaintively. 'I really don't know what I think.'

Volodya came back inside and said dreamily, 'Maybe there'll be an air raid tonight. There are lots of searchlights!' And then, his eyes bright and shining, 'Grandad, will our pussy cross the Volga with us, or will she stay here with you?'

After a brief splutter of delight, Varvara said in her gentle, singing voice, 'Volodya, how can you ask? Puss will take care of the housework for him. Then she'll go and work beside him in the factory. And then she can pick up the ration coupons and go to the shop.'

'Enough of all that!' said Andreyev with sudden anger. 'You be quiet now.'

Just then the long bony cat jumped up onto the table. 'Down, you little serpent!' Varvara shouted crossly. 'I haven't left yet!'

Andreyev glanced at the clock on the wall and said with a little smile, 'Misha Polyakov's just volunteered for the militia, for a mortar company. Perhaps I should do the same.'

Varvara took her husband's tarpaulin jacket down from a nail and checked that the buttons were still sewn on tight. 'A fine example to follow,' she said. 'Poor old Polyakov's on his last legs already.'

'What do you mean? Misha's a strong fellow.'

'Yes, yes … The moment he sets eyes on Misha Polyakov, Hitler will turn tail.' Varvara knew very well how much it upset her husband to hear criticism of his old comrade-in-arms from 1918, when they had fought together against the Cossacks at Beketovka.[185] But she had always been puzzled and annoyed by the friendship between her sensible, serious husband, who weighed every word he said, and this Polyakov who never stopped joking and playing the fool. And so she went on ridiculing him. 'His first wife left him thirty years ago, when he was still a young man. He was a skirt-chaser – women were all he ever thought about. As for his second wife, if she's still with him, it's only because of the children and grandchildren. And as for Polyakov calling himself a carpenter, the man's no use at all. He can't make a thing. His wife Marya's got a nerve too. Know what she likes to say? "The doctor," she says, "has forbidden Misha to smoke and drink. And if he does still drink, it's your Pavel Andreyevich who's to blame. If Misha goes to visit Pavel on one of his days off, I know he'll come back home sozzled." Well, I can tell you, I just laughed in her face. "Your Misha," I said, "doesn't need any help from Pavel. From what I've heard, he has quite a reputation in his own right. His fame as a boozer has spread as far as Sarepta."'

Varvara sometimes wondered how it was she wasn't afraid to argue with her husband during these turbulent days. His temper had often been violent. Now, though, he was quieter. It seemed he understood that, if she was quarrelsome, it was only because she was so very anxious about leaving her home and her husband.

Andreyev had usually been ready to forgive other people their weaknesses, but he had not always shown much patience towards his own family. In some respects, though, he had seemed strangely uninterested in his home: if Varvara bought something new, well, that was all right by him. If something precious got broken, that didn't really matter either. But once, Varvara had asked him to bring her a few copper screws from the steelworks. 'What?' he replied curtly. 'Are you off your head?' Later that day she noticed that some pieces of cloth she'd put aside for mending her winter coat had disappeared from the chest. When she mentioned this, he said, 'I needed them for cleaning the compressor.' And then he added, 'It's difficult. We never have any old rags for wiping away the oil. And the compressor's new, it's delicate.'

The incident had stayed in her mind over the years. And her husband was still the same as ever. The other day a neighbour had called round and said, 'Has your old man brought you some flour? Mine's brought me two kilos. It was being given out at the steelworks.'

'Why didn't you bring us our flour ration?' she had asked. 'It was the same last week – you didn't bring us any sunflower oil.'

'I meant just to wait till the queue had disappeared,' he replied casually. 'But then it turned out there wasn't any flour left.'

*

That night, as so often, Varvara lay awake for a long time, thinking and listening. Then she got out of bed and walked silently from room to room in her bare feet. She stopped by a window, raised the blackout curtain and gazed into the clear, enigmatic sky. Next, she went over to little Volodya and looked for a long time at his prominent dark forehead and his half-parted lips. He looked like his grandfather: stocky, far from handsome, with coarse, wiry hair. She pulled up his underpants, which had slid down to his hips, kissed his warm thin shoulder, made the sign of the cross over him and went back to bed.

During these long sleepless nights she had thought about many things. She had lived many years with Andreyev. It was no longer a matter of years – it was her life. Whether for better or worse, she was unable to say. Varvara had never admitted this – not even to the very closest of her friends and family – but during the first years of her marriage she had been deeply unhappy. It was not the marriage she had dreamed of in her girlhood. Her friends had said, 'You'll be the wife of a ship's captain, you'll be a real lady.' She had dreamed of living in Saratov or Samara,[186] being driven in a cab to the theatre, going with her husband to dances in the Assembly of the Nobility. Instead, she had married Andreyev. He had said more than once that he would throw himself into the Volga if she refused him. She had just laughed, and then all of a sudden she had agreed. 'All right, Pavel,' she had said, 'I'll marry you.'

A few short words – and an entire life.

Pavel Andreyev was a good man, but he was very unsociable. Difficult, taciturn people like him are often very concerned with their homes; they want to save up money and acquire possessions; they busy themselves with every detail of the housekeeping. But Andreyev wasn't interested in possessions. Once he had said to her, 'What I'd really like to do, Varya, is take a boat and sail to the Caspian Sea, and then go further and further, to distant lands. Otherwise I'll die, and I'll hardly have seen the world at all.'

Varvara was not like her husband. Doing well in the world, being able to show off to others, mattered a great deal to her. And she had much to show off. Not one of her neighbours had such fine furniture. Not one had such a lovely summerhouse in their garden, such splendid fruit trees, such pretty flowers in their window boxes.

Nevertheless, she was the daughter of an engineer and she had lived all her adult life in the workers' settlement around an important factory. She understood that her husband was unusually gifted and she was ready to say this to anyone, to proclaim that there was no better and more intelligent worker in any of the three giant Stalingrad factories – or even, for that matter, in the Donbass, the Urals, or Moscow. By now Varvara understood very well that to be considered the number-one worker in a huge workers' city was an incomparably greater honour than being the owner of a port café.

She took pride in his friendship with the Shaposhnikov family and she liked to talk about how warmly and respectfully they all treated him. She liked to show her neighbours the greetings letters she and her husband received every New Year from Alexandra Vladimirovna.

One year the director and the chief engineer had come round on the First of May. Seeing their two cars stop by the main entrance, the neighbours had been consumed by curiosity; they were all peeping through their garden gates or pressing their faces to the windows. Varvara's heart had burned with pride, though her hands somehow turned icy cold. As for Andreyev, he had welcomed his exalted guests as calmly and straightforwardly as he always greeted old Polyakov on their days off, when he called in for some vodka on his way back from the bathhouse.

And so their lives had gone by – but had anyone asked Varvara whether she loved her husband, she would merely have shrugged. It was a long time since she had given any thought to the question.

*

It was the same almost every night. First, she would think about her husband. Next, she would feel tormented by longing for her son; she could almost hear his quiet voice, almost see his childlike eyes. And then she would think cross, spiteful thoughts about her daughter-in-law Natalya.

Natalya was loud, wilful and quick to take offence. Varvara was convinced that Natalya must have somehow tricked Anatoly into marrying her; she was not his equal in any way – neither in intelligence, nor in looks, nor as regards her family, who, until the Revolution, had been small businessmen. Varvara's thinking followed a logic all of its own; she considered Natalya to have been responsible both for Anatoly's attack of dysentery in 1934 and for the severe reprimand he had once received for absenteeism, after a May Day holiday that had coincided one year with Easter Day. When Natalya went with Anatoly to the cinema or the football stadium, Varvara would accuse her of forgetting about Volodya. If Natalya made Volodya a new outfit, Varvara felt no less cross: why should poor Anatoly have to go about in torn underwear and a jacket with holes at the elbows while his wife thought only about their little boy?

But Natalya was anything but meek, and Varvara certainly did not always come out on top in their battles. Varvara may have been overly critical of Natalya, but Natalya was no less quick to find fault with her mother-in-law.

Natalya got a job in a children's home and was there from early morning until evening. After work, she often visited friends. No detail of her behaviour escaped Varvara's scrutiny: evenings she didn't want anything to eat when she got home; evenings when there was vodka on her breath; what dress she put on to go where; when she had her hair permed; words she mumbled in her sleep; when she came back with a packet of cigarettes instead of the usual home-grown tobacco; the distant, rather guilty tenderness with which she sometimes addressed little Volodya. There was nothing that did not provide grounds for suspicion.

Andreyev tried once to make the two women see sense, to get them to understand the importance of treating each other gently and fairly. Once he called them both Hitlers. On another occasion he lost his temper, raised his fist and smashed the pink teacup and saucer he had drunk from for the last eighteen years. He threatened either to throw them both out of the house or to walk out and leave the two of them on their own. But he must have realized that he was exhausting himself to no purpose; neither reason nor violence was going to bring about any change.

At first Varvara used to tell him that women's quarrels were none of his business. When he learned to keep his distance, however, she felt still more unhappy. 'What's the matter with you?' she would ask. 'Why on earth don't you say anything to the girl?'

She and Natalya would soon be setting out on a long and difficult journey together. But it was not easy to think about the future – it looked very bleak indeed.

7

Each shift worked eighteen hours. The tall iron box of the open-hearth shop shook from the constant din – from the rumble and thunder of the work in the neighbouring shops and the factory yard. There was the noise of the rolling mill, where the steel rang out and clattered, suddenly discovering its bright young voice as it cooled from a mute liquid into shimmering grey-blue sheets. There was the crash of the pneumatic hammers pounding red-hot ingots and sending out showers of sparks. There was the loud ring of the ingots falling onto loading platforms where thick metal rails had been laid out to protect the wood from the still-hot steel. As well as the constant thunder of metal, there was the roar of motors and fans, and the grinding of the chains and belts dragging the steel along on its journey.

The atmosphere in the steelworks was hot and dry, without even a molecule of moisture. A dry white powder, like the finest snow, flickered silently in the dim light around the row of stone furnaces. Now and again a sudden gust from the Volga flung rough, prickly dust into the workers' faces. When the molten liquid was poured into moulds, the half-dark of the shop floor would fill with swift sparks; during the brief second of their beautiful and useless life these sparks looked like a swarm of crazed white gnats, or petals of cherry blossom being swept away by the wind. Some would land on the workers – and then it seemed as if, rather than fading to nothing, these sparks were being born there, on the shoulders and arms of these flushed, overheated figures.

Workers due for a rest would put their cloth caps beneath their heads and spread their wadded jackets over some bricks or cooled ingots: there was no earth or soft wood inside this iron box – only stone, steel and cast iron.

The incessant din was soporific. A sudden silence, on the other hand, would have alarmed these men. Silence here could only mean death, a storm or trouble of some other kind. Noise, in this factory, meant peace.

The workers had reached the limits of human endurance. Their faces had no colour; their eyes were inflamed and their cheeks hollow and sunken. Nevertheless, many of them felt happy – these long hours of heavy labour, day and night, gave them a sense of freedom and the inspiration that comes from struggle.

In the office they were burning the archives – outlines of future plans and reports on past achievements. Just as a soldier engaged in mortal combat ceases to think about past dramas or about what awaits him next year, so the huge steelworks now existed only in the present day.

The sheets of steel smelted by the Red October workers were immediately being transformed – in the nearby Tractor and Barricades factories – into the armour plating of tanks and the barrels of guns and heavy mortars.[187] Day and night, tanks were leaving the Tractor Factory and going straight to the front; day and night, trucks and road tractors sent up clouds of dust as they transported more ordnance towards the Don. There was a close bond, a clear unity, between the gunners and tank men fighting off the still-advancing enemy, and the thousands of workers – men and women, young and old – labouring in factories now only thirty or forty kilometres from the front line. This was a true defence in depth.

Early in the morning the director appeared in the shop. He was a stout man in a blue tunic and supple kid boots.

The workers had used to make jokes about him, saying that he shaved twice a day and polished his boots before each shift, three times every twenty-four hours. Now, though, his cheeks were covered with dark stubble and he was certainly not polishing his boots any more.

Until recently, the director had been expected to know what the steelworks would be doing in five years' time. He had been expected to know the quality of the raw materials they would receive in the autumn and in the following spring. He had been expected to know about their future electricity supply, about impending deliveries of scrap iron, and about the food, clothes and other products expected in the special stores for his workers. He travelled regularly to Moscow. He received telephone calls from Moscow and met regularly with the first secretary of the *obkom*. He was responsible for everything both good and bad: apartments, promotions, financial rewards for achievements at work, and official reprimands and dismissals.

The engineers, the chief accountant, the technical manager, the directors of the individual shops all used to say, 'I promise to ask the director'; 'I'll pass on your request to the director'; 'I expect the director will help.' Or, in the case of some misdemeanour: 'I shall ask the director to consider your dismissal.'

The director walked across the shop floor. When he came to Andreyev, he stopped.

The other workers gathered around.

And then Andreyev asked, 'How's the work going? What's the situation now?' – questions asked more often by a director than by a worker.

'More difficult with every hour,' replied the director.

He said that the steel from Red October, turned into the bodies of tanks, was now confronting the Germans only fourteen or fifteen hours after leaving Stalingrad, that an important army unit with a crucial mission had lost vehicles and other equipment during an air raid, and that a great deal now depended on Red October overfulfilling its plan – the soldiers needed its steel. He added that it was impossible to find more workers – everyone suitable had already joined up.

'Are you tired, comrade?' he asked, looking Andreyev straight in the eye.

'Is *anyone* resting today?' asked Andreyev. And then, 'Should we be staying on for the second shift?'

'Yes,' said the director.

He was not giving an order; at that moment he was something other than a director. His strength was not a matter of his being in a position to fine or reward, to demote or to recommend for a medal. These things didn't mean anything any longer – as he well understood.

He could tell this from the faces of the people standing around him. He also knew that not all of them were ideal workers, in love with their work. There were people who worked simply because they had to, without enthusiasm. Some were apathetic and indifferent; some had already decided that the steelworks had no future; and there were some whose only concern was not to get into trouble with their superiors.

The director looked at Andreyev.

Andreyev's face had the same gleam as the soot-covered girders supporting the ceiling. His furrowed brow was illuminated by a white flame.

It was as if Andreyev embodied everything that mattered most both in work and in life as a whole. All personal concerns and anxieties had now yielded to something much deeper.

'If you need us to stay,' Andreyev replied, 'then we stay.'

An elderly woman in a tarpaulin jacket, with gleaming white teeth and a greasy red scarf wound round her head, said, 'Don't worry, my boy, if you want us to work two shifts, then that's what we'll do.'

404

They all stayed on.

Everyone worked in silence. No one was yelling out orders; there were none of the usual bad-tempered explanations being given to men who didn't know what they were doing.

There were moments when Andreyev had the impression that people were speaking to one another without words. There was a young lad called Slesarev; he had narrow shoulders and was wearing a stripy vest. When Andreyev turned to look at him, he glanced round and hurried towards the entrance, pushing some trolleys with empty moulds. This was exactly what Andreyev had been about to ask him to do.

Somehow total exhaustion went hand in hand with an unusual ease of movement.

Everyone in the shop – not only the Party and Komsomol members and the other most selfless workers, but also the sullen evacuees with no understanding of work, the mischievous young girls with plucked eyebrows who were always peering into little round mirrors, the mothers of families who were constantly checking if anything new had appeared in the store – everyone was now gripped by the same passion.

During the lunch break a thin-faced man in a green soldier's tunic came up to Andreyev. Andreyev glanced at him blankly but then realized that this was the secretary of the Red October Party committee.

'Pavel Andreyevich, you're to come to the director's office at four.'

'Why?' Andreyev asked angrily, thinking that the director was going to try to persuade him to leave Stalingrad.

After looking at him for a moment in silence, the secretary said, 'We received orders this morning to prepare to blow up the steelworks. I've been asked to choose the right men.' Clearly deeply upset, he reached into a trouser pocket for his tobacco pouch.

'You're joking,' said Andreyev.

8

Mostovskoy phoned Zhuravlyov, an *obkom* worker he knew, and said
he wanted to go to Red October: could Zhuravlyov help?

'Good!' Zhuravlyov replied. 'You'll find comrades of yours there,
Leningrad workers evacuated from the Obukhov factory.'

Zhuravlyov phoned both Red October and the Tractor Factory to
say that Mostovskoy would be coming. Then he sent his driver to collect Mostovskoy and ordered him to wait, once they'd got to the steelworks, for as long as Mostovskoy wished. Only an hour and a half
later, however, the driver reappeared. Mostovskoy had said he no longer needed him: after the meeting he wanted to visit a worker he knew,
and then he would walk back home.

Before the evening meeting, while they were waiting for the first
secretary, an instructor from the Tractor Factory committee told the
others about Mostovskoy's visit.

'You were right,' he said. 'A meeting with an old revolutionary was
just what our workers needed. It couldn't have gone better. People
were weeping when he talked about his last meeting with Lenin, when
Lenin was already ill.'

'And there's no one with a sounder grasp of theoretical matters,' said
Zhuravlyov, who had a penchant for theory.

'Yes, he couldn't have spoken more simply. Even the young apprentices were listening open-mouthed – everything he said was so clear
and straightforward. I was there when he arrived, just as the first shift
was coming to an end. The Party organizers announced that anyone who wished could go and join him in the club. Almost everyone
did. Hardly anyone went home – only those who are well and truly
politically backward. It was a splendid meeting. Then everyone went
into the main hall. Mostovskoy didn't speak long. He began with the
words, "You're all feeling tired by now," but his own voice was clear
and strong. There was something unusual about the way he spoke.'
The instructor thought for a moment, then added, 'He made everyone's
heart beat faster. Mine certainly did.'

'Were there any questions?'

'A great many. All about the war, needless to say. Why are we retreating? What's happening about the second front? Will we need to evacuate the city? How can we provide support for workers in other countries? There were, of course, people only interested in their pay and their rations – but that's not important. Everyone – no matter how young or old – listened attentively.' The instructor lowered his voice and said, 'Admittedly, there was one unfortunate moment. In reply to one worker, he said that there was no question of the factories being evacuated or of anything interrupting their work. He cited the examples of the Obukhov and Red Putilovite factories in Leningrad, saying that not even a year-long blockade had put a stop to their work.[188] And there we were – about to hold a closed meeting to discuss preparing the factories, in view of the deteriorating military situation, for extraordinary measures.'

'Well, what do you expect?' said Zhuravlyov. 'He didn't know about your closed meeting and you hadn't given him any special instructions. But what made him say he didn't want the car?'

'I was about to tell you. After his lecture, we were expecting him to join us for a light meal in the director's office. But he said he wanted to go and visit one of the workers, Pavel Andreyev. He dismissed the driver, said goodbye to us all and went on his way. From his gait, you'd have thought he was no more than fifty. I saw him through the window. The workers all gathered around him and then they all set off together.'

9

That morning Varvara had given little Volodya his tea and then got ready to go to the bathhouse.

Going to the bathhouse usually made her feel calmer. She liked talking to friends in the warm, quiet half-light. And the sight of their pink-skinned young daughters and granddaughters brought back memories of her own youth, which was sad yet also pleasurable. At least for half an hour, Varvara expected to be able to forget about the impending journey and her many griefs.

But even in the bathhouse there had been no escaping the war, and Varvara's misery had not been relieved for even a minute. There were a number of young girls who were serving in the Red Army; the changing room was full of green skirts, soldiers' boots and soldiers' tunics with triangles on the collar tabs.[189] There were two stout young women who seemed to have only just arrived in Stalingrad. She had not seen anyone whom she knew.

This bathhouse had been an important part of Varvara's life for several decades, but to these girls it was just one among many. They talked about other bathhouses they had been to during the last year – in Voronezh, Liski and Balashov. In a week or two, probably, they'd be washing in some bathhouse in Saratov or Engels. They laughed so loudly that it made Varvara's head ache. As for the two stout women, they talked quite obscenely about all kinds of extremely private matters. Varvara began to feel quite grubby, afraid she'd end up dirtier than when she came in.

'Oh well, it'll all be written off by the war,' one of them said loudly, with a toss of her wet perm.

The other, looking at Varvara, grinned nastily and asked, 'Why are you staring at me like that, Granny? Not going to inform on me, are you?'

'No,' she replied, 'I'd rather give you a good talking-to myself.' And then she wound a towel round her head. Instead of washing her hair as usual, she would keep it dry and leave the bathhouse as soon as she could.

Soon after she left, there was an air-raid alert, just as she was passing a patch of wasteland where some anti-aircraft guns had been sited. The guns opened fire with an ear-splitting roar. Varvara began to run, but she stumbled and fell. She was still hot and damp from the bathhouse and so a lot of dust and other muck clung to her. She returned home looking very dirty indeed.

Natalya had just returned from work. She was standing on the porch, eating some bread and cucumber.

'What happened?' she asked. 'Did you fall over?'

'I'm worn out,' said Varvara. 'I've no more strength.'

Natalya didn't reply. She just turned round and went back into the kitchen.

To Natalya it seemed that no one in the house understood her. If she spent time with friends or went to the cinema, it was because she was trying to take her mind off her own unhappiness – and she was unhappy because, day and night, she missed her husband. She had started smoking. She repeatedly took on the heaviest work she could find. Once she spent almost forty-eight hours at a stretch in the children's-home laundry, washing 280 sheets, pillowcases and items of children's underwear – anything to take her mind off her sorrows. Had she been feeling carefree and well, she would not have started smoking or spent so much time visiting friends. But the only person who understood her was her new friend Klava, one of the children's-home nurses.

Varvara, however, particularly disapproved of Klava. Mother and daughter-in-law couldn't understand each other and, despite their shared anxiety over Anatoly, didn't want to understand each other. Varvara went to the church to pray and paid several visits to a fortune-teller. But neither God nor the gypsy woman could help her to unravel a knot first knotted in times immemorial. The mother who had given her son life and the wife who had given life to this son's child – both had the right to primacy in the home. A shared right, however, is no right at all, and both women understood, or half understood, the stark truth that in the end there is no right but might.

Varvara cleaned herself up in the hallway, wiped the dirt off her shoes with a rag and went through into the main room. She asked her grandson, 'Is Grandad not back yet?'

Volodya mumbled something incomprehensible. Screwing up his eyes, he was standing by an open window and gazing up into the sky, at the fluffy white trail left at some enormous height by an invisibly humming plane.

'A reconnaissance plane,' he said. 'It's taking photographs.' He had been chatting to the anti-aircraft gunners.

'Of course he's not back,' she said to herself. 'If he were, I'd have seen his cap on the nail. He must have stayed on for the morning shift.'

There was no getting away from the bitterness of her present life. She did not want Natalya to see her tears and so she went out into the garden to weep among the cheerful red tomatoes. But Natalya was already there – sitting on the ground and weeping.

After lunch, some strange old man knocked on the door. At first Varvara thought he was an evacuee looking for somewhere to live, but he said quite straightforwardly, 'Greetings, Mother, I've come to see Pavel Andreyevich.'

'Mother!' she thought crossly. 'I think you mean daughter, you old cretin.' She had seen at once that Mostovskoy was an old man; her quick eye had not been deceived by his strong voice and his brisk movements. She let him in, though she feared that what had lured this old fellow to their apartment was the hope of vodka.

But after only a few minutes, after he'd asked her about her children and her life in general, she was talking freely to him. Far from feeling suspicious, she felt as if she had been wanting for ages to open her heart to him and pour out her troubles. Before going into the room, he had spent a long time carefully wiping his feet on the mat in the hallway. He asked if she minded him smoking, saying that if she did, he could go out onto the porch. In the end, when he asked for an ashtray, instead of putting out the tin lid used by Pavel Andreyevich, she handed him the fine ashtray in which she kept her supply of buttons, thimbles and hooks.

After looking around the room, he said, 'How nice you've made it in here. It's beautiful!'

He was simply dressed and he had no airs and graces. After a while, however, she realized that he was far from being a lowly worker or peasant. Who was he? An accountant? An engineer? A doctor from the hospital? She couldn't place him. Then it dawned on her that this must be someone her husband knew not from Red October but from the city. Perhaps a relative of the Shaposhnikovs.

'Do you know Alexandra Vladimirovna?' she asked.

'I do indeed,' he said, and he shot her a quick glance, impressed by her perceptiveness.

Then Varvara got more and more carried away. She told Mostovskoy about her husband: how wrongly he behaved, how little he cared about their lives, their home or their belongings. She talked about her son. Nearly every mother thinks her children are the best in the world, she said – but not her. She was well aware of her children's failings. She had two married daughters, both living in the Far East – and she could see their faults quite clearly. Anatoly, however, was another matter – he just didn't have any faults. As a child he had been calm and quiet. Even as a little baby, he had slept right through the night. She had fed him in the evening – and after that he hadn't once cried out or called for her. Come morning, he had just lain there quietly when he awoke, his eyes wide open.

From talking about Anatoly as a baby in swaddling clothes, Varvara jumped straight to his marriage – as if there had been only a month or two in between. Probably that's the way it always is – it may well be that, until the end of her days, a mother can never clearly distinguish between the fair-haired infant and the forty-five-year-old with greying temples and a wrinkled forehead.

How could she have imagined that her son would marry a woman who had no redeeming features at all?

From Varvara's stories Mostovskoy learned a great deal about the treachery of women; there was much that he had not read about even in Shakespeare. He was struck by the intensity of the passions at play in what he had imagined to be a small, quiet and united family. This family was clearly not going to bring him comfort or reassurance; it was, rather, *his* role to comfort *them*.

Andreyev appeared, greeted his guest, sat down at the table and began to cry. Varvara, who had been laying the table, rushed off to the kitchen and stood there dumbfounded, a tomato in one hand and a knife in the other; never before had she seen tears in her husband's eyes. She felt that death had entered her home and that their last hour must have come.

It was agreed that Mostovskoy would stay the night. The two old men sat together at the table. They went on talking well into the small hours.

When Mostovskoy got back home in the morning, Agrippina Petrovna handed him a note from Krymov. Krymov wrote that his unit would be stationed in Stalingrad for some time, but that he now had to return to the front. Next time he was in Stalingrad, he would call round again straightaway. As a postscript he had written, 'Mikhail Sidorovich, you cannot imagine how I long to see you.'

10

On Sunday morning the Shaposhnikovs received a letter addressed to Seryozha. Zhenya held up the envelope and asked, 'Shall I open it? It's a woman's hand. The military censors must have passed it. Now it's the turn of the domestic censors. Seems it's from some Dulcinea. So, shall I read it to you, Máma?'

She opened the envelope, took out a small sheet of paper and began to read. Suddenly she cried out, 'Oh, my God, Ida Semyonovna has died.'

'What from?' Marusya asked at once. She was afraid she would die of cancer and kept imagining she already had symptoms. Whenever she heard about the death of a woman her own age, she would immediately ask if it had been from cancer. Spiridonov had said to her more than once, 'You and your crabs – you've amassed quite a collection. Ever thought of opening a seafood bar?'

'Pneumonia,' said Zhenya. 'But what do we do now? Forward the letter to Seryozha?'

Ida Semyonovna was Seryozha's mother. The Shaposhnikovs had never been fond of her.

Even when Ida and Dmitry were still living in Moscow, she had often chosen to leave little Seryozha with Alexandra Vladimirovna for long periods. Before starting school, he had sometimes stayed with her for four or five months at a stretch.

And when Ida was exiled to Kazakhstan, near Karaganda, Seryozha had moved in with his grandmother once and for all. His mother had written to him only occasionally.

Seryozha had always been taciturn. He never volunteered anything about his mother and, when his grandmother asked about her, he had always replied rather curtly: 'She's all right, thank you. She's in good health. She's working in the club and giving lectures on hygiene.'

But there had been one occasion long ago when Marusya had criticized Ida, in his presence, for spending too much time by the seaside and too little time with her son. He had let out a strange, high-pitched, inarticulate cry – no one had been able to make out a word – and run out of the room, slamming the door as hard as he could.

Alexandra was silently reading and rereading this short note written by a hospital nurse. 'During her last days,' she said thoughtfully, 'Ida Semyonovna was talking about Seryozha all the time.' She slowly returned the letter to the envelope and said, 'I don't think there's any need to forward this to Seryozha yet.'

'Certainly not,' said Marusya. 'That would be cruel and pointless ... But what do you think, Zhenya?'

'I don't know, I really don't know,' Zhenya replied.

'How old was she?' asked Marusya.

'The same age as you,' said Zhenya, looking at her fiercely.

11

Spiridonov had been summoned by Pryakhin to an *obkom* meeting. There were many possible reasons for this. It might be just to discuss the general situation or such matters as the power station's anti-aircraft defences.

It might, on the other hand, be for a dressing-down. There had been an accident with a turbine and there had been an occasion when the city's main bakery had been left for two hours without power; this had caused serious delays to bread deliveries. There might have been a complaint from the shipyard about his refusal to allow them extra electricity from one of his substations. It might be a dispute arising from his complaint about being issued with substandard fuel, or it might be to do with his back-up cables not being properly prepared.

There were many things he could say by way of excuse or explanation: equipment was wearing out; many skilled workers had volunteered for the militia; he had too few electricians; and the factory substations were being far from helpful. He had asked the chief engineers of the Tractor Factory, the Barricades and Red October to provide him with work plans, so he could stop them all demanding extra power at the same time, but they had ignored his request. They were still all piling in at once – and if he couldn't meet their demands, it was he who was to blame. Satisfying three such monsters was no joke. Between them, in the course of an hour, they could consume more kilowatts than five cities.

But Spiridonov knew that reasoning like this did not always go down well with the *obkom*. It was only too likely that someone would say, 'So, should we be asking the war to wait while Spiridonov sorts these things out?'

It would have been good to call in at his home. There was time enough, and he was missing his family; after not seeing them for two days, he always began to worry. But he knew he was unlikely to find anyone there during working hours and he told his driver to go straight to the *obkom*.

Outside the building were sentries from the new militia. They wore belted jackets and were carrying rifles hanging from canvas straps. They reminded him of the Red Guards from Petrograd who had been among the defenders of Tsaritsyn during the Civil War. There was one man with a large grey moustache who could have stepped straight out of a painting.

Spiridonov felt stirred by the sight of these armed workers. His father had served in the Red Guard and had died defending the Revolution. And as a young boy, he himself – armed with a Berdan rifle – had done sentry duty outside the building of the district revolutionary committee.

He recognized the sentry by the main entrance. Until recently, he had worked as an assistant electrician in the Stalgres machine room.

'Greetings, fellow worker!' said Spiridonov. He took a step forward, but the man replied sternly, 'Whom do you wish to see?'

'Pryakhin,' said Spiridonov. 'And are you trying to tell me you don't recognize your old boss?'

The man's face remained impassive. Blocking Spiridonov's path, he said, 'Your papers?'

He scrutinized Spiridonov's Party card for a long time, looking up twice to compare the photograph with the man in front of him.

'Seems you're a born bureaucrat,' said Spiridonov, beginning to feel angry.

'You may pass,' said the sentry, still keeping the same straight face, except for a mischievous twinkle in the very depth of his eyes.

'Some people seem to think war's just a game,' Spiridonov said to himself as he went up the stairs.

Barulin, Pryakhin's taciturn assistant, usually wore a tie and a coffee-coloured jacket. Today, though, he was dressed in khaki breeches and a military tunic, with a strap over one shoulder and a revolver in a holster at his hip. The *obkom* staff making their way into the waiting room were also wearing tunics. Most of them had, in addition, acquired map cases and haversacks.

The corridors and the waiting room were full of commanders. A lean, handsome colonel walked straight through into Pryakhin's office. He was wearing shiny, squeaky boots and brown leather gloves that he took off as he passed by. The other commanders all got up and stood to attention. Barulin did the same, even though he was a civilian. The colonel recognized Spiridonov and smiled at him. Spiridonov got to his feet and gave him something close to a military salute. They had first

415

met in an *obkom* house of recreation and Spiridonov associated this colonel with more carefree times – with fishing, bathing in the river and leisurely morning strolls, still both in their pyjamas.

In his immaculately tailored jacket and kid gloves, the colonel seemed the very image of a professional soldier, but one night when they were out fishing together he had told Spiridonov his life story. He was the son of a Vologda carpenter; he had worked as a carpenter in his youth and he still had a Vologda accent.

Then the chairman of the city Osoaviakhim[190] came in. He was a peevish man who lived with a constant sense of grievance, convinced that the other officials did not take his work seriously enough and failed to treat him with proper respect. Today, though, his usual stoop had disappeared and there was a new businesslike confidence in his voice and demeanour. Followed by two young lads carrying posters – 'A Hand Grenade and its Mechanism', 'A Rifle', 'A Sub-Machine Gun' – he went up to Barulin, showed him the posters and said, 'Zhuravlyov's already given his approval.'

'You can take them to the printer's then,' said Barulin. 'I'll speak to the director straightaway.'

'But please understand that it's urgent – for the militia regiments, before they get sent into battle!' said the Osoaviakhim chairman. 'I needed posters last year and it took me a month to get them to do me a mere hundred. They were busy with school textbooks.'

'Your posters will be printed at once,' said Barulin. 'It'll be their next task.'

The Osoaviakhim chairman rolled up the posters and left the room with his entourage. He glanced absent-mindedly at Spiridonov, as if to say, 'I know who you are, my friend, but right now I have more important things on my mind.'

The telephones were all ringing incessantly.

There were calls from the Political Administration of the Front HQ, from the director of the city's anti-aircraft defences, from the chief of staff of the brigades now constructing fortifications, from the commander of the militia regiment, from the city hospitals' administration, from the fuel-supply administration, from an *Izvestia* war correspondent, and from two factory directors whom Spiridonov knew well – one was now producing heavy mortars, the other Molotov cocktails. There was a call from a factory fire-brigade boss. The war had indeed reached Stalingrad and the Volga. Here, in this familiar waiting room, this was more apparent than ever.

Today the waiting room seemed little different from his office at Stalgres. His office had always been full of noise and bustle: conversations with agitated foremen, supplies directors and the heads of individual workshops; telephone calls from the boiler room; a visit from some blustering bureaucrat; some complaint or other from Spiridonov's always dissatisfied driver. People were constantly rushing in to tell him of some new problem: the steam pressure had fallen, the voltage had dropped and a client was making furious accusations; an engineer had dozed off on the job; a supervisor had overlooked something important. All this without a break, morning till night, to the accompaniment of the constant ringing of internal and external telephones.

Spiridonov had understood that it was not like this everywhere. In Moscow, he had more than once been received by the people's commissar. The calm of the waiting room and the commissar's office had been a revelation – a far cry from conditions at Stalgres, where his every conversation was interrupted by telephone calls or excited whispers about the latest drama unfolding in the canteen.

The people's commissar had questioned him for a long time, speaking slowly and carefully, as if he had no more important concern in the world than the efficient functioning of Stalgres. And even in Stalingrad the *obkom* secretary's waiting room had usually been relatively peaceful, although the secretary was responsible to Party and state not only for dozens of major enterprises but also for Volga shipping and the whole of the province's harvest. But now the whirlwind of war had burst in. Only a few months ago, throughout the province, people had been bringing virgin land under cultivation, laying the foundations of power stations, building schools and mills, drawing up reports of repairs to tractors, recording the number of hectares now under plough and meticulously collecting data for the *obkom* about the sowing of crops. Today, however, buildings and bridges were collapsing, the province's stores of wheat were burning, and bellowing cattle were fleeing the machine guns of Messerschmitts.

The war was no longer confined to articles, news bulletins or stories told by evacuees. Victories and defeats were now a matter of immediate life and death – for Spiridonov, for his family, for everyone close to him, for his turbines and motors, and for the buildings and streets of his city.

Filippov, deputy chairman of the executive committee, came over to Spiridonov. Like everyone else, he was now wearing a military tunic and carrying a revolver at his side.

For the previous eighteen months Filippov had had it in for Spiridonov because of his refusal to supply electricity to a new construction site of particular concern to him. They barely greeted each other when they met and at plenums Filippov would criticize the Stalgres leadership for what he called their 'penny-pinching accounting'. To his friends, Spiridonov would say, 'Yes, I enjoy the constant support of comrade Filippov. He only narrowly failed to win me a severe reprimand.'

Today, however, Filippov came straight up to him, asked, 'How are you doing, Stepan?' – and gave him a firm handshake. Both men were moved, realizing that, in comparison with the tragedies of the day, their mutual hostility was something very petty indeed.

Filippov looked towards the door of Pryakhin's office and asked, 'Are you going in soon? If not, we could go to the canteen together. Zhilkin's brought in some good beer, and the sturgeon's excellent.'

'Only too glad,' Spiridonov replied. 'I've got plenty of time.'

They went to the canteen reserved for the *obkom* staff.

'Things aren't looking good,' said Filippov. 'Today, my friend, I heard that the Germans have taken Verkhne-Kurmoyarskaya. That's the village where I was born. It's where I first joined the Komsomol. I'm sure you understand ... But you're from Yaroslavl, aren't you? You're not a Stalingrader yourself ...'

'We're all Stalingraders now,' said Spiridonov.

'We are indeed!' said Filippov, impressed by these simple words. 'We're all Stalingraders – today's news bulletin was very grim.'

To Spiridonov it felt as if everyone around him had suddenly become very close. All were friends and comrades.

The head of the military section, a bald fifty-year-old, walked through the canteen. 'Mikhailov!' Filippov called out. 'Like a beer?'

Mikhailov had never, in peacetime, been one to allow work to burden him. Men who barely slept at night, men struggling to fulfil factory production targets or kolkhoz harvest plans, would smile wryly at mention of his name and say, 'Yes, Mikhailov certainly isn't one to be late for his lunch.' Today, though, Mikhailov replied, 'Beer! You must be joking. I've been two nights without sleep. I'm just back from Karpovka. In forty minutes I'm off to the factories. And then at two in the morning I have to report.'

'A new man,' said Spiridonov. 'I've never seen him like that.'

'He's a major now,' said Filippov. 'He got his second bar only yesterday. Thanks to Pryakhin.'

Spiridonov had always detested careerists who dropped those who had once been their friends. He himself still loved and remembered all his former comrades – boys from his village, young electricians he'd known, fellow students from the Workers' Faculty. Now, though, he felt more tenderness towards them than ever.

And he was also aware of something very different – of an alien, hostile force bearing a leaden hatred toward the world he so loved: factories and cities, friends, colleagues and family, the old waitress now so carefully bringing him a pink paper napkin.

But he had neither words nor time to say any of this to Filippov.

*

Back in the waiting room Spiridonov asked Barulin if he'd be seeing Pryakhin soon.

'You'll have to wait a bit longer, comrade Spiridonov. Mark Semyonovich has to go before you.'

'How come?'

'That's just the way it is, comrade Spiridonov.'

Barulin's tone was impersonal – and usually he addressed Spiridonov by his name and patronymic: Stepan Fyodorovich.

Spiridonov was aware of Barulin's remarkable ability to distinguish very important visitors from the merely important, to distinguish the important from the unimportant, and then to divide the latter into three distinct categories: necessary and urgent, necessary but not urgent, and those who could happily be left to sit and wait. Barulin would show the very important visitors straight into his boss's office, announce the arrival of the important ones without delay, and ask the unimportant to wait. And his conversations with the latter varied greatly in tone. He would ask one man how his children were getting on in school, talk business to another, give a quick smile to a third, pore silently over his papers in the presence of a fourth and say reproachfully to a fifth, 'This, comrade, is not a smoking room.'

Stepan Fyodorovich understood that today he had been demoted from important to unimportant, but he did not feel resentful. Far from it – he was thinking, 'Barulin's a good lad – he keeps at it day and night, day and night!'

419

12

When Spiridonov entered Pryakhin's office, he understood at once that Pryakhin had not changed; he was still the man he always had been.

Everything about him, his nod of the head, his attentive yet seemingly absent-minded gaze, his particular way of laying his pencil on his inkstand as he prepared to listen to someone – all were the same as ever. His voice and his movements were calm and confident.

He had a characteristic way of introducing 'the state' into a discussion about some problem or other. When the directors of factories or kolkhozes complained to him about some difficulty, about how they were struggling to meet a particular demand in the given time, he would say, 'The state needs metal. The state is not asking whether this is easy or difficult for you.'

His large bowed shoulders, his broad, obstinate forehead, his alert, intelligent eyes – all seemed to declare that he was the mouthpiece of the state. His hand was sure, sometimes severe; there were many directors and chairmen who had felt its weight.

He knew not only about people's work but also about their personal lives. Sometimes, during a meeting where the talk was all of tons, percentages and work plans, he would ask, 'Well, have you been fishing again?' Or, 'So, are you still quarrelling with your wife?'

As Spiridonov went in, he imagined for a moment that Pryakhin might get to his feet, come up to him, throw his arms round his shoulders and say in an emotional tone, 'Yes, brother, these are hard times. But do you remember, back in the days when I was working for the *raikom* ...?'

But Pryakhin was as severe and businesslike as ever, and Spiridonov found this oddly calming and reassuring: it seemed the state was still calm and confident, and not in the least inclined to flights of lyricism.

On one wall, instead of charts and tables detailing tractor and steel production, there now hung a large map of the war. Stalingrad province's vast spaces, instead of being given over to wheat, vegetables, orchards and flour mills, were now cut up by primary and secondary

420

lines of defence, anti-tank ditches and other defensive constructions, some concrete, some made simply from earth and wood.

Pryakhin's long red-baize-covered desk no longer displayed steel ingots, jars of wheat, and giant cucumbers and tomatoes from the Akhtuba floodplain. In their place were more recent products of local industry: hand-grenade sleeves, detonators, firing pins, a sapper's spade, a sub-machine gun, and tweezers for disarming an incendiary bomb.

Spiridonov spoke briefly about Stalgres and its work. He said that, unless they were provided with better-quality fuel, he would have to close part of the station in three months' time for repairs. This was not an exaggeration. Spiridonov went on to say that there were stores of high-quality fuel in Svetly Yar. If granted permission, he would take personal responsibility for fetching this fuel, originally intended for Kotelnikovo and Zimovniki.

Spiridonov knew that Pryakhin genuinely admired the Stalgres turbines. When he visited the power station, he always spent a long time in the engine room, questioning the technicians and senior electricians, showing a particular admiration for the most complex and sophisticated units. One day, standing in front of the red and blue indicator lights on the white marble switchboards that directed lightning-swift rivers of electricity to the three giant factories, the shipyard and the city itself, he had said to Spiridonov, 'I take my hat off to you. All this is truly magnificent!'

Given the latest military developments, Spiridonov had been certain that Pryakhin would support his proposal. Instead, Pryakhin shook his head and said, 'Always the good housekeeper, Spiridonov proposes to turn the current military situation to the advantage of Stalgres. The state has its line – and Spiridonov has a line all of his own.'

Pryakhin looked silently at the edge of the table.

Spiridonov realized that he was going to be assigned some new task; this was why he had been summoned.

'So,' Pryakhin continued, 'the People's Commissariat has, as you know, supplied us with a plan for dismantling Stalgres. The City Defence Committee has asked me to inform you that it is, in reality, almost impossible to dismantle the turbines and boilers. You're to continue working until the last possible moment, but you must, at the same time, make all necessary preparations to dynamite the turbines, the boiler room and the oil transformer. Understood?'

Spiridonov was appalled. He had considered it unpatriotic to think about evacuation and only the very closest of his Stalgres comrades knew that his family would soon be leaving. He had told them only in an undertone, afraid of the rumours that might spread if anyone overheard. He did indeed have a copy of the officially approved evacuation plan in his safe, but he had always thought of this plan as merely hypothetical. The few times his engineers had brought up the subject, he had responded angrily, 'Get on with your work and stop spreading panic.'

He had always been an optimist. When the war first started, he had not believed that the Red Army would keep on retreating. Day after day he had clung to the belief that the Germans were about to be halted.

And more recently he had consoled himself with the thought that Stalingrad was not like Leningrad. Leningrad had been encircled, but here the Germans would penetrate no further than the outlying districts. There would, of course, be air raids, and even shelling from long-range artillery. He had had moments of doubt after talking to soldiers and refugees, but any alarmist talk from his own family had upset him. And now – here in the *obkom*, of all places – he was being told not about evacuation, not about skirmishes on the city's outskirts ... He was being ordered to prepare to dynamite Stalgres.

Shaken, he asked, 'Ivan Pavlovich, are things truly as bad as that?'

Their eyes met. Momentarily, Pryakhin's calm, confident face seemed distorted by some deep anguish.

Pryakhin took his pencil from the inkstand and noted something on his desk calendar.

'I understand,' he said. 'For the last twenty-five years, comrade Spiridonov, you and I have been engaged in construction. We're not used to thinking about demolition. But similar instructions have just been given to the factories – to the three giants. Did you come here in your own car?'

'Yes.'

'Drive to the Tractor Factory then. They'll be discussing this at a meeting there. Take a couple of sappers along with you – and perhaps Mikhailov as well.'

'Three's too many,' said Spiridonov. 'The suspension's not up to it.' He had already decided he must call Marusya straightaway. As an education-section inspector, she needed to visit the Tractor Factory children's home and for several days now she'd been asking him for a car. He could take her there himself, and on the way he could let her know what he had just heard.

'All right, Mikhailov can go in an *obkom* car,' said Pryakhin, as he rose from his chair. 'But remember that Stalgres must now work harder than ever. As for this conversation – it's a state secret, with no bearing whatsoever on your day-to-day work.'

Spiridonov hesitated. He would have liked to ask about arrangements for the evacuation of families.

Both men were now on their feet.

'See, comrade Spiridonov,' Pryakhin said with a smile. 'You thought you were saying goodbye to me when I left the *raikom*, but we still keep on meeting.' And then, in his more official voice, 'Any questions?'

'No, everything's clear enough,' Spiridonov replied.

'You'll need the best possible underground command post,' Pryakhin called out as Spiridonov left the office. 'You'll be getting more than your fair share of bombs.'

13

When the car stopped outside the children's home, Spiridonov said to Marusya, 'So, here you are. I'll come back for you in a couple of hours, after the meeting.' And then, in an undertone, after a quick glance at the two other passengers, 'I need to talk to you about something extremely important.'

Marusya got out of the car. She had enjoyed the fast drive and she was bright-eyed and flushed. The soldiers in the car had been telling jokes, and she had been laughing.

But when she got to the front door and heard the hum of children's voices, her face took on a more troubled look.

Tokareva, the children's-home director, was not doing her job properly. It was a large and – so they said in the city education section – difficult orphanage. The children were of all ages and many nationalities. There were several children from the families of Volga Germans,[191] two Kazakh girls with just a few words of Russian, a little girl from Kobrin who spoke only Polish, and a Jewish boy from a small village who spoke only Yiddish and Ukrainian. Many of the children had been brought to the home in the course of the last year, after terrible air raids during which they had lost their parents. Two of these children had been diagnosed with psychological problems. It had been suggested to Tokareva that she send them to a psychiatric hospital, but she had refused.

The city education section had received complaints: the orphanage staff were not always coping with their work and there had been infringements of labour discipline.

As Marusya was walking towards the car, the section's deputy head had come hurrying after her. He had handed her a letter he'd received only a few minutes earlier: a complaint from two of the orphanage staff about the unfortunate behaviour of one of the assistants and about the director's inexplicable refusal to dismiss this assistant. Klava Sokolova, the assistant in question, had sung and wept, in an inebriated state, in front of the children; and a truck driver, who had come to the home in a three-tonner, had twice stayed the night in her room.

424

Marusya now had to look into all this. She sighed grimly, nerving herself for a conversation that was sure to be painful both for Tokareva and for herself.

She entered a spacious room, its walls covered by children's drawings, and asked the woman on duty, who looked about twenty, to call Tokareva. Marusya looked at her disapprovingly as she hurried towards the door; she disliked the young woman's fringe.

Marusya walked slowly about the room, taking a good look at the drawings. One was of a dogfight. In a whirl of black smoke and flame, black German planes were raining down from the sky; huge Soviet planes were flying calmly among them. The Soviet pilots' faces were outlined in red, the planes' wings and fuselages were red, and the planes' five-pointed stars were a denser, heavier red.

Another drawing showed a land battle. Huge red guns, belching red flame, were firing red shells; fascist soldiers were perishing amid explosions that flung heads, hands, helmets and a huge number of German boots high into the sky, higher even than the Soviet planes. The third drawing showed giant Red Army soldiers launching an attack; the revolvers in their mighty hands were bigger than the fascists' puny black cannon.

Separate from all these hung a large framed watercolour of young partisans in the forest. The fluffy, sunlit birch trees were executed perfectly, and the slim young girls had tanned knees – the artist, who must have been one of the older children, clearly had both real talent and a good grasp of the subject matter. Marusya immediately thought of her daughter. Vera was almost grown up now, and the young men would be starting to notice her. As for the young lads in the watercolour, they were all well built, blue-eyed and pink-cheeked. The girls had almond-shaped eyes, pure and transparent as the sky over their heads. One girl had waves of long hair down to her shoulders, another had plaits wound around her head, and a third had a wreath of white flowers. Marusya liked this watercolour, in spite of its one obvious fault: the faces of some of the young boys and girls were almost identical, all in profile, and with the same turn of the head. It seemed that the artist had been impressed by some particular face and had then attached this face to bodies of either sex, adding either short hair or long plaits. Nevertheless, the painting was impressive and moving; it was an expression of an ideal, of something noble and pure.

And it brought to mind the many arguments she had had about art with Zhenya: she, of course, was right, and Zhenya was wrong.

425

Zhenya painted what mattered to Zhenya, whereas this artist painted what mattered to everyone. And Zhenya had no right to accuse her of bombast and falsity. She would have liked to take this painting back home and show it to her. Zhenya would hardly be able to criticize the work of an artist guided only by the pure inspiration of a child's soul. Anyway, what was this truth of Zhenya's? There were two truths, not one. There was a vile, dirty, cruel and humiliating truth that made it harder to live, and there was this truth of a pure soul, born to put an end to Zhenya's vile and humiliating truth.

Yelizaveta Savelievna Tokareva came in – a stout woman with grey hair and a cross face. After working for many years in a bakery she had moved to administrative work at the *raikom*. Then she was appointed deputy director at the bakery where she had formerly kneaded dough. But she did not get on well in this post, apparently unable to impose her authority. After a month she was dismissed – and given a new job as director of this children's home. She liked working with children and had just completed a special course. Nevertheless, here too things were not going well for her. The education section kept having to send inspectors. Tokareva had received an official reprimand, and a month ago the second secretary had summoned her to the *raikom*.

Marusya shook hands with her and said she had come to discuss some recent complaints.

They walked down a cool, newly washed corridor. It smelled pleasantly fresh.

From behind a closed door came the sound of children singing. Tokareva, glancing at Marusya out of the corner of her eye, said, 'This is the youngest group. It's too early to teach them to read and write. They do singing instead.'

Marusya opened the door and saw a group of little girls standing in a half-circle.

In another room, she saw a little boy sitting at a table on his own and drawing in a notebook with a coloured pencil. He was probably about five, with red cheeks and a snub nose. He looked sullenly at Tokareva, then turned away. Pouting angrily, he went on drawing.

'Why's he sitting here all on his own?' asked Marusya.

'He's been very naughty,' said Tokareva. And then, in a loud, serious voice, 'His name is Valentin Kuzin. He drew a swastika on his tummy in indelible ink.'

'That's terrible,' said Marusya. But once they were back out in the corridor, she began to laugh.

Tokareva evidently had a weakness for drapes and curtains. In her room she had white cloths of one kind or another in the window, on her desk, on her bed and by the washstand. Above the bedhead, arranged in a fan shape, were a number of family photographs – elderly women in kerchiefs and men in black shirts with bright buttons. There were also a few group portraits: probably, some Party activists on a training course and Stakhanovite workers at the bakery.[192]

Marusya sat down at the desk, opened her briefcase and took out a sheaf of papers. First she asked about Sukhonogova, the deputy store-keeper. One of the assistants had happened to go past her house and had seen her little boy parading around in shoes from the children's home. 'Why have you not acted on this?' Marusya asked. 'This was reported to you a long time ago.'

Without looking at Marusya, Tokareva said, 'I've been to Sukhono-gova's house and looked into this incident in detail. It truly isn't a matter of theft. The boy's boots were falling apart and towards the end of winter he was unable to walk to school. Sukhonogova took his boots to be mended and borrowed some of our shoes for two days. As soon as she got the boots back from the cobbler, she returned the shoes without the least wear and tear. He's a boy, she says, who just won't stay at home. If it's not skating, it's skiing. And so he'd worn out his boots. And none of us had any shoe coupons just then. And what with the war, and her husband being away in the army for over a year now ...'

'My dear friend,' Marusya replied severely, 'I don't doubt Sukhono-gova's need, but that's no excuse for her to borrow without authorization from the children's-home store. As for it being wartime, that's no excuse at all. Anything but! Now more than ever, every state kopek is sacred, every state lump of coal, every state nail ...' For a moment Marusya stumbled, and this made her feel angry with herself. She went on, 'Think what sufferings are now being inflicted on people. Think of the rivers of blood now flowing in the struggle for our Soviet land. Do you not understand? This is no time for sentimentality and special exemptions. Yes, the slightest misdemeanour from my own daughter and I'd subject her to the very harshest punishment. I'll leave you to draw your own conclusions from this conversation, but I advise you to act without delay.'

'Yes, of course, I'll do as you say,' Tokareva said with a sigh. Then, taking Marusya aback, she asked, 'And what about the question of evacuation?'

'You will be notified,' Marusya replied, 'in due course.'

'The children keep asking about it,' Tokareva said apologetically. 'Some were brought here by soldiers. Some were picked up by people who were already refugees themselves. Others somehow made their way here alone. At night, when the sky's full of planes, the children know better than we do which planes are German and which are our own.'

'Oh, that reminds me,' said Marusya. 'How's little Slava Berozkin? I sent him to you myself. His mother's just been asking about him.'

'He's not so well. He's had a cold the last few days. Let me take you to the sickbay – you can have a word with him there.'

'Later. When we're done with business.'

Marusya questioned Tokareva about the various recent incidents in the home. It turned out that there hadn't, after all, been so very many.

One fourteen-year-old boy had run away during the night, making off with eight towels he had stolen from the storeroom. A second, who had always done well in his lessons, was discovered by a teacher in the flea market, begging for money to go to the cinema. When questioned, he admitted that he didn't really mean to go to the cinema at all. He was trying to save up some money for a rainy day. 'What if the Germans bomb the home?' he said. 'What'll become of me then?'

Tokareva was not especially bothered by incidents of this kind. 'They're good children,' she said resolutely. 'If you explain to them what they've done wrong, they feel genuinely sorry. They're nearly all good, honest children. True Soviet children! And we do, by the way, have an entire Internationale of them now. In the past there were only Russians, but now we've got children from Ukraine and Belorussia. We've got Romanies, we've got Moldavians. Who haven't we got? To be honest with you, even I wouldn't have believed they'd all get on so well together. And if sometimes they come to blows, well, what do you expect? After all, children are children – and anyway, adults in football stadiums are no better. I even get the feeling that they're growing more united than ever. Russian, Ukrainians, Armenians, Belorussians – all becoming a single family.'

'That's wonderful!' said Marusya, deeply moved. 'Everything you're telling me is truly remarkable.' She was in the state of happy excitement that came to her whenever she felt that everyday life was merging with her ideals. There were tears in her eyes and she was breathing hot and fast. There was, she felt, no greater happiness than this. She had certainly never known any greater happiness with her family or in her love for her husband and daughter. It was because of the intensity of her

428

feelings at times like this that she felt so angry and upset when Zhenya, who never understood anything at all, referred to her as cold-hearted.

Marusya had expected this visit to be difficult and unpleasant. Issuing official reprimands or requesting someone's dismissal were not tasks she undertook lightly. She did such things only when duty required, when there was no other option. If at times she seemed harsh and implacable, like a prosecuting counsel, this was because it was such a struggle for her to overcome her instinctive dislike of severity.

And it had certainly never occurred to her that she might experience moments of real joy in the children's home, that she might be moved by the work of a young artist, or by something that Tokareva told her.

The official part of the meeting was nearly over. Tokareva had been suspected of nepotism, but it was clear that this suspicion was entirely unfounded. On the contrary, she had, in fact, recently dismissed a relative of one of the *raikom* officials. This woman, one of the matrons, had ordered the kitchen to prepare her a special meal, from products set aside for sick children.

Tokareva had given her a warning, but the matron, understanding this as her boss's expression of anger at not being included, had ordered the kitchen to prepare a special meal for two. Tokareva had then dismissed her. This had angered the *raikom* official to whom the matron was related.

In her mind Marusya went through the many positive things she had seen: the cleanliness of the rooms and the bed linen; the general kindness of the staff; and the quality of the meals, which were more substantial than in many other such homes.

'We certainly shouldn't dismiss her, but we must find her a reliable deputy,' Marusya said to herself, making a few notes in her notebook and imagining what she would soon be saying to the head of the education section.

'And who painted that picture of the partisans? Your young artist has real talent,' she said. 'We should send the picture to Kuibyshev, I'd like our comrades in the People's Commissariat to see it.'

Tokareva blushed, as if it were she who was being praised. She did, in fact, very often say, 'Something horrible has happened to me again' or 'Something very funny has happened to me today' – and it would then emerge that she wanted to talk not about her own life but about the good or bad deeds of her children, a child's illness or recovery from illness.

'The artist is a little girl,' she said. 'Shura Bushueva.'

'An evacuee?'

'No, she's from nearby, from Kamyshin. She painted it from her imagination. The evacuees, the children who've seen fighting, have done drawings too, but I really didn't want any of *their* drawings up on the walls. They're ghastly – all dead bodies and blazing buildings. There's one boy who lived under the Germans. He drew Russian prisoners of war eating rotten horsemeat. No, I can't bear to look at drawings like that.'

They walked down the corridor and out into the yard. The bright sun made Marusya screw up her eyes. At the same time, she put her hands over her ears because of the din of merry, discordant voices. Twelve-year-olds in football shirts, raising clouds of dust, were kicking a ball around with desperate determination. A shaggy goalkeeper in blue ski trousers was leaning forward, resting his hands on his knees and watching the ball's every move. His eyes, his half-open mouth, and even his legs, neck and shoulders all declared that nothing in the world was more important, right now, than this game.

Some smaller boys, armed with wooden rifles and plywood swords, were running along beside the fence. Advancing towards them was an orderly column of soldiers, all wearing three-cornered hats made from newspaper.

A small girl was skipping nimbly over a rope that two of her friends were twirling for her. Others were waiting their turn, watching intently, silently moving their lips as they counted the number of successful jumps.

'It's for *them* we're fighting this war,' said Marusya.

'I think our children must be the best in the world,' Tokareva declared with conviction. 'I've got boys here who are true heroes. That one over there, Semyon Kotov, the goalie – he was a scout for a front-line unit. He was caught by the Germans. They knocked him about, but he didn't say a word. And now he keeps begging to return to the front. And see those two girls?'

Two little girls in blue dresses were walking through the yard. One was fair-haired; the other, who was holding a cloth doll, had quick dark eyes and a tanned complexion. Her head bowed towards her doll, she was listening to her fair-haired friend. The friend was speaking quickly and with barely a pause. The two women couldn't hear what she was saying, but it looked as if she was angry.

'Those two are inseparable,' Tokareva continued. 'They were brought here from the reception centre together and they stay together from morning till night. The fair-haired one's an orphan, a Polish Jew – Hitler's slaughtered all her family. And the other one, the one with the doll, is from a family of Volga Germans.'

They entered the wing that housed the workshops and the sickbay. Tokareva took Marusya into the workshop, a large half-dark room imbued with the cool damp – so pleasant on a stifling summer's day – that is to be found only in old buildings with thick stone walls. The workshop was empty, except for a boy of about thirteen sitting at the furthest table. He was peering into a hollow brass tube. When the two women came in, he looked at them crossly.

'Zinyuk,' Tokareva asked the boy, 'what are you doing here all on your own? Don't you like football?'

'I don't want to play football. I've got a lot of work to do, I've no time for games,' the boy said, and went back to examining his tube.

'My small university,' said Tokareva. 'Zinyuk keeps asking if he can go and work in a factory. I also have construction engineers, mechanical engineers and aircraft designers – and there are other children writing poems and painting pictures.' And then, quietly and somewhat unexpectedly, she added, 'What a terrible business it all is ...'

They went through the workshop and out into the corridor.

'This way,' said Tokareva. 'Here's the sickbay. As well as Berozkin, there's a Ukrainian boy we all thought was dumb. Whatever we asked him, he never answered a word. And so we thought he was dumb. And then one of our nurses, or rather, one of our cleaners, began to take care of him. And – it seems she has a way with children – all of a sudden he began to speak.'

14

It was a small room and there were patches of sunlight creeping slowly across the wall, their warmer white standing out against the limewash. There were some wild flowers in a potbelly jar on a little table, but another patch of sun, broken up by the glass into a spectrum of pure, airy colour, eclipsed the pale greens, blues and yellows of these flowers from the dusty steppe.

'Do you remember me, Slava?' asked Marusya, as she went over to Slava Berozkin's bed. He had the same features and the same colour eyes as his mother Tamara. And his eyes had the same sad look.

Slava looked thoughtfully at Marusya and said, 'Yes, Auntie, I remember you.'

Marusya did not know how to talk to children. She could never find the right tone. Sometimes she would talk to six-year-olds as if they were only three, sometimes as if they were already adult. Children would correct her, saying, 'We're not babies, you know.' Or they would yawn and ask her to repeat long words they didn't understand. Now, with Tokareva standing beside her, after a discussion that had at times been difficult, Marusya wanted to show that she could be kind and warm-hearted; she didn't want Tokareva to think her unfeeling. With a smile on her face, she asked, 'Well, how are you finding it here? Have any swallows flown in to see you?'

The boy shook his head and asked, 'Have there been any letters from Pápa?'

Realizing her mistake, Marusya quickly replied, 'No, not yet, no one knows his address. But Máma sends her love – she misses you very much.'

'Thank you – and how's Luba?' Slava thought for a moment and added, 'I like it here. Tell Máma not to worry.'

'Do you have some friends here now?'

Slava nodded. Realizing that he was not going to receive any reassurance from the adults and that it was, rather, up to him to reassure them, he added, 'I'm not really that sick, you know. The nurse has promised to let me get up the day after tomorrow.'

He did not ask to be taken away from the children's home, since he knew that life was not easy for his mother. He did not ask her to come and visit him, since he knew it was out of the question for her to take a whole day off work for the journey. Nor did he ask if she had sent him a present of anything sweet, since he knew that was equally impossible.

'What would you like me to tell your máma?' asked Marusya.

'Tell her I'm well,' he said sternly.

As she was saying goodbye, Marusya ran her hand over his soft hair, and over the thin, warm back of his neck.

'Auntie!' he burst out, 'I want Máma to take me back home!' And his eyes filled with tears. 'Auntie, tell her I'll do everything I can to help, and I will eat very, very little, and I'll go and stand in queues for her.'

'Your mother will take you home with her as soon as she possibly can – I give you my word,' Marusya replied, shaken.

Tokareva then took Marusya behind the partition, to a bed by the window. A dark-eyed young woman in a white gown was spoon-feeding a little boy with a shaven head. When she raised the spoon to his mouth, the movement uncovered the whole of her beautiful dark forearm.

'And this is Grisha Serpokryl,' said Tokareva.

Marusya looked at the boy. He was ugly, with large fleshy ears, a knobbly skull and blue-grey lips. He was swallowing down the por-ridge obediently, but with effort, as if he were being forced to eat lumps of dry clay. The contrast between his grey, pale skin and his brilliant, burning eyes was so extreme as to seem painfully unnatural. Only the mortally wounded have such feverish eyes.

Grisha's father had had a cataract, and for this reason he had not been conscripted. Once, during the first weeks of the war, a commander had wanted to spend the night in their hut, but after looking inside, he had shaken his head and said, 'No, I'll go and find somewhere a bit less cramped.' For Grisha, however, that hut had been finer than any palace or temple on earth. There this timid, strange-looking boy had known love. His mother, who had one leg shorter than the other, had limped up to him when he lay asleep on the stove and covered him with a sheepskin coat. His father had wiped his nose with his rough palm. Two or three months before the war his mother had baked him a special Easter cake in a little tin and had given him a decorated egg; and for the First of May his father had given him a yellow belt with a white buckle that he had bought in the district town.

Grisha knew that the other boys in the village made fun of his mother because of her limp, and this made him love her all the more. On the First of May his parents had dressed him up in his smartest clothes and taken him out visiting; he had felt proud of them, and proud of himself and his new belt. His father was strong and important, and his mother elegant and beautiful. He had said, 'Oh Máma, oh Pápa, you look splendid. You look so smart.' They had looked at each other and smiled sweetly and uncertainly.

There was no one who knew how intensely, how tenderly, he had loved them. He had seen them after the air raid – lying there covered with charred sacking ... His father's sharp nose, a white earring in his mother's ear, a thin strand of her fair hair ... And in his mind his mother and father were united for ever, lying dead side by side or exchanging sweet, embarrassed looks when he said how splendid they looked – his father in his new boots and a new jacket, his mother in a brown dress with a starched white kerchief and a bead necklace.

Grisha could not tell anyone his pain, nor could he understand it, but it was more than he could bear; the two dead bodies, and the two sweet, embarrassed faces on that First of May holiday formed a single knot in his heart. His brain clouded over: if he was being burnt by pain, this could only be because he was moving, because he was pronouncing words, because he was chewing and swallowing. He froze, paralysed by this pain now clouding his mind. And so he could easily have died, silently, refusing food, carried to his death by the horror with which the world and everything in it – the wind, the songs of birds, the sound of children talking, shouting and running about – now filled him. The teachers and nurses had been unable to do anything for him; neither books nor pictures, nor rice porridge with apricot jam, nor a goldfinch in a cage were of any help. The doctor ordered him to be sent to a clinic, so he could be fed through a tube.

The evening before Grisha was due to leave, one of the cleaners went into the sickbay to wash the floor. She gazed at the boy for a long time, then suddenly fell to her knees, held his shaven head to her breast and began to keen and wail, 'My child, my child, there's no one who needs you, no one in the whole wide world to pity you.'

And he had let out a cry and begun to shake.

She had carried him in her arms to her own room, sat him on her bed and sat there beside him for half the night. Grisha had talked to her, and he had some bread and tea.

'How are you doing, Grisha?' Marusya asked. 'Are things getting a little easier for you?'

The boy did not answer. He stopped eating. Instead, he stared patiently at the white wall.

The woman put down the spoon and stroked Grisha's head, as if to say, 'Don't worry. Just wait a little. This auntie will be gone soon.'

And Marusya, sensing all this, quickly said to Tokareva, 'All right, let's not get in their way.' Out in the corridor, she sighed loudly and quietly checked her pulse, afraid she might be having a heart attack.

They went back through the yard. Marusya said, 'Seeing children like him, you really do sense the horror of war.'

But in Tokareva's office, wanting to calm herself down, to dispel the anguish she now felt, Marusya said sternly, 'So, to sum up: discipline and more discipline. As you know, this is war, and these are difficult days. This is no time for laxity!'

'I know,' said Tokareva, 'but I find the work difficult. I'm not really managing. I haven't got things under control, and I don't know enough. Maybe it would be better if I went back to the bread ovens. To be honest, that's what I sometimes say to myself.'

'No, no, that's not true. To me, the home seems to be in a very good state. I was deeply moved by that cleaner, the woman who's been nursing Serpokryl. I can tell you straightaway that in my report I'll be drawing attention to all the positive, healthy elements of the home, to its generally healthy atmosphere. As for the failings, you can correct them easily enough.'

Marusya wanted, as she left, to say something particularly kind and encouraging. But there was something irritating about the look on Tokareva's face, and about her half-open mouth, as if she were about to yawn. And as Marusya was putting her various documents back in her briefcase, she came across the letter she'd been handed as she left the education section. Shaking her head, she said, 'Only it seems we still haven't got to the end of the various questions relating to your cadres. This Sokolova really does have to be dismissed: she sings songs in an inebriated state and some man comes to visit her at night. How can you turn a blind eye to such things? A strong, healthy collective – nothing is more important. You really must get a firm grasp of these basic matters.'

'Yes, of course, but it's the same woman … You saw her yourself, the woman who was feeding Serpokryl. She's the only person he'll speak to.'

'The same woman?' Marusya repeated, not understanding. 'The same woman? Well, what of it? I—'

She looked at Tokareva and broke off mid-sentence. It was as if she had been walking along a broad path – and, out of nowhere, an abyss had opened before her.

Tokareva stepped closer to Marusya, laid a hand on her shoulder and said quietly, 'It's all right, don't worry.' And she gently ran her hand down the senior inspector's arm.

But Marusya was unable to hold back her tears. And she was muttering, 'It's so hard, so hard to understand. Why, why is it so hard?'

15

One morning in August 1942, Ivan Pavlovich Pryakhin entered his office and paced about it for several minutes, from the door to the window and back again. Then he flung open the window – and the room filled with noise. It wasn't just the usual city hubbub. There was a struggling car engine, the tramp of feet, the rumble of wheels, the neighing of horses, the angry voices of the horses' drivers, the grinding and clanking of tanks and, now and again – obliterating all these terrestrial sounds – the piercing howl of a fighter in a steep climb.

Pryakhin stood for a while by the window, then went over to the large safe in the corner. He took out a stack of papers, sat down at his desk and pressed the bell. Barulin appeared immediately.

'So, how did you get on?' asked Pryakhin.

'Very well, Ivan Pavlovich. Once we'd crossed the Volga, I took the road to the right and we got there almost without trouble. There was just one moment when we nearly ended up in the ditch. We were driving without headlights. We grazed the back axle.'

'Has Zhilkin got everything organized?'

'Yes. And he couldn't have chosen anywhere better. Safe – not too close to the railway. Zhilkin says he hasn't once seen a German plane overhead.'

'And the countryside there? What's it like?'

'There's one hell of a lot of it … That is, there's all the countryside you could ask for. Of course, it's a full sixty kilometres from the Volga, but there's a pond. Zhilkin says the water's clean. And an orchard. With an above-average apple harvest – I made inquiries. Needless to say, a reserve battalion was stationed there – and I'm afraid they did help themselves a bit … So, just give the command and we'll move the whole *obkom* straightaway.'

'Are people starting to arrive for the meeting?'

'Yes, they are.'

Just then came a knock on the door. A voice called out, 'Open up, boss, there's a soldier to see you!'

437

Pryakhin tried to put a name to the voice: who could be speaking to him with such self-assurance?

The door opened and Colonel General Yeromenko walked in with his usual limp. He greeted Pryakhin, then rubbed his forehead, straightened his glasses and asked, 'Has Moscow phoned you?'

'Greetings, Commander! But the answer's *no* – I'm expecting a call any minute. Please sit down.'

Yeromenko sat down and began to look around the office. He picked up the heavy inkwell, weighed it in his hand, nodded his head respectfully and returned it carefully to its place. 'Quite something,' he said. 'Before the war I was trying to get hold of one like that for myself. I saw one at Voroshilov's.'[193]

'Comrade General, we're holding a meeting here in fifteen minutes. For Party workers and factory directors. Please say a few words to the comrades about the situation at the front.'

Yeromenko looked at his watch. 'Certainly, but I won't have much in the way of good news.'

'Has the situation deteriorated during the night?'

'The enemy has crossed the Don near Tryokhostrovskaya. According to my reports, only isolated sub-machine-gunners got across, and they have already been eliminated. But I doubt this. There were also determined attacks further south. I fear some isolated comrades may not have been reporting the full truth. I understand them: they're afraid of the Germans, but they're afraid of their superiors too.'

'So the Germans have broken through our line of defence?'

'What line of defence?'

'We've been constructing defences all year. The whole city, the whole province has been working on them. A quarter of a million cubic metres of earth has been moved. It was a strong line of defence, I think, but it seems that our forces have been unable to exploit it to the full.'

'Out in the steppe there's only one effective line of defence – and that's men and firepower,' said Yeromenko. 'The one plus is that our ammunition stores are still intact. Artillery fire, that's the only thing that keeps the enemy back. Thank heavens we still have ammunition.' Once again he picked up the inkwell and weighed it in his hand. 'Quite something. Almost an optical device, I'd say. Is it crystal?'

'Yes, probably from the Urals.'

Yeromenko leaned forwards toward Pryakhin and said dreamily, 'The Urals, autumn. There's fine shooting out there. Geese, swans. But not for us. For us soldiers it's just blood and mud. Oh, if only they'd send me two fresh infantry divisions, two full-strength divisions!'

'I understand, but we must start to evacuate the factories, before it's too late. In a single day the Barricades produces enough guns to equip an artillery regiment. The Tractor Factory sends out a hundred tanks each month. These factories are our giants, our titans. Is there still time to save them?'

Yeromenko shrugged. 'If one of my army commanders comes and says, "I'll defend my sector, but please allow me to move my command post further back," then I know he doesn't really believe he can hold out. And the divisional commanders then come to the same conclusion: "That's it, now we're retreating." The same thing happens with the regiments, the battalions, and the individual companies. Deep down, everyone ends up believing they're about to retreat. It'll be the same here. If you want to stand your ground, then stand your ground. Don't allow a single vehicle to move east. Don't look behind you – that's the only way. And if anyone crosses to the east bank without authorization, you must have them shot.'

Pryakhin replied at once, in a loud voice, 'For you, comrade General, a defeat means the loss of a line of defence, of a commanding height, of a hundred vehicles – but here in Stalingrad defeat means the loss of an industry of national importance. Stalingrad is no ordinary line of defence.'

'Stalingrad …' At this point Yeromenko got to his feet. 'What we are defending here, on the Volga, is not an industry. What we are defending here is Russia herself!'

'Comrade Commander, I've put my heart and soul into building these factories and this city. And this city is named after Stalin. Do you think it was easy for Kutuzov to abandon Moscow? Remember the council of war at Fili? I was reading Tolstoy again yesterday. There were many people then who saw Moscow as a final line of defence.'

'It's good that you're doing your homework. Nevertheless, we fought on the outskirts of Moscow, and we'd have gone on fighting even inside the city.'

Pryakhin was silent. Then he said, 'For us Bolsheviks, while we still live, there can be no final line of defence. We stop fighting only when our hearts stop beating. Nevertheless, no matter how hard this may be for us, it is our duty to take the current military position into account. The enemy has crossed the Don.'

439

'I've made no official statement to that effect. Our intelligence data is being checked as we speak.' Yeromenko then leaned forward again and asked, 'Have you evacuated your family from Stalingrad?'

'The *obkom* is about to transfer a number of families to the east bank, including my own.'

'Quite right. What's happening now is not for families. It's more than many soldiers can bear – let alone women and children. Send them to the Urals! Those bastards won't be able to bomb them there. No – not unless I let them get through to the Volga!'

The door opened a little. Barulin announced, 'The directors and workshop heads, all present.'

And the organizers of the city's economic life, the Party officials, factory directors and workshop heads made their way in and sat themselves down on chairs, armchairs and sofas. As they exchanged greetings with Pryakhin, some said, 'I've carried out your orders,' or 'The Defence Committee's instructions have been passed on to the workshops.'

Spiridonov was last to come in. Pryakhin said to him, 'Comrade Spiridonov, I need to have a few words with you in private. Stay behind after the meeting.'

As if he too were now a soldier, Spiridonov acknowledged this: 'After the meeting – understood!'

Gently making fun of him, someone else said, 'Our Spiridonov would make a fine Guards commander!'

When everyone was settled and the noise made by their chairs had subsided, Pryakhin said, 'Everyone here? Then let's start. Well, comrades, Stalingrad is now a front-line city. Today we must check how well each of us has prepared our sector for the conditions imposed by the war. How prepared are our people, our enterprises and our workshops? What have we achieved so far as regards the transition to new working conditions, and the evacuation of our factories? Here with us is the commander of the Stalingrad Front. The *obkom* has asked him to speak about the situation at the front. Comrade Commander!'

Yeromenko smiled. 'It's easy enough now to find out about this for yourselves. Just get on a lorry heading west. A few minutes' drive – and you'll be at the front.' Yeromenko then looked around the room, caught sight of Parkhomenko, his adjutant, who was standing by the door, and said, 'Give me the map – not the working map, the one you were just showing to the journalists.'

'It's already been taken across the Volga. Allow me to go and fetch it in a U-2.'

'You must be joking. You carry too much weight for one of those maize-hoppers. The plane would never get off the ground.'[194]

'I fly like a god, comrade Commander,' Parkhomenko replied, adopting the same jocular tone as his boss.

But this seemed only to annoy Yeromenko. He glared at Parkhomenko, then addressed the meeting as a whole, 'Come over here, comrades, we can use this map on the wall. It'll do just as well.'

And, like a geography teacher surrounded by pupils, intermittently moving either a pencil or his index finger over the map, Yeromenko began his account: 'You're strong men, I've no wish either to frighten you or to comfort you. And the truth has never yet harmed anyone. So, this is the situation today. Here to the north the enemy has reached the right bank of the Don. This is his 6th Army, which comprises three army corps and twelve infantry divisions. There's the 79th Division, the 100th and the 295th – I could almost call them old friends by now. There are also two divisions of motor infantry and two armoured divisions. All this is to the north and the west. Commanding these forces is Colonel General Paulus. So far he has achieved more successes than I have, as you well know. Now – to the south-west. Here we have a tank army threatening to break out from Kotelnikovo. Supporting it is another German army corps and one of the Romanian corps. Their aim, it seems, is to advance on Krasnoarmeisk and Sarepta. Here's where they want to attack, along the Aksay river and the railway line from Plodovitoye. The enemy's intentions are very simple – to concentrate their forces, make their preparations and strike. Paulus from the north and the west, and this tank army from the south and the south-west. Apparently, Hitler has publicly declared that by 25 August he will be in Stalingrad.'

'And what forces do we have to pit against this colossus?' someone asked.

Yeromenko laughed. 'That's not something you're supposed to know about. All I can say is that we have the forces, and we have the ammunition. We will not yield Stalingrad.' And then, turning to Parkhomenko, he said in a voice choked with rage, 'Who the hell dared send my belongings across the Volga? I want every last thread, every last scrap of paper brought back by this evening! Is that clear? And I can tell you – someone will pay for this!'

441

Parkhomenko stood to attention. The men standing nearby looked at Yeromenko questioningly. Just then Barulin hurried up to Pryakhin's desk and said in a loud whisper, 'You're being called to the telephone.'

Pryakhin got quickly to his feet and said, 'Comrade Commander, this is a call from Moscow. Please come with me.'

Yeromenko followed Pryakhin towards the door.

16

The door, which was covered in black oilcloth, had barely closed behind Pryakhin and Yeromenko when everyone began talking. At first the conversation was subdued, but it soon became livelier. Several men went over to the map and began examining it closely, as if trying to find traces left by Yeromenko's finger. There was much headshaking as they exchanged views: 'Yes, the Germans have assembled quite a host!' 'But if our forces try to hold out on the east bank of the Don, it'll be the same old story – the Germans will be on a high cliff and we'll be down by the water'; 'And then it'll be the same here on the Volga'[195]; 'I've heard the enemy's already established a bridgehead this side of the Don'; 'If you're right, it's only too clear what'll come next'; 'When he started listing the German divisions, it was like being stabbed in the heart'; 'We're not children, we need to know the truth.'

Marfin, the short, thin, hollow-cheeked *raikom* instructor, said sharply, 'You never fail to attend *obkom* meetings, Stepan Fyodorovich, but you seem to think the *raikom*'s beneath you.'

'I am indeed at fault, comrade Marfin,' Spiridonov replied. 'Still, I do have a lot on my shoulders. Evacuating a *raikom*'s not so difficult. You pack up your records, remove the red and green felt from a few tables, put everything into a truck – and off you go. What do you think it's like for me? I can't just carry my turbines out onto a truck.'

They were joined by two other men: the head of one of the main Tractor Factory workshops and the director of a cannery.

'The man himself, producer of a million tractors and great guzzler of electricity!' said Spiridonov.[196]

'Why have you still not sent me any electricians, Spiridonov? The factory's working day and night. I'll pay them the highest rate.'

In a low voice the cannery director said, 'You'd do better, comrade Tractor, to pay them with places on the launches ferrying people to the east bank.'

'You think too much about those launches,' said Marfin. 'I fear, comrade Cannery, that you may have caught yellow fever.'

The man from the Tractor Factory shook his head and said, 'My soul aches day and night. At present we're overfulfilling the plan. But if we move everything beyond the Volga, the collective will fall apart. We'll never re-establish it out in the steppe. The workers are staying day and night on the shop floor – and what am I doing? Drawing up lists of names for evacuation. And making preparations for special measures I can't bear to even think about! I'd rather die than go on talking about this evacuation. And Spiridonov's taken to giving me all the electricity I ask for. He was a lot less generous before the war – there were always "objective reasons" ...'

He turned towards Spiridonov and said crossly, 'But this evacuation fever's contagious, isn't it? What do *you* think?'

'You're absolutely right. Comrade Pickled Gherkins here has already had his family evacuated, and I keep thinking I should do the same. The thought's gnawing away at me, I can't deny it. What do *you* think, Marfin? Is there a cure for contagious evacuation fever?'

'There is, and it's very simple,' Marfin replied. 'But it's a surgical intervention – not just a pill.'

'You're a hard man!' said Spiridonov. 'Comrade Cannery King, did you see the way Marfin looked at you then? Watch out. He might decide to cure you any moment.'

'I can cure him all right. Spreaders of panic are the last thing we need. At a time like this, they must be dealt with at once.'

Then everyone fell silent. The door was opening.

Pryakhin and Yeromenko returned to their chairs. After clearing his throat several times and waiting for complete silence, Pryakhin resumed in a severe tone, 'Comrades! During the last few days, the deteriorating situation at the front has given rise to a pernicious tendency: we are preparing too much for evacuation and thinking too little about what our factories must do to defend our country. It is as if there has been a tacit agreement that we will all soon be crossing to the east bank.' Pryakhin looked around the room, paused, gave a little cough and continued, 'This, comrades, is a grave political error.'

He got to his feet, put his hands on the desk and leaned forward a little. Very slowly, with emphasis, as if printing each word in the largest and boldest of scripts, he said, 'No one defends an empty city. Alarmists, panic-mongers and anyone concerned only with saving their own skin will be dealt with mercilessly.' He then sat down and continued in his usual, somewhat colourless voice, 'Such are the orders given us by our motherland, comrades, in the most terrible hours of the struggle.

Every factory, every enterprise is to continue working as usual. There is to be no talk of special measures or evacuation. Is that clear? Clear to everyone present? This means that there should not be – and will not be – any further conversation about such matters. We must work. We must work and work. There is not a minute to be lost, since every minute is precious.'

He turned to Yeromenko.

Yeromenko shook his head and said, 'This is no time for lectures. I will say only that my orders from the Stavka are to hold Stalingrad no matter what the cost. Simple as that. I've no more to say.'

There was a brief silence. This was broken by a sullen, ominous rumble. The windows in the neighbouring room burst inwards and there was the sound of broken glass tinkling onto the floor. Papers lying on Pryakhin's desk were blown about the room. 'An air raid!' someone yelled.

In his most commanding tone, Pryakhin said, 'Stay calm, comrades. Remember – the work of every enterprise must continue without a minute's interruption.'

The rumble quietened, then grew louder again, shaking the walls of the office. The cannery director, standing in the doorway, said, 'Our ammunition dump in Krasnoarmeisk has exploded!'

Next came the voice of Yeromenko, furious and still more commanding, 'Parkhomenko, my car!'

'Your car – understood, comrade General!' said Parkhomenko. He rushed out of the office.

Yeromenko walked quickly towards the door. Everyone stepped aside for him.

As the last men were leaving, Spiridonov glanced at Pryakhin and began to walk towards the door too: Pryakhin probably now had more urgent concerns than the private conversation he had mentioned earlier. But Pryakhin called out after him, 'Where are you going, comrade Spiridonov? I asked you to stay behind.' Then he went on, with a knowing smile, 'A comrade from the front, an old friend of mine, was asking yesterday whether I'd come across the Shaposhnikov family here in Stalingrad. He seemed particularly concerned about your wife's younger sister.'

'Who was this friend of yours?' asked Spiridonov.

'Nikolay Krymov. I think you know him.'

'I do indeed,' said Spiridonov. He looked around at the window, wondering if there was going to be another explosion.

'Krymov's coming round tonight. He hasn't said anything, but I really do think she ought to come and see him.'

'I'll pass this on,' said Spiridonov.

Pryakhin put on his side cap and an army raincoat. Without looking at Spiridonov and probably without giving him another thought, he walked quickly towards the door.

17

That evening, in a large room in Pryakhin's apartment, Pryakhin and Krymov sat together drinking tea. On the table, beside their cups and the teapot, were a bottle of wine and some newspapers. The room was in a chaotic state – the sofa and the armchairs in the wrong place, the bookcase doors wide open, and the floor littered with leaflets and newspapers. Next to the sideboard were a pram and a rocking horse. A large rosy-cheeked doll with tousled blonde hair was sitting in one of the armchairs, with a toy samovar and some tiny cups on a little table in front of her. Leaning against this table was a sub-machine gun, and lying across the back of the armchair was a soldier's greatcoat, along with a brightly coloured summer dress.

Amid all this clutter, the two tall men, with their calm movements and measured voices, seemed out of place. Wiping the sweat from his forehead, Pryakhin was saying, 'The loss of the ammunition dump is a real blow. But there's something else I need to talk to you about. This city will soon be a battleground, no doubt about it. One worry we could do without is nurseries and children's homes. So, the *obkom* has ordered them to be evacuated – unlike our factories, which are not to stop work for one minute. And I've had my family evacuated too – I'm here on my own now.' He looked around the room, then at Krymov. 'Well, well, well,' he said with a shake of the head. 'A lot of water has flowed under the bridge.'

He looked around the room again and said, 'My wife's very house proud. She notices every cigarette butt, every last speck of dust – but now that she's gone … Look!' And he gestured around the room. 'Devastation! And this is just one apartment! What can it be like in the rest of the city? A city with great furnaces! A city renowned for its steel! We have workers here who know enough to be elected to the Academy of Sciences! And our guns! Have a word with the Germans – I'm sure they'll have something to say about the quality of our artillery. But I want to tell you about Mostovskoy. He really is one hell of an old man! I went to see him, to try and persuade him to leave. He just wouldn't listen! "*Why?*" he says. "I've had enough of being evacuated, I'm not

447

moving another inch. And should the need arise," he goes on, "I could be of use underground. Yes, I could teach you youngsters a thing or two about clandestine work – I put in a good few years of that before the Revolution." And he spoke so forcefully that in the end it was he who talked me round, rather than me him. I gave him some contacts and personally introduced him to one of them. No, I've never met anyone like him!'

Krymov nodded. 'I've been thinking a lot about the past too. And I certainly remember Mostovskoy. At one time he was living in our own small town, as an exile. And he liked to meet young people – I was only a boy then. To me he was like a god. I believed in him like a god. One day he and I went for a walk together, just outside the town. And he read the *Communist Manifesto* aloud to me. There was a little hill, and a summerhouse often used by lovers. But it was autumn when he and I were there. It was raining, and now and again the wind blew the rain inside. There were dead leaves flying about – and there he was, reading aloud to me. And I was so excited. I was overwhelmed. On the way back it got dark. He took my hand and said, "Remember these words: 'Let the ruling classes tremble before a Communist Revolution. The proletarians have nothing to lose but their chains. And they have a world to win.'" And there he was, with holes in his galoshes – I can still hear him squelching along. I wept.'

Pryakhin got to his feet, went up to the wall, pointed to the map and said, 'And that's just what we did. We won the world. Look! Here we are – Stalingrad! See these three factories? These three titans! Come November, Stalgres will have completed its first ten years. And here's the city centre, and the workers' settlements, the new buildings, the asphalted streets and squares. And here are the parks on the outskirts – the city's ring of green.'

'This morning those parks came under fire from German mortars,' said Krymov.

'And building this city wasn't all plain sailing!' Pryakhin continued. 'It took blood and sweat. The opposites that came together – it's hard to grasp such contradictions. There were prisoners, former kulaks, and, working right beside them, young boys and girls, Komsomol members still at school who'd left their home and family and travelled a thousand miles to help build a great factory. The cold, of course, was the same for everyone. Forty degrees below, and a wind to knock you off your feet. At night, in the workers' barracks, you could hardly breathe … Smoke, oil lamps, torn, tattered clothing hanging down from the

448

bed boards, the foulest of foul language, sentries rattling their rifles … It was as if we were cave dwellers, back in the Stone Age – yet look what it brought us! Fine buildings and theatres, parks and factories, our new industrial might … But there in the barrack you'd hear someone cough and see their bare feet hanging down. You'd look up and see some bearded old fellow, clutching his chest, his eyes shining in the half-dark. His neighbour would be fast asleep, letting out terrible groans. And I'd have to track down the work superintendent and ask why he was behind schedule with digging the foundation pits. And I knew, of course, that the man was doing all he could. He was no sentimental Christian socialist and he was at his wit's end himself.'

'And what happened?' asked Krymov. 'Did you fulfil the plan?'

'Of course! I told the work superintendent he'd better get up off his arse. Otherwise I'd have him expelled from the Party and he'd be out there with the rest of them, hacking away at the frozen earth with a crowbar. What else could I say to the man? Life was difficult. Difficult. Difficult as it gets … So you might think it was more fun to be creating parks and orchards. Cherries, apple trees … Apples of every kind – Antonovka, Oporto, Crimean, Rosemary Russet … Well, we invited an old scientist to the city. He was a famous man. He used to get letters from admirers all over the world – Belgium, the south of France, America. He was full of enthusiasm, excited at the thought of establishing sweet orchards on sand and clay, on the outskirts of a city of dust and sandstorms. In all the history of horticulture, he said, there'd never been a project on such a scale. The Hanging Gardens of Babylon, in comparison, were a mere kitchen vegetable patch. And he was such a sweet old man – it was as if he smelled of apples himself. We made our plans and got down to work. The scientist drove out to visit the site. Once, twice, a third time. I could sense his enthusiasm souring. Conditions were harsh. There were Komsomol volunteers, but alongside them were whole brigades of former kulaks. In the end the scientist left – he couldn't cope. And without him we made our share of mistakes. Young apple trees died in the frosts. I sent young men to tribunals and, to be honest, I sent a good few into exile myself. And then, last spring, we invited this scientist back. We put him in a car and drove him out to see our ring of green. The orchards were in blossom, thousands of Stalingraders were going out to see them. No barracks, no mounds of filth – just heavenly gardens. Butterflies, streams, the sound of bees. Where there had been only ravines, dust, barrack huts, and rusty wire. As he was leaving, he said, "Really, I don't understand a thing. I don't understand the limits of life's goodness. I don't understand where evil comes to an end, where it changes to good." Back in the old days, the least wind off the steppe used to shroud the city in dust – but now it brings with it a breath of apples. Just like that sweet old man. Yes, what we made there is quite something. A ring of green, hundreds of thousands of workers enjoying the fresh air. Sixty kilometres of park and garden.'

'First, a ring of sand and clay,' said Krymov. 'Then, a ring of green. And now, a ring of iron and steel. Remember that song from 1920? "Our foes crowd in from every side. / We stand here in a ring of fire."'

'I do. But let me finish. The old man was astonished. More than that, the world was astonished! And in the meantime three new factories have come online, the Tractor Factory's annual production is now up to 50,000 units, several thousand hectares of bog have been drained and the fertility of the Akhtuba floodplain has overtaken that of the Nile Delta. And you know as well as I do how all this was accomplished. We pitted poverty against poverty. With our teeth, with our twisted, frozen fingers we tore out a new future for ourselves. Former kulaks built libraries and institutes under armed guard. In bare feet or bast shoes they created monuments to the working class. Sleeping in barns and barracks, they constructed aircraft factories. We raised Russia – all her trillion tons – to a new height. Compared with us Bolsheviks, Peter the Great was a mere child – though it may be decades before people fully grasp what a geological shift we've effected! And what is it that the fascists are trampling underfoot? What is it they're burning? It's our own sweat, our own blood, our own great work, the unparalleled achievement of workers and peasants who fought against poverty with their own bare hands, whose only weapon against poverty was poverty itself. And this is what Hitler wants to destroy. No, never before has the world seen such a war.'

For some time Krymov looked at Pryakhin in silence. Then he said, 'I'm thinking how much you've changed. I can hardly believe it. I remember you as a young lad in a greatcoat, and now you've become a man of the state. You've been telling me about all you've built. And you've certainly climbed high in the world yourself, up into the stratosphere. But what can I say about my own life? I was a member of the international workers' movement. I had friends in every country – friends who were workers and Communists. And now I see fascist hordes – Germans, Romanians, Italians, Hungarians and Austrians – approaching the Volga, the same Volga where I served as a commissar twenty-two years ago. You tell me you've built factories and planted orchards. I can see you have a family and children. But as for me and my own life … Why did my wife leave me? Can you tell me? I'm sorry, brother, I'm saying the wrong thing. But you've certainly changed. I can hardly believe it!'

'People are always growing and changing,' Pryakhin replied. 'It's nothing to be surprised about. But I recognized you at once. You're the same man you've always been. In your cotton tunic and your boots with worn-down heels, though you could certainly get yourself something better. The man I remember from twenty-five years ago, on his way to the front to subvert the tsar's army.'

'You're right. Times change, but I don't. I don't know how to change. I've been criticized for this. But what do *you* think? Is that a plus or a minus, a good quality or a bad quality?'

'Always the philosopher! Another respect in which you haven't changed!'

'Don't make fun of me. Times change – but a human being's not a gramophone. I can't just play whatever record another man chooses. I'm not made that way.'

'A Bolshevik must do what the Party – and therefore the people – requires him to do. If his understanding of the needs of the time is in accord with the Party's, then he will do the right thing.'

'I led 200 men out of encirclement. How? Because I had the faith of a revolutionary, for all my grey hairs. Because these men believed in me! They followed me! For them I was Karl Marx and Dmitry Don-skoy.[197] I was both a Red Army general and a village priest. We were behind German lines. We had no radio. The Germans were telling the villagers that Leningrad had fallen and that Moscow had surrendered: no Red Army, no front, everything finished … And I made my way east with 200 men – ragged, with dysentery, swollen from hunger, yet still hanging on to their grenades and machine guns. Every last one of us still bearing arms. At a time like that, people don't follow a man who's no more than a wind-up gramophone. Nor would a man like that try to lead them. Don't tell me you'd send just anyone behind German lines!'

'True enough.'

Krymov got to his feet and paced about the room.

'Yes, my friend, it *is* true.'

'Sit down, Nikolay. Listen! We have to love life, all life – the earth, the forests, the Volga, and our people, and our parks and gardens. It's as simple as that, we have to love life. You're a destroyer of the old, but are you a builder of the new? And moving from the general to the particular, what about your own life? What have you done to build that? Sometimes, when I'm at work, I think about how I'll soon be back home. I'll see the children and I'll bend down and kiss them! That's something good. A woman, a wife, needs a great deal – and she needs children … And now the fascists are at the gates of this city we've struggled so hard to build. We can't allow them to wreck it. They have to be stopped.'

The door opened and Barulin came in. After waiting for Pryakhin to finish, he cleared his throat and said, 'Ivan Pavlovich, it's time you left for the Tractor Factory.'

'Very well,' said Pryakhin. He looked at his watch and stood up. 'Comrade Krymov, Nikolay, sit down, take your time. Yes, have a rest. Stay as long as you like. There'll be someone on duty here till I get back.'

'I'm going too. Has my car arrived?'

'Yes,' said Barulin. 'I've just come in off the street – I saw it waiting outside.'

Pryakhin went over to Krymov and said, 'You know, I really think you should stay here a little longer. Sit down for a while!'

'What's going on? Why this earnest advice?'

'I know what you're like. You won't go to the Shaposhnikovs yourself, not for anything in the world. You're too proud. But you need to talk to her, you really do.' He bent down and said in Krymov's ear, 'You love her, you know you do.'

'Wait a moment,' said Krymov. 'Just why do you want me to stay?'

'Because she'll be here any minute. The Shaposhnikovs know that you're here. I'm certain she'll come.'

'What do you mean? Why? I don't want to see her.'

'You're lying.'

'All right, I do want to see her. But what's the point? What can she say to me? Why would she come? To comfort me? I don't want to be comforted.'

Pryakhin shook his head. 'I really think you should talk to her. If you love her, you must fight for your happiness.'

'No, I don't want to. Anyway, it's not the right time. If I stay alive, maybe we'll meet some other time.'

'That's a great pity. I thought I could help you to rebuild your life.'

Krymov went up to Pryakhin, put his hands on his shoulders and said, 'Thank you, my friend.' He smiled and added quietly, 'But it seems it's impossible, even with the help of an *obkom* first secretary, to arrange my personal happiness.'

'All right,' said Pryakhin. 'It's time we were off.'

He called Barulin and said to him, 'If a young, beautiful female comrade comes and asks for comrade Krymov, please apologize on his behalf and say he was called back to his unit on urgent business.'

'No, comrade Barulin, please do not apologize. Just say that Krymov's gone, and that he did not leave a message.'

'It seems you really have been wounded,' said Pryakhin, as he made his way towards the door. 'Badly wounded.'

'Yes,' said Krymov, 'very badly indeed.' And he followed Pryakhin out.

18

In the late afternoon of 20 August, after finishing work, old Pavel Andreyev went to see Alexandra Vladimirovna. She wanted to give him some rosehip tea, for the vitamins, but he was in a hurry. He wouldn't even sit down.

'You really must leave Stalingrad,' he said. He went on to say that some tanks had been brought to them that morning for repairs and that the lieutenant in command of one of the tank crews had told him that the Germans had now crossed the Don.

'And you?' asked Alexandra. 'Are you leaving?'

'No.'

'And your family?'

'They leave the day after tomorrow.'

'And if the Germans come? If you're cut off from your family?'

'If I'm cut off, then I'm cut off. Comrade Mostovskoy's staying, and he's older than I am,' said Andreyev. He then repeated, 'But you really must leave, Alexandra Vladimirovna. The situation is serious.'

After Andreyev had left, Alexandra began taking out shoes and items of underwear from the cupboard. She opened a trunk full of winter clothes scattered with mothballs. Then she returned the shoes and underwear to the cupboard and began putting books, letters and photographs into a suitcase. Feeling more and more anxious, she rolled one cigarette after another. Her home-grown tobacco behaved like a green log in a stove, hissing, crackling and letting out sparks.

By the time Marusya got back, the room was full of smoke.

'What are people saying in town? Have you heard any news?' asked Alexandra. She went on, in a preoccupied tone, 'I've decided to start on a little packing. But I just can't find the letter about Ida Semyonovna. I'm upset. Seryozha will want to see it.'

Marusya tried to calm her mother. 'No, I haven't heard anything new. It's probably just those explosions – they must have scared you. Stepan's been at an *obkom* meeting. Everyone's staying in the city, and the factories are to go on working as usual. Only hospitals, nurseries and children's homes are being evacuated. The day after tomorrow

I'm accompanying the Tractor Factory children's home to Kamyshin. I'll sort out the premises and other arrangements with the *raikom* and then come back by car two days later. We can discuss everything then, but I can assure you there's no need to rush.'

'All right – but please help me find this letter. Where on earth can it be? What will I say to Seryozha?'

They began going through papers and letters, looking in every drawer of Alexandra's desk.

'I wonder if Zhenya's got it. Ah, here she is.'

Looking at Marusya, Zhenya made a pained face as she came in. The room was so full of smoke she could hardly breathe, but she didn't dare say anything. Not long ago she had told her mother that she shouldn't smoke any of her awful, poisonous tobacco after they'd put up the blackout curtains – and her mother had flown into a rage.

'You didn't take the letter about Ida Semyonovna, did you?' asked Alexandra.

'Yes, I did.'

'Heavens, I've just turned the whole place upside down. Give it to me.'

'I've already sent it to Seryozha,' Zhenya said rather loudly. She felt childishly embarrassed, and this made her angry.

'You put it in the post?' said Alexandra. 'But it might get lost. And anyway we decided it was best not to send it yet. A shock like that when you're only seventeen, alone in the trenches, surrounded by strangers ...'

'I didn't put it in the post,' said Zhenya. 'I gave it to someone who'll deliver it in person.'

'How could you!' Marusya shouted angrily. 'We agreed not to tell him. It was a joint decision! Idiot! Cruel, infantile, anarchistic idiot!'

'I did what was right,' said Zhenya. 'Seryozha's chosen to put his life on the line. We can't keep treating him like a baby. And just because you're now a candidate member of the Party, you don't need to keep calling us all petty bourgeois or anarchists!'

Marusya felt too furious even to look at Zhenya – she wanted so badly to say something vicious and wounding.

'All right, girls,' said Alexandra Vladimirovna. 'Enough of that. Party member or not, you're each as bad as the other. Marusya, you really haven't heard any cause for alarm, either in the factory or in the city?'

'Absolutely not. I've already told you about the general mood in the city.'

'Strange. Andreyev came round only an hour ago. Some commander had brought his tank along for repairs and he advised everyone who could to cross to the east bank. He said the Germans have crossed the Don.'

'Just some rumour,' said Marusya. 'It makes no sense. Everyone's quite calm.'

'No,' said Zhenya. 'It's not just some rumour. And what about Vera? Isn't she back yet? That's worrying too.'

'Maybe they've already started evacuating the hospitals?' said Alexandra. 'But hang on – Vera's working late today anyway.'

Alexandra went to the kitchen. No one had turned on the light there, and so the window hadn't been blacked out. She opened it and listened for a long time. There was a rumble of trains from the station, and flashes of summer lightning in the dark sky. Back in the room again, she said, 'The shooting sounds much louder and clearer than it used to. Oh, Seryozha, Seryozha!'

'There's no need to panic,' said Marusya. 'Especially since the day after tomorrow will be Sunday,' she added, as if the war took a rest on Sundays.

Late in the evening Spiridonov came round. 'Things are going badly,' he said, lighting a cigarette. 'You must all leave immediately.'

'Then you must warn Ludmila,' said Alexandra. 'Send her a telegram.'

'Forget it,' he replied irritably. 'You and your intelligentsia affectations.'

'Stepan!' Marusya exclaimed. 'What's got into you?'

She had often used exactly these words about her mother, but hearing her husband repeat them was another matter.

But Spiridonov's face had changed. He seemed lost – just a simple boy from a village.

'What am I going to do with you all?' he said. 'The Germans are right here. How are you going to get to Kazan all on your own? Anything could happen – I may never see you again.'

He insisted that they should all start packing straightaway.

'You must speak to Mostovskoy,' said Alexandra. 'Impress on him how serious things are. And you absolutely must warn Tamara. You've got an all-night pass, so you can go right now. And please calm down a little.'

'Stop ordering me about!' Spiridonov shouted. 'I came here to warn you, not to be given instructions. And I don't have an all-night pass – I've been infringing the curfew.'

'Calm down,' Alexandra repeated. 'We've had enough of your hysterics.' She straightened the sleeves of her dress, then added, as if Spiridonov weren't there, 'I always thought of Stepan as a true proletarian, with nerves of steel, but it seems I was wrong.' Turning to him again, she said condescendingly, 'Maybe you'd like a few drops of valerian?'

Marusya said quietly to Zhenya, 'Máma really is very angry.'

Máma's rages were nothing new. The two sisters could remember how, when they were little, the whole family would take cover and wait for the storm to pass.

Muttering and gesturing angrily, Spiridonov went to his wife's room.

In a loud, clear voice, Zhenya said, 'Guess who I went to see this evening? Nikolay Grigorievich Krymov!'

Simultaneously, and in the same tone of voice, Marusya and Alexandra said, 'Nikolay Grigorievich! Well, how did it go?'

Zhenya laughed. Speaking very fast, she said, 'Very well indeed. Could hardly have gone better. I was turned away at the door.'

Marusya and Alexandra exchanged silent looks. Spiridonov came back in, went up to his mother-in-law and asked, 'May I have a light?' After letting out a large cloud of smoke, he said quietly, 'I may have been over-insistent a minute ago. Please don't be angry. Best to get some sleep now and we can have another think in the morning. I have to go to the *obkom* again first thing. We'll get the latest information, I'll send Ludmila a telegram, and I'll have a word with Tamara and Mostovskoy. I do understand your feelings.'

Marusya immediately guessed what lay behind her husband's abrupt change of mood. She went to her room and opened the cupboard. Stepan had indeed taken a large swig of vodka – or, as he now called it, a dose of anti-bombitis.

Marusya sighed, opened her medicine chest and, silently moving her thin lips, began counting out drops of strophanthin.[198] She now took her heart medicines secretly – since applying to join the Party, she had come to see her use of strophanthin and lily of the valley as a petty-bourgeois weakness.

She heard Zhenya, who was still in the dining room, say, 'All right, so it's agreed that I'll travel in my skiing clothes.' And then, with no apparent connection, 'Well, we're all going to die sooner or later.'

Stepan laughed and said, 'You, with your ineffable beauty – never will I allow you to die!'

Usually Marusya felt irritated when Stepan joked with Zhenya like this. This time, though, she did not mind. 'My family, my dear ones,' she said to herself, and tears spilled from her eyes. The world was full of sorrow; with all their weaknesses, these people were more precious to her than ever.

19

In the second half of August, units of the Stalingrad people's militia, drawn from clerks and factory workers, Volga sailors and dock workers, took up defensive positions on the city's outskirts. A regular division of internal troops also received orders to prepare for combat.[199]

This regular division had no combat experience, but it was full strength, well armed and well trained; soldiers and commanders alike were professionals, not volunteers or recent conscripts.

As the militia regiments moved towards the city's western outskirts, units from the front were retreating towards them. These battered units, exhausted by constant fighting and a long, difficult retreat, were what remained of two infantry armies – the 62nd, to the west, and the 64th, further south. They were now positioned on the east bank of the Don, on the defensive line constructed by the townspeople of Stalingrad.

Before crossing the Don, these units had been some distance apart from one another, linked only tenuously. Now they stood close together, ready to fight side by side.

The German forces, however, were also drawing together as they approached Stalingrad. As before, they outnumbered the Russians and were better equipped, both in the air and on the ground.

Seryozha Shaposhnikov had by then completed one month of military training in a militia battalion just outside the city, in Beketovka. One morning his company was woken early and ordered to march west, bringing up the rear of their regiment. By noon, they had reached a gully to the west of the factory settlement of Rynok. Their dugouts and trenches were in a low-lying part of the steppe; Stalingrad itself was no longer visible. In the distance they could see only the small grey houses and grey fences of the village of Okatovka and a little-used back road running towards the Volga.

After marching thirty kilometres under the hot steppe sun, through long, coarse, dust-covered grass that clung to their legs like strands of wire, Seryozha and his comrades, still unused to army life, were exhausted. The march had seemed endless and every stride had required effort. All a man can think of during a march like that is whether or not he has the strength to reach the next telegraph pole, and the steppe had appeared infinite – certainly too vast to be measured by the gaps between telegraph poles.

Nevertheless, the regiment reached its assigned position. Sighing with relief and pleasure, the men slid down into the trenches and dug-outs constructed several months earlier. They took off their boots and stretched out on the dirt floor, in a dusty golden half-darkness that shielded them from the sun.

Lying with his eyes shut beside a log wall, Seryozha experienced a sweet sense of peace and exhaustion. He had no thoughts at all; his bodily sensations were too strong, and there were too many of them. His back was aching, the soles of his feet were inflamed, the blood was hammering against his temples, and his cheeks had been burnt by the fierce sun. His whole body felt heavy, as if cast from metal, yet at the same time so light as to be almost weightless – a fusion of opposites possible only at moments of extreme fatigue. And this acute sense of exhaustion engendered in him a certain boyish sense of self-respect. He was proud not to have fallen behind, not to have complained or begun to limp, not to have begged for a place on the cart. He had been at the very end of the column, next to an elderly carpenter by the name of Polyakov. As they marched through the Sculpture Garden and the factory district, women had shaken their heads and said, 'A grandad and a child – those two will never make it to the front line.'

Polyakov had grey hair and his face was all wrinkles and dense grey stubble. Beside him, skinny little Seryozha with his sharp nose and narrow shoulders did indeed look like a fledgling.

Both the child and the grandad, however, showed endurance and determination, and they finished the day in better shape than many of their comrades. Neither developed blisters.

Polyakov had drawn strength from pride, from the need of an ageing man to prove that he is still young. Seryozha had drawn strength and perseverance from the eternal quest of the young and inexperienced to appear strong and mature.

It was calm and quiet in the dugout. The only sounds were the men's heavy breathing and the occasional rustle of a clod of dry earth sliding down the wooden wall.

Then came the sound of a familiar voice. Kryakin, their company commander, was bellowing out commands. He was drawing nearer.

'Already, come to torment us again!' exclaimed Gradusov, one of the other militiamen. 'He was marching alongside us. I'd thought he'd want some rest too, that he'd leave us alone for a while.' He went on, almost tearfully, 'But I'm not getting up – no, not even if the man threatens to shoot me.'

'You'll get up all right!' said Chentsov, another of the men lying nearby. He appeared to take pleasure in saying this, as if he himself would be allowed to stay where he was.

Gradusov sat up. He looked at his comrades, all still lying down, and said, 'Yes, we've been burnt by the sun, well and truly.'[200]

Gradusov's plump neck and freckled arms had gone scarlet rather than brown, and he looked as if he had been scalded. His large, freckled face had also gone scarlet. He was clearly in pain.

Kryakin was now just above them. 'On with your boots!' he called out. 'And fall into line!'

Polyakov had appeared to be asleep, but he quickly got up and began putting on his foot cloths. Chentsov and Gradusov were already pulling on their boots, groaning repeatedly. Their feet were badly blistered and their foot cloths rigid from dried sweat.

Only a moment ago Seryozha had been thinking that no power in the world could prompt him to move; he would sooner die of thirst, he had said to himself, than get up and try to find water. But now, quickly and silently, he too began putting on his foot cloths and boots.

Soon the company had formed up, and Kryakin was walking down the line, calling the roll. He was a short man with high cheekbones, a wide mouth and large nose, and bronze-coloured eyes that seemed fixed in position; if he needed to look to one side, he turned his whole head and torso. Before the war he had been a district inspector for the fire brigade, and some of the soldiers had come across him in the course of their previous jobs. They remembered him as rather quiet, even shy, always smiling and ready to oblige; he had usually gone about in a green tunic worn with a thin belt, and black trousers tucked into his boots. Now, though, he was a company commander – and all his traits and quirks, all his particular understandings of the world, which had formerly hardly mattered to anyone, were now of immense importance to dozens of men, both young and old. He did his best to seem like a man used to ordering others about – but, being weak and unsure of himself, he could only do this by being harsh and brutal. Seryozha had once heard him say to Bryushkov, one of the platoon commanders, 'You must learn how to speak to your men. I heard you say to one of them, "Why is one of your buttons missing?" That's not good – you should never use the word *why*. The man will immediately

461

come out with some reason: he's lost his needle, there's no thread and he's already reported this to the sergeant ... You should address them like this.' And he bellowed out, 'Replace button!'

Kryakin's bellow was like a blow to the chest.

Although barely able to stand upright himself, Kryakin had ordered his men to line up. He berated some for standing out of line and others for their poor articulation during roll call. Next, he checked their weapons and found that Ilushkin appeared to have lost his bayonet.

Ilushkin, tall and sullen-looking, stepped hesitantly forward. Kryakin addressed him: 'What am I to reply if asked by higher command, "Commander of the 3rd Company, where is the bayonet, entrusted to your safekeeping, from rifle number 612192?"'

Ilushkin tried to glance out of the corner of his eye at the men behind him. Not knowing how to reply, he remained silent. Kryakin questioned Ilushkin's platoon commander and learned that during a brief halt Ilushkin had used his bayonet to hack down some branches; he had wanted to keep the sun off his face as he lay on the ground. Ilushkin then remembered: yes, he must indeed have forgotten to replace his bayonet at the end of the halt.

Kryakin ordered him to go back and retrieve his bayonet. Rather slowly, Ilushkin set off towards the city. Quietly but gravely, Kryakin called out after him, 'Step to it, Ilushkin, step to it!'

In Kryakin's eyes there was a look of sober, severe inspiration. By keeping his exhausted company standing in the full heat of the sun, he believed he was making both them and himself into better men.

'Gradusov,' he said, 'take this report to the battalion commander. He's in that ravine over there, 450 metres distant.' And he opened his orange map case, took out a sheet of paper folded in four and handed it to Gradusov.

Gradusov returned twenty minutes later, at a brisk pace, and cheerfully handed Kryakin a small grey envelope. After dropping down into the dugout, Gradusov told his comrades that the battalion commander, after reading the report, had said to his chief of staff, 'What the hell does that oaf think he's up to? Reviewing his men in the open steppe – does he want to call up enemy planes? I'll write him a note – his last warning.'

During that first day, life in the open steppe had seemed impossible; there was no water, no kitchen, no glass windows, no streets, no pavements – only purposeless bustle, secret despair and the shouting of orders. There were no mortars where there were mortar bombs, and no mortar bombs where there were mortars. It had seemed that no one was giving any thought to the company, that they would remain in the steppe for ever, forgotten by everyone. But then, come evening, barefoot young lads and girls in white headscarves had appeared from Okatovka. There was singing, laughter and the strains of a concertina. Soon the tall feathergrass was littered with white pumpkin seed husks. And suddenly the steppe became habitable. There in the gully, among the bushes, was a rich and pure spring of water; someone brought buckets and then a used petrol barrel. The briar roses on the gully's steep slopes and the rough, twisted branches of the low-growing steppe pears and cherries were quickly festooned with calico shirts and foot cloths. Watermelons, tomatoes and cucumbers appeared. Snaking its way through the grass, connecting them to the city they had left behind, was a black signals cable. And on the second night some three-tonners drew up, bringing Molotov cocktails, mortars and mortar bombs, and machine guns and cartridges, all straight from the factory workshops. Field kitchens arrived – and, an hour later, two artillery batteries. There was something moving about this sudden appearance, in the night steppe, of bread from the main Stalingrad bakery and weapons produced by Stalingrad factories. The weapons felt friendly. Only a few weeks ago, many of the militiamen had themselves been working at the Tractor Factory, the Barricades and Red October. When they put their hands on the gun barrels, the deadly steel seemed to be bringing them greetings from their wives, neighbours and comrades, from their workshops, streets, bars, flower beds and kitchen gardens, from a life that now lay far behind them. And the bread, covered by sheets of tarpaulin, was as warm as a living body.

That night, the political instructors began distributing copies of *Stalingrad Pravda*.

By the end of the second day the men had settled into their trenches and dugouts, trodden paths to the nearby spring and discovered for themselves what was good and what was bad about life in the steppe. At times they almost forgot that the enemy was approaching; life might go on like this for ever, in quiet steppe that was grey, white and dusty in daytime, and a deep blue in the evenings. But in the night sky they could see two distinct areas of light – one from the giant Stalingrad factories, the other from fires now blazing in the west – and they could hear not only the factories' distant rumble but also the explosions of bombs and shells near the banks of the Don.

20

Seryozha had left his home and everything he was accustomed to. He was living among people he had not known before, and in a world governed by codes of conduct that were unfamiliar to him. At times he was undergoing considerable physical deprivation.

In new and difficult situations, even adults discover that many of their ideas turn out to be mistaken and that their knowledge of the world is inadequate. As for Seryozha, he sensed at once how little the real world had in common with what he had been told about it at home and at school, with what he had read in books and deduced from his own small observations. What was truly surprising, however, was something very different. Once he had known real exhaustion, once he had experienced at first hand the harsh ways of the sergeant and sergeant major, once he had seen something of the simplicity of the soldiers' life and become attuned to the eloquence of their foul language, spoken both in jest and in anger – once he had got used to all this, he found that his own inner world still stood firm, strong and sound as ever. His respect for work, truthfulness and freedom, everything given to him by school, teachers and comrades, everything he had learned from books and from life itself – all this remained intact. None of it had been destroyed by the storm that had swept him up. Here amid the steppe dust, amid the soldiers' night-time talk and the orders yelled out by commanders, he found it strange and difficult to remember Mostovskoy's white hair and his grandmother's stern eyes and white collar. Nevertheless, he had not lost his sense of inner direction. His path still lay straight before him, neither broken nor bent.

As they drew nearer to the front, the hierarchies within the company had begun to change. During the first chaotic days, in barracks, when proper classes and exercises had yet to be organized and much of their time was frittered away in drawing up lists and then confirming them, with often fruitless discussion of possible ways of obtaining leave of absence, Gradusov had been a dominant figure. He was smart, nonchalant and worldly-wise.

Within an hour of enlisting and making his way to the barracks, Gradusov was confidently repeating, 'No, I won't be hanging around here for long. I'll get myself sent off on some mission.'

And he did indeed display a remarkable gift for getting secondments. He turned out to know people everywhere – in the Militia HQ, in the District HQ, and in the medical and quartermaster sections. After obtaining leave of absence for four hours, he came back from the city with some pencils and good-quality writing paper for the regimental HQ secretariat. He gave the political instructor a safety razor made from English steel. And he brought the regimental second in command a present from the housewives of the Beketovka district: a pair of box-calf boots. But for the obstinacy of the company commander, he'd have probably got himself transferred to either the medical or the quartermaster section. Kryakin, however, twice refused to release him, explaining his reasons in a note to the commissar. The regimental commander just shrugged and said, 'All right then, let him stay in his company.' He had been thinking for some time that Gradusov would make a good personal messenger.

Gradusov developed such a hatred of Kryakin that he hardly thought any longer about the war, about his family or about the future. But he could talk and think about Kryakin for hours on end. When Kryakin stood there in front of the company and opened the map case Gradusov had once given to him as a present, Gradusov could barely contain himself.

Gradusov seemed untroubled by contradictions. He would talk proudly about his years as a factory worker, about his recent work in the provincial housing construction bureau and about patriotic speeches he had given at meetings. He would denounce cowards and people who were only out for themselves – and then say how stupid he had been not to get himself exempted from conscription. He would express his contempt for traders and former merchants – and then boast about his successful acquisition of a tweed suit, a fur coat for his wife or some corrugated iron. Or he would tell everyone how smart his wife had been in her own business dealings. While visiting her family in Saratov, she had sold tomatoes from their kitchen garden, bought fabrics and cigarette-lighter flints and then, on her return to Stalingrad, sold these scarce items at a profit. After listening to these stories, Gradusov's comrades would say, 'Yes, it's all right for some, isn't it?' Deaf to their irony, he would respond, 'Yes, we had a good life once. Eat – or be eaten!'

He liked to joke about how Seryozha and Polyakov had both cheated their way into the militia, one by adding a year to his age, one by subtracting a year.

Later, however, when they got down to serious drill and real military discipline, during political-instruction sessions or when they were learning about mortars and machine guns, Gradusov ceased to impress. The man who stood out now was Chentsov, a lean, dark-eyed postgraduate student from the Construction and Engineering Institute.

Chentsov was a Komsomol member, though he had recently applied to join the Party. Seryozha was close to him not only in age, but also in many other respects.

They both disliked Gradusov, and they hated the silly rhyme he so loved to repeat: 'Everything's swell – all gone to hell.' He seemed to think these words excused him from all moral obligations.

In the evenings Seryozha and Chentsov often talked together for a long time. Chentsov would question Seryozha about his studies, then abruptly ask, 'So, have you got a girl waiting for you in Stalingrad?' Sensing Seryozha's embarrassment, he would add condescendingly, 'Don't worry – everything still lies ahead of you.'

He often talked about his own life.

He was an orphan. In 1932, after completing his seven years at a village school, he had come to Stalingrad and got a job as a messenger in the main office of the Tractor Factory. Then he had gone to work in a foundry and also begun attending evening classes in a technical college. During his third year at the college he had passed the entrance exams for the Construction and Engineering Institute and been accepted as a correspondence student. In his diploma dissertation, which was largely devoted to the work of the foundry, he had proposed a new formula for the furnace burden. This proposal, which would allow all the raw materials to be of Soviet origin, led to his being called to Moscow and offered a place as a graduate student in a scientific research institute. When the war began, he had been due to go to America for a year, along with a group of other young engineers.

Seryozha liked Chentsov's calm, practical good sense and self-confidence, the interest he took in all aspects of the company's day-to-day life and his ability to tell people what he thought about them straightforwardly, without embarrassment. There were no technical questions he did not understand and his advice and explanations to the mortarmen, as he helped them prepare their firing data, were clear and authoritative. Seryozha enjoyed listening to Chentsov's accounts of his work at the research institute, his stories about his childhood and the distant village where he had been brought up, and about how timid he had felt when he first started work at the foundry.

Chentsov had a remarkable memory. He could still remember all the questions from his final exams, three years ago.

Not long before the war, he had married, and his wife was now in Chelyabinsk. 'She's finishing her teacher training there,' he said. 'And she's the best student in every subject.' Then he laughed and said, 'We'd just bought a gramophone. We were about to start learning ballroom dancing – and then, the war.'

He was always interesting – except when he spoke about books. He had once said of Korolenko, 'He's a remarkable writer and patriot. He fought for our truth in tsarist Russia.' This had made Seryozha feel awkward. He hadn't thought anything of the kind when he read *The Blind Musician*. He had simply begun to cry.[201]

Seryozha was surprised that Chentsov, who had a good knowledge of many foreign writers as well as of the Russian classics, had not read Gaidar's children's books.[202] And Chentsov had never even heard of Mowgli, Tom Sawyer and Huckleberry Finn. 'How could I have found the time when they weren't even on the syllabus?' he exclaimed indignantly. 'You try completing a five-year degree course in three years at the same time as doing a full-time job in a factory! I was only getting four hours' sleep a night as it was.'

Both in the barracks and during exercises he was quiet and conscientious. He never complained about feeling tired.

His gifts were particularly obvious during study sessions. His answers to the commanders' questions were quick and always to the point. The other militiamen liked him – except that one day he went and informed the political instructor that the clerk was issuing unwarranted leaves of absence. This, naturally, was held against him. Galiguzov, formerly a dock worker and now the commander of a gun crew, said, 'No doubt about it, comrade Chentsov, you're a born bureaucrat.'

'I volunteered for the militia to defend the homeland, not to cover up other people's stupidities,' said Chentsov.

'And the rest of us?' said Galiguzov. 'Do you think we're not willing to sacrifice our lives for the motherland?'

Shortly before they moved out to the steppe, the rapport between Seryozha and Chentsov had soured. Seryozha's boyish outspokenness seemed to alarm Chentsov.

'Don't you ever feel like smashing Kryakin's face in?' Seryozha had asked, addressing a group of his comrades. After waiting in vain for an answer, he had said resolutely, '*I* do – the man's a shit.'

The others had laughed, but in the evening one of them said to Seryozha, 'You shouldn't say things like that about the company commander. You could be sent to a penal battalion!'[203]

And Chentsov joined in, saying, 'Yes, this should be reported to Polit-instructor Shumilo!'

'A fine comrade you are!' said Seryozha.

'It would be the act of a true comrade. You need to be taught a lesson or two, before it's too late. You've been educated pretty well, but you lack political awareness.'

'I think—' Seryozha began, both embarrassed and angry.

'You think the world of yourself,' Chentsov yelled furiously, 'but you're just a snotty-nosed brat.' Seryozha had never seen him like this before.

But once they had left Stalingrad and moved to the steppe, it was the turn of Polyakov the carpenter to come into his own. The Shaposh-nikovs would, no doubt, have been astonished to learn that Polyakov considered their dear Seryozha anything but well educated. All day long Polyakov criticized Seryozha and told him what to do: 'If you're going to sit down for a meal, you should first take your cap off ... No, not a *bucket* of water – a *pail* of water ... What are you doing – call *that* a way to cut bread? ... Whatever next? Flinging out your garbage just as a man's coming down into the dugout! ... No, no, no, there are no dogs round here – they're not going to clean up the bones you throw out! And I'm not a donkey – don't keep saying "Hey!" to me!'

Polyakov imagined that Seryozha placed a loaf of bread the wrong way up not only because military life exempted him from ordinary rules of human behaviour but also because he lacked respect for simple working people. It did not occur to him that Seryozha might never have been taught rules and customs known to every little boy in the workers' settlement where he himself had grown up. His own philosophy of life was unsophisticated but fundamentally decent: a belief that working people have the right to be free, happy and properly fed. He could speak eloquently about bread still warm from the oven, about cabbage soup with sour cream, and about the joys of drinking cold beer in summer or, in winter, coming in out of the cold into a clean, well-heated room, sitting down at table and downing a glass of vodka: 'Cool to the lips, warm to the heart!'

Polyakov loved his work. When he spoke about his tools, about planks of ash and beech, about working with oak and maple, it was with the same sensuous joy, the same gleam in his small, bright eyes – embedded deep in his many wrinkles – as when he talked about drinking vodka with his dinner. He thought of his work as a way of giving pleasure to people, of making their lives easier and more comfortable. He loved life and life had evidently returned his love, treating him generously and not hiding its charms from him. He went regularly to the cinema and the theatre and he had planted a small orchard beside his house. He loved football and some of the other soldiers already knew who he was, having often glimpsed him at the stadium. He had a small rowing boat of his own, and he usually went on fishing trips during his holidays, spending two weeks in the reeds by the east bank of the Volga, enjoying the silent excitement of fishing and the magical riches of the water – water that could be cool and sad in the misty silence of dawn, soft and golden as sunflower oil on a moonlit night, or sparkling and boisterous on a day of sun and wind. He fished, slept, smoked, made fish soup, fried fish in a pan, baked fish between burdock leaves, drank vodka and sang songs. He would return home tipsy, smelling of smoke and the river, and for many days to come he would discover stray fish scales in his hair and be emptying tiny pinches of white sand from his pockets. There was a particular fragrant root that he liked to smoke and, when he needed new supplies, he used to make a special journey to an old man he knew in a village forty kilometres away.

When he was young, Polyakov had seen a great deal; he had served in the Red Army, both in the infantry and the artillery, and he had taken part in the defence of Tsaritsyn. He would point to an overgrown ditch, now almost filled in by sand, and swear to the other soldiers that this was the very trench in which he had sat twenty-two years earlier, his machine gun trained on the White cavalry.

Politinstructor Shumilo took it into his head to organize an evening discussion, so that the old veteran could talk about the defence of Tsaritsyn. Soldiers were invited from the other units, but the discussion did not turn out as planned. Intimidated by the sight of dozens of people all come to listen to him, Polyakov stuttered for a while, then fell silent. After a moment or two, he recovered himself, sat down on the ground and, as if just chatting over a glass of beer with one of his mates, continued with wild vivacity. With astonishing recall of every detail, encouraged by the smiles of his audience, he talked about what they had been given to eat, listing the exact quantity of millet, the number of sugar lumps and the weight of their rations of corned beef and dried rusks. He spoke with particular feeling about a certain Bychkov, who, twenty-one years ago, had stolen a bottle of moonshine and a pair of new boots from his haversack.

Shumilo had to take over and give a proper lecture about the defence of Tsaritsyn, although he himself had been only two years old at the time.

The other soldiers did not forget this evening, and Polyakov became the butt of much banter. And the regimental commissar, for his part, would sometimes say to Shumilo, 'Well, who do you think we should send as a lecturer? Polyakov?' And then, with a wink, 'Yes, there are no flies on that old fellow!'

After the Civil War, Polyakov had worked in Rostov and Yekaterinoslav, and then in Moscow and Baku. He did indeed have much to reminisce about. He spoke freely and directly about women, but with a straightforward admiration, a kind of fearful astonishment that was somehow very appealing.

'You're still children,' he would say, 'still wet behind the ears. But the power of a woman is something to be reckoned with. To this day, a beautiful girl sets my ears ringing and makes my heart miss a beat.'

During the company's fifth day in the steppe two cars arrived: a green Emka and an elegant black saloon. Their passengers turned out to be members of the State Defence Committee, along with the colonel in command of the Stalingrad garrison. They went straight to HQ, leaving the soldiers chatting excitedly.

The visitors soon emerged from HQ and began to inspect the trenches and dugouts and to talk to the soldiers. The colonel examined the machine-gun nests at length, settled himself behind one of the guns, took aim and even fired a few rounds into the air. Then he moved on to the mortarmen.

'Stand to attention!' shouted Kryakin, before saluting. The lean, elegant colonel at once called out, 'At ease!' Seeing Polyakov, he smiled and went over to him.

'Well met, my good carpenter!'

Polyakov stood to attention again and said, 'Good day, comrade Colonel!'

Bryushkov, the platoon commander, felt relieved: Polyakov's response had been correct to the letter.

'Your position here?' asked the colonel.

'Mortar loader, comrade Colonel.'

'Well, brother Slav, will you fight off the Germans? You won't let the professionals down?'

'Not if I'm properly fed,' Polyakov replied brightly. 'But where are these Germans? Are they close yet?'

The colonel laughed and said, 'Well, soldier, let's have a look at your famous tin!'

Polyakov took a round tin from his pocket and gave the colonel some tobacco from his special root. The colonel took off his gloves, rolled a cigarette and puffed out a cloud of smoke. In the meantime, his adjutant quietly asked the other soldiers, 'Is there a Shaposhnikov here?'

'He's gone to fetch our rations,' said Chentsov.

'I've got a letter for him,' said the adjutant, 'from his family in the city.' Waving an envelope in the air, he said, 'Shall I leave it at HQ?'

'Leave it with me, we're in the same dugout,' said Chentsov.

After the visitors left, Polyakov said to his comrades, 'I've known him a long time. He's a good sort. A man like us – for all his smart gloves and high rank. Not long before the war I was laying a parquet floor in his office. He came to take a look at my work, then said, "Pass me the sander. I want to have a go too." And he knew what to do with the machine all right. He told me he's from Vologda. His father was a carpenter, and his grandfather too, and he even worked six years as a carpenter himself, before all his military schools and academies.'

'His Chevrolet is a dream,' Chentsov said thoughtfully. 'What an engine – it really purrs.'

'The number of houses I must have built in Stalingrad,' Polyakov went on. 'It's hard to imagine. And the garrison HQ – I did a parquet floor for them too. The best beech, beautifully sanded.' When Polyakov talked about all the schools, hospitals and club rooms he had helped construct, when he listed all the buildings where he had laid floors or installed doors, windows and partition walls, it was as if the whole city belonged to him – as if this spirited, cantankerous old man were the master of all Stalingrad. And now here he was out in the steppe, behind the barrel of a heavy mortar turned to the west: what lay behind Polyakov was his own realm – so who in the world could defend this realm better?

Everyone in the various militia HQs and command posts felt cheered by the colonel's visit. And two days later, a new division took up position nearby. Clouds of dust rose over the steppe and there was a constant rumble of trucks. The steppe roads were packed with close columns of infantry; with sub-units of sappers, machine-gunners and anti-tank riflemen; with large-calibre motor artillery; with batteries of heavy mortars; with heavy machine guns and anti-tank guns. There were three-tonners full of shells and mortar bombs, their suspension barely able to cope. Field kitchens rattled past; field radio stations and ambulances stirred up yet more dust.

Polyakov and his militia comrades watched excitedly as these new battalions deployed, as signallers passed by, trailing their long cables, and rapid-firing cannon were installed in their fire positions, their long barrels all pointing west.

To a soldier preparing to meet the enemy it is always a joy when new comrades take their place at his side, close by and ready for combat.

21

Gradusov was summoned to regimental HQ. Late in the afternoon he came back and, without a word to anyone, began packing his knapsack. With a mock-sympathetic smile, Chentsov asked, 'Why are your hands shaking? Being transferred to the paratroopers, are you?'

Gradusov looked around. He seemed almost drunk with excitement. 'People haven't forgotten about me after all,' he replied. 'I'm being sent to Chelyabinsk, to help build a military factory. My family will accompany me. All agreed just like that!'

'Ah!' said Chentsov. 'Now I understand. Your hands are shaking with joy. I'd thought it was fear.'

Gradusov smiled meekly. Rather than taking offence, he still expected others to delight in his success. 'Just think,' he said, unfolding a document he had in his hand. 'A man's life depends on a slip of paper! That's it now! Yesterday the best I could hope for was a position as a clerk, but now I'm off to Siberia. With luck, I'll get a lift on a truck to Kamyshin tomorrow. Then to Saratov by train. There I'll join my wife, and my son – and off we all go to Chelyabinsk. Farewell, comrade Kryakin, you won't be able to get at me there!' He laughed again, looked at his comrades, waved his document in the air, put it in one of his tunic pockets, did up the button and then, to make doubly sure, fastened the pocket with a large safety pin. He ran his hand over his chest and said, 'There – all in good order!'

'Yes,' said Polyakov. 'You're lucky to be able to see your family. I wish I could do the same – I'd love to spend an hour with my old woman.'

Gripped by a magnanimous pity towards those he was leaving behind, Gradusov opened his knapsack and said, 'Here you are, my friends – my army kit! I won't be needing it where I'm going now. Help yourselves!' Taking some neatly folded foot cloths and holding them out towards Chentsov, he said, 'Please, take these! Brand new, clean as napkins.'

'No,' said Chentsov. 'I don't want your brand-new napkins.'

But Gradusov was feeling more and more intoxicated by his own generosity. He took out a razor in a white cloth and said, 'This is for you, Shaposhnikov, something to remember me by – even if you do seem to have a grudge against me!'

Seryozha did not reply.

'Take it, Shaposhnikov, feel free!' Seeing Seryozha hesitate, he added, 'Don't worry, I've got another one back at home, an English razor. This one here is my old one – I didn't bring my new one in case someone made off with it.'

Seryozha was unsure whether or not it was right to say something hurtful to a man offering him a gift. He even wondered about saying that he didn't need a razor because he hadn't yet started to shave – not an easy thing to admit when you're already seventeen. But in the end he said, 'No. I don't want it. I look on you now ... as a deserter.'

'No, Seryozha!' Polyakov interrupted angrily. 'You're not a teacher, and we all have our own lives to live.' He turned to Gradusov and said, 'Give it to me. It can be our kolkhoz razor, our collective property.'

Polyakov took the black razor case from Gradusov and put it in his pocket. 'What are you all getting so upset about?' he asked brightly. 'So what if there's one militiaman less in our company! I've just been outside. I've seen our new divisions deploying. There's a whole host taking up position. They just keep on coming – no beginning and no end to them. Parade-ground uniforms, box-calf boots, ruddy cheeks. Strapping young men, real warriors. What's the matter with you all? We can get by without Gradusov!'

'True enough,' said Gradusov.

'Where do you think you're going now?' asked Polyakov, seeing Gradusov put on his knapsack. 'It's almost dark. You'll lose your way in the steppe and end up getting shot by one of our sentries. Stay here till morning. The field kitchen will be here any moment – why miss out on your rations? We're getting meat soup tonight – good and rich. Come morning, you can go on your way.'

Gradusov gave him a quick look, then shook his head. He didn't say a word, but everyone understood what he was thinking: 'No, my friends, I'm sorry – but what if the Germans attack during the night? Soup or no soup – it could be the end of me!'

Gradusov left. There may have been men who envied him, but there was no one who did not, in some way, feel superior to him.

'Why did you accept a gift from him, comrade Polyakov?' asked Chentsov.

'Why not?' replied Polyakov. 'It'll come in useful. Why let the fool go off with a good razor?'

'I think you were wrong,' said Seryozha. 'And you shouldn't have given him your hand. I didn't.'

'Shaposhnikov's right,' said Chentsov. Seryozha gave him a warm smile – this was their first moment of understanding since their quarrel.

Aware of this, Chentsov went on, 'You got a letter today. Was it anything important? No one else has had one yet.'

Seryozha looked up again and said, 'Yes, I did get a letter.'

'Are you all right? Is something wrong with your eyes?'

'They're sore,' said Seryozha. 'It must be the dust.'

*

Dark steppe, and two diffuse glows in the sky – from the furnaces of the Stalingrad factories and from the fighting to the west of the Don. Silent stars and wanton new interlopers – red and green German rockets, temporarily blinding men to the stars' eternal light. In the dark up above – the troubling hum of planes, maybe Soviet, maybe German. The steppe is silent, and to the north, where there is no source of light, earth and sky have merged – dark, sullen and anxious. Sultry heat – rather than bringing peace and cool, the night is full of alarm. It is a night of steppe warfare. Any slight rustle is frightening, but silence is no less frightening. The darkness to the north is terrifying, but the uncertain glow from beyond the Don is worse still – and drawing nearer.

A seventeen-year-old boy with narrow shoulders stands with his rifle at a company advance post. He stands there, doing nothing, thinking and thinking. But what he feels is not childish fear, not the fear of a lost, helpless bird; for the first time in his life he feels that he is strong, and the warm breath of this vast and severe land – this land he is here to defend – fills him with love and pity. He too is severe, strong, frowning and resolute, a defender of the small and the weak, of a land now lying hushed and wounded.

He raises his rifle and shouts hoarsely, 'Stop or I shoot!' He stares at a shadow in the feathergrass. The shadow freezes. The grass rustles. The boy squats down and calls softly, 'Fear no fear, timid hare!'

*

Later that night Chentsov let out a terrible scream, throwing everyone nearby into a panic. Dozens of men jumped to their feet, seizing their weapons. It turned out that a whip snake had got onto the bedboards and then under his tunic. Then Chentsov had rolled over in his sleep and begun to squash the snake. The snake had struggled to break free, first slipping under Chentsov's neck and then down his trousers.

'Like a steel spring, only made of ice,' said Chentsov, his nostrils flaring. 'It's incredibly strong.' He was holding a match between his trembling fingers and gazing with horror into the far corner of the dugout, where the snake had disappeared.

'He just wanted to warm up a bit. He gets cold at night, all naked like that,' said Polyakov, yawning.

It soon became clear that a great many empty dugouts had been settled by whip snakes – and these snakes had no intention of leaving their new homes.

There they were, behind the board walls – rustling, whispering, slithering about.

The city dwellers were scared stiff of them. Some were frightened to sleep in the dugouts, even though these whip snakes were entirely harmless, like ordinary grass snakes. The tiny steppe mice were a more serious problem. They tried to get to the soldiers' dried bread; they gnawed holes in sacks; they found their way to the sugar lumps packed in small white bags. The doctor told the soldiers that these mice could infect them with a serious liver disease called tularemia.

During the war, the mice bred in great numbers; in combat zones the grain was often left unharvested in the fields and so the mice took charge of the harvest themselves.

Early one morning the soldiers witnessed a mouse hunt. The whip snake lay motionless for a long time, while a mouse scampered about ever closer, then set to work on Chentsov's knapsack. Suddenly the snake struck. The mouse let out a terrible squeal, gathering into that squeal all the horror of imminent death, and the snake rustled back with the mouse to its home behind the boards.

'He can be our steppe cat,' said Polyakov. 'He can live with us and catch mice. Don't go stabbing him with your bayonets. He truly won't harm us – he's a serpent in name only.'

The whip snake understood Polyakov's words and stopped hiding away. Trusting him and the other men, it came and went, slithered about its business and, when it was tired, lay down by the wall, behind Polyakov's belongings.

One evening, as the late sun penetrated the dugout, catching the drops of amber resin exuded from the board walls and illuminating the earthen half-dark with dusty columns of oblique light, the soldiers saw something extraordinary.

Seryozha had been rereading the letter about his mother for the hundredth time. Polyakov touched him gently on the arm and whispered, 'Look!'

Seryozha looked up distractedly. He did not even wipe away his tears, since he knew that in the half-dark no one would see them.

A helmet hanging up in a corner was swaying and ringing, lit by a dense, compressed column of light. It took Seryozha a moment to realize that the helmet was being rocked by the snake. In the evening light the snake was the colour of copper. Looking more carefully, Seryozha realized that the snake was very slowly, with great effort, slipping out of its skin. The new skin looked bright and glistening, almost sweaty, like a young chestnut. Everyone in the dugout was holding their breath. Any moment now, it seemed, the snake would groan, or let out some complaint; getting out of its stiff, dead casing was obviously hard work.

Quiet half-darkness, pierced by a brilliant light, and something none of them had ever seen – a snake, trustfully shedding its skin in the presence of human beings. The men sat there enthralled. It was as if the evening light had entered inside them. Everything round about seemed equally quiet and thoughtful. And then came a wild yell from the sentry:

'Sergeant, the Germans!'

This was followed by two loud thumps. The dugout trembled, gasped and filled with grey dust.

The German long-range artillery, now positioned on the east bank of the Don, was ranging in on them.

22

On a hot, dusty August night General Weller, commander of a German grenadier division, a thin-lipped man with a long bony face, was sitting behind a large desk in a spacious village schoolroom.

He was looking through the papers in front of him, making notes on the operations map and tossing the reports he had already read onto a corner of the desk.

The main part of his work, he believed, was already accomplished. What remained were only minor details, of no real consequence to the future course of events.

The general was exhausted; he had put a great deal of time into planning the forthcoming operation. Now that the plans were complete, his thoughts kept returning to the summer campaign as a whole. It was as if he were preparing to write his memoirs, or to summarize his thoughts for some military textbook.

The last act of this drama – this epic drama being performed by grenadiers, tank crews and motor infantry on the huge stage of the steppe – would soon be concluded on the banks of the Volga. There was no precedent for this campaign in all the annals of warfare and the thought of its imminent conclusion was profoundly exciting. The general could sense the edge of the Russian lands; beyond the Volga lay Asia.

Had the general been a psychologist and a philosopher, he might have suspected that what for him was a source of joy and excitement must, inevitably, give rise to very different, dangerously powerful feelings in the hearts of the Russians. But he was not a philosopher – he was a general. And today he was giving free rein to a particular sweet thought he had long treasured. Fulfilment, for him, was nothing to do with rewards and honours. Fulfilment, he believed, lay in the union of two poles – power and subordination, military success and the meek execution of orders. In this play of omnipotence and obedience, this synthesis of power and subordination, he found spiritual comfort – a bitter-sweet joy.

Weller had toured the river crossings and seen burnt-out Soviet trucks, overturned tanks and guns smashed by shells and bombs. He had seen HQ documents being blown about the steppe, while horses ran wild, dragging their broken harnesses behind them. He had seen wrecked Soviet planes, their engines and broken-off, red-starred wings half-buried in the ground. To him, the dead, twisted Russian metal seemed still to bear traces of the horror that had gripped Timoshenko's troops as they retreated towards the Volga. The previous day, a bulletin from Supreme Command had announced that 'The 62nd Soviet Army has been encircled in the Great Bend of the Don and destroyed once and for all.'

During the night of 18 August, Weller reported to Army HQ that in the north-eastern loop of the Great Bend of the Don, to the north-west of Stalingrad, his advance units had forced a crossing and established a bridgehead on the east bank, in the Tryokhostrovskaya and Akimovsky districts.

The next stage of the plan, about which Paulus had informed him a few days before, was not complicated. After concentrating tanks and other motorized units on this bridgehead, they were to advance swiftly as far as the Volga, occupying the factory district in the north and cutting off the rest of Stalingrad from the river. The distance to be covered was extremely short; at this latitude, the Don and the Volga were not more than seventy kilometres apart. Hoth's panzer divisions, advancing along the railway line from Plodovitoye, were to launch a simultaneous attack from the south. And Richthofen would carry out huge air raids shortly before the two ground attacks.

Now and then, looking at the map, Weller wondered if there might be something paradoxical about this whole operation: to the north, the German army lay exposed to the whole immensity of Russia. Paulus's left flank could be crushed by a vast weight – by millions of tons of earth and a seemingly infinite mass of people.

At a time when the German armies were reporting success after success, Soviet forces had once, unexpectedly, crossed the Don and crushed the Italian division whose role was to cover the Germans' extended left flank.

But the Soviets appeared to have attached little importance to this sortie across the Don. Their newspapers did not even devote much attention to the capture of the Italian division's artillery and the fact that, as they withdrew to the east bank, they had taken 2,000 Italian prisoners with them. In the Serafimovich and Kletskaya sectors the Soviets were, admittedly, defending their bridgeheads on the west bank of the Don with an obstinacy beyond comprehension. But this too was strategically irrelevant: many important German operations had been effected with unprotected flanks.

Weller noticed a prisoner – probably a Georgian or an Armenian – being marched past outside; there was a light-coloured patch on his sleeve where a commissar's star had been ripped off. The man was barefoot and filthy. His face was covered with black stubble and he walked with a limp, a rag twisted around his wounded leg. The look on his face did not even seem human; it was blank, exhausted and indifferent. Then he looked up. For a moment his eyes met Weller's – and all Weller could see in them, rather than a plea for mercy, was a dark weight of hatred.

Weller quickly looked back at his desk, at the operations map showing the movement of German divisions. The key to the war, he believed, lay in this map – not in the hate-filled eyes of a captured commissar.

In much the same way, an axe, used to slicing effortlessly through smooth, even logs, might overestimate its own weight and sharpness and underestimate the force of cohesion in a stubborn, gnarled tree trunk. And then, after plunging through the trunk's outer rings, it will come to a sudden stop, gripped fast by the tree's tight, knotted strength. And it seems at this point that the black earth herself, beaten by rains and burnt by fires – an earth that has endured harsh frosts, the anguish of spring and terrible July storms – is lending her strength to this stubborn tree whose twisting roots have pierced into her depths.

Weller paced up and down the room. A floorboard close to the door creaked each time he stepped on it.

An orderly came in and placed some reports on the desk.

'This floorboard creaks,' said Weller. 'We need a carpet in here.'

The orderly hurried out. The floorboard creaked once again.

'*Was hat der Führer gesagt?*'[204] Weller asked another young orderly, who appeared a few minutes later. Somewhat out of breath, he was carrying a large, rolled-up rug.

The orderly looked searchingly at Weller's stern face. Somehow he guessed what the general wanted to hear.

'*Der Führer hat gesagt: Stalingrad muss fallen!*'[205] he said confidently.

Weller laughed. He walked across the soft carpet. Once again the floorboard let out an angry, obstinate creak.

23

On the same hot and dusty evening, Colonel General Paulus, commander of the German 6th Army, was sitting in his office at Army HQ. He too was thinking about the imminent capture of Stalingrad.

The windows, which faced west, were hung with heavy dark blinds. Only tiny pinpricks of light in the dense fabric bore witness to the now setting sun.

Paulus's adjutant, Colonel Adam, tall and heavy-footed but with the chubby cheeks of a young boy, came in to report that General Richthofen would arrive in forty minutes.

The two generals would be discussing their joint air and ground operation. Its vast scale was a matter of concern to Paulus.

Paulus believed that in the fifty-day battle he had begun on 28 June with the 6th Army's sudden thrust into the area between Belgorod and Kharkov he had already achieved a decisive victory; his three army corps, composed of twelve infantry divisions, two panzer and two motor infantry divisions, had crossed the steppe and reached the west bank of the Don. They were close to Kletskaya and Sirotinskaya; they had taken Kalach and would soon take Kremenskaya.

Army Group Command considered that – after Paulus had taken 57,000 prisoners of war and captured 1,000 tanks and 750 pieces of artillery (figures published by Supreme Command, somewhat to the surprise, admittedly, of some of Paulus's staff) – the Soviet defences had been entirely smashed. And Paulus knew that he was the architect of this great German victory. During this long summer Paulus had been granted an extraordinary degree of all-encompassing success.

He knew that a number of men in Berlin – men whose opinion mattered to him – were waiting impatiently for what would come next. His eyes half-closed, he imagined his coming triumph: back in Berlin after the glorious conclusion of this eastern campaign, he would step out of his car, climb some steps, walk through to the lobby and in his simple, soldier's uniform, walk past a crowd of the high and mighty, of important officials and generals on the Berlin staff.

There was just one thing that still troubled him. He needed another five days – five days at the most – but he was being ordered to begin the operation in two days' time.

Then Paulus's thoughts turned to Richthofen and his extraordinary belief that ground forces, during an attack, should be subordinate to air forces. The man's arrogance was unbelievable.

Richthofen's easy victories in Yugoslavia and Africa must have gone to his head.[206] And as for his insistence on wearing a soldier's side cap and his plebeian habit of relighting an extinguished cigarette instead of lighting a new one ... Not to mention his voice, and the way he could never let a colleague finish what he had to say, and his love of offering explanations when he should, rather, be listening to explanations given by others ... It seemed that Richthofen had much in common with the ever-fortunate Rommel, that lucky dog whose popularity was inversely proportional to his knowledge, his capacity for thought and his under-standing of military culture. And then, most galling of all, there was Richthofen's free and easy way, a habit he seemed to have made into a principle, of ascribing to his 4th Air Fleet successes achieved by the laborious work of the infantry.

Rommel, Sepp Dietrich and now this Richthofen – all of them upstarts, ignoramuses, heroes of the day, posers corrupted by successes that had come all too easily to them. Men who certainly knew how to advance their own political career but who knew little else. Men who had not even begun to think about military matters when he himself was already graduating from the academy.[207]

And Paulus went on looking at his map, which showed the vast mass of Russia pressing down on him, threatening the left flank of his 6th Army.

Richthofen arrived, looking preoccupied. There was dust all over him – under his eyes, on his temples and around his nostrils; it was as if his face were covered in grey lichen. On his way to Paulus's HQ he had met a tank column, evidently moving towards the assembly area. The tanks were going at full speed, the air was full of their grinding and clanking, and the dust they raised was so dense and impenetrable that they might have been huge ploughshares, lifting the earth itself into the air. Billowing around them was a dense reddish-brown sea, and only their turrets and gun barrels were visible. The tank men looked exhausted – somewhat hunched, peering sullenly out of their hatches, gripping their metal edges to steady themselves. Rather than wait for this steel column to pass by, Richthofen had ordered his driver to pull off the road and continue across the open steppe. On arriving at Paulus's HQ, he had gone straight to his office, without even washing.

Paulus, who had the thin hook-nosed face of a thoughtful hawk, got up to greet him. After a few words about the heat, the dust, the congestion on the roads and the diuretic properties of Russian watermelons, Paulus handed Richthofen a telegram from Hitler. In practical terms the telegram was relatively unimportant, but Paulus was secretly smiling to himself. Richthofen leaned forward a little, resting his hands on the table, and carefully read the telegram through; he was, no doubt, thinking not about its literal meaning but about its deeper implications. Hitler had chosen to discuss with Paulus, the general commanding the 6th Army, questions relating to the deployment of reserves that, in principle, were subordinate to Weichs, Paulus's immediate superior. One phrase indicated a certain dissatisfaction with Hoth, commander of the 4th Panzer Army deployed to the south of Stalingrad; Hitler clearly shared Paulus's view that Hoth was moving too slowly and incurring losses as a result of his excessive caution. And then came a few lines that Richthofen was sure to find very annoying indeed: since the 6th Army were to play the main role in the coming operation, Richthofen's air fleet was to be under Paulus's command, not that of Reichsmarschall Göring and his Luftwaffe.

After reading the telegram, Richthofen carefully placed it in the middle of the desk, as if to say that such documents are not subject to debate or criticism but must be acted upon without further discussion. 'The Führer does not only determine the general course of the war,' he said. 'He even finds time to manage the deployment of individual divisions.'

'Yes, it's astonishing,' said Paulus, who had heard more than a few complaints from colleagues about the Führer stripping them of all initiative, making it impossible for them even to change the sentry outside an infantry battalion command post without his personal authorization.

They spoke about the successful crossing of the Don near Tryokhostrovskaya. Richthofen praised the work of the artillery and heavy mortars and the courage of the soldiers of the 384th Division, first to set foot on the east bank of the Don. This crossing had created a bridgehead for the impending advance on Stalingrad of one panzer division and two motor infantry divisions. By dawn all these divisions would be in position; it was their movement north that had delayed Richthofen.

483

'I could have done all that a couple of days ago, but I didn't want to alert the Russians,' said Paulus. He smiled and added, 'They're expecting an attack from the south, from Hoth.'

'Yes,' said Richthofen. 'But I think they can wait a few more days.'

'I need five days,' said Paulus. 'What about you?'

'My preparations are more complex, I shall ask for a week. After all, this will be the knockout blow,' said Richthofen. 'Weichs keeps hurrying us on. He wants to impress, to win further promotions. But we're the ones who'll be taking the risks.'

He bent forward over a plan of Stalingrad and, running his finger over the neatly drawn squares, explained just how the city was to be set on fire, how much time would elapse between successive waves of destruction, what bombs he would drop on residential areas, river crossings, the harbour and the factories, and how best he could prepare the key area – the northern suburbs where, at a predetermined hour, Paulus's heavy tanks and motor infantry were to surprise the Russians. He asked Paulus to give him as precise a timing as possible.

So far, the discussion between the two generals had been constructive and detailed, and neither had so much as raised his voice. But Richthofen went on, sometimes with a degree of detail that Paulus found infuriating, to speak about the logistic complexities of the impending air raid; he spoke at extraordinary length about the methodology for co-ordinating a convergent attack from dozens of airfields located at different distances from the target. Not only did the flight paths and flight times of hundreds of aircraft of different designs and speeds have to be synchronised with one another, but they also had to be co-ordinated with the progress of heavy and lumbering tanks. All this was an attempt on Richthofen's part to score a point in the long-running covert rivalry between the two generals. They did not disagree openly, but each was well aware how he constantly irritated the other. The problem, as Paulus saw it, arose from Richthofen's unshakeable belief that it was to the air force that Germany owed her remarkable victories and that the role of ground forces had been merely to consolidate this success.

The generals were deciding the fate of a huge city. Among their concerns were the possibility of ground or air counter-attacks and the strength of the Soviet anti-aircraft defences. They were also concerned about the opinion of Berlin: how would their respective achievements be assessed by the General Staff?

'You and your Air Corps,' said Paulus, 'provided magnificent support for the 6th Army two years ago, when it was under the command of the late Reichenau during the invasion of Belgium. I hope that your support for my Stalingrad breakthrough will be no less successful.'

His apparent solemnity was belied by his eyes, where there was a hint of mockery.

Richthofen looked at him and said bluntly, 'Support? Who do you think supported whom? Most likely, it was Reichenau supporting me. And as for Stalingrad, who knows? It may be your breakthrough, or it may be mine.'

24

In the morning Colonel Forster came to say goodbye to General Weller before flying back to Berlin. This corpulent, grey-haired staff officer, now aged about sixty, had known Weller for many years. They had first met when Lieutenant Colonel Forster was in command of a regiment and a young Lieutenant Weller was on his staff.

Weller was attentive and welcoming, wanting to emphasize the respect he still felt for this colonel who had once been his senior. He knew that Forster had left active service for some time and that he had shared the views of Ludwig Beck, the now disgraced former chief of the General Staff, and that he had even helped draft Beck's memorandum about how catastrophic it would be for Germany to engage in another war. Beck's most emphatic warning had been about the dangers of a war with Russia; he had made out that Germany was certain to be defeated. Only in September 1939 had Forster written to the higher authorities, asking them to make use once again of his considerable experience. Thanks to the support of Brauchitsch he had been recalled from the reserves.

'What impressions will you be taking back to Berlin with you?' Weller asked. 'You know how much I value your opinion.'

Forster looked at Weller with his cool, pale blue eyes and said, 'It's a shame I'm leaving today. It would be better, I think, to be arriving today. But what I have seen leaves me in no doubt: we are about to achieve our strategic aim.' Visibly moved, he ran his hand over his grey Hindenburg crew cut, went up to Weller and said with solemn emphasis, 'Let me just say, as straightforwardly as I would have said eighteen years ago, well done, Franz!'

'They're fine soldiers,' said Weller, touched by these words.

'I'm not talking only about the soldiers,' said Forster, and smiled. With Weller, he did not feel even a trace of the burdensome irritation he felt in the presence of most other up-and-coming young officers.

Once, in 1933, at a critical moment for Germany, the two officers had met at a seaside resort. They had talked about how disgusted they both felt with the leaders of the new party. They had called Göring a glutton and drug addict, and Hitler a psychopath. They had talked about his hysterical bloodlust, his laughable 'intuition', his insane ambitiousness – which somehow went hand in hand with cowardice – and the doubtful provenance of his Iron Cross. Forster had spoken at length about the inevitable failure of any attempt at a military vengeance for the shame of Versailles; he had spoken about the ignorance of political charlatans who think that demagogic bluster can substitute for military logic and who choose to ignore everything that German generals had learned in the course of a lost war. Neither man had forgotten any of this, but the Reich's unwritten code did not allow even close friends openly to recall conversations so dangerous and misguided.

But now, a hundred kilometres from the Volga, on the eve of a victory unprecedented in world history, Weller suddenly asked, 'Do you remember those long-ago conversations of ours in the park, not far from the sea?'

'Grey hair and age do not always judge right,' Forster said slowly. 'I shall always regret that I did not realize my mistake sooner. Time has proved me wrong.'

'Yes, thanks to this war there are new factors that military strategy must take into account,' said Weller. 'Beck argued that Russia's breadth, its vast spaces, would afford us an advantage in the first stages of a war – but that the country's depth would then prove our undoing. He has been proved wrong.'

'That is now clear to everyone.'

'If you come back in two weeks, you'll find me here,' said Weller, pointing to a house marked with a cross on a plan of Stalingrad. 'Though Richthofen has, admittedly, told Paulus that he will be asking for the operation to be postponed by a week rather than by five days. He will be taking personal responsibility for that request.'

As he saw Forster to the door, he said, 'You told me you were looking for a relative of yours, a lieutenant. Did you find him?'

'I found out his whereabouts,' Forster replied. 'Lieutenant Bach, my future son-in-law – but I didn't get to see him. He's already on the east bank of the Don, on the bridgehead.'

'A fortunate young man,' said Weller. 'He'll get to see Stalingrad before me.'

25

In the summer of 1942, after the fall of Kerch, Sevastopol and Rostov-on-Don, the Berlin press changed its tone; grim restraint gave way to joyful fanfares. The successes of the ambitious Don offensive put an end to articles about the severity of the Russian winter, about the size of the Red Army and the power of its artillery, about the fanaticism of the partisans and the stubborn resistance of Soviet forces in Sevastopol, Moscow and Leningrad. These successes displaced the memory of terrible losses, of crosses on soldiers' graves, of the alarming urgency of the last Winter Relief campaign, and of how train after train, day and night, had brought back wounded and frostbitten soldiers from the Eastern front. These successes silenced those who saw the whole eastern campaign as an act of madness, those who worried about the strength of the Red Army and were still troubled by the Führer's failure to keep his promise to capture Moscow and Leningrad by mid-November 1941 and so bring the war to a swift, victorious conclusion.

Life in Berlin was now all bustle and noise.

The telegraph, the radio and the newspapers constantly reported new victories on the Eastern front and in Africa. London was now half-destroyed; U-boats had paralysed America's war effort; Japan was winning victory after victory. There was excitement in the air – an expectation of new, still greater victories, heralding a final peace. Every day trains and aeroplanes arrived with yet more of Europe's high and mighty: industrialists, kings, crown princes, generals and prime ministers from all the continent's capitals: Paris, Amsterdam, Brussels, Madrid, Copenhagen, Prague, Vienna, Bucharest, Lisbon, Athens, Belgrade and Budapest. The Berliners watched all this with amusement, studying the faces of the Führer's voluntary and involuntary guests. As their cars drew up outside the grey facade of the New Reich Chancellery, these important figures became like trembling schoolboys, frowning, fidgeting, glancing from side to side. There were endless newspaper reports of diplomatic receptions; of lunches and dinners; of military and trade treaties and accords; of meetings held in the Reich Chancellery, Salzburg, Berchtesgaden or Hitler's field HQ. Now that German troops were approaching the lower reaches of the Volga and the Caspian Sea, Berliners had begun to talk about Baku oil; about a future link-up between the Wehrmacht and the Japanese army; about Subhas Chandra Bose, India's future gauleiter.[208]

Trains from Slav and Latin countries arrived hour after hour, bringing more workers to Germany, along with cereal grains, wood, granite, marble, sardines, wine, iron ore, oil and butter, and a variety of metals.

There was a sense of victory, a hum of triumph in the Berlin air. Even the green of the ivy and vine leaves, of the lindens and chestnuts in the parks and on the streets looked more splendid than usual.

This was a time of illusion, a time when many were taken in by the fantasy that ordinary people and a supposedly all-conquering totalitarian state shared a single destiny. Many believed what Hitler proclaimed as truth: that the blood flowing in Aryan veins united all Germans under the banner of riches and glory, of power over the entire world. This was a time of contempt for the blood of others, a time of the official justification of unimaginable atrocities. It was a time when losses of every kind – the deaths of countless soldiers, the many children made orphans – were justified by the prospect of the imminent and total victory of the German nation. And yet, at the close of each day, another life would begin; hidden monsters would make their presence felt. Night was a time of fear and weakness, of lonely thoughts, of exhaustion and longing, of whispered conversations with your closest friends and immediate family, a time of tears for those killed on the Eastern front, of complaints about hunger and need, about backbreaking labour and the arbitrary power of officials. It was a time of doubts, of subversive thoughts, of horror at the implacable power of the Reich, a time of troubled premonitions and the howl of English bombs.

These two streams flowed through the life of the German nation as a whole, and through the life of every individual German – whether they were minor officials, workers, professors, young women or kindergarten children. The split was complete and extraordinary; it was difficult to imagine what it might lead to. Would new, unprecedented forms of life come into being? Would this split be annulled after the victory, or would it endure?

26

In the New Reich Chancellery the working day was beginning. Early though it was, the sun was already warming the building's grey walls and the stone slabs of the pavement. Afraid of being late, employees were hurrying in: typists, stenographers, clerks, archivists, receptionists, the women who worked in the canteen and the café, and junior officials from the adjutant's office and the Reich Ministers' Secretariat. Big-boned Nazi women strode down the corridors, swinging their arms, keeping up with the young men in military uniform; this was a time when the Chancellery's female employees were the only women in Berlin ever to be seen without a shopping bag for provisions. They had been ordered not to bring any large bags or packages to their workplace, since it was imperative that the staff of so august an institution should maintain their dignity. People said that this order had been issued after a collision between Goebbels and a librarian carrying bags full of cabbage and jars of pickled beans and cucumbers. In her confusion, the librarian had dropped her handbag and a paper bag full of peas, and Goebbels, in spite of the pain in his leg, had squatted down, placed his files of papers on the floor beside him and begun to gather up the scattered peas, saying that this reminded him of his childhood. The librarian had thanked him and promised to preserve the peas as a keepsake, as a reminder of the kindness and straightforwardness of the lame doctor, of the fact that he was truly a man of the people.[209]

Chancellery employees coming from Charlottenburg or from the direction of Friedrichstrasse understood at once, as soon as they left their tram or U-Bahn station, that Hitler was in Berlin and would be going to the Reich Chancellery. White-haired senior officials walked on with poker faces, as if to show they had no wish to see anything they weren't meant to see. But the young exchanged winks as they walked past the additional military and police posts and saw the many men in civilian dress, all with oddly similar expressions, each with a gaze that could penetrate the leather of a briefcase as swiftly and easily as an X-ray. For the young, all this was amusing and entertaining – Hitler had seldom visited Berlin during the last few months. He was now spending most of his time either in Berchtesgaden or in his field HQ five hundred kilometres from the combat zone.

At the main entrance to the Chancellery, senior guards were checking passes and documents. Behind them stood members of the Führer's personal bodyguard, looking slowly and searchingly at everyone who passed through.

The office had tall French windows looking onto the garden. These were now half-open and there was a smell of freshly watered greenery. The office was huge, and it took some time to walk from the fireplace at the far end, beside which stood a writing desk and an armchair upholstered in pink silk, to the anteroom door. In the course of this walk one would pass a terrestrial globe the size of a beer keg, a long marble table covered in maps, and the French windows opening onto the terrace and garden.

Out in the garden, thrushes were calling to one another with quiet restraint, as if afraid of expending too soon the strength they would need for a long summer's day. Inside the office, now walking past the French windows, was a man in a grey trench coat and breeches. On his chest – over a simple white shirt with a turndown collar and a tightly knotted black tie – were an Iron Cross, a wounded-in-action medal, and a special Party badge with a gold border around the swastika. His rather feeble, drooping shoulders, which seemed all the narrower in comparison with the almost womanly breadth of his hips, had been skilfully padded. There was something discordant about his general appearance – he seemed somehow to be both thin and plump. His bony face, sunken temples and long neck belonged to a thin man, while his bottom and thighs seemed to have been borrowed from someone stout and well nourished.

His suit, his Iron Cross testifying to military courage, his war-wounds medal testifying to the suffering he had undergone, the Nazi badge with a swastika that symbolized the racial and state unity of the New Germany – all this was familiar from dozens of photographs, drawings, newsreels, stamps, badges, posters and leaflets, bas-reliefs in plaster and marble, and cartoons by David Low and the Kukryniksy.[210]

Yet even someone who had seen hundreds of different images of this man might have been slow to recognize the real Hitler, with his sickly face, his pale, narrow forehead, his inflamed, protruding eyes with swollen lids, and his broad, fleshy nostrils.

That night, the Führer had slept little and woken early. His morning bath had not restored his spirits. It may have been the exhausted look

491

in his eyes that made his face seem so very different now from how it appeared in pictures and photographs.

While he was asleep, lying in his long nightshirt under a blanket, mumbling, snoring, chewing his lips, grinding his large teeth, turning from side to side, drawing his knees up to his chest – while he was asleep, this man in his fifties had much in common with any other middle-aged man with a shattered nervous system, an impaired metabolism and heart palpitations. It was indeed during these hours of ugly, troubled sleep that Hitler was closest to being human. He grew less and less human when he woke, got out of bed with a shiver, bathed, put on his underwear and military breeches – already laid out by his staff – combed his dark hair from right to left and checked in the mirror to make sure that the entire image – hair, face, bags under the eyes and all – was in accord with the sacrosanct model now as obligatory for the Führer himself as for his photographers.

Hitler went out through the French windows and leaned his shoulder against the wall, which was already being warmed by the sun. He seemed to enjoy the feel of the warm stone, and he pressed his cheek and his thigh against the wall too, wanting to absorb from it some of the sun's warmth.

He stood there for a while, obeying the instinctive desire of any cold-blooded creature to warm itself in the sun. His facial muscles relaxed into a sleepy, contented smile; there was something about this pose, which he thought rather girlish, that he found pleasurable.

His grey trench coat and breeches blended with the pale grey of the Chancellery stone. Now that it was at rest, there was something indescribably horrible about this weak, ugly creature with its thin neck and drooping shoulders.

Hearing quiet steps, Hitler quickly turned round.

But the man approaching was a friend. He was tall, well built, and he had a distinct paunch. He had rosy cheeks, plump, slightly protruding lips and a small chin.

The two men went back into the office. Reichsführer Heinrich Himmler, head of the SS, walked with his head bowed, as if embarrassed at being visibly taller than the Chancellor.

Articulating each word clearly, and raising his pale, moist hand, Hitler said, 'I don't want any explanations. I want to hear the simple words: *operation completed.*'

He sat down at the table and gestured brusquely to Himmler to sit opposite him. Narrowing his eyes behind the thick lenses of his pince-nez, Himmler began to speak. His voice was calm and gentle.

Himmler was well aware of the bitterness inherent in any friendship between those standing at the summit of a granite state. He knew that it was not any particular knowledge, intelligence or other gift that had elevated him – a poultry-farm manager and employee of a company that produced synthetic nitrogen – to such heights.

His terrible power sprang from only one source – his passion to execute the will of the man whom, as if they were both still students, he had just been addressing as *du*. The more blind and unquestioning his obedience within this office, the more limitless his power outside it.[211] Such a relationship, however, was not easy to maintain. Only by means of constant alertness could Himmler demonstrate the appropriate flexible, emotionally committed obedience. He needed to avoid all suspicion of freedom of thought, but it was equally important to avoid any suspicion of obsequiousness, that sister of hypocrisy and betrayal.

His devotion had to adopt complex, varied forms, not only that of straightforward obedience. At times it was better to be querulous or sullen; at times it was better to argue, to be rude, stubborn, or contrary. Himmler was speaking to a man he had first met long ago, at a dark time of pitiful weakness. It was important that Hitler should constantly, every minute, sense in some part of his soul the long-standing nature of the bond between them, that this bond should matter more to him than anything that belonged merely to the present moment. But it was equally important that Hitler should feel the exact opposite: the absolute insignificance, today, of such a link from the distant past. Really, this link served only to emphasize the depth of the abyss between them; never, under any circumstances, could it suggest that the two men might in any respect be on equal terms. And in every one of his conversations with the Führer, Himmler had to call up both of these opposites. This was a world where reality was without reality, where the only reality was the mood of the Führer, his whim of the moment.

Now Himmler was making out that he was obliged – in the Führer's own interest – to argue with him. He, Himmler, understood Hitler's deepest wish. This wish might seem terrible. It was born, however, not only from long-past yet indelible personal suffering but also from a selflessly noble hatred – the impassioned survival instinct of the race whom the Führer now represented. Still, a rage that does not distinguish between an armed enemy and a helpless baby or adolescent girl is indeed dangerous. In all likelihood, he alone among the Führer's close associates fully understood what strength of will was required to struggle against the seemingly helpless and weak; he alone knew the dangers of such a struggle. It was a rebellion against millennia of human history, a challenge to mankind's humanistic prejudices. The weaker and more helpless the victim appears, the more difficult and dangerous the struggle. Among those close to the Führer there was no one else who understood the true grandeur of the special operation, now already under way, that in the language of the enfeebled might be called organized mass murder. The Führer should have no doubt that Himmler was proud to share with him the awful weight of this burden. But no one else, even among the Führer's most devoted friends, need know all the bitterness of this work. Himmler alone should glimpse the depths the Führer had revealed to him, since he alone could discern in them the truth of a new creation.

Himmler was speaking quickly, in an excited, impassioned tone, conscious all the time of the weight of Hitler's gaze.

Himmler knew only too well Hitler's way of appearing to be absorbed in his own thoughts and not to be listening at all – and then, bewilderingly, pouncing on some important and subtle point. Hitler's unexpected smile at such moments was frightening.

Himmler put his hand on the papers lying on the desk.

The Führer had seen the plans, but he himself had just come back from the empty spaces that lay to the east. There, among uninhabited pine forests, he had seen the severe simplicity of the gas chambers, their steps and doorways adorned with flowers ... The sad music of the last farewell to life and the tall flames in the middle of the night ... Not to everyone is it given to understand the poetry of the primeval chaos that blends life and death together.

It was a complex and difficult conversation. For Himmler, every such tête-à-tête with Hitler had one and the same hidden purpose. Whether they were talking about the future of the German nation, the decadence of French painting, the excellence of a young sheepdog the Führer had given to him as a present, the extraordinary fruitfulness of a young apple tree in the Führer's garden, the bulldog face and fat belly of that drunkard Churchill or the unmasking of Roosevelt as a 'secret Jew', Himmler's hidden agenda was to consolidate his own position, to establish himself as closer to Hitler than the three or four other men who appeared to enjoy his ephemeral trust.

But progress towards this goal was no simple matter. When the Führer was cross with Goebbels or suspicious of Göring, it was best to disagree with him, to argue in his colleagues' defence. Conversation with Hitler was always complicated and dangerous. There were no limits to his suspiciousness. His moods changed swiftly and his decisions were beyond all ordinary logic.

Now too Hitler interrupted, repeating, 'I want to hear that the work has been completed. I want to hear the simple words: *all completed!* I do not want to have to return to this question when the war is over. What do I want with your flower-adorned steps and your clever little plans? There are enough gullies and ravines in Poland, aren't there? And enough idlers in your SS regiments?'

He leaned forward, gathered up the papers lying on his desk, held them for a while in the air, as if giving his anger time to build up, then threw them back down on the table.

'To hell with your clever plans and your idiot mysticism! I don't need your flowers and your music. Who told you I was a mystic?[212] I've had enough of all this. What are you waiting for? Have they got tanks? Machine guns? Air support?' And then, more quietly, he asked, 'Do you really not understand? Do you want to torment me when I need to gather all my strength for the war?' He got up from the desk and moved closer to Himmler. 'Shall I tell you the source of your slowness and your love of mystery?' He looked down at Himmler, at the pink, translucent skin he could see beneath Himmler's thinning hair, and went on with a laugh of disgust, 'Do you really not understand? You who know the pulse of the nation better than anyone – do you really not understand your own self? I know only too well why you want to hide everything in dark forests and obscure mysticism. It's because you're afraid! And that's because you don't believe in me, in my power, in my success, in my struggle! You did not believe in me, I remember, in 1925. And it was the same in 1929, in 1933, in 1939, and even after I had conquered France! Feeble souls, when *will* you believe? And you – will you really be the very last to understand that there is only one real power in the world? Is every blockhead in Europe going to grasp this before you? Even now, when I've brought Russia to her knees – when everyone can see she will stay on her knees for the next 500 years – do you still not believe? I don't need to hide my decisions. Stalingrad will be ours within three days. I hold the key to victory in my hands. I am strong enough. The time for secrets has passed. What I conceived, I shall carry out – and no one in the world will dare hinder me.'

He pressed his hands to his temples, tossed back the hair hanging over his forehead and repeated several times, as he looked around him, 'I'll give you flowers! I'll give you music!'

27

Colonel Forster was now waiting in the Chancellery reception room. He had flown back with a message from Paulus.

This would be Forster's first face-to-face meeting with Hitler. He felt both happy and frightened.

This time the previous day he had been drinking coffee, looking out of the window at an old woman wearing a ragged man's jacket. She had been walking down the street with a grey sheep. And then he himself had been walking down that same street – the dusty, ridiculously broad street of a large Cossack village.

In the evening, the plane had landed at Tempelhof, but Forster had been unable to go back home straightaway. Security officers had kept several planeloads of passengers waiting, refusing to allow them through to the exit. Some of the men waiting were generals and they had angrily demanded explanations. The security officers had said nothing. And then a gleaming black limousine swept past, followed by three open cars. Contravening every regulation, the cars drove straight across the airfield, from a plane that had stopped some distance away. One of the other passengers said, 'That's Himmler, we saw him at the airport in Warsaw.'

And Forster had felt a chill of fear – as if sensing a power still greater than the power now forcing its way to the Volga, smashing its way, in fire and smoke, through the Russian defences. He got home only late that night.

He was greeted by his wife and his daughter Maria.

To joyful cries of 'Oh, Pápa!' he opened his suitcase and took out the various presents he had brought back with him – clay pots for milk, wooden salt cellars and spoons, beads and embroidered towels, the little dry gourds that Ukrainian villagers called *tarakutski*. Maria, who was studying at art school, adored such exotic items and she immediately added them to her collection, which already included examples of Tibetan embroidery, colourful Albanian shoes and bright Malayan matting.

'Isn't there a letter for me?' asked Maria, when her father bent down again over his suitcase.

'No – I never got to see your student.'

'Wasn't Bach at HQ?' she asked.

'No, your student is now a tank man.'

'Oh my God – Pieter a tank man! Why? When the war's nearly over.'

Just then Forster was called to the telephone. A soft voice informed him that a car would come for him in the morning and that he should have his report ready. Forster understood who he would be reporting to: the man speaking to him was one of the Führer's senior aides-de-camp.

'What's the matter?' his wife asked. Her husband had seemed happy to be seeing his family again, but now he was looking inexplicably agitated.

He embraced her and said quietly, 'Tomorrow's a big day for me.'

Regretting that this big day couldn't have been postponed, she said nothing.

Something rather strange happened in the morning: for the second time in twenty-four hours Forster encountered an important figure he had never before been anywhere near.

As he approached the long, two-storey building of the Reich Chancellery, which extended the length of an entire block, Forster consciously set about registering things he could tell his wife and daughter about when he got home. His eye sharpened by excitement and curiosity, he noticed the small black plaque with a golden eagle by the main entrance; he counted the number of steps up to the porch; he measured the huge area, perhaps three quarters of a hectare, of pink carpet; he touched the grey, fake-marble walls; he thought how similar the countless bronze lamp brackets were to the branches of trees; he looked at the sentries standing by the inner arch. Motionless, in grey-blue uniforms with black cuffs, they could have been cast from steel. And then, from out on the street, through an open window, came the sound of a few curt orders, like muffled shots, followed by the jingle of a presenting of arms and some quiet words of acknowledgement.

A huge, shiny limousine came to a smooth stop outside the main entrance; it was the same black limousine that Forster had seen the day before, at Tempelhof. The two open cars behind it turned round almost without slowing. Members of the SS Reichsführer's personal bodyguard leaped out with practised agility.

A minute later, the SS Reichsführer, a smile on his plump lips, walked briskly past Forster and under the arch that led to Hitler's office. He was wearing a billowing grey cloak and a huge cap.

Forster sat for some time in an armchair, waiting to be called, feeling more and more agitated. There were moments when he felt he was about to have a heart attack; he was almost suffocating and there was a blunt, heavy pain under his shoulder blades. He felt oppressed by the silence and the impersonal calm of the secretaries: what did any of them care about this colonel just back from Stalingrad?

An hour or so passed.

Something changed in the atmosphere of the waiting room; Forster sensed that Hitler was now alone in his office. He took out his handkerchief and carefully wiped his damp palms. He felt he was about to be summoned. But another twenty minutes went by, minutes of terrible stress. Forster wanted to prepare his answers to the questions he might be asked, but all he could think about was the coming interview's very first moments; all he could do was rehearse in his mind, again and again, the click of heel against heel, and his initial salutation. 'Like a sixteen-year-old cadet before his first parade,' he thought, and ran his hand through his hair. Then he wondered if everyone had simply forgotten about him. He would sit there for another six hours and then someone would smile at him and say, 'It's probably not worth your waiting any longer. We've received a radio message that the Führer's just arrived in Berchtesgaden.'

He wanted to call home, to tell his family not to talk about where he had been today.

A ruby light lit up on a marble panel.

'Colonel Forster,' said a quiet and seemingly reproachful voice.

Forster got up, gasping for air. Wanting to get his breath back, he tried to walk very slowly. He couldn't see the person leading him towards the oak door; all he could see was the door itself, which was tall and gleaming.

'Faster!' whispered the same voice, now sounding brutal and commanding.

The door opened. Nothing, of course, went as Forster had imagined.

He had imagined he would salute, then walk briskly over to Hitler's desk. Instead, he stayed by the door, while Hitler approached from the depths of the office, treading silently on the thick carpet. At first the Führer seemed extraordinarily similar to his image in paintings, stamps and photographs, and for a second Forster felt as if both he and Hitler were acting in a film, which was being screened in daylight. But the closer Hitler drew, the more his face came to differ from all those millions of identical images. It was alive, pale, with large teeth.

Forster saw Hitler's thin eyelashes, his moist bluish eyes and the dark bags beneath them.

Forster thought he could see a smile on the Führer's large anaemic lips, as if he still remembered the old colonel's subversive thoughts and could sense how desperately anxious he felt now.

'You look as if the air of the Eastern front has done you good,' said Hitler.

Forster was astonished by the ordinariness of this quiet voice; he had imagined that it could only come out with sounds like shards of broken glass, with fanatical invocations like the speech that had once mesmerized an audience of 20,000 in the Berlin Sports Palace.[213]

'Yes, my Führer, I feel splendid,' said Forster. His voice was submissive, trembling with emotion; inside him, though, a kind of echo kept repeating, 'My Führer, my Führer, my Führer.'

This, of course, was a lie. He had felt ill on the plane and, fearing a heart attack, had taken a nitroglycerine tablet.[214] Back home, tormented by shortness of breath and heart palpitations, he had not slept until morning; during the night he had looked at his watch dozens of times and had kept getting up and going to the window, listening out in case his car was already waiting below.

'During the night I received a request from Paulus,' Hitler began. 'He wants a postponement of five days. Only an hour before that I'd heard that Richthofen is complaining. Richthofen has completed his preparations, even though they're more complex than Paulus's, and he wants to start now. I am disappointed with Paulus.'

Forster remembered how Richthofen had told Paulus he would be asking Hitler to delay the start of the operation by an entire week. By doing the opposite, he was clearly hoping to damage Paulus's standing. But Forster knew that it was not for him to speak the truth in this office: did anyone still have that kind of courage? 'Yes, my Führer, infantry preparations are indeed a great deal simpler,' he said.

'Let's go and have a look at the map,' Hitler said quietly.

He walked ahead of Forster, a little stooped, his arms at his side, his hair cut short like a soldier's. Running across the back of his neck was a patch of pale bare skin with a few sore spots left by the razor. At this moment, there was a sense of natural equality between the two men; both were walking silently over the same carpet. This was very different from what Forster had noticed two years earlier, at the parade in celebration of the victory over France. The Führer had walked with the same quick gait – the gait of an ordinary, anxious man, not that of a ruler – and he had been followed by a crowd of generals and field marshals in helmets and smart forage caps. Even though the generals had been pushing and jostling, clearly feeling no need to observe the usual discipline of a military parade, it had seemed that between them and Hitler lay a vast abyss – an abyss to be measured in kilometres rather than metres. Now, though, Hitler's shoulder was almost touching Forster's.

In the centre of a long table standing parallel to the windows lay a map of the Eastern front. To the right of this lay another map; from the amount of blue and yellow on it, Forster understood that this was the Mediterranean theatre – Cyrenaica and Egypt. He glimpsed pencil marks against Mersa Matrouh, Derna and Tobruk.[215] Forster found it strange to be looking at this table, at the windows, at the globe, at the armchair, at the tall doors with mirrors and at the fireplace with its huge grating. He had seen all this in photographs in magazines, and now he was confused: had he already seen this room in a dream – or was he, now, dreaming that he was seeing the room?

'Where was Paulus's HQ yesterday?' Hitler asked.

Forster indicated a point on the map and said, 'The HQ was scheduled to relocate this morning to Golubinskoye, on the bank of the Don, my Führer.'

Hitler leaned his hands on the table.

'You may begin, Colonel,' he said.

Forster began his report.

His sense of anxiety only continued to deepen. Hitler was staring sullenly at the map, his mouth slightly open. Forster felt that everything he was saying, about the operational schedule and the coefficients of bringing up the reserves, probably sounded irrelevant and superfluous; it might be merely irritating the Führer. Forster felt flustered, like a stammering child in the presence of an adult with other things on their mind. As a young man, he had imagined true military leaders as being ever attentive to news from the front, seeking for answers to strategic dilemnas not only in the reports of generals but also in simple stories told by soldiers. He had imagined them looking into the eyes of young lieutenants and hoping to learn the secret of victory from the thoughts of cart drivers and old veterans. He had clearly been wrong.

Forster lowered his voice and began to speak more slowly, not daring to stop completely. Hitler coughed and, without turning his head, asked, 'Are you aware that Stalin is there, by the Volga?'

'We have no information to that effect, my Führer.'

'No information?'

Only the previous day, Forster had imagined that the order to take Stalingrad on 25 August was born from precise calculation and a careful analysis of the military situation. He had imagined the Führer taking into account the panzers' fuel reserves, the mobility of the support columns, and the quantitative and qualitative superiority enjoyed by the German air force. He had imagined that the Führer had a precise grasp of the dynamic force encapsulated in each infantry division, of the speed with which ammunition and reserves could be brought up to the front, of the efficiency of the liaison and signals sections. He had imagined the Führer as having at his command an almost infinite amount of information. He had thought that when the Führer said, '*Stalingrad muss fallen!*' he was taking into account the effect of meteorological conditions on the state of the roads in the Don steppe, the sinking of British convoys attempting the voyage to Murmansk, the fall of Singapore and Rommel's impending attack on Alexandria.

Now, though, Forster realized that the words '*Stalingrad muss fallen*' had nothing to do with the reality of the war. They were simply an expression of Hitler's wish.

Forster had been afraid that Hitler would interrupt him, that he would ask a great many questions. He had heard about Hitler's impatience, his way of posing seemingly random questions that made one lose the thread of one's thoughts. When the Führer was particularly irritable, speakers had sometimes been thrown into total confusion, with no idea how they were meant to reply. But now Hitler was saying nothing at all.

Forster did not understand that he was seeing the Führer at a moment when no one else's opinion was of the least interest to him. Hitler did not at such moments read bulletins or radio messages. His thoughts were not determined by the movements of armies; on the contrary, Hitler believed it was his thoughts – and his thoughts alone – that determined both the general course of events and their precise timing.

Something made Forster think that it was best to talk to the Führer about aspects of the military situation that did not depend on him, that lay outside his control. And so he spoke about the size of the Soviet forces deployed in the south-east, about the reserves recently discovered by reconnaissance aircraft, about the infantry and tank units moving at night towards Saratov, about the measures the Red Army was most likely to adopt for the defence of Stalingrad, and about the possibility of a Soviet counter-attack from the north-west, against the 6th

Army's left flank; there had, he said, been a few barely noticeable signs that the Soviets might be planning something of this nature. Wanting to get the Führer's attention, Forster exaggerated his concerns, which he didn't really see as at all important. He thought he was showing great diplomatic skill, but everything he said merely irritated Hitler.

Unexpectedly, Hitler gave him a questioning look.

'Are you fond of flowers, Colonel?'

Never having had the least interest in flowers, Forster was taken aback. Still, he answered without hesitation, 'Yes, my Führer, I'm very fond of flowers indeed.'

'I thought so,' said Hitler. 'Colonel General Halder is also a passionate botanist.'[216]

Was Hitler suggesting that it was best for old veterans to find other occupations for themselves? Was he saying that Forster was a man of limited vision and that he should retire from active service?

'The issue of Stalingrad has been resolved. I shall not alter the schedule I have laid down,' said Hitler. Now for the first time Forster heard in his voice the grating, metallic tones he had so often heard during radio broadcasts. 'What the Russians have decided is of no interest to me. Let them know what I have decided!'

It became clear to Forster that Hitler was not going to listen to the most important thing of all: the impending breach of the Soviet inner defensive ring through which German troops would advance to the banks of the Volga. Forster considered this plan perfectly judged and eminently practicable. Hitler just replied irritably, 'Paulus is a competent general, but he does not understand that time is important. Every day, every hour is important to me. Unfortunately, it is not only my generals who fail to understand this.' He went over to his desk, looked with disgust at some papers, pushed them to one side with his little finger, then tapped them several times with a pencil, repeating, 'Flowers, flowers, music among the pines! Fraudsters – all of them!'

Forster felt ever more terrified – the man striding about the room, who now seemed to have forgotten all about him – was alien and incomprehensible. One moment he was walking away from Forster; next he was striding swiftly towards him. Forster stood there, head bowed: what if Hitler suddenly remembered about him? What if he suddenly started to yell and stamp his feet? The seconds went by in silence.

Hitler stopped and said, 'I've heard your daughter is in poor health. Give her my greetings. Is she doing well at art school? I'd love to do some painting, if I only had time. Time … Time … I'm flying back to the front today. I too am only a guest in Berlin.'

Hitler smiled, his lips strangely grey. He held out a cold damp hand to Forster, saying he regretted that it was impossible for him to pursue this conversation.

*

Forster walked to the corner of the street, where his car was waiting. He had, it seemed, sensed the power of the Führer; it had made him tremble. 'Give her my greetings, give her my greetings!' he repeated to himself. As he got into the car, he for some reason remembered how, yesterday afternoon, as they were flying over a pine forest and some sandy wasteland to the east of Warsaw, warning rockets had forced the pilot into an abrupt change of course. Forster had glimpsed a thread-like single-track railway, running between two walls of pine trees to a construction site where hundreds of men were swarming about amid boards, bricks and lime. Something of strategic importance was evidently being built there.

The navigator had bent down towards Forster and, addressing a senior passenger in the free and easy manner of an airman in his own element, had pointed down to the forest and whispered, 'Himmler's building a temple down there for the Warsaw Jews. He's afraid that we may tell the world too soon about the joyful surprise he's preparing for them.'

Forster sensed that in his quest for world domination the Führer had lost touch with all ordinary human understanding. At such icy heights good and evil no longer existed. Suffering meant nothing. There could be no mercy, no pricks of conscience.

But such unaccustomed thoughts were arduous and difficult to assimilate. After a few seconds Forster allowed himself to be distracted. He began to look at the smartly dressed people in cars, at the children standing in line with their milk cans, at the crowds emerging from the darkness of the U-Bahn or going down into it, at the faces of women of all ages going about their daily tasks, carrying paper bags, briefcases or handbags.

He needed to decide in advance which of his feelings and observations he could talk about at the General Staff, which to his acquaintances, and which only to close friends. And at night, in their bedroom, he would tell his wife in a whisper about how frightened he had felt.

503

He would tell her how different Hitler looked from his image in photographs; he would tell her how he stooped, how grey he looked, how he had dark bags under his eyes.

In his mind he went through every sentence of his report, all his replies to Hitler's questions, and he was startled by something terribly simple. Nearly everything he had said – about how well he felt, about Paulus and Richthofen, about his love of flowers – nearly everything he had said, he realized, had been a lie. From beginning to end he had been play-acting. His words, his tone of voice, his facial expressions had all been equally false. He felt that some vast incomprehensible force had compelled him to lie. Why? He could not understand it.

Forster would recall later how, when no one was thinking about such things, he had warned Hitler about the danger of a Soviet counterattack. He was genuinely taken aback by the clarity of his own foresight. But he no less genuinely forgot that, at the time, he had not taken what he said seriously. He had not believed in this danger; he had merely been trying to get the Führer's attention at a moment when nothing in the world, other than his own thoughts and decisions, seemed to mean anything to him.

28

The capture of Stalingrad would mean the achievement of certain strategic ends: the rupture of communications between the north and south of Russia, and between the central provinces and the Caucasus. The capture of Stalingrad would allow German armies to make broad advances both to the north-east, bypassing Moscow, and to the south, thus achieving the ultimate goal of the geographical expansion of the Third Reich.

To Hitler, however, the capture of Stalingrad meant more than this. It was of crucial importance to his foreign policy, since it was likely to bring about significant changes to German relations with both Japan and Turkey. And it was no less important to his domestic policy; as a foretaste of the final victory, it would reinforce his position within his own country. The capture of Stalingrad would redeem the failure of the blitzkrieg intended to bring about a German victory within eight weeks; it would compensate for the defeats outside Moscow, Rostov and Tikhvin and for the sacrifices of the past winter that had so shaken the German people. The capture of Stalingrad would strengthen Germany's power over its satellites; it would silence the voices of disbelief and criticism.

Lastly, the capture of Stalingrad would be Hitler's triumph over the scepticism of Brauchitsch, Halder and Rundstedt, over Göring's hidden arrogance, over Mussolini's doubts as to his ally's superior intelligence.

For all these reasons, Hitler irritably rejected all talk of postponement – at stake were the outcome of the war, the future of the Third Reich and the prestige of the Führer himself.

But Hitler's peculiar logic and the reality of events at the front had nothing to do with each other; neither was of any relevance to the other.

29

On a hot August morning Lieutenant Pieter Bach, a slim, tanned thirty-year-old commander of a German motor infantry company, was lying in the grass on the east bank of the Don and looking up at a cloudless sky. After a long advance across the steppe and the difficulties of a night-time river crossing, Bach had bathed and put on clean underwear. He at once felt a sense of peace. He was, of course, used to abrupt changes in his sense of himself and the world; there had been more than one occasion during the last year when, worn out by the heat and the roar of engines, longing for a drink of water – even from a filthy swamp – he had suddenly been transported into a world of cool cleanliness, a world where he could bathe, enjoy the smell of flowers and drink cold milk. He was no less used to the reverse, to exchanging the peace of a village garden for the iron stress of war.

Accustomed as he was to such changes, Bach was still able to enjoy this moment. He was able to think calmly, without any of his usual irritation, about the nitpicking criticisms that Preifi, his battalion commander, had made during a recent inspection, and about his difficult relations with Lenard, the SS officer who had recently joined their regiment. None of this troubled him; it was as if he were remembering the past rather than thinking about what would determine his life today and tomorrow. He knew from experience that the capture of a bridgehead was always followed by a halt of three or four days, while more forces were brought over the river and preparations were made for the next attack. This impending period of rest seemed blissfully long. He did not want to think about his soldiers, about his still unwritten report, about their lack of ammunition, about the worn tyres of his company's trucks, and the fact that he might be killed by the Russians.

His thoughts turned to his recent period of leave. He had failed to make the most of it and it would be a long time before he was allowed home again. In spite of this, he felt no regrets. Back in Berlin, he had felt a strange mixture of pity and contempt for other people – even for close friends, even for his own mother. He was irritated by their excessive concern over everyday hardships, even though he understood that their lives were not easy and that it was entirely natural for them to want to talk about such matters as air raids, ration cards, worn-out shoes and the shortage of coal.

Soon after returning to Berlin, he had gone to a concert with his mother. He had barely listened to the music at all; instead, he had studied the audience. There were a great many old people and hardly anyone young – just one skinny boy with very large ears and an ugly seventeen-year-old girl. The sight of the men's shiny jackets and the wrinkled necks of the old women had been depressing; it was as if the concert hall smelled of mothballs.

During the interval, he had greeted a few people he knew. He had spoken to Ernst, a well-known theatre critic; his son, a former schoolmate of Bach's, had died in a concentration camp. Ernst's hands were shaking and his eyes watering; and he had a sclerotic blue vein bulging out on his neck. He was evidently having to do his own cooking; he was like an old peasant woman, his fingers brown from peeling potatoes.

He spoke with Lena Bischof – the ugly, grey-haired wife of Arnold, one of his *gymnasium* comrades. She looked slovenly; there was a wart with a coiled hair on her chin and she was wearing a crumpled dress with a ridiculous bow tied at the waist. Lena told him in a whisper that she had pretended to separate from Arnold, since his grandfather was a Dutch Jew – not that this had ever been of any significance to him. Until the start of the Russian campaign, Arnold had lived in Berlin, but in November he had been sent to work in the east, first to Poznan and then to Lublin. Since then Lena had not had a single letter from him. She did not even know if he was alive – he had high blood pressure, and sudden changes of climate could be the end of him.

After the concert was over, the audience quietly went their separate ways. There were no cars waiting outside on the street. The old men and women just shuffled hurriedly away in the dark.

The following day he saw Lunz, a friend from his student days who had a withered arm. He and Lunz had once wanted to start a journal together, intended for people of culture: professors, writers and artists. Lunz was exhaustingly verbose, but he did not ask Bach a single question about the war and Russia; it was as if there were nothing more important in the world than the fact that, as a member of the elite, Lunz was entitled to superior rations and was living well.

Bach turned the conversation to more general topics – and Lunz replied reluctantly, in a whisper. Either there were now few things that interested him or he no longer trusted Bach. To Bach it seemed that people who had once been strong, intelligent and interesting now emanated an aura of quiet horror, as if they had been stacked away in a storeroom to gather dust and cobwebs. Their knowledge was now outmoded and their moral principles and scrupulous honesty were no longer of any use to anyone. They had no future and they had been left behind on the shore. And it had seemed all too likely to Bach that, when the war was over, he too would become one of these 'former people'.[217] It might have been better to end his days in a camp – instead of becoming one of the living dead, he'd have died with a sense of exaltation, knowing he had stayed true to the struggle.

He had seen Maria Forster every day. There was a similar sense of unease in her home; there too the air was full of discontent and resentment. Bach had not seen her father, who was working until late at night in the General Staff, but he had thought to himself that, were he a Gestapo officer, he would have no trouble divining the man's secret thoughts; his family were constantly making fun of army ways, laughing at the ignorance of newly appointed field marshals and prominent generals and telling jokes about their wives – and there could be no doubt about who had first told them these stories.

Maria's mother, who had studied literature as a young woman, said that Frau Rommel and Frau Model were grossly uneducated. They spoke incorrect German; they came out with the crudest of slang; they were rude, boastful and ignorant, and it would be utterly inconceivable to let them loose at an official reception. They ate like the wives of petty shopkeepers. They had grown fat; they didn't take part in any sporting activities and had almost forgotten how to walk. As for their children, they too were rude and spoilt; they were doing badly at school and all they really cared about was alcohol, boxing and pornography. In short, Frau Forster was full of rage and contempt. Nevertheless, Bach had a feeling that, should a field marshal's wife want to become friends with her, Frau Forster would gladly forgive her her ignorance, her large fat hands, and even her incorrect pronunciation.

Maria was no less discontented. She thought that art in Germany had fallen into decay – actors had forgotten how to act and singers had forgotten how to sing. Books and plays were a semi-literate mixture of bad taste, sentimentality and Nazi bloodlust. The subjects were always identical and, when she picked up a new book, she felt she was reading for the hundredth time something she had first read in 1933. The art school where she both taught and studied was in thrall to deadly boredom, ignorance and conceit. The most talented people were not allowed to work. German physics had lost its greatest genius, Albert Einstein, but much the same had happened, if to a lesser degree, in every other realm of art and science.

Once, when he and Lunz were drinking together, Lunz had said to him, 'Obedience, blind stupidity and the ability to change one's spots – these are the civic virtues now required of a Berliner. Only the Führer has the right to think, not that he has any great love of thinking – he prefers what he calls intuition. Free scientific thought has been trashed. The titans of German philosophy are forgotten. We have abandoned all shared categories; we have renounced universal truth, morality and humanity. All art, science and philosophy now begin and end with the Reich. There is no place in Germany for bold minds and free spirits. Either they have been neutered, like Hauptmann, or they have fallen silent, like Kellermann.[218] The most powerful of all, like Einstein and Planck, have simply soared into the air and flown away.[219] It is only people like me who have remained stuck in the swamp, in the reeds.' At this point Lunz had stumbled. 'Only please forget all this. Don't tell anyone, not even your own mother, what I've just been saying. Do you hear? You probably can't even begin to imagine the vast, invisible net that envelops us all. It catches everything in its mesh – the most casual words, thoughts, moods, dreams and looks. A gossamer net woven by iron fingers.'

'You talk as if I was born yesterday,' Bach had replied.

Lunz had drunk a lot that evening and couldn't hold back. 'I work at a factory,' he said. 'Up above the machine tools are huge banners with slogans: "*Du bist nichts, dein Volk ist alles.*"[220] Sometimes I think about this. Why am I nothing? Am I not *Volk*? And you too? Are you not *Volk*? Our era loves grand statements – people are hypnotized by their apparent profundity. What nonsense they are. *Das Volk*! It's a word the authorities love. They make out that *das Volk* is extraordinarily wise. But only the Chancellor understands what *das Volk* truly wants – that it wants deprivation, the Gestapo and a war of aggression.' And then, with a little wink, he went on, 'Another year or two, you know, and you and I will crack too. We too will make our peace with National Socialism, and we'll wish we'd seen the light a bit sooner. It's the law of natural selection – the species and genera that survive are those that know how to adapt. After all, evolution is simply a process of continual adaptation. And if man stands at the top of the ladder, if he is the king of nature, it's simply because the human beast is more adaptable than any other brute beast. He who fails to adapt perishes. He falls from the ladder of development that leads to divinity. But you and I may be too late – I may find myself in prison, and you may be killed by the Russians.'

Bach could remember this conversation clearly. It had made him uneasy. He had thought and felt the same as Lunz and had not contradicted him. 'We are the last of the Mohicans,' he had replied. Yet he had said this with a frown. Once again he had felt irritated. Mixed up with Lunz's thoughts was a troubling, humiliating sense of impotence. Lunz's thoughts belonged to a world of shabby old-fashioned clothes, of frightened whispers, of old people's eyes glancing anxiously at windows and doors. And they went hand in hand with the most primitive envy. The envy he had sensed in Maria, and, still more, in her mother's carping and grumbling – an envy of those who live their lives centre stage, of those who can exhibit their paintings, who go hunting with Göring, who receive invitations to Goebbels' villa, who fly to congresses in Rome and Madrid and are lauded in the pages of the *Völkischer Beobachter*.[221] Were Colonel Forster to be promoted to some important post, his family's spirit of revolt might evaporate only too quickly.

Bach had left Berlin deeply dispirited. He had so longed for his weeks of leave – for peace and quiet, for time to talk with his friends, to sit and read in the evenings, to speak freely to his mother about his innermost thoughts and feelings. He had wanted to tell her about the unimaginable cruelty of war, about how it felt to live every hour in total subordination to the coarse, brutal will of a stranger. This, he had wanted to say, was a greater torment than the fear of death.

Instead, he hadn't known what to do with himself when he got home. He had felt depressed and unsettled. He had felt irritated when he talked to people and he had been unable to read more than a few pages at a time. Like the concert hall, the books all smelled of mothballs.

As he left Berlin on his way east, he felt a sense of relief, even though he had no desire to go to the front and didn't in the least wish to see either his soldiers or his fellow officers.

He had returned to his motor infantry regiment on 26 June, two days before the start of the summer offensive. Now, on the quiet bank of the Don, he felt as if that had been only a few days ago. Since the offensive began, he had lost all sense of days, weeks and months. Time had become a hot, dense, motley lump, a confusion of hoarse screams, dust, howling shells, smoke and fire, marches by day and by night, warm vodka and cold tinned food, fractured thoughts, the cries of geese, the clink of glasses, the rattle of sub-machine guns, glimpses of white kerchiefs, the whistle of Messerschmitts, anguish, the smell of petrol, drunken swagger and drunken laughter, the fear of death, and the screeching horns of trucks and armoured personnel carriers.

There was the war, a huge smoking steppe sun – and a few distinct pictures: a bent apple tree laden with apples, a dark sky pierced by bright southern stars, the glimmer of streams, the moon shining over blue steppe grass.

This morning Bach had come back to himself. He was looking forward to these three or four days of rest before the final breakthrough that would take them to the banks of the Volga. Calm, sleepy, still able to enjoy the cool touch of the water, he looked at the bright green reeds and his slim, tanned hands and thought about his weeks in Berlin. He needed to link these two opposite worlds – worlds separated by an abyss yet existing side by side in the cramped space of a man's heart.

He rose to his full height and stamped his foot against the ground. He felt as if he were kicking the sky. Behind him lay thousands of kilometres of a strange land. For years he had thought himself robbed, spiritually beggared, one of the last Mohicans of German freedom of thought. But why had he set such store by his former way of being? Had he really ever been so spiritually rich? Now, as the smoke and dust of the last few weeks yielded to this clear awareness of an alien sky and a vast, equally alien but now-conquered land underfoot, he felt in every cell of his body the sombre power of the cause in which he was implicated. He could feel, it seemed, with his skin, with his whole body the furthest reaches of this alien land he had crossed. Perhaps he was stronger now than in the days when he glanced anxiously at the door as he whispered his secret thoughts. Had he truly understood what the great minds of the past would have made of the present day? Were those great minds now aligned with this resounding, triumphant force or were they on the side of those whispering old men and women who smelled of mothballs? And was it even possible that there was a smell of mothballs about the whole nineteenth century, the century whose faithful son he had considered himself to be? Perhaps those who had known the charm and poetry of the eighteenth century had looked on his beloved nineteenth century as cynical and atrocious?

Bach looked round; he could hear approaching footsteps. The duty telephonist hurried up to him and said, 'Lieutenant, the battalion commander's on the phone. He wants to speak to you.'

The telephonist glanced at the river and let out a barely audible whistle. So much for his chance of a swim in the river – he had already understood from his friend, the battalion telephonist, that their halt was now over. They were to prepare to move on.

30

People have tried many times to find in Hitler's psychological make-up an explanation for the part he played in history. We now know a great deal about Hitler. Nevertheless, neither vengeful rage, nor a love of cakes with whipped cream, nor a sinister ability to play on the basest instincts of the crowd, nor a love of dogs, nor a combination of paranoia and furious energy, nor an inclination towards mysticism, nor intelligence combined with a memory of great power, nor a fickle capriciousness in his choice of favourites, nor cruel treachery and the exalted sentimentality that accompanied it, nor any number of other traits – some ordinary, some exceedingly repulsive – can ever be enough to explain what he achieved.

Hitler came to power because, after the First World War, as the country inclined towards fascism, Germany *needed* such a man.

After being defeated in 1918, Germany was looking for Hitler, and she found him.

Nevertheless, a knowledge of Hitler's character will help us to understand the process by which he became the head of the Nazi state.

In his life, in his character and in everything Hitler did, there was one important constant: failure. Astonishingly, it was his repeated failures that constituted the foundation for his success. A mediocre student, who twice failed the entrance exams for the Vienna Academy of Fine Arts; a failure in his relationships with women; a failed politician, who began his political career as an intelligence agent for the German army, informing on the activities of the party he later went on to lead.

Deep in his heart he always felt the uncertainty of a young man who did badly at school and who, in a world of free competition, was denied entry into even the most modest provincial artistic circles.

Failure propels people along many different paths. It drives some to a state of sullen resignation and others to religious mysticism. Some fall into despair; others turn embittered and envious; others become hypocrites, adopting a false air of humility; still others become suspicious and timid. Some start manically concocting the most hare-brained

513

plans. Some find security in sterile contempt, some in wild ambition; others turn to robbery and crime.

Both before and after he came to power Hitler was essentially the same person – a petty bourgeois, a philistine and a failure; the immense power he wielded allowed him to display on a pan-European stage all the propensities of an embittered, mistrustful, vindictive and treacherous psyche. The peculiarities of his character brought about the death of millions.

Hitler's coming to power did not in any way lessen his sense of inferiority, which was too deeply rooted. His apparent arrogance was no more than a mask.

Hitler embodied and gave expression to the peculiarities of a German state broken by the First World War.

For five or six decades the German state had known little but failure. Its striving towards world mastery had led nowhere. German imperialism had failed to win markets by peaceful means.

In 1914, attempting to win markets by other means, Germany began a war – but this too proved a failure. The German strategy of swift strikes and pincer movements proved misguided, and the German army was defeated.

Meanwhile, Adolf Schicklgruber,[222] still unnoticed by anyone, was setting out on his own path of failure, parallel to Germany's. Hatred of freedom, hatred of social and racial equality, were becoming ever more important to him.

His appeal to Nietzsche's concept of the *Übermensch* and master race coincided with Germany's turn, after its repeated experience of failure, to the idea of some wild and criminal super-supremacy. The ideas adopted by Hitler, as he trod his little path, were exactly what the defeated country needed. We can now see more clearly than ever that the superman is born of the despair of the weak, not from the triumph of the strong. The ideas of individual liberty, internationalism, the social equality of all workers – these are the ideas of people confident in the power of their own minds and the creative force of their own labour. The only form of violence countenanced by these ideas is the violence inflicted by Prometheus on his chains.

In *Mein Kampf*, Hitler stated that equality benefits only the weak, that progress in the world of nature is achieved solely through the destructive force of natural selection, and that the only possible basis for human progress is racial selection, the dictatorship of race. He confused the concepts of violence and strength. He saw the vicious despair of impotence as a strength and failed to recognize the strength of free human labour. He saw the man sowing a vast wheat field as inferior to the thug who smashes him over the back of the head with a crowbar.

This is the philosophy of a loser who has fallen into despair, who is unable to achieve anything through labour but who is endowed with a strong mind, ferocious energy and a burning ambition.

This philosophy of inner impotence, to which so many reactionary German minds succumbed, was in accord with the philosophy of industrial and national impotence that had seized hold of the country as a whole. This philosophy proved equally attractive to individual dregs and failures, unable to achieve anything through their own labour, and to a state that had begun a war with the aim of world domination and ended it with the Treaty of Versailles.

So, from the failures of Schicklgruber was born the success of Hitler; so Hitler's inner impotence led directly to his years of brief, terrible, senseless power over the nations of Europe. His understanding of postwar Germany was unsophisticated yet penetrating, and in his quest for power he was able to draw on a reckless energy and a wild demagogic fury. He managed to bring together the personal amorality of postwar Germany's many losers – shopkeepers, officers, waiters, even some despairing industrial workers – with the state amorality of a defeated imperialist power, ready to follow a path of unabashed criminality. More consistently than any ruler in history, he appealed to the basest of human instincts, to which he himself was in thrall; he was born of these instincts and, day after day, he helped bring them to birth in others. But he also knew the power of virtue and morality – and he saw it all the more clearly for being a stranger to it. He knew how to appeal to mothers and fathers, to the feelings of farmers and workers. He suppressed the resistance of the revolutionary forces of the German working class and he made short shrift of the democratic intelligentsia. He silenced all dissent, transforming Germany into an intellectual desert.

He deceived many who might have stood against him; they mistook his lies for truth, and his hysteria for sincerity. They saw his religion of hatred as a love of Germany, his powerful animal logic as a token of genius, and his criminal dictatorship as a promise of freedom.

Even after assuming unlimited power, Hitler sensed that he still remained weaker than those whom he hated. He knew that, however many people he had managed to deceive, the constructive, creative forces of German labour and the German people did not stand behind him. He saw that neither hunger, nor slavery, nor the camps, nor any other abuse of power could grant him a sense of superiority over those he had defeated through violence. Then, in the grip of the most powerful hatred on earth – the hatred a conqueror bears towards the indestructible strength of those he has conquered – he began murdering millions of people.

His powerlessness manifested itself in many ways. He lied to the German people, saying that his aim was to combat the unjust provisions of the Treaty of Versailles while in reality he was preparing an unjust war. He deceived two million unemployed, giving them work building roads of military importance while persuading them that this heralded the beginning of an era of peaceful prosperity. Post-war Germany had been like the deranged mechanism of a large clock, with hundreds of cogwheels and levers spinning, whirring and clicking at random and to no purpose. Hitler's role was to be the malign cog that united all the disparate parts of this mechanism: the despair of the hungry, the viciousness of the rabble, a thirst for military revenge, a bleeding, inflamed sense of German nationhood and the general fury at the injustice of the Treaty of Versailles.

To begin with, Hitler was no more than a splinter of wood, floating with the current, then snatched up, as if by a wave, by the post-war dream of military revenge. Then, in 1923 he struck lucky; Emil Kirdorf, the devilish old coal-king of the Ruhr, became his financial backer.[223] This was at a time when Hitler and his entire National Socialist Party could fit inside a Munich beer hall or the cells of a Munich prison.

Tragically, many people believed that by working for Hitler, they were working for Germany. Through violence, treachery and deceit, he was able to exploit German science, German technology and the enthusiasm of German youth. He enabled the whole vast national mechanism to function once more – by declaring that German capitalists without markets and German workers without work were, in reality, a super-race, destined for power and glory. He was able to give complete expression to the paradigm of a fascist state.

And so it came about that Hitler's failures were the precondition of his success. As head of the fascist state, he was swept onto the world stage. At first, he was the instrument of individuals, then of unimportant and isolated groups, and then of industrial barons and the German General Staff. Finally, he became the instrument of the principal reactionary forces of world politics.

But in the summer days of 1942 he thought of himself, with a secret, slightly furtive joy, as the embodiment of free, all-powerful will. At times he imagined himself as immortal. There was nothing he could not do. He dismissed the idea of any kind of reciprocity between himself and the world. He was blind to the huge forces that determine the course of events. He did not see that by the time of his greatest success and seemingly most absolute freedom of action, when his will alone appeared to determine whether his battering ram would fall on the West or the East – he did not see that, by this time, he had become a slave. In August 1942, it seemed that his will was being realized, that he was indeed inflicting on Soviet Russia the deadly blow he had spoken about to Mussolini at their 29 April meeting in Salzburg. He did not understand – nor did he ever understand – that his will was no longer free; it was his absolute lack of free will that had led him to embark on a campaign where every additional kilometre of conquered territory brought the fascist empire closer to its end.

Physicists usually feel free to ignore the infinitesimally small value that expresses the earth's gravitational attraction to a stone. They do not deny the theoretical reality of this attraction, but it is only the stone's gravitational attraction to the earth that they need take into practical account. Hitler, at the height of his success, wanted to do the opposite; he wanted to ignore the gravitational attraction of a stone, or a grain of sand, to the earth. A mere grain of sand himself, he wanted to restructure the world according to the laws of his own will and intuition.

The only means at his disposal was violence. Violence towards states and nations; violence in the education of children, violence towards thought and labour, with regard to art, science and every emotion. Violence – the violence of one man over another, of one nation over another, of one race over another – was declared a deity.

In this deification of violence Hitler was looking for supreme power; instead, he toppled Germany into an abyss of impotence.

Never had the world seen such a glorification of racial purity. Defending the purity of German blood was proclaimed a sacred mission. Yet never in all German history was there more mixing of blood than during the years of the Third Reich, with vast numbers of foreign slaves flooding German factories and villages.

Hitler believed that the state he had created, founded on unprecedented violence, would endure for a thousand years.

But the millstones of history were already at work. Everything of Hitler's would be ground to dust: his ideas, his armies, his Reich, his party, his science and his pitiful arts, his field marshals and gauleiters, he himself and the future of Germany. None of Hitler's failures proved more catastrophic than his success. None brought more suffering to mankind.

Everything Hitler proclaimed was overturned by the course of history. Not one of his promises was fulfilled. Everything he fought against grew stronger and put down deeper roots.

*

There is more than one path by which an individual can take their place on the stage of history and remain in the memory of mankind. Not everyone goes through the main door, following the path of genius, labour and reason. Some slip quietly through a half-open side entrance; others break in at night; others are simply swept onto the world stage by a wave of events.

The measure of a historical figure's true greatness is their ability to divine and give expression to a central, though still barely visible, line of human development, a line that will determine the evolution of human society for generations to come. Someone with this ability is like an experienced swimmer; at first, they appear to be swimming against the current, but, as they swim on, it becomes clear that the opposing forces were mere eddies and backwaters. With perseverance, they get the better of these surface currents. Their own strength and the deepest, most powerful current then join together and the swimmer is able to move freely and powerfully.

Many years – and many miles – later, this current in turn comes to seem secondary. Another swimmer, another great figure appears, able to sense in the hidden depths the first stirrings of some powerful new movement.

A swimmer of this kind, able to distinguish between the false and the real, between surface eddies and the mainstream of history, is no mere splinter of wood. He is, of course, moved by the currents, but he decides for himself which to fight and which to follow. And with the passage of time it becomes clear to almost everyone that he has followed the truest and most important current.

The path followed by the blind madmen of history is very different.

Can we call someone a great man if he has not brought into people's lives a single atom of good, a single atom of freedom and intelligence?

Can we call someone a great man if he has left behind him only ashes, ruins and congealed blood, only poverty and the stench of racism, only the graves of the countless children and old people he has killed?

Can we call someone a great man because his unusual intelligence, able to detect and co-opt every dark and reactionary force, proved as virulent and destructive as the bacteria of bubonic plague?

The twentieth century is a critical and dangerous time for humanity. It is time for intelligent people to renounce, once and for all, the thoughtless and sentimental habit of admiring a criminal if the scope of his criminality is vast enough, of admiring an arsonist if he sets fire not to a village hut but to capital cities, of tolerating a demagogue if he deceives not just an uneducated lad from a village but entire nations, of pardoning a murderer because he has killed not one individual but millions.

Such criminals must be destroyed like rabid wolves. We must remember them only with disgust and burning hatred. We must expose their darkness to the light of day.

And if the forces of darkness engender new Hitlers, playing on people's basest and most backward instincts in order to further new criminal designs against humanity, let no one see in them any trait of grandeur or heroism.

A crime is a crime, and criminals do not cease to be criminals because their crimes are recorded in history and their names are remembered. A criminal remains a criminal; a murderer remains a murderer.

History's only true heroes, the only true leaders of mankind are those who help to establish freedom, who see freedom as the greatest strength of an individual, a nation or a state, who fight for the equality, in all respects, of every individual, people and nation.

31

The day began the same as every other day. Yardmen out in the square stirred up clouds of dust, sending them towards the pavement. Old women and small girls went out to queue for bread. In hospital, military and city canteens, sleepy cooks banged pans about on cold stoves, then squatted down by the warm ashes below, hoping to find an ember they could use to light an extra-large morning cigarette. Flies took lazily to the air; they had been sleeping on walls still hot from kitchen chimneys, and they were annoyed with the cooks for starting work so early.

A young woman with tangled hair, holding her nightshirt against her chest, flung open a window, smiling and screwing up her eyes as she looked out at the clear morning. Night-shift workers went by, oblivious to the morning chill, still deafened by the din of their workshops. Army truck drivers awoke, yawning and rubbing stiff hips and shoulders after spending the night in city yards, asleep in their vehicles. Cats mewed meekly at doors, asking to be allowed back inside after their night-time escapades.

Down by the river station thousands of people were waiting for a ferry to the east bank. Slowly and reluctantly they woke up, yawned, scratched themselves, ate a little dry bread, clattered teapots, looked suspiciously at their neighbours and felt in their pockets to check that everything important was still there: money, documents and ration cards for their journey. An old woman with a waxen face passed by, on her way to the cemetery; she went every Sunday, to visit her dead husband. Elderly fishermen with rods and crayfish pots made their way down to the river. In the hospitals, assistant nurses were carrying out white buckets and preparing bandages for the wounded.

The sun climbed higher. A woman in a blue housecoat was gluing a copy of *Stalingrad Pravda* to a wall. A group of actors had met up by the yellow stone lions outside the city theatre; their loud laughter was attracting the attention of passers-by. A cashier went into the cinema, about to start selling tickets for *The Bright Path*.[224] First, though, she spoke to a cleaner and asked her to find the jug she had lent the day before to the usher, so that the usher could collect her ration of sunflower oil. Then they both complained about the director, who was being slow to pay them their salary and who had shamelessly, in front of the whole collective, made off with twenty litres of malted milk recently delivered to the canteen for a children's matinee.

The entire, anxiety-filled city – now an army camp as much as a city – was taking a deep breath, getting ready for the day's work.

A Stalgres engineer, slowly chewing a small piece of bread, bent down towards a turbine, listening to its even hum. His thin face and narrowed eyes looked calm and alert.

A smelter, a young woman, frowned as she looked through her safety glasses at the white whirlwind raging in an open-hearth furnace. Then she walked away a little, ran her hand over the drops of sweat on her forehead, took a small round mirror from the breast pocket of her canvas overalls, straightened a lock of blonde hair that had slipped out from beneath her red, soot-blackened kerchief, and laughed. Her severe, dark face was transformed; her eyes and her white teeth gleamed.

A dozen workers of different ages were setting up an armoured turret outside the Red October steelworks. When the massive object finally yielded to their efforts and settled into its assigned position, they all let out what seemed like a single protracted sigh. Their tense faces relaxed into a shared expression of satisfaction and relief. One of the older workers said to the man beside him, 'Time for a smoke. Give me some of your baccy – it's good and strong.'

Among the bushes not far away someone was shouting commands: 'Fire position – edge of ravine! Machine gun – forward!' As part of a training exercise, some newly recruited militiamen began to drag a heavy machine gun into position. Patches of sunlight dappled the dark tunics and jackets on their bent backs.

Two women were talking at the district Party committee building on the corner of Barrikadnaya and Klinskaya streets. One was the young Party secretary of a small printing press; the other, who had grey hair and a wrinkled face, was a member of the committee bureau. 'Olga Grigorievna,' the former was saying quietly, 'you say we need to mobilize people for defence work. Well, our printers haven't needed any mobilizing. They're doing all they can already. The night-shift workers are digging trenches during the day, and the day-shift workers during the night. They bring their own spades. There's one worker, Savostyanova, whose husband's at the front. She brings her little boy along with her. She gives him something to eat at the press and then takes him with her to the trenches. The poor boy's scared stiff of air raids. He won't stay at home on his own for anything in the world.'

Two pretty young women were sitting on a bench by the main door of a white four-storey building. One, the wife of the house manager, was darning a little girl's dress; the other was knitting a sock. The former loved to gossip; the other wasn't saying anything, but she was smiling and watching the speaker alertly, enjoying her stories.

'There's nothing I don't know,' the house manager's wife was saying. 'All their little games: who's doing what, who's using whom, who's bedding whom. So, there on the first floor we have the Shaposh-nikov family. The old grandma's not so bad – I've got no complaints about *her*. It's true she's always criticizing my husband – nothing in the building's ever quite good enough for her. All the same, she's not a bad sort, even if she is full of prejudices. A woman from another age, I suppose. But as for her dear daughters – excuse me, but they beggar belief! Marusya, the eldest, works in children's homes. You should see what comes out of her briefcase when she gets home in the evening – bread rings, pastries, sugar, little pots of real butter, things the likes of us haven't seen for the last six months. Yes, she steals straight from the children's mouths. Her husband ditched her. What do you expect – with a mug as ugly as hers? And her husband's quite a man – works as an engineer in the Tractor Factory, eats in the bosses' dining room and gets special rations. Naturally, the woman moved heaven and earth to get him back. And as for her young sister Zhenya … What men see in her I don't know. Though she's certainly a sharp dresser. She has her brassieres specially made for her by a woman who makes dresses for the wife of our NKVD boss. And the young lady simply doesn't know shame! At times I want to tell her straight out, to say to her face, "Think I haven't seen you out here, sitting on this bench being pawed by that colonel of yours?" Some nights I'm on air defence watch, by the main entrance. I hear things that make me go inside and sit in the stairwell – anything not to have to hear more. And then there's Vera, Marusya's daughter. She's as foul-mouthed as they come. You should have heard her cursing and swearing when she came home from school with the boys. Now she works in the hospital – probably servicing the lieutenants … And then, on the same floor, just opposite that lot, we've got the Meshcheryakovs. I can tell you for sure that they won't be leaving Stalingrad. No, they can't wait for the Germans to come! Their maid's from a village. She asked me the other day, "What's a regime?" "What makes you ask?" I say. "'Cos of the man

I work for," she says. "Every time he looks at the newspaper, he says, 'Yes, this really is the end of the regime!'" But the Meshcheryakovs don't do too badly for themselves as things are. Sugar, grains, oils and fats – they're never short of good food.'[225]

The house manager's wife continued unstoppably, ever confident that she knew the truth and unshakeably certain that all human beings, without exception, are weak, dishonest and hypocritical.

People like her are can see only human vices and weaknesses. This makes it impossible for them to understand how the victory was won, who it was who performed such great deeds and endured such great suffering. Years later, when these world-shaking events have receded far into the past, people like her look back at those days and see only sombre burial mounds bearing witness to superhuman achievements. Then they come to think that everyone alive then was a hero, a spiritual giant. This noble but naive view of the past is no less misguided.

The German axe was raised high in the air, suspended not only over the city of Stalingrad but also over the dream of justice, over devotion to freedom, over loyalty to the motherland, over man's joy in labour, over maternal feeling and all sense of the holiness of life.

Stalingrad's last hour, the last hour of the pre-war city, was little different from any of its previous days and hours. People pushed handcarts full of potatoes, queued for bread and talked about items in shops. In the market people sold or bartered army boots, milk and yellowish sugar. Factory workers worked as usual. And those we are used to calling simple, ordinary folk – a Stalgres engineer, clerks, doctors, students, a young woman smelter, manual workers, rank-and-file Party workers – had no idea that in a few hours many of them would be performing deeds that future generations would refer to as immortal, and that they would do this as naturally and straightforwardly as they had until then gone about their everyday work.

It is not only heroes who love freedom, take joy in labour, know maternal feelings and feel loyalty to their country. And here, perhaps, lies humanity's greatest hope: great deeds can be accomplished by simple, ordinary people.

*

On the other side of the front line German officers opened their battle orders. Airfield mechanics shouted, 'Ready for take off!' Tanks finished refuelling, engines began to throb and turret gunners got into position;

infantrymen with sub-machine guns took their places in armoured personnel carriers, signallers checked their radios for the last time. Friedrich Paulus, like a mechanic who has just set hundreds of wheels of every size in motion, leaned back from his desk and lit a cigar, waiting for the axe of war to fall on Stalingrad.

32

The first planes appeared at about four in the afternoon. Six bombers were approaching the city from the east, at a high altitude. They seemed barely to have passed over Burkovsky Hamlet, not far from the Volga, when there was the sound of the first explosions. Smoke and chalky dust rose up from the bombed buildings. The planes were clearly visible. The air was transparent and the sun was shining, reflected in thousands of windows. People looked up and watched the planes disappear swiftly towards the west. A loud, youthful voice called out, 'Just a few strays – not even worth an alert!'

This was immediately followed by a long dismal wail from steamship hooters and factory sirens. This cry, prophesying death and disaster, hung in the air, as if conveying the anguish of all the city's inhabitants. It was the voice of the entire city – the voice not only of people but also of stone, of buildings, of cars, trucks and machines, of telegraph poles, of the grass and trees in the parks, of electric cables and tram rails; it was a cry let out not only by living beings but also by inanimate objects. All now sensed their coming destruction. Only a rusty iron throat could have engendered this sound, which expressed in equal measure animal horror and the anguish of a human heart.

It was followed by silence – Stalingrad's last silence.

Planes were coming from every direction – from east of the Volga, from Sarepta and Beketovka to the south, from Kalach and Karpovka to the west, from Yerzovka and Rynok to the north. Their black bodies slipped freely and easily through the feathery clouds in the pale blue sky; it was as if hundreds of poisonous insects had emerged from secret nests and were now all heading towards their victim. The sun in its divine ignorance brushed these creatures with its rays, and their wings shone milky white. White moths and the wings of Junkers – there was something painful, almost blasphemous about the similarity.

The buzzing of engines grew continually louder, denser, more viscous. The sounds of the city faded, as if drooping or curling up; only this buzz kept intensifying, growing darker and still denser, its slow monotony conveying all the furious power of the engines. The sky was now covered with exploding anti-aircraft shells, their grey smoke like the heads of dandelions gone to seed. Enraged, the flying insects flew swiftly on. Taking off from airfields on both sides of the Volga, Soviet fighters climbed swiftly towards them. The German planes were flying in several tiers, taking up the full volume of the blue summer sky. For a while, the flak and the Soviet fighters seemed to disrupt their orderly progress. Damaged bombers caught fire, releasing long trails of smoke as they fell from the sky or broke up in mid-air. Bright parachute canopies opened over the steppe. Nevertheless, the bombers flew on.

As the planes coming from north, west, east and south met over Stalingrad, they began their descent. It seemed, however, to be the sky itself that was descending – sagging, as if under dark, heavy storm clouds, under the vast weight of metal and explosives it now bore.

Then came a new sound – or rather two new sounds: the piercing whistle of hundreds of high-explosive bombs falling towards the ground and the screech of tens of thousands of incendiary units tumbling out as their containers gaped open.[226] This new sound, which lasted for three or four seconds, penetrated every living being. Hearts of those about to die, hearts of those who survived – all hearts clenched tight in anguish. The whistling grew fiercer, more insistent. There was no one who did not hear it: women who had been standing in queues and were running back home to be with their children; people who had managed to hide away in deep cellars, protected from the sky by thick stone slabs; people who dropped down on the tarmac in the middle of streets and squares; people who leaped into slit trenches in parks and pressed their heads against dry earth; patients in psychiatric hospitals; wounded soldiers lying under chloroform on operating tables; babies, red in the face as they cried angrily for their mothers' milk; half-deaf, feeble-minded old men.

The bombs reached the ground and plunged into the city. Buildings began to die, just as people die. Tall, thin houses toppled to one side, killed on the spot; stockier, sturdier houses trembled and swayed, their chests and bellies gashed open and exposing what had always been hidden from view: portraits on walls, cupboards, double beds, bedside tables, jars of millet, a half-peeled potato on a table covered with an ink-stained oilcloth.

Bent water pipes and bundles of cables and iron girders between floors were laid bare. Water was flowing everywhere, like tears and blood, making puddles on the streets and pavements. Heaps of red brick appeared; the thick dust coming off them made them look like heaps of steaming red meat. Thousands of buildings went blind, leaving the pavements covered with broken glass like a shining carpet of tiny fish scales. Huge tram cables fell to the ground with a grinding clatter, and plate-glass windows flowed out of their frames as if turned to liquid. Hunched, buckled tram rails were now sticking up from the streets. More fragile structures, however, seemed strangely untouched by the shock waves. A tin arrow with the words 'Cross here!' and a pale blue plywood kiosk for the sale of soft drinks were still standing. The many panes of glass of a frail telephone booth still shone. Everything most immovable – everything made of stone and iron – had become fluid; everything into which people had instilled the power and idea of movement – trams, cars, buses, locomotives – had come to a stop.[227]

The air was thick with brick dust and pulverized chalk. It was as if the city had been enveloped by mist and this mist was now spreading down the Volga.

The fires started by tens of thousands of incendiary bombs began to blaze. A huge city was dying, overwhelmed by fire, smoke and dust, amid thunder shaking the earth, the sky and the water. And yet, terrible though all this was, it was not as terrible as the eyes of a six-year-old child crushed by an iron girder. There is a power that can raise huge cities from the dust, but no power in the world can lift the almost weightless eyelashes that have closed over the eyes of a dead child.

Only people on the east bank of the Volga, ten or fifteen kilometres away, in Burkovsky Hamlet, Upper Akhtuba, Yami, Tumak and Tsyganskaya Zarya could see the fire as a whole and grasp the extent of the disaster. Hundreds of explosions merged into a single monotonous roar and, even there on the east bank, the iron weight of this roar made the earth shake. Oak leaves trembled and the windows of the little wooden houses rattled. The chalky mist, now lying like a white sheet over the city's tall buildings and across the Volga, continued to spread, creeping as far as Stalgres, the shipyard repair workshops and the outlying districts of Beketovka and Krasnoarmeisk. Then the mist gradually disappeared, blending with the yellow-grey murk of the fires.

From a distance people could see how swiftly the fires in neighbouring buildings were joining together. Building after building joined in a single blaze and whole burning streets fused into a single, living, moving wall. In some places tall columns rose up from this wall, along with swelling cupolas and fiery bell towers. Red gold, smoky bronze, it was as if a new city of fire had appeared over Stalingrad. Near to the shore, the Volga was steaming. Black smoke and flame slid over the water. Fuel tanks had been hit; the fuel had found its way to the river, and this too was on fire. A great cloud of black smoke was billowing up from it, growing denser and blacker. Caught by the steppe winds, the smoke thinned out and spread slowly across the sky. Weeks later, it still hung in the air, visible even at a distance of fifty kilometres. Swollen and bloodless, the sun made its daily journey through a pale murk.

The flames of the blazing city to the north were seen in the twilight by ferrymen crossing the Volga at Svetly Yar and by women on their way to Raigorod with sacks of grain. Old Kazakhs in carts, on their way to Lake Elton, saw a strange gleam to the west; their camels, sticking out their slobbery lips and extending their dirty swan necks, kept looking back at it. Fishermen in Dubovka and Gornaya Proleika saw a light to the south. And Colonel General Paulus's staff officers stood in silence on the bank of the Don, drawing on their cigarettes as they watched the patch of flickering light in the dark sky.

What did the strange blaze in the distance portend? Whose defeat? Whose triumph?

Radio, telegraph and ocean cables were already promulgating the news of the Germans' massive strike. Politicians in London, Washington, Tokyo and Ankara worked all through the night. Ordinary labourers of every race were studying newspapers. There was a new word on the front pages: Stalingrad.

It was a catastrophe. As during floods, earthquakes, avalanches and steppe or forest fires, every living thing wanted to leave the dying city.

First to leave were the birds. Helter skelter, staying close to the water, the jackdaws crossed to the east bank; they were overtaken by grey flocks of sparrows, alternately drawing close together and spreading far apart.

Unbelievably large rats – magnates and patriarchs that had probably not left their lairs for many years – sensed the heat of the fire and the trembling of the earth. Emerging from the cellars of food stores and harbourside granaries, momentarily blinded and deafened, they rushed hither and thither in confusion. Then, as instinct took over, they dragged their tails and fat grey behinds down to the water and made their way along boards and ropes onto barges and old, half-submerged steamers lying close to the shore. Ignoring the rats and mice, cats took refuge in pits and crevices between the rocks.

A horse overturned its cart, tore its harness, bolted along the shore and straight into the water, still dragging its reins and traces behind it. Crazed-looking dogs leaped out of the smoke and dust, ran down the slope towards the river, threw themselves into the water and began to swim towards Krasnaya Sloboda and Tumak.

Only the white doves and blue rock pigeons, chained to their dwellings by an instinct still more powerful than that of self-preservation, went on circling over the burning buildings. Caught by fierce currents of incandescent air, they perished in smoke and flame.

33

Varvara Alexandrovna Andreyeva was due to leave on Sunday, with her daughter-in-law Natalya and her grandson Volodya. Natalya had persuaded Tokareva, the children's-home director, to allow Varvara and little Volodya onto the boat allocated to the children's home. By Friday, everything had been packed into sacks and bundles, sewn up securely and taken down to the port by handcart, along with the baggage from the children's home.

On Sunday morning Varvara and her grandson arrived at the agreed meeting point in the port. After saying goodbye first to her husband – who had to go to the steelworks – and then to her house and garden, she had felt demoralized and defeated. Up to the very moment of departure she had gone on worrying: about the firewood, which hadn't been locked away securely enough; about how long her house would be standing empty while her husband was out at work; about there being no one to keep an eye on the tomatoes in the vegetable patch; about how someone was sure to pilfer their apples before they were even fully ripe; about the many items she had failed to properly sew, darn, wash or iron; about the sugar and fats ration that she would now never collect; about which of her belongings she needed to take with her and which she did not. It now seemed as if all her belongings were essential: her iron, her meat grinder, the embroidered rug over the bed, and her old, re-soled felt boots.

Her husband had accompanied her and Volodya to the corner of the street. She had kept telling him about the many things – some important, some of no importance at all – that he simply mustn't forget about. But when she looked around and saw his broad, slightly humped back, when she looked for the last time at the apple tree's leafy crown and the grey roof of her home – all her petty worries fell away. And with a feeling close to fear she realized that there was no one in the world nearer and dearer to her than her old friend and companion. Pavel Andreyev had looked back one last time and disappeared around the corner.

Sitting on the ground by the landing stage were hundreds of people with thin sallow faces: young mothers with children in their arms, unkempt old greybeards in winter coats, the soles of their boots tied on with string. The young mothers' faces looked empty and drained, as if everything had disappeared but their shining eyes; the belts of their fashionable coats were hung with kettles and flasks. Their children looked pale and weak.

She saw fifteen-year-old girls in blue ski trousers, with heavy hiking boots on their feet and knapsacks strapped across their thin shoulders. There were women her own age or still older, their heads uncovered, their grey hair uncombed and dishevelled. They were sitting with their brown, sinewy hands on their knees, watching the dark, oily water carry away pieces of swollen watermelon peel, a dead fish with white eyes, rotten logs and greasy scraps of paper.

While she still had a home of her own, she had felt cross when she heard these strangers asking the way to the bathhouse, to the port, to the rations-card office or to the market. It was as if they brought disaster with them, as if they were infecting the earth itself with tears, hunger and homelessness. Local women standing in queues – herself among them – had complained angrily, 'They're locusts – they gobble up everything. And look what they've done to the prices!' Now, though, to her surprise, it was these same refugees who were able to console her in her seemingly inconsolable pain. All had lost husbands, sons and brothers. All had left their own homes; all had left their stores of firewood and potatoes. All had left behind them unpicked vegetables and unharvested fields; many had left stoves that were still warm.

She talked to a high-cheekboned old woman from Kharkov and marvelled at the similarity of their fates. The woman's husband was a workshop supervisor. In autumn 1941 he had been evacuated to Bashkiria with his factory. She had then gone to Millerovo, where she had lived for six months with the parents of her eldest son's wife. Now her two sons were at the front and she was going to join her husband in Bashkiria, along with her daughter-in-law and her grandson. And the young woman sitting next to Varvara, the wife of a commander, said that she and her two children and her mother-in-law were going to live with her sister in Ufa. And an old Jew, a dental technician, said that this was the third time he had been uprooted. First he had moved from Novograd-Volynka to Poltava, then from Poltava to Rossosh, where he had buried his wife, and now he and his two granddaughters were on their way to Central Asia. His daughter, the little girls' mother, had died of hepatitis before the war, and their father, an engineer in a sugar factory, had been killed in an air raid. While the old man was recounting all this, the girls clung to his jacket and gazed at him as if he were a heroic warrior, even though he looked so frail that you could knock him down with a feather.

The other people on the landing stage had come from towns and villages Varvara had never heard of and they were on their way to many different places – Krasnovodsk, Belebey, Yelabuga, Ufa, Barnaul – yet they had all, essentially, suffered the same fate. The country's fate and the fate of her people were one and the same; Varvara had never before sensed this so clearly.

Time continued to pass. Steamers dappled with grey and green camouflage paint, their funnels draped with withered branches, set off from the port. 'Just like at Whitsun!' Varvara said to herself.[228] Volodya had already made friends with some of the other boys and she kept losing sight of him and having to call him back. The clear blue sky was troubling, and she kept gazing up at it. She was growing more and more anxious, and her only solace lay in thinking about her husband.

She was still unable to understand why he hadn't wanted to leave with her, what made him so determined to carry on working until the very last day. She felt more and more impatient and frightened, but at the same time she felt an ever-greater respect and tenderness towards her old husband. She understood that he hadn't just acted out of obstinacy or pride. She longed to see him, however fleetingly. But then, once again, she would be overwhelmed by a fear that left no room for any other feelings.

A few small cumulus clouds appeared in the sky. Dark water splashed and gurgled. Paddle wheels struggled noisily against the current. There was anxiety everywhere. It was, of course, all the fault of her daughter-in-law. Probably, she had told her to go to the wrong landing stage and the steamer with the children was already well on its way to Kamyshin.

Not until around midday did Volodya leap out in excitement from behind the stacks of baggage and shout, 'They're here, Grandma! They're here! Máma's here too!'

Varvara hurriedly picked up her bags and followed her grandson. There they all were: along with the children, the orphanage staff were walking down the steep cobbled slope to the river. The children were walking in pairs, the eldest in front. Some wore red ties and all had knapsacks and bundles over their shoulders. The adults were shouting and waving their arms about, and the dozens of small hurrying feet were clopping along like hooves.

'Which way?' Varvara asked agitatedly. 'Hey, Volodya, where are you? Come here – or we'll get left behind!'

Varvara was afraid that Tokareva – an imposing woman with a large bust and an angry face – might, at the last moment, refuse to take her on board. And so she kept rehearsing what she would say: 'Yes, yes, I'll do all I can to help the children. I can darn and sew, I can do whatever needs doing.'

As it neared the shore, their launch was caught by a current. As if mocking Varvara for her impatience, it overshot the pier. The helmsman switched the engine on again, and the launch made its way slowly back upstream. The same thing happened a second time, and a third time. Then the elderly captain, a short man with a wrinkled face and a faded forage cap, seemed to lose his temper. After he had yelled and cursed, with the help of a brass megaphone, at the sailors, the helmsman and even the launch itself, everything all of a sudden went smoothly. 'Nothing like a few good curses,' Varvara said to herself. 'You shouldn't have held back for so long!'

A ladder with rope rungs was put in place. Two sailors and a policeman with a rifle began to let the passengers on board. There was the sound of children's boots knocking against the deck, and the rustle of canvas shoes.

'Oi! Granny!' shouted the policeman. But Tokareva called out from the deck, 'It's all right. She's one of us!'

There was a comfortable-looking spot at the bow, near some crates, but Varvara was afraid the launch might hit a mine. Anyone near the bow would be blown into the air just like that. And so she chose a place at the stern. There was oil everywhere, and the deck was littered with chains and boards, but she could see a small dinghy, and a lifebelt hanging close by.

'Grandma,' said Volodya. 'Why don't I stay behind with Grandad?'

'I'll tie you up like a goat,' she replied, hitching up her skirt to try and keep it out of the oil. 'Or maybe you can go and look at the engine. We'll be off in a moment.'

But the launch took its time.

A truck was supposed to be bringing the linen, the tinned food, the plates and dishes and the children who were too ill to walk, but it was badly delayed, not arriving until after three o'clock. The driver made out that this was because of damage to the suspension, but he had, in fact, been driving with broken springs for the whole of the previous week. His day had begun with a little job he had agreed to do 'on the side'; in exchange for some light tobacco, he had delivered a sack of barley from the market to someone's home. Then he'd needed more petrol. He and one of his mates at the garage had chatted about the military situation for a few minutes – or maybe three quarters of an hour. Then they'd had a little to drink. This had put the driver in a good mood and he'd bought some tomatoes and some dried fish. Only then had he gone to the children's home and collected the two boys from the sickbay and all the boxes and trunks. While he was helping to load the launch, the driver picked up a patterned towel that fell out of a bag and tucked it under his seat. He then said goodbye to the director and wished her a good journey.

Last of all, he waved to his friend Klava Sokolova, who was standing on one side of the launch. He had spent the night with her several times and it was she who had persuaded him to take the boxes and trunks to the landing stage. 'Write, Klava!' he called out, looking at her large breasts, which were resting on the rail. 'I'll come and see you in Saratov.'

Klava laughed, showing her white teeth.

Without waiting for the launch to cast off, he started his engine and drove away. The truck stalled as he was climbing the slope and he had to tinker with the carburettor for a few minutes before he could get started again.

As he continued up the slope, he could hear the engine struggling.

Then he heard the howl of a falling bomb. He pressed his head to the steering wheel, sensed with all his body the end of life, thought with awful anguish, 'Fuck that' – and ceased to exist.

34

———◆———

Everyone and everything were now on board; agitation and bustle on the quayside had yielded to agitation and bustle on the deck. In their excitement the children didn't want to leave the deck for even a second, and only a few girls and the very youngest children went down to their cabins.

Marusya was to accompany the children as far as Kamyshin, where she needed to speak to people from the education section and the Party committee.

She sat down for a while in the cabin with the two boys from the sickbay – Slava Berozkin and the obstinately silent Ukrainian – and fanned her face with her handkerchief.

'A few more minutes and we'll be on our way!' she said to Tokareva, who had come in just after her. She was proud that it was thanks to her that the children had been allocated this launch. 'Let's just hope we get to Kamyshin without any hitches.'

'I'd never have managed without you,' said Tokareva. 'This heat's really killing me. But maybe it won't be so bad once we're out on the water.'

'I've just realized,' Marusya said thoughtfully, 'that my whole family could have come too. What a shame! They could have come with us to Kamyshin, boarded the steamer there and gone all the way to Kazan.'

'Come up on deck with me,' said Tokareva. 'The captain promised we'd leave on the dot of four. I want to take one last look at Stalingrad!'

Once the two women were out of the way, Slava Berozkin reached out to touch his silent companion's shoulder and said, 'Look!'

But the silent Ukrainian did not turn his shaven, knobbly head towards the rectangular porthole beneath which the river was splashing by.

Just outside the porthole there had been a tall, wet post, covered with green mould. This first post was now receding, and another was drawing nearer. The pier's stout decking came into view, then the feet of people standing close to the railing, then the railing itself, then a strong brown arm with blue veins and an anchor tattooed in blue, then the tar-encrusted sides of a barge – and then a cliff and the steep streets climbing up into the city. A minute later, the whole city – dust-covered trees, the stone and board walls of buildings of every size – began to move slowly down the porthole. In the top right corner there appeared a crumbling clayey slope, yellow-green petrol tanks, a railway line and some red coaches, and huge, smoke-veiled factory buildings. Waves splashed noisily and chaotically against the hull, and the entire boat began to creak and tremble, shaken by the engine's vibrations.

This was Slava's first journey by boat; he desperately wanted to talk and ask questions. He wanted to know how many knots the launch was making; he imagined huge knots, each the size of a cat's head, on a thick rope stretching the entire length of the river. He wanted to discuss whether or not the launch had a keel and could withstand a storm at sea. Did they have enough lifeboats and lifebelts? Did they have cannons and machine guns? What if they met a German submarine? He could take aim at the fascists himself, but he didn't know for sure whether submarines sailed up rivers or whether they just kept to the sea.

And there were other things on his mind, concerns far from childish: he had kept hoping that his mother and sister would be able to come with him, that there'd be room on the boat for them too. He had been meaning to talk about this to Tokareva and the woman from the education section: little Luba wouldn't take up any more space – she could sleep on his bed. He could then sleep on the floor, with her little shoes as a pillow. As for Máma – she could help with the laundry and cooking. She was a good cook and she worked quickly. Pápa had always been surprised when he came home after some regimental exercise: he'd barely had time to clean his boots, have a wash and change his tunic – and there was dinner, already on the table. And then his mother was very, very honest; she wouldn't take even a teaspoon of sugar or the smallest pat of butter for herself – everything would go to the children. He had already rehearsed all the arguments he could use. And he would help his mother to peel potatoes and turn the meat grinder ... He remembered how, during the night, he had dreamed that everything had turned out fine: Luba was asleep on his bed and he was lying on the floor. Máma came in. He felt the warmth of her hands and he said to her, 'Don't cry, Pápa's alive, he'll be back soon.' But even in the dream he knew this was not true. Pápa was lying in the middle of a field, his arms stretched out beside him ... A moment later his mother had white hair, and she was living with Luba in Siberia, and then he himself was there in the hut with her, stamping his heavy, frozen boots and saying, 'We've routed the Germans – so here I am now and I'll never leave you again!' He opened his knapsack, took out some biscuits, some fatback and some jars of jam. Then he felled a pine with a few blows of the axe and quickly chopped a pile of logs for the fire. Soon the hut was warm and full of light (he had brought electricity with him too). There was a large tub full of water and he was roasting a wild goose in the stove. He'd shot it himself, on the banks of the Yenisey. 'Máma, darling Máma,' he said, 'I'm not going to marry, I'm going to stay with you all my life.' And he stroked her white hair and wrapped his greatcoat around her legs.

Meanwhile waves were knocking with bony fingers against the thin planks of the hull. The launch creaked and trembled. Grey water flowed past the porthole; it looked wrinkled, as if frowning. He was alone. How would his mother find him now? Where was his father? Where was the end of this turbid river? His hands were gripping the frame of the porthole so fiercely that his nails had turned white. He looked out of the corner of his eye at Serpokryl: had his silent neighbour realized that he was crying? But Serpokryl seemed to be crying too; his shoulders were trembling and he'd turned his head to the wall.

'Why are you crying?' Slava asked, sniffing loudly.

'They k-k-illed P-Pápa.'

'And your máma?' asked Slava in astonishment. He had never before heard Serpokryl's voice.

'They k-k-killed Máma too.'

'Do you have a sister?'

'No.'

'Why are you crying then?' asked Slava – although he well understood that Serpokryl had more than enough to cry about.

'I'm sca-a-ar-red,' Serpokryl said into his pillow.

'What of?'

'Everything.'

'Don't be scared,' said Slava, his heart suddenly filling with love. 'Don't be scared. You and I are together now. I won't ever leave you.'

Quickly tucking his shoelaces inside his shoes, he went to the door. As he hurried out, he said, 'I'll tell Klava to give you your rations. We're getting bread, two sweets and fifty grams of real butter.'

A few minutes later he came back and said, 'Here. This is for you.' And he took from his pocket a small red wallet. In it lay a piece of paper with his pre-war address, in large capital letters.

537

Up on the deck, some of the children were looking at the city and the port, and two boys – Golikov from Oryol and Gizatulin the Tatar – were fishing for pike. They'd prepared a line in advance, making a spoonbait out of a piece of old tin and a safety pin. Dark-haired Zinyuk, who loved engines of every kind, had managed to get into the engine room and was admiring the boat's diesel engine.

Several children were standing behind a snub-nosed boy with ginger hair who was sketching the Stalingrad shoreline in his exercise book. Some of the youngest girls were holding hands and singing. The look on their faces was stern and severe, and they were opening their mouths very wide:

> A glitter of steel and a thunder of guns,
> As tank after tank grinds its way to the west.

The girls' singing was ineffably touching. Their birdlike voices were thin and trembling, out of keeping with the solemn words. And all around them the swiftly flowing Volga sparkled and splashed in the sun.

'My darlings, my darlings,' said Marusya. She had been watching the girls and she felt a deep tenderness towards them, but her words were also addressed to all the other children from the home, to her daughter, to her mother and husband, to old Varvara Andreyeva, who was sitting in the stern and knitting a stocking, to everyone on the shore, and to the buildings, trees and streets of the city where she had been born and brought up.

But Marusya did not want to give free rein to her feelings. Even though it felt awkward, she forced herself to say to Tokareva, 'So you've still got Sokolova with you, have you? See the way she's carrying on with that sailor? Laughing and joking with him in front of the children. Neighing like a horse. And she's clearly a bad influence on Natalya Andreyeva.'

Then Marusya heard shouting back on the shore. She also heard a low, monotonous hum, gradually breaking through the noise of the boat's engine and the splash of the water. It was as if a black net had been thrown across the river.

She saw the crowd on the quayside rush towards the landing stage. She heard a piercing shriek. A cloud of dust enveloped the shore and began to creep slowly towards the water. Then the crowd flowed back from the landing stage, dispersing along the railway line and the slopes up to the city.

Noiselessly, as in a dream, a murky-green column with a curly white head rose high out of the water and then collapsed, sending spray all over the launch. Then more tapering columns appeared, ahead, behind and all around the launch, rising high into the air and collapsing in clouds of spray and foam.

German high-explosive bombs were exploding in the water all around them.

Everyone looked in silence at the water, at the shore, and at the sky, now black and humming. Then came a loud cry, 'Máma!'

The sound of orphaned children crying out for their lost, murdered and disappeared mothers was unbearable. Tokareva seized Marusya by the hand and asked, 'What can we do?'

She imagined that the severe senior inspector – always energetic and resolute, always so intolerant of human weakness – could help her to save the children.

The desperate captain kept changing direction, first heading back, then turning towards the far shore. Then the engine went dead. Turning sideways to the current, the launch began to drift lazily and sleepily back to the port. The captain flung his cap down on the deck in fury.

Marusya could see everything, but she was somehow unable to hear sounds, as if she had been struck deaf. She saw the women from the children's home, the children's faces, the captain's shiny bald head, the open mouths of some shouting sailors, the columns of water, boats moving every which way, but everything was happening in an awful silence. And she couldn't bring herself to look up – it was as if an iron hand lay on the back of her head.

Forgotten for thirty years, a picture had emerged from the depths of her memory: she was a little girl, crossing the Volga with her mother. The ferry had run aground and the passengers were being taken to the shore in a dinghy. She was very small and wearing a large straw hat. A sailor took her to the side of the launch, lifted her up and said very gently, 'Don't be afraid, don't be afraid. There she is, there's your máma.' And then it was not her but Vera whom the kind sailor was lifting over the side of the boat, and she forgot about herself and thought instead about what would become of her daughter. As for her husband, she had always thought he needed her protection, but now she saw him as strong and decisive. Oh, if only he were with her now! But no, no, she was glad that Vera and Stepan, and her mother and sisters were not with her. Whatever was fated, was fated. But if only she could glimpse them one last time, just for a moment.

Then she was standing beside Klava, at the stern. Klava was helping the children into a dinghy. She was shouting at everyone – at Tokareva, at Varvara, at the sailors and even at Marusya. Sensing her strength, the children were clinging to her.

'What do you think you're doing?' Klava was shouting. 'The sick ones first! That's right, the little mute one! Yes, Berozkin, here! And now the little girl!'

She was cursing and swearing. Her eyes shone. She seemed confident and inspired, as if intoxicated by her lack of fear. Many, many eyes were looking at her with pleading trust; amid the broad Volga and the howl of bombs she was a pillar of strength. 'A real seahorse!' said an amazed sailor.

'Throw them that basket!' she shouted at Tokareva. 'There are blankets in it. Don't just stand there, you great lump!'

She helped Marusya into the dinghy. 'No need to be frightened now!' she called out to the children. 'You've got the inspector with you!'

Marusya was now only just above the water; she could sense its breath, its silent depths. The children had gone quiet, gripping the dinghy's sides as they peered into the turbid water. Suddenly Marusya felt more hopeful.

She wanted to kiss the hull – it was salvation. She could see everything clearly now, as if in a vision: the dinghy would take them to the far shore; she would hide the children in the willows there, wait till the air raid was over and then return to Stalingrad in the same dinghy.

Sitting on the floor of the dinghy were the two little boys. Slava Berozkin was hugging the mute Ukrainian. For some reason Slava was barefoot. He was repeating, 'Don't be afraid, don't be afraid, I won't leave you.'

Little Volodya Andreyev was wanting to jump straight down off the launch. His mother Natalya was having to hold him back. 'What are you doing, you little horror?'

'Quick, Natalya. Into the dinghy!' said Klava. 'With your boy!'

Natalya looked at her mother-in-law's paper-white face. Her hands looked stiff and numb; she was still clutching her knitting.

'You take my place,' said Natalya. 'You be a mother to him.' In reply Varvara put her arms around her daughter-in-law and embraced her almost convulsively.

'Natalya!' she said in a strangled voice, putting so much love, so much tenderness and repentance into the three syllables that Natalya was dumbstruck. The word seemed to have come not from Varvara's lips but from her heart, like a jet of blood.

But the sailor did not allow Varvara and Volodya into the dinghy: there was no more room.

'Cast off now!' shouted the sailors. 'Row across to the meadows, to Krasnaya Sloboda!'

Listing to one side, the dinghy set off diagonally across the river. The launch drifted slowly back towards the terrifying Stalingrad waterfront.

All of a sudden the engine came back to life, to the accompaniment of joyful shouts. The captain picked up his cap, gave it a good shake, put it on his head and, with trembling fingers, began to roll a cigarette. 'One drag!' he muttered. 'Just one good drag!'

There was a whistle of iron over the Volga. A thick bubbly column of greenish water leapt up just in front of the dinghy's bow, then crashed down on top of it. A moment later, in the middle of the river, amid foaming white water, the dinghy's tarred black bottom was shining gently in the sun, clearly visible to everyone on the launch.

35

Alexandra Vladimirovna finished her letter to Seryozha, the last she would be writing before her departure. She blotted the page, read through it again, took off her glasses and carefully wiped them with a handkerchief. Then she heard screams out on the street.

She went out onto the balcony and saw a black, droning cloud of planes approaching the city.

She hurried back inside and went straight to the bathroom. She could hear splashing and the contented grunts of Sofya Osipovna, who had returned only half an hour earlier from a long stint in the hospital. She knocked on the door and, articulating each syllable, said, 'Sofya, get dressed at once! An air raid – a huge air raid!'

'Are you sure?' replied Sofya.

'Quick! I'm not a panic-monger.'

With more noisy splashing, Sofya got out of the bath, muttering, 'More like a hippopotamus getting out of its pool.' After a loud sigh, she went on, 'And there I was, hoping to sleep till tomorrow. I've been up for the last forty-eight hours!'

Sofya was unable to make out what Alexandra said in reply. The first bombs were already exploding. She flung open the door and shouted, 'You run downstairs. I'll follow. But mind you leave me the keys!'

It was no longer a matter of individual explosions; all space was now filled by a single dense, protracted sound. When Sofya entered the living room a few minutes later, she found shards of glass and chunks of fallen plaster all over the floor. The lamp had been knocked off the table and was swinging from its flex like a pendulum.

Alexandra Vladimirovna was standing by the open door in her winter coat and a beret, looking long and intently at the tables and bookshelves, at Zhenya's paintings on the walls and at the empty beds of her daughters and grandson. As Sofya threw on her greatcoat, she glimpsed her friend's sad, pale face. It had not been easy for Alexandra, on her own, to create a home for her children – and she was leaving it for ever. There she stood, now an old woman, but still endowed with the same calm strength as on previous occasions when she had parted with everything she loved and to which she was accustomed: as a young student, leaving her wealthy father's fine home; setting off on long journeys to Siberia and to the River Kara; and on the November night when she crossed the Bessarabian frontier.

'Quick!' Sofya shouted. 'You shouldn't have waited!'

Alexandra turned towards Sofya and said, with a sudden smile, 'Have you got some tobacco?' And then, with a kind of despairing bravado, 'Oh, all right, let's go!'

A sharp, powerful blow shook the ground below, and the house gasped and trembled, as if in its death throes. More plaster scattered onto the floor.

They left the apartment. Closing the door behind her, Alexandra said, 'I thought these were just rooms, just an apartment – but I was wrong. Farewell, my home!'

Sofya stopped on the landing. 'Give me the key. I must get Marusya's suitcase and Zhenya's shoes and dresses.'

'No!' said Alexandra. 'They're only things.'

They set off down the empty staircase. Their steps were slow and shuffling. Sofya had to support Alexandra with one arm, while holding onto the rail with her other hand.

They left the building, then stopped in shock. The two-storey house opposite had been destroyed: part of the front wall had collapsed into the middle of the street, while the roof now lay in the front garden, across the fence and the trees. The ceiling beams had fallen into the rooms below, and the doors and windows had been blown clean out of their frames. All over the street were piles of stone and broken brick. The air was cloudy, from a mixture of white dust and yellow, acrid smoke.

'Lie down on the ground!' yelled a desperate male voice. 'It's not over yet!' Then came several more explosions. But the two women continued quietly on their way, stepping slowly and cautiously between the stones, dry flakes of mortar creaking beneath their feet.

*

The bomb shelter was crowded and there were heaps of bundles and suitcases all over the floor. There were only a few benches, and most people were either sitting on the floor or still on their feet, packed close together. The electricity had gone out, and the flames of the candles and oil lamps seemed wan and tired. Every least pause in the bombing brought more breathless tenants, rushing down into the cellar in the hope of salvation.

The atmosphere in the shelter was grim. It was one of those awful times when a crowd sees its vast size only as a danger, not as a strength, when everyone in the crowd senses how everyone around them feels as helpless as they themselves and this makes their own sense of helplessness seem all the more terrible. People know the same fear during a shipwreck, when non-swimmers may endanger the lives of swimmers, and soldiers feel the same when they are encircled, when they have been driven into a forest and have thrown down their arms. The words 'Every man for himself!' then sound like the height of wisdom.

Those who lived in the building above were whispering agitatedly to one another, looking angrily at the outsiders.

A dark-eyed woman in a grey astrakhan coat wiped a handkerchief over her temples and said, 'There were such crowds at the entrance my husband couldn't get through. I kept shouting, "Let him in – his life is important to our country!" And there were bombs falling all the time. Another moment – and it could have been the end of him.'

The woman's husband, rubbing his hands as if he'd just come in out of the cold, said, 'And if there's a fire, this will be a real Khodynka.[229] None of us will get out alive. We really must keep the entrance clear!'

Then Meshcheryakov, the Shaposhnikovs' neighbour, said in a booming voice, 'We need to instil order. This isn't a shelter for the whole street – it's for the commanders and scientific workers who live up above. Where's the house manager? Vasily Ivanovich!'

The outsiders, some of whom had only just rushed in, looked timidly at the rightful masters of the shelter and began to pick up their belongings, trying to make themselves less obtrusive.

An elderly man in a military tunic said, 'It's true – we need to consolidate.'

There was a brief silence. The air seemed more stifling than ever, the smoking candle and lamp wicks still more dismal.

'Listen,' Sofya began in her deep voice. 'This is a catastrophe – it's no time for *ours* and *yours*. Bomb shelters are for everyone. Entry isn't by ration cards.'

Alexandra Vladimirovna was looking furiously at Meshcheryakov. This was the man who only a month ago had accused her of being spineless, of showing excessive concern over matters of workplace safety.

'Comrade,' she said, 'my daughters will also have taken refuge in the first shelter they could find. Do you want them to be thrown out too?'

'Citizen Shaposhnikova,' Meshcheryakov retorted, 'this is no time for demagogy.'

This was not the way Meshcheryakov usually spoke to her. If he passed her on the stairs, he liked to take off his hat to her with extravagant politeness and say in broken Polish, 'I kiss your dear hand, Alexandra Vladimirovna!'

'If I were her,' said the house manager's wife, 'I'd keep my mouth shut. She's sent her daughters across the Volga, and she's got an illegal tenant. And now there's no room for the men and women who first built this shelter. Yes, she should keep her mouth shut! But we've all of us come across her sort. They wear the right uniform, but you don't see much of them at the front.'

'Whose are these things here? Who does this bundle belong to?' asked Meshcheryakov. 'Throw all this stuff outside!'

Alexandra leapt to her feet and said, in a voice that was quiet but full of rage, 'Cut it out! Or you'll be thrown out yourself. I'll call soldiers.'

A young woman with a little boy in her arms, her eyes shining in the half-dark, shouted, 'I'll tear your eyes out, you rat – then you'll know who this bundle belongs to! We have Soviet laws now. And they don't allow you to injure children!'

'You're waiting for Hitler, you swine,' shouted another woman. 'But you're waiting in vain!'

'Máma, Máma!' cried a weeping girl. 'Don't go away – we'll be buried alive like Grandad!'

Then the whole cellar seemed to brighten. As if with light, it filled with voices, and for a while these voices even drowned out the noise of the bombs.

'The fat brute – anyone would think he's a German. He thinks Hitler's here already. But we're Soviet citizens. We're all equal. He's the one who should be thrown out to die – not our children!'

Alexandra Vladimirovna reached out to the young woman with the little boy and gently tugged at her sleeve. 'It's all right. Please don't worry. And here's somewhere you can sit down.'

Meshcheryakov stepped back a little. 'Comrades, you didn't quite understand me. I wasn't meaning to throw anyone out. I just wanted to clear a passageway. For the common good.'

Afraid he was about to be lynched and trying to make himself inconspicuous, he sat down on a suitcase. The house plumber, who was standing nearby, said crossly, 'What the hell d'you think you're doing? That there suitcase is plywood. With that fat arse of yours you'll go straight through it.'

Meshcheryakov looked in astonishment at the man who only two days before had been working in his apartment, grateful to be given a tip after mending a bathroom tap.

'Maximov, you should address me a little more—'

'Get off that case, I said!'

Meshcheryakov got to his feet. He realized that the world had changed. People no longer saw one another as they had the day before.

'What are you doing?' Alexandra said to the young woman sitting beside her. 'You're squeezing the child to death. He can hardly breathe. Put him down for a while!'

The woman shook her head. 'I'm hugging him tight so we get killed together. His legs are withered, he can't walk. If I die, it'll be the end of him. His father's dead already – we've had a letter from the front.' She bent her head towards her son and kissed him repeatedly. She was still far from calm, but her eyes were now full of tenderness.

When the bombing grew louder, everyone fell silent and the old women began making the sign of the cross and calling in a whisper on God.

But when the bombing quietened, people started talking again and there were even eruptions of true Russian laughter, the sound of people able to burst into joyful, spontaneous laughter even at the bitterest times.

'Look at old Makeyeva,' a woman with a broad face was saying. 'Before the war, all she ever talked about was how she wanted to die. Again and again, "I'm eighty years old now – why should I keep on living? The sooner I go, the better." But at the sound of the first bombs, there she is in the shelter. Yes, she left me standing!'

'It was dreadful,' said her neighbour. 'My legs turned to jelly. I wanted to run, but I couldn't. And then I was suddenly running as fast as I could, holding a plywood board over my head. A minute before, I'd been chopping spring onions on it. Next thing, I was hoping it would protect me from bombs.'

'I've lost everything,' said the woman with the broad face. 'All my belongings. And I'd just re-upholstered the sofa. I'd covered it with cretonne. And then … all in a few seconds … I was lucky to get out alive.'

'All right. That's enough of you and your sofa – people are burning to death.'

No one left the cellar and it was a while since anyone new had appeared. Nevertheless, they all seemed to find out in no time at all about everything that was going on in the world, both on the earth and up in the sky: which buildings were on fire, where there'd been a direct hit on a bomb shelter, where Soviet flak had brought down a German plane, which point of the compass the last wave of bombers had appeared from.

A soldier standing at the top of the stairs was shouting, 'Machine-gun fire. From around the Tractor Factory!'

'Sure it's not ack-ack fire?' asked a second soldier.

'No, it's ground combat all right.' The first soldier listened for a moment, then added, 'Yes, mortars – and artillery too. No doubt about it.'

Then came more bombers – followed by another wave of explosions.

'Dear God,' said the woman in the astrakhan coat, 'please just bring all this to an end.'

'Let's go,' the first soldier said to his comrade. 'Or we'll be trapped here like mice.'

Then Sofya Osipovna leaned over towards Alexandra Vladimirovna, kissed her on the cheek, got to her feet, threw her greatcoat over her shoulders and said, 'I'll be on my way too. Maybe I can get to my hospital. I'll just roll myself a cigarette.'

'Yes, my dearest,' said Alexandra, 'you go to your hospital.' Reaching beneath her coat, she quickly unfastened her enamel brooch and pinned it to Sofya's tunic. 'You take care of these violets now,' she said gently. 'Do you remember? Viktor's mother gave this to me the spring I got married. When we were both staying with her in Paris. You were still just a girl. Two enamel violets – I took them to Siberia with me.'

In the dark cellar, this memory of a distant spring, of the two women's youth, seemed painfully sad.

They embraced in silence and kissed. From the way they looked each other in the eye, it was clear to everyone that they were close friends and that they were parting for a long time, maybe forever.

Sofya Osipovna began to walk towards the exit. The house manager's wife said, 'She's running away. The Jews are all running away. They know they won't last long under the Germans. Only I don't understand what makes a Russian woman give her her cross.'

'It wasn't a cross,' said a woman standing beside her. 'It's a brooch.'

'All right, all right,' said the house manager's wife. 'But whatever you choose to call it, it won't be any help to her now – not with a nose like that.'

Craning her neck, Alexandra Vladimirovna watched Sofya Osipovna's broad shoulders disappear into the gloom. She knew, with startling clarity, that she would never see her again.

36

Zhenya was down by the river when the first bombs fell. The ground shook, and she thought for a moment that Kholzunov the pilot, gazing up into the sky with his bronze eyes, had trembled and stepped down from his granite pedestal.[230] There was a second thunderbolt, this time unleashed by the earth; the whole world reeled, and the large corner building, which housed a haberdashery she often visited, collapsed slowly onto the pavement, exhaling clouds of chalky dust. Something struck her in the chest – warm, dense, compacted air. People on the quayside were running about and shouting. Two soldiers flung themselves down on a flower bed. One yelled, 'Lie down, you idiot woman – or you'll get yourself killed!'

Mothers were snatching up babies from prams and running, some towards the river, others away from the river. Zhenya, though, felt strangely calm. She could see everything around her very clearly: the collapsing buildings, the black and yellow smoke, the short, geometrically straight flames from the explosions. She could hear the triumphant howl of bombs tearing towards the earth; she could see people rushing along the quays, crowding onto the boats and ferries.

But it was as if her eyes and her heart lay underwater, as if she were watching the furious, raging world from the bed of a deep, quiet pond.

A young lad with a knapsack on his shoulder ran across the street in front of her, then fell. His green peaked cap flew towards the gate he'd been trying to reach. Zhenya glimpsed him – and immediately forgot him.

A mad woman, wearing only an unfastened bathrobe, was standing in the middle of a smoke-filled street, powdering her nose and cheeks with a coquettish smile.

A bald, stout man, with no jacket and with his braces hanging loose, was holding up a bunch of thirty-rouble notes and waving them in the air. He was offering the money to God and cursing him in the foulest of language; he too was out of his mind.

She saw a ragged young man running up the street from the port with a yellow suitcase: his movements were supple and catlike, as if he had paws rather than feet. She knew at once that he had stolen the suit-case. Through the smashed windows of a ground-floor room she heard the sounds of a gramophone playing a foxtrot and she saw people with glasses in their hands, singing, shouting and stamping. She saw injured men and women being lifted out of a window and she saw someone quickly pulling a pair of boots off a man who had been killed.

Later, as she tried to recall all this, she realized that she had lost all sense of time; it was during the third day of the bombing that she had seen the young man with the knapsack, not during the first hours.

She was looking intently around her, trying to take everything in. It was as if someone had spoken a word that had transported her to some past century, to a time of sombre and majestic upheavals. She saw her-self as a figure on the canvas of Briullov's *Last Day of Pompeii*, amid collapsed walls and columns, beneath a black sky slashed by forks of lightning. She thought of Pushkin's *A Feast in Time of Plague*, of the circles of Dante's hell and of the Last Judgement. She was certain that none of this was really happening. When she got home, she would recount her strange visions.

Everyone who saw Zhenya during these hours thought that she had lost her mind: how could this tall young woman be walking along so slowly and deliberately, with such a calm look in her eyes?

It is not uncommon for people in a state of deep shock, who have just heard terrible news, to go on polishing their boots with an air of great concentration, to quietly finish their bowl of cabbage soup, to calmly complete the line they are writing or the patch they are darning.

What brought Zhenya back, what allowed her to sense the horror of what was happening around her, was not the flames of burning houses or the dust and smoke swirling above them. Nor was it the blows struck by the crazed hammer now taking swing after swing at stone, iron and human beings. What brought Zhenya back was the sight of an old, poorly dressed woman lying in the middle of the boulevard, her hair matted with blood. Kneeling beside her was a chubby-faced man in a smart grey raincoat. Slipping his arms beneath the old woman and trying to lift her up, he was repeating, 'Máma, Máma, what's hap-pened? Máma, what's the matter with you? Máma, Máma, say some-thing to me!'

The old woman reached out and gently stroked the man on the cheek. As if her wrinkled hand were the only thing in the world, Zhenya at once saw everything it expressed: the mother's gentleness; her tears; her gratitude for her son's love; the plea of a being now helpless as a baby; her forgiveness of her son's failings; her desire to comfort her son, who was young and strong yet unable to help her; her need to say goodbye to life, along with the desire to keep on breathing and seeing the light of day.

Zhenya stretched out her hands to the cruel, snarling sky and yelled, 'What are you doing, you bastards? What are you doing?'

Human suffering. Will it be remembered in centuries to come? The stones of huge buildings endure and the glory of generals endures, but human suffering does not. Tears and whispers, a cry of pain and despair, the last sighs and groans of the dying – all this disappears along with the smoke and dust blown across the steppe by the wind.

Only after this moment did Zhenya feel afraid that she might die. She began to run back towards her home, doubling over at every explosion, dreaming that Novikov would suddenly appear and lead her out of the fire and smoke. Knowing he would be calm and strong, she was looking for him among the people running down the street, even though she knew he was in Moscow. But the fact that she was thinking of him – of *him*, and at a time like this, meant a great deal. It was, perhaps, the declaration Novikov so wanted to hear from her.

Later, Zhenya felt surprised that she had not once thought about Krymov, even though she knew he was in Stalingrad. And she had, until that day, been thinking about him constantly; it had seemed that she would feel guilty and anxious about him for the rest of her life. Their recent non-meeting, however, had left her with a feeling of calm indifference.

She was now close to her apartment block. On all five floors the windows had been knocked out, and curtains – some white, some coloured – were blowing about in the wind; even from a distance she could make out the ones she herself had sewn – white, edged with blue silk. In one apartment she could see flowerpots – palms and fuchsias. Everywhere she had been, Zhenya felt an awful emptiness. But here, close to her home, there was something still more awful about the drone of the planes and the din of the bombs.

And Zhenya, with her artist's eye – her ability to see inner, unexpected similarities – suddenly saw the building as a huge five-storey ship emerging from a misty, smoke-filled harbour into a raging sea.

She stopped and looked around, wondering how best to make her way through the debris. Someone called out and pointed her in the right direction, and she went down into the bomb shelter. At first the darkness seemed impenetrable, and the air stifling. Then Zhenya began to make out dim oil lamps, pale faces and white pillows. She saw a water pipe sparkling with moisture. A woman down on the ground said, 'Watch where you're going – you're about to step on a child!'

When a nearby explosion shook the five heavy storeys of stone and iron above them, the cellar seemed to stir and rustle. Then it went quiet again. It was as if the hundreds of bowed, silent heads had given birth to a stifling darkness.

The explosions were quieter down in the cellar, but the slight trembling of the reinforced-concrete ceiling made them more frightening still. Ears learned to distinguish the piercing buzz of the bombers' engines, the thunder of explosions, the sharp cracks of the anti-aircraft guns. Each time they heard the howl of a bomb – ominously quiet at first but growing continually louder – they all held their breath, bowing their heads in anticipation of a blow. And during these howling seconds, each composed of hundreds of infinitely long and entirely distinct fractions of seconds, there was neither breath, nor desires, nor memories; there was no room in people's bodies for anything except the echo of this blind iron howl.

Quietly groping her way through the darkness, Zhenya found a free spot and sat down on the floor. The stone suspended over her head, the water pipes, the depth of this dungeon – everything seemed threatening, and there were moments when the cellar seemed more like a grave than a shelter, when she wanted to run back up to the surface, to escape the deaths waiting for her in the dark, to escape to a death in daylight. And she wanted to find her mother; she wanted to push people out of her way, to beat a path through the darkness; she wanted to tell everyone her name, to put an end to the loneliness she felt among people who couldn't see her, people whose faces she couldn't see and whose names she didn't know.

But the minutes, each of which could have been the last, slowly turned into hours, and unbearable tension gradually gave way to quiet anguish.

'Home, home,' a child's voice repeated monotonously. 'Máma, let's go home.'

'And so here we sit,' said a woman, 'waiting for the end, *humiliated and insulted*.'[231]

Zhenya tapped her on the shoulder and said, 'No – insulted, but not humiliated.'

'Sh! Sh! There are planes up above,' said a man's voice behind her.

'Dear God,' said Zhenya, 'it's like being in a mousetrap.'

'Put out that cigarette. People can hardly breathe as it is.'

Feeling sudden hope, Zhenya shouted, 'Máma, Máma, are you there?'

Dozens of voices replied, 'Sh! Sh! Don't shout like that!'

As if in confirmation of this absurd fear that the enemy could detect their buried voices, they heard a thin sound overhead. At first barely audible, it grew quickly louder. A harsh roar filled all space, forcing everyone to the ground. The earth let out a loud crack. The entire cellar shook from the blow of a one-ton hammer, dropped from a height of over a mile; stones showered down from the walls and ceiling, and everyone gasped in shock.

It seemed as if darkness would bury them all for ever, but at that very moment the electric light came back on, shining on the people now rushing towards the exit. The walls and the whitewashed ceiling were still in place; evidently, the bomb had exploded very close, but not directly above them. The light shone only briefly, but these few seconds of bright, clear light were enough to relieve everyone from the worst fear of all – their sense that they had been abandoned in the bottom of a dungeon. No longer were they cut off from the world; no longer were they mere grains of sand in a storm.

Zhenya caught sight of her mother. There she was, hunched, grey-haired, sitting by the cellar wall. Kissing her mother's hands, kissing her shoulders and hair, she said, 'It's Stepan, Máma! It's our Stepan Fyodorovich! He gave us light from Stalgres! Oh, I so want to tell Marusya and Vera. He gave us light at a terrible moment, at the most terrible moment of all! We won't be broken, Máma. No, our people will never be broken!'

Could Zhenya ever have imagined, as she ran down the street, that she would, that same day, feel not only terror, but also love, faith and even pride?

37

Vera was in the hospital, on the stairs between the second and third floors. Suddenly she stopped dead.

The entire building had shuddered. Windowpanes were imploding and chunks of plaster falling to the floor. Vera shrank, covering her face with her hands; she was afraid that flying shards of glass might scar her lips or her cheeks and that Viktorov would never want to kiss her again. Then came more explosions, one after another. The sounds were drawing nearer – any moment now a bomb would fall on the hospital.

A voice up above her called out, 'Smoke! Where's it coming from?'

'Fire!' several voices shouted back. 'An incendiary!'

Vera ran down the stairs. It seemed to her that the roof and the staircase were about to come crashing down and that people were shouting at her, trying to catch her, to stop her escaping.

Running down the stairs along with her were cleaning women, assistant nurses, the head of the hospital club, two young women from the pharmacy, the doctor with a moustache from admissions and dozens of wounded from different wards. Above them, on the top floor, they could hear the hospital commissar. Authoritative as always, he was giving orders.

Two of the wounded threw their crutches away and slid down the bannisters on their bellies. They appeared either to be playing some game or to have gone crazy.

Faces Vera knew well now looked completely different; they had turned white and she could hardly recognize them. She thought she must be suffering vertigo and that her vision must be distorted.

At the foot of the stairs, she stopped again. Fixed to the wall above the words 'Bomb Shelter' was an arrow, and everyone was running in the same direction, following this arrow.

A nearby explosion flung Vera against this same wall.

'If I hide in the shelter,' she thought, 'my department head's sure to send me back up again, to the top floor, maybe even onto the roof.' Instead of entering the shelter, Vera ran out onto the street. Once, before her family moved to Stalgres, she had gone to a school on this street. It was here that she had bought toffees, drunk fizzy water with syrup, fought with the boys, whispered secrets to girlfriends, imitated Auntie Zhenya's peculiar gait, or hurried along, swinging her bag, because she was afraid of being late for the first lesson.

There was broken brick everywhere, and there was no glass in the windows of her school friends' apartment blocks. In the middle of the street were a burning car and a soldier's charred body – his head on the roadway, his feet on the pavement. He looked uncomfortable and she wanted to prop up his dead head, but she ran on.

A quiet little street she knew well – her own little life, now trampled and burnt. Vera was running back to her mother and grandmother, and she knew that this was not to help them, not to save them, but to throw herself into her mother's arms, to howl, 'Máma! Why? Why? Why did you bring me into this world?' – and weep as she had never wept in all her days.

But Vera did not run back home. She stopped and stood for a moment amid the dust and smoke. There was no one beside her, no mother, no grandmother, none of her superiors. The decision she had to take was hers alone.

What made this little girl turn back towards the burning hospital? Did she hear a pitiful cry from a ward where the wounded were still waiting to be taken to the operating theatre? Was she seized by a childish rage at her own cowardice? Did she then feel an equally childish determination to overcome this cowardice? Or was it a sense of mischief, the same love of wildness that had once made her read adventure books, fight with the boys, and clamber over fences to steal from other people's gardens?

Or did she remember the discipline of the workplace, the disgrace of desertion? Or did she just act at random, without motivation? Or was it an act that, in a natural and predictable manner, subsumed into a single resultant force all the good instilled in her during her life?

Vera walked back, along the burning street of her life. It was no surprise to her to find that Titovna the bad-tempered cleaning lady and Babad the short-sighted doctor had carried a wounded soldier out on a stretcher, laid him down in the yard and returned to the burning building.

There were many others trying to rescue the wounded. Among them were the hospital commissar; Nikiforov, an orderly who had always seemed rather slow and sullen; a handsome, cheerful political instructor from the convalescent ward; and Ludmila Savvichna, a forty-five-year-old senior nurse whose attempts to remain appealing to men, largely through spending a great deal of money on powder and eau de cologne, had always amused Vera.

There was also Doctor Yukova, who was always kind and talkative; Anna Apollonovna the housekeeper, suspected of drinking hospital alcohol; and Kvasnyuk, a hospital technical assistant who had also, very recently, been admitted as a patient. He had been injured in a collision with a three-ton truck carrying watermelons but was being discharged early for selling a hospital blanket; he had spent part of the money on vodka and sent the rest to his family. There was a young assistant professor, Viktor Arkadievich, who wore a signet ring and whom the nurses saw as a cold, arrogant Moscow dandy; and many, many other doctors, orderlies and assistant nurses whom Vera had always thought rather uninteresting.

Vera understood at once that all these very different people had something in common, something that bound them together. She even felt surprised that she had not been quicker to see this.

The absence of certain other members of staff, who one might have expected to be present, did not surprise her.

As for those who were working away in the fire and smoke while bombs exploded all over Stalingrad, they were certainly well aware of Vera's faults. Once, a patient had needed her when she had just sat down for a few minutes to read a few more pages of Alexandre Dumas – and Vera had said, 'Oh, for the love of God, let me finish the chapter!' Once, after finishing her own portion, she had eaten the whole of someone else's portion of the main dish in the hospital canteen. She had several times left work early, without asking permission. She had had an affair with one of the patients. All in all, she was considered cheeky, obstinate and generally troublesome. Nevertheless, no one was surprised when Vera joined them in the burning hospital.

Wiping the sweat off her dirty face, Ludmila Savvichna, said to Vera, 'So much for the duty doctor and the hospital director – they've just vanished into thin air.'

Vera went up into the burning building. When she got to the second floor, someone shouted, 'Don't go any higher. You won't find anyone still alive up there!'

She went on, up the very same staircase down which she had run in panic only half an hour earlier. She made her way to the third floor, through hot smoke. She did this out of a desire to prove to others, to people not afraid of death, that she too was not afraid of death – and that she was quicker and more daring than any of them. But then Vera groped her way, coughing and blinking, into a room where the ceiling had collapsed and that was now full of whirling, burning smoke. When a thin man who had fallen onto the floor stared into her eyes and reached out towards her, his hands almost as pale as the white smoke, she felt such overwhelming emotion that she wondered how there could be room for it in her heart.

Two of the four men left to die in this ward were still alive. Vera remembered how the orderlies had always complained about the hopeless cases being kept so high up – carrying the corpses down three flights of stairs was no easy matter.

She understood from the way these two men looked at her that they had been suffering something still grimmer than the agony of impending death. They had thought they had been abandoned. They had been hating and cursing the human race for forgetting those who must never be betrayed and forgotten, those whose mortal wounds have left them as weak and helpless as a newborn infant.

Vera's heart filled with motherly love. She understood what her presence meant to these men.

She began to drag one of them out of the ward. The other asked, 'Will you come back?'

'Of course,' she said. And she did.

Then she had to be carried out of the building. She heard a doctor say, after a quick glance at her face, 'Poor girl. Burns on her chin, her cheek and her forehead. And I fear her right eye may be damaged. Put her on the evacuation list.'

During a brief lull in the bombing, Vera, lying in the hospital garden, saw with her undamaged eye how the old, familiar world had once again blotted out the world revealed to her in the fire. People emerging from the shelter began bustling about and giving orders, and now and then she heard a familiar sound: that of the hospital director shouting loud reprimands.

38

Whether they were on the east bank or in Stalingrad itself, everyone imagined that the giant factories must be going through some cataclysm of destruction.

It never entered anyone's head that all three of these factories – the Barricades, Red October and the Tractor Factory – might still be working as usual, continuing to repair tanks and to produce artillery pieces and heavy mortars.

Everyone operating machine tools, carrying out autogenous welding, working power hammers and presses or adjusting jammed parts of tanks brought in for repair – everyone, of course, experienced difficulties. These difficulties, however, were easier to endure than the agony of awaiting one's fate in a cellar or bomb shelter. It is easier to face danger when working. War's manual labourers – sappers, gunners, mortarmen and infantrymen – all know this. Even in peacetime they had found meaning and joy in labour; they knew it could be still more of a comfort at a time of deprivation and loss.

Andreyev's parting from his wife had been painful. He could remember her timid, bewildered expression – a child's rather than an old woman's – as she looked for the last time at the curtained windows and locked door of their empty house and at the face of the man she had lived with for forty years. Once again Andreyev saw the back of Volodya's head, and his dark neck, as Varvara set off with him towards the river port. Tears clouded Andreyev's eyes, and the dark, smoky shop floor dissolved in a mist.

Repeated explosions echoed around the steelworks. The cement floor and steel ceilings shook. The stone beds of the furnaces, full of molten steel, trembled from the roar of anti-aircraft guns. Nevertheless, the bitterness of parting and the pain of witnessing the death of a whole way of life – a pain yet more agonizing when you are old – were accompanied by an intoxicating sense of strength and freedom, akin perhaps to what some old man from the Volga might have felt nearly three hundred years earlier as he left his house and family to fight alongside Stenka Razin.[232]

557

It was a strange feeling, a kind of joy Andreyev had never known before – different from what he had felt when he was first allowed to return to work at the beginning of the war, and no less different from the hours of inexplicable happiness he had experienced from time to time in his youth.

It was as if he could see tall fragrant reeds and the pale bearded face of a man gazing through morning mist at the wild, breathtaking expanse of the Volga.

And, with all the grief, with all the strength of a master worker, he wanted to shout, 'Here I am!' – as more than one peasant and worker had shouted during the Civil War, looking down over this same river, ready to sacrifice his life to the cause.

Andreyev looked at the factory's high glass roof, now covered in soot. Seen through the glass, the pale blue summer sky looked grey and smoky, as if the sun, the sky and the whole universe were also factories, layered with their own grime and soot. He looked at his fellow work-ers; these hours might be the last they all spent together. Years of his life had gone by here and he had put his heart and soul into his work.

He looked at the furnaces. He looked at the crane sliding carefully and obediently high above people's heads. He looked at the small shop-floor office, at the apparent chaos of the huge workshop, where in reality everything was as carefully ordered as in the little house with the green roof, the home that his wife had created but now abandoned.

Would Varvara return to the house where they had lived for so many years? Would he ever see her again? Would he ever again see their son, and their grandson? Would he ever again see this shop floor?

39

As always when some catastrophe tests people to the utmost, many of the inhabitants of Stalingrad behaved in unexpected ways.

It has often been said that, during a natural disaster, people cease to act like human beings, that they become puppets, driven by some blind instinct of self-preservation. And there were indeed people in Stalingrad who pilfered what had been entrusted to them, who looted vodka shops and food depots. There was pushing and shoving, and sometimes fighting, as people tried to board ferries. There were some whose duty was to remain in Stalingrad but who chose to cross to the east bank. There were others who liked to make out they were born warriors but who on this day showed only the most pitiful weakness.

Such observations are often made in a sad whisper, as if they constitute some unpalatable but inescapable final truth. In reality, however, they are only a part of the truth.

Amid the smoke and thunder of exploding bombs, steelworkers at Red October remained by their open-hearth furnaces. The main Tractor Factory workshops – the hot shop and the assembly and repair shops – worked on without a minute's break. At Stalgres, the engineer in charge of the boiler did not leave his post, even when he was showered from head to foot with shattered brick and glass and a splinter from a heavy bomb took out half of the control lever. There were more than a few policemen, firemen, soldiers and militiamen who died trying to extinguish fires that could not be extinguished. There are many accounts of the wonderful courage of children and of the calm, clear wisdom shown by elderly workers.

At times like this, misconceptions are exposed for what they are.

The burning streets of Stalingrad were a testing ground for a true measure of man.

40

Soon after seven o'clock in the evening, a staff car drove at speed onto a German airfield near a small grove of stunted, dust-covered oaks and braked sharply beside a twin-engine plane. The plane's engines were already running; the pilot had started them when the staff car first reached the airfield. Wearing a flying suit and holding a side cap in one hand, General Richthofen, commander of the 4th Air Fleet, emerged from the car. Ignoring the greetings of the technicians and mechanics, he strode up to the plane and began to climb the ladder. He looked strong and vigorous, with a broad back and muscular thighs. Sitting in the seat usually occupied by the radio operator, he put on an aviator cap with headphones and then, like all airmen preparing for a flight, took a quick, casual look at the people he was leaving behind on the ground. He fidgeted for a moment, then settled into position on the hard low seat.

The engines howled and roared. The grey grass trembled, a huge plume of white dust shot out, like glowing steam, from beneath the plane.

The plane took off, gathered height and flew east. At an altitude of 2,000 metres, the plane was met by its escort of Fockers and Messerschmitts.

The fighter pilots would have liked to chat and joke on their radios in their usual way, but they knew that the general would hear what they said.

Half an hour later Richthofen was flying over the burning city. Lit by the setting sun, the cataclysmic scene was clearly visible 4,500 metres below him. In the fierce heat, white smoke had risen high into the sky; this bleached smoke, purified by height, had spread out in wavy forms much like white clouds. Below these white clouds rolled a heaving, seething ball of thicker, heavier smoke; it was as if some Himalayan peak were slowly dragging itself out of the earth's womb, spewing out thousands of tons of hot, dense ores of different colours – black, ash-grey and reddish-brown. From time to time a hot, bronze flame would shoot up from the depths of this vast cauldron, scattering sparks for thousands of metres.

It was a catastrophe of almost cosmic dimensions. The giant blaze had spread almost to the border of the Kazakh steppes.

There were moments when the earth itself could be seen, with small black mosquitoes above it, but dense smoke instantly covered everything over.

The Volga and the surrounding steppe looked grey and wintry, blanketed by a sombre fog.

The pilot felt suddenly anxious; through his earphones he could hear Richthofen almost gasping for breath. Then he heard him say, 'Mars ... this must be visible from Mars. It's the work of Be-el-ze-bub.'

In his numbed, slave's heart the Nazi general could sense the power of the man who had elevated him to these terrible heights, who had entrusted to him the torch with which German planes, on this last border between Europe and Asia, had kindled a blaze that would enable German tanks and infantry to advance towards the Volga and the giant Stalingrad factories.

These minutes and hours seemed the greatest triumph of totalitarianism's most merciless idea – that of pitting TNT and aircraft engines against women and children. To the fascist pilots defying the Soviet flak and soaring over this cauldron of smoke and flame, these hours appeared to signal the fulfilment of Hitler's promise: German violence would triumph over the world. Those down below – listening to the planes' sinister hum, suffocating in smoke as they sheltered in cellars or among the incandescent ruins of their homes – appeared to have been defeated for ever.[233]

But this was not so. A great city was perishing, but this did not mean that Russia was being enslaved – still less that she was dying. Amid the smoke and ashes the Soviet people's strength, love and belief in freedom was still obstinately alive, even growing stronger – and this indestructible force was already beginning to triumph over the futile violence of those trying to enslave it.

41

By 23 August, two German panzer divisions, one division of motor infantry and several infantry regiments had crossed the Don near Vertyachy Hamlet.

These troops, now concentrated on the bridgehead, were ordered to attack Stalingrad immediately after the air raid.

The German tanks broke through the Soviet defences and advanced swiftly towards the Volga along a corridor between eight and ten kilometres wide. This breakthrough was swift and entirely successful. Bypassing defensive fortifications, the Germans advanced due east, towards a city now choking in fire and smoke, torn apart by thousands of high-explosive bombs.

The German tanks continued their advance, ignoring both Soviet supply columns and the many civilians on foot who, at the sight of the Germans, fled into the steppe or towards the cliffs above the Volga. In the afternoon, the tanks appeared on the city's northern outskirts, around Rynok and Yerzovka. Soon, they reached the Volga itself.

Thus, at 4 p.m. on 23 August 1942, the Stalingrad Front was bisected by a narrow corridor. German infantry divisions entered this corridor immediately after the tanks. The Germans were now on the west bank of the Volga, only one and a half kilometres from the Tractor Factory, at a time when most of the Soviet 62nd Army was still struggling to stand its ground on the east bank of the Don. These troops were in danger of encirclement.

Already shaken by the sight of the blazing city, people on the main road to Kamyshin suddenly glimpsed German heavy tanks. Close behind them were columns of motor infantry, half-hidden by dust.

German staff officers were following the progress of these columns intently. All relevant radiograms were decoded at once and transmitted to Colonel General Paulus.

There was tension at every link in the chain, but everything portended success. By evening it was known in Berlin that Stalingrad was a sea of fire, that German tanks had reached the Volga without meeting resistance, and that fighting had begun at the Tractor Factory. One last push – it appeared – and the Stalingrad question would be resolved.

42

On an area of wasteland and kitchen gardens a little to the north-west of the Tractor Factory, groups of Red Army mortarmen – members of an anti-tank brigade recently withdrawn from the front – were engaged in training exercises.

They could hear a low hum from the factory, reminiscent of the murmur of an autumn forest. Now and then small flames shone through the murk of the soot-covered windows. And there was a trembling pale blue light from the welding workshops.

Senior Lieutenant Sarkisyan, the commander of the heavy-mortar unit, was strolling slowly about. Clearly the man in charge, he was watching his men's movements and listening to what they said, pausing for a while, then going on further. There was a look of contentment on his swarthy, slightly bluish face. He was wearing a new gabardine tunic with a smart celluloid undercollar and – instead of the simpler cap he had worn at the front – a new artilleryman's cap with a black band. Locks of wiry black hair poked out from beneath it. Sarkisyan was stocky and extremely short. Like all short men, he did his best to look taller. He didn't smooth down his curly hair; and if conditions allowed and he was not at the front, he wore a fur hat in winter and a tall peaked cap in summer.

After hearing a slouching mortarman's casual reply to a question from his platoon commander, Sarkisyan muttered, 'A likely story!' and walked on further. There was an angry look in his dark-brown eyes.

The exercises were not going well. The men were giving careless answers to questions and calling out the wrong ranging data. They seemed especially reluctant to get down to the work of digging trenches. The moment Sarkisyan was out of sight, they started yawning, wondering whether or not they'd get a chance to sit down and have a smoke.

After many days of feverish tension, both commanders and soldiers had slipped into the languid state characteristic of men recently withdrawn from combat. No one wanted to remember the past or think about the future; no one felt like doing anything at all. But the young senior lieutenant had a fiery, southern temperament, and he had no patience with any of this. When he finally walked away from a mortar crew, he would leave them glaring at his thick neck and protruding ears. This, after all, was a Sunday and everyone else was resting. Anti-tank artillery crews, anti-tank rifles, anti-aircraft gunners, ammunition-supplies workers, HQ staff – all were free to do as they pleased. Everyone knew that the brigade commander and commissar had declared a day of rest. Sarkisyan, however, had taken his unit to the vegetable gardens, ordered them to dig trenches and to drag heavy mortars and part of their ammunition supplies to this new location, beside a deep gully. Senior Sergeant Generalov, in a good mood after a full night's sleep and a quick visit to the bathhouse followed by a Zhiguli beer, understood – simply from reading their lips – what one group of men were muttering to one another. 'All right,' he shouted good-naturedly, 'that's enough of your effing and blinding!'

Lieutenant Morozov, who had a bandaged arm, came up to Sarkisyan; he had been on duty at Brigade HQ but had just been relieved. He was walking arm in arm with the commander of the anti-aircraft battery responsible for the defence of the Tractor Factory. The two men had been fellow students at military school and had met again, unexpectedly, at the factory.

'Well, comrade Senior Lieutenant, I can tell you we really have said goodbye to the front now. There's just been a bulletin from Military District HQ. Seems we won't be staying here much longer – we're being sent to regroup somewhere north of Saratov. They gave the exact location, but it's slipped my mind.'

He laughed. Sarkisyan laughed too, and had a good stretch.

'You may even get some leave,' said Svistun, the anti-aircraft gunner. 'Especially you, comrade Lieutenant – you've got a wound that's not healing.'

'I probably will,' Morozov replied. 'I've already asked. My superiors have no objections.'

'No such luck for me,' said Svistun. 'The Tractor Factory is considered an object of national importance.' And he broke into curses.

Sarkisyan looked at Svistun's red cheeks, winked at Morozov and replied, 'What do you want with leave? You're as good as in a holiday resort already. There's the Volga nearby. You can go to the beach every day. There's plenty of watermelons.'

'I've had all the watermelons I can eat,' said Svistun. 'I'm fed up with them.'

'And as for his girls!' said Morozov. 'He's got quite a collection. Rangefinder operators, instrument technicians, you name it ... All clean and scrubbed up. All with ten years of schooling. Neat curls and pretty little white collars. When I first went in, I had to rub my eyes. No, Svistun, you don't need leave – you've got all a man can ask for right here. And you were famous for your conquests even back at military school.'

Svistun gave a little laugh and said, 'All right, enough of you and your stories!' It seemed he preferred not to brag of his successes.

Morozov turned to Sarkisyan and said quietly, 'Rest should mean rest. Now I'm off duty, why don't we all go into Stalingrad together? What's got into you, comrade Senior Lieutenant? Why all these exercises when you're safely back in the rear? Everyone's taking the day off. The lieutenant colonel and his adjutant have gone fishing. The commissar's writing letters.'

'All right,' said Sarkisyan. 'But the factory will be getting a beer delivery today – I heard from the canteen director.'

'The stout one?' asked Morozov.

'Maria Fominichna's a good woman. She always says when there's going to be beer,' said Svistun, who clearly knew the factory canteen well. 'And you should bear in mind that the cask beer's better than the bottled – and cheaper too!'

'Maria,' said Sarkisyan, his eyes gleaming. 'At eighteen hundred hours she finishes work and we'll be going out together. But till then, it's exercises – that's my decision, and I'm sticking to it.'

'Comrade Senior Lieutenant, Maria is ageing goods. She must be at least forty by now,' said Morozov reproachfully. 'You and your fatties – why don't you try something different?'

'I'd say she's a good bit over forty,' added Svistun.

It was around three o'clock in the afternoon. It was a quiet, hot Sunday and these men could hardly have imagined that in only an hour they would be first to confront the German tanks, that shots from Sarkisyan's heavy mortars and Svistun's rapid-firing, long-barrelled anti-aircraft guns would mark the beginning of a great battle.

They talked a little longer, then went their separate ways, having agreed to meet two hours later in the factory canteen. They'd have a beer and then drive into the city to watch a film. Sarkisyan could provide a car and Svistun the fuel.

'In this instance the fuel problem is not difficult to resolve,' said Morozov, who liked to sound learned.

But Sarkisyan, Morozov and Svistun never did meet again. By early evening Lieutenant Morozov was lying on the ground, half-covered in earth, his skull smashed and his chest torn open. As for Svistun, he was in battle for thirty hours on end. Some of his guns engaged with the German tanks; the others struggled, amid flames, smoke and dust, to keep off the German bombers. He lost all contact with HQ, and Lieutenant Colonel Herman, his regimental commander, thought that his guns and gun crews, lost in the black smoke, had been completely destroyed. Only slowly did he realize, from the sound of shooting, that the battery must be still active. The battle saw the death of many of the pretty young girls – the instrument technicians and rangefinder operators – whom the three lieutenants had joked about only a few hours before. Svistun himself was eventually dragged out on a tarpaulin ground sheet, with severe stomach wounds and burns to his face.

But at this hour of the afternoon – as Sarkisyan returned to quietly inspecting his mortar crews and Morozov and Svistun set off, arms around each other's shoulders, towards the factory, laughing and reminiscing about their time in military school – everything remained quiet, on the ground and in the sky.

It was the ammunition-bearers who first saw the German bombers.

'Look! Up there!' shouted one man. 'Like ants. All over the sky. Coming from the Volga, coming from everywhere!'

'And heading straight for us. That's it – we're fucked.'

'Sure they're not ours?'

'No way. Only the bloody bombs – they'll be ours soon enough!'

The factory sirens started up, but their piercing howl was drowned by the dense drone of engines now filling the sky.

The soldiers looked up, watching the black cloud. Chaotic though its movement seemed, their practised eyes quickly determined that the Germans' main blow was being directed at the city itself.

'They're turning, the bastards. Descending ... Diving ... They're diving! They've dropped their bombs.'

Then came a bleak, icy whistle – followed by deep, low explosions merging into a single powerful sound that made the earth tremble.

A young shrill voice yelled, 'Watch out – this time they're coming for *us*!'

The soldiers scattered into trenches, pits and ravines, and lay still, pressing their caps to their heads as if this might protect them from high-explosive bombs. The anti-aircraft guns opened fire.

The first bombs fell.

Wrenched back from his thoughts about beer and an evening in town, Sarkisyan looked around him. He was terrified of German bombers and air raids always made him feel lost and confused. He would look up at the sky in anguish: where were the planes heading now? Who would be their next victim? 'Not what I call war,' he would say. 'Just flying bandits.'

Ground combat was another matter. During ground combat, he felt strong, cunning and ruthless. Fighting an enemy on the ground, he no longer had that vile sense of the top of his head being naked and exposed.

'Fire positions!' he yelled, trying to silence his anxiety through fury.

The first wave of planes had dropped their bombs and departed, and the second wave had yet to appear; for now, there was only smoke, blowing swiftly towards the Volga. To the south, Sarkisyan could hear the rumble – now louder, now quieter – of anti-aircraft fire, and the sky over the city was dotted with the little white puffs left by shell-bursts. In the thin smoke from the buildings on fire below, a dark cloud of twin-engine insects was circling high over Stalingrad. Soviet fighters were attacking this furious, venomous swarm.

The mortarmen clambered out of their pits and trenches and went over to their mortars, not bothering to shake off the earth, knowing they might have to take cover again any moment. All heads were turned south towards the city, all eyes looking up at the sky. But Sarkisyan, his lips puckered and his eyes rounder than ever, kept turning to look behind him. As well as the snarling rumble in the air, he thought he could hear a harsh, iron purr he knew only too well.

'Can you hear something?' he asked Sergeant Generalov, who was frowning, though still as rosy-cheeked as ever.

Generalov shook his head and, cursing loudly, pointed up at the sky. 'They're heading this way again, straight for the factories.'

But Sarkisyan was no longer looking up at the sky, no longer listening to the concerted fire of the anti-aircraft guns defending the factory. Standing on tiptoe, he was looking as far as he could to the north, away from the city. Just beyond a broad gully leading down to the Volga, amid dusty grey bushes and stunted trees, he thought he could make out the sullen, low brow of a heavy tank.

'Take cover – they're heading this way!' Generalov shouted, pointing up at the sky.

Sarkisyan gestured impatiently. 'Run to the gully,' he said. 'I think there's something coming – on the far side. I want to know what it is.' He gave Generalov a gentle shove in the back. 'Fly! Like an eagle!'

Ordering his platoon commanders to train their mortars on the far side of the gully, he climbed up onto the moss-covered roof of an old, abandoned house. From there he could see sheds, kitchen gardens, an empty road, paths leading to the gully, the gully itself and everything beyond it. A column of tanks – he thought there must be at least thirty – was advancing along a broad yellow track towards the Tractor Factory.

They were a long way away, and Sarkisyan was unable to distinguish their colour or markings. Their armour, no doubt, was covered by thick layers of dust – and there was also the curtain of dust now being raised by their tracks and blowing about in the wind.

He could see Generalov approaching the gully, alternating between a run and a fast walk. No, there could be no real doubt … These were Soviet tanks – reinforcements coming down from Kamyshin. Only that morning the brigade commander, just arrived from Front HQ, had told Sarkisyan that the Germans had stopped at the Don and were unlikely to attempt a crossing any time soon. The Don was simply too broad …

Nevertheless, Sarkisyan did not trust these tanks.

Like everyone who has spent a long time at the front, Sarkisyan lived in a state of constant wariness. During the night he would prick up his ears at the slightest sounds – quiet footsteps or a barely perceptible hum of engines. He was used to watching intently as a truck drove through a village in a cloud of dust, to scrutinizing the contours of a solitary plane flying low over a railway, to stopping what he was doing and holding his breath as he watched a small group of men walk through a field. All this was now a part of him, a way of life that had entered his blood.

He could see dust over Lotoshinsky Gardens, where he had gone the day before to eat grapes. And from the garden near the Mokraya Mechetka rivulet – where an anti-tank battalion and several units of people's militia from the factories were positioned – he could hear frequent, if indistinct, rifle shots and a few short bursts from machine guns. The militia seemed to have opened fire. Who were they firing at?

Then Sarkisyan glimpsed intermittent flashes on the far side of the gully, among the tall grass and bushes. He heard the staccato of machine-gun fire. He caught sight of Generalov again. Flinging his hands in the air, the sergeant disappeared into the gully. A minute later, he was running back towards the mortars, bending down, swerving, falling to the ground and leaping to his feet again. Stopping for a second, he yelled, 'F-r-r-r-itzes!'

But it was already only too clear, from his every movement, that the approaching tanks were German panzers.

And Sarkisyan, small and majestic, standing erect on his moss-covered roof, saluted his stern fate. His voice both hoarse and exultant, he bellowed out a command not to be found in any military textbook: 'Open fire on the fascist fuckers!'

So ended the unit's brief period of rest in the quiet of the rear.

The Germans had at that moment been looking for a way across the gully. The sudden salvo from the mortars, along with rifle and machine-gun fire from the factory militia, brought their advance to an abrupt halt. The first line of the Soviet defences on the northern sector of the Stalingrad Front was holding.

*

Krymov was writing to his brother, lost in thought as he tried to imagine life in the Urals, which he had never visited. Everything he had ever read or heard about the region came together to form a strange, composite picture. This picture included granite mountain slopes covered in birches whose leaves were now turning; quiet lakes surrounded by age-old pines; the light-flooded workshops of giant machine-building plants; asphalted streets in Sverdlovsk; and caves where, amid dark masses of rock, semi-precious stones gleamed with all the colours of the rainbow. His brother's little house – located in this place where lakes, mountain caves, asphalt streets, and huge factory workshops existed side by side – was somewhere unusually good, quiet and calm.

A political instructor burst in, calling out, 'Comrade Commissar, the enemy!' Krymov's little room, which his orderly had tried so hard to make nice and comfortable, and his thoughts about his brother, about the Urals and its lakes and forests – everything evaporated at once, like drops of water falling onto a burning-hot iron.

Returning to the war felt as simple and natural as waking up in the morning.

A few minutes later, Krymov was out in the wasteland, where Sarkisyan's mortars were firing on the German tanks.

'Report!' he shouted grimly.

Red-faced, excited by his successes, Sarkisyan replied, 'Comrade Commissar, an enemy armoured column is approaching. I've just taken out two heavy tanks!'

It would be a good thing, he thought, to get a certificate from the brigade's adjutant to the effect that this had indeed been the work of his mortar unit. There had been an incident on the Don when Sarkisyan had knocked out an enemy self-propelled gun and it had been his neighbour, the commander of an artillery battery, who had been mentioned in despatches.

But one glance at Krymov was enough to make Sarkisyan forget such petty concerns. Never, even in the most critical moments, had he seen such a look on Krymov's face.

The Germans had reached the bank of the Volga, the outskirts of Stalingrad. They had broken through to the giant factories. There were German aircraft all over the sky. Their hum filled all space, and there was a vicious link between this menacing hum and the tanks grinding their way across the earth. Enemies in the air, enemies on the ground – and the link between them was strengthening. It was growing broader and deeper. The Germans had to be stopped. This link had to be broken. Nothing else mattered.

Krymov was in a state of supreme tension akin to inspiration. He was able to summon all his mental powers.

'Telephone cable to that house!' he ordered the deputy chief of staff. Turning to Sarkisyan, he asked, 'Your ammo supplies?'

After hearing Sarkisyan's reply, he said, 'Good. It's a long way to the ammo dump. We won't be retreating, so we must take all our ammo forward, to the fire positions.'

With a quick glance at Krymov, a soldier said, 'Well said, comrade Commissar!' Gesturing towards the Volga, he added, 'Anyway, where's there to retreat to?'

Quick glances and brief words were all that was needed. The commissar and the mortarmen understood one another immediately.

Krymov turned to the brigade commander's adjutant, who had just run up to him, and said, 'All HQ staff and admin workers to ammunition transport! There aren't enough bearers.'

Krymov smiled at another of the mortarmen and said, 'So, Sazonov, this time you look ready to stay at your post.'

'I certainly am, comrade Commissar. Back there by the Don things were different.'

'I understand,' Krymov replied.

The soldier said something else, but in the chaos of rifle shots, shell bursts and exploding bombs Krymov was unable to hear.

Krymov ordered a messenger to take a note to the commander of the anti-aircraft regiment. German panzers, he wrote, had appeared in the immediate vicinity; he was to establish communications with the anti-tank brigade and engage with these panzers immediately. But before the messenger even reached the commander, Krymov heard the sound of rapid, powerful gunfire. The anti-aircraft gunners had already opened fire on the panzers.

Dozens of men saw the commissar move from one mortar crew to another. Hundreds of eyes met Krymov's – fleetingly, slowly, excitedly, calmly, boldly.

Gun-layers glanced at him after a successful shot. Ammunition-bearers looked up at him before they'd even straightened their backs and wiped the sweat off their foreheads. Crew commanders saluted hurriedly before replying to a brisk question. Signallers held out their telephone receivers.

As they fought outside the Tractor Factory, the mortarmen felt all the tension and terror of combat. They were pleased with the speed and accuracy of their fire. They were aware both of the planes above and of the artillery now shelling their fire positions. They were troubled by their own occasional mistakes and by the shallowness of the slit trenches they had dug only a few hours earlier. They did not look ahead or think about the future: should a German shell fall nearby, there'd be time enough to drop to the ground before it exploded. But there was something new about this unexpected battle, something that distinguished it from earlier steppe battles. This was not simply the anger felt by men who had been longing for even the briefest of rests but were now being forced to fight yet again. It was more a matter of their realization that they had been driven back to the banks of the Volga. They were fighting on the border of the Kazakh steppes – and this filled them with a sense of grief and anguish.

Krymov sensed the strength of the link between everyone involved in these first few hours of the Battle of Stalingrad. The underlying intention of all his orders, of every word he spoke, was not only to establish reliable communications between the gunners and their commanders, between HQ and the various sub-units, between the brigade, the anti-aircraft regiment, the factory militia and Front HQ, but also to bring about the deeper human connections that are just as essential and without which victory is impossible. Krymov had learned a great deal during the long Soviet retreat – both from the moments of success and from the many defeats.

Very soon, at Krymov's instigation, telephone cables had been laid between Brigade HQ and the anti-aircraft-regiment HQ – and also to the factory-militia HQ and a nearby tank battalion that was still undergoing training.

Time and again the telephonist passed Krymov the receiver, and gunners, mortarmen and tank crew all heard the commissar's calm, clear voice.

'Comrade Commissar!' said Volkov, the commander of a machine-gun platoon, as he ran into Brigade HQ. 'We're almost out of cartridge ribbons. I thought we were safe in the rear. I never dreamed we'd be fighting again so soon.'

'Send some men to militia-regiment HQ. I've already spoken to the commander – he'll sort you out.'

The phone rang again. Krymov said into the receiver, 'The trenches need to be good and deep. Not temporary shelters. We must dig in – we'll be here for some time.'

The simultaneous ground and air attack had been intended to cripple Soviet communications. It had not succeeded.

*

The sight of German tanks nearing the Volga was appalling. The German tank men had been confident that their sudden appearance at river crossings and at a factory on the outskirts of the blazing city would sow confusion and panic, but in the event it was they who were taken by surprise; they had not expected to be met by such powerful and concerted fire. When, after direct hits, two tanks went up in flames, the officer in command concluded that the Soviet forces had not been caught unawares. They must have known of the German plans, guessed the route the tanks would follow to the Tractor Factory and the northern river crossings, and prepared their defence.

The officer radioed his HQ, saying he had ordered a halt. His tanks and motor infantry were preparing for a protracted exchange of fire.

It goes without saying that many important events contain an element of chance, sometimes fortunate, sometimes not. An event's true meaning, however, cannot be understood in isolation – only in relation to the spirit of the time. Chance details are of only secondary importance; they do not alter the course of history.

The time was coming when the laws of life and war would cease to transform millions of individual German actions into an invincible, crushing force. From now on, even favourable chances would dissipate like smoke, bringing the Germans no real benefit, while even the very slightest instances of bad luck, the least important of mischances, would have serious, irreversible consequences.

43

After the huge air raid, everything about the city seemed strange. Everything that had changed seemed strange, and everything that had not changed seemed strange. It was strange to see families eating out on the street, sitting on boxes and bundles beside the ruins of their homes, and it was no less strange to see an old woman doing her knitting by the open window of a still-intact room, next to a rubber plant and a sleeping long-haired Siberian cat. What had happened was unthinkable.

Piers had disappeared. Trams no longer ran and telephones were no longer ringing. Many important institutions were no longer functioning.

Cobblers and tailors had disappeared, as had outpatient clinics, pharmacies, schools, watchmakers and libraries. Radio loudspeakers on the streets had fallen silent. There was no theatre or cinema, no shops, markets, laundries, bathhouses, seltzer-water kiosks or beer halls.

The smell of burning hung in the air, and the walls of buildings that had burnt down had not yet cooled. They gave off a hot breath, like ovens.

The sound of artillery fire and the explosions of German shells drew ever closer. At night there was the sound of machine-gun fire to the north, around the Tractor Factory, and the dry crack of small-calibre mortars. It was no longer clear what was normal: a yardman sweeping the street while an orderly queue formed at a bread shop or a crazed woman with blood on her manicured fingernails, tossing aside bricks and sheets of clattering corrugated iron as she diligently dug her way down towards the body of her dead child. Everyone knew that the city's northern outskirts had been taken by German troops. More terrible surprises were expected. It seemed impossible for the present day to be like the previous day, for any day to turn out like the day before. Stability was unimaginable.

The only thing that did not change was the life of Front HQ, which only a few days earlier had seemed so provisional, so out of place in the city. Soldiers from the HQ guard battalion still rattled their mess tins as they ran to the kitchen. Signals officers still tore down the streets on motorcycles, and Emkas covered in dust and mud, with crumpled sides and star-shaped cracks on their windscreens, came to a halt in city squares, in front of traffic policemen holding red and yellow flags.

And every day saw a new city growing up amid the ruins of the old peacetime city. This new city – a city of war – was being built by sappers, signalmen, infantrymen, artillerymen and people's militia. Brick, it turned out, was the material from which one builds barricades. Streets existed not to allow the free movement of traffic but to prevent it; they were laid with mines, and trenches were dug straight across them. The right thing to put in the window of a house was not a pot of flowers but a machine gun. Gateways and inner yards were intended for artillery pieces and tank ambushes; and the little nooks and crannies between buildings were designed to be sniper nests, hiding places for grenade throwers and sub-machine-gunners.

44

During the evening of the fifth day after the air raid, Mostovskoy happened upon Sofya Osipovna, not far from his home.

In a greatcoat with a charred hem, her face now pale and thin, she looked very different from the stout, jolly woman with the loud voice whom Mostovskoy had sat next to on Alexandra Vladimirovna's birthday.

Mostovskoy did not immediately recognize her. The sharp, mocking eyes he so clearly remembered were now flitting about, glancing at him distractedly, then turning to the grey smoke still creeping about the ruins.

A woman in a colourful bathrobe, tied with a soldier's belt, and an elderly man wearing a white cloak and a battered soldier's sidecap walked past the gate, pushing a handcart full of household belongings.

The man and woman with the cart looked at Sofya and Mostovskoy. At any other time, they would have appeared extraordinary. But now it was probably the elderly Mostovskoy, with his usual calm attentiveness to everything around him, who seemed out of place.

Much has been written about the smells of meadows and forests, of autumn leaves, of young grass and fresh hay, of sea and river water, of hot dust and living bodies.

But what about the smells of fire and smoke in wartime?

Behind their apparent grim monotony lie many differences. The smoke from a burning pine forest – a light, scented mist, floating among the tall copper trunks like a pale blue veil. The damp, bitter smoke of a fire in a deciduous forest – cold and heavy, clinging to the ground. The fume-laden flames from a torched field of ripe wheat, heavy and hot, like the grief of a nation. The smell of fire racing across dry August steppe. Blazing stacks of straw ... The dense, fat, rounded smoke of burning oil ...

That evening the city was still smouldering; its breath too felt heavy and hot. The air was dry, with heat still coming off the walls of the buildings. Lazy, sated flames flickered here and there, consuming the last remnants of everything flammable. Wisps of smoke were creeping out through gaping windows or the spaces where there had once been roofs.

In the half-dark cellars red-hot piles of collapsed brick and plaster gave off a dark, uncertain glow. And the patches of sunlight on the walls, the rays of sun shining through gaps in the walls, the purple evening clouds – all seemed a part of the great fire, as if they too had been lit by man.

The tumult of smells was disturbing. Among them were the smells of hot mortar and stone, of scorched feathers, of burning paint and of burning coal extinguished by buckets of water.

A strange empty silence hung over the always noisy and talkative city, but the sky seemed somehow less distant, less separate from the earth than usual. It had drawn near to the streets and squares; it had drawn near to the city just as the evening sky draws near to open fields, to the steppe, the sea or the northern forest.

Mostovskoy was overjoyed to see Sofya Osipovna. 'You wouldn't believe it!' he said. 'The ceiling in my room is intact. There's still glass in the windows – probably the last glass in Stalingrad. Come on over!'

The door was opened by a pale old woman with eyes red from crying.

'Agrippina Petrovna, the head of my household,' said Mostovskoy.

They entered his room. Everything was clean and tidy, in contrast to the chaos elsewhere.

'First, tell me about our friends,' said Mostovskoy, motioning Sofya to the armchair. 'Marusya was killed during the first of the air raids. I heard from one of my neighbours, Zina Melnikova. But what about the rest of the family? Where's Alexandra Vladimirovna? Their building's been flattened – I've seen it myself – and no one's been able to tell me anything at all.'

'Yes, poor Marusya is dead,' said Sofya. And she went on to tell Mostovskoy that Zhenya and her mother had set off for Kazan, but that Vera had chosen to stay in Stalingrad. Vera didn't want to leave her father on his own and she had moved in with him at Stalgres. She had suffered slight burns to her neck and forehead. There had been concern about one of her eyes, but it was now completely healed.

'And that angry young man?' asked Mostovskoy. 'Seryozha, I think.'

'Would you believe it? I met him yesterday quite by chance, at the Tractor Factory. His unit was being marched somewhere – we couldn't talk long. I just managed to tell him about his family. And he told me he'd been in combat for five days on end, that he was a mortarman, and that his unit was now on its way back to resume the defence of the Tractor Factory.'

With an agonized look, Sofya went on to tell Mostovskoy how during the last few days she had attended to more than 300 wounded civilians and soldiers, dressing their wounds or carrying out operations, and that a great many of the operations had been on children.

She said that relatively few people had been wounded by shrapnel. Most of her patients had been struck by debris from collapsing buildings. Some had suffered injuries to their limbs; some to their skull or ribcage.

Her hospital had been evacuated across the Volga and was going to move to Saratov. She was staying behind for one more day. One of her tasks was to visit the factory district. Some of the hospital equipment was stored there. Now it had to be transported across the Volga, to Burkovsky Hamlet.

And she had, in fact, been on her way to call on Mostovskoy. Alexandra Vladimirovna had insisted that she promise to pass on a message. She wanted him to come and live with her family in Kazan.

'Thank you,' said Mostovskoy, 'but I'm not intending to leave.'

'I think you should,' said Sofya. 'And I can get you to Saratov on our hospital truck.'

'Comrades from the *obkom* have offered to help,' Mostovskoy replied, 'but I'm not intending to leave yet.'

'Why not?' asked Sofya. 'Why stay here when every civilian left in the city is moving heaven and earth to get across the Volga?'

Mostovskoy coughed rather crossly – and Sofya understood the likely reasons for his decision to stay behind and why he might prefer not to discuss them.

Agrippina, who had been listening, let out such a deep, loud sigh that both Mostovskoy and Sofya looked round at her. Turning to Sofya, she said pleadingly, 'Citizen, can I come too? I've got a sister in Saratov. And I'll hardly have anything with me – just a basket and one little bundle.'

Sofya thought for a moment and said, 'All right, I think we can find room for you in one of our trucks – but first thing tomorrow I have to go to the factory district.'

'Then stay here tonight. Get a proper night's sleep. You won't find anywhere better. Round here this is the only building still standing. Most people are living underground – the cellars are all packed solid.'

'That's a tempting idea,' Sofya replied. 'My one dream is to sleep. I've slept six hours in the last four days.'

'Of course!' said Mostovskoy, 'I'll make everything as comfortable as I can for you.'

'No,' put in Agrippina. 'That'll be awkward for your friend and uncomfortable for you. You must sleep in *my* room. Sleep as long as you like – and come morning we can set off together.'

'There's just one thing,' said Sofya. 'All our cars and trucks are on the east bank. We'll have to hitch a lift.'

'We'll be all right, we'll find a way,' said Agrippina, now looking much happier. 'The factories are no distance at all. What matters is to get to Saratov. And the hardest part of the journey is crossing the Volga!'

'Well, comrade Mostovskoy,' said Sofya, 'so much for your twentieth century. So much for its humanity and culture. A long way the Hague Conventions have got us! All I see is unprecedented atrocities. Certainly not much sign of the protection of civilians and humane methods of waging war ...' Sofya gestured towards the window. 'Look! What kind of faith in the future do you see in these ruins? Technology may be progressing, but what about ethics? What about morality and humanity? They're in some kind of Stone Age. Fascism is a new savagery. It's taken us back 50,000 years.'

'You're in a bad way,' said Mostovskoy. 'Get some sleep before the bombing starts up again. You need it.'

But this night too went by without Sofya being allowed to sleep. Just as it was getting dark and they heard the first German bombers in the misty, smoke-veiled sky, there was a sharp knock at the front door.

A young soldier came in and said, 'Comrade Mostovskoy, a message from comrade Krymov.' He handed Mostovskoy an envelope and then turned to Agrippina: 'Can you give me some water? I'm tired. Heaven knows how I ever managed to find this building.'

Mostovskoy read the letter and said to Sofya, 'This is difficult. I'm being called to the factory. The *obkom* secretary's there, and it's essential I see him.' Then he turned anxiously to the soldier: 'Can you take me now? Is that possible?'

'Yes, of course. But we must go straightaway, before it's completely dark. I'm not from round here. I blundered about for a whole hour trying to find you.'

'All right,' said Mostovskoy. 'And how are things at the front?'

'A bit quieter, I think. Comrade Krymov's been called to the Front Political Administration – he's leaving his brigade.' The driver took the mug of water Agrippina was holding out to him, drank it down, shook the last few drops out onto the floor and said, 'Let's go. I don't like leaving the car.'

'You know what?' said Sofya. 'I'll come with you. Otherwise, who knows how we'll find our way there tomorrow? I'll get my night's sleep when the war's over.'

'Then please take me too!' Agrippina said tearfully. 'I can't stay here all on my own. I promise I won't get in your way. And when you've done what you have to do, you can take me to the other bank. Otherwise I'll never get across.'

Mostovskoy turned to the driver. 'What's your name, comrade?'

'Semyonov.'

'Can you take all three of us, comrade Semyonov?'

'My tyres aren't too good. But we'll get there.'

They left in the gathering dusk, since Agrippina took some time to sort herself out. Agitated and out of breath, she explained to Mostovskoy where she was leaving everything, from her pots and pans to her supplies of salt, water, kerosene and potatoes. And then there were many items that had to be moved into Mostovskoy's room: her feather bed, her pillows, a bundle of linen, a pair of felt boots, her samovar.

Mostovskoy got in beside Semyonov, and the two women sat in the back. Semyonov could drive only very slowly – the streets were littered with heaps of stone. Still-smouldering fires, invisible during the day, glimmered in the dark like will-o'-the-wisps. There was a sullen glow from pits and basements. The sight of these strange lights and fires, in burnt-out stone boxes that had once been homes, was unsettling.

As they drove down the deserted streets, past the hundreds of dead houses, the enormity of what had befallen the city became ever clearer, ever more tangible. The city was dead, yet there was no sense even of the peace of the cemetery – both the earth and the sky were gripped by the silent tension of war. There was nothing but small stars of bursting flak, the restless, shifting tent formed by the beams of searchlights, and the constant, far-off lightning of exploding bombs and artillery shells.

None of them said anything. Even Agrippina stopped her constant sobs and laments.

Mostovskoy pressed his face against the side window, trying to make out the silhouettes of the charred buildings. 'I think this is where the Shaposhnikovs lived,' he said, turning to face Sofya Osipovna.

Sofya did not answer. She was asleep, her head drooping forward onto her chest, and her heavy body swaying with each bump they passed over.

They came to a road cleared of debris. To either side were small houses surrounded by trees and, every now and then, the dark figures of soldiers on their way to the factory district. Semyonov turned off to the left, saying to Mostovskoy, 'I'm taking a shortcut. It'll save time, and it's a better road.'

They came to a large area of wasteland, drove through some sparse groves of trees and then saw more houses. A man emerged from the dark, stepped out onto the road and gesticulated at them.

Semyonov drove on without slowing down.

His eyes half-closed, Mostovskoy was thinking about Krymov: what a joy it would be to see his old friend!

Then he thought for a while about what he would say to the *obkom* secretary: 'We need to discuss every conceivable form my work may take. It is not impossible that the Germans will capture the city, or part of the city.' His decision to stay behind was unshakeable. Yes, there was much he could teach the young about the art of conspiracy; the most important thing was to stay calm and to keep one's goal clearly in sight, no matter what the difficulties or dangers. Surprisingly, the trials and hardships of the last few days seemed only to have made him feel younger; it was a long time since he had felt such strength and inner confidence.

Then he too dozed off; there was something soporific about the dim shadows passing swiftly by. All of a sudden he opened his eyes, as if someone had shaken him violently awake. They were still on the road. Sounding concerned, Semyonov said, 'Have I gone too far to the left?'

'Perhaps you should stop and ask?' said Agrippina. 'I was born and brought up here, but I don't know this road.'

Then they heard machine-gun fire, loud and distinct – probably from the ditch by the side of the road.

Semyonov looked at Mostovskoy and muttered, 'We may have gone too far.'

The two women began to stir. Agrippina shouted, 'What have you done? You've taken us to the front line!'

'I've done nothing of the kind,' Semyonov replied crossly.

'We must turn back,' said Sofya. 'Or we'll end up in the hands of the Germans.'

'No,' said Semyonov, braking and gazing into the darkness. 'We need to turn to the right. We've gone too far left.'

'Turn back!' Sofya said in a commanding voice. 'Call yourself an army driver? More like some village woman!'

'That's enough orders from you, comrade military doctor,' said Semyonov. 'There's only one person driving this car, and that's me.'

'Yes!' said Mostovskoy. 'Let the driver decide.'

Semyonov turned off onto a smaller road. Once again they saw fences, low trees and the grey walls of houses.

'Well?' asked Sofya.

Semyonov shrugged. 'All right, I think – only I don't remember this bridge.'

'We must stop,' said Sofya. 'The first person you see, you must stop and ask.'

Semyonov drove on for a while without a word, then said with relief, 'Good. I know where we are now. One more right turn and we'll be at the factory.'

'All right, my anxious passenger?' Mostovskoy said condescendingly.

By way of reply, Sofya gave a kind of angry snort.

'So, first Semyonov must drop me off at the factory,' said Mostovskoy. 'And then he can take you to the river crossing. I really must see the secretary soon, or he'll be going back into the city.'

Semyonov braked sharply.

'What's happening?' cried Sofya.

'There's a man with a red light,' said Semyonov, pointing to a group of men standing in the middle of the road. 'We're being signalled to stop.'

'Oh my God!' said Sofya.

Men holding sub-machine guns surrounded the car. One pointed his gun at Semyonov and said with quiet authority, in broken Russian, 'Hands up! Surrender!'

There was a moment of silence, a stone-like silence during which the four people in the car, now barely able to breathe, realized that the chances and mishaps of the last few hours had turned into something of another order. Now an irrevocable fate, these mishaps would determine their entire lives.

All of a sudden Agrippina wailed, 'Let me go. I was only a servant. I cooked and cleaned for him for a few crusts of bread.'

'*Still, Schweinehunde!*' shouted one of the soldiers, pointing his gun at her. Ten minutes later, after a rough search, the four detainees were taken to the command post of the German infantry battalion whose advance outpost had halted their stray car.

45

During his time in Moscow, Novikov was staying with Colonel Ivanov. They had been fellow students at the Military Academy, and Ivanov was now serving in the operations department of the General Staff.

Novikov saw very little of Ivanov, who worked day and night. Sometimes Ivanov slept in his office, not coming home for three or four days on end.

Ivanov's family had been evacuated to Shadrinsk, in the Urals.

When Ivanov did come home, Novikov would at once ask if he had heard anything new. Then they would look at the map together.

After hearing about the massive air raid and the German breakthrough to the factory district, he was unable to sleep. One moment he saw Zhenya running through smoke and flames; the next moment he saw black German howitzers and self-propelled guns on the banks of the Volga, firing on the blazing city. He wanted to rush to the central aerodrome and fly to Stalingrad at once, on the fastest possible aircraft.

He spent the night pacing about the room, looking out of the window and studying the map spread out on the table, trying to divine the future course of the battle that had just begun.

Early in the morning he rang Viktor Shtrum. He was hoping Viktor might say, 'Zhenya and the rest of the family are all in Kazan. They've been there for several days now.' But no one answered. It seemed that Viktor was no longer in Moscow.

At such a time, few things are more difficult than having nothing to do – and Novikov was not working. On arriving in Moscow, he had gone straight to the cadres section of the People's Commissariat of Defence. There he had been told to leave his telephone number and wait to be called. The days had gone by, and no one had called him. Novikov had no idea what his next appointment was likely to be. General Bykov, his immediate superior at the Southwestern Front, had merely handed him a sealed envelope with his personal dossier; he had said nothing about the reason for this sudden summons to Moscow.

The day promised to be infinitely long, and Novikov was afraid he'd be unable to get through it alone and with nothing to occupy him. He put on a new jacket, polished his boots and set off to the Commissariat of Defence.

There he waited for a long time in the crowded, smoke-filled reception room, where he heard one story after another about injustices suffered by unfortunate majors and lieutenant colonels. Eventually he was called to the window and issued with a pass.

He was received by the same admin-section captain, with a medal 'For Merit in Combat', who had stamped his documents when he first came to Moscow. After asking Novikov where he was staying, he said, 'But you really needn't have come today. We've got nothing for you. I don't think the section head has even been told about you yet.'

A second, rather skinny, captain came in, said a few words of greeting and adjusted a small flag on a school map hanging between the windows.

The two captains then chatted briefly about the situation in Stalingrad. Their understanding of war also seemed to belong to a schoolroom.

The admin-section captain advised Novikov to go and see Lieutenant Colonel Zvezdyukhin, the commander responsible for his file. He might be able to tell him a little more.

The captain picked up the telephone, checked that Zvezdyukhin was in his office, told Novikov how to get to him and sent him on his way.

Lieutenant Colonel Zvezdyukhin, a stooped man with a pale face, ran his long white fingers over the cards in his index drawer and said, 'I have not completed the report, comrade Colonel, because the necessary attestations from Front HQ have yet to arrive.' He looked at the card and added, 'I've noted that the request was sent off without delay, the day following your arrival. The documents, therefore, will be received five days from now. I shall then report to my superior forthwith.'

'Might the commander be able see me today?' asked Novikov. 'Could you help make this possible?'

'Only too glad, comrade Colonel,' Zvezdyukhin replied with a smile. 'I'd be only too glad, if that served any purpose, but questions of this nature cannot be decided on the basis of mere verbal explanations. We need documents. Nothing can be determined without documents.'

He gave a particular weight to the word *documents*. Against the background of his habitual monotone the word sounded almost succulent.

Understanding that these wheels turned at their own slow speed and that there was nothing he could do to change this, Novikov said goodbye to Zvezdyukhin, who promised to call as soon as he had any news.

When Zvezdyukhin glanced at his watch and signed Novikov's pass, Novikov felt sad that their conversation had been so brief. On any other day, Novikov would probably have got very angry with Zvezdyukhin, but his sense of loneliness was now so unbearable that he felt grateful to anyone who relieved it for even a moment. He had even felt grateful to the sentry who checked his pass and the clerk who first issued it.

Back out on the street, Novikov went into a kiosk and tried again to phone Viktor Shtrum; again there was no reply. For the next few hours he walked about the city. A passer-by would have thought he was a man in a hurry, dealing with some urgent task; no one would have imagined that he was simply going for a walk. Until then he had gone out very seldom; strolling around Theatre Square or sitting on a boulevard would have felt shameful. Women would have seen him and thought, 'Who's this fine colonel? Strolling about on boulevards while our husbands fight on the front line!'

When Ivanov asked why he didn't go to the cinema or for a walk in the surrounding countryside, Novikov said, 'You must be joking. How can one laze about at a dacha when the country's at war?'

'Personally, I'd give a lot for an evening in the fresh air,' said Ivanov. 'For some fresh air and a bottle of cool beer.'

Novikov called at Viktor's. The elderly concierge was sitting outside the main entrance. Novikov asked if the tenant of apartment nineteen was at home.

'No, he left,' the old woman replied. She laughed for some reason, then added, 'Yes, he's been gone for ten days now.'

Next, Novikov went to the post office and sent a telegram to Alexandra Vladimirovna, though he doubted he would receive a reply. There and then he wrote a postcard to Viktor in Kazan, asking if he had any news of his family in Stalingrad.

He realized that his tone left little doubt as to his true feelings, but then Viktor would almost certainly have guessed these already.

Since he had no more tasks and no wish to return to an empty apartment, he spent the rest of the day walking, probably covering about twenty kilometres. He walked from Kaluga Street to Red Square, from there to the Krasnopresnensky Gate, and then along the Leningrad Highway towards the airport. He watched transport planes climbing into the sky – some, no doubt, on their way to Stalingrad.

From the Leningrad Highway he went through Petrovsky Park to the Savyolovsky railway station, and then back along Kalyaev Street to the city centre.

He did not stop once; walking briskly helped to calm his nerves. From time to time he remembered his feelings on the first day of the war, his sense that life was preparing difficult trials for him and that he must brace himself in anticipation. He remembered how, as bombs crashed down on the fighter regiment HQ, he had forced himself to buckle his belt properly and fasten the buttons on his tunic. Once again he began to feel resolute, ready to confront his destiny.

By the time Novikov returned to Ivanov's empty apartment, it was dark.

During the night he was woken by the telephone. He picked up the receiver, expecting to have to repeat the words he had already said so many times: 'Colonel Ivanov is not at home tonight. Please phone him at work.' But it was Colonel Novikov, not Colonel Ivanov, whom the caller asked to speak to.

And from the caller's very first words, Novikov realized that his future was being decided at a higher level than he had imagined – and certainly not in the room where Lieutenant Colonel Zvezdyukhin examined index cards bearing the dates on which he had sent out requests for attestations. Novikov was being summoned to the General Staff.

This night-time telephone call lasted only a minute, but Novikov was to remember it again and again.

At the General Staff he learned that his memo had been passed on to the Supreme Command; it had been considered important.

During the next two days Novikov had several conversations with senior members of the Armoured Directorate. On the third day a car came to collect him around midnight; he was to be interviewed by General Fedorenko, the head of the directorate.

As he sat in the car, Novikov wondered if, just as his fate as a soldier was being decided, a terrible personal tragedy might be about to befall him. What a joy it would be to receive a telegram saying that the Shaposhnikovs – and Zhenya – were all safe and sound. But there was no answer to his telegram, and no news from Kazan.

The general talked to him for about two hours; they had so much in common, so many shared thoughts and ideas, that Novikov felt as if they had known each other for years. The general turned out to be well informed not only about Novikov's service as a tank commander but also about his recent work on the Southwestern Front staff.

There were moments when it seemed strange that this good-natured, round-faced elderly man could be the head of a formidable branch of the armed forces, destined to play a crucial role in a great war, and that he could cite such illustrious names as Rybalko, Katukov and Bogdanov[234] as casually as a head teacher might mention teachers of history, natural sciences and the Russian language.

Nevertheless, Novikov was well aware that this conversation, however relaxed and pleasant it might feel, had not been set up on a mere whim. The head of the Red Army Armoured Forces Directorate clearly had his reasons for calling Novikov in the middle of the night and listening to him so attentively, not once even looking at his watch. Novikov, however, was scrupulously honest. He did not say a single word simply to please or impress the general; he did not try to present himself as better than he was.

Eight days went by. Novikov appeared to have been forgotten. No one called round; no one telephoned. He began to think he must have made an unfavourable impression. Sometimes he woke in the night, watched the pale blue searchlight beams moving about the dark sky and recalled some remark of his that now seemed particularly unfortunate: 'No, I hadn't thought about that'; 'No, I didn't know'; 'I tried to understand, but I couldn't.'

What came to mind most often was a conversation about the use of mass tank formations. Fedorenko had asked, 'What are your views on the training and preparation of new tank formations?' Novikov had replied, 'I think the first priority in the near future is the use of mass tank formations in active defence.' Fedorenko had laughed and said, 'On the contrary! The foundation for the combat training of tank companies, battalions, regiments, brigades, corps and entire armies must be the use of mass tank formations in an offensive! That's our task for tomorrow.'

One after another, Novikov recalled every detail of the conversation. As if mirroring his agitated state, the searchlight beams swayed, trembled, went still and then swept silently across the whole of the wide sky.

Novikov sent two more telegrams to Stalingrad and one to Kazan, but no one answered. His anxiety deepened.

On the ninth day after the interview, a car drove up to the building. A thin, narrow-shouldered lieutenant got out. Seeing him hurry towards the main entrance, Novikov realized that he was about to learn his fate and went out to meet him. As he was opening the door, the lieutenant rang. He smiled and asked, 'Were you expecting me, comrade Colonel?'

'Yes,' answered Novikov.

'You are being summoned immediately to the General Staff. I'm to take you by car.'

On his arrival, he received written orders: Colonel P. P. Novikov was instructed to proceed to a sector of the Urals Military District and supervise the formation of a tank corps.

For a second Novikov thought these orders must have been meant for some other Novikov. His deepest wish, something he had always looked on not as a realistic possibility but as the wildest of dreams, was set out so clearly and simply that it seemed it must be a mistake. His own surname seemed to belong to someone else.

He reread the orders. In two days he was to fly to the Urals.

He longed to speak to Zhenya – straightaway, before he spoke to anyone else. Not only did he want to share his news; he also wanted her to understand the constancy of his love – to understand that he loved her as much at a moment of proud success as at one of trial and failure.

Later, when he recalled this day, Novikov would feel surprised how quickly and straightforwardly he came to take for granted what for so long had seemed inconceivable.

Two hours after receiving his orders, he was discussing a variety of practical concerns in the Armoured Directorate, speaking on the telephone to one of General Khrulyov's adjutants and arranging to meet the head of the tank school. His head was full of ideas; dozens of notes, questions, telegraph addresses, telephone numbers and other figures had appeared in his notebook. And dozens of questions that, until the previous day, had seemed purely theoretical were now matters of life and death, issues of burning importance to which he needed to apply all the intellectual and emotional energy at his command.

Questions of recruitment; the numbers required to complement each battalion, regiment and brigade; the speed with which both operational and radio equipment could be delivered; fuel allocations; financial matters; food and uniform supplies; study plans and instruction methods; billets and living quarters – there were countless issues to be resolved, some simple, some complex, some of only minor importance and others that were very important indeed.

The day before he was due to leave Moscow, Novikov stayed until late evening in the office of the general in charge of ordnance; he was discussing tank fuel and lubricating oils with a group of military engineers. And his final meeting with General Fedorenko was scheduled for midnight.

In the middle of a discussion about the ash content of different fuels, Novikov asked the general for permission to make a phone call. He dialled Ivanov and found him at home.

'Still hard at it, are you?' said Ivanov.

Novikov told Ivanov that he would come by at dawn to say good-bye. Then, expecting the answer *no*, he asked, 'Any letters or telegrams for me?'

'Hang on a moment,' said Ivanov. 'Yes, there's a postcard.'

'Who's it from? Look at the signature.'

There was a brief silence. Ivanov was clearly struggling to decipher the handwriting. Finally, he said, 'Shturm, or maybe Shtrom, I'm not quite sure.'

'Please read it to me!'

'"Dear comrade Novikov, yesterday I returned from the Urals, where I was called on urgent business."' Ivanov coughed and said, 'I must report that the handwriting is atrocious.' He then continued, '"I am writing with sad news ... We have heard from Alexandra Vladimirovna that Marusya was killed during the first day of the bombing."' Ivanov hesitated, struggling to make out the next words. Novikov, however, assumed that Ivanov didn't want to tell him that Zhenya had died too.

At this point Novikov's usual self-restraint failed him. He forgot that he was in the office of a general from the Armoured Directorate and that four men he barely knew couldn't help hearing every word he said. His voice trembling, he cried out, 'Keep reading, for the love of God!'

The engineers fell silent, looking at Novikov.

'"Zhenya and her mother have reached Kuibyshev, where Zhcnya will remain for the time being. We received a telegram from her yesterday,"' Ivanov continued. The engineers all began talking again – Novikov's face was transformed. His sense of relief was obvious. And Novikov himself was aware how, the moment he heard about Zhenya, the tight hoop round his heart sprang open and, with no obvious connection to anything said before, he thought, 'I mustn't forget to mention Darensky.'

Shtrum went on to say that they had no news of Spiridonov and Vera. Ivanov was still reading rather slowly, and Novikov had time to think, 'It could be quite a battle to get Darensky posted to Corps HQ. Maybe I should start by trying to get him into a Brigade HQ.' Then, with an inner smile, he said to himself, 'You too, brother – it seems you too have your share of the administrative soul.'

Ivanov finally got to the end and said jokingly, 'Message transmitted by telephone. Duty officer – Colonel Ivanov.'

'Received by Novikov,' Novikov replied, and he thanked his colleague. By the time he hung up, he felt entirely calm, as if already accustomed to the good news he had just heard. 'Yes, of course. How could it have been otherwise?' he was thinking. But he knew very well that it could easily have been otherwise.

An elderly major from the technical department was going to be flying with him. 'You've been to the Urals before, haven't you?' Novikov asked him. 'What route do we fly?'

'Via Kirov,' the major replied. 'One can go via Kuibyshev – but sometimes they have fuel shortages there. One can get stuck. Not long ago I had to spend over twenty-four hours at the airport.'

'Understood,' said Novikov. 'Kirov it is – no need to take risks!' And to himself he said, 'Thank God Zhenya can't hear me – or I'd be in hot water.'

Shortly before he was due to meet Fedorenko, Novikov was sitting in the waiting room, listening to the quiet conversations of the other commanders and glancing now and again at the duty secretary, who was sitting behind a desk with a large number of telephones.

During the last few days, Novikov had begun to see both people and events rather differently. Past events now appeared to him in a new light, and he saw new connections between them.

A series of tragic defeats had led the Soviet forces to retreat to the Volga, but other developments pointed in a very different direction. Soviet workers and engineers were bringing ever closer the day when Soviet tank production would overtake that of the Germans.

In almost every conversation, every phone call, every order and memorandum, Novikov sensed something new, something he had not felt at the front.

He heard a military engineer speak on the phone to the director of a tank factory located far to the east. He heard a bald, wrinkled major general telephone the director of a firing range to discuss the orientation of future research work. He heard people talk at meetings about the impending increase in steel production, about the commanders who would graduate this winter from the Dzerzhinsky Academy and about changes soon to be introduced to the tank schools' curriculum.

The engineer general sitting beside Novikov said to him, 'We have to build a second workers' settlement straightaway or, come winter, people will have nowhere to live. And when we open a second assembly workshop next March, this settlement will have to become a town.'

And Novikov thought he understood what lay behind this sense of movement and change. Throughout this last year he had seen the war as linear; all that counted was the front line – its movement, its curves and bulges, and the holes sometimes punched in it. The war's only reality had been a narrow strip of land and the narrow strip of time within which reserves in the immediate rear could be deployed on this land. Nothing mattered but the correlation of forces on the front line during a strictly limited time span.

Now, though, Novikov understood that war had another dimension: it had depth. Its true reality was not to be measured in tens of kilometres or hundreds of hours. The real planning was being undertaken at a depth of tens of thousands of hours. What truly mattered were the tank corps and the artillery and aircraft divisions now taking shape in Siberia and the Urals. The war's reality was not only the present day; it was also the brighter day that would dawn six months or a year from now. And this day still hidden in the depth of space and time was being prepared in countless ways and countless places – it was not only today's defeats or victories that would determine the future course of the war. Novikov had, of course, understood all this before, while still at the front – but his understanding then had been merely theoretical, not a part of his inner being.

This future – these battles of the year ahead – was already being brought nearer through the development of new production-line methods, through the expansion of quarries and mines, through discussions between designers, engineers and technical experts, through improvements to military-school curricula and through teachers' assessments of the work done by students at tank, artillery and air academies.

What did Novikov know about the battles of 1943? Where, on what borders would they be fought?

The future lay behind a curtain of dust and smoke, hidden by the din of the battle above the Volga.

But Novikov understood that he was now one of those thousands of commanders to whom the Supreme Command was entrusting the outcome of tomorrow's war.

His meeting with General Fedorenko was different in tone from the previous meeting; Novikov sensed this at once. Fedorenko was brisk and businesslike and he made several critical remarks. At one point he said crossly, 'I was expecting you to have done more by now. You must move faster.' Novikov, however, saw all this as positive: Fedorenko had accepted him as one of the family – as a fellow tank man.

While they were talking, Fedorenko's adjutant came in to report the arrival of Dugin, the commander of an illustrious tank formation.

'I'll receive him in a few minutes,' said Fedorenko. And he looked intently at Novikov, surprised by the sudden smile on his face.

'An old colleague, comrade General.'

'Ah,' said Fedorenko, clearly not wanting to discuss his subordinates' past. 'So, any questions?' And he looked at his watch.

Novikov asked for Darensky to be appointed to his Corps HQ staff. Fedorenko asked a few quick questions, all of them to the point, thought for a moment and said, 'We can decide that later. Ask me again before you move up to the front line.'

As Novikov left, Fedorenko did not ask him if he felt up to the task. That would have seemed wrong. They both understood that Novikov now *had* to be up to the task.

Glad to see each other, Novikov and Dugin talked in the waiting room for several minutes.

They had served together before the war. Novikov remembered Dugin as a connoisseur of mushrooms; he loved foraging for them and was a true artist when it came to salting them. Now, though, Dugin was a formidable commander who had pushed back the German assault troops advancing on Moscow. Novikov looked at the thin, pale face of his former peacetime companion. It was hard to take in that this was the face of a war hero.

'And how are you getting on with your boots?' Novikov asked quietly. A comrade had told him that Dugin had vowed to keep on wearing the same boots, not allowing himself a new pair until the day of victory.

'Well, I haven't had to mend them yet,' Dugin replied with a smile. 'So, the story's got around, has it?'

'As you can see.'

Just then, the adjutant asked Dugin to go through.

'Straightaway,' Dugin replied. He then said to Novikov, 'And you'll be in command of a corps?'

'I will indeed,' said Novikov.

'Married?'

'Not yet.'

'Doesn't matter – you will be. And see you again soon. Maybe we'll fight side by side.'

And they said goodbye.

At six o'clock in the morning Novikov arrived at the central aerodrome. As his car drove through the gates, he turned to look back at the grey strip of the Leningrad Highway, at the dark green of the trees, at the city he was leaving behind him – and he recalled how unsure of himself he had felt three and a half weeks earlier, as he walked out through these same gates. Could he have ever imagined, as he stood in the queue by the window where passes were issued, as he spoke to Colonel Zvezdyukhin, that his cherished dream was about to be realized – that he was to be appointed a front-line tank commander?

They drove on into the aerodrome. In the pale light of the summer dawn the statue of Lenin gleamed white. Novikov felt hot in his chest; he could feel his heartbeat.

The sun rose as Novikov and the other commanders made their way out to the plane. The broad concrete runway, the dusty yellow grass, the glass in the cabin windows, the celluloid files in the hands of pilots and navigators walking towards their planes – everything gleamed, as if smiling in the sunlight.

The pilot of the green Douglas walked up to Novikov, gave him a free and easy salute and said, 'It's clear skies all the way, comrade Colonel. We're ready to fly.'

'Let's fly then,' said Novikov, and he sensed how the other commanders were, now and again, glancing at him in the inquisitive, slightly tense manner with which junior commanders steal a look at the commander of a division, a corps or an army. Novikov knew this look well, but he had always seen it directed at others, never at himself. Many people, he now realized, were going to take note of him – his general appearance, his clothes, even the little jokes he made.

Say what you like about modesty, but when a powerful, twin-engine plane is first placed at your disposal, when you realize that people are looking at you, when the flight mechanic comes up to you, salutes and asks if you might prefer to change seats so the sun won't be in your eyes – like it or not, you sense a tingle go up your spine.

*

Novikov began to read some of the documents he had been given in the directorate.

He looked several times through the window at the sparkling thread of the River Moscow, winding towards the Volga, at the calm green

593

of oak and pine forests, at the autumn birch and aspen groves, at the bright green of the winter crops in the morning sun, at the curly clouds and the plane's grey shadow sliding along below, never deviating from its course.

He returned the papers to his briefcase and drifted off in thought. For some reason he began to remember his childhood: a miners' settlement, clothes drying on lines in the yards, women shouting at one another. He recalled the mixture of envy and delight he had felt when his elder brother Ivan had come back from his first day down the mine. Their mother had come out into the yard with a stool, a tin tub and a bucket of hot water, and he had soaped Ivan's black neck. He remembered the sad look on their mother's face as she slowly poured out the water, one mugful after another.

Why were his mother and father no longer alive? They would have felt proud of their son, now about to take command of a tank corps. Still, he might well be able to spend a day with his brother; his mine was not far from where the tank corps was being formed. He would find his brother washing in the yard. He would see a tin tub on a stool. His brother's wife would drop the mug she was holding and shout, 'Vanya! Vanya! Your brother!'

He also recalled Marusya's thin, swarthy face. Why had her death made so little impression on him? Learning that Zhenya was alive, he had forgotten about Marusya. Now he felt an aching sense of pity. But then this pity dissipated and the image of Marusya faded away. Novikov's thoughts ran on ahead. They overtook the plane on its journey east, then returned to different times in the past.

46

Viktor returned to Kazan from Chelyabinsk at the end of August. Instead of spending three days there, as he expected, he had stayed for three weeks.

He had worked very hard indeed. At any other time it would have taken him two months to give so many consultations, check so many complex schemes and discuss so many different questions with engineers and laboratory heads.

He had felt a constant sense of surprise that his theoretical understandings should turn out to be of obvious importance not only to physicists and chemists in the factory laboratories but also to the work of engineers, technicians and electricians. The original problem – the problem Semyon Krymov had first telephoned him about – had been resolved within forty-eight hours, but Semyon had persuaded Viktor to stay until his recommendations had been put into effect and fully tested.

Throughout these two months Viktor felt acutely conscious of the closeness of his relationship to this vast factory. Everyone who has worked in the Donbass, in Prokopievsk or the Urals will know such a feeling.

The shop floors, the factory yard from which the newborn metal first sets out into the world – and even the theatre, the barber's, the chief engineer's carpeted dining room, the grove by the quiet pond with autumn leaves on its surface, the shops and streets, the few separate cottages, the long barrack huts – everything round about lives and breathes the life of the factory.

The factory determines whether there is a smile or a frown on the engineers' faces. It determines the nature of people's work and their standard of living. It determines their meal times and their hours of rest. It determines the ebb and flow of crowds in the streets, the timetable of local trains and the decisions of the city soviet. Streets, shops, squares, tram rails and railway lines – all feel the pull of the factory. People think about it and talk about it. Either they have just come from the factory or they are on their way to it.

The factory is everywhere, present all the time – in every mind and heart, and in the memories of the old. It is the future of the young – a source of joy, hope and anxiety. It breathes and it makes a lot of noise. There is no getting away from its warmth, from its smell, from its din. It's there in your nostrils, on your skin and in your eyes and ears.

In answer to Semyon's request, Viktor had outlined a simpler routine for installing the new equipment.

During the final assembly of the instruments and apparatus, Viktor spent two whole days and nights at the factory, snatching the occasional few minutes of rest on a small sofa in the shop-floor office. Like every one of the electricians and metalworkers involved, he felt under intense pressure.

The evening before the first trial, Viktor, Semyon and the factory director went round the workshops to carry out a final check.

'You seem remarkably calm,' said Semyon.

'You must be joking,' said Viktor. 'The calculations still look faultless, but that doesn't make me any less anxious.'

Instead of going back with Semyon, he chose to stay in the factory all night.

Along with Korenkov the shop-floor Party organizer and a long-faced young electrician in a blue overall, he climbed the iron staircase to the upper gallery, to the location of one of the main switching units.

Viktor's impression was that Korenkov never went home. If Viktor went past the Red Corner and looked through the half-open door, he saw Korenkov reading a newspaper aloud to the workers. If he entered the workshop, he saw Korenkov's small stooped figure, lit by the flames of the furnaces. He saw him in the laboratory, and outside the factory store, waving his arms about as he encouraged a growing crowd of women to form an orderly queue. Tonight was no different; Korenkov was still working away.

From the upper gallery, the ribs of the huge fire-breathing furnaces appeared almost sculpted and the casting ladle full of molten metal looked like the surface of the sun, bubbling with atomic explosions, surrounded by a bright mane of sparks and shifting protuberances. It was a sun that human eyes – for the first time – were looking at not from below, but from above.

After they had checked the switching unit, Korenkov suggested that Viktor go back down to the ground floor.

'What about you?' asked Viktor. 'What are you going to do?'

'I want to have a look at the wiring on the roof. I'm going up there with the electrician,' said Korenkov – and he pointed to a second iron staircase, spiralling up into the roof like a corkscrew.

'I'll join you,' said Viktor.

From up on the high roof they could see not only the factory itself, but also the entire settlement and its surroundings.

In the dark, the factory gave off a reddish glow. Hundreds of electric street lights flickered around it, and it was as if the wind were alternately blowing them out and making them flare up.

This inconstant light touched the water in the pond, the pine forest and the clouds. All nature seemed to be in the grip of the tension and anxiety introduced to this calm realm by mankind.

Many things were invading nature's night-time silence – not only this flickering light, but also the piercing hoots of locomotives, the whistle of steam, and the roar of metal.

It was the opposite of what Viktor had felt during his first evening in Moscow, when a quiet twilight from a world of village streams, empty plains and sleeping forests appeared to have invaded the blacked-out streets and squares of a world city.

'You wait here,' Korenkov said to Viktor. 'I'll help the electrician fix the end of the wire. The contact's a bit shaky.'

Viktor held the wire in the air. Korenkov, some distance away, gesticulated at him and called out, 'Towards me! Towards me!'

Viktor misunderstood and began to pull the wire towards himself. Korenkov shouted out crossly, 'What are you doing? I said, "Towards me!"'

When they were finished, Korenkov crawled back, smiled at Viktor and said, 'There was a lot of noise. You couldn't hear what I was shouting. Come on, let's go back down again.'

Viktor asked Korenkov whether he might be able to conduct a trial smelt. Korenkov said this would be difficult and asked Viktor why he needed this special grade of steel. Viktor told him a little about his work and specified the technical requirements the steel for his apparatus must meet.

Then Viktor went to the factory laboratory, and from there to the shop office. It was the relatively quiet hour before the change of shift.

A young steelworker, whom Viktor had seen several times on the shop floor and whose work he had observed, was sitting at a desk, writing something in a thick office book and glancing now and then at a stained sheet of paper.

Seeing Viktor, he pushed his tarpaulin mittens aside to make some space on the desk and went on writing.

Viktor sat down on a little wooden sofa.

The young man finished what he was writing and rolled a cigarette. 'How have things gone today?' Viktor asked.

'All right, I think.'

Korenkov came in. 'Ah, glad to see you, Gromov!' he said. 'Here for a smoke?'

He glanced at what the young man had just noted and said, 'That's quite something, Gromov!'

'Thanks!' said Gromov. 'I guess I deserve a cigarette. Soon there'll be two or three extra tanks on their way to the front.'

'Extra – but certainly not superfluous,' Korenkov said with a laugh.

The three men began to talk. Gromov told Viktor how he first came to the Urals. 'I'm not from these parts, I was born in the Donbass. I came here a year before the war. Everything here seemed wrong. I wished I hadn't come. It was a nightmare. I wanted to go back home. I wrote letter after letter, begging for work. I wrote to Makeyevka, to Yenakiyevo, to all the main works. And do you know, comrade Professor, when it was I came to love the Urals? It was when we first saw real hardship. Conditions before the war hadn't been bad at all. We had a room, and there was food. But I hated it – all I wanted was to return to the Donbass. But after the autumn and winter of 1941, after me and my family got to know cold and hunger – after all that, somehow I came to feel at home here.'

Korenkov looked at Viktor and said, 'It was a grim winter for me too. My brother was killed at the front and my mother and father ended up in occupied territory. And this whole city was packed with evacuees. My wife fell ill. It was cold, and there wasn't a lot to eat. The construction sites were at work day and night – we built whole new workshops. But equipment evacuated from Ukraine was still just lying around outside. And people were living in dugouts. And I couldn't stop thinking about my parents in Oryol. What were they going through, I kept asking myself, under the Germans? I'd tell myself they were alive, that I'd be seeing them again. But then I'd remember their age. My father's seventy, my mother's only two years younger. And my mother had heart trouble – and swollen legs – even before the war. The thought that I'd never see them again felt like a knife in my heart. And so it goes on. Grieve all you like, but you have to keep going.'

Viktor listened without saying a word. His anguish was so apparent that Korenkov stopped and said, 'But why am I telling you all this? I'm sure you've seen your share of suffering too.'

'I have, comrade Korenkov,' Viktor replied. 'And it's not over yet.'

'So far, at least, I've been lucky,' said Gromov. 'My family are all here, safe and sound.'

'You must give me your address, comrade Shtrum,' said Korenkov. 'I'll write to you about this trial smelt. Give me the technical specifications in as much detail as possible. We'll do our best. I'm confident that Krymov and the director will have no objections. Far from it! But I'll make it my personal responsibility. You can even include my name in your list of acknowledgements: Korenkov.'

'You're a remarkable man,' said Viktor, visibly moved. 'I thought you'd just forget all about it.'

'Comrade Korenkov never forgets,' said Gromov with a smile. And he shook his head – perhaps in approval, perhaps in disapproval.

At the start of the morning shift, the new control apparatus underwent its first complete test – with satisfactory results. At eleven the test was repeated – this time with perfect results; the minor faults noted during the first test had all been put right. A day later, the factory was able to return to its normal routine.

Throughout his stay Viktor had been lodging with Semyon Krymov, but they had little chance to get to know each other. Semyon came back home only late at night, and when they did meet they talked mainly about work. Semyon had had no letters from his brother and he was very worried about him.

Olga Sergeyevna, Semyon's wife, was a rather thin, pretty woman with big eyes and a pale face. Unwittingly, Viktor caused her a lot of grief. She did her best to cook tasty meals for him, but he hardly ate anything at all. He seemed absent-minded and taciturn, and she decided that the professor was a cold, dry fellow, with no interest in anything but his work.

But once, walking past Viktor's room during the night, she heard a quiet sob. She stopped. Feeling confused, she started back to her room, meaning to wake her husband. Then she hesitated, thinking she must have imagined it: the thought of this dry professor sobbing in the middle of the night was simply too absurd. She stood outside the door again – and could hear nothing at all. She went back to her room, thinking it had been some strange auditory illusion. But it had not been an illusion – Viktor's work was not all that mattered to him.

Viktor returned to Kazan in late August. The plane took off in the morning; the navigator announced with a smile, 'Goodbye, Chelya-binsk!' – and disappeared into the cockpit. And at two in the afternoon he reappeared, smiled and said, 'And here is Kazan!' All very quick and simple – as if he were an accomplished conjuror, slipping Chelyabinsk up one sleeve and taking Kazan out of the other. Through the little square window beside him Viktor was able to see the whole of the city: the tall red and yellow buildings crowded together in the centre; the motley roofs; the little wooden houses on the outskirts; people, cars and yellowing vegetable gardens; frightened goats, trying to escape the low-flying plane and the roar of its engines; the railway station and the silvery veins of its many spur tracks; the tangle of dirt roads leading out into flat plains and misty forests. It was the first time that Viktor had been able to take in every aspect of Kazan at once, but this had the effect of making the city seem dull, as if stripped of its mystery. 'How strange,' he thought, 'that the beings dearest to me in the world should live in this heap of stone and iron.'

He and Ludmila met just inside the front door. In the half-dark her face seemed pale but youthful. For a few moments they looked at each other in silence. There was no other way to express the mixture of sad-ness and joy they both felt.

It was not for the sake of happiness that they needed to see each other, nor to console or be consoled. During these brief moments Viktor felt many, many things – everything that can be felt by a man capable both of loving and of doing wrong, a man who can be overwhelmed by powerful emotion yet still manage to carry on with his daily life.

Everything in Viktor's life was in some way connected to Ludmila. Grief and success, a handkerchief he had forgotten at home, misunder-standings with friends, a misjudged remark during a scientific discus-sion, an occasion when he didn't feel like eating – Ludmila was present everywhere.

And if his life was important, if it differed from other lives, it was because even its smallest, seemingly mutest events took on mean-ing, and acquired a resonance of their own, from Ludmila's presence in them.

They went through into the main room, and Ludmila began talking about their Stalingrad family and relatives. Alexandra Vladimirovna and Zhenya were now in Kuibyshev. There had been a letter from Zhenya only the day before; she herself was going to stay on in Kuibyshev, but Alexandra Vladimirovna would soon be on her way to Kazan. She'd be coming by boat, and she might be with them in two or three days. Vera had decided to remain in Stalingrad with her father. That was all Ludmila knew; there was no longer any post to or from Stalingrad. Then Ludmila said, 'Tolya writes fairly often. Yesterday I received a letter he sent on 21 August. He's still in the same place. He's eating lots of watermelons, he's in good health, and he feels bored. And Nadya should be back from the kolkhoz either today or tomorrow. It seems I was right. She's worked hard and it's done her good. She's in fine spirits.'

'When did you last see Sokolov?' Viktor asked.

'He came by the day before yesterday. He was very surprised when I told him you were in Chelyabinsk.'

'Has there been some difficulty?'

'No, he says everything's fine. He just wanted to see you. And Postoev dropped by a few days before. He laughed at your being such a homebody. He said you hadn't wanted to stay even twenty-four hours in the hotel. But what did you do for food? Did you eat anything that wasn't out of a tin?'

Viktor shrugged. 'Seems I'm still on my feet.'

'Tell me about Chelyabinsk. Was it interesting there?'

Viktor began to tell Ludmila what he'd done at the factory. Neither he nor her said a word about Marusya or Anna Semyonovna – but they were both thinking about them all the time, no matter what was being said, and they both knew this.

And only late that night, when Viktor came back from the institute, did Ludmila say, 'Vitya, dearest Vitenka,[235] Marusya's dead ... and I got your letter about Anna Semyonovna.'

'Yes,' he replied. 'I've lost all hope. And I heard about Marusya only a few weeks afterwards.'

'You know me. I don't like to let myself go, but yesterday I was going through a few of our belongings. In one suitcase I found a wooden box Marusya gave me when she was nine and I was twelve. Engraved on it, in pokerwork – there was a craze for it that year – were some maple leaves and the words, 'To Luda, from Marusya.' And it was as if I'd been stabbed in the heart. I howled all night.'

*

Since his return to Kazan, Viktor's anguish had only deepened. No matter what he was thinking or doing, his thoughts constantly, relentlessly returned to his mother.

Getting on the plane for Chelyabinsk, he had thought, 'She's gone. And now I'm flying east, I'll be further away from where she lies.' And during the flight back, as they approached Kazan, he thought, 'And she'll never know that we're here in Kazan.' In the midst of his joy and excitement at seeing Ludmila again, he said to himself, 'When I last spoke to Luda, I was thinking I'd see Máma again once the war was over.'

The thought of his mother, like a strong taproot, entered into every aspect of his life, big or small. Probably it always had done, but this root that had nourished his soul since childhood had previously been elastic, yielding and transparent, and he had not noticed it, whereas now he saw it and felt it constantly, day and night.

Now that he was no longer drinking in what he had been given by his mother's love but giving everything back in confusion and longing, now that his soul was no longer absorbing the salt and moisture of life but giving it back in the form of tears, Viktor felt a constant, incessant pain.

When he reread his mother's last letter; when he divined between its calm, restrained lines the terror of the helpless, doomed people herded behind the barbed wire; when his imagination filled in the picture of the last minutes of his mother's life; when he thought about the mass execution she had known was imminent, that she had guessed about from stories told by a few people who had miraculously escaped from other shtetls; when he forced himself, with merciless obstinacy, to imagine his mother's feelings as she stood in front of an SS machine gun, by the edge of a pit, amid a crowd of women and children – what he felt then was overwhelming. But it was impossible to change what had happened, what had been fixed for ever by death.

He did not want to show this letter to anyone. He did not want to speak about it even to his wife, his daughter or his closest friends.

The letter contained no mention of Ludmila, Nadya or Tolya. His mother's only concern was her son. There was just one brief mention of Alexandra Vladimirovna; one night she had dreamed about her.

Several times a day Viktor passed his hand over his chest, over the jacket pocket where he kept it. Once, when the pain seemed unbearable, he thought, 'If I hide it away somewhere, I might slowly start to calm down. As things are, this letter's like an open grave.'

But he knew that he would sooner destroy himself than part with this letter that had, by some miracle, managed to find its way to him.

Viktor reread the letter again and again. Each time he felt the same shock as at the dacha, as if he were reading it for the first time.

Perhaps his memory was instinctively resisting, unwilling and unable fully to take in something whose constant presence would make life unbearable.

Everything around him seemed the same as before – yet there was nothing that had not changed.

Viktor was like someone seriously ill trying to carry on as usual. The sick man still works, talks, eats and drinks, even laughs and makes jokes, but everything around him has become different – work, people's faces, the taste of bread, the smell of tobacco, even the heat of the sun.

And everyone around him also senses that something has changed, that there is something different about the way this man works, talks, argues, laughs and smokes – as if some thin, cold mist now separates him from them.

Once Ludmila asked Viktor, 'What are you thinking about when you talk to me?'

'What do you mean? I think about whatever we're talking about.'

And at the institute, when he told Sokolov about his successes in Moscow, about all the new possibilities opening up, about his meetings with Pimenov, about his discussions with the Party scientific section, and about the astonishing speed with which all his proposals were acted on, Viktor was unable to escape the feeling that someone with tired, sad eyes was watching him, listening and shaking her head.

And when Viktor thought about his time in Moscow with the beautiful Nina, his heart did not start to beat faster. It was as if it had all happened to someone else and was of no real interest. Was it really necessary to write to her and think about her?

*

Alexandra Vladimirovna arrived in the evening. No one had known when to expect her. It was Nadya, just returned from the kolkhoz, who opened the door to her.

When she caught sight of her grandmother, who was wearing a man's black coat and carrying only one little bundle, Nadya leaped at her and flung her arms around her neck.

'Máma, Máma, it's Granny!' she called out. As she kissed her, she asked all in one breath, 'How are you feeling? Are you well? Where's Seryozha? Where's Auntie Zhenya? Any news of Vera?'

Ludmila came rushing out. Too breathless to speak, she kissed her mother's hands, eyes and cheeks.

Alexandra took off her coat, went through into the main room, smoothed down her hair, looked around and said, 'Well, here I am. But where's Viktor?'

'He's at the institute, he'll be back later,' replied Nadya. 'Our grandmother Anna Semyonovna's probably dead. The Germans have killed her – a letter reached Pápa.'

'Anna?' cried Alexandra. 'My darling Anna?'

Seeing her mother go pale, Ludmila said, 'Nadya, you must learn to say things more gently.'

Alexandra stood silently by the table, then walked about the room a little and stopped in front of a small desk. She picked up a little wooden box and looked at it. 'I remember this box,' she said. 'Marusya gave it to you.'

'Yes,' replied Ludmila.

Mother and daughter looked at each other, both wrinkling their brows.

'We've lost Marusya,' said Alexandra. 'Viktor's lost Anna – and here I am, still alive. But since that's how it is, I have to keep going.' She turned to Nadya and asked, 'Which class are you in now, kolkhoz worker?'

'I'm in the top class,' said Nadya, through her tears.

'Máma, do you want some tea, or would you rather wash first? We've got hot water.'

'I'll wash first. Then we can all have tea together.' Alexandra held out her hands, palms up, and said, 'I need a towel, soap, underwear and a dress. I own only the clothes I stand up in – everything else has gone up in smoke.'

'Yes, Máma, of course! But why isn't Zhenya with you? She must have lost everything too.'

'Zhenya's going out to work now. After what happened she said to me, "I'm going to go out and work, as Marusya said I should." She met someone she knew in Kuibyshev, and he found her a job as a senior draftsman in a military design bureau. Right up her street. And you know our Zhenya – she doesn't do anything by halves. Now she's got a proper job, she's at it eighteen hours a day. But don't worry – I'll soon be earning my keep too. I'll start looking for work tomorrow. Does Viktor know any factory directors I could speak to?'

'Certainly, but there's time enough,' said Ludmila, as she took some underwear out of a suitcase. 'First you must rest. You've been through a lot – you need to get your strength back.'

'All right, show me where I can wash,' said Alexandra. 'But just look at Nadya – she's so tall now! And tanned. And she looks unbelievably like Viktor's mother. I've got a photograph of Anna when she was eighteen. Her mouth, the look in her eyes – Nadya couldn't be more like her.'

She put her arms around Nadya's shoulders, and they all went through into the kitchen, where there was a basin of hot water on the stove.

'What luxury – an ocean of hot water!' said Alexandra Vladimirovna. 'On the steamer even one small cup of hot water was enough to make our day.'

While Alexandra washed, Ludmila prepared dinner. She spread out a tablecloth – one she took out only on holidays and children's birthdays. She put out all her supplies. She put out the pies she'd baked from white flour to celebrate Viktor's and Nadya's return. She put out half the sweets she'd hidden away for Tolya.

Then Ludmila brought in the little bundle her mother had left by the front door. She untied it. Next to the carefully laid table, it looked strangely touching: half a brick of stale soldier's bread, turning grey with age; a little salt in a matchbox; three unpeeled boiled potatoes; a tired-looking onion; a sheet from a child's cot that her mother must have been using as a towel.

Then there was a sheaf of old letters, wrapped in newspaper that was falling apart at the folds. Ludmila glanced quickly through the yellowing pages, recognizing her father's compressed, slanting hand and the handwriting of her sisters when they were little. She saw a page from one of Tolya's school exercise books, covered in his straight, even writing. She saw a postcard from her mother-in-law and two letters from Nadya. Scattered among all these letters were family photographs. It was strange and painful to look at these faces she knew so well. Some of these people were no longer alive, others had been scattered far and wide – but here they all were, all gathered together.

Ludmila felt a surge of tenderness and gratitude towards her mother, whose presence of mind had saved these old letters and photographs from the fire – and who always had room in her heart for all her loved ones, bringing together both the dead she never forgot and the living she was always so ready to help.

Her mother's love was as precious, as simple and necessary as this chunk of ageing bread.

Alexandra came out of the kitchen. In her daughter's housedress, which was too big for her, she looked thinner than ever. She looked younger now, with more colour in her cheeks and droplets of sweat on her forehead, yet she also looked sadder and more exhausted.

She looked at the table her daughter had laid and said, 'From famine to feast!'

Ludmila embraced her mother and led her to the table.

'How many years older than Marusya are you?' Alexandra asked. And then she answered her own question, 'Three years and six months.'

As she sat down, she said, 'It all seems as if it were only yesterday. Zhenya took it into her head to bake a pie for my birthday. And everyone was there – Marusya, Zhenya, Seryozha, Tolya, Vera, Stepan, Sofya Osipovna and Mostovskoy and Pavel Andreyev – all sitting down at table together. And now the house has burned down – and the table too. Here, it's just you, me and Nadya. No Marusya ever again, though I still can't believe it!' She spoke the last words very loudly. After that they all fell silent, for a long time.

'Pápa will be here soon,' said Nadya, unable to bear the silence any longer.

'Oh, Anna, dear Anna,' Alexandra said very softly. 'You lived alone and you died alone.'

'Máma,' said Ludmila, 'you just can't imagine what a joy it is to see you!'

After they had eaten, Ludmila persuaded her mother to go to bed. She sat down beside her and they talked, very quietly, until midnight.

It was one in the morning when Viktor returned from the institute. Everyone was asleep.

He went up to Alexandra's bed, looked for a long time at her white hair and listened to her slow, rhythmic breathing. He remembered a sentence from his mother's letter, 'Yesterday I dreamed of my dear Alexandra.'

The corners of her mouth trembled and she appeared to frown, but the sleeping woman didn't moan or cry; she almost smiled.

Viktor went quietly to his room and began to undress. He had imagined he would find it difficult to be with Ludmila's mother again, that the sight of his mother's dear friend would bring on yet another wave of anguish. But it was not like that at all; he felt only tenderness. It was like a moment in winter when, after a long period of harsh dry cold, when iron fetters seem to bind the earth and the trunks of trees, when the sun is a wan mauve, barely visible in the icy mist – it was like an unexpected breath of life in midwinter, when moist, almost warm snow gently brushes the earth, and, in the January dark, all nature seems to experience a premonition of the miracle of spring.

In the morning Viktor had a long talk with his mother-in-law. She had heard no news about all too many of her friends and acquaintances, and she was anxious about them.

She began to tell him about the terrible air raid, about the fire, about the tens of thousands made homeless, about people who had died, about her conversations with soldiers and workers on the ferry, about how many wounded children she had seen, about how she and Zhenya had walked through the Volga steppe with two other women each of whom was carrying an infant in arms. She talked about the sunrises, sunsets and starry nights she had seen in the steppe. She talked about the courage and endurance with which people were confronting these bitter times, about their faith in the triumph of a just cause.

'You won't be cross if Tamara Berozkina suddenly turns up on your doorstep?' she said. 'I've given her your address.'

'This is your home,' Viktor replied. 'You don't need to ask.'

He saw that her daughter's death had deeply shaken her but not depressed or enfeebled her. She was moved both by an iron determination and by love for others; she worried constantly about Seryozha, Tolya, Vera, Zhenya, Spiridonov and many others whom Viktor didn't know. She asked him to find out the addresses and phone numbers of factories where she might be able to find work. When he suggested she rest for a while first, she replied, 'What are you saying, Vitya? Who could rest after what I've just been through? I'm sure your mother went on working until her last day.'

Then she asked him about his own work. He became more animated and began to talk more freely.

Nadya went off to school. Ludmila went out too; the hospital commissar had asked her to call round. Viktor, however, stayed behind with Alexandra. 'I'll go to the institute after two, when Ludmila's back. I don't want to leave you on your own,' he said. Really, though, he simply wanted to spend more time with her.

Late in the evening, Viktor was alone in his laboratory. He needed to check a photoelectric effect on one of the sensitive plates.

He turned on the inductor current, and the bluish light of a vacuum discharge flickered down the thick-walled tube. In this dim light, which was like a pale blue wind, everything familiar seemed to quiver with excitement: the marble of the switchboards, the copper of the switches, the pale glow of the quartz, the dark lead plates of the photo screens, and the white nickel of the stands.

And suddenly he felt as if he were lit from within by this same light, as if a stark, radiant bunch of all-penetrating rays had entered his brain and chest.

What he felt was very powerful, but it was not a presentiment of happiness; it was a sense of life, of something greater than happiness.

Everything seemed to fuse together: his childhood dreams, his work, the sense of burning anguish that now never left him, his hatred of the dark forces that had burst into all their lives, Alexandra's accounts of her last days in Stalingrad, the beseeching look of the kolkhoz woman in the railway station in Kazan, and his faith in the free, happy future of his motherland.

At this difficult hour, this hour that was so difficult both for his people and for his own heart, he felt that he was not powerless, not at the mercy of fate.

He sensed that the determination and perseverance of a researcher was not enough on its own. To maintain the strength required for his life of labour, he needed to draw on other resources too.

And a momentary vision of a mankind that was happy and free – master of both earth and sky, disposing wisely of the most powerful energy in the world – flashed before him in the bluish, almost wind-like light of the cathode lamp.

47

Ivan Pavlovich Novikov, a shaft sinker, was walking back home after the night shift.

His room was in a family barrack one and a half kilometres from the pit. Some of the ground was swampy and birches had been felled to make a corduroy road. Novikov's heavy boots seemed to make the earth sigh, and here and there dark water oozed up between the white trunks.

The autumn sun cast spots of light on the earth and the already brown grass. The many-hued birch and aspen leaves shone, greeting the morning. The air felt quite still, yet leaves here and there began to tremble; it was as if thousands of butterflies – small tortoiseshells, red admirals, swallowtails – were about to take wing and fill the transparent air with their weightless beauty. In the shade beneath the trees, fly agaric mushrooms held up their red umbrellas; amidst the lush, damp moss, lingonberries glowed like rubies on green velvet.

The forest's morning beauty had probably changed little over the last thousand years; it was composed of the same colours and the same moist, sweet smells. It was strange that this beauty should now exist side by side with the hum of the factory, with white clouds of steam escaping from the pithead, with the dense yellow-green smoke hanging over the coke furnaces.

The pit had left its imprint on Ivan's face, giving it a look of severity, even grimness. There seemed to be a constant frown on his forehead; thick slate dust had turned his dark eyelashes still darker and particles of coal had eaten into his skin, deepening the wrinkles around the corners of his mouth. Only his clear blue eyes remained cordial and welcoming, untouched by the darkness of work underground, by the coal and silicon dust that ate away at the miners' skin and lungs.

As a boy he had worked as an assistant in an underground stables. After that, he had worked in the lamp cabin, refilling the oil lamps. Then he had dragged a sledge along the low, hot galleries of a mine working very thin seams of coal; then as a pony driver on the main horizontal gallery, taking trams laden with coking coal to the central

609

shaft; and then, for two years, on the surface, in one of the Yuzovka pithead workshops, using dynamite to break up slabs of old iron to be loaded into the open-hearth furnaces. From there he went to the bar-stock workshop; standing beside his mill, he had looked like a medieval knight in chain mail and a metal visor.

Long before the war, however, he had gone back to working underground. Now a brigade leader, he had been in charge of everything from building new pump and storage rooms to digging new shafts, galleries, drifts and gravity planes. He had also been responsible for hole blasting and deep drilling.

His younger brother had graduated from the military academy several years ago. Many of his contemporaries had also made their mark in the world. Smiraev, who had worked alongside him as a trammer when the two of them were mere boys, was now a deputy minister; another man his age had become mines administration director for the area; a third was in charge of a food-processing plant in Rostov-on-Don. Styopka Vetlugin, his best friend from childhood, was now a member of the miners' trade union central committee, living in Moscow. Chetvernikov, who had also once worked beside him, had completed a correspondence degree at the metals institute and was now working somewhere either in Tomsk or Novosibirsk.

Many of the young lads he had once taught, who had called him Uncle Vanya, had also gone up in the world. One was a deputy to the Supreme Soviet; another worked in the Komsomol central committee and had once come to visit Ivan in a ZIS-101. And there were many others who had done well for themselves, more than he could remember.

But not once had Ivan's brother Pyotr – or any of these former schoolmates, fellow workers or juniors now working in such exalted spheres – ever thought of condescending to Ivan. Not once had anyone said, 'Still stuck at the coalface, are you? No hope of a change?' And Ivan, for his part, had always seen himself as strong and successful, a man who had done well in the world.

It was, in fact, Ivan whose friendliness and warmth to these others concealed a hint – though no more than a hint – of condescension. He had always thought of his work as the most important thing in his life; the title of worker meant a great deal to him. And he took it for granted that others – his brother, or old friends now living in Moscow – should glance questioningly at him as they told him about their lives, seeking his advice or approval.

Ivan began to climb the slope towards the barracks. Taking a short-cut between two loops in the road, he reached the top of the hill, then stopped to get his breath back.

In a distant hollow he could see the factory workshops, the pit-head structures, the slag heaps and the rails of the broad-gauge line that served the pit and the factory. He admired the pearly smoke over the coke furnaces, and the puffs of steam. As they rose into the sunlit morning sky, they reminded him of a large flock of well-fattened geese.

A powerful locomotive, its proud breast gleaming like a mirror, was letting out quiet hoots as it moved between the spur tracks, and Ivan looked with sudden envy at the driver, who was waving angrily at the pointsman. 'A real warrior of a locomotive!' he thought. 'Yes, it would be good to work on an engine like that.' And he imagined himself driving a huge freight train, carrying guns, tanks and ammunition. It was a stormy night and Ivan's train was doing seventy kilometres per hour. The rain lashed at the cab window, but his train was still tearing along, the broad southern steppe trembling beneath it.

Ivan was a born worker and he knew it. His greed for work, his profound curiosity about labour of every kind, had not diminished over the years. He would get carried away – thinking how interesting it would be to try his hand as a copper smelter, or as an engineer on a sea-going steamer, or to go to eastern Siberia and work in the gold mines.

He wanted to see how people live and work all over the earth. But he could not imagine himself as a mere traveller, idly observing cities, forests, fields and factories. And for this reason, no doubt, his dream of wandering was always linked to a dream of working as a locomotive driver, or as a mechanic on a plane or an ocean-going ship. And Ivan had done much to realize this dream; he had seen a great deal in his life. He was lucky in that his wife, Inna Vasilievna, was always ready to pack up and go, to accompany her husband to distant parts. Within a year or two, however, they always wanted to go back home – and they would return to the Donbass, to their village, to their pit.

They went to Spitsbergen;[236] Ivan worked for two years under-ground, and Inna taught Russian language and arithmetic to the Soviet children there. They lived for fifteen months in the Karakum Desert, where Ivan helped dig for sulphur and Inna taught adults. They also worked at a lead plant in the Tian Shan Mountains; Ivan worked as a borer, while his wife ran the adult literacy school.

During the last years before the war, however, they lost interest in travel. After many years without children, Inna finally gave birth to a little daughter – a frail child who was constantly falling sick. And, as often happens with couples who have had to wait for a child, there was something excessive, almost desperate about their love for this little girl and their constant fears with regard to her health.

Ivan looked at the workers' settlement on the eastern slope of the hill and felt a sudden warmth in his heart. In his mind's eye he could see little Masha, with her fair hair and her pale face. He would enter the barrack and she would come running out to meet him, wearing only her knickers. She looked pale – ever so slightly bluish. And she would call out, 'Pápa's back!'

How could anyone understand what he felt? He would take her in his arms, run one hand over her soft, warm hair, and gently carry her to their room. And she would kick about with her bare feet, push against him with her little fists, look him straight in the eye, tilt her head to one side and burst out laughing. It was almost too much for him. How could there be room in his heart for these little hands full of living warmth, these tiny fingers with nails like the scales of the very smallest of carp – and for the grinding howl of a drill, the muffled explosions of buried dynamite, the red, smoky fire flaring over the coke ovens? How could this warm, clean breath, these clear eyes coexist in his heart with the troubles and hardships of war, with the exhausted faces of the evacuees, with the blazing fires of that winter's night when he and her and Inna had boarded a train and left the village that was their home?

48

He came back in to find Inna hurriedly clearing the table and getting ready to go out to work – school would be starting in twenty minutes. She looked at her husband, picked up the pile of children's exercise books she'd been marking, and put them into her briefcase. Then she put an empty can and a glass jar into a bag; after lessons, she meant to go to the store. Speaking quickly, she said, 'Vanya, there's a kettle of hot water under the pillow and bread in the drawer of the bedside table. If you want *kasha*, there's a pot outside.'

'Where's Masha?'

'With the neighbours. Old Doronina will heat up some soup for her lunch. And I'll be back by five.'

'Still no letter from Pyotr?' Ivan asked, and let out a sigh.

'You'll get one in the next few days,' said Inna. 'I'm sure of it.'

She began to walk towards the door but then turned round, went up to her husband and put her hands on his broad shoulders. The gentleness of her smile made her weary face, for all its tiny wrinkles, look young and pretty.

'Go to bed, Vanya. Go to bed. Not even you can carry on working like this without a break,' she said quietly.

'I'm all right,' he answered. 'I need to go to the pit office. Masha can come with me.'

She took her husband's large rough hand, held it against her cheek and laughed. 'So then, workers of the world?' she said loudly. 'All on course? You won't let your drills run wild? Oh Vanya! Dear, dear Vanechka!'

Ivan went with his wife to the main door and watched her go on her way. The schoolgirls walking beside her were swinging their oil-skin briefcases, and she too swung her bag and her briefcase. Short, narrow-shouldered, walking with quick steps – from a distance, she too could have been a schoolgirl. And Ivan remembered his wife over the many years he had known her: as a young girl with a pigtail, fearlessly berating her father when he went on a pay-day bender; as a student at the pedagogical technical school, reading *Taras Bulba* aloud to him as they sat near the pond; wearing tall fur boots and a fur coat, holding a pile of exercise books to her chest as she walked through the snows of Spitsbergen, the harsh clarity of the street lamps alternating with the marvellous light of the aurora borealis; reading a Sovinform Bureau bulletin in a freight car during the long hungry days of their journey east, from Stalino to the Urals.

'Yes, I'm a lucky man,' he said to himself.

Just then there was a barely audible, mouse-like rustle behind his back – and his daughter flung her arms around his leg.

He bent down and picked her up. His head began to spin – perhaps from joy, perhaps from the strain of night after night of working underground.

After he'd had some tea, Ivan sat Masha on his shoulders, went out onto the street and set off towards the pit office.

The dugouts along the hillside, the long squat barracks, and even the individual houses for the engineers, foremen and leading Stakhanovites – all bore the imprint of the hardships of war. It was clearer than ever how little difference there was between the lives of the front-line soldiers and the lives of their brothers and fathers working in the mines and factories of the Urals.

This Urals workers' settlement had come into being, during the bitterly cold winter of 1941, as swiftly as the dugouts, trenches and bunkers of rifle divisions and artillery regiments had materialized amid similar hills and forests to the west.

The cables hanging between tree trunks, the telephone lines linking the houses of the director, the chief engineer and the secretary of the mine Party committee both to the pithead buildings and to the office, shop floors and control room, were similar to the field telephone cables that linked divisional HQ commanders to their front-line units and to workshops, food stores and support services in the rear. And the factory newspaper posted at the door of the pit's Party committee office, with its short articles on the achievements of mine workers, resembled the pages of a divisional newspaper brought out in a hurry at the height of a German offensive.

And just as divisional newspapers call on new recruits to study grenades, machine guns and anti-tank rifles, so a leaflet issued by the Party committee called on former housewives and kolkhoz workers to familiarize themselves with the workings of coal cutters, percussion drills and both light and heavy jackhammers. It was imperative that they learn to recognize when a cutter is unstable, when a motor sounds abnormal, when a cable has too much play and when a power drill is overheating.

The similarities between a front-line position and this Urals settlement made the sight of the local children all the more affecting. Fair-haired and dark-haired, timid or loud-mouthed, serious or mischievous – there they all were, playing beside the dugouts, on the slag heaps, above the quarries, amongst the autumn leaves.

Ivan stopped beside a wall newspaper.

'We've done it!' he said, after reading that senior shaft sinker Ivan Novikov's brigade – shaft sinkers Kotov and Devyatkin and timber-men Vikentiev and Latkov – had now made up for various delays and, according to every indicator, caught up with the most advanced brigades.

He read the article through, trying to hold Masha's feet still, patiently repeating now and again, 'Masha, Masha, what's got into you?' Masha, for her part, was trying to kick the newspaper.

When she at last succeeded, her big toe landed bang on her father's name, which was printed in large script.

'Masha, Masha! Kicking your father like that! How could you?'

'I didn't kick you,' Masha replied with conviction. And she stroked the cap on her father's head.

Nothing in the article was incorrect, but there was not a word about any of the most important things: that Ivan's subordinates were all exceptionally difficult and incompetent; that Kotov and Devyatkin had previously been in a labour battalion[237] and were desperate to return to working above ground, and that Latkov was a bully and a troublemaker – once he had even turned up for work drunk. Vikentiev, admittedly, was a professional miner, and mine work was something he understood and loved. But even he was not easy to work with; he was captious to the extreme, constantly finding fault with the trammers, none of whom had ever worked in a pit before. There was an evacuee from Kharkov, a woman by the name of Braginskaya, whom Vikentiev had reduced to despair. This had been inexcusable: her husband, an economist, had been killed at the front, and she was trying her best.

Even Ivan himself might have found it hard to explain how it was that the lazy Devyatkin, always wanting to sit down for a minute and eat another crust of bread, and Braginskaya, the thin, sad-eyed russi-fied Pole, and the troublesome Latkov ended up fulfilling their norm in these difficult, sometimes dangerous conditions. Did this simply hap-pen of itself? Or was it Ivan's doing? He was responsible, certainly, for various improvements to the conditions: ensuring better ventilation, increasing the depth of the blast holes from one and a half to two metres, eliminating delays in the supply of pit posts and empty trucks ... Probably, though, there was more to it than that.

Ivan looked crossly at the workers passing by. Why did none of them stop to read this newspaper? Were they all illiterate, or what?

As he approached the barrack that housed the mines administration, he caught sight of Braginskaya. 'What are you doing here?' he asked. 'You should be at home, resting.'

Braginskaya looked strange up on the earth's surface, in a beret and high-heeled shoes. Down below, when she was wearing rubber boots and a tarpaulin jacket, with a kerchief around her head, it had felt entirely natural to address her as 'Auntie'. 'Hey, Auntie, bring us a few empty trams!' Now, though, that would have felt wrong.

'I went to the clinic to make an appointment for my son,' she explained. 'I really can't cope. Yesterday I asked Yazev for an attestation. I was hoping to send my boy to the boarding school in the city. He'd get three meals a day there. But Yazev refused. So I'm still fighting on two fronts – at work and at home.'

She held up a page of the factory newspaper. 'Have you seen this?'

'I have,' said Ivan. 'And I'm sorry they didn't include your name.'

'Why should they?' she replied. 'It's enough that there's something about the brigade. Although ... Well, it would have been nice if they had ...' Embarrassed by what she had said, she put her hand on Masha's arm and asked, 'Your daughter?'

Her arms still around her father's neck, Masha said loudly and defiantly, 'Yes, I'm his daughter, he goes underground, and I'm not giving him up to anyone. I won't let go of him.' After a pause, she asked in an admonishing tone, 'Auntie, why are you angry? Because you weren't in the newspaper?'

Braginskaya murmured, 'My Kazimir let go of his pápa – and now his pápa will never come back.'

'You're a silly girl, Masha,' said Ivan. And then, 'You've been riding me long enough. It's time you went under your own steam.'

And he took the little girl from his shoulders and set her down on the ground.

49

Ivan looked at the three dust-covered cars parked outside the office. One, an Emka, belonged to Yazev, the mine director; the second, a ZIS-101, was the car used by the *obkom* secretary; and the third, a foreign make, probably belonged to the director of the military factory next to the railway station.

'I was called here, but I fear I'm wasting my time. It seems the bosses are having a meeting,' Ivan said to the mine-director's driver, whom he knew.

'What makes you think that?'

Ivan explained: 'Three cars at once means an official meeting. The bosses catch sight of one another – and that's that. Meetings are like gravity – there's no getting away from it. The bosses just have no choice.'

The driver laughed. The girl behind the wheel of the foreign car smiled. The driver of the *obkom* ZIS frowned disapprovingly.

Just then Yazev looked out from his office window and said, 'Ah, Novikov, come and join us!'

Ivan walked down the corridor, glancing at some of the announcements posted on the walls. Section head Rogov told Ivan that a representative of the State Defence Committee was visiting and that he had convened a technical discussion. 'He's with the director now,' Rogov continued. Winking, he added, 'Have no fears, brother.'

Ivan looked around in bewilderment. 'But what about Masha? Where can I leave Masha? I thought they only wanted me for a few minutes – to sign some document or other.'

Masha took a firm hold of her father's hand and issued a warning, 'Don't leave me on my own, Pápa – or I'll scream!'

'Why? You'll be with Auntie Niura the cleaning lady – she's your friend,' Ivan whispered pleadingly. But at that moment the office door opened, and the director's young secretary said impatiently, 'Come on, Novikov. Where've you been all this time?'

Ivan picked Masha up in his arms and went into the office.

Yazev, a handsome, tight-lipped thirty-five-year-old, in a smart tunic with a broad, shiny leather belt, was pacing about his office, his box-calf boots letting out satisfying creaks. Several other men were sitting around his desk. One, built like a warrior, was wearing a frayed general's jacket; he had bags under his eyes and tousled hair hanging over his large forehead. The second – in a grey summer jacket and a pale blue shirt with no tie – had the sallow face of a man accustomed to working all night. He wore spectacles and was sitting in Yazev's chair. Lying on the desk in front of him were an open briefcase, piles of documents and large sheets of crumpled blue tracing paper. Lapshin, director of the coal trust, a man with yellow teeth and a constant frown, and Motorin, the grey-haired secretary of the pit Party committee, sat on chairs pushed back against the walls. Motorin, with his lively brown eyes, was usually loud and forthright; now, though, he looked preoccupied and confused.

Standing by the window was a tall thin man in a black jacket with a turndown collar. Ivan knew him from a meeting the previous May. He was Ivan Kuzmich, the *obkom* secretary responsible for industry.

'Georgy Andreyevich, this is shaft sinker Novikov,' said Yazev, addressing the pale man in spectacles. He then frowned and said in a low voice, 'Why have you brought the child here? It was the mine director who summoned you, not the director of the nursery.' He pronounced *nursery* strangely, placing the stress on the final 'y' and somehow making the word sound ridiculous and offensive.

'I think she may be a little old for the nursery,' said the *obkom* secretary. And then, 'How old are you, my girl?'

Masha did not reply. Her eyes large and round, she looked enigmatically out of the window.

'Soon she'll be four,' said Ivan. 'And I thought you only wanted me here for a minute, to sign a statement about a malfunction in the supply of compressed air. Anyway, the nursery and the kindergarten are both closed – they're in quarantine.'

'Why's that?' asked the man in spectacles.

'There have been cases of measles,' said Motorin. He coughed guiltily.

'This is the ninth day they've been closed,' Ivan added.

'That's a long time,' said the man in spectacles. Frowning a little, he asked, 'And just what is this malfunction? Is it really necessary to sign some protocol? Wouldn't it be better simply to sort out what's wrong?'

Looking at Ivan, he said, 'Sit down, take the weight off your feet!'

Feeling annoyed with Yazev, Ivan said, 'How can I? The master of the house hasn't yet asked me to.'

'Sit down! You too are a master of the house!'

618

Ivan glanced at Yazev, shook his head, and smiled so slyly that everyone present began to laugh.

Ivan disliked the mine director. He remembered their very first hours in these parts: the bitter cold as they got out of the train; the snow squeaking, almost squealing underfoot; Inna sitting on their bundles of belongings, enveloped from head to toe in a wadded blanket and holding little Masha in her arms; newly kindled bonfires in a hollow not far from the railway; and Yazev standing beside his car in a white sheepskin coat and tall white boots while everyone crowded around him. The workers had just learned that their barracks were not yet properly set up and they were questioning him anxiously: what had happened to the stoves he had promised them? How, in the middle of the night, with their cases and bags, were they to get their young children to walk the eight kilometres to the settlement? Yazev had replied with fine words about the deprivations of wartime, the need to make sacrifices and what life was like now for soldiers on the front line. Coming from a man like Yazev, these words had sounded false. There had been a cold, distant look in his eyes and he had been wearing thick mittens embroidered with little fir trees. And his car had been full of parcels and packages, all neatly made up and carefully fastened.

Early in the morning, as Ivan approached the half-finished barracks, with two heavy bundles over his shoulder, supporting his wife with one arm and holding little Masha wrapped in her blanket in the other, a three-tonner loaded with furniture and household utensils had passed by. It had been only too obvious who this furniture must belong to.

That had been over nine months ago, and Ivan had had no face-to-face encounters with Yazev since that day. Nevertheless, his sense of antipathy towards him had not abated, and he stored away in his memory every little thing that fed this antipathy. What upset Ivan most was Yazev's general lack of feeling; he simply took no interest in his workers. Everyone agreed that it was impossible to get to see him – and that, even if you did, no good ever came of it. Not only would he refuse your request but he would also yell at his secretary, 'Has the war suddenly come to an end or something? Why are you letting people bother me with such trivialities? What about improving productivity? Why does no one come to consult me about that?'

In any enterprise there are, of course, a small number of people who like to bother their bosses with stupid and pointless requests. But for the main part people turn to a factory or workshop director only when they are desperate. And anyone who knows anything about workers' lives

619

understands the importance of their seemingly minor requests. Instructions to the nursery to take in a little child, a transfer from a bachelor barrack to a family barrack, permission to go to the boiler room and fill a jug with water that has been boiled, help with moving an elderly mother from her village to a workers' settlement, changing the store where you're registered so you don't have to walk so far to pick up your rations, permission to take a day off work so you can accompany your spouse to a city hospital for an operation, a request for a coal bunker – these things may appear trivial and tedious, but a worker's health and peace of mind depend on them, and so, therefore, does his or her productivity.

Looking at Yazev's calm, handsome face, Ivan felt ill at ease. He might be a competent director, but Ivan still didn't like him.

Ivan said quietly to Masha, 'Let's put you here.' And he moved her a little, so that Yazev's bright, cold eyes could no longer see her.

Georgy Andreyevich, the pale, bespectacled representative of the State Defence Committee, said, 'Comrade Novikov, I have a few questions for you.'

The general in the frayed jacket – evidently the director of the military factory – sighed loudly and said, 'Really there's only one question. The new seam needs to be opened up and exploited without delay.' Leaning against the desk and staring straight at Ivan, he went on, 'Ahead of schedule, we have completed the construction of a factory that will produce armour plating for tanks. According to the plan, it is you who should be supplying us with both coal and coke. But you are failing to do this. We need your coal today, but the seam has not even been opened yet. You are late.'

'On the contrary,' said Yazev. 'We are not behind with the plan – we are, in fact, overfulfilling it. The new seam will be opened on schedule.' Turning to Lapshin, the director of the coal trust, he added, 'That's right, isn't it? You provided me with the plan, and I am fulfilling it.'

Nodding in agreement, Lapshin replied, 'The works are on schedule. The mine is fulfilling the plan.' Turning to the general, he said crossly, 'That's no way to speak to people, comrade Meshkov! We have objective documentation, approved by the Party organs.' He then glanced at the *obkom* secretary and said, 'Isn't that so, Ivan Kuzmich?'

Ivan Kuzmich, however, replied, 'All that you say is true. Except that there *is* a problem. You're not keeping up with General Meshkov. He really does need the coke – and he needs it today.'

'I understand,' said Lapshin. 'But who is to blame? And what are you saying? Are we overfulfilling – or underfulfilling – the plan? Which is it?'

'Who is to blame?' asked General Meshkov, standing tall and looking more than ever the warrior. 'Clearly, Meshkov is to blame. No doubt about it. Meshkov's to blame for everything. And – along with Meshkov – the navvies who dug the foundation pits, the concrete layers, the bricklayers and electricians, the fitters and punchers, the riveters and welders, the entire working class, it appears. So don't hang back, comrade Yazev and comrade Lapshin – take us to court for constructing the factory in half the time decreed by the plan!'

Looking at the other men's laughing faces, Yazev frowned and said, 'Comrade General, you may soon be named a Hero of Socialist Labour,[238] but that doesn't make it any more possible for the mine to give you coal today. Here is a worker, a senior brigade leader, a shaft sinker. Ask him what *he* thinks! He'll tell you that the workers are going all out, putting their heart and soul into the work – but that they cannot do more. In spite of everything, they are still only human. The mine cannot give you coal today.'

'And when *can* it give me coal?'

'In accordance with the plan – at the end of the fourth quarter of 1942.'

'No,' said Ivan Kuzmich, 'that's not acceptable.'

'Then what is to be done?' asked Lapshin. 'The entire schedule, the provision of labour, materials and workers' rations – everything has been calculated in accord with the plan. And we didn't just dream this plan up. I ask a great deal of Yazev, but I can't provide him with qualified cadres. I have to speak frankly. And where can he find them himself? In the taiga? We have no borers, rippers or timbermen. And even if we did, Yazev would be unable to provide them with jackhammers and power drills. And even if we had the jackhammers and power drills, we'd still be constrained by the insufficient capacity of the compressor pump and the power station. So tell me – what is to be done?'

Georgy Andreyevich took off his glasses and studied the lenses. 'Comrade miners,' he said, 'the questions you keep asking are those that once preoccupied our revolutionary intelligentsia: "Who is to blame?" and "What is to be done?"'[239]

He put his glasses back on and looked around him; his eyes were now both sombre and penetrating. 'Questions of guilt and blame are for the public prosecutor to determine. But rather than trouble him needlessly, let us agree upon a new schedule for the exploitation of this deep-lying seam. We have only one plan, and it is a very simple plan: to defend the independence of the Soviet state.' With sudden force, he added, 'Understand? This is a simple plan – and it has not been dreamed up on a whim. Please reorganize your schedule in accord with this plan.'

Just then an elderly cleaner came in, bringing a teapot and glasses.

Turning to Motorin, Georgy Andreyevich said, 'It's horribly smoky in here – harmful to a child's lungs.' Then he looked at Masha and said, 'Perhaps you should go outside for a while, with Auntie?'

Masha was feeling bored and unhappy. She had heard more than enough about coal horizons, jackhammers, power drills and compressor pumps. Her father was always saying things like: 'Where can I find timbermen?'; 'The compressor pump isn't powerful enough'; 'For rock like this we need heavy-duty jackhammers.' And now she was hearing the same long, difficult words here. She yawned and said, 'It's not harmful here – it's boring.'

She held out her hand to the cleaner and made as if to leave the room. When she got to the door, she stopped and looked quickly round at her father, as if unsure of her rights and wanting to reaffirm them.

As for her father, he too was finding this discussion difficult. On the face of it, Yazev had said exactly what he wanted to say himself. All the same, he found himself wanting to disagree. Yazev's reasons for arguing with the general were personal; he did not feel the least real concern for the workers whose efforts to fulfil the plan he had described with such eloquence.

Then Yazev turned to Ivan and said, 'Let's ask comrade Novikov, one of our best shaft sinkers, how he gets his work done without a single experienced worker to call on. His brigade is made up of housewives, young lads from a technical school and kolkhoz workers who had never before set eyes on a mine, let alone helped sink shafts. Really I think we should all go down to the pit bottom, so you can see for yourselves the work that Novikov's doing. He's performing miracles! And you should see what kind of people he has for muckers and trammers. I saw one of his trammers just now – a Pole by the name of Braginskaya. She's in poor health. Her husband, a former office worker, was killed at the front. She was born and bred in the city and she's never even dug a garden before, let alone worked down a mine. How much can you ask of a woman like her? All these things must be taken into account, Georgy Andreyevich. You yourself have praised my work. My achievements have been noticed by the State Defence Committee. If I undertake to fulfil the plan, then that's what I do. And so, for all these reasons I'm not afraid to ask you to reconsider your proposal. But first, let's hear what our shock-worker has to say.'[240]

Ivan had noticed a frown on Georgy Andreyevich's face as he listened to Yazev. Abruptly, Yazev added, 'And let me tell you straightforwardly, Georgy Andreyevich – there's no need to preach at me. I understand that war is war. On our first day here, in December 1941, in the bitter cold, when our first train was unloaded onto the snow, I told everyone that this war requires sacrifices of them. And I am capable of reminding people about this – no one has ever called me soft-hearted.'

Then General Meshkov turned to Ivan. In a very different tone, as if the two of them were old friends, he said, 'We're in the same position as you are, comrade Novikov. Our workforce is the same mix – a few experienced workers, and a great many housewives and recruits from elsewhere. But it's not a matter of how things are for me and my factory. What matters is that new tank corps are being formed. I saw the commander of one of these new units only the other day.' Speaking more slowly and with emphasis, he continued, 'My God, when I think of what is at stake in this work ... But I must press on – yes, that's what the Party requires. All Yazev says is true and just. But we have no choice.'

Then Georgy Andreyevich said, 'Comrade Ivan, what do you think?'

In the course of only a second Ivan Novikov remembered what seemed like dozens of important things he wanted to say. He wanted to give vent to his anger with Yazev: how could he speak about Braginskaya with such feeling, yet refuse to help place her son in a boarding school? How could he tell his workers that they must remain in unheated barracks while installing such fine stoves in his own apartment? Ivan wanted to say that the workers' rations were inadequate, that many of them still had to live in damp dugouts and that by the end of the shift some could hardly stand upright. He wanted to describe the young soldier he had seen being buried at a small station in the Urals. He had died in a hospital train, been carried out on a stretcher and buried in frozen ground; he had looked like a fledgling. Ivan wanted to talk about his love for his daughter and how she kept falling ill here, unable to cope with the Urals climate. He wanted to say how his father had lain dying, hoping that Pyotr, his younger son, would be able to come and see him one last time. But Pyotr had been unable to obtain leave from his unit. He hadn't been able to say goodbye to his parents' grave – and now it was being trampled on by the Germans.

His heart was beating fast. He had a lot to say – and these men would listen to him.

Quietly, slowly, he said, 'I think we can do it. Give us our new plan.'

50

A heavy battery lamp in one hand, Ivan was walking towards the pit-head. It was late in the evening and he had just been to the office to collect his work order. Before that, while he was still at home, something astonishing had happened. Just as Inna predicted, he received news from his brother. His gasp of joy as he read the telegram had been so loud that it woke Masha. He had been feeling more and more anxious, wondering whether or not Pyotr was still alive – and now here he was, not far away, and perhaps about to come on a visit.

The patch of light from his lamp floated along beside him. Coming from the bathhouse, the office and the lamp cabin were hundreds of other swaying patches of light, all moving towards the pithead. A second stream of swaying lights – miners who had just come off shift – was flowing in the opposite direction, away from the pithead. Few people were talking; everyone was getting ready, each in their own way, to part from the earth's surface. However much someone may love working underground, these last moments before the descent always plunge them into a silent, meditative state; we are all attached to our everyday world and it is hard for us to leave it for even a few hours.

The swaying lights all told their different stories. A constellation of five was clearly a single brigade, each member behaving the same above ground as underground. One light, a little ahead of the others, was the brigade leader; then came three keeping close together; then one who seemed to be flitting about – falling behind, hurrying along and overtaking the others, falling behind again … This was probably some young lad in boots too big for him, half-asleep one moment and then trying to get a grip on himself. Next came a dotted line of solitary lights. Then a number of pairs – friends walking side by side, exchanging a few words, then falling silent. They would enter the cage together and go their separate ways underground. At the end of the shift, they would meet again at pit bottom, their teeth and the whites of their eyes gleaming in the dark.

*

A shining cloud flows out of the lamp cabin. Moving faster and faster, it spreads and fragments. At the pithead a new dense cloud has taken shape, pulsing and breathing, then slipping through doors that can't be seen in the dark. Up above in the autumn sky the stars gleam and twinkle, and there seems to be some link, some warm living connection between the lights of the miners' lamps and the stars' pale flickering. No wartime blackout has darkened the stars.

One hot summer night many years ago, Ivan had gone with his parents to a neighbouring pit. His mother held little Petya in her arms; his father was lighting the way, gently swinging his miner's lamp; Ivan was walking behind them. When his mother said she was exhausted and that she couldn't go on carrying such a weight, his father said, 'Vanya, you hold the lamp – and I'll hold little Petya.' But it was now many years since the death of their parents – and little Petya had become an imposing, taciturn colonel, and Ivan could no longer remember why they had all been walking to this other pit. To a wedding? Or because his grandfather was dying? But his memory of first touching the oil lamp's rough hook – of the lamp's weight and its quiet, living light – was as clear and vivid as ever.

He had been so short that he had had to bend his arm at the elbow – otherwise the lamp would have knocked against the ground.

*

All that could be seen in the dark were these swaying lights. It is possible that, during this thoughtful silence before the descent, everyone was dimly remembering moments from long ago and then thinking about the present day and the war, aware that childhood memories were now inseparable from the graves of loved ones.

Ivan went up to the cage. Instead of the freshness of the autumn night, he felt on his face the soft, dank breath of the mine.

People watched in silence as the greasy cable, gleaming in the electric light, slid quietly up out of the black gloom of the shaft. Gradually the cable began to slow, yellow-brown patches of oil separating from the silvery white of the spiralling metal thread. Still more slowly the cage itself emerged from the gloom; the bright eyes of men and women returning to the surface in wet, dirty tarpaulin overalls met the eyes of those about to go down.

Those who had just come up sensed the night's freshness mingling with the close air of the mine. Tired of hanging over the abyss, they waited impatiently for the banksman to release them, to let them set foot again on the earth.

'Eight young lads, eight lasses,' said Devyatkin, who was standing beside Novikov. Latkov laughed and shouted, 'Off to the registry office with them!'

Ivan had noticed that those new to pit work always found it impossible to stay calm as they prepared to go down. Latkov, sullen, wrinkled Kotov, the usually serious Devyatkin – all betrayed their agitation in one way or another. Latkov cracked jokes, in a loud voice clearly not that of someone simply feeling relaxed and happy. Kotov, on the other hand, always fell silent, looking down at the floor, as if saying, 'This is a bad business, and there are sights best left unseen.'

The women were usually more scared than the men the first time they went down – some even cried out and screamed – but they got used to it more quickly. Ivan even felt angered by the way they went on chattering, even inside the cage, about everyday, surface concerns like rations and fabrics. And the young ones would talk about films or tell stories along the lines of 'So I told him, and he told me, and then Lida asked, but he just laughed and lit a cigarette and didn't say a word in reply.' Women – Ivan realized – must be very different from him; they simply did not understand the seriousness of the work.

The chain rattled, and the banksman, another evacuee from the Donbass, winked at Ivan and signalled to the engineman.

'Oh, oh, Máma, give us a parachute!' Latkov yelled in a silly voice. As if needing support, he flung one arm round the shoulders of Natasha Popova, the winch operator.

She threw off his arm. 'Cut it out, you idiot!' she shouted crossly. 'Stop playing the fool!'

But Latkov was not simply playing the fool. Deep down he felt afraid. What if the cable were to choose this minute to snap? They might not be on the front line, but it was still 180 metres to the bottom of the shaft.

The descent was so fast that it made people feel a little dizzy. Ears always felt blocked and there would be a sudden lump in one's throat. But the cage rumbled on; the shaft's stone lining zipped past as if it were a smooth grey ribbon. There was more and more water on the walls, and warm, heavy drops spraying onto people's clothes and faces.

The cage slowed as it approached the upper seam, where coal was already being dug. The shaft lining now seemed less like a mica ribbon and more like a mosaic of rough-hewn stones of different shapes and colours.

The cage came to a stop. With a quick nod to Ivan, a number of people got out: a face worker, a timberman, two female winch operators, the driver of the electric locomotive and a coal-cutter operator – one of Ivan's neighbours in the family barrack.

The banksman gave the signal – and the cage began its descent to the lower level, where Ivan and his brigade were opening a gallery to a four-metre-thick seam of coking coal.

Ivan had spent three months of the previous winter sinking this deepest part of the shaft. As the cage moved down, he examined the shaft lining. There was no doubt about it: he and his men had done a good job.

The cage even seemed to be moving more smoothly. The drops from the walls felt pleasant, like drops of warm, summer rain when the sun comes out and a rainbow appears. And the air at pit bottom felt drier and cleaner than on the upper level.

Ivan had certainly done his share of hard work here. In midwinter, he had had to contend with an incoming stream. It had been like icy rain, falling onto his hot, sweaty back and slicing straight through him. Even now it was painful to think about. The shaft had been stifling, filled by a filthy fog from day after day of blasting through rock. He used to come back up to the surface exhausted and soaked to the bone. Beneath a howling blizzard he would run to the lamp cabin; the lamp's icy handle would stick to his fingers, burning them as if it had come straight out of a furnace. He would hand in his lamp and run on to the bathhouse.

He remembered his fifteen months in the Karakum Desert, working down a sulphur mine. While he was there, he had longed for the Russian winter. People would close all the doors and windows and lie about on the clay floors of their homes, wrapped in wet sheets and drinking green tea – but there was no escape from the suffocating heat. And he had to work underground – in the heat and dust, and with no real ventilation. And on top of all that, there was the smoke from repeated explosions. It was a wonder he had been able to breathe at all. At the end of the shift, it was out of one furnace and into another: nothing but dark rock and white sand stretching far into the distance. It was as if the whole earth were burning, gripped by some fever. The night sky, though, was unforgettable: anthracite-black, with huge stars, white and pale blue like anemones in the spring. If you were to strike at the anthracite with a pick, starry flowers would fall from the sky. Yes, the Karakum had been quite something.

*

They had reached the cross-cut. Devyatkin was tapping the support props. There was a gleam from the thin rails.

'It's certainly good solid flint here,' said Latkov. 'Comrade Novikov has signed us up for quite a task. Heaven knows when we'll get to the coal.' He seemed to be joking, but there was an edge to his words.

Kotov joined in, his voice deep and hoarse, 'I heard the surveyor say we'd be lucky to get this job done by December. Especially on our present rations.'

'Yes,' said Devyatkin. 'Comrade Novikov's promises may cost us dear. Before the war, there was a Pole who worked at our factory. He liked to say, "Promises, promises – cheap to speak, but dear to keep."'

'Where was he from?' asked Braginskaya.

'Why?'

'My uncle used to say the very same words.'

'My own uncle,' Latkov began dreamily – and he launched into some strange story.

Ivan, meanwhile, was taking note of the work done by the day shift. Here there was a damaged timber – it would need reinforcement or the roof might fall in. Here the wall had buckled a little. And here there was strong lateral pressure – the base of the timber set was unstable. The director had, of course, promised to bring compressed air to the adjacent cross-cut, but the pipe still came to an end exactly where it had come to an end yesterday. No more lengths of pipe had been brought down from the surface. Nor had Ivan seen any in the store. They'd undertaken to bring some from the station, but maybe there hadn't been any available trucks. Someone had at least brought a power cable, but what use was that when there was still no additional power supply? At present there was barely enough power even for the machines already at work on the upper level. The coal-cutter alone consumed a crazy amount.

They turned into another cross-cut, and Devyatkin said, 'Here we are – this is where we got to yesterday.'

'Yes,' said Latkov, 'and we did a good job. The props are lined up like soldiers on parade. Firm and solid. And this is where I nearly got buried. Remember, Kotov? We'd finished blasting and I was putting in a post.'

628

'Really?' said Kotov, 'I'd completely forgotten.' In fact, he remembered very well – he simply wanted to annoy Latkov. Then he turned to Ivan and said crossly, 'I'd expected our neighbours to have got their compressed air by now, but there's no sign of any new pipes. Neither down here, nor at the pithead.'

'Ah,' said Ivan. 'You've noticed too.'

But Kotov merely frowned. He felt he was doing the wrong kind of work. Not long ago he'd been in charge of procurement at a poultry-processing centre – and now here he was, stuck at the bottom of a pit. As for Devyatkin, he'd worked in a galalith factory, making the bodies for fountain pens. Then he'd worked in another factory, operating a press and punching out components. He was an experienced worker, but once, in the hostel, he too had said, 'When I look up at that roof, when I remember there are houses up above me, and pine trees, when I think about all that – no, I can't bear it ...'

Kotov, ever contrary, had said, 'All right – if you're scared of the pit, then volunteer for the front!'

'Maybe I will,' said Devyatkin.

The two men were walking side by side, glancing now and then at Ivan's broad back as he walked quietly towards the coalface. He was the gentlest and most good-natured of men, but Latkov seemed unable to stop needling him: 'So, Novikov, I hear you signed some document in the office yesterday, giving your word that we'd get to the coal by the first of the month. Did you ask *us* what we thought? Or will you be going it alone? Or will Party Secretary Motorin be working alongside you?'

'You know very well who I'll be working with,' Ivan replied calmly.

'Think we all have eight hands and a few extra skins?' asked Devyatkin.

'Before agreeing to take on more work, you should see the rations I received from the store yesterday,' said Kotov.

'Why?' Ivan replied. 'Do you think mine are any different?'

'Like it or not, Novikov, you're a born bureaucrat,' retorted Kotov.

'I don't think so,' said Ivan. 'I've been a worker all my life. You're the one who wants to get back to your office.'

Latkov saw two lights flickering in the distance and said, 'Look, Niura Lopatina and Vikentiev are at work already. They've got political consciousness all right – soon they'll be brigade leaders themselves!'

51

More and more clearly, they could sense how close they were to the coal seam. It was as if the coal were growing angry, turning vicious, knowing it was about to be disturbed. Now and then there were small escapes of gas while they were boring, and the jet of water they used to clean out the boreholes was splashing about alarmingly. Sometimes the gas escapes were strong enough to shoot out small pieces of rock.

A blower appeared in the roof; an invisible stream of gas was escaping into the gallery. There was an ominous whistle and, when they brought the lamp up close, they could see glistening particles of swift-moving shale dust. Niura Lopatina's blonde hair quivered when she moved her head close to the crack, as if someone were blowing on it. Before they started work, the grey-haired gas foreman came to carry out a check, and the flame in his indicator lamp swelled up alarmingly. The miners exchanged looks and the foreman said gravely, 'Did you see what that flame did, comrade Novikov?'

'Of course I did,' Ivan replied calmly. 'The coal's not far away – it's breathing.'

'You know what that flame means?'

'Of course I do. It means we're nearly there.' Turning to Kotov and Devyatkin, Ivan said, 'So, before we bore any more blast holes, we'll drill a deep exploratory hole with a hand-operated machine. Once there's a proper vent, we can bore more blast holes. That way there'll be no risk.'

'Yes,' the foreman replied. 'That's what the ventilation director said. "Haste," he said, "makes waste."'

'Worse than waste,' said Ivan. 'It can kill.'

'Is it dangerous down here?' asked Braginskaya.

Ivan shrugged. He had worked on the western slope of Smolyanka 11, a deep, hot and difficult mine prone to gas escapes that could lead to a whole gallery being buried under hundreds of tons of coal dust and rubble. It was certainly dangerous down there. A bad rock fall – and it would be a week before you could dig out the bodies. After that, the gallery would be closed off once and for all. And he had helped sink the shaft of Rutchenkovo 17–17. Those were the worst blowers he'd ever seen. The howl of escaping gas was so loud you couldn't hear people speak. Outbursts had smashed the shield of the borer. Yet in the end it had worked out – they'd got through to the seam. But as for this new blower … He couldn't make promises. A severe outburst could do a lot worse than send a quiver through Lopatina's blonde hair. They were, after all, working underground – this wasn't a sweets factory. What could he say to reassure Braginskaya? Only that it was a great deal more dangerous where his brother Pyotr was working. And then Braginskaya, as if understanding Ivan's silent smile and involuntary shrug, said in embarrassment, 'I'm sorry. I realize no one asked questions like that where my husband was working.'

Ivan looked at the faces of the hushed workers, each thinking thoughts of their own. He looked at the part of the working that had yet to be timbered, at the low roof, at the borer, at the dark, threatening sheen of the rock face, at the empty tram waiting to take out the rock they extracted, at the props with their fresh damp smell of pitch. For a second he saw little Masha's face, red and feverish, and her shining, wide-open eyes. He saw his wife, frowning anxiously. Almost diffidently, he said, 'Well, I suppose we should start work.'

Slowly, as if reluctantly, he went up to the borer and began checking the mechanism.

There is a particular beauty about this first moment of work, about this very first movement, as a worker finds his balance, as he overcomes the inertia of rest, apparently unaware of his own strength yet fully believing in it, not feeling any sense of pressure or tension but knowing he soon will.

A locomotive driver feels this as he gets ready to take a powerful freight locomotive out of the depot and his heart senses the first slight push of the piston. A lathe operator knows this at the beginning of his shift, when he senses the first birth of movement in a machine tool that has been standing idle. A pilot knows it, when his first almost meditative routine makes the propeller begin to rotate, sleepily and uncertainly.

A furnaceman, a ripper, a tractor driver, a metalworker taking hold of his wrench, a carpenter picking up his axe, a miner switching on his rock drill – all these people know, love and appreciate the beauty of these first movements that give birth to the rhythm, the power and the music of their work.

That night the work was particularly difficult. The ventilation was poor. The fan recently installed near the blower was malfunctioning and the damp heat was enervating. When blasts were carried out at a working nearby, the greasy, caustic smoke spread into the cross-cut. There was a pale blue mist around the workers' lamps and there were times when they could hardly breathe. Their throats burned and they were covered in sweat. All they wanted was to sit down for a few minutes. The thought of the fresh air high above them seemed like a mirage, a vision of a cool spring seen by a traveller in a desert.

Ivan set about drilling a deep exploratory borehole. At first, this went relatively smoothly. Calmly, sleepily, if a little crossly, the drill ground its way through the rock. It too seemed troubled by the heat and the lack of air, but it did not get jammed.

Latkov was helping Vikentiev to position the pine props and to bring him the tie beams he needed to complete the roof.

'That one's only half-finished,' said Vikentiev, pointing to the base of one of the props. 'Gone blind, or what?'

'It's the heat,' said Latkov. He went on, with feeling, 'There's nothing worse for a Russian than real heat. Cold's not so bad.'

'I wouldn't be so sure,' said Vikentiev. 'Last winter I worked on the surface in the Bogoslovsky district. Forty degrees below, and a fog like frozen sour cream, not lifting for weeks on end. Open-cast mines – when the wind comes off the Chelyabinsk steppe, that's when you learn what cold can do to you. Being out in the open isn't so easy. I caught pneumonia. No, we're better off down below.'

Kotov and Devyatkin were helping Ivan. They kept looking at him, wondering when he would stop adding extension rods to the drill bit. Devyatkin's temples and forehead were covered with dark drops of sweat; he was no longer wiping them away. Gasping for breath, he said, 'I know we've only just started, but I need a rest.'

'Keep going, Gavrila,' said Kotov. Finding it difficult to turn the hand crank on his own, he stopped and wiped his face with his sleeve. Ivan looked back and said, 'Keep at it – or the bit will jam! Devyatkin, you're soaking!'

'It's still running smoothly, thank God,' said Kotov.

'Why thank God?' said Ivan. 'You don't find coal smoothly.'

There were moments when Ivan, bending forward, focused on the drill and its progress, imagined he was still in the Donbass and that there was no war. The rock formation here was similar to that around the Smolyanin seam, and the dank air was like the air in the lower galleries of Smolyanka 11. At the end of the shift he would leave, go a short way on a bus and then walk back to the building where he had lived for so many years. He inhaled the moist, close air and took pleasure in the feel of the sweat on his forehead.

A sudden jet of water mixed with small pieces of rock struck him in the chest and shoulders with such force that he staggered, momentarily winded. Kotov and Devyatkin looked at him anxiously. In response, Ivan took a deep breath, shouted hoarsely, 'Don't stop now – we must keep the bit moving!'

Somewhere in these dark depths lay the seam and Ivan's drill bit was feeling its way towards it.

Within him, in all its fullness, he felt the strongest, truest force in the world – that of a working man. And he expended it generously, with no backward looks.

At this point, something happened that everyone present, astonished by what they witnessed, tried later to explain in their own way. Gentle, courteous Ivan Novikov was transformed. This man who so rarely raised his voice; who affably laughed off all Latkov's attempts to needle him; who always stood meekly in line both in the food store and when he was waiting to be taken up in the cage at the end of the shift; who quietly took his little daughter for walks down the settlement's single mud street; who was happy, if his wife had to go out, to check the washing on the clothes line or to sit outside the front door and peel potatoes – this man was transfigured. His bright eyes darkened; his movements, usually calm and slow, became swift and sharp; even his quiet voice became brusque and commanding.

Latkov inadvertently made everyone laugh. Appearing to think of Ivan as a Cossack leader, he yelled, 'Careful, comrade Ataman – there might be a fall!'

And Niura Lopatina came out with something oddly similar. As she and Braginskaya were taking out a heavy load of rock, she looked back, saw Ivan in the lamplight, spattered with water and black mud, and said, 'He's a second Yemelyan Pugachov!'[241]

Pushing away the strands of hair stuck to her forehead, Braginskaya replied, 'There must be some pagan god in him – I've never seen such a man.'

A little later, when they sat down for a rest after completing this first borehole, Niura Lopatina said, 'Kotov, did you hear Braginskaya just now? She said our brigade leader's a pagan god!' They all turned to look at Ivan. His ear to a crack in the rock, he was listening out for the whistle of escaping gas.

'Dunno about gods,' Kotov replied good-humouredly. 'Some damned devil more like.'

'The man's certainly no slouch,' said Devyatkin.

Sullen, skinny Vikentiev, with his constant cough, had once resented Ivan. He had felt angry that he, born in Siberia, should be subordinate to a foreigner, a newcomer from the Donbass. But even he said, 'You have to hand it to him. He's a true miner. He knows what's what down below.'

*

Ivan went up to the others and said, 'Well, comrades, we've made a vent. Now it's time to get down to a little work.'

Each member of the brigade had their particular task.

Braginskaya and Lopatina carried out the slabs of coal and piled them into the trams. Slowly, overcoming the resistance of the wheels, which were initially reluctant to turn, they pushed the loaded trams along to the main gallery. Latkov went to fetch the pine props and Vikentiev sorted through them, shaping them with a saw or an axe, and then putting in place the timber sets that secured the top and sides of the working. Kotov and Devyatkin worked alongside Ivan, breaking up with their picks the rock he loosed with his sticks of dynamite.

Each of these people had their particular thoughts, hopes and fears. Vikentiev thought about his wife and children, now in Anzhero-Sudzhensk. His wife had just written to say that she no longer had the strength to go on living apart from him – but what could he do? There were no more family rooms in the Chelyabinsk hostel. He thought about the seams he had worked in the Kuzbass, and how much richer they were than the thin, ashy Donbass seams that Novikov always spoke about with such pride. All the same, Novikov was a good brigade leader. With him around the work was never dull – it had soul. And Vikentiev also thought about his eldest son. In the autumn he'd probably be called up – he was already going to classes at the military commissariat. And he and his son wouldn't even be able to say goodbye – he certainly had no chance of getting any leave himself. And he thought about his wife: 'Liza, Liza, if only Liza were here … When I get back from work, she could apply cupping glasses. That would knock this damned cough on the head.'

And Latkov was thinking it was a pity he'd quarrelled with Niura Lopatina, and a pity he hadn't asked for meal coupons for canteen number one – everyone said the director was an honest man, that he didn't filch any of the supplies. And he shouldn't have gone to the flea market and swapped his boots for a leather jacket – his mates were making fun of him and saying he'd been swindled. But it was good to be working with an experienced timberman – he'd already learned all the main joints: dovetail, tongue and groove, mortise and tenon, and plain butt joints. At this rate, he'd soon have his name on the Board of Honour! Too bad he hadn't signed up for the evening course for coal-cutter operators. If only he were like Ivan Novikov, a man who put his heart and soul into whatever he did and fought his way past every obstacle! As for the bottle of moonshine he'd paid 150 roubles for on Saturday evening, it had brought him no joy. He hadn't liked the men he drank it with and the commandant had threatened to throw him out of the barrack. Yes, he just kept on getting everything wrong. He failed to think something through, then he wished he'd done it differently, then he went and got it wrong all over again. But perhaps he should just forget about those wretched boots ... And forget about that ignorant kolkhoz Niura ... Perhaps he should just go to the commissariat and say, 'I renounce my exemption. Please send me to join the defence of Stalingrad.'

Devyatkin, for his part, was thinking, 'This just isn't the right place for me. I'm a press operator, not a miner. I'll hitch a lift to the military factory and talk to the men in the workers' settlement there. I'm sure they'll say they need people in my line of work. Then I'll go and ask to be taken on. After all, I don't have a family to think about. I don't need a place in a hostel – I'm sure to find something somewhere. Except they probably won't let me leave this pit. That bureaucrat in charge of cadres is bad news, and I need her permission ... And then there's my father – I need to send him 200 roubles. Yes, I will, of course I will. Have I ever said that I won't? I'll never get any promotion here. On the shop floor it would be another story. I've got a lot of experience – I'd be noticed at once. Yes, I'd show them a thing or two – I'd be as good a worker as Ivan Novikov ... If it weren't for the war, I'd be married by now. But she went and signed up as a nurse. She's probably forgotten all about me. There'll be soldiers around her all the time, you can bet your life on it! Before the war I was a member of the guitarists' club ... Still, it may be all for the best. War's not so bad if you're single ... No ... My, life's been ruined, and that guitar of mine no longer even exists.'

Braginskaya was remembering for the thousandth time the day she said goodbye to her husband, at the main railway station in Kharkov ... No, that's just not possible. There must have been some mistake. Another man with the same surname. But no, there had been no mistake. She was a widow now, a widow – a word she could never get used to. A widow, a widow, a widow, and Kazimir was an orphan.

And he, her husband, was lying there all on his own, in the earth, under a willow. Who, in the spring of 1941, could have imagined all this? Who could have imagined that he would be gone for ever and that she would be working deep underground and wearing a tarpaulin jacket, far away to the east? In the summer they'd been planning to go to the Black Sea, to Anapa. Before they left, she would have had a perm and a manicure. When they got back, little Kazimir would have started at a school for musically gifted children … There are times you forget everything, when it seems there's nothing more important than this coal and your shovel. And then, again, the Kharkov railway station, that warm, close morning, and puddles gleaming in the sun and rain, and that last sweet, confused, would-be-encouraging smile he had given her, and all those different hands waving from the carriage windows: 'Goodbye, goodbye!' Had she merely imagined that life? Two rooms, an ottoman, a telephone, a bread basket on the table, all those different breads – white bread, bread from sifted flour, bread rings[242] and yesterday's bread that no one wanted to eat. And now, backfill, tie beams, coal hewers, a tram going off the rails, blast holes, cutting and boring … And the way Ivan says, 'The coal's waiting. Shall we get down to work?' – and then smiles that wonderful smile of his.

Kotov was frowning, wondering how things were now in Karachev, the town near Oryol where he'd been born. He could almost feel the breeze, first thing in the morning, coming off the Bryansk forest. And he was thinking about his eighty-two-year-old mother: 'No, I'll never see Máma again – no, not with the fascists roaming around the village. As for dear Dasha, she doesn't have a clue. Why is it, she asked yesterday, that Vikentiev brings back 900 roubles while you only get 486? Does she think I'm a trained miner, with years of experience? She's a fool – she always has been a fool, and she always will be a fool. I'll tell her it's time she started working herself. Standing in line outside stores and chit-chat-chattering isn't what I call work – and certainly not in wartime. You're strong and fit, so work as a trammer! I've been kind to her, she's never wanted for anything. Still, she used to make a fine borsch, back in Karachev … And when I had to go to Oryol, Petya would drive, and I'd be up in the cab beside him. Orchards everywhere. Apple blossom. And the sky … No, there's nowhere better on earth.'

Niura Lopatina was thinking, 'It's probably all for the best. Latkov's a lout. Máma was right – there's no one to beat our village lads. I don't understand what the likes of Latkov are always moaning about. Work below ground, work above ground – it's all much the same. I like the young girls in the hostel. Once a week to the cinema. And magazines, and the radio. No, I won't find anyone better than my Sasha ... Latkov's a loudmouth. It's all right for him – he's got himself exempted. While my Sasha's ready to die for us, he's defending Stalingrad. Yet he's so gentle, and he has principles, and he never says a coarse word in front of a woman. Latkov's not like that – you can see at once he's from a children's home. I'm better off on my own. I send money to my mother and father every month. And I'll go to evening classes and study to be an electrician. Yesterday I spoke to a Komsomol representative and she promised to register me for the course. I just hope my brother comes back alive. And Sasha, and Uncle Ivan, and Uncle Petya, and Alyosha Nyurin. But no, that's not likely. I heard from Máma that Luba Rukina's already received a notification of death. And Sergeyeva received two on the same day. While back here, far from the front, we get men like Latkov. To this day he's afraid of the mine – I can see it in his eyes. Foul language is another matter – he's not afraid of that. Yes, he's not like the lads from our village.'

Everyone seemed to be carrying out their individual tasks – yet, now and then, in the stifling air, it was as if you could hear the buzzing of bees, a delicate, joyful music that stirred every heart, no matter how young or old. Everyone working there was bound by this strong, singing link. Their tasks, their movements, the slow steps of the trammers, the dull blows of the picks, the grinding sound of the shovels, the hiss of the saw, the boom of the back of an axe striking an obstinate strut that doesn't want to take on the burden of supporting the roof, the measured, regular breathing of the man operating the borer – all these came together to form a single living force. Everything was living as one and breathing as one.

And the fair-haired man with the kind eyes and the broad cheek-bones, the man with hands strong enough to lift a heavy iron beam and delicate enough to adjust the hairspring of a watch – this man could sense everything. Without even turning his head, he sensed with some sixth sense the threads that linked him to all his fellow workers.

But later, as they made their way to the lamp room, groaning with exhaustion, thinking about their homes and their difficult lives, there was much they found strange and mysterious. Why could they only feel their own good, wise strength when it was united with the strength of others? How could they feel so free when they had yielded their freedom to others? It was not easy to understand how subordina-tion to their brigade leader could allow the very best in them to open and blossom.

52

Late in the evening, everyone gathered for a brief meeting at the pit-head. Those on the night shift had been told to come to work twenty minutes early. The day-shift workers were streaming out from the cage.

Party Secretary Motorin had gone down the mine earlier to tell them about the meeting. Some had grumbled, saying they were exhausted enough already. Motorin had replied, 'You'll be all right. The autumn nights are getting longer. Plenty of time to sleep – you can see everyone you need to see in your dreams.'

The night was dark, windy and starless. There was a rustle of leaves from the trees nearby and the more constant, even sound of the pine forest. There were brief spells of rain; the cold droplets falling on people's hands and faces seemed like a foretaste of the foul weather to come, of autumn mud, of the snowstorms and snowdrifts of winter. The oblique beam of the pithead searchlight picked out the heavy, ragged clouds up above, making it seem as if it were they that were rustling, not the trees.

A number of engineers and Party leaders were standing on a simple wooden platform. There was a quiet hum from the sea of miners around them, and the black faces of the day-shift workers merged with the black of the night.

There were repeated small flashes as people lit cigarettes. Their sense of pleasure – inhaling the warm, bitter smoke along with the damp cool of the night – was almost palpable.

There was something peculiar and deeply affecting about this picture. The cold autumn night and the rain; the dark of the sky and the dark of the earth; the electric lights of the railway station and a coal mine close by; the faint pink stains cast on the clouds by the many other mines and factories round about; the muted hum of the forest, composed of the sullen breath of century-old tree trunks, the silky rustle of pine needles, the creak of pine branches and the sound of pine cones knocking against one another in the wind.

And within this frame of rain and darkness shone an extraordinary concentration of light. There was more light here than the sky could ever have glimpsed, even on its starriest nights.

First to speak was Motorin. He felt strange and awkward. He had spoken in public any number of times – underground, at pit bottom, during short briefings, at workers' meetings, public rallies and gatherings of Stakhanovites. Talks and debates were his bread and butter. The memory of his very first speech, at a provincial Komsomol conference, now made him smile. He had mounted the rostrum, but the sight of hundreds of alert, animated faces disorientated him. He had stammered a few words, felt ashamed of the way his voice was trembling, spread his hands in despair and returned to his seat, accompanied by good-natured laughter and indulgent applause. When Motorin told his children about this occasion, he found it hard to believe that it had really happened. Today, though, he found it only too easy. There was a lump in his throat, he was out of breath and his heart was beating wildly.

Either his nerves were giving out – from general exhaustion and too many nights without sleep – or else it was because of the report he had heard from an officer just arrived from Stalingrad. This officer had told the Party committee about the heavy fighting in the south-east, about how large areas of the city had burned to the ground, and about the Germans breaking through to the Volga. Red Army soldiers had been trapped on the shore, with their backs to the water. Laughing Germans had shouted out, 'Hey, Russky, glug-glug!' And then, just before this meeting, Motorin had received yet another grim Sovinform Bureau report.

'Comrades,' he began in a weak, trembling voice. Still struggling to get his breath back, he thought for a moment that he would be unable to speak.

For no apparent reason, he found himself imagining his father. Barefoot, wearing a blue shirt, his father had gone to the pit to say goodbye to his fellow workers; his eyes were bloodshot and his long grey beard was unkempt. Raising one hand, he had said, 'Dear workers and friends …'

His voice still lived in Motorin's memory. Carefully and obediently, with the same intonations, Motorin said, 'Dear workers and friends …' He paused, then quietly repeated, 'Dear workers and friends …'

Lost in the crowd around the platform, shaft sinker Novikov let out a quiet sigh and took a step forward. He wanted to be able to hear better and to see the speaker's face; there was something important, long familiar to him, in this voice.

Dozens of other men and women did the same. It was hard, because of the wind in the trees, to make out the speaker's words. Nevertheless, his voice touched something deep inside them.

Devyatkin and Kotov edged forward. So did Latkov, Braginskaya and Niura Lopatina.

Swaying gently, hundreds of lamps moved at once. With everyone pressing towards the platform, the light surrounding Motorin seemed brighter and more intense.

His carefully prepared speech – about productivity, extraction rates and linear metres of coal – vanished into the air. With no idea what he was going to say, he went on, 'I've remembered something from when I was very small. The mine owner had fired my father and locked us out of our room. He'd thrown all our belongings onto the street. It was the room where my two sisters and I were born and it was autumn, just like now. Guards came, and policemen. We had to go – but how could we? This place was our home. It was where we had lived and worked, where my grandfather and grandmother were buried. I looked at my father. I heard him saying his goodbyes. All that was a long time ago. Now I have grey hair too, but I can't forget. I just can't.'

Motorin glanced at the lights all around him. He was surrounded by people, yet he felt as if he were talking to himself. In a tone of surprise he asked, 'Comrades, do you understand why I'm telling you all this?'

But he was not surprised to hear many people reply, 'Yes, we do.'

Now sounding calm and confident, though this calm was really an expression of intense inner excitement, he continued his speech. He raised his lamp in the air, dug about in his pocket, pulled out a crumpled slip of paper and began to read the latest Sovinform Bureau bulletin:

Fighting continues on the north-western outskirts of Stalingrad. The enemy, ready to pay any price to break the resistance of the city's defenders, is launching repeated attacks. During the night small detachments of Hitler's forces succeeded in penetrating several streets. Fierce street fighting is leading to hand-to-hand combat.

He knew now that everyone understood why, before reading this bulletin, he had spoken about his father; he no longer felt the need to ask.

He was speaking slowly and quietly, but everything he said was entirely clear. And just as before, he felt as if he were talking to himself,

640

and yet, at the same time, giving voice to the thoughts of all those around him.

Ivan Novikov felt as if he were not only listening but also speaking. Except that he couldn't quite understand why his voice sounded different from usual. He felt that he, Novikov, was repeating words he had pronounced long ago: that there was no task beyond the power of the working class as they fought to defend their home. And at the same time he was thinking about little Masha. Why was she still feverish? Maybe it wasn't just malaria. Maybe she had TB?

High in the dark autumn sky, swift clouds reflected faint, trembling pink shadows – traces left by the breath of the many mines and factories round about, a reminder of the tens of thousands of mines, factories and railway-station workshops between the Volga and the Pacific, a reminder of all the workers who, like Novikov, Braginskaya, Motorin and Kotov, thought constantly about the dead, about those who had gone missing in action, about the war and all the hardships of wartime life, a reminder of the countless people who, like Novikov, Braginskaya, Motorin, Kotov and old Andreyev in burning Stalingrad, knew that their strength as workers was invincible, that it would overcome everything.

PART III

1

On 25 August, the Germans began to advance on Stalingrad from the west, from Kalach. To the south, German tanks and infantry had already broken through the Soviet front near Abganerovo and advanced as far as the Dubovy ravine, beyond Lake Sarp.

To the north, German troops now occupied the village of Rynok, near the Tractor Factory. Stalingrad was thus under threat from north, south and west.

On 31 August, the Germans launched a new assault on Bassargino-Varaponovo; units of the 62nd Army were forced to retreat to the second of the city's three rings of defences. By 2 September, however, further German attacks had forced these heavily depleted units to withdraw to the innermost ring of defence, an arc passing through workers' settlements known to everyone in the city: Orlovka, Gumrak and Peschanka.

These attacks – eight German divisions, advancing on a narrow front – were supported by a thousand aircraft and the firepower of 500 tanks. In the open steppe, our troops were especially vulnerable to attacks from the air.

The German artillery was favourably positioned on the higher ground to the west; their observers had an unimpeded view not only of the Soviet front line but also of supporting units further back. They were able to direct accurate fire onto almost all the approaches to the Soviet combat positions.

The terrain was equally favourable to the German infantry regiments. The many gullies and ravines stretching down to the Volga, the riverbeds – including those of the Mechetka and the Tsarina, which went dry in summer – all provided excellent cover for their advance.

Not only all that remained of the 62nd Army, but also all the reserves at the Front commander's disposal were thrown into the battle.

Fighting beside them were people's militia units – factory and office workers now transformed into machine-gunners, tank men, mortarmen and artillery men.

For all the stubbornness of the defenders, the Germans continued to advance. Their numerical superiority was simply too great. There were three German soldiers for every Russian soldier, two German guns for every Russian gun.

The fifth of September saw the beginning of a major offensive by the Soviet armies positioned to the north and north-west of Stalingrad.

The fighting was bitter. Advancing through open steppe, the Soviet forces suffered considerable losses. From morning until night German aircraft hung over the Soviet infantry like a dark cloud; Soviet artillery and tank concentrations were bombed even more heavily.

The offensive appeared to have been a failure: the Soviet forces failed to break through the corridor the Germans had established between the Don and the Volga. Fierce battles for a number of commanding heights brought no decisive success. Minor territorial gains, for which the Soviets paid a high price, were erased by counter-attacks from German tanks and dive-bombers. Nevertheless, the offensive compelled the Germans to divert a significant part of their forces to the north, away from their main objective. In this respect, it succeeded.

The offensive was a success in one other respect, unrecognized by most of those who took part in it: it won time, helping the city's defenders to hold out until the arrival of reinforcements.

Time is always the enemy of opportunists and a friend to those who stand on the side of history. It exposes false strength and rewards true strength.

But time's precious power is revealed only when people see it not as a generous gift of fate, but as an ally who makes stern demands.

The Red Army's reserves, aware of the importance of every hour and making no distinction between day and night, were moving swiftly towards Stalingrad.

Among the units that saw their baptism of fire during the 5 September offensive, on the high western bank of the Volga, near the village of Okatovka, was the division in which Lieutenant Shaposhnikov now served as a gunner. And among the units marching along the Volga's low eastern bank, towards Stalingrad, was Major General Rodimtsev's infantry division; Pyotr Vavilov was one of his foot soldiers and Lieutenant Kovalyov was one of his company commanders. The Stavka had ordered Rodimtsev's division to be the first to enter the besieged city. The division's name and fame would remain inseparable for ever from the name of Stalingrad.

2

Barely had they dragged their guns to the top of a vine-covered hill when a messenger ran up and ordered everyone to their fire positions; concentrations of German forces had appeared in the gardens and vineyards of the surrounding hills.

Tolya Shaposhnikov was covered in dust and sweat after helping to drag the guns up the steep clay scree. His new orders were to supervise the ammunition supply.

The ammunition trucks were still down by the Volga, unable to manage the steep climb.

Tolya raced down a mossy grass-covered slope, the warm wind whistling in his ears. Without slowing, in a cloud of red dust, he continued down the steep cliff to the water.

Up on the hill, the sun had been dazzling; in the shadow cast by the cliff it seemed to be already evening. Further out, away from the cliff's shadow, the Volga sparkled like mercury, alive and resilient.

After positioning a chain of soldiers to pass the shells up the slope, Tolya got onto the truck and began to help unload. 'I don't want anyone thinking that all I can do is give orders,' he muttered, as he moved crates of shells towards the side of the truck.

He felt he had done the wrong thing by going to artillery school; he would have found it easier to serve as a rank-and-file soldier. With his strong build and surly face, he looked tough and ungiving, but both his superiors and his subordinates had quickly understood that Tolya was, in fact, unusually shy and good-natured. When it came to issuing orders, he grew confused and indecisive. He would stammer and stumble through long strings of 'Please ... could you possibly ...', then rattle out the important words so fast that no one could understand a thing. Feeling both sorry for Tolya and irritated with him, his battery commander Vlasyuk had done his best to be encouraging: 'Shaposhnikov! Stop mumbling and muttering! You're an artilleryman – and the artillery is the god of war! Speak with authority!'

Tolya was only too glad to do small favours for his comrades and superiors – copying a report, fetching the post, filling in as duty officer.

His comrades would joke: 'A shame Shaposhnikov isn't here. You could have asked him to take your place at HQ. That would have made his day!' Or: 'Ask Shaposhnikov, he'll be here any moment.' And then, with a smile, 'He loves a spell on duty – and a nice walk to HQ in the heat of the day.'

At the same time, they appreciated his gifts. Everyone – and his fellow gunners above all – valued his outstanding mathematical and technical ability. He could quickly sort out any problems they had with their equipment. He could make complex and abstract physical laws comprehensible to the stupidest of men. With the help of the simple little diagrams he drew, even those who had always relied entirely on rote learning quickly came to a true understanding of how best to calculate the correct aim – taking into account distance, wind speed and wind direction – when firing at a moving target.

All the same, it was hard not to laugh at Tolya. The moment anyone began to talk about girls, he would start to cough and blush. Nurses from the medical battalion, who looked on the artillery commanders as the best educated in the division, would ask his fellow lieutenants, 'Why's your friend so stand-offish? He never says a word to any of us. If he sees us coming, he steps to one side. If we ask him anything, he gives us a one-word answer and hurries away.'

On one occasion Shaposhnikov said to Vlasyuk, 'A young person from the opposite sex was asking about you at HQ.'

After that, his comrades nicknamed him 'Young Person from the Opposite Sex.'

To the rank-and-file soldiers, however, he was known as 'Lieutenant, Could You Possibly?'

*

Everything looked grand and majestic. The vast, empty river glimmered in the sun. One might have expected an eternal silence over its timeless waters, but there was noise everywhere.

Pushing loose pieces of sandstone aside, road tractors were dragging guns and ammunition trailers along the narrow strip of land between the high cliffs and the water. Machine-gunners and foot soldiers with anti-tank rifles were clambering up the slope, away from this confined space and towards the open steppe. Other companies and battalions followed at their heels.

The sky, usually so blue, silent and splendid, was torn apart by the din of aerial combat. Engines howled among the fluffy white clouds;

there was the clatter of machine guns and the crack of quick-firing cannon. Sometimes planes swept low over the water before climbing up into the sky again; battles were being fought at every level.

From the steppe came the sound of terrestrial combat – the counter-attack launched by the Red Army's reserve regiments against Paulus's most northern units.

To the men down by the river, in ominous shadow, it felt strange that the warm steppe, where the sun shone so bright and carefree, should be seeing such bloody fighting.

Armed men continued to climb the slope. Every face bore the same expression of agitation and resolve, a paradoxical combination of the fear felt by a soldier going into battle for the first time and the fear of falling behind your comrades – a fear that compels you to quicken your step as you near the front line.

This was the most important day of Tolya's life.

An hour earlier, his unit had passed through Dubovka, beside the Volga. Here for the first time he had heard the whistle and thunder of falling bombs. He had seen smashed houses and streets covered in broken glass. A cart had passed, bearing a woman in a yellow dress. She was lying down and her blood was dripping swiftly onto the sand. An elderly man with no jacket was walking along with one hand on the side of the cart, sobbing loudly. Away from the road, behind fences, dozens of well-poles swayed and creaked in the wind; they looked like the masts of crazed little boats.

Early that morning he had drunk milk in the quiet little village of Olkhovka and had seen young geese grazing in a broad, damp field of bright green grass.

During a brief halt in the night, he had walked thirty or forty metres from the road, the dry wormwood rustling beneath his boots, lain down on his back and looked up at the starry sky. He had heard the soldiers talking to one another but had carried on gazing at the flickering stellar dust.

Yesterday afternoon there had been the stuffy fume-laden heat of the cab of a large truck, a hot dust-covered windscreen, and the rumble of the engine. A year ago: a small oilcloth-covered writing table in Kazan, a school exercise book he used for a diary, the book he was reading, and his mother's warm palm on his forehead as she said, 'Go to bed now!'

Two years before that: skinny little Nadya, wearing only her knickers, running barefoot up the steps of the dacha terrace and yelling, 'Tolya's a fool, and he's stolen my volleyball.' And further back still:

a child's model-aircraft kit; tea with milk and a candy before going to bed; a sledge with a hard seat, covered by a cloth with a fringe; and a fir tree on New Year's Eve. Viktor Pavlovich's grey-haired mother had held Tolya on her lap and, very softly, sung, 'A fir tree was born in a forest,' – and, in his thin little voice, he had joined in, 'There in the forest, the fir grew tall.'

All this was compressed into a tiny, compact lump, like a hazelnut. Had any of it ever existed at all?

The only reality now was the thunder of battle, still some distance away, but drawing nearer and growing louder.

Tolya felt confused. It was not that he was afraid of death or suffering; it was more that he was afraid of the test to which he would soon be subjected. Would he pass this test? Some of his fears were childish, others more adult. Would he be able to give orders in the heat of battle? Or would his voice crack? Would he let out little squeaks like a baby hare? Would his commander call out, 'What a mummy's boy!'? Would he suddenly flinch for no reason at all, while his gunners watched condescendingly? He didn't, at least, need to worry about his guns. He knew his guns all right – what concerned him was whether or not he knew himself.

Now and then he thought about his mother, but, rather than feeling homesick, he felt angry and resentful. Could she not have foreseen that he would be put to this test? Why had she always indulged him, protecting him from the cold, the rain and any hard labour? Why all those candies, cookies and New Year trees? She should have started to make a man of him from the very start. She should have imposed a regime of cold baths, coarse, simple food, factory work, long hikes in the mountains, and so on. And he should have learned to smoke.

And he kept looking up towards the top of the cliff, to the source of all these explosions and rumbles, to where the sun shone with such crazy brightness. He was so timid. He was always losing his voice. How could he command strong men who had already seen combat?

Tolya knocked on the roof of the cab and the driver poked his head out of the window. 'Comrade driver,' Tolya called out, 'move to one side now. We need to start on the next truck.'

Tolya was just getting down from the truck, telling himself that the unloading and delivery of shells was an important, responsible job, when he saw a sergeant from the command post running, sometimes leaping, down the slope. He was yelling to the soldiers handling the shells, 'Where's the lieutenant?'

A minute later he was standing in front of Tolya, saying, 'Comrade Lieutenant, the battery commander has been wounded by machine-gun fire from a plane. The comrade major orders you to take command of the battery.'

Tolya and the sergeant began to scramble up the slope. The sergeant, gasping for breath, told Tolya what had happened in his absence. The neighbouring division's infantry had gone forward. Their battery had not been bombed, but it had been strafed by fighters; there were several wounded. The steppe was white from propaganda leaflets dropped by the Germans. It was now only four kilometres to the German front line.

As he listened, Tolya gazed at the red dust once again swirling under his feet. He looked around: the Volga was now far below.

They came to their hill. It was steep and slippery, covered in moss and small pebbles. The sergeant went in front, sometimes pressing his hands against his knees to help his balance. The sudden sunlight on Tolya's face was harsh and dazzling.

Tolya never came to understand why and at what point he turned calm and confident. Was it when he reached the guns and saw their powerful, merciless barrels, camouflaged by dry grass and vine twigs, trained on the heights occupied by the Germans? Was it when he saw his men's joy and relief at the sight of their new commander? When he looked at the steppe, at the German leaflets now covering it like a white rash, and was struck by the clear and simple idea that everything he most hated, everything most hostile to his homeland, to his mother, sister and grandmother, to their freedom, happiness and life, lay there in front of him and that it was in his power to fight this enemy horde? Or when he received his battle orders and audaciously, almost merrily, decided to advance his guns far forward, to take up fire positions on the very crest of the slope. His guns, after all, were the Front's left flank. His own flank was covered by nothing less than the Volga; he could not be outflanked.

Never had Tolya felt as strong, as important to others as he did now. Never had he known that he could act with such daring, that there could be such joy in taking a bold decision, or that his voice could sound so loud and confident.

As the gunners were pushing their guns to the crest and Tolya was telling the sergeant major where to position them, a lieutenant colonel from Division HQ drove up in his jeep. He went straight to Tolya and asked, 'Who ordered you to advance the guns so far forward?'

'I gave the order myself,' Tolya replied.

'There's no one to cover you. Do you want to fall into the hands of the Germans?'

'No, comrade Lieutenant Colonel. I want the Germans to fall into *my* hands.' And Tolya quickly explained the advantages of this forward position. The guns were sheltered by a small copse, protected to the east by the Volga and to the south by a steep cliff – and they commanded a large area of steppe that the German tanks would have to cross. 'Their tanks are concentrated behind those orchards. They're in our sights, comrade Lieutenant Colonel. No need for calculations – we can lay for direct fire!'

The lieutenant colonel, narrowing his eyes, looked at the new fire positions, at the ravine snaking down to the Volga, and then at the steppe, where he could see groups of advancing Soviet infantry and small clouds from exploding mortar bombs.

'All right,' he said, now sounding less like a senior commander. 'I can see you're no fool. Been fighting since the very beginning, have you?'

'No, comrade Lieutenant Colonel, today's my first day.'

'Then you're a born gunner!' said the lieutenant colonel. 'So, don't lose contact with HQ. I can't see your telephone cable. Where is it?'

'I said to place it over there, down the slope. It's less likely to be damaged by shrapnel.'

'Good man, good man!' said the lieutenant colonel, and returned to his jeep.

Soon the major telephoned and ordered Tolya not to open fire until he received the order. He warned him that enemy tanks might appear to his right and that they must be held back at all cost. Should the tanks break through, there would be nothing between them and the ammunition and other equipment now being brought up to support the advancing Soviet infantry.

Listening to Tolya's replies, the major suddenly doubted whether he really was speaking to Lieutenant Shaposhnikov – he sounded uncharacteristically strong and bold. Had some German intercepted his call?

'Shaposhnikov, is that you on the line?'

'Yes, comrade Major.'

'Who have you taken over from?'

'Senior Lieutenant Vlasyuk, comrade Major.'

'Your name?'

'Tolya, I mean Anatoly, comrade Major.'

'Very good. Somehow I didn't quite recognize your voice. That's all for now.'

The major put the receiver down. He assumed that Tolya had found his new courage in vodka.

The day proved extraordinarily long, infinitely full of events. Afterwards, Tolya would feel he had more to say about this day than about the whole of his life before it.

The battery's first salvo sounded magnificent. Everything round about froze. The steppe, the huge sky, the blue Volga – all listened intently, caught the sounds up and multiplied them with repeated echoes. Steppe, sky and river – all put their heart and soul into these echoes. They were broad and solemn as peals of thunder, full of dense sadness and sullen anger, an impossible fusion of furious passion and majestic calm.

Without meaning to, the gunners fell silent for a moment, shocked and excited by the thunder of their guns – more muted over the Volga, louder over the steppe.

'Battery, fire!'

Again the steppe, the sky and the Volga acquired voices. They threatened, complained, exulted and sorrowed; they felt the same things as the gunners.

'Fire!'

And fire duly appeared. Through his binoculars Tolya could see grey smoke enveloping the trees and vineyards. He could see grey-blue figures bustling about and camouflaged German tanks crawling this way and that way like frightened beetles and woodlice. He saw a flash of white flame, short, straight and stark – and then billows of black smoke whirling about the orchards, merging, climbing high into the sky, sinking heavily back down. And again – a sharp blade of white flame, slashing through the dense veil of smoke.

One of the gun-layers, a high-cheekboned Tatar, looked at Tolya and smiled. He didn't speak, but his quick glance conveyed a great deal: his joy in their success; his awareness that he was not alone and that his fellow gunners were also delivering accurate fire; his appreciation that Tolya was a good commander and that there were no better guns in the world than the ones they were firing.

The field telephone buzzed. This time it was Tolya who was slow to recognize the excited, overjoyed voice of the major: 'Well done, my lad! Well done! You've set their fuel stores on fire. Our divisional commander has just called. He's told me to pass on his congratulations. And our infantry is advancing now. Take care not to fire on our own men.'

Along the entire front from the Volga to the Don, Red Army infantry regiments, supported by artillery, tanks and aircraft, had taken the offensive.

Dust and smoke hung over the steppe. And there was a constant din – the thunder of artillery, the hum of tanks, the drawn-out 'U-u-r-a-a!' of Red Army soldiers storming German positions, the commanders' whistles, the dry explosions of mortars, the crackle of sub-machine-gun fire and the howl of dive-bombers.

Up in the air the fighting was on an equally vast scale. There was the roar of fighter engines. Soviet planes soared almost vertically and then, like the flash of a knife, tore across the sky. They attacked Junkers approaching the battlefield; they broke up the sinister merry-go-round of dive-bombers.

Above the Volga, Yaks and LaGGs skirmished with Messerschmitts and Focke-Wulfs. Everything about these dogfights – the manoeuvring, the shooting, the engagements and disengagements – happened too swiftly for the men on the ground to follow. And the speed and fury of these fights seemed to be determined not by the power of engines and guns, or by the speed and manoeuvrability of the aircraft, but by the hearts of the young Soviet fighter pilots; it was their passion, their audacity that was manifest in the fighters' sudden climbs, dives and turns. A bright quivering spot, barely visible in the vast ocean that was the sky, would metamorphose into a powerful machine; people below would see bluish wings with red stars, the flames of tracer bullets and a pilot's helmeted head – and a moment later the plane would have soared out of sight. Sometimes there would be a wild roar from the steppe as Soviet foot soldiers, momentarily forgetting all danger, leaped to their feet and waved their caps in the air to salute the victory of one of their pilots. Sometimes hundreds of men would let out a long wail as a Soviet pilot baled out of a blazing plane and Messerschmitts attacked the frail bubble of his parachute.

There was one rather startling incident. Perhaps because Tolya's battery was well camouflaged and positioned so very far to the south, a disorientated Soviet fighter pilot mistook them for Germans. Flying low over the cliff top, he strafed the battery with a round of machine-gun fire. Three Messerschmitts promptly saw off this fighter and then, for a full twenty minutes, patrolled over the battery. Next, probably because they were getting low on fuel, they must have radioed for a relief. Three new German planes took over and continued circling over the battery, conscientiously protecting the Soviet guns from harm. At first the gunners had felt alarmed. Thinking that the Germans were about to strafe them or drop anti-personnel bombs, they kept looking anxiously up at the sky. Tolya shouted, 'Comrades, they're protecting us – they think we're Germans. Don't do anything to show them we're not!' The answering peal of laughter was so loud that the Germans could almost have heard it up in the sky.

On any other day this incident would have given rise to an endless string of stories and jokes. On this first day of combat, however, it was quickly forgotten.

The battery's success in shelling both tanks and infantry engendered the sense of elation that, on the front line, can so suddenly take over from anxiety and hopelessness. German ground observers evidently made the same mistake as the pilots; they too were confused by the battery's forward position. No one took a bearing on the battery and no one bombed or shelled it. The battery's success, achieved at no real cost, filled everyone with supreme confidence and a sense of mocking contempt for the enemy. And, as happens at such moments, the gunners generalized from their own experience, mistakenly imagining that Soviet troops were advancing along the whole of the front, that they had broken the German defences, that in an hour or two the battery would be ordered forward and that in a day or two the Soviet armies to the north-west of Stalingrad would link up with the armies within the city. They would drive the Germans back. As always, there were men who claimed to have spoken in person with some lieutenant or wounded captain just arrived from a sector where the Germans were fleeing in panic, abandoning guns, ammunition and schnapps.

3

In the evening everything quietened down. Tolya Shaposhnikov rested for a while beside a telegraph pole, hurriedly eating some bread and tinned meat. His lips felt rough, as if they belonged to someone else, and the bread made a strange rustling noise in his parched mouth. His ears rang and his head felt as if it were full of cotton wool. The day had left him deeply exhausted, but this was not unpleasant. In his mind he kept hearing his own words of command, as if he were still shouting them. His cheeks were burning and even though he was almost lying down, propped against the telegraph pole, he could feel his strong, rapid heartbeats.

He looked down at the thin strip of sand by the Volga; it was hard to believe that he had been standing there only a few hours ago, feeling anxious and confused as he helped to unload cases of ammunition. Now, though, it did not in the least surprise him that his first day of combat had gone so well. He had kept calmly and confidently abreast of a swiftly changing situation. His divisional commander had congratulated him. For the first time in his life, his voice had sounded loud and clear and people had attended to his every word. If in the past he had felt inadequate, it was simply because he had not known his own strength. Now, though, this was something he could take for granted. His strength, his intelligence, his will – all these were truly his. They were a part of him, of Tolya Shaposhnikov; he had not just found them under a bush, nor had he borrowed them from someone else. If there was anything to be surprised about, it was the fact that he had not understood this a year ago, or yesterday, or even this morning.

Lieutenant Shaposhnikov was indeed still himself. To think that someone has suddenly been transformed is always a mistake. No one who really knows another person will ever say in bewilderment, 'I can't believe it – he's changed overnight!' It is more accurate to say, 'Circumstances have suddenly changed, and this has allowed what was always present within him to reveal itself.'

Nevertheless, such changes remain astonishing.

Tolya imagined going along with his comrades to visit the girls in the medical battalion. He would shine in every way; he would be wittier than anyone and he would tell the most interesting stories.

At school Nadya's fellow pupils would ask, 'This Shaposhnikov in today's newspaper – is it your brother?' And his father would show the newspaper to his institute colleagues.

The nurses in the medical battalion would say, 'Lieutenant Shaposhnikov – he's so witty! And the way he dances!'

If you lie for a long time by a telegraph pole in the steppe, you start to hear music – a complex and varied music. The pole absorbs the winds and begins to sing. Like a samovar coming to the boil, it quietly hums, whistles and gurgles. The slate-grey pole has been tempered by wind, sun and frost. The pole is a violin, with telephone cables for strings. And the steppe knows this, and likes to play music on it. It's a joy to lean back against a telegraph pole and listen to this steppe violin, to listen to your thoughts and the rhythm of your breathing.

That evening the Volga was full of colour. It turned deep blue, then pink, and then shone like grey silk, as if covered by light, pearly dust. The water gave off a cool evening peace, while the steppe still breathed out heat.

Wounded men and women in bloodstained bandages were walking north along the shore. Half-naked figures were washing their foot cloths by the silky water, checking the seams on their underclothes for lice. Road tractors ground their way along the stones a little further inland, beneath the high cliffs.

'Air alert!' called the sentry.

The air was clear and warm, and it smelled of wormwood.

Life was so beautiful.

As it turned dark, the Germans went on the offensive. Lit by a sinister light, the world became unrecognizable and frightening. Flares dropped by German planes hung high over the Soviet positions, swaying in the sky like great jellyfish. Mute yet vigilant, they eclipsed the quiet light of the moon and stars, illuminating the Volga, the steppe grass, the gullies and vineyards, and the young poplars on the clifftop.

Tolya could hear the sullen hum of powerful Heinkel bombers and the quick chatter of Italian fighters. The earth shook from exploding bombs; the air quivered from the whistle of shells. German rockets hurled still more flares up into the sky. In their poisonous green light, the steppe and the Volga looked like a papier-mâché model. People's faces and hands seemed lifeless, as if made of cardboard. There were no longer hills, valleys and a living river – only numbered heights, terrain intersected by gullies running west to east and a water barrier running north to south. The tender, bittersweet smell of wormwood now seemed out of place; it did not belong to this strategic planning officers' maquette.

There was the roar of German tank engines, the sound of German infantry marching through feathergrass.

By then the Germans had located Tolya's battery. One after another, shells tore into the vines. There were cries from the wounded; men rushed to take cover. Then the German tanks moved forward and Tolya ordered his men to their fire positions. They opened fire, but they now had to pay dearly for their easy initial successes. The battery was being targeted not only by German artillery but also by mortars, firing from hills on the far side of the gully. And there were sudden rounds of machine-gun fire, like storms of thunder or hail.

Sliced through by a shell, the singing telegraph pole fell to the ground.

It seemed to Tolya that there would be no end to this night battle. The sultry darkness gave birth to more and more enemies. The drawn-out whistle of falling bombs; repeated explosions that made the ground shudder all around him; German tanks, more and more German tanks, with their guns and machine guns; sudden salvoes of shells that raised clouds of earth, leaves and pebbles and left him stunned and blinded.

And again and again, the ominous hum of the Heinkels.

There was grit and dry earth in Tolya's mouth, rasping between his teeth. He wanted to spit it out, but his mouth was so dry he couldn't spit. His voice had grown hoarse; sometimes he could hardly believe it was really him, shouting commands in such a deep, hoarse voice.

The harsh light in the sky faded. The darkness became impenetrable; it was only from the sound of their breathing that he knew there were men nearby. A church in the Transvolga steppe was a mere blur of white on black. A minute later the harsh light flared up again, and Tolya felt it was this dry, deathly light that was tickling his throat and drying his windpipe.

He had no strength left for anything but his guns. There was room in his soul for only one feeling, only one vague dream – to survive until morning, to see the sun.

And Tolya Shaposhnikov did indeed see the sun. He saw it rise above the eastern steppe, above the tender, pearly, pale-pink mist lying over the Volga.

The young man opened his parched mouth to call out the order, and the roar of his guns, which had repelled all the Germans' night-time attacks, greeted the sunrise.

*

Two paces away from Tolya there was a sudden dazzling flash. A powerful fist struck him in the chest. He tripped on a used shell case and fell to the ground. A voice shouted, 'Quick, here! The lieutenant's wounded!'

Men were bending over him, but Tolya couldn't make sense of their looks of concern and pity. They'd misunderstood – it must be some other lieutenant who'd been wounded. In a moment he'd get to his feet, shake off the dust, go down to the Volga, wash in the cool, soft wonderful water and resume his command.

4

A number of commanders and soldiers were waiting by a checkpoint at a steppe crossroads, hoping for a lift from a passing vehicle.

Each time a vehicle appeared in the distance, they all picked up their packs and hurried towards the traffic controller.

'What's got into you all?' he would repeat crossly. 'It's no use all crowding up at once. I've told you already – there'll be transport for all of you.'

A middle-aged major in a neat but faded tunic smiled – as if to say that he wasn't born yesterday and was well aware that it was no use trying to teach manners to quartermasters, generals' adjutants, admin clerks and traffic controllers.

A large post had been hammered into the ground, with arrows pointing to Saratov, Kamyshin, Stalingrad and Balashov.

East, west, north or south, the dirt roads all looked identical.

The dry, grey grass was coated in yellow dust. Kites were perching on the telegraph poles, gripping the white insulators with their talons. But the men waiting at the checkpoint knew that the roads were by no means identical; they knew very well which ran east and north, which south-west, and which towards Stalingrad.

A truck stopped by the barrier. It was carrying wounded soldiers and commanders. Their bandages were dark from layers of dust and, in places, still darker from black, congealed blood.

'In you get, comrade Major!' said the controller.

The major threw his pack inside, put one foot on a back wheel and climbed in. As the truck moved off, he waved goodbye to a captain and two senior lieutenants. The four men had been lying on the grass together, eating bread and tinned fish. He had showed them photographs of his wife, daughter and son.

The major looked around at his new set of chance companions – grey with dust and pale from loss of blood. He yawned, then said to a soldier with his arm in a sling, 'Kotluban?'

'Yes,' the soldier replied. 'We'd already got to the front line. Then someone decided to reposition us – the Germans had a field day.'

659

'It wasn't far from the Volga,' said a second wounded soldier. 'They made mincemeat of us. Everyone said we shouldn't have been brought forward till night. In daylight, in open steppe, we were in full view of the enemy. We were like frightened hares, wondering where we could hide. It looked like none of us would survive.'

'Mortar bombs?'

'Yes, fucking mortars.'

'Well, at least you'll be getting a rest now,' said the major.

'Yes,' said the soldier, 'we'll be all right.' Then he pointed to a young man stretched out on some straw and added, 'But I don't think this lieutenant will be doing any more fighting.'

The lieutenant's arms and legs were flopping about helplessly, subordinate to every bump and pothole the truck passed over.

'They should make him more comfortable,' said the major. 'Orderly!'

The lieutenant gave the major a long, intent look. He grimaced in pain, then closed his eyes.

His sunken cheeks, the way his lips appeared almost sealed together, the severity of his expression – all made it clear that he no longer wanted to look at the world, that there was no longer anything he wanted to say or ask about. The vast dusty steppe and the ground squirrels running across the road meant nothing to him. The lieutenant didn't care when they got to Kamyshin, whether or not he'd be given a hot meal, whether he'd be able to send a letter from the hospital or whether it was a German or a Soviet plane droning in the sky above them. He no longer cared whether the Germans had taken some height or other his company had been defending. He no longer even cared whether or not the war ever came to an end.

There he lay, gloomily sensing how the warmth of life – the one precious gift he possessed, now lost for ever – was slowly cooling inside him.

Medical orderlies say of men like him, even if they are still breathing and groaning, 'This one's ready.'

That night Kamyshin had been the target of an air raid. The wounded in the truck looked anxiously at the houses with gaping windows, at the men and women gazing fixedly up at the sky, at the streets glistening with glass, and at the pits dug by half-ton bombs dropped from a height of 1,000 metres onto small houses with grey and green roofs.

The wounded, naturally, were eager to get straight onto a boat for Saratov; they didn't want to hang about in a town like this. Carefully, as if their bandaged arms and legs were treasures entrusted to them for safekeeping, they shuffled them to the edge of the truck. Then they began their slow descent to the ground, gasping and groaning, looking expectantly at the nearby military doctor in kirza boots and a skimpy white gown with minuscule sleeves.

'What am I meant to do with this crowd?' the doctor said crossly to his orderly. 'The corridor's jam-packed as it is. And if we don't get bombed tonight, we're sure to be bombed tomorrow night. They should have been sent straight on to Saratov.'

As he climbed out, the major glanced at the wounded lieutenant. His face now grimmer than ever, the lieutenant gave him another intent look.

The major waved everyone goodbye and set off down the main street, wondering why it is that dying men always stare one straight in the eye.

He walked slowly, looking sadly at the little streets and squares of this war-battered town where his beloved Tamara had once gone to school. Long ago, a skinny young thing with a long plait wound round her head, she must have walked this same way. She had probably had trysts with young boys in the little garden he could see high over the Volga and that was now packed with refugees and bristling with anti-aircraft machine guns. And there were wounded soldiers in grey gowns, slyly swapping bread and sugar for vodka and home-grown tobacco.

Then he remembered about his rations. He asked a traffic controller the way to the store.

'I don't know, comrade Major,' said the controller, and waved his flag.

'Where's the commandant's office?' asked the major.

'I don't know, comrade Major,' said the controller. To ward off a cross retort, he added, 'We're new here. We arrived during the night.'

The major went on further. His experienced eye quickly determined that either a Corps or an Army HQ had recently arrived in the town.

A sentry with a sub-machine gun was standing outside a house with columns. A number of commanders, probably waiting for their passes, were standing by a wicker gate, watching a waitress going about her business. She was gliding along, holding a tray covered with a white napkin against her high breasts.

She had round, rosy cheeks, strong, pale calves and bold black eyes.

The major let out a long, drawn-out sigh. The commanders in their green side caps and dusty boots, with their packs and map cases, sensed the depth of meaning in this sigh and smiled.

Some of the men, those who had come a long way and were very hungry, wondered what lay beneath the white napkin. Most of them, though, looked at the young woman.

The major went on further. Behind an orchard he could see a radio mast. Signallers were laying down cables and there was the staccato knocking of a small engine. Several large trucks were parked near a dilapidated crimson building – 'The Comintern Cinema' – with half its windows knocked out. A captain in horn-rimmed glasses was waving his arms about and shouting at the drivers.

The major realized that this was the printing press of an army newspaper. He also understood that this was a reserve army, one that had not yet seen combat. Everyone was bustling about in a particularly agitated way. They were all in pristine uniforms. The commanders were carrying heavy drum-magazine sub-machine guns of little use to them at HQ. The trucks' camouflage was immaculate. And drivers, sentries, signallers and commanders alike were all repeatedly glancing up at the blue August sky.

At first the major had felt intimidated by the presence in this small town of so many high-ranking commanders. Now, however, he looked at these men newly brought up from the rear with a sense of indulgent superiority.

He had fought in the summer of 1941 in the forests of western Belorussia and Ukraine. He had survived the black horror of the war's first days; he knew everything and had seen everything. When other men told stories about the war, this modest major listened with a polite smile. 'Oh, my brothers,' he would think. 'I've seen things that cannot be spoken about, that no one will ever write down.'

Now and again, though, he would meet another quiet, shy major like himself. Recognizing him – from little signs known to him alone – as a kindred spirit, he would talk more freely.

'Remember General N.?' he might say. 'When his unit was surrounded, he plodded through a bog in full uniform, wearing all his medals, and with a goat on a lead. A couple of lieutenants he met asked, "Comrade General, are you following a compass bearing?" And what did he answer? "A compass? This goat is my compass!"'

The major came to a spot on the cliff overlooking the Volga and sat down on a green bench. He saw no reason to go about military affairs in a hurry – the war, after all, would not come to an end any time soon. He never forgot about meals and he liked to sit in the sun and smoke his pipe, giving free rein to his memories and to a quiet sadness.

If he had to travel somewhere by rail, he would wait at the station for a train that was less crowded. If he needed lodgings for the night, he would go out of his way to find a welcoming landlady. And it was essential that she should have a cow.

It was a hot day, without a breath of wind. The Volga stretched far into the distance, shining under the clear sun. The bench, the cobbled street, the roofs and dark log walls of the houses, the layers of dust on the sun-scorched grass – everything gave off its own particular smell, as if stone, tin, dry dust and an old, dead tree were living, sweating beings. And the major could see across to the east bank, with its dense reeds and willows. The sand looked bright and was, no doubt, very hot; minuscule soldiers, who must have just got off a ferry, were plodding laboriously across it. It would be good to lie down naked for a while and then get into the water. He could swim for half an hour, then lie down again in the shade and have some beer; first, of course, he would have tied a couple of bottles to a cord and lowered them to the bottom of a cool pool.

There was just a hint of mist in the far distance, as if a few drops of milk had been added to the pale blue air. As if tired and saddened by the splendour of this hot August day, the Volga flowed slowly on towards Lugovaya Proleika, Dubovka, Stalingrad, Raigorod and Astrakhan. She understood that she had no need to hurry.

The major looked around to see if there were any high-ranking commanders nearby, then quietly undid three buttons on his tunic.

'There are cantaloupes in the market,' he said to himself, 'and watermelons too. But the wretched kolkhoz workers will want goods, not money. I could swap some of my sugar, but I can hardly go to the market in this uniform ... Oh, if only Tamara were here – she always knows what to do.'

Thinking about his family, who had all disappeared without trace in the first days of the war, he took a photograph out of his pocket and gazed at it for a long time.

A barefoot boy came by. There were holes in the elbows of his shirt and a huge lilac patch on his tarpaulin trousers.

'Hey, you there!' the major called out.

Like any thirteen-year-old, the boy had sins on his conscience. He looked at the major mistrustfully, wondering if he had done anything to anger any commanders.

'What do you want?' he asked.

'Tell me how I can buy a watermelon,' the major said affably.

'In exchange for tobacco,' the boy replied. He went up close to the major and added, 'Half a packet.'

'All right then. Go and fetch me one. Good and ripe, with black pips. This is the best tobacco!'

'Boum Valley, I can see. Very good, comrade Major.'

The boy set off down the path. The major took out his tobacco pouch and some neatly cut squares of paper, covered with numbers written in purple ink. He rolled a thick cigarette, blew down the mouthpiece, which was made from aircraft glass, and squinted down the hole. He took out his German lighter and lit up.

He returned the lighter to his pocket, noting with concern that the flint was now near the end of its life.

Just then a pink-faced quartermaster came by. He stopped and looked at the major. He almost walked on but then looked at the major a second time.

'Excuse me, comrade Major,' he began. 'You're not Berozkin, are you?' And then he rushed up to him, shouting, 'Yes, yes, it's Ivan Leontievich!'

'Just a moment,' said the major. 'Ah! Aristov! My former supplies boss! Well, a lot of water's gone under the bridge since we last met!'

'That's right, Ivan Leontievich. I was posted to the Belorussian Military District on 11 February 1941.'

'And where are you serving now?

'I'm head of an army supply section. Till now, our army's been held in reserve.'

'A supplies boss for a whole army – you've done well for yourself!' said Major Berozkin. He looked Aristov up and down and said, 'Sit down. Roll yourself a cigarette. What are you doing, still standing there?'

'No,' said Aristov, offering Berozkin a cigarette from a packet. 'Here – have one of mine!' He laughed and asked, 'Remember the earful you gave me in Bobruisk for not registering the hay I took from the kolkhoz?'

'I do indeed,' said Berozkin.

'Those were the days,' said Aristov. 'We lived well then ...'

Berozkin looked Aristov up and down and concluded that he wasn't living at all badly even now. He had plump cheeks; his uniform was good-quality gabardine and he was wearing an elegant khaki cap and box-calf boots.

Everything about him was equally smart: a lighter with a little amethyst button, a small amber cigarette holder with an embossed gold beetle, a shiny-topped fountain pen peeping out of his tunic pocket, a map case – made from the very best red leather – hanging at his side and a penknife in a little suede case. Aristov took the penknife from his pocket, fiddled with it and then put it back again.

'Let's go to my billet,' said Aristov. 'It's not far.'

'I have to wait here a bit longer,' said Berozkin. 'A boy's doing an errand for me. I sent him off to the market, to barter half a packet of tobacco for a watermelon.'

'Heavens!' said Aristov. 'There's no need to send little boys on errands! I've got any number of watermelons – real giants, laid in for the military soviet.'

'I promised I'd wait here,' said the major. 'Just give me a minute.'

'Comrade Major! Let this damned boy of yours keep the water-melon for himself – I'm sure he'll be grateful!'

And Aristov picked up Berozkin's green knapsack.

During his long military career Berozkin had all too often had reason to feel resentful towards admin and supplies-section officers. 'Lucky guys,' he would say with a slow shake of the head. 'There's clearly no supplies problem for a supplies officer.'

Now, though, he was only too glad to follow Aristov.

And as they went on their way, Berozkin began to tell his story. His war had begun at five in the morning on 22 June 1941. He alone in his division had managed to withdraw his guns and even rescue a dozen fuel trucks and two batteries of 152-millimetre guns aban-doned by a neighbouring unit. He had walked through swamps and forests, contested hundreds of heights and fought on the banks of doz-ens of rivers large and small. He had taken part in combats near Brest, Kobrin, Bakhmach, Shostka, Krolevets, Glukhov, Mikhailovsky Ham-let, Kromy, Oryol, Belyov and Chern. During the winter he had fought by the Donets and taken part in the Savintsy and Zaliman offensives, the breakthrough towards Chepel and the advance on Lozovaya.

He had been wounded by shrapnel and treated in hospital. He had received a bullet wound and been treated again. Now he was on his way to rejoin his unit.

'And so here I am,' he said with a smile.

'But, Ivan Leontievich,' asked Aristov, 'how come you've done so much fighting yet got nothing to show for it?' And he pointed to Berozkin's tunic. It was bare of medals and looked as if it had gone grey from age.

'Oh,' Berozkin said slowly, 'I've been recommended four times for medals and orders. But I always end up being transferred before they get to fill in all the different forms and attestations. The same with promotion to lieutenant colonel – before they're done with the documents, I get moved on. Everyone says a motor infantry unit is like a band of gypsies. Here today – and God knows where tomorrow!' He smiled again, then went on with feigned indifference, 'Men who graduated from the academy with me in 1928 are in command of divisions now. They've all got two or three medals on their chest. Mitya Gogin's already a general – he's in Moscow, on the General Staff. If I ran into him now, I'd be saluting smartly and saying, "Comrade General, your orders have been carried out, may I be dismissed?" And about turn. And so here we are – that's the life of a soldier for you.'

5

They entered a neat little yard, and a sleepy-looking soldier quickly straightened his crumpled tunic, shook off the straw stuck to his trousers and gave an energetic salute.

'Asleep again?' said Aristov crossly. 'Lay the table.'

'At your command!' the soldier replied. He took Berozkin's green knapsack and went inside.

'The first time in the war I've seen a fat soldier,' said Berozkin.

'He's a smart man,' Aristov replied. 'He used to be an admin clerk, but we discovered he was a first-class chef. First, I'm trying him out here. Then we'll send him to the military soviet canteen.'

They went into a half-dark entrance room with board walls painted pale blue in accord with Volga tradition. There they were met by Aristov's landlady – a stocky elderly woman with a grey moustache.

She wanted to bow to her new guest. Instead, broad and short as she was, she half lost her balance and tottered forward.

Berozkin saluted politely and glanced around the room. There was a hibiscus, a table with an embroidered tablecloth and a double bed with a neat white blanket.

'You've landed a good billet!' he said to Aristov.

'It's no use making life hard for yourself, comrade Major. And rest's all the more important when you're at the front.'

'Of course,' said Berozkin. Looking round the room once again, he thought, 'Yes, I wouldn't mind serving on a front like this myself.'

He took his soap dish and towel from his knapsack, removed his tunic, asked the landlady to pour some water onto his hands and began soaping his strong, red neck and shaven, already balding head. He asked the landlady her name.

'Till now, I've always been called Antonina Vasilievna,' she said in a slow, singing voice.

'And so you always will be,' Berozkin replied. 'But keep going, don't stint on the water!'

Berozkin slapped his cheeks and the back of his neck, puffing, snorting, grunting and chuckling in his enjoyment of the slow stream of cool water.

Then he went through into the main room, sat down in an armchair and fell silent, relishing the sense of peace and comfort that comes to a soldier suddenly whisked from a world of dust, wind, noise and eternal movement into the quiet half-light of an ordinary human dwelling.

Aristov also fell silent. They watched the fat soldier lay the table. The landlady brought in a large dish of splendid beef tomatoes.

'Here you are! Eat all you want – there's no salt or vinegar, so we won't be able to put them away for the winter. But tell me, comrade Commanders, when will all this grief be over?'

'When we've smashed the Germans,' Aristov replied with a yawn.

'There's an old man here in Kamyshin,' said the landlady, 'who can tell the future. He told me the war will come to an end on 28 November. So it says in his book. And the Volga's spring floods said the same. And he has two roosters – one's black and the other's white, and they keep fighting.'

'What does your old man know?' said the fat soldier, putting a plate of ham and a bottle of vodka on the table.

Berozkin looked with childish delight at the vodka and at the lavish spread on the table. As well as the ham and tomatoes, there was caviar, lampreys, pickled mushrooms, cold mutton and a meat jelly. Turning to the landlady, he said, 'You should stay away from those old charlatans, Antonina Vasilievna. They're only after your chickens and eggs. Back in Kupyansk there was an old man who said what day the war would come to an end. And when the day came, there was a massive air raid. The women set on him and pulled out his beard.'

'Quite right!' said Aristov. 'Telling the future's not Marxist.'

'I'm in my sixty-fourth year now,' said the landlady. 'My father lived to be eighty-four, and my father's father to be ninety-three. We're all from these parts, but not once in any of our lifetimes have French or German invaders broken through to the Volga. But this summer some fool has let the Germans through to our Russian heartlands. I keep hearing things about German technology. They say Hitler's planes are more powerful than ours. And they say he's got some special powder. You just add it to water and it's as good as petrol. Well, that's as may be. But only this morning I spoke to an old woman from Olkhovka. She'd come to the market to barter flour. She told me a prisoner of war – a German general – had been kept in her hut and she heard him say he'd received orders direct from Hitler: "If we take Stalingrad, all Russia will be ours. But if we fail, we'll be pushed right back to our borders." What do you think? Will we hold Stalingrad?'

'No doubt about it!' said Aristov.

'It's war,' said Berozkin. 'Nothing's for sure. But we'll do what we can.'

Aristov slapped himself on the forehead. 'I've just remembered,' he said. 'I've got a truck going to Stalingrad tomorrow – to a distillery. Lieutenant Colonel Darensky will be in the cabin. And then there'll just be two others – my storekeeper and some boy, a lieutenant straight from military school. Someone asked me to help him out. So you can spend the night here in my billet and then they'll come and pick you up in the morning.'

'Perfect,' said the major. 'Somehow there's always a quick way to the front.'

The two men sat for a few minutes in silence – a silence familiar to anyone used to drinking with friends. They wanted to talk heart-to-heart. They knew they couldn't do this until they'd drunk their first glass and so they preferred to stay silent.

'There, comrade Commanders!' said the fat soldier. 'Sit down!'

Berozkin sat down at the table, gave Aristov a cheerful look and said, 'You're a good fellow, comrade Senior Lieutenant!'

Wanting to flatter Aristov, he chose to address him as a senior lieutenant, not as a quartermaster. Major Berozkin was well aware of the army's unwritten laws. If a lieutenant colonel has been put in command of a division, his subordinates address him not as 'comrade Lieutenant Colonel' but as 'comrade Divisional Commander'. If a captain is in command of a regiment, his subordinates address him as 'comrade Regimental Commander'. Conversely, if a man with four red bars is in command of a regiment, everyone addresses him as 'comrade Colonel'. No one would be so tactless as to highlight the discrepancy between his rank and his relatively lowly position by addressing him as 'comrade Regimental Commander'.

They downed a glass, had a bite to eat and downed a second glass.

Berozkin looked at Aristov and said, 'Tell me, do you remember my wife and children?'

'Of course I do! In Bobruisk, you lived on the ground floor with the other commanders, while I lived in the wing of the same building. I saw them every day. Your wife used to go to the market with a blue bag.'

'That's right. I bought it in Lvov,' Berozkin replied and shook his head sadly.

He wanted to tell Aristov all about his wife: how they had bought a mirror wardrobe the day before the war, what excellent borsch she made and how well educated she was. She knew French and English and she was always taking books out of the library. He wanted to tell him what a little hooligan young Slava was, how he was always fighting and up to mischief, how once he'd rushed in and said 'Pápa, you must give me a beating. I just bit the cat!'

But he was unable to say any of this. Aristov took over the conversation.

Aristov's attitude towards men like his former commander was complex. On the one hand, he felt fear and respect. On the other hand, he felt surprised and amused by their village simplicity, by their ineptitude with regard to practical matters. 'Oh, my brother,' he thought, looking at Berozkin's faded tunic and kirza boots, 'If I'd done a tenth as much fighting as you have, I'd be a top general by now.'

And so he served Berozkin generously, but without allowing him to get a word in.

'The general in command would be helpless without me,' he said. 'He orders sturgeon for lunch, so that's what he gets. And that's only two hours after we reach the Volga! The member of the military soviet smokes a pipe – so he gets his packet of Golden Fleece every day. Not once has he had to do without. The chief of staff can't drink vodka because of his ulcer. "At your command, comrade Colonel, whatever you need!" Back then we were up north, near Vologda, in the middle of nowhere – but the chief of staff still gets his Riesling! He even gets a little suspicious, summons me specially and tells me I'm a dangerous man. So, what's my secret? Well, it's no good waiting for the regular supplies – you can wait till kingdom come. No, you need imagination, you need initiative, you need to act boldly. Tomorrow, for instance, I'm sending a truck to Stalingrad. And we all know there's a distillery there, and that there's been a fire. Well, who's to say there aren't still bottles to be found in that building? No, it's no good just sitting and waiting. And if there's anything you need yourself, Ivan Leontievich, just say. I'll do all I can for you. I'll fill in documents, I'll send out trucks, I'll take risks. And I'll expect you to do the same for me. And men who know me say there's no document they trust more than my word. Just once there was a senior commissar who had it in for me. He got me demoted and removed from my post. Some Armenian was put in my place. Within a week the supplies section was falling apart. The military soviet would ask for Narzan mineral water – and there wasn't any. They'd ask for this, that and the other – and it was always the same answer. The Army commander was furious. He personally ordered me to be reinstated.' He looked at Berozkin and said, 'Some beer, comrade Major?'

'Well,' said Berozkin, pointing to the laden table. 'You've certainly managed things well.'

'I do nothing I shouldn't,' Aristov replied, and his clear blue eyes looked straight into Berozkin's. 'Certainly not! I've got nothing to hide. And anyway, the HQ commissar lives almost next door.'

Berozkin drank some more beer and smacked his lips. 'Good stuff!'

He touched the tomatoes, hoping to find one that was fully ripe but not going soft. Then he felt embarrassed, thinking sadly how Tamara used to tell him off for doing exactly this. She didn't like him fingering the tomatoes or cucumbers on a shared dish.

Just then there was a buzz from a field telephone standing on a chest of drawers. Aristov picked up the receiver. 'Quartermaster Aristov here!'

The call was clearly from a high-ranking commander. Aristov looked tense and was standing very upright, using his free hand to straighten his tunic and brush off crumbs. His only part in the conversation was to repeat four times, 'Orders understood!' Then he replaced the receiver and hurriedly put on his peaked cap.

'Excuse me! Eat all you want, and feel free to lie down and rest. This is urgent – I have to leave you.'

'Yes, of course,' said Berozkin. 'Only please don't forget about the truck tomorrow morning.'

'Don't worry!' And Aristov hurried to the door.

By then Berozkin had already drunk a fair amount. To remain without company was unthinkable. He went over to the door of the small room to which the landlady had retired and called out, 'Grandma, come and join me!'

The old woman came out.

'Sit down, Antonina Vasilievna,' said Berozkin. 'Have a glass with me, to keep me company!'

'Only too glad!' she replied. 'In the old days people would have been shocked to see a woman drink. But now we women all drink, young and old alike. Yes, round here we make our own vodka and drink our own vodka. What do you expect in this vale of tears?'

She knocked back a glass of vodka and ate a tomato.

'So, how have things been here? Are you being bombed badly?' Berozkin asked – just as countless majors, captains, lieutenants and rank-and-file soldiers had asked women of every age in front-line villages and towns all over Russia.

And, like all these other women, she answered, 'We're being bombed all the time, my dear.'

'That's bad,' Berozkin said sadly. Then he asked, 'Grandma, do you happen to remember a General Saltansky? He used to live here in Kamyshin.'

'I do indeed,' she replied. 'My old man was a fisherman, and I used to take the fish round to his family.'

'Did you know the whole family?'

'I certainly did. His woman died during the other war. And there were two daughters. Tamara was the younger and Nadya the elder. Nadya was always falling ill. They used to take her abroad for treatment.'

'You don't say!' said Berozkin.

'Are you from these parts?' asked the landlady. 'Do you know the Saltanskys?'

'No,' said Berozkin, after a moment's thought. 'I don't.'

The landlady knocked back a second glass.

'May God grant you return home alive!' she said, and wiped her lips.

'What were they like?' said Berozkin. 'Tell me about them.'

'About who?'

'About the Saltanskys.'

'The general was a difficult man. Everyone here was afraid of him. He was a real general, always ordering everyone around. But his wife was a good woman, she had a kind heart. She cared about other people. She did what she could to help them and she was always giving big gifts to the children's home.'

'And the two daughters? Did they take after their mother?'

'Yes, they were good girls. Both rather skinny, and without airs and graces. They used to wear brown frocks and go out for walks down Saratov Avenue. Sometimes they went to Tychok – there was a little park there, overlooking the Volga.' The landlady sighed, then went on, 'Their old cook, Karpovna, was a neighbour of mine. She died last Sunday, there was an air raid in the afternoon. She was on her way back from the market. She'd bartered a kerchief for some potatoes, and a bomb landed right at her feet. She used to tell me all about the Saltanskys. Nadya died during the Revolution. Tamara couldn't get a job and they wouldn't let her join a trade union. But then she found herself a good man. A carpenter, I think, someone simple and modest.'

'Really?' said Berozkin. 'A carpenter?'

'That's right. They say he got into trouble for marrying her. His comrades said he should find someone else – there were plenty of other young women in Russia and he'd do better to ditch her. But he just repeated, "I love her, and that's that." And so they married and had a good life together, with children.'

'Well, well, well!' said Berozkin.

'But now our lives are in ruins,' said the landlady. 'It's just one death after another. I've received a "killed in action" letter for two of my sons, and it's a year since I last heard from the third. "Missing in action", no doubt. And so I get by. I barter a few things at the market and some-times I've got lodgers helping me out.'

'Yes,' said Berozkin. 'A lot of blood has been shed.'

He got up from the table and sat down again by the window. He took a small white metal tin from his knapsack, spread out a sewing kit on his knees, found a thread that matched his tunic and set about darning a hole in the elbow. He worked quickly and skilfully, screwing up his eyes now and then to check what he'd done.

'You're a deft hand with a needle, my boy,' said the landlady. Now he'd taken off his army tunic, this man in a neat shirt, with a balding head, grey-blue eyes, high cheekbones and a tanned face looked like a simple working man from the Volga. At first she had addressed him more formally, as *Vy* rather than *Ty* but now this felt awkward and wrong.[243]

'Yes, I know how to sew all right,' he said quietly, and smiled. 'In peacetime my comrades used to make fun of me and say, "Our captain's a dressmaker." I can cut out a pattern. I can backstitch on a machine, and I can make a dress for a child. My wife was no good with a needle, so I took care of the children's clothes myself. It was a joy. And once I made a summer dress for her. She wore it two years. The other com-manders' wives all liked it so much they copied the pattern. I can still remember measuring my Tamara. I couldn't stop laughing. And she was stroking my hands and saying, "Golden heart and golden hands!"'

'Were you a tailor before you joined up?'

'No, I've been a soldier since 1922.'

He put his tunic back on, buttoned his collar and walked across the room.

Addressing him once again as *Vy*, the landlady said, 'I can see the kind of man you are. Men like you are the backbone of our state.' With a knowing wink, she went on, 'But as for that mate of yours – what does he know about fighting? If everyone fought like him, the Fritzes would already be in Siberia. He thinks spirits are the backbone of the state. And to him the state's just a giant office.'

The major laughed and said, 'There are no flies on you, Grandma!'

673

'And why would there be?' the landlady replied tartly.

Berozkin went out for a walk. He went to the house opposite, where a little girl was hanging out some yellowing soldier's underwear. 'Where did old Karpovna live?' he asked.

The girl looked round and said, 'She's gone. And her apartment's been boarded up, and her daughter-in-law's taken everything to her village.'

'And where's Tychok?'

'Tychok?' the girl repeated. 'Don't ask me.'

Berozkin walked on further. He heard the girl laugh and say, 'Someone wanting Karpovna. Must be after her belongings. And then he asked about some Tychok or other.'

Berozkin walked as far as the corner, took a photo from his tunic pocket, looked at it, heard the plaintive sound of an air-raid alert and went back to Aristov's apartment for a rest.

It was night before Aristov returned. He bent down over Berozkin, shone his flashlight at him and asked, 'Are you asleep?'

'No, I'm not,' Berozkin replied.

'Well, I've been rushing about all day. General Zhukov's arriving tomorrow. Straight from Moscow, by Douglas. There's been a lot to get ready.'

'No joke,' Berozkin replied sympathetically. 'But I'll be more than grateful if you can get some provisions ready for me too.'

'The truck will be here at nine o'clock in the morning,' said Aristov. 'And don't worry about the food – I'm not the kind of man to forget his former boss.'

Aristov began to pull off his boots. He let out a little groan, bustled about for a minute, then fell silent.

There was a sound, some kind of sob or sigh, from behind the partition wall.

'What on earth's that?' thought Berozkin. Realizing it was the landlady, he got up, walked in his socks to the door of her room and asked rather severely, 'What's up? Why are you crying?'

'Because of you,' she replied. 'Two of my sons are dead, and the third's gone missing. And now you. You're on your way to Stalingrad. A lot of blood will be shed there. And you're a good man.'

Berozkin didn't know what to say. He walked about for a while, sighed and went back to bed.

6

Lieutenant Colonel Darensky had completed his medical treatment and was on his way to the Stalingrad Front's Rear HQ.

The treatment had not helped; he felt no better than beforehand.

He was troubled by the thought of returning to the reserves, where he knew he would be a long time with no real work.

On his way he had to stop off in Kamyshin, now the HQ of an army just brought up from reserve. His friend Colonel Filimonov, deputy to the artillery chief of staff, arranged a lift for Darensky in a truck going to Stalingrad the following morning, along the east bank of the Volga.

After lunch, Darensky felt the onset of his usual stomach pains and went back to his room. He lay down and asked his landlady to heat up some water and fill up a bottle for him. The pains proved relatively slight, but he was still unable to sleep. Then there was a knock at the door – Filimonov's adjutant, inviting him to come round.

'Tell Ivan Korneyevich,' said Darensky, 'that I can't come. I'm not well. And please remind him about the truck tomorrow morning.'

The adjutant left. Darensky lay there with his eyes closed, listening to some women outside the window. They were criticizing a certain Filippovna, apparently a malicious gossip who had been telling people that Matveyevna had quarrelled with her neighbour Niura 'because of some senior lieutenant'.

Darensky winced; he was in pain and he felt bored. To amuse himself, he imagined the most improbable of scenes – the army commander and his chief of staff calling round, sitting at his bedside and questioning him with touching solicitousness.

'Well, my dear fellow, how are you doing?' the chief of staff would ask. 'You know, you do look rather pale.'

'You need a doctor, you really must see a doctor,' the army commander would say, looking around the room and shaking his head. 'And you must come and join me in my own quarters, Lieutenant Colonel – I'll have your things moved. Why lie here all on your own? You'll be better off staying with me.'

'No, no, it's all right. It's nothing serious. I need to be on my way tomorrow – that's all that matters.'

The commander and his chief of staff each took one of his arms. Their adjutants followed, carrying Darensky's suitcase and knapsack. And as they all walked through the town, they crossed paths with everyone who had ever annoyed Darensky or done him harm. A vile person who had once denounced him in writing. Then Skurikhin, who had occasioned Darensky no end of difficulties by ferreting out and making public something that Darensky himself had entirely forgotten: that his father, an engineer and the author of a textbook about the resistance of materials, had held a high rank in the tsarist civil service. A senior inspector of the Moscow City Soviet housing section, a balding Jew, who had once refused Darensky's request for accommodation with the words, 'My dear comrade, we have people more important than you who've been waiting their turn for two years now.' And a man who'd upset him only today – the pink-faced junior quartermaster who'd refused him entry to the senior commanders' canteen and only given him coupons for the general canteen.

Yes, there his tormentors were – all now smiling pathetically. All looking at the medals glittering on the commander's chest as he asked Darensky how he was feeling and whether there was anything he and his chief of staff could do to make him feel more comfortable. To hell with the lot of them … And Ulanova the ballerina was there too, asking, 'Who is this lieutenant colonel? He must be severely wounded – his face looks tanned but it's still terribly pale.'

Nevertheless, the hours went by, and no generals appeared. Instead, the landlady came in, checked whether or not he was asleep, and began to sort through a pile of newly ironed linen beside the sewing machine.

As it got dark, Darensky felt more depressed than ever. He asked the landlady to turn on the light. 'In a moment,' she replied. 'First I must put up the blackout. We don't want to call up the Antichrist.'

With extraordinary diligence she began draping shawls, blankets and old blouses over the windows. It was as if she thought Junkers and Heinkels were bugs and flies that might slip through cracks in the rickety old window frames.

'Grandma, I need to get down to work!'

The landlady muttered that she was running short of kerosene. First he'd wanted hot water – now he needed light.

This made Darensky angry. The woman evidently had food squirrelled away and was doing quite well for herself, but she was extremely

676

stingy – she had asked him to pay rent for the room and she charged more for milk than he had paid in Moscow.

As if that weren't enough, she'd kept pestering him to find her a truck. She wanted to go to the village of Klimovka, seventy kilometres away, and fetch the flour and firewood she'd stored there last autumn. As if he could get hold of a truck just like that …

*

Darensky began looking through his notes from the first days of the war.

'A battalion commissar was making out that Kutuzov's retreat was brilliant strategy. I had the thought that Kutuzov's retreat might have been no different from ours, and that His Highness Lev Tolstoy might simply have thrown fine robes over the bloody body of war. If so, he did the right thing – yes, he did! The army is holy – and so is the motherland! A commander is an apostle, and his authority must be absolute. There is only one question – discipline! And only one answer – discipline! The great Stalin can save us – and he will! Yesterday I read the text of his speech in a leaflet. What calm, what confidence!

'Everyone's suddenly an expert. Every conversation is about grand questions of strategy. Novelists, poets, film directors, still more important figures – they all get criticized … Yesterday, in the operations section, a major waved a book in the air and said, "Like to know what this fellow predicted? That we'd smash the Germans in the first ten hours!" … I've just been reading about Gastello – a true Russian hero![244] Now we've survived a blow like this, nothing can frighten us. France has collapsed. She's lying on the ground as if dead, legs twitching. But the French armies were fully mobilized. They had sound defences and were ready to go on the offensive themselves. So, we Russians should congratulate ourselves. There's been no knockout blow. We're still on our feet.

'Morale, in general, is low. Men seem more frightened of German flares than they are of shells. There's constant talk of spies sending up flares, of encirclements, of German paratroopers and motorcyclists penetrating deep behind our lines. I'm sure this paranoia will soon evaporate and that our men will make the Germans pay a thousand-fold for what they have done.

'Our men have no songs. And they aren't interested in women. Only cooks and clerks seem not to have forgotten that they are men. The army retreats in silence. I heard that K. surrendered of his own free will. Just waved a white handkerchief in the air. I remembered the day in 1915 when we saw Pápa off to the war. Máma was wearing a black veil. We took a cab and the driver was a woman. Today, in an army newspaper, I read, "Badly battered, the enemy continued his cowardly advance." Certainly an interesting way to put it ... What will happen come winter? They expect to be finished with Russia in ten weeks. No way! Still, the bastards are smart tacticians.

'I read a propaganda leaflet. Apparently, German officers have been taking pedigree dogs with them, in their cars. Some nerve – it's hard not to admire them!

'Bayonet attacks are all very well, but we need something different. Mobile artillery, rapid deployment of tanks!

'Today the corps commander invited me to his table. Throughout the meal all I heard was criticism of commanders afraid of encirclement.

'What's Guderian up to with his panzers? Is he aiming to meet up with Kleist?[245]

'I saw Red Army soldiers marching on foot and German prisoners being transported by truck. I stopped a truck and ordered the prisoners out. They were genuinely surprised. They truly believed that representatives of a higher race had the right to be driven, while their captors plodded along on foot. A strange lot, these Fritzes ...

'I'm certain that the old Russian army would have collapsed after a blow like this. And the whole tsarist regime with it. But we endure. So we'll go on enduring. And we'll win!

'I've been thinking about Alexander Nevsky, Suvorov and Kutuzov.[246] Oh, if only Pápa were still alive!'

'Yes,' Darensky said to himself as he closed his notebook. 'No doubt about it – I've certainly got a head on my shoulders!'

The injustice he had suffered still rankled deeply. Why, he kept asking himself, had he been posted to the reserves? And then he would answer his question: 'Because I was right. Because I assessed the situation correctly when that was not what Bykov wanted. But where's Colonel Novikov, what's happened to my one defender? Well, I suppose you could say it was wrong of me to be right ... Anyway, I'm certainly not like Bykov myself. I know a good man at first glance and I know how to value him.'

Darensky remembered the year 1937. He remembered his time in prison, the night-time interrogations and the investigator. He remembered the moment in 1940 when, after being summoned from the camp

678

to Moscow, he was told that his case had been reviewed and he had been judged innocent.

He remembered the month he had spent unloading barges in Kozmodemyansk[247] while he waited for his documentation. He remembered the wonderful day when he put on military uniform once again.

'If they gave me a regiment,' he thought, 'I'd be a good regimental commander. And if they entrusted me with a division, I'd command that just as well. But I'm sick to death of Bykov and his pettifogging archival work.'

As he fell asleep, he imagined himself sitting in a front-line command post. Bykov, now only a major, would come in. 'At your command, comrade General,' he would say. Recognizing Darensky, he would turn pale.

After this, there were a number of possible variations. Darensky's favourite scenario had him greeting Bykov with the words, 'Ah, an old friend! So we meet again!' And then, after a brief silence, 'Sit down, sit down! And, as they say, let bygones be bygones! Here, have some tea and a bite to eat – you must be hungry from the journey! And we must have a think about your duties here. What would you prefer?'

And he would see his former boss almost tremble from gratitude.

Surprisingly, the man who had done him such harm no longer seemed like an enemy.

Darensky was probably no vainer or more ambitious than most people, but since his pride had been trampled on so very often, he found it difficult to get over such episodes as his quarrel with Bykov.

So it was that this serious thirty-five-year-old lieutenant colonel consoled himself with fantasies of childish triumphs.

7

It was morning. One after another, trucks and infantry platoons were approaching the river at Kamyshin, waiting to cross to Nikolaevka on the east bank.

The hot August air shimmered over fields of yellow-brown wheat stubble and the wilted leaves of melon plantations.

Traffic controllers sheltered from the sun beside buildings, waving their flags and shouting at the drivers of approaching trucks, 'Stop! Are you blind? The barge has already left! Don't crowd so close together!'

The drivers leaned out of their windows, wondering where best to pull up. Depending on which road they'd taken – down the clay slope or through the fields of black earth – their dust-covered faces looked either yellow or dark grey.

Anti-aircraft gunners lay in shallow trenches beside the thin, raised barrels of their guns, trying to ward off the sun with tarpaulin ground-sheets. Soldiers sat in the backs of the trucks, touching the black bodies of the bombs lying beside them and joking sleepily, 'You could fry eggs on these – let's hope they're not about to explode!'

This convoy of dusty trucks, all bearing heavy loads of 200-kilo bombs, was on its way to airfields in the Transvolga steppe.

One of the drivers let out a mischievous cry and stepped on the accelerator. His truck left the wooden platform and moved towards the water, its overloaded suspension knocking and jolting. The traffic controllers all rushed forward, shouting, 'Stop! Get back!'

One of the controllers, a very tall man, raised his rifle butt in the air, as if to take a swing at the radiator. The driver hurriedly explained something, pointing to the rear axles.

Two more controllers ran up. Everyone began shouting at once. It seemed this would go on for ever, but the driver took a metal tin from his pocket and the three controllers, after tearing off pieces of newspaper, took some tobacco from this tin, rolled themselves cigarettes and lit up. The driver took the truck down to the water, positioning it so as not to hinder any vehicles coming from the east bank on the next barge. Then he lay down in the shade, on some large stones.

Agreeing that he would be first to board, the controllers drew on their cigarettes.

A very new black pickup appeared. Sitting beside the driver was a thin-faced lieutenant colonel who looked so bad-tempered and haughty that the controllers just let out cross sighs, not daring to say a word.

On the bench in the back were three other commanders: a major, smoking a proper cigarette from a packet; a lieutenant, a smart great-coat flung over his shoulders, whom the soldiers immediately identified as from the supplies section; and another lieutenant, a handsome young man who must have just graduated from military school. He was wearing a new uniform and he had a pained look in his eyes.

The controllers took a few steps back. They heard the lieutenant colonel say, 'Keep an eye on the sky, comrades.'

One of the controllers said mockingly, 'They know how to look after themselves all right. Ready-made cigarettes and tea in a thermos!'

A detachment of Red Army soldiers marched right down to the water's edge. The men in front were looking around for their commander. They slowed their steps. They had not been ordered to halt, but they were hardly going to be able to get across the Volga on foot. As for their commander, he was some distance away, getting a light from one of the controllers and asking whether the crossing was being bombed.

'Halt!' he finally shouted. 'Halt! Striding straight into the water – what the hell's got into you all!'

The soldiers sat down on stones near the water and put down their knapsacks, rifles and greatcoat rolls. Instantly a distinct smell wafted into the air – the smell of strong tobacco, fresh sweat and sweat-impregnated clothes peculiar to an infantry unit on its way to the front line.

The soldiers were a motley crowd: thin city dwellers, unused to long marches; broad-cheeked Kazakhs, pale from exhaustion; Uzbeks wearing tunics and side caps instead of long gowns and brightly coloured skullcaps, and with a pensive look in their velvet eyes; freckled young lads hardly any taller than their rifles; kolkhoz workers; fathers of families; men accustomed to heavy physical labour, their sinewy necks and muscles now standing out firmer than ever, as if to exemplify the austere life of a soldier. There was an Armenian with thick, black hair; a young man with a twisted mouth; and an agile, stocky fellow with a ruddy face and a broad smile; the long, arduous march seemed to have affected him no more than river water affects the well-oiled wing of a young drake.

681

Some went straight to the water's edge, then squatted down and filled their mess tins. One man set about washing his handkerchief, causing a black cloud to spread through the clear water; another first washed his hands and then splashed water over his face. Some sat on the ground, chewing on dried rusks, scratching inside their trousers or beneath their tunics, or rolling cigarettes, trying not to let others see their tobacco pouches. Most of the men, however, lay down, some on their backs and some on their sides, closing their eyes and going so still that, but for their look of utter exhaustion, they could have been taken for dead.

There was just one dark-skinned, lean but broad-shouldered man in his forties who remained on his feet, gazing for a long time at the river. It was absolutely smooth, like a flat, heavy slab of rock. All the fierce heat of this August day seemed to have emanated from this huge mirror at the foot of the high sandy cliff. In the cliff's shadow the mirror was a velvet black; where the sun beat straight down on it, the mirror was slate grey, with a hint of blue.

The soldier looked long and intently at the meadows on the far bank, from which the barge had already moved off again. He looked upstream and downstream and then turned round to look at his comrades.

The driver got out of the pickup and went up to the soldiers by the river.

'Where have you lot just come from?' he asked.

'Some of us have been digging trenches, some have been doing other auxiliary work,' the standing soldier replied, hoping to win the driver's sympathy. 'We've marched quite a distance, men are collapsing from sunstroke. Can you spare some baccy, comrade driver, and some pages from *Red Star*? One of the dates it was printed on super-fine paper!'[248]

The driver took out his tobacco pouch and some slips of newspaper. 'On your way to Stalingrad, are you?' he asked.

'Who knows? Right now it's back to Nikolaevka. Our division's being held in reserve there.'

A second soldier, annoyed that he hadn't been quicker to cadge a smoke himself, said, 'There's nothing worse than being separated from your unit. No hot meals, only dry rations. And it's two days since they last gave us any baccy.' Turning to the first soldier, he went on, 'Leave a few drags for your comrade!'

Without moving or even opening his eyes, a third soldier said, 'Wait till we get to Stalingrad. You'll get your hot meal there all right.' As he spoke, his teeth looked very white.

'Yes,' said the second soldier. 'Blood will be shed there. That's for sure.'

The pickup truck with the commanders, the trucks with the bombs and several kolkhoz carts drawn by oxen all went onto the barge. Barely had the crossing commandant ordered the infantry platoons to embark when there was a burst of activity in the sky above them. Soviet fighters were patrolling over the Volga and the sands to the east, filling the air with the roar of their engines. The soldiers looked around, slowing their step, expecting to be ordered to wait, but the crossing commandant merely urged them on and shouted, 'Quick! Get on board!'

Either this man with the red armband was eager to see the last of this huge barge laden with 200-kilo bombs or else he had seen so many air raids that they meant nothing to him.

There were several hundred men on the barge and they all instinctively tried to get as far away from the trucks as they could, crowding towards the bow and the stern, looking warily at the bomb containers' cylindrical grills and at the two lifebelts hanging on the bridge. Some of the men, no doubt, were wondering which of them would manage to seize one of these lifebelts and dive into the water.

There is no fear worse than a new fear; being bombed on water seemed infinitely more frightening than being bombed on land. It was clearly the same for all of them – both for the foot soldiers and for the commanders in the pickup. And it really was simply a matter of the novelty of this particular fear. The sailors were eating juicy tomatoes and smacking their lips. A sad-looking boy was holding a fishing rod, keeping a watchful eye on his float, and an elderly woman with red hair, sitting close to the helmsman, was knitting either a stocking or a mitten.

'Well, comrade Lieutenant, how are you feeling?' asked the major, blowing down his cigarette holder. 'Are you a good swimmer? Will you be needing a lifebelt?'

The lieutenant colonel got out of the pickup. Pointing to the tightly parked trucks with their loads of bombs, he said, 'If a bomb hits those trucks, the lieutenant will be better off with a parachute!'

After that, his face turned very stern again. He did not want his little joke to prompt the major to get too familiar with him.

Infringing the usual rules of behaviour for men of his age, the young lieutenant said with absolute frankness, 'I'm terrified, I can't deny it. What are all those fighters doing in the sky?'

'Clear enough,' said the major. 'There must have been a radio notification of approaching German bombers. They'll catch us right in midstream.' Remembering the tomatoes Antonina Vasilievna had given him as he left, he put his hand to his knapsack.

The fighters went on hurtling about the sky. There were MIGs, LaGGs and American Airacobras.[249]

The barge moved painfully slowly. The small tug seemed to be at the end of its strength. The west bank was slipping further and further away, but the east bank still seemed beyond reach, infinitely distant. The soldiers kept an anxious eye on the barge's progress, while repeatedly scanning the western sky, afraid that German bombers might appear at any moment.

'What's got into our fighters? Why are they circling around like that?' muttered one of the younger soldiers.

'They're guarding the melon plantations,' replied an older soldier, the man who had remained on his feet when they first reached the river. 'The plantations on the east bank are very special. Understood?'

'Very funny,' said a younger soldier. 'And you say you're a family man. You won't be laughing when we're all in the water.'

No one on the barge knew, or could have known, that the fighters were waiting to escort a passenger plane on its way from Moscow to Stalingrad.

8

The crew of the Douglas arrived at Moscow's central aerodrome at dawn.

The pilot, a major with a crumpled, capricious-looking face, and the navigator, who was pale and stooped, walked side by side. Each had a huge map case on a long strap, thrown casually over one shoulder and knocking against his thighs.

'Say what you like, she's a fine woman,' said the pilot. 'And as for her legs!'

'I'm not saying a word against her,' said the navigator. 'Only that she drinks. You can't deny that.'

Following behind were a radio operator and two senior sergeants.

The duty officer went out to meet the pilot and said with a smile, 'Ah, comrade Major!'

'Greetings, Lieutenant Colonel!' said the pilot, and walked on, his boots squeaking on the stone tiles.

He was well used to the small anxieties that went with having an important passenger. He inspected the soft seats with their starched covers, straightened the strip of carpet that ran down the aisle, used the sleeve of his jacket to polish the already sparkling window where his passenger usually sat, and went through to his cabin.

Twenty minutes later, General Zhukov, deputy people's commissar for defence, arrived in his car.

The plane took off to the south-east. The men behind Zhukov sat in silence, looking at the back of his large, closely shaven head. What was the general thinking as he gazed out of the window?

For a long time Zhukov sat very still. Only when the plane approached the Volga, which looked like a long blue shawl with torn edges, did he turn to the man behind him and ask, 'So, will you be treating me to some sterlet?'

'Of course, comrade Army General,' the general replied, getting quickly to his feet. 'And it'll be the very best. Malinovsky's 66th Army has been doing some fine fishing!'

Zhukov went back to looking out of the window. He had often had occasion to look down at the world and observe its contours. The world he saw now – the thin threads of tracks and roads, villages and small towns divided into square or rectangular blocks, the copper rectangles of harvested fields and the green rectangles of winter crops, the Volga flowing between patches of sand, pale blue backwaters and long green smears of rushes – the startlingly geometric world he saw now was as familiar to him as the day-to-day world of the earth's surface, with its cows, sheep and birds, with its snot-nosed little boys, with its dust and smoke, with its grasses and its crooked willows, with its multitude of unexpected features that so often hindered the orderly deployment of troops.

Below him now lay long beds of rushes. What a place to go shooting – it must be home to thousands of ducks!

The Douglas began to descend. The fighter escort, which they had picked up in Balashov, alternated between banking up steeply and descending in slow, sweeping curves. Then the Douglas was flying low over the Volga. In the middle of the river was a huge barge packed with trucks. Foot soldiers were moving slowly along the shore, many of them looking up at the plane. A long queue of trucks was waiting to cross.

Provisioning the troops deployed on the west bank, inside Stalingrad, was going to be painfully difficult.

Zhukov remembered discussions in the General Staff about preparations for the Soviet counter-attack. He closed his eyes and saw two fiery arrows on a map – one pointing down from the north, one curving up from the south.

Then he sighed loudly, imagining Field Marshal Bock looking at his own map and marking in where the Germans had broken through to the Volga.

He turned again to the major general sitting behind him, spat out the words, 'So you think you can fry sterlet on the Volga while you abandon tanks and guns on the Don!'[250] and swore furiously.

The soldiers on the barge saw a twin-engine plane flying low over the river, escorted by several fighters. The fighters already patrolling the area moved higher or to either side, with a swiftness that made the Douglas seem slow and lumbering.

'Look, Vavilov!' cried a young man, pointing to the Douglas. 'Must be someone important. Who do you think it is?'

And another soldier, looking up at the fighters, listening to a din which testified that the power of their engines truly was equal to that of a herd of 15,000 neighing and stamping horses, said coolly, 'Must be the corporal we left behind yesterday at the supply depot.'

9

They stopped for the night in Verkhne-Pogromnoye. Major Berozkin and the lieutenant from military school were to sleep in a barn. Lieutenant Colonel Darensky was offered a bed in a peasant hut, and the driver and the supplies-section officer were to sleep in the truck, close to a slit trench in the yard.

It was stiflingly hot. They could hear artillery fire to the west and there were swirls of glowing smoke to the south. There was a constant rumble from downstream – as if the waters of the Volga were falling from a high cliff into some underworld – and the whole flat mass of the Transvolga steppe was trembling. The hut's windows rang, the door creaked gently on its hinges, the hay rustled and small lumps of clay dropped from the ceiling. Somewhere nearby a cow was breathing heavily, getting to its feet and lying down again, disturbed by the noise, and by the smell of petrol and dust.

Infantry, guns and trucks were all moving down the main street. The blurred light of vehicle headlamps fell on the swaying backs of men on foot, on rifles glinting through clouds of dust, on the burnished barrels of anti-tank rifles, on mortars broad as samovar chimneys. Dust hung in the air and swirled around men's feet. There seemed no end to the flow of people, all utterly silent. Sometimes a stray flicker fell on a head in an iron helmet, or on the thin face, almost black with dust but with gleaming teeth, of an exhausted, stumbling foot soldier. A moment later another vehicle's headlamps would pick out a platoon of motor infantry in the back of a truck – helmets, rifles, dark faces and fluttering tarpaulins.

Powerful three-axle Studebakers growled past, towing seventy-six-millimetre guns with barrels still warm from the heat of the day.

Grass snakes and whip snakes, shaken by all the noise, tried to slip across the road and away into the steppe. Dozens of thin crushed bodies lay dark against the white sand.

The sky was equally full of noise. Junkers and Heinkels crept between the stars. U-2 'maize hoppers' rattled along just above the ground, soon to glide over the German lines and release their bombs.[251]

687

Tupolev TB-3 heavy bombers – four-engine mammoths – lumbered along at an invisible height.

For the men below, it was as if they were standing beneath a vast dark blue bridge painted with stars, as if thousands of iron wheels were rumbling past over their heads.

Smoothly rotating searchlights from steppe airfields marked out night-time landing strips. On the far horizon a shining kilometre-long pencil drew pale blue circles with silent but frenzied zeal.

There was no beginning or end to the columns of men and vehicles. Headlamps shone and were instantly extinguished, scared by angry shouts from the foot soldiers, 'Lights off! Bombers!'

Black dust swirled over the road. High in the sky hung a shimmering glow – a glow that had now hung over Stalingrad, over the Volga and the surrounding steppe, for several nights.

The whole world had seen this glow. It fascinated and horrified those now moving towards it.

> Blessèd the man who's visited this world
> At moments of great destiny.

Would Tyutchev have remembered these words of his, had he, on this August night, been marching towards the city on the Volga where the world's fate was being decided?[252]

*

Meanwhile, soldiers from the Southwestern Front, defeated in the battles west of the Don, were plodding towards Stalingrad from the south, following dirt roads and small paths through the steppe. Some had dirty bandages around their left hands[253] and were staring dispiritedly down at the ground. Some were feeling their way with sticks, as if blind. Some were crying out with pain, trying not to put any weight on bloody foot sores eaten away by sweat and filth. In their eyes could be seen all the horror of war – and their memories of a bridge over the Don, of half-dead men trying to run across slippery red planks. After the Don, these soldiers had crossed the Volga, some on boards, some on car tyres, some clinging to wrecked boats. They could still hear the howls of the wounded they had seen standing on the stairs or by the windows of burning hospitals. They could still hear the wild laughter of men who had lost their minds and were shaking their fists at a sky heavy with German bombers. Their cheeks still burned from incandescent air. Day and night, these soldiers walked on, driven by horror.

Further away in the steppe, under the warm August sky, lay refugees from Stalingrad: women and girls in felt boots, in fur coats or warm fur-trimmed jackets, in greatcoats snatched from cupboards as families abandoned their homes. Children lay asleep on bags and bundles. The smell of city mothballs mingled with the smell of steppe wormwood.

Still further away, in gullies and ravines hollowed out by spring floods, flickered the lights of small fires. Wanderers, deserters and members of workers' battalions who had lost their units after an air raid were darning threadbare clothes or cooking pumpkins pilfered from kolkhoz gardens. Some were picking off lice, screwing up their eyes and concentrating as intently as if there were no more important task in the world. Every now and then they wiped their fingers over the dry ground.

*

The driver and the supplies officer were standing out in the yard with the mistress of the hut.

They gazed in silence at the troops hurrying towards Stalingrad in the middle of the night. There were moments when they seemed to be watching not columns of individual soldiers but a single huge creature with a huge iron heart and eyes fixed grimly on the road ahead.

A man in a helmet slipped away from his company and ran up to the gate.

'Mother!' he cried, holding out a slim pharmacy bottle. 'Water! The dust's killing me. My insides are burning.'

The old woman fetched a jug and began to pour water into the narrow throat of his bottle. The soldier stood and waited, looking first at the imposing supplies officer and then at his company, which had now passed by.

'You need a proper flask,' said the supplies officer. 'Whoever heard of a soldier with no flask?'

'It was hard enough to get hold of this,' the soldier replied. 'And someone's already tried to steal it.'

He straightened his tarpaulin belt. His voice was somehow both thin and hoarse, like a fledgling's as it cheeps for food. And his thin face, his sharp nose, his pitiful eyes peeping out from under a helmet too big for him – everything about him recalled a bird peeping out of a nest.

He corked up his bottle, drank down a mug of water and ran off again, in boots that were also too big. Muttering 'One anti-tank unit, two with mortars – and then us,' he disappeared into the dark.

The supplies officer on his way to Stalingrad in search of vodka said, 'That young fool won't last long.'

'No,' said the driver. 'Fighters like him don't fight for long.'

10

Lieutenant Colonel Darensky went into the hut and told them to move his bedding. He would sleep not on the bed but on the bench, his head to the icons and his feet to the door.

A young woman, the mistress's daughter-in-law, said impassively, 'The bench, comrade Commander, is very hard.'

'I'm scared of fleas,' said Darensky.

'We don't have fleas,' retorted a ragged old man sitting by the door. He looked like some wanderer taken in for the night, but he must have been the owner of the hut. 'Though we do meet the occasional louse,' he added.

Darensky looked around. The dim light of an oil lamp with no glass made everything seem still more poor and austere. 'And yet there's someone in a front-line trench,' he said to himself, 'who remembers this stifling hut. He keeps thinking about this old man, this scrawny woman, these small windows and the black boards of this ceiling. To him there's nowhere more precious in the world.'

Darensky was too overexcited to sleep; the glow in the sky, the constant hum and drone of planes, the mighty flow of troops through the night had made too deep an impression on him. He felt ever more conscious of the importance of the impending battle – just now he had wanted to share his thoughts with his chance companion, this quiet major. But Darensky was deeply reserved; a frank, serious conversation with someone he hardly knew always left him disturbed. There was, moreover, something about this major he found particularly irritating, though he couldn't quite say what it was. It was to avoid talking to him that he had gone inside the hut.

Darensky paced about between the stove and the door, then looked with sudden curiosity at an armchair standing against the wall. It had a black oilskin cover and a metal armrest. It was, obviously, from a bus. Then he remembered seeing the old woman pouring water for the goat into a strange vessel out in the yard. It had been a cast-iron lavatory cistern, dug into the ground. 'Yes,' he said to himself. 'There's been a powerful centrifugal force at work in the country. It takes quite a whirlwind to transport a bus seat to a village hut in the Transvolga steppe. And as for goats and camels drinking from something so urban as a lavatory cistern ...'

The young woman sorted out the bedding, then went outside.

'Where's your old woman gone?' Darensky asked the owner of the hut.

'She's down in the trench,' he replied. 'Women are afraid of sleeping inside. Once the bombs start, she's like a ground squirrel. She peeps out, hides away, then peeps out again.'

'And you? Aren't you afraid of bombs?'

'What's there to be afraid of?' said the old man. 'I fought against the Japanese, and then I fought against the Germans. This time I've sent twelve men to the Red Army – four sons and nine grandsons. What's the good of hiding in trenches? Two of my sons are full colonels – I'm not joking. But soldiers come by and dig up all our potatoes. They've gone off with our last pumpkin. Yesterday two of them came to barter a tin of meat and stole a new kerchief. And my old woman gives away everything we have – she can't refuse the wounded anything. There was one son of a bitch who nicked my box of matches – and she'd already given him the milk and pumpkin porridge meant for our supper. She'd wept at the mere sight of him. Yes, that's the way she is – she looks on every last soldier as her own son. And one of those Asiatics stole a sheep from our neighbours and slaughtered it. What do you think of that, comrade Commander, is that right? And cattle are being ferried across the Volga to our steppe, and kolkhoz chairmen are bartering calves for bottles of moonshine. They slaughter calves every day. Is that right, comrade Commander, when a cow is worth 40,000? Men are dying every day, but some people are doing very well out of this war. Well, comrade Commander? Answer me that!'

'I need to sleep,' said Darensky. 'We're leaving for Stalingrad at dawn.'

Just then there was a powerful explosion – a bomb close by on the road. The hut shuddered. The old man got to his feet and picked up his sheepskin coat.

'Where are you off to?' asked Darensky, laughing.

'Where? To the trench. Didn't you hear?' Bent almost double, the old man ran out of the hut.

Darensky lay down on the bench and quickly fell asleep.

11

All through the night, between trembling searchlights, accompanied by the rumble of distant artillery, the troops marched on towards the glow of the blazing city. To their right lay the Volga; to their left – the steppes and salt deserts of Kazakhstan.

The mood of the marching columns was grim and grave – as if the men no longer felt thirst or exhaustion or feared for their lives.

Here, on the edge of the Kazakh steppe, the fate of a nation was being decided. The steppe, the sky and the stars, which tracer bullets were endlessly climbing towards – all seemed to understand this.

The bronze monuments of Lvov, Odessa's seaside promenade, Yalta's palms, Kiev's chestnuts and poplars, the stations, parks, squares and streets of Novgorod, Minsk, Simferopol, Kharkov, Smolensk and Rostov, Ukraine's white peasant huts and fields of sunflowers, the vineyards of Moldova, the cherry orchards around Poltava, the waters of the Danube and the Dnieper, the apple trees of Belorussia, the wheat fields of the Kuban – all Russia and Ukraine now seemed to these Soviet soldiers like a haunting vision, an unforgettable memory.

Camels harnessed to peasant carts half-closed their eyes and slowly chewed their long lips as they watched the endless flow of human beings. Owls, blinded by headlamps, flew about wildly, beating their dark wings against the beams of light.

There was no need for political instructors and commissars to give speeches. Gunners, soldiers with anti-tank rifles and machine guns on their backs, kolkhoz workers and factory workers – everyone understood that the war had now reached the Volga and that behind them lay only the Kazakh steppe. Like all truths of great importance, this truth was very simple; there was no one who did not understand it.

It was no longer possible to march along the hilly west bank of the Volga; the Germans had advanced all the way to the shore. On the east bank, the Soviet soldiers could see only brackish steppe and camels chewing thistles. And a vast expanse of water now separated them from the west bank, from its willows and oaks, from the villages of Okatovka, Yerzovka and Orlovka. And this expanse was widening; the groves of trees, the villages, the kolkhozes, the fishermen, the boys now living under German occupation, the spaces of the Don and the Kuban were moving ever further away.

From the low-lying east bank, Ukraine seemed unreachable. And there was nothing to greet them here but the rumble of guns and the flames of the burning city – a greeting that pierced the soldiers' hearts.

12

Darensky woke shortly before dawn. He listened for a moment – the rumble of guns and the hum of planes had not stopped. Usually the hour before dawn is war's quiet hour – the time when night's darkness and fear draw to an end, when sentries doze off, when the severely wounded stop screaming and at last close their eyes. It is the time when fever subsides and sweat comes out on the skin, when birds begin to stir, when sleeping babies stretch towards the breast of their sleeping mothers. It is the last hour of sleep, when soldiers cease to feel the hard, lumpy ground beneath them and pull their greatcoats over their heads, unaware of the white film of frost now covering their buttons and belt buckles.

But there was no longer any such thing as a quiet hour. In the darkness before dawn planes were still humming and troops still passing by. There was the rumble of heavy vehicles and the sound of artillery fire and exploding bombs in the distance.

Unsettled by all this, Darensky got ready to go on his way. By the time he had shaved, washed, brushed his teeth and filed his nails, it was already light.

He went out into the yard. The driver was still asleep, his head on the corner of the seat and his bare feet poking out of the window. Darensky knocked on the windscreen. The driver did not wake up, so Darensky sounded the horn.

'Time we were off,' he said, as his numb driver began to stir. 'Get the pickup out on the road.'

Darensky walked past the slit trench, where the old man and his family were sleeping on straw, covered by sheepskin coats. He went on into the vegetable garden.

In the distance, through a lattice of yellowing leaves, he could see the gleam of the Volga. The rays of the rising sun, now just clear of the horizon, ran almost parallel to the ground. The clouds had turned pink. Only a few – not yet caught by the sun – remained a cold ashy grey. The high cliffs of the west bank had emerged from the dark, and the patches of limestone shone like fresh snow.

Each minute brought more light. Not far away was a dense flock of sheep, some white, some black. They were bleating quietly, stirring up thin clouds of pink dust as they moved over the tawny, hummocky ground.

Their shepherd had a large staff over his shoulder and his cloak billowed behind him.

It was a touching sight. In the low sun's broad rays, the sheep looked like small boulders moving between the hummocks, and the shepherd with his staff and cloak might have been drawn by Gustave Doré.

Then the flock drew nearer, and Darensky saw that the shepherd's cloak was a tarpaulin and his heavy staff was an anti-tank rifle. He was walking along the edge of the road, and the sheep were nothing to do with him.

Darensky returned to the pickup.

'Ready now?' he asked.

The lieutenant, a timid, skinny young man, said, 'The major's not here yet, comrade Lieutenant Colonel.'

'Where is he?'

'He went off to find some milk for breakfast. It seems the cow here's not in milk.'

'I don't believe it!' said Darensky. 'Milk and cows – I don't believe it. When every minute's precious!' He paced silently about the yard for several minutes, then burst out, 'How much longer will I have to wait for your dairyman?'

'He'll be back any moment,' the lieutenant said guiltily. He had rolled himself a cigarette, but he threw it onto the ground.

'Which way did he go?'

'Over there,' said the lieutenant. 'Permission to look for him?'

'Don't bother,' said Darensky.

He now felt crosser than ever with the major. Like many irritable people, he often vented his frustration and anger almost at random, on whoever happened to be present.

And when Berozkin appeared with a watermelon under one arm and a litre bottle filled with milk, Darensky almost choked with rage.

'Ah, comrade Lieutenant Colonel,' said Berozkin, placing the watermelon on the passenger seat, 'did you sleep well? I've brought us some milk – fresh from the cow!'

Darensky glared at him, then said with cold fury, 'Just look at yourself – you look more like a pedlar than a commander. It's because of pedlars and petty traders like you that we were routed in 1941. Here we are, not far from Stalingrad. Every minute counts – and you wander about the village bargaining for milk!'

The blood mounted to Berozkin's tanned face, turning it darker still. After a few seconds, he replied quietly, 'I apologize, comrade Lieutenant Colonel. Our lieutenant was coughing all night. I thought some fresh milk would do him good.'

'All right,' said Darensky, now embarrassed. 'But let's be off now!'

Darensky was afraid of Stalingrad. He thought he was making his way to the front too slowly, but what really troubled him was that he would be there extremely soon.

Darensky glanced at the major. Until now, what irritated him had been the man's imperturbable calm – but now he looked tense and shocked. His jaw had dropped, and there was a bewildered, almost crazed look in his eyes. Involuntarily, Darensky looked around: what had the major just seen? Were they about to encounter something terrible? Had German parachutists landed this side of the Volga?

But the road, gashed by wheels and tank tracks, was empty. All Darensky could see were some refugees, trudging along past the huts.

'Tamara! Tamara!' called Berozkin – and a young woman in shoes held together with string, with a bag over her shoulders, suddenly froze. Beside her stood a little girl who looked about five years old. She too was carrying a bag, sewn from a pillowcase.

Berozkin walked towards them, still holding the bottle of milk.

The woman stared at the commander coming towards her with a bottle of milk, then cried out, 'Ivan! Vanya! My darling Vanya!'

And this cry was so frightening, so charged with complaint, horror, grief, reproach and happiness that everyone who heard it flinched, as if from a burn or some other sudden physical pain.

The woman ran forward and flung her arms around Berozkin's neck, her body racked by silent sobs.

And the little girl in sandals stood beside her, gazing wide-eyed at the bottle of milk in the large, bronzed, big-veined hand of her father.

Darensky realized that he too was shaking. This chance meeting in the steppe was not something he ever spoke about. But even thirty years later, when he was a lonely old man, he would feel the same overwhelming anguish when he remembered this moment – when he remembered how this man and woman had first looked at each other, and how he had glimpsed in their faces all the savage grief and homeless happiness of those terrible years.

697

It was then, he came to believe, that he first truly took in all the bitterness of the war – standing in the sands beyond the Volga and hearing a homeless, dust-covered woman with beautiful eyes and the thin shoulders of an adolescent girl say, in a loud voice, to a broad-faced forty-year-old major, 'Our Slava's dead. I failed him.'

Berozkin led the woman and the little girl to the hut. Then he came out again, went up to Darensky and said, 'Excuse me, comrade Lieutenant Colonel, I'm holding you up. Please go on your way without me. I've just found my family.'

'We'll wait,' said Darensky. He went to the pickup and said to the supplies officer, 'If this were my truck, I tell you I'd take this woman to Kamyshin, even if it meant throwing out the other passengers.'

'No,' said the supplies officer. 'I have a mission to carry out, and these two could be talking all day and all night. A good-looking young woman, a major who's got what it takes, and it's a year since they last saw each other. They've got more than enough to keep them busy.' He winked at the silent driver and at the young lieutenant, who was looking at Darensky with profound admiration, and began to laugh. His laughter was the abrupt, staccato laughter of a professional teller of jokes.

Darensky realized that it would indeed be better if they went on their way. There was, after all, nothing he could do for the major. 'All right,' he said, 'start the engine. I'll fetch my things.'

He entered the dark hut, looking down at the ground, and reached out for his suitcase. He heard the old woman say something, with a sob. He saw a look of pain on the face of the old man, who was standing there holding his hat. He saw the pale, excited face of the young daughter-in-law. This chance meeting in the steppe had affected all of them.

He tried not to look at Berozkin and his wife, thinking it must be unbearable for them to be among so many strangers and to be the focus of their attention.

'We'll go on our way, comrade Major,' he said loudly. 'Allow me to wish you all the best. You'll be staying here for a while, I think.'

He shook Berozkin's hand. Going up to Tamara, he again felt overwhelmed by emotion. She held out her hand. Darensky felt his eyes fill with tears as he bowed his head low and carefully raised her delicate, little girl's fingers to his lips. There were dark grooves on them, from cutting potatoes, and it was a long time since they had been washed.

'Excuse us,' he said, and hurried out of the hut.

13

It was a meeting that wrenched their hearts. Tenacious as thistles or steppe grass, overwhelming grief at once choked every stirring of joy.

Most terrifying of all was the lack of time; it was impossible for the family to stay together for more than a day.

Caressing his daughter, Berozkin felt overwhelmed by grief for his son. Luba could not understand why, whenever her father took her in his arms or stroked her hair, he suddenly frowned, as if he were angry. Nor could she understand why her mother, who had grieved so much for her father, kept crying now that she had found him again.

One night, Máma had dreamed that Pápa had come back. Luba had heard her talking and laughing in her sleep. But now that they had found each other, all Máma could do was repeat, 'No, no, I must stop crying. Why am I so stupid?'

Nor could Luba understand why her parents were so quick to talk about parting, why they were noting down addresses, why her father said he would put them on a car or a truck going to Kamyshin, why he asked Máma if she had any photos, since his old ones had almost faded away by now.

Her father fetched his things from the barn and laid out a spread on the table. Only once in her life, at the Shaposhnikovs', had Luba seen anything like it. There was fatback, and tinned meat and vegetables, and sugar, and butter, and salmon roe, and sausage, and even some chocolates.

Máma sat at the table like a guest, and her father prepared everything himself. And then Máma began tasting food from the tins and breaking off pieces of bread, and Luba kept asking, 'Can I have some sausage? ... Can I eat a little fatback?' 'Of course you can,' said her father. He handed her some bread and butter, and she put a piece of fatback on top and began to eat. It was very tasty, so tasty that she started to laugh. Then she looked at her father. He was watching Máma, who was eating very quickly, her fingers trembling as she put pieces of sausage and tinned meat in her mouth – and there were tears in his eyes. What was the matter? Was her father upset that they were eating all his supplies of food? Luba froze with resentment, but then, in her little heart, she understood what he was going through. And instead of feeling happy to have found a protector, she wanted to protect and comfort her father in his grief and helplessness. Looking into the darkest corner of the hut, where she thought the forces of evil were hiding, she said sternly, 'Don't touch him!'

Máma talked about all that the Shaposhnikovs had done for them in Stalingrad, and about how she and Luba had survived the fire. After the apartment burned down, she hadn't gone back there for five days. The Shaposhnikovs had looked for her and Luba, but in the end they had to leave; they had gone to Saratov by truck, and from there to Kazan by steamer. They left her an address and a long letter. She and Luba managed to cross the Volga by ferry and then they had set off on foot.

And then Máma began to tell their whole story from the very beginning, and Luba got bored, since she knew it all already: they had no winter coats; they were bombed four times; their basket of bread disappeared; they travelled for twelve days in a cattle wagon, in midwinter; there was no bread; Máma sewed, did people's laundry and dug vegetable beds; bread cost a hundred roubles a kilo; in one town Máma was issued a ration of sugar and butter and she swapped it for bread; it was easier to get bread in the villages than in cities. They lived in one village for three months, and the children were always full; not only did they have bread every day, but they also had milk. She was going to barter her ring and brooch for rye flour, but they got stolen, and after that she had to take Slava to a children's home. At least they gave him bread there. Bread, bread, bread. Four-year-old Luba well understood the meaning of this momentous word.

'Máma,' she said, 'can we keep some sweets for Slava?'

Her mother started shaking and sobbing again, silently, in a way Luba had never seen before. Then she started to hiccup, and Pápa said in a strange, sleepy voice, 'This is war. It's the way things are. It's the same for everyone.'

Then Pápa began to tell his own story. He mentioned old friends, some of whom Máma remembered, and Luba noticed that Pápa kept repeating the word 'killed', just like Máma repeated the word 'bread'.

'Killed, killed, killed,' he kept saying. 'Mutyan was killed on the second day, when we were still near Kobrin. And remember Alexeyenko? He was last seen in the forest near Tarnopol, lying on the ground with a stomach wound, with German sub-machine-gunners close by. And

Morozov – not Vasily Ignatievich, but the Morozov who acted in the play with you – he was killed during the counter-attack near Kanev, on the Dnieper. A direct hit from a mortar. And Rubashkin too – I've heard he was killed near Tula. He was taking his battalion across the highway when they were strafed by a Messerschmitt. A large-calibre bullet straight in the head. He was a good man. Remember how he taught us to salt mushrooms? And Moiseyev too. He shot himself – I heard from a man who saw him do it. It was July last year. He was surrounded, caught in a bog, and he could barely move – wounded in the leg. He just took out his revolver and that was that … And so here we are … I must be the only regimental commander from our division who's still alive. But guess who I bumped into yesterday? Aristov, my old supplies boss! Remember him? He looked as if he was just back from a holiday by the sea. I'll give you his address and write him a note. He's a good fellow, he'll do all he can for you and then send you on your way to Saratov. He has trucks setting off for Saratov every day.'

'And what about you?' asked Máma. 'Heavens, I wrote so many letters! There's nowhere I didn't inquire. You know about everyone, but no one could tell me anything about you.'

'Me?' Pápa replied with a shrug. 'I've just been with my guns. We've kept at it, but we've still retreated a long way. Well, we must be sure not to lose each other again – that's the main thing.'

He went on to say that he was on his way back to his regiment. The division had been in reserve. But when he came out of hospital, he found the division had been brought forward. Now he was trying to catch up with it.

And then he added, 'Tamara, let me wash your clothes for you. You need a rest.'

'Heavens, after all you've been through!' she replied. 'Still the same as ever – my kind, wonderful man. My sweet flint!' And they both smiled – that was what she had used to call him before the war.

Then Luba began to fall asleep, and her father said, 'She's tired.'

And her mother said, 'We've been walking for ten days. And she gets very frightened by all the planes – she can tell the German ones from their sound. She keeps waking at night, crying and screaming. And now she's just eaten a lot, which she's not used to.'

While she was asleep, her father picked her up in his arms. She remembered him carrying her out to a barn that smelled of hay. In the evening she woke up and had another meal. There were Germans planes in the sky, but she didn't feel frightened. She just went up to

Pápa, put his big hand on her head, and stood there quite calmly, listening to the noises above her.

'Sleep, Luba, sleep,' said her mother – and Luba fell asleep again.

It was a strange night, both happy and bitter.

'We've found each other again. You've come back from the dead – and now we have to part again, for ever. No, it's not possible.'

'Don't sit like that. Make yourself comfortable. And drink some more milk. Really, you're so thin now. Sometimes I'm not quite sure if it's really you.'

'He's gone. Lying at the bottom of this terrible river. It's night down there. It's cold and dark, and there's no power in the world that can help him.'

'I'll give you my underclothes. That'll be better than nothing. And I've got some new boots, box calf, good quality. I've only worn them twice and I really don't need them. And I'll make you up two pairs of foot cloths – soon it'll be winter.'

'The last time I saw him, he kept asking, "When will you take me home?" But how could I know? Fool that I am, I just felt happy to see he was a bit less thin.'

'I'll sew my field-mail address to your skirt. That'll be safer than your jacket – your jacket might disappear.'

'I must look quite scary. I'm nothing but skin and bones. Aren't you ashamed of me?'

'Your legs are so thin, and I can see blood on your feet. You've walked a long way.'

'What are you doing, my love? Kissing my feet when all I want is to wash off the dust.'

'Did he still remember me?'

'No, no, I can't spend any more time on my own. I can't, I really can't. I'm going to follow you – even if you drive me away with a stick.'

'Luba – think about Luba.'

'I know, I know. Tomorrow Luba and I will get in a truck going to Kamyshin.'

'Why aren't you eating anything? Here – have this biscuit. And wash it down with some milk, even if it's only a sip.'

'I can't believe it. It's you, it's really you. And the same as always. You even say the very same words – "Here ... even if it's only a sip."'

'I may look the same now, but you should have seen me last September. Hollow cheeks, face overgrown with stubble ... I remember thinking that my Tamara wouldn't want to look at me.'

'Howling and whining up in the sky above us, day and night, all year long. I suppose you must have been close to death many times?'

'No, not really, nothing much. No more than everyone else.'

'What does he want? What does the monster want?'

'In the villages, women say to their children, "Don't cry. If Adolf hears you, he'll fly straight here in his plane."'

'My sweetest of dandies. Cleanly shaved head, neat clean nails and a clean white collar. When I glimpsed you just now, it was like a thousand-pound weight off my heart. And I've told you everything, from beginning to end. But don't think I'm like this with anyone else. Usually I keep things to myself. Anyway, who'd want to listen to me? No one but you, no one in the world but you.'

'You must promise to eat better. You'll have a military rations card now. And you must drink some milk every day. All right?'

'This is so wonderful. It's you. Well and truly you.'

'I knew we'd be meeting. I knew it yesterday.'

'Remember when Slava was born? The car had broken down. We left the maternity home on foot. You carried him in your arms. No, this is our last meeting, I know it. We'll never see each other again, and she'll end up in a children's home.'

'Tamara!'

'Did you hear that?'

'Doesn't matter. It landed in the river.'

'Dear God, but that's where he's lying ... Vanya, you're crying, aren't you? Please don't. Everything will be all right, it really will. We'll see each other again, I promise you, and I'll drink milk. Poor you, you've been through so much, and all I've done is talk about myself. Look at me, look at me, my dearest. Let me wipe your nose – and your eyes. Oh, my silly, my little one, how do you ever manage without me?'

And in the morning they parted.

14

The 13th Guards Rifle Division was passing through the village of Verkhne-Pogromnoye, on its way from Nikolaevka to the front line.

Transport had been provided, but there were not enough trucks for everyone. Battalion Commander Filyashkin called Lieutenant Kovalyov and told him that his company would have to go on foot.

'Will there be trucks for Konanykin's men?' asked Kovalyov.

Filyashkin nodded.

'I see,' said Kovalyov.

He disliked Konanykin and was in the habit of drawing constant comparisons between his own company and Konanykin's.

If the regimental commander congratulated him for achieving excellent results in a shooting exercise, he would ask the secretary, 'And how did Konanykin do?'

If he was issued a pair of box-calf boots, he would ask, 'That's fine – but I hope you won't be wasting boots like these on Konanykin. He can make do with kirza!'

If he was reprimanded because too many of his men developed blisters after a long march, his main concern was the percentage of men with blistered feet in Konanykin's company.

The soldiers usually referred to Konanykin as Long-limbs – he really did have unusually long legs and arms.

Kovalyov was upset that he and his men would be plodding through the dust when the rest of the division was being taken by truck. If anyone was to cover this distance on foot, it should, of course, have been Long-limbs.

After Filyashkin had outlined the company's route, Kovalyov said he expected to complete the march only an hour or so after the trucks.

'But it seems to be always like this, comrade Battalion Commander,' he added, when the official part of the conversation was over. 'If anyone has to go on foot, it's me. There always seem to be trucks for Konanykin.'

Shifting to a less formal tone, Filyashkin explained that it was because Kovalyov's company – unlike the other companies – had still

704

been on the west bank when trucks were being allocated. 'But how are your men doing?' he asked. 'Not too many blisters?'

'They'll cope,' said Kovalyov. 'If they must march, then march they will.'

He went and ordered the sergeant major to get the company ready, hurried to his billet to collect his things and say goodbye to the landlady, and then ran on to have a quick word with medical instructor Lena Gnatyuk.

The medical section were already in their truck, about to depart. Standing beside the truck, Kovalyov said, 'I know Stalingrad. I spent a day there in June, on my way back from hospital. I stayed with a friend's family.'

Leaning over the side of the truck, Lena Gnatyuk called out, 'Good luck, comrade Lieutenant. Be sure to catch us up soon!'

The truck started off. Everyone began laughing and talking at once. Lena waved her hand toward the grey houses and called out, 'Farewell, land of melons!'

Kovalyov's company had only just crossed the Volga. They were given two hours to have something to eat and to change their foot cloths. Some of the men did not even receive their tobacco and sugar rations. Nevertheless, they set off shortly after the trucks.

After the first forty kilometres, everyone fell silent, no longer even dreaming aloud about shade or water.

By evening the column had grown long and straggly, extending several hundred metres from head to tail. Kovalyov had given permission to two soldiers, who were limping badly, to sit on top of the cart, on the baggage, and to three others to hold on to the edge of the cart.

The two men sitting on top were letting out constant groans; they also kept treating the carter to tobacco. The men staggering along beside the cart kept glaring at them and saying to the carter, 'Throw them out! They're faking – can't you see?'

'That's for the lieutenant to decide,' the carter replied.

Above a narrow bridge hung a sign, '10 Tons'. Below a large plywood arrow pointing to the left were the words 'Detour for Tanks'.

The driver of a three-axle truck hooted desperately, wanting to overtake the column, but no one responded. The soldiers seemed oblivious to everything around them. The driver opened his door and leaned out, intending to call down furious curses on these deaf soldiers. Seeing their weary faces, he muttered, 'Infantry – Queen of the Battlefield' and turned off to the left.

The two men at the head of the column were Vavilov and Usurov.

705

From time to time Usurov looked back at the men hobbling along in the dust behind him and smirked, enjoying his feeling of superiority.

Kovalyov was walking along the edge of the road, flicking the dust off the top of his boot with a long stick. In the cheery voice required of a commander, he asked Vavilov, 'Well, my good fellow? How's it going? Still on your feet?'

'We're doing all right, comrade Lieutenant,' Vavilov replied. 'We'll get there.'

Senior Sergeant Dodonov came up and said, 'Comrade Lieutenant, Mulyarchuk is undermining discipline. He's demanding a halt.'

'Tell the political instructor to have a word with him,' said Kovalyov.

Usurov looked at the camels harnessed to carts beside the road, and said loudly, not looking towards Kovalyov, 'So now we're fighting alongside these snake-necked creatures. Look where our kolkhozes have got us!'

'Yes,' said Vavilov, 'these creatures scare me too.'

Two men at the tail of the column were neither speaking nor looking around them. Their eyes were red and their lips cracked. They did not even feel exhaustion, since their exhaustion was too extreme, filling their sinews and veins, drilling into their bone marrow. They walked at a constant speed. Had they stopped for a moment, they would have found it almost impossible to get going again.

Then one of them grinned and said in Ukrainian, 'There's still some-one behind us, you know. Our company joker's limping along the other side of the bridge.'

And the other replied, 'Yes, so much for our brave Rezchikov. I thought we'd lost him completely.'

'No, he's still limping along.'

And they walked on in silence.

Towards evening Kovalyov declared a halt. He could barely stand upright. Everyone immediately lay down by the side of the road.

Coming the other way, from Stalingrad, were groups of refugees: men wearing hats and greatcoats, children carrying pillows, women staggering under heavy burdens.

'How far do you think you're going to walk with all that?' a young soldier asked one of the women. She had a bundle strapped to her back, and a bucket and a large bag hanging against her chest. Walking behind her were three little girls with bags on their shoulders.

She stopped and looked at him. Brushing a lock of hair from her forehead, she said, 'To Ulyanovsk.'

706

'You'll never get to Ulyanovsk carrying all that,' said the soldier.

'And my children?' she replied. 'I've no money, and they have to eat.'

'I call it greed,' said the soldier, remembering the night he'd thrown his gas mask into a ditch because it was hurting his shoulder. 'People weigh themselves down with clutter, and then they can't bear to throw it away.'

'You're an idiot,' said the woman. Her voice sounded distant and lifeless.

The soldier she had called an idiot took a large piece of dry, crumbling bread from his knapsack. 'Here you are!' he said.

The woman took the bread and began to cry. Her three little girls all had large mouths and pale faces. After looking quietly and seriously first at their mother, then at the soldiers lying on the ground, they too began to cry.

The family went on their way. The soldiers saw the mother breaking the bread with her free hand and sharing it out between the girls.

'She didn't keep a crumb for herself,' said Zaichenkov the former accountant.

'That's mothers for you,' someone pronounced with authority.

Next, the soldiers saw the girls approach a small boy. He looked about three, he had a large head and stout little legs, and he was eating a huge, unwashed carrot, spitting out bits of earth. As if by prior agreement, the girls all stopped. One slapped the boy in the face, the second pushed him in the ribs, while the third snatched his carrot. Then the girls went on their way again, mincing along on their slim legs. The boy sat down on the ground and watched.

'And that's solidarity for you,' said Usurov.

The soldiers took off their boots. The smell of sun-warmed wormwood at once gave way to the smell of an army barracks.

Very few of them waited for the water to boil. Some dipped their cubes of millet concentrate in warm water and ate with slow concentration; others lay down and fell asleep straightaway.

'Sergeant Major,' asked Kovalyov, 'are the stragglers all here now?'

'Here comes the very last,' replied Sergeant Major Marchenko, 'our company entertainer.'

Instead of grumbling and complaining, as everyone expected, Rezchikov called out brightly, 'Here I am. Engine and horn all in good order!'

Kovalyov looked at him and said to Kotlov, 'These men are a tough lot, comrade Politinstructor. We're almost keeping up with the trucks. They passed us only an hour ago.'

Kotlov moved away a little, sat down and began to pull off his boots – he had painful blisters.

Kovalyov sat down beside him and asked quietly, 'Why do you not conduct political work on the march?'

Kotlov examined his bloodstained foot cloths and replied angrily, 'The soldiers were all telling me to get onto the cart. They could see the state of my feet. But I marched on and I even sang songs and got the men to join in – that was my political work for the day.'

Kovalyov looked at the stains of black blood and said, 'I told you, comrade Politinstructor, that you needed boots a size larger. But you took no notice.'

Then Rysev came up and said, 'That was easy going – we were marching light. Now imagine doing that with thirty kilos on your back, with a mortar or an anti-tank rifle, and cartridges. But people manage.'

Those who had not gone to sleep straightaway were now drifting off. The others were gradually waking, rummaging in their knapsacks and taking out pieces of bread.

'I could do with some fatback,' said Rysev.

'Fatback!' said Marchenko. 'If only we could be back in Ukraine! Here the sun's burnt everything black. Villages, huts, even the earth – all black as coal. And as for these camels! When I think of our village, our orchards, our river, our girls singing under the trees in the meadows … And then I look around and all I see is this steppe, and huts that look like tombs … It chills my heart – it's as if we've reached the end of the world.'

An old man came up to the soldiers. He was wearing a coat and galoshes and carrying a bright red oilcloth bag. He smoothed down his white beard and asked, 'Where are you lot retreating from?'

'We're not retreating, Grandad. We're on our way to the front.'

'We're advancing,' said Marchenko.

'Oh yes,' said the old man. 'I've seen how you lot advance. Another month of your advancing – and the war will be over. If it isn't already.'

'What makes you say that?'

'Well,' said the old man, 'you've reached the Volga. Where are you going to fight now? Fritz won't want to go any further. What would he want with land like this?' And he gestured towards the sea of grey and rust-brown all around him.

He took a slim pouch from his pocket and began rolling an extremely slim cigarette. There was more paper in it than tobacco.

'Can you spare us a few crumbs?' asked Mulyarchuk.

'Not likely,' the old man replied – and returned the pouch to his pocket.

This angered Usurov. 'And who might you be?' he asked. 'Let's see your papers!'

'No! You can ask me that in the city. But a man doesn't need documents out in the steppe.'

'You can't do without documents. Without documents a man doesn't exist.'

'To hell with you. Go ask those there goats for their documents,' said the old man. And off he went into the steppe – tall, unhurried, shuffling through the dust in his galoshes. Turning round for a moment, he added, 'Woe to those living on earth!'

'He should be detained,' said Marchenko.

'No getting any baccy out of him,' said a soldier.

Everyone laughed.

'Soft in the head. Did you see his galoshes?'

'What d'you mean? He spoke good sense.'

'I've heard our divisions have been putting up a good fight. On the Don, I think. It took Fritz by surprise. Only he found a way to outflank them.'

'The sight of this steppe makes my heart ache.'

'I've never seen anything like it. The sun rises – and everything looks white. You think it's snow, but it's salt. Yes, it's a bitter land.'

'The way the camels twist their lips, it's as if they're laughing at us, thinking, "You idiots!"'

'These Germans are quite something.'

'No, they're not. Wait till you've met them. We put them to flight at Mozhay all right. When they're pushed, they run faster than we do.'

'Oh yes. That's why we're here with the camels.'

'A march like this – and you don't want to go on living. But you don't want to die either.'

'Think the war cares what you want?'

'Go on, Rezchikov, tell us a story.'

'First, a smoke.'

'No. Story first, then the smoke. Otherwise you'll fob us off with some old chestnut. It'll be "Give us a drink, Granny," said the soldier. "I'm so hungry there's nowhere to lie down for the night."'

'No,' Rezchikov replied abruptly. 'This is no time for stories. I tell you – we'll fight them off. Yes, we will! Then we can drink and feast all we want!'

'Very good,' said a serious voice. 'But we're not feasting now. Let's at least get some sleep. And look – look at all that!'

And they all looked in the direction of Stalingrad. The sky was covered by dense, billowing smoke – dark red from the blaze below and the setting sun.

'Our blood,' said Vavilov.

15

A chill, pre-dawn wind stirred the grass, raising clouds of dust over the road. The steppe birds still slept, puffing up their feathers. After the heat of the day and a warm night, this chill was unexpected.

To the east the sky turned pale grey. The faint light was hard, cold, somehow metallic. It was not true sunlight, only sun reflected off clouds, and it seemed more like the dead light of the moon.

Everything about the steppe seemed hostile. The road was grey and bleak. It was impossible to imagine peasant carts creaking slowly by, children running along in bare feet or people on their way to weddings and cheerful Sunday bazaars – this road seemed made only for guns, trucks loaded with crates of shells and soldiers going to their death. The telegraph poles and haystacks still hardly cast shadows; it was as if an artist beginning a new painting had sketched them in with a hard black pencil.

There were no real colours. Instead of the brown-green of grass, the yellow-green of hay and the river's cloudy pale blue, there was only dark and bright – much as at night, when black objects stand out only because they are still blacker than their surroundings. The soldiers all had pale faces, dark eyes and sharp noses.

Those already awake were smoking or rewinding their foot cloths. Their exhaustion was now giving way to apprehension, to an awareness that they would soon be in combat. One moment this felt like a cold lump under the heart, another moment like a blast of heat in the face.

A tall woman with narrow shoulders and a thin face walked quietly up to the men and put a wicker basket down on the ground.

'Here you are, my boys!' she said, and began handing out tomatoes.

No one thanked her or seemed in the least surprised. Everyone simply took the tomatoes, as if they were a part of their regular rations.

The woman was equally silent. She watched the soldiers eat.

Kovalyov went up to her, reached into the empty basket and said, 'My eagles have cleaned you out.'

'My hut's close by, just behind that mound,' said the woman. 'Come along and I'll give you some more.'

Kovalyov smiled; it had clearly never occurred to her that a lieutenant cannot simply stroll about the steppe carrying baskets of tomatoes. He called out to Vavilov, 'Here, accompany this citizen back to her hut!'

Vavilov and the woman set off. They walked side by side, their shoulders occasionally touching. Vavilov found this upsetting. It made him think of his last night at home, of how Marya had walked beside him in the same dawn light. The woman was in her early forties and she reminded him of Marya in many ways. Her height, her gait, even her voice – all were similar.

She said quietly, 'Yesterday we saw a German plane. I had some soldiers here with me. They'd been wounded, but not severely. All of a sudden the plane dived straight at the hut, straight as a spear. Those lads could have brought it down, but they just hid in the long grass. I stood in the middle of the yard, shouting, "Quick! Go for it – I can almost knock the bastards down with my poker!"'

'Why do you give us tomatoes?' asked Vavilov. 'We've brought the Germans all the way to the Volga, right to your doorstep. You shouldn't be feeding us – you should be cursing us, driving us off with your poker.'

They entered the warm half-dark of the hut. When Vavilov glimpsed the fair head of a small boy, his heart almost missed a beat. The stove, the table, the seat by the window, the thin-faced woman now looking straight at him, the sleeping bench and the fair head of the boy just getting up from it – everything seemed so familiar he could almost have been back home.

He noticed a gap in the bottom of the door and asked, 'And where's the man of the house?'

The boy whispered, 'Don't ask. You'll upset Máma.'

But the woman said calmly, 'He was killed in February, near Moscow. Not long ago they brought a German prisoner here. I asked him, "When did you get to the front?" "In January," he answered. "So it was you killed my husband," I said. I wanted to hit the man, but the guard said it was against the law. "Let me hit him against the law," I said. But the guard didn't let me.'

'Do you have an axe?' asked Vavilov.

'Yes.'

'Give it to me then. I must mend your door. Come winter, there'll be an icy draught.'

His sharp eyes noticed a board lying by the wall. The woman handed him an axe, and everything about it that reminded him of his own axe

712

made him feel sad. And everything that was different – this axe was far lighter, and the handle was thinner and longer – made him no less sad, since it reminded him how far he was from his home.

The woman guessed what he was thinking. 'Don't worry,' she said, 'you'll get back home in the end.'

'I don't think so,' he answered. 'It's not far from a man's home to the front, but it's a long way from the front to his home.'

Vavilov began trimming the board.

'I don't have any nails,' the woman said.

'I'll manage,' he answered. 'I'll make a peg.'

As he worked, she filled the basket with tomatoes and said, 'I'm counting on staying here with little Seryozha till winter. Then the Volga will freeze over. If the Germans get across to this bank, we'll leave home and make for Kazakhstan. Seryozha's all I have now. Under Soviet power, he'll make his way in the world, but under the Germans he'll never be anything more than a shepherd.'

Vavilov thought he could hear Kovalyov approaching. He put down the axe and straightened up. It was galling, even humiliating, to realize that he could get into trouble simply for carrying out necessary work.

'Yes, the Germans really have turned everything upside down,' he said to himself. After a quick look round, he picked up his axe again.

*

A few minutes later, as he was walking back, he felt anxious again. And the lieutenant did indeed say, 'Had a quick snooze, did you?'

And Sergeant Major Marchenko came out with a dirty joke, to which no one responded.

As Kovalyov ordered his company to resume their march, a man on horseback appeared. It was the adjutant to the regimental chief of staff, draped in map cases.

'Who ordered this halt? It's only another eighteen kilometres.'

'My battalion commander gave the order,' Kovalyov lied. He wanted to say that his men were tired, but he was afraid of being thought lacking in resolve.

'I shall report to the lieutenant colonel,' shouted the adjutant. 'He'll give you hell for this. Well, now you'll have to march fast. You're to reach your destination by ten hundred hours, without fail.'

The adjutant then shifted to an entirely peaceable tone; he was, in fact, an old friend of Kovalyov. He said that they'd spent the night in peasant huts and had fried eggs with fatback for supper. His only regret was that he had been woken at two in the morning; the divisional commander had ordered him to round up the laggards.

'I had to call on Filyashkin to check on your route. Guess who was spending the night in his hut? Medical instructor Lena Gnatyuk!'

Kovalyov shrugged.

And once again dust rose over the steppe. Grey and yellow clouds appeared here and there, eventually forming a veil that enveloped all space, as if a new fire from beyond the Volga was on its way to meet the fire of Stalingrad.

The earth, impregnated with salt, was hard and dry. The sun blazed down and a harsh dry wind whipped dust into everyone's eyes. It was like powdered glass.

Vavilov looked around at his comrades, at the steppe, at the smoke over Stalingrad, and said aloud to himself, as if coming to some clear and simple understanding, 'Still, we'll send them packing.'

By ten in the morning Kovalyov's company was approaching Srednaya Akhtuba, a small town built entirely from wood. They had long ago drained every last drop from their flasks and bottles. And suddenly they received new orders – the entire division was to proceed straight to the Volga.

Two cars sped past the dense columns of infantry. The soldiers glimpsed the frowning faces of senior commanders. Sitting beside the driver of the leading Emka was a young general, his right hand raised to his peaked cap in a continuous salute to the men he was passing.

A motorcycle tore past – a signals officer in blue overalls and a leather helmet with dangling earflaps. Next came Filyashkin, the battalion commander, in a light cart. 'Kovalyov,' he called out. 'Forced march! Proceed along your new route!'

And it was as if a chill wind had passed down the ranks, a premonition of the fighting to come.

People often express surprise at the ability of ordinary soldiers to keep up with the overall military situation. These men did not, of course, know that a signals officer in an armoured car had just brought General Rodimtsev, the divisional commander, a sealed envelope containing new battle orders from Yeromenko. They did not know that they were to proceed, via Srednaya Akhtuba and Burkovsky Hamlet, to Krasnaya Sloboda, and then cross the Volga forthwith, to Stalingrad.

Nevertheless, they knew very well that, during the night, the Germans had broken through into the centre of the city, that they had reached the Volga at two points, and that their artillery was now firing across the river, shelling the embarkation point at Krasnaya Sloboda.

If 10,000 soldiers are marching along the same road, nothing will escape them. They will question everyone: women with bundles who have just crossed the river; a worker walking along a sandy track, pushing a handcart on which a boy with a bandaged head sits among piles of parcels; an HQ signals officer repairing his motorcycle engine by the side of the road; wounded soldiers with sticks, greatcoats flung over their shoulders, plodding slowly east, away from the Volga; children standing beside the road and watching. And there is nothing the soldiers will fail to notice: the look on the face of the general speeding by; which way the signallers are taking the telephone cable; where exactly the truck with crates of soft drinks and a cageful of hens turned off from the main road; where the German dive-bombers now high in the air are heading; what kind of bombs the Germans dropped during the night; why a bomb hit a particular truck (the driver must have switched on his headlights as he was crossing a damaged bridge); and which side of the road had the deeper ruts – going towards the Volga, or away from it.

In short, there is no reason for surprise. If soldiers want to know something, they can certainly find it out.

'Pick up the pace!' commanders shouted, feeling the same grim anxiety as their men. But somehow it no longer felt so difficult to keep on marching. Shoulders ached less; rigid boots no longer rubbed so harshly against blisters. Exhaustion was blotted out by the fear of death.

A woman in a kerchief stood by the side of the road, a mug in her hand and a bucket of water by her feet. Soldiers were slipping out of the column or jumping down from their trucks and running up to her.

But no one was drinking her water. Men were merely exchanging a few words with her, then hurrying back.

The woman's face was tense, unmoving, stone-like. Someone from the rear of the column shouted out to a mate, 'Hey, what's up? Why didn't you drink?'

A sour, angry voice answered, ''Cos she's charging ten fucking roubles a mug.'

A tall soldier ran out from the column. He had several days of dust-covered beard on his face.

'A fine time to be trading!' he shouted, kicking the bucket so hard that it flew into the air and landed upside down on the far side of the roadside ditch.

715

'Who'll feed my children?' cried the woman.

'Filthy parasite!' yelled the soldier. 'I'll murder you!'

The woman let out a scream and fled, without so much as a backward look.

'Vavilov! And he always seemed so quiet and gentle,' said Rysev. 'He shouldn't have done that. She was doing it for her children.'

Zaichenkov, who was walking beside Rysev, replied, 'And who do you think we'll be dying for? For everyone's children.'

*

Major General Rodimtsev's Guards division was moving swiftly towards Stalingrad.

Their initial orders had been to follow a longer route, reaching the Volga only some distance to the south of Stalingrad. But in the last few hours the situation within the city had become critical and these orders had been countermanded. The division was to head instead for Krasnaya Sloboda, the embarkation point directly opposite the city.

For Rodimtsev and his staff, this change of plan – the second in only a few days – was exasperating. Men longing to rest, exhausted by the heat and dust of a long march, now had to march north. Only a few hours earlier, they had been marching south along the same road.

No one, neither commander nor rank-and-file soldier, foresaw that the name of their division would remain for ever associated with the city into which they were about to cross.

16

Front HQ had been withdrawn to the east bank. It was now located in the small village of Yama, eight kilometres from Stalingrad.

Yama was within range of the German heavy mortars, and all sections of the HQ were under constant fire. It seemed a senseless place to have chosen.

Once the decision had been taken to withdraw to the east bank, there might indeed seem to be little advantage in being eight, rather than twenty, kilometres from the Volga. And there were certainly disadvantages. The most serious was that German shells and mortar bombs were as deadly on the east bank as on the west bank. One day a shell landed in the HQ canteen during lunch, killing and wounding several commanders.

Telephone lines were frequently severed. There were occasions when generals summoned subordinates and the latter failed to appear. One mistrustful general assumed that a commander was simply being fearful, waiting for the shelling to quieten down. Vowing to give the man hell, he sent out his adjutant. The adjutant came back with the news that the commander had been wounded just outside the general's dugout and taken off to the aid station.

Even the most conscientious and level-headed members of the staff wasted a great deal of time in discussion: who had been wounded? When and where? What were the effects of such and such an explosion? How much damage had been caused by shrapnel?

Some of the staff dwelt on the more amusing side of these dramas: generals who had farted when a shell exploded, or who had cursed and sworn in the presence of a woman doctor; the chef who directed his kitchen from a distance and seasoned the dishes for the HQ canteen without leaving his trench; the waitress who flinched at the whistle of a shell and emptied a bowl of soup on some major; the fire-breathing colonel who had always insisted that his section should be a part of advance HQ but who now wanted it further back.

Others complained bitterly: why were they being exposed to enemy fire? Why were men being killed and wounded for no reason? And look at the Germans – their HQs were always several hundred kilometres from the front line!

Nevertheless, Yeromenko, the Front commander, had not acted without reason. There was logic behind his choice of this village as the location for a large military establishment, with all its sections and subsections, with its typists, clerks, topographers, stenographers, quartermasters, waitresses, messengers and secretaries.

Yeromenko had been reluctant to relocate his HQ. He had stayed in Stalingrad as long as he possibly could.

There had been fighting in the suburbs. The Volga crossings were being bombed day and night; they were being strafed by Messerschmitts. The war was entering the city, but Yeromenko had refused to move.

German storm troopers with sub-machine guns were infiltrating the streets at night. HQ staff regularly heard the sound of machine-gun fire. One evening, Colonel Sytin, whom Yeromenko had recently appointed commandant of the Stalingrad fortified area, reported the presence of German sub-machine-gunners 250 metres from Front HQ.

'How many?' Yeromenko asked.

'Could be two hundred.'

'Count precisely and report back!'

Sytin clicked his heels, said, 'Report back, Colonel General,' and left.

Soon afterwards Sytin returned, composed as ever, and confirmed his original figure.

'I see,' said Yeromenko.

And Front HQ had stayed put.

Communications between Front HQ and Shumilov's 64th Army, deployed further south to defend Sarepta, became increasingly difficult.

Yeromenko had been placed in command not only of the Stalingrad Front but also of the Southeastern Front. Communications with the latter had become hard to maintain. Nevertheless, Yeromenko stayed in Stalingrad.

Only when it became physically impossible for Front HQ to remain on the west bank did Yeromenko give the order to relocate to Yama.

Ordinary logic suggested that there was no reason not to move another nine or ten kilometres further east. But the logic of this harsh time – the most difficult months of the entire war – dictated otherwise.

Yeromenko withdrew to the east bank not because he wished to retreat but in order to organize the defence of Stalingrad. And Yama afforded a clear view of the city – its blazing buildings could be seen from every bunker and dugout.

There was, perhaps, even an advantage in being exposed to German shells and mortar bombs.

When divisional commanders and commissars returned to the west bank after visiting Front HQ, their comrades and subordinates would ask, 'Well, how's life on the east bank? Was it nice and comfy at HQ? Had a good rest?' Battalion commanders and regimental commissars would say this with a smile – the mocking smile with which those on the front line, those closest to death, speak and think about those at a greater distance from death.

And the commanders just returned from the east bank would reply, 'Far from it! While I was walking from operations to admin, the Germans landed four mortar bombs on HQ. And HQ really is very close – they can see everything that happens here.'

It is possible, surely, that those responsible for the location of Front HQ – for keeping it in the city as long as possible and then moving only as far as Yama – were aware of the effect their decision might have on their forces' morale. There may, in addition, have been more personal motives; they may have wanted to guard against accusations of cowardice. But then they also wanted to prove their lack of cowardice to themselves. The personal feelings and anxieties of most individuals were now aligned with the interests of the country as a whole; instead of contradicting them, they gave expression to them.

17

Yeromenko's two adjutants, talking quietly to each other, were working at a desk in a spacious bunker, its walls boarded with fresh, almost white pine. A sullen-looking general with three stars on his collar was sitting in a distant corner, waiting to be received.

One of the adjutants, a tall, pink-faced young man with two orders pinned to his tunic and a new peaked cap with a bright red band, was looking through a file of yellow telegraph forms; this was Major Parkhomenko, Yeromenko's favourite. The other, a fair-haired man by the name of Dubrovin, was sitting under a bright electric lamp, bent over a large-scale map on which he was entering the latest developments. There were two points – to the north of the Tractor Factory and in the city centre, near the River Tsaritsa – where the blue pencil marking the German front line now merged with the blue of the Volga. Dubrovin was smiling; he had just sharpened his blue pencil and the line he had drawn was fine and accurate.

Dubrovin half got to his feet, peered over his comrade's shoulder as if to look at the telegrams and whispered, 'Who is it?'

'Chuikov – he was one of Shumilov's senior commanders. Now he's being posted to Stalingrad, to command the 62nd Army,' Parkhomenko said in a whisper, continuing to sort through the telegrams.

Sensing that he was being talked about, Chuikov cleared his throat and brushed the dust off the sleeve of his tunic. He slowly turned his large head, and then, no less slowly, looked the adjutants up and down.

Like any commander accustomed to unquestioning obedience from his subordinates, Chuikov looked at the insolent adjutants of his superiors in a very particular way. His look contained not only a hint of mockery but also a certain philosophical sadness, as if to say, 'A pity you're being corrupted here. In my hands, you'd soon be the perfect adjutant – prompt and obedient.'

From behind the wooden door, a thin, hoarse voice called out, 'Parkhomenko!'

Parkhomenko went through the low door into Yeromenko's office. A minute later he came back, clicked his heels and said respectfully, though perhaps not quite respectfully enough, 'Comrade Lieutenant General, please go through.'

With a twitch of his massive shoulders, Chuikov got to his feet. Then he walked quickly and quietly through.

Yeromenko was at his desk. In front of him were a nickel-plated teapot, a half-drunk glass of tea, an empty fruit bowl and an opened, but otherwise untouched packet of biscuits. On the other half of the desk was a map of the city, covered with arrows, circles, triangles, numbers and abbreviations.

Chuikov went in. Standing to attention by the door, he reported in a deep bass, 'Comrade Front Commander – Lieutenant General Chuikov, at your command.'

'That'll do,' Yeromenko said with a chuckle. 'Think I didn't recognize you?'

Chuikov smiled and said more quietly, 'Hello!'

'Sit down, Chuikov, please sit down,' said Yeromenko.

He leaned over towards Chuikov and cleared some space on the desk, pushing away an ashtray filled with cigarette butts and a few apple cores. He then blew on the tablecloth to remove the ash.

Yeromenko had first encountered Chuikov before the war, during exercises in the Belorussian Military District. He was well aware of his brusqueness, of his swift, sometimes impetuous decisiveness.

At the end of July, Chuikov had been in command of the Southern Operational Group. This group had met with little success, and on 2 August it was incorporated into Shumilov's 64th Army. This setback, however, did not trouble Yeromenko. He knew that no long military career consists only of victories.

The two men's lives had followed similar paths. Each had regularly heard news of the other even though several years went by without them meeting. Yeromenko heard about Chuikov's successes and failures during the war against Finland and he knew about his work as a diplomat in China. He found it hard to imagine Chuikov as a diplomat. Chuikov seemed, rather, to be a man born for the trials of war, endowed with courage, endurance, will power and unshakeable determination. In the grim days of early September 1942, Yeromenko had proposed Chuikov for the command of the 62nd Army – and the Stavka had ratified this appointment.

'Well,' said Yeromenko, 'it seems the two of us have a little work to do. And this,' he added, laying his large palm on the map of the city, 'is your domain.' And then, with a smile, 'I know of your experience as a diplomat, but we won't need diplomacy here. Here are the Germans, and here are our own men. Simple as that.'

Yeromenko looked at the map, then at Chuikov. In a cross voice he suddenly asked, 'Afraid of getting fat, are you? Do you do gymnastics every morning?'

'I don't think the Front commander does,' smiled Chuikov, putting his hand on his belly.

'Not much I can do about it,' Yeromenko said sadly. 'First, I'm not a worrier. Second, I'm getting older. Third, I spend all day and night underground. And then there's my leg wounds.'

Yeromenko told Chuikov what resources he would have at his disposal and what was being asked of him. From his tone of voice, he could have been an elderly kolkhoz chairman going over the tasks for the coming month.

'You'll know what's what soon enough,' he said, tracing one finger over the map as he outlined the position at the front. 'You'll see for yourself. But you'll be fighting in the city, not in the steppe. Keep that in mind. And you can forget that the Volga has two banks. The Volga has only one bank – a west bank. Understand? There's no longer any such thing as an east bank!'

Yeromenko disliked grand words. He knew that men did not leave their usual concerns behind them just because they were on the front line. This straightforwardness made him popular with the soldiers. At a critical moment, addressing hundreds of men standing anxiously to attention, when the young captains and majors expected him to come out with high-flown oratory, his face would soften and he would talk to the soldiers about boots, tobacco, and their faraway wives, faithful or unfaithful.

Yeromenko looked at Chuikov intently and said, 'So, do you understand? You know what's expected of you? As for me, I don't doubt your courage. You're not a man to give way to panic.'

Chuikov sat very erect, looking straight in front of him. The blood mounted to his strong neck, his cheeks and his slightly weather-beaten forehead. He knew what was at stake. Thinking about how 62nd Army HQ had already been on the verge of crossing to the east bank, he smiled a little. Had he been chosen for this command because someone thought he was the man for the task – or was it simply that he was considered expendable?

With a nod of the head, Chuikov said, 'I assure the Front military soviet and the entire Soviet people that I am ready to die honourably!'

Yeromenko took off his glasses, frowned and said crossly, 'We're at war – dying's easy enough. As you well know. You've been brought here to fight, not to show how well you can die.'

With another emphatic nod of his curly head, Chuikov repeated doggedly, 'I shall hold Stalingrad – but if it comes to it, I shall die honourably.'

When it came to saying goodbye, both men felt awkward. Yeromenko got to his feet and said slowly, 'Listen, Chuikov ...'

It seemed he was about to embrace Chuikov, as if in blessing, before sending him on this terrible mission. But in reality Yeromenko felt irritated. He was thinking, 'Anyone else would be doing their damnedest to squeeze more out of me. They'd be asking for more men, for tanks, for artillery ... But this fellow doesn't ask for anything.'

Yeromenko continued, 'And I must warn you. No recklessness. Look before you leap.'

Chuikov grinned, which made his face look still more severe, and replied, 'I'll do my best, but I can't change my spots.'

He went back through the underground waiting room. As if to an unspoken command, the two adjutants jumped to attention.

Chuikov walked past them without turning his head and climbed up the steep wooden steps, his shoulders sometimes brushing the earthen walls.

It took him some time to get used to the bright daylight. Screwing up his eyes, he looked around him – at the oak groves, at the grey wooden houses, at the fields of the Akhtuba floodplain.

The Volga gleamed in the sun. Beyond it, Stalingrad appeared strangely white – the destroyed city looked elegant, festive and alive. It might have been built from marble.

But Chuikov knew very well that the city was dead.

Shading his eyes with one hand, Chuikov continued to look at the city. Why did these ruins seem so alive? Was it a mirage? A vision of the past? Could it even be a vision of the future? What awaited him among these ruins? How would the coming weeks and months turn out?

Looking round to the east, he bellowed to his adjutant, 'Fyodor, the car!'

They could hear his bellow even down in the bunker.

Dubrovin said gravely, 'That Fyodor must have a hard time of it. And people say adjutants don't see real combat.'

18

Lieutenant Colonel Darensky arrived at Southeastern Front HQ, in the village of Yama.

His former colleagues, however, were nearly all in the village of Olkhovka, to the north-west of Stalingrad. A new Front was being formed there – the Stalingrad Front.

Only towards evening did Darensky meet someone he already knew – a lieutenant colonel he had worked beside not long ago. This lieutenant colonel explained that, although Yeromenko was now commanding both the Southeastern and the Stalingrad Fronts, it was only the former that was to remain under his command. This Southeastern Front comprised Shumilov's 64th and Chuikov's 62nd Armies, both directly assigned to the defence of the city, and also several armies deployed in the southern steppe, in the area of salt lakes between Stalingrad and Astrakhan. The new Front – comprising the armies to the north of the city – would probably soon be under the command of Rokossovsky, who in the winter of 1941 had commanded an army near Moscow.[254]

When Darensky asked about the military situation, the lieutenant colonel shrugged and said, 'Bad, very bad indeed.'

He went on to say that he wished he'd been posted to the HQ of the new Front, in Olkhovka. 'From there you can get to Kamyshin, maybe even Saratov. But here in the Transvolga it's just camels and thorns. And I don't much like the people here. Everyone's somehow … Well, you'll see for yourself. Where we were before, I knew everyone and everyone knew me.'

Darensky asked about Novikov, and the lieutenant colonel answered, 'I heard he was summoned to Moscow.' He winked and added, 'But you'll still be able to find Bykov.'

After asking where Darensky was sleeping, he found him a billet in a hut with a group of signals officers. The junior commanders were living in huts, and the more senior commanders in dugouts. After his first night in the hut, it was agreed that Darensky should stay there until he received his new posting.

The signals officers (the most senior was a major, the others were lieutenants and junior lieutenants) were decent fellows – and they treated Darensky with respect. When he first arrived, they brought him hot water so he could wash, made him some tea and gave him the best bed. One of them took him outside with a flashlight and pointed out the spot they used as a latrine.

Some months later, when he happened to look through a list of signals officers no longer working in the operations section, Darensky noted that every one of these officers had been killed in the line of duty. At the time, however, he had felt nothing but irritation with them. He had arrived full of enthusiasm and lofty ideals and had felt shocked by the signallers' apparent dullness and pettiness. This had upset him more, even, than the stench, the fleas and bedbugs, the lack of space in the hut, and the danger from shell bursts.

The signallers seemed to lead strangely empty lives. There was one lieutenant who, after completing a job, could sleep for fourteen hours on end. His hair all matted, he would occasionally go out into the yard, then come back in and return to bed. The others spent their free time playing cards or dominoes, bashing the dominoes down on the table in a way that enraged Darensky. They spent an extraordinarily long time trying to divine whether it would be rice or millet *kasha* for supper, and whether they would be given tea with or without milk. They argued incessantly, accusing one another of stealing soap, toothpaste and boot polish. And when one of them was sent on a mortally dangerous mission to the burning city, he would remind the others to be sure to collect his breakfast ration of sugar and butter – and then set off as if this trip were the most ordinary task in the world.

While he was putting on his boots and his belt, his comrades just carried on with whatever game they were playing: 'You don't much like clubs, do you, but you'll be getting one now … We won't be seeing any more trouble from those pesky knaves. And here's an ace of spades for you to pick up – how do you like that?'

To Darensky they seemed like passengers on a long-distance train. If the lights suddenly go out, there are a few sighs – and everyone lies down to sleep. If they come on again – people sit up, open their little suitcases and go through their belongings. One man will feel the blade of his razor; another will sharpen his penknife. And then they return to their cards or dominoes.

The signals officers read the newspapers carefully and at length, but Darensky was annoyed by the casualness with which they referred to important essays as 'notes', and half-page articles as 'a few lines'.

They barely talked about their work, even though every night-time crossing of the Volga, under almost constant fire, must have been full of terrifying moments.

Darensky would ask, 'How was it?'

And they would reply, 'Bad. No let-up.'[255]

Conversations were equally dull when friends dropped by:

'How are things?'

'All right. The colonel's off on a mission today. Be sure to go round to the quartermaster's. They've just received an issue of fur waistcoats, and the major says that operations-section staff are first in the queue.'

'Any news of the supplementary ration?'

'Seems it's not here yet.'

One of the lieutenants, a strong, handsome young man by the name of Savinov, was strangely envious of front-line company and battalion commanders. 'The division or army commander hands out orders and medals the moment the fighting's over. It's not like that for us. A recommendation has to be passed by the Front decorations section. Then the commander must sign, and then the member of the Military Council. Up on the front line, you have your own hairdresser. The cook will give you whatever you ask for. Jellied meat, fried liver – you name it ... You can get a trench coat made to measure. And as for the pay you get in the Guards ...'

Savinov appeared not to realize that all these advantages, imaginary and real, came at a price: long marches; superhuman exertions; having to endure extreme cold and heat; blood; wounds; death.

Darensky also found it irritating that these officers said so little about women, and that what they did say was so boring. Darensky, for his part, was always ready to admire women, to be astonished by them or to condemn their frivolity and cunning. Like all true womanizers, he could feel excited by the greyest, plainest and dullest of women. The presence of any woman was enough to bring him to life, to make him witty and animated.

And in male company there was no topic of conversation he found more interesting than that of women.

Even in his depressed state, he had already been twice to the signals section to admire the sweet faces of the telegraph and telephone operators and the girls who handled the post. Whereas the handsome Savinov, when he was at leisure, could think of nothing better to do than take some tinned fish from his suitcase, twiddle the tin about in his hands, let out a sigh, open the tin with his penknife, use this same penknife to harpoon small morsels of fish and keep eating till he'd polished off the whole tin. He would then crush the jagged lid, exclaim, 'Not bad at all!', place a sheet of newspaper at the end of his bunk and lie down with his boots on.

Darensky was aware that his irritation with the signallers was unwarranted. He did, after all, only see them when they were resting after risking their lives on some dangerous mission. And more importantly, he was feeling low; his excitement and thirst for activity had yielded to apathy.

His interview with the plump, red-haired colonel in charge of the Front HQ cadres section had upset him.

The colonel had small, attentive eyes with flecks of red-brown, and a slow, singing Ukrainian manner of speech. As they talked, he went methodically through the large file in front of him, which had notes and underlinings, in blue and red pencil, on every page. The man sitting only a few feet away appeared not to interest him; it was as if his voice got lost in the half-darkness and never reached him. What mattered, what he studied with something close to reverence, were the typed lines of Darensky's service record, the neatly handwritten additional notes, Darensky's responses to questionnaires and the details of his personal biography.

Now and again he would raise an eyebrow, frown thoughtfully or give a little shake of the head. Darensky would wonder anxiously which page of his service life was evoking such doubt or perplexity.

The colonel asked him all the questions that are customary at such interviews.

Darensky felt angry and overwrought. He wanted to say to the colonel that there were more important things than these petty details. Why he had been excluded from such and such a list, why he had not been entrusted with such and such a mission, why there were minor inconsistencies in his responses to questionnaires – none of this really mattered. Why did this man not take more interest in Darensky's true self, in his desire to give all his strength to his work?

It looked as if he would be offered administrative work in the rear – not the operations posting he so longed for.

'And your wife?' asked the colonel, tapping some document with his finger. 'Why isn't she mentioned here?'

'Because we separated before the war. At the time of that – what people call – unpleasantness. When I was in the camp. That, really, was when our marriage broke down.' And then, with a little smile, 'Not *my* initiative, needless to say.'

This conversation about matters of little military import took place to the accompaniment of shell bursts, the rumble of long-range artillery, quick bursts of anti-aircraft fire and the heavier, deeper sound of exploding bombs.

When the colonel asked the date of Darensky's reinstatement in the Red Army, there was such a loud explosion somewhere close by that both men involuntarily ducked and looked up at the ceiling, wondering whether loose earth and oak logs were about to crash down on them. But the ceiling remained in place, and they went on talking.

'You'll have to wait a little,' said the colonel.

'Why?' asked Darensky.

'Just a few points I need to clarify.'

'Very well,' said Darensky. 'Only I beg you – please don't post me somewhere in the rear. I'm an operations officer, a combat officer. And please don't drag all this out for weeks.'

'Your request will be taken into account,' said the colonel, in a tone that filled Darensky with despair.

'So,' asked Darensky, 'shall I come back tomorrow?'

'No, no. Don't bother. Where are you billeted?'

'With the signals officers.'

'I'll send someone round in due course. Otherwise, is everything in order? Do you have a pass for the canteen?'

'Yes,' said Darensky. 'No difficulties there.'

He went back to his hut and looked at the hazy city on the far side of the Volga. Things could hardly be going worse. He would be stuck in the rear for months. The signals officers would cease to notice him; soon he would be begging to join in their card games and their attempts to divine what kind of *kasha* would be served that day and whether or not they would get milk with their tea. The waitresses would say behind his back, 'Ah, our poor out-of-work lieutenant colonel again.'

Back in the hut, he lay down on his bunk. Without taking his boots off, and without looking at anyone, he turned to the wall and closed his eyes, clenching his teeth so tight it seemed they would splinter.

In his mind, he went slowly over every word of the interview. He remembered the look on the colonel's face. It was all very unfortunate. There was no one here who knew him, no one who knew his abilities. The colonel had only his papers – and the picture they presented was far from perfect.

Someone gave him a gentle nudge on the shoulder.

728

'Comrade Lieutenant Colonel, go and have your supper,' said a quiet voice. 'There's rice pudding with sugar today, and the canteen will be closing soon.'

Darensky lay there without moving.

A second voice said crossly, 'Leave the comrade lieutenant colonel alone. Can't you see he's resting? And if he looks ill in the morning, go to the medical unit and find him a doctor.' And then the same voice added very quietly, 'Better still, go and fetch the lieutenant colonel his dinner. Maybe he's in a bad way. It's 600 metres to the canteen, and that's quite a distance. I'd go myself, but I have to cross to the other bank. A package for Chuikov. You can pick up my dinner too – dry rations, and don't forget the sugar.'

Darensky recognized the voice – Savinov's. He let out a sigh and felt sudden tears behind his tight-shut eyelids.

The following morning, as the men who hadn't been sent anywhere during the night were washing, cleaning their boots or darning their collars, an orderly came in. Somewhat out of breath, he looked around, quickly identified the most senior commander present, and rattled out, 'Comrade Lieutenant Colonel, may I ask which of you is comrade Lieutenant Colonel Darensky? You're to go forthwith to the cadres section. The colonel wants to see you before breakfast. May I be dismissed, comrade Lieutenant Colonel?'

The cadres-section colonel immediately told Darensky that he was being posted to the Artillery HQ. It was an important and responsible position – the kind of work Darensky had never even dared hope for.

'Colonel Ageyev orders you to report to Artillery HQ at fourteen hundred tomorrow,' the colonel said sternly.

'Report to Artillery HQ at fourteen hundred – understood!' replied Darensky.

Correctly guessing Darensky's thoughts, the colonel went on, 'And there you were, thinking that those wretched bureaucrats would keep you hanging on for ever. Well, we didn't do so badly after all. We may be bureaucrats, but we do understand that time's precious during a war.'

That evening, Darensky talked heart to heart for the first time with the young signals officers and felt astonished that he'd taken so long to realize what splendid fellows they were: modest, courageous, straightforward, well read, hard-working, outgoing and friendly.

They went on talking and playing cards late into the night and Darensky continued to discover more and more virtues in them. There was no end to their merits.

He could hardly believe how happy he now felt. Here in this peasant hut in the dismal, saline steppe beyond the Volga, amid the sullen rumble of artillery, beneath the constant hum of aircraft, he at last felt he could breathe freely. His dreams were being realized. He had been given an important, responsible job. He had no doubt that his boss would be gifted, intelligent and experienced and that his future colleagues would be clever, conscientious and quick-witted. Every difficulty in the world had melted away.

So it is when things go well for someone. Darensky's own life was now unusually successful and full of meaning; the situation at the front no longer so profoundly menacing.

19

Colonel Ageyev's hair was entirely white, but he was alert and energetic. He saw artillery training as the foundation for an understanding of all things military – and of everything else in life too. His subordinates liked to joke, 'If our colonel had the chance, he'd incorporate artillery training into floriculture, dacha construction, and the repertoire of the Moscow Art Theatre.'

In 1939, he had felt deeply wounded when his son decided to study humanities at university. And a year later, his daughter, whom he had been taking on Sundays to the firing range 'to listen to real music', married a film director. Ageyev said sadly to his wife, 'What have you done to the girl? You've ruined her.'

He had his own idiosyncratic theory about artillerymen: 'Our Russian gunners are tall, big-boned and robust, with large skulls and large brains.'

He himself was short, frail and frequently ill. His feet were so small that his wife had to buy his shoes in the children's department of the army store – a dreadful secret that his adjutant had divulged to everyone at Artillery HQ.

Ageyev was generally considered a good artillery commander. People respected him both for his knowledge and for his bold, incisive way of thinking.

Some, however, while not denying his gifts, disliked him for other reasons.

He could be brusque, sarcastic and often uncontrollably argumentative.

He particularly detested careerists and people who like to pull strings. Once, during a meeting of the military soviet, he accused a colleague of servility. His language was so abusive that the incident was reported to Moscow.

Just before Darensky's appointment, Ageyev had been faced with a difficult and important decision: whether or not to bring the heavy artillery across the river.

First he had driven up and down the sandy east bank, with its dense willow thickets and copses of young trees, and concluded that this was the perfect site for heavy artillery. It was God's gift to gunners.

Then he had crossed to the west bank on a small motorboat, visited divisional and regimental HQs, inspected artillery batteries located in squares and among ruined buildings and concluded, with no less certainty, that it was impossible for heavy artillery to function in these conditions.

The Germans were close by. Snipers and small groups of sub-machine-gunners were infiltrating the centre of the city at night, slipping between ruined buildings and firing at his gun emplacements and command posts.

In conditions like these it was impossible to find appropriate targets for heavy artillery. Cumbersome, large-calibre guns were being trained on small, quickly moving targets or isolated machine-gun nests and mortar emplacements.

The gunners' hard work was being wasted. Protecting their guns, guarding them against surprise attacks, was taking up too much of their time.

Communications were being disrupted. With so many streets blocked by rubble, it was often impossible to keep the guns properly supplied with ammunition.

Ageyev reported all this to Yeromenko with his usual directness. He criticized others for 'playing it safe' and for 'just parroting orders'. After declaring 'I never have been and never will be afraid of responsibility,' he demanded that the heavy artillery be transferred at once to the east bank.

Ageyev could scarcely have chosen a worse moment to say this. Reports from the front line were more alarming than ever. The Germans had reached the city outskirts and were now launching attacks on the city itself. The regiments defending the city were depleted in number. Rodimtsev's Guards division was still on the east bank.

Guards mortar regiments, anti-tank guns, heavy artillery, vast numbers of trucks for the transport of troops and ammunition – huge forces were being brought up from the reserves. Nevertheless, they were still some distance away. And the Germans, aware of their approach, seemed all the more determined not to delay their final assault.

Alarm was turning into panic. Several commanders had been making repeated requests, under pretexts of every kind, to be withdrawn to the east bank.

Ageyev's request – unlike dozens of apparently similar requests – was justified. More than that, it was of crucial importance.

Colonel General Yeromenko was right to refuse the requests made by other commanders. Unfortunately – since the world is not perfect and even the most senior generals can make mistakes – he suspected Ageyev too of what was then being called 'evacuationism'.

No other member of HQ staff was present when Ageyev made his report. All we know is that Ageyev left Yeromenko's office after only a few minutes. He returned to his bunker, threw his file down on the table and made a very strange sound through his nose. During the night he took two doses of valerian and, unable to calm himself, went through the whole of his campaign library.

Yeromenko's adjutants later told friends from the operations section that not one of the 'evacuationists' received so severe a dressing-down as Ageyev.

In their words, 'Ageyev got it where the chicken got the axe.'

What Ageyev did the next day was proof of a remarkable capacity for self-sacrifice. He showed extraordinary devotion both to his work as a gunner and to the common cause.

He returned to the west bank and at his own risk and peril ordered the construction of rafts to transport two heavy artillery batteries across the Volga. He gave strict orders to all his commanders to remain in the city. Communications between the commanders and the soldiers manning the guns on the east bank were maintained through a wire taken across the Volga and smeared with pitch, later to be replaced by a proper cable.

A day was enough to confirm that Ageyev had done the right thing. His guns were able to keep up a steady, uninterrupted fire. There were no difficulties with ammunition supplies and the gunners were never under any threat themselves.

Telephone communications were reliable. Instead of worrying about German snipers, the gunners were able to devote all their attention to their work. And the commanders on the west bank, no longer fearing for the safety of their guns, were free to liaise with neighbouring infantry units and then inform their men about major enemy troop movements worthy of their attention.

Soviet heavy artillery fire had previously been scattered and ineffectual; it was now accurate, concentrated and crushing.

Withdrawing the remaining heavy artillery batteries to the east bank was a matter of vital importance. It would not be a retreat; on the contrary, it would allow the artillery to play a leading role in the defence of the city.

Ageyev set off once again to Yeromenko. As he left his bunker, he discreetly crossed himself.

733

Aware that all this could end very badly for him, he did his best to be diplomatic. He held back from making his usual criticisms of people who always 'play it safe'. He reported that he was transferring all available mortars and light artillery to the city, along with many members of his own HQ staff. After that, he described the excellent work being done by the two heavy artillery batteries now on the east bank, emphasizing that their command posts and commanders all still remained in the city, 'on the very foremost front line'.

Yeromenko put on his glasses and began to reread Ageyev's draft order – now lying on his desk for a second time – for the transfer of the heavy artillery to the east bank. Yeromenko had, by then, received reports that Rodimtsev's Guards division was approaching Krasnaya Sloboda.

'But how come those batteries are already there?' he asked in his thin, almost girlish voice, jabbing at the document with one finger.

Ageyev coughed and wiped his face with a handkerchief. Because his mother had once taught him to speak only the truth, he replied, 'I transferred them myself, comrade General.'

Yeromenko took off his glasses and looked Ageyev straight in the eye.

'As an experiment, Andrey Ivanovich,' Ageyev added quickly.

Yeromenko looked silently at the document lying in front of him. He was frowning, breathing heavily.

These few lines on a thin sheet of paper counted for a great deal.

Long-range artillery, concentrated on the east bank of the Volga and subordinate to the Front commander! Large-calibre guns, heavy mortars, Katyusha rocket launchers! All this constituted a force of enormous power, both concentrated and manoeuvrable.

Ageyev began counting the seconds. Forty-five – and Yeromenko had still not spoken.

'The old man's going to have me shot,' Ageyev said to himself, thinking of Yeromenko, eight years his senior, as an old man.

He took out his handkerchief again, looking sadly at the orange silk with which his wife had embroidered his initials.

Yeromenko signed the order, saying, 'Good thinking!'

'Comrade Colonel General, this is profoundly important,' Ageyev began, deeply moved. 'I give you my word that you have guaranteed our success. We will bring to bear an unprecedented degree of firepower.'

Yeromenko silently pushed the order aside and reached for a cigarette.

'May I be dismissed, comrade General?' said Ageyev, in a different tone. He was now wishing he'd said a word or two about one of the staff generals who, in his view, had been shirking responsibility.

Yeromenko cleared his throat and breathed in noisily. With a slow nod of the head, he said, 'Very well, get on with your work now!'

A moment later he added, 'The military soviet's trying out a new bathhouse tonight. Come along around nine!'

'Seems things are all right now!' said one of the adjutants. The two of them looked almost disappointed when Ageyev came out from the office with a smile, waved goodbye and began to climb the earthen steps.

It was at this propitious moment that Darensky joined Ageyev's staff.

20

During his first night at Artillery HQ, Darensky was twice summoned by his new boss.

Restless and anxious as he always was, Ageyev felt upset when his staff slept at night, ate lunch during their lunch break or rested after finishing work.

He ordered Darensky to go at dawn to the right flank to confirm that the guns had been safely transferred and were adequately camouflaged in their new fire positions. He was to visit the supply points and check that ammunition delivery was proceeding smoothly. He was also to telephone the regimental and battery commanders in Stalingrad and check that there was good communication both by radio and by wire.

As Darensky left, Ageyev said, 'Stay in contact. Report every three or four hours. You can reach me through 62nd Army support services. If you find any senior commanders at the fire positions, send them straight back to Stalingrad. Bear in mind that intelligence has informed us of a major enemy troop concentration to the south, opposite the Kuporosnoye gully. Tomorrow will be our first serious test – the Front commander has requested a massive artillery barrage.'

It was two hours until dawn, but Darensky did not feel like sleeping. He walked only slowly back to his bunker.

There was a dim glow over the Volga from the buildings still burning in Stalingrad. Searchlights lit up the sky and there was a constant hum of aircraft. Darensky could also hear the sound of artillery fire in the city, and intermittent bursts from machine guns. Sentries emerged now and then out of the dark and asked, as a formality rather than with any sense of urgency, 'Who goes there?'

Darensky had been longing for danger, responsibility, exhausting work and nights without sleep. Now his dream was being realized.

Back in his bunker, he lit a candle, put his watch down on the table, took from his knapsack some paper and an envelope he had already addressed and began writing a letter to his mother. Every now and then he glanced at his watch, wondering when he would hear his jeep draw up.

'This may be the first letter in which I don't tell you about my hopes and dreams, simply because these have all been realized. I won't go into detail about my journey. It was much the same as any other wartime journey. A great deal of dust, bedbugs and other insects. All too many night-time alerts. Filthy station platforms. Cramped, airless spaces of every description. And very little in the way of soup, drinking water and room in the carriages. There was one occasion, needless to say, when my stomach ulcer played up, but it really wasn't anything serious – I only mention it because I gave my word not to keep anything back from you. I reached my destination without difficulties, but my first few days went badly. I fell into despair – I was convinced I'd either be left hanging about in the reserves or else given some dead-end job in support services. But things are different here. Instead of worrying about awkward details in my documents, they appointed me to an important, responsible post at Artillery HQ. And now I'm working day and night, drunk on the joy of it. I'm writing to you just before dawn. I haven't had any sleep at all, and soon a jeep will be coming for me. I truly don't know how to describe my present state. My colleagues are wonderful – friendly, cultured and intelligent. My boss gave me a warm welcome. Recently he did something truly remarkable – you don't have to be under fire to prove you're a hero.

'So, I feel fully alive. I feel happy and I know that my work is important. We're doing well. The men are fighting like lions. Morale couldn't be better. Everyone is confident of victory.

'I recently heard, by the way, that shoulder boards are being reintroduced – gold for combat officers and silver for quartermasters. They're already being sewn in factories in the rear.[256]

'And yesterday I drank some vodka. With it I had some fatty pork and black bread – and my ulcer didn't make the least murmur of protest. I seem to have completely recovered my health.

'I could carry on writing forever, which in the end would bore you. I beg you to take good care of yourself and not to upset yourself by worrying about me. Be sure to write – my field post office is on the envelope. Let me know about everything. Have you got enough firewood to see you through the winter? Once again, don't worry about me. Remember that I've never felt so well and happy as I do now.'

He sealed the envelope, took another sheet of paper and wondered whether to write to Angelina Tarasovna, the senior typist now at Don Front HQ, or to Natalya Nikolaevna, the young hospital doctor who had accompanied him to the station two weeks before.

But then he heard the sound of his jeep. He got up and put on his overcoat.

21

The staff at Front HQ were awaiting the arrival of Major General Rodimtsev's Guards division with desperate anxiety.

Their anxiety, however, was nothing in comparison with that felt by the commanders and soldiers in Stalingrad itself, on the west bank of the Volga.

On 10 September, the Germans launched a massive assault. Supported by bombers, the 6th Army and the 4th Panzer Army attacked from north, west and south.

More than 100,000 men, 500 tanks, 1,500 artillery pieces, and 1,000 aeroplanes took part in this attack.

To the north, the German advance was covered by the 8th Italian Army; to the south – by other divisions of the 6th Army.

The main thrust came from the south, from Zelyonaya Polyana, Peschanka and Verkhnyaya Yelshanka, and from the west, from Gorodische and Gumrak. At the same time, the German forces to the north increased the pressure on the Tractor Factory and the workers' settlements around Red October.

Ever more powerful blows forced Chuikov's 62nd Army slowly back, towards the Volga. The strip of land Chuikov still held was growing thinner.

The attacks from the south were repelled, but on the afternoon of 13 September, the forces advancing from the west broke through into central Stalingrad.

Street after street passed into German hands.

The space between the German front line and the Volga was melting away. Then a fierce counter-attack halted the German advance for several hours.

The 62nd Army remained in control of only a small area. To the north, they held the three giant factories: the Tractor Factory, the Barricades and Red October. Immediately to the south of these factories, they held a strip of land running alongside the river. This strip of land, about a dozen kilometres long and not more than two or three kilometres wide, was crossed by a number of gullies and ravines, all more or less at right angles to the river. In it were located a meat-packing plant, several workers' settlements, railway lines leading to the giant factories, and some oil tanks, now covered by huge green, black and khaki splodges and squiggles. Beneath the transparent autumn sky, this attempt at camouflage made the oil tanks more conspicuous than ever.

The dominant natural feature in the area was the hill referred to by the military as Height 102 and by the city's inhabitants as Mamaev Kurgan. It was only a few weeks, however, before the civilians, growing accustomed to military maps, were calling it Height 102, and the military, now looking on Stalingrad as their home, were calling it Mamaev Kurgan.

South of the oil tanks, towards the city centre, the strip of land held by Chuikov grew narrower still. Some central streets were already in the hands of the Germans and as you went further south – towards the mouth of the Tsaritsa and the grain silo – Chuikov's strip of land dwindled to nothing. The Germans had reached the Volga.

The large industrial area on the city's southern outskirts – the Stalgres power station, Factory 95, Beketovka and Krasnoarmeisk – was held by the 64th and 57th Armies, but by mid-September the Germans had come between these armies and Chuikov's 62nd Army.

And German forces around Yerzovka and Okatovka had, by 23 August, isolated the 62nd Army from the Soviet armies to the north-west of the city.

The 62nd Army thus held about fifty square kilometres of ground. There were German divisions to the north, west and south, and behind them lay the Volga.

Chuikov had to relocate his command post three times. When the Germans first attacked Height 102, he moved to a disused mine tunnel above the River Tsaritsa. And two days later, when the Germans got too close to this second command post, he would be forced to move to a cliff above the Volga, behind Red October, near the oil tanks.[257]

There is no need for military knowledge or vivid imagination. A glance at the map is enough to enable anyone to imagine the state of mind of the 62nd Army's commanders as the Germans' steel grip tightened around them.

Exhausted, depleted infantry divisions, battered tank brigades, some military cadets, a few units of Volga marines and people's militia – this is all Chuikov had at his disposal to counter an attacking force 100,000 men strong.

In the morning of 14 September, Soviet units launched a second counter-attack in the central sector of the front. The Germans were pushed back a little. Soon, however, thanks to powerful tank and air support, they continued their advance into the central part of the city.

By three o'clock in the afternoon they had seized the main railway station and occupied a great deal more of central Stalingrad.

22

Chuikov's bunker was shaking. Bombs had been exploding nearby for some time.

Chuikov was sitting on a bench covered by a grey blanket, resting his elbows on a small table and running his fingers through his hair. His eyes inflamed from lack of sleep, he was staring at a plan of the city. Thick lips, crinkly, tangled hair, a large, fleshy nose, lively dark eyes beneath prominent brows – these lent his rugged face a very particular expression. It looked grim and commanding, yet also attractive.

Chuikov sighed, shifted his weight a little and blew on his wrist, which was itching painfully. He was suffering from severe eczema, equally tormenting at night, when he worked feverishly and without interruption, and during the deafening air raids of the day.

The light bulb suspended over the table was swaying. The pale, still-damp boards lining the walls and ceiling creaked and sighed loudly, as if in pain. A revolver hanging on the wall in a yellow holster also began to swing, like a pendulum, then shook, as if preparing to fly off its nail. A spoon on a saucer beside a half-drunk glass of tea tinkled and trembled. And the swaying light bulb made the shadows of other objects move about the wall, quivering and shuddering, climbing towards the ceiling or plunging down to the floor.

There were moments when this cramped bunker seemed like the cabin of a steamer on a rough sea and Chuikov felt almost seasick.

The bunker's thick ceiling and double doors blurred the individual explosions, turning them into an incessant din, into a viscous substance endowed with weight and mass. This substance weighed on your temples, scratched at your brain, burned your skin and made your eyes ache. It penetrated deep inside you, scrambled your heartbeat and interfered with your breathing. It was more than mere sound; it incorporated the feverish shivering of stone, wood and the earth itself.

This was how mornings usually began – from dawn to dusk the Germans would pound one or another sector of the Soviet front. Chuikov ran his tongue over his dry lips and gums; he had been chain-smoking all night. Still staring at the map, he bellowed out to his adjutant, 'How many today?'

The adjutant couldn't hear a word, but Chuikov's first question of the day was always the same, and so he answered, 'Twenty-seven, I think.' Then he bent down and said into his commander's ear, 'The fuckers are ploughing the earth. They're diving almost to the ground, in relays. There are bombs falling 150 metres away.'

Chuikov looked at his watch. It was twenty to eight. Usually the Stukas stayed until eight or nine in the evening. Only another twelve or thirteen hours left. Eight hundred minutes, he calculated. Then he yelled, 'Cigarettes!'

'Tea?' asked the adjutant. Seeing Chuikov frown, he quickly said, 'Ah, cigarettes!'

A stout man with a broad, balding forehead entered the bunker. This was Divisional Commissar Kuzma Gurov, the member of the army military soviet. He wiped his forehead and cheeks with his handkerchief and said, somewhat breathlessly, 'I was almost blown out of bed. The German alarm clock went off on the dot of seven thirty.'

'You're in a bad way, comrade Gurov,' Chuikov shouted. 'Is your heart all right?'[258]

Gurov's fellow political workers did not see a great difference between the man they remembered as director of the Military-Pedagogical Institute and the divisional commissar they encountered in Stalingrad. Gurov himself, however, thought he had changed completely, and sometimes he wished his daughter could have seen her dear 'Pápochka' in spring 1942, as he escaped in a tank from encirclement, or now, as he made his way, escorted by a sub-machine-gunner, to an army command post under constant bombardment.

'Hey!' Chuikov shouted down the half-dark corridor. 'Bring us our tea!'

A young woman in kirza boots, who understood what kind of tea was required on a morning like this, brought in plates of caviar, smoked tongue, and salted herrings and onion. Seeing her place two small faceted glasses on the table, Gurov said, 'Make it three. The chief of staff will be here in a minute.' Then, pointing to his head and rotating one finger to indicate what the constant bombing had done to his brain, he said to Chuikov, 'How long since we last saw each other? Four hours?'

'Less,' Chuikov replied. 'The meeting didn't finish till after four. And Krylov stayed behind for another forty minutes. There was a lot to talk about – no men, no equipment, but we have to patch up the gaps all the same.'

Gurov looked crossly at the swaying light bulb and raised a hand to still it.

'Poverty is no vice,' he said. 'Especially since we will soon be rich, very rich indeed.' He smiled. 'Yesterday I went to see Major Kapronov, the commander of an infantry regiment. He and his staff are sitting underground in a huge sewer, eating watermelons. And he says, "These things are diuretic, so here I am in a sewer. No need to walk far." And all around him is sheer hell – it's a good thing he can laugh.'

Chuikov struck his fist on the table. He was shouting from pain and fury, not because of the din outside. 'I'm asking for the impossible – the superhuman – from my commanders and soldiers. And what can I give them? A single light tank, three or four guns, a company to guard a command post! And what men they are, what fighters!' He struck the table a second time. Plates and glasses jumped about, as if yet another bomb had exploded nearby. 'If we don't get reinforcements soon, I'll have to hand out grenades to my HQ staff and lead them into combat myself. What the hell! Better than sitting here in this mousetrap or floundering about in the Volga. And people will remember. They'll say I did what I could to reinforce the troops entrusted to my command!'

Placing his hands on the table, he looked at Gurov and frowned. After a moment's silence, he began to smile. Born in the corners of his eyes, overcoming the sullen fold of his lips, this smile slowly lit up his whole face. He put his hand on Gurov's shoulder and said, with a little laugh, 'You'll lose weight here, comrade Divisional Commissar ... Yes, Kuzma, you certainly will.'

The day before, to seal their friendship, they had exchanged the traditional three kisses, but they were still hesitant, a little unsure how to address each other, shifting between the formal *Vy* and the informal *Ty*.[259]

'I know,' said Gurov with a smile. 'And it won't only be the Germans making me lose weight.'

'True. It'll be me and my gentle good nature. Never mind, it'll be good medicine for your heart.' He bellowed down the phone, 'Get me Krylov!' And then, still down the phone but in a different tone, he continued, 'Enjoying the morning bombardment, are you? Is that what's keeping you? Or have you dozed off? Come along now, or our tea will get cold.'

A spoon tinkled on a saucer. Gurov stilled it and said soothingly, 'All right, you can stop shaking now!' Then he raised his hand, trying once again to still the swaying light bulb.

Krylov, the chief of staff, came in. Everything about him gave off an unusual sense of calm. His large head and smoothed-down hair, a forehead without a single wrinkle, his large, rather tired brown eyes, his freshly shaven cheeks that smelled of eau de cologne, his pale hands and oval fingernails, the thin white stripe above the collar of his jacket,[260] his quiet movements, the thoughtful smile with which he looked at the food and drink set out on the table – all these testified to a man of unshakeable, fundamental calm.

Unlike the others, he did not need to shout; somehow his voice was always audible above the general din. Either he spoke only at moments of relative quiet or else his voice had some special timbre that allowed it to carry above all the thunder of war. Or perhaps his inner calm was so strong that it always rose to the surface, like oil on water, regardless of storms round about.

He had spent the last year in one besieged city after another, and he was clearly accustomed to constant bombardment – a hammerer, accustomed to the crash of a hammer.

In the autumn of 1941 he had been chief of staff of the army defending Odessa; then, for 250 days, chief of staff of the army defending Sevastopol. Along with Petrov, the commanding officer, he had escaped in a submarine when the Germans captured the city. And now he had been appointed chief of staff of the army defending Stalingrad.

Gurov was smiling; he evidently took pleasure in contemplating Krylov's calm face. 'How are things further south?' he asked.

'The heavy artillery on the east bank are doing a grand job. They're giving the Germans hell – a good thing they were relocated. They keep it up all day long, a steady fire on the southern outskirts. Katyushas too. But my colleagues calculated 1,100 sorties by German planes.'

'To hell with their calculations,' Chuikov replied crossly.

'Time on your hands – measure the sands!' joked Krylov. He went on, 'Our KVs repelled a tank attack.[261] Our losses yesterday were less than the day before – but probably only because we've got less tanks to lose. The general picture's clear enough. But that doesn't make it any better. The Voroshilov district's been flattened. There are air attacks everywhere and ground attacks along the same axes as before – from Gumrak, Gorodishche and Beketovka. From papers found on the German dead, we know they sent in two new divisions yesterday. In the south we're holding our ground. During the night, the enemy concentrated tanks and infantry around the Tractor Factory. It seems they're

745

regrouping, as if they think they've completed their task in the city centre. They're flying a lot of sorties over the factories now.'

'And what am *I* to do?' asked Chuikov. 'While the enemy regroups for a decisive attack, how am *I* meant to regroup? Where can I find the men? I have my duty. My duty to myself! But we've lost the railway station. We've lost the grain silo and the State Bank building. We've lost the House of Specialists.'

There was a silence. The explosions, growing swiftly louder, drew ever closer to the bunker. A plate near the edge of the table fell to the ground and appeared to break into pieces without a sound, as in a silent film.

Krylov put down his fork, half-opened his mouth and narrowed his eyes. Both the earth and the air were vibrating; it was unbearable, like a red-hot needle being plunged into the brain. The men's faces froze. Then the entire bunker shook and squealed. It was like a concertina being stretched, pulled out of shape, then crushed by wild, drunken hands.

All three men looked up. Here it was. Death.

Then came a silence, a silence that deafened and dazed.

Gurov took out his handkerchief and began to fan his face. Krylov put his large pale hands to his ears.

'I put my fork down on the table,' said Krylov. 'I imagined everyone laughing if they dug me out with a fork in my hand.'

Chuikov gave him a sideways look and said, 'Admit it now. It wasn't as bad as this in Sevastopol, was it?'

'Hard to say ... but you could be right.'

'Hah!' said Chuikov. This 'Hah!' was an expression of joy, bitter pride and triumph. Chuikov was evidently jealous with regard to Sevastopol. He wanted to feel that no one in the war had taken on a burden greater than his. And this, of course, may well have been true.

'Sevastopol was child's play,' said Gurov, with a knowing smile. 'We all know what an easy time General Petrov had of it.' Chuikov laughed, pleased that Gurov understood his feelings.

'Things seem to be quietening down,' said Chuikov. 'Let's drink to Sevastopol.'

As he spoke, there was another howl up above them. A dreadful blow shook the bunker. There were sharp cracks from the timber frame. Some of the boards split, and sawdust and other debris rained down on the table.

A cloud of dust drowned everything – faces and objects alike. There was only the sound of explosions, now to the right, now to the left, blurring together into a kind of drumming.

When the dust began to settle and Chuikov, coughing and sneezing, was able to look around him – at the table, at the ash-grey pillow, at the miraculously still-shining light bulb, at the telephone now lying upside down on the floor, at his comrades' pale, tense faces – he merely smiled and said, 'So here we are, for our sins – in Stalingrad!'

There was such childish surprise in his smile, such human, soldierly simplicity in his words that the others began to smile too.

Chuikov's adjutant, looking bewildered and rubbing his bruised head with his hand, came in and reported, 'Comrade Commander, one member of HQ staff has been killed and two wounded. The commandant's bunker has been destroyed.'

'Re-establish communications immediately!' Chuikov said brusquely, once again looking harsh and severe.

'Compared to this,' Gurov said wryly, pleased with his words from a few minutes earlier, 'Sevastopol was child's play.'

'Stalingrad's a hard place to construct a defence,' said Chuikov. 'Short, straight streets, and all sloping down to the Volga. Makes it all too easy for the German guns.'

The duty officer came in. 'Let me see,' said Chuikov. He reached out for the file of messages, not giving the man time to report in the proper manner.

'The 13th Guards Division is now under my command,' he said clearly and solemnly. 'They're approaching the Volga.' Gurov and Krylov leaned forward, wanting to look at the telegram too.

'Damn it all!' said Chuikov, jumping to his feet. '"Today we will reach the crossing." If only they could have crossed yesterday! I'd never have let the Germans so deep into the city!'

'Just one day,' said Gurov. 'That's what students always say about their exams – if only they could have had just one more day to prepare. We're no different.'

'I want all remaining tanks down on the quays, to cover the crossing,' said Chuikov. 'But not a single man to be taken from combat units! The tanks to be manned by staff commanders.'

'A full-strength division,' said Krylov. 'It should get us out of what seemed, only a minute ago, to be one hell of a pickle.'

'Rodimtsev has come to rescue me,' said Chuikov, with a grim smile.

*

The first half of September 1942 saw three events of particular importance for the defence of Stalingrad: the Soviet offensive to the north-west of the city, the concentration of heavy artillery on the east bank, and the transfer of Rodimtsev's Guards division, and other fresh divisions, to the west bank.

The fighting to the north-west drew several German and Italian divisions away from the city. This made it possible for Chuikov to hold out until the arrival of reinforcements, at a time when the German High Command was expecting, within days or even hours, to be able to announce the capture of Stalingrad.

The Front commander fully understood the value of his new concentration of firepower; it was as if he had a pistol in his hand and could point it at the enemy just like that. And it would be hard to overestimate the importance of Rodimtsev's role. But the artillery commander was not a favourite of the Front commander. Nor was Rodimtsev much loved by Chuikov. Men with strong characters do not like those who rescue them during a moment of weakness and help them to become strong again. This is an inescapable fact of life.

23

Rodimtsev's division did not waste a minute. As soon as the men were out of their trucks, the sergeants were opening crates of cartridges, sacks of dried rusks and boxes of tinned and dried food, and then handing out fuses, cartridges and grenades, along with rations of sugar and foodstuffs.

Without further delay, the men began to climb onto launches, barges and ferries. The soft sound of footsteps on wet sand gave way to the dry staccato of boots on planks and boards – it was as if they were embarking to the accompaniment of a muted, yet ominous rumble of drums.

A ragged yellow fog spread over the water – from smoke candles being burned at the landing stages. Gaps in this fog allowed glimpses of a sunlit city. High on the cliffs of the west bank, it looked clean and white, elegantly patterned, almost castellated. It could have been all palaces, without a single ordinary house or hut. But there was something strange and terrible about this white city. It was blind and voiceless. Its windows did not shine in the sunlight, and the soldiers could sense the death and emptiness behind this eyeless, blinded stone.

It was a bright day. Carefree and generous, the sun was joyfully sharing its riches with everything on earth, great or small.

Its warmth penetrated everywhere – into the boats' rough gunnels, into soft deposits of tar, into the green stars of side caps, into sub-machine-gun drums, into the barrels of rifles. It warmed belt buckles, the glossy leather of map cases and the holsters of the commanders' pistols. It warmed the swift water, the wind over the Volga, the osiers' red twigs, their sad yellow leaves, the white sand, the copper cases of shells and the iron bodies of mortar bombs waiting to be ferried across the river.

Barely had the first boats reached the middle of the river when anti-aircraft guns began to fire from the bank. Flying south to north, at full throttle and only feet above the water, was a squadron of Messer-schmitts, yellow-grey with black swastikas, their engines howling, their machine-gun fire sounding like the caws of sinister birds.

The leading plane banked sharply and once again, howling and cawing, tore towards the barges and small boats scattered across the river. And then, after the planes, came shells and mortar bombs, all with their different voices, followed by wild gurgles and splashes.

A heavy mortar bomb fell on a small boat. For a moment it was hidden by fire, dirty smoke and a veil of spray. Then the smoke cleared and the men on the other boats and barges saw their fellow soldiers silently drowning. Already deafened and crippled by the explosion, they were dragged to the bottom by the weight of the cartridges in their packs and the grenades tied to their belts.

Rodimtsev's division was nearing Stalingrad. Is it possible to convey what these thousands of soldiers felt and thought as they gazed at the ever-growing expanse of water now separating their boats from the low east bank, as they listened to the splashing waves and the shells and mortar bombs, as they saw the white city slowly emerge from the haze?

Throughout these long minutes the men were silent; only occasionally did anyone say even a word. There was nothing the men could do; they could neither shoot, nor dig trenches, nor rush into the attack. They could only think.

There were young men and fathers of large families, city dwellers, men from workers' settlements around huge factories and men from villages in Siberia, Ukraine and the Kuban. What was it these men shared? What brought them together? Is it possible to find a common element in the whirl of hopes, fears, loves, regrets and memories of these thousands of soldiers?

24

When they cast off, Vavilov made his way to the side of the barge – his instinct was to stand as close as he could to the shore.

After so much noise – the constant hooting, the rumble of trucks, the stamp of boots and the shouts of the crew – the silence felt strange. There was only the lapping of water against the hull and, now and again, the sound of the tugboat's engine.

He could feel a moist breeze on his hot, sunburnt face, on his dry, cracked lips and his inflamed, dust-clogged eyelids.

Vavilov looked at the river, and at the shore, still almost within reach. The other soldiers were also looking around them, not saying a word. The barge was moving unbearably slowly, but the distance from the shore was increasing rapidly – Vavilov could no longer see sand on the riverbed and the water had turned grey and metallic. Yet the city wrapped in white haze was no closer; it felt as if this crossing might take more than a day.

Sometimes the barge was caught by a sudden current, and the cable shook and jerked. Then, when the tug turned a little, the cable slackened and dropped into the water – and it seemed that a sharp pull might snap it once and for all. The barge would float downstream, away from the silent city. They would come to quiet shores where there was only white sand and birds. Then there would be no shores at all. They would sail out to sea – there would be only blue water, and silence, and clouds. For an instant this was what Vavilov wanted – to slip away into peace, silence and solitude. If only for a day, if only for an hour, he wanted to push the war away from him.

There was a jerk on the cable that made his heart miss a beat, but the barge continued on its slow course towards Stalingrad.

Usurov was standing beside Vavilov. He gave his knapsack a shake and said,

'Empty – just a change of underwear, a sliver of soap, and a needle and thread. Nothing I can't hold in one hand. I got rid of everything else on the way.'

Usurov had not spoken to Vavilov since the incident with the shawl. Vavilov looked at him uncertainly. Was Usurov wanting to make peace with him?

'Too heavy to carry, was it?' Vavilov asked.

'No, it wasn't just that. When I left home, it was heavier than my wife could lift. But I've thrown all that rubbish away. Possessions aren't going to get me anywhere now.'

Vavilov realized that Usurov wanted to talk seriously; this was not just idle chatter. Gesturing toward the west bank, he said, 'True. No flea markets there any longer!'

'Yes,' said Usurov, contemplating the huge city. It stretched for dozens of kilometres along the Volga – and there were no markets, no cafés or beer joints, no bathhouses, no schools or kindergartens.

Moving closer to Vavilov, he said quietly, 'We're entering into mortal combat. We don't need any of this rubbish.' And he gave his empty knapsack another shake.

The barge was now halfway across the Volga. To Vavilov, these words, spoken by a man far from sinless, felt like a refreshing breeze. He felt sadder yet calmer.

There was not a cloud in the sky over Stalingrad – a city with grief and misery on every street, where there was no smoke or noise from the factories, no goods being sold in the shops, no quarrels between husbands and wives, no children attending schools, no one singing to the accompaniment of a squeeze box in a garden outside their workplace.

Just then the Messerschmitts appeared. Shells and mortar bombs burst in the water. The air was torn apart by the whistling of shrapnel.

Then something strange happened to Vavilov. First, along with everyone else, he rushed to the stern. He wanted to be closer, even just a step closer, to the shore they had left behind. He tried to guess the distance: could he swim for it? Everyone around him was jammed so close together that he could hardly breathe. The smell of sweat and stale air, of soldiers' boots and dirty underwear was stronger than the breeze off the Volga; it was as if the heavens had disappeared and they were standing beneath the low ceiling of a railway carriage. Some of the men were talking, but most were silent. Eyes were darting about anxiously.

The city the tugboat was pulling them towards was grim and forbidding. The sands of the east bank looked calm and sweet – as if even the dust there were kinder.

He remembered their long march: the last stretch before they reached the Volga; before that, the never-ending road from Nikolaevka. It was like some hellish vision: whirling dust; inflamed eyes staring out, as if from under the earth, from beneath dust-plastered foreheads; patches of white salt on the steppe; the serpentine necks of camels; their strange cries and their bald, naked thighs; refugee women with grey hair; the desperate faces of young mothers carrying small, howling babies.

He remembered a young Ukrainian woman who must have lost her mind; she was sitting by the road with a knapsack on her shoulders, gazing with mad eyes at the dense yellow dust whirling over the steppe and shouting, 'Trokhym! The earth is on fire! Trokhym! The sky is on fire!' An old woman, probably her mother, was gripping her hands, as if to prevent her from tearing her clothes.

The road stretched still further back. He saw his sleeping children, his wife's face as they said goodbye, as he set off towards the red dawn.

And still further back – past the cemetery where his mother and father and elder brother were buried, through fields where the rye stood green and merry like the days of his youth. And then into the forest, towards the river, towards the city ... There he was again – he could see himself walking along, strong and cheerful, with Marya at his side, and little Vanya trying to keep up on his bandy legs.

Everything dear to him, he realized with anguish, lay to the west, where the tugboat was dragging them. There ahead of him were life, his native earth, his wife and children. Behind him lay only orphanhood and yellow dust. The roads of the east bank would never take him back home; if he were to follow them, his home would be lost for ever. Here, on this river, two paths had met – only to part once and for all, as in the fairy tales he had heard as a child.

Vavilov left the crowd huddled in the stern and walked along the side of the barge, watching the splashes from shell bursts.

The Germans did not want him to go back home. They had driven him into the Transvolga steppe. They hurled shells and mortar bombs at him. They were attacking him from the air.

The city was already close. Everything was now clearly visible: half-collapsed walls; streets filled with rubble; windows like gaping eye sockets; the remains of charred rafters; warped sheets of tin hanging from roofs; beams and girders sagging between the floors of large buildings. On the quay, close to the water, was a car with wide-open doors – as if it had been about to enter the river and then changed its mind at the last minute.

Nowhere could Vavilov see any people.

The city kept growing, broadening, revealing its details, drawing the soldiers deeper into its sad, severe silence.

The barge had already entered the shadow of the high cliff and the buildings standing on top of it. This broad, slanting band of water was dark and calm; the shells were all flying high overhead.

The tug began to turn upstream. Caught by the current, the barge moved swiftly towards the shore.

By then many more men had moved to the bow and the port side. Standing in the cold, stern shadow of buildings gutted by fire, they looked sadder and more thoughtful than ever.

'Home again,' someone said in a low voice. 'Russia!'

And Vavilov understood that here in Stalingrad he was being given back the key to his native land, the key to his home, to everything most holy and dear.

For Vavilov this was all clear and simple – and thousands of other soldiers may well, in their heart of hearts, have felt something similar.

25

The 13th Guards Division completed the crossing at dawn on 15 September. Rodimtsev reported only minor losses: in spite of heavy mortar and artillery fire, they had successfully crossed to the west bank.[262]

Rodimtsev himself embarked a little later, in the afternoon. The signals-battalion boat set off at the same time, only a few metres behind him.

Everything shone and sparkled: the ripples in calm backwaters; the waves where the river's two streams met below Sarpinsky Island; the medals and the gold star on the young general's chest; the empty yellow can, lying on the bottom of the boat, that they used for bailing out water. It was a crystalline day, rich in warmth, light and movement.

'Vile weather!' said the grey-haired, pockmarked artillery colonel sitting beside Rodimtsev. 'If we can't have rain, they could at least let us have a little haze. As it is, the air's like glass. The only good thing is that the sun's in the Germans' eyes.'

The German gunners, however, did not seem bothered by the sun. With their second shot they scored a direct hit on the boat carrying the signals battalion.

There was one survivor. He had been sitting at the bow. The blast sent him straight into the water and he managed to swim back to the east bank. Everyone else was drowned. All that remained of them was a lone side cap rocking on the water and a mess tin with flaking green enamel, its lid firmly closed.

When this lone signaller reached the shore, a small car sped down to the sand and General Golikov, the Stavka representative at Front HQ, ran down to the water and yelled, 'Is the general alive?'

The signaller was shaking the water out of his heavy sleeves. Deafened by the explosion and overwhelmed by the miracle of his own survival, he stammered out, 'I'm the only one left. I was thinking we were sure to be hit – and then it happened. Heaven knows how I'm still alive. I didn't even know which way to swim.'

Only an hour later was Golikov informed that Rodimtsev had crossed safely and reached his command post.

This temporary command post was located five metres from the shore, among heaps of brick and charred logs, in a shallow pit covered by sheets of corrugated iron.

Rodimtsev and Divisional Commissar Vavilov, a stout, pale-faced Muscovite, stumbled a little on the many stones. Outside the command post stood a soldier in well-worn boots, a sub-machine gun across his chest.

As he went in, Rodimtsev bent down and asked, 'What about communications with the regiments?' He had been worrying about this both during the crossing and while still on the east bank.

Major Belsky, the chief of staff, looked up. Adjusting his side cap, which had slipped to the back of his head, he reported that there were good communications with two of the three regiments. The third had disembarked further north and communications had yet to be established.

'And the enemy?' asked Rodimtsev.

'Still attacking?' asked Vavilov, sitting down on a large stone to get his breath back. Seeing the calm, workaday look on Belsky's face, he nodded in satisfaction; he admired Belsky, both for his imperturbable good nature and for his capacity for hard work. Belsky was the subject of many fanciful stories. One such story had a German tank positioned on top of the HQ bunker, slowly crushing it with its tracks, and Belsky, half crushed himself, shining his flashlight onto the map and drawing a neat diamond, with the note: 'Enemy tank on divisional command post.'

'Belsky the bureaucrat', people liked to joke.

And now, with his feet on the floor of the pit and his chest at ground level, he pushed aside a sheet of corrugated iron and looked at Rodimtsev. His eyes calm and serious, he seemed no different from a week earlier, when he came to report to Rodimtsev on clothing allowances.

'The man's worth his weight in gold,' Vavilov said to himself, as he listened to Belsky's report.

'I'm setting up our new command post in a sewer,' said Belsky. 'It's big – we'll almost be able to stand upright. There's flowing water, but I've ordered the sappers to put in some decking. And the main thing is we'll have ten metres of earth over our heads – quite something.'

'Quite something,' Rodimtsev repeated thoughtfully. He was studying the city plan Belsky had just handed him. The positions occupied by the division were already marked in.

The regimental command posts had been set up twenty or thirty metres from the shore. The battalion and company command posts, along with the guns and mortars, were located in pits, in a gully and in some bombed-out buildings on top of a cliff. There were also small infantry units nearby.

Aware of the danger to which they were exposed, the soldiers were determinedly constructing bunkers or digging trenches and foxholes in the stony soil.

Rodimtsev had no real need to study the city plan – the positions of the artillery pieces and the two infantry regiments were all clearly visible even from the edge of the water.

'Long-term defensive positions,' said Rodimtsev, gesturing towards where the soldiers were working. 'And you didn't even say a word to me.'

'We don't even really need telephone cables,' said Belsky. 'We can shout out orders to the regimental command posts – and they can pass them on to the battalions and companies.'

He looked at Rodimtsev and broke off. Seldom had he seen him looking so grim.

'Nice and cosy,' said Rodimtsev. 'All huddled together, and only a few steps from the water!'

Rodimtsev began to pace about the shore, which was littered with slabs of stone, charred logs and sheets of corrugated iron.

A number of paths led up the steep, stony slope into the city, towards the tall windowless buildings on the cliff above them.

It was relatively quiet, with only the occasional mortar bomb whistling past, making everyone lower their heads. Now and then a yellow-grey Messerschmitt would fly low over the Volga, letting out bursts of machine-gun fire and tapping insolently away with its small quick-firing cannon.

Most of the men, however, were used to the sound of machine guns and mortar bombs. It was the silences that terrified them. Everyone in the division, from General Rodimtsev to the rank-and-file soldiers, understood that they were positioned on the main axis of the German offensive.

The young HQ commandant appeared and brightly reported that the new command post was now fully equipped.

Rodimtsev scowled and snapped out, 'What's that round hat on your head? You look like you're on your way to a village wedding. Where's your side cap?'

The smile disappeared from the man's broad face. 'Understood, comrade Major General,' he replied.

Rodimtsev set off towards the new command post, accompanied by his staff.

Soldiers were bustling about, carrying logs, planks and bits of metal towards their trenches and bunkers. 'Anyone would think they're beavers,' Rodimtsev said to Vavilov, who was already out of breath again. 'Who else constructs long-term defences right by the water?'

Ten metres from the shore was the dark mouth of a sewer. 'Here we are,' said Vavilov. 'Our new home.'

The west bank of the Volga must have seemed a terrible place indeed on this radiant day. As they said goodbye to the sun, the clear sky and the splendour of the river, as they entered a black pipe where the walls were covered in mould and the air was stale and musty, Rodimtsev's staff began to look calmer and to breathe more freely.

Soldiers from the commandant's company were carrying in tables, stools, lamps and boxes of documents; signallers were sorting out telephone cables.

'You've got a magnificent command post, comrade General,' said an elderly signals officer, who had been passing on Rodimtsev's orders to his battalion commanders ever since the defence of Kiev. 'We've made a special place for you, a kind of office, here on these boxes. There's even some hay, in case you want to lie down.'

In reply, Rodimtsev nodded sullenly.

He walked along the pipe, tapped on the wall and listened to the murmur of the water underfoot. Then he turned towards Belsky and said, 'Why bother with telephone cables? Here we all are in our bathing huts – we can just call out to one another.'

Belsky understood that something was troubling Rodimtsev, but he kept respectfully silent; it was not for him to ask questions of his commander.

Seeing the grim look on Rodimtsev's face, Vavilov began to frown too.

Nobody in the division knew more than Vavilov about men's strengths and weaknesses. He knew that many people were watching Rodimtsev. He could imagine only too easily what signallers, telephonists, messengers and adjutants would soon be saying in regimental and battalion command posts: 'The general just keeps pacing about. He hasn't sat down once.' 'He's in a rage with everyone – he's even given Belsky an earful. He's on edge, well and truly on edge.'

All this made Vavilov angry. Rodimtsev should have been more careful. He should have known that his subordinates would now be whispering, 'Things are looking bad. We're done for – no doubt about it.' But then Rodimtsev was clearly not blind to such matters. Vavilov had often admired his ability to respond to anxious looks with a casual smile. On one occasion, when a messenger reported, 'German tanks are advancing towards the command post,' he had calmly replied, 'Prepare the howitzers for direct fire. And now let's get on with our dinner!'

Once the field telephone was in order, Rodimtsev called Chuikov and reported that the division had crossed.

'You must understand,' said Chuikov, 'that we have to attack. There's no time for the division to rest.'

Thinking there wasn't much chance of anyone resting at a time and place like this, Rodimtsev replied, 'Understood, comrade General!'

Rodimtsev went out into the fresh air, sat down on a stone, lit a cigarette, looked at the far-away east bank, and fell into thought. As at earlier critical moments in the war, he felt both calm and burdened.

In a soldier's side cap, with a green quilted jacket thrown over his shoulders, he was sitting at a distance from the general bustle of the human anthill. Aged thirty-seven, though he looked a great deal younger, he appeared to be gazing at the world around him with a kind of absent-minded sadness. Few people would have taken this lean, good-looking, fair-haired soldier for the major general in command of the first division of reinforcements to enter the half-occupied city.

During the hours that Rodimtsev had been out of contact with his division, the life of thousands of men, like water seeking the easiest path downhill, had followed its own, entirely natural course.

Wherever they are – waiting for a train at a railway junction, sitting on an ice floe in the Arctic Ocean, or even when they are fighting a war – people do what they can to make themselves warm and comfortable.

This is everyone's natural desire. Much of the time, this natural desire and military necessity are in harmony. Soldiers dig pits and ditches to shelter their bodies from splinters of steel, and then they lie down in them to shoot at the enemy. Sometimes, however, this life instinct – this instinct for self-preservation – crowds out all other concerns. A man digs a pit or a trench, lies down in it for protection and forgets about his rifle. In his simplicity he imagines that he has been given a sapper's spade for only one purpose: to protect himself from bullets and shrapnel.

Sitting on a large stone, Rodimtsev took a cursory look at the reports from the regiments about the successful construction of their defensive positions.

From the perspective of the self-preservation of the division, of the self-preservation of individual regiments and battalions, these measures were entirely rational. But even a man as clever as Belsky appeared not to have grasped that, at a time like this, the self-preservation of an individual division, deployed a few metres from the edge of the water, was not what really mattered.

'Belsky!' Rodimtsev called out. A moment later, he said, 'This position you've taken up here on the shore – we need to give it a bit more thought.' He paused, to give Belsky time to think, then continued, 'What can we do? One regiment's completely cut off from us. We've no communications with them worth speaking of. And here we are, five metres from the water. What'll happen if we have to defend ourselves? Can't you see? We'll be drowned – drowned in the river like a litter of puppies. First the Germans will flatten us with their mortars, then they'll drown us.'

'What are we to do, comrade General? What's your decision?' Belsky asked in his calm, quiet manner.

'What are we to do?' Rodimtsev asked quietly, as if infected by Belsky's habitual calm. Then, loudly and emphatically, he went on, 'We must attack! We must break into the city! We've no other option. They're stronger than us in every way. We have only one advantage – surprise. We must make the most of it.'

'Absolutely!' Vavilov joined in, already imagining that this was what he had been thinking himself. 'They didn't send us across the Volga just to dig pits!'

Rodimtsev looked at his watch.

'Two hours from now I shall report to the army commander that I'm ready to advance. Summon the regimental commanders. I need to prepare them for their new task: to advance at dawn! Our reconnaissance data is non-existent. Set divisional intelligence to work immediately. Contact army intelligence. Where's the enemy front line? Where are their artillery pieces? Check communications with our artillery on the east bank. Prepare every unit to attack, not to defend. Distribute plans of the city to every commander and commissar. In a few hours they'll be fighting in the streets. There's no time to waste.'

He was speaking quietly yet authoritatively, as if pushing Belsky gently in the chest.

Vavilov shouted to his orderly, 'Call the regimental commissars. They're to report immediately.'

Rodimtsev and Vavilov caught each other's eye. They both smiled. 'Not long ago,' said Rodimtsev, 'we used to go for a quiet walk in the steppe at this time of day.'

760

All the human activity round about at once began to change direction. Rodimtsev had put in place the first stones of a dam intended to divert his men's energies down a different channel. A few minutes ago he had been sitting alone on the shore, apart from the general bustle. Now he was imposing his will all around him – and not only on his own staff and his regimental and battalion commanders. There was no one – no platoon commander, no rank-and-file soldier – whose actions Rodimtsev had not redirected. Bunkers and trenches were no longer a matter of urgent concern.

More and more often, in regimental and battalion command posts, men were repeating, 'The general confirmed'; 'The general countermanded'; 'The general forbade'; 'Number one says we must act fast'; 'Number one will be coming to check.'

And the soldiers were working things out for themselves. It was only too clear that, in the course of the last hour, something important had changed.

'You can put down that spade – we're done with digging. Now we're all being given more ammo.'

'Have you lot been given Molotov cocktails? We're getting two grenades each. And the guns are being moved forward.'

'Rodimtsev's here now. We're to storm the city.'

'Know what Rodimtsev just said to our major? I heard from a signaller. He yelled, "Think I brought you all this way just to dig pits?"'

'The first platoon are all getting their hundred grams – and two bars of chocolate.'

'Hmm. If they're doling out chocolate, we're in trouble. We must be about to attack.'

'Fifty extra cartridges each.'

'Seems we'll be attacking at night. I don't like it. How'll we know where we're going?'

At twilight, Rodimtsev, accompanied by two sub-machine-gunners, set off along the shore, right by the water's edge, to report to Chuikov.

It was quiet, with only the occasional sound of a few rifle shots – probably sentries afraid of the gathering dark, wanting to drown out the sound of falling stones and the repeated creak of sheets of tin.

An hour and a half later Rodimtsev returned, with Chuikov's signature on the order for the offensive. By then the darkness was total.

Silence set in. Night spread out over the Volga in all its splendour: with the deep blue-black of the sky; with gently lapping waves; and

761

with swift breezes that brought in turn the steppe's dry heat, the stifling air of the streets and the moist, living breath of the river.

Millions of stars gazed down at the city and at the river, listening to the murmur of water against the shore, listening to people's grunts, sighs and whispers.

Rodimtsev's staff left their huge sewer. They looked at the river, at the sky, and at the silhouettes of Belsky, Vavilov and Rodimtsev himself. The three men were sitting by the water on a log half covered in sand.

All three were thinking similar anxious thoughts, glancing at the broad barrier of water and trying to make out the Transvolga steppe beyond it.

Rodimtsev took out a cigarette, lit it and took several drags.

Belsky asked quietly, 'How was it, comrade General, with our new commander?'

Rodimtsev appeared not to hear, and Belsky did not repeat his question.

Rodimtsev drew a few more times on his cigarette, then tossed it into the water. Vavilov said quietly, 'Here's to our housewarming party!'

Seemingly lost in thought, Rodimtsev said, 'Yes, precisely. And so life goes on.'

One might have thought that each man was in a world of his own, not taking in what the others were saying, but they did, in fact, understand one another very well.

All three had been fighting since June 1941. Together they had been through countless hardships and looked death in the face many times. Together they had seen cold autumn rain, hot July dust and winter snowstorms. They had talked about so many things that now they barely needed to speak. A word, half a word, even a brief silence was enough.

Then Rodimtsev answered Belsky's question: 'Well, there's no doubting he's a commander. Maybe it's because they've been bombing him all day, but he certainly has a temper on him.'

They listened for a long time to the silence, perhaps sensing that it was the last silence they would hear in this city.

Still gazing out at the river, Rodimtsev then said something very surprising – the last thing a subordinate expects to hear from his commander immediately before an offensive: 'I feel sad, Belsky. I've never felt so sad before. No, not even when we lost Kiev, or at Kursk. We've come here to die, it's only too clear.'

Some dark object slid down the river, painfully slowly, and there was no knowing whether it was a boat without oars, the swollen corpse of a horse or part of a barge destroyed by a bomb.

Behind them the burned-down city was silent. The men gazing at the Volga looked round every now and then, as if sensing some oppressive presence observing them out of the darkness.

26

Chuikov had been informed about the crossing by early evening. Rodimtsev had reported in person at twenty-two hundred hours, and Chuikov had signed the order for the attack. Then, at midnight, he received the head of the special department and the chairman of the army tribunal. They had come with reports on two commanders who, in spite of the 'Not One Step Back' Order, had transferred their HQs to Zaitsevsky and Sarpinsky islands. Breathing heavily, Chuikov took a pencil and pulled the documents towards him.

'That's all for now,' he said. 'You are dismissed.'

He paced grimly about his bunker for some time, then sat down in a chair, ruffled his hair and, sticking out his lower lip, stared intently at the pencil with which he had signed the papers. He sighed, paced about a bit longer, unbuttoned his collar, pinched his neck and ran one hand over his chest and the back of his head.

The bunker was airless and full of smoke. Chuikov made his way towards the exit, through the tunnel where his adjutant lay asleep. The greatcoat covering the man had slipped off onto the floor. Chuikov turned on his flashlight. The man's lips were half-open and his childish face looked very pale. Chuikov wondered if he was ill.

Chuikov picked up the greatcoat and laid it back over the sleeping lieutenant's thin shoulders.

'Máma, Máma,' the lieutenant called out in a strangled voice.

Chuikov stifled a sob and walked quickly out of the bunker.

27

Men's shadows flickered uncertainly in the dark before dawn. There was the occasional clank of weapons. Rodimtsev's Guards division was getting ready to move forward. The political instructors were quietly calling to their men, bringing them together for a short meeting, pointing out the way with their flashlights.

Soldiers sitting on heaps of bricks were listening to Regimental Commissar Kolushkin. He was speaking in a low voice and the men at the back had to strain to hear. There was something important and moving about this meeting amid rubble and ruins, on the slope just above the Volga. A faint band of light to the east heralded the arrival of a cruel day.

Instead of keeping to the speech he had planned, Kolushkin was telling the soldiers about his own life in Stalingrad. He talked about how he had worked on the construction site of one of the factories and how, shortly before the war, he had been given an apartment not far from where he was now sitting on a charred log. His old mother had fallen ill and she had insisted they move her bed to the window, so that she could see the Volga. The soldiers listened in silence.

When Kolushkin finished, he suddenly made out the imposing figure of Vavilov, leaning against a brick wall.

'Damn it,' he said to himself. 'Why did I ramble on like that? Now I'll get it in the neck. Vavilov will ask what all that had to do with today's offensive.'

Vavilov shook him by the hand and said, 'Thank you, comrade Kolushkin, you spoke well.'

28

When the German High Command announced on the radio that Stalingrad had been captured by German troops and that the Red Army
was continuing to resist only in the factory district to the north, they
fully believed this to be the objective truth.

The city's entire administrative centre, the railway station, the theatre, the bank, the central department store, the *obkom* building, the
city soviet, the *Stalingrad Pravda* editorial office, most of the schools,
hundreds of half-destroyed multistorey residential buildings – all this,
the heart of the new city, was in German hands. In central Stalingrad
the Soviet troops still held only a narrow strip of land beside the river.

As for Soviet resistance in the giant northern factories and in the
southern suburb of Beketovka – the Germans had no doubt they would
soon snuff it out.

The Soviet line of defence had been broken. Their centre was cut off
from their left and right flanks. There was no liaison between them and
it was impossible for them to undertake any joint action.

All the German officers and soldiers were confident of victory. No
one even thought it necessary to secure the ground already taken.
Many senior officers saw it as a foregone conclusion that the Red Army
would withdraw from Stalingrad in the next few days, or even hours.

Rodimtsev's attack was, therefore, unexpected. This was one of the
reasons for its success.

His right-flank regiment first attempted to regain Mamaev Kurgan,
the height that dominated the city, then fought its way through to the
positions held by the other two regiments and succeeded in restoring
an unbroken front line.

Dozens of large buildings were recaptured. Rodimtsev's central regiment advanced furthest of all. One of its battalions took the railway
station and the adjoining buildings. And the German advance in the
southern part of the city was halted.

Rodimtsev then ordered his men to take up defensive positions and
to keep fighting. Half-surrounded or entirely surrounded, they were to
fight to the last bullet.

He made it clear to his commanders that he would look on the slightest hint of a withdrawal as the gravest of crimes. Chuikov had said the same to him, and Yeromenko had said the same to Chuikov.

The order had come down from above, yet it was also an expression of the soldiers' own state of mind, born of their own determination. And the success of Rodimtsev's attack, though certainly facilitated by surprise, was a natural consequence of the logic of events.

29

It was Senior Lieutenant Filyashkin's battalion that did best of all.

Moving through narrow streets and patches of wasteland, the battalion advanced 1,400 metres west. Meeting almost no resistance as it reached the railway station, it captured coal sheds and signal boxes, bombed-out warehouses carpeted with flour and grains of maize, and the half-ruined buildings of the station itself.

Filyashkin, a man of about thirty, with reddish hair and small eyes now bloodshot from lack of sleep, set up a temporary command post by the railway embankment, in a concrete booth with smashed windows.

Wiping the sweat from his face and scratching at his left ear, which had been damaged by a shell burst, he was writing a report on lined office paper to Yelin, his regimental commander. He was overjoyed by his success – taking the main railway station was no small matter – but frustrated that the other battalions were so far behind. With his flanks unprotected, he could not advance further.

Shvedkov, the battalion commissar – until recently a *raikom* instructor in the province of Ivanovo – was overexcited by his first taste of combat. 'Why are we stopping?' he asked in a loud voice. 'We must build on our success. Our men are straining at the leash. They want to advance further!'

'Where to? We've advanced further than anyone else as it is!' replied Filyashkin, jabbing one finger at his plan of the city. 'Do you want us to head for Kharkov? Or straight for Bérlin?'

He pronounced Berlin with a strong stress on the first syllable.

Lieutenant Kovalyov, commander of the third company, came in. His side cap had slipped onto one ear and a lock of hair poked out from beneath it. Each time he turned his head at all sharply, this forelock jumped about, like a metal spring.

'How's it gone?' asked Filyashkin.

'Not at all badly,' said Kovalyov, trying to keep his voice deep and hoarse. 'I despatched nine of the buggers myself.' And he smiled with his eyes, his teeth, his whole being, as only children usually smile.

He had killed three Germans. Two more had fallen to the ground, but he did not know whether or not they had died. He wondered why he had said nine. He must have just wanted Filyashkin to know what a daring young fellow he was. That Lena Gnatyuk had spent the night with Filyashkin was neither here nor there.

Kovalyov then reported that Politinstructor Kotlov, whose personal courage had been an inspiration to all of them, had been wounded and taken back to the rear.

Lieutenant Igumnov, the grey-haired battalion chief of staff, was looking silently at the map. Before the war he had worked in a district Osoaviakhim soviet.[263] He looked down on the younger commanders, whom he thought frivolous and boastful. He considered Filyashkin too much of a womanizer and he disliked being subordinate to a battalion commander no older than his eldest son.

Then Konanykin – Long-Limbs – appeared. He was dark-haired, like a gypsy. His movements and gestures were quick and abrupt. One of the squares on his collar tabs had been cut from a piece of red rubber; another had simply been drawn with indelible ink.

'There are Germans all around us,' Igumnov muttered crossly. 'This isn't a social club.'

'Report, comrade Konanykin!' said Filyashkin.

Konanykin reported his company's successes and the number of casualties sustained. He also handed over a written report, in large handwriting.

'Well, I've certainly given the Fritzes something to think about,' said Filyashkin. He turned to Igumnov and said, 'Come on, let's have a bite to eat!'

Pointing towards silent buildings now occupied by the Germans, Kovalyov said, 'I passed through Stalingrad in the summer. I was with a friend, another lieutenant. We stayed with his family – and we had quite a time of it. I can confess now, comrade Senior Lieutenant: we stayed an extra day without leave. There was a girl I really fancied – my friend's sister. About twenty-five. Unmarried, a real beauty. Never seen a girl like her. Gorgeous, cultured.'

'I'm glad she was cultured!' said Konanykin. 'But did your advances meet with tactical success? Did you give her what for?'

'Oh yes,' said Kovalyov. 'I certainly did!' This, of course, was a lie – his way of making out to Filyashkin that he wasn't really so very interested in medical instructor Lena Gnatyuk. He'd gone for walks in the steppe with her and he'd given her his photograph – but that was simply because they'd been in reserve and there hadn't been much to do.

Filyashkin yawned and said, 'Why do you think I want to hear about Stalingrad? I've been here too, after finishing military school. I didn't see anything so special about the place. And as for the winds they get in winter ... I almost got blown off my feet.'

He handed Kovalyov a mug.

'Thank you, comrade Senior Lieutenant, but I won't,' said Kovalyov.

Filyashkin and Konanykin drank their regulation hundred grams[264] and then recalled an incident when they were billeted in a village hut. A lieutenant, a very quiet, shy young man, had drunk some moonshine – for Dutch courage – and then climbed up onto the stove.[265] But instead of the young mistress he thought was expecting him, he had found her elderly mother-in-law. And she really had 'given him what for'. He had tumbled onto the floor and ended up with a black eye. All this had desperately embarrassed him. During the rest of their stay in the village, he had done his best to hide away in the kitchen garden.

The two commanders had been in Stalingrad only a few hours – they had no shared memories of the city. All they had to reminisce about was their months spent in reserve, in the Transvolga steppe. And for them and for many who followed them, Stalingrad never did have time to become a memory; it became, instead, the highest and last reality, a today with no tomorrow.

A messenger returned with a note from the regimental commander. They were to strengthen their defences. There were signs that the enemy was preparing to counter-attack.

'But what about food? We've only got two days' rations,' Shvedkov and Igumnov said with one voice.

Konanykin looked at Filyashkin and smiled. His smile was so clear and carefree; it conveyed such a readiness to meet fate, such an understanding of the simplicity of his fate, that Igumnov's heart missed a beat: he might have grey hair, but in the presence of this lieutenant he was a mere boy.

Filyashkin marked out on his map the sectors each company was to defend. The company commanders copied these to their own maps and noted Filyashkin's other instructions.

'May I be dismissed?' asked Kovalyov, standing to attention.

'Dismissed!' Filyashkin answered briskly.

Kovalyov clicked his heels and did a sharp about-turn, saluting at the same time.

The ground beneath him was littered with pieces of broken plaster and brick. He stumbled and almost fell. Embarrassed, he did a little jump and began to run, as if, rather than stumbling, he had been hurrying to obey orders.

'Call that an about-turn?' Filyashkin shouted crossly.

Such sudden transitions from straightforward friendliness to an exaggerated severity are perhaps less surprising than they first seem. The relations between these young commanders of different rank were complex. On the one hand, they faced danger together, sang songs together and even read family letters together; on the other hand, a superior enjoys being able to pull rank on a subordinate. Sometimes this severity stems from fear of seeming a mere boy, not yet mature enough to be a commander. In someone young, and democratically inclined, such a fear is only too natural.

It is only after many years of experience that men acquire the ability to be indulgent towards a subordinate, to behave gently while in a position of power. And most men only acquire this ability after coming to believe that the exercise of power is their natural and inevitable right – and that subordination is the inevitable lot of most other men.

Filyashkin adjusted the binoculars hanging from his neck and said, 'One of us must go to the regimental command post. Our belongings are still there. And the commander's incorporated one of my companies into his reserve. If we don't do something soon, it'll get dispersed.'

He looked at Igumnov and Shvedkov. They understood that he was wondering which of them to send.

Their faces changed. A word or two from Filyashkin would decide their fate.

The silence outside was ominous; the apparent peace foretold death. Their regimental command post now seemed like a haven of safety, as if it were located way back in the rear.

'Send me – I'm an old man,' Igumnov wanted to say, as if in jest. Sensing with disgust how false this would sound, he frowned and bent down impassively over his map.

As for Shvedkov, he was already well aware that the battalion was doomed. His suggestion that they should advance further had been preposterous. Their initial success had left them in an impossible position.

But he too, of course, remained silent, examining his pistol.

Filyashkin was generally mistrustful of people, and he had taken a particular dislike to Shvedkov; he had little time for former reservists who had gone straight into active service. Shvedkov had been appointed a senior political instructor the day he enlisted, while he himself had served three hard years before being promoted to senior lieutenant. Filyashkin was equally critical of his chief of staff, whom he saw as a tedious old man. He had more respect for Konanykin, who had just been to a three-year village school and then done active service as a rank-and-file soldier. Konanykin, however, kept challenging his authority, which irritated him.

'Watch it, Konanykin!' Filyashkin had once snapped at him.

'Watch what?' Konanykin had snapped back. 'I'm not frightened and I'm not watching out for anything. I'll be killed soon anyway. Do you think it's any easier to lead convicts into battle than to be in a penal battalion oneself? Do as you like – I don't care!'

In the end, Filyashkin said, 'Shvedkov, why don't you go?' With a little smile, he added, 'Otherwise you'll die, and then you'll receive a reprimand from the political section for failing to report!'

He had settled on Shvedkov, since he had not seen Lena Gnatyuk since the long march and Shvedkov might get in the way of him seeing her today.

Filyashkin then returned to his more immediate tasks. He picked up a sub-machine gun and, so as not to attract the attention of an enemy sniper, slipped a greatcoat over his map case. Then he said to Igumnov, 'I'll go and check our positions.'

Unnerved by the silence outside, Igumnov replied in a loud voice, 'Comrade Battalion Commander, there's a deep cellar under the station building – just right for an ammo dump. The company commanders can send men there when they run short.'

'No,' said Filyashkin, with a shake of the head. 'That's the last thing we need. Ensure that all hand grenades and cartridges are distributed to the men straightaway.'

The Germans were still not shooting, and this made the sullen, distant rumble to the north all the more frightening. Like any experienced soldier, Filyashkin was afraid of silence. He remembered the silence around Chernovtsy on the night of 21 June 1941. The regimental HQ building felt stifling and he had gone outside for a smoke. It was very quiet indeed and the windows shone in the calm moonlight. He was duty officer for the night. His relief was supposed to take over at six o'clock, but now Filyashkin felt as if no relief had ever shown up and he'd had to stay on duty for the last fifteen months.

The empty, slate-grey Stalingrad square; the bent, twisted poles and dangling wires; the gleaming rails without the least hint of rust; the silent sidings; this proletarian earth, gleaming with black oil, trodden down by railway workers as they checked couplings and greased pistons and axles; this earth that had trembled for so long beneath the weight of huge freight trains – all this was silent, as if everything here had been calm and sleepy since the beginning of time. Even the air itself, usually gashed by guards' whistles and the hooting of locomotives, seemed strangely intact and spacious. Everything about this quiet day reminded Filyashkin both of the last hours of peace and of his childhood home. Aged seven and the son of a track inspector, he had loved nothing more than to escape his mother's watchful eye and wander about the tracks.

Crouching beside the station wall, he opened his map case and found the note from Yelin. Without removing it from its yellowish celluloid envelope, he reread it. It brought him no comfort; Yelin, too, understood that the present calm was deceptive.

Everything, it seemed, would be the same as on that moonlit night in June 1941; the silence would be ripped apart, yielding to fire and the roar of planes. But no – what happened then would not be repeated. Today, Filyashkin would not be caught off guard. Today he was on the alert; he was different from the man he had been fifteen months ago. And maybe that young lieutenant hadn't even been him at all – maybe it had been somebody else out there in the moonlight. He was now strong and capable. He knew what was what; the sound of a shell burst was enough to tell him the calibre of a gun. He didn't need to read reports or speak on the phone to his company commanders – he always already knew where the Germans were targeting their mortars and machine guns and which of his companies was under the most pressure.

He felt cross with himself for feeling so anxious.

'There's nothing worse,' he said to the orderly walking beside him, 'than being moved forward from the reserves to the front line. If you've got to fight, it's better to just keep on fighting without a break.'

30

The battalion prepared a perimeter defence.

Premonitions are often deceptive. People with real experience of war treat them warily. Someone wakes in the night, certain they are about to die; they have seen the book of their fate and everything has been spelled out to them. Sad or embittered, or perhaps reconciled to their lot, they write a last letter, look at the faces of comrades, or at the earth beneath their feet, and slowly go through the few personal belongings in their knapsack.

And the day passes quietly by, with no shelling, with not a single German plane in the sky.

Or someone begins the day calm and hopeful, thinking about what they will do when the war is over – and by noon they are choking in blood, half-buried under stone and rubble.

After occupying the main railway station, Filyashkin's men were cheerful and confident. 'Now we can go back home,' said one of them, looking at a cold locomotive. 'We just need to get up a head of steam. I'll be the driver. Get the commandant to reserve you a seat.'

'We certainly won't run out of coal. There's enough to get me back to Tambov,' said a second man. 'Let's go buy some pies for the journey!'

After cutting embrasures in the walls with axes and crowbars, they did what they could to make themselves comfortable. One man regretted the absence of hay or straw. Someone very house-proud and organized put up a shelf so he had somewhere to keep his knapsack and mess tin. Two others were examining a tin mug crushed by a brick, wondering if it was worth removing the small chain attached to it.

'You take the chain,' said one of them, 'and I'll have the mug.'

'You're very generous,' said the second man, 'but why not take the chain too?'

Someone else found a convenient windowsill, took out a small mirror and began to shave. His dust-covered beard squeaked beneath his razor.

'Give me a little soap!' said someone else. 'I need a shave too.'

'There's hardly any left. Look!' Seeing the hurt look on his comrade's face, the man went on. 'Oh, all right, here you are – but save me one last sliver!'

The men in the penal unit attached to Konanykin's company were equally calm and good-tempered. Expecting to be staying in the station for some time, they set about their tasks with care.

One man, though, looked at the smashed ceiling and the collapsing partition walls and said resignedly, 'The Guards companies get the first-class waiting room. The Guards companies get the room for mothers with small children – and all we get is this!'

Another man, with narrow shoulders, curly hair and a surprisingly pale face, had just set up his anti-tank rifle. He squinted, took aim and, with a tired smile, said to his number two, 'Out of the way, Zhora – you're in my line of fire. We don't want any accidents!'

Kovalyov's company was also hard at work, smashing holes in the brickwork and digging trenches in the heavy Stalingrad ground – a mixture of earth, crumbled brick, white tiles and decomposing pieces of tin that looked almost like lace.

Waist-deep in a trench, Usurov asked, 'Vavilov, why aren't you eating your chocolate? It's really tasty. How about a swap? Your chocolate for half a packet of baccy?'

'No,' said Vavilov, 'I'm keeping it for my children. My little Nastya's never seen chocolate like this.'

'It'll go mouldy before you get to see her again.'

'I might not get killed. I might just get wounded. Then I'll be sent home for a while – and Nastya won't mind if it's gone a bit off.'

'Well, say if you change your mind.'

Usurov smiled. He remembered how, long ago, his father had tried to get him to chop wood and he had run away and hidden. Now, watching Vavilov's big hands and calm movements, observing the strong, carefully placed blows to which the stone quickly yielded, as if in collusion with Vavilov, Usurov forgot their previous differences and felt a sudden affection for this tall, severe man who reminded him of his own father.

'I love working with my hands,' he said, even though he hated manual labour and had never taken much interest in anything except his pay.

While they were still on the east bank, the sight of the red glow over Stalingrad had appalled the men; it had seemed impossible for anyone to survive in the city for even an hour. Now, though, they felt reassured. They were digging trenches and they had thick stone walls to shelter behind. And there was silence, and the earth itself, and the sun in the sky. Everyone felt calmer, happier, confident that all would go well for them.

Lieutenant Kovalyov's nose was peeling; in places it looked pink and tender. 'How are you doing, my eagles?' he called out. 'No slacking – the enemy's close by.'

Kovalyov felt confident in his men. He had just accompanied Filyashkin on a tour of the company's sector. The two men had inspected the trenches, the machine-gun nests and the forward outposts. As he left, Filyashkin had said, 'You've constructed your defences well.'

Kovalyov felt no less confident in his own strength and experience. He went to his command post, a cave dug out beneath the half-collapsed wall of a freight warehouse and located deep in the company's rear, a good fifteen to twenty metres from the front line. Their preparations were now almost complete. Everyone had been issued cartridges, hand grenades and Molotov cocktails. The anti-tank guns were in place; the machine guns had been checked and their ammunition belts loaded. Everyone had received their ration of sausage and dried rusks. The telephone cable to the battalion command post was protected by rubble and debris. The platoon commanders knew their instructions. Senior Sergeant Dodonov, who had made out he was ill and asked permission to go to the regimental medical unit, had been given a severe reprimand.

Kovalyov opened his kitbag. To forestall mocking looks, he spread out a map of the sector and pretended to study it as he took out his few belongings – silent witnesses to his short, poor and pure life. A tobacco pouch with a red star, made for him by his elder sister Taya from the sleeve of a colourful, once smart dress. He could remember this dress from when he was only eight. Taya had worn it for her wedding to Yakov Petrovich, an accountant from the district town. When people asked Kovalyov, 'Goodness, where did you get such a fine pouch?' he would reply, 'My sister gave it to me when I was still at military school.'

Next, he looked at a small calico-bound exercise book with worn edges. In faded, once gilt letters, it bore the title NOTEBOOK. His teacher had given it to him when he began his last year at the village school. In it, in a large, splendid hand, Kovalyov had written down poems and popular songs: 'A sultry summer', 'My proud love', 'A people's war, a holy war', 'Katyusha', 'My soul is a thousand years old', 'My little blue shawl', 'Farewell, beloved city' and 'Wait for me'.

776

On the very first page was a poem by Lermontov. The lines 'Eternal love is not possible, / Any other love is not worth the trouble' had been boldly yet neatly underlined in both blue and red pencil.

Between the pages lay four tickets for the Moscow metro, and tickets for the Tretyakov Gallery, the Museum of the Revolution, the Moscow zoo, the 'Union' cinema and the Bolshoy Theatre – souvenirs of Kovalyov's two days in Moscow in November 1940.

Then he took out a second notebook – summaries he had made of tactics lectures at military school. He was proud of this notebook; he was the only member of his group to have been graded 'Excellent' for tactics.

Next came a photograph, wrapped in cellophane, of a girl with fierce eyes, a snub nose and a rather masculine mouth. On the back, in indelible ink, was written,

> Laughter and joy are easy to share,
> But a friend in need is rare indeed –
> And the only friend who deserves your care.
> *Remember me – Vera Smirnova.*

In tiny capitals, inside a small rectangle drawn in the top right-hand corner, were the words, 'In place of a stamp, a passionate kiss.'

Kovalyov smiled a little sadly and returned the photograph to its crackly cellophane. Then he took out his more material belongings: a wallet with a wad of red thirty-rouble notes; a purse containing two spare squares for his collar tabs; his spoils of war – a German razor and a German cigarette lighter; a red plastic pencil; a compass; a little round mirror; an unopened packet of cigarettes; and a huge, particularly impractical penknife in the shape of a tank.

He looked around, listened both to the continuing rumble in the distance and to the silence nearby, opened the packet of cigarettes with one fingernail and lit up. Then he turned to Sergeant Major Marchenko – his right-hand man now that Politinstructor Kotlov was wounded – and said, 'Have a smoke!'

Glancing at the treasures spread out beside him, he added, 'I couldn't find the fuses for my grenades. I've had to turn out the whole bag.'

'Why bother?' said Marchenko. 'We've got more than enough fuses.' He carefully pulled out a cigarette. Before lighting up, he rotated it between his thumb and forefinger and examined it from all sides.

31

Only in Stalingrad did Pyotr Semyonovich Vavilov come to understand what war truly meant.

A huge city had been killed. Some buildings, however, remained hot from the fire. As he stood on sentry duty in the dusk, he felt the warmth still breathing deep in the stone. To him it seemed to be the living warmth of those who until recently had lived in these buildings.

Before the war Vavilov had visited several different towns and cities, but it was only here, amid these ruins, that he understood the vast amount of labour that went into building a city.

Back in his village, Vavilov had found it extraordinarily difficult to obtain a small pane of glass, a batch of factory-made bricks, window catches for the hospital windows, awnings to put over the school doors, or an iron girder for a mill they were building. Nails were in such short supply that they were accounted for individually rather than by weight. It had been difficult to obtain dry, seasoned wood, rather than still-damp spruce, for the school roof. A new floor for the village school had been a source of constant anxiety and taken an inordinate amount of time to complete. A building roofed with corrugated iron had seemed like a mansion.

The ruined buildings of Stalingrad revealed the wealth that had gone into their construction. Thousands of sheets of twisted corrugated iron lay scattered over the ground; stretches of street hundreds of metres long were covered by dead mounds of precious brick; pavements glittered, as if covered in fish scales. To Vavilov it seemed that the glass now carpeting the pavements would have been enough for the windows of every village in Russia. Wherever he looked, there were screws, door handles, bits of chewed-up iron and nails made soft by the wild, drunken flames. Huge steel rails and girders lay torn and twisted.

Much sweat had gone into hewing rough stone, into extracting copper and iron from their ores, into turning sand into glass and bare rock into rows of steel girders. Thousands of teams of masons, carpenters, painters, glaziers and metalworkers had worked here year after year, from dawn until dusk. Everything – the brickwork, the masonry, the layout of stairwells – had required skill, strength and labour.

Now, though, the streets were cratered by bombs, and some of these craters were the size of a haystack. And these countless pits and craters exposed a second, underground, city – water pipes, central-heating boilers, concrete-lined wells, thick telephone cables and intricate webs of electricity cables.

An unimaginable amount of work and material had been destroyed, in some monstrous act of desecration. In the Transvolga steppe Vavilov had already met many of the people who had once lived in these buildings: orphans, old men, crazed, shaking old women and young women carrying babies. There was no knowing how many more women, children and old people now lay in stone tombs under these mounds of brick.

'This is Hitler,' Vavilov said aloud.

The three words went on echoing in his mind: 'This is Hitler.'

For Hitler, strength was a matter of violence – one man's ability to exercise violence over another. To Vavilov – and millions like him – it was a matter of the power of living breath over dead stone.

What we call the soul of the people is determined by a shared understanding of strength, labour, justice and the common good. When we say, 'The people will condemn this', 'The people will not believe this' or 'The people will not agree', it is this shared understanding that we have in mind.

This shared understanding – these simple and fundamental thoughts and feelings – is present both in the people as a whole and in each individual. Often only latent, this understanding comes to life when someone feels him- or herself to be united with a larger whole, when someone can say, 'I *am* the people.'

Those who say that the people worship strength must differentiate between different kinds of strength. There is a strength that the people respect and admire, and there is a strength that the people will never respect, before which it will never abase itself.

32

All through the morning pulverized, shell-shattered brick hung in the air. Mingling with dust flung up by steel-soled boots and exploding shells and mortar bombs, it formed a flickering cloud.

German observation officers climbed to the higher floors of half-destroyed buildings. In the quivering midday air, they looked out through smashed windows and caught sight of the Volga. The huge river was astonishingly beautiful, its delicate blue reflecting a cloudless sky, its sea-like expanse sparkling in the sun. Its moist breath on their sweat-covered faces felt pure and tender.

On the streets beneath them, German infantry battalions continued to move forward between empty stone boxes still hot from the fire. Tanks, armoured cars and self-propelled guns negotiated sharp corners, squealing and grinding. Motorcyclists circled drunkenly around city squares, their uniforms unbuttoned and with no covering on their heads.

City dust merged with smoke from field kitchens, the smell of burning with the smell of pea soup.

Sub-machine-gunners shouted and gesticulated gaily as they herded prisoners of war in dirty, bloody bandages to the western outskirts, along with crowds of civilians – bewildered women, children and old people.

Infantry officers kept clicking their cameras. Not trusting their memories, they noted down details in small notebooks destined to become family heirlooms – testimonies to a glorious day, to be bequeathed to grandchildren and great-grandchildren.

Soldiers with ash-grey cheeks and dry lips entered empty apartments; sometimes their steps echoed on intact parquet floors. They peered into cupboards, shook blankets and knocked rifle butts against walls.

And as had happened before, amid all the rubble, they miraculously managed to find bottles of vodka and sweet wine.

The streets were full of the shrill music of mouth organs. From behind smashed windows could be heard wild singing, loud laughter and the stomp of dancing soldiers. Here and there the soldiers had found gramophones and were playing records by Soviet singers. Amid the raucous excitement, Lemeshev's tenor and Mikhailov's bass sounded lonely and sad.

And there was both sadness and surprise in the voice of a young woman singing, 'And just what he thinks of me, what makes him wink at me, is anyone's guess.'[266]

As they reappeared on the streets, the soldiers were still stuffing their calfskin knapsacks with loot from abandoned apartments: stockings, blouses, reels of thread, towels, vodka glasses, cups, knives, spoons of all sizes. Some patted their bulging pockets. Some, looking from side to side, ran through the square; a ladies' luxury shoe factory was rumoured to be just round the corner.

Drivers filled their trucks with carpets, rolls of fabric, sacks of flour and crates of spaghetti. Tank men and armoured-car drivers had opened the hatches of their vehicles and were tossing in bedspreads, quilted blankets, women's coats and curtains just ripped down from windows.

From the streets close to the Volga could be heard mortar fire and the rattle of machine guns and sub-machine guns, but few men were listening.

Up on the highest balcony of a three-storey building facing east, a non-commissioned officer in camouflage overalls and a face veil was shouting imperiously into a telephone mouthpiece, '*Feuer! Feuer! Feuer!*'[267] In obedient response to his commands and gestures, guns beneath the trees on the boulevard let out deafening roars; forked tongues of yellow and white flame leapt from their muzzles.

An armoured staff car drove up at speed, turned sharply in the middle of the square and came to a stop. A thin general with a hooked nose, a scarred face and yellow gaiters on his bandy legs got out and took a few steps. His monocle catching the light, he looked up at the sky, glanced at the buildings around the square, gestured impatiently with his gloved hand, said a few words to an officer who ran up to him, got back into his car and set off in the direction of the railway station.

This was how the Germans had imagined the last day of the war – and it seemed they had not been mistaken.

After long weeks in the steppe, the smell of burning, of red-hot stone and melting asphalt, was intoxicating. The hot flickering mist seemed to have penetrated deep inside them. Even their heads were on fire.

Time and again the Germans had seen the Volga on maps – an incorporeal, pale blue vein. And now here it was – the Volga herself, full of

781

life and movement, splashing against the stone embankment, rocking logs, rafts, boats and pontoons on her broad breast. And there could be no doubt what this meant: the Volga meant victory!

Yet not every German was looting and celebrating. Paulus had driven a wedge into the heart of the city, but there was still fighting where this wedge bordered streets held by Soviet troops. Tanks fired point-blank at doorways and windows. Gun teams struggled to drag their guns up to bombed-out buildings on the high cliffs over the Volga. Signallers sent up coloured flares. Machine-gunners fired burst after burst into dark cellars. Snipers crept along the edges of gullies. Twin-fuselage spotter planes hung in the air. Soviet radio monitors on the east bank had to listen again and again to the guttural cries of the German artillery observers. Their commands seemed to be echoing across the Volga: *'Feuer! Feuer! Gut! Sehr gut!'*[268]

33

Captain Preifi, the commander of a grenadier battalion, chose the ground floor of a still-intact two-storey house as the location of his command post.

The house stood immediately to the west of the massive carcass of a bombed-out tall building. Preifi reckoned that, should the Russians conduct artillery fire from the east bank, the house would be well protected.

His battalion had been first to enter the city. During the night of 10–11 September, Lieutenant Bach's company, following the course of the River Tsaritsa, had reached the west bank of the Volga. Bach had reported that the company's advance outposts were now positioned beside the water. Their large-calibre machine guns were subjecting the main road on the east bank to constant fire.

There had been previous occasions when the battalion had been first to enter a conquered city and the soldiers were accustomed to marching along deserted streets, to the particular smell of burning buildings, to the crunch of smashed brick and glass beneath their boots, to general astonishment at the sight of their grey-green uniforms, to the way some people said nothing, some tried to hide away and others smiled falsely as they tried to come out with a few words in German.

They had, many times, been the first Germans that the local inhabitants had encountered. And so they saw themselves as the embodiment of all-conquering force, of a force that destroys iron bridges, transforms huge buildings into heaps of rubble and evokes horror in the eyes of women and children.

So it had been throughout the campaign.

Nevertheless, entering Stalingrad had felt different; it had meant more to them than entering other cities. Before the attack, the deputy corps commander had come to talk to them all, and a propaganda-department representative had filmed them and distributed an information sheet. A *Völkischer Beobachter* correspondent, an important and knowledgeable figure who had himself endured all the hardships of the previous year, had interviewed three veterans. As he was leaving, he had said, 'Dear friends, tomorrow I shall witness, and you will take part in, the decisive battle. To enter this city means we have won the war. Beyond the Volga, Russia comes to an end. We will meet no further resistance.'

All the newspapers – not only the army newspapers but also those brought by plane from faraway Germany – bore huge headlines: '*Der Führer hat gesagt: "Stalingrad muss fallen!"*'[269] The colossal losses the Soviets had suffered were listed in bold. There were figures for numbers of prisoners of war, for tanks and guns and for aircraft captured at airfields.

Soldiers and officers alike believed that the final, decisive day of the war had now dawned. They had, admittedly, believed this more than once before, but the mistaken hopes of the past served only to confirm that their present convictions were well founded.

'After Stalingrad we can all go home,' everyone was saying.

It was rumoured that the Supreme Command had already decided which divisions would remain as an army of occupation.

Bach had pointed out to Preifi that there were huge spaces yet to be taken. Moscow was still holding out. There were Soviet armies still held in reserve. And then there was England and America.

'Nonsense,' Preifi had replied. 'If we take Stalingrad, the remaining armies will scatter, and England and America will make peace with us straightaway. We can go back home, leaving only a few units to serve as a garrison and to flush out any last partisans. But we must take care not to end up in one of those units ourselves. The last thing we want is to moulder away for years in some foul-smelling provincial Russian town.'

During the night Bach crept down to the Volga and scooped up some water in his helmet. At dawn, when the battalion had consolidated its position and the shooting had quietened, he took the water to the command post and offered it to Preifi.

'Very good,' said Preifi. 'But the water hasn't been boiled and it may contain Asiatic cholera bacteria. To be on the safe side, we'd better mix it with Stalingrad alcohol.' He winked and added, 'A little water and plenty of alcohol.'

They did as he suggested. After they had clinked glasses and drunk, Bach raised one hand and said, 'Let's have five minutes' silence. We can each write a quick postcard to our families, saying that we've drunk from the Volga.'

'What an excellent, truly German thought!' Preifi replied.

Bach wrote to his fiancée about the southern stars looking down on the black river. The Volga's moist breath was the breath of history.

Captain Preifi wrote that, as he raised the mug of Volga water to his lips, he had imagined himself in the bosom of his family. He had felt he could smell the fresh, still-warm milk that his wife would bring him one clear morning in the coming spring. It was a joy to be thinking of his nearest and dearest during these splendid days.

Rummer, the battalion chief of staff, who saw himself as a profound strategist, wrote to his elderly father about the glorious breakthrough the Wehrmacht would soon make to the east, into Persia and India. There they would meet up with the Japanese advancing from Burma and Indochina. A chain of steel would then encircle the globe – and it would endure for a thousand years.

'The enemy's last stronghold has now fallen,' he wrote. 'And so I have drunk to the coming meeting with our allies.'

Only Lieutenant Fritz Lenard, a company commander like Bach, did not write to anyone. A gentle-looking young man with a small pink mouth, a high, pale forehead and unblinking blue eyes, he paced about Preifi's large collection of war trophies. With a half-smile on his face, occasionally shaking his curls, he was reciting lines of Schiller under his breath.

Lenard inspired something close to fear in the other officers. Even Preifi, a giant of a man with a loud voice and formidable organizational energy, felt wary of him.

Before the war Lenard had worked as a propagandist. Then he had served as an SS *Sturmführer*. At the beginning of the war with Russia, he was transferred to the staff of a motor infantry division.

It was whispered that he had been responsible for the arrest of two officers. He had accused Major Schimmel of concealment of his racial origin, of having Jewish blood on his father's side. The other officer, Hoffmann, had allegedly been in secret contact with a group of internationalists interned in a camp. According to Lenard, Hoffmann had not only corresponded with them but had also contrived, with the help of relatives in Dresden, to send them money and parcels of food and clothing from army stores.

On one occasion, appearing to forget his rather junior rank, Lenard had replied insolently to General Weller, the divisional commander. The general had had him transferred to the front line. There he had proved to be a good company commander. He had been mentioned several times in despatches and had been awarded an Iron Cross.

Lenard often chatted to his soldiers. He read poems to them and was attentive to their needs. He seldom used a car, preferring to sit in the back of a truck with his men.

The other officers knew that Lenard and his company had taken part in two special actions – the torching of a village on the Desna that had been harbouring partisans, and the liquidation of 5,000 Jews in a Ukrainian shtetl.

Few of the other officers truly liked Lenard, but many – even those senior to him in rank, position and age – sought out his friendship.

Bach kept his distance, even though he saw Lenard as the most intelligent and cultured of his fellow officers. Preifi's concerns, by contrast, were exclusively economic; the only thing he ever wanted to talk about was the question of which items of food and clothing it was best to send back to Germany. Preifi concluded every conversation by asserting the importance of an all-round approach to the organization of parcels. At first, he had thought he should send linen and wool. Then he had decided to send food: coffee, honey, clarified butter. Only after some time – after crossing the Northern Donets – had he grasped the importance of meeting his family's requirements comprehensively and simultaneously.

He liked to show the other officers his campaign packaging system. Wearing a white gown, his batman would filter clarified butter through a pharmaceutical funnel, pour it into large metal cans and then hermetically seal these cans. His batman had many talents. He was an expert solderer; he could make tough, hard-wearing sacks; and he had a conjuror's ability to compress dozens of metres of cloth into unimaginably small packages. All this brought great joy to the giant Preifi, occupying most of his thoughts when he was free from the demands of the war.

Rummer, the chief of staff, was an alcoholic. Bach found him irritatingly verbose. Like most narrow-minded people, he was extraordinarily self-assured. When he was drunk, he liked to hold forth about questions of strategy and international politics.

The younger officers had little interest in conversation. Their only concerns were women and alcohol. But on this extraordinary day, Bach was desperate to talk. He wanted to share his thoughts with someone intelligent.

'In a fortnight,' said Preifi, 'we'll be in the heart of Asia, in the realm of silk gowns, of priceless Persian rugs and Bukhara carpets.' He laughed. 'But say what you like, I've already found something special here in Stalingrad. Yes, you lot have missed out.' He lifted the corner of a tarpaulin thrown over a roll of grey cloth. 'Pure wool, I've checked. I put a match to one thread – it shrank and went hard. And I've called in an expert – the regimental tailor.'

'A real treasure,' said Rummer, 'and you must have about forty metres there!'

'No, no, no,' said Preifi. 'Eighteen at the most. And if I hadn't taken care of it, someone else would have. It was homeless and ownerless – like the air.'

In Lenard's presence, he preferred to downplay the scale of his operations.

'Where are the women who used to live in this house?' asked Lenard. 'One of them is a real beauty, a true Nordic type.'

'They were taken to the western outskirts, along with the other inhabitants. Orders from the divisional chief of staff,' said Rummer. 'He thinks the Russians may soon counter-attack.'

'A shame about the woman,' said Lenard.

'Wanting to converse with them, were you?'

'To the old fat one, no doubt?'

'Well, Lenard wouldn't be interested in the young beauty, would he?'

'The fat one's not so very old,' said Preifi. 'She has a rather oriental face.'

This made everyone laugh.

'Quite right, Captain,' said Lenard. 'I wondered if she was Jewish.'

'I'm sure that will be ascertained soon,' said Rummer.

'All right,' said Preifi. 'Time you went back to your companies.' He replaced the tarpaulin over his roll of cloth. 'And don't get in the way of any bullets. I'm a changed man – I've turned into a coward. What could be more stupid than to go and get yourself killed a day or two before the end of the war?'

Bach and Lenard went out onto the street. Their command posts were located in a long one-storey building; Bach was in the southern half, Lenard in the northern.

Lenard said, 'I'll come and join you. There's a covered passage between the two halves of the building – I won't have to go out onto the street.'

'Please do,' said Bach. 'I've got some alcohol, and I've had enough of conversations about war loot.'

'If we carry out a landing on the moon,' Lenard replied, 'the first thing our captain will ask is whether they make good cloth there. After that it's just possible he might ask whether or not there's any oxygen in the atmosphere.' Tapping the wall with one finger, he went on, 'I think this wall must have been built in the eighteenth century.'

The walls were astonishingly thick – stout enough to support another seven floors, even though this was only a one-storey building.

'Russian-style,' Bach replied. 'Senseless and scary.'[270]

The telephonists and messengers were in a large room with a low ceiling. The two officers went through to a smaller room where they could be on their own. One window looked out onto the embankment, a small section of the river and a monument to some Soviet hero. From the other window they could see the high grey walls of the grain silo and the factory buildings in the southern part of the city.

They spent almost half their first day in Stalingrad together, drinking and talking. 'Our national character continues to surprise me,' said Bach. 'All through the war I've been longing for my home and family. But today, now I've finally come to believe that the war is nearing its end, I feel sad. It's not easy to say which has been the happiest time of my life, but it may well have been last night. Armed with grenades and a sub-machine gun, I crept down to the Volga. It looked black and wild. I scooped up some water with my helmet, poured it onto my head – which was almost on fire with excitement – and looked up at the black Asian sky and its Asian stars. There were drops of water on my glasses, and I suddenly understood that this was truly me, that I had come all the way from the Western Bug to the Volga, to the Asian steppe.'

'We have defeated not only the Bolsheviks and the vast spaces of Russia,' Lenard replied. 'We have also rescued ourselves from the impotence of humanism. We have conquered both within and around us.'

'Yes,' said Bach, suddenly moved. 'Only Germans could be talking like this, in a company command post in a recently captured city. This need for a universal perspective is our German privilege. And you're right: we covered those 2,000 kilometres without the help of morality.'

Leaning forward over the table, Lenard said cheerily, 'And I challenge anyone to stand on the bank of the Volga and say that Hitler has led Germany down the wrong path.'

'I'm sure there are people who think that,' Bach replied no less cheerily. 'But understandably, they prefer to keep silent.'

'True, but who cares? It is not sentimental old lady teachers, snivelling intellectuals and specialists in children's diseases who determine the course of history. It is not they who speak for the German soul.

Lachrymose virtue counts for nothing. The important thing is to be German. That is what matters.'

They each drank another glass. Bach felt an overwhelming desire for a frank, sincere conversation. Somewhere deep down, he understood that if he were sober, he would not say what he was about to say, that he would come to regret his loose tongue, that it would cause him pointless, tedious anxiety. But here, on the Volga, everything seemed permitted, even a frank conversation with Lenard.

Anyway, Lenard was different now. Months of rubbing up against ordinary German soldiers and officers had changed him. There was something attractive in his bright eyes with their long lashes.

'For a long time,' said Bach, 'I thought that Germany and National Socialism were incompatible. Probably it was because of the world I was brought up in. My father, a teacher, lost his job; he said the wrong things to the children he taught. To be honest, I too felt sceptical about Nazi ideas. I did not believe in the racial theory and I have to confess that I was expelled from my university. But now I have reached the Volga! There is more logic in this long march than in books. The man who led Germany through Russian fields and forests, who crossed the Bug, the Berezina, the Dnieper and the Don – now I know who he is. Now I understand. Our philosophy has moved out of the libraries. It's no longer confined to the pages of academic tomes. What had long lain dormant, hazily expressed in *Beyond Good and Evil*, and in the writings of Spengler and Fichte – this is what is now marching across the earth.'[271]

Bach was unable to stop, even though he was well aware that his eloquence was born of insomnia, the tension of recent battles, and almost half a litre of strong Russian vodka. Thoughts were streaming out of him the way waves of heat stream from incandescent steel.

'You see, Lenard, I used to think, to be honest with you, that the German people did not want special actions carried out against women and children, against the elderly and defenceless. And only at this hour of victory have I understood that this battle is taking place at a level beyond good and evil. The idea of German power is no longer merely an idea; it has become a power in its own right. A new religion has come into the world. It is cruel and brilliant and it has eclipsed the morality of mercy and the myth of international equality.'

Taking a handkerchief from his pocket, Lenard went over to Bach, wiped a drop of sweat from his forehead and put his hands on his shoulders.

'You are speaking sincerely,' he said slowly, 'and that is what matters most of all. All the same, you are mistaken. It is our enemies who make out that our philosophy is a negation of love. How wrong they are! The snivelling fools equate the trembling of the impotent with love. In time you will see that we too are tender and sensitive. You must not think that we know only cruelty. We too know love. And it is our love – strong men's love – that the world needs. I would like us to be friends, dear Bach!'

There was an expectant look on Lenard's face. Bach took off his glasses. Lenard's face misted over; it was now merely a bright blur, without eyes.

'This is real,' said Bach, squeezing Lenard's hand. 'And I value what is real. Now, how about going for a swim in the Volga together? Wouldn't that be great? "Two Germans have bathed in the Volga!" we could write in our letters back home.'

'Bathe in the Volga? We'd get shot straightaway,' said Lenard. 'Better just to put your head under a cold tap – you've had a lot to drink.'

Sobering up a little, Bach looked at Lenard in alarm.

He had a sudden thought: if Lenard ever tried to turn his recent confession against him, his best defence would be to make out he'd been hopelessly drunk. It had, after all, been a momentous day.

'You're right,' he muttered. 'I've had a lot to drink. Tomorrow morning I probably won't remember a word of my babblings.'

As if divining his anxieties, Lenard laughed and said, 'What do you mean? You spoke beautifully – your words deserve to be printed in tomorrow's newspapers.' Taking Bach's hand again, he added, 'But how did I let that Nordic beauty slip through my fingers. I must track her down. I can't forget her. It's as if she's standing right here in front of me.'

'I never saw her,' said Bach, 'but the soldiers are talking about her too.'

'She's the only kind of war trophy *I* value,' said Lenard.

That night Bach had a painful headache. Beneath a bright electric light he wrote in his diary:

'I think I'm coming to understand something important. It's not a matter of denying old-fashioned humanism; it's a matter of taking our understanding to a higher level. Today Germany and the Führer are resolving a question of fundamental importance. Good and evil are not fixed categories; they are capable of mutual transformation. Like thermal and mechanical energy, they are not opposites but different forms of a single essence. They are conventional signs; it is naive to assume they are in opposition. Today's crime is the foundation for tomorrow's virtue. The nation's energy assimilates good and evil, freedom and slavery, morality and amorality. It brings them together and makes them into a single pan-Germanic force. It may be that we have now, here on the Volga, found a simple and definitive answer to a fundamental question.'

34

The companies commanded by Bach and Lenard settled into the cool, spacious basement of a large building. The broken windows let in light and fresh air. The soldiers diligently carried down pieces of furniture from apartments not damaged by fire. The basement looked more like a warehouse than an army bivouac.

Each soldier had his own bed, covered with a quilt or blanket. They also carried down little tables, armchairs with fine, ornately carved legs and even a three-leaved mirror.

In one corner of the basement Stumpfe, a popular figure who was the battalion's senior soldier, created a kind of model bedroom. He brought down a double bed from a top-floor apartment, spread a pale blue blanket over it and placed two pillows in embroidered pillowcases by the headboard. He stood bedside tables, covered with small towels, on each side of the bed, and laid a carpet on the stone floor. Then he found two chamber pots and two pairs of old-people's fur-trimmed slippers. And he hung ten framed family photographs, taken from different apartments, on the walls.

The photographs he chose were all rather comic. One was of an old man and an old woman, probably working class, dressed up for some important occasion. The old man wore a jacket and tie; he looked uncomfortable and was frowning severely. The old woman wore a black dress with large white buttons. She had a knitted shawl draped over her shoulders and she was sitting with her hands folded in her lap, looking meekly down at the ground.

Another, much older photograph was of the same couple (the experts were all in agreement) on the day of their wedding. She was wearing a white veil, with small bunches of wax orange blossom; pretty but sad, she looked as if she were preparing for difficult years to come. The groom stood beside her, resting one elbow on the back of a tall black chair; he was wearing patent-leather boots and a black three-piece suit, with a watch chain attached to the waistcoat.

The third photograph showed a wooden coffin lined with lace paper. Inside the coffin lay a little girl in a white dress; standing around it, their hands on the coffin's sides, were various strange-looking people: an old man in a long calico shirt with no belt; a boy with his mouth hanging open; a man with a beard and several old women in kerchiefs, their faces fixed and solemn.

Without taking his boots off or removing the sub-machine gun hanging from his neck, Stumpfe collapsed onto the bed. His legs trembling, he called out in a high-pitched, affected voice, as if imitating a Russian woman, '*Lieber Ivan, komm zu mir!*'[272] The entire company roared with laughter.

Then he and Corporal Ledeke sat down on the chamber pots and began to improvise comic dialogues: first, 'Ivan and His Mother'; then, 'Rabbi Israel and His Wife Sarah'.

Very soon, soldiers from other regiments were coming to attend repeat performances. Preifi appeared too, somewhat tipsy, along with Bach and Lenard.

Stumpfe and Ledeke went through the whole programme again from beginning to end. Preifi laughed more loudly than anyone, helplessly rubbing his hands against his huge chest and saying, 'Stop, stop! You're killing me!'

In the evening the soldiers hung blankets and shawls over the windows, lit the large pink- and green-shaded oil lamps, filled with a mixture of petrol and salt, and sat down around a large table.

Only six of them had served throughout the Russian campaign. The others were from divisions previously stationed in Germany, Poland and France. Two had been in Rommel's Afrika Korps.

The company had its aristocrats and its pariahs. The Germans made fun of the Austrians, but they also often made vicious fun of one another. Those born in East Prussia were considered ignorant hawbucks. The Bavarians laughed at the Berliners, saying that Berlin was a Jewish city, a melting pot for riff-raff from Italy, Romania, Hungary, Poland, Czechoslovakia, Mexico, Brazil and any number of other countries, and that it was impossible to find a single true German there. The Prussians, the Bavarians and the Berliners all despised the Alsatians, calling them foreign swine. Men repatriated from Latvia, Lithuania and Estonia were referred to as 'quarter-German'; all the miserable weaknesses of the Slav East were thought to have entered their blood. As for *Volksdeutsche* from central and eastern Europe, they were not considered German at all. There were official instructions to keep an eye on them and not to entrust them with important tasks.

The company's aristocrats were Stumpfe and Vogel, both former SS. They were among the many thousands of SS who, on the Führer's orders, had been transferred to the Wehrmacht to boost morale.

Stumpfe was generally seen as the company's life and soul, as its moral backbone. He was tall and – unlike most corporals and rank-and-file soldiers – round and plump in the face. He was bold, smart and lucky, and he had an unrivalled ability to go round a half-destroyed Russian village and conjure up enough good foodstuffs for a parcel to send back home. He only had to look at an 'Easterner' for honey and fatback to appear. All this, naturally, impressed and delighted his fellow soldiers.

He loved his wife, his children and his brother. He wrote to them regularly and his food parcels were as rich and nutritious as those sent by officers. His wallet was full of photographs, which he had shown more than once to everyone in the company.

There were photos of his rather thin wife – clearing a dining table piled with dishes; leaning against the fireplace, wearing pyjamas; sitting in a boat, her hands on the oars; holding a doll and smiling; and going for a walk round the village. There were also photographs of his two children: a tall boy and a pretty little six-year-old girl with blonde hair down to her shoulders.

The other soldiers sighed as they looked at these photographs. And before returning a photograph to his wallet, Stumpfe would gaze at it long and devotedly; he could have been contemplating an icon.

He had a gift for telling stories about his children; Lenard once said to him that, with his talents, he should be performing on stage. One of his best stories, about preparing the family Christmas tree, was full of sweet, funny invented words, sudden cries and gestures, childish hypocrisy, childish cunning and childish envy of other children's presents. The story's effect on its audience was often unexpected. While Stumpfe was speaking, people would be laughing out loud, but when he came to the end they often found themselves moved to tears.

But it was not only Stumpfe's stories that were paradoxical. He embodied in his own being qualities one might have thought irreconcilable. This lover of his wife and children was capable of extraordinary, devil-may-care violence. On the rampage, he truly did become a devil; it was impossible to restrain him.

In Kharkov, dead drunk, he once climbed out of a fourth-floor window and walked right round the building on a narrow ledge, pistol in hand, firing at anything that caught his attention.

On another occasion, he set fire to a house, got up onto the roof and, as if in charge of an orchestra, began to conduct the flames and smoke and the wails of the women and children.

Stumpfe ran amok a third time on a moonlit May night in a Ukrainian village. He threw a hand grenade into the middle of some trees in full blossom. The grenade got caught in the branches and exploded only four metres away. Leaves and white petals rained down on him, while one piece of shrapnel punctured an epaulette and a second ripped open the top of one of his boots. Stumpfe suffered only mild concussion, but it was two days before he recovered his hearing.

There was something about his face, about the sudden glassy glitter in the depths of his large, calm eyes, that terrified the 'Easterners' he so despised. When he entered a hut, sniffed disdainfully as he looked slowly around him, pointed to a stool and ordered an astonished child or dazed old woman to wipe it clean with a white towel, they understood that it was best to do as he said.

Stumpfe's grasp of the psychology of Russian peasants was remarkable. After observing a woman for five minutes, he could win bets as to the quantity of honey, eggs and butter in the hut and whether or not there were treasures hidden beneath the floorboards: new boots, cloth or woollen dresses.

He was quicker than any of his comrades to learn words of Russian and was soon able to organize all his requirements without recourse to a phrase book or dictionary. 'I've simplified the Russian language,' he liked to say. 'In my grammar there is only one mood: the imperative.'

His fellow soldiers loved hearing him talk about his past; he had witnessed a great deal.

As a young man, he had worked in a sports shop. After losing his job, he spent two summers working on farms, in charge of a threshing machine. In 1926 he worked for three months in the Ruhr, in the Kronprinz coal mine. Then, after obtaining his licence, he became a professional driver. He began by delivering truckloads of milk and then worked as a chauffeur for a well-known dentist in Gelsenkirchen. A year later he became a taxi driver in Berlin. After that, he worked for a year as an assistant concierge in the Hotel Europa, and then as a kitchen supervisor in a small restaurant frequented by lawyers and industrialists.

He was happy to see his hands becoming soft and white and he took good care of them, wanting to erase any last trace of the harm done to his skin by some of his former jobs.

In the restaurant Stumpfe had his first real encounter with a world that had always intrigued him. On one occasion he calculated that a single deal – buying a portfolio of shares just before they shot up in value after a long slump – enabled a customer to make a profit equivalent to what he himself, in his previous job, would have earned over a period of 120 years – or 1,440 months, or 40,000 days, or 300,000 working hours, or 18 million working minutes. The customer had made this deal between two sips of coffee, using the restaurant telephone; it had taken him less than two minutes.

Some miraculous power was at work here – and this power intrigued Stumpfe.

Breathing the atmosphere of wealth, hearing omniscient waiters talk about which of their customers had bought a new Hispano-Suiza,[273] which had just built a villa and which had bought a pendant for a well-known actress – all this was a source of both pain and pleasure.

Stumpfe's younger brother Heinrich had the same round face and was equally tall. In 1936 he joined the political police. He often said to Stumpfe, 'Soon things will change. The two of us will see real life.'

Heinrich told his elder brother in whispers about a game still bolder and grander than anything talked about in his restaurant. With the backing of fortune, a single audacious move could raise you to dizzying heights.

There was a three-leaved mirror in the dimly lit restaurant lobby. Sometimes Stumpfe would stop in front of it, adopting the look of fastidious ennui he sometimes saw on customers' faces. He was in good shape: 177 centimetres tall, eighty kilos in weight, soft hair and smooth, pale skin. He had no doubt that he deserved something better than the life he was leading.

Meanwhile Alfred Rosenberg and Julius Streicher, Reichsmarschall Göring, Joseph Goebbels and the Führer himself were all proclaiming that the wisdom of the world's greatest sages and the labour of its greatest labourers meant nothing in comparison with the greatest treasure of all – the blood that flowed in the veins of every true German. Countless lecturers, journalists and radio presenters repeated the same intoxicating message. Stumpfe's head, planted on top of a huge, lazy, greedy torso, began to spin.

During the Eastern campaign Stumpfe came to believe more strongly than ever in his racial superiority – but this afforded him no joy. The nearer they got to the end of the war, the clearer it became that he was not in any real way benefiting from this superiority; he was still only a private soldier and he could fit all his belongings into a small knapsack. He wanted more than the opportunity to send regular food parcels back home.

Stumpfe was widely respected. The non-commissioned officers were well aware that the other soldiers listened to what he had to say, and that he often played the role of arbiter in their disputes. He was brave and was often chosen for reconnaissance missions; men liked to go with him, saying they felt safer with him than with Corporal Munk, who was a trained scout. He fearlessly entered villages occupied by Russian troops. One night he even set fire to a command post guarded by a Red Army sentry.

Stumpfe's comrades enjoyed his sense of humour. He had nicknames for almost everyone in the company; he was quick to notice people's peculiarities and could mimic them to perfection. He had a whole repertoire of campaign sketches and anecdotes: 'Sommer Four-Eyes receives a dressing-down from the battalion commander'; 'Vogel puts together a modest breakfast – twenty fried eggs and a small chicken'; 'In front of her small children Ledeke the determined womanizer wins the love of a Russian peasant woman'; 'Meierhof enables a Jew to understand that it is in his interests to leave this world sooner than the god of the Jews had decreed.'

Among the most fully developed of these sketches was an entire cycle devoted to a certain Schmidt: 'Schmidt marries but, working for a whole year on the night shift, is unable to sleep with his wife'; 'Schmidt receives a badge from his factory in recognition of his twenty years as a metalworker and tries to exchange this badge for a kilogram of potatoes'; 'Schmidt stands solemnly before the ranks to listen to the order demoting him from corporal to private soldier.'

Thanks to Stumpfe, Schmidt had become a butt of ridicule for the whole regiment, but there was nothing obviously comic about this unfortunate, middle-aged private. He was stout, as tall as Stumpfe, and slightly stooped. Much of the time he was silent and somewhat glum. But Stumpfe managed to capture even the least obvious of his quirks and mannerisms: his slight shuffle; his habit of half opening his mouth as he darned his clothes; the way he puffed and sniffed when he fell into thought.

Schmidt was the oldest soldier in the company and had fought in the First World War. It was rumoured that in 1918 he had joined the deserter movement organized by some scoundrel with a name like Labiknecht or Leibnecht. The younger soldiers were unsure of the name, but they knew from school that he was an agent of the Jewish Sanhedrin.[274]

Schmidt's gloomy obtuseness was deeply irritating and Stumpfe was unable to look at him without feeling angry. Too old to be a private soldier, he had joined the Wehrmacht as a non-commissioned officer. After his demotion, his work qualifications should have led him to be demobilized, but for some reason he remained in the company. He was a born loser. His constant misfortunes won him only contempt and he was always chosen for the most unpleasant tasks. He had a gift for showing up just when someone was needed to clean the officers' latrines or to clear up some other filth. He carried out such tasks with his usual quiet conscientiousness, with a kind of brainless indefatigability.

The sketch about Schmidt's demotion was based on a real event from the first weeks of the Russian campaign. Before being moved to the front line, the company had been guarding a prison and a prisoner-of-war camp. Schmidt had tried to avoid his guard duty by pretending to be ill and had been caught out by the regimental doctor – he was, it appeared, an inveterate deserter.

As a private soldier, however, Schmidt did his duty, was a good shot and showed no signs of cowardice. When the company was withdrawn to regroup and refit, he diligently sent food parcels back home. Yet he remained ridiculous – a blockhead, as Stumpfe never tired of repeating.

35

Stumpfe, Vogel and Ledeke were sitting together at a round table, lit by a lamp with a pink shade.

Bound by the ties of difficult work, shared danger and shared merriment, the three friends had few secrets from one another.

Vogel, a tall, lean youth, still a schoolboy when the war began, looked at Stumpfe and Ledeke, who were almost dozing, and asked, 'And where is our friend Schmidt?'

'On sentry duty,' replied Ledeke.

'It seems the war will soon be over,' said Vogel. 'But this really is a huge city. I got lost on my way to the regimental command post.'

'Yes,' said Ledeke. 'I've become a coward lately. The closer we are to the end of the war, the more terrible it would be to get killed.'

Vogel nodded. 'Yes, we've buried a lot of men. It really would be stupid to die now.'

'I find it hard to believe I'll soon be back home,' said Ledeke.

'You'll have plenty to tell people, especially if you catch a particular illness,' said Vogel, who disapproved of womanizers. He slowly ran his hand over the ribbons attached to his medals. 'As for me, I may not have as many of these as some of our HQ heroes, but at least I can say that I earned them honourably.'

Stumpfe had not spoken until then. Smiling wryly, he said, 'There's no writing on your medals – and medals earned in combat look no different from the ones given out at HQ.'

'*Unexpectedly, Stumpfe falls into despondency*,' said Ledeke. 'Stumpfe's like me. He doesn't want to take risks just before the end.'

'Is something the matter?' asked Vogel. 'I don't understand.'

'Why would you?' said Stumpfe. 'You'll return to your father's razor-blade factory and you'll live like a god.'

'But you'll be doing all right for yourself too,' Ledeke put in irritably.

'Because of a few parcels?' Stumpfe asked angrily, thumping his hand on the table. 'I don't think one or two parcels will get me very far!'

'And that little purse you wear on a chain?'

'Think I've got some great treasure in it? It's only now, at the end of the war, that I can see what a damned fool I've been. Dancing on the roof of a burning hut while others were making themselves rich!'

'It's all a matter of luck,' said Vogel. 'I know someone who was posted to Paris. Somehow he ended up with a diamond pendant. When he was back home on leave, he showed it to a jeweller. The jeweller just asked, "How old are you?" "Thirty-six," my friend replied. "Well, then," said the jeweller, "even if you live to a hundred and have many children and grandchildren, none of your family need ever know want." And the pendant had just fallen into my friend's hands.'

'Your friend was a lucky man,' said Ledeke. 'Stumpfe's right – you don't find diamond pendants in the huts of Russian peasants. We'd have been better off on the Western front. Or if we'd been tank men. They can take what they like – quality cloth, fine furs. We're on the wrong front and in the wrong branch of service.'

'And we're the wrong rank,' added Vogel. 'If Stumpfe were a general, he'd be looking a lot happier. They send truck after truck back home. I used to chat to their orderlies when I was on guard duty at Army HQ. You wouldn't believe it. They used to argue about which of their bosses had sent back the most furs.'

'*Pelze ... Pelze ...*' said Ledeke.[275] 'It's the only word you ever hear at HQ. But when we get to Persia and India, it'll be carpets.'

'You're a pair of fools,' said Stumpfe. 'Unfortunately, I've realized today that I've been a fool too. Fur coats and carpets are neither here nor there.' He looked around, then went on in a whisper, 'It's a matter of my children's future. I took part a while ago in a special action in some miserable little shtetl. That's where I came by these little trinkets – this gold coin, this watch, this little ring. Well, imagine what treasures come the way of *Einsatzgruppen* carrying out liquidations in Odessa, Kiev or Warsaw! Do you follow me?'

'I'm not so sure about these special actions,' said Vogel. 'My nerves aren't strong enough.'

'A pfennig from every Jew who's stopped breathing,' said Stumpfe. 'That's all.'

'Then you won't do too badly,' said Ledeke. 'The Führer's fully behind these special actions. It'll be whole wagonloads of pfennigs.'

They laughed, but Stumpfe, usually only too ready to laugh and joke, was in a serious mood.

'I'm not an idealist like you are,' he said to Vogel, 'and I fully admit it. You're like Lieutenant Bach – a man of the nineteenth century.'

'That's true,' said Ledeke. 'Not everyone has a rich family. It's easy enough to come out with fine words if your father owns a whole factory.'

'I've made up my mind,' said Stumpfe. 'I'm going to have a word with First Lieutenant Lenard. Maybe he can get me transferred – and I can make up for lost time before it's too late. I'll tell him I can hear a call, that it's my inner voice. He's a poet – he likes that sort of thing.'

Then Stumpfe took out another of his photographs. It showed a huge column of women, children and old men walking along between lines of armed soldiers. Some were looking towards the photographer; most were looking down at the ground. In the foreground stood an open-top car. The young woman inside was wearing a black fox stole, which brought out the paleness of her skin and the gold of her hair. Some officers standing nearby were watching the column of people. The woman had plump white hands and she was holding up a small dog with a big head and shaggy black hair, apparently wanting it too to look at the people. She could have been a mother showing some unusual sight to a small boy in order to be able to tell him, years later, what he had once witnessed.

Vogel studied the photograph for a long time. 'It's a Scottish terrier,' he said. 'We've got one very like it at home. Every time she writes, my mother passes on his greetings.'

'Quite a woman!' Ledeke sighed.

'My sister-in-law,' said Stumpfe. 'And the man leaning against the car door is my brother.'

'He looks very like you,' said Ledeke. 'At first I thought it *was* you. But he's got SS lapels and he's a higher rank.'

'The photo was taken in Kiev, in September 1941. Near a cemetery, but I've forgotten the name of the place.[276] My brother did well out of that Purim.[277] If your dad ever wants to expand his factory, my brother can certainly lend him a few pfennigs.'

'Let me have another look at her,' said Ledeke. 'There's something of the ancient world about her, especially with this procession of death in the background. A Roman lady in the Coliseum.'

'Before the war,' Stumpfe continued, 'my brother was an actor in an operetta company and his wife was a ticket-seller. If you'd come across her then, you'd hardly have noticed her. Eighty per cent of a woman's beauty comes from her clothes, the way she does her hair, the elegance of her surroundings. When the war's over, I want my wife to be able to look like this too. My brother's in the General Government now.[278]

Reading between the lines, I understand from his letters that they've established something remarkable there – a real factory for processing Jews. What happened on the outskirts of Kiev was mere child's play. He's told me that, if I can get a transfer he'll find me work at his factory. And don't worry – I've got nerves of steel!'[279]

'But what about comradeship?' Vogel burst out. 'Apart from anything else, there *is* such a thing as comradeship. Soldierly comradeship, the comradeship of the front line. Wanting to bugger off on your own after fourteen months that have bound us closer than brothers! I call it vile!'

Always easily influenced, Ledeke joined in with Vogel. 'Yes, we three have been through a lot together. And I'm not sure your plan will work anyway. There's no guarantee they'll accept you. Somewhere like that, they won't just be taking whoever shows up. Whereas if you stay here in Stalingrad, you're sure to be decorated. When the war comes to an end, there'll be no Germans further east than we are. And there'll be a special gold medal – for Stalingrad and the Volga. A medal that will bring us more than just honour.'

'Will it buy us a castle in Prussia?' Stumpfe retorted. He blew his nose.

'Ledeke, you're missing the point!' said Vogel. 'I'm talking about feelings – and you're like a peasant selling beets in the market. These things should be kept separate.'

And suddenly the three friends were quarrelling viciously.

'Fuck you and your fucking feelings!' Stumpfe yelled at Vogel. 'You're a rich bourgeois. *I'm* afraid of having nothing to eat when I get home.'

Shocked by the look of hate on his comrade's face, Vogel said, 'It's not quite like that, you know. Ministry of Industry inspectors have been giving my father hell. He looks more like a frightened worker than a wealthy capitalist.'

'I hope they really do give him hell! You too! You're all parasites and you should be flayed alive. The Führer will show you what's what!' Stumpfe then looked at Ledeke.

But Ledeke, rather than agreeing in his usual way with one of the others, said, 'To be honest with you – now that the war's almost over – all this talk about the unity of the German nation is bullshit. The bourgeoisie will go on stuffing themselves. Nazis and SS, men like Stumpfe and his dear brother, are sure to do all right for themselves too. If anyone gets flayed alive, it'll be stupid workers like me and my peasant father. So much for German unity! When the war's over, our roads will part.'

'Comrades, what's come over you?' said Vogel. 'What's happened? You've lost your minds.'

Stumpfe looked at Vogel intently. 'All right, all right,' he said in a conciliatory tone. 'Enough of all this. But please get one thing into your heads. If I don't go through with this plan of mine, it'll be because I care about my friends.'

A soldier came in. He'd just been relieved from sentry duty at the entrance to the company's basement.

'What was that shooting just now?' came a sleepy voice from the half-dark.

The soldier put down his sub-machine gun with a loud clatter, had a quick stretch and said, 'The duty lieutenant told me that some Russian unit has captured the railway station. But it's not on our sector.'

One of the soldiers laughed. 'They're probably so scared they lost their way. They meant to go east but ended up going west by mistake.'

'You're probably right,' said Ledeke. 'East and west mean nothing to them.'

The soldier sat down on his bed, brushed some muck off the blanket and said crossly, 'Listen. I've had to say this twice already. Before I go on duty tomorrow, I'll be putting a grenade under this blanket. I can't believe how little respect anyone has for other people's belongings. I want to take this blanket back home with me – and someone's marched all over it without even taking their boots off.'

Calming down at the thought that he would soon be able to have a good rest, he pulled off his own boots and said, 'There may be shooting going on around the station, but Lenard's having a party. They've found a gramophone, they've got guests, and they've dragged in some weeping maidens. Even Bach's joining in – seems he's decided to lose his innocence before the end of the war. Shooting in one sector – and song and dance in another!'

'They'll capitulate any day now,' said a voice from the darkness. 'I can feel it in the air. Home! The mere thought of home makes my heart miss a beat.'

36

Karl Schmidt was on sentry duty, just inside the courtyard of the building Captain Preifi had chosen for his battalion command post. The flickering light from the still-burning buildings made Schmidt's thin, wrinkled face seem hard and sullen.

A large white cat was walking along the cornice, looking around anxiously.

Schmidt checked whether or not anyone was watching, then called out in a hoarse voice, '*He du, Kätzchen, Kätzchen!*'[280] But this Stalingrad cat didn't understand German. She stopped, wondering if the man standing by the wall was dangerous, then flicked her tail, leaped with a loud clatter onto the iron roof of a nearby shed and disappeared into the dark.

Schmidt looked at his watch. He would be on duty for another hour and a half. But he did not mind being alone in this quiet yard; he had come to love solitude – and not merely because of being subjected to Stumpfe's constant ridicule.

Silent pink shadows – petals, half-circles, ovals – were flitting across the wall, as if it were a cinema screen. A nearby building must have started to burn more brightly; probably some wooden floors had just caught.

It was extraordinary how much people changed. Ten years ago, his wife had often got angry and upset with him for never staying at home in the evenings; he would come back from the factory, change his clothes, snatch something to eat and go straight out again, either to a meeting or to a beer cellar. Every evening would be taken up by political discussion. But if he could go home now, he'd happily lock the door and not go out again for the next year.

In the first place, most of the people Schmidt used to see were no longer around. His fellow factory-committee activists and the senior officials from the trade union had mostly either emigrated or been sent to camps; a few had adapted and become Brownshirts. And Schmidt didn't particularly want to see anyone anyway. Everyone lived in fear; all anyone wanted to talk about was the weather, buying a new

Volkswagen on credit, what the woman next door was cooking for dinner, how stingy some of their mutual acquaintances had become, who gave their guests real tea and who palmed them off with acorn coffee. And if a friend visited at all often, then you could be sure the *Blockleiter*[281] would soon be looking through a crack in your door or putting his ear to the wall of your room. What were these strange types up to? – he'd be thinking. Why were they sitting and talking for hours on end? Why weren't they reading *Mein Kampf*?

Nevertheless, Schmidt was unsure whether or not people really did change.

This, he realized, was a difficult question. Who could he ask? Who could he talk it over with? Only that Stalingrad cat – but even she was keeping her distance.

Maybe that vile Stumpfe was right? Maybe he, Schmidt, really was just a stupid blockhead? But had he always been a blockhead? Or had he only become a blockhead under the Nazis? Or was he a blockhead in the eyes of the Nazis, but not in the eyes of others? There was a time when Schmidt had been seen as a leader – and not only in the factory where he worked. He had gone to Bochum for a trade union congress and been elected as a delegate representing 10,000 people. And now he was a blockhead – the laughing stock of the company.

Schmidt kicked a piece of brick out of his way and began to pace the length of the wall. When he got to the corner, he stopped and gazed for a while at the abandoned buildings and their dead, burnt-out window sockets. He felt cold, lonely and anguished. He knew this feeling only too well; at moments like this it seemed that everything – the light of the sun and stars, the depth of the sky, the breath of the open fields – had become tormenting and oppressive. It was worst of all in the spring, when the stars, the soft breeze, the young leaves, the murmur of streams – when everything spoke of freedom.

His son had once read aloud to him a passage from his botany text-book. Apparently there were bacteria – 'anaerobic bacteria' – that did not need oxygen. Instead, they breathed nitrogen, and they lived happy, well-nourished lives around the roots of leguminous plants. It seemed there were also people like that – anaerobic people who could breathe Hitler's nitrogen. But he was not one of them. He was suffocating. He could not get used to nitrogen. He needed oxygen; he needed freedom.

Schmidt found it hard to get away from the tall forehead and pale face of the man who had declared that he was Germany and that Germany was him. This face was now everywhere, looming over the innocent blood, over the sparkling brass of celebrating bands, over the drunken laughter, over the barks of guards and the howls of old women and children.

Why was it that he, Karl Schmidt, a German soldier who loved his country, the son of a German and the grandson of a German, felt only horror when he heard news of German victories?

And why did he feel such particular anguish tonight, on sentry duty in this ruined city, watching bright shadows flit across the walls of dead buildings?

Real loneliness was very painful indeed.

Sometimes he worried that he had forgotten how to think, that his brain had petrified, that it was no longer human. And there were other times when he felt frightened by his own thoughts, when he felt that Ledeke, Stumpfe and Lenard could simply look into his eyes and read everything in his mind. Or he might mutter something incorrect in a dream. His neighbour would hear him, wake some of the others and say, 'Here, listen to what this red Schmidt has to say about our Leader.'

Here, though, in this dark courtyard, where he had been alone throughout his watch, he felt calm; neither Lenard nor Stumpfe, nor anyone else could be reading his thoughts now.

He looked at his watch again: his relief was due soon.

For all his loneliness, Schmidt knew that there were, in fact, other blockheads in the division. There were other men who thought like he did. But how could he make contact with them? Not even the stupidest of blockheads would voice thoughts like his openly. Nevertheless, such blockheads existed. They were capable of thought, and maybe even of action. But how could he find them?

The door half-opened and the guard commander came out. His uniform was unbuttoned and in the glow from the burning buildings his shirt looked pale pink.

Looking out from the doorway, he called quietly, 'Hey, Sentry Schmidt!'

Schmidt walked over to him. The guard commander, whose breath smelt of vodka, said with unexpected gentleness, 'Listen, my friend, you're going to have to stay here a little longer. Your relief is Hofmann, and it's his birthday today. He's a little tired, he doesn't quite feel himself. All right? After all, it is still summer. You're not too cold out here, are you?'

'All right,' said Schmidt.

*

A few hours later, Stumpfe walked over to the squat building where the officers were billeted. The sentry outside was someone he recognized.

'How are things going?' asked Stumpfe. 'How's the commander? Is he in a good mood? I need to make an important request.'

The sentry shook his head.

'They were having quite a party,' he said. 'Vodka and women and all. But at the very climax, so to say, the officers received an urgent summons from the colonel, and they're not yet back.'

'Has Moscow surrendered?'

The sentry didn't hear this. Instead, he gestured towards the door and winked. 'I'm guarding the young women,' he said. 'First Lieutenant Lenard told me, "We have to carry out a small operation. Just half an hour or so. We have to clear some Russians out of the station." He ordered me to take good care of the girls and promised to be back by noon.'

A few minutes after this, the battalion was ordered to prepare for combat. And German tanks and artillery began to move towards the station.

37

At two in the afternoon the Germans attacked the station. Lieutenant Colonel Yelin was drawing up a report for General Rodimtsev, his divisional commander, about the actions in which his regiment had taken part during the last few days. He was also listening with one ear to an argument between his adjutant and the head of the regiment's medical unit about which were the sweeter watermelons – those from Astrakhan or those from Kamyshin.

Yelin understood what was happening immediately, before hearing from his battalion commanders. The bombs and the fierce mortar and artillery barrage could mean only one thing.

He rushed out of the bunker and saw a pale cloud of chalky dust rising over the station. Mixing with swirls of greasy smoke, it formed a thick smog, swaying over the wrecked buildings.

Then came the sound of rifle fire, on their left flank and in the centre of the sector assigned to their division.

'Here we go,' Yelin said to himself. And thousands of other Red Army soldiers had the same thought; they had all known this would happen.

The tension of the last few hours had been especially painful for those who had just crossed from the east bank. It was as if they had chosen to stand on a railway line, braced for the impact of runaway trucks on a downhill gradient. A terrible blow was inevitable.

Yelin had been through a great deal and his hair had gone white in the course of the last year. He believed this was due to the excessive demands of some of his superiors and the negligence of some of his subordinates.

He was all the more upset because it was Filyashkin's battalion that was bearing the brunt of the attack. He considered this battalion his weakest link; it had only recently been placed under his command and he did not know its commanders at all well.

A messenger called him back to the bunker. Filyashkin was on the telephone: he was being bombed and shelled and he could hear the sound of approaching tanks. He was sustaining casualties and was preparing to repel the German attack.

'Yes, I already know!' Yelin shouted into the receiver. 'Take care of your machine guns. Don't even think of retreating. I'll support you. Can you hear me? I'll provide full artillery support! Are you there? Are you there?'

But Filyashkin did not hear Yelin's promise of supporting fire – the line had gone dead.

Yelin called Rodimtsev. He reported that the Germans were directing their main thrust against Filyashkin. 'The battalion recently placed under my command,' he added. 'It was formerly part of Matyushin's regiment.'

Yelin then turned to his chief of staff. 'We've been ordered to hold the station at all cost. There'll be supporting fire from the divisional artillery. Heaven knows what the Germans are cooking up now. I just hope we don't end up going for a swim in the Volga.'

The chief of staff nodded, thinking to himself that it was a pity they didn't have a boat.

Yelin summoned his battalion commanders, to check that they were ready to conduct an active defence.

The consequences of a swift German success would be disastrous. Most of the Soviet reinforcements were still in transit. Only Rodimtsev's division was already on the west bank. If they forced Rodimtsev into the Volga, the Germans could prevent the rest of the reinforcements from ever crossing to Stalingrad.

Rodimtsev telephoned the commander of his right-flank regiment. Then he summoned the divisional artillery commander and the commander of the sapper battalion. After giving them their orders, he sent Belsky to inspect in person the streets along which enemy tanks were most likely to approach. Then he telephoned Chuikov, 'Permission to report, comrade Lieutenant General. The enemy has launched an attack. He is concentrating his tanks and bombing and shelling my left flank. His objective is clearly the railway station.'

Rodimtsev was no less aware of the seriousness of the threat: his right flank was exposed. If the Germans achieved a quick and easy success on his left flank, they would immediately turn to his right flank. The entire division would be endangered.

As he listened to Chuikov's staccato reply, Rodimtsev looked at the stone vault of the sewer and the distant light of the opening. Was he really, he wondered, destined to end his days in this dark pipe?

'Stand firm!' Chuikov was saying. 'Not one step back! If anyone retreats, they go before a tribunal. I'll shoot them! Understand? In two hours Gorishny will begin the crossing. He will cover your right flank. The front line will then be secure. The situation will stabilize. As for "retreat" or "withdrawal" – forget the words!'

But Rodimtsev had no wish whatsoever to retreat. More than anything, he wanted to attack at once.

Chuikov was, of course, every bit as concerned as Rodimtsev. Rodimtsev's division had just crossed. Gorishny would cross soon. Still more reinforcements were approaching. It would be a catastrophe if the front were to break now.

What mattered was to keep fighting, to prolong the battle, to tie down the enemy's forces. The Germans clearly liked to complete one operation before starting another; they preferred not to leave loose ends. A drawn-out battle on Rodimtsev's left flank would give the rest of Chuikov's forces a breathing space. Things had already become easier for the defenders of the factory district. The pressure on them had eased. The dive-bombers had moved elsewhere.

But if the Germans managed to isolate Rodimtsev's division, if they prevented him from digging in, from consolidating a front line that was still little more than a dotted line on a map, if they found a way to exploit their numerical superiority and freedom of manoeuvre … Chuikov was hamstrung by his lack of reserves. He had been expecting this attack for some time, but he had been hoping against hope that the Germans would delay.

Chuikov telephoned Yeromenko.

'Chuikov reporting,' he began grimly. 'The enemy, after aerial bombardment, has attacked my left flank, mobilizing artillery and mortars, and concentrating his tanks. His objective, I assume, is to isolate Rodimtsev and break through to the Volga.'

'Don't assume!' Yeromenko replied impatiently. 'Act! Counterattack! And provide Rodimtsev with full artillery support.' Then came a strange noise – Chuikov realized that Yeromenko was eating an apple.

'There's smoke everywhere, you can hardly see a thing,' said Chuikov. 'But I'll call up the artillery straightaway.'

'Don't waste time!' Yeromenko snapped. Then came a moment of silence – Chuikov realized that Yeromenko was now lighting a cigarette. 'But don't fire on your own men – we don't want a second front here in Stalingrad. As for Rodimtsev, if he cracks, you're in trouble. On your right flank, there are two large divisions about to cross. And two more soon afterwards. So, get to work!'

'Understood, comrade Colonel General,' said Chuikov. He put down the receiver and picked it up again straightaway. 'Pozharsky!' he bellowed. 'At once!' While Pozharsky, the artillery commander, made his way to the phone, Chuikov glanced at Gurov, who was sitting beside him, and said, 'Fritz is giving the station one hell of a bombardment, no doubt about it. Round here, things have turned quieter. All the same, I'd rather it was us they were shelling.' Raising his voice, he said, 'Pozharsky, got your map in front of you? Good. Note the following!'

On the other side of the Volga, Yeromenko was also leaning over a map.

The Germans had done nothing for two days. If only they'd waited a little longer … Was this an isolated operation or the beginning of a general offensive? If only he'd had time to complete the redeployment of Shumilov's 64th Army. He'd wanted Shumilov to attack whenever the Germans attacked Chuikov, thus reducing the pressure on Chuikov's left flank and centre. As for the reinforcements on their way from the Don front, they were still some distance away …

'Why the hell did they have to attack today?' Yeromenko said to his chief of staff. 'Even our artillery can provide little support. If only the bastards had waited till I'd got Gorishny safely across the water. What if they really go for it now?' The chief of staff remained silent. Yeromenko went on, 'They're pulling out all the stops. You can tell even from here.'

A minute later Yeromenko was on the phone to his artillery commander, Colonel Ageyev, 'Support the left flank and the centre. What's that? Difficult to establish the enemy's position? Yes, of course. But there's no bloody choice. Step to it!'

A report written on the page of a notebook went from a regimental command post to a divisional command post. From there it moved on to the army command post, where it was typed out. Next, a signals officer carried the report, along with three carbon copies, across the Volga to Front HQ. Another signals officer called Moscow by radio telephone. Teleprinters at the Front signals centre began to clatter. A thick packet with five seals was put ready for a special courier; he would leave at dawn, by Douglas, to deliver it to the General Staff.

The burden of this report was very simple: after a brief lull, the Germans had resumed their offensive.

Temporarily deafened by all the explosions, Yelin well understood the responsibility that had fallen to him. He shouted to the telephonist, 'Get me Filyashkin! This minute!'

The telephonist replied bleakly, 'The line's dead, stone dead.'

Yelin's adjutant came down into the bunker. Several pale, anxious messengers watched as he passed by.

'Comrade Lieutenant Colonel, three messengers have been killed already. It's impossible to get through to Filyashkin. The station's surrounded. The battalion's conducting a perimeter defence.'

'Radio?' Yelin asked abruptly. 'What about radio?'

'No reply, comrade Lieutenant Colonel.'

'So his transmitter's broken,' said Yelin.

The battalion was cut off. It had lost contact with the regiment, the division, the army, and the Front as a whole. For all Yelin knew, Filyashkin might already be dead.

The Germans were clearly prepared to go to any lengths to eliminate the battalion. The mortar and artillery fire around the station was intense and unrelenting, and this was all the more apparent during the brief moments of respite elsewhere on the front. The rest of Rodimtsev's division understood only too well what their surrounded comrades were now going through.

Yelin said to his commissar, 'Filyashkin, now – what do you think of him? We've repelled this last attack, but can *he*? We'll give him all possible support. We'll counter-attack, and we'll provide supporting fire. But he's only just been transferred to my command – I can't be held accountable for him. I don't think I've ever even seen the man.'

The commissar replied, 'I'd just sent Shvedkov back, with the parcel we've received from the women of America – and then the attack began. It's good that Shvedkov will be with them – he's a true Communist. In one company they've got men from a penal battalion serving along with the other soldiers – I gave Filyashkin a good dressing-down. I told him to draw up proper lists and have them transferred.'

Yelin telephoned Matyushin, the commander of the neighbouring regiment. They agreed to reinforce the defences at the junction of their two sectors. Then Yelin asked, 'What's your opinion of Filyashkin's battalion? I hardly know them. Really, they're your men.'

'Certainly not,' said Matyushin, realizing what Yelin was up to. 'It's your battalion – it's nothing to do with me any more. Anyway, they're just men like any other men – what matters is how well they're commanded.'

38

After organizing his defences, Filyashkin had secretly cherished the hope that the Germans would not attack the railway station; like most people, he could not help wanting to stay alive.

One scenario saw him withdrawing to the Volga – under orders, of course, since Yelin would realize the senselessness of trying to defend a position when both your flanks are wide open. The battalion would conduct a fighting retreat and then be withdrawn to the reserves. Another scenario saw him being taken to the east bank, slightly wounded, by medical instructor Lena Gnatyuk. There turned out to be no room in any of the hospitals and so he and Lena bivouacked in a fisherman's hut. Lena took care of him and changed his dressings; they slept together on top of the stove and at dawn he went fishing in the River Akhtuba. In yet another scenario he was pronounced unfit for active service and sent to teach in the Ryazan Infantry Academy, eighteen kilometres from his home village; Lena, however, had to stay with the battalion, since Filyashkin had a wife and two children and taking her back home with him was out of the question.

Each of the 300 men in the battalion created their own picture of a fortunate outcome to the war; their lives would be happy and fulfilling – happier, it went without saying, than in the past. Some thought about moving from their village to the district town, others about moving out to a village. Some thought about their wives, vowing to treat them more gently. Some wondered how their wives were managing now: if they were in difficulty, they should go to the market and sell a pair of trousers or a smart jacket. When the war was over, it would be easy to earn enough to replace them. Some thought about their children; one resolved to do all he could to help his young Masha qualify as a doctor.

It was Filyashkin who was first to understand that his dreams were doomed to die with him. Everything was only too clear. He had lost telephone and radio contact with his regiment. Tanks, and then infantry, had broken into his rear. The German mortar and artillery fire was devastatingly accurate. It wasn't just that you couldn't run or even crawl anywhere – you couldn't even poke your head out from behind a wall. Filyashkin loaded and cocked his pistol, releasing the safety catch. After that, he felt less heavy at heart.

'We've been cut off,' shouted Igumnov. 'They've severed our lines of communication.'

'Yes,' Filyashkin replied, 'we're our own masters now!' He glimpsed a smile on Igumnov's usually tense, anxious face. He had turned pale, but this somehow made him look younger and fresher, as if he had just washed.

Filyashkin then saw Igumnov take some letters from his tunic pocket, tear them into small pieces and scatter them on the floor. He understood at once: his chief of staff didn't want the Germans to be fingering letters from his wife and children when they searched his dead body.

Igumnov ran a comb over his grey crew cut.

'Fuck it all!' Filyashkin yelled in sudden fury. 'I'm a commander and there are commands to be given.'

He sent a signaller to find the break in the cable connecting him with the regiment. He issued new orders to his company commanders. For the time being they were to keep their machine guns and anti-tank rifles hidden; he did not want to risk them being damaged before the Germans tried to storm the building, which was sure to be soon. They were to take care of their messengers, and to disperse their men over as wide an area as possible, so as not to sustain premature casualties. He asked about the soldiers' morale and repeated once more that anyone who took to his heels would be shot.

For a moment the telephone came to life. Filyashkin got through to Yelin, who again promised to provide the battalion with full artillery support, but their conversation was cut short; the line went dead once and for all, cut by either a shell burst or a German sapper.

Filyashkin gave orders and explanations, licked his dry lips and slapped himself on the forehead and the back of his head to try and rid himself of his deafness. Everything he said was founded on one clear and simple resolve: no matter what, his battalion was not going to budge. It would stand its ground and it would fight to the bitter end. The battalion's withdrawal, Filyashkin understood very well, would lead to the whole regiment being drowned in the Volga.

His men had been held in reserve a long time and some had never seen combat at all. Nevertheless, Filyashkin felt certain that they all shared his sense of determination. He was no longer troubled by doubts and fears; retreat was impossible – behind him lay only a steep cliff and a deep river. He and his men had seized hold of this little corner of earth and dug themselves in. Nothing was going to dislodge them.

All the same, when Shvedkov returned from the regimental command post, just before the artillery barrage began, Filyashkin called out to him, 'Go and see how things are with Konanykin. He's got men from a penal unit in his company. We need to keep an eye on their morale.'

39

The first mortar bomb fired at Konanykin's company landed on the edge of a trench where three soldiers were sitting. All three were showered with earth. Two had been bending forward over their mess tins; they froze, as if gripped by some invisible hand. The third, who was thin and somewhat stooped, also remained where he was, leaning calmly against the wall of the trench.

'The bastards won't even let us have a bite to eat,' said one man, looking at the earth in his mess tin, as if the Geneva Conventions forbade mortar and artillery fire during mealtimes.

The second shook the earth from his shoulders, lovingly wiped his spoon against the palm of one hand and muttered in bewilderment, 'I thought that was it, I really did.'

The third collapsed without a word. The full weight of his body and dead, blood-covered head landed on his comrades' feet.

Then came another quiet, terrifyingly tender and innocent whoosh as several more mortar bombs flew over the trench.

Out of the smoke and the din of explosions emerged a piercing groan. Voices called, 'Pull him out! … No … What's the use?'

Then – another whoosh, and more explosions.

'Covered by enemy fire' – these words perfectly convey what it is like to be subjected to a sudden barrage of fire. The barrage covered the men, like a net or like sacking.

Splinters flung against bricks gave birth to small clouds of red dust, then lost their lethal force and dropped quietly to the ground. As they flew through the air, each splinter made its own particular sound, depending on its weight, speed and shape. One, which must have had curly, jagged edges, sounded like someone playing a comb or a kazoo. Another howled, ripping through the air like a large steel claw. A third, probably tube-shaped, somersaulted along, as if puffing and splashing.

As for the big-bellied mortar bombs themselves, they let out complex, constantly modulating whistles; they were like metal spindles, drilling a hole in the air, then deftly enlarging this hole with their broad, strong shoulders.

And these sounds made by invisible pieces of iron – all these squeals and howls, all these lisps, whines and whispers – were the voice of death.

Small, separate puffs of smoke, some grey, some reddish-brown, merged into a single huge cloud. Swirls of dust from bricks, earth and plaster merged into a dense grey fog. Blending together, the smoke and the dust hung between earth and sky, still further isolating the encircled battalion.

The Germans were preparing to send in their tanks. They did not, however expect their artillery fire to liquidate the entire battalion – not even the fiercest barrage can kill hundreds of men who have dug themselves into the ground or taken shelter in deep trenches and stone burrows. The barrage was directed less against soldiers' lives than against their souls, against their wills. No matter how deep a man has dug himself into the ground, an artillery barrage can penetrate his soul. It can drill into nerve ganglia that not even the deftest of surgeons can reach with a scalpel. It can invade a man's inner being through the labyrinth of an ear, through nostrils or half-closed eyelids; it can grasp a man's skull and shake up his brain.

Hundreds of men lay there in the smoke and fog, each entirely alone, each conscious as never before of his body's fragility, of how at any moment his body might be lost irrevocably. And this was indeed the aim of the barrage – to plunge each individual into his own solitude. Relentless thunder would prevent a soldier from hearing the words of his commissar; smoke would make him unable to see his commander; the soldier would feel isolated from his comrades, and in this awful isolation he would be conscious only of his own weakness. And this barrage lasted not for seconds, not for minutes, but for two whole hours, mangling men's thoughts and destroying their memories.

Now and then men would lift up their heads for a second, glimpse their comrades' motionless bodies and wonder if they were alive or dead. And then they would lie down again with only one thought in their minds: 'I'm still alive, but what's this swishing sound I can hear? Is it my death?'

The barrage broke off when, according to the enemy's understanding of human nature and the laws of resistance of psychic material, overwhelming anxiety and tension should have yielded to depression and a resigned indifference.

The ensuing silence was cruel and malign. It allowed the men to recollect their past and to feel a kind of timid relief: in spite of everything, they were still alive. The silence awoke hope, yet it also engendered a terrible despair. Its message was only too clear: that this was merely a fragile moment of respite – a swift ray of light on the blade of a drawn knife – and that the minutes to come would be still more merciless than those that had just passed. Their political instructors had evidently talked a load of baloney and now they were doomed; if they had any sense, they would run. Quick – before it was too late – they should crawl away and hide.

Such thoughts need only a moment, and the enemy was too experienced to allow the silence to continue a moment longer than necessary. Silence, after all, can also engender resolve. The silence was quickly followed by the sound of metal grating on stone, by a sullen clanking and grinding and the sound of exhausts and revving engines. The German tanks were advancing. And from somewhere a little further off came the sound of wild, confident yells.

The battalion remained silent. It seemed that the powerful, experienced enemy had achieved his aim, that he had broken the will of the Soviet soldiers, that he had stunned and silenced them, that he had indeed crushed their souls.

Suddenly there was the crack of a rifle shot, the blast of an anti-tank rifle, then a second anti-tank rifle, and then the explosions of hand grenades, long bursts of machine-gun fire and hundreds more rifle shots. The living – it appeared – were alive.

The Germans had hoped to fragment the encircled battalion. They knew that a defensive position is like a living body; if it is cut apart, its life drains away. Confident that their artillery fire would have destroyed the resilience of the Soviet defence, deadening its living tissue and making it weak and anaemic, the Germans expected their attack to meet with rapid success. But their tanks were unable to slice into the battalion's body. Like a lance point hitting a strong, ringing shield, they fell back, their incisive power blunted and weakened.

Vavilov thought he had been the first to fire. Fifty or sixty other men, however, were equally certain that it was they, and no one else, who broke the battalion's silence.

Vavilov also believed that the first sound of all had been his furious yell. It was this, rather than his shot, that had broken the silence. His voice was at once picked up by hundreds of other voices – and everything around thundered and burst into flashes of fire. He saw German soldiers rushing about in confusion. Vavilov seldom cursed or swore, but the men beside him heard him let out a long volley of curses.

He felt astonished that the tiny buzzing insects running after the tanks could have brought about so much destruction, grief and misery.

There was an alarming, impossible discrepancy between the enormity of the tragedy and the small agitated creatures that had brought it about.

40

Konanykin was a seasoned fighter. When the Germans began to shell his company, he said aloud to himself, 'Understand, comrade Lieutenant?'

Along with an orderly, he crawled to the crate of hand grenades, now the most precious object in the world, and dragged it to his command post.

As he passed the men from penal battalions, he said in a calm, cheerful voice, 'Stand firm, lads, you'll all be amnestied now!'

His rough but good-natured joke, pronounced with unimaginable calm, did much for their morale.

Throughout the barrage Konanykin had been keeping a close eye on these men, whom he had placed near his command post. One had kept stroking the green body of a hand grenade; a second had been frantically taking rusks from his pocket and stuffing them into his mouth, evidently finding this comforting; a third had repeatedly been trembling all over and then, all of a sudden, going dead still; a fourth had been kicking away at a brick with the toe of his boot, as if trying to chisel a hole in it; a fifth was opening his mouth very wide while blocking his ears with his fingers; a sixth was constantly whispering to himself, probably either praying or swearing.

'Just my luck,' Konanykin said to himself. 'Filyashkin was meant to be getting these heroes transferred, but now I'll have them fighting alongside me.'

Konanykin had no love for these men. One had deliberately shot himself. Another had run from the battlefield. All of them regularly infringed military discipline and created difficulties for Konanykin. One had lost his military-service book. Yakhontov – a common criminal with fair hair and pale blue eyes – had fallen behind during the long march; he had finally shown up, having got a lift in a passing truck, just as Konanykin was writing an official report about his desertion. Another man had a particular gift for winning the sympathy of village women and getting them to give him large quantities of rotgut. His platoon commander had written in a report that 'This soldier's conduct in matters pertaining to vodka is most excessive.'

Now, though, Konanykin was unable to summon up his usual irritation either with Filyashkin, who had failed to get these men transferred, or with the men themselves. Instead, he felt pity for them.

Someone tapped Konanykin on the shoulder. He looked round and saw a pale figure coated in dirt and sweat. It took him a moment to recognize Battalion Commissar Shvedkov.

'What are your losses? How's the men's morale?' Shvedkov asked, breathing hotly into Konanykin's ear.

'Morale's strong. We'll fight to the end.' Konanykin then cursed and swore as a shell exploded close by.

Konanykin now felt an uncharacteristic confidence in people and a great warmth towards them. Usually he divided the male population of the Soviet Union into two halves: those who had been professional soldiers before the war began, and those who had not. Now, though, he no longer made this distinction.

When Shvedkov finished questioning him, wished him all the best and crept off towards Kovalyov's company, Konanykin said to himself with feeling, 'He's a fine man, a true fighting eagle, even if he has only been serving a few months.'

And it seemed entirely natural to him that Shvedkov, who had left before the attack for the relative safety of the regimental command post, should have returned to the battalion and was now creeping along the ground under fire, speaking straightforwardly and from the heart to soldiers and commanders alike.

But Konanykin's new feelings towards people were never put to the test; he was killed a few minutes before the end of the artillery barrage.

41

The grey sharp-edged tank had a broad, sloping forehead adorned with a black cross. Somewhat jerkily, it mounted a low bank of bricks, then came to a standstill, as if to get its breath back and examine its surroundings.

It was hard to believe that its cautious, mistrustful movements – the slow, silent rotation of its turret, the stirring of a predatory steel pupil in the eye of its machine-gun port – were being directed by people. The tank seemed a living being, with its own eyes and brain, with claws and terrible jaws, with muscles that never tired.

A fair-haired Soviet soldier was preparing, with icy concentration, to fire his anti-tank rifle. With an almost impossible slowness he began to raise the butt. The barrel moved down and the backplate dug into his shoulder, which felt reassuring. He pressed his cheek to the cool butt and glimpsed, through the V of the backsight, the tank's low, sloping, simian forehead, powdered with pink brick dust. Next, he saw the tank's closed rectangular hatch. Then the side armour came into view, with its dotted line of bulging rivets; then the silvery caterpillar track and some splashes of oil. The ball of the soldier's index finger, till then barely touching the trigger, gently took the first pressure, and the trigger began to yield. There was sweat on the soldier's chest; he knew that he now had in his sights the most vulnerable part of the tank's steel hide.

The tank began to move again and the turret spun slowly round. As if sniffing out its prey, the gun turned smoothly towards the soldier lying behind the mound of bricks.

Holding his breath, the soldier increased the pressure on the trigger. His weapon fired. The recoil was like a powerful punch to his shoulder and chest.

He had put all his strength, all his passion into this shot – yet he missed.

The tank shuddered, as if belching, and white, poisonous fire flashed from its gun. A shell exploded behind the soldier and to his right. The soldier opened the breech, inserted another black-nosed armour-piercing cartridge, took aim, fired – and missed. A small dust cloud rose from a heap of stone a few metres away from the tank. The tank let off a round of machine-gun fire and a flock of iron birds tore harshly through the air, just above the soldier lying flat on the ground. In despair, drawing on his last reserves of emotional strength, the soldier reloaded and fired once more.

A bright blue flame flashed across the tank's grey armour. The soldier lifted his head: was he imagining it or had he truly seen a blue flower flare from the grey steel? But then he saw thin yellow smoke coming out of the hatch and turret, accompanied by cracks and rumbles; it sounded as if machine-gun cartridge belts were detonating inside the tank. All of a sudden, a flaming black cloud shot up from the tank, and there was a deafening explosion.

For a moment he felt unsure whether it was really he who had brought about the explosion, whether this black cloud really did have anything to do with the blue flame he had glimpsed on the tank's armour. Then he closed his eyes, bent his head to his rifle, and gave the barrel a long slow kiss, feeling the blue steel, with its smell of gunpowder, against his lips and teeth.

When he lifted his head again, the tank was still smoking. It had been blown apart by its own ammunition. There was a gash in one side, the turret had slid down onto the tank's forehead and the drooping gun now pointed towards the ground.

Forgetting all danger, the soldier got to his feet and repeated in a loud, passionate whisper, 'Me! Look! That was me!'

He lay down again and called out to his neighbour, 'Please, lend me another cartridge!'

Never, perhaps, in all his complex, motley, often less-than-honest life had he known such happiness. Today he was fighting not for himself, but for everyone. And the world that had deceived him so often – the world he had so often wanted to deceive – had ceased to exist.

Death was nearby. He was confronting death in single combat. Zhora, his number two, had died already. Konanykin, his battalion commander, had been killed by shrapnel a few minutes before the tanks attacked. His section leader was almost dead too, crushed beneath a huge heap of brick, unable to give orders or even let out a groan. He was alone, with only his gun.

Who did he remember at this moment? Did his thoughts turn to his mother and father?

This man had never known his mother and father. Before the Revolution they had lived in Petersburg, where his father had worked as a civilian official in the Admiralty. During the Civil War his parents had tried to escape the country, via Crimea, but they had both died of typhus at Melitopol railway station, in south-eastern Ukraine. Aged two, he had been taken to a children's home. He grew up knowing nothing of his past. Although once, in the hostel of a school for future railway workers, he had a strange dream: he was standing on a slippery parquet floor, wearing a small lace-edged apron and holding in his hands the long warm ears of a dog. The dog's clouded eyes were looking straight into his own, and its rough tongue was licking his cheek. A woman threw up her hands in horror and carried him away, pressing him against the slippery silk on her breast. While he kicked his legs and yelled, she wiped his cheeks with a warm sponge.

He studied, then dropped his studies and got a job. He married, left his wife, left his job, went off his head and took to drink. One night he and two friends broke into a grocery store; they were arrested the next morning. The beginning of the war found him in a labour camp. He petitioned to be enlisted – and was sent to the front, granted the opportunity to earn his pardon.

Today he had destroyed an enemy tank and received a shrapnel wound in the leg. He knew he would now be pardoned. But that was not what he thought about as he saw a second tank moving forward between the ruined buildings.

Calm, sure of his strength and still rejoicing in his success, he began to take aim. He was confident of a second triumph but, before he could pull the trigger, he was hit by machine-gun fire. Finding him still alive, with a fractured spine and his stomach gashed open, two orderlies dragged him away on a greatcoat.

42

That evening, when things quietened down, Filyashkin tried to count up the casualties. But he soon realized that it would be simpler to count the number of men still alive.

Apart from himself, the only surviving commanders were Shvedkov, who had just got back from reviewing the trenches; Company Commander Kovalyov; and Ganiev, the Tatar platoon commander.

'Overall, our losses are around sixty-five per cent,' Filyashkin said to Shvedkov. 'I've ordered the sergeant majors and sergeants to take command of their units. They're good fighters, they won't panic.'

The command post had been destroyed in the first minutes of the German assault and Filyashkin and Shvedkov were sitting in a pit roofed with logs from a shed beside the station. The last few hours had blackened their faces, gluing their cheeks to their cheekbones and leaving a dark crust on their lips.

'What should we do with the dead?' asked the sergeant major. He was up above them, on all fours, looking down into the pit.

'I've already told you,' said Filyashkin. 'Take them down to the cellar.' He went on crossly, 'I knew it – we're already short of F1 and RGD grenades.'

'The commanders separately?' asked the sergeant major.

'Why?' Shvedkov replied tersely. 'They were killed together, so let them lie together.'

'Very good,' said the sergeant major. 'Anyway, it's hard to tell the commanders apart now. Men's collars and tabs have been torn off and everyone looks much the same.'

'Two of our machine guns have been destroyed,' Filyashkin said in a preoccupied tone. 'And five anti-tank rifles and three mortars are now out of action.'

The sergeant major crept off. Used cartridges lying on the ground squeaked and tinkled.

Shvedkov opened a school exercise book and began to write. Filyashkin stuck his head up out of the pit, looked around and sat down again. 'They won't start up again until morning,' he said. 'What are you writing?'

'A political report for the regimental commissar,' said Shvedkov. 'I've described the various acts of heroism, and now I'm listing the dead and the circumstances of their death. Only I've got muddled. Was it Igumnov who was killed by a bullet, and Konanykin by shrapnel? And which was killed first? I can't remember. Was it seventeen hundred hours when Igumnov was killed?'

They both glanced at the dark corner where Igumnov's body had been lying until a few minutes ago.

'No use writing a chronicle,' said Filyashkin. 'You won't get it to the regiment now. We're cut off.'

'True,' said Shvedkov. Nevertheless, he went on writing. Then he said, 'Igumnov's death was particularly stupid. He half got to his feet to call a messenger – and that was the end of him.'

'All deaths are stupid,' said Filyashkin. 'There's no clever way to get killed.'

Filyashkin did not want to talk about dead comrades; he was well aware of the value of the stern, sometimes life-saving grace of emotional numbness during combat. If he were spared, he would recall his comrades in years to come. One quiet evening, he would feel a lump in his throat. Tears would well up in his eyes and he would say, 'He was a good chief of staff. A splendid, straightforward fellow. Yes, I remember him as if it were yesterday. When the Germans attacked, he tore up some letters he kept in his pockets. It was as if he knew. And then he took out a comb and ran it over his hair, and he looked at me.'

But in combat the heart goes cold and stone-like, and it's best to let it stay that way. In any case, no heart can comprehend all the blood and death of battle.

Shvedkov looked through what he'd written, sighed and said, 'They're fine lads. Our political work hasn't been wasted. They're brave, and they've got cool heads. One man said to me, "Don't worry, comrade Commissar, we understand our work and we'll do our duty!" And another said, "Better men than us have met their deaths already."'

There were two explosions nearby.

Shvedkov looked up. 'Are they starting up again?'

'No, they'll carry on like this until morning,' Filyashkin said condescendingly. 'A few shots every now and then, just to stop us from sleeping. But it's been hard work! Between five and six I machine-gunned a good thirty of the shits. There was no end to them.'

'Let me record the details,' said Shvedkov, moistening his copying pencil.

'Drop it,' said Filyashkin. 'What's the use of your scribbling?'

'What do you mean?' replied Shvedkov – and he began to write. Then, suddenly remembering, he said, 'Comrade Battalion Commander, I've been entrusted with a gift for our heroic girls.' He was aware that, but for this confounded gift, he might not have been sent back so promptly. He might still be sitting in the political-department bunker, drinking tea and writing a routine report. But this thought did not occasion him either regret or annoyance. He looked questioningly at Filyashkin and asked, 'Who should we give this to? Gnatyuk, perhaps? She's shown true heroism today.'

'You know best,' Filyashkin replied, with exaggerated casualness. Shvedkov called a soldier and ordered him to summon Gnatyuk. 'As long as she's still alive,' he added.

'Of course,' the soldier replied morosely. 'There's not much I can do if she isn't.'

'She's alive all right, I've checked,' Filyashkin said with a smile. He shook the dust off his sleeve and wiped his face. He was constantly sniffing; the air was full of bitter smoke, thick, greasy soot and pulverised plaster – the disturbing, intoxicating smell of the front line.

'How about a drink?' said Shvedkov, who hardly ever drank.

Everything had turned upside down during these last few hours. The delicate and sensitive had become coarse, and the coarse and gross had softened. The thoughtless had turned thoughtful, and the usually punctilious were waiting for death with gay, despairing abandon, spitting on the floor, and laughing and shouting as if they were drunk.

'Well, how do you feel about the life you've led?' Filyashkin asked out of the blue. 'The hour's drawing near when we have to account for ourselves. Is everything in your Party history as it should be? Are there any incidents in your past that might compromise you? If so, speak freely. Let me write off your sins.'

'What's got into you, comrade Filyashkin? I don't understand such talk, especially from a battalion commander.'[282]

'You and your scribbling – you're very strange,' said Filyashkin. 'Anyone would think you expect to stay alive' – he thought for a moment before coming out with what, down in the pit, seemed an inconceivable length of time – 'for another six months. Why don't we talk instead? Tell me – do you think I did wrong with Lena Gnatyuk?'

'I do. But who knows? I could be mistaken,' Shvedkov replied. 'If need be, the Party commission will correct me. But it's not the conduct I expect from a commander – and that's what I've written.'

'You're right, you're absolutely right. I'll say it myself. There's no need to wait for any Party commission. I did wrong and I know it.'

Feeling a sudden surge of warmth towards Filyashkin, Shvedkov said, 'Oh, come on, let's have a drink together! The regulation hundred grams,[283] while it's still quiet.'

'No, I'd rather keep a clear head,' Filyashkin replied. He laughed; Shvedkov had criticized him only too often for drinking too much.

Up above them appeared the face of Lena Gnatyuk.

'Permission to come down, comrade Battalion Commander?' she asked.

'Yes, quick, before you get yourself killed!' Filyashkin replied. He moved aside to make room for the young woman. 'Give her her present, Commissar. I'll be a witness.'

Before going to the command post, Lena Gnatyuk had spent some time trying to clean herself up. But the water from her small flask could do little to wash away black dust and soot that had penetrated deep into her skin. She had given her nose a good firm rub with a handkerchief, but that had not made it any cleaner or paler. She had polished her boots with a scrap of bandage, but that had not made them shine. She had tried to tuck her dishevelled plait under her side cap, but her hair was stiff and unruly from the many layers of dust; she looked like a little village girl with loose strands slipping out onto her ears and her forehead.

Her tunic was too tight for her full figure and it was smeared with black blood. Her trousers were too big for her and had slipped down onto her hips. She was wearing large, broad-toed boots and she had several bags hanging from her shoulders. Her fingernails were short and black, and she was trying not to show her hands, which had carried out much good, merciful work. She felt awkward and ugly.

'Comrade Gnatyuk,' Shvedkov said solemnly, 'I have been asked to pass on this gift to you in recognition of your devoted service. It is a present from the women of America to our girls fighting on the Volga. The parcels were delivered by special plane, straight from America to the front.'

He held out a large rectangular parcel, wrapped in crisp parchment paper tied with a plaited silk cord.

'I serve the Soviet Union,'[284] she replied in a hoarse voice as she took the parcel from the commissar's hands.

In his ordinary, everyday voice, Shvedkov said, 'Open it now. We're curious too. We want to know what the American women have sent you.'

Lena removed the cord and began to unwrap the parcel. The crinkly paper squeaked and rustled. There were many different items inside, some very small, and she squatted down to prevent anything falling out and getting lost. There was a beautiful woollen blouse, embroidered with a red, blue and green pattern; a fluffy bathrobe with a hood; two pairs of lacy trousers with matching shirts adorned with little ribbons; three pairs of silk stockings; some tiny lace-embroidered handkerchiefs; a white dress made from fine lawn, also trimmed with lace; a jar of some fragrant lotion; and a flask of perfume tied with a broad ribbon.

Lena looked at the two commanders. There was a moment of silence around the station, as if to prevent anything from disturbing the grace and delicacy of her expression. Her look said a great deal: not only that she knew she would never now become a mother but also that she took a certain pride in her harsh fate.

As she stood there in the pit, in her soldier's boots and badly fitting uniform, about to refuse these exquisite gifts, Lena Gnatyuk looked overwhelmingly feminine.

'What use is all this?' she said. 'I don't want it.'

The two men felt troubled. They understood something of the young woman's feelings – her pride, her understanding that she was doomed and her mistaken belief that she looked awkward and ugly.

Shvedkov felt the edge of the woollen blouse between his fingers and said in embarrassment, 'This is good wool. It's not just any old cloth.'

'I'll leave everything here. It's no use to me,' Lena repeated. She put the parcel down in a corner and wiped her hands on her tunic.

Filyashkin examined the contents of the parcel and said, 'These stockings aren't so very strong – they'll ladder in no time at all. But they're pretty. You could wear them to a ball.'

'And when will I be going to a ball?' Lena retorted.

At this point Shvedkov got angry, which helped him to resolve a thorny international issue of a kind he had not encountered before.

'All right then. If you don't want them, don't take them. Quite right! What's got into those people? Do they think Stalingrad is some kind of holiday resort? Are they making fun of us? Silk stockings and bath-robes – whatever next!' He glanced at Filyashkin and said, 'I'll go and have a look round now. I need to have a word with the men.'

'All right, you go ahead, and I'll follow,' Filyashkin said hurriedly. 'I've just checked the area around here. Move carefully – there are German snipers only 150 metres away. The least sound – and you're a goner.'

'Permission to leave?' Lena asked as Shvedkov crept away.

'Just a moment,' said Filyashkin. He always felt awkward when he was first left alone with a young woman, exchanging the tone of a commander for that of a lover. 'Listen, Lena,' he went on, 'this is important. Forgive me. During the march I behaved grossly and presumptuously. Stay here so we can say a proper goodbye. We may not live through another day. There's nothing that won't be written off by the war.'

'As far as I'm concerned, comrade Battalion Commander, there isn't anything to be written off,' Lena replied. Taking a deep breath, she went on, 'First, there's no need for anyone at all to forgive you. I'm not a little girl, I know what's what and I'm responsible for myself. When I went to your hut, I knew very well what I was doing. Second, I won't be staying here – I must return to the aid post. Third, I've got my own uniform and I don't need any of these gifts. Permission to leave?'

Her last sentence no longer sounded like a conventional formula.

'Lena,' said Filyashkin. 'Lena ... do you really not understand?' His voice sounded very strange. Lena looked at him in astonishment. He got to his feet, as if to say something important, but then he just said with a smile, 'All right then.' After pointing towards the west, he went on in a calm, flat voice, 'Don't let yourself be taken prisoner. Keep that captured pistol at hand, the one I gave you, just in case ...'

She shrugged and replied, 'And fourth, I can shoot myself just as well with my own revolver.'

And she left, not looking back at the senior lieutenant, nor at the fine, useless rags now lying on the ground.

43

In the twilight, as she made her way to the aid post, Lena Gnatyuk came to the 3rd Company's command post.

A sub-machine-gunner challenged her, but he recognized her at once and said, 'Ah, Senior Sergeant, please pass.'

She felt momentarily disorientated: was Senior Sergeant Gnatyuk really the same being as the young girl who, two years earlier, in Podyvotye, in the province of Sumy, had worked as a brigade leader during the beet harvest? Was she really the girl who had come back home in the evening and called out merrily to her mother, 'Come on, Máma, give me some food! I'm starving!'?

Kovalyov was asleep, leaning against a large beam that propped up the basement ceiling. There was a candle nearby, stuck on top of an upturned brick. Hand grenades lay scattered about the floor, like netted fish thrown onto the ground.

Kovalyov's sub-machine gun lay on his lap. His blackened hands were clasping his cherished kitbag against his stomach.

Lena walked over to him, stumbling on the empty sub-machine-gun magazines that littered the floor.

'Misha, Misha!' she called out. She touched him on the sleeve, then took his hand. Out of habit, she felt his pulse.

'What is it?' he asked. He opened his eyes but didn't move. 'Is that you, Lena?'

'Are you tired?' she asked.

'Just resting a little,' he replied. As if excusing himself, he went on, 'Yes, the sergeant major's on duty, and I'm resting.'

'Misha!' she repeated quietly. 'I've come to say goodbye.'

'Off to the rear, are you? To the other bank?'

'To the other world, more likely. Like all of us.'

Kovalyov yawned.

'Misha,' she said quietly.

'Hm?'

'Are you angry with me?'

'Why do you ask?'

'Misha, you don't understand.'

'Let me be, Lena,' he replied. 'Really, there's nothing to say. I've got a girl waiting for me back at home. What's there to say goodbye about?'

She suddenly clung to him, laying her head on his shoulder.

'Misha, we may only have one more hour,' she said hurriedly. 'What I did that night doesn't mean anything. I was being stupid – surely you can see that? There were so many wounded today. They kept bringing in more and more of them – and I rushed over every time in case you were there ... Something came over me that night. I don't know why, sometimes people just don't know what they're doing. Ask any of the girls from the medical unit – they all know how much I love you. I've just come from the battalion command post. I didn't even want to look at the man. Please, please, I beg you – believe me! Believe me! Don't be so obstinate! Why won't you understand?'

'Maybe I don't understand, comrade Gnatyuk ... But you understand too much. With me, you get what you see. I'm simple, I've no secrets. Go ahead, understand all you like. But I don't need to 'cos, unlike some folks, I don't cheat.'

And as if seeking support for his difficult decision, Kovalyov held his kitbag still closer, stroking it with his palm.

For a few moments they said nothing. Then, in a loud voice, he said, 'You have permission to leave, comrade Senior Sergeant.'

He wanted to put an end to this conversation, and these were the words that came to him. He could feel in every cell of his body, in his back and in the nape of his neck, how deeply wrong these wooden words sounded.

There were two soldiers lying on the ground. They both sat up and looked around sleepily, wondering who had just been reporting to their company commander.

44

Yakhontov was lying on a pile of greatcoats removed from the dead. He was not moaning or groaning. His eyes dark, his pupils dilated by suffering, he was gazing almost greedily at the sky, which was dotted with stars.

'Go away, you're hurting me!' he yelled in a whisper to the orderly trying to move him. 'Let me be, your hands are like stone!'

Next, he could see the face of a woman, and he could sense her breath. Tears were falling on his forehead and cheeks. He thought they were drops of rain.

Then he realized that they were tears. If they seemed hot, and if the hand now stroking him seemed hot, it was because life was departing from him. The touch of a living body felt hot to him, just as it might if he were a piece of cold metal or wood. And he thought it was because of him that the woman was crying.

'You're good and kind. Don't cry, I'll feel better in a while,' he said, but the young woman didn't hear this. He thought he was pronouncing words, but all she heard was a gurgle.

Lena Gnatyuk did not sleep that night.

'Don't shout, don't shout, the Germans are very close,' she said to a soldier with two broken legs. Stroking his forehead and cheeks, she went on, 'Be patient. In the morning we'll send you to the army hospital. They'll put your legs in plaster.'

She went over to another of the wounded. The soldier with the broken legs called out, 'Mother, come back, I need to ask you something.'

'In a minute, my son,' she replied. To her, and to everyone there it seemed entirely natural for a man with grey stubble to be calling her 'Mother', and for her, aged twenty-four, to be calling him 'my son'.

'Will they sedate me?' he asked. 'It won't hurt when they put me in plaster?'

'It won't hurt. Be brave. Be brave until morning.'

In the dawn light, as it went into a dive over the railway station, the nose and wings of the Stuka turned pink. A high-explosive bomb fell in the pit where Lena Gnatyuk and two orderlies were caring for the wounded. Every last breath of life was cut short.

A cloud of dust and smoke, reddish brown in the light of the rising sun, hung in the air for a long time. Then a breeze off the Volga dispersed it over the steppe to the west of the city.

45

By eleven o'clock in the morning the situation around the railway station was truly hellish. Amid dust and smoke from fierce mortar and artillery fire, amid black clouds from exploding bombs, to the accompaniment of whining aeroplane engines and the rattle of Messerschmitt machine guns, the battalion – or rather its last remnants – continued to fight off the German attack.

Out of their minds from pain, men lay in pools of blood or crawled about, desperately searching for shelter. Cries and groans mingled with the sound of yelled-out commands and bursts of fire from machine guns and anti-tank rifles. But each time the German artillery fell silent, each time the German foot soldiers, bent almost double, ran forward – each time the Germans thought the battle was over, the mute, dead, ploughed-up ruins of the railway station and its surrounding buildings came back to life.

Filyashkin was lying on a pile of used cartridges, holding down the trigger of a machine gun. He glanced round at Shvedkov, who had a sub-machine gun. Shvedkov was a poor shot, but he was firing away diligently.

The Germans were attacking yet again.

'Stop!' Filyashkin called out to himself, realizing that he needed to move the machine gun to a new location. Seizing hold of the barrel, he shouted to his number two, a young soldier who was looking at his commander with devotion and reverence, 'Quick – help me drag it over here, beside this wall!'

While they were setting up the machine gun, Filyashkin was wounded in the left shoulder. He thought this was a very slight wound, a mere cut.

'Bandage my shoulder!' he said to Shvedkov, unbuttoning his tunic collar. 'Use some of that tat Lena Gnatyuk didn't want.' But then he pushed Shvedkov's hand away. 'No, they're at it again,' he said, and began aiming his machine gun. 'I began as a machine-gunner,' he muttered, 'and now I'm a machine-gunner once more.' Then he turned to his number two, to ask for another ammo belt.

Filyashkin was issuing commands to himself and then carrying them out himself. He was, at one and the same time, sub-unit commander, forward observer and machine-gunner.

'Enemy 300 metres ahead and to the left!' he shouted in the role of observer.

'Aim at attacking infantry, half a belt, continuous fire!' he shouted in the role of commander. Gripping the backplate handle, he slowly moved it from left to right.

The sight of some grey-green Germans leaping up from behind a mound made him almost choke with fury. Rather than thinking that he had to defend himself against a sly, crafty, advancing enemy, he saw himself as the attacker.

A single simple thought, like an echo from the grinding fire of his machine gun, now took up all Senior Lieutenant Filyashkin's consciousness. This thought furnished him with an explanation for everything of importance: his success and disappointments, his feeling of condescension to those of his peers who were still mere lieutenants, and his envy of those who had already reached the rank of major or lieutenant colonel. 'I began as a machine-gunner and I'm ending as a machine-gunner.' This simple, clear thought was an answer to all that had troubled him during the last few hours. To machine-gunner Filyashkin, everything bad and painful in his life had ceased to matter.

Shvedkov never managed to bandage Filyashkin's shoulder with strips of cloth torn off a bathrobe. Filyashkin suddenly lost consciousness, smashed his chin against the back of the machine gun and fell dead to the ground.

A German artillery observer had been watching Filyashkin's machine gun for some time. When it went quiet, he suspected a ruse.

Shvedkov never kissed the battalion commander's dead lips. He never had time to mourn him, nor to feel the burden of command he should have assumed after Filyashkin's death. Shvedkov was killed by a well-aimed shell that landed right in the embrasure of his little hiding place.

*

Kovalyov was now the battalion's senior commander, but he did not know this – he had lost contact with Filyashkin at the beginning of the German attack.

Kovalyov no longer looked in the least like the shock-headed, bright-eyed young man who, two days before, had been rereading inscriptions on photographs and verses copied down in a school exercise book. Not even his own mother would have recognized this exhausted-looking man as her son – with his hoarse voice, inflamed eyes and locks of grey, dust-layered hair glued to his forehead.

He was severely concussed and his ears were clicking and ringing. His head felt as if it were on fire. Blood was pouring from his nose, tickling his chin and soaking his chest, and he had to keep wiping it away with his hand.

Walking had become difficult. He had fallen to the ground several times, crawling some distance on all fours before he could get back onto his feet.

Despite the hours of shelling and repeated infantry attacks, his company had suffered somewhat fewer casualties than the battalion's other companies and sub-units.

Kovalyov had gathered his remaining men into a tight circle and they were keeping up a surprisingly dense, concentrated fire. When the Germans attacked, it was as if the dead took up arms again and were standing shoulder to shoulder with the living.

Through the dust and smoke he could see tense, grim faces. His men were firing their sub-machine guns, flattening themselves against the ground while shells exploded around them, leaping to their feet again and shooting, then falling silent as they watched the grey-green creatures advance from all sides.

These moments of silence as the enemy drew nearer brought with them a complex mixture of fear and joy.

Backs, arms and necks tightened. Fingers gripped the levers of hand grenades, pulled the safety pins and waited. All the tension the men felt as the Germans approached was concentrated in their grip.

And then the air would fill with dust and the din would make it impossible to think.

To Kovalyov the sound of the Soviet grenades was entirely distinct from that of the German grenades – as distinct as the voices of people from Nizhny Novgorod, with their long, accented 'o's, from the guttural cries of Berliners and Bavarians. And even if the defenders' yells were inaudible in the din, there was no doubt that the anti-tank grenades booming over the railway station, over the city as a whole and even over the Volga, were yelling out the most terrible of Russian curses.

The dust would disperse. From the stony murk would emerge piles of rubble, dead bodies, smashed German tanks, a gun lying on its side, a collapsed bridge and abandoned, eyeless houses. And as the German infantry once again got ready to attack, their artillery would return, with renewed determination, to its task of pounding people and stone.

Kovalyov lived through a great deal in these minutes.

Sometimes his consciousness would dim and nothing remained but a sense of speed and desperate determination, as if there were no longer anything in the world but grey running figures and the grinding of tanks. The Germans would advance in small groups, usually on a diagonal. Sometimes it seemed they were only pretending to advance and that their real aim was to retreat. It looked as if someone were pushing them from behind and they were charging forward to escape this invisible pressure, then running about from side to side before they scattered and turned back. Kovalyov would want to put an end to their deceptive game. Calmly and carefully, he would choose his target, his sharp eyes swiftly determining whether an enemy had dropped flat, found shelter, fallen down dead or was just slightly wounded.

Sometimes the men running towards Kovalyov seemed mere cardboard figures, harmless and with no will of their own; sometimes he had a clear vision of men seized by the horror of death. Sometimes not only his mind but his whole body – legs, arms, shoulders and back – would sense that these men, no matter how great their numbers, had only one aim, that they were moved by a frenzied determination to reach the small pit by an overhanging wall where a Red Army company commander lay hidden, concussed, covered in blood, his index finger aching from the stiff trigger of his sub-machine gun. Then he would feel tense and furious; his breath would come only in short gasps and everything would disappear except for his tally of bullets, his thoughts about the new magazine lying beside him and his concern about how far the German soldiers might run while he was reloading: might they reach the crooked pole with strands of wire hanging down from it? Might they even get to the shack with no roof?

Kovalyov shouted, and his voice merged with the sound of his sub-machine gun. It seemed as if it were his own hands, and the fury within him, that were making the barrel so hot.

Now and again the tension would let up. There would be a glimpse of clear blue sky and a sudden silence – not the feverish silence, worse than the thunder of guns, that heralded a German attack, but a peaceful, restorative silence he wanted to last for ever.

And then a random, or not so random, memory would flash to the surface of his mind. It was early in the morning and a young girl with pale bare arms was rinsing her linen on the bank of a river; on her left arm he could see a slight scar from a smallpox vaccination. She had twisted a wet sheet into a rope and was beating this rope against a dark wooden board. Each blow gave rise to multiple echoes and sent sparkling waterdrops flying into the air. The girl glanced at Kovalyov; her half-open lips were smiling, but there was something challenging in her eyes. He could see her breasts sway as she bent forward and straightened up again, and he could sense the living warmth of her body, along with the smell of young grass and cool water. She was aware how greedily he was looking at her, and this both pleased and upset her. She liked him, and somehow it was both strange and funny that the two of them were so very young.

And then another memory. Lieutenant Shaposhnikov, his pale, thick-lipped travelling companion from only a few months ago, was lying on an upper bunk in a railway carriage. He was coughing, trying to smoke but not knowing how, holding one hand beneath his cigarette to stop the ash falling onto the passengers sitting on the lower bunk. And then the two of them were sitting at a table with a rich spread of food, in a wealthy city apartment, in this same Stalingrad – this same 'inhabited point' – somewhere to the north-east of the little wall he was now lying beneath, and a beautiful young woman was looking at him with amusement. Several other people were also looking at him: a stout military doctor with a major's bars on her collar tabs; two old men – one with a large nose and a broad forehead, the other with thick black hair and a rather sullen expression; and a dark-eyed, twitchy young man who had recited some poems. He had copied them down in his exercise book.

These people had been kind and charming, but he now felt both irritation with them and an uncertain sense of his own superiority over them.

If that beautiful woman with the pearl-white neck could see him now, she would understand why he'd got so upset and angry. What they had been talking about was death – nothing less than death. No one at that table had had the right to make silly, clever jokes about the Red Army's long retreat. The way they'd looked at him as if he were a child, the condescending tone of their questions. As if all they could see was that he was from a village, that he was still young and that he'd only just graduated from his training course.

His heart and soul, however, really were those of a child. His experience of life, his dreams and anxieties, his moments of rudeness, his clear faith and his doubts – everything about him was still adolescent. And he was now living through a bitter, merciless fulfilment of his adolescent dreams. In the last hours of his life he had grown up;

he had become the stern, unshakeable figure he had so longed to see when, long ago, before going to bed, he had frowned enigmatically into a little pocket mirror backed with crinkly red paper. And his new strength and manliness would have been evident to anyone who could see him – not only to his friends and fellow villagers, not only to his mother and the girl who had once given him a photograph stamped 'with a passionate kiss', but even to his fiercest enemies.

Wanting to share his feelings with some other person, wanting to save them from being lost for ever, Kovalyov took out his little exercise book, touched the photograph wrapped in cellophane and glanced at the poems copied in a large beautiful hand by a young man who was now someone else. He pulled out a sheet of paper and began to write a report.

> *1130 hours, 20-09-42.*
> *Report*
> *To Guards Senior Lieutenant Filyashkin.*
> *The current situation:*
> *The enemy is constantly on the offensive, trying to surround my company and to infiltrate sub-machine-gunners behind our lines. He has twice sent tanks against our positions, but his attacks have been repelled. Not until they can trample over my dead body will the Fritzes achieve their aim. My guardsmen are standing their ground, ready to die the death of the brave but not to let the enemy through our defences. Let the whole country know of the heroism of the 3rd Rifle Company. While the company commander is alive, not one of the fuckers will pass. They'll have to wait until the company commander is killed or seriously wounded. The commander of the 3rd Company now finds himself in a difficult situation. He is unwell, physically weak and suffering from loss of hearing. His head spins. There is bleeding from his nose and he keeps falling to the ground. In spite of everything, the 3rd Guards Rifle Company is not retreating. We shall die as heroes, for the city of Stalin. May the Soviet land prove to be the enemy's grave. I trust not one of these vermin gets through. The 3rd Company will give all its Guards' blood for Stalingrad. We will be the heroes of the city's liberation.*

Having signed the report and folded it in four (while he was writing, the white paper turned dark brown from the blood on his palm), Kovalyov called Rysev and said, 'Deliver this to the battalion commander!'[285]

Then he opened a small metal locket hanging on a chain around his neck. It was a present from his parents, in case he was seriously wounded or killed. Above the official details – name, rank, position, unit, address and blood group, he wrote, 'Whosoever dares examine the content of this medallion, I ask him to direct it to my home address. My sons! I'm in the next world. May you avenge my blood. Forward to victory, my friends, for the motherland, for the glorious cause of Stalin!'

Kovalyov was not even married and he had no idea why he wrote to sons who did not exist. But he needed to. He wanted a sombre, honourable memory of him to endure in the world. He was a husband of the war. He did not want to accept that the war was cutting his life short, that he would never know fatherhood or be a husband to a woman of his own. He was writing these words a few minutes before his death. He was struggling for his own future time. Aged only twenty, he did not want to yield to death. Here too he remained stubborn, determined to conquer.

Rysev returned from the battalion command post, surprised to be still alive.

'There's no one there, comrade Lieutenant,' he reported. 'There's no one to hand the report to. Everyone's dead. There's not a single messenger left.'

But Rysev was unable even to hand the report back. Kovalyov lay dead, his chest on his kitbag, his hand on his loaded sub-machine gun.

Rysev lay down beside him and took hold of the sub-machine gun, nudging Kovalyov's body a little to the right with one shoulder. He could see that the Germans were getting ready to attack again. They were gathering in small groups, darting behind burnt-out tanks and gesticulating to one another. As well as the sound of shell bursts, he could now hear, coming from somewhere off to the side, the busy rattle of their sub-machine guns.

Rysev counted the remaining grenades and took a quick look at Kovalyov. He could see a short dark notch on his forehead, between his eyebrows. The wind was catching his fair hair. His eyes were half hidden beneath his delicate eyelashes and he was looking sweetly and knowingly down at the ground, smiling at something that he alone knew, that no one but he would ever know.

'Instantaneous – on the bridge of the nose,' Rysev said to himself, appalled by death's swiftness, yet also envious.

46

Kovalyov was the last of the commanders to be killed, forty-eight hours after the battalion had captured the railway station.

The sergeants, too, were also nearly all either dead or seriously wounded.

Paralysed by fear, Senior Sergeant Dodonov lay flat on the ground. No one spoke to him or took any notice of him.

Sergeant Major Marchenko also lay motionless, blood flowing from his nose and ears; he had been severely concussed by the same shell that had killed Kovalyov.

But Kovalyov's death did not lessen the determination of the rank-and-file soldiers. While they were still alive, Konanykin, Filyashkin, Shvedkov, Kovalyov and the political instructors and platoon commanders had fought like ordinary Red Army soldiers – and this had seemed entirely normal and to be expected. After the commanders had all been killed, a rank-and-file soldier assumed command, and this seemed equally natural.

In everyday life there are many people who have what it takes to be a leader, although their gifts are not always apparent. Their greatness lies not in their ability to respond adroitly to superficial social changes but in their strength of character, in their capacity to remain true to themselves. When life's dramas are being played out at the very deepest level, it is these people who come forward, whose modest strength is suddenly recognized.

Nobody appointed or elected Vavilov as their commander, but it was in no way surprising that the battalion's remaining soldiers should recognize his abilities, that they should understand him to be as strong and capable a leader as the army commander himself.

Even before the war there had been moments of crisis when it was Vavilov who ended up taking charge. This had happened when he and his fellow workers were ploughing virgin soil. It had happened in the forest, when a team of loggers was felling pines, and it had happened on a windy autumn day, when the whole village was threatened by a forest fire. The other villagers were concerned only with putting out fires in their own huts and Vavilov had taken command, ordering them to attend to the kolkhoz grain store and to the school, which was already smoking. He had also once raised his axe over the head of the boatman. The village idiot, Andryushka Orlov, was on the verge of drowning and the boatman had been reluctant to go out and save him.

Now too, and without even thinking about it, others began to turn to Vavilov for advice, and to gather around him. And when Vavilov ordered them to share all they had, nobody hid biscuits in their pockets or kept quiet about the water still left in their flasks.

Vavilov divided the soldiers into small groups. He had eaten bread with these men and he had marched beside them. He knew everyone's strengths and weaknesses, and his sense of who to put in command of each group was unerring.

He further tightened the ring of defence, placing the men where they had clear sight lines and stout walls to shelter behind.

For his own group, at the centre of the ring, he chose Rezchikov, Usurov, Mulyarchuk and Rysev. Whenever one of the other groups was under particular pressure, he quickly went to their aid.

He set aside a reserve supply of cartridges, magazines, grenades and fuses, and he positioned the machine-gun crews behind a thick concrete wall that only the very heaviest of shells could penetrate.

In only a few days the soldiers had learned the grim art of urban warfare. Just as they understood the functioning of a labour team, they now understood the functioning of a storm group. They had worked out its ideal size and the laws that determined its success. Each man was important, but his importance could only be realized if the group worked well together.

They knew which were their most valuable weapons: the F-1 hand grenade, the sub-machine gun and the company machine gun. They christened the F-1 the 'Fenka' – the unwritten name by which it later became known to every Soviet soldier. Vavilov also discovered the brute power of a sapper's spade.

Rezchikov, sullen and gloomy during the long march on the east bank, had recovered his spirits. The ever-sensible Zaichenkov, whom no one had ever heard swear, had become a wild firebrand, cursing after every word. Usurov, once greedy, quarrelsome and acquisitive, was now obliging and generous; he had given half his tobacco ration and all his bread ration to Rysev. But no one had changed more dramatically than the sickly and seemingly slow-witted Mulyarchuk. He was now barely recognizable. Even his face had changed; the wrinkles on his forehead, which had given him a look of constant bewilderment, had fused into a furrow of intimidating severity; his raised white eyebrows now met at the bridge of his nose, blackened by dust and soot. He had twice been trapped in a trench by a German tank, and he had twice crawled out and, from an unimaginably short distance, destroyed the tank with a blast grenade. In the end he had collapsed back into the trench, severely concussed and coughing up earth and blood.

Some of those once most reserved had become big-hearted and emotionally generous. Some of those once most cheerful and carefree were now grim and taciturn.

Vavilov, however, remained the same as always. He was the man his wife, family and neighbours had known; the man who had sat in his hut in the evenings, dipping his bread in a mug of milk; the man who had worked in field and forest, or out on the road.

War shows us many things. While life is easy for them, the weak in spirit can appear strong and resourceful; they can fool not only others but also themselves. A sudden difficulty, though, can reveal their weakness. There are others who appear quiet and timid and who enjoy little success in life; they are thought weak and often end up mistakenly believing themselves to be weak. But when put to the test, they reveal their true strength, astonishing everyone around them. And then there are people of the highest mettle of all, people who remain true to themselves even while undergoing the most terrible ordeals; their smile, their gestures, the clarity of their minds, their calm voices, their gravity, their openness, their smallest quirks and the fundamental laws of their being – all remain the same during a storm as during times of calm.

Come nightfall, the soldiers still occupying the station buildings were overwhelmed by exhaustion. They fell asleep in mid-conversation, to the sound of gunfire and shell bursts.

And then, at two in the morning, in total darkness, they were faced with something new and terrible: a night attack.

The Germans did not send up flares. They crept along the ground, coming from every point of the compass. All night long the carnage continued. The stars disappeared behind clouds and the darkness deepened – perhaps to keep men from glimpsing the hate and fury in one another's eyes.

Everything became a weapon: knives, spades, bricks, the steel heels of boots.

The darkness was full of screams, of groans and wheezes, of pistol shots, rifle shots and short bursts of machine-gun fire, of the last bubbles and gurgles of departing life.

The Germans attacked in overwhelming numbers. Wherever there was the sound of a fight, there would suddenly be a dozen of them against one or two Russians. The Germans fought with knives and fists. They went for the throat. They were frenzied, furious.

They called out to one another as seldom as possible, since every word of German elicited a shot from a Red Army soldier hiding in the ruins. It was the same when they used red and green flashlights to signal to one another – quick shots would immediately force them to turn off the flashlight and fall to the ground. And a minute later there would be another scuffle, with gasps, groans and the grating of metal.

Nevertheless, the Germans were evidently following a clear plan.

The ring of defence continued to tighten. Pits and foxholes that had sheltered Red Army soldiers went quiet; a few minutes later there would be furtive winks of red and green light and whispers in a foreign tongue. And then a vicious, desperate cry, a clatter of stone and the sound of shots from some other place. And a minute later, a green light would flash out from this new place.

Yellow lightning, a solitary hand grenade, a flurry of movement, a piercing whistle – and then silence, followed by a quick green wink and an answering red wink. Another silence, another sudden yellow flame, as if someone had flung open the door of the village smithy and immediately slammed it shut. Another grenade, a long-drawn-out 'A-a-a-a!' – and then the living cry would break off, as if plunged into silence. And a careful, watchful green light would flash closer still.

To everyone listening from a distance, it was clear that the battalion's struggle was almost over.

But whispers of Russian could still be heard. A few men were still quietly stacking stones and reinforcing walls, preparing to continue the fight at dawn.

Their position was surrounded by pits and craters. In the darkness, it was impregnable.

Rysev was lying on one side. Breathing heavily, he whispered to the men lying close beside him, 'They cornered me like a wolf. I got away by the skin of my teeth. Just a slight wound to my left shoulder. As for Dodonov, I heard the slippery bastard creeping away to surrender.'

'Maybe they killed him?' said Rezchikov.

'No, I checked everything. I could see his sub-machine gun and his grenades – but there was no Dodonov. The fucking shit.'

In the dark he groped for Vavilov's hand and said, 'It's good to be with men I can trust.'

'Don't worry, we won't leave you,' said Rezchikov.

'You mustn't,' said Rysev. 'I'm wounded.'

Rysev had lost a lot of blood and his head was spinning. There were moments when he forgot where he was. He would mutter away for a while, then fall silent.

'Vera, come here,' he would call in a calm, clear voice. And then, after a brief silence, 'Vera, what's keeping you?'

He couldn't understand why his wife was being so slow. For a while he said nothing. Then a new thought came to his feverish mind, 'Semyonovich ... Pyotr ... What do you think? Will they open a second front soon?'

'Sh!' said Vavilov. 'Be quiet.'

'I want to know if they're going to open a second front. Yes or no?' Rysev whispered angrily. Then, at the top of his voice, 'Can't you hear me? I want to know. Or are you that blind you think it doesn't concern you?'

Rezchikov put his hand over Rysev's mouth. 'Stop it, you fool!'

'Leave me alone, leave me alone,' muttered Rysev. He was choking, trying to push his mate's hand away.

The Germans heard. A few bursts of blood-coloured tracer fire whizzed overhead and some Germans called out anxiously to one another by their first names. Then everything went quiet. Most likely, the Germans had decided it was just a dying man calling out in delirium. Which it was.

'Who's there?' Vavilov asked abruptly.

There was the quiet knock of a falling stone. Someone was creeping towards them.

'It's me, it's me!' came the voice of Usurov. 'And you're still alive! I thought the Germans had finished you off.' After a pause, he added, 'Give me a smoke!'

'First, cover yourself with your greatcoat,' said Vavilov.

Usurov lay down beside Rysev and very slowly, repeatedly snuffling and clearing his throat, pulled his greatcoat over his head.

'How do I recognize them in the dark?' Usurov wondered aloud, sticking his head out from under his greatcoat. His need to talk to his comrades must have been stronger than his wish to smoke. He put out his cigarette and said in a quick whisper, 'One of them was creeping along. There was something different about him. He didn't move quite like us and the noise he made was different too, more like the noise of an animal. But I didn't dare shoot, I just used my hands.'

Mulyarchuk was building walls, working quickly and quietly.

'You're a good builder,' whispered Rezchikov, not wanting to hear what Usurov was saying.

'I used to be a stove maker,' Mulyarchuk replied. 'I was thinking just now how good life used to be. After work, I would go straight back home. I lived in the district town.'

'It's quietened down now,' said Vavilov. 'Probably they'll stay quiet till dawn. But don't talk too loud!'

'Are you married?' Usurov asked Mulyarchuk.

'No, I lived with my mother, in Polonnoye,' Mulyarchuk answered, glad to feel that his life was of interest to someone. He went on, 'My mother's a good woman. And I was a good son to her, I gave her everything I earned. But she worried a lot. If there was an evening meeting or if anything held me up, she'd come out and look for me. I didn't drink and I didn't go out with women. I was a stove maker in the district-town kolkhoz.'

'I was a widower, and there were no children,' said Rezchikov. Like Mulyarchuk, he now spoke about himself in the past tense. 'Oh, brother, how I loved vodka! I loved vodka like a cat loves milk, and the women loved me. They never said no.'

'Let's just sit here together,' said Usurov. 'We've got until dawn. And forget that wall – we can't keep death away now.'

'True,' said Vavilov. 'I just thought we should keep working, to make death less frightening.'

'But we're fucked,' said Usurov. 'Maybe we should just shoot ourselves?'

'What I think,' said Vavilov, 'is that we should all sit here together, till dawn. And why shoot ourselves? We're not out of ammunition yet.'

'Tell us one of your stories, Rezchikov,' said Usurov.

'I've been telling stories all my life,' said Rezchikov. 'I've not got much longer. Let me be quiet for a minute before death.'

Articulating each syllable, wanting his words to be remembered, Mulyarchuk said, 'My mother was called Marya Grigorievna, and I'm Mikola Mefodievich.'

It upset Mulyarchuk to think that, unless he told them now, his comrades would never know about the beauty of the small town of Polonnoye in summer and the excellence of the local sugar refineries. Nor would they know that his mother was a kind and good woman and a skilled dressmaker. In a mixture of Russian and Ukrainian, he went on, 'My mother could sew anything she turned her hand to, but she did most of her work for the peasants nearby. Coats and quilted jackets for the men in winter; *sachki* – that's winter jackets for the village women; and the bright-coloured waistcoats they call *korsetki*; and *lyshtvi* – embroidered skirts for the holy days; and then plain skirts, light summer jackets … Yes, there was nothing she couldn't do … As for me, I made stoves. Big stoves, little stoves, stoves with sleeping benches … Eight years I worked – in Polonnoye, Yampol and the villages round about. People said I made good stoves.'

Calmly, without fear of the Germans, Vavilov struck a match and lit a cigarette. Everyone saw two black tears flow down his grimy cheeks.

'Go on, Mulyarchuk,' he said. 'Say more! I was going to rebuild our own stove, during the summer.'

Usurov bent down to get a light from Vavilov. The light fell on his huge palms.

'Wounded in the hands?'

'No, that's not my blood. I felled two of them with a spade. While I was creeping towards you.' With a sob, Usurov added, 'We're like wild beasts now.' Then, listening intently, and almost gasping, he said, 'There's no sound from Rysev, he's stopped breathing.' He stood up, sat down again and looked around. 'The sky's like a fur coat. The clouds are never this thick in Samarkand, not even in July.' He touched Rezchikov anxiously. 'Don't sleep, don't sleep. Sit and talk a little longer.'

'Don't be afraid, Usurov,' said Vavilov. 'Better men than us have died already. I just wish I could see my home again, just for a minute. But death's nothing, it's no different from sleep.'

'And you've still got a bar of chocolate to give to your daughter,' Rezchikov said with a smile.

A Soviet flare appeared over the Volga. It ripened like an ear of wheat – first wax-coloured, next a milky white, then yellow. Then it drooped, faded and scattered its grains. And the night turned even blacker.

The men waited silently for the dawn, exchanging only an occasional word. There is no knowing what they thought, or whether they even dozed for a few minutes. Later, though, they were on guard, watching avidly, anxiously and submissively as light came silently into being, out of the darkness that filled both heaven and earth.

The earth around them turned a more solid black, while the still-dark sky began to separate from it, as if the earth had drawn off a little of the sky's darkness and this darkness was peeling away, settling on the earth in silent flakes. There was already not one dark in the world but two: the calm, even dark of the sky and the dense, crazed dark of the earth.

And then the sky lightened a little, as if touched by ash, while the earth went on filling with darkness. The line separating sky and earth began to break up, to lose its straightness; small bumps and notches appeared on the earth's surface. But this was not yet light on earth; it was darkness being made more apparent as the sky grew brighter. Then clouds appeared. One of them – the highest and smallest – let out something like a sigh, and a hint of pink, living warmth touched its cold, pale face.

Down by the Volga, half-sleeping soldiers from other battalions of the 13th Guards Division heard a sudden commotion from the railway station: hand grenades, rounds of machine-gun fire, shouts of Germans, rifle shots, mortar bombs, the rumble of a tank.

'Still fighting,' they said in amazement. 'They're a tough lot!'

But not one of these Soviet soldiers saw the sun's slant rays fall for a moment on a middle-aged man as he climbed out of a black pit, threw a grenade, and looked all around him, his bright, alert gaze out of keeping with his torn clothes and the black, bristly stubble on his sunken cheeks.

Vying with one another, German machine guns greedily opened fire on this man. He stood there in a cloud of bright yellow dust. When he was no longer to be seen, it was as if, rather than collapsing in a dead bloody lump, he had dissolved in the dusty, milky, yellowish mist swirling in the morning sun.

47

German burial teams worked all through the following day, collecting the bodies of German soldiers and officers and loading them onto trucks.

On a deserted hill on the city's western outskirts, surveyors marked out grave sites. Special detachments prepared coffins, crosses, turf, pebbles and bricks; they brought in sand to sprinkle on the paths of the new cemetery.

The crosses were perfectly aligned; the distance between each two graves, and between each two rows of graves, was always the same. And the trucks kept on coming, raising clouds of dust as they brought in the dead, along with empty coffins and sturdy, factory-made crosses impregnated with a chemical compound to protect them from damp.

On small rectangular plaques, a team of painters stencilled in black Gothic script the first name, surname, rank, and date of birth of each of the dead.

There were hundreds of different names and surnames, hundreds of different birth dates, but every plaque bore the same date of death – the day of the storming of the railway station.

*

Lenard and Bach wandered about the ruins, looking at the bodies of the Soviet soldiers.

Lenard sometimes touched these bodies with the toes of his elegant boots, wondering if they might contain some secret. What, he wanted to know, was the hidden source of the grim, monstrous obstinacy of these men now lying dead on the ground? They looked strangely small, with their grey or yellowish faces, in their green tunics and rough boots, with their black or green puttees.

Some lay with outstretched arms; others were sitting; others had curled up in a ball, as if feeling the cold. Many lay beneath a thin sprinkling of stone and earth. There was a kirza boot with a broken heel, sticking out of a shell hole. A thin, wiry man had collapsed with his

850

chest pressed against the overhang of a wall. His small hand was still gripping the lever of a grenade, but his skull was shattered; he must have been killed as he rose to throw the grenade.

'This pit is like a whole storehouse of corpses,' said Bach. 'To start with, they must have been bringing all their dead here. Look – it's like a social club. Some are sitting, others lying down, and this one here could be delivering a speech.'

Another pit was more like a bunker; it must have served as a command post. Among shattered beams, the two officers found a broken radio transmitter and the splintered green case of a field telephone.

A commander lay with his head against a machine gun with a crushed, twisted barrel. Close beside him lay a man with a commissar's star on his sleeve. Hunched by the entrance was an ordinary soldier, probably a telephonist.

There was a haversack lying on the ground by the commissar. With a look of distaste, Lenard picked it up between thumb and finger and ordered a soldier to take the map case off the officer leaning on the machine gun. 'Take it along to HQ,' he added. 'Our translator should have a look at it.'

'This is very different from one of our abandoned trenches,' said Bach, holding a handkerchief to his nose. 'Ours are usually surrounded by piles of newspapers and magazines, but here there's only a pile of shit.'

'They may not have wiped their arses,' Lenard replied, 'but I've noticed something more important. This was a command post. These men were officers and, judging by the way their corpses have swelled up, they were killed on the first day of fighting. We've always assumed that Russian soldiers lack initiative. But it appears that the rank-and-file soldiers here at the station kept on fighting like stubborn beasts – even without their officers.'

'Let's go,' said Bach. 'The smell turns my stomach. I won't be able to eat tinned meat for days.'

They caught sight of a small group of German soldiers.

'Look,' said Bach. 'The comradeship of soldiers!'

He gestured towards Stumpfe, who had put his arm around Ledeke and was pretending to push him onto a corpse that had one arm sticking up in the air.

'You're a sentimental fool,' Lenard burst out in sudden irritation.

'What do you mean?' replied Bach. He felt startled. Was Lenard sneering at him because of his long confession during that first night

851

in Stalingrad? He had been a fool to talk like that to a Nazi, to an SS lieutenant rumoured to be a member of the Gestapo. 'I don't understand,' he said. 'Don't you think that comradeship between soldiers is a wonderful thing?'

Lenard did not reply. He was unable to say that this same Stumpfe, whom everyone so loved, had recently handed him a written denunciation of Ledeke and Vogel, accusing them of voicing subversive opinions.

The two officers went on their way, while the soldiers continued wandering about the ruins.

Ledeke glanced down into a semi-basement with a collapsed ceiling. 'This must have been an aid station,' he said.

'Look, Ledeke, a woman!' said Vogel. 'Specially for you!'

'There's quite a stench.'

'Don't worry. Soon they'll round up some civilians to come and bury all this.'

Ledeke glanced casually at the dead bodies and said, 'We won't find anything much here. I doubt we'd find even a decent towel or a handkerchief.'

Stumpfe, however, continued working away, kicking mugs and mess tins to one side and diligently checking through the meagre contents of haversacks.

In one haversack he found a chocolate bar wrapped in a clean white cloth.

Among some notebooks, papers and letters in a lieutenant's kit-bag, he found a penknife, a small mirror, and a quite decent razor. He paused, then threw them away.

But eventually his diligence was rewarded. When Lenard and Bach left the commanders' dugout, Stumpfe went down into it himself. In one corner he came across a package half-buried by clay.

It turned out to contain elegant women's clothing. Everything was brand new; none of it had even been tried on. Stumpfe was overjoyed. He even began to sing.

'Look!' he shouted. 'Look what I've found here! A bathrobe! A shirt with lace edging! Silk stockings! A bottle of perfume!'

48

Marya Nikolaevna Vavilova woke up early in the morning, sometime before five, and quietly called out to her daughter, 'Nastya, Nastya, time to get up!'

Nastya stretched, rubbed her eyes and began to get dressed. Frowning crossly and lamenting how tired she still felt, she began to comb her hair. To help wake herself up, she tugged violently on the comb.

Marya cut some bread for little Vanya, who was still asleep, poured out some milk and covered the mug with a towel, not wanting the cat to help herself to the milk before Vanya got up. Then she went over to the trunk and put away the awl, the bread knife and the matches – dangerous items in which Vanya had been known to take a special interest during his long, lonely mornings. She wagged her finger at the cat and looked expectantly at Nastya, who was still drinking her milk.

'Time we were off!' she said.

'For heaven's sake, let me at least finish my bread!' said Nastya, sounding like an old village woman. She let out a sigh and added, 'Ever since you were appointed brigade leader, you've been unbearable.'

Marya went towards the door, looked around the room, came back again, opened the trunk, took out a piece of sugar and put it under the towel along with Vanya's bread and milk.

'What's got into you?' she said to Nastya. She didn't need to look at her to realize that she was upset. 'You're not little any longer. You'll manage.'

When they were outside, Marya looked at the road ahead and said quietly, 'It's four months to the day since your father left.'

Seeming to understand what her mother was thinking, Nastya said, 'Do you really think I begrudge Vanya his sugar? He can have all the sugar he wants. I don't even like sugar any longer.'

After the close air of the hut Marya found it a joy to be walking along a country track still moist with dew, to look at places beloved since childhood, and to allow any last trace of tiredness to dissolve in the rhythm of her stride.

In the light of the September sun, the winter wheat looked thick and silky; stirred by the east wind, it seemed like a single creature, alive and young, testing its strength, rejoicing in life, light and the pleasing cool of the air. The shoots' feathery tops were almost transparent, allowing the rays of sunlight to pass right through them. A greenish light shimmered over the whole field.

Each tiny shoot had its tender, timid charm. Each stout, whitish stalk was straight as an arrow and endowed with a stubborn strength. Each stalk had laboured hard to fight its way up; its green shoulders had pushed aside clods of earth equivalent to huge blocks of granite.

And everything about this young wheat – its green charm, its translucence, its freedom from care – was in sharp contrast to the brown grass round about, to the yellowing aspen and birch leaves and the general autumnal sadness. This piercing green was the only young life in a fading world of grey, lifeless gossamer and small clouds already pregnant with snow. Tall fir trees stretched their heavy branches over the track, but their sullen, dusty green was of a different order.

Nevertheless, for all its bright richness, this winter wheat was not like the shoots and blossoms of spring. Its close ranks, its tautness and density signalled an alert wariness. It was preparing for what was to come; long before it was fully grown, it would encounter storms and blizzards.

The young shoots were like soldiers, standing shoulder to shoulder, ready to confront whatever fate threw at them. And when an absent-minded cloud passed over the sun and its broad shadow drifted silently across the fields and onto the winter wheat, the shoots turned so dark as to be almost black, their wary, grim strength now more apparent than ever.

As for the men and women at work at this early hour, they felt not only the emptiness of the autumn spaces and the chill wind of approaching winter – they also felt all the sorrow of war.

Young girls, mothers of families and old women with kerchiefs around their heads were now reaping the summer wheat. Nearby, on a field already harvested, old men were stacking the dry sheaves on carts, shouting at the small boys who were helping them.

This picture of harvesting in the mild morning sun, beneath the spacious clarity of the autumn sky, seemed to breathe peace and tranquillity. The threshing machine sounded the same as always. The cool, slippery, heavy grain made the same quiet rustle. The young girls' sweating faces had the same animated look. The dry smell of the warm sheaves, the grey-blue dust, the crunch of straw underfoot, the pearly sheen of wisps and flakes of straw floating about in the air – all seemed normal and familiar.

But Marya knew only too well that everything here spoke of war. Women in men's boots, an elderly man in army trousers and an army tunic, a fourteen-year-old boy in a side cap still bearing the faint shadow of a five-pointed star, two younger boys in overalls sewn from old camouflage cloth – each was the wife, mother, sister, father or child of a soldier. Their clothes were a sign of the enduring link between those on the front line and those who remained in the villages.

In peacetime, a wife sometimes wore her husband's jacket and a son sometimes took over his father's felt boots. It was no different now; if they were issued with new uniforms, those whose work was the war would pass on their old uniforms to their family.

And were it not for the war, would there have been so many old men and women working out in the fields and on the threshing floor? Many of them should have retired long ago. And there were boys and girls who should have been sitting in classrooms. Because of the war, the school term was beginning a month late for children in their last two years at a village school. And there were no tractors humming away. Nor were there any of the trucks that usually came to the fields at this time of year. Trucks and tractors alike had also left for the war.

And Vasya Belov, a bold, self-confident mechanic, was no longer standing beside the threshing machine. He was now a turret gunner and his place had been taken by Klava, his seventeen-year-old sister, who had a child's thin white neck and clumsy, fumbling fingers discoloured by engine oil. At this moment there was a frown on her face and she was shouting at her grey-haired assistant, 'Kozlov, have you dozed off, or what? Give me the key!'

It was because of the war that Degtyarova had stood for hours by her gate, hoping for letters from her husband and sons. And it was because of the war that Degtyarova had just slowly straightened her back, wiped the sweat from her forehead and looked with anguish at all the mown wheat still lying helplessly on the ground.

Weep, Degtyarova, weep – you have loved ones to weep for.

Could Marya have guessed how much responsibility she would take on in the course of a mere four months?

When her husband left for the war, she had been racked by anxiety about her home and her children. Would she be able to support them? Would she manage to feed them properly?

But she had soon become responsible for more than her family, her hut and her supply of firewood.

How had this happened? Had it begun during the kolkhoz meeting when, for the first time in her life, she spoke in front of dozens of people? They had all listened intently. She had watched with a sudden, calm confidence as their changing expressions bore out the importance and truth of her words.

Or had it been out in the fields, the day she argued with the kolkhoz chairman? He had come to criticize the work of the women's brigade and she, speaking with slow, deliberate emphasis, had pulled no punches in setting him straight.

The last months had been difficult, but she had worked harder than anyone and there was nothing anyone could reproach her for.

Kozlov came up to her and said, 'A shame you don't have more help, Bombardier Brigade Leader. If our sons and younger brothers were here, if we had drivers and mechanics, and tractors and trucks, we'd be done with the harvest and threshing in no time at all, before the end of the month. You and your women make a deal of noise, but you might as well be ploughing the air. You'll still be reaping and threshing when the first snows fall!'

Marya looked at Kozlov. He had narrow eyes and a prominent Adam's apple. She wanted to come out with a sharp retort, but she restrained herself. She knew he resented having to work as an assistant to a young girl. When he got back home in the evening, his wife sometimes greeted him with the words, 'So, Mister Assistant Thresher, has your Klava said you can come back home?'

And once, when he started carping at his wife and grandchildren, little cross-eyed Luba, the youngest of the girls, said to him in a quiet, low voice, 'Careful, Grandad – or we'll tell Klava!'

And so Marya merely smiled and said gently, 'We've done what we can – and we can't do more.'

But they had done a remarkable amount. A tractor had broken down in the middle of ploughing. The kolkhoz mechanic was now at the front and someone else, a man recovering from wounds, had been sent to them as a substitute. He overdid it, reopened his wound – and failed to repair the tractor. But they finished the ploughing all the same. Some days they used cows, and some days the women pulled the plough themselves.

And the winter wheat had already come through – they certainly weren't letting the land lie empty and idle.

Now, though, there was the harvest to attend to. And they would have to work hard to complete the threshing before the first snows.

Marya gripped some of the crackly stems of ripe wheat, bent them against her sickle, sliced through them and laid them on the ground. Her quick, measured movements, both generous and spare, seemed one with the wheat's harsh rustle. As if echoing this monotonous sound, a single thought was circling round in her head: 'You sowed, and now here I am, reaping what you sowed. You sowed, you sowed, and here I am, gathering in your harvest. You sowed, you ...' This sense of a living connection with her husband made Marya feel quietly sad.

'Will Pyotr come back? We didn't hear from Alyosha for months on end, but now we get letters regularly. Alyosha's alive, thank God, and he's well. One day there'll be a letter from Pyotr too. He'll come back! He'll come back!'

The wheat rustled, whispered, looked agitated, then quietened down again, waiting and thinking.

The ring of the sickle, and the rustle of the wheat.

The sun had climbed higher, warming Marya's neck and the back of her head just as in summer. Even beneath her jacket, she could feel the sun's warmth on her shoulders. And she could hear the thin, high voice of a swift September fly.

'You'll come back and you'll want to know everything. I worked hard, I didn't spare myself. I didn't spare Nastya either. No one can reproach me. There were times when the poor girl cried and asked to be transferred to another brigade. We lived honestly with you and we live honestly without you. I can look you straight in the eye – I've nothing to be ashamed of.'

The quiet clink of her sickle – and a spark of joy flaring up in her heart, scorching her with hope, with faith in a happy future.

Once again, echoing the rustle of wheat – wheat clutched in her hand, wheat sliding down to the ground: 'It was you, you who sowed this field ...'

Still bent down, shading her eyes with her hand, Marya looked at the winter wheat shining green in the distance. 'And you will come back, you, you will reap what I have sown.' Her whole being was filled with faith in this simple, natural, enduring connection, a connection strong enough to outlast life and death. She could, it seemed, have kept on reaping until evening, not once straightening her spine, not noticing the ache in her back and shoulders, not noticing the blood pounding against her temples.

Scattered about the field she could see the white kerchiefs of the other reapers. They had fallen behind. Only Degtyarova was still keeping up with her.

Weep, Degtyarova, Degtyarova, weep – life has proved hard for you ...

A cold wind began to blow. The wheat made more noise. It rippled and swayed, as if in anguish.

'He wrote to me all the time. He was always writing. And now it's over three weeks without a single letter.'

Marya straightened up and looked about her – at the fields, some already harvested and some not, and at the broad strip of dark forest in the distance. The grey-blue space around her was cold and transparent, and the bright sun on the fields and copses brought neither warmth nor peace to the soul.

'Who can I ask? Who's going to answer? Who can turn this blade away from my heart?'

Degtyarova was standing a few yards away, frowning thoughtfully as she looked at the swaying ears of grain.

'Why do you keep crying?' Marya asked.

Degtyarova looked round at her, said nothing for a few moments, as if she hadn't heard or understood, then said quietly, 'I think you're crying too.'

49

No one would ever again cross paths with any member of Filyashkin's battalion. All were dead and can play no further part in this narrative. Nevertheless, they constitute one of its longest threads.

The dead – most of whose names are forgotten – lived on during the Battle of Stalingrad.

They were among the founders of a Stalingrad tradition that was transmitted from heart to heart, without words.

The fighting around the station had continued for three days and nights. The grim, unrelenting rumble was a clear message to the other Soviet soldiers, spelling out what lay in store for them.

Reinforcements went on crossing the Volga at night. There on the bank, without anyone looking at any lists, without administrative formalities of any kind, they were immediately assigned to one regiment or another. Sometimes these soldiers died in battle almost immediately. During their few hours in Stalingrad, however, they came to understand as much as Khrushchev, Yeromenko and Chuikov, and they fought in accord with a strict but unwritten law that had matured in the consciousness of the nation and been proclaimed to the world at large by the Red Army soldiers who died at the railway station.

50

Regimental Commander Yelin reported to Rodimtsev that his battalion had carried on fighting for three days after being encircled, had not retreated one step and had been annihilated to the last man.

Yelin forgot that only a few days earlier he had referred to 'the battalion recently placed under my command, formerly part of Matyushin's regiment'. Now, as he reported how they had fought to the death, he called them simply 'my battalion'. He used this phrase three times.

While Filyashkin's battalion was still fighting, Colonel Gorishny's division had crossed the Volga and taken up position on Rodimtsev's right flank. One of Rodimtsev's regiments was transferred to Gorishny's command. It then took part in an attack on Height 102 – Mamaev Kurgan.

Initially the regiment suffered heavy losses and failed to gain any ground. Angered by this apparent failure, Gorishny said that the regiment was insufficiently prepared for the challenges of urban warfare.

'It happens again and again,' his chief of staff replied. 'You're handed a regiment at the last minute – and then you have to answer for it straightaway.'

Gorishny was a tall, stout man with a strong Ukrainian accent. He seemed slow and calm, but his family had disappeared without trace and this had left him in a state of constant anguish. Later that day, he said to his chief of staff, 'You can't capture a height like that with a mere regiment. It's sheer hell on those slopes. It would be hard enough with an entire corps.'

Meanwhile, in the sewer that served as the command post for the 13th Guards Division, Belsky was saying to Rodimtsev, 'Gorishny's regiment has lost a lot of men, and he's failed to establish proper liaison with the artillery.'

In spite of a hurricane of fire, the regiment in question had, in fact, just launched another attack and reached the crest of Mamaev Kurgan. Had they known this, the divisional commanders and their chiefs of staff would have spoken differently.

In general, however, issues of personal vanity – and disagreements about who was responsible for a particular unit's successes or failures

– were of little concern during these first weeks. The fighting was too intense; it required all the commanders' mental powers, all their will, all their time and – only too often – their lives.

Only some time afterwards, in late November and early December, as the tension began to ease, did such matters come to the fore. Every mealtime then became an opportunity to debate who had been exposed to most enemy fire, who had defended the most critical sector, who had yielded a metre and who had not, whether it was Gorokhov or Lyudnikov who had been pushed back into the tightest little corner, and when and for how long a particular regiment or battalion had been transferred to someone's command.

This was when the arguments about who first recaptured Mamaev Kurgan began in earnest.

Rodimtsev's men considered, not without reason, that it had been one of their regiments.

Gorishny's men considered, with no less reason, that it had been their division, since the regiment in question was, at that time, under Gorishny's command.

Those who regained the height had no need to discuss anything; they knew very well that they, and they alone, had recaptured Mamaev Kurgan – they had not seen any other Soviet forces on the crest. As for the many dead, they had all played their part and might well have had something to say, but the dead had no voice in these debates; all that concerned anyone was how the glory should be shared among the living.

Another dispute – although this only flared up after the war was over – was about the relative importance of the infantry on the west bank and the artillery on the east bank. Those who had been on the west bank made out that the architects of the victory were the storm groups, the rank-and-file soldiers with hand grenades, the machine-gunners, snipers, sappers and mortarmen. The artillery may have provided support – albeit not always in time, not always accurately, and even, now and again, firing on their own men – but they did not play a decisive role.

Those who had been on the east bank argued that the infantry, for all its courage, could never have fought off the monstrous onslaught of the German army. Especially towards the end of the defensive battle, the Soviet infantry was a spent force. The Soviet front had become a line drawn on a map rather than a material reality, and what halted the Germans was the power and concentration of the Soviet artillery.

But for the Volga, lying between the infantry and the artillery, this dispute could never have assumed such apparent importance. Similar disputes arose at other stages of the war but, in the absence of any such clear demarcation line, they died down; neither side could easily find evidence to back up its case. Here, though, the demarcation line was only too clear. On one bank stood Stalingrad – and the infantry. On the other bank stood a new, fire-breathing city, so densely packed that battery commanders argued with one another over a few square metres of sand, over a small patch of ground sheltered by willows.

The long barrels of the anti-aircraft guns were like a forest of steel. Camouflaged in shallow creeks lay ships from the Volga naval flotilla, armed with large-calibre cannon. Huge aerodromes had appeared, providing secure bases for the hundreds of Yak and LaGG fighters flying across the Volga, for the P-8 light bombers whose role was to attack the German support services and communication lines, and the Tupolev TB-3 heavy bombers that roared into the night sky. And this concentration of the most advanced military technology was located in a small area; it was well organized and under effective central control. A radio report about a German attack would be followed, only a few seconds later, by the command 'Fire at square X!' The whole fire-breathing city would then come to life. Thousands of shells would crash down, a minute later, on a small area designated by the same grid reference on the maps of the commanders of artillery, mortar and rocket regiments. Everything there, animate and inanimate, would be blown into the air or pounded into the ground.

The Volga's great breadth has confused matters. The river may have looked like a dividing line, but in reality it marked a perfect joint, welding together the two halves of the Soviet forces, uniting the firepower of the east bank with the west bank's unflagging courage. The Volga enabled gunners and foot soldiers to co-operate with unusual effectiveness.

Were it not for the infantry's courage, the artillery could have done nothing. It was because the infantry held its ground that the artillery was able to manifest its monstrous concentration of firepower.

But it is equally true that, without the shield provided by the artillery, the infantry could never have withstood the countless German attacks. Without artillery support, the infantry's extraordinary courage – and their determination not to retreat – would have led simply to their annihilation.

Neither the artillery's material might nor the infantry's fighting spirit could have achieved anything on its own. It was the union between them that led to the Soviet victory.

51

In the middle of September, the Germans began shelling the Stalgres power station. The station was, at the time, operating normally – it was a fine day, and the white clouds of steam from the boiler room and the smoke from the chimney were clearly visible.

When the first 103-millimetre shells hit the cooling towers and exploded in the yard, and when one of the shells smashed through the engine-room wall, someone phoned from the boiler room to ask Spiridonov if they should stop work. Spiridonov, who was standing by the central control panel, ordered them to continue as usual. Stalgres supplied power to Beketovka, to the command post and signals centre of Shumilov's 64th Army and to the front-line radios. It recharged the batteries of trucks and other vehicles and it also supplied the Stalgres workshops now being used for the repair of tanks and Katyusha rocket launchers.

Spiridonov then telephoned his daughter and said, 'Vera, go to the underground shelter at once.'

In an equally authoritative tone Vera replied, 'Nonsense, I'm not going anywhere.' She added, 'Come and have lunch – the soup's almost ready.'

That day marked the beginning of a prolonged battle between the workers of Stalgres and the German bombers and gunners. The workers' courage and obstinacy astonished even the most hardened Red Army soldiers.

Day after day, the moment the first smoke rose from the main chimney, the German artillery opened fire. Shells crashed through the main walls; sometimes splinters whistled through the engine and turbine rooms. Shattered glass littered the stone floors, but the smoke still curled stubbornly up from the chimney, as if laughing at the German guns. As for the Stalgres workers and engineers, they saw nothing to laugh at, but their determination did not waver. Day after day, fully aware that this would attract the attentions of the German heavy artillery, they diligently raised the pressure in the boilers. Sometimes workers standing by furnaces, switchboards and water-level controls saw

German tanks on the crest of the surrounding hills, moving towards the Obydino church. There were moments when tanks seemed about to break through to the power station itself and Spiridonov had to order the electricians to prepare to detonate 'the soap boxes' with which all the main units were mined. These boxes of TNT caused no small anxiety to anyone who remembered about them during artillery barrages: should one of them be hit by a shell, the whole building would be blown to smithereens.

The families of the remaining Stalgres workers and engineers had been evacuated to the east bank, and everyone working at the power station now also lived there, under martial law. Their work had not changed, but they lived the lives of soldiers. And there were no human ties that were not altered by this new communal existence, by this combination of ordinary work and military discipline, to the accompaniment of shell bursts and the howls of German aircraft. No matter how long people had known one another – on shop floors, in offices, in meetings and committees of every kind – their relationships developed in unexpected ways.

With the fragility of human life now so apparent, the value of every individual emerged more clearly than ever.

Nikolaev, the fair-haired Party organizer, was well aware of the extent of his new responsibilities. But he had never taken a deeper interest in the minutiae of people's lives than during these terrible September days. He told Kapustinsky, one of the engineers, that he should not smoke on an empty stomach if he had an ulcer. He talked about the kindness and magnanimity of Suslov, one of the electricians. He pointed out that Golidze the guard, though certainly quick-tempered, was cheerful, responsive and generally good-natured; and that Paramonov, the duty technician on the second floor, knew a great deal about literature and should, perhaps, study humanities instead of thinking only about transformers. He insisted that Kasatkin the accountant liked a good joke, was fond of children and was not in any way a bad person; if his view of family and marriage was alarmingly bleak, this was simply because he had been unfortunate in his personal life.

Differences of age, profession and social standing – differences that so often make it difficult for people to draw close to one another – ceased to be of importance. The Stalgres workers and engineers became a single family.

Sometimes Spiridonov felt that whole years had passed since his wife's death. Every day of this last month had brought more deaths;

every hour had brought crises. Day after day, fearing he was unlikely to see the sun rise again, he had given his all to dealing with difficulties that appeared overwhelming. And his memory of Marusya was like a flame. Every now and then it scorched him – and he would take a photograph of her from his pocket and gaze at it, unable to believe that he would never see her again.

Was it really possible that he would never again talk to her, or ask her advice? Never again discuss some escapade of Vera's with her? Never again joke with her, fly into a temper or rush home to see her? Never again take pride in one of her newspaper articles? Never again bring back some cloth for a new dress and say, 'No, don't be angry with me, it hardly cost a kopek!'? Never again go to the theatre with her and grumble, 'Marusya, it'll soon be the third bell. As usual, we're going to be late'?

As for Vera, she had undergone surgery but had recovered well. She had fully regained her sight in both eyes and the only trace of her burns was a small pink spot on one cheekbone. The faint scar left on one eyelid by her recent operation was barely noticeable.

There was a new tenderness between Vera and her father, and this was a source of great joy to him.

Spiridonov did not talk to Vera about what he was going through, and she almost never spoke to him about her mother, but everyone who knew them could see that their relationship had changed.

Vera was now remarkably thoughtful and caring towards her father. In the past, she had treated domestic matters with mocking contempt. Anything to do with health, rest and nutrition had been beneath her, but she now checked constantly whether her father had had enough to eat, whether he had drunk his tea and whether he had had at least a few hours of sleep. She would make his bed for him and bring him hot water for washing. There was no longer the least hint of the accusatory manner so common in young people's attitudes to their parents: 'You may like to think you've got something to teach me, but I'm not so sure. To my mind, you've got more than enough problems yourself.' Instead, Vera chose to close her eyes to her father's weaknesses and to say in a comradely tone, 'You've had a hard day, Pápa, you need to get some vodka inside you!'

She now admired everything about him, and she was proud of how he managed to keep the power station in operation in spite of the constant shelling. She also discovered that, for all his heroism, he was often surprisingly helpless with regard to more everyday matters.

Aware of all this, Spiridonov began, without fully realizing it, to look on her differently. Until recently, everything she did had caused him anxiety. He had seen her as a foolish, unreliable child, always likely to put her foot in it. Now, though, he saw her as a clear-headed, sensible adult. He asked her advice, talked freely to her about his doubts and mistakes and felt a little apprehensive if, instead of going back to have lunch with her, he snatched a bite to eat with some of the engineers or Party workers. In view of the severity of wartime conditions, this would be accompanied not with the regulation hundred grams of vodka, but with 150 grams.[286]

They now lived not in a spacious apartment but in a small room in a semi-basement below Spiridonov's office. It had thick walls and windows that looked east, into the power-station yard and away from the German artillery.

Immediately after the fire, Spiridonov had found a temporary home for Vera a few kilometres from Stalgres, in a small house belonging to one of his accountants. The house was in a safe place, just above the Volga and far from the main road and any of the factories. He repeatedly begged Vera not to return to Stalgres. He wanted her to go to Kazan and live with her aunt Ludmila, but she refused point-blank. Nevertheless, she was pleased by her father's concern; it made her feel she was a little girl again, as in the irrevocably lost days of peace, and this was both sweet and painful.

Sometimes she *did* want to go to Kazan and live with Ludmila. She wanted to see Nadya and her grandmother. She wanted not to hear gunfire and shell bursts. She wanted not to wake in the night, wondering in horror if she could hear German soldiers outside. Nevertheless, something in her heart told her that she would find life in Kazan still harder. Not only would it mean leaving her dead mother; it would also mean losing all hope of ever seeing Viktorov again. She was certain he would come to Stalgres to look for her, or send her a letter there, or at the very least ask some comrade to pass on his greetings. Whenever she looked up and saw Soviet fighters, her heart missed a beat: could it be Viktorov, high in the sky above her?

She asked her father to find work for her in Stalgres, but he kept delaying, not wanting to expose her to danger.

Then she said that, unless he arranged something soon, she would go to the medical unit of the nearest division and ask to be sent to the front, to a regimental aid post. He promised to find her a job in one of the workshops in the next few days.

One morning, Vera went to the abandoned building that had once housed the Stalgres engineers. She went up to the second floor, to the apartment with wide-open doors and smashed windows where she had lived with her parents. She went into her mother's room, sat on the metal frame of the bed and looked around. The carpet, the paintings and the photographs had all gone, but pale rectangles on the walls showed where they had once hung. And then everything – her sense of loss, her guilt at how rude she had been to her mother during the last months of her life, the roar of the Soviet artillery, even the sky's deep blue – everything was suddenly more than she could bear. She got to her feet and ran down the stairs.

Vera crossed the square to the checkpoint at the main entrance to Stalgres. For a moment she imagined that her father was about to come out, put his arms around her and say, 'Ah, here at last – someone's just brought you a letter!' But the guard told her that Spiridonov had left a few minutes ago, on his way to Army HQ with some major. And there was no triangular letter for her.[287]

She walked through into the yard. Then she saw Nikolaev coming towards her. He was wearing a soldier's tunic and a worker's cap.

'Verochka, has Spiridonov come back yet?'

'Not yet,' said Vera. 'Why? Has something happened?'

'No, no,' said Nikolaev. 'Everything's all right.' Pointing at the smoke rising from the chimney, he added, 'Vera, there's no smoke without fire. Don't wander about the yard. The Germans will start shooting any minute.'

'What of it?' she replied. 'I'm not afraid.'

Nikolaev took her by the arm and said half jokingly and half crossly, 'Come on now. In the director's absence, I have to assume the responsibilities of a father.' He went with her to the main office, then stopped by the door and asked, 'What's the matter? Something's wrong – I can see it in your eyes.'

'I want to start work.'

'That goes without saying. But it's more than that.'

'Sergey Afanasievich, surely you understand?' Vera said sadly. 'You know what's happened, don't you?'

'Yes, of course,' he replied, 'but there's something else, isn't there? You look lost.'

'Lost? I'm not in the least lost and I never will be.'

Just then a shell whistled by. It exploded on the eastern side of the yard.

Nikolaev hurried off to the boiler room. Vera stayed where she was, by the office door. The entire yard seemed changed by this shell. Earth, iron, the walls of the workshops – everything had become tense and grim, like people's souls.

Her father returned only late in the evening.

'Vera!' he called out. 'Are you still up and about? I've brought back a very dear guest.' She ran out into the corridor. For an instant she thought she saw Viktorov, standing beside her father.

'Hello, Verochka,' came a voice from the dark.

'Hello,' she said slowly. It was a voice she knew, but it took her a moment to recognize who it was: Pavel Andreyevich Andreyev.

'Pavel Andreyevich, come in! I'm so glad to see you!' There were tears in Vera's voice; in only a few seconds she had experienced a whirlwind of emotions.

Spiridonov excitedly explained how he'd met up with Andreyev. They'd been driving along and all of a sudden he'd seen him on the side of the road – walking up from the river towards Stalgres. And so he'd picked him up. 'Really, Vera, you wouldn't believe it! Two days ago, he and his fellow workers were ferried to the east bank, under fire from German machine guns. The steelworks is being evacuated to Leninsk. His wife, his daughter-in-law and his little grandson are already there. But instead of going to join them, Pavel Andreyevich walked to Tumak and got into a boat with some soldiers. And now here he is!'

'Can you find work for me, Stepan Fyodorovich?' asked Andreyev. 'Here in Stalingrad I'll feel myself again.'

'Shouldn't be difficult,' replied Spiridonov. 'There's more than enough that needs doing.' Turning to Vera, he added, 'Look at him – he's indomitable. Clean-shaven – and he hasn't even lost weight!'

'A soldier was having a shave this morning, just before we crossed. I asked him to shave me too. But how are things here? Do you get many bombs?'

'We get more trouble from shells. As soon as they see smoke from the chimney, their artillery starts pounding away.'

'There's no end of bombs at the factories,' said Andreyev. 'You can't stand up straight for one moment.'

Vera placed a teapot and some glasses on the table. Glancing in her direction, Andreyev said quietly, 'So Vera's in charge now, is she?'

Spiridonov smiled and said, 'I battled with her for a long time. I kept telling her to go to her aunt in Kazan, but in the end I capitulated.

There's no getting round her. She's like you – she says she can't live anywhere else. Pass me the knife – I'll cut some bread.'

'Remember how Pápa always used to slice up the pie?' asked Vera, wondering whether or not Andreyev already knew about her mother.

'Of course I do,' said Andreyev, with a nod of the head. 'But I've got some white bread in my bag and it's already going a little hard. It needs eating.' He untied his bag, put the bread on the table, and said with a sigh, 'The fascists have pushed us to the edge of the abyss, Stepan Fyodorovich, but we'll crush them yet.'

'Take your jacket off, it's warm in here,' said Vera. 'Did you hear about my grandmother's home? It burned to the ground.'

'I know. And our little house has gone too. It was destroyed on the second day of the air raids. A direct hit by a large bomb. It smashed the trees too, and the garden fence. Everything I own now is inside this bag. But never mind – I'm still alive and I've got no white hairs yet.' He smiled and added, 'At least I didn't listen to my dear Varvara Alexandrovna. She told me not to go out to work – she wanted me to stay at home and guard our belongings. If I'd done as she said, that house would have been my grave.'

Vera poured out the tea and moved the chairs up to the table.

'And I've heard news of your Seryozha,' said Andreyev.

'What news?' father and daughter asked with one voice.

'Yes, how could I forget! There was a man from the factory militia in the boat with me. He'd been wounded, but he said he'd been in the same mortar battery as my friend Polyakov, who used to work as a carpenter. I asked about the other men in the battery and he told me their names. One was Seryozha Shaposhnikov – 'a young lad from the city', he said. I'm sure he was your Seryozha.'

'But how *is* our Seryozha?' Vera asked impatiently.

'All right. Alive and kicking. The militiaman didn't say much about him, just that he's a brave lad, and that he and Polyakov are good friends. People joke about the two of them being inseparable – the oldest man in the battery and the youngest.'

'Where are they now? Where's their battery?' asked Spiridonov.

'Here's what he told me. First, they were in the steppe for some time. Then they fought their first battle. Then they were at the foot of Mamaev Kurgan. And then they withdrew to the workers' settlement by the Barricades Factory. That's where they are now, in a building with good strong walls. They fire their mortars from the cellars and they're well protected from bombs.'

'But how *is* our Seryozha?' Vera repeated. 'How does he look? Has he got enough clothes? Is he in good spirits? What does he have to say for himself?'

'I don't know what he has to say for himself, but I'm sure he's all right for clothes, wearing the same Red Army uniform as everyone else.'

'Yes, of course. Sorry – I was being stupid. What I mean is – is he all right? Not wounded, not suffering concussion? Nothing the matter with him?'

'So the man said: alive, healthy, not wounded, and not suffering concussion.'

'Please, Pavel Andreyevich, say all that again. From the beginning: a brave lad, good friends with Polyakov, not wounded, and not suffering concussion. Go through all that again, Pavel Andreyevich, I beg you.'

Andreyev smiled. Speaking very slowly, lengthening each syllable to give weight to his words and make them last longer, he repeated everything he'd heard from the wounded militiaman about Vera's cousin Seryozha.

'We must tell Grandma as soon as we can. She'll be worrying about him. She's probably lying awake all night.'

'I'll do what I can,' said Spiridonov. 'I'll ask at Army HQ. Maybe they'll let me send a telegram to Kazan.'

He took a flask from a drawer of his desk and poured out two large glasses of vodka – for himself and Andreyev – and a third, smaller, glass for Vera.

'Not for me,' Vera said quickly.

'Not even half a glass, Verochka,' said her father, 'to drink to an old friend?'

'No, no, I really don't want to. I mean, I can't.'

'How things change!' said Spiridonov. 'When you were a little girl, there was nothing you wanted more than to down a glass on your birthday. Everyone laughed and said you'd turn into a drunkard. And now, all of a sudden, "I don't want to. I mean, I can't."'

'Seryozha's alive and well!' said Vera. 'That's wonderful!'

'We don't have long, Pavel Andreyevich,' said Spiridonov. He looked at his watch. 'I'll have to go back to work soon.'

Andreyev got to his feet. He raised his glass, his large hand entirely steady, and said in a loud, strong voice, 'Marya Nikolaevna. Our dear Marusya. Memory eternal!' Spiridonov and Vera rose to their feet, looking at the old man's stern, solemn face.

Before he left, Spiridonov tried to persuade Andreyev to stay the night, but Andreyev insisted on going to the room where the guards slept. Spiridonov also suggested that, to begin with, Andreyev should work at the checkpoint, examining and issuing passes.

Spiridonov came back again only late at night. He tiptoed to his bed.

'I'm not asleep,' said Vera. 'You can turn on the light.'

'I don't need to. I'm only lying down for an hour – I won't even undress. I have to go straight back to work.'

'How have things been today?'

'A shell hit the boiler-house wall. Two burst in the yard and some of the windows in the turbine hall have been smashed.'

'Anyone wounded?'

'No. But why aren't you asleep?'

'I don't feel like it. I can't. It's stifling in here.'

'I heard at HQ that the Germans have broken through to the Kuporosnoye Gully again. You must leave, Vera. I'm afraid for you. You're all I have now. I must answer to your mother for you.'

'You know I'm not leaving, so why keep on about it?'

They remained silent for some time, both looking into the darkness, the father conscious that his daughter was lying awake, the daughter conscious that her father was worrying about her.

'Why are you sighing?' asked the father.

'I'm glad about Pavel Andreyevich,' said Vera, not answering the question.

'Nikolaev came up to me and said, "What's up with our Verochka? Something's the matter with her." What is it? Are you worrying about your fighter pilot?'

'Nothing's the matter with me.'

'I was only asking.'

There was a brief silence. Spiridonov could sense that Vera was still wide awake.

'Pápa,' Vera said all of a sudden, in a loud voice, 'I've got something to tell you.'

Spiridonov sat up. 'Yes, my girl.'

'Pápa, I'm going to have a baby.'

Spiridonov got up, walked around the room, coughed and said, 'Well ...'

'But please don't turn on the light.'

'I wasn't going to.' Spiridonov went to the window, lifted the blackout curtain and said, 'That's ... I really ... I don't know what to say.'

'Why? Are you angry?'

'When are you due?'

'Not till winter.'

'Ye-es,' Spiridonov said slowly. 'It really is stifling in here. Let's go out into the yard.'

'All right, I'll get dressed. You go on out, Pápa. I'll join you in a moment.'

Spiridonov went out into the yard. It was a cool, starry night, with no moon. The large insulators of the high-voltage cables to the transformer were white and shining. Through gaps between the Stalgres buildings he caught glimpses of a dark, dead city. From the factory district to the north came occasional lightning flashes of artillery and mortar fire. Then a blur of light flickered briefly over the dark streets, as if a huge bird were sleepily flapping a pink wing; a night bomber must have dropped a large bomb.

The sky was full of sounds and movement. There were green and red threads of tracer fire. And high above him, at that impossible height that is both height and abyss, shone the autumn stars.

Spiridonov heard his daughter's light steps behind him. Then she was standing beside him. He could sense her alert gaze.

Turning towards her, he looked at her intently, shocked by the sudden force of his feelings. In her sad, thin face, in her dark, staring eyes, he saw not only the weakness of a small helpless being, a child waiting anxiously for her father to speak; he could also see a remarkable and beautiful power, a power with the strength to triumph over the death now storming across the earth and through the sky.

He put his arms around Vera's thin shoulders and said, 'Don't be afraid, my daughter – we'll manage. We won't let your little one come to harm.'

52

Altogether, the fighting in the centre of the city and on the southern outskirts lasted for approximately two weeks.

On 18 September, Yeromenko ordered the 62nd Army to counter-attack, to prevent the Germans from transferring troops to the factory district in the north. Soviet forces deployed to the north-west of Stalingrad attacked at the same time.

Neither offensive met with success. The Germans still held their positions by the Volga, splitting the Soviet front line.

On 21 September, five German divisions – two tank, two infantry and one motor infantry – attacked the city centre. The main blow fell on Rodimtsev's 13th Guards Division and the two infantry brigades. The fighting was fiercer still on the following day.

Rodimtsev repelled twelve attacks. The Germans eventually forced him to withdraw from the city centre, but Rodimtsev counter-attacked, throwing his reserves into the fight and regaining some of the ground he had lost. And from that day, though unable to recapture the city centre, Rodimtsev kept an unshakeable hold on the stretch of ground further east, along the shore of the Volga.

The focus of the battle then crept slowly northwards, away from Rodimtsev's positions and towards the factory district. Throughout October, the main German offensives were directed against the three giant factories.

More reinforcements kept arriving. Rodimtsev's division was followed by Gorishny's; Gorishny was followed by Batyuk. Gorishny deployed to the right of Rodimtsev; Batyuk to the right of Gorishny. Sokolovsky joined them. All three divisions were positioned close to Mamaev Kurgan, near the meat-packing plant and the water towers.

More new divisions deployed further north. The divisions commanded by Guriev, Gurtiev, Zheludyov, and then Ludnikov, all took up position in the factory district.

Further north still, on the extreme right flank, were the brigades commanded by colonels Gorokhov and Bolvinov.

The density of the defending forces was constantly increasing; an entire full-strength division now defended a single factory. General Guriev's Guards division was positioned in Red October; Colonel Gurtiev's Siberian division in the Barricades; and General Zheludyov's Guards division in the Tractor Factory, where he was later joined by General Ludnikov.

These vast numbers of men had all been ferried across from the east bank and were deployed in a narrow strip of land parallel to the Volga. Only here and there was the distance from the front line to the river greater than 1,000 or 1,200 metres; more often it was between 300 and 500 metres.

All supplies and equipment had to be ferried across the Volga. Otherwise the Soviet forces were entirely cut off.

German spearheads had reached the Volga in two places. A northern spearhead separated Stalingrad's defenders from the Don Front. A southern spearhead separated them from General Shumilov's 64th Army.

Stalingrad's defenders were armed with all kinds of light weapons: easily manoeuvrable mobile cannons, small-calibre mortars, machine guns, sub-machine guns, ordinary rifles, sniper rifles, hand grenades, anti-tank grenades and Molotov cocktails. Sapper battalions had at their disposal a large quantity of TNT, along with anti-personnel and anti-tank mines. The entire Soviet position had become a single, carefully engineered structure, covered by an intricate network of trenches, communication trenches, dugouts and bunkers.

This new city – this strong, resilient network of cellars, staircases and bomb craters, of water pipes, sewers and underground tunnels, of gullies and ravines running down towards the Volga – had quickly become densely populated. In it were located the 62nd Army HQ, divisional HQs, the command posts of dozens of infantry and artillery regiments, and a still greater number of infantry, engineer, machine-gun, chemical and medical-battalion command posts.

All these HQs and command posts were connected with the troops and with one another by telephone cables, radio transmitters, and a system for sending messengers and signallers on foot.

The Army and divisional HQs were in radio communication with the east bank – both with Front HQ and with their own heavy artillery.

The electromagnetic waves travelling between radio transmitters and radio receivers connected the front line not only to Front HQ and the fire positions of heavy and medium artillery, but also to rear positions and support services extending almost infinitely far to the east. These included fighter and bomber airstrips, the blast furnaces of Magnitogorsk, the tank factories of Chelyabinsk, the coking ovens of Kuznetsk, the collective and state farms of Siberia and the Urals, and the fisheries and military bases of the Pacific coast.

The scale of the battle was clear even to those taking part in it only from afar: railway workers; men working in support services; fuel-supply workers delivering fuel to cars, trucks and tanks; ammunition workers supplying divisional depots with tens of thousands of mortar bombs and hand grenades, with the shells devoured every day by the thousands of artillery pieces, and with millions of cartridges for rifles, anti-tank rifles and sub-machine guns.

Firepower testified to strength of spirit. There was a direct correlation between the thousands of tons of shells, grenades and cartridges delivered to Stalingrad and the furious self-sacrificing struggle of the men expending these mountains of steel and explosives in battle.

The scale of the battle was clear to people living in the Transvolga steppe, thirty or forty kilometres from the river. There was a constant glow in the sky. The rumble of gunfire grew louder or quieter but, night or day, it never fell silent.

The scale of the battle was felt by lathe operators, by troubleshooters at ammunition plants, by train despatchers and railway-station porters, by miners, steelworkers and blast-furnace operators.

The scale of the battle was felt in printing presses, in radio and telegraph offices, in the editorial offices of the thousands of newspapers published in different parts of the country, in the depths of forests and in remote polar stations. It was equally apparent to injured veterans, to old women working on collective farms, to children at village schools and to famous academicians.

The battle was an overwhelming reality not only for people, but also for birds flying through the smoke-filled air and for the fish in the Volga. Huge catfish, ancient pike, and giant sturgeon all kept close to the riverbed, trying to escape the deafening bombs, shells and torpedoes and the violent eruptions of the water itself.

Ants, beetles, wasps, grasshoppers and spiders in the surrounding steppe were no less aware of the battle. Field mice, hares and ground squirrels slowly became used to the smell of burning, to the sky's new colour, to the earth's constant trembling. Even several metres below ground, lumps of clay kept falling from the walls and ceilings of their burrows.

Livestock and domestic animals in the Transvolga steppe were as agitated as during a wildfire. Cows dried up; camels screamed and dug in their heels. Dogs howled all night, lost their appetite and hung their heads; hearing the whine of German aircraft, they whimpered and tried to shelter in holes and cracks in the ground. Cats stayed indoors, pricking up their ears mistrustfully in response to the rattling and tinkling of windowpanes.

Many frightened birds and animals fled the area altogether, moving north towards Saratov or south into the Kalmyk steppe, towards Astrakhan and Lake Elton.

The tension of this battle was felt by millions of people in Europe, China and America. It came to determine the thoughts of diplomats and politicians in Tokyo and Ankara; it influenced the tone of Churchill's secret conversations with his advisers and the spirit of appeals and decrees signed by President Roosevelt.

Soviet, Polish and Yugoslav partisans lived and breathed this battle – as did members of the French resistance, prisoners of war in the German camps, and Jews in the Warsaw and Biatysłok ghettos. For tens of millions of people the fire of Stalingrad was the fire of Prometheus.

An awesome and joyful hour for mankind was approaching.

53

In September the Supreme Command ordered the disbandment of the anti-tank brigade that had first confronted the German tanks on Stalingrad's northern outskirts.

Towards the end of the month, after spending two weeks in the reserves, Nikolay Krymov received a new posting: he was to give lectures on politics and international affairs to the soldiers and commanders of the 62nd Army.

He found a billet in Srednaya Akhtuba. This dusty little town, full of small wooden buildings, now housed the propaganda department of the Front Political Administration.

At first, life in this town seemed tedious, anodyne and oppressive. But then Krymov was summoned one evening and ordered to make his first trip to Stalingrad.

From across the Volga could be heard an unceasing rumble. It was always present – in the dark of night, in the clear hours of morning, and during a quiet, contemplative sunset. Flickers of light from distant artillery ran across the grey board walls and the blacked-out windows; red noiseless shadows skittered across the night sky; sometimes a bright white flame – lightning engendered not by the heavens but by man on earth – called out of the night a hill covered with small houses, or a grove of trees by the flat bank of the River Akhtuba.

A group of young girls was standing by the gates of a house on a corner; a fourteen-year-old boy was quietly playing the accordion. Four of the girls – two couples – were dancing together, lit by an uncertain, faltering light; the others watched in silence. There was something ineffable about this conjunction of the distant rumble of battle with soft, timid music; the light that shone on the girls' blouses, that fell so gently on their arms and their blonde hair, was death-dealing fire.

Krymov stopped; for a moment he forgot his immediate tasks. The soft music and the dancers' restrained, thoughtful movements were endowed with a bitter charm, a strange sadness and poetry. What he saw and heard was a far cry from the usual, frivolous merriment of the young.

In the pale light of the distant fire, the dancers looked serious and intent. They were looking towards Stalingrad, and Krymov could see on their faces how inseparable they felt from the boys now shedding their young blood there. Their faces expressed the sadness of being alone, a tentative yet indestructible hope of a meeting to come, and the girls' faith in their young charm and in happiness. As well as the pain of separation, he could see something else, something both girlishly strong and girlishly helpless, something great and simple for which there were no words and that could be expressed only by a bewildered smile or a sudden sigh from the heart. And Krymov, who during the past year had lived through so much and thought through so much, stood there without moving, forgetting everything as he gazed at the dancers.

As he prepared his lectures, Krymov had looked through a pile of foreign newspapers delivered by plane from Moscow. The word 'Stalingrad' appeared in the headlines of newspapers from all over the world, in huge capitals; it was present in news bulletins and editorials, in telegrams and despatches. Everywhere – in England, China, Australia and the Americas, in India and Mexico, on Spitsbergen and Cuba, in Greenland and in South Africa – people were talking, writing and thinking about Stalingrad. And the foreign schoolgirls who bought pencils, notebooks and blotting paper with emblems of Stalingrad on them, the old men going to the pub for a glass of beer, the housewives meeting at grocery and vegetable shops, in cities and villages at every latitude, on every continent and island of the globe – these people of every age and nationality wanted to discuss Stalingrad not out of idle curiosity but because Stalingrad was now a part of their daily reality. The city had woven itself into school lessons, into working families' weekly food budgets, into their calculations of what they would have to pay for potatoes and swedes, into all the plans and hopes without which no sentient person can live.

Krymov had noted down quotations exemplifying the extent to which the diplomatic positions of neutral powers, the workings of international treaties, and important speeches by prime ministers and ministers of war were now being determined by the flames and thunder of Stalingrad. He knew that the word 'Stalingrad' had appeared, written in coal and red ochre – the black and red ink of the masses – on the walls of apartment blocks, workers' hostels and camp barracks in dozens of cities throughout occupied Europe. He knew that this word was on the lips of partisans and paratroopers in the Bryansk and Smolensk forests; that it was an inspiration to the soldiers of the Chinese People's Liberation Army; that it had the power to stir hearts and minds even in the death camps, igniting hope and the will to fight where one might think that there was no possibility of hope. Krymov knew all this very well; in his lectures he would be emphasizing, more than anything, the universal significance of the bitter fighting in which they were now engaged. Krymov was moved by these thoughts and he could already sense in his heart the strong, stern words he would soon be speaking.

But now, listening to the accordion, watching the girls who had gathered like a little flock of birds by the board wall of a small Akhtuba home, he felt emotions for which there are no words.

54

As he got into the cab of the truck in his usual way, pushing his bulging knapsack to one side so that he could lean back against the seat, Krymov realized that he was about to encounter something the like of which he had not experienced during the whole year of the war.

With a sense of trepidation, he looked at his driver's anxious, frowning face and said, as he had so often said to Semyonov, 'All right, let's be off.'

He then sighed, thinking, 'Not a sign of Mostovskoy, and not a sign of Semyonov. It's as if they've both been swallowed up by the earth.'

A full moon was rising. The street and the little houses were lit by the strong, even, un-white light that artists and poets have tried so doggedly to capture and that may perhaps always elude them because there is something contradictory in the very essence of moonlight, not only in the feelings it evokes in us. In it we recognize both the power of life, which we associate with light, and the power of death, clearly present in this celestial dead body's cold and stony brightness.

The truck went down the steep slope to the River Akhtuba, which looked as dreary as a canal, crossed the pontoon bridge, passed a little copse of thin, sickly trees, and turned onto the main road towards Krasnaya Sloboda.

Along the road stood tall panels, bearing inscriptions: 'For us there is no Land beyond the Volga!', 'Not One Step Back!', 'We will Defend Stalingrad!' Other panels listed the exploits of Red Army soldiers who had destroyed German tanks, self-propelled guns and artillery pieces and killed large numbers of shock troops.

The road was broad and straight, and tens of thousands of men had recently passed along it. Arrows with broad black circles around them indicated: 'To the Volga', 'To Stalingrad', 'To the 62nd Crossing'. No road in the world could have been simpler, cleaner, sterner and more demanding.

The road would be no less straight – Krymov said to himself – during moonlit nights after the war, and people would follow it as they transported cloth, grain and watermelons to the river crossing.

Or they would take little children along it, on their way to visit grand-mothers in Stalingrad. And Krymov drifted off into thought, trying to divine the feelings of the men and women driving along this road in years to come. Would they think of the soldiers who had marched from Akhtuba to the Volga in September and October 1942? Perhaps not. Perhaps they would not recall them at all. But, dear God! What was it? What made him, all of a sudden, catch his breath? What made him so sure that, even thousands of years from now, people would feel a chill in their hearts as they looked at these osiers and willows? Look! Here! Yes, this was the road soldiers had once marched along. This was the road followed by battalions, regiments and divisions. Their mortars had banged and clattered; the muzzles of their rifles had glittered in the sun; the light of the full moon had fallen on the burnished barrels of their anti-tank rifles.

And only the autumn trees, only silent copses had witnessed those tens of thousands of men, their homes now far behind them, marching towards the Volga crossing, and to that most bitter ground.

No one, no one had come to meet them. No one, no one had seen all those young and old faces, those pale and dark eyes, all those thousands of men from steppe, town and forest, from the Black Sea and the Altay Mountains, from Moscow, from smoky Kemerovo and bleak Vorkuta.

Here they had marched in their long columns: young lieutenants walking along the side of the road, sergeant majors and sergeants surveying the ranks, battalion and regimental commanders marching in step with their soldiers ... Here some young adjutant had come running past, his map case dangling at his side, to deliver an order.

What strength, what sadness. What emptiness all around these men. Yet the whole of Russia had been watching them.

On a Saturday evening in fifty or sixty years' time, a group of young men and girls would pass by in a truck, laughing and joking, on their way to Stalingrad from the Akhtuba steppe. The driver would stop and get out to check the carburettor or fill up the radiator. And suddenly it would fall quiet in the back of the truck. Why? Was it the wind stirring the dust on the road, rustling the treetops? Or was it something more like a sigh? Or the thud of footsteps? And then it would become quieter still – you could hear a pin drop. Why? What was it that so wrung their young hearts? Why were they looking so anxiously down the straight, empty road? What was it? A dream, a steppe mirage?

Krymov could no longer distinguish between his own thoughts and feelings and those of the people he imagined looking back from the future.

Tell me, why are you weeping? Why do you listen so sadly,
Hearing these stories of Trojans and Greeks, of long-ago battles?
All was decreed by the Gods – to make songs for far-off descendants.[288]

Perhaps in 800 or 1,800 years, when this road and these trees no longer existed, after this land and this life had fallen asleep for ever, covered by a new land and a new life of which we can know nothing – perhaps some old greybeard would walk slowly by, stop for a moment and say to himself, 'There were trenches here once. Long ago – in the days of the Great Revolution, of the great construction projects and terrible invasions – soldiers came this way, marching towards the Volga.' And he would remember a picture from a children's textbook: soldiers marching through the steppe with simple, kind, stern faces, in old-fashioned clothes and old-fashioned boots, with red stars on their caps. The old man would stop. He would prick up his ears. What was it? A sigh? The thud of footsteps? Men marching?

When they reached the scattered houses of Burkovsky Hamlet, the driver turned off onto a narrow track running through a dense young forest. 'A little detour,' he said. 'The main road gets bombed day and night.'

Instead of slowing down after leaving the main road, the driver accelerated. The truck creaked and groaned as its wheels bounced over tree roots or dropped into ruts.

The sound of gunfire was getting louder, no longer drowned out by the engine. The roar of the Soviet artillery was distinct from the sound of exploding shells; it seemed to be some inner instinct, more than the ear, that told these sounds apart. Calmly indifferent to the roar of the Soviet guns nearby, nerves tensed and hearts missed a beat in response to the German shells. The brain, for its part, would carry out swift calculations: shell or mortar bomb? Large or small calibre? Had the shell passed overhead or fallen short? Or had a German artillery piece now accurately bracketed them?

As they drove on, the trees became visibly shorter. As if trimmed by huge scissors, they stood there without leaves or branches. What Krymov saw around him was not a forest but a palisade – thousands of stakes and poles stuck into the ground. German shells had spawned hundreds of thousands of shell splinters, and these had torn off bark and sliced through leaves, branches and twigs. The forest was transparent. In the moonlight shining through it, it was a skeleton forest, a forest that no longer moved or breathed.

Now Krymov could see flashes of gunfire, earthen parapets, freshly made clearings, the pale wooden doors of dugouts, camouflaged trucks half-buried in the ground. And the closer they drew to the Volga and the 62nd Crossing, the greater the tension – a tension that seemed to emanate not from Krymov or his driver but from the entire surrounding world: the earth's sandy pallor, the silence of the leafless forest, the trembling moonlight and stars.

All of a sudden, they left the forest behind them. The driver braked sharply, held out a pencil and a sheet of paper, evidently prepared in advance, and said, 'Sign this, comrade Battalion Commissar. I'll be off now.' He clearly did not want to stay by the crossing a moment longer than necessary.

And off he drove.

Krymov took a few steps and looked around. Stacked in a hollow beneath a high earth wall were crates of shells, sacks of bread, piles of winter uniforms and large wooden boxes of tinned food. Dozens of men were quietly carrying these crates and sacks towards a long wooden platform.

In a narrow gap between dense willow thickets and the far end of the earth wall lay the Volga, bright in the moonlight. Krymov went up to the traffic controller, an elderly soldier with a large round face, and asked, 'Where can I find the crossing commandant?'

Just then came a flash of light and the sound of powerful explosions from the forest behind them. The soldier turned towards Krymov, waited for a moment of quiet and said, 'Under those trees over there you'll find a small dugout. There's a sentry standing outside it.' He paused, then asked, 'On your way to the city, comrade Commander?'

There were more explosions, still more deafening, to their right, to their left and behind them.

Krymov looked around him. No one was dropping to the ground or running to take shelter. The men at the foot of the earthen wall were carrying on with their work. The elderly soldier had not even moved; he was quietly waiting for Krymov to reply to his question. In a no less friendly and relaxed tone, Krymov said, 'Yes, I'm on my way to Stalingrad. Someone should have received a phone call about me.'

'Then you'll be going on the motorboat,' said the soldier. 'The barge won't be crossing tonight. It's too bright and clear – a night for finding needles in haystacks.'

Krymov set off towards the commandant's dugout. Before he reached it, shells whistled and screeched overhead, then exploded in the forest nearby. Dense smoke whirled through the air; everything crackled and crunched. It was as if a great shaggy bear made of smoke had got up on its hind legs, roared, spun round and started crushing the trees. Yet everyone just carried on with their work, as if this had nothing to do with them, as if their life might not be snapped off at any moment, like a thread of spun glass.

Krymov did not yet fully understand the mood of exaltation now taking hold of him, nor was he entirely conscious of his astonishment at the calm, matter-of-fact majesty with which everyone he met was going about their business. Nevertheless, he looked greedily and joyfully around him, slowly taking in that something in the world had changed.

During the past year he had met all too many people like his sullen, chain-smoking driver, who had done a swift U-turn and then put his foot on the gas, desperate to get away from the crossing. Might that driver – Krymov asked himself – be the last of this dispiriting breed?

Quick anxious looks, abrupt laughs and silences, the gross rudeness of people trying to hide their sense of panic. The bowed shoulders of tired men walking along the dusty roads of the first year of the war. Wide eyes gazing up at the sky: were those bastards up there still at it? The hoarse, enraged, pistol-waving lieutenant at that pontoon bridge over the Don … Scraps of overheard conversation: 'They're not far away', 'They've sent up rockets', 'They've dropped paratroopers', 'They've cut the road', 'They've encircled our forces'. Talk about German spearheads and pincers, about the might of the German air force, about German generals issuing orders that stated the day and hour when Moscow would capitulate and then went on to emphasize the importance of soldiers brushing their teeth regularly and their being provided with seltzer water at halts.

Later, Krymov would often recall his first glimpse of the soldiers at the 62nd Crossing working away in the moonlight.

Krymov entered the dugout, which was still shaking from the nearby shell bursts. A fair-haired, broad-chested, strong-looking man in a fur waistcoat was sitting on a new little white stool at a new little white desk. He introduced himself: 'Perminov, commissar of the 62nd Crossing.'

He told Krymov to sit down and said that there would be no barge that night but that he would be taken to the city by motorboat, along with two commanders due to arrive soon from Front HQ.

After asking if Krymov would like some tea, he went over to a small iron stove and came back with a shining white teapot.

As he sipped his tea, Krymov asked Perminov how things were at the crossing.

Perminov must have been about to write a report. He moved a small inkwell and a few sheets of paper to one side. He seemed glad to talk, though he did not waste words.

He had recognized Krymov as a veteran, a man who knew what was what. There was an immediate rapport between the two men.

'Are you well dug in?' asked Krymov.

'We're doing all right. We've got our own bakery. And a decent bath-house. The kitchen functions. All underground, of course.'

'Is it mainly bombs?'

'Yes, at least in daytime. The Stukas cause real damage. The others aren't so bad – they drop most of their bombs in the water. We can't go outside till dark, of course. The Germans keep hard at it.'

'Do they come in waves?'

'It depends. Sometimes it's waves. Sometimes, the odd lone wolf. But they keep at it. Dawn to dusk. So we hold talks and lectures during the day. And we sleep. While the Germans keep ploughing away.'

Perminov gestured dismissively towards the heavens, where the Germans were so pointlessly ploughing away. 'And then it's mortar and artillery fire all night long – as you can hear.'

'Medium calibre?'

'Mainly, but now and again it's their 210s. And sometimes they try out their 103s.[289] They do all they can, there's no denying it. But where does it get them? We fulfil our plan. They can't stop us. Though there are, of course, barges that don't get across.'

'Many losses?'

'Only from direct hits – we're well dug in. But they did damage the kitchen yesterday. A hundred-kilogram bomb.'

Perminov leaned across the table. Lowering his voice, as if wanting to boast to a friend about his close, harmonious family, he said, 'My men are astonishingly calm – sometimes I can barely believe it. They're mostly from the Volga, many of them from Yaroslavl. Not so young. Most of the sappers are getting on for forty. But the way they work under fire – you'd think they were just building a school back home in their village. Not long ago we were constructing an assault bridge – from here to Sarpinsky Island. Well, you know what the Germans are like.' Perminov gestured again towards the sky over the Volga. 'They realized what we were up to with our carpentry and they opened fire for all they were worth. But our sappers just carried on. You should have seen them, comrade Commissar – it was quite something! They thought things through and took their time. They stopped now and again for a smoke. No botched work, nothing done in a rush. I saw one man pick up a log, squint at it and measure it. Then he shook his head, rolled the log to one side, picked up a second log, measured it against a string, notched it with his fingernail and began to trim it. And the Germans didn't let up for one moment. Concentrated fire on the whole sector.'

A look of pain crossed Perminov's face. Then he recovered himself and said, 'But who are we to talk? Compared with the west bank, this is a holiday camp. It's over there, in Stalingrad, that you see real war! That's what I hear again and again from my sappers: "What we've got here is nothing. In Stalingrad, it's real war."'

Soon after this, the two commanders from Front HQ arrived – a young captain and a lieutenant colonel. At three in the morning the duty sergeant came and said that the boat was ready and that they should embark. A tall young soldier came in too, holding two large thermoses. He asked Perminov for permission to cross to the west bank.

'I'm taking fresh milk to our commander. Doctor's orders. Someone goes every other day – but our boat was sunk a few hours ago.'

'Which division are you?' asked Perminov.

'13th Guards,' the soldier replied, and blushed with pride.

'All right,' said Perminov. 'Go ahead. But how was your boat sunk?'

'It's a bright night, comrade Commissar, a full moon … A mortar bomb, mid-river. No survivors. I waited and waited. Then I decided to come here.'

Perminov climbed up out of the dugout along with Krymov and the others. He looked up at the bright sky and said, 'Well, I can see a few clouds, even if they aren't very big ones. But don't worry. It'll go fine. Your pilot knows what he's doing. He's a young lad from Stalingrad.'

Turning to Krymov, he added, 'Why not stop for a few hours on your way back? You could give a lecture to our men too!'

Krymov and the three other passengers set off in silence behind a messenger. Rather than taking them past the stores of supplies, he led them along the edge of the forest. They passed a smashed-up three-tonner and some graves with small wooden obelisks and five-pointed stars. The moon was so bright that the names of the dead sappers and pontooners, written in indelible ink, were clearly visible.

As they walked by, the soldier with the thermoses read aloud, 'Lokotkov, Ivan Nikolaevich,' and added, 'My namesake, laid to rest.'

Krymov felt his anxiety growing. It seemed unlikely, on this bright night, that he would get across the Volga alive. Back in the dugout, he had been thinking, 'Will this be the last stool I sit on? Is this the last mug of tea I'll ever drink?'

And when he saw the Volga gleaming between the dense willows, he said to himself, 'Keep going, Nikolay. These may be the last steps you're fated to take on this earth.'

But fate did not allow Krymov to take these steps in peace. A heavy shell exploded in the willows close by. A red, ragged flame shot up amid a huge cloud of smoke. Momentarily deafened, all five men dropped onto the fine cold sand close to the water.

'Quick, into the boat!' shouted the messenger, as if it were safer there than on land.

No one was hurt. But everyone's head was ringing, clicking, buzzing and fizzing.

They jumped aboard, their boots banging on the planks.

A man in a greasy padded jacket, with a thin, young face, bent down towards Krymov. In the gentlest of voices, he said, 'Don't sit there, you'll get oil on your clothes. You'll be more comfortable over here.' He then turned to the messenger, who was still standing by the willows, and said, in the same calm voice, 'Vasya, get me today's paper in time for my next trip. I've promised a copy to the lads in Stalingrad. Otherwise, they'll have to wait till tomorrow.'

'What a man!' thought Krymov. He wanted to sit closer to the pilot and ask him all about himself. What was his name? How old was he? Was he single or married?

The lieutenant colonel held out his cigarette case to the pilot and said, 'Light up, hero! And tell me – how old are you?'

The pilot smiled and said, 'What's that got to do with anything?' And he took a cigarette.

887

The engine began to knock. Bending willow branches slapped against the side of the boat, then straightened again with a swish. The boat left the creek for the open river. At first there was only the smell of petrol and hot oil, but that soon yielded to the calm, fresh breath of the night-time Volga.

55

Krymov listened intently to the purr of the engine, hoping it would not suddenly cut out. He had heard more than one account of boats with stalled or shell-damaged engines being swept by the current to the central landing stage, straight into the hands of the Germans.

His companions appeared to share his anxiety. The young captain asked, 'Got any oars, just in case?'

'No,' the pilot replied.

The lieutenant colonel, looking at the pilot's thin face, and at his long thin oil-soaked fingers, said gently, 'Our pilot's a master – he doesn't need oars.'

The pilot nodded. 'Don't worry, it's a good engine.'

Krymov looked around. Captivated by what he saw, he forgot his worries.

Breathing and shimmering on the Volga lay a field of silver, gently tapering towards the south. The small waves of the boat's wake streamed behind the stern, like magic pale blue mirrors. An immense sky, bright and weightless, dusted with stars, spread over the river and the broad lands stretching both east and west.

Such a picture – a night sky, the solemn splendour of a great river, mighty hills and plains lit by moon and stars – is usually associated with silence, majestic calm and either stillness or slow, smooth movement. But this Russian night over the Volga was far from quiet.

Over the hills of Stalingrad, above the white, moonlit buildings stretching along the Volga, trembled the incandescent light of artillery fire. A little to the north, like grim fortresses, loomed the black buildings of the giant factories. From the east bank came the slow rumble of the Soviet artillery, shaking the earth, the sky and the water. From high above came the constant drone of heavy night bombers. The pale blue of the autumn night was threaded by thousands of red lines of tracer shells and bullets. Some threads were isolated; others were in dense clumps. Some were like short spears, plunging into the ground or the walls of buildings; others were long enough to cover half the sky. The German bombers were trying to knock out the Soviet anti-aircraft defences. Semi-automatic weapons down on the ground hurled up cones of red and green tracer bullets, and these formed a complex pattern as they met the cones of tracer shells and bullets flung down by the bombers.

Heavy bombs exploded on the moonlit streets like flashes of pink summer lightning. Iron screeched and whistled over the Volga. Mortar bombs burst in the swift water, and blue flames flared and faded amid suddenly seething golden-white foam.

At first glance this vast, rumbling smithy, full of fire and movement and extending for dozens of kilometres, seemed beyond all comprehension. But that was not so. On the contrary, it was surprisingly easy to make out the main forces involved – the twin hammers and anvils of the battle. It was equally easy to follow many of the swifter, more ephemeral contests and skirmishes – between two buildings, between two windows, between an anti-aircraft battery and a circling bomber. Everything was laid out clearly – in all its dynamics. There on the dark blue tracing paper of the night sky was a living, breathing sketch of the war; dotted lines of tracer fire, bursts from machine guns and the flames of explosions marked out the strongholds and force fields of a huge battle.

The flashes of artillery salvoes were especially dense in a hilly sector a little to the north of the three giant factories. Sometimes the flashes came at regular intervals, like a precisely stamped chain; sometimes they came in bundles; sometimes the entire sector flickered and shone with modulating lights. The German artillery batteries were hard at work, evidently preparing the ground for an infantry attack on the factories.

And then hundreds of parabolas of fire rose from the east bank, a broad red arc climbing over the forest and the Volga. The men in the boat heard a prolonged, barely describable howl; it could have been dozens, or even hundreds, of huge locomotives simultaneously letting off steam.

After reaching their apogee over the Volga, the rockets hurtled towards the ground. Bursts of flame leaped from the German heavy-artillery positions on the hills. Iron drums drowned out all other sounds. Compressed by the explosions, then expanding convulsively, the air transmitted the crashing of iron hail. Each stone of this hail was enough to crush a reinforced concrete wall.

When the glowing smoke cleared, Krymov could see that the German batteries were no longer firing. A well co-ordinated salvo of Katyushas had silenced them once and for all.

With eyes, ears and joyful heart, Krymov understood all that had just happened. He saw sharp-eyed observers calling out aiming data, radio operators transmitting this data across the Volga, frowning divisional and regimental commanders waiting for the order to fire, a grey-haired artillery general in his bunker watching the second hand of his clock, and soldiers running back from their rocket launchers as the Katyushas took off.

In the boat, everyone lit cigarettes and began to talk. Only the soldier with the milk sat there silently and motionless, holding the thermoses to his breast; he could have been a wet nurse cradling two babies.

When the boat reached the middle of the Volga, a battle broke out between two dark factory workshops. From a distance the high walls of these bastions looked very close to each other. There was a flash from one of them, and a burst of tracer fire plunged into the wall of the opposing workshop. A German gunner appeared to have opened direct fire on a building occupied by Red Army soldiers. A quick spear then flashed from the dark wall of the Soviet bastion and pierced the wall of the German workshop. A few seconds later, the air was full of fiery spears and arrows. There were bursts of tracer fire from machine guns; rifles were firing tracer bullets that seemed like incandescent flies. The dark walls were like great thunderclouds, with forked lightning flashing between them.

It occurred to Krymov that these workshops were indeed full of electricity, that the tension between the two opposing elements could be measured in billions of volts.

Krymov forgot that the frail boat might sink at any moment. He forgot that he could not swim; he forgot his recent forebodings. He felt surprised that his companions were crouching, and that one of them had covered his eyes with his hand. This was, of course, a natural reaction – hundreds of invisible steel strings now stretched across the water, only a little above their heads, humming alarmingly.

This vivid picture was not only stern and majestic; it was also strangely affecting. The thunder and flames of battle had not extinguished the colours of the moonlit autumn night. The swaying, shimmering field of silvery wheat spreading across the water was still intact. Nothing violated the sky's thoughtful silence and the melancholy of the stars.

The quiet and exalted world of the Volga night seemed, in some impossible way, to be one with the war. All that was most incompatible had come together; wild audacity and martial passion had merged with a sense of peace and resigned sadness.

Krymov remembered the girls he had seen dancing in Akhtuba. He remembered how moved he had felt by them, and for some reason this evoked another, more distant memory: the day he told Zhenya that he loved her. She had looked at him for a long time without saying a word. But this memory no longer made him feel sad.

As the boat drew nearer to the west bank, the water grew calmer. The shells and mortar bombs were now passing high overhead.

The pilot cut the engine and the boat came to rest against some large stones. The four passengers went ashore and began to climb the path towards the Army HQ bunkers.

After the tension of being on the water, it was a joy to feel solid earth underfoot, with its stones and its lumps of clay.

Behind him Krymov heard the quiet knock of the engine. The boat was on its way back to the east bank, about to return to open water that was repeatedly being torn apart by explosions.

Krymov realized that, as they jumped out, he and his companions had forgotten to say goodbye to the pilot. Maybe this was why the pilot had smiled when the lieutenant colonel asked him his age. It had been the same with the engine; at first they had all listened intently, noticing every slightest misfire, but as they approached the shore they were no longer even aware whether or not the engine was still running.

But Krymov was now in the grip of new impressions; he was walking on the earth of Stalingrad.

Timeline of the War

1 September 1939 Germany invades Poland. This is generally accepted as marking the beginning of the Second World War.

22 June 1941 Launch of Operation Barbarossa. German forces invade the Soviet Union. It is this date that most Russians see as marking the beginning of the war, which they almost always refer to not as 'the Second World War' but as 'the Great Patriotic War'.

9 July 1941 German forces capture 300,000 Soviet troops near Minsk.

27 July 1941 German forces complete the encirclement of Smolensk.

8 August–19 September 1941 Battle of Kiev. Soviet Southern Front is encircled and more than half a million soldiers are taken prisoner. General Zhukov had wanted to withdraw earlier, but Stalin had refused to allow this, saying, 'Kiev was, is, and will be Soviet!'

29–30 September 1941 Beginning of Babi Yar massacre outside Kiev. Execution of 33,000 Jews on these two days alone.

September–October 1941 Nikolay Krymov leads an ad hoc grouping of 200 men out of German-held territory and across the front line. He joins Major General Petrov's 50th Army to the north of Bryansk.

October 1941–January 1942 Operation Typhoon. The Germans advance on Moscow.

2–21 October 1941 Battles of Vyazma and Bryansk. Three Soviet armies are encircled – but their continued fighting delays the German advance on Moscow.

10 October 1941 Zhukov is named commander of all forces defending Moscow.

20–22 November 1941 German forces take Rostov.

5–6 December 1941 The German advance is halted and the Soviets begin a successful counter-offensive.

12–28 May 1942 Krymov is appointed commissar of an anti-tank brigade. Second Battle of Kharkov ends in a disastrous defeat; the Germans take at least 240,000 prisoners in what is called 'the Barvenkovo mousetrap'.

7 June–4 July 1942 German forces besiege and eventually capture Sevastopol.

28 June 1942 Launch of Operation Blue – the German summer offensive intended to capture the oil fields of the Caucasus. Initial success leads Hitler to insist on the additional goal of capturing Stalingrad.

12 July 1942 Establishment of the Stalingrad Front, under General Timoshenko.

17 July 1942 Forward units of General Paulus's 6th Army engage with the 62nd Army by the River Chir, a tributary of the Don.

23 July 1942 General Gordov takes over command of the Stalingrad Front.

24 July 1942 Forward units of General Paulus's 6th Army reach the Don, near Kalach.

28 July 1942 Stalin issues Order 227 – 'Not One Step Back'. This included the sentence, 'Panic-mongers and cowards should be exterminated on the spot.'

5 August 1942 Establishment of the Southeastern Front, under General Yeromenko.

7–8 August 1942 The Germans encircle much of the 62nd Army, on the west bank of the Don.

9 August 1942 General Yeromenko also takes over command of the Stalingrad Front.

21 August 1942 German forces cross the Don. No Soviet forces remain west of the Don, except for bridgeheads at Serafimovich and Kletskaya.

23 August 1942 First massive air raid on Stalingrad. German forces reach the Volga at Rynok, north of Stalingrad, thus isolating the remnants of the 62nd Army from the Soviet forces to the north-west of Stalingrad. Grossman and his companions set out from Moscow. The journey to Stalingrad takes them five days. On the way, Grossman pays a second visit to Yasnaya Polyana.

25 August 1942 Mining of main Stalingrad factories lest the Germans capture the city.

28 August 1942 Mass flight of civilians from Stalingrad. This went unmentioned in most Soviet accounts of the battle.

29 August 1942 General Zhukov is sent to the Stalingrad Front as representative of the Stavka (the Supreme Command).

8 September 1942 The Germans reach the Volga at Kuporosnoye, to the south of Stalingrad, isolating the 62nd Army from the 64th Army positioned still further south. Yeromenko moves the Front HQ to the east bank of the Volga.

12 September 1942 General Chuikov takes over command of the 62nd Army.

14 September 1942 German forces enter central Stalingrad. Rodimtsev's 13th Guards Division begin crossing the Volga at 5 p.m.

15 September 1942 A battalion of Rodimtsev's division recaptures the main railway station.

21–22 September 1942 Intense fighting in central Stalingrad. Rodimtsev is forced to withdraw to a thin strip of ground parallel to the river.

1 October 1942 The Germans capture the Tractor Factory, reaching the Volga and splitting Chuikov's 62nd Army in two.

19 November 1942 Beginning of Operation Uranus, a major Soviet offensive.

23 November 1942 Soviet forces encircle Paulus's 6th Army.

2 February 1943 The last German forces in Stalingrad surrender.

Afterword

THIS TEXT

Stalingrad is one of the great novels of the last century, but it does not exist in any definitive text. Its textual and publication history is, in fact, still more complicated than that of *Life and Fate*. Grossman began his first version in 1943 and completed it in 1949. A selection of eleven chapters – heavily edited – was published later that same year, under the title *By the Volga (chapters from the novel Stalingrad)*. They are mostly about military matters and there is no mention of Viktor Shtrum or the Shaposhnikov sisters. The first ten of these chapters were included – in fuller versions – in the novel's various published editions. The remaining chapter, however, was included not in *Stalingrad* but in *Life and Fate* – yet another testimony to the fact that Grossman, at least at this point, saw the two novels as a single work.

In his struggles to meet his editors' changing demands, Grossman then partially or completely rewrote *Stalingrad* at least four times between 1949 and the novel's first publication, serialized in the journal *Novy Mir*, in late 1952. The novel was then published as a book: first by the military publishing house *Voenizdat* in 1954 (reprinted in 1955); and then, in 1956, by the literary publishing house *Sovetsky Pisatel'* ('Soviet Writer'). The 1952, 1954/55 and 1956 editions differ a great deal from one another, and they all differ still more from the various typescripts. Even the title was changed, against Grossman's wishes, shortly before the novel's first publication. Grossman's original title was *Stalingrad*, but the novel was published under the title *For a Just Cause* – a phrase from the speech made on the day of the German invasion by Vyacheslav Molotov, the Soviet minister for foreign affairs.

Clearly anticipating difficulties from the beginning, Grossman recorded all official conversations, letters and meetings to do with the novel in his fifteen-page 'Diary of the Journey of the Manuscript of the Novel *For a Just Cause* through Publishing Houses'.[290] Anatoly Bocharov, the author of the first monograph on Grossman, summarizes this 'journey of the novel' as follows: 'Changes were made between 1949

897

and 1952 in the course of meetings of editorial boards, after comments from a large number of reviewers and consultants, editors and literary bosses of all kinds. Battered, exhausted, patched and repatched – it was only by some miracle that the author managed to save his text from destruction by demagogy, blinkered thinking and excessive caution.'[291]

The tone of these editorial meetings was set in an exchange in December 1948 between Grossman and Boris Agapov, one of the members of the *Novy Mir* editorial board:

Agapov: I want to render the novel safe, to make it impossible for anyone to criticize it.

Grossman: Boris Nikolaevich, I don't want to render my novel safe.[292]

Even though Konstantin Simonov (chief editor of *Novy Mir* until February 1950), Alexander Tvardovsky (Simonov's replacement as chief editor) and Alexander Fadeyev (general secretary of the Union of Soviet Writers for most of the period from 1937 until 1954) seem genuinely to have admired *Stalingrad*, publication of the novel was repeatedly postponed. The demands made by Fadeyev and Tvardovsky range from the most trivial to the most sweeping. At one point Tvardovsky is said to have suggested that Grossman should make Shtrum the head of a military commissariat rather than a physicist; in reply, Grossman asked what post he should give Einstein.[293] On another occasion Grossman was asked to remove all the 'civilian' chapters. The novel was set in type three times, but on each occasion the decision to publish was countermanded and the type broken up – although it seems that, at least on two of these occasions, a very few copies were, in fact, printed. The 30 April 1951 entry in Grossman's diary reads, 'Thanks to the splendid, comradely attitude of the technical editors and printing-press workers, the new typesetting was carried out with fabulous speed. I now have in my hands a new copy: second edition; print run – 6 copies.'

The reason for the extreme caution shown by Grossman's editors is that the Soviet victory at Stalingrad had acquired the status of a sacred myth – a myth that legitimized Stalin's rule. There was, therefore, no room for even the slightest political error. Tvardovsky and Fadeyev felt it necessary to ask for approval from a variety of different bodies: the Writers' Union; the Historical Section of the General Staff; the Institute of Marx, Engels and Lenin; and the Communist Party Central

Committee. They were afraid of offending important generals. They were afraid of offending Khrushchev, who appears in the earlier versions in his role as the most senior political commissar at Stalingrad. They were, no doubt, still more concerned about Stalin's own reaction.

In December 1950 Grossman himself wrote to Stalin. His letter ends, 'The number of pages of reviews, stenograms, conclusions and responses is already approaching the number of pages taken up by the novel itself, and although all are in favour of publication, there has not yet been a final decision. I passionately ask you to help me by deciding the fate of the book I consider more important than anything else I have written.'[294] Stalin, it seems, did not reply. Nor did Georgy Malenkov, one of Stalin's closest henchmen, to whom Grossman wrote in October 1951.[295] Nevertheless, after a last flurry of new suggestions for the title, which included 'On the Volga', 'Soviet People' and 'During a People's War',[296] the novel was finally published in the July–October 1952 issues of *Novy Mir*. In a letter to Fadeyev, Grossman wrote, 'Dear Alexander Alexandrovich [...] Even after being published and republished for so many years, I felt more deeply and intensely moved, on seeing the July issue of the journal, than when I saw my very first story ['In the Town of Berdichev'] in *Literaturnaya gazeta*.'[297]

*

As well as the novel's three different published editions, there are eleven versions – some complete, some partial – in the main literary archive in Moscow (RGALI). The first of these is a manuscript, almost unreadable because of Grossman's poor handwriting and the huge number of corrections he made to it. The next version has – inexplicably – gone missing; it is not even known whether it was a manuscript or a typescript. The third version, therefore, is the first readable version we have. It is a fairly clean typescript, with handwritten revisions, and it does not appear to differ greatly from the original manuscript; it is bolder and more vivid than the later versions and it deserves to be published in full.

The fourth and fifth versions incorporate both editorial suggestions and changes introduced by Grossman himself. These versions are less bold, but all the main plot lines are still present. An important feature of the fifth version is the addition of a moving chapter – the account of Tolya Shaposhnikov's last day before being mortally wounded – that is not in any of the previous versions. The sixth version is the most orthodoxly Soviet of all; most of the chapters about Viktor Shtrum and the Shaposhnikovs have been cut and much about Stalin and his historical role has been added. Interestingly, Grossman's editors appear to have realized that their caution had weakened the novel; subsequent proofs and published editions are based not on this version but on the less heavily edited fifth version.

The later versions in RGALI are galleys and page proofs for the projected (but cancelled) publication of the novel in *Novy Mir* in 1950, for the actual publication in *Novy Mir* in 1952 and for the first book publication in 1954. The most interesting of these versions is the so-called 'ninth version' – about a dozen chapters that were added, in 1951, to the unused 1950 galleys. It is here that Chepyzhin and Ivan Novikov (the coal-miner brother of Colonel Novikov) appear for the first time.

We know that it was not Grossman's own choice to introduce these two characters. In January 1951 Alexander Fadeyev told Grossman and Tvardovsky that the Central Committee had expressed a 'high opinion of the novel' and proposed that the Union of Writers and *Novy Mir* jointly 'decide the question of publication'. Soon after this Fadeyev sent Grossman a number of demands. He was to add new chapters about the heroic wartime work being carried out in mines and factories in Siberia and the Urals, insert the current official view on the wartime alliance with England and America (see below, note on chapter 23), and entirely remove the figure of Viktor Shtrum. This last demand was clearly motivated by official anti-Semitism. Grossman replied, 'I agree with everything, except Shtrum.' Tvardovsky then suggested an artful compromise: to make Shtrum subordinate to a world-famous Russian physicist. Grossman accepted this suggestion and introduced the figure of Chepyzhin.

It would be wrong, however, to assume that these new sections are any the less valuable for being forced on Grossman. Grossman had a remarkable gift for turning an apparent compromise to his own advantage. He himself had worked as a safety engineer in a Donbass mine. His first novel, *Glückauf*, is set in the Donbass, and it is clear from his memoir *An Armenian Sketchbook* that he recalled his time in the Donbass with pride. There is no reason to think that he was reluctant to add these chapters. They are extremely vivid and Grossman's picture of the wartime Soviet Union would be incomplete without them.

Many of the pages devoted to Chepyzhin are equally vivid. The account of his lectures is almost certainly another of Grossman's tributes to the physicist Lev Shtrum. The recent rediscovery of the life and work of Lev Shtrum lends an added poignancy to such passages as the following: 'These formulae seemed full of human content; they could have been passionate declarations of faith, doubt or love. [...] Like a valuable manuscript, this blackboard should surely have been preserved for posterity.'[298]

*

An editor or translator must decide which of Grossman's many versions to follow. The simplest course would be to follow the 1956 edition. This is the best of the three published editions. The year 1956 marks the beginning of Khrushchev's 'Thaw' – the relatively liberal period following Stalin's death in 1953 – and Grossman was able to reinstate many passages omitted in 1952 and 1954. He made only a very few small changes when the novel was republished in 1959 and 1964, and the plot line of *Life and Fate* begins where the 1956 version ends, with no conflicts or inconsistencies. Until today, all Russian republications and all translations of *Stalingrad* have followed the 1956 edition.

The chief disadvantage of following this edition is that – though more complete than the two earlier editions – it still omits many of the wittiest, most perceptive and most unusual passages of the unpublished third version. The boldness of this early typescript cannot be emphasized enough. It was as daring of Grossman to think of publishing it in the late 1940s as to think of publishing *Life and Fate* in the late 1950s. To continue to omit many of the finest passages of Grossman's writing would be unforgivable.

A secondary problem with the 1956 edition is that, at some points, it is weakened by the anti-Stalin censorship characteristic of the decades following Stalin's death. The most glaring instance of this particular variant of Soviet censorship relates to Grossman's treatment of Stalin's Order of 28 July 1942, shortly before the beginning of the Battle of Stalingrad. This still-controversial Order, with its slogan 'Not One Step Back', forbade any further retreat, under any circumstances, and decreed the death penalty for 'laggards, cowards, defeatists and other miscreants'. In the third version, and in both the 1952 and 1954 editions, Grossman portrays Krymov reading Stalin's Order with profound elation. This brief chapter is the climax to a long sequence of chapters in the course of which Krymov has grown ever more enraged by what he sees as an unthinking general acceptance of a seemingly endless Soviet retreat. It is crucial to the novel's structure. Nevertheless,

901

since Stalin's role is seen – on this occasion – as entirely positive, the chapter was omitted in 1956. There is little doubt that Grossman would have wanted to reinstate it.

*

The third version of *Stalingrad* deserves to be published in full, both in Russian and in other languages – just as publishers now publish early drafts of such works as *War and Peace*. Unfortunately, for all its brilliance, this version is only a draft; it is not a finished novel. One plot line – Viktor's affair with Nina – simply fades out with no explanation. There are other inconsistencies. It was not until the fifth version of the novel that Grossman clearly differentiated Novikov and Darensky; in the first four versions, instead of two characters, there is only one, sometimes called Novikov, sometimes called Darensky. Some long passages relating to this composite character are repeated verbatim, hundreds of pages apart.

There are also conflicts between this third version and the plot line of *Life and Fate*. In the third version, Vera does not become pregnant and Ivannikov hands Mostovskoy his essay on senseless human kindness while they are both still in Stalingrad. In *Life and Fate*, on the other hand, Vera has given birth to a child and Ivannikov (renamed Ikonnikov) shows Mostovskoy his essay not in Stalingrad but in a German POW camp, probably Dachau.

A further reason not to consider this version definitive is that many of Grossman's later revisions were entirely worthwhile. He was required to delete many fine passages, but he also omitted passages that are verbose, confusing or over-detailed. He added not only the mining chapters and the account of Tolya's day in command of an artillery battery but also the chapters about Marya Vavilova working in the fields, Alexandra being shown around the Stalgres power station and Mostovskoy and Sofya falling into German hands.

*

The third version and the 1956 edition are the two most important texts of the novel, yet neither is satisfactory on its own. We have, therefore, drawn on both of them for this translation. With regard to the general plot and the order of the chapters, we have followed the 1956 edition, but we have reinstated several hundred passages – some of just three or four words, some of several pages – from the third version. And where entirely new chapters – e.g. the coal-mining chapters – were added at a later stage, we have also drawn on whichever was the earliest typescript in which these chapters appear.

In an attempt to guard against excessive subjectivity on our part, we have tried to keep to two guidelines: not to reinstate any passages that would result in plot conflicts, and not to reinstate any passages unless we had good reason to think that it was Grossman's editors – rather than Grossman himself – who were responsible for their omission from the published editions. There were, of course, borderline cases – passages that Grossman might have chosen to omit for the sake of concision, but where it was equally possible that his editors might have found something questionable.

The task of faithfully 'restoring' Grossman's novel – as one might restore a damaged painting – is, no doubt, theoretically impossible. In practice, however, it is less difficult than one might imagine. The first step was to carry out a detailed comparison of the three main published editions. This gave us a clear idea of the nature of the disagreements between Grossman and his editors, allowing us to see both what most perturbed the editors and which passages mattered so much to Grossman that he went out of his way to reinstate them when given the opportunity.

These three editions constitute a unique resource for the study of Soviet censorship. There are, of course, instances where the omissions (mostly in 1952) and reinsertions (mostly in 1954 or 1956) relate to matters of obvious political sensitivity – criticisms of kolkhozes and mentions of military defeats or of labour camps. More often, however, the differences between the editions are less a matter of substance than of tone. Many of the passages omitted in 1952 could not possibly have been construed as anti-Soviet; they must simply have been considered too silly or frivolous for a novel about so epic a subject as the Battle of Stalingrad. During the last years of the Stalin regime, only the most dignified of styles was acceptable. Soviet soldiers or officials could not be portrayed as behaving childishly or selfishly at a moment of critical military importance. And there was a strong taboo on any overt mention of petty crime. In the third version and in 1956, Seryozha's mess tin was 'stolen' (*ukrali*) the day he graduated from military school; in the more heavily edited 1952 and 1954 editions, it 'disappeared' (*propal*). The same substitution was made in the scene at Kazan station, when a kolkhoz woman has her money and documents stolen. The taboo on mentions of lice, fleas, bedbugs and cockroaches seems to have been equally strong. There is no doubt that Andrey Sinyavsky, one of the first and most important of Soviet dissidents, was right to define socialist realism as a twentieth-century version of neoclassicism.[299]

A passage about Major Berozkin illustrates this strikingly:

He had fought in the summer of 1941 in the forests of western Belorussia and Ukraine. He had survived the black horror of the war's first days; he knew everything and had seen everything. When other men told stories about the war, this modest major listened with a polite smile. 'Oh, my brothers,' he would think. 'I've seen things that cannot be spoken about, that no one will ever write down.'

Now and again, though, he would meet another quiet, shy major like himself. Recognizing him – from little signs known to him alone – as a kindred spirit, he would talk more freely.

'Remember General N.?' he might say. 'When his unit was surrounded, he plodded through a bog in full uniform, wearing all his medals, and with a goat on a lead. A couple of lieutenants he met asked, "Comrade General, are you following a compass bearing?" And what did he answer? "A compass? This goat is my compass!"'

The general acts correctly and courageously; he does not take off his uniform and medals, even though these may attract the attention of German soldiers. And he is intelligent and resourceful; a goat is more likely than a compass to lead him safely out of the bog. Nevertheless, it is undignified for a Soviet general to entrust his life to a goat. There is also an interesting ambiguity in these paragraphs: is Berozkin unable to speak about what he saw in the summer of 1941 because of its 'black horror', or because some of it is too strange or seemingly absurd to fit the official picture?

The final paragraph, in any case, was omitted in 1952 and 1954. Grossman was, fortunately, able to reinstate it in 1956. But the third version includes many other examples of his best writing that he was *never* able to publish. It has been a joy to include them in this translation, and so to restore to the novel much of its original sweep, humour and vigour. Like Anton Chekhov, whom he loved, Grossman is, amongst much else, a great comic writer.

*

Most of Grossman's characters remain broadly the same in the third version and the published editions. There are, however, a few important differences.

First, there are three characters who had to be completely or partially removed from *Stalingrad*; later, Grossman included all three in *Life and Fate*. In the third version, Jenny Genrikhovna, the former German governess to Ludmila and Marusya, is living with the Shaposhnikovs in their Stalingrad apartment. To have the novel's central family giving shelter to a German, as the Wehrmacht approached Stalingrad in the summer of 1942, was extraordinarily daring on Grossman's part. It is no surprise that he had to remove all the passages about Jenny Genrikhovna. We would have liked to reinstate them, but this would have led to plot conflicts with *Life and Fate*.

The second character whom Grossman moved to *Life and Fate* is Vladimir Sharogorodsky, the poet and Russian historian who – like Jenny Genrikhovna – is a part of Zhenya's social circle in Kuibyshev (*L&F*, I, 25). Sharogorodsky was too much an aristocrat, and too fiercely anti-Soviet, to be included in the published editions of *Stalingrad*, but, unlike Jenny Genrikhovna, he plays an indispensable role in the plot. He introduces Ivannikov/Ikonnikov to Mostovskoy and so enables Anna Semyonovna's last letter from the Berdichev ghetto to reach Viktor's family. Unable to remove Sharogorodsky from the novel completely, Grossman split him into two separate figures: the Sharogorodsky we meet in *Life and Fate*, and Gagarov, the more acceptable, less anti-Soviet version of Sharogorodsky whom we meet in the published editions of *Stalingrad*.

The third character whom Grossman had difficulty including in *Stalingrad* is Ivannikov himself. In the third version he is an important presence, the bearer of two important documents both of which are a response to the Shoah. Not only does he carry Anna Semyonovna's last letter across the front line, but he also shows Mostovskoy his essay on senseless kindness. Mostovskoy reads this essay and is shaken by it.

Grossman evidently realized that Ivannikov's essay was unpublishable and removed it from *Stalingrad*, possibly already hoping he might be able to include it in *Life and Fate*. The essay appears in the fifth version of *Stalingrad* but not in the sixth, and there is no mention of it in any of the stenograms of editorial meetings. But Ivannikov, like Sharogorodsky, plays a necessary role in the plot and it was impossible for Grossman to remove him entirely. Instead he just reduced his importance. The reader does not meet Ivannikov; he merely hears about him from Gagarov. And there is no mention at all of his essay.

In *Life and Fate*, Ikonnikov – as Grossman renames him – regains his importance. His essay is included in full and he argues with Gardi the Catholic priest and Mostovskoy the Old Bolshevik, insisting that, with regard to personal moral responsibility, their points of view are indistinguishable. Both Gardi and Mostovskoy believe they can be absolved from responsibility for their actions. Gardi trusts in the forgiveness of God, and Mostovskoy believes his actions are determined by historico-economico-political forces so all-determining as to be equivalent to what a Catholic understands by God. Ikonnikov, in contrast, takes a position we could call Protestant; he insists that he has free will, and is therefore responsible for his actions, no matter what degree of force he is subjected to. Ikonnikov then proves he means what he says, condemning himself to death by refusing to work on the construction of a gas chamber.

*

Socialist realism favours consistency and decorum. Positive characters should be entirely positive and negative characters entirely negative. And there is little room – still less in a novel about the Battle of Stalingrad – for pettiness, excessiveness and frivolity. Nearly all Grossman's characters, therefore, are somewhat less complex, somewhat more stereotyped in the published editions than in the third version. As Grossman originally conceived them, they are more fully developed and have more rough edges. Vera is ruder. Zhenya is more unpredictable. Abarchuk is more fanatical and Marusya takes up a still more hard-line position when reprimanding Tokareva the orphanage director and arguing about art with Zhenya. Viktor and Ludmila quarrel more bitterly and Viktor's affair with Nina is sexual, not platonic. Vera's friend Zina Melnikova possibly has an affair with a German officer. And on the part of the minor characters, there are more instances of bad behaviour, drunkenness and petty crime.

In most cases there is little doubt what Grossman would have preferred. The quarrels between Viktor and Ludmila, for example, are of obvious importance both for *Stalingrad* and for *Life and Fate*. Alexandra Vladimirovna is two-dimensional in the published editions of *Stalingrad*; in the third version, Grossman tells us more about her past and this makes her a more rounded and convincing character. Grossman was evidently compelled to omit not only the mentions of her wealthy merchant father but also the passages about her life in Western Europe. The published versions of the Zina Melnikova chapters are yet more unsatisfactory; since most instances of her suspect behaviour have been deleted, it is hard to see why the Shaposhnikov sisters so disapprove of her.

Wherever possible, therefore, we have restored the more interesting and unexpected details from the third version. With regard to Viktor's affair with Nina, however, we have stayed closer to the 1956 edition; as with Jenny Genrikhovna, it was impossible to follow the third version without confusing the plot.

*

In his December 1950 letter to Stalin, Grossman wrote that there were already almost as many pages of internal reviews, stenograms of meetings, etc., as there were pages in the novel itself. A comprehensive study of the four main typescripts and three published editions could easily end up still longer. We shall limit ourselves to a brief mention, chapter by chapter, of the most striking differences.

PART I

1–2. These chapters were omitted in 1952 and 1954. They are identical in the third version and the 1956 edition.

3–5. Similar in all variants. Some of the bleaker aspects of the lives of Soviet peasants – the details of Vavilov's backbreaking work, the family's grief over the dead cow, the meagreness of the food Vavilov takes away in his knapsack, even the mention of the cockroaches under the floor – are from the third version. The grim paragraph beginning 'Vavilov saw the war as a catastrophe' is also from this version. So are Pukhov's sharpest criticisms, his positive attitude towards the Germans and the passage about the loss of his sons. And so is much of the portrait of the corrupt kolkhoz chairman.

A condensed version of these chapters was included in *By the Volga* (1949).

6. The mention of Sofya and Alexandra having got to know each other in Paris and Bern are from the third version – one of many instances where the published editions omit mention of the older characters' lives in Western Europe. We have also followed this version for the details of the food consumed at the dinner. In the published editions, the meal is more modest, with no butter, sturgeon or caviar and only one half-litre of vodka.

7. In general, Grossman's editors seem to have wanted to tone everything down, to make everything smoother and more even. Anything comic or absurd in the third version is less so in the published editions. In the published versions of this chapter, for example, there is no mention of Seryozha's ambition to eclipse both Newton and Einstein.

And – as already mentioned – in the third version and in 1956, Seryozha's mess tin was 'stolen'; in 1952 and 1954, it 'disappeared'.

8. Most of Mostovskoy's sociological analysis of Alexandra's room is from the third version. In the published editions, he just says that the books (Marx, Hegel and Lenin) and the two portraits remind him of his apartment in Leningrad. He does not mention either her merchant father or her prosperous son-in-law. And in the published editions Alexandra is unshakeably positive. Instead of ending one of her speeches to Mostovskoy with the words 'Some kind of darkness has fallen on us', she says, 'No, no, we'll stop the fascists. Of course we'll stop them.'

9. For Mostovskoy's speech about Antaeus, we have followed not the 1956 edition, but the 1952 and 1954 editions. In 1956, Stalin has been edited out and Mostovskoy begins, 'I am sure you remember the myth about the giant Antaeus.' This makes little sense. Mostovskoy would not suddenly bring up a Greek myth had Stalin not recently mentioned this myth in a public speech. The deletion of the mention of Stalin is a clear instance of Grossman's editors struggling, after Khrushchev's criticisms of Stalin in 1956, to minimize the number of references to him.

For Alexandra's reminiscences about pies, we have followed the third version. However unwittingly, she makes it all too clear that exile was a great deal more pleasant under the tsarist regime than in Soviet days. This passage was omitted in 1952 and 1954; it was included in 1956, but heavily abridged. Mostovskoy's memories of his Easter meal in prison were also omitted from the published editions.

In the published editions, Vera's friends borrow copies not of Conan Doyle or Rider Haggard, but of *How the Steel was Tempered* by Nikolay Ostrovsky (1904–36). A classic of socialist realism, this novel was first published serially in 1932–34. Copies would not have been difficult to obtain. Conan Doyle was genuinely popular at this time, in spite of some degree of official disapproval.

For the last two pages of this chapter, from 'There was a general silence' to 'everyone turned to look at him', we have followed the third version. Grossman was clearly enraged by the suspicion with which the Soviet establishment looked on the hundreds of thousands of men encircled by the Germans during the first year of the war; many were sent to penal battalions, sentenced to years in the camps or shot. The 1952 and 1954 editions omit Kovalyov's words about bureaucrats collaborating with the Germans; the 1956 edition includes this passage, though much toned down.

Andreyev's bleak words about truth are from the third version.

10. Here we have followed the 1956 edition. In the third version Seryozha, when playing with the cat, imitates not Marusya's voice but that of Jenny Genrikhovna. And the 1952 and 1954 editions omit the lines about Seryozha pretending to headbutt the cat and calling him a 'little ram!' Evidently this was considered too silly for a novel on a theme as important as the Battle of Stalingrad.

11. Pavel Andreyev's criticism of Mostovskoy's internationalism as being like the teachings of Christ is from the third version.

12. The mention of the anarchist philosopher Mikhail Bakunin is from the third version. Even the mentions of Lake Geneva and Marx's grave in London, present in the typescript, were first published only in 1954; in 1952 it was evidently considered safer to omit all references to Mostovskoy's years as an exile in Western Europe, as if this might have made him too much of an internationalist and less truly Russian.

13. For Agrippina not eating anything with her vodka, her words about prayers 'being said in every one of the churches' and her envious complaints about Mostovskoy, we have followed the third version. In the published editions there is no mention of his trips to the Caucasus, and his pension is only a thousand roubles. And the

last paragraphs are blander, omitting the word 'whore', the suggestion that this woman may be signalling to the Germans, and the threat of shooting.

14. Similar in all variants.

15. The mention of the nature of Sitnikov's wound – and of the suspicion with which he was evidently treated – is from the third version. The description of Viktorov lying on the stretcher also follows the third version; in the published editions, the comparison with the clubbed turkey is omitted, and his underwear is 'worn', not 'soiled'. A condensed version of this chapter was included in *By the Volga* (1949); here his underwear is 'unwashed'.

16. This chapter about Alexandra first appears only in the fifth version. It may represent a compromise on Grossman's part; his editors may have demanded that he emphasize Alexandra's empathy with Soviet workers. It would be wrong, however, to dismiss the chapter for this reason. As always, Grossman was determined to write truthfully, and some of his truthfulness was clearly found unacceptable. The paragraph about the 'vicious powers' of chemistry, for example, was omitted in both 1952 and 1954.

The startlingly bold paragraph about Dmitry Shaposhnikov, present in the fifth version, was also first published only in 1956. In the earlier editions, Dmitry dies of a heart attack brought about by 'major unpleasantnesses' (*krupnye nepriyatnosti*) at work. His wife – Seryozha's mother – then goes to work in the far north; after Seryozha twice catches pneumonia, she agrees to let him live with Alexandra in Stalingrad.

In the fifth version Grossman states that Dmitry was working on the White Sea Canal. Grossman's editors may have required him to omit this for political reasons, but mention of the canal would, in any case, have been anachronistic; Dmitry was arrested in 1937 and the White Sea Canal, the first of Stalin's major slave-labour projects, was built between 1931 and 1934. Nevertheless, the 1956 edition still preserves a faint trace of the White Sea Canal: 'empty shore […] *white* foam […] seagulls […] *white* head'.

17. This chapter is not present in the third version; we have not yet established in which version it first appears.

18. An entire page of this chapter, from Marusya's 'You should paint posters', is from the third version. Neither the argument about truth, nor Zina's stories about Kiev, nor the discussion of the possibility of Alexandra staying in Stalingrad appear in the published editions.

19. Similar in all variants. Some of Novikov's apologies and the humorous mentions of his readiness to subordinate himself to Zhenya are from the third version. A Soviet colonel was evidently not supposed to subordinate himself to a woman.

20. The paragraph about Novikov's extreme correctness – his being as 'scrupulously fair as a pair of pharmaceutical scales' – is from the third version.

21. The emphasis on Novikov's sense of shame is from the third version. This version also includes several pages from Novikov's notebook. Some of Novikov's reflections were later given to Darensky and incorporated in the published editions (III, 6) as a part of *his* notebook.

22. Similar in all variants.

23. At the beginning of the chapter we have omitted almost a page from the published editions – a long summary of military developments that does not appear in the third version. In 1952 and 1954 the Soviet defeats mentioned in this account are excused by the Allies' failure to open a second front; this assertion of the Soviet official line was omitted in 1956.

The cockroach 'scuttling across the map' and the secretary 'conscientiously minuting decisions never to be put into effect' are from the third version. The page beginning

'The speed of the retreat', with the vivid image of Novikov as a cinema operator, is also from this version – as is the reference to Heraclitus near the end of the chapter.

24. Some of the account of Major Berozkin's regiment – that it is advancing west under orders from Major Berozkin (!), and that the women looked at his men as if they were 'holy martyrs' – is from the third version. Novikov's criticism of Bykov – that he is like a scientist explaining just how and why a boat is going under when he should be trying to plug the holes in the hull – is also from this version.

25. This chapter, present in a slightly different form in the third version, was first published only in 1956. But in 1956 Cheprak is a great deal more positive as he says goodbye to Novikov. Instead of saying, 'That'll be the end of you', he says, 'I think that's a good decision.'

26. Three important passages are from the third version: the report of Timoshenko bathing in the Volga, the lines about his men having 'lost all faith in themselves and their future'; and the two paragraphs about the symbolic importance of this 'mass baptism in the Volga'.

27. Similar in all variants – though the published editions omit many interesting details: e.g. the scientist who talks about his life being 'essential to science', Ludmila's pine-needle baths and courses of 'photo-, electro- and hydrotherapy', and Varya's bartering in the market.

28. This chapter was first published – heavily edited – in 1956. Among the details we have taken from the third version are the students' jokes about the importance of having the right social origin; the passage about Sofya and Alexandra spending time together in Paris; Abarchuk's joke – if that's what it is – about having sex with a monkey; his belief that it was impossible to eradicate the contagion of bourgeois ideology from the psyche of anyone with a bourgeois parent or grandparent; his guarded yet ominous words about what should be done with such people; and Alexandra's remark about people who 'don't know how to reconcile love of humanity and love for an actual person'.

29. Similar in all variants, though the seemingly innocuous paragraph beginning 'Her love for her son' was first published only in 1956. No doubt, it was considered too silly to be included for a novel on such an epic theme.

30. Here we have followed the 1956 edition. The third version is similar, but more detailed. Viktor's mother's love and concern for his well-being is still more obsessive. Olga Ignatievna's apartment is still more exotic, her aquarium still more splendid. Part of the argument between Viktor and the director of the Physics Institute – the six paragraphs from '"Ivan Dmitrievich," Viktor had said' – was omitted in 1952 and 1954.

31. The quarrel between Viktor and Ludmila is a great deal more serious in the third version than in the published editions. Here we have stayed closer to the third version, taking from it the eight sentences from 'Sometimes I need your heart' to 'quarrels and disagreements'.

32. The first three paragraphs were omitted in 1952 and 1954, evidently because they emphasize Viktor's Jewish background. Here and elsewhere, the third version puts more emphasis than the published editions on the importance to Viktor of his relationship with his mother. The long paragraph about his mother's readiness to sacrifice herself for him, for example, was omitted from all the published editions.

The comparison of nuclear energy with a sleeping bear or a vast fish is also from the third version; Grossman's editors probably saw such comparisons as too extravagant, too far from the realism they were required to promote.

33. In the 1952 edition there is great emphasis, throughout the chapter, on Chepyzhin's breadth of interests, his worldwide fame and his importance to his students; in this first publication of the novel Chepyzhin played not just a 'big' (as in 1956), but a 'decisive' role in the formation of Viktor's scientific world view.

The ten paragraphs at the end of the chapter, from 'Viktor remembered a conversation about Chepyzhin with Krymov', first appeared in 1954. Though Grossman had introduced Chepyzhin only to meet Fadeyev's demands, several reviewers of the 1952 edition criticized Grossman for giving so much space to Chepyzhin's 'homespun philosophizing'. Krymov's attack on Chepyzhin may have been introduced to counter this criticism.

34. Some of the items in Viktor's suitcase, including the boiled water and the half-litre bottles of vodka for bribes, are from the third version. Several of the less dignified episodes in the first half of the chapter are also from this version. These include Viktor's account of his train journey during the Civil War, people's unsympathetic responses to the woman from the kolkhoz, and the account of the pugnacious drunk. Because of other changes to the structure of this and later chapters, it was impossible to reinstate another interesting episode from this version: Postoev's discovery, in the train, that he too has been robbed; that the suitcase with his provisions, including the roast chicken, is now empty.

The lines from 'And after Stenka Razin' to 'baffling to the mind' were omitted in 1952 and 1954. It was evidently unacceptable, during the first decade after the war, to suggest that, after serious discussion of the likelihood of the Germans reaching the Volga, Russians could have slipped so quickly into singing light-hearted songs.

35. About thirty lines of this chapter are from the third version. These include the passages about the birthday greetings telegrams, Anna Semyonovna's need to work and be financially independent and the words of Yiddish she quotes in her letters. The omission of these passages from the published editions must have been another of the compromises required of Grossman. In order to keep Viktor Shtrum in the novel, he clearly had to give less space to his personal life and his Jewish background.

36. The entire account of Viktor and Ludmila's quarrel is from the third version, as is much of what Maximov says about the stifling of free speech in Czechoslovakia. In the published editions, Maximov has not actually written his article but has merely come to talk to Viktor about fascism. And his last words – about how gardening could save the world from fascism and war – are omitted.

The account of Viktor listening to Stalin's speech is not present in the third version. In the 1952 and 1954 editions, it takes up about two pages, while in 1956 it takes up only five lines. Since this speech is historically important, and since Grossman was clearly, in 1956, under strong pressure to minimize Stalin's role in the war, we have inserted from the 1954 edition the two paragraphs beginning 'Stalin had then asked'. It is possible that Grossman might have wanted to restore more of this speech; it is hard to judge.

The description of Viktor's autumn 1941 train journey to Kazan, present in the third version, was omitted in 1952 and 1954. Its realism was, no doubt, seen as too negative.

37. All three published editions omit the emphasis on the importance of the Hotel Moscow's supplies of vodka. The 1952 and 1954 editions omit the account of Postoev's dealings with the hotel manager; his shameless assertion of his entitlement to privilege must have disconcerted Grossman's editors.

By far the most important of the four scientists mentioned by the hotel manager is the biologist and plant breeder Nikolay Vavilov, one of the many victims of Stalin's purges. Vavilov was arrested and sentenced to death in 1941 – in part because of his contacts with foreign scientists and in part because of his disagreements with Trofim

Lysenko, a charlatan who was a favourite of Stalin's. Vavilov's death sentence was commuted to twenty years of imprisonment, but in 1943 he died of starvation in prison. In 1955 his sentence was posthumously reversed and by the 1960s he was hailed as one of the most important of Soviet scientists.

Grossman's several versions of this passage differ a great deal from one another. In the third version, he writes, 'The hotel manager could remember with astonishing exactness the numbers of the rooms in which Fersman, Vedeneyev and Lysenko had stayed, though he seemed to have little idea which of them was a geologist and which a metallurgist.' Grossman includes three names but only two professions – as if preferring not even to dignify Lysenko with the title of a biologist.

The much shorter 1952 version of this chapter entirely omits this paragraph. But in the 1954 and 1956 editions, the name of Lysenko is replaced by that of Vavilov. Given that Vavilov was rehabilitated only in 1955, this was daring on Grossman's part. As in the third version, there is a mismatch between the number of names mentioned and the number of professions. Here, though, this mismatch serves a different purpose. It is Grossman's way of hinting that there may be something he is unable to say straight out. Vavilov certainly *does* deserve to be called a biologist, but in the eyes of the state he is a criminal.

There is no mention in the third version of Viktor and Postoev talking and reading during the night. In the 1952 and 1954 editions we are told that the two men are reading, but not that they are reading Sherlock Holmes. At this time of extreme Russian nationalism, it may have been unacceptable for them to be reading a foreign book.

38. Here we have followed the 1956 edition. The third version is similar, though the description of Viktor's apartment is more detailed.

39. The paragraph about Viktor's absent-mindedness is from the third version, as are some of the physical details – the rough skin and callused hands – that show Viktor what heavy, exhausting work Anna Stepanovna has been doing. The sentence about Viktor bowing to her and kissing her hand is also from the third version.

40. Similar in the third version and the 1956 edition. Much of the first four paragraphs were omitted in 1952 and 1954. Grossman's emphasis on the precarious condition of the Russian state during the summer of 1942 was clearly unacceptable. The paragraph about support services' HQs being located within the city is from the third version, as are many of the more reflective passages.

41. For this chapter, we have followed the 1956 edition. In the third version, Nina says more about the vileness of her husband. He forced her to have an abortion, and he and his mother trade tinned food on the black market. In the third version, Nina is artful and seductive, though Viktor believes her to be naive and innocent, seeing himself as a noble warrior ready to defend her. Viktor and Nina spend the night together. They are, it seems, alone in the building, in an exalted world of their own; everything harsh, petty and mundane has disappeared into the bomb shelter.

42. One of the chapters that Fadeyev required Grossman to add for the novel's first publication in 1952. Grossman's typescript of this (in the so-called 'ninth version') and the 1952 edition are almost identical, but the 1954 edition differs a great deal. The 1954 and 1956 editions differ only slightly.

On 2 February 1953, ten days before the publication in *Pravda* of Bubyonnov's denunciatory article, there was a meeting in the *Novy Mir* editorial office, attended not only by the editorial staff but also by writers, critics and military figures. Understanding which way the wind was blowing, Tvardovsky and everyone present criticized several aspects of the novel, including its inadequate portrayal of the role of Stalin. Still more criticism, however, was directed at the novel's 'historico-philosophical concept'.

Grossman's attackers and defenders united in advising him to omit the 'far-fetched' philosophical passages. And six weeks later, at a meeting of the Union of Writers' Presidium, Fadeyev referred to the 'reactionary, idealist, anti-Leninist philosophy' put in the mouth of Chepyzhin.

It may be difficult for a reader today, unversed in the Marxist–Leninist orthodoxy of the time, to grasp what was so heretical about Chepyzhin's thoughts. The literary critic Venedikt Sarnov has suggested, very plausibly, that the most serious issue of all is simply that Chepyzhin is thinking for himself. Both Chepyzhin and Grossman are guilty of thinking for themselves about political and philosophical matters on which only Stalin and the Party had the right to pronounce.[300]

The changes introduced in 1954 were clearly a response to the criticisms made at this editorial meeting and in subsequent published reviews. The chief difference is that in the 1954 and 1956 editions it is Viktor who wins the argument, while in 1952 it is Chepyzhin. The 1952 variant of the chapter ends with Viktor subordinating himself to Chepyzhin: 'What I wanted to talk to you about today was not just the methodology of my work. I have to confess that I was very pleased when you brought up more general questions of life. And I suddenly understood more clearly than ever than you are my teacher not only with regard to the problems of physics.'

Grossman introduced the figure of Chepyzhin to meet Fadeyev's demands. It was agreed that he could keep Viktor Shtrum in the novel if he made him the student of a world-famous Russian physicist. It is ironic that this made the novel vulnerable to criticism on other scores.

43. Not in the third version. It is still unclear in which version it first appeared.

44. A great deal of this chapter – around fifteen paragraphs, including the account of Krymov's personal battle with 'the life instinct', the paragraph with the mention of Tolstoy, and much of the description of the wounded soldiers and the pontooners – is from the third version. This chapter marks the beginning of a series of chapters that see Krymov thinking constantly, with growing anguish, about the Soviet retreat. This was a sensitive issue; it is not surprising that there is much here that Grossman was unable to publish.

45. For the description of the evening steppe we have followed the 1956 edition; in the third version, this passage is longer. We have, however, followed the third version for several sentences about the refugees, and also for the chapter's final paragraph. In the published editions this is more upbeat. The 1956 edition reads, 'Thousands of people, thousands of men, women and children, all of them filled with an implacable hatred of fascist evil, were heading east beneath the broad copper and bronze of the setting sun.'

46. Not in the third version. It is unclear in which version it first appeared.

47. Like many of the chapters summarizing military developments, this is not in the third version.

48. This chapter went through a great many changes. Among the passages we have taken from the third version are the quotation from Lermontov, the mention of men from Chernigov deserting to the Germans, and the paragraphs about General Vlasov, along with other references to the catastrophic encirclement at Kiev. The paragraph beginning 'And – as if summoned by the approaching dark forces' was omitted in 1952 and 1954. The last five or six pages of this chapter – from 'became manifest, in word and deed' to 'separate escape' – were evidently added relatively late; they are present in 1954 and 1956, but not in the third version or the 1952 edition.

49. Much of this chapter is about yet another panicked Soviet retreat. It seems likely that Grossman's editors insisted that he add some more upbeat passages to balance this.

On the first page, for example, the words 'Krymov learned what had happened during the days of his wanderings' are followed by this: 'The front line had been breached and the Germans had advanced rapidly, but before them had appeared a new Front, the Bryansk Front, with new armies and new divisions; and behind the Bryansk Front had appeared still more armies and divisions. The Soviet defences were growing ever deeper and stronger; they now extended for hundreds of kilometres.' We have omitted this and two similar paragraphs – all present in the published editions but not in the third version.

The tribunal chairman does not appear in 1952 and 1954. In the third version and the wartime notebooks there are six traitors for him to judge; in the 1956 edition only three.[301] The 'contemptuous smirk' (*brezglivo usmekhnulsya*) with which one of Yeromenko's subordinates looks at Krymov – a man who had been in German-held territory and was therefore automatically suspect – appears in the third version, but not in the 1952 and 1954 editions.

In 1952 and 1954 Yeromenko himself makes no appearance, though some of his words are attributed to the major general.

In the published editions, but not in the third version, Krymov's recollections of Belorussia end with a sentence probably foisted on Grossman by his editors: 'But during the last twenty-five years a new force had entered the life of Belorussia. In village, town and forest Krymov had encountered Belorussian Bolsheviks – the soldiers, craftsmen, workers, engineers, teachers, agronomists and kolkhoz brigade leaders now at the head of the partisan bands fighting for the people's freedom.' The 1952 and 1954 editions include a similarly orthodox paragraph about Bolsheviks in Ukraine, omitted in 1956.

The old woman's account of praying to God and then cursing the Devil is from the third version. It closely follows a wartime notebook entry that concludes, 'These hearts, like the righteous ones in the Bible, illuminate with their strange light our entire people. There are only a handful of them, but they will be victorious.'[302]

The poem by Tyutchev, like most other passages of poetry, is from the third version.

50. In the third version, this chapter takes the form of a letter Krymov writes to Zhenya.

51. In the third version Krymov spends only ten days in Moscow and doesn't attend the celebration of the Revolution in Red Square. In 1952 and 1954, on the other hand, Grossman devotes over a page to the speech by Stalin at the end of this chapter. Here we have followed the much-abbreviated 1956 account of the speech.

52. Like other summaries of military developments, this chapter first appeared in one of the later typescripts. But Grossman's brief mention of two disastrous defeats – the Battle of the Kerch Peninsula and the Second Battle of Kharkov – was first published only in 1956; the taboo against mention of the defeats of the first year of the war was relaxed only gradually.

53. The various versions of this chapter differ a great deal. In the third version, Grossman emphasizes the importance of English and American armaments production. In the published editions, however, this passage is replaced by a criticism of the Allies for failing to open a second front. In 1952 and 1954, this criticism takes up almost a page, but in 1956 only a few lines – yet another confirmation that Grossman only introduced it on the insistence of his editors. We have, therefore, omitted most of the criticism and restored the lines about Allied armament production. We have also omitted a few passages such as the following: 'It was during these battles that the Party Central Committee, the army political officers and other Party members gradually forged discipline, that they organized the Red Army's moral and fighting strength.' There is little doubt that Grossman added such passages under duress.

In the third version there is a long discussion of the differences between the war against Hitler and the war against Napoleon. Grossman considers that Kutuzov truly wanted to avoid fighting; in his day, the vastness of Russia was enough in itself to defeat an invader. Stalin, however, wanted to keep fighting throughout the retreat. He understood that for Hitler, with his mechanized army, Russia's vastness was not an *overwhelming* problem. And the Red Army fought doggedly whenever it had its back to the wall – as in the Battle of Moscow, the sieges of Leningrad, Sevastopol and Odessa, and Stalingrad itself.

For the main part, however, our translation of this chapter follows the 1956 edition, which includes striking passages not present in the third version.

54. Similar in all variants, but many of the more dissonant, undignified or simply comic moments are from the third version. These include Sofya's words about fashions in marriage; Zhenya wanting to laugh while Krymov's comrades sing the Internationale; Krymov being driven to work in a car that spends ten days of each month in the repair workshop; and Zhenya feeling the same sense of pity for Krymov as for the murdered fox cub.

55. Similar in all variants. We have followed the third version for the passage about the statue of Kholzunov; in the published editions Zhenya and Novikov do not appear to be hoping that he will hear them. We have also followed the third version for the quarrel between Bykov and Novikov. In the published editions this is less serious, with no mention of tribunals.

56. For nearly all of this chapter we have followed the third version. In the published editions, Zina is generally less colourful. She does not spend any time under German occupation and the story she tells to exemplify her ideal of true love is tamer; the engineer heroine merely abandons her studies and leaves her husband for an actor. In the third version, however, Vera does not become pregnant. Since she is portrayed in *Life and Fate* with a small baby, we have followed the 1956 edition for her exchange with Zina about pregnancy.

57. In the third version, Mostovskoy argues not with Gagarov – who first appears only in the fourth version – but with Vladimir Sharogorodsky, a former aristocrat. Sharogorodsky is essentially the same character as Gagarov, but he is openly and uninhibitedly anti-Soviet. The two men argue fiercely. Mostovskoy lists, one by one, all the criticisms directed against the Soviet regime by Mensheviks, by members of the Social Revolutionary Party, by anarchists and by bourgeois émigrés; he even includes their views on the Nazi–Soviet non-aggression pact and the execution of important Red Army generals during the purges. He then says that it is for the Soviet people to decide. If they think these criticisms just, they will do away with the Soviet regime; if they think them unjust, they will defend the regime. Sharogorodsky says that the Communists will have to answer for their failings – 'just as we [i.e. the tsarist regime] had to answer for our failings'. The chapter ends with Sharogorodsky telling Mostovskoy that a former partisan called Ivannikov is eager to see him; he wants to give him both a letter from Shtrum's mother and something he has written himself.

58. The engineers' conference is similar in all variants, except that Krymov's engineer brother does not appear in the third version. A few of the more shocking details – workers swelling up from hunger or dying of scurvy – were omitted in 1952 and 1954. The 1956 edition, on the other hand, omits several mentions of Stalin. In one of Andrey Trofimovich's speeches, for example, the earlier editions read, 'Stalin resolved to construct' while the 1956 edition reads 'the State Defence Committee resolved to construct'. Here we have followed the earlier editions. The omission of Stalin's name,

in direct speech during a formal meeting, is a clear example of the anti-Stalin censorship characteristic of the Khrushchev era.

Like many of the novel's more comic moments, Postoev's question at the end of the chapter was omitted in 1952 and 1954.

59. For this chapter, we have, for the main part, followed the 1956 edition, since following the third version would lead to plot conflicts. In the third version, Viktor kisses each of Nina's fingernails in turn, while Nina laughs and counts, 'One, two, three', etc. Then they spend the night together. In 1952 and 1954, however, Viktor does not even kiss her; he just takes her by the hand. The Soviet Union, especially in the last years of the Stalin regime, was a prudish world; the hero of an epic novel could not be allowed to commit adultery.

60. In the third version, this chapter is longer, mainly because it includes several pages of Viktor arguing with himself about lies, honesty and the ethics of adultery. We have included only one of these somewhat verbose pages – the eleven paragraphs from 'A man man with one leg'. Some of the thoughts in these pages reappear in *Life and Fate*, when Viktor is thinking about his love for Maria Sokolova.

In the third version, Viktor expects Nina to join him at his dacha the next morning. The 'Nina' thread, however, simply breaks off at the end of the chapter, unresolved, Grossman does not even tell us whether or not Nina arrives at the dacha. For this reason we have stayed close to the 1956 edition for this chapter and chapter 59.

61. Like other chapters about mines and factories in Siberia and the Urals, this is not in the third version.

62. Krymov's bitterness and fury – his indignation at other commanders for their resigned acceptance of a seemingly endless retreat – is more extreme in the third version than in the published editions. His reflections on the life instinct and his fantasies about how best to punish 'flighters' are all from this version.

We also follow the third version for the last four paragraphs of the chapter. In the published editions, the general is more measured. He does not threaten to have Malinin shot and there is no mention of fuel reserves being blown up. Instead he says, 'If Malinin no longer has any petrol, then he's to give the commissar the petrol from his own vehicles – and he and his Talmudic accountants can continue their way on foot.' Among other details taken from the third version are the unnamed commander's complaint about the canteen boss eating fried chicken and the adjutant's lament over the lost 'museum-piece' carpet.

63. Similar in all variants. Three sentences about the treacherous limitlessness of the Russian steppes are from the third version.

64. Similar in all variants.

65. We have followed the third version for the paragraph of gossip about the commanders; the spicier items are omitted from the published editions. The horrors of collectivization and the subsequent famine made many peasants welcome the German invasion, at least initially. The most interesting differences between variants of this chapter are in the old man's speech beginning 'In 1930 we slaughtered ...' In the 1952 and 1954 editions, he says, 'In 1930 we slaughtered all the pigs and we drank for two weeks on end. Two rich men went mad. And then one old man – he owned more land than anyone in the village, he had eight horses and four women working for him as labourers – drank two litres, went out into the steppe, lay down in the snow and fell asleep.' The implication of all this is that only the wealthiest, most exploitative peasants were opposed to collectivization – and this, of course, made the passage more acceptable to Grossman's editors. Here we have followed the 1956 edition, which is identical to the third version.

Most of the last page and a half of this chapter – Krymov's thoughts about how much energy he has expended over the years arguing with people like this old couple, the old man's view of himself as a witness and a historian, and the old woman's assertion that it is only the Jews who have anything to fear from the Germans – is from the third version.

66. The passage about Lieutenant Orlov's suicide is from the third version. This chapter touches on sensitive issues; it was, of course, almost impossible to say outright that some sections of the population had welcomed the Germans. Most of the account of the black-bearded man, the shifty youths and the silent Cossack – the two pages beginning 'He was drunk' and ending 'you'd have thought not one of them had been drinking' – was omitted in 1952 and 1954. The Cossack woman's promise to marry Krymov in church is from the third version.

67. This chapter is present in the third version and the 1952 and 1954 editions but was omitted in 1956. The Order in question is Stalin's Order 227 of 28 July 1942, with its slogan 'Not One Step Back'. See page 901 of this Afterword.

68. Similar in all variants.

69. For the sentence about Mulyarchuk and his lice we have followed the third version. The published editions read, 'Mulyarchuk would be the only man on whom lice were discovered.' In the third version, the passage about Vavilov's love of work is still longer; for Grossman, the love of work is an important theme – not something forced on him by his editors. A condensed version of this chapter, mostly focusing on Vavilov, was included in *By the Volga* (1949).

PART II

1. Another of the summaries of military developments that first appeared in one of the later versions.

2. Similar in all variants. In the third version, Grossman cites Tolstoy as an example of the 'deep simplicity' of true art.

3. The 1952 and 1954 editions do not include any of the general reflections about Yeromenko. Even the third version includes only a few of them.

4. For this chapter we have stayed close to the 1956 edition. We have taken just three passages from the third version: the image of Bolokhin's foot cloths and books of poetry being transformed into some ancient, homogeneous material; the paragraph about the repentant HQ journalist who nearly gets himself killed; and the paragraph about the cynical and pessimistic journalist who wants to buy a camel harness. The 1952 and 1954 editions differ little from the 1956 edition, except that Yeromenko is not named. Yeromenko was notoriously vain; he may have objected to some aspects of Grossman's portrayal of him, largely positive though this is.

5. The list of books read by Andreyev, including the mention of Alexandre Dumas' two novels, is from the third version. As in other chapters, several of the wittiest and most interesting passages were omitted from the published editions. Among them are the paragraph about Andreyev entering the officially required melt data instead of the real data; the paragraph about Bebel's *Women and Socialism*; and the paragraph about the similarities between family relations and inter-state relations.

6. The sentence about Andreyev calling his wife and his daughter-in-law 'Hitlers' is from the third version. Part of this chapter was included in 'The Andreyev Family' in *By the Volga* (1949).

7. Similar in all variants.

8. Similar in all variants, though in the third version Mostovskoy is indignant at being asked to give a formal talk. He would have preferred just to walk about and chat to the workers.

9. Some vivid details near the end of this chapter – the knife, the tomato and the words about death entering the home – are from the third version.

10. Similar in the third version and in 1956. There is no mention in 1952 and 1954 of Ida being exiled; we are only told that she lived in Kazakhstan and the Urals.

11–12. Similar in all variants, though the third version is a little prolix.

13. For the main part we have followed the 1956 edition. In the third version, Marusya's rants about discipline are still more obsessive, making her almost a caricature. We have, however, taken several short passages from this version. Most important of these is Marusya's internal argument with Zhenya about truth. We have also followed this version both with regard to such details as the Russian POWs being fed rotten horsemeat and in its greater emphasis on the children being from so many different nationalities. Internationalism of any kind was suspect during the last years of the Stalin regime.

The mention of the boy stealing towels is present both in the third version and in the 1956 edition. In 1952 and 1954, however, it is replaced by a sentence about a boy picking a fight during a game of football; Soviet children, evidently, could not be described committing even the pettiest of thefts.

14. Similar in all variants, except that, in the third version, Marusya is still more deeply upset in the final scene.

15. As in II, 4, Yeromenko is not named in the 1952 and 1954 editions.

The name 'Pryakhin' is fictional. In his notebooks Grossman records Yeromenko saying that Chuyanov (the real-life First Secretary of the *obkom*) 'doesn't know a fucking thing' (*ni khuya ne znaet*), and that the fortifications he constructed were 'fucking useless' (*khuyovye*).

The mention of Tolstoy and the Fili Council of War is from the third version. Two of the less serious moments – the discussion of the attractive setting to which the *obkom* is to be relocated, and Yeromenko's interest in Pryakhin's inkwell – were omitted in 1952 and 1954.

16. Similar in all variants.

17. For most of Pryakhin's long speeches we have followed the third version. His emphasis on the use of forced labour would have seemed bold in the early 1960s, let alone in the late 1940s; it is no surprise that the published editions are far blander, though the 1956 edition includes one brief mention of 'former kulaks' (*raskulachennye*). The 1952 and 1954 editions include an extra twenty lines, not present in the third version, of laboured Soviet rhetoric.

18. Broadly similar in all variants. The mention of Marusya's candidate membership of the Communist Party is from the third version. The omission of this from the published editions makes Alexandra's remark beginning 'Party member or not ...' seem unmotivated.

19–20. These chapters are similar in the third version and in 1956. We have taken a few details from the third version: Kryakin's apparent inability to move his eyes, some of the bribes with which Gradusov curries favour with the commanders, Chentsov's planned trip to America and some of Polyakov's recollections from his 'lecture'.

21. Similar in all variants.

22. There is no mention in the third version of any General Weller; his place is taken by Paulus. As elsewhere, some of the most vivid details, such as the glimpse of the wrecked Soviet planes with their 'broken-off, red-starred wings half-buried in the

ground', were omitted from the published editions. There are important differences between the earlier (1952 and 1954) and the later (1956 and after) editions of the paragraph beginning 'Had the general been a psychologist and a philosopher'. *All* these changes have the effect of allowing the general's thoughts to seem relevant not only to Nazi Germany but also to the Soviet Union. In the two earlier editions, instead of the laconic 'Fulfilment, for him, lay not in rewards and honours,' there is a much longer sentence: 'Fulfilment, for him, lay not in rewards and honours, but in the severe soldierly simplicity with which he was elevating the glory of Germany.'

23. This chapter was omitted in 1952, but it is similar in the third version and in the 1954 and 1956 editions.

24. Here we follow the 1956 edition. As in other chapters, many of Weller's thoughts and speeches are, in the third version, given to Paulus.

25. Similar in all variants – but there are important differences in the penultimate paragraph. The following phrases were omitted in 1952 and 1954: 'backbreaking labour and the arbitrary power of officials ... horror at the implacable power of the Reich ... the howl of English bombs'. The chapter's last two sentences – about what would happen 'after the victory' – were also omitted. This is telling; in view of the consolidation of Stalinism after the Soviet victory in 1945, there is little doubt that Grossman was thinking more of the Soviet Union than of Germany – and it also seems that his editors must have been aware of the possibility of this interpretation.

26. Similar in all variants. In the account of her collision with him, the librarian praises Goebbels for being 'truly a man of the people'. She uses the word *narodnost'* (literally, 'peopleness' or 'being of the people') – a very Soviet word indeed. This, naturally, was omitted from the published editions.

The mention of Churchill is from the third version.

27. Similar in all variants, except for the last two pages. In the third version, Forster does not bring up the possibility of a Soviet counter-offensive.

28. This chapter, not present in the third version, was first published in 1954.

29. Few differences between the various versions.

30. This chapter was omitted in 1952 and 1954; serious discussion of the nature of a dictator and dictatorship was probably thought dangerous. For the main part, our translation follows the 1956 edition, which is similar to the third version. The long opening paragraph first appeared only in 1959 (a rare instance of a change introduced after the 1956 edition).

31. About half the monologue by the house manager's wife is from the third version. Among the sentences omitted from the published editions are those about Zhenya's bras, Marusya stealing from the children's homes, and Vera 'servicing' the lieutenants in hospital.

32. Similar in all variants. We have reinstated a few vivid details omitted from the published editions: e.g. the image of the heaps of red brick seeming like heaps of steaming red meat.

33. Some of the bleaker details are from the third version. The published editions also omit mention of two of Varvara's many fears: that Natalya may have sent her to the wrong landing stage and that the boat may hit a mine. Much of the paragraph about the jobs the truck driver does 'on the side' was omitted in 1952 and 1954. A small part of this chapter was included in 'The Andreyev Family' in *By the Volga* (1949); this version ends with the dinghy sailing off to the east bank – not with it sinking.

34. Similar in all variants. A few details, such as Sokolova's cursing and swearing, are from the third version.

35. As in other chapters, we have taken the references to Alexandra's past from the third version; they were omitted from the published editions. Several instances of particularly mean and selfish behaviour were also omitted. Among the passages we have reinstated are the sentence about the woman shouting out that her scientist husband's life is important to the country and several of the fiercest exchanges between Sofya and Alexandra, on the one hand, and Meshcheryakov and the house manager's wife, on the other hand.

36–37. Similar in all variants. But several of the grimmer or more bizarre moments in the third version – the incidents of petty theft, Zhenya's strange imaginings – were omitted from the published editions. Part of chapter 37 was included, under the title 'The Fire', in *By the Volga* (1949).

38–39. Similar in all variants. The mention of vodka shops and food depots being looted was omitted from the published editions. Towards the end of chapter 39, we have omitted the following sentence, present in all the published editions but not in the third version: 'There are accounts of Communists and Komsomol members, of Red Army commanders and political instructors doing everything in their power to save the burning city and the people who lived there.'

40–41. Similar in all variants. The joke about 'the bloody bombs' is from the third version – black humour like this was not acceptable.

42. Similar in all the published editions. In the third version, however, the second half of the chapter is entirely different. Instead of taking part in the fighting, Krymov reports to Yeromenko at HQ. Khrushchev, Malenkov and Vasilevsky are also present. Grossman portrays Yeromenko as being unjustifiably rude to Krymov.

43. Similar in all variants. A few details, such as the description of the woman's fingernails, are from the third version.

44. This chapter first appeared only in the fifth version.

45. This chapter was added at a later stage; it is not present in the third version.

46. Another chapter that was added at a later stage.

47–51. These chapters were added for the novel's first publication in 1952. One of Fadeyev's demands had been that Grossman should add a section about the work being done, in support of the war effort, by miners and factory workers. There are a number of highly rhetorical passages in the typescript version of this section. These remain in 1952 and 1954 but are absent from the 1956 edition; it seems likely that it was Grossman who chose to delete them, recognizing their verbosity. The only other significant difference between the typescript and published variants of these chapters is the treatment of Masha. Ivan thinks about her a great deal more often in the typescript than in the published editions. In the typescript Ivan is more of a human being – not only a Stakhanovite model worker. In this translation we have reinstated all mentions of Masha.

PART THREE

1. Another of the military-historical chapters added at a later stage.

2–3. The account of Tolya's day in command of the artillery battery first appears in the fifth version. This episode was included, as a single chapter, in *By the Volga* (1949), though the last two paragraphs – the account of Tolya's being wounded – are omitted. The chapter thus ends on a positive note: 'the roar of his guns [...] greeted the sunrise'.

4–5. Details taken from the third version include the image of Tolya's arms and legs as 'subordinate to every bump and pothole'; the Kamyshin doctor's complaint about the hospital being overcrowded; the more expensive items – the ham, lampreys and caviar – in the lavish spread provided by Aristov's landlady; the mention of the old man whose beard gets pulled out; and Berozkin's account of making a dress for his wife – evidently considered a task beneath the dignity of a Red Army commander.

Aristov's words about providing the chief of staff with Riesling are also from the third version. The 1956 edition reads, 'The chief of staff is on a special diet because of his ulcer. "At your orders, comrade Colonel, whatever you need!" We may be out in the steppe, far from any collective farms, but he still gets the very best milk products. He even gets a little suspicious, summons me specially and tells me I'm a dangerous man if I can find sour cream in the middle of nowhere.'

The vignette of the general with the goat was omitted in 1952 and 1954.

In the published editions, Tamara's father is simply 'a man called Sokratov'.

A condensed version of Part III, chapters 4–7, 9 and 12–13 was included, titled 'On the Road of War' and 'By the Volga' in *By the Volga* (1949).

6. Two long passages – Darensky's fantasy about being cared for by the commander and chief of staff, and the extracts from his notebooks – were first published only in 1956. The first dozen lines of the notebook extracts, from 'A battalion commissar' to 'what confidence', are from the third version. With regard to the two paragraphs about Darensky's time in prison and a labour camp, the 1952 and 1954 editions differ surprisingly little from the 1956 edition. The words 'camp' and 'prison' do not appear, but there is no doubting where Darensky has been. Grossman's euphemistic way of putting it is 'Darensky lived through a great deal of unpleasantness before the falseness of the accusation against him was finally proven.' In the third version, Darensky is released after sending a letter to Stalin.

7. Similar in all variants. As elsewhere, we have taken from the third version a few of the more comic details omitted from the published editions – e.g. the lines about the company that seems about to march straight into the Volga.

8. This chapter, except for the last three paragraphs, was omitted in 1952 and 1954 – almost certainly because, after the war, Stalin saw Zhukov as a potential rival. He downplayed his role in the Soviet victory and demoted him. The chapter is almost identical in the third version and in 1956.

9–11. The quote from Tyutchev and the sentence immediately after it are from the third version. Among other passages taken from this version are the paragraph about the defeated soldiers crossing the Don, the mention of wanderers and deserters picking off lice, the image of the 'centrifugal force' that casts a bus seat and a lavatory cistern into the steppe, and much of the old man's litany of complaint about thieving soldiers and kolkhoz chairmen 'bartering calves for bottles of moonshine'. The old man's admission 'Though we do meet the occasional louse' was omitted in 1952 and 1954. In the third version, chapter 11 ends with an emphatic declaration on Grossman's part that everyone – from Stalin to the rank-and-file soldiers – shared a clear understanding that the Red Army now had to stand its ground, that any further retreat was no longer possible.

12. We have taken several details from the third version. In the published editions Darensky's fury with Berozkin is less extreme; he does not accuse him of being like a pedlar. Nor do his eyes fill with tears as he says goodbye to Berozkin and Tamara. And the penultimate sentence, about Tamara's hands being dirty and disfigured, is omitted – another instance of the Soviet insistence on the observation of decorum.

13. Similar in all variants, except that in the published editions the paragraph beginning 'Killed, killed, killed' is less varied in tone; the sentence about salting mushrooms and the description of Aristov looking as if he had just returned from holiday are both from the third version. There was also a change to the penultimate paragraph. In the

published editions Tamara just wants to wipe Berozkin's eyes; in the third version, which we have followed, she also wants to wipe his nose. This too was clearly seen as an unacceptable infringement of decorum.

14. Two episodes were omitted in 1952 and 1954: the account of the three girls stealing a carrot from the small boy and the conversation with the old man who says he doesn't need documents out in the steppe. The sentence about the camels twisting their lips 'as if they're laughing at us' is from the third version.

15. Here we have followed the 1956 edition. In the third version there is nothing about the woman's hut reminding Vavilov of his own home. And the woman has no children. When Vavilov asks her why she hasn't driven him and his comrades off with a poker, she says, 'I feel pity for you, my sons. You may be poor soldiers and you may not be very brave, but I love you all the same. My old man passed away long ago. I've got no children, so there's only you for me to take care of. And a woman always loves her children, whether they're good children or bad children.'

The passage about the woman selling mugs of water is present in the third version but was first published only in 1956, with one change. In the third version she charges ten roubles per mug; in the 1956 edition, only one rouble per mug.

The sentence about the soldiers' exhaustion being 'blotted out by the fear of death' is from the third version.

A condensed version of Part III, chapters 15, 23, 24 and 31, titled 'The Crossing', was included in *By the Volga* (1949).

16. Like many passages about Yeromenko, much of this chapter was omitted in 1952 and 1954. The mention of farting and cursing generals is from the third version.

17. This chapter was omitted in 1952 and 1954. The third version and the 1956 edition are similar, except that in the third version Chuikov is received not only by Yeromenko but also by Khrushchev. The mention of the adjutant's pleasure in the 'fine and accurate' line with which he indicates the German advance is from the third version – as is Chuikov's rueful thought about being considered expendable.

18. In the 1956 edition Darensky is surprisingly forthright about his time in the camp. In the third version and in 1952 and 1954 he says, 'At the time of that unpleasantness'; the context, however, makes his meaning entirely clear.

Several details, such as Darensky's fear that he too will join in the signallers' petty obsessions about different kinds of kasha, are from the third version. The passage about Darensky's womanizing, however, does not appear in the third version; Grossman evidently added it later. Originally, Darensky and Novikov were a single character; Grossman's making Darensky into a womanizer may have been one of his ways of differentiating the two commanders.

19. The mention of Ageyev discreetly crossing himself as he leaves his bunker is from the third version, as is the adjutants feeling 'almost disappointed' at the end of the chapter.

20. Some details in Darensky's account of the journey – e.g. the bedbugs 'and other insects' and the fouled station platforms – are from the third version.

21. Like other military-historical summaries, this is not in the third version.

22. For Gurov's speech beginning 'Poverty is no vice', we have followed the third version. In the published editions Gurov goes on to list improbable numbers of men from various regiments who have applied to join the Party. This list is shorter in 1956 than in the 1952 and 1954 editions – which suggests that Grossman might have preferred to omit it completely. According to a recent article by Oleg Budnitsky, 'Mass entrance into the Party and Komsomol was far from being a chaotic movement from below. It was initiated from above.' ('A Harvard Project in Reverse', in *Kritika*, vol. 19, no. 1 (Winter 2018), p. 192). Grossman would certainly have been well aware of this.

For the third paragraph from the end of the chapter we have followed the 1956 edition. In the third version, this paragraph reads as follows: 'The first half of September 1942 saw two events of particular importance for the defence of Stalingrad: the concentration of heavy artillery on the east bank, and the transfer of Rodimtsev's Guards division to the west bank.'

The final paragraph is from the third version.

The third version contains an additional chapter about Chuikov. Until Stalingrad, according to Grossman, Chuikov had enjoyed no great success and the other commanders had at first been rather contemptuous of him. Soon, however, they understood that 'Chuikov had not simply been imposed on them from above. On the contrary, it was as if he had been created for the most terrible battle humanity has ever known.'

23–24. Similar in all variants. We have, however, omitted this paragraph from the beginning of chapter 23: 'And there on the east bank of the Volga, political instructors and commissars read aloud to their men the Front military soviet's decree no. 4, "Fight to the Death!" and distributed copies of the 4 September issue of *Red Star* with its front-page article "Repel the German Advance on Stalingrad!" They also gave quick, five-minute talks about acts of heroism, citing the examples of Boloto, Oleinikov, Samoilov and Belikov, the anti-tank riflemen who between them had destroyed fifteen tanks in a single battle near Kletskaya.' Given the desperate urgency of getting the division across the Volga, it is unlikely that there would have been time for even five minutes of political instruction. Since this paragraph is not in the third version, it seems likely that it was Grossman's editors who required him to insert it, in order to underscore the importance of the role played by the Party and the political commissars.

25. Here too we have omitted approximately fifteen lines, not present in the third version, about political instruction. Vavilov gives orders to his battalion commissars, and they in turn tell the political instructors how to conduct short meetings with their men: 'Everything must be short and simple. We defended Tsaritsyn from the Whites – we will defend Stalingrad from the Germans. Familiarize everyone with the plan of the city.'

The soldier's remark about chocolate is from the third version. In the published editions it is less pointed; in 1952 and 1954 the soldier just says, 'Yes, brother, we'll get our chocolate all right.'

The chapter's penultimate paragraph, in which Rodimtsev says that he has never felt so sad before, is present in the third version but was first published only in 1956 – with the omission of the words 'it's only too clear'.

A condensed version of this chapter, titled 'Before the Battle', was included in *By the Volga* (1949).

26–28. Similar in all variants.

29. Here we have taken a few short passages from the third version: the paragraph ending with the mention of Lena Gnatyuk spending the night with Filyashkin; the paragraph about the lieutenant being given a black eye in a village hut; and the last two sentences of Grossman's reflections on Filyashkin's moments of 'exaggerated severity'. In the published editions Konanykin's retort to Filyashkin towards the end of the chapter is less bold, with no mention of convicts. He just says, 'Do you think it's easier to lead soldiers into battle than to be a soldier oneself?'

30. Similar in all variants – except that, in the published editions, the discussion of the bar of chocolate is shorter.

31. For the paragraph about Vavilov's difficulty in obtaining building materials of any kind we have followed the third version. There are many small changes in the published editions, all of which go to create a softer, more comfortable picture.

The last four paragraphs of the chapter – about people worshipping strength – are present in the third version but were first published only in 1956. This suggests that they were important to Grossman but that his editors were uncomfortable with them. Grossman's style here is also somewhat verbose and opaque. It is possible that he had in mind the Russian people's attitude to Stalin as much as the German people's attitude to Hitler – but that he could not afford to make this too clear.

32. Similar in all variants.

33. The words 'some people said nothing, some tried to hide away and others smiled falsely as they tried to come out with a few words in German' are from the third version. Bach's reference to England and America is also from this version; in the published editions he says, 'And then there was Siberia and the Urals.'

34. The sentence about Stumpfe setting fire to a command post guarded by a Red Army sentry is from the third version, as is the mention of his competency in Russian. More importantly, the third version contains two references to Nazi antisemitism which Grossman was, no doubt, required to omit. First, the 'comic dialogue' between a rabbi and his wife. Second, the German soldiers' belief that the Communist Liebnecht (*sic*!) was an 'agent of the Jewish Sanhedrin'.

35. Some of Vogel's words about 'soldierly comradeship' are from the third version. Grossman's editors were evidently uncomfortable about German soldiers attaching such importance to so Soviet a concept as 'comradeship'.

36. Another of the chapters added for the novel's first publication in 1952. Fadeyev had asked Grossman to insert a passage about German resistance to Hitler; the Soviet authorities needed to emphasize this in order to legitimize the Communist regime they had imposed on East Germany.

Grossman's response exemplifies his ability to make creative use of editorial interference. In the third version and in 1952, Schmidt thinks, 'Or he might mutter something incorrect in a dream. His neighbour would hear him, wake some of the others and say, "Here, listen to what this red Schmidt has to say about our Führer."' Here Grossman simply transliterates the word 'Führer'. In 1954 this sentence ends with the words, 'listen to what this red Schmidt has to say'. And in the 1956 edition it ends with the words 'listen to what this red Schmidt has to say about our Leader'. This time, however, the word for 'leader' is *vozhd'* – the usual Soviet way of referring to Stalin. This whole passage, therefore, can be read as a statement not only about life in Nazi Germany but also about life in Soviet Russia. The fact that Grossman revised this sentence not just once but twice is a particularly clear indication of how consciously he was addressing this issue.

37. Similar in all variants. The words 'I'll shoot them!' in Chuikov's 'staccato reply' to Rodimtsev are from the third version, as is Yeromenko's black joke about not wanting 'a second front here in Stalingrad'.

38. Some parts of Filyashkin's fantasies about spending time with Lena Gnatyuk are from the third version. Like many other bleak details, the lines about women needing to sell items of their husband's clothing were not included in 1952 and 1954.

39. In the following sentence the word 'lovingly' is taken from the third version: 'The second [soldier] shook the earth from his shoulders, lovingly wiped his spoon against the palm of one hand and muttered in bewilderment, "I thought that was it, I really did."' A reader may wonder why Grossman – or one of his editors – should have bothered to delete such a seemingly innocuous word, or why a translator should bother to reinsert it. This word, however, is *not* unimportant. Brandon Schechter's title for Chapter 3 of his book about the Red Army's wartime supplies and equipment is 'The Government's Pot and the Soldier's Spoon: Rations in the Red Army'. He writes, 'Virtually

nothing that soldiers carried belonged to them. Their clothes were the property of the government. [...] However, the spoon was something that the individual soldier owned. [...] the spoon and cup were among the few items from the civilian world that soldiers would carry throughout their service. Spoons were frequently individualized with initials and artwork [...] all of their food was designed to be eaten either with a spoon or bare hands. The spoon became a mark of a real soldier. Vera Malakhova, a front-line surgeon, recalled an embarrassing moment near Odessa. While joining a group of soldiers sitting down to a meal, she realized that she lacked something the men around her all possessed: "What sort of a blankety-blank are you? Just what sort of soldier are you? Why don't you have a spoon?" [...] A soldier reduced to a minimum carried a spoon and a rifle. [...] Spoons were *the* implement of individual consumption and a deeply prized, rare piece of personal property.'

Later in the chapter, the powerful image of the brief moment of respite being like 'a swift ray of light on the blade of a drawn knife' is from the third version.

40. Much of the paragraph about the members of the penal battalion is from the third version. The published editions are blander, with no mention of the soldier who shot himself, the soldier who ran from the battlefield or Yakhontov's apparent desertion.

41. The two paragraphs from 'This man had never known his mother and father' are far shorter in 1952 and 1954. There is only the sentence 'Aged two, he had been taken to a children's home', and the last four sentences, from 'He studied' till the end of the paragraph.

42. For this chapter we have followed the third version. The published editions are similar, except for the addition of ten tedious lines from Shvedkov's notebook, recording acts of heroism and the soldiers' expressions of gratitude to their political instructors.

43–44. Similar in all variants.

45. For the beginning of this chapter we have followed the third version. The published editions contain an additional six paragraphs, about an unsuccessful Soviet attempt to relieve Filyashkin's battalion. It seems likely that Grossman's editors required him to add this passage, so as not to give the impression that the Red Army abandoned Filyashkin lightly.

The two references to making a bandage from the fine clothes sent by the women of America are from the third version. The last words of Kovalyov's message – 'for the glorious cause of Stalin!' – were omitted from the 1956 edition.

46. Like many of Grossman's most vivid images, the words 'the last bubbles and gurgles of departing life' are from the third version. The exchanges about death, from Usurov's 'We can't keep death away now' up to Rezchikov's 'Let me be quiet for a minute before death' are also from this version.

47. The exchange between Bach and Lenard about shit and arse-wiping is from the third version.

48. Another of the chapters that Grossman was required to add for the novel's first publication. The typescript of these chapters and the published editions are almost the same except for the last half-page, which is shorter in the published editions. We have taken two passages from the typescript: the sentence beginning 'He wrote to me' and the four short paragraphs beginning 'Who can I ask'.

Another small change exemplifies both the extraordinarily detailed attention given to Grossman's text and the authorities' determination to downplay the suffering undergone by women. In the typescript and in 1956, the women had to pull the plough 'some days'; in 1952 and 1954 only 'two days'.

49. The second and third sentences of this chapter, from 'All were dead' are from the third version. Grossman's editors may have considered them too paradoxical.

50. Similar in all variants. In the third version – but not in the published editions – this is followed by a chapter of more general reflections about the first eighteen months of the war. Using the language of physics, Grossman states that the kinetic energy of a modern, highly mobilized army is such that no defensive line – no fortress or Maginot Line – can possibly halt it. Nothing can halt it except technology and moral strength, working together. During the first year of the war there were several occasions – e.g. the defence of the Brest fortress and the long siege of Sevastopol – when the Soviet forces showed their moral strength. It was not until the Battle of Stalingrad, however, that they were able to combine both moral and technological strength.

It is hard to judge whether the decision to omit this somewhat verbose chapter was Grossman's or his editors. It seems likely, though, that Grossman could have reinstated at least part of it in 1956 if it had felt important to him.

51. This chapter first appears in the sixth version, the most orthodox version of all, probably written in 1949.

52. Similar in all variants.

53–55. Another section that Grossman was obliged to add for the novel's first publication in 1952. There is nothing in the third version, or any of the early typescripts, that corresponds to these powerful chapters.

Robert Chandler and Yury Bit-Yunan

Note on Russian Names and List of Characters

A Russian has three names: a Christian name, a patronymic (derived from the Christian name of the father) and a family name. Thus, Alexandra Vladimirovna is the daughter of a man whose first name is Vladimir, and Viktor Pavlovich is the son of a man called Pavel. The first name and patronymic, used together, are the normal polite way of addressing or referring to a person; the family name is used less often. Close friends or relatives usually address each other by one of the many diminutive, or affectionate, forms of their first names. Luda, for example, is a diminutive of Ludmila; Nadya of Nadezhda; Petya of Pyotr; Varya of Varvara and Vitya of Viktor. Masha and Marusya are both diminutives of Marya; Less obviously, Zhenya is a diminutive of Evgenia; Vanya of Ivan; and Tolya of Anatoly. There is also a great variety of double diminutives: Vitenka is a double diminutive of Viktor, and Vanechka is a double diminutive of Ivan.

LIST OF CHARACTERS

To keep this list to a manageable length, we have not, for the main part, included minor characters who appear only in a single chapter: e.g. most of the Stalgres power-station workers and the staff at the hospital where Vera and Sofya Levinton work. The arrangement of these lists is not intended to be consistent. When there is a clear hierarchy, e.g. within a military unit, the most senior figures come first. Otherwise the names are in alphabetical order, except that members of a particular sub-group – e.g. a small family within an extended family – are grouped together.

All Russian words bear a strong stress on one syllable. Where this is not obvious, we have used italics to indicate where the stress falls.

Real historical figures are indicated by an asterisk *.

1. CIVILIANS

The Shaposhnikov Family

Alexandra Vladimirovna Shaposhnikova	the family matriarch
Ludmila Nikolaevna Shaposhnikova	Alexandra's eldest daughter
Abarchuk	Ludmila's first husband, arrested in 1937
Lt Anatoly ('Tolya') Shaposhnikov	Ludmila's son by Abarchuk
Viktor Pavlovich Shtrum	Ludmila's husband, a physicist
Nadya	Viktor and Ludmila's daughter
Anna Semyonovna	Viktor's mother
Marusya Spiridonova	Alexandra's middle daughter
Stepan Fyodorovich Spiridonov	Marusya's husband, director of the Stalgres power station
Vera Spiridonova	Stepan and Marusya's daughter
(Zina Melnikova	a close friend of Vera)
(Sergeant Viktorov	a fighter pilot, becomes Vera's lover)
Dmitry Shaposhnikov	Alexandra's son, arrested 1937, sent to work on White Sea Canal
Ida Semyonovna	Dmitry's wife
Seryozha Shaposhnikov	Dmitry's son, adopted by Alexandra
Yevgenia Nikolaevna Shaposhnikova ('Zhenya')	Alexandra's youngest daughter
Nikolay Grigorievich Krymov	Zhenya's former husband, a Red Army commissar
(Colonel Pyotr Pavlovich Novikov	Wants to marry Zhenya. Is given command of tank corps)

Friends of the Shaposhnikovs

Pavel Andreyevich Andreyev	worker in a steel factory
Sofya Osipovna Levinton	a surgeon in a military hospital
Mikhail Sidorovich Mostovskoy	an Old Bolshevik (Agrippina Petrovna is his landlady and Gagarov is an old friend)
Tamara Berozkina	a refugee, often visits the Shaposhnikovs

Pavel Andreyev's Family and Circle

Varvara Alexandrovna	his wife
Anatoly	adult son of Pavel and Varvara
Natalya	Anatoly's wife
Volodya	little son of Anatoly and Natalya
Misha Polyakov	an old comrade of Andreyev

Tamara Berozkina's Family

Ivan Leontievich Berozkin	her husband, an infantry major
Slava	their son
Luba	their daughter, aged five

Viktor Shtrum's Colleagues

Dmitry Petrovich Chepyzhin	Viktor's former teacher, an academician
Anna Stepanovna Loshakova	laboratory assistant
Ivan Ivanovich Maximov	a biochemist, recently returned from Czech-oslovakia
Pimenov	acting director of the Physics Institute from spring 1942
Leonid Postoev	eminent physicist, an academician
(Alla Postoeva	Postoev's daughter)
Pyotr Lavrentievich Sokolov	a mathematician, Viktor's colleague
Ivan Dmitrievich Sukhov	director of the Institute until Spring 1942

Stalingrad Obkom (Province Party Committee)

Ivan Pavlovich Pryakhin	First Secretary
Barulin	his assistant
Major Mikhailov	head of the military section
Filippov	deputy chairman of the executive committee
Zhilkin	director of the obkom canteen

Stalingrad Children's Home

Yelizaveta Savelievna Tokareva	director
Klava Sokolova	an assistant (a friend of Natalya Andreyeva)
Slava Berozkin	son of Ivan and Tamara Berozkin
Grisha Serpokryl	a traumatised, supposedly mute orphaned boy

Pyotr Vavilov, his Family and Circle

Pyotr Semyonovich Vavilov	kolkhoz worker, posted to Filyashkin's battalion
Marya Nikolaevna	his wife
Alyosha, Nastya and Vanya	their children
Masha Balashova	a young neighbour, friend of Nastya
Natalya Degtyarova	a neighbour

Senior Engineers and Factory Directors in Moscow

Andrey Trofimovich	the most senior figure at this meeting, per-haps a deputy minister
Chepchenko	director of a metals factory recently evacu-ated to the Urals
Semyon Krymov	brother of Nikolay Krymov, chief engineer in a Siberian factory
'Smezhnik'	a nickname, meaning 'Partner Factory'
Sverchkov	factory director, from the Urals

Ivan Novikov and the Coal Mine

Ivan Pavlovich Novikov	brother of Colonel Novikov, experienced miner, senior shaft sinker
Inna Vasilievna	his wife, a teacher
Masha	their sickly little daughter
Braginskaya	a Russified Pole, a trammer
Gavrila Devyatkin	a shaft sinker
Kotov	a shaft sinker, from Oryol
Ivan Kuzmich	*obkom* secretary responsible for industry
Ilya Maximovich Lapshin	director of the coal trust
Latkov	a timberman
Niura Lopatina	a former kolkhoz worker, now a trammer
General Meshkov	director of a factory producing armour plating for tanks
Motorin	secretary of the pit Party committee
Rogov	a section head
Vikentiev	an experienced Siberian miner, now a timberman
Yazev	director of the mine
Georgy Andreyevich	representative of the State Defence Committee

2. MILITARY

With Nikolay Krymov Escaping from Encirclement

Petrov	an army doctor
Sizov	Krymov's chief scout
Skoropad	his provisions manager
Air Force Major Svetilnikov	his chief of staff

With Nikolay Krymov at 50th Army HQ

Major General Petrov	commander of 50th Army
Brigade Commissar Shlyapin	his commissar

With Nikolay Krymov in the Southwestern Front

Semyonov	his driver
Senior Sergeant Generalov	
Lt Colonel Gorelikov	his brigade commander
Kostyukov	brigade chief of staff
Lt Morozov	
* Senior Lt Sarkisyan	commander of a heavy mortar division
Selidov	a gun-layer
Svistun	commander of an anti-aircraft battery at Stalingrad

With Pyotr Novikov on the Staff of the Southwestern Front

* Marshal Semyon Timoshenko	C-in-C of Southwestern Front
Major General Afanasy Georgievich Bykov	Novikov's immediate superior
Battalion Commissar Cheprak	secretary of the military soviet
Lt Colonel Vitaly Alexeyevich Darensky	a talented officer, of aristocratic background
Ivanchin	member of the military soviet (i.e. most senior commissar)
Angelina Tarasovna	the best typist

At The General Staff in Moscow

* General Yakov Fedorenko	head of the Red Army's Main Armoured Directorate
Colonel Ivanov	a friend of Novikov, serving on the General Staff
* General Andrey Khrulyov	Deputy People's Commissar for Defence (from August 1941)
Lt Colonel Zvezdyukhin	an officer in the cadres section

Army Journalists

Bolokhin	*Red Star* correspondent, loves Symbolist poetry
Zbavsky	correspondent for *The Latest Radio News*

Officers in Stalingrad

* Lt General Andrey Yeromenko	C-in-C of Stalingrad Front
Ageyev	his artillery commander
* Major General Vasily Chuikov	commander of the 62nd Army
* Divisional Commissar Kuzma Gurov	member of the military soviet
* Major General Nikolay Krylov	Chuikov's chief of staff
* Pozharsky	his artillery commander
* Major General Guriev	a divisional commander
* Colonel Gurtiev	a divisional commander
* General Zholudev	a divisional commander
* General Ludnikov	a divisional commander
* Lt Colonel Batyuk	a divisional commander
* Colonel Gorishny	a divisional commander
* Major General Rodimtsev	commander of 13th Guards Division
Major Belsky	his chief of staff
Vavilov	his divisional commissar
Lt Colonel Matyushin	a regimental commander
* Lt Colonel Yelin	a regimental commander
Senior Lt Filyashkin	battalion commander
Battalion Commissar Shvedkov	his commissar
Lt Igumnov	battalion chief of staff
Senior Lt Konanykin	commander of Filyashkin's 1st Company

Lt (*Misha*) Koval*yov*	commander of Filyashkin's 3rd Company
Kot*lov*	his political instructor
Sergeant Major *Ma*rchenko	Kovalyov's right-hand man after Kotlov is wounded
Senior Sergeant Do*do*nov	a telltale, eventually a deserter
Senior Sergeant Lena Gna*tyuk*	medical instructor
Mulyar*chuk*	formerly a stove maker
Re*z*chikov	the company joker
*Ry*sev	a former paratrooper
Us*ma*nov	an Uzbek
Us*u*rov	formerly a driver, in Central Asia
Pyotr Se*my*onovich Va*vi*lov	a former kolkhoz worker
*Za*ichenkov	a former accountant

SERYOZHA SHAPOSHNIKOV'S MILITIA COMRADES

Bryush*kov*	a platoon commander
Chen*tsov*	a former postgraduate student of engineering
Gali*gu*zov	commander of a gun crew
*Gra*dusov	formerly a minor official in a housing construction bureau
Il*ush*kin	a muddle-headed soldier
*Krya*kin	the company commander
Polya*kov*	a former carpenter, a friend of Pavel Andreyev
Shu*mi*lo	the company's political instructor

3. THE GERMANS

* General Friedrich Paulus	commander of the 6th Army
* Colonel Adam	his adjutant
* General Franz Weller	commander of a grenadier division
* General Richthofen	commander of the 4th Air Fleet
Colonel Forster	a staff officer
Lt Pieter Bach	engaged to Forster's daughter Maria
Preifi	a battalion commander
Lenard	an SS officer
Ledeke, Stumpfe and Vogel	three friends
Karl Schmidt	a private soldier and former Communist

Further Reading

During the last twenty years a great deal has been published about the war on the Eastern Front and the Battle of Stalingrad. Richard Overy's *Russia's War* (Penguin, 1998) and Antony Beevor's *Stalingrad* (Viking, 1998) were among the first such books to reach a large readership. Listed below are a few of the other books I have found particularly helpful:

Antony Beevor, *The Second World War* (Weidenfeld & Nicolson, 2014).

Chris Bellamy, *Absolute War* (Pan, 2009).

Rodric Braithwaite, *Moscow 1941* (Profile, 2006).

Frank Ellis, *And Their Mothers Wept* (Heritage House Press, 2007) – a comprehensive account of Soviet and post-Soviet fiction about the Second World War.

K. I. Finogenov, *December 1942–February 1943, Front-line Diary of the Artist K. I. Finogenov* (Moscow–Leningrad, 1948) – eighty superb drawings, done under the pressure of immediate experience. It is astonishing that this volume has never been republished.

John and Carol Garrard, *The Life and Fate of Vasily Grossman* (Barnsley, 2012).

David Glantz and Jonathan House, *Stalingrad* (University of Kansas Press, 2017) – detailed and scrupulously researched military history.

Vasily Grossman, *A Writer at War*, ed. Antony Beevor and Luba Vinogradova (Harvill Press, 2005) – extracts from Grossman's wartime notebooks, with a useful commentary.

Vasily Grossman, *Gody voiny* (Moscow, 1989) – an almost-complete text of the wartime notebooks; it is censored only very slightly.

Jochen Hellbeck, *Stalingrad: The City that Defeated the Third Reich* (Public Affairs, 2016) – a selection of interviews carried out by Soviet historians in 1943 with survivors of the battle, Russian and German, military and civilian.

Michael K. Jones, *The Retreat* (John Murray, 2009).

Michael K. Jones, *Stalingrad: How the Red Army Triumphed* (Pen and Sword, 2010) – clear and vivid.

Catherine Merridale, *Ivan's War* (Faber & Faber, 2006) – a sensitively written, psychologically informed evocation of the experience of the rank-and-file Red Army soldier.

Alexandra Popoff, *Vasily Grossman and the Soviet Century* (Yale University Press, 2019).

Brandon Schechter, *The Stuff of Soldiers: A History of the Red Army in World War II Through Objects* (Cornell University Press, 2019) – a remarkable, almost encyclopedic account of the practical, material side of the lives of Red Army soldiers: their rations, their uniforms, their weapons, etc.

*

The most important recent Russian publications, by far, are the articles and books published by Yury Bit-Yunan and David Fel'dman. Semyon Lipkin's engaging and well-written memoir has influenced most subsequent writing on Grossman, but it is sadly unreliable.

Acknowledgements

I am especially grateful to Jochen Hellbeck for first encouraging me, many years ago, to translate this great novel; to Ian Garner, Alexandra Popoff, Brandon Schechter and Tatiana Dettmer for allowing me to draw on unpublished work of their own; to Yury Bit-Yunan, Darya Paschenko and Pietro Tosco for their help in obtaining archival material; and to Antony Beevor, Maria Bloshteyn, Rodric Braithwaite, John Burt, Tom Cowdrey, Steve Crawshaw, Boris Dralyuk, Philip Horowitz, Michael Jones and Garrett Riggs, all of whom have read through complete drafts of this translation and made helpful suggestions; and to David Black, Elizabeth Cook and Martha Kapos, who have listened to me read many chapters aloud and have helped me to clarify a number of awkward passages.

Many, many others have also answered my countless questions about language, military terminology, Soviet clothing and diet, etc. Among them are Denis Akhapkin, Tarik Amar, Michele Berdy, Loren Billings, Edyta Bojanowska, Stuart Britton, Oxana Budjko, Dmitry Buzadzhi, Inna Caron, Ilona Chavasse, Vitaly Chernetsky, Ralph Cleminson, Andy Croft, Stephen Dalziel, Lydia Dhoul, Stephen M. Dickey, Jim Dingeman, John Dunn, Anna Finkelstern, Anne Fisher, Paul Gallagher, Maria Gapotchenko, Ian Garner, Irina Gnedko, Stuart Goldberg, Svetlana Grenier, Gasan Gusejnov, Ellen Hinsey, Geoffrey Hosking, Alina Israeli, Tatiana Kaplun, Bryan Karetnyk, Pavel Khazanov, Brendan Kiernan, Ani Kokobobo, Anna-Maria Leonard, Mikhail Lipyanskiy, Yelena Malysheva, Steve Marder, Melanie Mauthner, Jenya Mironava, Alice and Alexander Nakhimovsky, Colonel Ian Vere Nicol, Andrew Nurnberg, Natasha Perova, Anna Pilkington, Karen Porter, David Powelstock, Olia Prokopenko, Daniel Rancour-Laferriere, Anna Razumnaya, Oliver Ready, Paul Richardson, Irina Rodimtseva, Alex Schekochihin, Peter Scotto, Richard Shaw, Miriam Shrager, Irina Six, Clifford Slaughter, Ludmila Snigireva, Sasha Spektor, Oleksandr Spirin, Lisa R. Taylor, Peter and Susan Tegel, Anne Thompson, Ken Timbers, Christine Worobec, Jurgen Zarusky. My gratitude, as always to all members of SEELANGS, a remarkably helpful and generous email group without which this work would have been a great deal more difficult. And my deepest apologies to anyone whose name I have forgotten to mention.

While translating this book, I have thought a great deal about my father, Colonel Roger Elphinstone Chandler, who died aged forty-seven, when I was fifteen. He had a particular interest in history and he was an officer in the Royal Artillery. *Stalingrad* would have meant a lot to him, all the more so in view of the particular sympathy and admiration Grossman appears to have felt for gunners.

Notes

INTRODUCTION

1 Jochen Hellbeck, *Stalingrad: The City that Defeated the Third Reich* (Public Affairs, 2015), pp. 433–4.

2 Alexandra Popoff, *Vasily Grossman and the Soviet Century* (Yale University Press, 2019), chapter 8.

3 Vasily Grossman, *A Writer at War*, ed. Antony Beevor and Luba Vinogradova (Harvill Press, 2005) p. xiii.

4 E. V. Korotkova-Grossman, *Vospominaniya* (Moscow, 2014), p. 4.

5 'Trud pisatelya', in *Literaturnaya gazeta*, 23 June 1945. Anna Berzer quotes most of this short article in Semyon Lipkin, *Zhizn' i sud'ba Vasiliya Grossmana // Anna Berzer, Proshchanie* (Moscow, 1990), p. 121.

6 Rachel Polonsky, *Molotov's Magic Lantern* (Faber & Faber, 2010), p. 146.

7 Gary Paul Nabhan, https://tinyurl.com/y7rcpzao, accessed 13 October 2018.

8 Part II, chapter 53.

9 There are photographs showing Lev Shtrum with Lev Landau. Lev Shtrum's daughter Yelena Lvovna, a physicist herself, worked in the Leningrad institute run by Abram Ioffe.

10 Yury Bit-Yunan and David Fel'dman, *Vasily Grossman v zerkale literaturnykh intrig* (Moscow, 2016), p. 45.

11 John and Carol Garrard, *The Life and Fate of Vasily Grossman* (Barnsley, 2012), p. 332.

12 I, for my part, am deeply grateful to Tatiana Dettmer for sharing her recent research with me. A Russian version of her 'The Physicist Lev Shtrum. Unknown Hero of a Famous Novel' has now been published by Radio Liberty: https://www.svoboda.org/a/29512819.html?fb_action_ids=10155749450641088&fb_action_types=og.comments

13 Bit-Yunan and Fel'dman quote Gorky's letter at length; *Vasily Grossman*, pp. 176–8.

14 Ibid., pp. 186–202.

15 See Vasily Grossman, *A Writer at War*, p. 114. Beevor uses 'The Ruthless Truth of War' as the title of the chapter in which he mentions this discussion.

16 For this understanding, which they develop at length in their three-volume biography of Grossman, I am indebted to David Fel'dman and Yury Bit-Yunan.

17 Berzer and Lipkin, p. 151.

18 Bit-Yunan and Fel'dman, *Vasily Grossman*, p. 334.

19 Dnevnik prokhozhdeniya rukopisi (RGALI, 1710, opis' 2, ed. khr. 1).

20 Ibid.

PART I

2

21 The Battle of Berezina (26–29 November 1812) took place during Napoleon's retreat from Moscow. Though they suffered heavy losses, the French succeeded

in crossing the River Berezina and so escaped being trapped. Nevertheless, some nations continue to use the word 'Berezina' as a synonym for 'disaster'.

22 Reinhard Heydrich (1904–42) was a high-ranking Nazi official and one of the main architects of the Shoah. On 27 May 1942, he was critically wounded in Prague by a British-trained team of Czech and Slovak soldiers. He died a week later. The Nazis carried out massive reprisals against the civilian population.

23 In late 1940 and early 1941 the British had routed the Italian Army Group in North Africa. In February 1941 Hitler had sent Rommel's Afrika Korps to support the Italians. Since then he had reinforced the Afrika Korps several times.

24 War, peace, world history, religion, politics, philosophy, the German soul (Grossman's own note).

3

25 Between the outer door or porch and the habitable room or rooms of a peasant hut was an unheated entrance room. This provided insulation from the cold and could be used for storing tools and firewood, or for housing animals.

26 A Russian stove was a large brick or clay structure taking up between one fifth and one quarter of the room it stood in. Its functions included baking and cooking, boiling water, heating the building, and drying linen and foodstuffs. A sleeping-bench might be attached to one side of the stove; a wide shelf above it could also be slept on; and people often slept directly on the stove's warm surface.

27 Foot cloths were lengths of material wound around the foot and ankle. Throughout the nineteenth and early twentieth centuries these were far more common in Russia than socks or stockings. By the 1950s, however, they were used only in the army and in labour camps.

28 A portmanteau word, meaning 'collective farm'. In 1929–30 Stalin forcibly collectivized nearly all Soviet agriculture, against massive peasant resistance.

29 A common refreshing drink, lightly alcoholic, usually made from stale bread.

30 The original meaning of the word 'soviet' is both 'council' and 'counsel'. The 'workers' soviets' in Petrograd and other cities became the Bolsheviks' main power base during 1917, and so the word became associated with the Communist Party. In the Soviet Union, governmental bodies at all levels – from that of a small village to that of the entire country – were known as 'soviets': 'village soviet', 'town soviet', 'province soviet', etc.

31 His surname is derived from the work *kozyol*, which means 'goat'.

5

32 Russian peasants – even those who were not believers – continued unofficially following the Christian calendar for many decades after the Revolution.

6

33 The Comintern (Communist International), an international communist organization, held seven World Congresses in Moscow between 1919 and 1935. It gradually lost its importance as Stalin abandoned the earlier Soviet goal of world revolution in favour of establishing socialism in one country. In 1943 it was dissolved.

7

34 Among the staples of the Red Army diet, especially when it came to field rations, were a dehydrated wheat or millet porridge and a dehydrated pea soup. Both needed only the addition of hot water.

35 Every unit of the Red Army, from company to Front (equivalent to a German Army Group), had both a military leader and a political leader. The military leaders were called 'commanders' until 1943, when the word 'officer' was officially reintroduced. The political leaders were called 'commissars', except for the most junior rank, which was 'political instructor' (*politruk*). Catherine Merridale writes: 'An individual *politruk* was likely to combine the functions of a propagandist with those of an army chaplain, military psychiatrist, school prefect and spy.' *Ivan's War* (Faber, 2006), p. 56.

36 This song featured in Eduard Pentslin's popular film *Fighters*, which premiered in 1940.

8

37 Nikolay Nekrasov (1821–77), the most popular poet of his time, was fiercely critical of serfdom and the autocracy. Nikolay Dobrolyubov (1836–61) was a literary critic and political revolutionary.

38 A Soviet rocket launcher, generally known by its nickname 'Katyusha'. Mostovskoy jokingly uses the word to refer to his rudimentary cigarette lighter.

39 The Academy of Sciences was – and remains – immensely important. There are two levels of membership: corresponding membership (the more junior level), and full membership. Even to be a corresponding member is a great honour.

40 Nikolay Chernyshevsky (1828–89) was a philosopher, revolutionary and literary critic, best known for his utopian socialist novel *What is to be Done?*. This greatly influenced Vladimir Lenin, one of whose political tracts bears the same title. Leo Tolstoy also used this title, for a pamphlet about personal moral responsibility. The writer and journalist Alexander Herzen (1812–70) is sometimes called the father of Russian socialism.

41 The title of a miniature play by Alexander Pushkin, one of his *Little Tragedies*.

9

42 The Irtysh flows through Kazakhstan and western Siberia. The Amu-Darya (once known as the Oxus) is the biggest river in Central Asia.

43 Most Soviet institutions were linked to at least one 'house of recreation'. Usually in an attractive spot in the country or by the sea, these were like holiday hotels for particular sections of society. Universities and factories, unions such as the Union of Soviet Writers – all provided their members with subsidized holidays in their house or houses of recreation.

44 A standard term for former members of the clergy, bourgeoisie or aristocracy.

45 Nikolay Gastello (1908–41) was a pilot whose plane was hit by flak and set on fire. He reputedly flew it into a column of German vehicles, destroying a large number of them, including tanks. He was made a Hero of the Soviet Union, posthumously.

46 Grossman evidently knew the Sherlock Holmes stories well. His daughter Yekaterina Korotkova remembers him recounting *The Hound of the Baskervilles* to her when she was a child: 'The sense of horror was both agonizing and splendid [...]

My father evoked the atmosphere of the story with such inspiration that I can sense its horror and beauty to this day. [...] I remember reading the book several years later and feeling slightly disappointed. In my father's retelling it was more interesting, more powerful and more frightening.' Korotkova-Grossman, *Vospominaniya*, p. 204. Korotkova – one of Grossman's most perceptive readers – has put her finger on a central feature of her father's greatness. Grossman's psychological understanding is acute. His work is important to historians, and to political and moral philosophers. But he is also a superb storyteller. Many chapters of his dilogy are imbued with a sense of horror that could be described as 'both agonizing and splendid'.

11

47 A phrase from the *Communist Manifesto* (1848), by Karl Marx and Friedrich Engels.

12

48 The Smolny Institute was Russia's first educational establishment for women, constructed in 1806–8. During the October Revolution it was the Bolshevik HQ.
49 The words 'Everything flows' (Πάντα ῥεῖ – *panta rhei*), later chosen by Grossman as the title of his last major work, are often, though probably wrongly, attributed to Heraclitus, a Presocratic philosopher. One of Heraclitus' best-known aphorisms is 'You cannot step twice into the same river.' In the third version of the novel Heraclitus is one of the philosophers Mostovskoy has written about for a dictionary of philosophy.

15

50 Shooting oneself in the left hand was a common way of trying to escape the fighting, so wounds of this kind aroused suspicion. For more about soldiers shooting themselves in the left hand, see Brandon Schechter, *The Stuff of Soldiers: A History of the Red Army in World War II Through Objects* (Cornell University Press, 2019), chapter 1.
51 The standard measure for a serving of vodka in a café or restaurant was a hundred grams. This was so common that the word 'vodka' was usually omitted. 'He drank a glass of vodka' can best be translated as 'He drank a hundred grams' (*On vypil sto grammov*).
52 The Union of Communist Youth.
53 The Yak (named after its designer Alexander Yakovlev) was produced from early 1940. A single-seat fighter, it was fast, manoeuvrable, well armed and reliable.

16

54 Chekhov's 'A Man in a Case' is a story about an obtuse and rigid-minded civil servant.

17

55 The constituent republics of the Soviet Union were divided into *oblasti* (provinces), which were in turn divided into *raiony* (districts). An *obkom* is the Party committee for an *oblast* and a *raikom* is the Party committee for a *raion*.

18

56 I.e. an internal passport, a document of crucial importance in the Soviet Union.

19

57 The Soviet Union was a highly militarized society and military terminology infiltrated most areas of life. Such terms as 'artists' (or writers') brigade' and 'shock-workers' (by analogy with 'shock-troops') were standard.

58 Sofya quotes Apollon Maikov (1821–97), a popular poet many of whose short poems have been set to music.

59 The GAZ-M1 car was produced from 1936 until 1942. The 'M' referred to Vyacheslav Molotov, later to become People's Commissar for Foreign Affairs, and the car was usually known by its nickname – the 'Emka'. The larger ZIS-101 was produced from 1936 until 1941.

60 A 'Front' was equivalent to a German 'Army Group'. According to Rodric Braithwaite, 'A Front contained up to nine mixed armies, up to three tank armies, one or two air armies and various supporting formations. A mixed army contained five or six rifle divisions and supporting arms.' *Moscow 1941* (Profile, 2006), p. 268, note 6. The word 'Front' was used only after the German invasion; the earlier equivalent was 'Military District'. Throughout this translation we distinguish between 'Front', as above, and 'front' or 'front line' in a more general sense.

61 Here and elsewhere Novikov addresses Zhenya rather formally, by her first name and patronymic. 'Zhenya' is the most common affectionate form of 'Yevgenia'. See Note on Russian Names.

20

62 From 1869, this town was called Yuzovka. In 1932 it was renamed Stalino, and in 1961, Donetsk. As a young man, Grossman had worked in the Smolyanka mine, as a safety engineer and chemical analyst.

21

63 Russians have always seen the war as beginning with the German invasion of the Soviet Union on 22 June 1941. See Timeline, p. 893

64 A Finnish defensive fortification line across the Karelian Isthmus. During the Winter War (1939–40) between Finland and the Soviet Union, it halted the Soviet advance for two months. Both Finnish and Soviet propaganda exaggerated the extent of the fortifications: the Finns wanting to improve national morale, the Soviets needing to explain the slowness of their advance.

65 After Germany and the Soviet Union invaded Poland in summer 1939, they split the country into three parts: a western part annexed by Germany; a central part, also under German control, that was officially called 'the General Government'; and an eastern part annexed by the Soviet Union. The river Bug was the border between the General Government and the Soviet area.

66 It may now seem surprising that Grossman was able to publish this passage about the Nazi officer (which appears in all the published editions), but it is in

accord with the official Soviet doctrine of the time. 'Falsifiers of History', an important document edited and in part rewritten by Stalin in 1948, claims that 'No forgers will ever succeed in wiping from history [...] the decisive fact that under these conditions, the Soviet Union faced the alternative: either to accept, for purposes of self-defence, Germany's proposal to conclude a non-aggression pact and thereby to ensure to the Soviet Union the prolongation of peace for a certain period of time, which might be used by the Soviet State better to prepare its forces for resistance to a possible attack on the part of an aggressor; or to reject Germany's proposal for a non-aggression pact and thereby to permit war provocateurs from the camp of the Western Powers immediately to involve the Soviet Union in armed conflict with Germany at a time when the situation was utterly unfavorable to the Soviet Union and when it was completely isolated. In this situation, the Soviet government found itself compelled to make its choice and conclude a non-aggression pact with Germany.' https://en.wikipedia.org/wiki/Falsifiers_of_History http://collections.mun.ca/PDFs/radical/FalsificatorsOfHistory.pdf 'Falsifiers of History', needless to say, does not mention the secret protocol to the non-aggression pact according to which Stalin and Hitler divided up the whole of central Europe, from Finland to Romania, with Stalin annexing the Baltic States and eastern Poland. One of Hitler's conditions was the transfer to German-held areas of all ethnic Germans living in Poland or the Baltic States. Most of these Germans were 'resettled' in 1939 or 1940, but a final resettlement was organized in spring 1941. See https://en.wikipedia.org/wiki/Baltic_Germans#cite_ref-20

67 Boris Dralyuk writes (private email, 2017), 'I see the self-correction as indicative of cognitive dissonance. Like any serious trauma, it upends Novikov's sense of reality to such a degree that he can neither process it at the time nor forget it later. It is the Nazi officer, of course, whom Novikov has in mind; his haughty face and bizarre uniform makes him look like a sinister fool. But Novikov may also be thinking of Hitler. And Grossman himself may – possibly – also be thinking of Stalin. All three are murderous, self-serious clowns.'

68 The 1940 German–Soviet Commercial Agreement stipulated that, in exchange for technical and military equipment, the Soviet Union should deliver large quantities of raw materials to Germany. The German war effort against the Soviet Union was partially supported by raw materials – above all, supplies of rubber and grain – obtained through this agreement.

69 A well-known play by Oleksandr Korniychuk (1905–72), a Soviet Ukrainian playwright, literary critic and politician.

70 A Red Corner was a special room in a Soviet hostel, factory or other institution, stocked with educational literature and reserved for reading. Before the Revolution the term referred to the corner of a room in a private house or peasant hut where the icons were kept (the word *krasny* originally meant both 'red' and 'beautiful' – a connection independent of Communism).

23

71 This marked the catastrophic end to the Soviet offensive first mentioned in chapter 4 of Part I, when Shepunov reads to Vavilov from a district newspaper.

72 Three of the main Soviet fighters of the time. The Yak was designed by Yakovlev. The LaGG-3 was named from the first letters of the names of its three designers: Lavochkin, Gorbunov and Gudkov.

73 In March 1940, at the end of the Winter War with Finland, the Soviet Union won the right to lease this southernmost point of Finland for thirty years and to set up a naval base there. In the event, this base existed only until December 1941.

24

74 Later known as the Po-2, this simple, versatile biplane was produced in large numbers between 1929 and 1953.
75 The Supreme Command in Moscow, established on 23 June 1941, was known as the Stavka. Its members were Stalin, Semyon Timoshenko (the defence commissar), Georgy Zhukov, Vyacheslav Molotov, Kliment Voroshilov, Semyon Budyonny and Nikolay Kuznetsov.

25

76 The Southwestern Front – then under the command of Marshal Timoshenko – was formally disbanded on 12 July 1942.
77 A traditional token of hospitality.
78 From 8 April 1942 Bagramyan was the Southwestern Front chief of staff, but on 28 June he was dismissed from this post – unfairly blamed for the catastrophic encirclement following the Soviet recapture of Kharkov.
79 The phrase 'Memory eternal!' is pronounced at the end of an Orthodox funeral or memorial service. It refers to remembrance by God, rather than by the living; it is a prayer that the soul of the departed may enter heaven and enjoy eternal life.
80 The Douglas C-47 Skytrain, generally considered the best transport plane of the Second World War, was supplied to the Soviet Union through lend-lease. It was also produced locally, under licence, as the Lisunov Li-2.

26

81 After the catastrophic Battle of Kiev (August and September 1941) the Southwestern Front was re-established with new forces. From September to December 1941 and from April to July 1942 it was under the command of Marshal Timoshenko. On 12 July 1942 it was disbanded and its forces transferred to the Stalingrad Front and the Southern Front.

27

82 Ivan Michurin (1855–1935) was an agronomist and plant breeder, a founding father of scientific agricultural selection. His belief that environmental influences could bring about changes to the genotype was the starting point for the pseudo-scientific theories of Trofim Lysenko (1898–1976).
83 In the Soviet Union, maids and servants were known as 'domestic workers'.

28

84 For the Orthodox Church, St Tatyana is the patron saint of students. Students traditionally celebrated her day by getting drunk.

85 This was founded in 1922. It collected funds to publicize the plight of political prisoners in capitalist countries and to provide material assistance to their families.

86 Someone who profited, or was thought to have profited, from a business venture during the period (1921–8) of relative economic liberalisation known as the New Economic Policy (NEP).

87 During the first decade after the Revolution, fervent Communists often gave their children politicized names like this. 'October', 'Vladlen' (Vladimir Lenin), and 'Marlen' (Marx–Lenin) are among the more common examples.

88 See note 39.

29

89 One of the stores for privileged sections of the population – in this case, families of members of the Academy of Sciences – where it was possible to obtain goods and products not generally available.

90 With no envelopes or postcards, Red Army soldiers used to fold a letter in such a way as to make it into its own envelope. All mail had to be checked by censors and these letters were folded rather than sealed. They were delivered free of charge; there was no need for stamps.

33

91 Two of the greatest Russian landscape painters, from the second half of the nineteenth century.

92 For Nekrasov, see note 37. For Herzen, see note 40. Nikolay Ogaryov (1813–77) was Herzen's closest friend and collaborator. In 1840, on the Sparrow Hills above Moscow, the two men famously swore not to rest until their country was free.

34

93 Pyrethrum is a natural insecticide, made from chrysanthemum flowers. Sulfonamide, the only effective antibiotic available before penicillin, was used to treat coughs and allergies.

94 From a song about Stenka Razin, the Cossack brigand who in 1670–71 led a major peasant rebellion. In the song he casts his young Persian bride into the Volga – as a sacrifice to the river – and to placate his comrades, who are jealous of her.

95 The first line of a famous quatrain by Fyodor Tyutchev (1803–73): 'Russia is baffling to the mind, / not subject to the common measure; / her ways – of a peculiar kind ... / One only can have *faith* in Russia'. Translated by Avril Pyman, *The Penguin Book of Russian Poetry* (Penguin, 2015), p. 111.

36

96 Between the signing of the Nazi–Soviet non-aggression pact (23 August 1939) and the German invasion of the Soviet Union (22 June 1941) all criticism of Hitler and Nazi Germany was suppressed. By speaking so openly, Maximov is endangering himself.

97 See note 82.
98 This paragraph is based on an actual dream of Grossman's. His mother Yekaterina Savelievna was killed in the first and largest of the mass executions of Berdichev Jews, on 14 September 1941. See Popoff, *Vasily Grossman and the Soviet Century*, chapter 6.
99 The Moscow metro had been designed from the start to provide shelter in time of war. At night, when Metro services were suspended, and during air-raid alerts in daytime, civil defence troops 'put wooden duckboards on the rails and closed off all apertures through which a bomb blast might penetrate [...] Invalids, children, and the elderly were accommodated in the trains and in the stations [...] The remainder went into the tunnels themselves for shelter. The stations were comparatively well lit. Water was available from drinking fountains on the platforms and from taps in the tunnels.' (Braithwaite, *Moscow 1941*, p. 189.)
100 Balloons sent high into the sky and trailing fine steel wires designed to wreck any aeroplane that flew into them.
101 *Perfectum* and *futurum* – Latin for 'past' and 'future'.

37

102 For more about the biologist and plant breeder Nikolay Vavilov, see Introduction, p. xvii–xviii, and Afterword, p. 911–2.
103 The first Russian translations of Sherlock Holmes appeared in 1903 and were followed by a wave of cheap imitations. Holmes remained popular after the Revolution, without encouragement from the Soviet authorities. For some time, the stories were passed around only unofficially. In 1945, however, 'The Man with the Twisted Lip' was published in a series titled 'The Little Library of the Journal of the Red Army Soldier' and it seems likely that close to 11 million copies of the complete works were published in the late 1950s.

40

104 The Razguliay district is named after a famous local tavern. Cheryomushki was the home of wealthy merchants and Sadovniki was a peasant district. Grossman evokes different aspects of Moscow life.
105 Kliment Timiryazev (1843–1920) was a famous Russian botanist and physiologist.

41

106 A well-known Russian children's song.
107 Madeira Massandra, a quality wine made since 1892 in Crimea.

42

108 In the 1940s some Armenian scientists claimed to have discovered the 'varitron', a new particle with a variable mass. 'Carl Anderson speculated that they may have been under such great political pressure to produce a "breakthrough" that they invented one that would satisfy the administrators but not damage physics, since no physicists would believe it.' D. A. Glaser, 'Invention of the Bubble Chamber and Subsequent Events', *Nuclear Physics B Proc. Suppl.* 36 (1994),

pp. 3–18, https://www.sciencedirect.com/science/article/pii/0920563294907641, accessed 10 July 2016.

109 In 1854, the poet Heinrich Heine (1797–1856) republished some of his earlier newspaper articles under the title *Lutezia,* the Latin name for Paris.

110 Friedrich Wilhelm Ostwald (1853–1932), one of the founders of physical chemistry, wrote on many subjects, including philosophy. Soon after the beginning of the First World War he was one of ninety-three prominent German scientists and cultural figures who signed a chauvinistic 'Appeal to the Civilized World'.

111 Also known as gas vans or gas wagons, these had an air-tight compartment into which exhaust fumes were piped while the vehicle's engine was running. Those held inside died of carbon monoxide poisoning. This method of execution was thought up and first put into practice by the NKVD in the late 1930s. It was then used in Nazi Germany, before being superseded by the far larger gas chambers of the death camps.

112 Bruno was a Dominican poet, mathematician and philosopher. Found guilty of heresy, he was burned at the stake in Rome in 1600. For Chernyshevsky, see note 40.

113 From 'A Contribution to the Critique of Hegel's "Philosophy of Right"' (1843–4), published in *The German–French Annals* (1844).

114 August Bebel (1840–1913) was one of the founders, in 1869, of the Social Democratic Workers Party of Germany. Lenin referred to him as 'a model workers' leader'.

44

115 Grossman expresses similar thoughts in a passage in his *Red Star* article 'Through Chekhov's Eyes': 'Every brave man is brave in his own way. The mighty tree of courage has thousands of branches [...] but selfish cowardice takes only one form: slavish submission to the instinct to save one's own life. The man who runs from the battlefield today will run tomorrow from a burning house, leaving his old mother, his wife and his little children to the flames.' *Gody voiny* (Moscow, 1989), p. 43.

116 'Mankind – the word has a proud ring'; in Soviet days these words of Maxim Gorky's were very well known indeed.

45

117 Oswald Spengler (1880–1936), a German philosopher of history, published his influential *The Decline of the West* in 1918.

48

118 After the war began, this new industrial centre in the Urals grew increasingly important. It was nicknamed Tankograd.

119 Mikhail Lermontov (1814–41), the celebrated Russian Romantic poet. See *The Penguin Book of Russian Poetry*, pp. 116–17.

120 The middle-aged general in glasses is General Andrey Vlasov. At the time of the Battle of Kiev, Vlasov was an up-and-coming lieutenant general in command of the 37th Army; along with part of this army, he managed to escape encirclement.

In July 1942, however, he was captured by the Germans. He agreed to collaborate and, in autumn 1944, founded the anti-Communist ROA (the Russian Liberation Army). After the war, he was found guilty of treason and was executed in August 1946. As a traitor, Vlasov was held in contempt. It was bold of Grossman even to mention his name; the three paragraphs from 'First, though, Krymov ...' were not included in any of the published editions.

121 In a notebook entry, Grossman puts this more strongly, writing that 'Men from Chernigov were deserting in thousands.' This entry was omitted from the 1989 publication of the wartime notebooks. Oleg Budnitsky, who is preparing a more complete edition of the notebooks, quoted it in a talk at Pushkin House, London, in April 2018.

122 The main street of central Kiev.

123 Babi Yar ('Woman's Ravine') is the name of the ravine on the outskirts of Kiev where 100,000 people, mostly Jews, were shot in the course of six months, over 33,000 of them during the first two days of the massacre, 29 and 30 September 1941. The route the old woman advises Krymov to take is, in reverse, the route along which the Jews were taken to Babi Yar from central Kiev.

124 Yelena Lvovna Shtrum, the daughter of the physicist Lev Shtrum, has spoken about how she herself escaped from Kiev at this time. All entrances to the main railway station had been closed, but there was a vast crowd of women and children in the square outside. Among them were Yelena (aged eighteen) and her two aunts (aged about thirty). Unlike many of the others, who were weighed down with luggage, they were carrying only a very few bags. One of the fences collapsed and Yelena and her aunts and other women at the front of the crowd occupied an empty goods train. Officials realized it would have been impossible to remove the women; they simply did not have the manpower. In Yelena's words, 'it would have taken two men to remove each woman'. The doors were then bolted, with about twenty women being shut up in each wagon. For twenty-four hours nothing much happened. The women defecated and urinated through a hole they had made by removing a plank from the floor. Eventually, the train crossed the Dnieper. After that, it travelled slowly east, taking two weeks to reach the Volga. Bread or swill was brought to the women at some of the stations. It was also sometimes possible to buy food being sold privately (private conversation, Cologne, 30 August 2018).

125 Grossman provides these words only in Ukrainian; he does not translate them.

126 Mikhail Kirponos, commander of the Southwestern Front, was killed during the defence of Kiev.

127 Ukrainians who collaborated with the Nazis and acted as local police.

128 The historian Michael Jones quotes at length from a diary kept by Ivan Shabalin, the courageous and clear-minded head of the political section of the 50th Army. Shabalin was killed in October 1941, while trying to break out of encirclement. Jones summarizes one passage as follows: 'Shabalin, an ambitious NKVD officer responsible for army education, realized that he no longer needed to give political lectures or issue instructions to the men around him. The comradeship binding his group of fighters together was enough in itself. And as Shabalin realized that, he felt a remarkable sense of peace.' *The Retreat* (John Murray, 2009), p. 67. Shabalin's diaries were first published only in 1974, ten years after Grossman's death; this makes the similarity between them and Grossman's account of Krymov all the more striking.

129 The Black Earth region is a belt of exceptionally rich, fertile soil in Ukraine and southern Russia.

130 Grossman met Shlyapin in September 1941, when he was sent as a *Red Star* journalist to the Bryansk Front. Grossman's first war novel, *The People is Immortal* (1942), is based on Shlyapin's account of his escape from encirclement.

131 Shlyapin quotes from Pushkin's verse fairy tale *Ruslan and Ludmila*.

132 Alexander Suvorov (1729/30–1800) is considered the greatest of all Russian generals. The Order of Suvorov, one of the highest of Soviet military decorations, was established on 29 July 1942; its first recipient was Georgy Zhukov.

133 A lieutenant general wears three stars, a colonel general wears four.

134 Heinz Guderian (1888–1954) was one of the most successful German tank commanders both in France in 1940 and on the Eastern front in 1941.

135 See Vasily Grossman, *A Writer at War* (Harvill Press, 2005), p. 47.

136 In July 1941 Yakov Kreizer (1905–69) became the first Red Army general to outfight the Wehrmacht in a large-scale engagement, stalling Guderian's superior forces and thus holding up German Army Group Centre in its drive towards Moscow.

137 Lines from what is usually seen as a children's poem, by Alexey Nikolaevich Pleshcheyev (1825–93), a political radical.

138 The old woman quotes from the beginning of Psalm 68: 'Let God arise, let his enemies be scattered: let them also that hate him flee before him. As smoke is driven away, so drive them away: as wax melteth before the fire, so let the wicked perish at the presence of God.'

139 Vasil Kolarov (1877–1950), a Bulgarian, was a key functionary in the Communist International. Maurice Thorez (1900–64) led the French Communist Party from 1930 until his death. Ernst Thälmann (1886–1944) led the German Communist Party throughout most of the duration of the Weimar Republic. Sen Katayama (1859–1933) co-founded the Japanese Communist Party.

140 The Hotel Lux housed many leading exiled Communists – from Germany and elsewhere. The hotel's international character aroused Stalin's suspicions. Between 1936 and 1938 a great many of its occupants were arrested.

141 Titled '14 December 1825', this poem by Tyutchev is about a failed revolt against the autocracy. The translation, by Robert Chandler, is from *The Penguin Book of Russian Poetry*, p. 104.

142 From Lenin's 'The Three Sources and Three Component Parts of Marxism' (1913): https://www.marxists.org/archive/lenin/works/1913/mar/x01.htm

50

143 The estate, seven miles from Tula, where Tolstoy was born and where he wrote both *War and Peace* and *Anna Karenina*. Since 1921, it has been a museum.

144 Krymov is, of course, remembering *War and Peace*. The 'old, sick prince' is Prince Bolkonsky, father of Prince Andrey and Princess Maria. His estate – Bald Hills – is modelled on Yasnaya Polyana.

145 Grossman has given Krymov many of his own experiences from these weeks. He himself made a similar journey in early October 1941, visiting Yasnaya Polyana and speaking to Tolstoy's granddaughter. A few days later General Guderian took over the estate, making it his HQ for his planned assault on Moscow. (See Grossman, *A Writer at War*, p. 54.) In early September 1942, on his way from Moscow

to Stalingrad, Grossman stopped a second time at Yasnaya Polyana, which the Russians had recaptured the previous winter.

146 This was one of the first engagements in which the Red Army deployed their new T-34 tank, generally recognized as the best all-round tank in the Second World War. Soon to be produced in vast numbers, this tank made a crucial contribution to the Soviet victory.

51

147 Two towns very close to Moscow.

148 The location of three major railway termini.

149 Probably: 'Follow me ... straight ahead ... Fire ... Direct hit.' But the German does not entirely make sense. This may be a mistake on Grossman's part, or it may be his way of conveying that this is how the Russian listeners hear the words.

150 Russia moved from the Julian to the Gregorian calendar only in 1918. Thus the anniversary of the October 1917 Revolution has always been celebrated on 7 November.

151 Lobnoye Mesto is a thirteen-metre-long stone platform, often mistakenly thought to have been a place of execution. A nearby bronze statue commemorates Kuzma Minin and Prince Dmitry Pozharsky who, in 1611–12, gathered a volunteer army and expelled the forces of the Polish–Lithuanian Commonwealth. This put an end to the period known as the 'Time of Troubles'.

152 *Kirza* is a type of artificial leather – multiple layers of textile impregnated with latex and other substances – that was widely used in the Soviet Union, mainly for army boots.

153 Until 1 August 1941, the bars on their collar tabs would have been red. They were changed to green in the interests of camouflage.

154 Semyon Budyonny (1883–1973) was a cavalry commander during the Russian Civil War and a close ally of Joseph Stalin. He was a popular figure but an opponent of mechanization. He declared that the tank could never replace the horse.

53

155 Some German officers thought much the same surprisingly early in the war. In July 1941, General Walther Nehring, commander of the 18th Panzer Division, wrote, 'The further our armoured spearheads advance into the depths of this country, the more our difficulties mount, while the forces of the enemy seem to gain in strength and cohesion' (Jones, *The Retreat*, p. 19).

54

156 Sergey Chekhonin (1878–1936) was a graphic artist, ceramicist and book designer. After leaving Soviet Russia in 1928, he lived in France and Germany.

157 The novelist Henri Barbusse (1873–1935) was a member of the French Communist Party. His sycophantic biography of Stalin was published posthumously, in 1936.

158 Ernst Busch (1900–80) was a German singer and actor who collaborated several times with Bertolt Brecht. After fleeing Nazi Germany in 1933, he settled in the Soviet Union. 'The Peat Bog Soldiers' ('Die Moorsoldaten') was written, composed and first performed by political prisoners in 1933, in a Nazi concentration camp in the moors of Lower Saxony. The song became a Republican anthem during the Spanish Civil War and a symbol of resistance during the Second World War.

159 This was established in 1933. The zoo was struggling to look after a large number of orphaned baby animals – some born in captivity and rejected by their mothers, others brought to the zoo by hunters who had shot their mothers. It was thought that the keepers would be able to care more easily for these cubs if they were all kept together. Each species had its own cage, and there was also a large shared space, which included a pool. The 'cubs' pen' soon became one of the zoo's most popular attractions. But in 1950 and in the early 1970s the shared space was twice reduced in size and the pen was finally closed in the late 1970s. Since then, the pen has been criticized as reflecting 'a Stalinist concept of education' (http://radiomayak. ru/shows/episode/id/1122701/, accessed 24 August 2016).

160 From a poem by Heinrich Heine: 'This is an old story, yet it remains always new.'

161 From Pushkin's *Eugene Onegin* IV, 14, as translated by Stanley Mitchell (Penguin, 2008) – though slightly amended.

162 Clothes produced by this factory were of notoriously poor quality.

55

163 Viktor Kholzunov (1905–39), born in Stalingrad, commanded a bomber squadron during the Spanish Civil War. Grossman saw this statue in August 1942, during his first days in Stalingrad. It evidently made an impression both on him and on his companion, Vasily Koroteyev. Both writers mention the statue several times in their writings (with thanks to Ian Garner for help with this note).

164 A chapter from Lermontov's *A Hero of Our Time* (1839–40).

56

165 Lvov is now a part of Ukraine and is known as L'viv. Schechter, *Stuff of Soldiers*, chapter 7, refers to Lvov and Riga as 'centres of fashion' during the two years between the signing of the Nazi–Soviet non-aggression pact in August 1939 and the German invasion of the Soviet Union in June 1941.

57

166 In an apartment block like Mostovskoy's, there would have been one central radio receiver. This would have received broadcasts from All-Union Radio, based in Moscow. The individual apartments had only speakers, connected by wire to the central receiver. There was no choice of channels or stations.

167 Pyotr Chaadaev (1794–1856) is best known for his eight 'Philosophical Letters' about Russia, only the first of which was published during his life. These are highly critical of nearly all aspects of Russian culture and society. The government's response was to declare Chaadaev insane.

168 A pre-revolutionary measure of distance, a little more than a kilometre.

58

169 This last short paragraph, like many of the novel's more humorous moments, first appeared in the 1956 edition.

59

170 A popular historical melodrama, made in England in 1941. Its central theme, the adulterous liaison between Admiral Nelson and Emma Hamilton, links it to the affair between Viktor and Nina.
171 See note 90.

65

172 Four *poods* is about sixty-five kilograms.

66

173 It was in Dno railway station that Tsar Nicholas II signed his abdication decree on 15 March 1917.

67

174 Stalin's still-controversial order, with its slogan 'Not One Step Back', forbade any further retreat, under any circumstances, and decreed the death penalty for 'laggards, cowards, defeatists and other miscreants'. See note to this chapter in Afterword.

69

175 See note 82.
176 Administrative officials – some of them German, others Ukrainian collaborators.
177 It is startling to read of vodka being measured by such a large measure as a kilo, but it was entirely normal to measure spirits by weight rather than by volume. See note 51.
178 The earlier name for Stalingrad. The city was renamed in 1925 in recognition of Stalin's role, probably somewhat exaggerated during the Stalin era, in defending the city during the Russian Civil War. In 1961, the city was renamed Volgograd.

PART II

3

179 A popular musical comedy released in 1940.

4

180 Alexander Blok (1880–1921) and Innokenty Annensky (1855–1909) were the two most important Russian Symbolists. Annensky's poetry is subtle and delicate. Blok's is less subtle, but deeply mystical. Both are a far cry from socialist realism.

5

181 Nikolay Ostrovsky's novel *How the Steel was Tempered* is a classic of socialist realism. Alexander Sheller-Mikhailov was a progressive novelist of the 1860s, lauded during the early Soviet era because of an essay in which he quoted large chunks of Marx's *Das Kapital*, effectively introducing the book to Russian readers. Andreyev dutifully reads a certain amount of the correct literature of the era – e.g. Stalin and Ostrovsky – but what he really loves is more imaginative and entertaining literature.

182 See note 114. The book is primarily an attack on the institution of marriage.

6

183 Founded by Volga Germans in 1765, Sarepta was renamed Krasnoarmeisk in 1920. In 1931 it became a district of Stalingrad.

184 There were three categories of disability pension. Those with the most serious disabilities were registered as category one.

185 A town not far from Stalingrad.

186 Saratov and Samara (called Kuibyshev from 1935 to 1991) are two of the oldest and most important cities on the Volga.

7

187 These three factories, located parallel to the Volga and connected by underground tunnels with secure telephone lines, played a crucial role throughout the Battle of Stalingrad. Even when largely destroyed and unable to function as factories, they proved to be ideal ground for fighting a defensive battle. Each factory was about a kilometre long and from 500 to 1,000 metres wide.

8

188 The Red Putilovite factory was the largest factory in Leningrad, producing mainly artillery and tanks. Though most of the equipment and personnel were evacuated to Chelyabinsk, the Leningrad site continued to repair tanks throughout the Blockade. The Obukhov factory also produced artillery and tanks.

9

189 Triangles were worn by corporals and sergeants.

11

190 The Society for the Promotion of Defence, Aviation and Chemistry. The declared aim of this 'voluntary' civil-defence organization, founded in 1927, was to promote patriotism, marksmanship and aviation skills. Stalin described it as vital to 'keeping the entire population in a state of mobilized readiness against the danger of military attack, so that no "accident" and no tricks of our external enemies can catch us unawares'. The society sponsored clubs and organized contests throughout the Soviet Union; within a few years it had around 12 million members.

13

191 Ethnic Germans who lived along the Volga, mainly in what is now the Saratov region to the north of Volgograd/Stalingrad. Encouraged by Catherine the Great (a German herself), they settled there in the eighteenth century. A Volga German Autonomous Republic was established in 1924, but this was abolished after the Nazi invasion. Seeing the Volga Germans as potential collaborators, the Soviet authorities deported approximately 500,000 of them to Siberia and Kazakhstan, where many died.

192 Alexey Stakhanov was a miner whose improbably vast output of coal – twelve tons a day – led to his being held up as a model for Soviet workers. The word 'Stakhanovite' was part of the official vocabulary of the era; there were, for example, regular congresses of 'Stakhanovite' workers.

15

193 Kliment Voroshilov (1881–1969) was a prominent political and military figure, one of the first five generals to be given the title 'Marshal of the Soviet Union'.

194 See note 74.

16

195 The Don, the Volga and several other rivers flowing south into the Black and the Caspian Seas have high, steep west banks and low, flat east banks.

196 Spiridonov exaggerates, but not absurdly. By June 1940 the Stalingrad Tractor Factory had produced over 230,000 tractors – more than half the tractors in the Soviet Union.

17

197 Prince of Moscow from 1359 to 1389, Dmitry Donskoy was the first Muscovite ruler to openly challenge Moscow's Mongol overlords.

18

198 A cardiac medicine, used more in Russia and Germany than in the English-speaking world.

19

199 The 10th NKVD Rifle Division, under Colonel A. A. Sarayev.

200 Gradusov alludes to 'Thoughts by the Grand Entrance', a poem by Nikolay Nekrasov (see note 37). A group of exhausted pilgrims and beggars, 'burnt by the sun', knocks at the door of a grand house, hoping for alms. They are turned away.

20

201 Vladimir Korolenko (1853–1921) was best known for his short novel *The Blind Musician* (1886), based on his experience of exile in Siberia.

202 Arkady Gaidar (1904 –41) was a popular children's writer, best known for *Timur and His Squad*, a story about an altruistic young Pioneer.
203 Penal battalions were formed from Gulag detainees and men sentenced by military tribunals. Most commanders looked on the lives of these men as entirely expendable, thinking nothing – for example – of sending them straight across minefields.

22

204 'What has the Führer said?'
205 'The Führer has said, "Stalingrad must fall."'

23

206 Richthofen's Air Corps played an important part in the Battle of Yugoslavia (April 1941) and in the subsequent Battles of Greece and Crete. Richthofen did not, in fact, take part in the North Africa campaigns.
207 Another of Grossman's few mistakes with regard to German history: for much of the First World War Paulus and Rommel were company commanders in the same regiment.

25

208 Subhas Chandra Bose (1897–1945) was an Indian nationalist. In 1943, when Singapore was under Japanese rule, he formed a government of 'Free India' there. He died in a plane crash.

26

209 Goebbels was born with a deformed right foot, and he walked with a limp. A would-be writer as a young man, he obtained a doctorate in philosophy from the University of Heidelberg in 1921.
210 David Low was a famous British cartoonist. The Kukryniksy was the collective name of three Soviet cartoonists who began to work together in 1924 and went on to win international recognition for their caricatures of fascist leaders.
211 The accuracy of Grossman's portrayal of Himmler is confirmed by recent historians. Christopher Clark, for example, reviewing a biography of Himmler by Peter Longerich, writes: 'Though he never became close to the dictator, he acquired a reputation as Hitler's most dedicated and ruthless servant. Himmler fashioned the SS (originally a small offshoot of the much larger SA) into an instrument of the Führer's will alone.' ('Theorist of Cosmic Ice', *London Review of Books*, 11 October 2012, pp. 11–12.)
212 Christopher Clark writes, 'Between 23 April and 2 May 1942, a series of meetings, some very protracted, took place between Himmler and his deputy, Reinhard Heydrich, and between Himmler and Hitler [...] Longerich concludes from the timing and intensity of these summit discussions that they ratified the transition from local and regional mass killings to a Europe-wide extermination programme' (ibid., p. 12). Grossman may have misdated the meeting he describes, but in other respects he was accurate. Clark refers to Himmler having 'forsaken Catholicism to embrace

a raft of esoteric post-Christian fads'. Hitler, on the other hand, was dismissive of occultism. In a major speech in September 1938, he claimed, 'National Socialism is a cool, reality-based doctrine, based upon the sharpest scientific knowledge and its mental expression ... The National Socialist movement is not a cult movement ... Its meaning is not that of a mystic cult.' Quoted by Richard J. Evans in 'Nuts about the Occult', *London Review of Books*, 2 August 2018, p. 38.

27

213 Hitler's first speech as Reich Chancellor, on 10 February 1933.
214 Nitroglycerine was used to treat chest pain and high blood pressure. It dilates the blood vessels and helps more blood reach the heart.
215 Tobruk, in Cyrenaica (part of Libya), and the Egyptian town of Mersa Matrouh were important in the North Africa campaigns of 1941–2. There was an Axis airfield at Derna.
216 Franz Halder (1884–1972) was chief of staff of the Army High Command from 1938 until September 1942. After receiving intelligence reports that Stalin could muster as many as 1.5 million men north of Stalingrad, Halder told Hitler that Paulus's 6th Army was in a potentially catastrophic position. In response, Hitler threatened to replace Halder. Halder resigned – to be replaced that same day, 24 September, by Kurt Zeitzler.

29

217 See note 44.
218 Gerhart Hauptmann (1862–1946), who won the Nobel Prize in Literature in 1912, chose to remain in Germany after the Nazis came to power. Some of his plays were banned but others went on being performed. His eightieth birthday in 1942 was celebrated on a grand scale. Bernhard Kellermann (1879–1951) was a novelist and poet; he welcomed the Russian Revolution in 1917 but remained in Germany throughout the Nazi era, publishing little.
219 Albert Einstein (1879–1955) emigrated to the USA in 1933. Max Planck (1858–1947), in fact, remained in Germany throughout the Nazi era.
220 'You are nothing, your people is everything.'
221 The Nazi Party's official newspaper, published daily from February 1923.

30

222 Hitler's father, Alois Hitler, was the illegitimate son of Maria Schicklgruber, an Austrian peasant woman. When Alois was five years old, Maria married Johann Hiedler – or Hitler – and Alois assumed this surname.
223 The industrialist Emil Kirdorf (1847–1938) helped promote Hitler's rise to power, though not, in fact, until 1927.

31

224 See note 179.
225 'Fats' (*zhiry*), one of the food categories on ration cards, could mean anything from good quality pork fatback to all kinds of surrogates and 'combined fats' (*kombizhiry*).

32

226 There are many accounts of the terrifying whistle made by high-explosive bombs as they fell. The small incendiary units, however, were still more devastating in their effects. An He-111 bomber could carry up to thirty-two containers, each holding thirty-six units. The container was designed to fall apart soon after being dropped from the plane, thus releasing the individual units.

227 Grossman arrived in Stalingrad soon after the air raid. A notebook entry reads, 'Dead. People in cellars. Everything burned down. Hot walls of buildings, like the bodies of people who have died in the terrible heat and not yet cooled down … Still miraculously standing – amid thousands of vast stone buildings now burnt down or half destroyed – a small wooden soft-drinks kiosk. Like Pompeii, caught by destruction in the fullness of life.' (*Gody voiny*, p. 344)

33

228 Decorating houses or churches with birch branches at Whitsun was a common practice in much of northern Europe.

35

229 During festivities following the coronation of Nicholas II, a mass panic on Khodynka Field in north-west Moscow led to the death of 1,389 people.

36

230 See note 163. Remarkably, Kholzunov survived the Battle of Stalingrad. At the end of January 1943, when the embankment was cleared of rubble, this statue was found to be still intact.

231 *The Humiliated and Insulted* is the title of one of Dostoevsky's earlier novels, published in 1861.

38

232 See note 94.

40

233 An estimated 40,000 people died during the first day and night of air raids on Stalingrad. (Merridale, *Ivan's War*, p. 150)

45

234 Three important Soviet tank army commanders.

46

235 'Vitya' and 'Vitenka' are both affectionate forms of 'Viktor'. See Note on Russian Names.

47

236 The second-largest town on this archipelago to the north of Norway is the Russian coal-mining settlement of Barentsburg.

48

237 Labour battalions were usually formed from categories of people under suspicion, e.g. nationalities that had been deported. They were assigned to particularly hard physical labour.

49

238 'Hero of Socialist Labour' was one of the highest Soviet honours, of equal status to 'Hero of the Soviet Union'.
239 See note 40.
240 See note 57.

51

241 Yemelyan Pugachov (*c.*1742–75), a Cossack leader and pretender to the Russian throne, led a major popular rebellion during the reign of Catherine II.
242 Similar to an Italian bread stick, but in the shape of a ring.

PART III

5

243 *Vy* and *Ty* are equivalent to the French *vous* and *tu*.

6

244 See note 45.
245 Evidently noted by Darensky shortly before the Germans encircled half a million Soviet troops during the Battle of Kiev.
246 Three great Russian military heroes, from the thirteenth, eighteenth and nineteenth centuries.
247 A port on the Volga, in what is now the Mari El Republic. There was a labour camp nearby.

7

248 The paper used for Soviet newspapers was coarse and poor quality – far from ideal for roll-ups.
249 Around 5,000 American Bell Airacobra P-39s were delivered into Soviet service, half of them flying via Alaska and Siberia, half of them transported in crates via Iran.

8

250 Part of the 62nd Army had been encircled on the west bank of the Don.

9

251 See note 74.
252 The first lines of an untitled poem well known to Russians. According to Grossman's daughter, Tyutchev was one of his favourite Russian poets, along with Pushkin, Lermontov and Nekrasov (Korotkova-Grossman, *Vospominaniya*, p. 214).
253 See note 50.

18

254 Between 1 and 6 August, Stalin made several changes both to the naming of the various Fronts and to the chain of command. For a summary of this confusing period, see David Glantz and Jonathan House, *Stalingrad* (University of Kansas Press, 2017), p. 99.
255 The Volga at this point is about one and a half kilometres wide. One of Grossman's notebook entries reads, 'An awful crossing. Terror. The ferry was packed with vehicles, carts, hundreds of people all crowded together – and it hit a sandbank. A Junkers 108 dropped a bomb. A huge column of water, vertical, pale blue. Terror. Not a single machine gun or anti-aircraft gun at the crossing. The quiet, bright Volga – awful as a scaffold.' *Gody voiny*, p. 345.

20

256 This reintroduction of the most ideologically charged part of tsarist military uniform was a significant moment in Stalin's abandonment of revolutionary internationalism and assertion, in its place, of traditional Russian patriotism. See Schechter, *Stuff of Soldiers*, chapter 2.

21

257 On 13 September Chuikov was on Mamaev Kurgan. On the 14th, he was in this tunnel by the River Tsaritsa. During the night of the 16th he moved to the cliff behind the Red October steelworks. My thanks to Michael Jones for clarifying these details (private email).

22

258 In September 1943 Kuzma Gurov died from a heart attack.
259 The move from the formal *Vy* to the informal *Ty* is a serious matter and was often marked by a threefold kiss, either on the cheeks or on the lips. It was not, in the mid-twentieth century, unusual for two Russian men to kiss on the lips.
260 Red Army soldiers and commanders were expected to sew a narrow strip of white cloth to the inside of their jacket collar, leaving just two to three millimetres showing above it. This both created the illusion of a shirt and helped preserve the collar.

261 The 'Kliment Voroshilov' heavy tank, named after the Soviet minister of defence, was generally referred to by its initials.

25

262 According to Michael Jones, Grossman's account of the 13th Guards Division crossing the Volga is slightly inaccurate. Jones writes, 'The crossing began on the early evening of 14 September, and the majority crossed during the night of the 14th, which was when the railway station was regained' (private email).

29

263 See note 190.
264 See note 51.
265 In winter people often slept on top of the stove. See note 26.

32

266 Lines from a song best known in a recording by the popular Lydia Ruslanova (1900–73). Ruslanova was arrested on trumped-up charges in 1948, and from January 1949 until her official 'rehabilitation' in July 1953 her recordings were banned. It may be for this reason that Grossman leaves her nameless and sounding 'sad and surprised'.
267 'Fire! Fire! Fire!'
268 'Fire! Fire! Good! Very good!'

33

269 'The Führer has said, "Stalingrad must fall."'
270 Grossman – though not Bach! – alludes to a famous sentence from Pushkin's *The Captain's Daughter*, 'God spare us from Russian revolt, senseless and merciless.' Both syntactically and rhythmically, the echo is precise. Bach may be coming to realize, if only half-consciously, that the Germans are about to encounter unshakeable, merciless resistance.
271 Friedrich Nietzsche's *Beyond Good and Evil* was first published in 1886. Like Oswald Spengler's *Decline of the West*, it was well known in Russia and the Soviet Union. The Nazis made selective use of the philosophy of both Nietzsche and Spengler, and also of the work of the philosopher Johann Fichte (1762–1814).

34

272 'Dear Ivan, come to me!'
273 A Spanish company, founded in 1904, that produced luxury cars.
274 Karl Liebknecht (1871–1919), a co-founder of the German Communist Party, is best known for his opposition to the First World War and his role in the Spartacist uprising of 1919. The idea of him being an agent of the Jewish Sanhedrin was, of course, Nazi propaganda.

35

275 Furs.

276 Stumpfe's brother evidently took part in the massacre at Babi Yar, outside Kiev. See note 123. There were two cemeteries nearby: a Russian Orthodox cemetery and a Jewish cemetery. The latter was closed in 1937.

277 A reference to the Bible, to the Book of Esther. Haman, vizier to the Persian king Ahasuerus, was plotting to destroy the Jewish people. Queen Esther, herself a Jew, manages to foil this plot. The festival of Purim commemorates her success.

278 See note 65.

279 The 'factory' in question is Treblinka. In 'The Hell of Treblinka' (an article first published in 1944), Grossman writes, 'We know about a huge young man named Stumpfe who broke out into uncontrollable laughter every time he murdered a prisoner or when one was executed in his presence. He was known as "Laughing Death".'

36

280 'Hey you, Puss, Puss!'

281 A *Blockleiter* (block leader) was a junior Nazi official, responsible for the political supervision of a neighbourhood. *Blockleiters* were supposed to act as a link between the Nazi authorities and the people as a whole.

42

282 Filyashkin is being ironic and facetious; as a professional soldier, he has suffered from the interference of commissars. At the same time, he clearly feels the need for some kind of ritual to mark the imminent end of his and his comrades' lives. Unconsciously, he turns to the only ritual with which he has any familiarity – that of the Orthodox church. Shvedkov, naturally, is irritated by Filyashkin's facetiousness. He may also sense Filyashkin's deeper feelings – which would be still more irritating for him.

283 See note 51.

284 A standard formula, pronounced in acknowledgement of the receipt of any official award.

45

285 This report is based on a report by a real figure, Company Commander Kolaganov. Grossman carried this report about in his map case throughout the war. He reproduced it first in his article 'Tsaritsyn – Stalingrad' and then in *Stalingrad*. For a discussion of the battle for the railway station, see Michael K. Jones, *Stalingrad: How the Red Army Triumphed* (Pen and Sword, 2010), pp. 121–7. Grossman's account telescopes three separate events into one: the defence of the railway station, which in reality lasted only twenty-four hours, and the subsequent defence first of the Univermag department store and then of the nail factory, which is where Kolaganov wrote his report. It seems likely that Grossman knew the true sequence of events and chose to employ dramatic licence.

51

286 See note 51.
287 See note 90.

54

288 From Book VIII of the *Odyssey*.
289 The 210 was the heaviest German artillery piece – the 210 mm Morser 18 howitzer. The 103 was a medium artillery piece, firing 103 mm shells.

AFTERWORD

290 RGALI, 1710, opis' 2, ed. khr. 1.
291 A. G. Bocharov, *Vasilii Grossman: zhizn', tvorchestvo, sud'ba* (Moscow, Sovetskii pisatel', 1990), p. 196.
292 Guber, *Pamyat' i pis'ma* (Probel, 2007), p. 64. 'Render safe' is our translation of *obezopasit'*.
293 Semyon Lipkin, *Kvadriga* (Knizhny Sad, 1997), p. 533.
294 Guber, op. cit., p. 67; also RGALI, 1710, opis' 2, ed. khr. 8.
295 Guber, op. cit., p. 67.
296 See 'Diary of the Journey of the Manuscript of the Novel *For a Just Cause* Through Publishing Houses'.
297 Natalya Gromova, *Raspad* (Ellis Lak, 2009), p. 337.
298 See Introduction, pp. xviii–xx.
299 See Abram Tertz / Andrey Sinyavsky, *The Trial Begins* and *On Socialist Realism* (University of California Press, 1992).

NOTE

300 See 'Voina i mir dvadtsatogo veka', http://www.lechaim.ru/ARHIV/177/sarnov.htm, accessed 21 October 2017.
301 Grossman, *A Writer at War*, pp. 31–5.
302 Grossman, *Gody voiny*, p. 285.

The Soviet retreat during the first fifteen months of the war, also showing Krymov's journeys

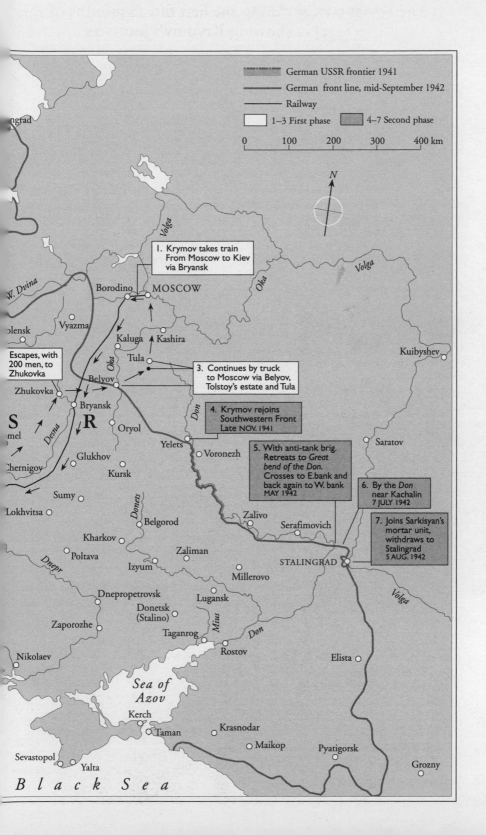

Map legend:

- German USSR frontier 1941
- German front line, mid-September 1942
- Railway
- 1–3 First phase
- 4–7 Second phase

0   100   200   300   400 km

N

1. Krymov takes train From Moscow to Kiev via Bryansk

Escapes, with 200 men, to Zhukovka

3. Continues by truck to Moscow via Belyov, Tolstoy's estate and Tula

4. Krymov rejoins Southwestern Front Late NOV. 1941

5. With anti-tank brig. Retreats to *Great bend of the Don*. Crosses to E.bank and back again to W. bank MAY 1942

6. By the *Don* near Kachalin 7 JULY 1942

7. Joins Sarkisyan's mortar unit, withdraws to Stalingrad 5 AUG. 1942

Place labels:

ngrad, W. Dvina, olensk, Vyazma, Borodino, MOSCOW, Volga, Oka, Volga, Kaluga, Kashira, Tula, Kuibyshev, Oka, Belyov, Don, Zhukovka, Bryansk, S, Desna, R, Oryol, Yelets, Voronezh, Saratov, mel, Glukhov, Kursk, Chernigov, Sumy, Lokhvitsa, Donets, Belgorod, Zalivo, Serafimovich, STALINGRAD, Kharkov, Zaliman, Poltava, Izyum, Millerovo, Dnepr, Dnepropetrovsk, Lugansk, Volga, Donetsk (Stalino), Mius, Don, Zaporozhe, Taganrog, Rostov, Elista, Nikolaev, Sea of Azov, Kerch, Krasnodar, Sevastopol, Taman, Maikop, Pyatigorsk, Grozny, Yalta, Black Sea

Stalingrad and surrounding area

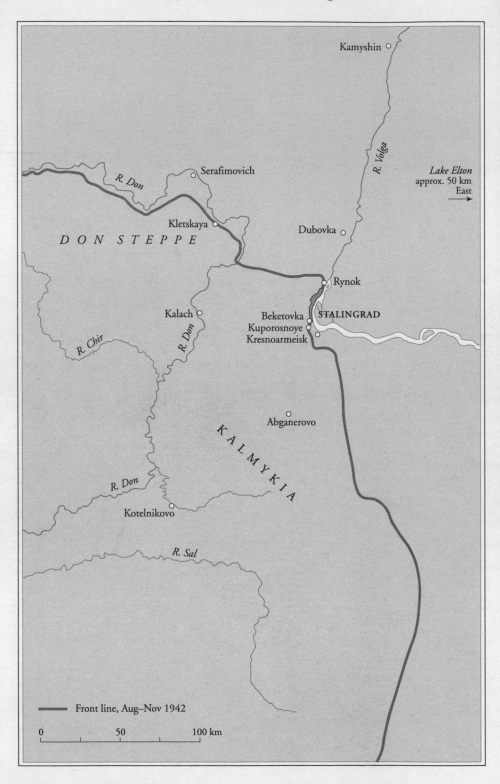

Kamyshin

R. Volga

Lake Elton
approx. 50 km
East →

Serafimovich

R. Don

DON STEPPE

Kletskaya

Dubovka

Rynok

R. Chir

Kalach

R. Don

Beketovka
Kuporosnoye
Kresnoarmeisk

STALINGRAD

R. Don

Abganerovo

K A L M Y K I A

R. Don

Kotelnikovo

R. Sal

—— Front line, Aug–Nov 1942

0   50   100 km

Stalingrad

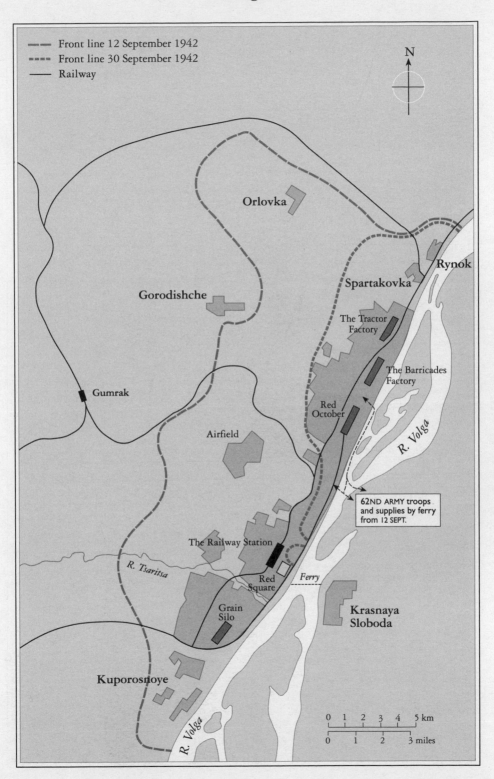

Front line 12 September 1942
Front line 30 September 1942
Railway

N

Orlovka

Rynok

Spartakovka

Gorodishche

The Tractor
Factory

The Barricades
Factory

Gumrak

Red
October

R. Volga

Airfield

62ND ARMY troops
and supplies by ferry
from 12 SEPT.

The Railway Station

R. Tsaritsa

Red
Square

Ferry

Krasnaya
Sloboda

Grain
Silo

Kuporosnoye

R. Volga

0 1 2 3 4 5 km

0 1 2 3 miles

VINTAGE CLASSICS

Vintage launched in the United Kingdom in 1990, and was originally the paperback home for the Random House Group's literary authors. Now, Vintage is comprised of some of London's oldest and most prestigious literary houses, including Chatto & Windus (1855), Hogarth (1917), Jonathan Cape (1921) and Secker & Warburg (1935), alongside the newer or relaunched hardback and paperback imprints: The Bodley Head, Harvill Secker, Yellow Jersey, Square Peg, Vintage Paperbacks and Vintage Classics.

From Angela Carter, Graham Greene and Aldous Huxley to Toni Morrison, Haruki Murakami and Virginia Woolf, Vintage Classics is renowned for publishing some of the greatest writers and thinkers from around the world and across the ages – all complemented by our beautiful, stylish approach to design. Vintage Classics' authors have won many of the world's most revered literary prizes, including the Nobel, the Man Booker, the Prix Goncourt and the Pulitzer, and through their writing they continue to capture imaginations, inspire new perspectives and incite curiosity.

In 2007 Vintage Classics introduced its distinctive red spine design, and in 2012 Vintage Children's Classics was launched to include the much-loved authors of our childhood. Random House joined forces with the Penguin Group in 2013 to become Penguin Random House, making it the largest trade publisher in the United Kingdom.

@vintagebooks

penguin.co.uk/vintage-classics